Allen William

Municipal Boundaries Commission (Ireland)

part III: report; minutes of evidence

Allen William

Municipal Boundaries Commission (Ireland)
part III: report; minutes of evidence

ISBN/EAN: 9783742805560

Manufactured in Europe, USA, Canada, Australia, Japa

Cover: Foto ©Andreas Hilbeck / pixelio.de

Manufactured and distributed by brebook publishing software
(www.brebook.com)

Allen William

Municipal Boundaries Commission (Ireland)

CONTENTS.

LIST OF WITNESSES.

a 2

REPORT.

TO HIS EXCELLENCY JOHN POYNTZ, EARL SPENCER, K.P., K.G.,

LORD LIEUTENANT GENERAL AND GENERAL GOVERNOR OF IRELAND.

MAY IT PLEASE YOUR EXCELLENCY,

His Grace the Duke of Marlborough, then Lord Lieutenant of Ireland, was pleased to issue a warrant, bearing date the 31st day of October, 1878, by which he nominated and appointed William Allen Exham, Esq., one of Her Majesty's Counsel in Ireland; William P. O'Brien, Esq., then Local Government Board Inspector, and Charles P. Cotton, Esq., Civil Engineer, Commissioners, to inquire into the municipal boundaries of the several cities and towns in Ireland, and to inquire and investigate whether the boundaries of any of the said cities or towns required to be extended, limited, or otherwise altered, and whether the wards in any of the said cities or towns required rearrangement, and generally to enquire into the municipal areas of the said cities and towns.

His Grace was afterwards pleased to issue a further warrant, dated the 22nd of February, 1879, by which the Commissioners were authorized to inquire into the existing incidence of taxation of the said cities and towns, and the debts due or owing by the municipal bodies of the said cities and towns, and charged on the municipal property thereof, and the taxes payable by the occupiers of houses and lands outside the present municipal boundaries of the said cities and towns, and in the immediate neighbourhood thereof, and into the terms and conditions as regards the incidence of taxation, and the charge of the said debts, upon which the boundaries of any of the said cities or towns should be extended, limited, or otherwise altered.

Mr. O'Brien ceased to be a Commissioner on the 14th day of February, 1879, in consequence of his appointment as a member of the Prisons Board, but up to that date he had taken part in some of the inquiries, and held others by himself, and we have his authority for informing your Excellency that he concurs in the opinions we have formed as to the extensions of the towns which were visited by him, and which are hereafter recommended and the reasons which have guided us in such recommendation.

On the 26th day of June, 1879, His Grace was pleased to appoint Mr. Henry A. Robinson (who had previously been the Secretary to the Commission) to be a Commissioner. On the 25th November, 1881, the Commission was deprived of its Chairman by the death of Mr. Exham.

We have now the honour to submit, for your Excellency's consideration, the following report.

Before visiting any of the towns, due publicity was given to the intended proceedings, and on the appointment of the Commission it was intimated, through the medium of the Dublin and local newspapers, that an inquiry would be held in every municipal town and township in Ireland, and all persons who were desirous of expressing their opinions were invited to forward their communications to the offices of the Commission in Dublin on behalf of themselves or any interests represented by them. Circulars were sent to all municipal bodies requesting information as to whether they, as representing the ratepayers of the town, were satisfied with the existing areas of their respective towns, and if not, to what extent, in their opinion, an extension or alteration of the existing municipal boundary was expedient, and as to what were the reasons which influenced them in desiring any such alteration. A copy of the queries and notice of the inquiry was sent to each municipal body. When the Commissioners had thus ascertained the views of the governing bodies, and had been furnished with the necessary statistics and the maps of the different towns, and the electoral division in which each town was situated, the first inquiry was opened in Drogheda within a month of the date upon which the Commission was issued. Appendix to Report No. 1 and No. 2.

The Commissioners collectively or individually visited the 111 towns mentioned in Schedule F in Mr. O'Brien's report, referred to in His Grace's warrant, and in addition the town of Arklow and township of Drumcondra, which were formed into townships subsequently to the date of that report, having received due authority so to do. The smaller towns were visited by one of the Commissioners only, but in the larger and consequently more important towns and townships care was taken that, as far as possible, the inquiry should be held before all the Commissioners for the time being. In an Appendix to this report will be found a list of the towns and townships visited, showing the dates at which the inquiries were held in each, and by whom such inquiry was held.

Of the 118 towns and townships so visited, your Excellency will perceive that the municipal form of government may be divided into four classes, as follows:—

No. 1.—Towns solely under the Towns' Improvement Act of 1854 (78).

Arklow.	Ballina.	Dromore.	Larne.	Newtownards.
Athy.	Boyle.	Enniscorthy.	Lisburn.	Parsonstown.
Ardee.	Carlow.	Ennis.	Lurgan.	Portadown.
Athlone.	Callan.	Fermoy.	Letterkenny.	Rathkeale.
Antrim.	Clonakilty.	Gorey.	Limavady.	Roscommon.
Aughnacloy.	Carrick-on-Suir.	Gilford.	Loughrea.	Skibbereen.
Bagenalstown.	Cashel.	Holywood.	Maryborough.	Strabane.
Balbriggan.	Cavan.	Killiney and Ballybrack.	Mountmellick.	Tullamore.
Ballymena.	Cootehill.	Kells.	Mullingar.	Trim.
Ballymoney.	Coleraine.	Kinsale.	Midleton.	Tandragee.
Belturbet.	Carrickmacross.	Keady.	Naas.	Thurles.
Ballyshannon.	Castleblayney.	Killarney.	Newbridge.	Tipperary.
Banbridge.	Clones.	Longford.	Navan.	Templemore.
Bangor.	Cookstown.	Lismore.	New Ross.	Tuam.
Ballybay.	Castlebar.		Nenagh.	Westport.
Ballinasloe.	Dundalk.			

No. 2.—Towns solely under the 9th George IV., c. 82 (11).

Armagh.	Dungannon.	Mallow.	Omagh.	Wicklow.
Bandon.	Fethard.	Monaghan.	Tralee.	Youghal.
Downpatrick.				

No. 3.—Towns and Townships under Special Acts of Parliament and the Acts incorporated with such Special Acts, respectively (14).

Blackrock.	Dalkey.	Enniskillen.	Kingstown.	Queenstown.
Bray.	Drumcondra.	Galway.	Newry.	Rathmines and Rathgar.
Clontarf.	Dungarvan.	Kilmainham (New)	Pembroke.	

No. 4.—Towns under the Municipal Corporation Act of 1840 and Special Acts (12).

Belfast.	Cork.	Kilkenny.	Londonderry.	Wexford.
Carrickfergus.	Drogheda.	Limerick.	Sligo.	Waterford.
Clonmel.	Dublin.			

Very considerable interest was taken in the proceedings at Dublin, Belfast, and Cork, and in fact, in all the corporate towns, but in the majority of the smaller municipalities the attendance at the inquiries was somewhat limited. This, however, may be accounted for in cases where an extension of the boundary was advocated by the fact that the people residing outside the limits of the township, although apprised by the local papers of the sitting of the Commission, were not in many instances aware that an extension of the existing boundary was suggested by the Municipal Body —but in each case it was intimated publicly at the inquiry, that all persons who would be affected by any extension, might forward any suggestions on the subject, which would be duly considered and to any communications so received, we have given every consideration and have set forth each of them as we consider necessary for your Excellency's information in the Appendix to this report.

A separate report has already been presented to your Excellency, in which are stated the views and suggestions of the two members of the Commission who inquired into the boundaries of Dublin and the surrounding townships, and also with respect to the townships of Blackrock, Dalkey, and Kingstown.

Of the 104 remaining towns, the governing bodies of fifty-seven announced themselves, in their replies to the queries forwarded to them, as being in favour of an enlargement of the existing area of taxation, as will be found in the Appendix to this Report, but with very few exceptions no definite extension was specified, the Municipal Bodies merely stating that it was their opinion that for the reasons hereafter alluded to an enlargement of the town boundary was desirable, but to what extent they were somewhat indifferent, and the evidence taken at the inquiries tends to show that they were generally unaware of what the result of any extension would be. It is, however, right to observe that in the few cases in which serious consideration had been given to the question, as may be seen from the evidence, the Municipal Bodies had entered most carefully into all the details bearing on the results to be anticipated by the adoption of their scheme.

The effect of an extension of the boundaries resulting as it would somewhat differently in towns constituted under special Acts and the 9th of George IV., chapter 82, from those under the Towns Improvement Act, we will proceed to remark first on the towns which have adopted the provisions of the latter statute solely, comprising seventy-six of the municipal towns in Ireland.

Much apprehension was expressed at some of the earlier inquiries, lest extern lands when brought within an extended boundary, would come under the designation of townparks and accommodation lands, and that thus the occupiers might lose the rights with respect to them which they had under the existing laws. The Commissioners refrained from giving any expression of opinion on this head, but the evidence was tendered in almost every instance, on the supposition, on the part of those who gave it, that the extension would not result in any interference with existing rights.

The first question that presented itself to the consideration of the Commissioners was, what general principle should guide them in fixing the boundary of a town, or in other words, in fixing the area which should contribute to the charges of its maintenance.

Property in the neighbourhood of a town derives a benefit from it depending on varying circumstances, but in all cases distance from the town-proper forms a preponderating element. It would be impossible to fix in any case a distance where such benefits began or ceased, but the practical limits may generally be estimated without difficulty.

We beg to refer to the evidence of Mr. M'Carthy Downing, which, we think, well expresses these principles, as follows:—That for a certain distance, varying from a mile to two miles round each of the towns, the occupiers of residences derived exceptional advantages from the proximity of those residences to the town; that the owners of land within the same area, derived a rent from them very much in excess of what lands of a similar quality would produce at a distance of three miles or more from the town; that the occupiers of those lands were enabled to pay this increased rent from the fact of the lands being so closely approximate to the town, and being able to sell their produce from day to day in, and to the residents of, the town; that the occupiers were able also to procure quantities of manure for the necessary cultivation of those lands; that the persons occupying the houses and lands within the above area largely took advantage of and used the town, and availed themselves of its accommodation and advantages for marketing, shopping, attending their places of worship, going to railways, sending their children to schools, and any other advantages which were afforded by the town to its own inhabitants; that the lighting of the town was considerably for their advantage, and in fact in some instances it was alleged to be of more use to them than to the inhabitants of the town themselves; that it was for their advantage that the town should be kept in a healthy and cleanly manner as they used it so largely, and while doing so must of necessity have caused injury to the streets of that town, and entailed additional expense on the funds which had to be provided for keeping it in proper order. It was contended that for these advantages, they, who derived such benefit should contribute something to the rates of the town, and that the entire of these advantages should not be provided for them exclusively at the cost of the ratepayers of the town itself.

Dungarvan, p. 23. Ev. 34. Ev. 44, 45. Ev. 34.

The persons to be affected by any proposed extension on the other hand in most instances based their opposition on the ground that they *objected* to it, and had no right to be brought into the town or put under taxation against their own consent, and they insisted that, as a large majority in most cases of the persons to be affected by any extension were opposed to it, we should not propose any such extension. They further stated that they derived no benefits from the town, which were not more than compensated by the advantages which the town derived from them, that it was they who principally kept up the town by spending their money amongst the shop-keepers, and they urged that it would be unfair for them to be made pay anything towards the taxes of the town. It was contended, in cases where the roads of the town were managed by the Grand Jury, that the ratepayers of the town could not fairly make any complaint as to the use of those roads by parties outside the town, inasmuch as their repairs were paid for out of the Grand Jury Cess, which was levied in common on the occupiers outside as well as on the ratepayers of the town and therefore were not kept exclusively at the expense of such ratepayers, and that a similar argument applied to anything that would cause expense on those roads, by scavenging or otherwise; this argument would apply to the majority of the towns, as the roads at present are only in a very few cases in the hands of the Municipal Body. It was further in many places stated by extern residents, that they had built their houses outside the existing boundary, so as to secure exemption from taxation, and that it would be unfair now to include them in an extended area which would involve them in additional taxation.

A further objection, which we have already alluded to, was raised early in the inquiry which though not strictly within the scope of our Commission to inquire into, we think it right to bring under your Excellency's notice. Our attention was called to the provisions of that portion of the Land Act of 1870, which exempts townparks, &c., from its operation, and it was objected in many places by the occupiers of lands which were sought to be brought in, that if an extension took place which embraced their lands, they would lose the benefits which they had by law under that Act. The objectors were informed that in all such cases, although we had no power to offer any recommendation on the subject, we would take especial care to report to your Excellency, that their evidence was in almost every instance given on the supposition, that any proposed extension embracing their lands would not result in any interference with existing rights. Indeed, had we not taken the evidence on this assumption, we are satisfied, that not only would such evidence have been withheld, but that the Municipal Bodies would themselves in the majority of cases, have declined recommending any extension of the existing areas which would bring in lands, and make them liable to any such consequences; the observations in this paragraph apply to the lands within and without all the towns and townships, the subject matter of this Report.

Your Excellency will perceive that we have hereafter recommended that all *lands* inside the present municipal areas, and those in the extended areas as proposed by us, should be placed on the same footing as regards taxation: and it will be for the consideration of the *Legislature* how far any different rule can be adopted in relation to the two classes of land, under the Land Acts or in any other respect.

Another objection was made to any extension in most of the towns under the Municipal Corporations Act, and in many of the larger towns under the Towns Improvement Act of 1854, to the effect that the districts proposed to be brought in, were to be considered as purely rural districts, and not as suburban ones, or districts at present largely built on or likely to be built on; and it was contended that, having regard to the decisions of Select Committees of the Houses of Lords and Commons on private Bills, brought in by municipal bodies in England and Scotland, for the extension of their boundaries, we should not recommend any extension of existing areas which would have the effect of bringing in such rural districts. Instances were stated to us in which it was contended that such Select Committees had refused any extension which would bring in districts of the same character as those with which we had to deal. We have carefully considered this last objection, and also that grounded on not bringing into existing townships persons outside its area against their consent, and we have declined to give effect to, or to entertain these objections on the following grounds:—

The members of the Select Committee, in pursuance of whose report his Grace's warrant was issued to us, had before them in successive sessions of Parliament, the question of Local Taxation in Ireland. We assume that they were aware of the decisions of the Select Committees referred to, and had they considered that the question of consent or non-consent was to be an element in our consideration, we cannot but think that some intimation would have been given to us on that point. They had themselves taken much evidence which showed that in many cases parties living outside existing areas, would strongly object to be brought into municipal areas, adjacent to the residences or lands occupied by them; and we can hardly imagine that, if the element of consent or non-consent was to determine the question, such an inquiry would have ever been entrusted to us. We may make a similar remark with regard to the objection as to the nature of the lands which are likely to be affected by any extension of the area, and also to the objection founded on the unfairness of taxing persons who had expended their money on the faith of their being outside the area of town taxation. It appears to us after considering the evidence given before the Select Committee and their Report upon it, and having also read the clause in the draft report of the late Mr. Butt, laid before the Select Committee in relation to this matter—(See foot note*), that our duty was to consider the propriety of extending or otherwise altering the boundaries of all the municipal towns in Ireland, comprised in the return "F" of Mr. O'Brien's Report, on general principles, wholly irrespective of any objections founded on the question of consent or the nature of the outside areas, and not on principles applicable to each town exclusively.

Bearing these views in mind, we have to state, for your Excellency's information, that we have come to the following conclusions as regards all the towns under the Towns Improvement Act:—

---

* Section 15, subsection 2nd. "A change of boundaries is desirable in almost all the corporate towns. Your Committee are of opinion, that this could best be carried out by a Commission like that which settled the boundaries of the English Parliamentary Boroughs, before the last Reform Bill. The immediate appointment of such a Commission would prepare the way for a General Act relating to the Municipal Institutions of Ireland. Their functions should, of course, extend to all towns in which Municipal bodies of any power exist.

1. That all *lands* within the present boundary of a town, and those within a certain distance outside it, varying with the circumstances of each town and its immediate neighbourhood are exceptionally valuable from their proximity to the town, and that the landlords of such lands derive a rent much larger than what lands of a similar quality would produce if situated farther off, or not so circumstanced.

2. That the tenants or occupiers of such lands are enabled to pay this increased rent solely in consequence of their situation, and the advantages thereby derived by them from the daily sale in the town of their produce and otherwise.

3. That the occupiers of *residences* within a like distance also derive exceptional advantage from their proximity to the town, and use it in the same manner as the occupiers of similar houses within the existing area.

4. That many of these advantages are supplied to such occupiers of houses and lands outside the existing area at present at the exclusive cost of the ratepayers of the town, which cost is increased by the use made of the town by the occupiers of such houses and lands. In nearly all the towns lighting is at present supplied to the extremity of the township boundary, and in many instances water at high pressure is also supplied. In many cases also the towns are scavenged at the expense of the ratepayers, much in excess of the work done by the Grand Jury contractor.

5. That a number of gentlemen of position and farmers of a superior class live within a short distance of the present boundaries of most of the towns, and that it would be most desirable that such parties should become voters, and eligible as members of the Municipal Body, and thereby have a voice and interest in the administration of the affairs of the town.

6. That within a like distance there is a large population, and it is desirable that they should be within the jurisdiction of the magistrates acting in or for the town.

7. That in several of the towns in this class some of the public institutions and buildings are outside of the present area, as will appear from the following list:—

Name of Town.	Public Institutions or Buildings outside present Boundary.	Name of Town.	Public Institutions or Buildings outside present Boundary.
Antrim, .	Workhouse and Railway Station.	Kinsale, .	Workhouse.
Aughnacloy, .	Fever Hospital.	Longford, .	Workhouse.
Ballymena, .	Workhouse.	Lismore, .	Railway Station and Workhouse.
Coleraine, .	Workhouse and Hospital.	Maryborough, .	Lunatic Asylum.
Castleblayney, .	Workhouse and Hospital.	Mullingar, .	Lunatic Asylum and Workhouse.
Clonakilty, .	Site for buildings not rated.	Naas, .	Sallins Railway Station.
Clones, .	Workhouse and Hospital.	Navan, .	Workhouse.
Cookstown, .	Workhouse and Hospital.	Rathkeale, .	Workhouse.
Ennis, .	Railway Station and Lunatic Asylum.	Skibbereen, .	Workhouse.
Gorey, .	Workhouse.	Trim, .	Railway Station and Workhouse.
Kells, .	Workhouse.	Tuam, .	Workhouse.

And we consider it desirable that in each case these institutions and buildings should be within the township boundary, even though the income of the town might not be materially increased thereby.

8. That a judicious administration of municipal affairs is necessarily a matter of convenience which would be experienced as much, or nearly as much, by the occupiers of houses and land in the immediate neighbourhood of the town as by the ratepayers themselves, and that the residents within a limited distance from the town are directly interested in any further improvements which the Commissioners would be enabled to carry out by means of an increased revenue.

9. That at present it would not be possible to extend all the advantages of the present municipalities over the entire of the new areas proposed to be embraced, and we have had regard to this fact in fixing the extension of the areas, and the increase and distribution of taxation which we submit for your Excellency's consideration.

10. In most cases the boundary suggested to us was that of a circle taken from some central point in each town, and varying in extent. The adoption of any such boundary would have the effect of subdividing farms and holdings, and even portions of houses would have to be assessed for municipal purposes, so that, while recognizing its desirableness on principles of equity, we were compelled to abandon it (save in a few cases hereinafter referred to) on the score of the inconvenience that it would entail, and in its stead we have adhered as nearly as possible to townland or other well and permanently defined boundaries in the selection of the extended areas as recommended by us.

Acting on the opinions which we have above expressed to your Excellency, we recommend an extension of the existing boundaries in all the towns under the Towns Improvement Act, save those of Ballinasloe, Cashel, Newbridge, Nenagh, and Strabane, in which it is not in our opinion desirable that any extension should take place.

In all the other towns in this class (seventy-one in number), we have come to the conclusion that an extension of the existing boundary is desirable, and, with respect to sixty-seven towns of the seventy-one, in marking it out on the maps which accompany this report, we have adhered, as fully as possible, to townland or other well-defined existing boundaries, such as public roads or watercourses, and in cases where we could not obtain such, we have adopted a line drawn between well-defined and recognised existing marks. With respect to the remaining towns in this class (four in number), we have been compelled, for convenience sake, to adopt, as a boundary line, a circle drawn from a point as nearly as possible in the centre of the town, and this circle we have shown on the map of each of those towns, viz: Dromore, Keady, Navan, and Trim.

We do not recommend any extension of the present boundary of the town of Cashel. No rates have been levied there since it was placed under the Towns' Improvement Act, as it has ample property to cover any expenditure necessary in the town, and the Town Commissioners are the owners of the property extending for a considerable distance beyond it, as trustees for the inhabitants of Cashel for the time being; and with respect to the towns of Ballinasloe, Newbridge, Nenagh, and Strabane, we consider that the present boundary could not be usefully extended or altered, save that we have lessened the inner area for full taxation in Ballinasloe and Nenagh, in accordance with the recommendations hereafter made.

We had next to consider the manner in which we should bring before your Excellency's notice, the existing boundaries of the towns in this class, with the alterations we suggest. When they were originally fixed under the Towns' Improvement Act of 1854, they were published in the *Dublin Gazette*, and set out by then existing metes, bounds, and descriptions. We found it to be very difficult in many cases, and impossible in some to fix the present boundaries from their descriptions in the then *Gazette* notices, owing to several of the fences, bye-roads, marks, and houses therein mentioned having disappeared. From the constant changes in fences and bye-roads, this difficulty would be probably increased from year to year in the future. In most cases the Town Commissioners had maps showing the boundaries of their towns, which had been acted on for several years, and the rates had been, from time to time, collected without question within the areas specified in such maps respectively. We, therefore, came to the conclusion that it would most facilitate your Excellency in considering our report, and those who may hereafter have to legislate on the subject, if we prepared maps, which are appended to this report, showing the existing boundaries of the several towns in this class with the extension of the boundaries which we propose in cases where we have recommended extension.

We have marked the existing boundary of each town with a green line, and the increased boundary with a red line. If the new boundaries thus recommended by us should ultimately meet with the approval of your Excellency and the Imperial Parliament, they can be easily copied on maps prepared at the Ordnance Survey Office at a small cost, and in that event we would suggest to your Excellency, that, when so finally arranged, copies should be deposited with the Municipal Body at their office in each town, and with the Clerk of the Peace at his office in the county in which each such town is situated; and that copies of such maps purporting to be signed by the Town Clerk of each town, or by the Clerk of the Peace, should be received as conclusive evidence of such boundaries respectively in all legal and other proceedings in which the question of the boundaries of each town may be raised. If, however, the boundaries we recommend should not be approved of by your Excellency, or should become a question for consideration before Parliament, we cannot but think that the matter can be more conveniently considered by your Excellency, or those whose duty it will be so to do, by having before you or them, on maps, the existing boundaries of the existing towns as well as we could ascertain them, and also the changes which we suggest.

We had also to consider in connection with this question of extension the all important question of taxation. Your Excellency is aware that under the Towns Improvement Act of 1854 (17 and 18 Vic., c. 103) the maximum improvement rate which could be levied in townships under that Act was 1s. 6d. in the pound, where the enactments of the Act with respect to water had been adopted, and 1s. in the pound where such enactments as to water had not been adopted, while by the 62nd section it was provided that "all lands used as arable, meadow, or pasture ground only, or as woodlands, or market gardens, or nursery grounds, and all lands covered with water and used as a canal, and any towing path to the same, and all lands used as a railway constructed under the powers of any Act of Parliament for public conveyance shall be assessed and liable in the proportion of one-fourth part only of the net annual value of such lands respectively."

In many instances the maximum of rating had been levied for several years, and we presume it had been found to be insufficient, for its limit was increased to

2s. by the 11th section of the Public Health Act of 1874, and which provided that where, in any town, in which the Towns Improvement Act (Ireland), 1854, was in force, the provisions of that Act with respect to water have been adopted, the amount of any assessment under section 60 of the said Act may, notwithstanding the limitations in the said section contained, amount to but shall not exceed the rate of 2s. in the pound. This clause was re-enacted by the 238th section of the Public Health (Ireland) Act, 1878, so that the maximum amount of the "Improvement Rate" is now 2s. in the pound in the class of towns mentioned in that section.

We are satisfied from the evidence given before us that rates payable in the proportion of one-fourth by the classes of property mentioned in the 62nd section above referred to are insufficient, and we consider that one-half rates should for the future fairly be paid in respect of those classes of property. We, therefore, recommend that the classes of property comprised within the 62nd section shall be assessed and liable in the proportion of one-half part of their net annual value respectively, and that the rate be divided between the landlord and tenant on the same principle as the Poor Rate is now divided. The effect of this would be not to increase the taxation on the occupiers of those classes of property (save in the cases where the occupiers and owners were the same persons), but to make the owners who derive such real advantages from the situation of their property, contribute a fair share towards the taxation of the town, which makes their lands thus exceptionally valuable to them. In recommending the division of the rates we are further acting on the recommendation contained to that effect in the Report of the Select Committee.

Your Excellency will perceive that with respect to the towns under the Towns Improvement Act the principle of differential taxation was adopted between houses and the classes of property mentioned in the 62nd section of that Act, and we recommend that a similar principle should also be adopted with regard to the houses in the outer area hereinafter alluded to, and all the classes of property comprised within the 62nd section above mentioned, which may be included within the new boundaries which we suggest to your Excellency. It would not be always possible, except at a great loss, to give to the entire area of a township the full benefits and advantages which are at present enjoyed by the ratepayers within the town proper. We have therefore fixed an inner area for full taxation and an outer area for differential taxation of houses and buildings.

We recommend that if in time to come the Town Commissioners are able to give to the occupiers of houses and buildings in the outer area, or any district thereof, the full advantages and benefits at present enjoyed and claimed by the ratepayers of the inner area, such occupiers should thenceforward pay the full Improvement rates from time to time to be levied in the town; and if any dispute were to arise as to whether or not such full advantages were afforded to them, it could be referred to a suitable appellate tribunal.

In order to show at a glance the area within which the differential rate should, in our opinion, be paid by houses and buildings, we determined, with respect to each of the towns in this class, the portion which, in our opinion, should derive the full benefit and advantages with respect to lighting and otherwise, and we have marked that district with a blue line on the maps above referred to. We recommend that all houses and buildings within that district (other than any which may at present be exempt by law from taxation) shall pay the full Improvement rate, and that all such houses and buildings outside the blue line shall only pay half rates, and that all the classes of property mentioned in the 62nd section of the Towns Improvement Act, whether within or without the blue line, shall pay half the Improvement rate.

In eleven towns in this class, viz.—Arklow, Belturbet, Bagenalstown, Ballinasloe, Loughrea, Naas, Nenagh, Parsonstown, Rathkeale, Templemore, and Westport, we have lessened the area, within which full taxation is to be paid. In one—Lismore—we have increased the same area, and in the remaining towns in this class we have allowed the present boundary to remain as that of the area for full taxation. A reference to the map in each case will show at once these boundaries in each town.

We have limited our recommendation as to the payment of a differential rate to the improvement rate, payable under the Towns Improvement Act, alone. Your Excellency is aware that the *sanitary* rate is at present unlimited in extent, whether property is situated in an urban or a rural district, and we see no reason to recommend, and do not recommend that there should be any differential rate, for any class of property, in respect of sanitary rates, payable within a town, either as it exists at present, or within the extended boundary proposed by us. If our recommendation in this respect is carried out, it would necessitate an alteration in the striking and levying of the rates in towns which are Urban Sanitary Districts and under the Towns Improvement Act, as the improvement and sanitary rates should be kept separate. With respect to the improvement rate the entire or the moiety of the rates, as the case might be, should be paid, but the full rates should be paid on all property in respect of the sanitary rate. This would place the payment of the sanitary rate in the urban and rural sanitary districts on the same footing.

Our reason for the recommendation contained in the last paragraph is caused by the present state of the law, to which we have to call Your Excellency's attention, viz., to the difference in the law at present existing with respect to the payment of sanitary rates, in urban and rural sanitary districts, as it will materially affect all classes of property, which are at present in a rural sanitary district, and which, if our recommendation is carried out, will in the cases of towns which are urban sanitary authorities, be brought within those authorities. At present in an urban sanitary district, the sanitary rate is included in the improvement rate, which the occupier pays, without being entitled to deduct any part of it from his landlord, while in the rural sanitary district, the occupier pays the sanitary rate, but is entitled to deduct half from his landlord on the same terms as his poor rate. If the law was to remain as it is, the occupiers of all property by being transferred from the rural to the urban district, might lose, by such transfer, a considerable benefit, while occupiers of the same class of property would be on a different footing in towns which were in a rural sanitary district. In both cases the lands and other property are valued on the same principle, and are equally valuable to both the landlord and tenant, and therefore it would appear to us that there should not be any difference in the law relative to each, and that both should be placed on the same footing. If it be right, as the Legislature has provided with respect to property in the rural sanitary district, that the sanitary rate should be divided between landlord and tenant, we think that a similar rule should apply to all the same classes of property in the urban sanitary district, and we therefore recommend to Your Excellency, that with respect to all classes of property within the boundaries of the new townships, as proposed by us, the sanitary rate should hereafter be paid by the occupier as a separate rate, or part of the poor rate, and that he should be entitled to deduct one-half from his landlord.

In some places evidence was given before us to show that considerable advantage would arise to the present ratepayers in the towns, and also to the occupiers of houses and lands in the adjoining districts, if the management of the roads was taken up by the Municipal Bodies, as they could be maintained by them at much less cost than that paid at present, by way of County Cess, to the Grand Jury. At Holywood the question was gone into at some length by Mr. Anderson, the Chairman of the Town Commissioners, who proved by figures taken from the Grand Jury returns, that a saving of nearly one shilling in the pound would take place if the Town Commissioners of Holywood had the management of the roads, and that this saving would more than pay the moiety of the improvement rate, which it was proposed that the occupiers of houses and buildings in the outside districts should pay if brought within the township. In Wexford it was shown that a saving to the extent of £400 a year had taken place for the benefit of that town since the Town Council got the management of the roads from the Grand Jury in the year 1874, and in several other places it was stated that a like saving would take place by a transfer to the Municipal Body of the management of the roads. We do not consider that it is within our province to offer any opinion on this point, which appears to have occupied the attention of the Select Committee, who have given their recommendations with respect to it. We may add that any recommendations of ours with respect to the improvement and sanitary rates, is not to be taken as in any manner applying to a road rate in lieu of County Cess in cases in which a town may hereafter obtain the care and management of its roads.

In considering the extension of the boundaries of all the municipal towns and townships, we have not lost sight of the clause in His Grace's warrant, following the report of the Select Committee, "that care should be taken to make municipal wards coterminous with wards for Poor Law purposes, and towns with Poor Law electoral divisions; and, if possible, to secure that every town, except Dublin, should be included in one Poor Law Union." The result of our investigation with respect to the Poor Law electoral divisions has satisfied us that, except in the cases next mentioned, it would be impossible to make any equitable extension based on any such consideration, and we were, therefore, obliged to abandon it. The present shapes of those divisions are extremely irregular—in many cases they run for miles beyond the township boundary, while in other cases they abut on it, or divide it, and are, therefore, unsuitable as township boundaries or areas of municipal taxation. In the cases of Ballymena, Coleraine, Dungannon, Ennis, Kells, Mullingar, Naas, and Sligo, the enlarged boundaries will coincide in each case with that of the electoral division. In Carrickfergus, which we do not purpose to alter, the boundary is co-extensive with the electoral division.

Strabane (which we do not propose to alter), is at present the electoral division, with the addition of the townland of Miltown, and the proposed enlargement of Wexford will include all the electoral division, and also four townlands outside it, on the north side of the River Slaney.

In no town or township (save Dublin and Belfast) have we proposed any alterations in the boundaries which would have the effect of bringing the town or township into more than one Poor Law Union, and in those cases we have pointed out how any difficulty arising therefrom may be met.

Of the seventy-six towns in this class, nine have wards, viz.:—Arklow, Athlone, Ballina, Banbridge, Carlow, Carrick-on-Suir, Dundalk, Longford, and New Ross. It will not be necessary or desirable that there should be any alteration of the existing wards in any of those towns save Banbridge. If the extension of the boundary proposed by us with respect to each of these towns is carried out, we advise that the houses and lands abutting on each of the existing wards shall be added to such wards, and no further alteration will be necessary, nor was it asked for in any of those towns. Banbridge has two wards, the eastern and the western, which return five and ten Commissioners respectively. Having regard to the extent and valuation of the increased area which we recommend, we think that the new district should be formed into a separate ward to be called the "New Ward," and that the numbers of Commissioners should then be seven for the Western Ward, four for the Eastern Ward, and four for the New Ward.

Loans have been obtained by some of the towns in this class for the purposes of the Act of 1854, and the Public Health Acts of 1874 and 1878. The rates of the existing towns are at present ample security for the money due in respect of such loans, and we do not advise that any exemption from the charges due on them should be made in favour of the property in the new boundary. To the extent of the differential rating which we propose with respect to such property, we think it derives and will derive a full benefit from being included within the township boundary, and we think that such property should be liable, with the other property in the township, to the debts of the township.

It may be necessary to consider in future legislation how far the clauses of the Towns Improvement Act, with respect to the regulation of towns, and to obstruction and nuisances in the streets, and to the suppression of vagrants and beggars, should be applied to the whole of the new area which we propose for the towns. It is not within our province to offer any suggestions with respect to this matter, but we have thought it right to call your Excellency's attention to it.

The next class of towns, eleven in number, are those under the 9th Geo. IV., c. 82. Your Excellency will perceive that the Select Committee have, in their report, recommended that this Act should be repealed, and that all those towns should be brought under the Towns Improvement Act of 1854. Assuming that this recommendation will be carried out, we do not think it necessary to call your Excellency's attention to the practical difficulties under which the Commissioners in those towns labour in carrying out that Act. All the observations we have already made with respect to the towns under the Towns Improvement Act, and the reasons which have guided us in defining their boundaries, apply with equal force to the towns under this Act. We, therefore, recommend an increase of the boundary of each of those towns, with the exception of Downpatrick, with respect to which the Commissioners requested us to diminish the existing boundary, which we declined to do. On the map of each of these towns we have marked the existing and proposed boundary in green and red lines, and the boundary of the inner area within which we propose that there shall be full taxation, with a blue line. In Youghal and Fethard we have increased the inner area, and we have been obliged to adopt a circular inner area for Fethard. In the remaining nine towns we have adopted the existing boundary as that of the inner area. With respect to the payment of rates, both improvement and sanitary, and both full and differential, we are of opinion that the recommendations hereinbefore made by us as to the towns under the Act of 1854 should be applied to those towns in a similar manner.

No wards exist in any of those towns. The observations we have already made as to not adhering to electoral divisions, apply to the towns in this class, save Dungannon.

In several of the towns in this class some of the public institutions and buildings are outside of the present area, viz.:—

Name of Town.	Public Buildings or Institutions outside present Area.	Name of Town.	Public Buildings or Institutions outside present Area.
Dungannon,	Workhouse.	Tralee,	Magdalen Asylum, Industrial School, and Workhouse.
Mallow,	Workhouse and Railway Station.	Youghal,	Workhouse, Barracks, Industrial School, Bridewell, and Railway Terminus.
Monaghan,	Barracks, Workhouse Hospital and Railway Station.		
Omagh,	Workhouse.		

For the reasons already mentioned we think it most desirable that all those buildings and institutions should be brought within the township area.

We have now to consider the towns and townships in the third class (fourteen in number), which have been formed under special Acts of Parliament and the Acts incorporated with them. Of these Clontarf, Drumcondra, Kilmainham, Pembroke, and Rathmines, have been dealt with in the separate report on the boundaries of Dublin, and also the townships of Blackrock, Dalkey, and Kingstown. The remaining six towns, viz.: Bray, Dungarvan Enniskillen, Galway, Newry, and Queenstown, are constituted as follows:—

BRAY.

Bray

17 & 18 Vic., c. 103. 29 & 30 Vic., c. 261.

Bray having been for some years under "The Towns Improvement (Ireland) Act, 1854," became a township under the Act 29 & 30 Vic., cap. 261, with which certain clauses of the former Act (including the 62nd) were incorporated. It has the management and maintenance of its own roads, which together with the proportion of the county at large charges to the Grand Juries of the County of Dublin and Wicklow are paid for out of the "Bray Township Rate," (which is limited by the 63rd section of the Act to the sum of 2s. 6d. in the pound) on all the property in the Township, save those classes of property mentioned in the 62nd section of the Towns Improvement Act, which only pay one-fourth rates. The other rates payable in Bray are the "Bray Township Water Rate," not exceeding 1s. in the pound, under the 64th section of the Act, and the "Sinking Fund Special Rate," under the 73rd section, which varies annually in amount, but by the 89th section of the Act the rates under this Act shall not exceed in any one year the sum of 3s. 6d. in the pound for any purpose whatever. For this the Township is supplied with lighting and high-pressure water, and the roads and footways have been made and maintained, and a good deal of sanitary work has been done. The county cess which has been paid outside the boundary may be taken at an average of 1s. 7d. in the pound. The present area of the township is 1,044A. 0R. 15P. and the annual valuation £23,304 13s. 0d.

Ev., 15, et seq. Ev., 25, 27. Ev., 28. Ev., 6, 7.

Complaints were made at Bray that the Town Commissioners did not sufficiently carry out their duties in providing proper lighting, and otherwise, over the whole township, and this was to an extent admitted by Mr. Brett, then their surveyor, who stated that they had not sufficient funds at their disposal to make all the improvements and do all the things they deemed necessary and advisable, and this he attributed to the insufficient area for taxation in the township, and the insufficient funds at the disposal of the Town Commissioners.

Mr. Brett, Evid., Bray, 183. Do., 192.

The Commissioners in reply to the queries sent to them by us stated that the general feeling of the ratepayers was that the present boundaries were unsatisfactory, and that an extension of them was desired, on the general grounds of benefit to the township.

Appendix to Report No. 3.

They subsequently passed a resolution approving of a certain extension on certain terms as to rates.

Appendix to Report No. 5.

We have to draw Your Excellency's attention to a most influentially signed letter from owners of property outside Bray, setting forth objections to any extension of the township boundaries.

With the arguments contained in this document we cannot concur. We have already expressed our opinion to the effect that, *primâ facie*, every town under a municipal authority has or should have its urban and suburban districts, or its inner and outer areas, with full and partial taxation respectively. We, therefore, recommend the extension shown on the Map, which will be found amongst those annexed to this report.

In considering the rates to which the outer area in this case should be subject, we find an element which was absent in the cases dealt with hitherto in this report, namely, that the extern property which would be brought in by the proposed extension would, *ipso facto*, be severed from the county in which it lies at present as regards its liability to the portion of county cess for baronial charges.

We are of opinion that a rate to defray these charges should still continue to be paid in full by the property brought in by any extension, besides a differential rate towards the general charges of the town.

We cannot see why, when the roads were taken up from the county, any property should have been partially exempted from being rated to their maintenance, as has been the case in Bray, by allowing the 62nd clause of "The Towns Improvement (Ireland) Act" to apply to the "Bray Township Rate," from which the charges corresponding to those of county cess are defrayed, and we think that the differential rating within the present boundary *for such charges* should cease.

A fair solution of the difficulty would be to separate from the "Bray Township Rate" a "Bray Road Rate" from which there should be no exemptions, and this we recommend.

This, it will be observed, differs from the suggestion contained in the resolution of the Bray Commissioners, that the extern property to be brought in should "pay the present county rate in full as now paid to the Grand Jury." The proposed road rate may be different from the county cess in amount, and there is evidence here, as in the cases of other towns, that it will be less. (Appendix to Report No. 3.)

We consider that the Bray Water Rate should not be levied on the outer area. (Evidence, 135, 156, 159, of seq.)

Under the Act of 1866 the Commissioners were empowered to borrow £10,000 for the purposes of the Act, including the construction of sea-embankments, market-house, and Bray Bridge Road. Under this Act and the Sanitary Acts they borrowed £7,600 for sewerage, water-mains, and Bray Bridge Road; of this a large portion is now repaid or secured by sinking fund. (Bray, Evid.)

The Bray Township Act of 1881 authorized the construction of sea walls, a pier, harbour, and outfall sewers; and by section 41 the Commissioners are empowered to borrow £50,000 for the purposes of the Act. (44 & 45 Vic., c. 143.)

The powers of constructing works under the Act of 1866 have lapsed. We consider that the outer area, which we propose, should contribute to the charge in respect of loans which have been incurred under the Act of 1866 and the Sanitary Acts, but we think that the inner area alone should be liable for the charges which may result from the exercise of the borrowing powers conferred by the Act of 1881.

The rates, excepting the Road Rate, to be levied and assessed in the outer area as already recommended by us in the case of towns under the Towns Improvement Act, 1854.

The proposed extension will add to the town about 3,300 acres, having a valuation of about £8,000.

We consider that the boundaries of the wards might be extended as shown on the map, so as to add to each of the present wards the adjacent portion of the extended area.

DUNGARVAN.

The municipality of Dungarvan is constituted under the "Towns Improvement (Ireland) Act, 1854," which was there adopted in 1855. (Ev., 2.)

The area is 1,349a. 3a. 31p., the valuation £8,793 10s. (1878), and the population 7,700. The Commissioners are the Urban Sanitary Authority. (Ev., 10, 153.)

By "The Dungarvan Harbour, Markets, and Improvement Act, 1863," sec. 32, the power then vested in the Grand Jury of making or maintaining roads was transferred to the Commissioners. Section 39 provides that the town shall continue to contribute its proportion of county-at-large charges. (26 Vic., c. 45.)

By sections 35 and 36 the Commissioners are empowered to raise a road-rate, being an equal rate in addition to those they were then authorised to raise under the Act of 1854, to be levied in the same way. By section 37 this rate is not to exceed 2s. in the pound in any one year, except that, with consent of ratepayers given as therein provided, it may be increased to 2s. 6d.

By section 4 the "Towns Improvement (Ireland) Act, 1854," is to be read, where not inconsistent, as if it were one with this Act.

The "road-rate," which at first amounted to the full 2s., was gradually reduced till it was 1s., at which amount it continued for five years previous to the inquiry. (Ev., 42.)

From 1863 to 1878 the "road-rate" was levied equally on all descriptions of property, the Commissioners having assessed it as if the differential rating of the 62nd section of the Act of 1854 did not apply to the "road-rate." In 1878 a ratepayer appealed against the assessment of the full rate on his agricultural land, and his appeal was successful. It would, therefore, appear that the Commissioners' view was erroneous and they have only the power to assess for "road-rate" at one-fourth rate on the properties named in the 62nd section of the Act of 1854. (Ev., 40, 41. See Mr. Anthony's letter, Appendix A. Town Clerk's letter, Appendix B.)

On this decision being given against them, the Commissioners applied to us to recommend a reduction of their area to that of the town proper. This we have not thought proper to do, as in passing their Special Act, Parliament thought it right that the Commissioners should be the Road Authority in their district; but we recommend that the road-rate should be made a full rate on all properties, it being manifestly in lieu of the portion of county cess formerly applicable to the maintenance and repair of the roads and bridges.

The improvement-rate has always been struck at its maximum amount of 1s. in the pound for lighting the town, paying the salaries of the officers, and for sanitary purposes. (Ev., 67, 68.)

An improved water-supply is said to be urgently required, and a Provisional Order (Ev., 69.)

DUNGARVAN. to obtain lands for the purpose was sanctioned by the Local Government Board, and
Ev., 108. confirmed by Act of Parliament; but the project has been abandoned, solely on account
Ev., 112. of the increase of taxation which would be caused by it. The estimated cost of the scheme was £6,000.

Ev., 147, 248. The length of roads within the borough is stated to be ten miles, and the cost of maintenance has varied from £438 to £230 per annum. There is, however, a divided opinion as to the way the roads have been maintained since they were taken up from the county.

The evidence tends to show that the roads can be properly maintained with the rate authorized by the Special Act, if levied in full on all properties, but not if the 62nd section of the Act of 1854 is to be operative.

Ev., 134, 174, 189, 250. The evidence shows that great advantages are derived from being within a distance of from two to two and a half miles of this important town.

We think that the boundary should be extended, as shown by the red line on the map.

We propose that all properties be assessed in full for the road-rate, and that the improvement-rate be assessed and levied on the present township as an "Inner Area" and on the district outside as an "Outer Area," as recommended above by us in the case of towns under the Act of 1854.

Ev., 90. The want of a new and proper water-supply is clearly shown by the evidence, and by the fact that the Local Government Board issued, and Parliament confirmed, a
Ev., 97, 98. Provisional Order to acquire property by compulsion for the purpose, and only want of
Ev., 108. funds has prevented the carrying out of the works.

We propose that the added area shall bear some portion of the expenses, and recommend that the expenses of the water-supply be defrayed by a domestic water-rate within the Inner Area and a public water-rate over the whole township, the latter being one-fourth of the amount of the former rate.

County Treasurer's Accounts. The county cess in the barony surrounding Dungarvan was about 3s. 5d. in the pound, of which 1s. 3½d. was for the Waterford, Dungarvan, and Lismore Railway Guarantee, and 4½d. for the county-at-large charges, leaving the assessment for roads 1s. 7½d.

The rates assessed within the town were—the road-rate, 1s. in the pound; the railway guarantee, 1s. in the pound, and county-at-large charges 5½d., and the improvement-rate 1s.—altogether 3s. 5½d. in the pound, and under our proposal the rating on the outer area would be 2s. 8½d. for the road-rate, railway guarantee, and county-at-large charges, and 6d. for improvement-rate—altogether 3s. 2d. in the pound, or if 3d. be added for a public water-rate it would be 3s. 5d., the same as paid at present; but, if our recommendation is adopted, portion of this will be paid by the landlord.

The area of the district proposed to be added is 4,285a. 1r. 11p., having a valuation of £5,040. We propose that the adjacent portions of this extension should be added to the two existing wards respectively.

ENNISKILLEN.

ENNISKILLEN.
32 & 34 Vic., c. 143. The municipality of Enniskillen is constituted under "The Enniskillen Borough Improvement Act, 1870," with which are incorporated several sections of the "Towns Improvement (Ireland) Act, 1854," but omitting the 62nd section.

By section 6 the boundaries of the borough were extended so as to be co-extensive with the boundaries of the Parliamentary borough. Sections 8 to 15, inclusive, provide for the annexation of adjacent districts, with the consents of the Lord Lieutenant and Grand Jury of the county.

By section 16 the charge of the roads within the borough is transferred from the Grand Jury to the Commissioners, and by subsequent sections the levying of county cess is to cease, but the borough continues liable to contribute to county-at-large charges in proportion to its valuation.

By section 29 the "Borough of Enniskillen Improvement Rate" is sanctioned, not to exceed in any year 2s. 6d. in the pound, and to be applicable to maintenance, construction, and repair of roads, and the carrying out of the provisions of the Act relating thereto.

Ev., 5, 31, 15. By section 42 a water-rate, limited in any one year to 1s. 6d. in the pound, is sanctioned.

The area of the township is 314a. 2r. 14p., the population in (1871) 5,836, and the valuation £11,388.

The Commissioners, being appointed under a special Act, are the Urban Sanitary Authority.

Ev., 29. The rates struck have since 1874 been 2s. for improvement-rate and 1s. 4d. for water-rate.
Ev., 27. These rates are levied equally on all descriptions of property.
Ev., 31. The county cess in the adjoining baronies has varied from 1s. 10d. to 2s. in the pound.

The lands in the neighbourhood of the town are let at very high rates. Enniskillen.

The Commissioners were not desirous of having any alteration in the boundary, but the Chairman stated that if there was to be an extension they would have adopted one "by townlands." Ev., 67. Ev., 17.

We recommend that the boundary be extended to include the townlands of Portora, Drumlyon, Colehill, Mullaneraw, Hascolo, Carrigan, Rossory, Derrychara, Breandrum, Drumclay, Kilmacormick, and Cornagrade. Ev., 78.

We think that all property within the area, as extended, should contribute equally to a road-rate, applicable to the maintenance, &c., of the roads in the same way as county cess.

We have marked an inner area, consisting of the present township with the addition of that portion of the townland of Windmill Hill, which is at present excluded.

The road-rate being taken out of the improvement-rate, we think the property within the inner area should contribute full rates for the other purposes of the improvement-rate, and the property in the outer area to contribute one-half rates, to be levied as recommended above in the case of towns under the "Towns Improvement (Ireland) Act, 1854."

The outer area not to be liable to the water-rate.

The area of the extension proposed is 2,036A. 3R. 26P., of which 408 acres is water, and its valuation is about £2,964.

GALWAY.

Galway.

By the Act of 6 & 7 William IV. (Local and Personal), c. 117, intituled "An Act for Regulating and Improving the Town of Galway, in the County of the same Town," certain charter tolls therein mentioned were abolished, and other tolls therein mentioned were substituted, which were vested in the Commissioners therein named, and their successors for ever, to be applied in the manner therein mentioned for the benefit and improvement of the said town and the environs thereof, within the distance of one mile from the collegiate church of St. Nicholas, as the said Commissioners should think fit. 6 & 7 Wm. IV., c. 117 (Local and Personal).

By the Municipal Corporations Act (1840), the body corporate of the Mayor, Sheriffs, Free Burgesses, and Commonalty of the town and county of the town of Galway was dissolved, and all real and personal estate of such body corporate in conjunction with the said town, was forthwith vested in the said Commissioners, under said former Act, upon the trusts therein mentioned, until a charter of incorporation should be obtained, and before the granting of any fresh charter, and the election of a council under its provisions, the powers of such Commissioners as to the said estate was to cease, and any accumulation thereof, forthwith to vest without any conveyance thereof in the body so incorporated. 3 & 4 Vic., c. 108.

By the Galway Town Improvement Act, 1853, 16 & 17 Vic., c. 200 (Local and Personal), the area of one mile from the church of St. Nicholas was extended to a circle of two miles from said church, and the Commissioners then acting for the town were incorporated with perpetual successors, under the name of the Galway Town Improvement Commissioners. 16 & 17 Vic., c. 200 (Local and Personal).

By the 70th section, the improvement rate is to be applied to—1st. cost of Act; 2nd. interest on loans; 3rd. sinking fund; 4th. making new streets, widening streets, the erection of markets, and in making sewers; 5th. paying all moneys due on improvement rate. By the 7th section, the town is divided into four Wards.

By the 3rd section of the Galway Town Provisional Order of 1871, confirmed by the 35 Vic., c. 2, the Commissioners were empowered in addition to all other rates which they had then power to levy, to make, assess and levy such equal rate, to be called the "paving and repairing rate," as might be necessary for the purpose to which the said rate was thereinafter made applicable, not exceeding in any one year 2s. in the pound of the full net annual value of the property included in "the improvement rate," to be apportioned as the poor law rate is apportioned between landlord and tenant. The Commissioners also levy a public water rate of 3d. in the pound, and a domestic water rate under the 72nd section of the Act of 1853. 35 Vic., c. 2. Ev., 6, 9. Ev., 38, 48, et seq.

The area of the municipality of Galway is now contained within a circle of two miles from the church of St. Nicholas, it is all comprised within the electoral division of Galway, which however is considerably larger, and has an excess of valuation of about £2,554 17s. a year. Ev., 8.

The area of the present town comprises 24,132 acres, and its valuation is £30,185. The county of the town of Galway extends for a distance of about four Irish miles, or five English, from the centre of the town, and comprises the residue of Ev., 2. Ev., 3.

GALWAY.

the electoral division of Galway, parts of the electoral divisions of Ballintemple and Carraghbrow, and the entire of that of Barna.

Ev., 66. Ev., 62. Ev., 33.

There are four wards in the town, which are conterminous with those for poor law purposes within the municipal boundary, but the latter wards extend further out in the electoral divisions. There is not any differential rating with respect to railways or agricultural land. All classes of property under the Acts of 1853 and 1875, pay full rates.

Ev., 65. Ev., 133, 134, 140. Ev., 115, et seq.

Two propositions were made to us at Galway: one made by the Commissioners, was to extend the municipal boundary to the full extent of the boundary of the county of the town—and the other, to extend it at least, so as to take in the whole of the electoral division; while Major Lynch, J.P., one of the Commissioners, strongly opposed any change in the present boundary. In considering the first proposal, we have not lost sight of the recommendation contained in the Report of the Select Committee, "that all fiscal powers of the Grand Jury in counties of towns should be transferred to the Town Council," which in this case would be the Galway Town Commissioners. We cannot however, approve of such an extension of the municipality, as would include the entire of the county of the town of Galway. The suggestion of Major Lynch was, that all the lands and railways comprised in the county of the town outside the limits of the present municipality, should be taken from the county of the town and added to the county of Galway. It is not within our province to offer any suggestions on this point, further than that it points out the way in which the recommendation of the Select Committee, above alluded to, might be carried out. We do not recommend any extension of the boundary so as to include the entire of the electoral division. It would be unequal and irregular, and we cannot see that it would serve any useful purpose. We, therefore, recommend that the present boundary should remain as it was fixed by Act of Parliament in 1853; and it is to be remarked, that no application for an extension of boundaries was made by the Commissioners, when they sought the Provisional Order in 1875. We see no reason for any change in the present boundaries of the wards. We do not recommend that any change should be made as to any of the rates at present payable by any classes of the rateable property in the town, further than that all sanitary rates should be divided between landlord and tenant, in the same manner as the other rates are at present divided.

NEWRY.

NEWRY.

17 & 18 Vic., c. 103. 34 & 35 Vic., c. 98. Ev., 17, 6. Ev., 1. Ev., 9, 10. Ev., 23, 20.

Newry is governed by the Towns Improvement Act of 1854, and the Newry Improvement and Water Act of 1871.

Newry was one of the first towns constituted under the 9th of Geo. IV. In 1865 it adopted the provisions of the Towns Improvement Act, and an area comprising 711A. 2R. 4P., was then defined as the municipal boundary.

The population of the borough, by the Census of 1871, was 14,078, and a considerable increase is believed to have taken place since that time.

The valuation, which in the year 1865, was £24,000, has now increased to £30,468.

By the Act of 1871 the roads within the borough are exempted from the jurisdiction of the Grand Jury and placed under the Town Commissioners. This Act also empowered the Commissioners to erect a town hall, to establish markets, fairs, and slaughter house, and to acquire and protect existing market rights, to make a public park, to erect public baths and wash-houses, and to supply water to the town.

The 31st sec. of the Act empowers the Commissioners to levy a maximum town rate of 2s. in the £ on all the rateable property within the borough, and by the following section a water rate to the extent of not exceeding 1s. in the £ may be struck.

The Commissioners are authorized to borrow £89,000, and have availed themselves of these powers to the extent of £74,000, £42,000 of which has been applied to the construction of waterworks and markets, and the remaining £32,000 to the purchase and improvement of gas works.

The £42,000 is being paid off in sixty half-yearly instalments, and the £32,000 by eighty half-yearly instalments; of the former loan £35,000 remained unpaid at the time of our sitting, and of the latter loan £31,516.

The Parliamentary boundary comprises an area of 2,548 acres.

Ev., 34, et seq.

The town is one of rising commercial importance, and building is largely increasing.

We recommend that the existing municipal boundary be adopted as the inner area, and this we have marked blue on the accompanying map, and that the boundary thereon, marked in red, be that of the outer area.

We think that a Road Rate should be created as we have proposed in the case of Bray township, and that the outer area should contribute with a differential rating to the charges of the town in the same way as in Bray, the exemptions in the case of Newry being the charges for water and gas.

The outer area we consider should be as defined by the red lines on the same map. There are three wards in the town, the north, south, and west ward. We recommend that the portion of the extension in the county Armagh be added to the West Ward, and that the remainder be divided equally between the North and South Ward. Newry.

The additional area contained in the proposed extension would be 3,008A. 3R. 8P., with a valuation of about £18,000.

QUEENSTOWN.

Queenstown.

Queenstown is governed by the Towns Improvement Act of 1854, and a Local Act entitled the Queenstown Improvement Act, 1863. Under this latter Act the jurisdiction over the roads within the borough is transferred from the Grand Jury to the Town Commissioners, who are empowered to strike a road rate, which is not to exceed 1s. 6d. in the pound. 17 & 18 Vic., c. 103. 26 Vic., c. 21. Ev., 4.

The Grand Jury are authorized to levy on the town its proportion of the county at large charges.

The Act also authorises the Commissioners to provide a mortuary; to erect public conveniences; and to appoint and maintain a staff of watchmen. The area of the township is 589A. 3R. 29P., and the valuation £19,232. The population by the census of 1871 was 10,334. Ev., 2, 3.

The Town Commissioners are the Sanitary Authority, and, under the Public Health Act, they have borrowed £3,850; of this sum they have expended, in their capacity as Burial Board, £400, and the remainder has been applied to the making of sewers and other sanitary improvements; £4,724 of this loan still remains to be paid off. We recommend that the existing municipal boundary shall be the limits of the inner area, and that the outer area should be as defined by the red lines on the accompanying map. This will give an increased area to the town of about 1,946 acres and an increased valuation of about £2,841.

The road rate is assessed and levied as the town improvement rate, and, consequently, certain properties under Sec. 68 of the Act of 1854, pay only one-fourth rate, we think the differential rating should be abolished, and all properties should contribute in full to the road rate; the other rates on the inner and outer areas being respectively as previously recommended for towns under the Act of 1854.

The cities and towns in the fourth class remain to be considered. Of these, Dublin with its adjacent townships form the subject of Part II. of this Report, and the Cities of Cork and Belfast are dealt with in Part IV.

CARRICKFERGUS.

Carrickfergus.

The municipal government of Carrickfergus consists of Commissioners appointed under the provisions of the 16th section of the Municipal Corporation Act, 1840, and the Select Committee in their Report have recommended that this town should be forthwith brought under the provisions of the Towns Improvement (Ireland) Act, 1854. We do not recommend any alteration in the boundary at present, but if the Towns Improvement (Ireland) Act, 1854, be adopted, the question should be reconsidered.

CLONMEL.

Clonmel.

The town of Clonmel is constituted under the Municipal Corporations Act, and under the Towns Improvement (Ireland) Act, 1854, which was adopted in its entirety, on the 15th October, 1855. In 1878, a Provisional Order was issued by the Local Government Board for Ireland, transferring the fiscal powers of the Grand Juries of the counties of Waterford and Tipperary, with regard to roads, bridges, footpaths, and public works within the borough, except such as concern the county at large, to the Corporation of Clonmel; the order was confirmed by an Act of Parliament in the following year. 3 & 4 Vic., c. 108. 17 & 18 Vic., c. 103. 42 & 43 Vic., c. 84. (Local).

The present area of the township is 331 acres; the population in 1871 was 10,112; and the annual valuation in 1879 was £15,325. Ev., 6, 7, 10.

There are two wards. East Ward, the valuation of which is £8,362, containing 155 burgesses; and West Ward containing 126 burgesses, and valued at £6,963. Ev., 11, 12, 152.

The municipal rate from 1874 to 1878, was 1s. 4d. in the pound each year, and in the latter year a rate of 4d. was struck under the Towns Improvement Act, to clear away an overdraft at the bank. Ev., 25. Ev., 150.

The County Cess in the borough in 1876, was 1s. 10d. in the pound, and in adjacent baronies it varied from 1s. 7d. to 1s. 7½d.

The Corporation passed a resolution approving of an extension of about one quarter of a mile all round the present boundary on the north side of the River Suir, and including the suburban townlands of Oldbridge, Glebe, Raheen, and Croan lower, on the south side Ev., 69, et seq.

Clonmel.

Ev., 120. Ev., 83.

of the river. In passing this resolution, the Corporation contemplated a reasonable supply of water and gas to the district to be taken in; and with regard to one part, Oldbridge, there was the particular reason for desiring to include it, that being a "most unsanitary place;" the proper sanitation of it, thereby "preventing a pestilence arising there, and spreading through the valuable portion of the town," was of great importance. This question of the sanitary control of Oldbridge being in the hands of the urban authority, was spoken to by nearly every witness, and we quite agree in its desirability.

Ev., 145, 186, 208, 249, 325, 331, 398, 447, 475.

It was pointed out, that great advantage would result from the railway station being brought within the jurisdiction of the Mayor and borough magistrates.

Ev., 139, et seq., 179.

The town is situated in two electoral divisions, Clonmel and St. Mary's, either or both of which are quite unsuited from their size and shape to be constituted the area of the borough.

We recommend the extension as shown by the red line on the map of Clonmel attached to this Report, with an inner area as marked by the blue line. The cost of roads, &c., and the county at large charges in the whole district should, we think, be assessed and levied as the borough rate, and other rates in the inner and outer area should be assessed and levied as we have recommended for towns under the Town Improvement Act 1854.

We think that the portion of the extension in the county Tipperary should be divided between and added to the existing wards, as shown by the dotted green line on the map, and that the increase on the south side of the river, together with so much of each of the existing wards as is situate in the county Waterford, should be formed into a new ward to be called the South Ward, and we suggest that this new ward should return one Alderman and three Councillors. The increment in area which we propose would be 1,496A. 3R. 16P., and its annual valuation about £4,273. The valuation of the proposed new ward on the south side of the river would be about £2,700, while that of the proposed East Ward and West Ward respectively, would be £8,534 15s., and £8,308 5s.

DROGHEDA.

Drogheda.

3 & 4 Vic., c. 108.

The borough of Drogheda is constituted under the Municipal Corporations Act of 1840.

Ev., 1. Ev., 2, 3.

The acreage within the present boundary is 531A. 3R. 27P., this area was originally defined by the Act of 1840, since which time no alteration in the municipal limits has taken place.

Ev., 11.

The valuation of the borough is £19,104, and the population in 1871 was 13,510.

Ev., 32, et seq. Ev., 254, 291.

The repair and maintenance of the roads within the borough is vested in the Grand Jury of the County of the Town of Drogheda, who exercise their functions over an area which is conterminous with the municipal boundary. The county cess levied by the Grand Jury of the town, averages about 1s. 6d. in the pound.

Ev., 332. Ev., 123.

The Corporation have within the last ten years carried out extensive sanitary improvements at considerable cost, which necessitated a sanitary rate being levied at the time, but no municipal rate has ever been struck, as the corporate income has been found sufficient to meet the expenditure.

Ev., 130, et seq.

The annual value of the property vested in the Corporation is about £4,000 a year, and it is anticipated that, as some leases fall in during the next few years, the rental will be largely increased.

Ev., 16, 78. Ev., 123.

The Corporation were of opinion that the municipal area was too circumscribed and that the present boundary should be extended to a radius of two miles from the centre of the town. The arguments in favour of this extension were not based on the necessity for an increased area of taxation; but principally that it was desirable that the Borough Magistrates should have power to exercise their functions over a wider area, as the railway station which was the traffic centre of the town, the workhouse, and several other places were outside the town, and consequently without the jurisdiction of the borough authorities.

Ev., 123.

Much inconvenience was felt to be the result of this. The principal traffic of the town is through the railway. Cars assemble there, and the station is thronged with people at the going and coming of every train, and if any dispute occurs, or any offence is committed, the case has to be brought before the Meath magistrates instead of being dealt with at once by the local magistrates, and it was alleged that offenders were frequently allowed to go unpunished in consequence of the trouble which was entailed by bringing them to a remote petty sessions court.

Ev., 123.

Similar inconveniences were pointed out in the case of the workhouse, as in the event of an inquest having to be held, the coroner of the county of Meath has to be com-

communicated with, and brought from a distance, although the borough coroner lives close at hand.

The Corporation anticipated that in the event of their acquiring the extended area they sought, the income derivable from their property would still prove adequate to meet the increased expenditure over the new area, and as no further sanitary improvements for the town were required, or in contemplation, the corporate property would still be found sufficient to maintain the present sanitary staff and arrangements. On the grounds of the general policy, that the suburbs of every large town within a certain distance beyond the built-upon portion or town proper, should be under the municipal jurisdiction for police and sanitary purposes, we propose a new boundary, which will extend to a distance of from one and a-half to two miles from the centre of the town, following, as far as possible, townland boundaries. The area would then be 7,091 acres, and the valuation about £13,500. Ev., 130, et seq. Ev., 147.

We have marked on the map an "inner area" for full taxation, in case, at any time, it should become necessary to strike a municipal rate.

We propose no alteration in the boundaries of the existing wards, but that the suburbs brought in should be divided into portions to be added to the wards to which they are adjacent.

KILKENNY.

The municipal boundary of the borough of Kilkenny as fixed by the Corporation Act, was retained as the boundary under the Towns Improvement Act, the provisions of which were adopted in 1856. 3 & 4 Vic., c. 108. 17 & 18 Vic., c. 103.

The area of the borough is 878A. 0R. 30P., and the valuation is £17,238 6s. Ev., 4.

The population is 12,710, and it is not believed to be increasing. Ev., 9, 14.

The Corporation have an income arising from rents and rentcharges, market and fair dues, amounting in the aggregate to about £4,236 a year. Hitherto the necessity has not arisen to levy a borough rate, or a rate for sanitary purposes, as the income derived from the corporate property has been found adequate to meet the requirements of the town. Ev., 30, 31. Ev., 168. Ev., 14, 42.

We beg to submit the following recommendations:—That the present boundary be taken as the inner area, over which the Corporation may levy a full rate, and that the outer area be adopted as defined by the red lines on the accompanying map. There are two wards in Kilkenny, St. John's and St. Canice's, and we recommend that the portions of the new area should be annexed to them in the manner described on the map. Ev., 20.

In the event of the suggestion of the Select Committee, that the fiscal powers of the Grand Juries of the cities of the towns should be vested in the Town Council being carried out, we think that a road rate should be struck over the entire area, in the manner we have described in the case of Bray.

The additional area which we propose to include within the municipal boundary will be about 6,071 acres, of which 41A. 3R. 39P. is water, and the valuation of the borough will be thus increased by £10,493.

LIMERICK.

The boundaries of the city of Limerick were fixed by the Municipal Corporations Act, 1840, and by the same Act the city was divided into five wards. 3 & 4 Vic., c. 108.

By the Limerick Corporation Act, 1853, the wards were re-arranged, and increased in number to eight. 16 & 17 Vic., c. 73.

By the Limerick Improvement Act, 1853, section 37, the fiscal powers of the Grand Jury of the City ceased, and were transferred to the Corporation; by the 39th and following sections a rate for General Purposes, for all purposes theretofore provided for by the Grand Jury, was authorized; but this rate is not to be applied to the making, enlarging, repairing, or paving any street, road, or passage within the borough. 16 & 17 Vic., c. 196.

By the 67th section portions of the Towns Improvement Clauses Act, 1847, are incorporated, including section 167 of that Act, by which every person occupying lands used as arable, meadow, or pasture ground only, or as woodlands or market gardens, or nursery grounds, shall be rated in the proportion of one-third part only of the net annual value. 10 & 11 Vic., c. 34.

By the 63th section the expense of making, maintaining, and cleansing the present or future sewers are to be defrayed out of the Improvement rate.

By the 77th section the Corporation are authorised to assess and levy an equal rate, to be called "The Improvement Rate," not exceeding in any one year five shillings in the pound, on the annual value of the property included in such rate.

LIMERICK.

By the 72nd section no other rates can be levied except a "borough rate" under 3 and 4 Vic., c. 108, sec. 133, and 3 and 4 Vic., c. 109, sec. 10, by the latter of which the amount of the borough rate is now restricted to 3d. in each year.

28 Vic., c. 8. By the Limerick Improvement Amendment Act, 1865, the Corporation was empowered to construct an embankment to reclaim a foreshore adjoining the lands of Courtbrack and Corkanree. By the 15th section the limits of the borough were extended so as to include the lands acquired and reclaimed by the Corporation.

Ev., 28. The rates struck from 1874 to 1878 are as follows:—

	General Purposes Rate.		Improvement Rate.	
	s.	d.	s.	d.
1874, ...	2	0	3	10
1875, ...	1	11½	4	2
1876, ...	1	3	3	7
1877, ...	1	10	4	1
1878, ...	1	3	4	6

No borough rate has ever been struck.

Ev., 112, 117, 118. The present area of the city is 2,074 acres; the annual valuation, £65,359, of which £64,610 is assessable; and the population (in 1871), 44,209.

Ev., 729. The area of the Parliamentary borough is much more extensive, containing 31,753 acres, and extending on the west and south about five miles, and on the east six miles, from the centre of the city.

Ev., 134–5. The electoral division of Limerick contains 6,321 acres, and is of the annual valuation of £78,763.

Ev., 107, 234. Ev., 16, et seq. A good deal of evidence was given in favour of an extension of the present boundary. The Corporation passed a resolution on the 10th January, 1879, seeking an extension to the limits of the Parliamentary borough; the intention being to take over the additional area from the County Grand Jury, on the terms of the Limerick Improvement Act, 1853.

We do not think such an extensive development is desirable, but we recommend an extension of the present boundary, as shown on the map with this Report, and embracing the townlands set out on said map, which will add to the existing area 4,333 acres, and to the valuation about £9,500. The boundary differs from that of the electoral division by the exclusion of some townlands at the north-west, which are more than two miles from the centre of the town.

We propose that the cost of maintaining the roads, &c., which is now borne by the Improvement Rate should be in future defrayed by a Road Rate, to be assessed and levied on all property, in the same manner as County Cess; and that the Improvement Rate in the inner and outer areas be assessed and levied, as recommended by us for towns under the Towns Improvement (Ireland) Act, 1854; railways being added to the list of differentially-rated properties.

LONDONDERRY.

LONDONDERRY.

11 & 12 Vic., c. 141. 18 & 19 Vic., c. 84. 27 & 28 Vic., c. 181. Londonderry is constituted under the Towns Improvement Act, and under the Londonderry Improvement Acts of 1848, 1855, and 1864.

By the Act of 1848, the Corporation were given the control and management of the roads within the municipal limits, and were empowered to levy an improvement rate not to exceed 4s. in the pound on the net annual value. The 70th section of this Ac provided that every house, building, or garden situated more than 100 yards from a

Ev., 40, 41. public lamp should only be liable to one-third of the rate.

The Corporation were authorized to borrow £40,000 by the Act of 1848, and by the subsequent Act their borrowing powers were extended to a further sum of £1,000 They have contracted loans up to the full limit, and the money has been applied t the establishment of public markets, a cemetery, and a water supply.

By the Act of 1864, the municipal boundary was extended to its present area, which comprises an acreage of 2,464.

Ev., 16. There are three wards in the borough—the North, South, and East wards, th valuation of which is as follows—North ward, £28,434; South ward, £17,198 10s. East ward, £26,165; making the total valuation of the Borough £71,798 10s. (h £58,200 of this amount the full rate is assessed, and the one-third rate on th remainder.

We have marked with a blue line the area which we believe is at present liable t the full rate, and in the view of the so recent legislation on the subject we do no propose to recommend any extension or alteration in the existing municipal boundar or in the boundary of the wards.

SLIGO.

Sligo. *3 & 4 Vic., c. 108. 32 & 33 Vic., c. 147. 43 & 44 Vic., c. 189. Ev., 5, 28.*

Sligo is constituted under the Municipal Corporations Act, 1840, and the Sligo Borough Improvement Act, 1869, and the Sligo Borough Improvement (Revival of Powers) Act, 1880.

By the Act of 1869 the boundary was extended and made conterminous with the Parliamentary boundary, which is a circle of a radius of one and a-half miles. This includes an area of 3,601a. 2r. 28p., which is an increase of 3,501 acres on the former area.

The population in 1871 was 10,670, and the valuation £15,250. The population in 1881 was 10,764. *Ev., 8, 9, 10.*

By the Act of 1869 the powers and duties of the Grand Jury of the county in relation to the applotting and levying of county-cess ceased, but the borough continued liable to contribute towards amounts from time to time presented by the Grand Jury of the county for purposes for which county-cess would have otherwise been leviable in proportion to the valuation of the borough to that of the county. By the 12th section the repairs of streets, roads, passages, footways and bridges are to be borne by the borough fund. By the 147th section the Corporation may, in case the borough fund is insufficient to meet the expenses charged on it, strike a borough rate on all property rateable to the relief of the poor. Land which is arable meadow, pasture only, woodland, market garden or nursery ground is assessable only in the proportion of one-half; houses and buildings situate more than 200 yards from a lamp, or 100 yards from a water main, shall not be liable to more than a maximum of 2s. 6d. in the pound, but it shall not be compulsory on the Corporation to supply such houses with gas or water. By section 148 the Midland Great Western Railway, having been at great expense to obtain a private water supply, are only to be rated in the proportion of one-fourth. By the 149th section the borough rate was limited to 4s. 6d. in the pound, or 5s. when arrangements for carrying out the waterworks were perfected. This maximum included the borough rate of 3d. under the 3 & 4 Vic., c. 108.

The Act also empowers the Corporation to make and maintain water works, to purchase the works of the Gas Company, to establish fairs and markets and to acquire market rights, to construct slaughter-houses, to provide fire engines, and to maintain a staff of firemen, &c.

By the Act of 1880 the powers as to waterworks of the Act of 1869, which had expired, are revived. By the 12th section the Corporation are empowered to strike a water-rate not exceeding 2s. in the pound to be levied and assessed in the same manner as, and in addition to, the borough-rate under the Act of 1869, the maximum of which is 4s. 6d. in the pound in any one year. The Midland Great Western Railway not to be rated at more than 5s. in the pound on their buildings, and in the proportion of one-fourth only on the railway.

The blue line on the map shows the former municipal area, and within which the houses may be rated to a maximum of 6s. 6d. in the pound for borough-rate including water-rate.

Within this area the supply of water free of charge to the inhabitants by the Corporation for domestic purposes is compulsory, outside it the Corporation are authorised but not required to give such supply.

The total liabilities of the Corporation amounted to £11,197 16s. 3d., and this debt stood in debentures, mortgages, and bonds, on which the Corporation at present pay interest at the rate of £5 per cent. per annum. *Ev., 112, et seq. Ev., 118.*

There are twenty-two miles of road within the present borough, and the cost of maintaining these is estimated at £20 per mile. *Ev., 176, 177.*

We are enabled in the case of Sligo to carry out the suggestion of the Select Committee by recommending that the area of the borough be made conterminous with the Electoral Division.

This will place an additional area of 3,067 acres in the hands of the Corporation, and will increase the valuation by £3,667. We recommend that the Corporation shall be empowered to assess and levy rates to the same extent over the enlarged area as they are now authorised to do over the present one.

There are three wards in Sligo, the North, West, and East Ward, and we propose that the extension should be apportioned between them in the manner set down in the map.

WEXFORD.

Wexford. *3 & 4 Vic., c. 108. 17 & 18 Vic., c. 103.*

The municipality of Wexford is constituted under the Municipal Corporations Act, 1840, and a Charter obtained in 1846, the Towns Improvement (Ireland) Act, 1854, and an Act passed in 1878, confirming (among others) a Provisional Order of the Local

Wexford. Government Board for Ireland, transferring to the Corporation the fiscal powers of the Grand Jury within the town.

36 Vic., c. 61 (Local). Ev., 17. Ev., 6, et seq.

The town, the boundary of which is coterminous with that of the Parliamentary Borough, contains 483 acres; with a population of 12,077; and is valued at £15,783 annually. It is divided into three wards.

Ev., 37.

Under the Act of 1840, a borough rate has been struck, varying from 1s. to 9d. in the pound, in the years 1876-7-8, and under the Provisional Order and Act of 1873, a rate has been struck, varying from 2s. to 1s. 10d. in the same years.

Ev., 110.

No improvement rate has ever been struck under the Act of 1854.

By the Provisional Order and Act. 1873, all rates ceased to be levied by the Grand Jury within the town, but the Grand Jury continues to receive the due proportion of county at large charges. By section 7 of the Provisional Order, the Corporation are empowered to make a rate not exceeding 2s. in the pound in any one year, to defray the expenses consequent upon and incident to the transfer of the charge of the roads, bridges, footpaths, and public works, and county at large charges. The application of the rates which have been assessed and levied under this Provisional Order and Act, *(Ev., 38, 71, 94, 156.)* has not been confined to the purposes above stated, but has extended to the "improvement of the town" and sanitary works, on which it would appear about £400 a year *(Ev., 73.)* has been spent, equivalent to the proceeds of a rate of 6d. in the pound. As this rate is assessed and levied as if under the Act of 1854, land and other property mentioned in the 62nd section of that Act, contribute to the maintenance of roads, only in the proportion of one-fourth. As we have previously stated in this Report, in the case of Bray township, we think that there should be no differential rating for maintenance *(Ev., 81.)* of roads, &c. In Wexford, at present, this is of little consequence, but if the extension we propose is carried out, it would be only right, in our opinion, that differential rating for this purpose should be abolished, and a Road Rate created, which should be confined to its proper purposes of maintaining roads, &c., and paying county at large charges to be assessed and levied as county cess is at present; and an improvement rate struck, if necessary, for the other requirements of the town.

Ev., 105, 128.

Opinion was divided in Wexford as to the desirability of an extension, the opponents of it being influenced chiefly by the operation of the 62nd section of the Act of 1854.

We are of opinion, that the boundary should be extended as shown on the map, to take in the entire electoral division of Wexford, and the townlands of Crosstown, Tincone, Ferrybank north, and Ferrybank south, on the north side of the river Slaney.

We propose the present area as the "inner area," and the extension above mentioned as an "outer area," the borough and improvement rates to be assessed and levied in the inner and outer areas as recommended by us in the case of towns under the Towns' Improvement Act, 1854, but the outer area not to be rated for the supply of water to the town.

The charge of the bridge across the river Slaney to remain with the Grand Jury.

We do not recommend any change in the present wards, but that, if the extension we propose is carried out, the present ward boundaries be continued along the same roads to the boundary of the electoral division, and that the four townlands on the north side of the river Slaney be added to St. Selskar's ward. The additional area brought within the town by the proposed extension would be 3,655A. 3R. 31P., with a valuation of about £5,284; and the valuation of the proposed wards would be as follows:—St. Selskar's ward, £5,955 4s.; St. Iberius' ward, £6,505 5s.; and St. Mary's ward, £7,270 5s., respectively.

Waterford.

WATERFORD.

The boundary of the city of Waterford was fixed by The Municipal Corporation Act, 3 & 4 Vic., c. 108, and is the same as that of the county of the city of Waterford.

Ev., 8. Ev., 5. Ev., 4. Ev., 21. Ev., 36. Ev., 41.

The area within the municipal boundary is 499A. 2R. 15P., and the valuation in 1879 was £88,739 5s. The population was stated to be about 24,000. No municipal rate has ever been levied. Under the Act authorizing the waterworks, rates will be levied, the public water-rate being limited to 3d. in the pound, and the domestic water-rate to 1s. in the pound. The portion of the city which lies on the north side of the river Suir is wholly exempted from these water-rates by a Provisional Order issued by the Local Government Board for Ireland on 1st June, 1876, which was subsequently confirmed by Act of Parliament, 39 & 40 Vic., c. 183 (Local and Personal).

Ev., 84. Ev., 70.

The City Grand Jury Cess at the time of the inquiry was 2s. 1d. in the £, and the County Grand Jury Cess in the baronies adjoining the city was, on an average, 2s. 10d. The maintenance of the roadways, &c., within the city is paid for out of the income of the Corporation, with the exception of one road, for which the City Grand Jury pays *(Ev., 83.)* £33 a year.

In 1875 the Corporation promoted a Bill in Parliament to **extend the area** to be coterminous with the electoral division, and to transfer to **them the fiscal** powers of the County Grand Jury in respect thereof.

Waterford Ev., 1..; Ev., 67; Ev., 52; Ev., 36.

The question of extending the boundaries had been considered by the Corporation, and the finance committee to whom it was referred adopted a boundary which would be an extension of about one half-mile beyond the present boundary on the south side, and of about one quarter-mile on the north side of the River Suir. It was calculated that the cost of the roads, &c., with £100 a year for additional sanitary supervision, would be met by a rate of 2s. 3d. in the £, showing a considerable advantage to the persons brought in. This extension would have brought into the city about 1,400 acres additional, the rateable value of which was £6,990. It was proposed that this extension should be subject to the public water-rate, but not to the domestic water-rate. The Corporation, on considering the report of the finance committee, resolved that no extension should be made.

Ev., 161.

The present boundary runs along the middle of Barrack-street; this gives rise to an anomalous state of things, namely, that the houses on one side of the street will be assessed for water-rates, but not those on the other side, and of two military barracks in this street—one is within and the other without the City.

Ev., 143.

There are several public buildings and a large number of residences immediately outside the municipal boundary.

We beg to direct attention to the evidence that the sanitary state of the suburban district will be better attended to if it be brought under the Urban Authority, who have better arrangements for attending to it than are at the disposal of the Board of Guardians who, as Rural Authority, have charge of the district outside the municipal boundary at present.

Ev., 196, 241, 315.

We recommend that the boundary of the city be extended to that of the electoral division, as shown by the external red line on the map which we have prepared, and on which we have also shown, by a blue line, the boundary which we propose for the inner area.

The fiscal powers of the Grand Jury of the County being transferred to the Corporation as regards the maintenance of roads, bridges, and footways, we recommend that a rate be struck, to be called a road rate, and that all property be equally assessed to it. All property within the inner area should be assessed to the public water rate; but as regards the domestic water-rate, it should only be assessed on premises within a fixed distance of which the water mains may be brought.

The electoral division contains 7,358 acres, with a valuation of £[illegible], **and a** population of about 27,000.

It was remarked at our inquiry that one beneficial effect of this extension of the boundary would be that the population of the city would be increased to beyond 25,000, so that the Artizans Dwellings Act would become applicable, and evidence was given that in such event the Act would probably be at once availed of, to the great benefit of the city.

Ev., 161.

[illegible] & 39 Vic., c. 36. Ev., 163, 163-5.

The city is at present divided into six wards:—

	Valuation.	Population.
Centre Ward,	15,612	136
Custom House Ward,	5,838	166
South Ward,	[illegible]	131
Tower Ward,	3,740	177
West Ward,	11,155	[illegible]

We think the new ward boundaries should be as shown on the map, the present boundary between West Ward and South Ward being altered so as to be the same as that of the Poor Law wards; and the area north of the river being divided and added to Custom House Ward and Tower Ward respectively.

(Signed),

CHARLES P. COTTON. (Seal.)

H. A. ROBINSON. (Seal.)

VERE ST. LEGER GOOLD, *Secretary.*

June 21, 1882.

APPENDIX TO THE REPORT.

APPENDIX No. 1.

Form I.

Notice of Enquiry.

Municipal Boundaries Commission, Ireland,
Four Courts, Dublin, 18

Sir,—In accordance with the instructions of the Municipal Boundaries Commissioners, I hereby give notice that they will attend at the Town Hall , on , the at o'clock a.m., when they will be prepared to receive such evidence as may be tendered to them on the subject of the existing Boundaries of the Town of , and as to the expediency of extending, limiting, or otherwise altering the same.

I am, sir, your obedient servant,
Vere St. Leger Goold, Secretary.

The Town Clerk.

APPENDIX No. 2.

Form of Queries sent.

Municipal Boundaries Commission (Ireland).

Town of

Population . Area . Valuation .

1. Whether the town is divided into wards for Municipal purposes, and, if so, into how many?

2. Are such wards conterminous with any wards in existence for Poor Law purposes, and, if not, in what particulars do they differ?

3. In what Electoral Division or Divisions is the town included?

4. Are the Municipal and Poor Law boundaries, as at present arranged, conterminous? and, if not, state in what particulars they differ.

5. What have been the poundage rates made for Municipal, Poor Law, and County purposes respectively, during each of the last five years, viz.:—

—	Municipal.	Poor Law.	County.
1876,			
1877,			
1878,			
1879,			
1880,			

6. Are the present municipal boundaries regarded with dissatisfaction by the ratepayers generally or by any section of them?

7. If so, what are the objections entertained to them?

8. What is the opinion of the Municipal Body on this subject?

9. Are there any changes in the existing boundaries which they would suggest as desirable, whether in the direction of extending, limiting, or otherwise altering them?

10. What are the particular grounds on which any such suggested changes are founded, and what advantages are anticipated from them if adopted?

11. Are there any general observations bearing on the objects of the present Commission which the Municipal Body desire to submit for consideration?

Abstract of Replies to Circulars sent to the several Municipal Authorities.

n.k.—Not known. n.r.—No reply. n.g.—Not given.

—	Valuation.	Area in Acres.	Population.	Extension asked for.	Reasons assigned.
[illegible]	[illegible]	About [illegible]	[illegible]	No.	—
[illegible]	[illegible]	[illegible]	[illegible]	Yes.	[illegible]
[illegible]	[illegible]	[illegible]	[illegible]	Yes.	[illegible]
[illegible]	[illegible]	[illegible]	[illegible]	Yes.	[illegible]
[illegible]	[illegible]	[illegible]	[illegible]	No.	—
[illegible]	[illegible]	[illegible]	[illegible]	No.	—
[illegible]	[illegible]	[illegible]	[illegible]	No.	—
[illegible]	[illegible]	[illegible]	[illegible]	No.	—
[illegible]	[illegible]	[illegible]	[illegible]	No.	Additional expenditure without corresponding benefit. [illegible]
[illegible]	[illegible]	[illegible]	[illegible]	Yes.	[illegible]
[illegible]	[illegible]	[illegible]	[illegible]	No.	—
[illegible]	[illegible]	About [illegible]	[illegible]	Yes.	[illegible]
[illegible]	[illegible]	[illegible]	[illegible]	Yes.	[illegible]
[illegible]	[illegible]	[illegible]	[illegible]	No.	—
[illegible]	[illegible]	[illegible]	[illegible]	No.	—
[illegible]	[illegible]	[illegible]	[illegible]	No.	—
[illegible]	[illegible]	[illegible]	[illegible]	Yes.	[illegible]
[illegible]	[illegible]	[illegible]	[illegible]	Yes.	[illegible]
[illegible]	[illegible]	[illegible]	[illegible]	Yes.	[illegible]
[illegible]	[illegible]	[illegible]	[illegible]	No.	—
[illegible]	[illegible]	[illegible]	[illegible]	Yes.	[illegible]
[illegible]	[illegible]	[illegible]	[illegible]	Yes.	[illegible]
[illegible]	[illegible]	[illegible]	[illegible]	Yes.	[illegible]
[illegible]	[illegible]	[illegible]	[illegible]	Yes.	Extension of area.
[illegible]	[illegible]	[illegible]	[illegible]	Yes.	[illegible]
[illegible]	[illegible]	[illegible]	[illegible]	No.	—
[illegible]	[illegible]	n.k.	[illegible]	No opinion.	—
[illegible]	[illegible]	[illegible]	[illegible]	No.	—
[illegible]	[illegible]	[illegible]	[illegible]	No.	—
[illegible]	[illegible]	[illegible]	[illegible]	Yes.	To increase the rating area.
[illegible]	[illegible]	[illegible]	[illegible]	No.	—
[illegible]	[illegible]	[illegible]	[illegible]	No.	—
[illegible]	[illegible]	[illegible]	[illegible]	Yes.	[illegible] in case of Commissioners becoming the Urban Sanitary authority.
[illegible]	[illegible]	[illegible]	[illegible]	No.	—
[illegible]	[illegible]	[illegible]	[illegible]	Yes.	[illegible]
[illegible]	[illegible]	[illegible]	[illegible]	No.	—
[illegible]	[illegible]	[illegible]	[illegible]	Yes.	[illegible]

ABSTRACT of REPLIES to Circulars sent to the several MUNICIPAL AUTHORITIES—continued.

—	[illegible]	[illegible]	[illegible]	[illegible]	Reasons assigned.
[illegible]	[illegible]	[illegible]	[illegible]	Yes.	Area of taxation too limited.
[illegible]	[illegible]	[illegible]	[illegible]	No.	—
Cork	[illegible]	[illegible]	[illegible]	Yes.	[illegible]
[illegible]	[illegible]	[illegible]	[illegible]	Yes.	[illegible]
[illegible]	[illegible]	[illegible]	[illegible]	Yes.	[illegible]
[illegible]	[illegible]	[illegible]	[illegible]	Yes.	[illegible]
[illegible]	[illegible]	[illegible]	[illegible]	No.	[illegible]
[illegible]	[illegible]	[illegible]	[illegible]	No.	[illegible]
[illegible]	[illegible]	[illegible]	[illegible]	Yes.	[illegible]
[illegible]	[illegible]	[illegible]	[illegible]	No.	[illegible]
[illegible]	[illegible]	[illegible]	[illegible]	Yes.	[illegible]
[illegible]	[illegible]	[illegible]	[illegible]	No.	To increase area of taxation.
[illegible]	[illegible]	[illegible]	[illegible]	Yes.	[illegible]
[illegible]	[illegible]	[illegible]	[illegible]	Yes.	[illegible]
[illegible]	[illegible]	[illegible]	[illegible]	No.	[illegible]
[illegible]	[illegible]	[illegible]	[illegible]	Yes.	[illegible]
[illegible]	[illegible]	[illegible]	[illegible]	—	[illegible]
[illegible]	[illegible]	[illegible]	[illegible]	Yes.	[illegible]
[illegible]	[illegible]	[illegible]	[illegible]	Yes.	[illegible]
[illegible]	[illegible]	[illegible]	[illegible]	Yes.	[illegible]
[illegible]	[illegible]	[illegible]	[illegible]	No.	—
[illegible]	[illegible]	[illegible]	[illegible]	No.	—
[illegible]	[illegible]	[illegible]	[illegible]	No.	—
[illegible]	[illegible]	[illegible]	[illegible]	Yes.	Area of taxation too limited.
[illegible]	[illegible]	[illegible]	[illegible]	Yes.	To increase the area of taxation.
[illegible] and [illegible]	[illegible]	[illegible]	[illegible]	Yes.	[illegible]
[illegible]	[illegible]	[illegible]	[illegible]	No.	—
[illegible]	[illegible]	[illegible]	[illegible]	No.	—
[illegible]	[illegible]	[illegible]	[illegible]	No.	—
[illegible]	[illegible]	[illegible]	[illegible]	Yes.	[illegible]
[illegible]	[illegible]	[illegible]	[illegible]	No.	—
[illegible]	[illegible]	[illegible]	[illegible]	No.	—
[illegible]	[illegible]	[illegible]	[illegible]	Yes.	[illegible]
[illegible]	[illegible]	[illegible]	[illegible]	Yes.	[illegible]
[illegible]	[illegible]	[illegible]	[illegible]	No.	—
[illegible]	[illegible]	[illegible]	[illegible]	No.	—
[illegible]	[illegible]	[illegible]	[illegible]	Yes.	[illegible]
[illegible]	[illegible]	[illegible]	[illegible]	Yes.	[illegible]
[illegible]	[illegible]	[illegible]	[illegible]	Yes.	[illegible]
[illegible]	[illegible]	[illegible]	[illegible]	Yes.	[illegible]
[illegible]	[illegible]	[illegible]	[illegible]	Yes. Conditionally.	[illegible]
[illegible]	[illegible]	[illegible]	[illegible]	Yes.	[illegible]
[illegible]	[illegible]	[illegible]	[illegible]	Yes.	[illegible]
[illegible]	[illegible]	[illegible]	[illegible]	No.	—
[illegible]	[illegible]	[illegible]	[illegible]	Yes.	[illegible]
[illegible]	[illegible]	[illegible]	[illegible]	Yes.	[illegible]
[illegible]	[illegible]	[illegible]	[illegible]	Yes.	[illegible]
[illegible]	[illegible]	[illegible]	[illegible]	Yes.	[illegible]
[illegible]	[illegible]	[illegible]	[illegible]	Yes.	[illegible]
[illegible]	[illegible]	[illegible]	[illegible]	No.	—
[illegible]	[illegible]	[illegible]	[illegible]	No.	—
[illegible]	[illegible]	[illegible]	[illegible]	Yes.	[illegible]
[illegible]	[illegible]	[illegible]	[illegible]	Yes.	[illegible]
[illegible]	[illegible]	[illegible]	[illegible]	No.	—
[illegible]	[illegible]	[illegible]	[illegible]	No.	—
[illegible]	[illegible]	[illegible]	[illegible]	No.	—
[illegible]	[illegible]	[illegible]	[illegible]	No.	—
[illegible]	[illegible]	[illegible]	[illegible]	Yes.	[illegible]
[illegible]	[illegible]	[illegible]	[illegible]	No.	—
[illegible]	[illegible]	[illegible]	[illegible]	Yes.	[illegible]
[illegible]	[illegible]	[illegible]	[illegible]	Yes.	[illegible]
[illegible]	[illegible]	[illegible]	[illegible]	Yes.	[illegible]
[illegible]	[illegible]	[illegible]	[illegible]	No.	—
[illegible]	[illegible]	[illegible]	[illegible]	No.	—
[illegible]	[illegible]	[illegible]	[illegible]	Yes.	[illegible]
[illegible]	[illegible]	[illegible]	[illegible]	No.	—
[illegible]	[illegible]	[illegible]	[illegible]	Yes.	[illegible]
Tralee	[illegible]	[illegible]	[illegible]	Yes.	[illegible]
[illegible]	[illegible]	[illegible]	[illegible]	No.	—
[illegible]	[illegible]	[illegible]	[illegible]	Yes.	[illegible]
[illegible]	[illegible]	[illegible]	[illegible]	Yes.	[illegible]
[illegible]	[illegible]	[illegible]	[illegible]	Yes.	[illegible]
[illegible]	[illegible]	[illegible]	[illegible]	Yes.	[illegible]
Wexford	[illegible]	[illegible]	[illegible]	—	[illegible]
Wicklow	[illegible]	[illegible]	[illegible]	No.	—
Youghal	[illegible]	[illegible]	[illegible]	Yes.	[illegible]

APPENDIX No. 3.

Towns under 17 & 18 Vic., c. 103.

Town.	Number of Electoral Divisions in which situate.	Town.	Number of Electoral Divisions in which situate.	Town.	Number of Electoral Divisions in which situate.
Arklow,	2	Castleblayney,	1	Mountmellick,	1
Athy,	3	Cushendall,	1	Mountrath,	3
Ardee,	1	Clones,	1	Midleton,	1
Athlone,	4	Cookstown,	1	Mitchelstown,	1
Antrim,	1	Clondalkin,	1	Naas,	1
Aughnacloy,	1	Dundalk,	1	Newbridge,	1
Bagenalstown,	1	Dromore,	1	Nenagh,	2
Ballyshannon,	1	Ennis,	1	New Ross,	1
Ballymoney,	2	Enniscorthy,	1	Navan,	1
Ballymena,	1	Fermoy,	1	Newtownards,	2
Ballinasloe,	3	Gorey,	1	Parsonstown,	1
Ballybofey,	3	Gilford,	2	Portarlington,	3
Banbridge,	1	Holywood,	1	Rathkeale,	3
Bangor,	1	Kilkee & Ballybunion,	1	Roscommon,	2
Boyle,	1	Kells,	2	Skibbereen,	2
Ballymahon,	1	Kinsale,	2	Stranorlar,	1
Bandon,	3	Keady,	1	Tullamore,	1
Birr,	3	Kilrush,	3	Trim,	1
Carlow,	1	Longford,	1	Templemore,	1
Callan,	2	Lismore,	1	Thurles,	1
Clonakilty,	1	Larne,	1	Tipperary,	1
Carrick-on-Suir,	1	Lisburn,	3	Tandragee,	1
Cashel,	3	Lurgan,	4	Tuam,	1
Cavan,	1	Letterkenny,	1	Westport,	1
Cootehill,	1	Limavady,	1		
Coleraine,	2	Lisnaskea,	1		

9th Geo. IV., c. 82.

Town.	No.	Town.	No.	Town.	No.
Armagh,	1	Fethard,	1	Tralee,	1
Bandon,	2	Mallow,	1	Wicklow,	1
Downpatrick,	1	Monaghan,	1	Youghal,	1
Dungannon,	1	Omagh,	2		

Special Acts.

Town.	No.	Town.	No.	Town.	No.
Blackrock,	2	Enniskillen,	1	Newry,	2
Bray,	2	Galway,	1	Pembroke,	2
Clontarf,	2	Kilmainham (New),	1	Queenstown,	1
Dungarvan,	1	Kingstown,	–	Rathmines & Rathgar,	5
Dalkey,	2				

3 & 4 Vic., c. 108.

Town.	No.	Town.	No.	Town.	No.
Belfast,	8	Dublin,	2	Sligo,	1
Clonmel,	3	Kilkenny,	1	Wexford,	1
Cork,	1	Limerick,	1	Waterford,	1
Drogheda,	2	Londonderry,	4		

APPENDIX No. 4.

Town.	Date Visited.	By whom Visited.
Arklow,	May 1, 1878,	Charles P. Cotton.
Athy,	February 13, "	W. P. O'Brien.
Ardee,	May 14, "	C. P. Cotton.
Athlone,	December 14, 1876,	Messrs. Cotton and O'Brien.
Antrim,	July 19, 1878,	H. A. Robinson.
Armagh,	July 25, "	Messrs. Cotton and Robinson.
Aughnacloy,	July 24, "	H. A. Robinson.
Bagenalstown,	February 11, "	Messrs. O'Brien and Cotton.
Balbriggan,	May 15, "	C. P. Cotton.
Ballymena,	September 23, "	Messrs. Brien and Robinson.

APPENDIX No. 4—continued.

Town.	Date Visited.		By whom Visited.
Ballymoney,	July 15,	1879,	H. A. Robinson.
Belturbet,	September 26,	„	H. A. Robinson.
Ballyshannon,	October 6,	„	H. A. Robinson.
Banbridge,	September 16,	„	W. A. Exham.
Bangor,	June 18,	„	C. P. Cotton.
Ballybay,	July 22,	„	C. P. Cotton.
Ballynahinch,	October 2,	„	H. A. Robinson.
Ballina,	September 4,	„	Messrs. Cotton and Robinson.
Boyle,	September 30,	„	H. A. Robinson.
Bandon,	January 3,	„	W. A. Exham.
Blackrock,	September 4,	„	W. A. Exham.
Bray,	May 8,	„	Messrs. Exham and Cotton.
Belfast,	August 6, 8, 9, 9, October 20, 21, 22, 24, 25, 27, November 26, 27,	„ „ „	Messrs. Exham, Cotton, and Robinson.
Carlow,	February 12,	„	Messrs. Exham and O'Brien.
Callan,	August 21,	„	H. A. Robinson.
Clonakilty,	January 2,	„	W. A. Exham.
Carrick-on-Suir,	March 10,	„	W. A. Exham.
Cashel,	March 11,	„	W. A. Exham.
Cavan,	September 27,	„	H. A. Robinson.
Cootehill,	September 18,	„	H. A. Robinson.
Coleraine,	July 14,	„	C. P. Cotton.
Carrickmacross,	September 17,	„	H. A. Robinson.
Castleblayney,	July 23,	„	H. A. Robinson.
Clones,	July 21,	1880,	W. A. Exham.
Cookstown,	September 16,	1879,	H. A. Robinson.
Castlebar,	September 4,	„	H. A. Robinson.
Carrickfergus,	September 24,	„	Messrs. Exham and Robinson.
Clontarf,	November 5,	„	Messrs. Exham and Robinson.
Clonmel,	May 26,	„	Messrs. Cotton and Robinson.
Cork,	January 7, 8, 10, December 8,	„ „	Messrs. Exham and Cotton.
Dundalk,	July 29,	„	Messrs. Cotton and Robinson.
Drumcondra,	June 23,	1880,	W. A. Exham.
Dromore,	August 7,	1879,	C. P. Cotton.
Downpatrick,	June 19,	„	C. P. Cotton.
Dungannon,	July 24,	„	C. P. Cotton.
Dungarvan,	December 31,	1878,	Messrs. O'Brien and Cotton.
Dalkey,	April 24,	1879,	Messrs. Exham and Cotton.
Drogheda,	November 20, '78, April 28,	„	Messrs. Exham, Cotton, and O'Brien.
Dublin,	April 7, 8, 9, 10, 15, 16, May 19, 20, 21, 22, 23, 24, July 3, 4,	„ „ „	Messrs. Exham and Cotton.
Ennis,	December 9,	1878,	Messrs. Exham and O'Brien.
Enniscorthy,	February 7,	1879,	Messrs. Cotton and O'Brien.
Enniskillen,	July 24,	„	Messrs. Cotton and Robinson.
Fermoy,	January 4; October 15,	„	C. P. Cotton.
Fethard,	August 13,	„	H. A. Robinson.
Gorey,	February 24,	„	Messrs. Exham and Cotton.
Gilford,	August 7; September 12,	„	H. A. Robinson.
Galway,	July 8,	„	Messrs. Exham, Cotton, and Robinson.
Holywood,	November 24, 28,	„	Messrs. Exham and Robinson.
Killiney and Ballybrack,	April 22,	„	C. P. Cotton.
Kells,	April 26,	„	C. P. Cotton.
Kinsale,	January 3,	„	W. P. O'Brien.
Keady,	September 9,	„	W. A. Exham.
Killarney,	December 26,	1878,	W. A. Exham.
Kilmainham (New),	November 4,	1878,	W. A. Exham.
Kingstown,	August 26; September 16,	„	Messrs. Exham and Cotton.
Kilkenny,	March 4,	„	Messrs. Exham and Cotton.
Longford,	October 1,	„	H. A. Robinson.
Lismore,	December 30,	1878,	Messrs. Cotton and O'Brien.
Larne,	June 17,	1879,	Messrs. Cotton and Robinson.
Lisburn,	June 14,	„	C. P. Cotton.
Lurgan,	June 16,	„	Messrs. Cotton and Robinson.
Letterkenny,	August 11,	„	H. A. Robinson.
Limavady,	July 16,	„	H. A. Robinson.
Loughrea,	December 21,	1878,	Messrs. Cotton and O'Brien.
Limerick,	July 4,	1879,	Messrs. Exham, Cotton, and Robinson.
Londonderry,	July 11,	„	Messrs. Exham, Cotton, and Robinson.
Maryborough,	March 8,	„	C. P. Cotton.
Mountmellick,	March 14,	„	C. P. Cotton.

APPENDIX No. 4—*continued.*

Town.	Date Visited.	By whom Visited.
Mullingar,	December 16, 1878,	Messrs. Cotton and O'Brien.
Midleton,	January 3; October 17, 1879,	C. P. Cotton.
Mallow,	December 23, 1878,	Messrs. Eakins and Cotton.
Monaghan,	September 26, 1878,	H. A. Robinson.
Naas,	December 21, 1878,	Messrs. Cotton and O'Brien.
Newbridge,	March 17, 1879,	C. P. Cotton.
Navan,	December 18, 1878,	Messrs. Cotton and O'Brien.
New Ross,	February 19, 1879,	Messrs. Cotton and O'Brien.
Nenagh,	August 28, "	H. A. Robinson.
Newtownards,	June 17, "	C. P. Cotton.
Newry,	July 24, "	Messrs. Cotton and Robinson.
Omagh,	July 23, "	Messrs. Cotton and Robinson.
Parsonstown,	May 31, "	C. P. Cotton.
Portadown,	June 18, "	C. P. Cotton.
[illegible]	November 8, "	Messrs. Cotton and Robinson.
Queenstown,	January 8, "	Messrs. Eakins and O'Brien.
Rathkeale,	March 12, "	C. P. Cotton.
[illegible]	September 20, "	H. A. Robinson.
Rathmines and Rathgar,	September 3, "	W. A. Eakins.
Skibbereen,	January 2, "	W. A. Eakins.
Strabane,	July 14, "	H. A. Robinson.
Sligo,	September 1, "	Messrs. Cotton and Robinson.
Tullamore,	May 16, "	C. P. Cotton.
Tralee,	December 18, 1878,	Messrs. Cotton and O'Brien.
[illegible]	March 13, 1879,	C. P. Cotton.
Thurles,	March 13, "	C. P. Cotton.
Tipperary,	May 30, "	C. P. Cotton.
Tandragee,	September 15, "	H. A. Robinson.
Tuam,	December 13, 1878,	Messrs. Cotton and O'Brien.
[illegible]	December 23, "	W. A. Eakins.
Westport,	September 6, 1879,	Messrs. Cotton and Robinson.
Wicklow,	April 8, "	W. A. Eakins.
Wexford,	February 4, "	Messrs. Robinson, O'Brien, and Cotton.
Waterford,	March 7, "	Messrs. Eakins and Cotton.
Youghal,	January 2, "	Messrs. O'Brien and Cotton.

APPENDIX No. 5.

COMMUNICATIONS received from MUNICIPAL AUTHORITIES and other Bodies and persons interested.

ARMAGH.

Town Commissioners' Office,
Armagh, May 31, 1879.

GENTLEMEN,—I have been directed by the Urban Sanitary Commission of Armagh to call your attention to the open sewers upon the outskirts of this city, which are within your rural sanitary district, and to request that you, in compliance with the 21st sec. of the 41st and 42nd Vic., c. 52, will be pleased to have them properly cleansed, and put in such a sanitary state, so as that the nuisance which they contain may not be a possible source of [illegible], during the summer [illegible], to the spread of disease.

The Commissioners hope that there will be no unnecessary delay in the execution of this important duty.

I am, Gentlemen, your obedient servant,
T. G. PEEL, Town Clerk.

To the Board of Guardians, Armagh Union.

Copy of RESOLUTION from the Meeting of ARMAGH TOWN COMMISSIONERS, held on the 5th December, 1878.

The persons instructed to ascertain, as far as possible, the boundaries of the old borough, and to report how far they would recommend same, or what other limits they would recommend the Commissioners to adopt, having made their report; and same having been approved of, it was unanimously resolved:

That the Commissioners determine [illegible] the city and of the suburbs and districts thereof, respectively, to which the purposes of the Act shall extend, to be as follows:—Adopting the boundaries of the old borough so far as same, with certainty, appear to be defined, viz., commencing at Umgola Spring Well, pursue the stream passing thereby till it falls into the Callan River, the course of which again pursue, keeping it on the left, until it is joined by the Mullinure Water, the course of which pursue, keeping it likewise on the left as far as [illegible], through said town, crossing the Newry-road, up to the [illegible] of the meadow held by Mr. Dobbin, which [illegible] follow until the point where it comes up to [illegible] against the Primate's demesne wall (the old borough boundary being included within the demesne), then in a direct line from the aforementioned point, over which there appears some [illegible] work, through the demesne, south of the Palace, keeping on the left [illegible] of the Palace, and outside the private pleasure-grounds, thence down an old ditch [illegible] of the old orchard and south of the farmyard, into which there flows a small stream which pursue and under the demesne wall [illegible] to the Keady-road, [illegible] as far as [illegible], which take and pursue so far as the [illegible] between the Rev. [illegible] and Dr. [illegible]'s houses, pursue that [illegible] between

Mr. Gardner's and Dr. Robinson's farms, as far as the Old Monaghan road, which take, turning up more to the left, as far as Umgola lane, at the head of which the wall commenced as it is situate.

Resolved—That the Chairman be requested to get made a proper map of the foregoing limits, as determined on by the Commissioners.

[illegible], Armagh,
August 16th, 1879.

Gentlemen,—In my evidence given at the sitting of the "Municipal Boundaries Commission," at Armagh, on 25th of July last, I [illegible] stating that [illegible] the Town Clerk's that the existing municipal boundary of the borough should be made coincident with the limits of the Poor Law electoral division of Armagh.

The advantages to the ratepayers would be, if the city were divided into wards, then the four Guardians of the electoral division would be chosen by the ratepayers—one Guardian to each ward, distributing the representation to each quarter of the city.

At the last and previous meetings of the Town Council, Mr. T. G. Peel, the Town Clerk, [illegible] and [illegible] the [illegible] Commissioners. He has for many years past [illegible] the four Guardians of the "Armagh electoral division," thus practically taking a whole city and division of nearly 10,000 people.

A meeting of the ratepayers of the city requested me to bring the above to your notice, so that by the division of the city into four wards, constituting one electoral division, the borough may be saved from the chaotic state it was in from July last 1878, to February 17th, 1879, during which the ratepayers had the "Corporation" in the High Court of Justice.

I have the honour to be, Gentlemen, your obedient servant,

ALEXANDER SHAW.

To C. P. Cotton and H. A. Robinson, esqs., of Her Majesty's Municipal Boundaries Commission.

BALLYMONEY.

Ballymoney, 18th July, 1879.

The Municipal Boundaries Commissioners.

Gentlemen,—We take the liberty of directing your attention to the area of rating in the Ballymoney Electoral Division of Ballymoney Union for sanitary purposes. The area of rating for such purposes, as laid down by the Local Government Board, is the townlands of Townparks and Glebe, and we would beg to inform you that our farms are situated a mile and a quarter from Ballymoney; that, consequently we derive no benefit from the expenditure of any moneys for making sanitary improvements; we would also draw your attention to the fact that our holdings are purely agricultural, as none of us reside in the town, or own any property therein. Before the Government valuation came into force in this union there was a townland in the old poor-law rate books known as Leamy, but since the introduction of the new valuation this townland was included in that of Townparks, and we would beg you would inquire into this matter, and on account of the reasons stated direct that the lands set forth in this old townland of Leamy shall be excluded from paying any portion of the special sanitary rate of the Ballymoney Division. We may state that at a special meeting of the Board of Guardians this application was considered, and no objection was made by any member of the board to the change we have proposed.

We are respectfully, &c.,

DANIEL KIRBY,
JOHN QUINN,
ANDREW M'ILROY,
JAMES KENNEDY,
THOMAS STEWART.

BALLYBAY.

Ballybay, County Monaghan,
5th September, 1879.

Gentlemen,—Referring to the inquiry held by you at this town on 24th July last, and the evidence then given, [illegible] the only person, in addition to the Town Clerk and some of the Commissioners, who gave any evidence before you. I then stated that I objected to the proposed small extension as proposed by the Commissioners, but recommended a larger extension as was, I think, suggested by the Town Clerk. I now beg to add that I have since then had several opportunities of talking to the people who own the lands in the district proposed to be added to the town boundary, and they are unanimously against being annexed to the town, [illegible] and thus [illegible] I consider it would be better to let the boundary alone, [illegible] only the small portion of lands proposed by Commissioners. As I am myself one that is very much interested in this matter, I hope you will excuse this letter, and take these facts into consideration before making your final report to Government.

I am, sirs, your obedient servant,

JOHN LAWSON.

To the Municipal Boundaries Commissioners, Dublin.

BOYLE.

Town Commissioners' Office, Boyle,
6th October, 1879.

At a meeting of Town Commissioners held this day, John D. MacDermott, Esq., Chairman, Clerk was directed to forward a copy following resolution:—

To Municipal Boundaries Commissioners, Ireland,
Four Courts, Dublin.

Resolved—That as we were not present at the recent inquiry by a Municipal Boundaries Commissioner, having been on the eve of a fair, and inconvenient to most of us, and our chairman being at Athlone Sessions, and as some statements were then made which are inaccurate, we deem it our duty to put the Municipal Boundaries Commissioners in possession of the following facts:—

That this town was put under the Towns Improvement Act in January, 1867, after the usual preliminary steps, including public advertisements, which steps extended over some months, and that the public meeting held by order of the then Lord Lieutenant, before two Justices of the Peace was unanimous in adopting the Act.

That prior to its adoption, the town was in a most neglected state, nothing being done for it except the repairs of roads by Grand Jury cess; that amongst the many defects then existing there was a conspicuous and dangerous one in the very centre of the town—namely, a crumbled down old wall, from the canal bridge to the military barracks, and separating the river from a roadway. That nobody acknowledged liability to repair said wall, which was for many years in a most disgraceful and dangerous state, so much so that a valuable life was lost owing to there being no protection between that roadway and the river. That soon after that melancholy death it was agreed by all the inhabitants, except about two persons, that the general want of improvement ought not to be allowed to continue any longer. That the wall referred to was rebuilt and raised, and was since kept in repair by the Town Commissioners, though in strictness same ought to have been done by others. The expense was about £30.

That there was no public pump or fountain then in the town, and the Commissioners had piping laid in the bed of the river, and conveyed the present spring water from St. Patrick's Well about a quarter of a mile into the centre of the town.

That whilst the piping was being laid one of the

[illegible] who [illegible] before the Municipal [illegible] Commissioners [illegible], the [illegible] of the [illegible], and who [illegible] to the [illegible] which [illegible] from the Town. [illegible]

That the town is [illegible] lighted by [illegible] public lamps, and [illegible]

That [illegible] important [illegible] Municipal [illegible] Commissioners [illegible] the Town Commissioners [illegible] the town [illegible] [illegible]

That the [illegible] Grand Jury, [illegible] to have [illegible] a week, and the present [illegible] [illegible] Commissioners have [illegible] Town [illegible] [illegible] some days in the [illegible].

That the Commissioners [illegible] the cattle [illegible] pigs [illegible] the streets. [illegible] the Grand Jury [illegible] [illegible] Commissioners [illegible] the [illegible] [illegible]

That the Board of Guardians [illegible] [illegible] Grand Jury [illegible] [illegible]

That at [illegible] public [illegible] in the town [illegible] Commissioners [illegible]

That the Commissioners had [illegible] the [illegible] of the town [illegible].

That in dry [illegible] the [illegible] through the [illegible] of the [illegible] bridge and [illegible] Commissioners [illegible] [illegible]

That the Commissioners [illegible] of having [illegible] the [illegible] [illegible] Commissioners [illegible] [illegible] by the police [illegible] public.

That the [illegible] market [illegible] the public [illegible] within [illegible] of a few miles of the town [illegible] supplied by the Commissioners.

That the town is [illegible] of [illegible]

in the [illegible] of the [illegible] number of small tenements in the town, very many [illegible] a state of things so detrimental to health and decency. That the attention of the sanitary [illegible] of the inhabitants, and in the [illegible] nothing has been effected [illegible] it is hoped will be.

That there [illegible] be no [illegible] of authority between us and any other body. [illegible] We have [illegible] the town, considering [illegible] that [illegible] being carried out [illegible] have improved the town considerably [illegible] with our [illegible].

Proposed by the Chairman, seconded by Mr. [illegible] and passed unanimously.

By order,

[illegible], T.C.

BALLINASLOE.

To the Municipal Boundaries Enquiry Commissioners.

The memorial of the Town Commissioners of Ballinasloe showeth—That at the holding of a recent inquiry with regard to [illegible] of municipal boundaries [illegible] of the town, some [illegible] ago, a number of [illegible] were opposed to an extension of the existing boundaries.

That since then the sanitary authority has been transferred from the Board of Guardians to memorialists.

That [illegible] of [illegible] the Public Health Act it is proposed to construct sewerage and waterworks for the township.

That memorialists are aware that [illegible] of those [illegible] opposed to an extension of the boundary some time ago [illegible] owing to the improvements which will take place [illegible] of [illegible] sanitary supervision.

Memorialists, therefore, pray that these [illegible] may be considered by the Commissioners, previous to the issue of their report, and, if considered necessary, that they will hold a supplemental inquiry to have the [illegible] of their [illegible], and memorialists shall, as in duty bound, ever pray.

Signed on behalf of the Board,

John Watts, Chairman.

Edward [illegible], Town Clerk.
Ballinasloe, September 24th, 1880.

BRAY.

Dublin Castle, July 15, 1879.

Gentlemen,—I have been requested to forward to you a memorial, signed by the [illegible] inhabitant [illegible], Justices of the Peace, and [illegible] residing [illegible] in the neighbourhood of Bray, protesting against the proposed enlargement of the boundaries of that township, and to request that it may be [illegible] [illegible] upon that subject.

I am, Gentlemen, your obedient servant,

[illegible] B. [illegible]

The Municipal Boundary Commissioners.

"We, the undersigned, owners of property and residents in the neighbourhood of Bray, [illegible] respectfully to the Boundary Commissioners [illegible] reasons for deprecating the proposed extension of the township, so far as our interests are concerned.

"In the first place, we must earnestly protest against the doctrine repeatedly enunciated, and apparently regarded as self-evident, during the recent sitting, viz., that, because we derive certain undefined advantages, whether in the shape of actual profit, or mere convenience from our proximity to the town, we are therefore equitably liable to be rated in consequence of those advantages.

"Not to insist upon the obvious consideration that whatever benefits we derive from the vicinity of the town are fully reciprocated and paid for by our expenditure and custom, we prefer to base our objection upon the broader ground, that it is a fundamental principle of local taxation, that each tax must represent a distinct and tangible local purpose and benefit, and that such a thing as taxation in the lump for objects not distinctly stated and defined, is without precedent and calculated to lead to infinite abuses.

"Were we to be annexed to the township on the terms referred to, we should be at this disadvantage, as compared with those who reside within the present township (and they derive at least as much benefit from the town as we do), that whereas they know exactly what they are taxed for, and can judge whether or not the money raised for each specific object is properly applied, we shall be paying the rate of 10½d. for an advantage so vague and shadowy that it never can be in any man's power to say whether it is too much or too little, whether it ought to be doubled or reduced to one-half; in fact it will not be so much a rate as a penalty.

"An example will illustrate the untenable nature of the position. Those who happen to reside near a railway station undoubtedly derive both profit and convenience from that proximity. Will it be contended that if, through mismanagement or any other cause, the company should find itself in pecuniary difficulties, those who have thus benefited by the line should be made legally liable to contribute towards its maintenance?

"We venture to affirm, in contradistinction to the principle we have noted, that the limits of the township should not be enlarged, except so far as to include those districts to which there is a reasonable prospect of soon extending the tangible benefits derivable from the township, such as gas, water, paved footpaths, &c., and that it would be an arbitrary and unwarrantable proceeding to annex outsiders, to whom the Commissioners have neither the means nor the intention of giving such privileges.

"Pembroke,
"Powerscourt,
"Monck,
"Plunket, Meath,
"George Hodson, Bart.,
"E. Synge Hutchinson, Bart.,
"Emily Reeves,
"Fitzwilliam Beall, J.P., D.L.,
"Henry Barton, J.P.,
"Fitzwilliam Charles Cockburn,
"G. Bookey,
"Thos. Lefroy, Q.C.,
"Richard R. Wingfield, J.P.,
"Edward Lambert Rathdowne, J.P.,
"Lewis Beall,
"Matthew P. D'Arcy,
"Henry Doyle,
"Richd. M. [illegible],
"A. G. Beall,
"William C. Domvile, J.P., D.L."

Copy of a Resolution passed at a Special Meeting of the Bray Township Commissioners, held on Friday, the 9th May, 1879:—

Resolved,—That we approve of the extension of the present township boundaries as proposed and shown on the map before us, on the condition named by Mr. Exham, Q.C., viz.:—That the portion proposed being taken into the township shall pay the present county rate in full, as now paid by them to the Grand Jury, and that they shall also contribute quarter the township rates on land, and the full township rates on house property, and that a copy of this resolution be forwarded to the Boundaries Commissioners.

Passed 9th May, 1879.

Edward Breslin, Chairman.

CLONAKILTY.

Town Commissioners' Office, Clonakilty,
8th January 1879.

Sir,—I am directed by the Town Commissioners of Clonakilty to forward to you the annexed copy of a resolution unanimously adopted by them at their meeting held on yesterday, the 7th instant:—

"That we approve of the extended boundary of the township as marked out by Mr. Exham, one of the Boundary Commissioners, at the meeting held in the Town Hall on last Friday—in the meantime requesting that the portion of the bay extending from the town to Ringsnier on one side, and to the townland of Youghall, on the other side be included in the township, in order that it may be used at some future time for sanitary or other purposes."

The Commissioners also enclose a schedule of the townlands comprised in the extended township with their areas, population, valuation, &c.

I have the honour to be, sir,

Your obedient servant,

John Davis, Clerk to the Commissioners.

Ware B. Lowry Cooke, esq., Secretary,
Municipal Boundary Commissioners, Dublin.

DUNDALK.

To the Commissioners appointed to inquire into the existing boundaries of the several municipal towns in Ireland.

Dundalk, 18th November, 1878.

Gentlemen,—In accordance with your published notice, we send herein our objections to the existing municipal boundaries of Dundalk.

I, Robert Black, Presbyterian clergyman of Dundalk, for myself object to the existing boundaries, as I receive no benefit whatever from the rates which I am compelled to pay to the highest figure as if living in the town, and the nearest gas lamp to my residence, "The Manse," is fully a quarter of a mile distant.

And I, Kane Dickie, of Fairhill, object to the existing municipal boundaries for the same reasons as said Robert Black, and also that my residence, Fairhill, is fully half a mile from the nearest gas lamp.

And I, Henry Coddell, Captain and Adjutant of the Louth Militia, of "Brighton Villa," object to the existing municipal boundaries of Dundalk for similar reasons to the said Robert Black and Kane Dickie, and I say that my residence, Brighton Villa, is a quarter of a mile from the nearest gas lamp.

And we all collectively object, because we derive no benefit from the rates, in the way of cleansing, paving or being supplied with water or gas, or in fact in any way whatever.

And the Commissioners refuse to give us any benefit or relief, and the post office authorities refuse to deliver our letters on account of the distance from the town, so that we really derive no more benefit from the rates than if we lived twenty miles from Dundalk.

And, therefore, we respectfully submit that the municipal boundaries should not extend on the west side beyond the Great Northern Railway line from

Dublin to Belfast, and that the rampart stream should be the municipal boundary on the north and south-west side.

Signed,

ROBERT BLACK,
KATE DENNIS,
H. CAMPBELL.

DUNGARVAN.

Ringville, Dungarvan, 14th April, 1879.

GENTLEMEN,—It having come to my knowledge, as well as others of the Town Commissioners, that at a meeting held on this day week that they ordered their Clerk to apply to me to alter the township boundary for road purposes to what he calls the town proper.

I must say that this order was made without notice, only those who attended the meeting knowing anything of it.

As to the case referred to in the Clerk's letters, and the decision (of Mr. Waters, our Quarter Sessions barrister) against them, I am not surprised at, as far as the Commissioners and the solicitors appointed by them to defend (for their own solicitor, Mr. Hunt, was against them), they seemed to take no interest in the matter, and as for the solicitor, I can not much say to say, he let it go by default.

Mr. O'Brien I am sure will recollect that reference was made to this matter at the inquiry which he held here, and after looking into our special Act he seemed to think the special Act quite clear as to our powers of raising for road purposes. Section 4 takes it from under the restrictions of the Act of 1834 (section 63), where expressly varied.

I take the liberty of enclosing a copy of our special Act.

I remain, Gentlemen, your very obedient,

M. A. ANTHONY.

To the Boundary Commissioners.

Dungarvan, April 8th, 1879.

GENTLEMEN,—I am directed by the Town Commissioners of Dungarvan to ask you to limit the present boundaries of the township to the limits of the town proper for road purposes, on the following grounds:— A landholder named Richard Curran, residing within the present boundary, appealed to the County Court Judge against the last road rate, made on the grounds that land should not be assessed for more than the one-fourth part of its value, and the Judge confirmed the appeal.

This change would necessarily involve a loss on the road rate of fully seventy-five pounds a year to the occupiers of houses who are already heavily taxed.

The Grand Jury cess is an equal cess on lands and buildings, and should be equitably so for repairs and maintenance of roads within the township, but as the law is evidently against such a rating within the township the Commissioners feel that, in justice to the ratepayers of the town, they, as the governing body, now ask you to make the required alteration which they know you are empowered to do.

I am, Gentlemen, your obedient servant,

EDMOND MORRISSEY, Town Clerk.

The Boundary Commissioners, Dublin.

GOREY.

Knockmullen, Gorey, March 22, 1879.

SIR,—I have the honour to forward to you the enclosed memorial, and to inform you that the signatures are strictly limited to *bonâ fide* ratepayers for the town of Gorey, and a radius of one mile. Fourteen of those who have signed pay collectively for about 150 weekly tenants. The poor law valuation attached has been supplied by the poor rate collector as nearly correct as possible.

I have the honour to be, sir,

Your obedient servant,

OLIVER OWEN.

To W. A. Exham, Esq., Q.C.

Gorey, County Wexford, Ireland,
March 22nd, 1879.

To the Municipal Boundaries Commissioners.

We, the undersigned ratepayers living in and near the town of Gorey, beg to state that we are perfectly satisfied with the existing boundaries of the township, and do not wish for any alteration of the same.

Signed by

JOHN C. GUISE, Major-General,
and 113 ratepayers.

HOLYWOOD.

Commissioners' Office, Town Hall, Holywood,
6th January, 1880.

SIR,—By direction of the Holywood Town Commissioners, I beg to forward to you extracts from minute book as below.

Commissioners' Meeting, 2nd June, 1879.

The boundary question having been fully considered, it was moved by Mr. Gray, and seconded by Mr. M'Lean, and passed. That the existing boundary should not be altered or extended.

Commissioners' Meeting, 15th December, 1879.

Mr. M'Lean gave notice that he would at next meeting move that any action or resolution come to by this board in this matter be rescinded.

Commissioners' Meeting, 6th January, 1880.

Moved by Mr. M'Lean, and seconded by Major Griffin, and resolved—That the resolution of the 2nd June last, on the non-extension of the boundary, be rescinded.

Moved by Mr. M'Lean, and seconded by Mr. M'Cann, and resolved, Mr. Patterson dissenting— That we approve of the boundary of the town of Holywood being extended in accordance with the lines on the map delivered to the Boundary Commissioners when in Holywood hearing evidence on the subject, provided the Town Commissioners are to be exonerated from any liability to light and scavenge the extended district, or any part thereof, until the Commissioners shall be of opinion that the taxation will be sufficient to meet the outlay, but with liberty to the Commissioners to levy a tax on the extended district not exceeding one-half the taxation to be levied on the lighted district.

Moved by Mr. Griffin, and seconded by Mr. M'Cann, and resolved—That if the boundary of the town be extended as proposed, the foreshore should be included to low water mark for the purpose of giving the Commissioners sanitary jurisdiction.

I am, sir,

Your obedient servant,

ARTHUR WATERS, Town Clerk.

Vere St. Leger Goold, Esq., Secretary,
Boundaries Commissioners.

To the Municipal Boundaries Commissioners.

The memorial of the undersigned, owners of property and residents in Cultra and Marino, showeth— That memorialists having heard that the Town Commissioners of Holywood propose that the limits of the Holywood township be extended to include the above districts, beg to protest against such extension for the following reasons, viz.:—

That as regards public lighting, which is the only tangible benefit at present within the power of the

Town Commissioners to borrow, memorialists do not consider it necessary, or that it would add materially to their comfort—that such as wish for it have gas in their houses, which is all that is necessary.

That in the matter of water supply—a question yet to be satisfactorily settled for Holywood itself—the rural parishes in these districts are quite sufficiently provided, and that if further water were needed it could be had more abundant and superior from the high ground in their neighbourhood than it is at all likely could be obtained from Holywood.

That there is nothing in those districts requiring the interference of the Town Commissioners with [illegible] authority, and that no works of a sanitary nature as proposed by Holywood could be made available for these districts.

Memorialists therefore pray that you will reject the proposal of the Holywood Town Commissioners.

Signed by
R. [illegible], The [illegible], Marino.
Wm. F. Duncan, Woodleigh, Marino,
and twenty-three other residents.

KILKENNY.

Memorial from Grand Jury.

We, the undersigned members of the Grand Jury of the county of Kilkenny, assembled on the 6th of March, 1879, disapprove most emphatically of the extension of the municipal borough of Kilkenny, which, if carried into effect, would increase the area of taxation of the county at large.

Signed by twenty-two members.

NAVAN.

Town Commissioners' Office, Navan,
7th January, 1879.

The Secretary to the Boundary Commissioners, Ireland.

Sir,—I am directed by the Navan Town Commissioners to forward herewith a copy of Resolutions adopted by them at their Meeting held on the above date, and to request that same be laid before the Municipal Boundary Commissioners, in accordance with their request.

Copy of Resolutions.

Proposed by Mathew Moore, Esq., seconded by Michael Rogers, Esq., and unanimously resolved:—

That we make application to the Local Government Board for the extension of the boundary of the township of Navan, [illegible] to a radius of one statute mile from the Market-square.

Proposed by Thomas Nugent, Esq., seconded by Mathew Moore, Esq., and unanimously resolved:—

That similar application be made with regard to conferring on the Town Commissioners the sanitary authority within the township, and a copy of the above resolutions be forwarded to the office of the Boundary Commissioners, in accordance with their request.

I remain, sir, your obedient servant,

Philip [illegible], Town Clerk.

Vere St. L. Goold, Esq.,
Secretary, Municipal Boundaries Commission.

SLIGO.

Sir,—I am directed to forward to you a copy of resolution passed unanimously at a special meeting of the Town Council of Sligo, held on 24th September, 1879, and to request you will be so good as to lay it before the Municipal Boundaries Commissioners for their consideration.

I am, Sir, your obedient servant,

James M'Kim.

To Vere St. L. Goold, Secretary.

Resolved—That having considered the subject of the extension of the municipal boundary of Sligo to the electoral division, the Council are of opinion that it would be desirable to make such extension.

That this resolution be communicated to the Municipal Boundary Commissioners, and request them to report accordingly.

Moved by Alderman [illegible], seconded by Alderman [illegible]. Passed unanimously.

Alexander Gillmor, Mayor, Chairman.

James M'Kim, Town Clerk,
September 24, 1879.

STRABANE.

Ramelton, 31st July, 1879.

Sir,—I beg to enclose herewith a copy of a resolution passed by the Grand Jury of the county of Donegal at last Assizes.

I am, sir, your obedient servant,

J. [illegible], Secretary to the Grand Jury.

To Vere St. L. Goold, Esq.,
Secretary, Municipal Boundaries Commission,
Four Courts, Dublin.

County of Donegal.
Summer Assizes, 1879.

Ordered—That the Secretary write to the Commissioners of Municipal Boundaries, stating that they have heard that the project of including the town of Lifford in the municipal boundary of Strabane, has been recommended to them, and that having considered the subject, the Grand Jury are of opinion that said project should not be carried out, as it would be injurious to the interests of the county town of Lifford, and no reasons have as yet been laid before the Grand Jury why the change should be made.

Robert G. Montgomery and Fellows.

TUAM.

Tuam, December 20th, 1878.

Resolution of Town Commissioners:—

At a meeting of the Town Commissioners held on this day, it was unanimously resolved, that taking into account the difficulties that present themselves in the arrangement of townland boundaries, the Town Commissioners are of opinion that the electoral division of Tuam would be the most advisable to the municipality, as it would avoid all interference with townland boundaries, and very considerably better the constituency of the municipality.

James [illegible], Town Clerk.

TIPPERARY.

Kingswell House, Tipperary.
25th June, 1879.

My Dear Sir,—I send a formal application supporting the application to extend the boundaries of district under Tipperary Commissioners, and I am satisfied it will receive at your hands every consideration.

Yours most truly,

J. Massy.

Chas. C. Cotton, Esq., C.E.

Kingswell House, Tipperary,
25th June, 1879.

Dear Sir,—In reference to the inquiry you lately held in the town of Tipperary to obtain information as to the necessity of an extension of the boundaries of the lands under the control of the Town Commissioners, I beg to inform you that the first intimation I had of such an inquiry was a statement I saw by chance in a Dublin paper that it had been held.

I am agent to Mr. [illegible], who owns by far a considerable portion of the town and the lands adjoining the west and south-west. I am also possessed of a considerable property in the immediate neighbourhood. I am chairman of the union (one of the largest in Ireland), and have been for upwards of seventeen years, and a constant resident within a short distance of the [illegible] Had I notice I certainly should have attended before you to give my decided opposition to any extension beyond, [illegible] the lands in the [illegible] of the present boundary, and I have spoken to several parties of influence who would have done the same, but they [illegible] had the [illegible] that such a meeting was to be held. They with myself were equally surprised how the matter had been kept so secret, and which accounts for the way it [illegible] attended [illegible] of whom having [illegible] can show [illegible] without [illegible] an extension.

I respectfully submit for the following reasons [illegible] that there should be no extension [illegible] beyond what I have stated:—

1st. In the year 1853, when the town was then [illegible] being placed under the provisions of the Towns Improvement Act, an extension of the present boundary was sought, but the then Lord Lieutenant [illegible] any extension whatever, as [illegible] by the letters of the late Sir Thomas Larcom to me, which I enclose. Since this I understand similar applications were made to the Lord Lieutenant, but with like result.

2nd. The Board of Guardians have from time to time expended large sums of money in the town for sanitary purposes, making [illegible] drains, erecting pumps, &c., &c.

3rd. The Grand Jury of the county have [illegible] large sums of county [illegible] for flagging, &c., &c., according to several [illegible] presentments.

4th. The Town Commissioners have lately [illegible] and are now in possession of a [illegible] by the late [illegible] of £200.

5th. [illegible] in a considerable sum to the Town Commissioners.

6th. The roads in the town and neighbourhood are made, kept up, and maintained by the barony; [illegible] the present [illegible] is now [illegible] at the [illegible] of the barony.

Should you consider it requisite I am prepared to attend and give evidence before you as to the correctness of this statement, and a number of people [illegible] are also prepared to do so.

Under these circumstances I respectfully submit you ought not to recommend any extension beyond what I have stated.

I remain, dear sir, yours faithfully,

J. Maher.

To Charles P. Cotton, Esq., C.E.

WATERFORD.

Waterford, November 29th, 1878.

Gentlemen,—I beg to submit some information and suggestions with reference to the boundaries of the county of the city of Waterford, in accordance with the invitation contained in your advertisement, and I ask you to consider this communication as an objection to the existing boundaries of the county of the city of Waterford, or the borough.

I am, gentlemen, very respectfully,

Joseph Fisher.

The Municipal Boundary Commissioners.

County of the City of Waterford.

The Charter of Charles I. describes the bounds of the county of the city of Waterford, which district [illegible] is still [illegible] the Parliamentary borough of Waterford. It comprises an area of 5,448 acres, and has at present a population of 31,929 persons. It formed the county of the city of Waterford for judicial, fiscal, and for Grand Jury purposes. The principal roads, bridges, and [illegible] therein were made by the city Grand Jury, and it was recognised as the county of the city of Waterford by the Grand Jury Act of 1836, but was [illegible] to the extent by the Corporate Reform Act, which was intended to deal solely with municipal matters, but which affected the [illegible] of the Grand Jury and [illegible] arrangements as [illegible]. The county of the city of Waterford was authorised by the [illegible] George III., c. [illegible] to close up all burial grounds within the [illegible] part of the city of Waterford, and to purchase a burial ground in the [illegible] portion, and a piece of land was purchased [illegible] under that Act and was [illegible]. The Corporate Reform Act divided the county of the city into [illegible] divisions, some portions are wholly within the city, some are partly within and partly without the city, and some wholly without it. This [illegible] special legislation in the Burial Board Act of 1856, and the Public Health Act of 1878. The latter [illegible] the Corporation the Burial Board for the city of Waterford, and [illegible] over to [illegible] burial grounds closed by order of the Lord Lieutenant and Privy Council, but leaves the burial ground purchased out of the Grand Jury [illegible] in the hands of the Board of Guardians. An extension of the boundary of the county of the city of Waterford would give the burial ground to its rightful owners, and would vest it in the Council selected by the citizens who purchased it.

Upon the passing of the Poor Law Act, 1 & 2 Vic., c. 56, the Poor Law Commissioners proceeded to define the electoral division of Waterford, and for a considerable portion of the circumference adopted the boundaries of the then county of the city of Waterford, but included a small portion [illegible] of the borough, and excluded a portion which was portion of the county of the city of Waterford. The electoral division contains an area of [illegible] acres, and a population of [illegible], being about 2,000 acres less than the former county of the city, but having a population only 1,026 less than that of the Parliamentary borough. The electoral division was divided into five wards, the area and valuation being as follows:—

	Area			Valuation		
	a.	r.	p.	£	s.	d.
Tower Ward,	[illegible]	1	6	[illegible]	[illegible]	0
Custom House Ward,	[illegible]	3	[illegible]	[illegible]	5	0
St. Patrick's Ward,	[illegible]	[illegible]	[illegible]	[illegible]	0	[illegible]
South Ward,	[illegible]	[illegible]	0	[illegible]	14	0
* West Ward,	1,[illegible]	[illegible]	10	[illegible]	[illegible]	0
Total,	[illegible]	[illegible]	[illegible]	[illegible]	3	0

Each ward elects [illegible] guardians, but there is a provision in the Public Health Act, enabling the Local Government Board to divide the [illegible] portions into [illegible] wards for the purposes of that Act. The electoral division is divided into two dispensary districts, with separate physicians, but the [illegible] Medical Charities Act is [illegible] by one committee, which meets at the dispensary at Lady-lane, in the city of Waterford. These physicians are sanitary officers under the Act, but their salaries as sanitary officers are partly paid by the [illegible] portion of the electoral division, and partly by the [illegible] portion.

The Corporate Reform Act, which was meant to remedy municipal abuses, formed the municipal borough out of part of the Parliamentary borough. The boundary lines were drawn in an arbitrary manner, being in some cases to the middle of streets; and, by a strange regulation, it [illegible] the Grand Jury [illegible], and made the municipal borough so formed the county of the city of Waterford for judicial, fiscal, and Grand Jury purposes. That portion of the former county of the city excluded from the present county of the city, which lies at the north of the river Suir, was formed into a new barony, in the county Waterford, and is called the barony of Kilculliheen. It contains only [illegible] acres, and is valued at [illegible], yet [illegible] of the main arterial roads approaching the city of Waterford [illegible]. This barony is [illegible], and ought to be under the jurisdiction, either by the city Grand Jury or the [illegible]

* The valuation of the West Ward includes [illegible] in the Waterford [illegible]

Corporation, the other portion of the former county of the city which was excluded from the existing county of the city was added to the baronies of Gaultiere and Middlethird. The effect of this has been to necessitate the appointment and holding of a county petty sessions, called St. Patrick's Hall Sessions, for the district thus excluded from civic rights, and, as the portion thus transferred from the city to the county is mainly urban, and the sessions are only held monthly, considerable inconvenience has arisen. Such buildings as the poorhouse, the lunatic asylum, the railway stations, the proposed dry docks, and other public buildings are outside the civic bounds. There is no legal provision for lighting these roads, nor does the Hackney Carriage Act apply, and it has been held that for the purposes of the Sunday Closing Act the "City of Waterford" extends to the Parliamentary bounds, and there are two co-ordinate jurisdictions in the same locality. The power of the Town Council, as urban sanitary authority under the Explosives Act, is limited to the municipal bounds.

Wards.—The county of the city of Waterford is divided for municipal purposes into five wards, but the bounds of these do not correspond with those of the Poor Laws, and considerable confusion arises from this want of identity. Their valuation is as follows:—Centre Ward, £5,011; Custom House Ward, £5,933; South Ward, £6,840; Tower Ward, £9,750; *West Ward, £11,165.

Each of these wards elects two aldermen and six councillors, and the Town Council consists of forty representatives; it is the urban sanitary authority, and is intrusted with burial, sanitary, and other purposes.

Under the Registration Acts a fourth district has been formed for the registration of births, deaths, and marriages, and the collection of vital statistics. This district contains an area of 17,939 acres, and containing a population of 30,828. This district is also referred to as the city of Waterford.

There are, therefore, four different areas, each of which is recognized as the city of Waterford.

1st. The county of the city, containing 493 acres, with a population of 23,349.

2nd. The electoral division, containing 7,348 acres, with a population of 28,952.

3rd. The Parliamentary borough, containing 8,444 acres, and a population of 29,979.

4th. The Registrar's district, containing 17,939 acres, with a population of 30,828.

It would be of general utility and convenience to extend the present civic boundaries and to adopt one of the existing divisions for all purposes. The Waterford Improvement Bill of 1874 proposed to adopt the electoral division as the area to be comprised within the county of the city, and to make it the Parliamentary borough, and it is probable it would also be adopted by the Registrar-General as the Registrar's district, and to adopt not only the Poor Law division as to wards, but also, to avoid confusion, the Poor Law nomenclature. This would change the Centre ward into St. Patrick's ward. The St. Patrick's Hall Petty Sessions might be given up, as all cases within the district would be heard at the city petty sessions, which are held every Friday. The Hackney Carriage Act could then be applied to such portions of the enlarged borough as might be considered advisable, and the lighting of the public roads adjacent to the city could be undertaken by the Corporation.

This change would add to the present county of the city the entire of the barony of Kilculliheen and parts of the baronies of Gaultiere and Middlethird, and would transfer to the civic authorities the cost of maintaining the roads (many of them arterial ones), the footways, and other Grand Jury expenditure. The valuation of the electoral division is £51,913 5s.,

* The West Ward valued as comprises £5,[illegible] for the tolls of the Waterford bridge.

and that of the county of the city is £38,739 5s. The district so added, valued at £13,174, would yield a revenue sufficient to meet the expenses which would be transferred from one district to the other. There are no municipal or civic taxes in the county of the city of Waterford. The proposed change would in no way affect the Poor Law taxation, and the districts proposed to be added to the county of the city of Waterford would be relieved from taxation. The Grand Jury cess, at the Summer Assizes, 1878, on the barony of Kilculliheen, was 1s. 5½d. in the pound; that in the barony of Gaultiere was 1s. 3d. in the pound; that in the barony of Middlethird was 1s. 6½d. in the pound; while that in the city of Waterford was only 10½d. in the pound. Thus, too, the districts which would be annexed to the city of Waterford would derive many advantages, and not the least would be the reduction in their taxation under the Grand Jury system. It would be manifestly unfair to the city to enlarge the bounds in such a manner as would throw upon it a burden inadequate to the receipts from Grand Jury cess, and it would be of great public utility to define the bounds in such a way that the term the county of the city, the Parliamentary borough, the electoral division, and the Registrar's district, should comprise and convey the same idea. The Labourers Dwellings' Act is confined to places with a population of not less than 25,000, and the present city of Waterford is exempt from its operations.

Waterford, February 1, 1879.

GENTLEMEN,—I wish to correct a statement in my letter of 29th November, with reference to the taxation of the county of the city of Waterford. The amount of presentments at the Summer Assizes of 1878 was £2,170 7s. 9d., being at the rate of thirteen pence in the pound. A sum of £418 11s. 9d. had been in the hands of the late Board of Superintendents. It was assigned to the credit of the presentments, and reduced the rate to 10½d. in the pound.

The valuation of the portions of the electoral division of Waterford which are not in the county of the city are as follows:—

	Valuation.	Barony Cess.
	£	£ s. d.
Barony of Gaultiere,	4,253	260 12 1
" Middlethird,	4,943	280 7 1
" Kilculliheen,	3,926	202 11 5
Total,	13,174	740 15 1
		County Cess.
County of the city of Waterford,	38,739	2,129 7 1
Total of Electoral Division,	51,913	2,870 1 11

The average on the entire district is equal to thirteen pence in the pound.

I understand the difference of boundary of the wards for Poor Law and for municipal purposes gives the Commissioner of Valuation and his assistants a great deal of trouble, which would be saved by uniformity of area.

I am, gentlemen, yours respectfully,

JOSEPH FISHER.

The Boundary Commissioners.

YOUGHAL.

At a Special Meeting of the Town Commissioners, held on the 3rd of May, 1850, pursuant to a resolution of 5th of April, 1850, it was resolved—

"That the limits of the town for carrying into effect two of the provisions of this Act, namely, Lighting and Cleansing, agreeable to the 21st section, be defined as follows, viz.—on the east, by the river; on the south, by Clifton and Belvue; on the north, by John Rasimore's house at the extremity of Tallow-street, up Cork Hill to the Barrack-master's gate, thence on the west by Ralsonslane, the Infirmary, Town Walls to the top of Windmill-lane, from Windmill-lane along the old Milk Market, to the westward of the town and on a line to Mr. Giles' wall."

MUNICIPAL BOUNDARIES COMMISSION.

MINUTES OF EVIDENCE.

DROGHEDA.—SATURDAY, NOVEMBER 30TH, 1878.

Before W. A. EXHAM, Esq., Q.C. (Chairman); W. P. O'BRIEN, and C. P. COTTON, C.E., Esquires, Commissioners.

Drogheda, Nov. 30, 1878.

Mr. JOHN J. F. GREENE examined.

Mr. John J. F. Greene.

1. [illegible]

2. [illegible]

3. [illegible]

4. [illegible]

5. Mr. O'BRIEN.—[illegible]

6. Mr. EXHAM.—[illegible] 430 odd acres, [illegible]

7. [illegible]

8. [illegible]

9. [illegible]

10. [illegible]

11. [illegible]

12. [illegible]

13. [illegible]

14. [illegible]

15. [illegible]

16. [illegible]

17. [illegible]

18. [illegible]

19. [illegible]

20. [illegible]

21. [illegible]

22. [illegible]

23. [illegible]

24. [illegible]

25. [illegible]

26. [illegible]

27. [illegible]

28. [illegible]

29. [illegible]

30. [illegible]

31. [illegible]

32. [illegible]

33. [illegible]

B

Drogheda.
Nov. 28, 1879.
Mr. John J. F. Greene.

34. The *Town Clerk*.—They don't repair them. The borough boundary extends as far as Mell; the Grand Jury do that.

35. Mr. O'Brien.—None of the Grand Jury functions have been transferred by Act of Parliament to the municipal authorities of Drogheda.

Witness.—The road from Lawrence's-gate in Lawrence-street, to Westgate, is repaired by the Corporation; and from West-gate to Mell it is repaired by the Grand Jury.

36. The *Town Clerk*.—Though it is within the borough, within the walls of the town, the Corporation repair the roads, and within the borough the Grand Jury repair the roads.

37. Mr. O'Brien.—Is that by arrangement?—It is done voluntarily.

38. Could you tell me the actual population living between the one-mile radius and the present boundary?—No, sir, I have not made it out.

39. But you would be able to do so?—Yes.

40. Mr. Exham.—And I suppose you don't happen to know exactly the number of houses, of buildings of all kinds, between the two?—No, I have not made a calculation of the one-mile radius at all.

41. Well now could you tell the number of houses that are within that two mile radius—houses or buildings generally?—I could not exactly tell the number, but I could point them out on this map.

42. Mr. Cotton.—Do we understand this blue line to indicate a townland line?—Yes.

43. Mr. O'Brien.—Then does not the blue line cut a townland?—No, except in two places where it was so large, comprising some 3,000 acres, so that we could not take it in. The only townland we cut in that way by the proposed radius was Mell; we proposed leaving out a small portion of Mell.

44. On what ground?—Because the remainder of the townland which we omitted was a most out-of-the-way place.

45. Was that the only point?—Yes. There was another at Killineer; we cut out about 100 acres, but we took in portion to make the boundary more equal—about 100 acres.

46. Mr. O'Brien.—But you shut out this portion of Mell?—Yes, there was about 1,050 acres. It would bring nearly five miles west. There is another townland, Newtownstalaban; we took in nearly the whole of it, and have cut about 60 acres for the same purpose of equalization. The only other place is the townland of Platin. If we did not take in some of that we would have a zig-zag line—so to make it even, we took the centre of the road, and equalized it. If we took the 1,400 acres in it, it would bring us out six miles.

47. Mr. Cotton.—If you took the one-mile radius what townlands would you cut?—If we took the one-mile radius we would cut two townlands, we would have to cut across Bryanstown and Leggetsrath. Then on the east side we would cut through Newtownstalaban in the same way.

48. Mr. Exham.—What does the red line on the map mark?—That is the old Parliamentary boundary. It is all by townlands, there are no cuttings.

49. Mr. O'Brien.—Can you say how the poor law boundaries would be affected if the one-mile radius were adopted. The present municipal district of Drogheda is entirely within two electoral divisions or districts, St. Mary's and St. Peter's?—Yes, it does not comprehend the entire of them.

50. The poor law electoral divisions extend beyond both those?—Yes.

51. Mr. Exham.—Have you been able to calculate the number of houses that are within the two-mile area proposed, the number of houses or buildings?—Yes.

52. I mean within the two-mile radius and outside the present municipal boundary. Do you know is it all agricultural ground—strictly speaking?—No, there are a great many gentlemen's seats in it.

53. How many gentlemen's seats are there—how many gentlemen's residences outside the present municipal boundary, and that would be, if I may use the phrase, captured within the two-mile radius?—Well, I would say, at least sixteen large places.

54. Rated over £10?—Oh, yes, over £100.

55. Mr. Exham.—Independent of those, are there many buildings—of course we know there is the railway station and the poor-house?—Yes, I except those and Mr. Whitworth's mill. What I have mentioned are gentlemen's seats.

57. Are there any small class of houses or terraces of houses?—Yes, there is Pitcher-street and Bredin outside the boundary, and part of Mell.

58. Mr. O'Brien.—What do you say is the area of the two-mile radius?—8,400 acres, exactly, it would be about 8,200 acres.

59. Mr. Exham.—Can you tell me, Mr. Greene, what are the present rates within the municipal boundary? The *Town Clerk*.—Municipal rates we have none.

61. Has there been any increase of buildings outside the municipal boundary of late?

Witness.—Oh, no, the only large building is Mr. Whitworth's mill.

62. Mr. Exham.—There has been no tendency manifested to build villa residences or places of that sort outside the boundary?—No.

63. Mr. O'Brien.—Tell me, Mr. Greene, how many of these buildings you speak of have been built since 1840?—Mr. Whitworth's mill is the only one.

64. Mr. Exham.—Mr. Whitworth's mill would be brought in by the one-mile radius as well?—Yes.

65. And how many of these gentlemen's places would come within the one mile radius?—They would all be left out, except Alderman Curry's, by the one-mile radius, all except Mr. Whitworth and Alderman Curry.

67. All these principal places except some fifteen or sixteen gentlemen's residences, would be taken in by the one-mile radius?—Yes.

68. How much of Mell would the one-mile radius take in?—It would take in a place called Bryanstown, but would leave out Kearn's place.

69. Mr. Exham.—If you went for a radius in a circle, just to take in a particular place, you would take in a lot of land which, strictly speaking, is not connected with land built on, or likely to be built on?

70. *Witness*.—The mile and a quarter radius would take in Marion Lodge and the whole of Greenhills, and the Old Grove-lane and some houses there, about twenty-five.

71. Mr. Exham.—Then if you took in the one mile and a quarter radius, you would take in the whole of Mell and the whole of Mr. Smith's, whereas if you extend that three quarters of a mile further, there would be only about fifteen or fourteen villa residences that would be taken in, and all the rest would be land?—Yes, when I speak of villa residences, I mean gentlemen's places where there is a quantity of land attached.

72. Then, speaking for the Corporation, I understand you to propose the two-mile radius. What do they propose to themselves by carrying the area out so far — merely to bring in a certain quantity of land, there are only fourteen or fifteen villa residences between the one-mile and the two-mile radius, while the quantity of land brought in is very considerable. Now what advantage do the Corporation think the present inhabitants of Drogheda would have by that?—Well, sir, a great many members of the Corporation are here and are prepared to give their views—so that I would not like to take on myself to speak for them.

73. I thought they might have communicated their views to you?—No; there was no arrangement of that kind. I simply prepared the map.

74. Now, that two-mile radius, so far as the electoral divisions are concerned, it would not alter them at all?—Well, Mr. Farrell would be the best person to ask about that.

75. Would it be your idea that it would be better to take a fixed line from the centre of the town all round, or to have a varying line by town-

Drogheda. Nov. 27, 18[illegible].

Mr. John [illegible].

[illegible]—Well, the only reason I have for [illegible] would be that it would be easier to give notice to the [illegible]. Everyone would be able to see and know the municipal boundary.

76. Would it not be a great inconvenience to make a boundary [illegible] a mile [illegible] of the boundary, and [illegible]—[illegible] I would be for [illegible] by [illegible].

77. Mr. Exham.—There is one very important [illegible] to be borne in mind. The [illegible] of the Committee of the House of Commons, from which the [illegible] has emanated, emphatically points out that for the future there should be, if possible, the one governing body, and they were of opinion that [illegible] powers of the Grand Jury in counties and [illegible], it [illegible] to be transferred to the Town Council." It is a curious [illegible] that "By the law, as it at present stands, when [illegible] outside the boundary, and who [illegible] within the limits of the Act, are brought in, they will only have to pay one-fourth of the [illegible] on one-fourth of the net annual valuation." If this land is brought in the rural districts [illegible] and put in the city [illegible]. The farmers that are brought in, according to the existing law, [illegible] they are brought in, no matter what they may pay now, pay only one-fourth of the taxation. I don't know if the Corporation have given this point full consideration, in putting forward this proposed extension.

78. Mr. O'Brien.—I had better read the section. Under the [illegible] section of the Towns Improvement Act, 1854, it is provided—

"For the purpose of any rate to be made or levied [illegible] provisions of this Act, or of any Act incorporated herewith, all lands used as arable, meadow, or grazing land only, or as woodlands or market gardens, or nursery grounds, and all lands covered with water, or used as a canal, or any towing path to the same, and all lands used as a railway, [illegible] [illegible] of any Act of Parliament, for public conveyance, shall be assessed and liable in proportion of one-fourth only of the net annual value of such lands respectively."

79. Alderman [illegible].—We did not consider that at all.

80. Mr. Exham.—It is a matter for serious consideration before arriving at a definite decision to take in this extended radius, that in such land is only bound to pay one-fourth of the taxation. Further, there can be no doubt that it is on this particular view that these matters must be considered. At present [illegible] recommendations of the House of Commons is that within the municipal boundaries there should not be a divided authority—one party doing one thing, [illegible] lighting, cleansing; and the Grand Jury [illegible]—but that all should be placed under the one governing body. The farmers, as I have said, who will be brought within this radius, would only have, under the section just read, to pay rates on one-fourth only of the net annual valuation. At present [illegible] pay [illegible]. They get off paying that if they come within the municipal boundary, and the Corporation take over the roads and by the existing law they might only be bound to pay rates on one-fourth of their valuation for all their lands. This is a very serious matter for a corporation to consider in a [illegible] of such an extended area as that. It seems to me that a great many [illegible] in future will be [illegible] of the fact that where they want to bring in land, the land they bring in will only be subjected to one-fourth the valuation. I can well understand a great many [illegible] will say, "We will go within the boundary, willingly and joyfully, for then we will get [illegible], and only pay the one-fourth of the taxation."

81. Mr. [illegible] (solicitor to the Corporation).—As to the poor law, that section would not apply.

82. Mr. Exham.—It would be a different thing in respect of the poor law, but would apply as the improvement rate.

83. Mr. O'Brien.—Assume that the land and that line represented by the one-mile radius is taken and adopted, it would be impossible to carry out the recommendation of the Parliamentary Committee—In dealing with this question care should be taken to make municipal wards conterminous with wards for poor law purposes, and [illegible] with poor law electoral divisions.

84. Witness.—I believe it would. There is no [illegible] that the mile radius would not suit.

85. Mr. Exham.—Would the adding of the [illegible] boundary be less if a radius of a mile and a quarter were adopted?—Well, I don't think it would.

86. Is not every portion of ground lying between the one-mile radius and the two-mile radius, which you propose, in point of fact, agricultural ground?—It is, in general, agricultural land.

87. All, I suppose, with the exception of what is contained within gentlemen's residences or grounds?—Yes; I should say all agricultural. When they were making the new borough, under the Reform Act, the Commissioners cut right through the townland.

88. Mr. O'Brien.—The municipal boundaries were made irrespective of townlands altogether.

Mr. John Farrell examined.

Mr. John Farrell.

89. Mr. O'Brien.—Are you the poor-rate collector?

90. Have you any office under the Corporation?—No, not now.

91. How many wards are there at present in the borough?—Three.

92. Are there guardians elected for these three wards, as well as members of the Corporation?—No; the guardians are elected for electoral divisions, and these divisions extend three miles or so from the union—from the workhouse.

93. Then, in point of fact, there are no wards, strictly speaking, for which guardians are elected, and which are conterminous with wards for municipal purposes?—No.

94. Can you tell me what is the valuation within the one-mile radius?—I could not, sir, because it goes outside our rate-books. Our rate-books give the valuation within the borough, but as the one-mile radius stands, I could not give it.

95. It divides townlands, in fact?—Yes; it divides both fields and townlands.

96. There are portions of only two electoral divisions, I understand, St. Mary's and St. Patrick's in the borough?—Yes.

97. Now, adopting that one-mile radius, would it take you into any other electoral division?—Yes, it would. A two-and-a-half-mile radius would extend beyond the electoral divisions. It would go into Mellifont and into Julianstown or Bey More. I should mention it would likewise take in Platin.

98. That is the two-and-a-half-mile radius?—Yes.

99. Mr. Exham.—What portions of the present borough are within the different electoral divisions if the river cuts them in two?—This portion (on map) is St. Mary's, and this St. Peter's.

100. Mr. Exham.—Am I right in saying that outside the present boundary, with the exception of the places that were mentioned—Mall, Whitworth's mill, the railway station, and a few other buildings, it is nearly all agricultural land?—Yes; generally speaking.

101. And excepting also what is comprised within the limits of gentlemen's villas?—Yes; generally

Drogheda. [illegible]

Mr. John Fagan.

speaking, it is all agricultural—generally speaking, it comprises small farms.

102. And I suppose tillage farms, a great deal of it?—Yes; nearly all occupied by tillage farmers.

103. And are there many small farmers amongst them?—Oh, yes; they are very numerous.

104. A large population?—Very numerous.

105. Now, as far as you know from going amongst them, is there any anxiety on the part of those small farmers to be brought within the borough?—I never heard them express a wish on it.

106. They are not so very anxious on the subject, then; anxious about lighting or benefits of that sort? —No. I may say they don't benefit by the lighting.

107. Mr. O'Brien.—Are not the lands within a certain radius of the town benefited by their proximity to the lighting and other advantages?—Yes; there is no doubt of this, that they have a most valuable market for their goods—the best in Ireland—there is no better market for their produce in the whole of Ireland.

108. And in that way they derive, indirectly, advantage from the lighting in coming into the town with their produce?—Oh, yes; being a market town, of course, those who come to profit by it. Formerly, I may mention, we had a "custom" here payable on goods. That is now all done away with.

109. So then, in fact, they have all the advantages without paying?—Yes, quite so.

110. And do you think that, in a diminished proportion, they should contribute for the enjoyment of those advantages?—Yes, where they profit by them, decidedly.

111. Mr. Exham.—Would you say that the people three miles out profit just as much as those nearer? —Yes, and I think you might go further.

112. I suppose, in point of fact, the small farmers flock in from some miles round?—Yes.

113. But I presume you would say the nearer the town—and the closer to these advantages—the better for those people?—Well, yes; but I would say that those four miles away would have equal advantages, or nearly so, with those a mile distant.

114. They are afforded, by being near the market, greater facilities for sales and purchases?—Yes; there are many facilities.

115. Would there be to those poor people any substantial advantage in giving gas to them, for instance? —Oh, no; there is no chance of that.

116. Or if there was a water supply to them at high pressure?—Oh, no.

117. I believe they have not been supplied in that way yet in Drogheda?—Oh, yes; many years since.

118. It would be no great advantage to them to get the water at high pressure—those small farmers?

Mr. Orme.—Oh, no; the water is confined to the borough—to the portion marked yellow on the map.

120. I don't suppose cleansing the streets or anything of that kind can interest them very much—they can't have any particular object in seeing that?

Witness.—No, sir.

121. The Mayor.—If we got an extension would the magisterial authority extend to that radius for quarter sessions—petty sessions?

Mr. Exham.—That is a thing I could not answer. That is for the Legislature to do, founded on the report of the Select Committee and dealing with the report we make.

122. Mr. O'Brien.—At present the effect of extending the boundary would be to give you a larger area for municipal purposes, but up to the present time the transfer of the grand jury functions to municipal corporations would be only by special legislation. By the Public Health Act of 1878, there was power given to the Local Government Board to give a provisional order which required the consent of the grand jury as well as the municipal body.

Alderman R. B. Daly.

Alderman Robert Bedford Daly, J.P., examined.

123. Witness.—I was not here early, and consequently I do not exactly know what matters have been brought under your attention. Captain Keogh, our Stipendiary, and Mr. Whitworth are here, and they will be able to tell you as to the railway station where all the cars from Drogheda assemble, and which is thus supplied with a great necessary from the town, and in many other ways is benefited, and which is so closely connected with its business, and yet it is out of the jurisdiction of the local magistrates; and, if a dispute occurs there, the police, I believe, frequently, rather than go to all the trouble and bother of bringing them before the county Meath magistrates, are inclined to let offenders go unpunished, and thus justice suffers. The fact is, they are tempted to overlook offences so as not to go through all this work and difficulty about matters that ought to be settled by the local magistrates. The same thing applies to the union workhouse. We have a coroner from the county Meath coming here to hold an inquest in our own workhouse, though, as Mr. O'Brien knows, it is just close to the town. These, sir, are anomalies that I am sure must be patent to even the Commissioners themselves. In the next place it may be mentioned that it adds no doubt to the prestige of a town to have a fair boundary round it, and that people who unquestionably derive the advantages that are given by the lighting, cleansing, and paving of the town, who use its churches and its schools, and so on, and who, in fact, have all the advantages connected with the town, while living in villa residences and elsewhere around, should fairly come within the limits of the town radius and be subject to all the rules and regulations connected with it. In an especial manner I should say that, as far as Drogheda is concerned, none of these persons need object or ought to object, for we have a chartered property of £4,000 a year, increasing year by year, and there is not one penny of borough rate laid on.

124. Mr. O'Brien.—What is the present amount of the property of the town?—£19,000 and odd is the valuation.

125. I mean the annual income?—It is about £4,000.

126. And what is your expenditure?—Oh, every penny of it.

127. Do you, in seeking an extension of your area, require additional funds for the proper execution of the municipal work. Is that one of your objects?—If we did execute further works, we might require additional funds, no doubt. There are things that would be better here for outsiders than in Meath. They are going to build a large courthouse in Navan, and of course the men outside will have to contribute to that. I would go in for a better courthouse here; and if a proper one were built, of course we would require some little addition.

128. You said that one of the advantages derived by those people outside was the fact that the churches and schools in Drogheda were availed of by them. Now, for what radius around Drogheda are, would you say, the inhabitants beholden to or dependent on the town of Drogheda in that respect?—I know that nearly all the Protestant and Catholic gentry come in here to the churches and send their children as a matter of course to school here.

129. Within what radius would you say does that apply?—About three miles, I should say. The people outside have, generally speaking, the advantages derivable from the town, and I don't think they would suffer one penny of taxation. Remember that we have

chartered property, unlike Newry or Dundalk, of £4,000 a year, and that it is likely to be doubled.

130. How is that?—By leases falling in.

131. Lately, do you mean?—Yes, some lately.

132. And you will get a higher rent?—Yes; when the leases fall in we get a better rent.

133. What increase now would you estimate that you would have during the next five years, say?—About £600 a year for the next five years.

134. Mr. Keenan.—Have you considered about the proposed radius?—Yes, I have.

135. Do you think that an extension to a two-mile radius would be fair?—Decidedly; I want myself for more.

136. Now, I would ask you have you considered this, if you do extend the boundaries would you propose to light and give water to those people whom you would by such extension bring in?—Not for what you have pointed out—not for one-fourth taxation. What I hold is that the man who would be brought in gets value at present. All that he gets done for his county cess is his roads being done, which we would do. We would take the doing of the roads; but as to the cleansing and lighting, he gets advantage of that at present.

137. Yes; but what of the man who comes in once a week to market, or, at most, twice a week; would you then say it was right and fair for them to pay the same as those persons living in the very heart of the city?—Well, if a rate had to be struck it would be a hard case, but there are no municipal rates.

138. If you were sure you would never have to ask for a municipal rate there would be an advantage to them, as they would get off better by paying a smaller county cess; but you can't forget that you cannot be sure of that—you can't foresee what may happen. The question is whether the persons brought in should not have the same advantages as to lighting, and so on?—We could not do that.

139. Would you not have the statement made—"here we are within half a mile of the borough boundary, and though we are paying all the taxes, there is no gas lamp for three-quarters of a mile of our houses"?—Well, the man who would say that would drive into the town to the railway, and so on, and would have all the advantages of the lights.

140. Take the case of a man living away out here, as from the town; from the time he goes out of the town he gets no advantage, at least the advantage of the lights cannot extend very far, would it be fair, then, to extend the borough boundary and make the case, that he drives in and indirectly gets advantages from the lighting and other matters?—I would hold that whatever you take in, whether less or more, within the municipal boundary should be liable to the same rate. You must recollect, besides, that the man so brought in has a chance of a red cloak and may be Mayor.

141. If you bring him in and put him under the liabilities you should give him the advantages you yourself possess up to his gate. You should give him water up to his door, for instance. I know of one place—a town in which the people on one side of the road get the lights, and have to pay for it, whilst the people on the other side pay nothing.

142. Witness.—In this case the people get the advantage of the light every day of the week.

143. The Mayor.—I would say, also, that when these people outside come within the boundary—when they become part of the borough—they would be represented, and would have a voice in the distribution of the lights and other advantages of the municipality.

144. Mr. Keenan.—The gentleman who has his office and place of business in the town, and who, for his own convenience, lives outside the borough, would you put him on a par with the farmer?—Yes; for he would get rid of the county cess that he pays in Louth or Meath if he were brought in. I quite admit that this is an exceptional town, and I would expect that you would give us an exceptional report, for a man coming in here has no municipal taxes to pay.

145. You say you spend all your income upon your own borough; now suppose that the area is extended to, say, two miles and that the whole maintenance of the roads within that two miles, and of all the streets, is put upon you, do you consider that you won't be obliged to put on a rate?—Well, the work is all done. We were called on to make sewers, which, of course, was calculated to run away with money; but it has been done, and we won't want to do it again.

146. Yes; you made sewers within your own radius. If you bring these people outside into the area, and make the two-mile extension, you will be called on as Urban Sanitary Authority to make sewers leading over that one-mile radius to your own sewers; you will be called on to keep all the roads in repair within that boundary; you will require to have them scavenged and cleansed, and so on. Now, the question is—suppose that the expenditure was such that you required to strike a rate; you must recollect that, under the provisions of the Act already read, if you have to strike a rate, these people so brought in come in at the one-fourth of the annual value. That is an advantage to them. But see how it affects the Corporation, on the other hand. How is it useful, is it judicious, for existing owners of property within the present borough to have that state of circumstances existing, for you may be obliged to put upon the people of Drogheda that which you say does not now exist—namely, a rate; and it may be that you will have to do that to assist those who are outside. It is in that view I ask you to consider as to the large radius. I can perfectly understand your taking it further in of, perhaps, one mile for the purpose of taking in the railway and outlying residences, and so on, as of extending it even more; but the suggestions I have thrown out on the point should receive careful consideration.—I must say, sir, for myself, and I think I may, in so saying, speak for a great many of us here, that it comes with surprise upon us, this point about the one-fourth of the valuation. By that it would seem that we would, in fact, be liable for everything.

147. Mr. Keenan.—We must, of course, call your attention to how the matter exactly stands, so that you act with your eyes open.—Under these circumstances I would rather go for the one-mile-and-a-quarter radius.

148. If you extend the boundary the man who is out here—far out on the extended radius—will be in the same position as the man in the centre of the town. You cannot strike one rate for one portion of the borough, and another for another. The moment the man out here is brought in you must give him all the benefit of the altered circumstances—the benefits of sewers, and so on. That man says to you, "You must give me all these advantages, and I only pay one-fourth of whatever rate you strike inside." Now, with that fact staring you in the face, the question for you to consider is—whether it would be desirable to have the enlargement of the borough boundary?

149. Witness.—It is a most important consideration.

150. The Mayor.—The matter comes with surprise upon us in the light you have put it.

151. Alderman Kenny.—Might I ask would grass lands come under the denomination of paying the one-fourth?

Mr. Keenan.—Certainly.

152. The Mayor.—We are claiming our own boundary. It is not like many other boundaries. We are claiming what has been taken from us. The red boundary on the map was the boundary belonging to Drogheda.

153. Alderman Kenny.—It is the Parliamentary boundary at present. What I understand is that in anything you extend beyond the borough of the town of Drogheda, and take in those parties, those parties when they come under the control of the Corporation, will be bound to pay only one-fourth.

154. The Mayor.—That is what we understand. But

Drogheda.
Nov. 22, 1873.

Alderman R. B. Daly.

Drogheda. Jan. 27, 1879. — Alderman E. B. Daly.

we should not be treated as people claiming something new. We ask the same extension of boundary that we had.

155. *Witness.*—Clearly from what Mr. Exham has said, instead of gaining anything, we are losing everything.

156. Mr. Exham.—Our object here is to see what is best to be done for all parties. It is not in the interest of outsiders, or those living within the town, that we act, but simply to find out what is the best course. It would, therefore, be foolish for us to adopt your view as to the two-mile boundary without at least showing you the consequences.

157. *Witness.*—It has certainly come with surprise upon us.

158. If we were inclined to recommend the adoption of the two-mile radius you would probably say afterwards, well, you might have shown us the consequences.

159. *Witness.*—Having heard the whole explanation, my evidence, and my wish is, that I would be understood to approve of the mile-and-a-quarter radius.

160. *The Mayor.*—The people of Drogheda also would like that so many people should not have to go to Trim and Dundalk sessions and quarter sessions, who might, if the radius was larger, come to Drogheda.

161. Mr. *Patrick M'Cullen.*—I think the outsiders are more content to remain as they are at present.

162. Mr. Exham.—It occurs to me that as considerable difficulty arises in this case, and as the Corporation here are taken by surprise, we will have no objection to come down on another day, and you will have an opportunity of considering what we have thrown out in the meantime.

163. Alderman *Knapp.*—That is a very prudent thing.

Mr. O'Brien.—If you desire an adjournment, which I think would be advisable, it would be well that you endeavoured to get a line which, adhering as closely as possible to the mile-and-a-quarter radius, would be still adhering to the townland boundary, for the intention of the committee is to make the municipal and poor-law boundaries coterminous. You should also get as nearly as possible the valuation of the line you propose.

164. Alderman *Knapp.*—We will be then better prepared.

165. Mr. Exham.—Now, Alderman Daly, as to this one-mile radius, what would you propose to do with the existing wards. Would you be disposed to make the new district added on into a separate ward, or would you be disposed to alter the existing wards. Would you, in fact, let the wards stand as they are at present, and let the new districts be made into one or two wards?—I would run them according to their natural position as regards the existing wards.

166. Mr. O'Brien.—Would three wards be enough?—Yes.

167. Mr. Exham.—Taking the mile-and-a-quarter radius, how many ratepayers would it bring in?—About 815 I should say.

168. Are the wards at present equally manned?—

169. *The Mayor.*—There is not more than a difference of twenty in each ward. Laurence's-gate is the largest.

170. Mr. Exham.—I see here Fair-gate ward, 84?

171. *The Town Clerk.*—It is 79 now.

172. Mr. Exham.—West-gate ward, 84; Laurence's-gate, 120. Now what I want to know is, do the Corporation think it advisable to make any alteration, and if so, what in the existing boundary of the wards?—Alderman *Knapp.*—My impression is that the extended radius should just be a continuation of the wards.

173. I see that Mr. Corbett asked "Has Laurence's-gate Ward the largest population as well as the largest number of burgesses?" The Town Clerk answered, "I think it is the richest ward of the three, and has, I think, the largest population, as well as the largest number of burgesses." Do the wards return the same number of representatives each?—Yes, two aldermen and six councillors.

174. Mr. Exham.—Does any member of the Corporation think it would be advisable to add any portion of these out-districts to the Fair-gate to make it up to the numbers of Laurence's-gate?

175. *The Mayor.*—It would only cause confusion. There is no fault found with there being a greater number of electors in one ward than in another.

176. Mr. Exham.—Probably that one-mile radius would throw more into one ward than into another, and make the disproportion of burgesses still greater.

177. Mr. Cotton.—It would increase that South Ward twice as much as the others. It is mostly St. Mary's, I think.

178. *The Town Clerk.*—The South Ward is part of Laurence's-gate and part of West-gate.

179. You increase the number of burgesses by these extensions; in Laurence's-gate say by about 50, in West-gate the same, and you have these wards getting an amount of representation equal to Fair-gate, which has only 79. Now would you, under these circumstances consider it to be advisable to have the wards increased or lessened in any way.

180 *The Mayor.*—In Fair-gate Ward I would suggest alteration. Outside West-gate, the voters of Trinity-street, on both sides, go with West-gate. I would suggest this alteration, that the electors on the north side should be put up with the Fair-gate Ward, and that those on the south side should stay as they are.

181. It is one of the things that ought to be considered, and it does occur to me when I see Fair-gate with 79, and West-gate with 120, that if I was an inhabitant of West-gate, I would say, "I don't think Fair-gate should get as many representatives at the Council as the other."

182. *Witness.*—After all that is a consideration for the Council.

The Mayor.—This inquiry shows the necessity of these alterations, when we go into the matter.

183. One reason for my mentioning the matter is that I know elsewhere there have been great complaints of the valuations of wards in connexion with this subject. In Cork the valuation of one ward is, I think, £30,000 odd, or so, and they get no more representation than two valued at £16,000. If you would be able to give me the valuations we would then be better able to judge of what was proposed to be brought in under the mile-and-a-quarter area.

184. *Witness.*—If you take in some of the large districts it would outweigh the valuation, and would make an immense difference. I think the Corporation would rather go to equalize the number of voters.

185. Mr. Exham.—It is a matter for the Corporation to consider what is to be done with the new district to be brought in, as to voters. They must be attached to existing, or formed into new ones.

Mr William Whitworth, M.P.

Mr. William Whitworth, M.P., examined.

186. Mr. Exham.—It is right to mention that the complaints were made in Cork in some wards where such a state of things as this prevailed. The wards were small and the valuation was less, and yet they returned the same number of Town Councillors to the Corporation as wards that had three times the number of voters, and three times the valuation. That matter was discussed by the Committee of the House of Commons, and this was one of the suggestions that emanated from them, and which I think, namely, that in this inquiry we were to try and see from the evidence if there, what was stated before us in our inquiry, any and what alteration in the wards was desirable.

187. WITNESS.—The proportion of [illegible] in that the numbers should correspond with the value.

188. Mr. EXHAM.—It does not appear what view they took, except that there should be a modification of boundaries.

189. Mr. O'BRIEN.—You should consider the matter well between this and the day we return, Aldermen, and tell us your views fully on it.

190. WITNESS.—It is desirable that there should be as great [illegible] as possible in that respect.

191. The MAYOR.—It is a matter the people of Drogheda have not [illegible] of.

192. Mr. EXHAM.—There are five or six Town Councillors in Fairgate Ward, which has only 78 voters, the present valuation of that ward being less than the large ward of 130 voters. Now the question is whether there should be any portion of the larger ward thrown into the smaller one, to make property more represented in the different wards.

193. The MAYOR.—There are large houses in the Laurence-gate Ward, and not in the others.

194. Mr. EXHAM.—Laurence-gate is the greater and the best provided. These two things we want to have the views of the Corporation upon.

195. Mr. *Patrick M'Quillan*.—I hold land within the mile-and-a-quarter radius, in Bryanstown. I am beyond the Parliamentary boundary, and vote for a member of Parliament. What I was going to say is, I believe it would be better if you would form whatever you take in between the present boundary and the old, into a separate ward. It would then be better represented than if you put it in with the old wards.

196. Mr. O'BRIEN.—Do you mean to have a separate ward going round in a circle?—Yes.

197. The TOWN CLERK.—It would not be done, and by increasing the ward you will be increasing the [illegible] very [illegible].

WITNESS.—I agree with a good deal of what has been said here as to the necessity of extending the boundary of Drogheda. I differ, however, with some of my fellow councillors in the Corporation as to the extent of the requirements as to such extension. I differ with some of them as to the extent of the new boundary to be asked for; but in order to make our proceedings unanimous I agreed to the two-mile radius. That opinion, however, is with Alderman Daly's, [illegible] by the information you have been kind enough to give. At the same time I must say that what we fought for an increase of boundary, is for the taxation purposes. I think that this increase of boundary is absolutely necessary, and if for no other reason but this, that a great many things come from outside our boundary—so the residents would not so have justice done if it is necessary to go so far that the citizens are very often taxed for [illegible]. That state of things is very much to be regretted, and it would conduce to the interests of justice that such places should be within the municipal boundary. I, myself, would think the mile-and-a-quarter radius would be enough. Beyond that I do not think I have any observations to make. I will only add that your observations ought to be taken carefully into consideration by the Corporation.

[illegible] &c.

198. Mr. EXHAM.—For magisterial purposes the mile-and-a-quarter radius would [illegible] bring in the places most desirable?—I think so. There are parts that are practically part of the borough, and they ought to be brought in, and if that is done it will unquestionably be a great point gained.

199. The MAYOR.—I [illegible], but I have really nothing to add to what has been already said.

200. Mr. EXHAM.—Under all the circumstances it is much better that the Corporation should take [illegible]. We commissioners, as I have said, to do our best for all parties. There will be no hurry in the matter of your considering the subject, for our time will be so much occupied that we could not be here before another month.

The Commissioners adjourned.

DROGHEDA.—SATURDAY, APRIL 26TH, 1879.

April 26, 1879.

The Inquiry was resumed to-day by Mr. EXHAM, Q.C., and Mr. COTTON, C.E.

Mr. J. J. [illegible], County Surveyor, examined.

Mr. J. J. [illegible].

1. Mr. EXHAM.—Have the Town Commissioners considered this matter of the extension of the boundaries since we last sat in Drogheda?—Yes, they have.

2. They passed a resolution, I believe, on the subject?—Yes, they did.

3. What was the effect of that resolution?—It is in favour of accepting the two mile radius.

4. Two miles from the centre of the town?—Yes.

5. And was that a unanimous resolution of the Corporation?—I could not exactly say.

6. Was the former unanimous, to the best of your recollection?—Yes, as well as I remember, it was. Perhaps one or two members spoke against it.

7. Have you, since we were here last, looked out on the map, and seen how the extension could be made following townland boundaries?—By the two-mile radius we cut three townlands.

8. Mr. COTTON.—Would you give us the names of the townlands you propose to include—those that are whole and those that are cut?

9. Mr. EXHAM.—I think you gave us that on the last occasion.

Mr. [illegible].—Yes, I gave a copy to the Secretary.

10. Mr. EXHAM.—Well, now, the blue line—the portion coloured blue on the map—what portion is that?—The blue line is the boundary of the proposed two-mile radius. We proposed to come as near to the townland boundary as we can possibly, but we cannot adhere to it in all cases.

11. Mr. COTTON.—Can you give us a tracing of that?—Yes, I shall send it on to you.

12. What does the red line mark?—The red line is the present Parliamentary boundary of the old borough.

13. Mr. EXHAM.—What is the Parliamentary boundary?—The red line, and the yellow portion is the municipal—the red is the old county boundary.

14. Then what the Corporation propose to do is to take in all that portion included within the blue line on this map, making a radius of two miles from the centre of the town?—Yes.

15. Mr. COTTON.—Did the Corporation come to any conclusion about the division of the area into wards?—They believed that there should be a subdivision into three wards as at present, and the extended portions taken into each.

16. Did they come to any conclusion as to how it should be done?—No; they did not.

17. Mr. EXHAM.—Have you got a list of the voters at present within the municipal district?

18. I have [illegible] in list of voters.

19. Mr. EXHAM.—I see from this that there are seventy-nine voters in Fair Gate ward at present, and in West Gate ward, ninety-five?—Yes.

20. Can you let me have the area and valuation of the wards, with the number of houses, &c.?—Yes; the 1871 [illegible] Fair Gate ward, the area is 132 acres, in Laurence Gate 156 acres, and West Gate 173, total 461. In Fair Gate ward there were 395 houses, of which 336 were inhabited, 58 uninhabited, and there were 56 buildings, under the head of out-offices, not corresponding. Laurence Gate, 1,285 houses, 1,146 inhabited, 87 uninhabited, two buildings.

DROGHEDA. April 26, 1876.

Mr. J. J. Greene.

and 265 out-offices or farmsteading. West Gate ward, 1,099 houses, 982 inhabited, 103 uninhabited, two building, and 169 out-offices and farmsteading. The total number of houses for the three wards was 3,279, of which 2,938 were inhabited, 300 uninhabited, four building, and 491 out-offices, &c.

21. Now, as to the population?—According to the return of 1871, there were in Fair Gate ward 3,099 persons—1,799 males, 1,377 females. Laurence Gate, 5,380 persons—2,420 males, and 2,960 females. West Gate, 4,416 persons—2,135 males, 2,280 females. In St. Mary's parish there were 803 families; in St. Peter's, 2,193, and Tullyallen, 171 (total 3,167). The municipal valuation of St. Mary's parish was £3,779 10s., of St. Peter's, £15,035 4s., and of Tullyallen, £310—total £19,104 14s.

22. Mr. Cotton.—That, I understand, was the valuation in 1871?—Yes; it is taken from the census book.

23. Mr. John Farrell, T.C.—There has been a great decrease in the valuation of the small tenements which are rated at about 30s., while there has been a large increase in those above £5.

24. How much would you say is the difference?—The decrease in the borough would amount to about £200. A great many small streets have disappeared altogether.

25. Mr. Exham.—Now, Mr. Greene, I think we got from you already, when we were here, what is the entire valuation of the new district, as we may call it?—Yes.

26. Mr. Cotton.—What would you propose yourself with regard to the division of the additional area into wards?—I think if they were divided into three distinct wards, and the lines of the present wards extended out to meet the boundaries formed, it would be sufficient.

27. Would that include one-third, about, of the additional population, and one-third the additional valuation in each?—Yes, at the same time they are very unequal at present. Laurence Gate ward has the largest number.

28. Mr. Exham.—Would you be able, Mr. Greene, in sending us the tracing, to mark out what you would suggest as a line to be added to the three wards?—Yes, you will be able to see it on the map. I will send you a tracing. It will be one marked green on the map.

29. Mr. Exham.—Now, Mr. Farrell, what is your view as to the division of the wards?—All the three wards will commence at the Court-house—the line separating West Gate ward from Laurence Gate ward will be a line through centre of Shop-street, Bull-ring, Barrack-lane, Duleek-street, Beamore-road, out in a straight line to boundary. All on the eastern side will be in Laurence Gate ward, and all on the western side will be in West Gate ward. The line from Tholsel up through centre of Peter-street, William-street, King-street, Palace-street, Newfoundwell-road, and in a straight line through said road to borough boundary, will divide Laurence Gate ward from Fair Gate ward. All east and south of said line to be in Laurence Gate ward, and all north and west in Fair Gate ward. The line at Court-house for the third division passes through the centre of West-street, Horsefair, George's-street, North-road, and on by centre of Dundalk-road to borough boundary, will divide the Fair Gate ward from West Gate ward—all on north and east to be in Fair Gate ward, and all on west and south in West Gate ward.

30. Mr. Cotton.—Would that add about one-third of the new area to each Ward?—I think Fair Gate ward would have the largest proportion of property, but there would be less rated occupiers.

[Mr. Greene here handed in a list of all the persons rated at £9 15s. and upwards, who would be within the proposed two-mile radius—336 in number.]

31. Mr. Farrell.—There are several people who hold in the town, and in different parts outside, so that the constituency will not be increased exactly by 336, because some people in the list are already rated occupiers in the town.

32. Mr. Cotton.—I was going to ask did the Corporation purpose to take up the powers of the County Grand Jury?

Mr. Greene.—I could not answer that.

33. Alderman Kearney.—I should suppose that would be their object.

34. Mr. Cotton.—Are we to take it the Corporation do wish to take up the duties from the two Grand Juries?

Alderman Kearney.—In certain proportions, I should say so.

35. Alderman Daly.—I think you may take it to be the wish of the Corporation, but there has been no formal resolution or expression of opinion, no vote of the Council yet, on the subject. I brought the subject myself before the notice of the Corporation, but we took no vote on it.

36. Alderman Kearney.—I think we may say we were unanimous as to the advisability of adopting the two-mile radius.

37. Mr. Exham.—As I learned from Mr. Greene, there was no absolute destruction??

Alderman Daly.—Yes; but there was not a vote taken.

38. Mr. Greene.—Even at the present time the Corporation has asked me to present at these Sessions for all the works carried on heretofore by the Grand Jury; and, in fact, though the Grand Jury gave the rates, the Corporation do the roads.

39. Mr. Exham.—Are you speaking of the Grand Jury of the county outside, who have charge of the extended area?—

Alderman Daly.—We will take them in, and the county outside will have no more to do with them then.

40. Mr. Exham.—You can tell me, Alderman Daly, is the county of the city of Drogheda exactly coincident with the municipal area?—Yes, both are exactly the same.

41. Am I right in saying, Alderman, that all the roads outside the present municipal district, and within the blue line, are at present kept in order by the two Grand Juries of the county Meath and the county Louth?—Yes.

42. Do the people living in those localities pay county cess?—Yes.

43. Have you any taxes in the town?—No municipal taxes.

44. And do you keep up our roads out of your own property?—No; we have the county cess and Grand Jury rate here, put on by the Grand Jury of the county of the town of Drogheda, and they give a rate in aid to the Corporation. There is a certain area called the "Gates," and within these old "Gates" the Corporation have been doing the work out of the borough fund; from that, then, out to where it joins the county, the roads have been put in repair by county rate, which is a rate in aid.

45. Mr. Exham.—Who strikes that rate?—The Grand Jury of the county of the town of Drogheda.

46. Alderman Kearney.—That is outside the Gates, between the counties of Louth and Meath. The city Grand Jury assess for the short distance, from the boundary to the adjoining county of Meath or Louth.

47. Mr. Exham.—Then, Alderman Kearney, how much does that amount to in the year—what is the city cess for that?—Well, it has been rather high for the last half-year, but it was in consequence of a large expenditure in making a pathway from the terminus of the railway; the utmost cess for keeping it in order is from 10d. to 1s. each half-year.

48. For the town?—For the county of the town it used to be from 10d. to 1s. I may say altogether that the average is about 10d.

49. Mr. Exham.—What I want to know is this: Do the Grand Jury of the county of the city of Drogheda levy or present for a county cess, or a cess in the nature of county cess, which hitherto has amounted to 10d., or varied from that to 1s., or 1s. 1d.—is that so?—Alderman Daly.—It used to amount to 3s.

a 1s. 6d., but the [illegible] Act [illegible] us of a portion of that, which is [illegible] lighting [illegible] of 1s. 6d. for every [illegible]

48. Well, now, if you bring in these outlying districts you will get a great lot of roads that you will have to keep in repair. Have you considered what it would be fair to those people living outside to pay—at present they pay the county cess, what is that?

Mr. Farrell.—[illegible] it averages about 1s. 9d. in the pound. We have a [illegible] which the [illegible] of Drogheda, and the county of [illegible]; the rate is [illegible]

49. What is it to Meath?

50. Farrell.—From [illegible]

51. Well, if those roads are brought in, what is your proposal as to the taxes the people living in this area are to pay?

Alderman Keegan.—There is nothing except the maintaining and lighting the roads [illegible]

52. Alderman Daly.—The Corporation property is every year increasing and will go up to about [illegible] a year. At present the Corporate property is over £4,000 a year for all municipal purposes, so that all the[illegible] within the new area [illegible] will only have to pay a rate in aid towards the roads.

53. Mr. Cotton.—How much will that be?—It will never come to more than 1s. 3d. in the pound; 1s. 6d. is the very outside that portion brought in will have to pay.

54. Mr. Exham.—Then you would be, in point of fact, bringing these [illegible] in this way [illegible] as at present, they were paying also the county [illegible] [illegible] included in the [illegible] The county at large charges are included in the 1s. [illegible] assessment. The benefit of the [illegible] Act will go [illegible] county, as well as the town, and also the [illegible] to lunatic asylums, and so on, and in this way would aid the county rate [illegible]

55. I know it won't go beyond 1s. 9d. They are now talking of building a new Court-house [illegible] it would come up to 2s. 6d.

56. Then, suppose all this outside land is brought in, and then, as I already called your attention to, the law [illegible] land within the municipality is only to pay [illegible] of its valuation, then you [illegible] will you be [illegible] to all this land. You will have to keep the roads in repair, and the rate the land will have to pay will be only an one-fourth of the valuation.

57. Alderman Daly.—We were under the impression that that only referred to the sanitary rate. The Corporation would be greatly gained by that. They would modify their opinion very much [illegible] in the [illegible] I should have [illegible] other towns where [illegible] this question, the [illegible] that had only reference to the sanitary rate.

58. Mr. Exham.—Oh, not at all. What do the railway company pay—do they pay full rates or only one-fourth of the valuation?

Mr. Farrell.—They pay the full rate for the building.

59. And for the line?—There is a valuation as on ordinary property, so much on the linear mile.

60. And they pay the whole of that rate?—Yes.

61. Alderman Daly.—This is the opinion in reference to this subject by Mr. Walker, Q.C. (Printed copy of opinion handed to Mr. Exham.)

62. Mr. Exham.—Mr. Walker in this opinion states that at present the paving, lighting, and cleansing are done out of the Corporate property.

63. Alderman Keegan.—So they are.

64. Mr. Exham.—I thought it was stated that there was a [illegible] There is a rate in aid applicable to the portion outside the borough, but anything inside is done by the Corporation.

65. Alderman Daly.—It is the outside portion—it was the [illegible] to which the rate in aid applies.

66. Mr. Cotton.—The Corporation [illegible] one mile and a half of streets within the town, and three miles and a half of highways, and the Grand Jury of the county of the town of Drogheda [illegible] about five and a half miles of roadway within the borough.

67. Then there are five miles outside [illegible] by the people?—Yes, by money [illegible] by the Grand Jury of the county of the town of Drogheda. Every person has to pay a share for the repairs.

68. In that case they are already [illegible] county at large charges?—Yes, to the county of the town of Drogheda.

69. That is, whatever the Corporation [illegible] the amount you are to pay for prisons, and so on?—Yes.

70. Mr. Whitworth, M.P.—I should think the [illegible] taken place [illegible] and, as a matter of fact, the only increase of taxation on the persons outside who may be brought in?

Alderman Keegan.—There will be a decrease.

71. Mr. Whitworth.—The Commissioners should understand there is not complete case of the boundary for taxation purposes.

72. Mr. Exham.—What I am inclined to think is, that it is not the Corporation who will get any advantage, but those people outside who will get a great advantage.

73. Mr. Whitworth.—That is my opinion. I was against the large extension, for the borough will gain, but so far as the outside are concerned there will be no difference in their taxation—certainly no increase in it, but rather the contrary.

74. Mr. Exham.—Mr. Walker, in his opinion, appears to have had the same idea as has been running in my mind—that the new area comes in just the same way as if it were part of the borough at this moment. Then, under the Towns Improvement Act, and I [illegible] it is under the Towns Improvement Act together with the Corporation Act, any land within the area only pays rates on one-fourth of the valuation. At present these lands that are outside your municipal boundaries are paying about 1s. 9d. or 1s. 10d., and in Louth 1s. 4d., and in Meath 1s. 5d.

75. Alderman Daly.—I have a great many more here besides the mayor, and Mr. Whitworth, and myself would, I believe, modify our ideas very much if this were [illegible] [illegible] with the law, but we have been led to think, from having [illegible] of the arguments before yourself, that it only referred to sanitary rate.

76. Mr. Exham.—That is a mistake. Suppose, then, the legislature were to [illegible] they were to pay one-fourth, you would not be inclined to take them in on these terms, unless they paid full rates?

Alderman Daly.—We would not take them in so far, we would modify the extension, we would take in the railway probably. May we take it, that that land, [illegible] will be otherwise, and that they will have to pay the usual rate as usual.

77. Mr. Exham.—We cannot say what may be in contemplation. It is impossible to say what the legislature will do. If we were to decide to report in favour of the extension, the legislature may say, "No, we won't have it."

78. Alderman Daly.—What I would wish to press upon the Commissioners as fair and reasonable is, that if a man comes in within the limits of our boundary, and is enabled to derive all the advantages of the municipal district, he ought certainly to pay the same rate—the same [illegible] rate—as the man in the town.

80. Mr. Exham.—I would say so, certainly. I can understand well the distinction between keeping up the town, and the improvement rate for scavenging, watering, and so on. Now, have you considered this question, and did you take it into consideration in obtaining Mr. Walker's opinion—whether, if this district is brought in, you are prepared for sewers, light, and water?

Drogheda. April 22, 1879.

Mr. J. J. [illegible]

Alderman *Daly*.—As far as it requires it. Up to the present, I may say, you had to grope your way up to the railway, and probably if the auditor knew that the lamps had been laid along that road he would surcharge us, for we are actually lighting beyond our limits—beyond our area. If we brought in the proposed extended district we would like to give the lights as far as possible, and several other similar advantages.

81. Mr. Exham.—Now, Alderman Daly, you say, so far as it would be requisite, you will give those privileges or advantages of water, lighting, &c. Now here is what Mr. Walker, in his opinion, says on the subject:—

"If the boundaries be extended, under the Act of '54, the ratepayers in the new area will have all the rights and privileges as to lighting, watering, &c., as the ratepayers within the boundary."

That is Mr. Walker's opinion, and it means this—that a man living at the very furthest point of the new area to be taken in can compel you to give him light, water, sewers, and scavenging, just the very same as the man living a door off from where we now are?

Alderman *Daly*.—He would have to pay improvement rate. The Water Company is not a public company; it is a private company.

82. Mr Exham.—You have no water works of your own?—No. Some time ago, Mr. Dickie, an attorney, was asked under the Towns Improvement Act, to pay town improvement rate; he refused, saying, "I am not getting light, or water, or anything else." He tried the question before the barrister, and the barrister made him pay.

83. *The Mayor of Drogheda*.—I may mention that a meeting of the ratepayers and members of the Council and persons interested was held, at which I presided, and it was agreed by a majority that the extension of two miles, as suggested, was advisable. If, however, what we have been given to understand relative to the one-fourth be the case, opinion on the subject would be doubtful, and the disposition would be to remain as we are, or to go in for a mile and a quarter extension. We would be guided as to the extension by the consideration as to whether they would pay rates on one-fourth of the valuation or the whole.

84. Mr. Exham.—We may take it, then, that it is the feeling of the Corporation, and, as the mayor says, of the majority of those who constituted the meeting over which he presided, that they should go for the two mile extension as marked by the blue line on the map, but on the understanding that the occupiers, the people occupying land there, shall, as far as the roads are concerned, pay the same road rate and the same for their county at large charges. The people in the town, as I understand it, pay at present something like 1s. 6d. (it is that now) in the £, for what is called a city rate, which is analogous to county rate. The people outside are paying in one county 1s. 9d., and in the other 1s. 8d. What I understand then is, as to the Meath area, by the extension he would be overtaxed with 3d. more, for it would be raised to 1s. 9d., but there would be a reduction in the case of the Louth area, for it would be reduced to 1s. 6d.

85. Alderman *Kenny*.—And likely to be reduced more.

86. Mr. Exham.—Yes, for as the Corporate property increases you will have money in hand to enable you to clean those roads.

87. Alderman *Daly*.—I may say that we are in for less than a mile and a quarter extension under any circumstances.

88. Mr. Cotton.—And do I understand that it is the wish of the whole of the Corporation to take up the whole of the Grand Jury powers over the district taken in?—That is the belief; that it would be well to do so.

89. Mr. Cotton.—And have the Grand Juries of Louth or Meath expressed any opinion on the subject?—No, they have not been asked.

90. Alderman *Kenny*.—The Grand Jury of neither county has expressed any opinion.

91. Mr. *Cooper*.—It has not been before them.

92. Mr. Exham.—They know, I suppose, that this inquiry is going on, and have an opportunity of giving expression to any view they may entertain on the subject.

93. Mr. *Cooper*.—The roads immediately contiguous to the boundary are very expensive to repair.

94. Alderman *Daly*.—I suppose it is the larger carts do that, carrying potatoes and turnips, and so on.

95. Mr. *Cooper*.—But that is qualified in this way—the barony is very large, and the cess is therefore light on those about where those roads are.

96. Mr. Exham.—What Mr. Cooper means is this—the county-cess comes off the entire barony, and if the county-cess was to be applied to particular townlands only, and not off the whole barony, the roads within this area would cost more than the rest of the barony, and he says if you take the roads you will find they will cost more for those roads than they are now costing, for they are helped by the other districts, and he means to convey, I suppose, that you will have to increase the general rate of taxation for those roads, but the answer is that you bring in a large valuation of the people of Drogheda to make up these roads.

97. Mr. *Cooper*.—But that valuation of the people of Drogheda is heavily taxed already.

98. Alderman *Daly*.—It has poor rate and county cess to meet, and that is all.

99. Mr. Exham.—You, in fact, you are very exceptionally situated in Drogheda?—Very fortunately so circumstanced.

100. Mr Exham.—And, as the Mayor has said, Alderman Kenny, you don't want those people outside should pay any taxes to the town, you don't want to make money by them?

Alderman *Kenny*.—Quite so.

101. Mr. Exham.—What then do you want with the extension at all.

102. Alderman *Kenny*.—Well, the power of our doing magisterial duties over the district that ought to be within our area, that is one reason, and for the purposes of sanitation, and so on. We would also have a greater area for jurors.

103. Alderman *Daly*.—The same answer could be given to your question as would be given by a gentleman who wants to extend his property—there is a prestige connected with an increased area, and then we would have the railway in, and have control over the care.

104. Mr. Cotton.—That circumstance about the care is a very exceptional and special one indeed.

105. Alderman *Daly*.—It is very important. All the district around, circumstanced as it is here, ought to be in the hands or under the control of the authorities of a town like this.

106. Mr. Exham.—Certainly, that about the care is a very strong argument. It was mentioned too, I think, on the last day, that if a death occurred in the [illegible], it is the coroner of Meath who would have to be communicated with to hold the inquest.

107. Alderman *Daly*.—I can understand how, perhaps, in other places where there are municipal taxes to be paid, objections may be raised, but here we know the property the Corporation has, and the advantage it will be to those who will be brought in. They will save all the bother of going off as jurors and so on.

108. Mr. *Cooper*.—Do you want to bring them in against their will?

Alderman *Daly*.—Oh, they would all give their consent if they understood it. There is all sort of talk outside about putting rates on these people which is all folly.

109. Mr. Exham.—I think we understand pretty fairly the views of the Corporation on the matter. Are there debts on Drogheda at present?

Alderman *Daly*.—None, except in respect of some money we borrowed to build the bridge. There is a sum of about £3,[illegible].

110. How long is that borrowed?

Alderman *Daly*.—I think about £7,000 was borrowed since 1856.

111. How was it incurred?

Alderman *Daly*.—The other portion was an old debt.

112. Who was the £7,000 borrowed from?—From Mr. Cairns, I think, the largest portion of it, at four and a half per cent.

113. And is it being paid off by sinking fund?—No, we are waiting till we get a large income. There is no hurry or pressure for the money.

114. Mr. Exham.—Now I think we know what is the feeling of the Corporation on this matter, and also, as the Mayor has said, of a large number of ratepayers of the town, and we take it with the qualification that has already been mentioned. Now, if there is anyone who wishes to give his view—anyone living in the area outside—we will hear him.

115. Mr. George *Harcourt*, J.P.—I am opposed to the extension.

116. Mr. Exham.—You live outside, and within this two mile extension proposed?—Yes.

117. What is the name of your place?—Kilsaran House.

118. And have you much land attached?—About 100 acres.

119. You, I understand, don't wish any extension to take place?—No, I do not. I am so situated that it appears they have come out of their way to take me in.

120. Alderman *Daly*.—Mr. Greene shut a little out at that point.

121. Mr. *Greene*.—We did not like to leave him out.

122. Mr. *Harcourt*.—This is in the barony of Drogheda.

123. Mr. Exham.—It is at present in the County Louth?—Yes. It is stated here that all that is levied in the town at present—that is for keeping up the roads—is 1s. 6d. in the pound, but it is more than that.

124. What has been the average rate, the average city rate, for five years?—2s. 6d. or 3s. 6d.

125. Alderman *Daly*.—The Sanitary Act came in, sir, and owing to letters in the newspapers and that, the authorities came down with great pressure on us, and called on the Corporation to make unnecessary sewers costing very large sums of money. That happened within those five years. That however is all done, and won't happen again. I mentioned this to show this gentleman that 1s. 6d. is a fair average, instead of say it is beyond it.

126. Mr. *Harcourt*.—It is impossible to depend upon it. It has jumped up in such a way that I am afraid something of the same sort will occur again.

127. Mr. Exham.—In any case, Mr. Harcourt, do you not use the town for all purposes?—Yes.

128. And is not your place much more valuable owing to its proximity to the town?—Well, but I am paying for that.

129. The *Mayor*.—Are you not a tenant of the Corporation?—Yes.

130. Mr. Exham.—But in all you are paying to the Corporation, you are paying nothing for the lighting of the town, keeping the streets clean, and so on, all of which is of great advantage and benefit to you and to your family, and don't you think you ought to pay something towards it?—No doubt in that view certainly; but something is one thing, but I am afraid the Corporation will jump up the same as last half year.

131. Alderman *Kenny*.—I would be sorry to think so.

132. Mr. *Harcourt*.—There is always new expense coming on.

133. Mr. Exham.—Take your own land and see what you are paying for it, or what you can get for it, and compare it with what would be the value of land of the same quality, say six miles off?—Yes, but the land beyond me again has similar advantages, and it is exempted.

134. Mr. Exham.—You are quite right, no doubt, in saying that two miles and a quarter is probably the same as two miles—that the advantages in the former case are much the same as the latter, but suppose you go to five miles, out to a place not so easy of access, would not your land be worth double that land situated some five miles off?—I don't think so.

135. Alderman *Daly*.—Oh! it is quite clear the lands adjoining the town are all double value, they are all town parks.

136. Mr. *Cooper*.—As to the advantages—I would ask, do not these people come in and spend their money in the town here.

137. Alderman *Daly*.—I can only say you are remarkably well off—there are very many places where you would be charged large sums for tolls, and fees, but here you have no impediment of the kind whatever.

138. Mr. Exham.—You are afraid, Mr. Cooper, your taxes would be increased?

Mr. *Cooper*.—I am quite satisfied of it.

139. Mr. Exham.—And your argument, Mr. Cooper, as I take it, is this, that you cannot tell with any certainty what may be done, and that this raising of the rates has been done so often, that probably it will be done tomorrow or the next day?

Mr. *Cooper*.—Precisely.

140. Mr. Exham.—Well, but if anything unforeseen should happen, for instance, if one of the bridges in Louth were to be swept away, your county rate would perhaps go up to 5s. in the £.

141. Alderman *Daly*.—I ask Mr. Cooper this question, he comes into Drogheda every Sunday to say his prayers (and we are very glad to see him), now, does he mean to say, that for the advantage he derives walking over the nice flags and so on, he would begrudge to pay a penny or two pence?

Mr. *Cooper*.—No, certainly not—I would not begrudge a penny or two pence; but I have explained why I object to the extension.

142. Mr. Exham.—We will take your evidence, if you please, Mr. Cooper.

Mr. John Cooper examined.

143. Mr. Exham.—You live within the proposed extended area of two miles?—Yes, and I have no objection to anything rational, but I am apprehensive of what Mr. Harcourt says. It may be perhaps ideal, but so many rises have taken place, that it is only natural to suspect more of a like nature. I also object to the extension on the ground that it was objected to by Mr. Heron in Dublin—Mr. Heron objected to bringing in Clontarf—that there was an agricultural district between Clontarf and the city boundary, and that they would not or should not go into Clontarf to take it in.

144. Mr. Exham.—You know Clontarf is a township already, and that makes a great difference.

Mr. *Cooper*.—As was pointed out by Mr. Heron, the principle followed in England and in Scotland was only to include such districts as were natural extensions of the town.

145. Mr. Exham.—Certainly, and that is where portion of a town had grown up around the old boundary.

Mr. *Cooper*.—But here there is no natural extension; it is all agricultural land, and it would be agricultural extension.

146. Mr. Exham.—If your principle on that point were to be applied, I don't think there would be much use in issuing the Commission. In Dublin you see there are five townships around the city, and the question is are they to continue five or are they to be brought into the city or any portion of them.

Mr. *Cooper*.—But the case there is quite different

from here. In Dublin these townships ought to be brought in because they are natural extensions of the city.

147. Mr. Egan.—In point of fact, the reason you object to being brought in is that it will or may cost you something—is not that it?

Mr. Cooper.—I don't mind a small thing, but here it might be a very considerable thing. Where gentlemen have the power of increasing rates they have a great desire and are very fond of doing things they might not otherwise think of—and of in fact inventing a great many things to do. If you had the power would you not like to put an iron bridge in place of a wooden one. Don't you think you ought to do so in such a case. Then you would raise our taxation. I am arguing to show that there may be a very considerable rise in the taxation.

148. Alderman Daly.—Take the case now of the new bridge, for which Mr. Osirne lent us the money, now, on the ground of fair play, don't you think you should have paid something towards the erection of that bridge?—I don't know whether that bridge was done economically or not.

149. Would it not be fair that you should pay something towards that bridge?—To be sure it would.

150. Mr. Egan.—It would be very hard—as to anything prospective—to say what might happen; if there was an agrarian outrage, for instance, in the barony in which you lived, and the Grand Jury measured the compensation at say £3,000, and it was levied off the barony, your county cess would go up to 6s. or 7s.

151. Alderman Daly.—We never these anyone here at all.

152. Mr. Cooper.—These cases may no doubt be possible, but there is a considerable amount of probability that the rates would be raised by the town, for it has been done so often before.

153. Alderman Daly.—But it will be all in your favour, Mr. Cooper.

154. The Mayor.—I may say I would be taken in by the two mile extension, and I would be glad to be taken in.

155. Mr. Cooper.—May I ask what is the amount of your valuation?—£40 a year.

156. Mr. Cooper.—Mine is 140 acres.

157. Alderman Daly.—But the whole of it won't be taken in.

158. Mr. Cooper.—There will be scarcely anything not taken in.

159. Mr. Egan.—Is it all in your own hands or is it let?

Mr. Cooper.—It is all in my own hands. I would not object to some of it being inside, but I do object to it all being taken in.

160. And do you think it would be reasonable and fair to make an extension of say a mile and a quarter?—I think it would be reasonable for the town.

161. And you as the owner of property do not object to that?—No, it is the difference of three-quarters of a mile that I object to, for it takes in all I have.

162. Now, suppose you were letting land tomorrow, and you had the same land five or six miles away from this great town, what would be the difference in the value per acre?

Mr. Cooper.—It is very difficult to say. If it was agricultural, growing crops, then no doubt the nearer to the town the more valuable it would be, but where it is merely grazing, four or five miles difference would be of very little account, for it would only be a question of driving cattle an hour or an hour and a half more, and I don't know if it would make any difference.

163. Alderman Daly.—It would make a difference of 100 per cent.

164. Mr. Cooper.—Would it make a difference of 5s. an acre?

165. Alderman Daly.—It would, £1 an acre.

166. Mr. Egan.—Suppose you were letting it, Mr. Cooper, would you not get from people who wished to supply milk to the town, and so on, much more than you would if it was six miles off?—Oh yes, I would get more in that case.

167. Mr. Egan.—And so, also, if you turn it into agricultural land, would it not be more valuable considering the proximity of the market for produce.

168. Alderman Daly.—I know in Newry two years ago they got a bill, and there is now not a single article of produce that does not pay so much by the barrel or stone, by way of toll, but here you get everything in without paying a halfpenny.

169. Mr. Egan.—What is your view, Mr. Cooper, about the mile and a quarter extension?

170. I would be quite satisfied with the mile and a quarter.

171. That is, you would be quite satisfied if they did not take you in?—I would certainly be glad to be out altogether.

172. The Mayor.—I live outside, but am in favour of extension.

173. Mr. Egan.—Though you would be taken in?—Yes.

Mr. Laurence Morris examined.

174. Mr. Egan.—Have you property outside the present boundary?—Yes.

175. Would you be taken in by the proposed extension of two miles?—Yes.

176. What is your view regarding the extension of the boundary?—Well, there is not one in my neighbourhood who would object to it, or would not be satisfied.

177. How far out do you yourself live?—I live about a mile from where we now sit.

178. So that either extension would take you in?—Yes, but I have property in the town also.

179. Have you been speaking on the matter to others?—Yes, I was, and some said they would rather the extension was two miles, Mr. Eager, for instance, is one, and he has, I think, 400, or from that to 600 acres.

180. Mr. Cooper.—He told me most distinctly he objected.

181. Mr. Moore.—He told me at the workhouse he was afraid the Commissioners would not take him in.

182. Mr. Egan.—Well, in any case if he objected there was plenty of notice given, and he had ample opportunity of attending here today, and expressing his opinions. If he wishes to write to us well and good.

183. Alderman Nugent.—I should say I have property outside.

184. Mr. Egan.—Is that between the mile and a quarter and two miles?—Yes.

185. And so far as you heard people outside speaking about the matter, have you heard them objecting?—Not latterly. Formerly they did—they did not understand their objection—they did not know their position.

186. But since the question has been ventilated have their opinions altered?—Yes, I have heard no complaints against the proposition—quite the contrary.

187. Mr. Egan.—Mr. Ferrall, how many electoral divisions, or portions of electoral divisions would be taken in, by this two mile extension?—Two. I say only two, for we have east ward, and west ward, but at the same time it is in the electoral divisions of St. Peter's and St. Mary's, divided by the river.

188. Then at present the town is in two electoral divisions?—Yes.

189. And the extension you propose will still be within the same electoral divisions?—Yes.

190. Mr. Cotton.—I would like to know if the Corporation have gone into the question of the expense of keeping the roads within this area, if they take

[illegible] they made any calculation as to the [illegible] of maintaining those roads?

[illegible]. Mr. [illegible].—I do not believe it would be any [illegible] expense, that I can see.

[illegible]. How do you mean any [illegible] expense?—Anything over what they cost at present.

[illegible]. Do you mean the roads would be maintained by the rate that is at present being paid?—Yes, [illegible] [illegible] who would do it.

[illegible]. Mr. [illegible].—Probably they would be kept [illegible] than the [illegible] roads.

Mr. [illegible].—Certainly they would be kept for the same [illegible] as at present.

[illegible]. Mr. [illegible].—And do you say that would be [illegible] increasing the rates on the people to be brought in?—[illegible] the people to be brought in [illegible] paying at present.

[illegible]. Mr. [illegible].—Ay, but they only pay the [illegible], they only pay [illegible] there.

Mr. [illegible].—I am sure they can't be kept up for the same rate.

[illegible]. Mr. [illegible].—Then if the Corporation take up these roads, and get the same money from the people in [illegible], [illegible] would be an increase in the [illegible] of [illegible]. You have made no calculation, I think you said, as to the cost?—I have been looking into the various points, and I do not think there would be an increase of rates.

[illegible]. But you have not, as I understand, made any calculation as to what it would be in the pound on this [illegible] valuation?—No.

[illegible]. Alderman *Daly*.—The argument will hold good in another way—if it is knocked off on one side [illegible] it will be [illegible] on the other—it will not be a special rate on any one part—it will be on the whole.

[illegible]. Mr. [illegible].—Some roads are much lighter than others. The cost is about [illegible] a perch for the Dublin road, while for the [illegible] road up to the [illegible] it is only [illegible].

[illegible]. Mr. [illegible].—Have you made any estimate of what the maintenance of that blue line—of the roads within it—would be?—No. I have the length of roads taken in, and the present prices.

[illegible]. What length of roads are included?

Mr. [illegible].—Twenty-three miles of roads, and they [illegible] very rough.

[illegible]. Mr. [illegible].—I have no objection to be brought in. I at present live outside the boundary.

[illegible]. Alderman *Daly*.—I may mention that the cattle of Westmeath and Louth are shipped here in Drogheda, without a farthing of charge being made.

[illegible]. Mr. [illegible].—Yes, but the shipping is your trade. It is the great trade of the town.

The inquiry then terminated.

ENNIS.—DECEMBER [illegible], 1878.

Before Mr. [illegible], Q.C. (Chairman), and Mr. O'[illegible].

CHAIRMAN.—We are here to-day in pursuance of the warrant issued to us by His Grace the Lord Lieutenant [illegible]. Acting under that warrant we [illegible] in the different municipal bodies, and, amongst others, to the Municipal Commissioners of Ennis, and we have received their replies, by which the Commissioners of Ennis give it as their opinion that the present boundary is too limited, and that it ought to be extended by [illegible] of at least two [illegible] miles in radius from [illegible]. They state that this is also the view of the people living inside the present boundary, and that the reason they seek this extension is that the present smallness of the area causes the taxation to press heavily on the people in the town, while the gentry and others living outside the town, who benefit by their proximity to Ennis, contribute nothing towards the expenses of keeping up the township, and the Commissioners consider that those parties should contribute according to the means for that purpose.

Having received that reply from the Commissioners, we are here to learn the opinion of all parties on the matter, and to inquire generally whether the present boundaries require to be extended, limited, or otherwise altered. In order, in the first place, to know what the boundaries are, we will examine Mr. O'[illegible], the Surveyor, and then we will ascertain what are the views, if I may so call it, of insiders and outsiders on this question.

Mr. FRANCIS O'[illegible] examined.

Mr. Francis O'[illegible].

1. Are you the Town Surveyor?—I am.

2. Are you authorized by the Commissioners to state their views and opinions as to an extension of the area of the town?—I am; and Mr. [illegible], one of our Commissioners, will tell you, I have been deputed by the Commissioners to give evidence before you; but there is a matter I would wish to call your attention to. I see by the *Freeman's Journal* report of your inquiry in Drogheda that the Committee of the House of Commons were of opinion that the areas of the boroughs should be, if possible, made coterminous with the Poor Law electoral divisions, and that the authority over the roads and bridges should be transferred to the municipal body. You are also reported to have stated on that occasion that, according to the 60th section of the Towns Improvement Act of 1854, simple lands and so forth would be only liable to pay the improvement rate on one-fourth of their valuation. I just wish to call your attention to that and to get your opinion on it, for if that is so it will then become a question with the Commissioners whether they will look for any extension of the town under these circumstances. There is no doubt the 60th section is to that effect, and we want to know.

3. Mr. O'[illegible].—I don't think the report states that Mr. [illegible] said the Committee held that view.

4. CHAIRMAN.—What I said at Drogheda was, that so far as we could judge from the report of the Select Committee of the House of Commons, the Committee thought it desirable that all municipal towns, and particularly the large ones, should, as much as possible, have one body to manage the affairs, including the management of the roads and sanitary matters, but it was not [illegible] any [illegible]. I will read what the Committee say exactly.—[Reads extract from Committee's report.] In Drogheda when they asked to have their town extended to a radius of two miles from the centre of the town, I asked them had they considered the effect of the 60th section of the Towns Improvement Act of 1854, by which all arable lands, market gardens, &c., were chargeable only to pay the rates under that Act on one-fourth of their Annual value, and I then mentioned what was the view of the Committee of the House of Commons, so far as we could judge from their report, and I asked whether, if an Act of Parliament was passed carrying out that recommendation, and then the area of the town was extended, they had considered the effect of the rate which the districts proposed to be added would have to pay under the 60th section of the Towns Improvement Act.

5. Mr. O'[illegible].—You are probably aware that under the Local Government Act of 1871, power was given to the Local Government Board to make alterations with respect to the management of the

Ennis
Oct. 2, 187[illegible].
Mr. Bernard O'Connor.

roads on the application of the Local Municipal Authority, but with the consent of the Grand Jury. It was found, however, that in every case except Wexford the consent of the Grand Jury was refused, so that the Act became practically a dead letter, and then an Act was passed to enable the Local Government Board to proceed by provisional order. It was to that section I was going to call your attention.

6. CHAIRMAN.—A town may get control over the roads whether its area is increased or not under the law as it now stands, but as to the question of the rates to be imposed or paid I can give no opinion, for that must be settled by legislation.

7. Mr. O'BRIEN.—That refers to the expenditure of the Town Commissioners and the Grand Jury powers; but under the 20th section of the Public Health Act of last session that provision has been extended to sanitary matters, and there is an arrangement in reference to particular lands making them liable to rating on only one-fourth part of the cess. The rural territory outside continues as a rural sanitary district, but under the Towns Improvement Act it will only be subject to one-fourth the rate?—The Town Commissioners are well aware of that, and the only question that arises is, assuming that the portion of the roads now under the control of the Grand Jury within the present or extended district were transferred to them: does this section repeal the section of the Towns Improvement Act and give them power to levy what the Grand Jury now levy on all lands?

8. Unless there be some special provision made to the contrary, I would think that the class of lands and other things you refer to would only be liable to one-fourth at all events, so far as relates to the improvement rate?—Under these circumstances I am directed by the Commissioners to give evidence that subject to a provision being introduced giving the Commissioners the same power as the Grand Jury now have for levying the full county cess upon the districts to be brought in, they are in favour of extending the boundary.

9. That is that they would only wish it subject to that condition?—Yes. It would result in a great loss to the Commissioners if we could only levy one-fourth of what the Grand Jury levy on arable and such lands.

10. Well, if the powers of the Grand Jury were simply transferred to the Municipal Commissioners, I should think there could be no doubt that the districts to be included would be subject to the same expenditure on the part of the Commissioners as the rest of the municipal boundary, but be subject only to one-fourth the rate, at least as regards improvement rate.

11. CHAIRMAN.—The Committee of the House of Commons say, "Your Committee think that the governing body in towns which are urban sanitary districts should be entitled, with the approval of the Local Government Board, to exercise the Grand Jury powers if they so desire it, to the exclusion of the Grand Jury;" and they go on to say, "subject to such local liabilities as may be equitable." The way I understand your position is this; if this outlying district is brought in, as you propose, you have power to go to the Local Government Board and say, give us all the powers of the Grand Jury, and you propose to do that, subject to the special condition, and it will be for the Local Government Board to say if they will sanction it and give you a special road rate on the district you bring in equal to the old county cess.

12. Mr. FAWCETT, Q.C.—That will be a matter on which the Commissioners will have the option of going to the Local Government Board, and they need not go unless they like.

13. CHAIRMAN.—And suppose you don't go to the Local Government Board and get some special authority to be done with the Grand Jury, I presume the Grand Jury will continue to levy their county cess on the lands in the town, the same as they do now, while, as regards the borough rate, the arable lands, &c., in the district brought in, will only have to pay one-fourth?—What I want to convey is this; that if portions of the Grand Jury powers are transferred, as to the making of roads and bridges, to the municipal body, and if the municipal body have only power to levy one-fourth of the road rate for the maintenance of roads within the borough, the Commissioners are of opinion that so far from the transfer being any advantage it would be a very serious loss to them. Under the 20th section of the Public Health Act of last year, presuming the Commissioners applied and the Local Government Board transferred the powers, would not all powers of the Grand Jury with respect to the levying of rates be transferred?

14. We could not tell that. The provisional order when confirmed is an Act of Parliament, and it would all depend upon the provisions in the order. It is for the Local Government Board to say whether they will grant the provisional order, and if so, on what terms. I thought it right to draw their attention at Drogheda to that matter, of which they did not seem to be thinking, and of which, as far as I can see from the answers given to the queries we issued, no municipality ever thought. We are here to ascertain, as far as we can, the views of all parties—I mean those inside and outside the present boundary, as to whether or not that boundary should be extended; and having heard all parties it will be our duty to report our opinion thereon. I want to know the existing boundaries of the borough of Ennis?—I have a map of them here.

15. Are they now the same as those originally fixed by the Boundaries Commissioners?—I believe they were never altered since.

16. Are the Parliamentary and the municipal boundaries conterminous?—They are. The municipal boundary at present is that fixed in the report of the Boundaries Commissioners in the year 1832. There has been no alteration in the boundary from that time to the present.

17. What is the area within the present borough boundary?—464 acres.

18. Mr. O'BRIEN.—Does that include any waste, for by the return published in my report I have the acreage as 469. That I got from the Valuation Office?—I think there are exemptions in that 464 acres. I have never calculated the acreage myself.

19. Then you are not prepared to contradict the Valuation Office return?—No, I am not; but I am aware that the practice is that any exemptions ought not to be included.

20. So that 469 may be taken as the correct acreage return?—Yes.

21. CHAIRMAN.—The valuation is how much?—£8,768 13s.

22. And the population?—6,503 in 1871.

23. Is the town in one electoral division?—Yes.

24. Does the electoral division extend beyond it?—It does.

25. Mr. O'BRIEN.—Do you know what the statistics of the electoral division are?—I can give the area and valuation of the whole. The area of the electoral division, as given me by the Clerk of the Union, is 7,644a. 0r. 29p., and the valuation is £13,174 15s.

26. To what distance does that extend from the town?—A little over two miles.

27. CHAIRMAN.—Are the municipal boundaries conterminous with townland boundaries?—No; the municipal boundary is very irregular. It cuts the town in several ways. A very considerable portion of the Municipal boundary is altogether undefined, except at the extreme points there is no line of demarcation.

28. How do they manage the assessment and payment of taxes?—I take it the way the matter stands is that the surveyor has calculated the quantity within the boundary, and then struck a fair proportion.

29. Mr. O'BRIEN.—How many townlands are cut by the municipal boundary?—Three.

30. Name them, please?—They are *Lifford*, Cloghleigh, and a very small portion of Clonroadmore.

31. CHAIRMAN.—Can you let us have the rates struck for the last five years?—For the year ending 1876 the municipal rate was 1s. 6d.

Ennis, Jan. 3, 18[illegible]. — Mr. Francis O'Connor.

32. Is that for municipal and sanitary purposes?—Yes. The poor law rate was 2s. 6d., the county cess 2s. 10½d.; total 6s. 0½d. In 1877 the municipal rate and sanitary was 1s. 6d., the poor law 2s. 1d., and the county cess 2s. 3½d.; total 6s. 0½d. In 1876 the municipal and sanitary rate was 2s. 6d., the poor law 2s. 6d., and the county 2s. 8½d.; total 6s. 8½d. In 1875, municipal and sanitary rate 1s., poor law 2s. 1d., and county cess 2s. 11½d.; total 7s. 6½d.; and in 1874, municipal and sanitary 1s., poor law 2s. 6d., county cess 3s. 0½d.; total 6s. 6½d.

33. Do we understand that the Commissioners recommend a uniform boundary line at a radius of two miles?—As near as practicable two miles.

34. *Point out on the map the line of boundary you propose?*—All that is coloured green. In laying down this line I was guided by the natural boundaries.

35. Does that adhere to the townland boundaries?—Yes, except in one case, and the reason there is that the townland is a rather long and narrow one.

36. Would there be any reason why it should not be included?—No, except that I was keeping as near the townland as possible, and this one runs out in a narrow line. When I laid out this boundary I did not know what the electoral division boundary was. I afterwards ascertained, and laid down the electoral division boundary. They are very nearly the same.

37. Would there be any difficulty in including the entire electoral division in the new boundary?—No. The Commissioners are perfectly satisfied to accept the electoral division, for in fact the extension they propose is nearly the same as it.

38. By the map you propose to bring in a portion that is outside the electoral division?—Yes; but I did not know what the electoral division was when I was preparing that. It was afterwards I found out the electoral division.

39. Would there be any difficulty in omitting the parts external to the electoral division, and making the boundary to the electoral division?—No. The Commissioners are ready to adopt either of them.

40. How many gentlemen's residences would be brought in, supposing the electoral division was adopted as the boundary?—Eight. They are—Brookville, Lifford, that house is immediately outside the present boundary; Newpark, Roslevan, Beech Park, Ashline, Oakfield, and Hermitage.

41. But then I see Green Hill House and Clareville House. What about them. Would they not be included?—One of them is not in existence now.

42. Here is a place called Abbeyview Cottage?—That is a very small cottage; but a college is to be built, and that would be included in the new boundary, and also the railway station.

43. Is the railway station outside the boundary?—Yes.

44. Are these then the only residences to be brought in?—Yes.

45. Mr. *Pearson*, Q.C.—There is an asylum to be brought in?—Yes.

46. Chairman.—I see a school also here?—That is a small one.

47. Mr. O'Brien.—Within what radius from the centre of the town would all these houses come?—Some of them will come within a very small radius, and others will go to a mile and three-quarters.

48. What is the remotest point of the electoral division from the centre of the town?—Three miles, or a little over three miles.

49. That is at one point only?—Yes, that is the extreme point of the area.

50. I should like to understand the view of the Commissioners on this point. Suppose the Grand Jury point were arranged to their satisfaction, and that the Grand Jury expenses were to be assessed as at present, but seeing that the state of the law absolutely requires that the sanitary expenses shall be in any case only one-fourth, would that influence the views of the Commissioners?—The Commissioners would be very desirous, so far as I can understand, that they should get the same taxing powers with reference to the maintenance of roads as the Grand Jury have at present, and to get charge of the roads, but they are aware that for sanitary purposes they can only get one-fourth by the existing law.

51. Then they are aware that it would mean a substitution of one-fourth on those outlying districts?—Yes, and of course they would object to take over the roads of the county if they could only levy one-fourth of the rate for them.

52. Chairman.—This proposed extension will take in a very fair proportion of the Limerick and Ennis Railway, and also of the Athenry and Ennis Railway. Indeed it will take in two miles of the Athenry and Ennis?—Yes, and about three-quarters of a mile of the Limerick and Ennis.

53. The railways are altogether free at present?—They pay nothing whatever.

54. Is the gaol outside the boundary or in it?—The gaol is within the boundary.

55. Have the Commissioners considered whether, if the municipality is increased, they are prepared to light and water the increased area?

56. Mr. *Pearson*, Q.C.—We have no objection to give them water, but certainly not light.—I think I may say on behalf of the Commissioners that if you do go out to the extent of this proposed boundary, they could not supply them with either water or light, for the expense would be enormous.

57. Mr. O'Brien.—Do the Commissioners consider that these people in this outside district, from their proximity to the town, derive benefits which could fairly be estimated, at all events, at one-fourth?—Yes. The people in the outlying districts enjoy all the advantages—and they are great advantages—of being near the town, and they should contribute to the expense of keeping it clean. It is a market town and these people bring in cattle to the market. There are fairs held in the town also, and there is a fair-green just outside here, and that fair-green is used twice a year and the streets after.

58. Chairman.—The Committee of the House of Commons call attention to the great nuisance caused by these fairs, and recommend that they should be stopped.

59. Mr. *Pearson*.—We also objected, and we called attention to it at the last inquiry before you, in the hope of having the matter remedied.

60. Mr. O'Brien.—Do the inhabitants of these outlying districts derive any advantage for their children by sending them to school in the town? Do they resort to the town for that purpose?—Well, not perhaps on the average basis, for I think they have National schools, but of course within a certain radius the people do resort to the schools in the town for their children.

61. Chairman.—In whose hands principally is the land within the electoral division? Is it held by gentlemen or small farmers?—They are small farmers. I think there is very little of it held by gentlemen. There is Cahercalla owned by Mr. Cullen.

62. Rev. Mr. *Egan*.—I wish, gentlemen, to ask one question. How does Mr. O'Connor make out that the fairs being held in the town are more benefit to the small farmers near the town, than to the farmers of the district generally?—I did not say that they are a benefit to the people of the immediate neighbourhood more than to the people of the county, for they are more availed of by the large farmers, but the people within the district derive benefit from the fairs being held so convenient to them.

63. I am very much affected, for the proposed change would bring in a college with which I am connected.

64. Chairman.—Perhaps, Father Egan, it would be better to allow Mr. O'Connor to finish his evidence, and then we will hear you afterwards on the question. Can you say, Mr. O'Connor, of your own knowledge whether these small farmers have considered the question of being brought within the municipal boundary?—No, sir, I cannot.

65. Have you any idea of the increase in population by this change?—No, I could not ascertain that. There is no record of it here in any way.

66. In your opinion do the people within the area of the electoral division derive exceptional advantage from their proximity to the town?—No doubt of it. There is a monthly market and there are fairs held here, and they are availed of greatly by the people within the electoral division area.

67. Do the farmers get benefit from the town itself in the way of revenue?—They do. They buy manure from the Commissioners and others in the town.

68. Are you able to say, from your knowledge, whether land of equal quality brings a better rent within the electoral division than that a mile further off?—Certainly, all lands convenient to towns do.

69. Are you able to say that with regard to this place?—Yes.

70. Does that advantage extend over the entire electoral division?—Yes, and I would not like to confine it to the electoral division, it may go a little outside it.

71. Are the Town Commissioners prepared to take upon themselves the management of the sanitary condition of the whole electoral division, even if the rate for sanitary purposes was only one-fourth?—They are fully prepared to do that. The Commissioners are at present not very fairly dealt with by the Grand Jury in reference to the cess levied upon them in the town compared with the advantages they derive from the Grand Jury. They do not lay out sufficient on the town. They do not give a fair expenditure for the amount contributed at all.

72. Have you calculated, supposing the whole of this electoral division was brought in, what the cost of the roads within the extended municipality would be—what the rates would be, and what it would cost for the county-at-large charges, suppose all parties paid their proportion as at present payable, for in working out those figures afterwards we might be able to arrive at a very fair way of dealing with all parties?—I did. I calculated it on the average cost for the last twenty years, and, assuming we got the whole electoral division, the cost of the roads within that would be 1s. 3d. in the pound on the valuation.

73. 1s. 3d. on the entire?—Yes.

74. Including the town?—Yes.

75. Have you calculated what the county-at-large charges would be, and your proportion towards them?—I could give it proportionately, for I made it out for another inquiry. I have taken the statement of the accounts between the Grand Jury and the town for the last twenty years, and I will divide it into two periods of ten years each. From 1857 to 1866, a period of ten years, the amount of taxes levied by the Grand Jury on the borough was £8,797 16s. 4d. The amount the Grand Jury expended in new works and the maintenance of roads within the borough, including also its fair proportion of the county-at-large charges, was £4,806 11s. 3d., leaving a balance of over-tax on the town of £1,991 5s. 1d. for that ten years. Within the next ten years, from 1867 to 1876, the amount of tax levied by the Grand Jury off the borough was £7,840 12s. 6d., and the total amount expended for new works and the maintenance of roads, including its proportion of the county at-large charges, was £8,001 4s. 9d., so that the town benefited in those ten years to the extent of £160 11s. 3d., but lost for the previous ten years £1,991, or nearly £2,000. I think I am correct in stating that the amount being so evenly and fairly kept between 1867 and 1876 is entirely attributable to the County Surveyor here. He is a very efficient and upright officer, but I think I will show you his hands are tied by the rule of the Grand Jury passed here some two years ago, and that in the future the town will be taxed to a far greater extent than it was some ten years ago. There was a resolution passed at the Summer Assizes in 1876, on an application then made to the Grand Jury, for the purpose of forming a drain in the town of Ennis. The drain merely drains the surface water that falls on the street. The drain became choked. The place, I think, you will recollect, for it was brought prominently before you on a former occasion. It is at Carmody's Hotel, and the sanitary officer reported that a great nuisance existed there. The Commissioners were censured very much, but I think I will show you it was all owing to the fault of the Grand Jury.

76. I don't think we can go into that. What I understand from you, Mr O'Connor, is that the Commissioners anticipate that the Grand Jury will be increasing the rates of the town?—Certainly, by the resolution they passed.

77. Well, no matter how they do it. Do you think they will do it?—Yes; and I think it a very unequal proceeding on the part of the Grand Jury with reference to the town. A resolution was passed with reference to this application about the drain. After heavy rain that portion of the street used to be flooded. A drain leading from this trap to the river got choked up, and the Commissioners got an application made to the Grand Jury for a presentment to clean out the drain, and they threw it out.

78. On what ground?—On the ground that it was sanitary expenditure, and should be charged to the rate for that purpose.

79. Would that affect the bringing in of the outside area?—No; but it shows the relations that exist between the town and the Grand Jury.

80. But you would get rid of that at once if you got the control over the roads?—Certainly; and I merely mention the matter to show that the Commissioners ought to get the control.

81. Mr. O'Brien.—Have the Commissioners taken any steps under the powers of the Act I referred to to get the powers of the Grand Jury transferred to their own body?—No, sir, not yet.

82. Chairman.—Do you say that 1s. 3d. in the pound is what you would require for the proper and efficient maintenance of the roads according to your calculation?—Yes.

83. Could you tell me how much besides the town should contribute to the county-at-large charges?—I did not go into that, and I don't know that I would be able to give it at present. I have it for the present borough.

84. Would it be anything equal to the 1s. 3d. in the pound?—No.

85. Do I understand you to say that the reason the Commissioners have not sought for the transfer of the Grand Jury powers in the present limited area?—The reason is that under the old Acts it required the consent of the Grand Jury, but under the new Act it is not so.

86. Are they aware that the law has been altered?—Yes, but the Chairman of the Commissioners has been unwell for some time, and has not attended the Board. It was intended to bring the matter forward, and it will be in a short time. I have here the resolution of the Grand Jury, passed at the Spring Assizes, 1876, to the effect, the construction of the drain there was a sanitary work for which the Commissioners were responsible. [Witness read the resolution.]

87. Are you aware that since the Sanitary Acts came into operation, that is the general view taken of the matter?—Yes; where it is a purely sanitary purpose; but what I maintain is, that this was not for a sanitary purpose; it was for surface water.

88. However, if the county-at-large charges were one-half of the other, it would leave it about 1s. 10½d., and the smallest rate is 2s. 8½d.?—That is a very exceptional rate, that 3s. 3½d.

89. There would be practically nothing in the pound saving on the average of the years you have stated?—There would be clearly.

90. And for that you say the roads would be so efficiently kept in order as under the Grand Jury?—Yes; I think so.

91. Mr. O'Brien.—I understood you to say that the Grand Jury did not do enough for the roads within the municipal boundary?—No; the Grand Jury do not. A great many of the applications for improvements are always thrown out by the Grand Jury.

92. I understand you complain not only of an undue amount being levied, but also that the work is not

[illegible] ?—No; but that there is not [illegible] done or given.

[illegible] Then there is work left undone that ought to be done?—Yes.

[illegible]. CHAIRMAN.—You say there is not as much done [illegible] for the town as they do for the parts [illegible]?—Yes; and there's too little undone that ought to be done.

[illegible]. Mr. O'BRIEN.—Which you say would be provided for if the town [illegible] got [illegible] to get it.

[illegible]. CHAIRMAN.—If there be any gentleman present who wishes to have Mr. O'Connor asked any question, and if he wishes to do so, we will ask it. I take it now that Mr. O'Connor is [illegible] here, and giving us the views of the Commissioners on the municipal boundary [illegible] ?—Mr. Perrson, [illegible], etc., and I am one of the Commissioners.

[illegible]. Mr. O'BRIEN.—Was there a resolution of the Commissioners on the subject?—There was.

[illegible]. CHAIRMAN.—Mr. O'Connor, I understood you, on the part of the Commissioners, to say they are perfectly ready to adopt the proposed boundary on the [illegible] of [illegible] only the residents of the existing [illegible] the [illegible] of the [illegible] in the sea, to be brought in; that they say it would not be fair that the parties living in the extended area should only pay one-fourth of the expense of keeping up the roads which [illegible] have been paying about [illegible] in the pound for county cess on the average of the last [illegible] years, while if the Commissioners got the management of the roads, they would be able to maintain them with a rate of [illegible], including the [illegible] of [illegible] charges, instead of [illegible], so that there would be a saving of from [illegible] in the pound to the [illegible] of those [illegible], and that their roads would be kept up as well, if not better than hitherto, and that the whole town would also be kept better cleaned?—Yes; the Commissioners have no [illegible] what they derive from taxation.

[illegible]. Mr. O'BRIEN.—They have adopted all the provisions of the Towns Improvement Act, except [illegible], and they are getting that?—Yes.

[illegible]. CHAIRMAN.—What will be the increase of taxation on the town in consequence of this proposed bringing in of water?—We anticipate there will be no additional taxation at all.

[illegible]. Then, in point of fact, the area will not be affected by any water rate?—No.

[illegible]. Mr. O'BRIEN.—How so?—The water would be more than self-paying.

[illegible]. CHAIRMAN.—If there any one wishes to ask any questions of Mr. O'Connor? If so, we will be happy to hear them.

Rev. Mr. Ryan.—I do not see that the farmers living immediately near the town—say within a mile of the town—really derive any greater benefit than the farmers living three or four miles off from the [illegible] and [illegible] held in the town.

[illegible]. CHAIRMAN.—Mr. O'Connor thinks they do. Possibly I will ask your opinion. According to Mr. O'Connor's view, the farmers who would be brought in, supposing we recommend the extension of boundary sought for, and it is carried out, would be actually benefited to the extent of [illegible] in the pound in some years, if they are withdrawn from the county.

Rev. Mr. Ryan.—That is as to one rate; but then as to the poor rate, how will they benefit?

[illegible]. CHAIRMAN.—They pay at present the full [illegible] rate as long as they are outside, but as the law now stands, they would only pay one-third if they were within the municipal boundary. As against that, they would have to pay one-fourth of the improvement rate in the town, which at the most is [illegible] in the pound; so they would only pay [illegible] of that, while they get off three-fourths of the sanitary rate, which ought to come to more than [illegible], and they would also have to pay less for the repair of the roads than they now pay for them.

[illegible]. Mr. Cullen (a ratepayer).—But there are [illegible] the [illegible] collected by the Commissioners, they are collected by the Commissioners off the occupiers, who have to pay the whole; but the rates on the land outside are collected by the poor rate collector, and there the landlord pays half, and the tenant or occupier [illegible] the town pays the whole.

[illegible]. CHAIRMAN.—If the land you speak of is brought within the municipal boundary, I presume the poor and sanitary rate will be divided in the same way.

[illegible]. Mr. O'BRIEN.—This [illegible], but [illegible] with them, not [illegible] in the pound, the question had been finally disposed of by the [illegible] of [illegible].

Mr. Cullen.—If we had to pay the whole of the sanitary rate outside the borough, I would have to pay [illegible] a year, for which I would get no benefit.

Mr. O'CONNOR.—If the extension were to proceed, the sanitary rate would be collected as the municipal rate would be, and more so than at present.

Mr. Cullen.—I am afraid the water will not be of the value you put upon it.

[illegible]. Mr. O'BRIEN.—Do the Commissioners wish [illegible] any one else to [illegible]?

Mr. Perrson, [illegible].—I think not. They have nothing to add to Mr. O'Connor's evidence.

[illegible]. CHAIRMAN.—Are we to understand that the boundary suggested by Mr. O'Connor is the unanimous recommendation of the Town Commissioners?

Mr. Perrson, [illegible].—Yes. They convened their meeting held for the purpose, and deputed Mr. O'Connor to speak for them on the question.

[illegible]. Mr. O'BRIEN.—Do they wish that [illegible] the electoral divisions should be followed [illegible]?—Mr. Perrson, [illegible].—Yes.

[illegible] Mr. Shepherd.—I would like to know on what ground Mr. O'Connor maintains that the roads would be kept for less than [illegible], if they were brought within the town boundary.

Mr. O'Connor.—I say that the town is over-taxed now by the Grand Jury.

[illegible]. Mr. Shepherd.—If you look back to what the Grand Jury has done for the town, you will see they have done a great deal.

[illegible]. Mr. O'BRIEN.—Mr. O'Connor has done so. He has given us a return for [illegible] years of the sums raised and the sums expended. In one period of ten years the Grand Jury received nearly £2,000 more than they expended, while in the other period of ten years they have expended £100 more on the town than they received.

[illegible]. CHAIRMAN.—Is there any one appearing here [illegible] of the railway companies?—Mr. O'Connor.—They can have no valid objection to offer, to their being brought within the boundary. They are a long time outside.

[illegible]. If they are they will only have to pay one-fourth of the improvement and sanitary rate. If, however, they are valued highly, on account of the land being occupied for railway purposes, they may be paying as much as anybody else, for this proposed boundary would be taking in three miles of their line; and they will have to pay on their valuation.

[illegible]. Mr. O'BRIEN.—I suppose we may infer from their not appearing here that they are not opposing.

[illegible]. Rev. Mr. Ryan.—I came here to get information. I only heard of this inquiry, and I had heard that the new college might be affected by the proposed change. Of course, I am quite satisfied with it if it doesn't increase the taxation of the new diocesan college.

Mr. O'Connor.—The college is immediately outside the present boundary.

[illegible]. Mr. O'BRIEN.—So that any extension would bring in the college?—Mr. O'Connor.—Yes.

[illegible]. And if there is to be any extension, the larger the better for the college?—Rev. Mr. Ryan.—Yes; and, for the sake of uniformity, it would be better to make the boundary [illegible] with the electoral division. I was under the impression that the total taxation in the new area would be much in excess of the present rating.

[illegible]. CHAIRMAN.—I have already said, to you, what the Committee of the House of Commons say on the

Rev. Mr. [illegible] by Mr. [illegible] O'Connor.

Ennis. Jan 6, 1880. Mr. Francis O'Connor.

subject of the transfer of Grand Jury powers to Town Commissioners and Commissioners, and there also should the alterations recently made in the law with regard to townships including the management of the roads, &c., within the townships, and the rates which may have to be paid, if any such change be made; and also to the imposition and payment of sanitary rates under the more recent legislation. Bearing this in mind, do you think that if there is to be an extension of the boundary it would be better to follow the electoral division?—Yes, Mr. Egan,—Yes. I think it better in this thing to have uniformity; and that appears to be the best principle to adopt.

112. Mr. O'Brien.—The Parliamentary Committee have reported, and there is no doubt their report will be followed by legislation on the subject, and they recommend that the lower rates should be divided by the poor rate.

113. Chairman.—We now wish to know are there any owners or occupiers of property within the proposed area who would like to give us their opinions either in favour of or against the proposed extension?

Mr. John W. Scott.

Mr. John W. Scott examined.

124. The extension, as marked on the map, is what is proposed by the Commissioners. I was not prepared to go into the calculations, and I am not prepared to dispute Mr. O'Connor's calculations; but I don't see any benefits, for instance, in the township's being there; in fact, I think they are very much better as they are.

125. Mr. O'Brien.—Are not the lands within a certain distance of the town increased in value by reason of their proximity to the town?—None of them are accommodation lands.

126. But are not the lands within say two miles of the town, and which therefore have greater facilities for using the town, more valuable?—Of course they are; but I think not more than those within three or four miles. Then you get out of the townparks, and these are not more useful than any others. The way I would be myself inclined to think Mr. O'Connor's calculations were wrong is as to the cost of keeping up the roads. I know that the contracts for keeping up the Ennis roads also include a considerable portion of the country roads leading to them, and the great traffic of those roads is in the town. I am not prepared to give the exact amount per perch the contract is taken at; but if you think it necessary, it will come out. Mr. Hill, the County Surveyor, is here, and he will tell you what extent of the country roads is included in the town of Ennis.

127. Chairman.—Of course the traffic in the town is much larger than outside it, but is not that traffic to a considerable extent caused by the surrounding gentry and people coming in and using the town?—Of course, but that applies to an area of ten miles. As to the question whether the roads in the proposed area are being kept up economically at present, perhaps Mr. Hill can tell us how many contractors are there in the main streets of Ennis?

Mr. Hill.—Only one at present.

128. Mr. O'Brien.—But don't you think it would be a hardship to keep the area in what it now is if the people within a radius of a couple of miles add considerably to the wear and tear of the roads and yet bear no part of the expense?—It would be simply a question of what the area should be, and I don't see why you should take two miles and not take four.

129. Chairman.—Here we have the electoral division, and if we are able to adopt these electoral divisions as the boundary for the town we will be carrying out the recommendations of the Committee of the House of Commons, that the municipal should be made conterminous with the electoral division. That is the reason why, in places like this, the electoral division is proposed as the boundary. We don't want to take an arbitrary line of two miles where we can take the electoral division. When the electoral division is so large, and so townlands are cut. To Mr. Scott.—Do you not think that all farmers who have farms about the town, and sell such articles as butter, poultry, &c., have greater facilities for supplying the town, and making money for themselves, than the man who lives three or four miles off?—Certainly only the money they save to the town. The money they use to the market, but it doesn't make much difference whether a man has two miles or four miles to go to and from his house. There you suppose of town parks and got in farmers who rent 15, 20 or 30 acres of land, it makes no difference whether it is two miles or three miles from the town.

130. But we must strike a line somewhere, and therefore suggest that it might be well to follow as nearly as possible the boundary line of the electoral division?—My idea would be to go as far as the townparks, but I think it is hard to bring in others beyond that.

131. Mr. O'Brien.—What radius do you consider it would be equitable to introduce?—I have not gone sufficiently into the question, and I should not like to define any definite limit to it.

132. What radius would you consider to be fair from the centre of the town?—I think a mile should be the extent. I think once you pass the mile you get out of the accommodation lands. With the class of people who have milk and butter for sale, whether they come three or four miles, does not make much difference. They come in for supplying the dairy wants of the town.

133. Then you think a mile should be the extent of the limit?—I think so. That comes within the distance that lands would be let as town fields and not as farms, and that is the principle adopted elsewhere.

134. Mr. O'Connor.—I wish to ask Mr. Scott is he aware that lands belonging to Clonroe Dwyer, a mile and a half outside the town—a couple of acres or so—were sold for £250 a short time ago?—What is given for land is no criterion whatever of the rental value, for if people want the land they will buy it.

135. Having regard to the report of the Committee of the House of Commons, and the terms of our warrant, we must consider whether the boundaries of towns require alteration, and the question is, what the extent of that alteration should be.

136. Mr. Shegogue.—The great majority of the lands consists of crag land, which cannot be improved in any way.

137. Chairman.—But then its valuation is low in that account, and the occupier would only pay on his valuation, and I presume that whoever valued it has taken the actual condition of each farm of land into account.

138. Mr. Shegogue.—I would like you to hear the expenses of improvements that have taken place in Ennis while the management of the present Town Commissioners.

139. Mr. O'Connor.—I gave that for a number of years.

Mr. George Hill, c.e.

Mr. George Hillyard, c.e., examined.

140. I am Deputy County Surveyor, and I live within the borough at present. The only thing I would ask Mr. O'Connor would be whether the road contract extends for a distance of four or five miles at present from Ennis?

141. Chairman.—Mr. O'Connor says that, according to his calculation, the roads within the present town and the extended area could be kept for 1s. 2d. in the pound. In your opinion, if the boundary is extended, how much per mile would the

contract be?—It is an average price at present, but it will take twice as much to keep the town part as the outside part.

142. Mr. O'BRIEN.—Is that not caused to a great extent by the county traffic?—I think so. My opinion is they could not be maintained for less than at present.

143. Mr. O'Connor.—I desire to call the attention of the Commissioners to No. 763 in the Grand Jury accounts. It is a contract for some roads in the town at 3s. per perch, while here is another account for the road between Limerick and Gort, at 1s. per perch. Is not Clare bridge more than two miles outside the town of Ennis?—Yes.

144. And is not Dulick only a mile outside the town?—Yes.

145. CHAIRMAN.—Mr. O'Connor says how is it that out a distance from the town costs 1s. a perch, and the other close to the town costs only 3s. per perch?—That is caused by the immense traffic from Clare Castle.

146. Mr. O'BRIEN.—Is there special traffic from Clare Castle?—Yes; coal and corn traffic.

147. CHAIRMAN.—You see there is a very small portion taken in if we follow the electoral division boundary toward Clare Castle. The difference between the two contracts may be easily accounted for. It appeared to me, when we were here before, that the roads in the town were never cleansed at all, which may account for some of them costing only 2s.

148. Mr. O'Connor.—I call your attention also to No. 780, the Ennis and Kilrush road, 2s. 6d. per perch. There is only a very small proportion of that in the borough at present. It goes out for a distance of nearly seven miles, and that is 2s. 6d?—And if you make it one contract for the portion in the town alone it will be 7s.

149. I maintain it will be less. He says if they are separated from the county they will cost more than at present, and I say they will not?—The traffic in the immediate neighbourhood of the town is three times as great as it is three or four miles off.

150. CHAIRMAN.—I would like to know what would be the cost of keeping up the roads within the electoral division which is marked here?—On an average?

151. Yes?—It would be very hard to tell. If we knew something about this matter before we might have made some calculations.

152. What could we do more than put the announcement of our appointment in all the leading newspapers in Ireland, and we invited everyone interested to write us their views. We also gave ample notice that we would hold this inquiry today.

153. Mr. O'Connor.—The notice appeared in all the local papers.

154. CHAIRMAN.—It was published a month ago, and we invited everyone to write to us in the meantime; and we sent these queries to the Town Commissioners, for we could not know otherwise whether the Commissioners would seek any extension of their present boundary.

155. Mr. O'Connor.—The Commissioners held a meeting to consider the matter, and the report of that meeting appeared in the public papers.

WITNESS.—I don't think the local papers had any reference to it.

156. Mr. Patrons, T.C.—It appeared in the local papers.

157. Mr. O'Connor.—The meeting of the Town Commissioners was held last Monday, and a report published in all the papers stating that I was appointed to act here on the part of the Commissioners.

158. CHAIRMAN.—We take it that the Town Commissioners represent the town people, and that they wish to have the electoral division boundary, and that being so, we want to know the views of the people who would be brought in according to the proposal of the Commissioners.

Mr. EDWARD STACPOOLE examined.

159. I think the extension of the area to the extent proposed is excessive. I think a mile would be excessive.

160. But in some places it doesn't go a mile?—Well, you would go out of the electoral boundary there.

161. By our warrant, which follows the report of the Committee of the House of Commons, we are to take care to make the boundaries of towns conterminous with electoral divisions, and it would appear to be very advantageous to follow it here if we can?—A great deal has been said about the convenience of people a distance from town; but if you extend it more in one direction than the other is it not unfair?

162. In 1828 the boundaries of the towns in Ireland were arranged by gentlemen most competent to do so. At that time the portion of lands covered with houses were only brought in as a rule, and there is the boundary as adopted then (pointing to the original boundary map), and now all parties appear to think there should be an extension.

163. Mr. O'BRIEN.—The electoral divisions have been formed on the same basis. One of the principles was to attach to the town as much of the rural territory as it could be assumed derived some advantage from its proximity to that town. And here you have the outcome of that feeling in the constitution of the electoral division of Ennis as at present?—I want to know whether they were not influenced very much by property in the original distribution or divisions?

164. That to some extent was kept in view in rural districts?—I don't know whether it will affect any one in particular, there are so many proprietors around Ennis, but it would tell particularly hard where a town division belonged to one person.

165. This town appears to be pretty fair and even in its division.

Rev. Mr. Ryan.—Much fairer than a great many.

166. Mr. O'BRIEN.—You think a radius of a mile would be excessive?—I think it would be ample. A mile would certainly be the extent of land used in connection with the town as town plots. A great quantity of this land is impracticable for tillage.

Mr. EDWARD MACKEY, Poor Law Collector, examined.

167. CHAIRMAN.—What is your opinion?—I say beyond a mile would be a great hardship on small tenants.

168. Mr. O'BRIEN.—Do you think it would be unfair to keep to a mile?—I think a mile would be a fair radius. A mile would come in just at Dulick Bridge.

169. Are there small tenants outside the mile radius?—Yes.

170. How much beyond it?—About a quarter of a mile farther would take them in.

171. Don't they derive advantage from their proximity to the town?—Yes; but their holdings are very small.

172. Mr. O'Connor.—Is it merely on one townland?—No; but taking the land about generally.

173. But you merely now refer to one townland?—I just refer to Ballycorree at present, and I come to the other side and take in Gaurus. Dulick is one side and Gaurus is the other.

Mr. M'Grath.—Gaurus is the poorest neighbourhood.

174. CHAIRMAN.—Do you suggest a mile all round?—Yes, I say beyond that would be a hardship.

175. Mr. O'BRIEN.—You admit that outside the mile there are a number of small holdings which you think it would be a hardship to burden, but you say at the same time that these people derive advantage from their proximity to the town?—Yes, to a certain extent. As far as their proximity to the town is concerned the housekeepers of Ennis purchase principally on Saturday what they require, and then they purchase from people twenty miles away as well as

Mr. Edward Stacpoole.

Mr. Edward Mackey.

Ennis.
Sep. 5, 1878.
Mr. Edward Macbeth.

half a mile. As a rule there is nothing doing during the week.

176. CHAIRMAN.—There are such articles as milk, for instance, that could not be purchased weekly?—Well, that is a daily matter and I am not speaking of that.

177. Mr. *Parsons*, T.C.—Would this affect the collection of your rates in any way?—I could not tell that yet.

178. CHAIRMAN.—Is not the town of Ennis supplied with milk principally by persons living within the division?—But will the farmers supply it. No one pretended you are to have a boundary in which you will include the big farmer and leave his neighbour, the small farmer, out, but I say if you exceed the mile you will do damage.

179. Do you say that the farmers living beyond the mile are the principal persons who are supplying the town?—Yes, small and large.

180. Mr. *Scott*.—As a matter of fact, the contractors for all the large institutions are within the electoral division.

181. Mr. *Parsons*.—Some of the contractors come within it.

182. Mr. *Harvey*.—Does Mr. Macbeth's farm come within it?—It would not be worth a farthing to me.

183. CHAIRMAN.—Is it your calculation that the rating would be diminished by this district being brought in?—No, I think if you take it beyond a mile you would not be lessening it.

184. But suppose we think that by adopting the electoral division boundary the taxes on all the land within the boundary would be lessened instead of increased, what would you say then?

185. Mr. *Scott*.—Do you believe, if the electoral division is adopted as the area, that the taxation outside the present borough boundary would be decreased or increased?—I think the sanitary would be increased.

186. Mr. O'BRIEN.—How do you arrive at that?—Suppose you take that in, what are you going to give the people for that taxation?

187. CHAIRMAN.—The law makes them pay one-fourth only of the sanitary rate, and they get the advantage of light without paying a penny for it, and the people of the town say it is unfair that they should get that advantage and pay nothing.

188. Mr. *Scott*.—If we believed there will be a decrease in the taxation we would all go with Mr. O'Connor, but there is water and other matters to be had in Ennis, and that will be charged on the whole division.

189. Mr. O'BRIEN.—It is said it will not cost anything.—Mr. *Scott*.—I am very glad to hear so.

190. Mr. *O'Connor*.—I may say that the calculation about the expenses of the roads, and so on, was made for another inquiry, and not for this inquiry at all.

191. Mr. *Scott*.—I am not saying anything about that, but I have a strong impression that the taxes will be increased on the rural part.

192. Rev. Mr. *Egan*.—A great deal depends on that, and every person living outside the present area would have strong reasons for objecting to the extension if the taxation would be increased by it.

193. CHAIRMAN.—But that would apply to property in the area within the mile. Take, for instance, the railway company, see all the money they are getting out of the town and all the goods they are bringing in, all the traffic they are creating on the streets, yet they are not paying a penny for all that. No one could say there must be no alteration if there is to be fair play at all. Of course everyone will say bring me in, provided you lessen my taxation, but don't bring me in provided you increase it.

194. Mr. *O'Connor*.—You speak about fairs and markets. Does not the fact of holding these fairs and markets in the town increase the cost of keeping the town clean?—There is no doubt about that; but so far as the markets are concerned, the Commissioners don't come within the precincts of the walls.

195. Mr. *O'Connor*.—But the streets suffer, and then there are the monthly fairs?—The Commissioners have nothing to do within the markets.

196. Mr. *Harvey*.—They have to clean the streets afterwards?—Yes.

197. CHAIRMAN.—Who cleans after the fairs?—The Commissioners do.

198. At the cost of the inhabitants of the town?—Yes.

199. And are not the persons who derive benefit from those expenditures the persons who come into town at those fairs?—Yes.

200. Why, then, should the town be made pay for the benefit the country people enjoy from them?

201. Mr. *O'Connor*.—Who receives the customs tolls?—Lord Leconfield.

202. But that is your fellow citizens there?—Yes.

203. CHAIRMAN.—As far as that is concerned, Lord Leconfield has given you a fair-green, and you can extend it [illegible]?—The Commissioners have power to [illegible] the green, but they will not do it.

204. Mr. *O'Connor*.—I maintain that the fair-green, as at present, would increase the dirt of the town.

205. Mr. *Parsons*.—I hope the mile will be given to the several towns in Ireland.

206. Mr. *Richard*.—I am in the town at present, and I never see a lot of [illegible] in it.

207. CHAIRMAN.—The Committee reported on the objectionable practice of holding fairs in the streets of towns. Even in some where good and convenient fair-greens exist, as in Ennis, the practice is permitted by the Town Commissioners to continue. The Local Government Commissioners report "that the general feeling of the inhabitants and their country neighbours is generally adverse to the continuance of these fairs, but they appear to be maintained in the interest of the publicans, who, amongst the Commissioners, generally form an important clique"?—Mr. *O'Connor*.—All the fairs are held within the fair-green, but the markets are held in the streets.

208. Is much of the land to be brought in owned by Lord Leconfield?—Mr. *Scott*.—No, hardly any—the fair-green and Roslevan.

209. There is Rosslevan House, Ashline Park, and Clonroad House?—Mr. *O'Connor*.—Those houses are not there now. Ashline is the only house there, and the owner lives in the town, and is one of the Town Commissioners.

210. Beechpark House—where is that?—Mr. *O'Connor*.—It is Mr. Marcus Keane's. He is not present, but he knows of the inquiry. His clerk inquired from me, and I told him his place would be brought in.

211. Kilmoully House—where is that?—Mr. *O'Connor*.—That belongs to Mr. Cullinan, who is here.

212. Mr. *Cullinan*.—If the half of my rate is paid by the landlord I would be very glad to have the boundary extended, but I would consider it a hardship to pay a sanitary rate for a place that is of very little value. My objection is only as to the distribution of the sanitary rate.

213. CHAIRMAN.—Have you considered that the one-fourth you would pay under the municipality would be probably less than what you pay at present?—Mr. *Cullinan*.—I have no doubt it would be considerably more. I live in the town of Ennis, and I might be lightened there. If they would divide the sanitary rate it would be very popular with all parties. The Commissioners of the town have expressed their opinion very often that the landlords ought to contribute half the sanitary rate.

214. In any arable lands, and so on, which would come under the one-fourth valuation, do you say that the landlord should pay half the poor rate and the sanitary rate?—Mr. *Cullinan*.—Yes, they should, as deriving more than half the value.

215. Do you say that the electoral division boundary would be fair?—Mr. *Cullinan*.—Considering it is a boundary, I would not object.

216. Although you would come in almost at the extreme end of it?—Mr. *Cullinan*.—Yes.

217. Being in the town itself, and knowing the whole district, in your opinion do the occupiers of the land within the electoral division derive substantial benefit by their proximity to the town?—Mr. *Cullinan*.—

Mr Michael M'Kenna.

221. Chairman.—What is your opinion?—I hold land within and without the present boundary, and I think the contemplated extension is one that would not at least, one less than that would be comparatively useless, for it would only take in land and leave out the residences of the gentry, who are certainly benefited by their proximity to the town just as much as the residents themselves. They avail themselves of it to the fullest extent, and have all the advantages the residents have, but if the boundary is only extended a mile, as Mr. Macbeth suggested, it would only take in land and leave out the houses altogether. I don't think Mr. Scott ought to complain at all.

222. Mr. Scott.—I believe I should come within the area of a mile.

Witness.—I would like to have them all in by this fair arrangement. It is the most equitable arrangement.

223. Chairman.—Of course you see at once the objection to any suggested circular line, for it would destroy the electoral division altogether?—The electoral division is a guide, and there is no doubt people would be benefited and they would pay the tax.

224. Do you think there would be an improvement in the constitution of the body of the Town Commissioners if the area was extended as proposed?—Certainly; for people would take a deeper interest.

225. Can you give me an idea of the addition to the constituency of this proposed boundary?—Mr. O'Connor.—It would be very considerable, but I could not say exactly.

226. Mr. Pearson.—It would be more than 200.

227. Chairman.—If you would just kindly find out the numbers you can send them up to the office?—Mr. M'Kenna.—I should say twenty at a guess.

Mr. Harvey.—I would say about 100.

228. Chairman.—The best way is to get from Mr. O'Connor a return of them?—Mr. O'Connor.—I can get all the occupiers and their valuation.

229. Mr. M'Namara.—When I said so I was making a mistake. I thought it was the qualification of the Commissioners was spoken of.

230. Chairman.—No.

Mr. M'Namara.—Then I agree with Mr. Pearson as to 200.

231. Chairman.—Is there any other of the gentlemen present who wishes to express his opinion. Here is Woodstock House, where is that?—Mr. Pearson.—That is another of Mr. Cullen's houses.

232. I heard some one say that Mr. Bagnesbyrne had some objection?—Mr. Pearson.—No. He is most anxious for the extension. He is at present in the middle of the borough.

233.—Some one told me he had a farm outside and was objecting?—Mr. Harvey.—He is rated in the town at over £300 a year.

234. Rev. Mr. Egan.—I would like to ask one question in reference to the taxation. I don't dispute any of the figures given; in fact, I did not know anything about the points, but it strikes me the use of borough extension at all must be necessarily to increase the taxation of the outlying districts that are brought in, otherwise, what is the object except to spread the present taxes paid in towns over a large area, and diminish the taxation in the town, and necessarily increase it outside?

235. Mr. O'Brien.—Not necessarily at all. One argument is that in consequence of the present limit of the area works that are absolutely necessary become oppressive on the limited area, and that if the boundary was extended they could be borne without any undue pressure; that there are works of public health at present which have been stopped and set aside because it would be oppressive to carry them out.

236. Rev. Mr. Egan.—Doesn't that mean that the taxation of the extended area is to be increased. Suppose the works are executed and the taxation is spread over the area, must the taxation not be increased?

237. Chairman.—It depends on circumstances; if they are able to keep the roads cheaper than the county it becomes a question of £ s d.

238. Mr. O'Brien.—The taxation becomes one question, but there are other questions to be considered, and if public works are obliged to be set aside because the public charge renders them impossible, why should they not be carried out, if by an extended area they become possible? and as all will obtain the advantage they should all contribute.

239. Chairman (to Mr. O'Connor).—How many houses are there down at Clare Castle?—Mr. O'Connor.—There are a good many, but they are of a very poor class.

240. Mr. Harvey.—Is Clare Castle Hill been included?

241. Chairman.—No, it is out of it, but it might easily be included.

242. Mr. Pearson.—If you take in Clare Castle you will be taking in the most poverty stricken part of the county, and no additional taxation would make up for it, for they couldn't pay.

243. Mr. O'Connor.—We might possibly invest the control of Clare Castle Harbour in the Commissioners, and the benefit would be more than any additional taxation. The port is at present in a very neglected condition, and it would be well if something could be done to improve it.

244. Mr O'Brien.—There are Commissioners who already have control over the port, and you could not touch it.

245. Mr. O'Connor.—No tax would provide for the Clare Castle portion, for they can't pay.

246. Chairman.—It just occurred to me that as there was a lot of houses there, they might be brought in.

247. Mr. O'Connor.—The greater portion of them pay no rent at all; it is conacreage. With reference to the roads, I find, according to the official return here, that there are 113 miles of roads in the barony of Islands outside the borough boundary, which are maintained, under contract, by the Grand Jury, and that within the borough boundary there are only nine miles, including lanes and alleys; yet, that the borough has to pay one-fifth of the whole tax levied on the barony of Islands. Although there are only nine miles of roads within the borough, and 113 in the barony, yet the borough of Ennis has to pay one-fifth of the whole tax levied by the Grand Jury on the barony of Islands; that barony goes out a very long way.

248. Chairman.—How many miles of road would there be within the new proposed boundary?—Mr. O'Connor.—I can give it afterwards, sir.

Chairman.—I would be glad you should. There being no other evidence we will close the inquiry.

The inquiry then terminated.

LOUGHREA.—WEDNESDAY—DECEMBER 11TH, 1878.

Before W. P. O'BRIEN, Esq., and C. P. COTTON, Esq., C.E.

Mr. MICHAEL S. KELLY examined.

1. Mr. O'BRIEN.—How long have you been Town Clerk?—I think twelve years.

2. This town is incorporated under the 17th & 18th Victoria, the Towns Improvement Act?—Yes.

3. For what purposes has the Act been adopted?—Lighting, cleansing, paving, and flagging.

4. For everything, in fact, except the water supply?—Yes.

5. Under the section of the Act under which you are incorporated, you have a rating power of 1s. on house property, and one-fourth of that on arable lands?—Yes, it is 6d. at present.

6. What is the present area of the district?—1,046 acres, 3 roods, 13 perches.

7. Does the township include portion of the lough?—I think it does.

8. Do you know the exact acreage of the lake?—No, I do not.

9. You make one rate each year?—Yes.

10. According to the returns you have given us, the rate for the last five years has been an uniform rate of 6d., with 1½d., or one-fourth, to be assessed on the arable land?—Yes.

11. There are no wards in the town?—None.

12. Does the township consist of entire townlands, or only portions of townlands?—Only portions of some, and the entire of others. There are six entire townlands, and portions of ten.

13. Are they all in the same electoral division?—Yes.

14. That is within the electoral division of Loughrea?—Yes.

15. But the electoral division comprehends a great deal more than that?—Yes; a great deal more.

16. How many townlands are there comprised in the electoral division of Loughrea?—Forty-two townlands.

17. What is the area and the valuation of those forty-two townlands?—I think I gave the return of 7,516 acres and 13 perches, and the valuation of £7,[illegible] 1s.

18. What is the radius of the present township, taking it from the centre of the town?—One mile.

19. One statute mile?—Yes.

20. Is that what you take as a basis of the township?—Yes; an area of one statute mile.

21. The opinion of the Commissioners is that the boundary ought to be extended?—Yes.

22. Are they unanimous on the subject?—Yes; perfectly unanimous about it.

23. And they think an area of two miles would be better?—Yes.

24. What is the radius of the electoral division from the centre of the town. Would two miles take in the whole of the electoral division?—No; I think not; but I am not aware.

25. Would the feeling of the Town Commissioners be favourable, as far as you are aware of it, to making the electoral division and the municipal boundary conterminous? One of the instructions of the Parliamentary Committee is that the poor law and municipal boundaries should be assimilated. Would the adoption of the electoral division boundary, as the municipal boundary of Loughrea, meet the views of the Commissioners, so far as you are aware of them?—That question was not considered; they have not decided that matter. They said they would get more enlightenment when you came round, but they will be satisfied with the two miles radius. They did not enter into the particulars at all.

26. The feeling is that they want an extension?—Yes.

27. What are the reasons, so far as you know, why the Commissioners think an extension of the present boundary would be desirable?—There is a moiety of their funds received at present from the Marquis of Clanricarde—namely, £75—and they apprehend he may stop that any day, and then they would have to increase the taxation.

28. Then, in point of fact, 6d. in the £ only represents half the expenditure, and they think it would be a heavy rate?—Yes; heavy on the limited area.

29. Are there, in addition to that, any desirable improvements which the Commissioners are restrained from effecting, in consideration of the amount of taxation they would involve?—Yes.

30. Could you mention any of them?—Yes; they could extend the flagging, and paving, and lighting, and we would get a fire engine, and a fire escape, which are indispensable for the benefit of the town. These are the principal things.

31. Have the Commissioners ever considered, or are they aware of the fact, that under the Public Health Act of last Session, section 7, although they are not the urban sanitary authority (their powers as such merging in the guardians of the union), yet there is power given them; notwithstanding the fact that the general law is that towns not having a population exceeding 6,000, shall be merged in the Board of Guardians, as the rural sanitary authority, to apply to the Local Government Board, who can, if they see fit, and after proper inquiry, transfer the sanitary authority from the Board of Guardians to the Commissioners of the township where there are Town Commissioners?—They are.

32. Have they ever considered the question of applying to have that power exercised on their behalf, and to have the sanitary authority transferred to them?—It was the subject of conversation, but they never brought the matter forward formally.

33. Are they also aware that under the same Act, section 204, another new power is given?—Formerly the functions of the Grand Jury over a town could only be transferred to the municipal body by special Act of Parliament. In the Local Government Act, 1871, however, power was given to make a transfer of this authority over roads and bridges, &c., to the municipal body, under a "provisional order," but that transfer required not only the consent of the municipal body and ratepayers, but also of the Grand Jury concerned, and in consequence of that, and the unwillingness experienced on the part of Grand Juries to confirm any such transfers, all the applications submitted failed, except in one instance. Are the Commissioners aware that in consequence of the failure, for the reasons just stated, of that provision, there is now a power given by the Act of last session that, even though the Grand Jury do not consent, the Local Government may transfer the authority over the roads and bridges, in certain cases, to the municipal body?—No; I think they are not aware of that.

34. Do you think that if that provision of the law was brought under their notice, the opinion of the municipal body would be favourable to the transfer, if practicable, of the entire control over the roads, bridges, and streets within the municipal district to themselves?—I don't know. I could not say.

35. They have never discussed it, so that you have no opportunity of knowing?—No.

36. Is there any reason to suppose this grant from Lord Clanricarde would be withdrawn?—The agent, Mr. Blake, who is chairman of our Board, says he only temporarily is he bound to give it.

Loughrea. Jan. 11, 1879. — Mr. Michael J. Kelly.

37. And on that you found your apprehension?—Yes.

38. Is there any other suggestion you would wish to make?—No; I think I have exhausted nearly all I have to say.

39. Mr. Cotton.—I want to know where that acreage was got from?—From the township valuation books.

40. There is no map showing it?—Not one, except the one you have before you.

41. But this is only roughly done. Could you get us a map with the boundary exactly marked on it?—We could get it marked in Dublin.

42. Could we get a map of the exact township boundary?—No; there is no such thing. There was one.

43. There was a map at the time the township was formed, for it is referred to in the memorial to the Lord Lieutenant?—Yes; but it was lost. There is a description of the township boundary in the memorial (produced). The description in the memorial is—

"Householders occupying dwelling-houses within the town of Loughrea, and rated in respect thereof to the relief of the poor, at a net annual value of £8 or upwards, pray your Excellency may direct that the provisions of the Towns Improvement Act, 1854, may be carried into execution in such town; and the boundaries which we propose for the purpose of said Act are as follows, viz.:—Commencing in the townland of Cosmaick, in the parish and barony of Loughrea, and county of Galway, at the point (No. 1) in the [illegible] where the eastern boundary of Henry Reilly's lane if produced southward would strike the margin of Loughrea, and proceeding northerly as said boundary to the centre of the [illegible]-road, and from thence in a direct line to the eastern extremity of the townland of Tullagh Lower, and from thence north and west, following the townland boundary as far as the dividing fence between the farms of Michael [illegible] and Wm. Kelly, in the townland of Caherlavine, thence northwardly along said fence to the Galway-road, and across said road to the boundary between Bryan Ryan and Peter [illegible]'s farm, in the townland of Gortavoher, thence in a north-easterly direction along said boundary, and through Bryan Ryan's holding to point (No. 6) in the townland of C[illegible], and through the last-named point along the southern boundary of Thomas Feeney's holding to the Bunaddy-road, and thence in a direct line from the townland of C[illegible] to the north-west angle of Monearmore (No. 7), and from thence easterly along the south boundary of Monearmore townland to its boundary or termination at the small stream which forms the boundary of Caherwalsh, and from thence southerly in a direct line to the northern extremity of the said boundary between Gortavoher and Caherwalsh townlands to the Ballinasloe-road (No. 10), thence easterly along the centre of the said road for a distance of twenty-eight perches to the western boundary of the Rev. John [illegible]'s holding, in the townland of Gortnamackanee (No. 11), and from thence southwardly along the said boundary to point in the townland boundary of Bunnagea (No. 12), and thence westerly for a distance of 15 perches along the said boundary to the dividing fence between Richard O'Neill and Jeremiah O'Leary's holding (No. 13), along said fence to the north-eastern extremity of same at No. 14. Thence in a direct line south-westerly through the holding of Patrick Sherwin, in the same townland of Bunnagea, to a point in the centre of Portumna-road (No. 15), opposite to the dividing fence between the holdings of James Fox and John Lynch, in the townland of [illegible], thence along said fence southwardly to the point No. 16, and westwardly along the same dividing fence between Jeremiah O'Leary and Patrick Sherwin's holding in the same townland, to the lane or passage which forms a boundary between [illegible] and Knockadine (No. 17), thence southerly along said lane for a distance of seven perches to the boundary between Jeremiah O'Leary and Patrick Sherwin's holding in the townland of Knockadine (No. 18), thence southwesterly along the said boundary, and continuance thereof, which forms the boundary between Patrick Sherwin's holding and the workhouse land, to the margin of Loughrea (No. 19), and from thence in a direct line through the Lough Rea to the point first described."

44. Mr. O'Brien.—Assuming that you were to take in a two-mile radius, would it include many inhabited houses?—I think not.

45. It would be chiefly arable land, which would only be liable to be rated to one-fourth?—Yes.

46. And the fact that it would be liable to only one-fourth would not indispose the Commissioners to include it?—No; they are quite willing to have it.

47. So far as you have had means of forming an opinion on the subject, do you think the views of the persons outside the present boundary would be adverse to being included in the township?—Really, I could not form an opinion on the subject. There has been no meeting of them, nor has the subject been brought before them.

48. Are there many townparks in Loughrea?—I don't know.

49. Are there many holdings by persons living in the town?—No; I don't know of any.

50. People who hold fields or accommodation lands?—Yes; there are.

51. They are within the existing boundary?—Yes.

52. There are no accommodation lands outside the boundary?—No.

53. Are the lands within two miles outside the town increased in value by reason of their proximity to Loughrea as a market town?—Yes; I think they are.

54. Do the children outside the one-mile radius and within the two-mile radius avail themselves largely of the schools in the town?—Yes; the Nunnery school.

55. To a large extent?—Yes; to a large extent.

56. And the people of the radius mentioned resort to Loughrea for markets and fairs?—Yes.

57. And so in that way they derive decided advantage?—Yes.

58. Are the lands within the radius of two miles of more value than lands situate at a distance greater than two miles from the town?—I think so.

59. Mr. Cotton.—Have the Commissioners ever had before them any map with the two-mile radius marked so that they could see what it would comprise?—Not that I'm aware.

60. It would be a very large area, about 8,000 acres, and larger than the electoral division?—Yes.

61. Mr. O'Brien.—You are aware the electoral division is composed of townlands?—Yes.

62. And that if you adopted it you would be following the recommendation of the Parliamentary Committee?—Yes.

63. And that your proposed area of two miles would cut the townlands?—Yes.

Mr. John Kenny examined.

Mr. John Kenny.

64. You are one of the Town Commissioners?—Yes.

65. The governing body, I think, consists of twelve members?—Yes.

66. The Act has been in operation in the town since 1857?—Yes.

67. You never had Commissioners before under the 9th George IV.?—There were some Commissioners about 30 years ago.

68. But they died out?—They did.

69. The present municipal district of Loughrea consists of the whole of six and portions of ten townlands?—I don't know about that.

70. Have the present limited area and valuation hampered the Commissioners in obtaining funds for carrying out improvements which they would otherwise think desirable?—I think they have, for the funds are too limited, and they are obliged to hold over things until the funds get strong again.

71. Were any important works been held over in

Loughrea. Jan. 11, 187[illegible]

Mr. John Kennedy.

consequence of the rating being too high?—When they first introduced water here I opposed it on the ground that it would make the rate too high.

72. That was before the Board of Guardians became the sanitary authority for the supply of water?—Yes.

73. Did you at any time adopt the water clause under the Act?—I am not certain.

74. You opposed the movement to avail yourselves of the clauses of the 17th and 18th Victoria, with reference to the water supply, before the guardians became the sanitary authority?—Yes.

75. Do you know of any other case in which works were stopped for the same reason?—Yes, sewage also. We would not be able to carry it out before the guardians took it up.

76. You heard me read the section of the Public Health Act which enables the Local Government Board now—notwithstanding the general law making the Boards of Guardians the sanitary authority for municipal towns of which the population doesn't exceed 6,000—to grant a provisional order vesting the powers of the sanitary authority in the Town Commissioners. Would the feeling of the Town Commissioners here be favourable to that?—As far as I can recollect, I always heard them express that opinion, and I often saw [illegible] by reason of it being taken out of their hands—for until the present sub-sanitary officer became our officer we felt it—but things are better now. Before that, however, the sub-sanitary officer would not do the things we wanted, and we felt it very much.

77. You think, then, the Commissioners would like to have control themselves of sanitary matters?—Yes, sir, in looking after lodging-houses, and compelling small families to keep their houses and yards clean. We could not get hold of this other sanitary officer at all.

78. Are the Commissioners aware that under the Towns Improvement Act, section 62, all arable lands, market gardens, &c., are only liable to be rated at one-fourth?—I am aware that that is the rating still.

79. You are aware that as long as the Board of Guardians are the local authority for sanitary expenditure within the district all arable lands are rated the same as other property?—Yes.

80. Would the view of the Commissioners in favour of having the area of the township extended be affected by the fact that, if they were made the sanitary authority, and if a two miles radius were introduced, those arable lands would only have to pay one-fourth instead of, as at present, the whole of the rate?—I think they would still approve of the radius being extended.

81. Notwithstanding that those lands outside would then only have to pay one-fourth?—Yes.

82. For instance, if there was an outlay to-morrow in the union for water works or sewerage works, all the lands, whether arable or otherwise, would be rated as other property; but if you became the sanitary authority, and carried out these works, those lands would be only liable to one-fourth of the rating. Would the fact that the law differs in that way, where the Act is administered by the Board of Guardians, cause the Commissioners to alter their view on this matter?—My own view of it is this: I wish the boundary to be extended, and I am a ratepayer also.

83. Notwithstanding the limitation I have mentioned, that the property brought in would be liable to only one-fourth of the rate?—Yes.

84. You heard me read section 204 of the Public Health Act, which gives power to all urban sanitary authorities to apply to have the control over roads, bridges, footpaths, &c., transferred from the Grand Jury to the municipal authority. Are the Commissioners aware that that provision exists?—I don't know, but it would be my feeling that it should be transferred.

85. Are the Commissioners aware that it is open to them to apply to have the power?—I am not aware.

86. It has never been, in fact, considered by them?—I heard nothing about it.

87. Your present radius is one mile?—Yes.

88. Between the radius of one mile and the radius of two miles are there many dwellings that would be brought in?—Not many to the west. There might be a little brought in, but not many.

89. Who are the chief occupiers of land between the one-mile radius, and the two-mile radius?—They are generally small farmers, except Captain Smith.

90. What is the name of his place?—Mason Brook.

91. Do you think the inhabitants outside the one-mile radius, and within the two-mile radius, derive advantages from their proximity to the town, which should fairly make them liable to some rating?—Yes.

92. Are their lands made more valuable by their proximity to the town?—Yes.

93. And by the fact that in the town they have a market for the sale of their produce, &c.?—They have a market for buying and selling market produce.

94. Do the children from the district outside the one-mile radius, and within the two-mile radius, avail themselves of the schools in the town?—Yes.

95. And they get some advantage from the water supply, &c.?—I know they all come here a couple of miles.

96. Loughrea is lighted with paraffin all during the winter months?—Yes.

97. Do the people coming to the market in the evening derive any benefit from the lighting, and so forth?—Yes, it is just as much to them as it is to us. It is for their safety and convenience as well as ours.

98. These lands, within the two-mile radius, are more valuable, in consequence of their proximity to the town?—Certainly; they pay more rent, too.

99. So you consider it would not be inequitable to bring all within a radius of two miles within the municipal district. You think they derive advantages which fairly compensate them for any taxes they might be asked to pay?—I believe they derive more of the advantages we have here just as much truly as ourselves.

100. You have heard me read a paragraph from the report of the Parliamentary Committee, in which one of the instructions is—that we should take care to make the municipal district coterminous with the electoral division, and having heard that instruction of the Committee, would it meet the views of the Commissioners if the Electoral Division of Loughrea were adopted and substituted for the present boundary?—I have heard them say so. I recollect when it was spoken of we all agreed, and they considered they were entitled to an extension of the district.

101. What is the extreme part of the electoral division?—I know Kilconickny goes nearly two miles in one direction.

102. What would be the farthest point from the centre of Loughrea?—I don't know whether the division goes to Dunsandle or not.

103. How far is that?—Two miles.

104. Then the electoral division would represent about a two-mile radius?—I don't know that the electoral division would go so far; I don't think, on reflection, that it would take in a radius of two miles.

105. Then the electoral division would be less than the two miles radius?—It would. There is Kilconickny, Kilreagh, and the Lake. I don't know whether they are in the electoral division or not.

106. On the whole it would meet the views of the Commissioners if the electoral division was adopted?—I think so.

107. Would the people brought in entertain any objection?—They might, some of them. Of course, I suppose every one of them would.

108. They have not come forward?—Unless there is power to carry the thing over their authority. I recollect when we wanted to introduce Commissioners here the country people came in and opposed it very much, but when Mr. Blake became agent to the Marquis of Clanricarde, he carried the thing almost independent of them, he thought it was wanted so much.

109. How many ratepayers have you at present within the municipal district?—I could not say.

110. Or how many would be transferred if the electoral division was adopted as the municipal boundary?—No; I think the Clerk of the Union could tell. The two parts near [illegible] a good deal of property [illegible] Lord Clanmorris's.

111. Why was the lake divided?—Because the outside part of it—the part outside the present boundary—is Lord Huntingdon's and Lord Clanmorris's.

112. But the entire electoral division is Lord Clanmorris's?—I think it is. Smith's Park belongs to the Nugents. Opposite is Lord Huntingdon's.

113. Lord Huntingdon's property doesn't come within the electoral division at all?—Yes, it appears it does.

114. Mr. Cotton.—Is there any object in having any portion of the lake in the town boundary?—It is no value, but a great deal. I suppose there are a great many hundred acres in the lake—200 or 300 acres. We would have taken fish if the lake was within the land.

115. Is Smith's Park in the Loughrea electoral division?—I think so.

116. Lord Clanmorris is the owner of the entire electoral division of Loughrea?—I think he is, except the place outside [illegible].

117. Mr. Walsh is chairman of the Town Commissioners?—Yes.

118. And he is in favour of the extension?—Yes.

119. Of course you are aware, if you apply to get the Grand Jury powers over roads, bridges, and streets transferred to you, it would give you very considerable additions to your responsibilities?—Yes; we considered there was a very dangerous bridge somewhere by the [illegible], which we tried to get [illegible] with the [illegible]; and we never could get it done.

120. You think the Commissioners would be able to look after their roads and bridges better than the Grand Jury?—I know we could; but as far as the funds, I don't know we would be able to spend as much.

121. Do you consider the Grand Jury spend as much as they have on the roads and bridges?—I would not say they do; all they spend here is, they do [illegible] the roads.

122. You don't know the difference between the amount of presentment and the expenditure?—I do not. I know we pay two county cesses in the year.

123. They amount now to [illegible] and [illegible] in the pound?—Yes; that is county cess at each.

124. You are now aware there is power to seek for a transfer of the authority over the roads and bridges, and that it is open to the Commissioners in certain cases to do so, that it is entirely optional with them?—Yes.

Loughrea, Mar. 11, 1898.

Mr. John Kennedy.

Mr. Patrick Ryan, Clerk of the Union, examined.

Mr. Patrick Ryan.

125. Can you tell me the number of ratepayers in the electoral division of Loughrea?—About 1,300. I would say about 700 rated occupiers.

126. In the whole electoral division?—Yes.

127. How many are included within the municipal boundary?—I could not say that.

128. Would you be able to tell me within [illegible]?—I could say [illegible] about 500.

129. You would be able to send me the exact valuation of the electoral division, and the number in the municipal boundary?—Yes.

130. Is the entire property in the electoral division Lord Clanmorris's?—No, it is not.

131. Who else hold property in it?—Mr. Burton Persse, Mr. Errington, and Mr. Nugent.

132. Lord Huntingdon's property doesn't come in?—No.

133. And Captain Smith's doesn't?—He is a leaseholder.

134. Mr. Cotton.—Does the electoral division go to the south side of the lake?—No.

135. Could you give me a list of the townlands within the electoral division?—Yes.

136. What extent would the electoral division of Loughrea represent from the centre of the town?—The electoral division is not uniform, it goes down towards [illegible] and the east.

137. How far does it go to the east?—Over two miles.

138. How far does it go to the west?—About a mile.

139. And to the north?—A mile and a half.

140. And to the south?—Just convenient to the town.

141. The area of the electoral division is 7,379 acres?—Yes.

142. Does that include the whole of the lake?—No, part of the lake is in the division.

143. How much of the lake does it include?—About two-thirds of the lake.

144. What is the acreage of the whole lake?—About 700 acres.

145. Have you any means of knowing whether the ratepayers outside the municipal boundary would have any objection to having the entire electoral division constituted into the municipal district?—I know they would not wish for increased taxation.

146. But would they consider it as an inducement to support it that they would have a voice in the election of municipal representatives, and the power of being themselves elected?—I should say that they would not place much value on that.

147. Would you say that all the people within the electoral division derive advantages from their proximity to the town?—I don't say all. Some in the far parts do not.

148. But don't they, to some extent, derive benefit from Loughrea as a market town?—Yes.

149. Don't their children come here for educational purposes?—A few do.

150. You say not so many do?—No.

151. Isn't land within the electoral division more valuable than land at a greater distance from the town?—Well, its being near the market, in a certain sense it is more valuable.

Mr. John Cummins, Town Commissioner, examined.

Mr. J. Cummins.

152. I am one of the Commissioners. We would like very much to have the area extended.

153. Mr. O'Farrell.—The feeling is unanimously in favour of extension?—Unanimously in favour of it.

154. What particular extension do you think the Commissioners wish to have?—They would wish to have the area extended about a mile.

155. They would wish it extended about a mile more than at present?—Yes.

156. What are their principal reasons why they wish to have that?—Well, the principal reason would be in order to save the tax on the inhabitants of the town.

157. And is their feeling that the people within the two miles radius derive advantages?—Yes, I consider they do.

158. Advantages that should make them subject to the rates?—Yes, we don't extend advantages to these places without having authority.

159. Would the feeling of the Commissioners, so

far as you know, be in favour of having the sanitary jurisdiction transferred from the Board of Guardians to the Town Commissioners?—I believe it would. I am almost certain it would.

159. Are they aware there is a provision in the Public Health Act of last session enabling the Local Government Board to do so?—I think so.

160. But they have taken no step yet?—No.

161. Would the feeling of the Commissioners be in favour of having the control over the roads and bridges transferred, if practicable, to the municipal authority?—I could not say.

162. Do you know are they aware there is power to do that in the case of Urban Sanitary Authorities?—No.

163. Mr. *Egan*.—Would that give the power of taxation over the whole?

164. Mr. O'Brien.—No. The arable lands brought in are only assessed, at present, on one-fourth. You think there is no doubt they are in favour of having the sanitary jurisdiction extended?—I have no doubt of it.

165. Are you aware that the outlying districts, which now have to bear their full share of the sanitary rate, will, if they are brought into the municipal district, be liable to only one-fourth?—I believe that's so.

166. And that would not alter the wish of the Commissioners?—No.

167. Mr. *Egan*.—Are you aware that if the tenants outside are transferred to the Town Commissioners, they will have to pay all the taxes, while at present the landlord pays half?—Yes.

168. Mr. O'Brien.—You know in the case of the poor rate the occupier deducts half from the landlord?—I am aware of that.

169. And that the rates made by the Commissioners are charged on the occupier?—Yes, and not on the landlord.

170. And even that would not change your opinion?—No.

171. Are the Commissioners aware that in their report the Parliamentary Committee have not only recommended an inquiry into the boundaries of towns, but also that the rates should be divided?—No, I could not say.

172. Then even if the incidence of the rate continued as at present they would still desire the change?—We would still desire it.

173. Are you aware of any matters that have ever been put aside or delayed in consequence of its being found they would constitute too heavy a charge on the present area?—No, I have not, for there never was any necessity for it.

Mr. John M'Carthy examined.

174. You are one of the Commissioners?—Yes, sir.

175. And you concur in the view of the other Commissioners in favour of extension?—Decidedly.

176. What are the grounds on which you are in favour of it?—I think there are certain advantages derived by those people within a certain distance of the town for which they should pay something.

177. What are, in your opinion, the advantages they participate in?—For instance, they have certain footpaths made out, and they resort here for their markets and fairs, and they derive more advantage than the people from a greater distance for lighting and so on.

178. Do the outlying districts derive any advantage in the way of schools in the town?—Yes, the majority send in their children to the local schools about the town.

179. Do you agree with the evidence of the other witnesses that the electoral division of Loughrea would be a fair line to take, the opinion of the Parliamentary Committee being that, if possible, the municipal and poor law areas should be made coterminous, and do you think it would meet the views of your body if the electoral division were adopted as the municipal district?—I believe that that is the wish of the Commissioners.

180. Assuming the feeling of Parliament to be, as expressed in the Committee's report, that care should be taken to make the municipal and poor law boundaries coterminous, would it be sufficient to meet the opinion of the Commissioners of Loughrea if the electoral division boundary was adopted?—The electoral division would not extend to the places Mr. Egan mentioned.

181. Are there places outside the electoral division that participate in the advantages and yet would be excluded?—I think there are. I think Carhune and other places would be excluded.

182. And the opposite side of the lake?—Yes.

Mr. Patrick Egan recalled, and further examined.

183. Mr. O'Brien.—You have heard the evidence given as regards the adoption of the electoral division?—Yes.

184. Are there any townlands lying in proximity to the town and deriving the same advantages that would not be included by adopting the electoral division boundary?—There are several—Carhune, Caheranna East, Gorteenpark, Glenaclara, and Grange.

185. In what electoral division are they?—Aille.

186. Within what radius are they?—About two miles.

187. It would be fair then, you think, to include those townlands in addition to the electoral division boundary were it followed?—Yes. In addition to the electoral division they should be included.

188. But are there not other portions of the electoral division of Aille at a considerable distance from the town?—Yes.

189. How far off?—About six miles.

190. So that you would not suggest that the whole of that division of Aille should be annexed?—No. Of course the lake represents so many acres of land lost to the town. Would you ask Mr. Campbell about transferring the powers from the Board to the Commissioners? Would the expense of waterworks follow the transfer if there is a loan obtained for the purpose?

Mr. O'Brien.—Yes, all liabilities would follow, and the Commissioners would have to take all the sanitary authority. Under the Public Health Act, 1878, section 7, the Local Government Board have power to grant a provisional order making the transfer, and if application be made to them they will deal with it.

Mr. Martin Tarpey, Town Commissioner, examined.

I concur in the views of the other Commissioners.

191. Mr O'Brien.—Are you in favour of having portion of the townlands of Aille brought in?—I agree with the Commissioners. Whatever they suggest I would make no objection.

The inquiry then closed.

TUAM.—THURSDAY, DECEMBER 12TH, 1878.

Before Messrs. W. P. O'Brien and C. P. Cotton, C.E.

Tuam. Dec. 12, 1878.

Mr. Wm. Gannon examined.

Mr. William Gannon.

1. Mr. O'Brien.—You are the Chairman of the Town Commissioners?—I am.

2. The town of Tuam is under the Act the 17th and 18th of Victoria, chap. 103, commonly known as the Towns Improvement Act?—Yes.

3. In what year was that Act adopted?—I cannot exactly say. I think it was in the year 1855, but the Minute Book will supply the exact date.

4. Had the town previously been under the 9th of George IV.?—It had.

5. It was transferred then to the Towns Improvement Act?—Yes. The Act of George IV. was adopted in Tuam in the month of July, and in November of the same year the town was placed under the 17th and 18th of Victoria, chapter 103.

6. Was the Act then adopted in its entirety for all purposes, including the supply of water, or only in part?—For all purposes.

7. Including a water supply?—Yes.

8. Mr. Cotton.—That map, I suppose, describes the boundaries?—This (pointing to the map in the Minute Book) is as proposed by Mr. Griffith. That is the boundary we were working in.

9. Are they the boundaries under which you are working at present?—Yes, I think so. They are.

10. Mr. O'Brien.—I believe in the existing municipality, as formed in 1855, that the area of the district, as determined at that time, is 903 acres?—I don't know.

11. Your Board have expressed an opinion that the area adopted at that time is too limited?—They have.

12. Now, will you state the grounds upon which they based that conclusion?—Well, first and foremost——

13. What is the radius in miles? How far does the existing boundary extend from the central point of the town?—It does not extend a mile on any side.

14. Does it extend more than half a mile?—Yes, it is more than half a mile.

15. It does not comprehend a radius of a mile from the centre of the town?—No, it does not in any case.

16. At the present time, the whole of the municipality is included within the Tuam electoral division?—Yes, the whole of it. The Tuam electoral division comprises a great deal more than the municipal area. The Tuam electoral division on one side goes out nearly three miles; on another side, I suppose it goes nearly two miles, and in other directions more than a mile, and in another direction not fully half a mile.

17. I suppose you are not in a position to state exactly what the area of the electoral division is?—No.

18. At all events it is very considerably more than the municipal area?—Considerably more.

19. Your Board having come to the conclusion that the existing limits require to be extended, what area do they contemplate ought to be substituted for the present one?—Some consider that it ought to be about the same as it was when the town was under the 9th of George IV.

20. What was that?—One mile.

21. A radius of a mile?—Yes. Others consider that the boundary ought to be a mile; and others that they should not extend so much, because it would compromise the rights of those who hold what are called town parks for accommodation for themselves. That is the only difference.

22. How many members are there on your Board of Town Commissioners?—Fifteen.

23. What is the opinion of the majority with reference to an extension of the present boundary—what is their view?—My impression is that the majority of the Board consider that it should be a mile. I am not, however, very positive of that, because the matter has not been sufficiently considered, and the point is not, that is my opinion.

24. The present area, I take it for granted, cuts the townlands in some cases?—Yes, it does; but not in very many. But the great thing that we complain of is that there is no defined boundary, because it does not follow the townland boundary, nor does it define anything clearly.

25. What was the guiding principle observed when framing the present boundaries?—I could not say.

26. At all events, as a matter of fact, they did not follow the townland boundaries. They are considerably out?—I would not like to say to what extent they are out.

27. At all events we may take for granted that the townland boundaries are not observed; they are not in several instances?—Yes.

28. Assuming that to be so, you have mentioned the view of the majority of the Board of Town Commissioners to be in favour of a radius of about a mile, and you have given us the radius of the existing electoral division which you said in one direction is three miles, in another direction two miles, and in another direction half a mile?—The northern is about two miles Irish, or very nearly it; the southern is about a mile and a quarter Irish. I am now taking the village of Clooniffmore, and then goes about a mile and a quarter from where we are now (the Town Hall)—on the east side it is three miles, and on the west it is something about very nearly a mile.

29. The boundary of the electoral division on the west is what?—The west is over two miles Irish. It takes in Kilbylane, and leaves the townland of Cloonmough outside.

30. Is the portion of the electoral division lying outside the existing municipal area studded with inhabited houses?—Outside the municipal district—yes.

31. Is it thickly populated?—There is a great deal of the population at Cloonmough.

32. There are numerous inhabited houses included between the electoral division boundaries and the boundaries of the municipal area?—Yes.

33. Of course you don't know what the number of ratepayers in the municipality, or in the portion between the municipal boundary and the electoral divisional boundary may be?—I do not know.

34. Do you consider, from your knowledge of the district, that the resident inhabitants of that portion of the boundary lying between the electoral and municipal boundaries—the portion surrounding the municipal and inside the electoral division boundary—do you think they derive advantages from their proximity to the town of Tuam?—Of course they do.

35. What, in your opinion, do those advantages consist of?—What you mean to say, I suppose, is that their land is enhanced in value by reason of its proximity to the market town?—Of course it is.

36. Is Tuam lighted with gas?—Yes.

37. And supplied with water?—Yes.

38. Do the people of the district to which I am referring, by reason of their frequently resorting to the town—do you consider that they, in some measure, participate in those advantages?—Yes.

39. Do they derive advantages from any of the schools of the town for their children?—Yes, they do.

40. Assuming the view of the Board of Guardians

Tuam. [illegible]

to be that it is desirable, on grounds of general policy, to assimilate the municipal to the poor-law boundaries, or, as it is called, to make them coterminous, do you think the Commissioners would see any objection to substituting for the present area the electoral division of Tuam as at present constituted?—I do not know. I think it would be rather wide. I think it would be unnecessary to send it out so far. I would not consider it necessary to send it so far out.

41. Are there many town-parks held by residents of Tuam? I mean accommodation lands?—There are, but not so many as there might be, because the proprietors of those places have taken them up and kept them for themselves.

42. As a rule, are these accommodation lands situated within the municipal boundary, or outside of it?—Outside.

43. What radius would bring them within the municipality?—It would not take a radius of a mile.

44. The radius you suggest would take in all these town-parks?—Yes.

45. It would bring in all the accommodation lands?—It would.

46. The Town Commissioners are not the sanitary authority for Tuam? You are not the urban sanitary authority; you have not the necessary population?—No.

47. I observe, from the return (the list of queries sent by the Municipal Boundaries Commissioners to the Tuam Town Commissioners, and the answers to them) which I have before me, that in answer to the question, "What were the poundage rates for municipal purposes within the last five years?" the column headed "municipal" remains blank for the five years. Have you never had any municipal rate?—Never.

48. What does your municipal expenditure annually amount to?—I really could not say.

49. Speaking roughly—lighting, paving, and everything—what is your total expenditure as Town Commissioners?—I am not sure. I should think about £300 a year.

50. In what way is that expenditure met, as you don't make any rate for ordinary municipal expenditure—in what way are the funds supplied?—By the receipts from tolls at fairs and markets.

51. Is the entire of your expenditure supplied in that way?—Yes.

52. What income do you derive from the sources you have named?—It varies, but on an average for the last ten or fifteen years—I do not recollect—but I think it amounted to £300 a year.

53. It has always proved adequate to meet the expenditure?—Yes.

54. Have you been restrained by insufficiency of income, at any time, from making municipal improvements, or improvements that you considered it desirable to make?—I promised, when the old corporation was put out, that we should never have a rate levied, and having done that I always resisted it, and there never was a rate, and one of the consequences of that was the whole of the flagging of the town had to be done piecemeal.

55. As a matter of fact are there any municipal improvements which were, on general grounds, deemed advisable—are there any of those remaining unattended, because it would involve the necessity of making a rate?—Yes, the water supply.

56. The Board of Guardians now supply you with water?—No, the water is supplied from the river.

57. Were you formerly prevented from taking any steps in regard to a water supply?—No, we were not, but I am anxious to state that we were prepared to get up a company, formed with the object of supplying the town with water, but there was a quarrel about it, and we became embarrassed and lost the opportunity.

58. There are then no particular improvements at the present time lying unmade, merely in consequence of an insufficiency of income to carry them out?—It does not strike me that there are. We are doing all by degrees.

59. How long is it that sanitary matters have not been under the control of the Town Commissioners?—Since 1874.

60. The Board of Guardians are the rural sanitary authority?—Yes; but the sanitary matters were in the hands of the Commissioners for some time.

61. Since the Local Government Act of 1872 it is charged to the Board of Guardians as the rural sanitary authority, but as the Commissioners may [illegible] under the new Public Health Act the general law of this country remains unchanged, namely, that in the case of all towns where the population does not exceed 6,000, unless they have been constituted urban sanitary authorities under that Act, the sanitary authority merges in the Board of Guardians—[illegible] under the 41st and 42nd of Victoria, chapter 52, section 5, power is now given to the Local Government Board, by Provisional Order—

"To [illegible] town [illegible] in which there shall be any [illegible] under any Act of Parliament, whether the number of the inhabitants of such district shall be more or less than 6,000, and to constitute it an urban sanitary district [illegible] all the provisions of this Act affecting urban sanitary districts, [illegible] any such town [illegible] in any adjoining urban sanitary district, which, when so included in such urban sanitary district, shall be subject to all the provisions of this Act constituting the urban sanitary authority of such urban sanitary district, [illegible] provisions of this Act affecting urban sanitary districts, and the said Board shall likewise have power by Provisional Order, [illegible] under this Act [illegible] an urban sanitary authority all the rural sanitary [illegible] which it is situated [illegible] provisions of this Act affecting rural sanitary districts. No such Provisional Order shall be made except on petition [illegible] by such Order, nor in the event of any objection being taken by any person affected thereby until after [illegible] local inquiry."

Are they aware that there is this power to transfer the sanitary authority to Town Commissioners when they so desire?—I am not aware.

62. Has any application been made by your body to avail themselves of the provisions of that section?—No, not recently. They have not done so, we have [illegible] Guardians, but such arrangements have [illegible].

63. You think they will [illegible]?—Yes, I know they are [illegible].

64. They are [illegible], as you are aware, the public sanitary expenditure [illegible] is charged equally on all descriptions of property, land [illegible], but that all properties are to be rated alike—they are aware of that?—Yes.

65. And both bodies are aware that under the [illegible] section of the Public Health Act of last session, a difference is made as to this in the rating of urban sanitary authorities. The section I may as well read to you, it is this—

"Provided that where any such rate shall be made and levied by any Corporation, Commissioners, or persons becoming at any time after the passing of this Act the Urban Sanitary Authority, all buildings [illegible] lands used as arable meadow or pasture ground only, or as woodlands or market gardens or nursery grounds, and all lands covered with water and used as a canal, and any towpath of the same, and all lands used as a railway constructed under the powers of any Act of Parliament for public conveyance, shall be assessed and liable in the proportion of one-fourth part only of the net annual value of such lands respectively."

Are they aware that, in the event of this transfer being effected from the Board of Guardians to those [illegible], one of the advantages would be to alter the incidence of sanitary taxation to the extent provided by the section of the Act of Parliament that I have just read to you?—I don't know that they are.

66. That being the law, would that alter, so far as you can tell, the views of the Commissioners on the subject?—I don't know, it would not alter mine

think it is but fair and proper that those who derive benefits from the proximity of the town should pay more.

67. You do not consider that that difference in the incidence of the rating would create any difficulty?—I really don't know whether it would or would not; but my opinion is that it should not; but of course I cannot speak for others.

68. Are you aware that under the 20[illegible]th section of the same Act there is power now also vested in the Local Government Board to transfer from the Grand Jury to municipal bodies, being also Urban Sanitary Authorities, the control of their roads, bridges, and footpaths, and all public works within the municipal area?—I do not know whether the people, speaking generally, are aware of that, but I myself am aware of it.

69. You do not know, I suppose, whether there is, as regards Tuam, a desire that there should be such a transfer?—I could not answer that question definitely. Some people have expressed a desire that there should be the transfer you have named, and others have expressed a contrary opinion.

70. You are not in a position to say whether the change is desirable or not?—I cannot say.

71. You cannot say whether the [illegible] of the Town Commissioners [illegible] would depend upon whether [illegible] be changed [illegible]

72. And do you include grass lands in that statement?—Yes, grass lands [illegible]

73. Then do I understand it to be your opinion that if the Grand Jury powers were transferred to the Town Commissioners all property should be rated alike?—Yes, I think so.

74. That it should be a single transfer, but that there should be no alteration in the mode of rating?—Yes.

75. Can you tell me what is the feeling of the ratepayers outside the municipal area who would be affected and brought inside the boundary, if the suggestion of the Commissioners to make the radius a mile were carried out? What is the feeling of the outsiders?—I don't know. I do not know what objection they could have to being brought inside the municipal boundary [illegible] I don't know whether I ought to speak with positive certainty with regard to it, [illegible]

76. You think the people outside would have no objection?—I don't think they ought to have any objection.

77. Is that property that you have mentioned [illegible] likely to increase or to diminish?—As a matter of fact, it has increased considerably.

78. To what extent?—It has increased since the time of the Act of George IV. [illegible]

79. You do not contemplate that there is likely to be any necessity for [illegible]?—No.

80. Under the circumstances the people outside should not object?—So I think. [illegible] a change in the whole face of the town. When the Commissioners were elected and acted under the provisions of the Act of George IV., we had no [illegible] in anything of that kind. All these things have been done since, [illegible]

81. As the area of the electoral division [illegible] do you think the people in the further portions of it would object to [illegible]?—I have not made any inquiries as to that. I could not give you any information on that point. I myself think it would be extending the boundary too far.

82. Mr. [illegible].—Is there any map [illegible]?—No; we had a map, but we lent it to the railway company, and we never got it back.

83. You have no map showing the existing area, and what you propose to substitute?—No.

84. Mr. O'Brien.—I presume in recommending a radius of a mile you proposed that the particular boundary should be strictly followed?—Indeed, in some places it might not be possible; for instance, if you take it in the Dublin-road. There a small portion of [illegible] property would be taken in, [illegible]

85. The view of Parliament being that the Poor Law boundaries should be [illegible] by the municipal boundaries—that being the case, do you consider you could [illegible] in carrying out their views as to making the townland the unit for municipal purposes in every instance?—I do not quite understand your question.

86. Do you see any difficulty, supposing a radius of about a mile to be taken, and seeing that the House of Commons Committee have expressly stated their desire that Poor Law and municipal boundaries should be the same, or, as it is called, coterminous, do you see any objection to [illegible], at all events so far that, in forming the new area, the townland should be followed in every instance?—I think so, where practicable.

87. Can you mention any particular instance in which there will be any practical difficulty in making the townland the boundary for municipal purposes and following it strictly?—Such an instance does not occur to me just now.

88. Mr. [illegible].—When you say a mile radius do you mean an Irish mile?—Yes.

89. I see on the map the village of [illegible]—would you include that?—[illegible] would include that. It would take all the [illegible] side of the village; it would take a portion of the village itself, but I think there would be more of the lands of that village outside the mile.

90. Mr. O'Brien.—In addition to the specific answers you have given to the questions put to you, is there any other suggestion you would desire to submit in relation to the matters which form the subject of this inquiry?—No; I think not.

TUAM. Dec. [illegible] Mr. William Burke.

Mr. John Lyons examined.

Mr. John Lyons.

91. Mr. O'Brien.—You are the Clerk to the Town Commissioners?—Yes.

92. How long have you occupied that position?—Something over two years.

93. Am I correct in assuming that the entire town of Tuam is included within the electoral division of Tuam?—It is, I believe.

94. Can you give us the statistics of the electoral division—the area, population, and valuation?—I could not do so.

95. I believe the area of the Tuam municipal division is 694 acres?—I believe so.

96. And the population 4,223?—Yes, sir.

97. And the valuation, according to the return furnished to me, is £3,916. The return of the valuation made by the Commissioners is £3,918, and I presume

Thurles. Jan. 13, 1878.

Mr. John Lyons.

the difference is owing to some revision. The return, as furnished to me by the Valuation Office, is £3,930 ?—Yes, sir.

98. You have had no rates of any kind ?—Never, sir.

99. You have never had a rate ?—Never.

100. Give us exactly what is the present expenditure and the present income of your municipal body ?—I have not the figures just at present, but I can get them for you.

101. Can you give them to us for each of the last five years ?—Yes.

102. During the year 1871 what was the municipal income ?—£313 10s. 9d.

103. What were the sources from which that was derived ?—It was derived chiefly from tolls and customs.

104. What was the expenditure of that year ?—The expenditure that year was £316 7s. 8d. There was a balance due to the Treasurer in that year.

105. What was the actual sum expended in that year ?—£316 7s. 2d.

106. That was in excess of your income ?—Yes, that was in excess of our income.

107. How was that excess provided for ?—It was provided for in this way—there was a sum of £218 5s. 6d. due by the Treasurer to the Commissioners from the previous year.

108. Was there anything exceptional in the expenditure that year, or was that year exceptionally high ?—I could not say.

109. What were the purposes to which that expenditure was applied ?—The payment of officers' salaries, to pay for rent of the fair green, to pay for gaslight, to pay for the rent of this Town Hall and the rent of two or three market places, to pay for flagging and paving operations, and the cleansing of the streets.

110. The cleansing of the streets ?—Yes, and also to pay for fuel.

111. What was the fuel for ?—It was for the Town Hall. That was what the expenses were.

112. You were not at that period the sanitary authority—the Town Commissioners were not the sanitary authority ?—No, they have not been the sanitary authority since 1871.

113. Take the next year, 1876—was there any difference in that year ? What were the receipts and what was the expenditure in 1876 ?—The receipts for 1876 were £478 15s. 8d.

114. What was the expenditure ?—I cannot say offhand.

115. Will you be able to furnish us with a return of the receipts and expenditure ?—Yes, sir, I will.

116. At the close of the year 1876 how did you stand ; were you in debt or in credit ?—At the close of the year 1876 the probable balance due to the Treasurer will be £324 16s. 3d.

117. After providing for your expenses ?—Yes.

118. Can you state how many townlands are wholly and how many townlands are partly included in the municipal district ?—I do not know.

119. Have you any statement showing the townlands included in the municipal area ?—We have a statement in the book showing that.

120. How many townlands are wholly situated within the municipal district ?—I could not say.

121. Don't you see in the book the heading "Part of" ?—Yes, I do. There are thirteen whole townlands and two parts of townlands included in the municipal district.

122. Then only two townlands are cut ?—That is it, according to the valuation return.

123. You are quite sure there are only two townlands divided ?—There are only two marked here in the book "part of"—Carraghorewn and Hallistraddle.

124. The other thirteen townlands do not appear to be divided ?—No, sir.

125. Do you think you can furnish us with a return giving the names of each of these townlands, and showing their valuation and area ?—Yes, sir.

126. The Town Commissioners have expressed an opinion in favour of having a larger area ?—Yes, sir, they have.

127. Did they agree upon any particular townlands which they proposed should form the new municipal area ?—They did not.

128. They have merely agreed in general terms to the principle that a radius of about a mile would be a reasonable one to adopt, but they have not gone into details or agreed as to what townlands should be included within that radius ?—They have not.

129. They have not had under consideration any proposal to apply for a transfer of the sanitary functions to the Town Commissioners ?—They have not had it under consideration. It has been spoken of in a cursory manner, but the subject has not been formally entertained by the Commissioners.

130. They have not either, I suppose, considered any proposal to seek for a transfer of the Grand Jury functions in the matter of the control over the roads and bridges within the town ?—They have not, to my knowledge.

131. According to the answer to query No. 6, the poor rates for the last five years have been 4s. 2d. and 3s. 4d. in two years, and 5s. 7d. in one year. Are you aware, or have you any knowledge as to what portion of that poor rate has been applied to sanitary purposes ?—I don't know.

Mr. Alexander Strachan.

Mr. ALEXANDER STRACHAN examined.

132. You are a landed proprietor ?—Yes.

133. Within the borough or outside ?—Within the borough.

134. Are you acquainted with the existing boundaries ?—I am very nearly.

135. According to the evidence of the Town Clerk it appears that there are thirteen whole townlands and two parts of townlands comprehended within the district. Is that correct ?—No ; it is incorrect.

136. In what respect, please, Mr. Strachan, is it incorrect ?—I will, if you will permit me, explain how the Town Clerk's evidence is incorrect.

137. Certainly.—The whole of Cormalea West is in it ; there is only part of Carraghorewn in it. Of the Dunmoyne townland there is only one-fourth in it, and of Farrinaleux only a part of it is in. There is only part of Farrinamartin in it, but the whole of Glebe is in it. There is only part of Hallistraddle, there is only part of Millahenny in it ; there is only part of Park Moor in it ; there is only part of Turtey in it, Townparks, first division, only part of it in ; Townparks, second division, all in ; Townparks, third division, all in ; Townparks, fourth division, I think that is all in, too—yes, that is all in.

138. Now as to the Townparks, fifth division ?—Well, only part of the fifth division of the Townparks is in.

139. Then there are several cases in which there are only parts of townlands included ?—Yes ; it could not be otherwise, because it would extend out in parts more than a mile and a half from the centre of the town. I am speaking of statute miles.

140. Would you be kind enough to mention any townland, suppose it was considered desirable that townlands should be adopted as the unit in the formation of the municipal area, can you mention any townland where a difficulty would arise in applying that principle, where it would be inconvenient to include a townland within the municipal district ?—In the very last townland I have mentioned—the fifth division of Townparks—that would arise.

141. What would the difficulty be ?—Supposing you take a mile from the centre of the town on the [illegible]

the municipal boundary, then it would take in very little of the 6th division of Townparks at all.

142. What would be the distance from the centre of the town to the remotest part of Division No. 5? —I think very nearly two English miles.

143. Is there any other townland where the same difficulty would arise?—It would arise in the case of the [illegible] division.

144. If that were included, what would be the remotest part from the centre of the town?—More than a mile and a quarter.

145. Any other townland where the same difficulty would arise?—It would arise in the case of the [illegible] lands of the bishop. It would also [illegible] him; it would take in all his lands.

146. What would be the remotest part of his lands from the centre of the town?—About a mile; nearly a mile and a quarter.

147. The only difficulty you see in introducing these townlands and their boundary into the municipality would be that it would operate unfairly in making the radius over a mile?— Not only that, but it would not include anything, in fact, only grass lands. There would be only two persons having votes included.

148. That is in the radius of a mile?—Yes, sir.

149. If the townlands were all introduced it would bring in more?—It would not bring in any more, but it would add more taxation to the parties.

150. Who are the two voters of whom you have spoken?—Mr. Lydon and Mr. William Clonan.

151. That is the only objection?—The difficulty you see there, is that it would exceed a distance of a mile from the centre of the town, and, while it would subject those to taxation, it would bring in only two additional voters. It might also bring in one from Kilblaney. I do not know of any more.

152. With respect to the distance, what distance do you consider Mr. Lydon's is from the centre of the town?—I think it is about an English mile.

153. What townland is that?—It is the townland of Tubber Jackob.

154. You say Mr. Lydon's land is about a mile?—Yes, about a mile.

155. What townland is it in?—Tubber Jackob.

156. Would the whole of Tubber Jackob be brought in in a mile radius?—Yes, very nearly the whole of it.

157. Have you any property outside the municipal boundary here?

158. Would that be included?—It would.

159. Are you in favour of the adoption of the mile radius?—No, sir; I am against it.

160. You are in favour of the present arrangement?—I would rather have a radius made around the town. I would propose that a half mile or three-quarters of a mile radius should be adopted.

161. You would be in favour of a fixed radius, irrespective of townlands—a hard and fast line representing a certain radius?—Yes, sir.

162. What radius would you propose?—Half a mile.

163. Is not the present radius half a mile?—It extends half a mile, but in some places only a quarter of a mile.

164. You think the present irregular boundary unsatisfactory, and would substitute for it a uniform one, with a radius of half a mile?—Yes.

165. And you consider that sufficiently large?—Yes; it would be sufficiently large.

166. Would that bring in a large rural population?—It would.

167. Would the entire lands be chiefly composed of townparks?—Yes.

168. Accommodation lands?—Yes, sir.

169. You think anything outside would not be desirable?—I think not.

170. Would the area you have said you are favourable to, would that take away any of the present municipality?—Very little.

171. Where?—Well, it would take off corners.

172. Would it take off any other part?—It would take off part of Mr. Kennedy's.

173. Where is Mr. Kennedy's?—At Cloonaghmore.

174. Would it take off anything else?—It would take off a small portion of [illegible].

175. Any other place in which it would take off anything?—It would take off a small portion of property in the hands of the Commissioners.

176. What is the townland?—It is in the first division of the townland of Parks.

177. What townland?—In the first division of Townparks.

178. Would it take off any other part now within the municipality?—I don't think it would.

179. Would it be included in it with any of the far end of Patrick Martin, and part of Killaveenty?—I think not.

180. Supposing that in the case of all these townlands in the present municipality it was decided that they should all be included for the purposes of carrying out the provisions of the [illegible] Commission—supposing all these townlands were to be included in the municipality, are there any other townlands that it would be necessary to include also?—There are a great deal all round.

181. Name any other townland, if these were brought in, that should follow?—The whole of Killaveenty should be brought in.

182. Is not that one of those partly in now?—Yes.

183. Assuming that the whole of those townlands that are now entering either wholly or partly into the municipal district, supposing it was decided to bring the whole of those townlands in, are there any other townlands which, in your opinion, it would be necessary to introduce on the same principle in making a uniform rule?—Tubber Jackob.

184. Are there any others?—And the land of the Vicar's Glebe.

185. Can you mention any other townland?—Ballymoate; that is part of Doon.

186. Then Doon should be introduced?—I think so, sir.

187. Can you mention any other?—Probably, if you included the whole of the Bishop's demesne, [illegible] would be included.

188. Can you name any other townland?—[illegible].

189. These townlands that you have just now enumerated are the only ones that occur to you?—These are all.

190. If these townlands were included with those already, wholly or in part, comprised in the municipal boundary, it would give a radius of about a mile and a half from the centre of the town, outside distance?—Yes.

191. Does it not appear to you that that would be unreasonable?—Yes, sir; it appears to me to be very unreasonable.

192. Do not the people within that radius of a mile and a half—do they not derive some advantages from their proximity to a good market town like Tuam? Tuam is a good market for the different descriptions of agricultural produce. Don't you think that that in itself must be a considerable advantage to them?—I do not see that.

193. Do the children of the persons living in these places resort to the town of Tuam for the purposes of education at the schools?—Some do, and some do not.

194. These people resort here, I suppose, on fair days and market days a good deal, and don't they participate a good deal in the advantages of having the town flagged and lighted, &c.?—Yes, they would, if it was done, but it is not done.

195. Is the land within that radius of greater value than land lying further off, in consequence of its proximity to the town—does not that fact enhance the value of land?—I don't think it does. The taxes are greater in the Tuam electoral division than in the divisions outside.

196. Assuming that the sanitary powers were transferred from the Board of Guardians, who at present exercise them, to the municipal body, and to—

Tuam. Jan. 13, [illegible].

Mr. Alexander [illegible].

Tuam. Jan. 13, 1879. Mr. Alexander Cumming.

entire part of their expenditure, would it not be an advantage to the outlying ratepayers to have them so transferred to the municipal body, because instead of having to contribute the full amount of the rate, they would, if brought in within the municipal district, have these funds supplied by the Corporate income for Corporate expenditure, or in case of a rate becoming necessary, they would only have to be rated to the extent of one-fourth—would not that confer an advantage on them?—I do not think it would.

197. Either having to pay no sanitary rate, or only part of the sanitary rate, would not that be an advantage over the present system, under which they have to pay the full rate?—I don't think it would.

198. Is there any other observation or suggestion that you would wish to make?—I only suggest that half a mile radius would be enough.

199. Mr. Cotton.—Assuming that the whole of those townlands that are enumerated here on the first page of the valuation return were all brought in for the purpose of carrying out the Parliamentary instruction, I ask you could you enumerate any townland, and apply the same rule—that it ought to be included on the ground that it would be so close to the centre of the town, and derived as much advantage as those included within the proposed boundary?—I think Drum is.

200. Are you aware that any part of Drum is within a mile of the centre of the town?—I think the very edge is.

201. Did you leave out the townland of Cloonbaugh?—No; it is included in the valuation return already.

202. Do not those having town parks and fields and grazing land generally derive benefit from their proximity to Tuam?—No; I don't think they do.

203. Don't they sell milk and butter and things of that kind in the town?—Some do, and some do not.

204. Is not Tuam supplied with milk and butter from those grazing lands?—Yes.

205. Within what radius are those grazing lands?—Within a radius of five miles.

206. Does any person at a distance of more than a mile and a half supply milk to the town of Tuam?—They do; but I cannot tell you who they are.

207. Who are they?—I cannot reply to that question, unless the answer is urgently demanded of me.

208. You may as well state who they are?—Well, the Bridges, of [illegible], they supply milk, and the Bridges, of Parke—and, indeed, all the people of Parke—supply milk to the town of Tuam.

209. Supply milk?—Yes.

210. To whom?—I shall not tell you more, sir, but I will furnish you with the names of the parties to whom they supply milk if you require that I should do so.

Mr. John Morris.

Mr. John Morris examined.

211. Mr. O'Brien.—You are, I believe, acting as Assistant Clerk of the Union?—Yes.

212. Your father is the Clerk of the Union, I believe?—Yes.

213. Are you aware what the area and rateable valuation of the electoral division of Tuam are?—The area is [illegible] statute acres, [illegible] roods, and [illegible] perches, and the valuation, according to the last revision, is £[illegible] [illegible].

214. How many townlands are included within the electoral division?—[illegible] townlands, and, including the [illegible], it makes [illegible].

215. I observe that during the last five years, Mr. Morris, the poor rates appear to have ranged between [illegible] and [illegible]; in 1874, [illegible]; in 1875, [illegible]; in 1876, [illegible]; and in 1878, [illegible]. During the whole of the period comprehended by that series of years the Board of Guardians have been acting as the Rural Sanitary Authority under the Local Government Act of 1872?—Yes.

216. Can you say what proportion of the rates made were rates to raise for sanitary purposes?—How much, I cannot tell. There has been about £[illegible] expended by the Guardians.

217. How much is made up of sanitary expenditure?—I cannot tell you for the town of Tuam. There was no rate specially struck for the town of Tuam.

218. Have you struck a special rate for sanitary purposes for the town of Tuam?—No; because the Town Commissioners expend their own money for it.

219. Would the guardians—would the [illegible], as I have [illegible], represent the entire [illegible]?—They do.

220. What was the rate devoted to sanitary expenditure?—There was 1d. in the pound struck in the rate for the whole union.

221. Do you make the whole union the area for all the sanitary expenditure? Have you no contributory districts?—We have now, because we are getting up special rates.

222. When did you make a special rate for sanitary purposes?—The year before last for Dunmore.

223. Was any portion of the rate of 1s. 7d. for the year 1878 levied, or was any part of that rate devoted to meet sanitary expenditure?—It included 1d. in the pound for general expenditure under the Sanitary Acts, but not specially for the town of Tuam.

224. Was there a special rate for Tuam?—No; there was not.

225. In Tuam you have not been carrying out any special sanitary works?—No; we have not.

226. What were the general expenses?—They were for the sanitary staff—for the sanitary officers.

227. Except that general 1d. in the pound for general purposes, you have had no special sanitary expenditure in the town of Tuam in 1878?—No.

228. Had you in 1877?—No.

229. Had you in 1876?—No.

230. Nor in 1875?—No, sir.

231. Had you in 1874?—No, sir; not in the division of Tuam.

232. That is all poor rate with the exception of the 1d. in the pound for general sanitary purposes?—That is all.

233. Are there any items of sanitary expenditure that have been pressed on the attention of the Guardians?—There have been nuisances so pressed on their notice.

234. What was the nature of them?—Cleansing the sewers—opening them, and cleaning them, where required.

235. You have not known proposed an undertaking any large works, such as water supply, sewerage, or anything of that kind?—No; we have not.

236. Are the Board of Guardians aware that there is now power to transfer the jurisdiction of the Board of Guardians under the Sanitary Act from the Board to the Urban Sanitary Authority under provisions of [illegible]?—They are.

237. Has the subject ever been considered by the Poor Law Board?—No; the Poor Law Board have not given the matter consideration, but the Town Commissioners have considered it.

238. Then you don't know whether the Board of Guardians are or are not in favour of such a transfer?—The fact is, they have not considered the matter at all.

Tuam, [illegible] 1878.

Mr. John Claran examined.

Mr. John Claran.

[illegible]. You are one of the Town Commissioners of Tuam?—I am.

[illegible]. You have heard the evidence given to-day by Mr. Strachan and others.

[illegible]. Do you desire to offer any observations in reference to it?—I would prefer, and I believe the Commissioners and the people of Tuam would prefer, that the boundaries should be extended a mile.

[illegible]. A radius of a mile from the centre of the town?—Yes.

[illegible]. To a mile?—Yes, sir. Of course you know I mean as near as we could go to that.

[illegible]. Do you propose a hard and fast line?—I do not.

[illegible]. You would leave us to correspond with the townland boundaries?—Yes, sir.

[illegible]. While taking a radius of a mile, as the guiding principle, you would not be in favour of a hard and fast line; you would leave us to have a fairly [illegible] and satisfactory demarcation made in favour of the townlands?—Yes, sir; I believe it would be of advantage to the people of the town and suburbs. I know that if Mr. Strachan's half-mile circle were adopted it would stop, as far as [illegible] goes, at the [illegible], and shut out a lot of houses on the [illegible] that should be included within the municipal boundary. The boundary he suggests would especially shut out his (Mr. Strachan's) land near the town.

[illegible]. Mention the situation of the lands of Mr. Strachan that would be shut out?—I do not know what the lands in [illegible] are that would be shut out. It would shut out his lands in [illegible].

[illegible]. Following that mile radius would shut out Mr. Strachan's lands in [illegible]?—Yes, sir. On the [illegible] road, it would partly shut out Mr. Strachan's lands, too.

[illegible]. At what distance from the town?—A little more than half a mile. At [illegible] road it would shut out Mr. Strachan's land, too.

[illegible]. At what distance from the centre of the town?—About half a mile. I believe also that the people in the suburbs, and within a mile or less of Tuam, enjoy great benefits from the proximity of the town.

[illegible]. Within what radius would you say that benefit is diffused?—Within four or five miles certainly. Of course the nearer to the town the greater the advantage. Mr. Strachan stated, I believe, that the people reaped very little advantage from the town, and he said that if the town was properly paved and lighted they would derive advantage. I say that they do now derive advantage from the town.

[illegible]. Are any of those neighbouring districts supplied with [illegible] from the [illegible] in Tuam?—Yes, sir.

[illegible]. To what extent or distance?—I employ men myself——

[illegible]. What distance do they come?—They come to half a mile from the town. I have also men coming in a mile and a quarter from the town.

[illegible]. Is that a common occurrence? Are there many labourers working a mile and a quarter from the town?—No, there are not; but within a mile there are a great many. I should like to be allowed to state that I have no object in making these statements of the [illegible] than that which would confer benefit on the town.

[illegible]. Mr. Strachan stated that these grass lands nearest the town derived no advantage to the town, as he said a large milk consumer in this town?—He is.

[illegible]. Do the owners of lands within a radius of a mile derive advantages from being able to supply milk to the town?—Yes. And besides that they have other advantages, for the holders of fields on the use of their [illegible] grass lands, and that is an advantage.

[illegible]. How many fairs are there in Tuam in the year?—Eleven. Tuam is the third largest fair in Ireland. The people of the town who have no lands, but who have to keep a cow for the milk for their children, pay very high for grazing land to gentlemen in the suburbs of the town, and, of course, besides that lands near the town are more valuable than those at a distance.

Mr. Thomas Egan examined.

Mr. Thomas Egan.

[illegible]. You are one of the Town Commissioners here?—I am.

[illegible]. Upon what point are you desirous of giving us information?—I think you were led to believe that the majority of the Commissioners and the people outside were in favour of having a boundary of a mile. I know a great many outside who would wish a radius of half a mile, and I can answer for some more of the Commissioners, who would prefer to have the boundary not extended more than half a mile.

[illegible]. Are you aware of the grounds upon which they prefer this radius of half a mile?—Well, no; but I heard them express views on the subject.

[illegible]. Did they base their views on any particular principle?—There is this in it: There are some people who may live three-quarters of a mile from the town. If a burning or anything of that kind took place, it would be very hard for them to have to pay their share of the taxation for that.

[illegible]. What do you mean by "a burning"?—I mean a malicious burning. It would be very hard on those people to have to pay their proportion of the taxation.

[illegible]. Is there any other objection?—I think that is a particular objection.

[illegible]. To going beyond half a mile?—Yes.

[illegible]. Would it not be equally hard on people within half a mile radius if they had to pay a still higher proportion of the taxation?—Yes, it would, but they are living within the circle of the town—I mean they would have more claim to have to pay. If you extended the boundary for twenty miles it would be very hard to have a man paying his share of the cost of a proceeding such as I have named.

[illegible]. Have you any other objection to urge?—I think before anything is done in relation to this question a public meeting should be called, and the wishes of the people should be consulted.

[illegible]. That as the proposal has only been made in vague and general terms, they should call a special meeting to consider exactly what proposal they desire to have adopted, and submit it with a map prepared according to the course they may have agreed upon?—Yes.

[illegible]. Mr. O'Brien.—I presume that will be done, and we shall await a special resolution from the Town Commissioners, accompanied by maps, and we shall give the fullest consideration to any views that the Commissioners may, on careful consideration, submit to us. I may venture to repeat again that our duty is of course to carry out the instructions of the Parliamentary Committee, and they have expressly laid it down that it is desirable that poor law and municipal boundaries should be coterminous. To do that at all—to make even a step towards it—it is absolutely necessary that townlands should be adhered to—for this reason, that, under the Poor Law Acts, the townland is the unit, and there is no denomination recognised smaller than a townland there. Electoral divisions are simply aggregations of townlands. You should bear this in mind, and that if effect is to be given to the wishes of the Parliamentary Committee it will be necessary that there shall be no unavoidable departure, at all events, from the lines of townland [illegible]. Bear this in view, and you can then consider what area should be fixed upon, and submit it to us?

Mr. Ganly.—Yes, sir.

270. Mr. Cotton (to witness, Mr. Thomas Egan).—You said you were in favour of having a half-mile radius?—Yes.

271. Are you aware that making a half-mile radius would restrict the present boundary, and cut off a large amount of property built on in the present area?—I am not. I said half a mile or three-quarters, but I am only a little too far.

Mr. Richard Kelly examined.

272. Mr. O'Brien.—You are a ratepayer in the town of Tuam, and proprietor of the *Tuam Herald* newspaper, I believe?—Yes.

273. You have been present at these proceedings during the day, and you have heard the evidence of the several gentlemen who have been examined?—Yes.

274. Is there any observation you wish to make as to that evidence, or any suggestion you have to offer?—So far as I am concerned personally, and as far as I can understand the wishes of the people of Tuam, they are very much in favour of an extension of the present boundary, and that that extension should at least be a mile—a mile radius from the centre of the town. The objections that I have heard urged to-day have come from interested parties up to the present. One of the arguments in favour of an extension of the present boundary is this—that it is so restricted that sometime ago when the Board of Guardians were looking out for a site for a burial ground, they were confined to a very narrow limit, owing to the restricted boundaries; and another reason why an extension should be sought for is that townparks are very valuable—nearly as valuable as house property to some people—and during the times of fairs they are let, and they are generally set at rents one and a half more than would be given for them if they were four miles from the town; and the people certainly living within two miles of the town of Tuam derive as much advantage from the benefits of the flagging, paving, and everything else in the town as the inhabitants do, except in the matter of gaslight.

275. What radius do you advocate?—At least a mile.

276. You would have no objection even to a wider area?—I think a wider would be preferable.

277. What would be the extreme limit?—I think the electoral division. I think nearly everyone living within the electoral division derives advantage from the town.

278. Do you think the people living outside the present municipal boundary, but within the electoral division would object?—I do not think they would.

279. Do those people avail themselves of the school accommodation afforded in Tuam?—I think a great portion of them come in for school accommodation, and numbers come in every Sunday for Mass, and though Mr. Strachan mentioned some cases where the people send their children to school a distance from the town, that is more or less the fault of those people, because the school accommodation of Tuam is very good. I also think that the present sanitary powers in the hands of the Board of Guardians should be transferred to the Town Commissioners.

280. You think that if transferred those powers would be better exercised?—I think so—not that the Town Board is in itself a better body for conducting such matters, but the members are interested parties.

281. They are more representative of town interests?—They are; besides that rural guardians cannot be expected to have the same interest in town affairs. Mr. Morris, the assistant clerk of the union, said that no special sanitary rate had been struck in Tuam. To my knowledge several sanitary works have been carried out in Tuam; whether those works were charged to other portions of the union or not, I am not in a position to say.

282. A special sanitary rate is made on a sanitary district, but under the Act of last Session it may include part of a townland. If there were any special sanitary expenditure, it should be charged to some definite sanitary district?—This year the sewers of Tuam were opened at an expense of about £30.

Mr. Morris re-examined.

283. Mr. O'Brien.—How was that expense of opening the sewers in Tuam charged?—I would not say that the sum was £30. It might be about £20. The rate should have been charged specially to Tuam, but it was not.

284. It was charged to the general union?—Yes.

285. There are certain portions of the expenditure "general," such as staff expenses?—Yes; I am aware of that.

286. When special sanitary expenditure takes place, such as the making of a sewer, the supplying of water—any sanitary work, in fact—there is a printed form sent down by the Local Government Board in which your members exhibit the amount proposed to be expended, the place where the work is to be done, and the townland proposed to be made contributory to the charge, and upon making that application, the Local Government issue a sealed order, and so forth. It appears that this year there was no contributory charge?—There were several expenses since 1871 not charged.

287. Mr. Kelly.—There have been each year several expenses not charged; and so far as I can understand, these expenses are kept by specially to be yet paid by the Town Board.

Examination of Mr. Kelly resumed.

288. Have you any further information to give us?—Another reason why the boundary should be extended, and that the present sanitary powers should be transferred to the Town Board is, that there are two or three things which the Town Board must take in hand, and which, if they have a restricted boundary, they cannot do. The first thing is a grave-yard, and it should be certainly the electoral division that should be charged with the expense of the grave-yard; and I think if the Town Commissioners have not the management of sanitary affairs, they cannot do, outside the municipality—it lies outside the townships—and the grave-yard at present in Tuam is in a disgraceful condition. It is overcrowded to such an extent, that a [illegible], it is necessary to remove first the bones of another that is in the ground.

289. Is there any other matter to which you wish to direct our attention?—I do not know of anything else.

290. As far as you are acquainted with the public opinion of Tuam generally, is it favourable to that extension?—Yes, only because the people brought within the area would be kept up much [illegible] the people at present within the restricted area.

Tuam. Jan. 10, 1876. Mr. Kelly.

[illegible]. Don't you think the grazing lands in the borders of the [illegible] derive great benefits from the [illegible]?—Yes; I have said so already.

[illegible]. In their [illegible] also, Mr. Kelly, that you are [illegible] of [illegible]?—I am anxious in any [illegible] or [illegible] as to any waterworks that might be contemplated. The water supply of Tuam is one of the very best. If the work of providing a [illegible] and adequate supply were taken in hand by the Town Commissioners it would be an injustice to the inhabitants of the town to levy a [illegible] rate for [illegible] purposes, because the waterworks would concern people within half a mile at any rate.

[illegible]. You think there is a decided want of an improved water supply?—Yes, [illegible] decidedly; the water supply at present is very [illegible]—[illegible] by two or three sources of pollution, each of which could be stopped if they made the necessary steps [illegible]. It goes through the [illegible] and [illegible] [illegible] them. If the [illegible] to be adopted I which [illegible] there would be only [illegible] should be left with. I [illegible] a board and that line should be drawn. [illegible] would be taken in within the mile radius; I think it would be but slightly [illegible].

[illegible]. Where [illegible] were only slightly encroached upon—where they were only [illegible], you would omit them?—Yes; but I think that at least it should be a [illegible] radius. I think another advantage that would be [illegible], and that should not be lost sight of, by the [illegible] of the sanitary powers to the Board of Town Commissioners would be that it would [illegible] an additional expense, as the present clerk would be the clerk of the Sanitary Board as it would be then formed. They are at present paying an inspector £[illegible] a year, which sum I consider amply sufficient for any other duties he might have to perform as [illegible] sanitary officer of the new Board, so that it would be a great advantage to consider, that the transfer of the sanitary powers would be inexpensive.

Mr. Glynn re-examined.

Mr. Glynn.

[illegible]. Mr. O'Brien.—I think it would be better for you to call a special meeting and to submit a definite proposal to it?—Yes.

[illegible]. And then give the gentleman who draws the map instructions to mark on it the present boundary and the proposed boundary, and to submit it to me?—Yes, sir.

[illegible]. Mr. Cotton.—And may I know with this line what the workhouse is not marked on the Ordnance map, and that it should be included in yours?—That is outside the present boundary.

[illegible]. At any rate in the map that you propose you might mark it on?—It is outside the present boundary.

[illegible]. Would it be within the proposed boundary?—It would.

[illegible]. Then it should be on the map?—Certainly.

Mr. [illegible] re-examined.

Mr. [illegible].

[illegible]. Mr. O'Brien.—I believe you wish to make a [illegible] of your former evidence?—Yes; I said in reference to the chargeability of certain [illegible] [illegible] on the union—I said they were charged on the whole union generally. I now recollect that they were charged on the Tuam electoral division.

There being no more witnesses for examination, the inquiry terminated.

ATHLONE.—SATURDAY, DECEMBER 14th, 1876.

Before Mr. W. P. O'Brien, C.B., and Mr. C. P. Cotton, C.E.

Mr. William Kelly examined.

Athlone. Dec. 14, 1876. Mr. William Kelly.

1. Mr. O'Brien.—You are town clerk for Athlone?—I am.

2. And have been for some years, I understand?—Yes.

3. This town is under the Town Improvement Act of 1854?—It is.

4. When was Athlone incorporated under that Act of 1854?—It was incorporated on the 17th of [illegible], 18[illegible].

5. Did you, on that occasion, adopt the Act in its entirety?—We did.

6. Previously to your coming under the Towns Improvement Act, had you been under the 9th George IV.?—Yes.

7. In adopting the Towns Improvement Act what principles were you guided by?—Well, under the former Act of George IV. the [illegible] boundaries were not so well defined as they were in 1854 when we became incorporated.

8. Mr. Cotton.—Of course you are aware that town boundaries are for a particular purpose?—I am.

9. Mr. O'Brien.—I observe that you obtained a local Act in 18[illegible]. What was the title of that Act?—It was the "Athlone Markets Act."

10. And the Towns Improvement Act was adopted in 18[illegible]. There was a memorial of course forwarded to the Lord Lieutenant?—Yes.

11. Have you got a copy of that memorial to the Lord Lieutenant?—No.

12. Mr. Cotton.—I take it, Mr. Kelly, those were certain [illegible] adopted for the Athlone Markets Act of 18[illegible]?—Yes.

13. Mr. O'Brien.—And the boundaries adopted under that Act are those that now exist under the Towns Improvement Act of 1854?—Yes.

14. I am right in assuming that you sent forward a memorial to the Lord Lieutenant previous to becoming incorporated under the Towns Improvement Act of 1854?—Yes.

15. Have you any record there of the memorial to the Lord Lieutenant?—None.

16. What was the principle which guided you in the selection or determination of the area?—The principle was to take in buildings.

17. Was there any such proposal?—Yes, there was a [illegible].

18. Did you take in any particular areas from the centre of the town?—Yes, we took in those places that were most inhabited.

19. In what electoral division is Athlone?—It is divided into two electoral divisions—Athlone East and Athlone West.

20. One portion is in Westmeath, and the other portion is in Roscommon?—Yes.

21. The reason of that was that the electoral division boundary and the county boundary, and it was thought advisable [illegible] to make electoral [illegible] and [illegible] boundaries correspond. In Athlone [illegible] that as municipal [illegible] it is divided into St. Peter's Ward and St. Mary's Ward.

22. Mr. Cotton.—Divided by the river?—Yes.

23. Mr. O'Brien.—They are much more largely included within the borough. Are the Commissioners desirous of any change in the municipal boundaries or

they at present exist?—No, they are not. I may mention that there was a special meeting held of the Commissioners with reference to the subject. The meeting was called for Thursday last. Each and every one of the Commissioners got full notice of the fact, and I think only nine attended.

24. How many Commissioners are there in each ward?—Nine.

25. How many do you say were actually present at the meeting?—Eight attended, and all desired that the municipal boundary should be left as it is.

26. You have gasworks?—Yes.

27. Whose property are they?—They are the property of the Commissioners.

28. Mr. Cotton.—Have you any copy of the memorial to the Lord Lieutenant, or of the letters in reply with reference to the application for a change?—No.

29. Surely the Town Commissioners' book of proceedings for December, 1854, can be got, and that would tell? [The minute-book was produced, but the required record was not found.]

Mr. Maxwell.—The memorial must have been sent between January and December, 1854.

Mr. Cotton.—The matter was considered at the meeting of 7th December, 1854.

Mr. O'Brien.—I find entered in the minute-book the following:—"The Clerk was directed to write to the Lord Lieutenant, requesting to know if His Excellency would sanction the appointment of the borough of Athlone under the Towns Improvement Act."

30. Mr. Cotton.—How could you prove that the Towns Improvement Act was adopted at all?—It must have been adopted when we were allowed to borrow large sums of money from the Board of Works.

31. What I want to get at is this, whether the boundaries under the Towns Improvement Act are the same as those under the Market Act?—They are just the same.

32. Mr. O'Brien.—What is the radius of the municipal boundary?—About a mile and a half.

33. Would there be any objection to extend it to include the entire of the townlands?—It would be no advantage, and is not desired.

34. What objection, in your mind, would there be to so altering it?—It would take in the much very and uninhabited area.

35. Would you see any difficulty in introducing the entire of the townlands, now partly included, into the municipal boundaries?—It has not been entertained that it would be desirable, and the people outside the present boundary would expect too much. Until the electric light was established or talked about they expected gas would be sent out to them.

Mr. Maxwell.—Moreover, I may say that outside the boundary the people are very poor. Towards the north of Athlone there is a great quantity of water, and there is a large lake. It would not be wise, I think, to think of taking them in.

36. Mr. O'Brien.—Are there any lands deriving benefit from the operation of the Towns Improvement Act in the neighbourhood of Athlone?—I believe not.

37. You have the gasworks—have you any other property?—Yes, we have the tolls.

38. What is your annual expenditure?—About £600.

39. How much do you gain by the tolls?—About £350 per annum.

40. The residue, I presume, is made up of rates?—Yes, and of the profits derived from the gasworks.

41. You are the urban sanitary authority?—Yes.

42. What is your town tax?—1s. in the pound and 3d. on arable land. 1s. 3d. would cover the entire want. There is 1s. on account of borough rate, and 3d. in the pound lamp rate.—£917 is the gross rating. We carry on no buildings or works.

43. You say no one desires a change?—No one desires that any alteration should be made in the existing boundary.

44. You think the present boundary is ample enough?—Yes, quite so. The radius is about an Irish mile.

Mr. Patrick Maxwell, j.p., examined.

45. Mr. O'Brien.—Mr. Maxwell, you are the chairman of the Town Commissioners of Athlone?—I am.

46. I presume you concur with what has been said by Mr. Kelly?—Yes.

47. How many members of the Town Board were at the meeting summoned for Thursday last?—Eight; and all agreed in the opinion that a change in the existing boundary was undesirable.

48. You fully concur with the body over which you preside in that opinion?—I do.

49. You don't think any change desirable?—No; I think that everything that could be done under the Towns Improvement Act has been done.

50. As a matter of general policy, now, would you not be inclined to think that the entire of the townlands, now partly included in the borough, should be incorporated within the municipal boundary?—No; I believe such a proceeding would cause trouble, and the few buildings on the land that would be so incorporated are very poor. A great portion of the land, as you have heard, lies under water. If [illegible] roads and [illegible] property built on them, then it might, no doubt, be very desirable to include them, but it is no use taking in water and bog land.

51. Your objection would be this, that the [illegible] of the boundary would add nothing to your property, and that the portion which would thus be added would [illegible] it?—Yes. I may mention, too, that the [illegible] [illegible] in that [illegible]. Over one hundred [illegible] [illegible] to come into the town, and [illegible] [illegible] years ago, when the [illegible] in [illegible].

52. You would have no difficulty in getting a map of the extended area, and marking it up on it?—We [illegible] [illegible] [illegible] and the [illegible] lands near the town would then be [illegible] included. We would wish to have the power of building on them.

53. Would you wish the Grand Jury's [illegible] of their powers over roads, bridges, &c., to be [illegible] [illegible] to—Yes. We would think it an advantage to have such works in our own hands.

54. Has there been under consideration the necessity of [illegible] [illegible]?—No, but we would wish to have it in our power. We would build a new market-house, for instance, if we had.

55. You do not think you get a sufficient return in the improvements effected for you for the money paid by you to the Grand Jury in the [illegible], on the [illegible].

56. It would be necessary for you, in order to do so, to make application to the Grand Jury, in the first instance, for a presentment, and then to apply to the Local Government Board, under section [illegible], 41 & 42 Vic., ch. 52.

Mr. Joseph [illegible], Clerk of the Union, examined.

57. Mr. O'Brien.—You are the Clerk of the Union?—Yes.

58. Have you any map in the workhouse showing the exact municipal boundaries of Athlone?—No, sir; there is no map there as good as that (the Ordnance Survey).

59. Well, the municipal district of Athlone now extends into two electoral divisions?—Yes.

60. How are those distinguished?—They are called Athlone East and Athlone West.

61. Has that change been made recently?—Yes; within the last year.

62. Before that, then, it was all included in one?—Yes.

63. Now I want you to give me the area and the valuation of the municipal district and the electoral divisions, giving first the east side?—I understand.

64. Take first the east side, the east division, what is the area and valuation of the part within the municipal district?—Within the municipal district, sir?

65. You give me the valuation.—The valuation on the east side is £4,774 10s.

66. Of the municipal part?—Yes.

67. And what is the area?—[illegible]a. 3r. 32p.

68. Well, now of the entire electoral division of Athlone East, what is the valuation?—It is £7,273 15s.

69. Well, now I want the same statistics as to the area of the entire electoral division?—It is 4,451a. 3r. 18p.

70. Of the entire of Athlone East?—Yes.

71. So that the entire electoral division of Athlone East comprehends considerably more than the municipal division?—Yes.

72. Now as to Athlone West—taking the part within the municipal boundary, what is the area of that?—Within the borough it is 544a. 2r. 17p.

73. And the valuation?—£4,511 10s.

74. And what of the whole electoral division?—5,[illegible]a. 1r. 31p.

75. And the valuation?—£7,[illegible].

76. So that in the west, as in the case of the east, the electoral division comprehends more than the municipal district?—Considerably more.

76. From the town what is the radius in each of these two divisions?—A mile would be the radius—that is of the whole of Athlone East and West.

77. Is there then no portion of either East or West more than a mile distant from the town?—No; it is not a full mile.

Mr. *[illegible]*.—I wish to call attention to this. It is a remarkable point that the land outside the municipal boundary is of a poor quality. You can see that here within it there are 544a. 2r. 17p., and the valuation of that is £4,811 10s., while outside in the electoral division, there are 5,467 acres, and notwithstanding the valuation is only £3,000 more, with 5,000 acres more. That shows, sir, that the value of land is extremely poor outside.

78. Mr. O'Brien.—Now what is the radius of the municipal district, taking the centre of the town?

Witness.—About three quarters of a mile would be a fair radius. I think that is about it.

Mr. *Vaughan.*—About one Irish mile.

79. Mr. O'Brien.—You are giving the general radius, but I want the radius from the centre of the town?—About one and a half English miles.

80. Mr. O'Brien.—What is the radius of the electoral divisions of Athlone?—I did not understand you to say the electoral divisions.

81. Yes; to the remotest part of the electoral division?—Well, I would say, two and a half English miles.

82. Then I take it that Athlone East and West extend two and a half miles from the town?—Yes.

83. And what do you say would represent the radius of the municipal district?—About one English mile.

84. So that the electoral divisions are double the municipal?—Yes.

85. We take it now that there is nobody desirous of having any change made in the municipal boundary.

The Inquiry then closed.

Athlone. Dec. 14, 1878.

Mr. Joseph Vaughan.

MULLINGAR.—DECEMBER 16th, 1878.

Before Mr. W. P. O'Brien, P.L.I., and Mr. C. P. Cotton, C.E.

Mullingar. Dec. 16, 1878.

Mr. Lawrence Keena examined.

Mr. Lawrence Keena.

1. Mr. O'Brien.—You are clerk to the Town Commissioners of Mullingar?—I am.

2. How long have you filled that position?—[illegible].

3. Now the town of Mullingar is constituted under the Towns Improvement Act of 1854?—Yes.

4. At what time was the Act adopted in Mullingar?—In the year 1856—on the 28th of April of that year.

5. Is that the date of the Lord Lieutenant's sanction of it?—Yes.

6. The town had not previously been under any form of municipal government?—No, sir.

7. That was the first time the town became subject to municipal government?—Yes.

8. Was the Towns Improvement Act on that occasion adopted in its entirety or in part?—Only in part.

9. For what purposes?—For lighting, cleansing, and [illegible].

10. But not for a water supply?—No, sir.

11. Then it was adopted for all purposes except a water supply?—Yes.

12. Your taxing limit has been 1s. in the pound, I believe?—Yes.

13. I observe from your answers to the queries submitted to you by us that during the last five years the rate was always, and still is, 1s.?—Yes, it is 1s.

14. You have gone up to your limit?—Yes.

15. You are not the sanitary authority. For sanitary purposes the town is managed by the rural sanitary authority, the Board of Guardians?—Yes, that is so.

16. Has any part of your expenditure been made applicable to sanitary purposes?—No, not since the Act of 1874.

17. Your expenditure having been 1s. in the pound, has that been found adequate for the discharge of the duties of the Commissioners, or have they been debarred from making improvements or doing works considered to be of material benefit to the town,—have they been prevented doing so by reason of the rating power being limited?—Yes, if they were to go for anything and all those things, 1s. in the pound would not be sufficient, but at the present moment it is sufficient for the purposes to which it is devoted.

18. What I want to know is this—are there any works of public utility which the Town Commissioners have felt themselves unable to carry out owing to the limit in their rating powers?—Not that I am aware of, since they ceased to be the sanitary authority.

19. Before that time they did feel it difficult?—Yes.

20. But since the Act of 1874 transferred the sanitary functions to the Board of Guardians they have found the 1s. rate sufficient for their purposes?—[illegible], but nothing more.

21. Have the Town Commissioners already had under consideration the question submitted by the Municipal Boundary Commissioners, as to whether the existing area of Mullingar was considered satisfactory or not?—They have.

22. I observe from your answer to Query No. 6 that it is stated that the boundaries are not considered satisfactory?—Yes.

23. Was there a resolution adopted by the Town Commissioners to that effect?—Yes; at the first meeting of the Board. That was their opinion at the time.

24. How many members were present on that occasion?—Five or six.

MULLINGAR. Jan. 15, 1879. Mr. Laurence Kenny.

25. What number constitute the Board altogether?—Fifteen.

26. Had notice been given to the Commissioners generally to attend?—Yes, sir, to attend to answer these queries.

27. They were all aware of the holding of this meeting and the object with which it was called?—They were all aware.

28. Did they adopt a formal resolution to the effect you have stated?—They did not adopt a formal resolution, they merely answered the queries submitted to them.

29. Will you kindly now give me the area and valuation of this town as it is at present—the area of the present township?—Why the area of the present township is something less than a mile.

30. In radius less than a mile?—Yes.

31. How many townlands and parts of townlands go into it—are comprehended in it?—There are five parts of townlands.

32. How many townlands are comprehended within the municipal district?—Five.

33. Five townlands comprehended within it?—Yes.

34. How many townlands are included in part?—Three.

35. Give the names, please?—Ballinderry (part of), Petitswood (part of), Robinstown, Levington, Robinstown Tyrrell (part of), Springfield (part of).

36. Within the municipal district there are seven entire and parts of nine townlands, you say?—Yes.

37. What is the area of the entire township as at present constituted?—Less than a mile.

38. The area in acres?—The area in acres is 1,2[illegible] acres 2 roods and 33 perches.

39. And the valuation?—The whole valuation is £7,237 5s.

40. That is not what you have given in the answers to the queries, and yet this figure is correct, according to the return of the Valuation Office?—Well, it is £7,237 5s.—that is correct. That was last year's. This is revised. The Valuation Office return was taken after it was revised. The valuation furnished to you must have been last year's.

41. And the revision since then made the difference you have mentioned?—Yes.

42. In what electoral division is the township of Mullingar constituted?—In the electoral division of Mullingar.

43. The entire of it?—Yes.

44. You have given the number of townlands and parts of townlands included within the municipal boundaries—how many townlands and parts of townlands are included in the electoral division? I presume the electoral division extends a good deal beyond the municipal boundary?—Yes, it does.

45. How many townlands are in the electoral division of Mullingar?—I cannot say; Mr. Walker, the Clerk of the Union, will be able to answer that question.

46. When the Commissioners adopted the answer which you have sent to the query about the extension of the boundaries, did they consider or agree to any particular extension—I think I understood you to say that the radius of the present municipal district is about a mile from the centre of the town?—Yes.

47. That is about the farthest point?—Yes.

48. Do you mean in English or Irish miles?—I think English miles.

49. Did the Commissioners consider this question—did they agree among themselves, or discuss what the alteration was that they were prepared to recommend?—I am not aware what was the exact nature of the agreement they came to at the time, but they all decided upon an extension.

50. When they came to a resolution in favour of an extension, did they agree upon what the alteration was that they would adopt, or decide to adopt?—Yes, sir, two miles radius from the court-house.

51. What they proposed was a two mile radius from the court-house of the town?—Yes, sir.

52. Without respect of townland or any other boundaries?—Yes.

53. Without respect of any other boundaries?—Just so.

54. And they have had a map prepared embodying that view?—Yes, sir.

55. In this map, I believe, the red line shows the existing boundaries, and the blue circle the proposed boundaries?—Yes.

56. Who prepared that map?—I did. I took a compass, and made a circle showing the proposed extension to two miles.

57. Mr. Cotton.—Who marked the red line—is it on an Ordnance map?—I did myself.

58. In that blue line that you have drawn there you have paid no attention whatever to townland boundaries?—No, sir; it was not my intention to do so.

59. As a matter of fact in several instances does it cut townlands?—It does.

60. Point out how many instances. Does it cut townland boundaries in several instances?—It does.

61. Mr. O'Brien.—Do you happen to know whether the whole of that two mile radius is included in the Mullingar electoral division?—It is not.

62. Where else?—Some of it is outside the Mullingar electoral division. It takes in part of four electoral divisions.

63. That is the blue line?—Yes.

64. It does not take in the whole of any one electoral division—does it—is the entire of an electoral division included in it?—No, sir; I am not aware that it is.

65. That blue line does not include the entire of any single electoral division, but includes parts of four?—Yes, just so.

66. Is the whole of the Mullingar electoral division included in the blue line?—The whole of the electoral division of Mullingar.

67. Mention the divisions of which it includes parts?—I do not know the particulars of the divisions.

68. The Board of Guardians are the Sanitary Authority for Mullingar?—They are.

69. Are the Town Commissioners to your knowledge aware of the fact, that under the 7th section of the Public Health Act of last session—what is called the new Public Health Act—are they aware that, under the 7th section of that Act, there is now power vested in the Local Government Board, on application from the Commissioners, to separate, by what is called a provisional order, the town from the rural sanitary district, and constitute it an urban sanitary district; are they aware of that power?—Yes, they are.

70. Has it been in their contemplation to make an application for the purpose?—Not directly.

71. They do not intend to make any such application?—Not at present.

72. Are you aware whether or not they have that in contemplation?—They have it in contemplation.

73. Then it has been under their consideration, but not formally?—Yes.

74. The general disposition of the Commissioners is favourable to it, so far as you know?—Yes.

75. Assuming that they were to apply for that transfer, to have the sanitary functions vested in them, would that alter their desire to extend the boundaries? Would they wish to extend the boundaries notwithstanding that?—They would, provided that they would not be liable to extra expenses, such as the repairing of the roads.

76. That has nothing to say to the sanitary business at all. Would they, even if they applied for and succeeded in their application for the transfer of the sanitary functions to them as the sanitary board—would that alter their desire for an extension of the boundaries?—I do not think it would.

77. They would still wish to have the boundary extended?—Yes.

78. Are they aware that if the boundaries were extended, and if the transfer did take place, and the radius was extended, as proposed, to a two mile one—are

[illegible] ... They are.

79. Are the Commissioners aware of that, and still, [illegible] they concede [illegible] of having the [illegible] taken place?—Yes.

80. And that the boundary should be extended?—Yes.

81. So that it would not affect their opinion in any way?—No.

82. The Commissioners, I presume, are aware that there is also a power [illegible] of the county [illegible] roads, bridges, [illegible] and [illegible] works [illegible] district?—They are aware of that.

83. As a matter of fact, do they desire any such boundary?—They do not desire any such boundary.

84. They do not desire to look after any boundary of that sort?—No.

85. Mr. [illegible].—Did you get the red boundary line marked on this map before it, from another map?—It was [illegible].

86. [illegible] map?—The former map was the survey; it was an Ordnance map.

87. Was [illegible] Ordnance map?—Yes. I had only one sheet, and the [illegible] that, and I had to send up for a second sheet, and paste them together.

88. What map was it that you took that red boundary from?—It is marked upon the original map.

89. Have you got that map?—I have, sir.

Mr. David [illegible] examined.

90. Mr. [illegible].—You are the Clerk of the Mullingar Union?—Yes, sir.

91. And have filled that position for a great many years?—Yes, I have.

92. You are [illegible] acquainted with the boundaries of the electoral division?—Perfectly.

93. You have heard the evidence [illegible] the Town Clerk has given [illegible] I believe Mullingar is entirely included within the electoral division of Mullingar?—It is.

94. [illegible] the evidence that we have already had [illegible] and portions of [illegible] townlands included within the [illegible] district?—I heard that evidence, but I think the Town Clerk is mistaken.

95. What is the actual fact?—I think the townland of Mullingar—

96. [illegible] give us the [illegible] would be the [illegible] Mullingar and [illegible] are the only two townlands entirely within the [illegible] boundary.

97. How many are partly within and partly without?—There are five parts of townlands.

98. And one whole townland?—No, I forget; there are three whole townlands.

99. What is the third?—Belvue.

100. You give it that there are three entire townlands and parts of five [illegible]?

101. You have [illegible] the [illegible]. Would you mention the five partly within the township?—Rathinastown Tyrrell, Robinstown, Loughan, Springfield, [illegible], and Ballinderry—all which surround the town.

Mr. [illegible] re-examined.

Mr. [illegible]

102. Mr. O'Beirne.—How is it that you make out [illegible]? Will you reconcile the townlands, because we have only eight [illegible] to Mr. [illegible], and you gave us [illegible]?—I am speaking of the [illegible] townlands.

103. And as to Mr. [illegible]?—There is Ballinderry, part of; [illegible], part of; Robinstown, Loughan, part of; Rathinastown Tyrrell, part of; Springfield, part of. There [illegible] and the town of Mullingar.

104. What [illegible] have you?—We have the whole of [illegible] and Mullingar, and the townparks included in the town of Mullingar.

105. What about Belvue?—That is "part of."

106. That is wrong?—Belvue! No, the whole of Belvue.

107. Then in point of fact you say, correcting your former answer, that instead of being the entire of seven and parts of four, that there are only parts of five and the whole of three?—Yes.

108. Then Mr. [illegible] is quite correct now?—Yes.

Examination of Mr. [illegible] resumed.

Mr. [illegible]

109. Mr. O'[illegible].—How many townlands are comprehended in the electoral division?—Twenty-three.

110. They lie in the entire electoral division?—Yes.

111. What is the radius of the electoral division of Mullingar?—I can only give you an approximation. I would take [illegible] on the map.

112. [illegible]?—I know it does not.

113. What is the radius of the Mullingar electoral division?—I think it is [illegible] miles.

114. Mr. [illegible].—What is the nearest and what is the farthest boundary?—The nearest boundary is [illegible], and the farthest is [illegible].

115. [illegible] around the town, or is it an [illegible]?—It is irregular.

116. What is the nearest part?—[illegible], about half a mile.

117. In point of fact it is not uniform?—No.

118. Mr. [illegible].—Taking the division, as at present constituted, what is the area and valuation of the entire electoral division?—The area is [illegible] acres.

119. What is the valuation?—£[illegible].

120. Are the residents of the division outside the municipal district fairly [illegible]?—No; there is a [illegible] population altogether.

121. Are they [illegible]?—They are [illegible].

122. The population is thin?—It is thin.

123. Would you say that the people within that radius, not included within the electoral division—would you say that they derive advantage from their proximity to the town?—I do not, [illegible].

124. Do you think those advantages would be pretty fairly met by [illegible] them [illegible] of the town expenditure?—I think they would—or more.

125. What advantages do you think they derive from their proximity to the town?—I know of my own knowledge that they make use of the town for [illegible] of [illegible] for their children.

126. The land, too, is more valuable within that radius than at a greater distance from the town?—Undoubtedly.

127. And having a market close at hand is a great source of value to the people?—It doubtless enhances the value of land, I think.

MULLINGAR.
Dec. 12, 1879.
—
Mr. Harton.

128. You heard it suggested, Mr. Harton, that an even radius of two miles round the town might be advantageously adopted. If that space included in the blue line were adopted how many electoral divisions would be then included partly or wholly in the municipal district?—Mullingar would, I believe, be wholly included. I think it would be wholly.

129. Are you clear upon that point?—Not quite, but I can tell you in a few moments. There would be part of Castle, there would be part of Owel, there would be part of Tullaghan, there would be a small portion of Hopestown, and there would be portion of Belvedere. There would be also part of Rathconnell—a very small portion. I see also a small portion of the Mullingar electoral division—two or three acres.

130. What townland is that in?—The townland of Irishtown.

131. The whole of Mullingar, with the exception of two or three acres of Irishtown townland would be included in the proposed municipal district—included in the blue line?—Yes. There would be another angle of six or seven acres in the townland of Ballinderry or Charlestown. There would be about as much more —the whole division would be within the blue line with the exception of those two bits.

132. There are six electoral divisions which would enter into the township partly or very nearly the entire of it?—Yes.

133. So that in point of fact there would be seven electoral divisions partly or wholly included in the proposed township?—Yes, sir.

134. You could not, I suppose, state what the area and valuation would be of the township as denoted by that?—No; except approximately. I did make a rough calculation.

135. What would be the total valuation? I want to get as closely as possible what the area and valuation would be, assuming the blue line were adopted? —I can give you the valuation at once.

136. Mr. Cotton.—That is what we want?—The valuation would be £13,619, including the Mullingar electoral division and the township.

137. Including everything within the blue line?—Yes.

138. Now give us the area?—As to the area, it is very known by the area of a circle. It would be about 8,000 acres.

139. The present municipal district is entirely within the Mullingar electoral division?—Yes, entirely.

140. Without a single exception?—Yes.

141. Would that blue line in every instance divide townland boundaries?—Yes.

142. With reference to the adoption of the blue line, I do not know if you were present when I read the paragraph in the Parliamentary Committee's Report, under which we are acting, and the views of which are to be carried out as nearly as possible—as far as can be done, consistently with other considerations —that municipal wards are to be made coterminous, and towns with poor law electoral divisions. Having regard to the expression of opinion contained in that paragraph, would not the adoption of the blue line involve a much wider departure from that principle than the existing one does?—Decidedly.

143. With a view to meet the views of the Parliamentary Committee, if the proposed two mile extension by reason of its including so many electoral divisions were considered objectionable, do you consider that the adoption of the electoral division of Mullingar would be an improvement on the existing boundary?—Well, it would; it would extend the area considerably.

144. I think you have already given us the figures? —I think so.

145. What is the entire area of the Mullingar electoral division?—4,620 acres; and if the proposed blue line were adopted it would be 8,000 acres.

146. And the population?—11,980—of the electoral division of Mullingar.

147. So that if the Mullingar electoral division were adopted instead of the existing one it would give a considerable increase of the area of valuation?—Of course it would; but that for rating purposes it would not be much; it would be all rural.

148. That would be in consequence of arable land, and that addition would be only liable for one-fourth of the taxation?—Yes.

149. So that it would not give so large an addition to the rating margin?—It would not.

150. Not so large as would appear at first sight?—Yes.

151. The Board of Guardians is the sanitary authority?—Yes.

152. Have they made any special rates for sanitary purposes with the municipal district of Mullingar?—Yes; a penny in the pound.

153. Do you mean for general or special?—For special.

154. How many special rates have you made?—Three only.

155. What were the years they were made in?—Last year and the year before.

156. That would be only two?—Three instalments, I meant.

157. You have only made one rate in each locality? —Yes.

158. And was 1d. in the pound the amount of the rate?—No; in one instance it was 2d.

159. Within the municipal district?—Oh, I was speaking of another district.

160. I am speaking of the municipal district?—In the municipal district we had two special rates.

161. What was the amount?—1d in the pound.

162. To what purposes were they applied?—Sewerage.

163. You have made no outlay for a water supply?—No, we have not.

164. Has there been any sanitary work pressed upon the attention of the Guardians which has been left in abeyance. Have they been called upon or urged to make any improvements?—No, nothing. The water question was not brought before them.

165. Is there any want of an improved water supply in the municipal district?—Yes; no doubt there is; all parties, I think, are agreed about that.

166. Then that is a purpose for which expenditure is called for?—Decidedly.

167. Would it be an expensive project if taken in hand?—I should say it would; there is no water available near the town except the canal, and I believe that cannot be had without an Act of Parliament.

168. There is absolutely a want of a water supply in the town?—Yes, decidedly.

169. Is there any want of sewerage or other sanitary works?—I may say, sir, that the sanitary officer of the town, Dr. Kelly, has recommended sewerage on a rather large scale.

170. Would that, if carried out, be a source of considerable expense?—Decidedly it would; a source of very large expense.

171. Have the Guardians been deterred by reason of the existing amount of the poor rate from undertaking any of these works in the town?—Not at all.

172. From the return that I have before me I find that the rating of the Mullingar division in 1874 was 3s. 6d; in 1875 was 3s. 3d.; in 1876 was 3s. 9d.; in 1877 was 3s. 6d.; and in 1878 was 3s. I think these were the amounts of the rate?—I should say so.

173. Have the Guardians, are you aware, ever taken into consideration the expediency of applying the provision contained in the 7th section of the Irish Public Health Act, of having the control of sanitary matters transferred from themselves to the Town Commissioners?—They have never considered it, so far as they are aware of it.

174. So far as you are aware, is it a proposition that would be likely to meet with their concurrence, or the reverse?—I should say from what I know of the feelings of the Board of Guardians that if the Guardians of the electoral division of Mullingar were in favour of it, no other Guardian would oppose it.

MULLINGAR. Dec. 14, [illegible]. Mr. William [illegible].

175. They have no particular desire to retain it?—I think not.

176. So far as you know the ratepayers in the outlying districts, would they be likely to object to being brought within the municipal district?—I think they would, simply on account of the rate. I think very naturally they would.

177. But you are quite clear, with the people outside, that there is a considerable portion of the district outside the municipal area where the [illegible] derive advantages from their proximity to the town without contributing to the expenditure?—Yes; I think there must be.

178. And you think it is reasonable and fair that they should contribute?—Yes; that is my opinion.

179. And the Commissioners have given them fair protection by lowering the amount to be rated on outside land at one-fourth?—I think so.

180. Assuming that it would be considered a fatal objection to the blue line being adopted that it divides so many electoral divisions, is there any other position you can suggest as being a desirable one to adopt for the purpose of extending the present limits?—No, sir; I have not considered the subject at all. I did not give the question any consideration at all until Mr. Keena came to me about it.

181. Do you consider that there is any practical objection to dividing townlands—in making the boundaries of townlands?—I think there could be no objection to that; it has already been done in the townships here.

182. And parts of townlands are now made rateable as a contributory district?—Yes; they can be so rated now.

183. You don't see any objection to it in a municipal boundary on general grounds?—I don't think there could be any.

184. Of course, the Poor Law never divide [illegible] townland in an electoral division or aggregation of townlands?—I am aware of that. The townland is a unit.

185. The Chairman.—Will you give us a list of the townlands, those lines, those electoral divisions that you have proposed?—Yes; I can give you both the electoral divisions and the townlands.

186. That are included in the blue line?—Yes.

187. Mr. O'Brien.—Of all the townlands that come, either wholly or in part, within the blue line?—Yes, sir.

188. Mr. Cotton.—I want the names of the townlands that are in each of these electoral divisions?—Yes.

189. Those that come within the blue line?—Yes; I will give them to you.

190. Merely the names?—Yes.

191. I want a complete list of the townlands that come within those electoral divisions in [illegible] the electoral divisions that are touched by the blue line?—I will give it to you.

Dr. Dillon Kelly examined.

Dr. Dillon Kelly.

192. Mr. O'Brien.—You are the Chairman of the Town Commissioners of Mullingar?—I am.

193. How long have you been Chairman, Dr. Kelly?—About twenty or twenty-one years.

194. Did you preside at the meeting when the Commissioners were considering the question of the municipal boundaries lately?—I think I did.

195. Do you remember exactly how many members were present on that occasion?—No; Mr. Keena can tell you.

196. Get the minutes, and [illegible]?—[Referring to minutes]—There were nine present.

197. There were nine persons on the occasion?—Yes.

198. They were unanimously in favour of having the boundaries extended?—I think they were.

199. There was no dissent?—I think not.

200. What was the extension which appeared to meet with their approval?—A two mile radius.

201. [illegible] to the general principle that a two mile radius would be a suitable one?—Yes.

202. Are the Town Commissioners, so far as you are aware, anxious to have the sanitary functions transferred to their own body?—I don't think they have considered it. I am not in a position to say whether or not they desire to have the sanitary functions transferred to them.

203. What are the reasons which chiefly influenced them in wishing that the present limit should be extended?—I cannot say exactly the reason, but they were unanimous for it.

204. You don't know what their reasons are?—I cannot say.

205. Do you know whether the people outside generally would be likely to be opposed to the extension that you have suggested?—I cannot tell that.

206. Do you consider that the people living within the radius—there are a good many persons outside the present municipal district within the blue line—there are a good many persons living there, are there not?—A good many.

207. Do you consider that the people living within the blue line—in the surrounding [illegible] between this and the blue line—do you consider that the people inhabiting that district derive advantages from the town of Mullingar?—Enormous advantages.

208. What advantages?—I mean in the way of commerce.

209. Are there any other advantages that you can think of?—None, except that.

210. Do not the children come to school to the town?—Yes, they do come to school.

211. Does that prevail to a large extent?—A very large extent.

212. Are the lands enhanced in value by reason of being within that radius?—Yes, very much.

213. Is agricultural produce more valuable in consequence of having a market so available and so close as Mullingar?—Yes; Mullingar is a considerable market town, with communication with every other county town in Ireland by railway.

214. You provide lighting for the town?—Yes, we do.

215. That is a great convenience to the people outside the town?

216. How is the lighting carried out? Do the Commissioners manufacture the gas themselves, or is it done by contract?—By contract.

217. Do you consider that the people living outside the town derive advantages from that?—I do consider they do, very much.

218. Assuming that objections were to be entertained to departing so far from the approved principle of the Parliamentary Commission to include as many electoral divisions as you propose to include within the blue line, is there any other extension which would meet less with that objection, that would commend itself to the Commissioners?—I know of none.

219. Would, for instance, the adoption of the electoral division of Mullingar be regarded with favour by the Commissioners, supposing the present electoral division were adopted as the municipal division?—I cannot give you an answer as to that.

Mr. Francis Nulty examined.

Mullingar. [illegible] 1879. Mr. Francis Nulty.

230. Mr. O'Brien.—You are one of the Town Commissioners of Mullingar?—Yes.

231. Assuming now that objection were made to the adoption of what appears to be the wish of the Commissioners, namely, to adopt the blue line—assuming that a valid objection was [illegible] to apply to that, because it involves a wider departure from the present arrangement than what the Preliminary Committee [illegible] advisable, namely, the [illegible] of the two boundaries, municipal and poor law, what would be the opinion of the Commissioners as to the adoption of the electoral division of Mullingar?—I think it would be favourable, if it was [illegible] all round.

232. Having the division [illegible] circumstances?—Yes; if [illegible], I think their opinion would be favourable.

233. If you could not get the blue line you would consider the other an advantage?—Yes.

234. But you would consider the other more desirable?—Yes.

235. You would rather have the blue line than the electoral division, and you would, in the event of being unable to obtain the blue line, rather have the electoral division than the present municipal boundary?—Yes, decidedly.

236. Would that meet with the general concurrence of the Town Commissioners?—I think it would; that would be my opinion.

237. If they were aware that the blue line could not be had, the general opinion is that they would be in favour of getting the electoral division?—Yes, I do think that is the opinion.

238. Have you had any means, from discussion with your brother Commissioners—have you had any [illegible] of knowing whether or not they are in favour of getting the power to have the sanitary functions transferred from the Board of Guardians to themselves?—I think they are all favourable to it.

239. In thinking that, are they aware of the [illegible] under the Board of Guardians [illegible] [illegible] [illegible] [illegible]—[illegible] they were that if the sanitary powers were transferred to the Town Commissioners [illegible] would be only liable to [illegible] [illegible]?—I think they are.

240. And that does not alter their opinion?—No, sir.

241. I understand from the Town Clerk that the [illegible] that there was a [illegible] [illegible] in [illegible] [illegible] functions of the Grand Jury to them, with regard to the control of [illegible], [illegible], [illegible] [illegible]. They do not desire that, I believe?—Exactly so; that is the only thing they would object to. I understand the Commissioners to be entirely opposed to having anything to do with the Grand Jury.

242. You do not want the Grand Jury functions, but you do desire the sanitary functions?—Yes.

243. That is not allowed, because under the [illegible] section of the Act, [illegible] [illegible] not be [illegible] [illegible] one-fourth of the [illegible]?—[illegible] is the [illegible]

Mr. Joseph Shaw examined.

Mr. Joseph Shaw.

234. Mr. O'Brien.—You are a Town Commissioner of Mullingar?—Yes.

235. On what point did you desire to give evidence?—In relation to the sanitary condition of the town. I am of opinion that it is absolutely necessary to transfer the sanitary functions from the Board of Guardians to the Town Commissioners, inasmuch as the—the Board of Guardians only meet once a week, and if an epidemic happened to break out they would not be available to take prompt measures, whereas the Town Commissioners are always more [illegible] [illegible], as they are always on the spot.

236. Are there any sanitary works, such as a water supply, sewerage, or any [illegible] works of any kind in contemplation that you consider pressing?—Both.

237. Both a water supply and sewerage?—Yes.

238. On an extensive scale?—Not on an extensive scale.

239. Still they are required?—Absolutely required.

240. Do you consider those works would be better carried out if they were transferred to the Town Commissioners by the Board of Guardians?—Yes.

241. Do you consider, assuming the transfer to be made of these sanitary functions—do you think it would be an essential element, for the purpose of enabling you to do what you consider necessary, that the present area should be extended?—Yes, quite so. Could we have the sanitary powers transferred with our present population?

242. Certainly. Under the [illegible] section of the [illegible] and [illegible] of Victoria, chapter 52—the Act of 1874. The general law of the country is this—the law under the Act of 1871 was this—in all towns within the population of the town exceeded 6,000 the sanitary functions were vested in the Board of Guardians, unless where there were Local Acts. That was the [illegible] [illegible] [illegible] rule. Under the Act of 1878 the general law remained untouched, but it contains, with reference to [illegible], a provision which did not appear in the Act of 1874. The [illegible] section of the Act of 1878 provides—"Has Mr. O'Brien read the section?" This is the [illegible] [illegible] [illegible] [illegible] [illegible] power, if you think fit to seek for the transfer, and there is the power given to the Local Government Board, if they consider the [illegible] [illegible] [illegible] case, in [illegible] [illegible] [illegible] [illegible] [illegible] [illegible] [illegible] of your own [illegible] population. Do you consider it that therefore [illegible] [illegible] it would be an essential element to get the present boundaries extended?—I do, sir.

243. You have heard what I have said as regards the objection to what the Commissioners think might be a fair limit—a two mile radius—you have heard what I have said as to the objection that might exist to that on account of its cutting many electoral divisions—assuming that that objection were held to be fatal, then it [illegible] to you [illegible] the electoral division would be the next best?—Yes.

244. You think that if a wider area could not be got the electoral division would be the next best?—Certainly.

Mr. William Fagell examined.

Mr. William Fagell.

245. Mr. O'Brien.—You are a Town Commissioner and a Poor Law Guardian?—Yes.

246. You are on both Boards?—Yes.

247. What is the matter on which you wish to give evidence?—I think it would be very desirable, and I am anxious to see the Commissioners with the sanitary functions vested in them, and I think it is very necessary to have the sanitary powers transferred to the Town Commissioners. Some time ago I myself inspected, as a Poor Law Guardian, some nuisances in the town, and made a report on them. None of them have been corrected. The Board of Guardians is principally composed of country gentlemen, who take no interest in sanitary matters connected with the town, but the Town Commissioners would, if they had the requisite powers, take an interest in those matters, and in a

these much needed reforms carried out. I think it would be the anxious wish of the Commissioners to have the sanitary functions transferred to them.

248. You have heard it said that there is a want of a water supply and of sewerage?—Certainly.

249. Those works would be better undertaken and better carried out by the Town Commissioners?—Yes.

250. Do you think it would be an additional element in their getting a transfer of the sanitary authority that the present area should be extended?—Yes, it is entirely too narrow.

251. The effect of that is that persons who derive advantages from the proximity of the town do not contribute any corresponding share in the expenditure?—Certainly not.

252. Do you think that the people living within the blue line derive any certain advantages from their proximity of the town?—They do, certainly.

253. Assuming that the blue line is objected to on the ground that I have mentioned, do you think the electoral division will be the next best?—Yes, I think so.

254. You will observe that the Parliamentary Committee having laid down this principle, there would be very great difficulty in introducing a change which would not carry out that recommendation, but that would on the contrary, involve a much wider departure from the present system?—I think the electoral division would be the best, and would involve much less trouble.

255. It would give a good fair demarcation, and it fairly represents the equity of the question [illegible] think so.

256. Is there anything else that you wish to state?—The Sanitary Board connected with the Board of Guardians have recently carried out large sewerage work, and in doing that they have done nothing in the way of cleansing, and have left behind a terrible amount of offensive matter, which might have the effect of causing sickness, whereas if the sanitary power was in the hands of the Town Commissioners, they could cleanse filters, and so remove what might become a source of sickness.

Mr. O'Brien.—Is there any person present who wishes to make any objection to the proposed change?

Mullingar. Dec. 16, 18[illegible]. — Mr. William Farrell.

Mr. Edward Coffey examined.

Mr. Edward Coffey.

257. Mr. O'Brien.—You are one of the Town Commissioners?—I am.

258. What evidence do you wish to give?—I say that the blue line where it goes should be coterminous with [illegible], and not [illegible] in parts of fields.

259. It appears to me the electoral division in several places?—There can be no great objection to that.

260. What I have been saying is this—we are certainly bound by our instructions, and the instructions which I read to you all have been founded on a recommendation from an influential Select Committee of the House of Commons, consisting of some of the most prominent Irish members of the House, and some English members also, presided over by the late Chief Secretary for Ireland; and after very careful investigation, they have arrived at the conclusion that in dealing with the question one should be taken in main municipal wards coterminous with poor law wards, and towns with poor law electoral divisions. Inconveniences may arise which then cannot be overlooked. In the present case the only departure is that the whole of the township is in the Mullingar electoral division, but it does not include the whole of St. [illegible]. The blue line, however, embracing several electoral divisions, and as far as carrying out the recommendation of the Parliamentary Committee, it would be a much wider departure from the present state of things. Would the Town Commissioners wish to consider this matter at a special meeting, and to submit any other proposal which would not involve a departure from the electoral division boundaries?—I think the blue line where it cuts a field or a townland—that that could be avoided by leaving out those portions.

261. Do you mean to say on that principle that the blue line could be substantially followed without cutting the electoral divisions?—The blue line could be so modified.

262. As to avoid cutting townlands, but it could not be so modified as to avoid cutting electoral divisions?—Certainly; except in one part, [illegible] of Mullingar.

263. The only proposition the Commissioners have submitted is the blue line—the two mile radius. I take it that if the blue line could not be adopted, they would take the electoral division?—Still the electoral division is not a fair one. The distance [illegible] to Mullingar [illegible], and it ought to [illegible]—

264. That is to say, you think that the electoral division is objectionable on the ground that it is not a uniform distance?—It was made at a time when landlords was brought considerably to bear on the formation—when gentlemen kept their own townlands as much as possible to themselves. Whereas the radius in one place would be [illegible], in the [illegible] there would be a [illegible] outside the boundary. That is a great objection.

265. You think that the objection to this electoral division is that it is not a uniform distance?—It is, yes.

266. Which would you prefer—the existing municipal district or the electoral division of Mullingar?—I would prefer the electoral division of Mullingar.

267. As a matter of choice between the present municipal district and the electoral division of Mullingar, supposing you chose between these two, which would you prefer?—Of course, we might get something larger by the electoral division.

268. Would you prefer the electoral division to the present municipal district?—Certainly.

269. But you would prefer the blue line to either?—Yes, I would.

270. Would the Commissioners desire to hold a special meeting to consider another revised boundary, taking into account the objection, as I have stated it, to the present proposition, and to get a map made, showing the boundary suggested, as well as the existing one?—I do not know that it is necessary.

271. You have heard objections urged on different grounds, and you understand one objection to the electoral division, and I have mentioned an objection to the blue line—would the Commissioners wish now to have the opportunity of having a special meeting to reconsider the entire question, and then to forward to us as [illegible] a specific proposal, pointing out any other arrangement of the boundaries that they would submit?—I think the Commissioners, from what I know, would adopt the blue line. At the same time, there would be some modification.

272. Having heard the objection that I have pointed out, would the Commissioners desire to avail themselves of the opportunity of reconsidering the entire question, and then submitting some modified proposal, which either like that would not be open to the same objection?—I would say that they will [illegible] in this extension. There could be some changes made in it, of course.

273. Is there any alternative proposition that they would be prepared to submit?—Except that of the electoral division of Mullingar—that they would submit to [illegible].

The inquiry then terminated.

TRIM.—DECEMBER 18TH, 1878.

Before Messrs. W. P. O'Brien and C. F. Cotton, C.E.

Mr. John Healy examined.

1. Mr. O'Brien.—You are Clerk to the Town Commissioners?—Yes, sir.

2. How long have you filled that office?—From the 6th of May, 1872.

3. The town of Trim is, I believe, constituted under the provisions of the Towns Improvement Act of 1854?—Yes.

4. What was the date of its being constituted under that Act?—November 6th, 1868. The Commissioners adopted a memorial to the Lord Lieutenant, praying His Excellency to ascertain certain [illegible] in the boundary.

5. The town at that time was under Commissioners appointed under the 9th of George the Fourth?—Yes.

6. And they then adopted a memorial to the Lord Lieutenant praying that the town might be placed under the Act of 1854?—Yes.

7. When was that adopted?—They also prayed that the radius of the town should be one Irish mile from the Town Hall as the centre of the town.

8. In general terms that the area should be a radius of a mile from the centre?—Yes.

9. Did you get a communication to specify more particularly what the boundaries were that you required?—Yes, they were settled by Mr. Griffiths.

10. Was that memorial specifying the boundary adopted?—Yes.

"At a meeting of the Commissioners and inhabitants of the borough to take into consideration the Lord Lieutenant's letter, dated the [illegible] February, [illegible] recommending an alteration in the boundaries of the borough, the Commissioners resolved to adopt the said boundaries."

11. What were those boundaries?—They are described in the memorial, as follows, viz.:—

"Commencing on the north side of the Kildare road, at the north-west angle of the townland of Townparks North, thence eastward along said road to the western boundary of the townland of [illegible]; thence northward along said boundary to the Athboy road; thence eastward along the southern boundary of Michael Hogan's field to the Kells road, about fifty yards; thence eastward and south-east along the boundary of John M'Cann's property, and its continuation to the fence between [illegible] property and Peter Moran's; thence eastward and south-east along the boundary of townland of Townparks by the [illegible] to the northern angle of [illegible] garden; thence southward along the northern wall of the River Boyne; thence south-east along the River Boyne to the western boundary of [illegible], and [illegible]; thence southward along said boundary to the Dublin road; thence westward by said road to rear of the [illegible] to the western boundary of the townland of [illegible]; thence along said boundary to the [illegible] opposite the [illegible]; thence along said road south-west about thirty yards; thence [illegible] along the [illegible] of the [illegible] buildings to about at the north-west end of [illegible] Crosbie's tenements; thence westward and northward along the [illegible] boundary of [illegible] and Henry [illegible] tenements to the Longwood road; thence westward along said road to the western boundary of Townparks South; thence northward along said boundary to the north-west angle of [illegible] at the [illegible] boundary; thence northward in a straight line crossing the River Boyne to the western boundary of the townland of Townparks North; thence northward along said boundary to the point first named."

12. About what radius did you give from the centre of the town?—It is very irregular.

13. About what would it be, speaking generally?—About three-quarters of a mile.

14. That is in some places three-quarters of a mile?—Yes.

15. What is the closest point to the centre of the town in that case?—The distance would be about a half a mile.

16. What would be the extreme point of the boundary to the centre?—You say it is not regularly circular?—It is marked on the map (produced). It would be about two furlongs.

17. What is the area of the present municipal district?—I can't tell the number of acres without the rate book, which will be here directly.

18. I have in the tabular statement [illegible] in my report, and that I got from the Valuation Office, at the time. It is given as 418 acres?—Yes, I should think so.

19. And the valuation is £[illegible]?—Yes.

20. So that substantially I presume that that return is correct?—Yes; £1,788 in the poor law valuation.

21. How many townlands enter wholly and how many townlands enter in part into the municipal boundary?—We have portion of the Commons lands.

22. Then, what townlands are entirely included?—There are no townlands wholly included.

23. It is all parts of townlands, and you have not the entire of any townland in the district?—No.

24. Are Townparks recognised as a townland?—No; but I could not say exactly.

25. How many Commissioners are there?—Nine.

26. Was the Towns Improvement Act adopted for all purposes?—Yes.

27. Including the supply of water?—Yes—water, lighting, cleansing, and everything.

28. You are not the urban sanitary authority here, and never, not since 1874.

29. You escaped in 1874 as the Board of Guardians, as the rural sanitary authority, your town having less than 6,000 inhabitants?—Yes.

30. From what source is your expenditure supplied; is it entirely by rates or otherwise?—By property. We have no rates; we never had any.

31. Is it entirely by corporate property?—Yes.

32. What is the nature of it?—It is all land.

33. What is the annual value of it?—We have 478 acres, 3 roods, 32 perches, Irish measure, and the annual income is about £[illegible].

34. You have **never had any municipal rate**?—Never.

35. Your income being about £[illegible], can you state what is your annual expenditure?—I have it in detail—the poor law tax is about £40, the income tax £6 or £10. We have interest to pay on a debt of £[illegible], and the property is mortgaged for, at the rate of [illegible] per cent. We have to pay for [illegible] about £[illegible] or £[illegible]. The Town Clerk's salary is £[illegible], and the fee to the agent for the collection of the rents of the town property, at 1s. 3d. in the pound, come to between £[illegible] and £[illegible].

36. Do you light the town of Trim with gas?—We do.

37. What does that cost?—The Commissioners have the gas-works in their own hands.

38. And they manage the gas-works themselves?—Yes, and they try to make a profit, and light the town besides.

39. So that, in point of fact, the gas-lighting covers its own expenditure?—It does at present.

40. Is the entire town situated in one electoral division?—Yes; in the electoral division of Trim.

41. I presume you are not aware of the area of the town and population of the electoral division of Trim?—I am not, sir.

42. But, I presume, there can be no doubt that the electoral division of Trim extends greatly beyond the present municipal boundary?—Oh, yes; Trim is only portion of the electoral division.

Yarm. Dec. [illegible] Mr. John Ridley.

43. Within the municipal [illegible] there is there no rural [illegible] [illegible] which [illegible] would be [illegible] sanitary or otherwise?—No, it is not purely [illegible].

44. [illegible] purely of course, you say?—Yes, and [illegible] purposes [illegible].

45. Have the Commissioners, so far as you are aware, had under consideration the question of the existing boundaries, with the view of seeing whether they might not be extended, [illegible], or otherwise altered?—No, not so far as I am aware.

46. Did you place the recommendation [illegible] the Commissioners [illegible] before them, asking them to reply in writing [illegible], [illegible] they considered the matter?—Yes, they considered it, [illegible] they [illegible] opinion on it.

47. Then you are not in a position to state whether they are in favour of having the boundaries extended, limited, or otherwise altered?—No, they did not give any [illegible] on the matter.

48. Do you know whether the opinion of the inhabitants outside the present municipal boundary is in favour of having the area extended or [illegible]?—I don't know, but with the exception of the body that [illegible] the town, they never come into the affairs of the town at all. They don't attend.

49. What is the municipal expenditure, taking one year with another?—As the local rates we had [illegible] £1,300, [illegible] [illegible] and [illegible], and in the [illegible] of the year we [illegible] [illegible] £100 [illegible].

50. Up to what date do you make your accounts?—Up to the 11th April.

51. Well, on the last account, closed on the 11th April this year, there was a balance to the credit of the Commissioners?—There was.

52. Have you a printed copy of that report?—We have a copy, but it is not [illegible].

53. You will be able to furnish a copy of it?—Yes.

[illegible] Tell me exactly what the correct balance was, [illegible] the [illegible] of the [illegible] to April last?—Yes; our receipts were £999 [illegible]. [illegible], [illegible] our expenditure left a balance of £[illegible] [illegible].

55. To the credit of the Commissioners?—Yes.

56. After providing for all expenditure?—Yes.

57. Then I may take it that your income is amply sufficient for all purposes, and that you have not had to abstain from carrying out necessary works in the town through the limited nature of your income?—No; certainly not.

58. And as to the year 1874, when you merged in the Board of Guardians, as the sanitary authority, you provided the [illegible] what you provide for now, but for all sanitary works undertaken within the town?—Yes.

59. It was only in 1874 you became merged in the Board of Guardians?—Yes; and we were engaged at that time in drainage works which were stopped in consequence.

60. Were there drainage works which you had then [illegible] carried out since by the Board of Guardians?—No.

61. And is the view of the Commissioners in favour of having them carried out?—Certainly.

62. Were they works of any large extent?—No; not very large; they were the secondary drains of the town.

63. What would be the probable cost of the drainage of the town?—The drainage of the town would cost about £600.

64. The Commissioners had not entered on the work?—Yes, we had, and there are two very good drains made already.

65. Would the £600 represent the entire cost?—Yes.

66. How much had been expended on these works by the Commissioners before they were merged in the Board of Guardians?—About £[illegible].

67. So that about £150 would still be required to complete the drainage works?—Yes.

68. And that would give a complete system of drainage to the town?—Yes.

69. Have the Guardians refused to carry out that scheme?—I don't know that they have refused, but they have not carried it out.

70. The Guardians [illegible] supply water for the town?—The water supply was carried on by us a little time after [illegible]; [illegible] the matter and the expenditure for some purposes [illegible] the Commissioners, and we had to [illegible] the Local Government Board that proceedings should not be taken, to [illegible] the [illegible], and we [illegible] paid back the money.

71. Has anything been done to improve the water supply by those [illegible] [illegible] of the [illegible] not in good order.

72. The supply is still from [illegible]?—Yes.

73. [illegible] you [illegible] aware that, under the Act of 1874, towns such as Tuam, each having a population of 6,000, [illegible] for sanitary purposes by the Boards of Guardians; but are the Commissioners aware that under the Local Act [illegible] a new provision has been introduced to enable the Local Government Board, on the application of the Town Commissioners, to transfer, by provisional order, the sanitary authority from such Boards of Guardians to the Town Commissioners?—They are aware; they had a letter from Mr. [illegible], the county member for [illegible], stating that the Attorney-General would add that clause.

74. Do the Town Commissioners contemplate availing themselves of that clause?—Yes, I think so; they talked the matter over.

75. The question has been under discussion, I take it [illegible].

76. And an opinion favourable to it has been expressed?—Yes; the Commissioners have been favourable to it.

77. But no formal step has yet been taken in it?—None.

78. But so far as you are aware the feeling of the Commissioners is favourable to having the authority back?—Yes.

79. Is it the opinion of the Commissioners that the different sanitary matters would be better attended to by the Commissioners than by the Board of Guardians?—Yes; they do not think the Board of Guardians do so for the town with as [illegible] [illegible] [illegible] the [illegible] of water, [illegible] [illegible] in [illegible] that would be used for the purpose.

80. You think the Guardians are of the same opinion?—I don't know about the Guardians, but the people think the Guardians would not have readily to make a rate when there is [illegible] to meet the [illegible] without putting rates at all.

81. You think the [illegible] is in favour of that?—Yes.

82. Are the Commissioners also aware that, under the Public Health Act of last Session, there is power to transfer certain jurisdiction now exercised by the Grand Jury, as to roads and bridges in the towns, to the urban sanitary body?—They are not; but the Commissioners [illegible] [illegible] [illegible] [illegible] [illegible] in such a bad way, we have [illegible] them. I had a letter from the county surveyor, asking for the Grand Jury, stating that the [illegible] were [illegible] to [illegible] for the streets. They should have [illegible]; and the Commissioners have had to [illegible] [illegible] of [illegible], for which they got nothing; and the Commissioners have made a rule that I should apply to the Grand Jury laying before them the account expended by the Commissioners, and [illegible] to get it refunded.

83. Do the Commissioners consider there is more received from the town at Grand Jury cess than is expended on it [illegible] of it?

84. Are they dissatisfied?—They are dissatisfied.

85. So far as you know they are not aware of the provision in the Act of last session, enabling the Local Government Board to transfer the authority of the Grand Jury as to roads and bridges?—They are not.

86. That is something have never taken the matter into consideration?—Only [illegible] with the Grand Jury.

Trim. Jan. 18, 18–.

Mr. John Kelly.

87. I will read you the section referred to, in case they desire to avail themselves of it, and then they will be aware of the exact state of the law. Originally no portion of the Grand Jury jurisdiction could be transferred to the town body without a special Act of Parliament, which was very expensive, and was therefore only availed of by large towns of the first class; but by the Local Government Act of 1871, a provision was introduced enabling the Local Government Board to transfer certain authority to the municipal body. That, however, required not only the assent of the ratepayers of the town, but subsequently, by presentment of the Grand Jury, and where that presentment was not passed, the proceedings lapsed, and in several instances where it was sought, the presentment was thrown out, and in only one town—Wexford—was the presentment passed; but the question has been dealt with in the Act of last session, section 200 (reads section). You will thus see that if you were constituted the urban authority under the seventh section, you are now given power to look for the transfer. You think the Commissioners would be glad to avail themselves of that power if they were aware of it?—I do.

88. But you have no means of knowing what the views are on the subject of the extension of the borough boundaries?—No. There are four Commissioners here, and they will be able to tell you.

Mr. T. Kennedy.

Mr. Thomas Kennedy, Chairman, Town Commissioners of Trim, examined.

89. Mr. O'Brien.—Have you been many years Chairman of the Town Commissioners?—Yes; last year and portion of this year, and I was Chairman other years too.

90. You have been Commissioner for a great many years?—About twelve years.

91. And you are acquainted with the working of the town?—Yes.

92. Have you ever amongst yourselves in any shape discussed the question of the desirability of having the municipal boundary altered in any respect?—There was no decision come to at last meeting.

93. But you have discussed it amongst yourselves?—We have.

94. Are you aware of the feelings of the Commissioners on the subject?—I think the majority of them are for leaving the boundaries as they are.

95. You think they would rather leave them untouched?—Yes.

96. You have only nine Commissioners?—Yes, nine.

97. How many Commissioners were present the day you were discussing the matter?—Six.

98. Were they unanimously in favour of leaving the boundaries as they are?—I think the majority of the Commissioners are—not the Commissioners present that day; they were in favour of extending the boundary.

99. Then the Commissioners are not united in opinion?—No.

100. But the majority of the six present were in favour of extending the boundary?—Yes.

101. What was the extension that seemed to commend itself to them?—There was no particular extension decided on at the meeting.

102. The radius of the present town is rather limited, it is three-quarters of a mile at the furthest point, and a quarter of a mile at the shortest point?—Yes.

103. Are you in favour of extension of the boundary?—I am not in favour of extension.

104. You are in favour of leaving things as they are?—Yes.

105. Are there not lands about the town which derive advantage from this proximity to the town?—I think not.

106. But don't you think there are lands near the town whose value is greater than lands at a greater distance from it?—Those adjoining the town are.

107. Aren't there many people on the lands about the town?—No.

108. It is chiefly grass lands?—Yes.

109. Are the accommodation lands held by the people of Trim included within the municipal district at present?—Only a portion of them.

110. And you say there are not many inhabited dwellings on these accommodation lands?—No.

111. There are not many people then who derive advantage from having a market so close to them for the sale of all kinds of farm produce?—No.

112. Or who benefit by having schools in Trim to which they can send their children?—No; not immediately. They are about a mile or a mile and a half away.

113. How many inhabitants would you say there are between the present municipal boundary and the radius of a mile outside it?—The number is very small. I could not say twenty.

114. Then there are not many persons living outside the present boundary who derive any advantage from their proximity to the town, in the way of schools, markets, or otherwise?—No.

115. You would not be in favour of extending the participation in the advantages of municipal government to the people outside the present boundary?—No, I think not.

116. Assuming you got the sanitary jurisdiction transferred to you, would your present income be amply sufficient for sanitary purposes besides?—It would.

117. Assuming that under the seventh section of the Public Health Act you became the sanitary authority, and that subsequently, by provisional order from the Local Government Board, you acquired the jurisdiction over roads and bridges, would your income be still sufficient for all purposes of that nature that would be likely to arise?—Yes, if we got a tax.

118. But suppose the duties were transferred to you, do you think the funds would be sufficient?—I think it would not, without a borough rate.

119. You think a rate would be necessary if you had charge of roads and bridges?—I think it would.

120. What rate do you think would be necessary?—I could not say.

121. In the event of a rate becoming necessary, would not that modify the views of the majority of the Commissioners as to the desirability of bringing in some of the grass lands?—Yes. The Grand Jury Rate is 1s. 3d. in the year.

122. On the Poor Law Valuation?—Yes.

123. What is the poor rate?—3s. in the Trim Electoral Division.

124. The whole rate is 3s.?—Yes.

125. How much is the sanitary rate?—11d.

126. That is the special sanitary rate?—Yes.

127. Of the 3s. poor rate, 11d. is for sanitary purposes?—Yes. 2s. 1d. poor rate and 11d. for sanitary rate.

128. And if the sanitary functions were referred to you, you say you would be able to provide for them without any tax at all?—Yes.

129. But you would not be able to do without a Grand Jury Rate?—Yes.

130. When you speak of 11d. being required for sanitary purposes, you mean that that was required to meet the sanitary expenditure for three years?—Yes.

131. It was one rate made since the Guardians became the sanitary authority?—Yes.

132. But the annual expenditure for sanitary purposes doesn't come to 11d.?—No.

133. Only about one-third of that would be required in the year?—Yes.

134. What were the sanitary works that were executed?—There were sewers cleaned up, and so

[illegible]

Mr. Patrick Malone examined.

[illegible]

TRIM. Dec. [illegible] Mr. P. [illegible]

[illegible]?—From the gaol wall to the model school, including the model school; the children walk up there.

181. That acreage would that improvement that would also take up to the Boyne on the north, and the road on the [illegible], which would represent roughly the [illegible] acres English.

182. Are there any other additions you would suggest?—Yes. We can't [illegible] the chapel gate, and I would like to extend the boundary up along the [illegible] road to [illegible] of the workhouse and the model school.

183. Going out the south by what point?—The workhouse point would be this south, and I think, for all purposes, it would be quite enough to include the whole of the road.

184. To the townland of Mornington?—Yes.

185. You would include the pool at the north side of Mornington?—Yes, so as to [illegible] to [illegible] and repair it.

186. You would only include the road?—Yes.

187. Are there any other additions?—There are all I would suggest.

188. You heard me read the various resolutions of town bodies as to, in certain cases, a transfer of the Grand Jury authority over roads and bridges. Are you in favour of having the Grand Jury powers, as to roads and bridges, transferred from the Grand Jury to you?—Yes, because we have always been making footpaths and repairing them out of the rates when we had control over them.

189. If all the Grand Jury functions were transferred, do you agree it would involve the necessity of making some rate?—Yes; and for this reason. Although the rental is only £700 now, it was [illegible] and years ago, when prices were lower; and we will be getting additional revenue from our land, and altogether we will be worth £1,000 a year.

190. When would that be?—Within the next four or five years; for the leases will expire, and be renewed at higher rents.

191. So that you think even if the Grand Jury duties were transferred to you, you would have funds enough?—I think so. I was originally for the little [illegible].

192. **But your views have since been changed?—** Yes.

193. Why have you changed your opinion on the subject?—Because we would have to repair roads if we got the functions of the Grand Jury.

194. And you would not be in favour of that?—Yes; it would be too heavy a liability.

195. It is only on that ground that you **object to** the mile radius?—Yes.

196. You only object to the extension of getting control over the roads and bridges?—Yes.

197. But you think the changes you have suggested would be sufficient?—I would be satisfied with them, because I know a few of the Commissioners are for making no alteration at all.

198. If you adopted the mile radius would that bring in a great many more ratepayers than at present?—Oh, yes; a great many more. [Produces map.]

199. That circle represents the mile radius?—Yes.

200. If that were adopted, what would be about the area of the district?—It would be over 2,000 acres.

201. That would be about the acreage included in the mile radius?—Yes.

202. How many additional ratepayers would that bring in?—It would bring in a good many.

203. Would that mile radius cut townlands?—Yes, nearly in every instance.

204. Would it all be still within the electoral division?—Yes.

205. You don't know the valuation it would give?—I think the valuation of houses and everything would be about £3,000.

206. Speaking roughly, about £3,000?—Yes.

207. Still, it would all be within the electoral division of Trim?—Yes.

208. Doesn't it seem to you that that would not be an unreasonable bulk to take?—It would impose a great deal of duties on the Commissioners that they would not like to have to discharge.

209. Can you give me an idea of how many ratepayers it would add to the constituency?—I think there are nearly 700 or 800, including town and all up that circle.

210. How many have you in the present municipal district?—About 300.

211. So that it would double the ratepayers?—Yes.

212. How many new ratepayers would it embrace?—Well, about double the number would then be included.

213. Don't you think it would be an advantage to give a larger number an interest in the good working of the municipal government?—No doubt it would.

214. Don't people within that radius derive advantages from their proximity to the town as a market in the sale of butter, eggs, and all that?—They are certainly within that circle.

215. They get higher value for their farm produce?—Yes.

216. And don't their children all come to the schools in town?—Yes.

217. Aren't there a good many out there not connected with the town?—We have about fifty or sixty of my own tenants who would come within the circle. About the sewerage, when the Sanitary Authority was transferred to the Board of Guardians, being a Commissioner myself, I never could do anything for the Town Commissioners as engineer, but the Board of Guardians at once employed me to get up plans and sections for the town, and to report on the amount of drainage that would be required to complete the sewerage of the town, and I made a report and estimates, and plans and sections, and they determined to apply for a loan of £500 to complete the sewerage, and pending this it became a question whether we could get the Sanitary Authority back, and we came to understand we could, and we began to suspend our operations, as we think the property could pay the expense, instead of having to pay for a loan of £500, the property being already mortgaged.

218. What were you going to do with the drainage?—Discharge it into the river through the old [illegible] falls.

219. Then you think both bodies would be in favour of having the authority transferred?—Yes. The town think it would be a great hardship to have a tax put on where we have a free property, and although I would make money as Engineer to the Board of Guardians, I would prefer, as a Town Commissioner, having the works done by the Commissioners. The Board of Guardians were about to do all that drainage when we started about.

220. You are aware you have to make an application in order to get the transfer of the authority?—I am afraid we will not get it next session, as the Kells men are in for a provisional order, and we will hardly be in time. I mentioned about the sewerage to show that the Guardians were not neglecting it.

221. Is there anything wanting in the water supply?—Dr. Cameron has been condemning all the pumps, even the splendid pump I have in my own garden.

222. He says they are impure, and in that case they will be looking for an improved supply?—Yes, Dr. Reilly suggested an improvement—that the main strip of Commons land which extends on the south to the Boyne and west of the town—that is all our own property—should be included, and whenever we might look for a water supply we might use that land for reservoir purposes. Dr. Reilly would wish as a Commissioner to have that strip of land included.

223. Then, it is probable you will have to make a reservoir for the water?—Yes.

224. At the next meeting of the Commissioners you will consider the subject, and forward a map showing what alterations you suggest?—Yes.

225. You can submit to us the existing boundary, the mile radius, and any changes you recommend?—Very well, sir.

Tuam. Dec. 14, 18[illegible]. Mr. P. [illegible].

Mr. Henry Parkinson examined.

Mr. Henry Parkinson.

226. Mr. O'Hara.—You are a Town Commissioner?—Yes.

227. You have heard the statements made by the Chairman and Mr. [illegible]; is there anything you wish to add? What is your own view?—My own view is that extension would result in [illegible] to the Commission, with [illegible] my friends.

228. That is, that you would be giving benefits without any [illegible]?—Yes.

229. You are in favour of getting the sanitary authority transferred?—Yes.

230. And also the transfer of the Grand Jury control over roads and bridges?—Yes.

231. Would the circumstances of the town's property not being equal to the [illegible] expenditure in that regard, and the necessity for keeping it [illegible], alter your view?—I did not take that into consideration.

232. What do you think now, if you found you could not do the duties without some additional tax, might that alter your view?—It might alter it.

233. That is if it involved a considerable rate, but the necessity for a moderate rate would not?—Yes.

234. Are you present [illegible] when you [illegible] to the extension?

235. Nearly without [illegible]?—Nearly so.

236. Don't you consider that lands lying within a radius of a mile have all more or less an interest in the town, and participate in its advantages?—Well, I suppose they do, more or less.

237. And they derive advantages from being close to the town?—I suppose they do.

238. Your main objection is that you have corporate property which renders the rates [illegible], and you would be sharing that without receiving any [illegible] [illegible]?—Yes.

239. But assuming that the Grand Jury functions were to be transferred, and that a new tax had to be struck in consequence—would that alter your opinion?—Yes.

240. But as things stand you object?—Yes.

241. But if you had the same power of taxation as the Grand Jury, you would not have any objection to share the property?—No.

242. It is looked upon as a matter of [illegible]?—Yes.

Mr. Laurence Sheridan, Clerk of the Union, examined.

Mr. Laurence Sheridan.

243. Mr. O'Brien.—Tell me the statistics of the electoral division of Tuam. What is the area?—5,775 acres, 0 roods, 21 perches is the area.

244. That is the area of the entire electoral division?—Yes.

245. What is the valuation?—£16,[illegible] 15s.

246. What is the area of the town district?—The district within the town is [illegible] [illegible] [illegible].

247. That probably includes some fields?—Yes, some and the [illegible].

248. What is the valuation?—£9,[illegible] [illegible].

249. Can you give me a list of the names of the townlands in electoral division?—Yes.

250. How many townlands are included in the electoral division of Tuam?—Seventy-three.

251. What is the entire area?—[illegible], [illegible]. [illegible].

252. How many townlands are partly included within the town?—Eleven.

253. How many are entirely included?—Commons third division; Commons, fourth division; and Town Parks, North.

254. Then there are only three wholly included?—Yes.

255. How many are partly included?—Black Friar; Charter school land; Commons first division; Commons, fifth division; Upper [illegible] [illegible] [illegible], first division; [illegible] [illegible], second division; [illegible] lands; and Town Parks, North.

256. What is the distance of the furthest point of the electoral division of Tuam from the town?—I could not exactly say.

257. Well, speaking as closely as you can?—It extends about a mile and a half.

258. Then the electoral division of Tuam doesn't extend a radius of a mile and a half from the town?—It does not.

259. Its furthest point is how far?—About a mile.

260. What is the rate in the town division at present?—Three shillings.

261. Have you imposed any special sanitary rate on the town?—There is a sanitary rate of [illegible]d., and the other rate is [illegible] [illegible].

262. You have had the sanitary jurisdiction of the town since 1874?—Yes.

263. Have you had any other rate during that time, except the present rate?—No other rate.

264. Then that [illegible] [illegible] against the sanitary expenditure of the entire period?—Yes. We had some difficulty about fixing the scale of incidence. Some of the Guardians wanted to put it on the whole electoral division, and others were not in favour of that.

265. Have the Board ever considered the question of transferring the sanitary jurisdiction to the Commissioners?—They have not; it was only considered in a casual way.

266. There was no formal discussion on the subject?—No.

267. Have you any idea of the opinion of the Board?—I think the Board would not be opposed to the transfer.

268. I suppose there has been some question about carrying out or completing [illegible] works of sewerage?—The Board passed a resolution, [illegible] that the Commissioners were [illegible] to petition the Local Government Board to get back the sanitary authority, and I was ordered to forward a copy of that resolution to the Secretary of the Board of Works, as we had made arrangements with the Board of Public Works for a loan to complete the work.

269. Then you don't think there will be any unwillingness to transfer the jurisdiction?—No.

270. Are you aware of what the people living outside the town boundary, but within the mile radius, think on the subject?—I could not exactly say what they think. If there was any additional tax, they would, of course, be opposed to it.

271. But if the Grand Jury functions over roads and bridges were transferred, and, by reason of the graduated scale, they would have less to pay, they would be in favour of it?—Yes.

272. They regard it much as a matter of pounds shillings and pence?—Yes.

JOHN BRATTON examined.

273. Mr. O'BRIEN.—You are one of the Commissioners of Trim town?—Yes.

274. Are you in favour of extending the boundaries or the reverse?—I am not in favour of extending the boundaries.

275. You are not in favour of sharing your property with your neighbours?—No.

276. If you had power to impose a tax you would not have the same objection to share the tax with your neighbours as you have to share the property?—No; but if we got the county cess we could do the roads for half the cost.

277. If it became necessary, in the event of you getting the control of the roads, and getting an use to put a tax on, would you not be in favour of having a wider district to levy the tax upon?—I would, sir.

Mr. *Henry Parkinson*.—We would derive very little advantage by extension.

278. Why?—Because there are so few owners of property, and so many of the holders of land live in the town.

279. You are aware that the area of Trim is exceptionally small?—Yes.

The inquiry then closed.

NAVAN.—DECEMBER 19TH, 1876.

Before Messrs. W. P. O'BRIEN and C. P. COTTON.

PHILIP MULLIGAN examined.

1. Mr. O'BRIEN.—You are Town Clerk of Navan?—Yes.

2. How long have you held that office?—Seven years until March.

3. The town of Navan is constituted under the Towns Improvement Act of 1854?—Yes.

4. In what year was the town placed under the Towns Improvement Act of 1854?—It was placed under it in 1854. I have no document so far back. The earliest minute that came into my possession was dated 1860.

5. You have nothing earlier than that?—No.

6. You have no copy of the memorial on which the town was constituted?—No. I am aware from the receipts and expenditure it was incorporated in 1847.

7. It could not have been constituted in 1847. The only Act it could have been constituted under prior to 1854 was the 9th of Geo. IV. The Towns Improvement Act was passed on the 10th August, 1854, and it must have been some date subsequent to that that this town was placed under the provisions of the Act?—I could not tell. I have no document to carry me back so far.

8. Had the town been previously under what is called the Lighting and Cleansing Act, the 9th Geo. IV.?—It had.

9. For what length of time?—I have no document to show. I have nothing but receipts and expenditure to show.

10. Do the receipts and expenditure show you at what time the town ceased to be under the 9th Geo. IV., and commenced under the Towns Improvement Act?—They do not. It is nothing but in the ledger form.

11. Is there nothing to show under what Act they were administered then?—No, sir.

12. How far back do these books go?—They go back as far as 1847.

13. And no further than that?—No.

14. And from that it may be inferred that in 1847 the town was placed under the 9th Geo. IV.?—Perhaps it might have been before that. There are books before that.

15. But you have no record beyond that?—No.

16. What is the area of the present municipal district of Navan?—434a. 0r. 11p.

17. In the returns of the Valuation Office it is given as 443 acres. Where do you take your return from?—Our valuation book.

18. What is the total valuation?—£4,684 is the rateable valuation, only taking one-fourth of the valuation of the land.

19. But what is the total valuation?—£5,994.

20. How is it that the return, as given in the valuation book, is £5,185 on the 10th May, 1876?—At any revision they never give the same return.

21. But £5,235 is the present valuation?—Yes.

22. Has the Towns Improvement Act been adopted here for all purposes, or only for limited purposes?—All purposes.

23. Did it include the supply of water?—Yes, and the Act of 1871.

24. But at present you are not the sanitary authority. You are merged, since 1874, in the Board of Guardians for sanitary purposes?—Yes.

25. And since that you have had no sanitary expenditure?—No.

26. The rates for the last five years appear to have been as follows, viz.:—11d. for the year 1876, 10d. for 1877, 10d. for 1876, 8d. for 1875, and 10d. for 1874. Previous to 1874 were larger rates assessed?—No; 9d. in the years before that.

27. Then, in point of fact, the largest made was in 1876, 11d.?—Yes.

28. Was there any special circumstance that made the rate higher last year?—Yes, the building of the house.

29. How much did that cost?—£900.

30. What are the other purposes to which the rates were applied?—For cleansing, paying salaries, and gas.

31. You light the town?—Yes.

32. Do you supply the gas yourselves?—No; it is a limited company supply the Town Commissioners.

33. And they contract for the supply to the public lamps?—Yes; heretofore it was by measurement.

34. Are you aware whether any special sanitary rate has been made by the Board of Guardians since 1874, in addition to these rates for the purpose of water supply and sewerage?—There was 1d., 1d., and 8d., but nothing this year.

35. When was the 1d.?—In 1875.

36. When was the 8d.?—The 8d. was last year.

37. The 8d. was in 1877 for sanitary purposes, and the 1d. and 1d. in the other two years?—Yes.

38. What purposes were they for?—Keeping sewers and making new sewers, and repairing old ones.

39. Has there been any outlay for water supply?—Yes; they erected new pumps.

40. Is there any sanitary work required to meet the necessities of the town besides the original water supply?—Yes; main sewers are very much wanted.

41. They are very bad at present?—Yes.

42. Would it require an effective scheme to supply them?—Not so much now.

43. Had the Guardians in contemplation to carry out any scheme?—They had; they have carried out some.

44. Had they in contemplation to carry out any large scheme?—I am not aware.

45. Are the Commissioners aware that under the Public Health Act of last Session there is now power vested in the Local Government Board, on the application of the Town Commissioners, if they see fit, to transfer the jurisdiction, as a sanitary authority, from the Board of Guardians to the Commissioners?—I am not quite sure, but I believe they are.

46. [illegible] ?—No [illegible].

47. [illegible] aware whether the feeling of the Commissioners is favourable to [illegible] ?—I am not aware; [illegible] I would not say.

48. [illegible] the power [illegible] under the Act of [illegible] to [illegible] the jurisdiction within the municipal division, [illegible] by the Grand Jury, [illegible] the Grand Jury to the Rural Sanitary Authority ?—I am not quite aware [illegible].

49. Are you aware whether the Commissioners consider the present area of the municipal district too limited, or otherwise ?—I am not aware it has not been under discussion.

50. Have you a map in your possession showing the present municipal district ?—I have only, except the municipal boundary [illegible].

51. In what electoral division is the municipality of Navan situated ?—It is in one electoral division. It is in the electoral division of Lower Navan.

52. What does the present municipal district comprise—how many townlands and parts of townlands are included in it ?—There is Navan, Athlumney, [illegible]

53. First give those that are altogether included. Do you know the townlands that are wholly, and then those that are partly, within the municipal district ?—I do.

54. I want to get a list of the townlands which are wholly included in the municipal district; and then I want to get a list of the townlands, parts of which only are included in the municipal district ?—[illegible] wholly included in the municipal district ?—No, sir; it is only parts of townlands.

55. How many townlands are partly included in the municipal district ?—Athlumney, [illegible] Castle, [illegible], Athlumney, and Dillonsland.

56. Is there any other townland partly included ?—No, sir, only these.

57. What would be the radius of that district ?—I would hardly say.

58. What is the most distant part of the municipality from the town ?—One mile, I should say.

59. What is the nearest part ?—I should say something less than a mile. Athlumney is the nearest.

60. [illegible] a mile [illegible] place called [illegible], that is in Athlumney.

61. What side is that on ?—The north-west.

62. What is the point where you say it comes nearest to the town ?—One end of Athlumney.

63. That is how far ?—About half a mile, or less.

64. Half a statute mile ?—Yes.

65. What is the area of the entire electoral division of Navan ?—There are [illegible] acres [illegible] in Dillonsland.

66. What is the total of the entire electoral division ?—[illegible]

67. What is the valuation ?—[illegible]

68. What is the [illegible] point of the electoral division from the town ?—I don't know.

69. Can you give any idea about it ?—I should say something about two miles to the farthest point.

70. What place is that that you say is two miles distant ?—It takes a northern direction [illegible].

71. Could you mention the point where it is two miles ?—Not exactly two miles.

72. How many townlands are included within the entire electoral division ?—Twenty-eight.

73. If you took a radius of a mile from the centre of the town, would it include a great many houses in addition to the houses included now ?—No, sir, not many; but if you took a radius of a mile and a half, it would take in a great deal of valuable property.

74. The mile radius would not ?—No, sir; it would make very little change.

75. As regards the radius of a mile and a half, that would not take in the whole electoral division of Navan ?—I think not.

76. Do the people you speak of, living between the existing boundaries and the radius of a mile and a half, derive advantage from their proximity to the town, [illegible] having a market close by them, and are their lands more valuable by reason of their nearness to the town ?—I think the land is more valuable.

77. Do their children resort to the town for school purposes ?—All except two divisions.

78. What are they ?—In the northern part of the town there are schools within a mile or a mile and a quarter.

79. In the other part of the radius there is no school ?—No, sir.

80. And they all come in to Navan to school ?—Yes.

81. And do the people come here to sell their butter, and so on ?—Yes, sir.

82. And in that way it is of special advantage to them to be so close to the town ?—It is.

83. What electoral division besides Navan comes closest to the town ?—Dunmoe.

84. Would that radius of a mile and a half bring in any other electoral division except Navan ?—It would bring in all Athlumney and [illegible].

85. I am talking of electoral divisions. That radius would not take in any electoral division except the one Navan is in ?—No.

86. Then, if you made a radius of a mile and a half, you would be still within the electoral division of Navan ?—Yes.

87. And you would not go into any other electoral division ?—I think not.

88. The poor rates appear to have ranged, within the last [illegible] years, between [illegible] and county cess [illegible] in the same period ?—Yes.

Navan, Dec. [illegible], 1888.

P. [illegible]

Nicholas Kelly examined.

Nicholas Kelly.

89. Mr. O'Brien.—You are Chairman of the Town Commissioners of Navan ?—Yes.

90. Have you been long chairman of the Commissioners ?—About a year and a half.

91. Have you been a Commissioner long ?—A good many years.

92. About how long ?—For fifteen or twenty years, I dare say.

93. Are you in a position to say when you [illegible] placed under the Towns Improvement Act ?—I could not say.

94. You were not a Commissioner when the town was under the old Act of the 9th Geo. IV. ?—No, sir.

95. It must be a good many years ago since you were under the Towns Improvement Act ?—Yes.

96. It occurred before you came on the Board, and you are a Commissioner for fifteen years or more ?—Yes, I think I am a Commissioner fifteen years.

97. There is no record showing the date ?—No, sir.

98. You have not the original memorial to the Lord Lieutenant ?—No, sir. The chairman we had at that time is dead, and nothing could be ascertained after his death. He was chairman from the beginning, I think.

99. Since 1874 the sanitary authority has existed in the Board of Guardians, your population being under 6,000. Are you aware that the law has been so far altered as to enable the Local Government Board to transfer that jurisdiction from the Board of Guardians to the municipal body on their application ?—I think they are aware of it.

100. Have you ever, amongst yourselves, in any way considered the advisability of asking for a transfer of these functions ?—Never.

101. Could you form any idea whether the general

NAVAN.
Oct. 16, 1879.
—
Nicholas Kelly.

feeling would be favourable to that or not?—Well, I could not say, for the matter has never been discussed.

102. Would they not prefer that the regulation of sewerage and water supply, and the cleansing of the streets and other sanitary works of the town, should be under their own superintendence rather than vested in the Board of Guardians?—Well, some time ago it was discussed at a meeting of the Commissioners, and they all appeared to think that if they had it they would be able to benefit the town a good deal more, and to pay better attention to it. Sewerage and things of that kind are hard to be got done, and on two or three occasions sewerage was badly wanted, and the Town Clerk waited on the guardians on one or two occasions about the matter.

103. And the guardians would probably be in favour of having the authority transferred?—Yes.

104. How many Commissioners have you?—Fifteen.

105. How many generally attend a meeting?—About an average of eight or ten.

106. You must have a quorum?—Yes.

107. And you think the feeling would probably be in favour of having the authority transferred to you?—I think it would.

108. Would that feeling be influenced in any way by the fact that, as part of the rural sanitary district, arable lands have to contribute their full quota at present, whereas under the Towns Improvement Act they are only rated at one-fourth? Would it make any difference that on the transfer, arable lands would be liable to only one-fourth?—I think it would be very little. There is very little land within the present radius of the borough, but if the radius was extended there would be far more land taken in.

109. Are they aware that under the 200th section there is also power vested in the Local Government Board to transfer from the Grand Jury to the sanitary authority the control over roads and bridges, &c.?—I think they are well aware of that.

110. Are the Commissioners in favour of having that transfer or allowing things to remain as they are?—I could scarcely say. It has never been discussed.

111. What is your impression, as to the feeling of the Commissioners?—I dare say if they got the entire rates as the Grand Jury have them.

112. Of course you should get the rates?—Could the Commissioners strike a rate?

113. Yes?—And should we keep a county surveyor?

114. You would have to take charge of the roads the same as the Grand Jury do now?—I don't know what is thought of that.

115. Are the Commissioners in favour of extending the boundary? The present area of Navan appears to be 436 acres; other municipalities are very different from that and there are great varieties of areas in the municipal districts of Ireland. Have you been able to collect whether the opinion of your body is in favour of extending the present limits or not?—I think they are a little.

116. Don't you think that under the present arrangement places are left out which derive advantages from being so close to the town?—I think they are.

117. What would appear to you to be a reasonable radius, taking the centre of the town as a starting point, so as to include the districts which should contribute in the same proportion as the advantages of municipal government are conferred?—I should say half a mile.

118. Half a mile outside the present boundary?—Yes.

119. You think that would be fair?—Yes.

120. That would give an entire radius of how much from the centre of the town?—About a mile and a half.

121. Statute measure?—Yes, sir.

122. The Committee of the House of Commons has expressed a strong opinion that as far as practicable the boundary of the municipal district should be made coterminous with the boundary of the poor law division. Would you consider the electoral division of Navan a desirable municipal boundary to adopt?—It would be too large.

123. Then that would be going too far?—Yes.

124. The advantages of municipal government would not go so far?—No.

125. But you would not object to a radius of a mile and a half?—No.

126. I presume in that mile and a half radius there are a good many inhabitants who derive advantage from their proximity to the town?—There are.

127. Who derive advantage by having such a market for their produce, and schools for their children, and who participate a good deal in the benefits arising from the lighting and cleansing of the streets?—Yes, to a very large extent, for the railway comes to one side of the town, and the parties living on the other side who chiefly use the railway have to pass through the town.

128. Are there any sanitary works which the Commissioners, if they became the sanitary authority and if they had a larger area to operate on, would be likely to proceed with?—Outside the present area?

129. No. Suppose you became the sanitary authority instead of the Board of Guardians, are there any sanitary works which you think are required for the benefit of the town?—I think there are.

130. Of what description?—Sewerage.

131. And the water supply?—I think it is very fair.

132. Are the Commissioners prepared to undertake that if they had a wider area to extend it over?—I think the present area would do as soon as any other.

133. I presume you have no source of income except the rates?—No.

134. No property of any kind?—No.

135. Nor tolls?—No; no tolls, or anything.

136. What is your present annual expenditure?—About £250 a year.

137. I see in my own report for 1876 it was about £373?—I don't think it was so much as that.

138. *Philip McElligott*, Town Clerk.—In 1877 the expenditure was £373 4s. 8d.

139. Mr. O'BRIEN.—Then £373 would about represent the average expenditure?—Yes.

140. As yet there has been no formal resolution adopted on the subject of extending the boundary?—No, sir.

141. You have no map showing the exact boundaries of the present district?—No.

142. You have got no description of the boundaries of any kind?—None whatever.

143. Mr. COTTON.—Do the railway stations come within the municipal boundary?—They do.

144. Both railway stations?—Yes, and a number of persons at each side of the stations.

145. Mr. O'BRIEN.—Is there any general suggestion on the subject you would wish to make to us?—No, sir; I don't know of any.

Navan, Jan. 13, 1876. Mr. T. Wagner.

of the [illegible] although they did not participate in all the advantages, still they indirectly derived so many that they would contribute something. You do not think if the [illegible] was extended, though they would not expect to get all the advantages, still they would be fairly [illegible] towards the rates. Do you consider that the inhabitants of [illegible] within a mile and a half of the town derive certain advantages from being close to the town?—I don't see how they would.

151. But is it not an advantage to have a good market for their farm produce?—It is a very good market.

152. Well, isn't that an advantage?—No doubt of it.

153. Do the inhabitants avail themselves of the town for sending their children to school?—Yes, on the [illegible] side.

154. In a more [illegible] they derive advantage from schools, and so forth, do they not?—Yes.

155. And they have to dispose of their produce?—Yes, no doubt.

156. And the land is made valuable near the town?—No doubt of it.

157. Taking it on the whole do you consider a radius of a mile and a half would be a reasonable one?—[illegible], it would.

158. And you think it would be desirable to extend the present boundary?—I did not myself consider it.

159. What is your opinion of the [illegible] on public grounds?—I would rather let it stand as it is.

160. You would not particularly urge it [illegible].

161. You consider the electoral division boundary would be too large to be adopted as the municipal boundary?—Yes.

162. On the whole you would rather let things stand as they are?—Yes, just as they are.

163. Would you be in favour of having the powers of [illegible] transferred to the Commissioners?—I would be an advocate for that.

164. If the control was transferred would you not wish to have a larger area?—No doubt of it.

165. And would you consider it desirable to have the Grand Jury control over roads and bridges within the town transferred to the Town Commissioners?—I have not considered that.

Mr. Kenny (Chairman), re-examined.

[illegible]

166. [illegible]

167. You don't know whether the amount expended on the town is equal to the amount contributed by the town?—No, sir, I do not. If they [illegible] it would be of advantage to get control of the roads, but if the Grand Jury expended the whole of the money, or more, which is not likely, it would be well to remain as it is.

168. But you are not in a position to say whether they spend more or less?—I am not aware.

169. I suppose you are not aware either whether the Grand Jury [illegible]?—No.

170. Mr. [illegible].—What I understood you to say is that if the amount expended by the Grand Jury is greater than the amount the Grand Jury get in the town, you would be [illegible] having the control transferred to you?—Yes.

171. But if, on the other hand, the Grand Jury are spending as much as they receive, you [illegible] to have the control?—[illegible].

172. You would not contemplate that if you contributed more than [illegible] you would get nothing from the Grand Jury?—No, but merely that we would get the same [illegible], and we would keep the roads, and if there was a difference we would [illegible].

173. Mr. O'Brien.—You would keep it?—Yes, and spend it for the benefit of the town.

174. If the [illegible] was transferred [illegible] you would only [illegible] as much as the roads would require?

Mr. Curran.—The Grand Jury rates would be [illegible].

175. Mr. O'Brien.—You would just have the same [illegible], and you would levy whatever rate would be necessary?—Well, under these circumstances, we would not wish for the transfer. I thought the rate would be [illegible], and if we could do the work for less the difference would go [illegible] for other purposes.

176. No, that is not what it means. You would [illegible]?—Under these circumstances, I would not desire the transfer at all.

177. Is your view, Mr. Wagner, the same as that expressed by [illegible]?

Mr. Wagner.—Yes, the same.

178. Mr. O'Brien.—Is there anything else you would wish to mention?

Mr. Wagner.—No, sir; nothing.

Mr. William Lawlor examined.

Mr. William Lawlor.

179. You are both a Guardian and a Town Commissioner of Navan?—Yes.

180. How long have you been a Commissioner?—Fifteen or eighteen years.

181. And how long a Poor Law Guardian?—Twelve years.

182. Since 1874 you are aware the Guardians have acted as sanitary authority?—I am.

183. Are you satisfied with the manner in which the Guardians discharge that duty?—I am satisfied.

184. Do you prefer it should remain vested in the Guardians?—Yes.

185. You think it is better?—I do.

186. Are you in favour of having the present boundary extended?—I am not.

187. You think it is large enough as it is?—I do, sir.

188. On what grounds do you think that?—One reason is, that by extending the boundary further on we would not gain much by it.

189. If you brought in a considerable tract of land would that not introduce a considerable amount of rateable property?—Yes.

190. And would that not lighten the taxation of the town?—It would.

191. And do you think the people living within that radius of a mile and a half derive many advantages from lighting and cleansing and the general work of the town, and by having a market for their produce, and resorting to it on business, and having schools there for their children?—Yes.

192. They derive advantages?—Yes.

193. And would you think they should not contribute?—I think it goes far enough.

194. And you would not be in favour of having them contribute anything?—No.

195. And you would consider the electoral division entirely too large to be adopted as the municipal boundary?—Yes, too large entirely.

196. Do you consider that the people living outside the present boundary would object to being brought into the town?—I could not say.

Mr. Kelly.—There are parties outside the present radius who use the streets considerably more than the parties living within the town.

197. Mr. O'Brien.—There are a good many accommodation lands held by the residents of Naas?—Not too much.

198. But they hold what are called accommodation lands?—They do.

199. Are these included within the municipal boundary?—Portion of them.

200. And portions are without the municipal boundary?—Yes.

201. And are they chiefly within or without?—Chiefly outside.

202. Would you consider it fair that these accommodation lands, held by the residents, should be brought in?—The people in the town have no land.

203. So far as it extends, would you consider it a reasonable thing that they should be liable in the reduced proportion?—One-fourth is a very small tax on them.

204. You think they derive advantages commensurate with that?—They do.

205. Within what radius are these lands included?—About a mile and a quarter.

206. Then a mile and a half would include the whole of them?—Yes. There is not much accommodation land about Naas.

207. Would you be able, Mr. Kelly, to get a special meeting of the Commissioners held for the purpose of adopting a resolution expressing finally the change they consider to be desirable in the existing boundary, and to submit it with the answers to the queries?—*Mr. Kelly.*—Certainly, sir.

The inquiry then closed.

NAAS.—SATURDAY, DECEMBER 21st, 1878.

Before Messrs. W. O'Brien, LL.D., and C. Cotton, C.E.

Mr. E. Malley examined.

1. Mr. O'Brien.—You are Clerk of the Union of Naas?—Yes.

2. Can you tell us what is the acreage and valuation of the electoral division of Naas as at present constituted?—The electoral division at present, sir, comprises 7,677a. 3r. 9p.

3. That is in the electoral division?—Yes.

4. What is the valuation, please?—The valuation of the electoral division is £11,338 16s.

5. How many townlands are there included in the electoral division?—There are twenty-three.

6. What is about the radius of that electoral division from the town of Naas. What is the most remote part of the electoral division from it?—I should say that the most remote point is Craddockstown East.

7. Now, what is the closest part of the electoral division—the closest of the boundary line of the division to the town of Naas?—Oldtown demesne is the nearest outlying townland.

8. Is the entire of the municipal district of Naas included in the electoral division?—Yes.

9. Now you have the entire of the townlands made out?—Yes.

10. How many are there do you say?—Twenty-three.

11. Well, how many entire townlands, and how many parts of townlands, are included in the municipal district?—There are eight entire townlands.

12. And how many parts of the townlands?—There are fourteen parts of townlands—that is twenty-two.

13. What is the acreage—but first I take it that with the exception of one townland entirely without—the municipal district includes all the electoral division?—Yes.

14. What is the acreage of the municipal district?—It comprises 1,093a. 2r. 31p.

15. In the return I got it is 1,341 acres. What is the valuation?—£7,611 2s.

16. The Board of Guardians are the Sanitary Authority?—Yes.

17. For the entire of Naas?—Yes.

18. The duties of the Sanitary Authority have been merged in the Board of Guardians since the passing of the Public Health Act of 1874. During the interval between that and the present time have any rates—any special rates—for sanitary purposes been assessed within the municipal district of Naas?—Yes, there have been, I think, every year. I am not perfectly certain as to the exact amounts.

19. Can you, then, say what rates have been paid each year?—Well, I would be quoting from memory. There has been a two-penny rate, and I think one year a three-penny rate—merely for keeping the pumps in repair.

20. Then you have undertaken no large sanitary works in that time?—No.

21. Has it been in contemplation recently, or is it now in contemplation, to undertake any large sanitary work within the municipal district?—Well, yes, it was in contemplation. There was a committee meeting, or rather there was a committee appointed by the Board of Guardians.

22. For what purpose was that committee appointed?—It was appointed for the purpose of arranging with Mr. Brett, the engineer, as to plans.

23. For what purpose?—It was for the drainage of the town, and the committee ceased to act, and it appears to be a dead-letter now.

24. Then I may take it that at the present time the question of introducing a proper system of sewerage is under consideration, but no particular plan or system has been adopted or settled on?—No.

25. Has any estimate been received as to the probable expense of the scheme?—Yes.

26. And can you tell us what was about the estimate of those works?—Yes, it was about £6,000.

27. That is the estimate of what the proposed system of drainage would require?—Yes.

28. Are you aware why it was that the committee did not act, and that no proposal or estimate was taken or adopted?—The general feeling was that the expenditure was too great for the town to bear—for the municipal district to bear.

29. But the necessity for the work, I suppose, is admitted on all hands?—Well, I believe there is a difference of opinion on that point too.

30. Do you mean that there is a difference of opinion as to the best scheme to be adopted, or that there is a difference of opinion as to the necessity for the work at all?—I think as to there being any necessity for any drainage scheme at all.

31. Well, has there been any project for an improved supply of water for the town?—No; there is plenty of water. The water supply is very good.

32. Then there has been no representation as to the supply of water to the town?—No.

33. What is the supply of water—where is it taken from?—There are public pumps, and also the canal.

34. How many public pumps are there?—There are five, and the canal, you know.

38. Are the Board of Guardians aware, or have they had under their consideration, with reference to the general law, an existing provision in 1878, [illegible] boards of guardians sanitary jurisdiction for all towns where the population did not exceed 6,000. Are they aware that in the Public Health Act of this session there is a section [illegible] which makes a most important modification of that, enabling the Local Government Board, by provisional order, on the application of a municipal authority, to transfer the sanitary jurisdiction from the board of guardians to the latter body?—I don't know if they are aware of it, but I am aware of it.

39. It was never under their consideration at a meeting?—No.

40. You are not then, in a position to say, with any confidence, whether the Board of Guardians would be desirous of transferring to the Municipal Body the sanitary jurisdiction over the town of Naas?—I should say the Board would be most happy.

39. You are aware, yourself that there is a clause to this effect. I shall read it. [Here Mr. O'Brien read section 7.] You yourself, are personally aware of that provision?—Yes.

40. And, as far as you are aware, the Board of Guardians would see no objection to the change?—I think not. They would be willing to have the jurisdiction or duties transferred.

41. Now, what have been the poor law rates on the electoral division of Naas during the last five years, during '78, '77, '76, '75, and '74?—Well, I could not properly tell from memory.

41. You will be able to let us know?—Yes, I can certainly; and will furnish it to you with pleasure.

42. We would like to have it for the years I have mentioned?—I could furnish them to you.

43. I only speak of 74, 75, 76, 77, and 78, and you will be able to supply us with the poundage rate?—Yes, for Naas; specifying for ordinary purposes and for sanitary purposes.

44. You have no map showing the boundary of the electoral division and of the town of Naas?—No, I have no map of any kind.

44. You have no further information to give?—No, I think not.

Naas.
Dec. 11, 1878.
Mr. S. Kelley.

Dr. Robert G. Hayes examined.

Dr. Robert G. Hayes

45. Mr. O'Brien.—You are chairman, Dr. Hayes, of the Town Commissioners of Naas?—I am.

46. Now, how long have you filled that position?—I have filled it frequently.

47. You have been a member of the body for a considerable time?—Yes. I have been a Commissioner ever since the establishment of the Town Improvement—since its adoption.

48. Naas is constituted under that Act?—Yes.

49. In what year was it placed under the Town Improvement Act?—Immediately after the passing of the Act.

50. In 1854?—Yes. We were one of the first who took advantage of it in 1854.

51. Had you been previously under the 9th of George IV.?—No; we never were under that Act.

52. What then?—The town was under what is called the "Old Corporation Act."

53. Were there Municipal Commissioners appointed then for the temporary custody of the corporate property?—No. There was a good deal of the corporate property we never got possession of.

54. There were not Municipal Commissioners then appointed to take up and administer the corporate property?—No. The fact is, I think Naas was rather peculiarly placed in that respect. The late Lord Mayo—not the late man, but the old man—got some inkling of the Act passing, and he managed to transfer the property altogether to what is called the Protestant Orphan Society.

55. So you had no Municipal Commissioners?—No.

56. Did you adopt the Act—the Town Improvement Act of 1854—did you adopt it in its entirety?—No, only portions. We afterwards took in lighting and other sections.

58. What were the purposes for which you adopted it at first?—Well, it is in the minutes.

59. Have you got the minutes?—It is in the minutes of the 22nd of May, 1855. Unfortunately the Town Clerk is ill and unable to attend.

60. However, you subsequently adopted it for all purposes?—Yes; all bar the many other purposes than at first.

61. Did you adopt it for other purposes, including water supply, to get the right of being enabled to put a rating power of 1s. 6d.?—No, I don't think so. There is plenty of water in Naas, both pump and canal.

62. Only for lighting, cleansing, and paving, then?—Yes.

63. Are you still fulfilling those functions; you light the town with gas?—Yes.

64. Now, is the gas supplied by the Commissioners themselves, or do they obtain it from a company?—No, we lease the premises to Mr. Daniel, of Dublin, and the Commissioners purchase it for the public lighting.

65. Now, I observe here an answer to one of the queries submitted to you.—I observe that you say that in 1878—it was stated there was no rate in 1877—the rating was 6d. on land and 1s. 6d. on houses?—No; it was the reverse.

66. On quitting; and I observe in 1878 there was 1s. on houses and 3d. on land?—Yes, that is according to the Act.

67. I am aware. I see that for the year 1877 there was no rate, and in 1874 there was 6d. on houses and 3d. on land. There is something about the burial rate marked down here; I don't know what it refers to.

Mr. Oarrok.—That refers to the last one.

68. Mr. O'Brien.—That is 1874. Did the rate in 1874 include a burial rate?—Yes, for we acquired a burial ground then for the town, and immediately after it was taken out of our hands.

69. Have you any source of income except what you receive by the rates?—Yes, we have the Grand in the public streets, the proceeds of those markets here, we charge for weighing potatoes, and so on.

70. What income do you derive from these sources you have mentioned?—Well, I see here returned (reading from a book) the potato market produces £24 13s. 1d.

71. During the year?—Yes, the year ending 15th of April last.

72. What other items?—Donor, £14 3s. 6d.; the manual, £36 14s. 6d.; making a total of £38 11s. 2d. Then there are the tolls at sheep fairs, £25 14s. 1d.

73. What is the total annual income, or the average income?—£265 10s. 1d.

74. Are there any other sources but those you have mentioned?—There are fines and penalties from the Petty Sessions Court, £27 12s.

75. For last year?—Yes.

76. Any other sources of income?—There are fines by Petty Sessions Court, £9 10s. 6d., making a total of £36 3s. 7d. on those two items.

77. What do you say is the total income from all sources?—£265 10s. 1d.

78. Exclusive of rates?—Oh, no.

79. Well, take the amount of rates collected from it?—The rates collected amounted to £149.

80. What is the total amount exclusive of rates?—£116 7s. 10d.

81. During the past year?—Yes.

Naas.
[illegible] 1879.
Dr. [illegible] G. Hayes.

82. From sources exclusive of rates?—Yes.

83. There was no rate levied during the past year—during 1878?—Yes, there was.

84. That must have been previous to 1878?—Oh, yes; it was for 1877, the year ending 30th April, 1878.

85. That is calculated but not made in 1878?—Yes.

86. And during the year represented in that, what did you get in rates?—£102 16s. 3d.

87. Now, for the last year, to which your accounts are closed, what is your total income and total expenditure?—The receipts were, exclusive of rates, £269 odd.

88. Can you give the items?—The first item here is: "Balance in favour of the Commissioners, £96 3s. 6d.," and, exclusive of that, the total amount, leaving out the rates, is £269 7s. 10d.

89. And what was the total expenditure?—It is £465 10s. for all purposes.

90. I thought you mentioned that as the total received?—No, expenditure.

91. Give any further sums received during the year?—There is rent for the Town Hall—we set the room, £34; licenses to hackney cars, £15 15s.; the total is £269 odd. There is grazing of sheep on fair green £11; dog license duty, £21 1s. 6d.

92. What is the annual expenditure for all purposes?—£465 10s.

93. Expenditure for last year?—Yes, less by £31 6s. 5d. in hand.

94. Then the whole expenditure is £435?—Yes.

95. For all purposes?—Yes.

96. What were the purposes?—There is £25 18s. salary of town clerk, weighmaster, town sergeant, market porters, &c. Lighting—gas for public illumination of lamps and town hall, £56 10s.; election expenses, £3 13s.; Local Government Board for audit, £4 16s.; rent taxes of town hall and fair green, £15 3s. 6d.; repairs, &c., town hall, £189 1s. 6d.; fuel, £3 18s.; printing, stationery, &c., £16 10s.

97. How did you close at the end?—There was £31 6s. 5d. in the Hibernian Bank balance.

98. That account has been audited?—Yes; by Mr. Finlay.

99. Well, there is nothing there of a sanitary kind. You have had no sanitary expenses to provide for?—No; that has been entirely taken out of our hands.

100. Up to 1874 you provided for sanitary expenditure?—Yes. It was the Commissioners erected all the public pumps in the town.

101. Now, you have heard me read the section of the Public Health Act of last session; but first let me ask how many Commissioners are there?—There are nine Commissioners.

102. Has it ever been under the consideration of the body the effect that the 7th section of the Public Health Act of last session could have, enabling the Local Government Board, by provisional order, if they think fit, to transfer the sanitary jurisdiction from the Board of Guardians to the Town Commissioners, and make them an Urban Authority?—Well, I don't think it has been actually under consideration. We have, of course, felt that the powers were taken out of our hands.

103. Were you aware that under the provisions of the Act of last session there is power to restore those functions?—Yes.

104. Had it ever been under the consideration of the Commissioners to make application to the Local Government Board to make the transfer I speak of?—No.

105. Do you consider that the opinion of the Commissioners would be favourable to having the sanitary authority transferred to themselves?—I rather think so.

106. Do you consider that the town body would be more likely to attend properly to the interests of the town than the Board of Guardians—a rural board?—Yes; I certainly think so. I think a body of gentlemen living in the town, and connected with the town, would have more influence and be more likely to attend well to its affairs than men living ten or fifteen miles away.

107. You think, then, they would be favourable to having the jurisdiction transferred?—I think so.

108. Now, they are aware probably that as things are at present arranged, any sanitary expenditure levied by the Board of Guardians, as rural sanitary authority, is charged upon all sorts of property in the same ratio, there being no distinction made between houses and lands. Are they aware that under the 226th section, where any such rate shall be made by any commissioners, corporation, or persons becoming urban sanitary authority after the passing of this Act, all lands used as woodlands, market gardens, nursery grounds, &c., or railways constructed under the powers of an Act of Parliament for public conveyance, shall be assessed, and liable in the proportion of one-fourth only of the net annual value of such lands. Are they aware of that provision?—No. I did not know that myself.

109. Would the fact of that difference having been made in the mode of levying sanitary expenses modify your view—does it change your own opinion as to the expediency of transferring the sanitary jurisdiction to the town body—would they still desire it, do you think, notwithstanding the difference in the mode of levying the sanitary expenses?—I think they would still desire it, unless such a tremendous expenditure as £8,000 came on, as in the case of Mr. Brett's plan. They would never be able for that.

110. Notwithstanding this difference in the law, introduced under the 226th section, you think they would approve of the transfer?—Yes.

111. You heard reference made by the Clerk of the Union to the scheme for the drainage of Naas, estimated to cost £4,000, but which it appears has fallen through on account of the opposition appealed to carry it into effect as to details referring to it. You heard that statement—are you aware yourself, as a resident of Naas, that there is a necessity for an improved drainage?—I admit there is.

112. You believe there is such a necessity?—If you will allow me I shall explain. This whole matter came before the Commissioners, and plans, drawings, and everything from the Board of Guardians were submitted to us. A special meeting was called to consider the whole matter, and I will read the result of that meeting——

113. What is the date of the meeting?—The 11th November, 1878.

114. That is in the present year?—Yes.

115. Specially convened?—Yes.

116. How many Commissioners were present?—Six.

117. What was the resolution adopted at the meeting?—The minutes state:—

"At a special meeting of the Town Commissioners called for this day to consider the proposed plans for the drainage of the town of Naas, notice of which was given at the last day, Dr. Hayes, J.P., Chairman, presided. The other Commissioners present were Joshua S. Casteld; Wm. Alex. Osb. J.P.; J. Fagan; Henry Sergeant; Richard Tracy. Dr. Smith, Sanitary Medical Officer, was present. It was proposed by Mr. Fagan, seconded by Mr. Sergeant, and resolved unanimously—That whilst we admit there is a necessity for the improvement of the sewerage of Naas, we would respectfully urge on the Guardians who have been charged with the carrying out of the proposed plans—(1) That a scheme of drainage to cost £8,000 for the construction, and a large sum per year for maintenance, is far beyond the present requirements of the town of Naas, and out of all proportion to the area of taxation if placed on the town property. (2.) That the experience of all similar works has proved that they are never completed for the estimated cost, but, as a rule, far exceed the sum estimated. (3.) That such an outlay would be destructive to the interests of the town of Naas, especially as the success of the proposed flushing of the sewers by means of tanks and syphons is of so doubtful a nature." The clerk was directed to forward a copy of the foregoing to the Guardians of the Naas Union."

Naas. Jan. [illegible] Dr. [illegible] Hayes.

118. How many Commissioners do you say were present at that meeting?—Six.

119. And there are nine Commissioners in all?—Yes.

120. Well, the resolution, I suppose, was forwarded?—Yes.

121. Well, now, the Commissioners who adopted that, we may take it they did not at all question the fact that some improved scheme was actually necessary?—Certainly. The great difficulty, I may mention, is the flushing of the sewers. Naas is peculiarly situated, some parts of it are high and some low, and unless you have a full flush of water you will never succeed.

122. May I ask, was the opinion of the Commissioners that if they had the conduct of the matter in their own hands they would be able to carry out a scheme at a more moderate outlay?—Well, no, I don't think they went into that.

123. What is the radius of the municipal boundary?—It is a mile and a half from this door; just a mile and a half.

124. Is it pretty equal in all directions?—Yes it is.

125. Mr. Cotton.—Is it a hard and fast line?—Yes.

126. Have you a map showing the boundary line?—Well, there is a map somewhere about. I have been asking for it.

127. Mr. O'Brien.—Have you a copy of the memorial to the Lord Lieutenant with reference to the town being placed under the Towns Improvement Act?—I have not.

128. You say the radius is about a mile and a half?—Yes.

129. Mr. Cotton.—It is exactly that, he says.

130. Mr. O'Brien.—You know the electoral division of Naas?—Yes, I do.

131. That would be considerably wider?—Yes, it would take in more townlands.

132. I see in the answers to the queries we sent you to the question, "Are the municipal boundaries and poor law electoral divisions coterminous?" you reply, "They are not coterminous. The town extends to a radius of a mile and a half, and the poor law boundary extends to a much larger area."

133. Now, do the lands that are included in the portion of the electoral division of Naas that are not included in the municipal district, do those lands derive advantage from their present proximity to the market of Naas, and are their goods in that way provided with advantages in the way of a ready sale, and do the inhabitants derive the benefits of the schools and churches of Naas from living in proximity to it?—That is unquestionable. The farmers derive decided advantages in that way from being near Naas. We have a couple of markets—two markets.

134. Now, having regard to this fact, that the Parliamentary Committee, in dealing with this matter, and in laying down the principle to guide us in forming boundaries, said:—"In dealing with the question care should be taken to make municipal wards coterminous with wards for poor law purposes, and towns with poor law electoral divisions." Now, the opinion of the Parliamentary Committee being that, where practicable, poor law electoral divisions and municipal areas ought to be coterminous, would it appear to you that there would be anything inequitable in substituting for your present division the entire of the electoral division of Naas?—No, I think not.

135. You are aware that arable lands would still be only liable to be rated at one-fourth the net valuation?—Yes.

136. And having regard to that, do you think it would be a fair measure of the advantages those portions not included contributing one-fourth to the municipal expenditure—would it be a fair measure of the advantage they derive?—I think it would.

137. And you think there would be nothing unfair in extending the area to the electoral division?—I think so.

138. And if that extension took place it would probably have the effect of modifying the objection of the Town Commissioners to the large outlay required for sewerage purposes?—Yes.

139. You think that?—Yes, it would give us a larger area.

140. And would bring it more within your power to carry out a better system of drainage?—Certainly. At the same time, I am bound to say the Commissioners are quite satisfied with the present boundaries. The only thing where a real inconvenience is felt is in respect of the car-drivers here. When they get to Sallins they are independent, and we can neither summon them nor exercise any control over them.

141. I see in the answer to Query No. 5, you say that generally the Commissioners are satisfied with the existing boundary, but the Commissioners would like to have the boundary extended along the public road, to get control over the hackney carmen at Sallins station.

142. Now, how far is the railway station at Sallins from Naas?—A mile and a half, Irish; it is beyond the boundary.

143. Is it within the electoral division boundary?—Yes, it is within the electoral division.

144. Then, by taking in the electoral division, the object which the Commissioners express in query No. 5—to have the hackney car-drivers brought under their control—would be effected?—Yes.

145. And that would be an additional inducement to the Commissioners to think it desirable to adopt the extension?—Yes; I should think so.

146. Now, what is the advantage they think they would derive from having that car station placed under their control?—They could maintain better order, and bring those carmen into discipline, so that the Commissioners could regulate them, and bring them up for offences.

147. Do you find there is a want of the desirable good order and regularity?—Oh, yes.

148. What are the abuses you complain of?—Well, a carman may abuse you, or over-charge you, and you can't summon him.

149. Those things do take place?—Yes.

150. Mr. Cotton.—Does that answer apply to the roadway or to the railway yard. Do you wish to have the railway brought into the boundary?—I think the railway people won't give up their right.

151. It appears to me that if you don't get the yard, you won't get the control you want. The carmen in the yard are inside the boundary of the railway.

152. Mr. O'Brien.—Would the substitution of the electoral division boundary introduce any portion of the railway?—It would.

153. A considerable portion?—Yes; the village at the other side is in North Naas.

154. I take it the railway derives advantage from having Naas as a feeder to it?—Yes.

155. They contribute nothing?—No.

156. The extension I have mentioned would bring them in?—Yes.

157. Now, as regards the county expenditure. What is the grand jury cess levied here? What is the average rate for Grand Jury purposes?—I really could not say.

158. Do they consider—do the Town Commissioners consider the outlay for roads, bridges, streets, &c., within the town boundary—are they satisfied the Grand Jury outlay is commensurate with the amount of county cess levied?—Well, we never found fault with the Grand Jury.

159. Are you aware whether the sums expended for Grand Jury purposes within the town district is commensurate with the sums raised in the shape of Grand Jury cess?—I have no means of saying. They repair the streets and keep the flagging in order. We ask it.

160. Are the Commissioners aware that, assuming you were constituted an urban sanitary authority, under the 9th section of the Public Health Act of

last session, that if you were once placed in that position, are they aware that under the 206th section it is provided [here Mr. O'Brien read section 206]?—Yes.

161. You don't think you would desire the transfer?—You mean as to the maintenance of the roads?

162. Yes?—Well, I think the Commissioners would rather remain as they are. We have very little to do.

163. As Commissioners, you have not much to do?—No; most of our work is taken out of our hands.

164. Even now the cleansing of the streets—under the Act of last session, repealing a certain section of the Towns Improvement Act—is vested in the Board of Guardians?—Yes.

165. Then, to summarise what you have been saying, I take it you think the feeling of your Commissioners would be in favour of having all the sanitary jurisdiction transferred from the Board of Guardians to themselves, and would not be anxious to take over any of the jurisdiction of the Grand Jury?—No.

166. And I take it that there would be no objection at all to the extension of the municipal boundary to the electoral division—to take in the electoral division?—Yes.

167. And that would secure first, control over hackney cars and carmen at Ballina, the abuses in connexion with which matter you have mentioned, and would also be attended with the advantage of making the railway contributory to the town expenditure, to which they at present pay nothing?—Yes.

168. Mr. Cotton.—What kind of control would it give you over the carmen at the railway?—Oh, none, if the railway company would not permit us to act—if they considered us as trespassers on their private property.

169. Mr. O'Brien.—Under the 85th section of the "Towns Improvement Act" you would have authority to make bye-laws, regulating the carmen, and so on. If the boundaries were extended to Ballina you could make such bye-laws as would regulate the proprietors and drivers of those hackney cars.

Dr. *Hayes*.—We have that at present, sir.

170. Yes, within the boundary—within your own district. But it would give you powers beyond your own district as at present constituted?—Quite so.

171. Mr. Cotton.—Does not that apply only to the public roads? You can have no control, I think, within the limits of the yard or private property of the railway company.

Mr. O'Brien.—Under the bye-laws you can punish any acts of misconduct committed by the drivers within your district.

Mr. Cotton.—Yes, I think, on private property, as this railway yard is.

172. Mr. O'Brien.—They can be punished for overcharging, or other misconduct, or breach of the bye-laws. Now, Dr. Hayes, is there anything you would like to add to what you have mentioned?—No, I don't know that there is anything more.

173. Now, as regards the map, would you be able to supply us with a map, showing the existing municipal boundary, and the boundary of the electoral division? You have no map at present?—We had, I know.

174. Well, you can get a map prepared for us by Mr. [illegible], showing the existing municipal boundary and the electoral division?—There will be no difficulty.

175. Mr. Cotton.—As to the car drivers—this is the point—"Drivers are not on any pretence to demand more than the legal fare, or refuse to hire where so employed." That only applies to the public streets. But the police have no right over the cars in the railway station.

176. Mr. O'Brien.—You can summon them for refusing to go for hire, if you tender the fare.

177. Mr. Cotton.—It is not a public hiring place.

178. Mr. O'Brien.—Oh, yes, there have been several such convictions. Now, I take it, doctor, your views are pretty closely representative of those of the general body?—I think so.

179. And there is nothing further you would wish to say?—No.

180. Have you been able to find the original minutes?—No, they are not here.

181. It would be well if we had the Lord Lieutenant's answer to the memorial.

182. Mr. Cotton.—It would be well, for we want to see the exact authority for the mile and a half radius.

183. Dr. *Hayes*.—It is a mile and a half. The radius was from the old post-office.

184. Mr. Cotton.—An English mile?—Yes.

The inquiry then terminated.

LISMORE—30TH DECEMBER, 1876.

Before Messrs. W. P. O'Brien and C. P. Cotton.

Mr. Maurice Healy examined.

1. Mr. O'Brien.—You are Clerk to the Town Commissioners and also Clerk of the Poor Law Union?—Yes, sir.

2. Lismore is constituted as a municipality under the Towns Improvement Act of 1854?—Yes, sir, the Towns Improvement (Ireland) Act.

3. In what year was the Act adopted?—In the year 1856.

4. How long have you been Clerk to the Town Commissioners of Lismore?—Since 1863—fifteen years.

5. What is the present area of the municipal district of Lismore?—129A. 2R. 37P.

6. I have it here in the Valuation Office return as 115 acres—how is that?—There is a discrepancy between what is returned on the valuation books and the ordnance survey.

7. What is the population of the municipal district of Lismore?—In 1871 it was 1,946.

8. What is the valuation of the municipal district?—At present the valuation is £3,172 10s.

9. Is the entire of the municipal district of Lismore comprehended in the same electoral division?—It is.

10. What electoral division?—The electoral division of Lismore.

11. What is the area of the electoral division of Lismore?—7,703 acres.

12. And what is the valuation?—£7,080 13s.

13. How many townlands are included in the municipal district?—One.

14. What is the townland?—The townland of Lismore town and one holding in Ballyanggarthig East.

15. What is the area of the holding in Ballyanggarthig East?—3A. 3R. 13P. It is merely a house and garden.

16. What is the area of the whole of the Ballyanggarthig townland?—223A. 3R. 11P.

17. In the electoral division of Lismore how many townlands are included?—Thirty-five.

18. The centre of the townland of Lismore is included in the municipal district of Lismore?—It is.

19. And the town is all in the same townland except the small portion of Ballyanggarthig?—Yes.

20. What is the radius from the centre of the town of the existing municipal district?—About a quarter of a mile from the centre.

21. Are there many inhabited houses lying within a radius of, say, a mile from the centre of the town not included in the present municipal district?—There are.

22. About how many would you say?—There might be about 100.

23. Outside the present municipal district, and within a radius of a mile?—Yes.

Lismore, Dec. 10, 1878. Mr. Maurice Roch.

[illegible] [illegible] communication [illegible] hold [illegible] to Lismore within the radius of a mile?—Yes; a large portion of it [illegible].

[illegible]

38. How far is the [illegible]?—It is [illegible] boundary of the borough boundary.

[illegible] quarter of a mile?—Yes.

[illegible] electoral division extend?—About two and a half miles.

[illegible] the Commissioners [illegible] boundary of the municipal district?—I think it would be practicable, and it would be advantageous.

[illegible]

41. In the opinion, what opinions did they express?—[illegible] Commissioners [illegible] in favour of allowing things to remain as they are.

[illegible] How many Commissioners are there?—[illegible] but there are only eight at present. There is a vacancy.

[illegible]

44. Were the [illegible] members who attended the meeting unanimously in favour of allowing things to remain as they are?—No; Dr. Lowe was not.

45. Did he dissent?—Yes.

[illegible] How many Commissioners did you call upon?—All, except one, and he was from home.

47. What opinion did they express?—That they were satisfied with the existing boundaries.

48. I asked you, a little while ago, assuming that a radius of a mile was taken, how many inhabited houses it would bring in, and how many townlands, which are in occupation of residents of the town. Do you consider that within that mile radius the residents derive advantages from their proximity to the town of Lismore?—They do derive advantages.

49. Has the Towns Improvement Act been adopted for all purposes?—Well, it has been adopted for all purposes.

50. Was it originally adopted for the water supply only?—Yes.

[illegible] Of course, since the Public Health Act of 1874, your functions as a Sanitary Board have merged in the Board of Guardians?—Yes; the Commissioners' functions are only merely the lighting and cleansing of the streets.

52. You have no water rate?—No.

53. There never was a water rate?—[illegible] [illegible] purpose of [illegible] because [illegible]

54. What year was that?—1858, I think.

55. Well, [illegible] rate?—No.

56. What are the rates?—They have been uniform [illegible].

57. Does that fully meet your expenditure?—It does.

58. Have you been debarred by that shilling limitation from effecting any improvements which were considered, on general grounds, to be desirable in the town?—Well, scarcely. There was only one instance in which an improvement the Commissioners wished was not carried out.

59. What was that?—It was the flagging of a small portion of the town.

60. Then they have been prevented from effecting improvements by reason of the limitation?—That is the only instance.

61. When did that occur?—Last year.

62. There is no other improvement they have been prevented from effecting?—No.

63. The town is lighted with gas?—Yes.

64. Is the lighting carried out by the Commissioners, or is it by contract?—It is by contract with a private company. The Commissioners contract with the lessee of the gasworks. The gasworks don't belong to the Commissioners themselves.

65. Do you consider that the inhabitants are excluded, and who live within the radius of a mile from the town, derive advantages from their proximity to the town as a market, and so forth?—They do.

66. And they participate, to some extent, in the town improvements?—Yes.

67. Are there schools in Lismore?—Yes.

68. And are the children of those people sent to the schools in Lismore?—Yes.

69. How often are markets held?—There are monthly markets, and during the winter season there are weekly butter markets held.

70. Is it a good market?—It is a fair market, but not very good.

71. Had the persons residing in the district here the advantage of the town as a market for the sale of their produce?—Certainly.

72. The whole of that property within the mile radius is the Duke of Devonshire's?—Yes; I think it is, or very nearly.

73. Do you consider there would be any unwillingness on the part of the occupiers of houses, who live outside the present municipal boundary, but within the radius of a mile, to be included in the municipal district?—I think there would.

74. You think they would object?—Yes, I do.

75. On what ground do you think they would object?—Simply on the ground of additional taxation.

76. If the radius was extended further than a mile—say a mile and a half—would that bring in a great many more inhabitants?—No, sir; it would not.

77. The radius of a mile would bring in most of the inhabited houses?—Yes. I think it would be absurd to have the radius extended beyond a mile, under any circumstances.

78. And you think the general feeling would be opposed to anything beyond a mile?—Any time any discussion took place on the subject, it was restricted much below a mile—probably a quarter of a mile would be nearer what was suggested.

79. Taking the radius of a mile, would that go into any other electoral division besides the electoral division of Lismore?—Yes; the Ballyin electoral division.

Lisburn. Dec. [illegible], 18[illegible] — Mr. [illegible].

80. How many townlands **are included in that** electoral division?—Fifty-five.

81. How many of those townlands would be brought in by the adoption of the mile radius?—None.

82. Nine townlands out of fifty-five?—Yes, sir.

83. You mentioned a while ago that about 100 inhabited houses would be brought in by the adoption of the mile radius. Now, how many of those 100 are included in the electoral division of Ballykeel, of which you are now speaking?—There would be portions of a third electoral division—Ballymagarrick—[illegible] I am not sure; I rather think it would be brought in.

84. How many of the 100 inhabited houses would be in the electoral division of Ballykeel?—From twenty to twenty-five.

85. About one-fourth would belong to Ballykeel?—Yes.

86. And the rest would be in the electoral division of Lisnagarvey?—Well, when you are done with me I will look, and [illegible] as to the number.

87. You are only giving the numbers in general terms?—Yes, as a rough guess.

88. The Board of Guardians have, since 1874, acted as sanitary authority?—Yes.

89. The population of the town being considerably under 6,000?—Yes.

90. Are the Town Commissioners aware of the fact that, under the Towns Improvement Act or [illegible] sion, power is now vested in the Local Government Board, on the application of the Town Commissioners, to transfer, if they see fit, the jurisdiction over sanitary matters from the Rural Authority to the Commissioners, and to constitute the Commissioners the Urban Sanitary Authority?—I am aware of it; and I think I mentioned the matter to some of the Commissioners, but I am not sure whether, as a body, they are aware of it.

91. They have never taken into consideration the advisability of having that course adopted?—I think the feeling of the general body would be against it, on the ground of the additional expense it would entail.

92. Have there been any special rates struck in the town since 1874 for sanitary purposes?—Yes, sir.

93. What were they?—[illegible]

94. Take the last five years, and say what were the rates for sanitary purposes?—In 18[illegible] it was [illegible], in 1878 it was [illegible], and in 18[illegible] it was [illegible]; and in one of those years there was work done which would [illegible] [illegible] to [illegible] the town.

95. What were the purposes for which **those rates** were made?—For sewers.

96. Not for water supply?—No.

97. Entirely for sewerage purposes?—Yes.

98. Is there any expenditure still required for sanitary works in the town?—Yes.

99. What is the nature of the sanitary work for which expenditure is still required?—Well, it is one that has been spoken of for some time—to extend the sewerage up towards the Chapel Hill portion.

100. Would that work be very expensive?—Well, portion of it is completed, and the part remaining would cost about £[illegible].

101. What is the cause of the delay in the completion of the work?—The Guardians think the [illegible] who would be accommodated by it should, and they [illegible] think the general feeling of the occupiers [illegible] [illegible].

102. Would the Guardians be in favour of the transfer of the authority to the Commissioners?—They would be indifferent.

103. They have no particular feeling on the subject?—No.

104. At present it doesn't involve any special taxation?—No, sir.

105. And the Guardians have not expressed any feeling on the subject?—I have no doubt if the Commissioners applied the Guardians would not object.

106. Are the Commissioners aware of the fact that if they were made the Urban Sanitary Authority, under section [illegible] of the Public Health Act, their powers under that section [illegible] of the Act, authorize the Local Government Board also to transfer to them, by provisional order, the control heretofore exercised by the Grand Jury over roads and bridges within the municipal district?—No, they're not aware of the [illegible] of that.

110. And you have no means of knowing whether, if they were aware that they could obtain that control, it would influence them in getting the transfer of the Sanitary Authority?—No, I don't think it would.

111. They are not dissatisfied with the present jurisdiction of the sanitary affairs by the Board of Guardians?—No, I am not aware that they are.

112. At present all rates for sanitary purposes are imposed equally within the district on all description of property. There is no graduated scale of rating?—There is no difference I know.

113. Are the Commissioners aware that if, under the Public Health Act, they became the Sanitary Authority, the sanitary rates may be charged on [illegible] [illegible]?—I don't think they are aware of it. I was aware of it.

114. You are not aware whether the power to apply that scale would induce the Commissioners to wish to have the sanitary functions transferred to them?—I think the general body of the Commissioners would not want to incur any additional expense simply for the purpose of having the sanitary control transferred to them.

115. Additional taxation would be required, you think?—The present taxation would show [illegible] for the Commissioners are out of debt. They were burdened with old [illegible], but up to the present year, but it is now wiped out, and so the present would be sufficient to meet the old purposes.

116. Even if the sanitary functions were transferred to the present would still be sufficient?—Unless it would be sufficient.

117. Including any necessary works that might be called for?—No; not for necessary works, but for the ordinary purposes it would be sufficient. I think for in the period for the future years would suffice for the present expenditure.

118. And it **would be sufficient for all ordinary** purposes?—Yes.

119. There are **nine Commissioners at present**?—Yes.

120. How many persons are there within the municipal district who are eligible to act as Commissioners?—I think there are only [illegible] altogether.

121. Are there nineteen, [illegible] [illegible] eligible, and who would be likely to undertake the duties?—Not who would be likely to undertake the duties.

122. But who are **perfectly eligible in all respects**?—Yes.

123. If a radius of a mile was substituted for the present boundary, would that introduce many additional persons who would be qualified to act?—Oh, it would.

124. How many would, you say it would bring in?—I suppose forty or fifty.

125. Who would be eligible to be Commissioners?—Yes.

126. What is the constituency of the town?—There are fifty-six voters on the present list.

127. Assuming that the boundary was to be extended to the mile radius, what would be the constituency then?—I think it would be 300.

128. Don't you think it would give a healthier impulse to the town government if both the constituency and the number of persons eligible were enlarged so as to bring in such a large number?—Well, it ought to have that tendency; but whether it would do so I can't say. I don't think there would be that amount of interest taken by the people outside. They would acquiesce in the general management at present.

129. You don't think they are dissatisfied?—I don't

Lismore, [illegible]

Mr. [illegible]

think there would be any agitation against the present arrangement?

127. Have you got a copy of the memorial originally addressed to the Lord Lieutenant in applying to get the town put under the provisions of the Towns Improvement Act?—No; I can [illegible] an entry here in the Minute Book of 2nd January, 1853: "Chairman read the letter of the Lord Lieutenant's [illegible] the town was placed under the Towns Improvement Act." There is no copy of the memorial.

128. Have you there the Lord Lieutenant's answer defining the boundary of the town?—No, sir.

129. I think you mentioned that, in addition to the townland of Lismore, the present municipal district includes portions of Ballysaggart townland?—Yes.

130. If the whole of that townland was introduced, how far would it extend from the centre of the town?—About half a mile, or something more. It is irregular.

131. It is a long strip that goes off about a mile from the centre of the town?—Yes.

132. Is there any other townland besides that that goes close to the present municipal boundary?—Oh, yes.

133. What townlands are they?—There are several townlands.

134. That are altogether at present excluded?—There are.

135. What are they?—There are eighteen that come pretty close, not much more than a mile.

136. Do you mean that the nearest point is about a mile distant from the town?—No; that the radius of a mile would take in about eighteen townlands.

137. It would take in the entire of them?—No.

138. It would cut them in some instances?—Yes.

Dr. [illegible] examined.

Dr. [illegible]

139. Mr. O'Brien.—You are Chairman of the Town Commissioners of Lismore?—Yes.

140. How long have you been Chairman of the Commissioners?—Since 1866, I think.

141. The boundaries have never been changed since the Act was adopted in 1853?—No.

142. You were not Chairman at the time the Act was [illegible]?—No.

143. And you don't know what were the principles that guided the Commissioners in originally fixing the boundaries?—No.

144. From your experience do you think the feeling of the Commissioners is favourable to having the existing boundary extended, or in any way altered?—I think it is in favour of allowing things to remain as they are.

145. You are aware the present area is only 130 acres?—Yes.

146. That is a particularly small area?—Yes.

147. And you think the feeling of the Commissioners would not be in favour of having a wider area adopted?—No; all the Commissioners I have spoken to would rather be in favour of allowing things to remain as they are.

148. What were the grounds on which they arrived at that conclusion?—In consequence of the separation of the sanitary [illegible] from the jurisdiction of the Town Commissioners, the expenses are very much diminished, and the rate collected is sufficient to cover those expenses; but if the area was extended so as to include the land in the neighbourhood of the town, the greater part of the land being in the hands of the people in the town, the increased taxation would come on the backs of those who now pay the principal portion of the rates.

149. Are there not also [illegible] living within a radius of a mile of the town who are not subject to the town taxation and yet derive advantages?—There are some, but I think Mr. Hardy has rather exaggerated the number.

150. You think there are not many?—There are a few.

151. How many do you make out, excepting the labouring class farmers?—Including those above the status of labourers who would be called upon to pay rates, I should say about fifty.

152. Well, assuming the number to be fifty, don't you think they derive, in numerous ways, advantages from their proximity to the town?—They derive some, but nothing at all equivalent to the town people.

153. And they derive advantages in having a market close to them, and in having schools provided for their children?—They do.

154. You know about the rate levied on [illegible]?—Yes.

155. Doesn't it appear to you that the reduced taxation of the district is a pretty fair measure of the advantages these persons derive from the town?—Yes, I think so.

156. Then you don't think there would be anything inequitable in including persons within the town who live within the radius of a mile?—I think they would [illegible] object to it.

157. On what ground?—On the ground that they do not get value for it.

158. You would not yourself consider that there was anything inequitable in requiring that persons deriving certain advantages should give a certain contribution towards the town expenditure?—No; but if I was there myself I would object.

159. On the ground of the additional taxation?—Yes.

160. You heard me read the opinion of the Parliamentary Committee in favour of having town boundaries and electoral division boundaries made coterminous. If it was proposed here to follow that opinion by substituting the electoral division for the present municipal boundary, would you consider there would be any objection to that?—I do.

161. What would be the objections that strike you to applying to that?—I think it would be going in direct opposition to the strong recommendation of the committee.

162. Oh, no. The Committee expressed an opinion that the town should be made coterminous with the poor law electoral division?—Yes.

163. Now, the town of Lismore is situated in the poor law division of Lismore?—Yes.

164. And suppose you confined it to the electoral division of Lismore, what would be the objection to it—if you take a radius of a mile?

165. No, but putting the mile radius out of the question, and if you, instead of that, took the electoral division as the boundary, what would be the objection?—I think it goes out in different directions, and you would be bringing in people who derive no advantages more than if they were six miles away.

166. How far does the electoral division go?—Nearly three miles in a southerly direction, and two and a half miles in a westerly direction.

167. In greater distance of which you consider they derive no advantage from the town?—None whatever.

168. Would it also have the effect of excluding, in other directions, the people who happen to be close to the town, and yet live in another electoral division?—Yes, it would.

169. So that there would be a twofold objection to the electoral division—that it goes too far in one direction, and leaves out in another direction people who should be included?—I don't know that anybody living at the other side of the river would derive any advantage whatever from being included in the township.

170. But that is outside the electoral division?—Yes.

171. If you took the electoral division, would you not exclude persons deriving much more benefit than some of those in the division, but who did not happen

Lismore. Rev. M. [illegible] Dr Curry.

to be in the electoral division of Lismore?—No, I don't think it would. I think there are persons in the electoral division of Lismore living near the town of Lismore who never contribute anything to the town.

172. Suppose you made the electoral division the municipal area, one objection you mentioned is that it goes so far in one direction that it would bring in some people who derive no benefit from the town, and leave out in other places people who derive advantages, and who are at present excluded, because they are not in the electoral division?—Yes, it would.

173. So that you would have persons excluded altogether who are much closer to the town than those included in the electoral division boundary?—Yes.

174. You are aware that under the 7th section of the Public Health Act of last session there is power given to the Local Government Board to transfer, by provisional order, the control from the Board of Guardians to the Commissioners respecting sanitary matters?—Yes, I am aware of that.

175. Did the Commissioners ever consider the expediency of getting a transfer?—The subject has been mentioned, but never seriously entertained.

176. And so far as you know, the opinion is not in favour of having the transfer?—No.

177. They would rather let things remain as they are?—Yes.

178. They would not be influenced by the power (if they were constituted the Sanitary Authority) of getting control over certain works?—That might have also been discussed, but we thought we were better as we were.

179. So that you think there is no desire to have either the Grand Jury or the sanitary functions transferred?—No.

180. You would rather remain as you are?—Yes.

Major Olpherts examined.

181. You are not a Commissioner?—No; I am a resident in the Ballysaggart townland; it is in the Ballyinn electoral division, and we derive no advantage whatever from the town.

182. How far is Ballysaggart from the town?—About half a mile and a quarter.

183. Then a radius of a mile would introduce it?—Yes, and it would introduce a great number of poor, who are not able to pay rates, and then derive no advantage.

184. Have they not the benefit arising from their proximity to the market?—Yes, but the market is nothing.

185. Haven't you the advantage of the schools for poor children?—We have a school in the place this very nearly as near.

186. But persons living within a radius of a mile round the town [illegible] more than persons living at a greater distance?—No doubt of that.

187. And if the roads are lighted they participate in that benefit?—It's most trifling.

188. But they have greater advantages from the town than the people living miles away?—I don't consider the ratepayers out there have any advantages.

189. You don't consider that you have any advantages of such a nature as would fairly make you liable to [illegible] ?

190. You are aware that if you were introduced, arable lands are only liable to one-fourth?—Yes.

191. Don't you consider that that would meet your objection, and that the fact of your only being obliged to pay one-fourth would be a fair equivalent of the advantages you derive?—No; and so far as the market is concerned, Lismore is no use to us. My market is Cappoquin, and I get my store there.

192. How far is that away?—About four miles.

193. Don't you consider that the people of Ballysaggart resort generally to Lismore as a market town?—I suppose they do.

194. How many inhabited houses are there in Ballysaggart?—There are a great many, but they are of a very poor class—cottiers—men holding only a small portion of ground.

195. And you don't think they would be able to bear any increased taxation?—I am sure they are not able to bear any taxation; even the taxation that is on them.

196. And the inhabitants would object?—I am sure they would. They are about the poorest people in the place. It is a miserable district.

Mr. John Healy examined.

Mr John Healy.

197. You are a Commissioner of the town of Lismore?—I am.

198. How long have you been a Commissioner?—Since the town was put under the provisions of the Act.

199. And probably you took part in the preliminary arrangements of getting the Act adopted?—Yes.

200. What was the principle that generally guided you in fixing the boundary then?—I think it was the old boundary.

201. You had been under the 9th of George IV.?—I believe we were not under the Act, but there was an old boundary, the boundary of the manor court.

202. You think the boundary adopted was the boundary that previously existed for the manor court?—Yes, with the exception of Dr. Curran's house, and that was included with his own consent.

203. You have heard the explanation given as to the objects of the inquiry: from your experience as a Commissioner do you think it desirable that the present boundary should be extended?—We were discussing that—myself and Dr. Curry—since last week, and we came to the conclusion that there would not be much advantage derived by the town people, but if the boundary could be extended a mile we would be in favour of it.

204. You would not be in favour of a small radius, but you would be in favour of extending the town boundary a mile?—Yes.

205. And you think the people living near the town derive advantage from their proximity to it?—Yes.

206. And you would not be in favour of anything more or less than a mile?—If I was in favour of anything I would be in favour of a mile, or even less. Down as far as the bridge, to Ballyinn I should say should be taken in.

207. How many townlands of that electoral division of Ballyinn would you take in?—About a mile.

208. How many townlands would that introduce?—I could not say exactly how many.

209. It would take in a considerable part of the electoral division?—No, not a considerable part.

210. Well, some part of it?—Yes.

211. You think some part of it should be introduced?—Yes, I do.

212. You would not be in favour of adopting the electoral division of Lismore as the municipal boundary?—No.

213. So you have a two-fold objection to that, that it goes too far in one direction, and omits places in another direction that you think should be included?—Yes; it is in Ballyin our servants are, and I think they benefit more than the people a mile out.

214. But you are not in favour of adopting the electoral division as the boundary, or anything beyond a mile?—No.

215. Are there any improvements which you have been restrained from making from a consideration that

Lismore. Dec. 19, 18[illegible]

Mr. John Hickie.

[illegible] would be a burden on the present township?—We were assisted by Mr. Gorey in making them. He gave assistance to help us.

216. Otherwise the works would involve too heavy a charge?—Yes; and the county gave us one fourth.

217. Since 18[illegible] you ceased to be Sanitary Authority for the town?—Yes.

218. You have heard me read the section of the Public Health Act of last session, which enables the Local Government Board, by provisional order, to transfer these functions from the Board of Guardians to the Town Commissioners?—Yes.

219. Have you considered whether it would be desirable that these functions should be transferred?—I think it would be desirable.

220. You think the Town Body would have more interest in the work?—I do.

221. And that the transfer would be desirable?—Yes.

222. If these duties were transferred would it increase your desire to see the area extended?—It would.

223. You are aware there is a further provision in the Act enabling the Local Government Board to transfer certain jurisdiction over the roads and bridges within the municipal boundary from the Grand Jury to the Town Commissioners. Would it appear to you to be advisable if you were made the Sanitary Authority that you should seek to obtain control over the roads and bridges also?—I think it would be.

224. You think you would be able to do the work better?—With more satisfaction.

225. Do you consider the sum at present expended by the Grand Jury is commensurate with the great they levy?—I think the work could be better done by the Commissioners themselves. They would have more interest in it, and, with regard to the sanitary question, the people think it very strange to see guardians coming over from other neighbourhoods to look after works that should be carried on by those in the locality.

Once there was a sewer to be made, and it was the Cappoquin Guardians who carried the making of the sewer through Lismore.

226. And you think the people of Lismore would be able to take a greater interest in such works than the people of Cappoquin?—Yes.

227. Would the people of Lismore be in favour of having the boundaries extended?—I think they would.

228. You have heard me ask Mr. Healy the number eligible to fill the office of Town Commissioner within the present township, and he has told us there are 18 eligible to fill the office of Commissioner, and that there are 86 entitled to vote. He has also told us that if the boundary was extended, it would bring in a larger number [illegible] of those who would be eligible to be Commissioners and of voters—does it appear to you that it would have a healthier effect and improve the state of affairs in the township if there was an extended area?—I think it would be an improvement.

229. You think it would give a healthier impetus to the town government, as you would have a larger number to select from and a larger number interested?—Yes.

230. You think that would be desirable?—Yes.

231. Mr. Cotton.—Suppose there was to be no extension on the north side of the river, would you still be in favour of an extension to the south?—I think the Ballyin people derive many benefits.

232. Would you still be in favour of an extension of the boundary to the south if there was no extension to the north side?—I think it should be equal general.

233. Suppose it was considered impossible to go into that second electoral division of Ballyin, and it was considered desirable to keep to the one electoral division, do you consider it desirable to go for the mile?—I think it would be better to have it more uniform.

Mr. Thomas Gorey examined.

Mr. Thomas Gorey.

234. Mr. O'Brien.—You are a Commissioner of Lismore?—Yes.

235. You have heard the different views expressed as to the extension of the township boundary; what is your own opinion?—I quite coincide with Mr. Hickie.

236. You would be in favour of having a mile radius?—Yes.

237. And you think the people within the mile radius should contribute?—Yes.

238. And you think it would give a healthier tone if there was a larger number of persons eligible to be Commissioners, and a larger number of electors?—Yes.

239. Mr. Hickie has also expressed the opinion that the sanitary functions should be transferred to the Commissioners from the Board of Guardians—is that your view also?—Yes.

240. On general grounds, you think that would be best?—I do.

241. You have also heard the opinion expressed by Mr. Hickie that if you were constituted the sanitary authority he would be in favour of having the control over the roads and bridges transferred to you from the Grand Jury—is that your view too?—Yes.

242. You would be in favour of having the control over them transferred to the town body?—Yes.

243. You think the work would be better done than at present?—Yes.

244. And you think you would take greater interest in the execution of the works?—Yes.

245. Greater interest than the Grand Jury take?—Yes.

246. In transferring the Grand Jury functions over bridges of course you would be responsible for them, and if any accident occurred, for instance, to the bridge at Lismore here you would be responsible—would that fact deter you from undertaking the functions, or would you think that a sufficiently probable contingency to deter you?—I don't think there is any fear of the bridge.

Dr. Lowe examined.

Dr. Lowe.

247. You are a Commissioner of the town?—Yes.

248. How long have you been a Commissioner?—[illegible] for me.

249. You were not a member when the body was first constituted?—No.

250. And you don't know what were the principles that guided them [illegible]. only from hearsay.

251. Do you consider the existing boundary satisfactory?—I do not.

252. Do you think it should be extended or [illegible]?—Extend it.

253. What, in your opinion, you would think desirable?—I have heard Mr. Hickie's statement, and I think it is very fair.

254. You are in favour of a mile radius?—Yes.

255. And you think the people within a mile derive benefit?—Yes.

256. And you think they derive advantages commensurate with the one-fourth taxation to which they would be subject?—Yes, and I heard Major [illegible] speak [illegible] [illegible] advantage, but I think he [illegible] [illegible] as any other person. [illegible] bridge [illegible], and we keep the [illegible] [illegible]. He is very rich, and we are very poor, and we would like to have the Major's money.

257. You consider the radius of a mile would be a fair boundary?—I do.

258. And you would not be in favour of adopting

the electoral division as the boundary of the town?—I don't understand that, and I will not give any opinion on it.

259. As at present advised you are in favour of the radius of a mile?—Yes, and particularly to the north.

260. You would take a radius of a mile all round?—Yes. There is a mill on the north that we wish to have in; it is a flour mill, and these gentlemen derive much benefit from the town. We are their commodity here.

261. What townland is it in?—Ballyinn, I think.

262. These mills you think should be introduced?—Yes, and we have the Duke of Devonshire's weirs which we should also have.

263. Where are they?—In Ballyinn also, and we have Lismore Castle.

264. Is that rated at present?—I believe there is some trifle paid for it. We have also two large corn stores.

265. Where are they?—They are outside the municipal area.

266. What distance are they from the centre of the town?—Not 1,000 yards.

267. And you consider that they should be taken in?—Yes, and there is the Canal, that produces £150 profit rent, and we must pay the expenses off the town, and get nothing from it.

268. What radius would bring that in?—The mile would, and we are most anxious to have Major Giles.

269. Are you in favour of having the sanitary functions transferred from the Board of Guardians to the Town Commissioners?—I think that is the greatest injustice Government ever did.

270. And you are in favour of having the sanitary functions transferred?—Certainly.

271. Are you aware there is power vested in the Local Government to transfer, if they see fit, the authority over sanitary matters?—I am very glad of it.

272. But you were not aware of it?—All the townspeople will be most delighted to have it again transferred to the Commissioners.

273. Under the Public Health Act, of 1874, which took away the sanitary functions from the Town Commissioners, and vested it in the Board of Guardians in towns where the population did not exceed 6,000, and here your population is only 2,000, the transfer to the Board of Guardians was absolute and universal, and the law so remained until last session of Parliament, and now stands in the same way, but in the Local Government Board Act there is power given to give back the authority to the Commissioners under a provisional order?—I am very sorry to tell you I think the Guardians are very lazy in doing their duty.

274. You would be in favour of the transfer?—Certainly.

275. You also heard me read another section of the Act, under which, if you were the sanitary authority, there is power given to obtain control over certain works now exercised by the Grand Jury. Do you think your Board, or are you yourself in favour of having the control of the roads and bridges in your own hands?—I think it would be desirable.

276. And you think you would do it better?—Much better, particularly if we had the rural guardians coming in to assist us.

277. You think an extension of boundary would be of advantage as bringing in the rural class of people?—It would give a more select class of people. I heard Mr. Hickey complain that the sanitary rate was imposed on the Town Commissioners without their will and against their will, to make a sewer through the South Mall, leading up from the church. It cost, I believe, £180. Now that is perfectly useless to the town, and we have been taxed by it, and if we had power to prevent that we would do so, but being under the government of a few gentlemen from Cappoquin they carried it against the will of the people.

278. You mention that as an illustration that the sanitary affairs are not as well managed by the Board of Guardians as they would be if the Town Commissioners had control over them?—I do. Whereas, here is Dr. Owen, an old respectable inhabitant of the town, and his place wants sewers, and he has to carry off the sewer water through the street down to the other sewers. This sewer that I mentioned has been granted at a cost of £120, while the other was refused.

279. Assuming that it would not be advisable to extend the boundary into Ballyinn?—I would be against that.

280. Would you consider it advisable to extend the boundary to Ballyinn?—By all means extend it to Ballyinn.

281. But if it was not extended to Ballyinn?—It would be almost useless. The benefit to the people of Lismore comes nearly altogether from Ballyinn.

282. Supposing it was put to you, you can't get an extension towards Ballyinn, but you can have an extension in any other direction, what would you say then?—I would say then the law is a one-sided one. I would consider it a mere pretence if it was not extended to Ballyinn.

283. You would consider any extension that did not take in Ballyinn unsatisfactory?—I would.

284. Is the railway station at present included in the town?—No.

285. In what townland is the railway station?—Townparks.

Mr. HEALY recalled.

286. The townland of Townparks is part of the Lismore electoral division?—Yes.

287. But it is outside the town boundary?—Yes.

288. How far is it from the centre of the town?—Scarcely a quarter of a mile from it.

289. It is entirely outside the town boundary at present?—Yes.

290. The station is attended by hackney cars from the town?—Yes.

291. Have you no by-laws?—No, sir.

292. Suppose the boundary was extended to take in the railway station, would the Commissioners consider it an advantage to have power to pass by-laws to regulate the conduct of the carmen?—I should say so.

293. At present they have no by-laws and no control over them?—No, not for that place; but they can regulate the hackney cars within the town.

294. At present they have no by-laws and no control?—No.

295. Would you consider it an advantage if you had by-laws, and if the railway station was included?—I would; but there are not many cars except from the two hotels.

Mr. JAMES O'BRIEN examined.

296. You are a Commissioner of Lismore?—Yes, sir.

297. How long have you been a Commissioner?—About six months.

298. You have heard the different opinions expressed to-day by different witnesses, is there anything you would wish to add?—No. I quite agree with Mr. Crotty, Mr. Hickey, and Dr. Lowe.

299. There is nothing special you wish to add?—No, sir.

300. You are in favour of adopting the mile radius?—I am.

301. You are in favour of that including Ballyinn?—Yes.

302. You would not be in favour of any extension that would not bring in Ballyinn?—No.

303. You are in favour of a transfer of the sanitary functions from the Board of Guardians to you?—Yes.

304. You think that would be an advantage?—Yes.

Mr. James O'Connor examined.

305. **You are a Town Commissioner of Lismore?**—Yes, sir.

306. How long have you been a Commissioner of the town?—For a few months.

307. You have heard the different opinions expressed—is there anything you would wish to add?—I would be for not extending the boundary at all.

308. You would be in favour of allowing things to remain as they are?—I do think the change would not be of advantage.

309. Don't you think it would be a benefit to have a larger area to extend the taxes over?—But I don't think the people would pay the tax; they would object to it.

310. In what part of the radius of a mile are the people unable to pay?—I don't think on the other side. There are a few gentlemen, but as a rule the farmers and others can't afford to pay.

311. But don't you consider that persons within a radius of a mile, to some extent at all events, participate in the general advantages which town governments offer?—They do; but we have a large market in the cattle market, and there is no other weekly market.

312. Don't they sell the different descriptions of farm produce in the town?—No; not in a satisfactory manner.

313. But still don't the people within a mile of the town sell eggs and butter, and that kind of thing?—Very little; and there is no regular market.

314. Don't think nobody is benefited by the schools in the town?—Some do, and others do not.

315. Don't you think there is some advantage derived by the people living within a mile of the town, which the people living three or six miles off don't enjoy?—I do.

316. Don't you think the advantages they derive would be fairly measured at one-fourth, if the tax?—Yes; I dare say they would.

317. Aren't you aware that arable lands throughout are only liable to one-fourth the rate?—Yes.

318. And don't you think that is a fair enough measure of the advantages they derive?—I don't say they would not object to pay that.

319. You don't think that that would be inequitable?—I don't think it would be.

320. You would not object to the mile radius under those circumstances?—Not if it was a benefit to the town of Lismore, but I don't believe it would be. I don't think it would bring in any additional Commissioners.

321. You don't think it would be desirable?—No.

Major Giles.—Mr. Lowe said the bridge was lighted with gas, but that's not so. They endeavour at the south side, and there is no light at the other side, although the gas works are over there.

Mr. O'Connor.—I would not be in favour of taking over the control over the roads and bridges.

322. Mr. O'Brien.—Would you be in favour of a transfer of the sanitary jurisdiction?—No; I would not.

Dr. Cooney.—The water supply is really supplied by the Duke, and the Town Commissioners simply give it a year to give them control and to prevent waste of the water.

Mr. Healy.—I find there are about forty-seven persons who would be eligible to be Commissioners in the mile radius.

323. Mr. O'Brien.—What would be the number of voters then would be immediately?—There might be about double that—about 150.

324. Do you know there would be 50 additional persons who would be eligible to act as Commissioners?—Yes.

325. And about 100 additional voters?—Yes.

326. Mr. O'Brien.—How would those numbers be affected if you left out everything north of the river?—There would be 33 included who would be eligible, and there would be 13 for Ballyduff.

327. And how many voters would be brought in if Ballyduff was left out?—About 80, that is persons rated under £4 in the mile radius.

328. Dr. Cooney.—I heard it stated that the gas would be adequate to the increase, but I don't believe that; for we are limited here, and we could carry out improvements owing to the limited amount of our revenue.

329. You think your limitation is too much?—We think.

330. You have no property of any kind except what you raise by taxation?—No.

331. The complaint is, the limited area your town?—Yes, and that they have the lands which the rate ought to bear.

332. Can you mention any way in which you were restricted from making up revenue of your limited funds?—There is a nuisance in the Mill, which we want to have removed, but we have only the rates here to meet, we could not have it done, and then we must apply always to the Duke to have anything carried out.

333. Do you pave the streets?—If we had the means we would pave and flag.

334. Have you been restrained from doing that?—We have no fund for doing it, and are paying in its lower funds.

Mr. Healy said there were some incumbrances which are now cleared off, and that that £4, would suffice for the ordinary expenditure, and that the margin between the £4 and 1s. would leave sufficient for the sanitary works. Mr. Healy would not like to be relieved in his salary. Even at our Lismore where children come in in hundreds, we accordingly had and upon a sub-commissioners are paid. Doing their duty, and we have no power over them.

335. There are works **under the Grand Jury?**—Yes.

336. And that is one of the reasons why you think the transfer of the Grand Jury powers desirable?—Yes.

Mr. Healy.—About £1,000 would be the valuation of the additional townlands brought in by the mile radius.

337. Can you separate them?—£2,750 would be Ballyduff and £1,600 for the other.

Dr. Cooney.—Portion of the town was drained and part paid by the Commissioners, and part by the sanitary, but since the amalgamation of the railway from Waterford to Lismore the Grand Jury have resolved not to pass any presentment except what is absolutely necessary, and therefore we have thought it useless to apply for any additional growth.

Dr. Lowe.—As it is, the Grand Jury have drawn all the rates we can take ourselves but not on the lands hereby.

Mr. O'Brien.—That is the law of the land.

Mr. Cotton.—What is the date of the meeting of your board, so that we may be able to get a return of the boundaries?—The 23rd January, 1883.

The inquiry then closed.

Mallow, Dec. 27, 1878.

Mr. Thomas W. Priestley.

MALLOW.—DECEMBER 27TH, 1878.

Before Mr. W. A. Exham, Q.C. (Chairman), and Mr. C. P. Cotton, C.E.

Mr. Thomas W. Priestley examined.

1. Chairman.—Are you, Mr. Priestley, Chairman of the Town Commissioners?—No, I am not; Dr. Barry is the chairman, but he is at present unwell, and I represent him on the present occasion. I was chairman of the Commissioners for some years.

2. Was anything done with regard to the striking of a rate, or have you struck a rate since we held our last inquiry here?—No.

3. Did you see, and have you answered, the queries that were sent to you from the office of the Municipal Boundaries Commission?—I really cannot say whether they were answered or not. I am now informed by the Town Clerk that they were answered.

4. Is it the opinion of the governing body here that there should be any enlargement of the boundary?—Yes; the Town Commissioners are desirous of an enlargement of the boundary.

5. Are they unanimous upon the point?—Yes, I believe they are. I have not heard of any dissension from it. I have not heard of anyone opposing it.

6. Can you say whether or not it is the feeling of the inhabitants outside and inside the present township that there should be an extension?—I believe it is.

7. What is the present boundary; is it what is coloured yellow on the map before me?—Yes.

8. Mr. Cotton.—Is the municipal the same as the Parliamentary boundary?—Not quite, though it certainly does approximate as closely to it as possible. In some particular instances, however, there is a little difference.

9. Do you know how it was fixed, or when?—No. As a matter of fact, I could not tell you.

10. Mr. Exham.—As far as you know, has there been any alteration of the boundary since the township was formed?—Not that I am aware of.

11. Can you tell us how and when the boundary was first adopted?—As a matter of recollection, I cannot. Mr. Nagle will be able to give you that information.

12. What is the valuation of the town now?—You can get that also from Mr. Nagle.

13. Is the township in one electoral division?—Mr. Nagle will tell that.

14. What is the extension that the inhabitants outside with the Town Commissioners in proposing?—The extension that they desire, and that has been, so far as I have been able to learn, apparently approved of by the parties who would be embraced within it, would be a mile—a radius of an English mile, as closely as possible—from the north-western angle of the Mallow military barrack square. Taken from that point to Colonel Williamson's back gate would give, as closely as I can tell, an English mile.

15. Where would Colonel Williamson's back gate be on this map?—It would not be on the map you have before you at all, but you will find it quite clearly shown on the Ordnance map. The southern pier of the back gate of Colonel Williamson's demesne, starting from that and following the circle, it would strike a point marked at the herbstone at Gould's Hill; continuing that circle around to the west, you take in part of Fermoy.

16. Whose place is that?—That is Mr. Croft's place. Still following that circle, you take in the Manor Mill.

17. Who does that belong to?—Mr. Webb; and you strike a house occupied by a man named Crean, an employé of Mr. Webb's. Still following that circle, you strike the western pier of Mr. Webb's back entrance to Quartertown Park. Still following that circle, you strike a point of the paling where it touches the river Blackwater. Crossing the Blackwater, and still following that circle, you touch the third tree on the lawn at Kilbrin.

18. Whose place is that?—Mr. Robert Waggett. Still following that circle, you take in—I do not know the points round there exactly.

19. Mr. Cotton.—You take in a mile the whole way round?—Yes; you take in a part of Gaalbally, Fairy Hill, Sentry Hill, Victoria, and Hawthorn. You also take in part of Kinkelbin, Annabella——

20. Are all those places you are now mentioning outside the present boundary?—Yes, every one of them; and also the railway premises.

21. Mr. Exham.—Then the railway station is at present outside the boundary?—Yes, entirely. The new villas are also outside at present. It would be hard for me to specify everything.

22. About what length of the railway would be taken in?—There would be about a mile and a half on the length within that circle.

23. That is of the two railways—the Fermoy and the other?—It would take in part of the Fermoy line. Crossing from Kinkelbin, and going north-east, you take in Lackanalooha, which is in the tenancy of Mr. Thomas Walsh. Still following that circle, you take in the Lease lands, Mr. Hooper's; you take in part of the Fermoy railway and the Spa Glen lands, Keatley's-close, the whole of the Castle lands; and, still following the circle, you take in Rosaly Cottage, Ballydahin, Mr. Brooke Brasier's place, and you take in part of Bear Forest—that is, Mr. Cooke's part of Bear Forest, known as Lower Bear Forest; also part of Gaalbally, including the house and demesne, and all that would bring you to the point from whence you started—the south pier of Colonel Williamson's back entrance gate. The circle I have detailed embraces all those that at present derive full benefit from the town, and who would derive the benefit of any improvement made by the Town Commissioners.

24. Are you now referring to the mile circle?—Yes.

25. Is Mr. Seward's house included in the mile?—No, it is outside.

26. Is Mr. Seward's a good house?—I should tell you the reason we agreed upon a mile is this, that in departing from the circle you must take in somebody and leave out somebody, and the reason we thought the mile would be more generally adopted, and the reason it was adopted accordingly, was because it favoured no one, but took in every person that came within the circle.

27. Would Mr. Webb's house be within that line?—It would; it is within the mile radius. I may tell you that the circle you have before you is a mile from the pump in the barrack square; but the point that I am taking is the north-western angle of the barrack square, which gives you the opportunity of embracing some valuable property that would be otherwise left out almost completely if the radius was taken from the pump. The barrack pump would leave out a great deal of the property that I have mentioned.

28. Mr. Cotton.—Have you considered the extension of the boundary going by townlands, and not by a circle?—Yes; I have a map of those here.

29. To what map do you refer?—That is taken from the Ordnance map.

30. I see the present proposed boundary was the last proposition submitted to Mr. Griffith?—Yes, that was submitted to Mr. Griffith twenty years ago, approved by him, and adopted at the time by a public meeting called for the purpose, but it never was carried out; it fell through owing to some informality in the proceedings in connection with it.

31. Mr. Exham.—Can we retain this map?—Yes; and I can send you a map, made by Mr. Lyons, which marks the townland boundaries; but the great difficulty to be contended against in connection with the

[illegible] of the townland [illegible] I think you have [illegible] through these fields and water-courses ; in fact, it would be almost practically impossible to carry out the townland boundary.

32. I do not understand that. If you adopt the boundaries of the townlands for the municipal district you will not have that difficulty?—I thought you meant the [illegible] lands. By the townlands you would not.

33. Do you say that this boundary, as marked on this map, which we will mark with the letter B, was [illegible] approved of by the inhabitants of the town [illegible] twenty years ago?—Yes.

34. Was that the time when you were trying to adopt the Towns Improvement Act at first?—Yes; it was.

35. Was this map sent to the late Sir Richard Griffith?—Yes.

36. And approved by him?—Yes.

37. Is that the red line which is shown here?—Yes.

38. Is that the line now proposed [illegible] correct?—Yes, practically it is; but it does away with the objection that might be raised to the other proposition of taking in any portion capriciously, and that was the reason we decided upon the circle. Colonel W[illegible] has said that he was one of the parties who objected at first to the extension.

39. Do you mean to this extension of twenty years ago?—Yes; he objected to the first proposition ; and the reason he gave was that he thought some parties were taken in that ought not to be, and other parties left out that should have been taken in, as they derived the same benefit from the town as those that were taken in, but he also said that by taking the circle all difficulty was obviated, and the objection was done away with.

40. Mr. C[illegible].—Supposing it was not possible to adopt a hard and fast line, such as a circle, can you give us any other boundary that would meet your views—any boundary by townlands?—Yes. Mr. [illegible] has made a tracing which, however, I do not [illegible] have with me, but I will send it to you. You can put in beside the other one, and whichever you think best you will, of course, adopt. They will [illegible] be the same, except that they—the townland boundaries—will follow hedgerows and other [illegible] more closely than the circle could possibly, because the circle crosses the [illegible].

41. Mr. [illegible].—Are you able to give us the increase in acres and in valuation this proposed extension would give?—I could not tell you that just now. I [illegible] send you that information.

42. About how many residences would be taken in by the proposed mile boundary?—It would take in [illegible] gentlemen's seats and residences, including the railway premises.

43. That is the circle?—Yes.

44. Are there many occupiers of houses valued over [illegible] a year, who would be taken in by the circle—small farmers, and such people?—No ; the land [illegible] would be principally gentlemen's seats and residences, who derive full benefit from the proximity of the town.

45. Do those who would be brought within the municipal district by the proposed mile boundary consent to it?—Every one of them seems to it except Mr. W[illegible], and he has not either consented to or dissented from it. He simply said he would consider the matter.

46. Have you spoken to him lately on the subject?—Yes, very lately. Several parties who objected before have come in to say that, on a reconsideration of the question, they think that the proposed boundary is the only equitable arrangement that could be made.

47. It is your opinion that all the persons who live within the proposed boundary derive benefit from their proximity to the town?—Exactly as much as any residents in it.

48. Have the Town Commissioners considered whether it would be desirable that they should have the management of the roads, or do the Grand Jury do that work well?—There is a great and serious difference of opinion on that subject.

49. Is that amongst the Town Commissioners themselves or the inhabitants?—Well, Sir [illegible] has not yet quite expressed his approval of it, and his approval I look upon as very important.

50. Then there is a difference of opinion as to whether the management of the streets, roads, and such like, would be better done by the Grand Jury or the Municipal Body?—Yes. I may mention, however, that everyone living within the proposed boundary who goes to divine church, chapel, club, post office, or any other public building, gets the benefit of the [illegible] of the town. All those buildings are in the town.

51. Is it a fact that a great portion of the town through considerable [illegible] work [illegible]?—Yes, considerably.

52. I am told that through the [illegible] there is a sewer wanted?—Take, for instance, the upper part of the town, which embraces the Protestant and Roman Catholic churches, the Wesleyan chapel, the post office, the telegraph office, the club, the three banks, and three medical establishments, all is without a sewer.

53. Is that portion entirely without a main sewer?—Yes.

54. Are all the premises that you have named abutting on the public road or street?—All of them on the highway—in the heart of the main streets.

55. Would the persons living in the district that you propose to bring in derive much benefit from having the principal street with a proper sewer?—Yes. They must always pass that portion of the street when on their way to church, mass, or meeting, or the [illegible].

56. Is not the lower part of the town exposed to considerable floods, and would not that part want improving, too?—I think we have almost gone as far as nature will allow us in that direction, because the level of [illegible] is of that kind that you could not sink it deeper without having back-water.

57. Can you say what would be the increase of population by bringing in the increased area you propose?—I [illegible] what it is at present.—Our population at present is [illegible].

58. What would be the increase?—I think fully 1,[illegible].

59. Then you would be nearly up to the numbers which would entitle you to be made the Urban Sanitary [Authority]?—Yes. I can say that we are aware it would make us the Urban Sanitary Authority, because we have gone into it, as a matter of fact.

60. And then you would have the full control over the sewerage, &c., and then, the different [illegible] would have no objection to pay?—Just so.

61. Have you considered this matter in view of the provisions of the Public Health Act of last session?—I should say that I do not know whether I clearly understand your question when I said that the outsiders would have no objection to pay on [illegible] of our being made the Urban Sanitary Authority, because many of those people are guardians at present, and members of the [illegible] sanitary authority; and, of course, that would, to a great extent, operate on their minds in any decision they might come to. Therefore, I cannot say whether they would object or not.

62. Have you considered this—supposing you are made the Urban Sanitary Authority, and that the district that you propose to bring in, by the boundary you are now submitting, is brought in, that the parties [illegible] in that district will only pay rates on one-fourth of their valuation, including the sanitary rate?—I know that.

63. Is it your opinion that it would be advantageous for the town, even in that view, that the extension should take place?—Exactly; but subject to that, and in coming to that conclusion it would be necessary to consider how far you should extend the improvements beyond the present boundary.

64. That would be a thing that you would have to consider yourselves. It may be that there would be very little sanitary work, and not much sewerage or cleansing work to be done, as the extension would chiefly bring in gentlemen's demesnes?—That is a matter of law that I could not offer an opinion on, as to how far we would be bound to put lamps outside the present town. It is a question of law how far we would be bound to light the district.

65. Are there not gentlemen's residences within say 100 yards of this boundary you propose, that, by extending it zigzag a little, would be taken in, who derive as much advantage from the town as those within the boundary you propose, and would it not be advisable to include their places within the boundary?—I think the disadvantage that would arise from going out of the way to take them in would more than counterbalance any advantage that would arise by taking such places in.

66. Does the proposed boundary take in the workhouse?—Part of it. It runs under the workhouse.

67. Does it take in part of the ground?—It just goes underneath it. It does not take in the workhouse.

68. Mr. Cotton.—Does it not take in the workhouse or any part of the ground?—It goes under the angle of the wall.

69. There was some mistake just now when you answered a question and was under the impression I spoke of plough lands. Have you considered the question of extending the boundary by the townland boundary?—That is a matter that Mr. Lyons gave a great deal of attention to, and, unfortunately, I am not in a position to speak definitely as to the conclusions at which he arrived about it, because it was under his consideration the last time I saw him and spoke to him on the subject. He seemed to think that some advantage would be derived from following certain landmarks that practically would come within the circle, but that technically would be a little departure from it, either inside or out. If it would be of any assistance to you, I would send you his ideas on the matter.

70. Mr. Exham.—Could you get Mr. Lyons, or some one, to give us a map, showing the exact present boundary?—I can.

71. You say it differs a little from the Parliamentary boundary?—Yes, there is some little difference, but I do not know what it is.

72. As far as this map before us goes it is the same?—It is practically the same, but if you wish to get it exactly accurate I can have it so prepared for you.

73. On a large scale?—Yes.

74. And also the townland boundaries which Mr. Lyons proposes?—Yes; a map showing Mr. Lyons's proposition, by townland boundaries; one showing the parliamentary boundary, and one showing the municipal boundary.

Mr. Edward Nagle examined.

75. Mr. Exham.—You are acting for the Town Clerk here?—I am.

76. What is the present valuation of the town?—The last new valuation that I got from the Town Clerk's office books was dated the 2nd of December, 1871. At that date the valuation was £6,314 5s., but it has been considerably increased since on account of new buildings. The Clerk of the Union will tell you what the present valuation is.

77. What is the area of the town?—3,000a. 0r. 0p.

78. And how large is the parliamentary area?—That is the parliamentary area.

79. Well, then, what is the municipal area?—The parliamentary and municipal areas to my mind are the very same. Everything within the parliamentary and borough boundary was assessed with a borough rate.

80. You have heard of this proposed extension of a mile round?—I have.

81. What would be the area brought in by that proposed extension?—I have never considered that.

82. Nor the valuation?—Nor the valuation either. That would be a most difficult matter to ascertain.

83. But in some way we will have to ascertain it?—I know you will.

84. We must get it as nearly as we can?—When Mr. Rogers, the Town Clerk, comes back we can get it for you.

85. Do you know Mallow since the first public meeting was held about the boundaries in 1851?—Yes, I do.

86. Do you recollect when the boundaries were adopted by the people here?—The Town Commissioners adopted that boundary in 1854.

87. And there was a meeting of the Town Commissioners?—Yes, and there was a meeting of the town people, but it was defeated on account of some informality.

88. Is it the feeling of the town that that should be carried out still?—Yes, it is.

89. Or a mile radius, which is something analogous to it?—Either would be acceptable, because either would be considered fair.

90. Can you state whether or not it would be generally acceptable to those who would be brought in by it?—I cannot say.

91. But, from your knowledge of this place, do you think that the people within that area will derive substantial benefit from their proximity to the town, and so on?—Certainly.

92. Then we have it that that line—in fact, either of those boundaries, if adopted—would make this place an Urban Sanitary Authority?—Yes; either would make this town an Urban Sanitary Authority.

98. There is a great deal of difficulty in that, because in some places we have been shown that if you take a line you would be within fifty yards of a gentleman's house, who derives as much benefit from the town as those living in it?—Well, I would go round it. But that is the very danger of breaking the line.

99. I do not suppose that the area to be taken in would be a bit greater by Map A than by Map B?—I would not object to a boundary like that.

100. Would you yourself, for one, and the others living within an area of about a mile, object to be brought within the town?—I can only answer for myself. I have not talked the matter over with anyone.

101. Would you yourself object?—Not, if I am convinced that it's for the good of the town and the public at large.

102. Do not the people whose residences are outside the town come into the town to church, mass, club, and so on?—They do. I quite agree with the evidence of the person who deposed to that. I think a man ought to pay for what he gets, wherever he is.

103. Practically, if that circle which Mr. Priestley has suggested, and of which you expressed your approval to him, and, as it has been explained to you, were adopted, would you have any objection, or have you since changed the opinion you expressed to Mr. Priestley?—No, I have not changed my opinion, though it takes in my house. Either line will take in my house.

104. It must bring in a large additional taxation, for it will take in three miles of railway, and that has generally a very high valuation?—Yes.

105. The signing line excludes the upper mill, but Mr. Priestley's circle embraces the upper mill?—Yes.

106. There is one thing we must see to—how it will affect the electoral division?—I think the municipal boundary ought to be made a hard and dry line, if possible, and not favour anyone.

107. The English mile circle would be all within one parish—that is the one that strikes your back entrance year, Colonel Wilkinson—an English mile from the south-west angle of the barrack square?—Yes.

Mr. Nagle [illegible].

108. Mr. [illegible].—How much is the contribution from the town to the county?—About £510 for the [illegible]. It averages [illegible] in the pound, and we do not get £170.

109. Do you mean to say that there is not more than £170 expended on the town, on the roads, scavenging, &c.?—Yes. There is but one road [illegible] through the town—the [illegible] through the town [illegible] and that takes at 3s. 11d. a perch [illegible] to only [illegible] a year for 330 perches through the [illegible] about of the town. Then there is another mile of roads approaching the town—that is 330 perches, at [illegible] a perch—that would be about £75 or £80 a year. Those are the facts.

110. Do you say that all that is expended on the roads of the town is under £80?—It is not so much at all. We have not got lighting for years, because all the [illegible] lighting every direction has been made to [illegible].

Mr. John A. Newman examined.

111. Mr. Haman.—I believe you have taken an interest in this matter, as a Grand Juror?—Yes, I have a small property in the town; and I have been on the Grand Jury very often; and I have always found it to be the feeling of the Grand Jury that if Mallow was put under the Towns Improvement Act that they would be glad to get rid of it.

112. But if you put the town under the Towns Improvement Act you would not get rid of it?—Well, we would be very glad to get rid of it. There is a very extensive amount of paving done, and there are constantly recurring works which the Grand Jury have to carry out—such, for instance, as making roads along walls. We would be very glad to get rid of Mallow. I do not think the Grand Jury would view any attempt made to transfer their powers to the Municipal Body.

113. What is your opinion about the proposed mile boundary from the barrack square? You have property in the town. Have you considered the question of the extension of the boundary?—Really, my property in the town is so small that I would hardly like to express an opinion; but I may say that I think it is a very fair suggestion.

114. To take a mile all round?—Yes. Still it would only affect me slightly in comparison with some property out of which I derive a head rent. It would affect me slightly in regard to property outside the town that would be taken in; but, at the same time, I think it would be only fair to adopt the boundary suggested by Mr. Priestley.

Mr. Joseph Hanson examined.

115. Mr. [illegible].—You are one of the Town Commissioners of Mallow [illegible].

116. And have taken a very active interest in the municipal affairs of the town and its management?—Yes, as far as in my power.

117. Do you approve of the extension of the boundary, as proposed by Mr. Priestley, in one mile radius [illegible].

118. Do you, however, think it would be very questionable how far it would be for the advantage of [illegible] party, particularly of the town, if they were obliged to [illegible] all the advantages of lighting and watering, [illegible], and scavenging, to the entire proposed municipal boundary, inasmuch as the rates payable out of the new district, consisting of townparks and arable lands, and such like, being liable to only one-fourth of the valuation—would not be adequate to provide for those expenses?—Yes; that is my opinion.

The inquiry then terminated.

TRALEE.—MONDAY, DECEMBER 30TH, 1878.

(Before Mr. W. A. EXHAM, Q.C. Chairman.)

Mr. JAMES COFFEY examined.

1. You are the Clerk to the Town Commissioners of Tralee?—I am.

2. Are the municipal and the Parliamentary boundaries the same here?—They are.

3. There are no wards in the municipal district of Tralee?—No, sir.

4. In what electoral division is the town included?—In the electoral division of Tralee.

5. Are the municipal and the poor law boundaries as at present arranged coterminous?—No; the electoral division is very much larger.

6. What have been the poundage rates made for municipal, poor law and county purposes respectively, during each of the last five years?—They have been as follows:—

	Municipal.		Poor Law.		County.	
	s.	d.	s.	d.	s.	d.
1878, . .	2	9	2	8	2	10½
1877, . .	1	9	2	0	3	8
1876, . .	1	3	3	10	2	2½
1875, . .	1	9	2	4	2	0½
1874, . .	1	6	2	10	2	10½

7. How is the municipal rate made up—is it so much for each thing—or do you strike only one rate?—We strike but one rate. The sanitary rate is a uniform rate but the borough rate varies according to the valuation.

8. Can you say yourself from your knowledge as Town Clerk whether the present boundaries are looked upon with satisfaction or otherwise by the ratepayers or inhabitants of the town?—They are considered too small entirely.

9. And can you say whether or not the Town Commissioners agree in that opinion?—They do.

10. Unanimously?—Yes.

11. There are I believe waterworks being got for the town of Tralee at present?—Yes.

12. And a provisional order was made by the Local Government Board with respect to those waterworks?—Yes.

13. That provisional order been confirmed by an Act of Parliament?—Yes.

14. The provisional order was made on the 27th of February 1878—is not that so?—Yes.

15. And the Act of Parliament confirming it is the 41st and 42nd of Victoria, chapter 163?—Yes.

16. Under that Act have the boundaries of the town been increased for the purposes of the Tralee waterworks?—Yes.

17. What is the present municipal area?—431 acres.

18. And the valuation?—£12,185.

19. And the population?—9,353 according to the last census.

20. Can you tell me what was the acreage added under the Waterworks Act?—I think the valuation was £493.

21. And the area is forty acres and thirty perches and the annual valuation of these forty acres is £3 15s is it not?—Yes it is.

22. And the property liable to assessment will be £391 15s, and half the annual rents £5 and that brings out the total?—Yes, sir.

23. Are you able to state what extension of boundary the Commissioners as a body propose?—I suggest a two mile radius from the centre of the town—that is from the corner of Denny-street.

24. Can you give me any idea of how many houses—I mean such as gentlemen's residences—that would embrace?—I should say about twelve gentlemen's residences besides the town of Blennerville in which one gentleman also resides. The workhouse would also be taken in.

25. Can you tell me how many small farms would be taken in by the increased boundary?—I should say, about one hundred.

26. Of your own knowledge as Town Clerk have and in your opinion do the persons residing in that district—the district embraced by the two mile radius—derive considerable benefit from the use of the town?—Most certainly they do.

27. Do these small farmers bring their produce and dispose of it in the town, do they sell their milk, butter, eggs, and so forth in the town?—Yes they do; but those gentlemen residing in the villas derive more benefit from their proximity to the town than the small farmers.

28. But do not the small farmers derive considerable benefit from their contiguity to the town also?—To be sure they do.

29. And I suppose the value of their land is greater because of its proximity to the town?—Yes.

30. More especially is that the case because of Tralee being an assize town with all its attendant advantages?—Yes.

Mr. ROBERT M'COWEN examined.

31. You are, I believe, one of the Town Commissioners?—I am.

32. How long have you filled the position?—About seven years.

33. I believe, you are one of the largest ratepayers in the town?—I am.

34. Can you say whether there is a desire on the part of the ratepayers within the present borough that the area should be increased?—There is a very general desire that it should be increased.

35. To what extent to your own knowledge do the people of the town—those generally interested—the ratepayers—think the boundaries ought to be extended?—Well we had the matter under discussion for some time. We considered the question as to the desirability of three separate boundaries—a one mile, a two mile, and a three mile radius—and it appeared to be the general opinion that the medium one of the three would be the most desirable, and that two miles would be a very suitable radius as it would bring in the important buildings of the district—starting from the corner of Denny-street as the centre of the town.

36. Can you say from your knowledge, whether the people who live within that proposed radius—the gentry and poor people derive a substantial benefit from their proximity to and their use of the town?—I think they do; they derive a very great advantage in manure, and also in frosty weather, in being able to get water, for in some instances, the people come in a mile and a half to get water.

37. Are these the poorer classes?—The farmers send in their water-carts for the purpose.

38. That is from the small farmers using it, and sending in their produce, and so on?—Yes, certainly.

39. Is the land attached to the gentlemen's residences increased in value also, from its proximity to the town?—Yes.

40. And also from the facilities afforded of getting manure, and all that sort of thing?—Yes, they avail themselves of the town for these purposes. It would

be of advantage to the town if the boundary was increased, in a sanitary point of view also, I believe.

Tralee. Jan. [illegible]. Mr. Robert [illegible].

41. Were you considered at all these aspects of the question which at present the people outside the municipal boundary and within the area you propose to include, are attached to the rural sanitary district, and as such whether your bringing them in, and their only paying one-fourth of the taxation under the Act of Parliament, would make any difference in your opinion to the townspeople in reference to an extension of the boundary?—Under the Towns Improvement Act, if they are brought in, they will only pay one-fourth of the taxation. Have you considered that you might have to execute any sanitary works for them, which would saddle the town with an outlay, and for which they would not pay in a corresponding proportion, because they would only pay one-fourth?—I don't think that would make much difference. Very probably we would have to supply them with water in some places which would be an advantage to them. I suppose when we get the waterworks in, we can accommodate them better.

42. As far as you know, amongst the outsiders that would be taken in, in the proposed area, is there a feeling on their part against being taken in?—I never heard any expressed against it. I think it would be an advantage to them and an advantage to the town to have all under the same sanitary authority. There are a good many complaints of neglect in the sanitary arrangements outside the town, and while the neighbourhood would be served by the plan which we propose to them, and which would be of immense benefit, the sanitary arrangements are unsatisfactory, and the town is injured by the want of sanitary arrangements outside the town, and there are a great many complaints.

43. You think the having all under one sanitary authority, and that sanitary authority of course the governing body of the town, would be an advantage for both parties?—It would undoubtedly in a sanitary point of view. There are constant complaints of the want of sanitary arrangements, especially between here and Blennerville, where dead horses have been [illegible] and left exposed, and thus created a nuisance [illegible] public nuisance. The two sanitary authorities oppose each other. It is at times the town that the guardians will not interfere, and often a thing is left for days unattended, whereas if the place was all under one sanitary authority we would have all these nuisances attended to and the nuisance removed. At present it is outside the borough and our sanitary officers won't attend to it.

44. Will not the place you speak of be brought in under the Waterworks Act, even if the boundary was not extended under the present Commission?—It would not.

45. You know what the rates have been for the last few years in the town. In your opinion would the rates be increased or be likely to be increased by the addition to the municipal boundary that you propose?—Well, I would expect them to be lightened. It is for that purpose we wish to get the increase I have been speaking of. That would be one of the reasons in my opinion in favour of extending the boundary.

46. You yourself are of opinion that the two mile radius will afford a satisfactory boundary?—Yes; I think the two mile radius will bring in everything—will bring in all the important places, and it is near enough to the town.

Mr. John Lunham examined.

Mr. John Lunham.

47. You are one of the Town Commissioners of Tralee?—Yes.

48. And I believe you have been a Commissioner for a great many years?—Yes, for forty years.

49. You are I believe a large ratepayer in the town?—Yes, pretty large.

50. May I ask you is it your opinion that there should be an extension of the boundary of the municipal district?—It is my opinion that there should be an extension of the municipal boundary.

51. And do you agree that it should be to the extent of two miles?—I think up to two miles would be a desirable extension, just as you have been already told.

52. Of course we cannot have a hard-and-fast line—a mile?—No.

53. Is it your opinion from your knowledge of the town that the persons who live within that extension [illegible] derive substantial benefit from the town?—They have [illegible] of it. It is a [illegible] advantage; [illegible] advantages they enjoy.

54. And I suppose the letting value of the land is increased from its proximity to the town?—Yes, decidedly increased.

55. As far as you have heard and from your experience of this place, is there any hostility on the part of the people outside not to be brought in?—I don't think there is, nor indeed can I say there is not. I think they are apathetic about it. I need put my foot [illegible] when there is anything in the shape of additional taxation proposed, the people always [illegible] back, but there can be no question about it, that it would be of advantage, and of advantage to them too, because we would have a larger governing body. We would have a larger board to conduct the public affairs of the municipality and the public health would be better looked after; for in the town we have been kept back from carrying out works that we consider are desirable. We have a resolution on our books in favour of making public sewers in the town and we have been kept back for the want of water. There was no use in putting them up until we had the power of flushing them with water.

56. What you say then as far as I understand you, is that at present on account of the limited extent of the municipal area, you cannot in fact satisfactorily carry out the sanitary arrangements of the town?—Not so satisfactorily; certainly not.

Mr. Robert Denny examined.

Mr. R. Denny.

57. You are a civil engineer?—Yes.

58. And I believe Mr. Denny you are the engineer for the waterworks that are being constructed for the town?—I am.

59. And as such it was you who prepared the plan, bringing in Blennerville and the other places under the Waterworks Act?—Yes, sir.

60. I believe you are resident in Tralee?—Yes.

61. And you know the districts around well in consequence of the position you hold as an engineer?—Yes.

62. Is it your opinion that there should be an increase of the boundaries beyond what was done under the Waterworks Act?—I think so; and the people for two miles around derive a great deal of benefit from the town.

63. That is, not only the gentry, but the farmers and poor people?—Everyone who lives within two miles of the town derives a great deal of benefit from the proximity of the town.

64. You have marked out on map "A" in a blue line the boundary you would propose?—Yes.

65. This is following as nearly as possible townland

TRALEE
[illegible], 18[illegible].
—
Mr. S. Denny.

boundaries with roads as distinct marks?—Yes; equalising the two mile radius as nearly as possible by roads and townland boundaries.

[illegible]. From your knowledge of the locality can you say whether or not [illegible] of all the gentry that are within the two mile radius object to the proposed enlargement?—I did not hear any objection.

[illegible]. Do you think the farmers as far as you know would object to any increase of the town, as far as they are concerned?—Well, I cannot say; I have not consulted with any of them, but if you ask me for my opinion, I [illegible] to say that I do not think they would object.

[illegible]. Is it your opinion that the sanitary arrangements of the town would be benefited by such a change as that proposed?—Of course they would; they would be considerably benefited.

[illegible]. Now I want to know this; would you be able, when the water supply is got into the town, and supposing the extension of the boundary took place as proposed—would you be able to supply the places taken in with water?—Supposing the boundary is extended to two miles?

[illegible]. Yes.—I could not say; our scheme is not calculated for that. It would be tremendously expensive. When these people are only brought into the town, they are [illegible] only for the benefit they derive from the town. They cannot expect when they pay only one-fourth of the taxation to get water. They could not expect that.

[illegible]. There is a difference between this town and others, because you are not under the Towns Improvement Act. You are under the Act of George IV., and there there may be a question what the law on that would be. But what you say is this, according to your present scheme, the waterworks would not be able to supply the whole district?—I would not undertake it at all. We would have, even if our mains were large enough, to expend considerably more money.

[illegible]. What would you propose to do with regard to the lighting of that district?—I would give you just the same answer as I have given with regard to the water. I do not think they should expect to have the district lit [illegible]. I do not think that any one of them would care to pay for gas when they have the [illegible] of paraffin, which is so cheap now.

[illegible]. You are speaking of lighting used in the house, but I was referring to the lighting of the roads. Have you considered that at all—or, if you bring those people in, and they are made to pay towards the taxation, have you considered whether or not they will derive any advantage, whether they will for instance have the benefit of the gas mains along the roads?—I think the answer I gave about the water may [illegible] with equal force to the gas. They cannot expect to derive any benefit from the gas when they are only paying one-fourth of the taxation.

[illegible]. Well, supposing they were to pay the full amount of the taxation?—That is quite another question.

[illegible]. Would you think that the town would have to pay very largely then?—It would be very expensive laying gas pipes for that distance.

[illegible]. Do you think the townspeople would be satisfied to pay the then?—I don't think they would.

77. As far as you know, do the Town Commissioners propose to give the included districts—to give the people who would be brought within that extended area any advantages beyond what they now have?—I don't know what other advantage they would get by it. I think they have been gaining advantages in years past and that they are enjoying them now. We have got lighting in the town, [illegible], [illegible], and everything of that sort and they avail themselves of the advantages of these places.

[illegible]. And then you think it is [illegible] an advantage to them in proportion, as it is to the inhabitants of the town who have their houses abutting on the streets?—Of course it is.

—

Mr. Samuel Murray Denny.
Mr. SAMUEL MURRAY DENNY examined.

[illegible]. You are the agent for the Denny family here?—Yes.

[illegible]. I believe a very large portion of the Denny estate would be taken in by this increased boundary?—Yes, and some other property that I am agent for also.

[illegible]. As far as you know do the gentry for whom you are agent object to this proposed extension?—No, they think it fair that they should pay the same taxes as other people, as their fair proportion of them, for the town of Tralee from which they reap a good deal of benefit.

[illegible]. Do you approve of the proposed boundary as marked on the map by Mr. Denny?—I think that is a fair extension. The taxation of the town of Tralee [illegible] is frightfully high, and the people in the neighbourhood of the town of Tralee get the benefit of these, and they pay nothing for it.

[illegible]. As far as you know the farmers on those estates [illegible] you are agent—would they object to this extension?—Very likely. I must mention, in connection with the [illegible] of the number, that Sir Edward Denny is one of the largest owners of property.

[illegible]. Even if you extended the boundary to a mile, are these living between the one mile and the two mile radius deriving as much benefit from the town as those living in the town?—I think it would be very unfair to carry the municipal area out only one mile, and not two miles. I think that would be very unfair.

—

Mr. Stephen Huggard.
Mr. STEPHEN HUGGARD examined.

[illegible]. You are a solicitor residing in the town of Tralee for a great many years?—Yes; I was a Town Commissioner for a long time, and I am now the Solicitor to the Town Commissioners.

[illegible]. I ask you as a resident here, is it your opinion that the boundary of the town should be increased?—Well, I think it ought to be increased.

[illegible]. In other words, whether or not do the lands lying immediately close to the town get exceptional value from their contiguity to the town, and from the facilities which the owners of those lands enjoy in the town for the disposal of their produce, and so on?—I think they do, and I have known occasions when gentlemen have been very anxious to make out that their lands outside the borough of Tralee were town-fields and town-parks, so as to exempt them from the operation of the Land Act.

[illegible]. Have you considered the extent to which the adjoining lands derive benefit from their proximity to the town?—Yes, I was a party to the laying out of the boundary as indicated on map "A."

[illegible]. Do you agree that a boundary taken in this way following the outline map "A" would be a fair one?—Do you think that boundary would be a fair one? In some places it would be a little outside, and in others a little inside the circle—if the blue line on map "A" is followed?—I think that that would be a very fair boundary.

[illegible]. If there is any alteration of the boundary at all, you would not have a circle because it would right little [illegible], and upset the valuation altogether. Your opinion is that, if there is any alteration at all, the one marked out by the blue line on the map I have shown you would be the most expedient one?—I think the extent indicated on the map you refer to could be very fairly taken into the borough of Tralee.

91. And that the people living within that increased area fairly ought to pay something towards the taxation of the town?—I think they ought to contribute to the taxation of the town.

92. Do you think the sanitary arrangements of the town would be improved at all by taking this district into the town, and having all as one urban sanitary authority, and not having a rural sanitary authority out here?—I think it would be very well to have a defined area surrounding the town all included in the one district, and ——

93. And to have the sanitary authority of the town the sanitary authority of the whole district?—Yes; I think it would be well to have them.

94. Do you think that the parties whom it is proposed to annex would be quite willing to be annexed?—I don't think they would.

95. I suppose not on account of having to pay some of the taxation?—Yes.

Tralee, Dec. [illegible]

Mr. [illegible] Hayward.

Mr. S. M. Hussey re-examined.

Mr. S. M. Hussey.

96. Can you tell me whether the proposed extension would make the municipal district all in one electoral division?—It would not. It would be impossible to have any substantial increase of the area of taxation of the town at present that would be advantageous, to be confined to one electoral division, with any regard to the question of equity.

97. How many electoral divisions would this proposed line fall in?—Five; portions of the proposed boundary would be in five electoral divisions besides Tralee:—Ballymacelligott(?), Dooa, Clogherbrien, Annagh, and Rathass, besides Tralee. The present municipal boundary is all within the electoral division.

Major William Brown, J.P., examined.

Major William Brown, J.P.

98. I believe you are Chairman of the Tralee Board of Guardians, and live at [illegible], in the district that is proposed to be annexed?—Yes.

99. You are living at present within about 300 yards of the present boundary?—Yes; I am very close to the present boundary, about 300 yards outside of it. I object to being included in the municipal area, and being, as a natural consequence, subjected to increased taxation, for which I think we will get no return whatever. It has been acknowledged by Mr. [illegible] that we cannot be lighted or cleansed, and the waterworks are [illegible] benefit [illegible] the water cannot be brought to us. The only advantage that appears to me to be offered to us is that we shall have an urban sanitary authority instead of a rural sanitary authority.

100. Don't you think all the houses included in the district proposed to be annexed derive exceptional advantages from their proximity to the town?—I think they derive some advantage, certainly. I must say that.

101. They use the roads of the town for all purposes?—They do.

102. As Chairman of the Board of Guardians, is it your opinion that the sanitary work would be better done if the powers were transferred to the governing body of the town?—I don't think it would, because I do not think the urban sanitary authority would have time to extend its labours to the large district now proposed to be included.

103. There is a very large number of small farmers, of course, within this proposed district. Do you think the value of the land is, and the value of the buildings are, increased by their proximity to the town, and their consequent advantages in the tenants being able to sell their milk, butter, vegetables, and all those things?—To some extent it is.

104. Then on a differential rate, is it your opinion this [illegible] portion of this outlying district should be taxed, [illegible] supposing it was taxed at a lower rate—"If you cannot give water, and gas, and all [illegible] things we should not be taxed the same as the people in the town." Is it your opinion that there should be a differential tax on [illegible] as compared with the town?—Well, in my opinion, that should be very small. I do not think that a man living two miles from the town has at all the advantage that would be supposed from his proximity to the market. A man living within one mile would have, to a certain extent, a market garden; but the other would not.

105. Have you any idea where, for instance, the [illegible] who supply the [illegible], the gaol, [illegible] I suppose, other public institutions—with milk, and those sort of things?—I think the [illegible] of them are [illegible] the boundary.

106. In one of the towns in which we sat all the great contractors to the public institutions lived outside the town, and had all the benefit of the town, and derived great benefits from their contracts, without contributing to the taxation of that town?—That is very likely. I do not think two or three miles distance is any bar to their supplying those institutions.

107. From the statement of some of the houses in the district proposed to be annexed I should fancy that they would be able to get the benefit of the water supply?—Yes, for my own house, and perhaps two or three more; but as to the public in those two or three townlands benefiting by the water supply, that is quite out of the question. The people in this townland have to resort to a [illegible] outside the town for their water for domestic purposes.

108. But I suppose that will be remedied when you get your water supply for the town?—Yes; I suppose so.

109. You heard it said to-day, I suppose, that even before the appointment of this Municipal Boundaries Commission was thought of at all, it had been [illegible] in the town by the Town Commissioners that there ought to be an extension of the boundary?—I have heard it, in a general way, but not with a view to this immediate inquiry.

110. Can you say whether there has been any objection raised to such a proposal?—I think there is a decided objection to it on the part of residents, and at the time of the [illegible] extension of the boundary, even to the extent of the [illegible] limit, there was [illegible] by Mr. [illegible], and there was great opposition to that proposed extension.

111. [illegible] the opposition [illegible] Mr. [illegible] the extension [illegible]?—[illegible] the part I mean. [illegible] was proposed to be included, and the [illegible] townlands of [illegible] and [illegible] were proposed to be included in the [illegible], but the [illegible] did not sanction the bringing in of those townlands. Indeed, I think they withdrew the proposal to include those townlands at the inquiry, on account of the opposition shown to it.

112. Have you given this matter any consideration at all?—At present the roads through the town are all managed by the county?—Yes.

113. Of course, you being the Urban Sanitary Authority, could get the management of the roads. Do you think it would be of advantage to the town if there was the inclusion of the area that is proposed, and if the town then took up the management of all the roads and the sanitary work and cleansing, and it all ought all that to be done by one body?—I don't think it would be possible that this should be so. Some time ago there was a proposition that the Town Commissioners should be the commissioners for the [illegible] of Tralee, but they declined. They cannot [illegible]

Tralee.

but they do not repair them. The divided authority is decidedly a disadvantage; but they were offered the opportunity of getting money as contractors under the county, but they declined to do it.

114. Mr. M'Cartan.—On two or three occasions the Town Commissioners applied to the Grand Jury to take up the management of the roads, and to exempt the borough from taxation, and the Grand Jury refused, and vetoed the application.

Mr. Thomas O'Regan.

Mr. Thomas O'Regan examined.

115. You are one of the Town Commissioners here?—I am.

116. And have you been on the Municipal Board for some time?—Yes.

117. Is it your opinion, and that of your brother Commissioners, as far as you know, that an extension of the borough is desirable?—Yes; I always heard them express that very strongly, and my reason for considering so is, that I am thoroughly convinced that a man living within a mile or a mile and a half or two miles derives an advantage from the town. I know nearly every one of them, and I see them mostly in the town as early and late as the inhabitants themselves, and they dispose of all they have in the town, and if the town is to be properly cleansed I think they should contribute to it, as they derive such advantages from its success.

118. I suppose they help to dirty them?—Yes, and the people of Tralee should not pay for their accommodation. They should get a little help.

119. Have you seen the proposed boundary, as marked on Map "A"?—I have seen it.

120. Do you think that would be a fair boundary, as far as we can adhere to it?—I know every single inch of the ground all round about the town.

121. Do you think this proposed line would be a fair line—the blue line in Map "A"?—I think so.

122. With regard to the sanitary matters, is it your opinion that the sanitary arrangements of the town would be improved in this extended area, by bringing this township portion in from the Rural to the Urban Sanitary Authority?—I think so.

123. As a Town Commissioner, knowing the town, is it your opinion that the work would be better done if it was all under the one individual authority?—Certainly.

124. And if you had the management yourselves of the roads?—Yes, certainly. It will be always a nuisance until the Commissioners get the management of the roads themselves. Any man looking at those roads will see that he should get a pair of cow-boots to cross them in wet weather. There is £1,000 a year going to the Grand Jury, and we get nothing. Their mode of repairing the roads consists of putting a handful of rocks on a road one day, and that is scraped off the next by the scavenger.

Mr. Coffey.

Mr. Coffey re-examined.

125. How much do you spend annually in cleansing and lighting?—About £250.

126. How much can you raise by taxation?—Part of the sum I have named is from the benefit derived from the making of the gas.

127. How much can you raise by taxation?—About £900.

Mr. John Shea.

Mr. John Shea examined.

128. You live at Blennerville?—Yes.

129. At present you are out of the area of taxation except for water?—Yes. I consented to the water, because I thought it most necessary, and it is all that is wanted.

130. Tell me, don't you think the town of Blennerville—the people living in that district—derive a great advantage from being so close to the town?—What advantage do we get? I cannot see that we get any advantage.

131. Have you not got the shops and all those conveniences in the town of Tralee at which you can purchase the things you want for your house, or for your business, if you are in business?—The shopkeepers in the town of Tralee are very glad to have us go to them.

132. But you are very glad to have them to go to as well, and beyond that, too, there are the roads going into the town?—But we pay county cess for them.

133. But don't you think, as an inhabitant of Blennerville, that your business and your place is more valuable than it would be if you had no town between you and Killarney, for example, in which to buy your things?—Conscientiously I can say no. Speaking for myself, conscientiously I can give that answer, because I never buy anything either here or there.

134. Is it not a fact that you derive your usual income from Tralee?—Yes—well, from the canal basin and harbour.

135. Don't you consider that Blennerville is substantially part and parcel of Tralee, with the canal, quay, and shipping coming up to it, and boats and all that sort of thing?—I suppose it is a suburb; but I don't think you can call it anything else.

136. How many houses are there at Blennerville?—About thirty.

137. What are their ratings? Are they all above £3 or £5 in rating value?—They are about £4, £5, and £6 on one side, and £4 or £3 on the other. There is a large mill-house and some stores there.

138. Is it the case that a number of persons doing business by day in Tralee live out at Blennerville?—Only three persons.

139. Are the houses at Blennerville occupied by shopkeepers?—There are five shops on the right-hand side and one on the left.

140. I suppose they supply themselves from Tralee?—Yes, I suppose they do.

141. There are some public-houses there, too, are there not?—I have included them; I call them shops.

142. I suppose the real reason for your opposition to an extension of the boundary is that you are afraid of having additional taxes put on you?—Most decidedly. I care as little about that as anyone else, but I don't consider that it's necessary, or that any advantage will be derived by the inhabitants of Blennerville by the change. As for telling me that Blennerville will be cleansed by being joined to Tralee—as for talking about that, it's all a mistake; it will never be done.

143. Don't you think it's an advantage to the persons living at Blennerville if they could have Tralee nicely kept? If you are walking yourself, would you not like to walk on a clean street instead of a dirty one?—But they will never do anything right here. It is not in their composition to do anything right.

144. You have no gas supply at Blennerville?—No.

145. Do you think, supposing you were brought within the municipal area, just the same as anyone living in the town, and you got the gas, and paid no more for the gas than the townspeople, and had to pay no more than the townspeople in the way of taxes—don't you think there would be advantages?—I don't think they would. I think burning petroleum is cheaper than gas.

146. You don't think, with the present price of petroleum, you would get any benefit from the gas being brought to you?—I do not. We have a far cheaper light. It is a hundred per cent. cheaper than gas.

The inquiry then terminated.

DUNGARVAN, Dec. 31, 1878.

DUNGARVAN—DECEMBER 31st, 1878.

Before Messrs. W. P. O'Brien and C. P. Cotton.

Mr. Edward Murphy examined.

Mr. E. Murphy.

1. Mr. O'Brien.—You are Clerk to the Town Commissioners?—Yes.
2. How long have you been so?—Since 1865.
3. This town is constituted under the Towns Improvement Act?—Yes, the Act of 1854.
4. In what year was the Act adopted here?—In January, 1856.
5. What was the exact date of the adoption of the Act?—18th January, 1856.
6. Had the town been previously under the provisions of the 9th of George IV.?—No.
7. What was the area of the town then?—Just as at present.
8. What was the acreage?—I cannot give it.
9. What is the valuation?—£4,899 10s.
10. In the returns furnished to you last year it was £4,944, but there was apparently difference—5,747 acres is given as the area?—Yes, that is about it.
11. Have you a record of the boundary at the time the town was fixed?—No, I have not a copy of the document to the Lord Lieutenant.
12. You have not the Lord Lieutenant's answer?—No, sir.
13. You have no record of the boundary?—No, sir.
14. How many townlands are comprehended within the municipal area?—Several small townlands.
15. Including some townlands?—Yes.
16. What is the number of townlands within the municipal boundary?—There are forty-eight townlands and parts of townlands.
17. How many townlands are included entirely, and how many partly within the municipal district?—Thirty-five whole townlands.
18. And how many are partly included?—Eight partly.
19. Then, there are eight cases where townlands are cut?—Yes.
20. Does the area extend pretty equally in all directions from the centre of the town?—Yes.
21. What is the radius—taking as the point to measure from—the centre of the town?—The present municipal district is about one mile.
22. One mile to each side?—Yes, sir.
23. Are you aware what was the principle followed in forming the boundaries?—I am not aware.
24. But it is about a mile in all directions?—Yes.
25. The Act was adopted for all purposes?—I think so.
26. Was it adopted for the water supply?—I have no record.
27. You are not aware whether it was adopted for the water supply?—No, sir.
28. The Town Commissioners are the sanitary authority?—Yes, sir.
29. Have the Commissioners also obtained a Local Act in addition?—Yes.
30. What was the date of it?—August, 1868.
31. What was the title of the Act?—The Dungarvan Harbour and Improvement Act, 1868.
32. What were the various purposes for which it made provision?—To take the roads out of the Grand Jury, to improve the harbour, and to take in markets.
33. Now, as regards the transfer of the Grand Jury powers, what were the functions that were transferred?—The care of the roads and bridges within the borough.
34. And the footpaths?—Yes, everything connected with the roads and bridges.
35. And the public works?—Yes.
36. Were the court-houses, &c., transferred?—No, sir.
37. Then, it was just the roads and bridges?—Yes, that is all.
38. I presume the municipal district includes a good deal of arable land?—Yes, it does.
39. You are aware that under the Towns Improvement Act, section 60, in the levying of rates all arable lands, meadow or pasture land, all market gardens, &c., shall be assessed at only one-fourth annually?—Yes, I am aware of that.
40. I am anxious to ascertain whether, under the Local Act by which the care of the roads, and bridges, and footpaths was transferred, the expense of keeping up the various works previously maintained by the Grand Jury was assessed only at one-fourth on the arable lands?—Lands and buildings under that Act of 1868 are assessed at the same rate.
41. Then you don't adhere to the one-fourth?—No.
42. And all the purposes provided for before by the Grand Jury are assessed at the same rate?—Yes.
43. And the limitation of one-fourth only applies to the Towns Improvement Act purposes?—Yes.
44. What is the arrangement with the Grand Jury—do they the rate, and you pay the same for county purposes?—No, they levy a rate for all purposes. We only levy for repairing the roads.
45. The small public works for which they have provided?—Yes.
46. In what electoral division is the municipal district of Dungarvan included?—In the electoral division of Dungarvan.
47. What is the area of the electoral division?—I don't know.
48. Nor how many townlands are included?—No.
49. I presume the electoral division is considerably larger than the municipal area?—Much larger.
50. To what extent does the electoral division extend from the centre of the town?—I dare say about a mile and a half or two miles.
51. This is more than two miles?—I can't say exactly, but I think not.
52. Have the Commissioners had under consideration the questions submitted to them by our Board, whether it is desirable that the existing municipal district should be extended, limited, or otherwise altered?—They had, sir.
53. How many Commissioners are there?—Fifteen.
54. Was it considered at a special meeting?—No, only at an adjourned meeting.
55. Was the meeting adjourned for that purpose?—It was not.
56. How many Commissioners were present when the matter was considered?—Nine or ten.
57. What was the date of that meeting?—14th November. It was adjourned that day, and they did not come to any decision.
58. Were you able to gather what were the views of the nine or ten present on that occasion?—Some of them were against the town coming at all, and others were.
59. As far as you understand, the feeling was that they did not wish to have any change at all?—Yes.
60. They were satisfied?—Yes.
61. What have been the rates made during the last five years, and what were the purposes for which they were made?—I will tell you by a account.
62. The town is lighted with gas?—It is.
63. How is the gas supplied—is it by the Commissioners themselves, or do they contract for the supply of the public lights?—They contract with a private company.

DUNGARVAN. Dec. [illegible]

Mr. E. [illegible]

64. It is by contract with the gas company?—Yes.

65. What is the improvement rate at present?—It has always been 1s.

66. It has always been so?—Every year, as long as I am here.

67. What are the purposes for which the rate is levied?—Lighting the town and paying the salaries of the officers.

68. Have you had any sanitary expenditure for the construction of sewers or for water supply?—No; we never made a sanitary rate. The sanitary expenses are paid out of the 1s rate.

69. You have undertaken no large sanitary works?—No.

70. Water supply nor sewerage?—No, sir.

71. The sanitary expenditure has been supplied by the shilling rate?—Yes.

72. As regards the roads that were transferred by the Act of 1863, how are they provided for?—There is a shilling rate, I think, for the last three years.

73. In addition to the other rate?—Yes, sir.

74. You call it a road rate?—Yes.

75. Is it levied with the other?—No.

76. You levy it by separate warrant altogether?—Yes.

77. There is a provision for that in the local Act?—Yes.

78. Is that the highest rate you ever had?—No; we had a 2s. rate at one time.

79. Your powers are unlimited?—They are limited to 2s.

80. You could make a rate for road purposes of 2s. and nothing more?—Yes, under special circumstances, we can make it 2s. 6d.

81. Just look at the section of the Act, and then you will be able to answer exactly?—Yes, sir; there is special power given, under a section of the Act, to make the rate 2s. 6d. where two-thirds of the ratepayers and Commissioners agree.

82. Then, since 1863, the annual rate for road purposes has been 1s, except one year?—It was 2s. one year, and it came down next year to 1s. 6d., and next year to 1s. 6d., and next year to 1s. 4d.

83. And when did it come down to the 1s.?—About three years ago.

84. Then, for the last three years it has stood at 1s.?—Yes.

85. And that is ample for doing the work effectually?—Yes, I think so.

86. Have any sanitary works been abandoned from or put aside from a feeling that the pressure on the ratepayers would be too heavy if they were undertaken—works, for instance, which were necessary for the sewerage or water supply?—Yes; they contemplated a water supply lately.

87. When?—It is just in hands.

88. Then a scheme is under consideration?—Yes.

89. Is it much required for the town?—Well, I should say it is.

90. The Commissioners think there is necessity for an improved water supply for the town?—Yes.

91. It is expected the scheme will involve a considerable expense?—Yes; very large expense.

92. What is expected to be the cost?—From £10,000 to £12,000.

93. That would make a considerable addition to the rate?—Yes.

94. Can you say it will cost £10,000 or £12,000? What do you base that estimate on?—On the estimate of the engineer.

95. Who was that?—Mr. Foster.

96. When was that estimate prepared?—About twelve months ago.

97. Was there a provisional order obtained?—Yes.

98. And that was ratified by Parliament?—Yes.

99. Then, there is an Act in existence authorising it?—Yes.

100. What was the estimate given when applying for the provisional order?—£10,000.

101. You are speaking of round numbers?—Yes, about £10,000.

102. Then they have taken no step yet to give effect to that Act?—No, sir.

103. When did it receive the consent of Parliament?—Last August.

104. The matter is under consideration now?—Yes.

105. And it is about to be effected?—Yes. There was a resolution passed in December, 18[illegible], by the Commissioners asking for a loan of £10,000 from the Board of Works. That resolution has been rescinded by a majority of the Commissioners yesterday.

106. What was the object?—To stop the waterworks.

107. Then, practically, they have rescinded the scheme, and abandoned the intention of proceeding with it at all?—Yes.

108. What has led to that—is it an apprehension of the expense?—Yes; it is apprehension of the expense.

109. It is not from any alteration in their views as to the necessity of the works?—No; some parties are for water and some against it.

110. Were they unanimous in rescinding the resolution?—Ten Commissioners met, three left, and the seven who remained were unanimous.

111. And the three who had left were against it?—They had not expressed an opinion in favour of it.

112. Notice had been given of that meeting?—Yes.

114. The seven who remained were unanimous, and the three who had left were against rescinding the resolution?—Yes.

115. You say there are fifteen members of the municipal body?—Yes.

116. How many persons within the district are eligible to fill the office of Commissioner?—I could not state the number except from the books.

117. You could make it out for us?—Yes.

118. Do you know how many electors there are within the municipal district?—I do.

119. Outside this radius of a mile, are there many inhabited houses the occupiers of which derive, in your opinion, some substantial advantages from their proximity to such a town as Dungarvan, in the way of having a market for supplying their wants at hand, and a market for the disposal of various forms of agricultural produce—having schools for their children to attend. Would you consider that there are lands outside that radius that participate, to some extent, in these advantages?—Yes, I think there are.

120. You think the mile doesn't cover all the people who derive advantage from their proximity to the town?—Well, I should say not. The people come to market from five or six miles.

121. Of course, the persons living within a mile and a half derive more advantage than the people living five or six miles off?—Yes.

122. Do the people in the country attend the town schools largely?—Yes.

123. What schools are there?—There are three or four public schools in the town.

124. From how far would you say the children are in the habit of resorting to the town for the purpose of attending schools?—From about two miles.

125. Would that be the limit?—Yes. I know there are National schools at a distance of about two miles from the town.

126. Then what is the limit from which you would say children are in the habit of resorting to the town schools?—I could not well tell.

127. But as far as you have been able to form an estimate?—I have seen some come more than a mile from the town.

128. What schools are?—The Christian Brothers' and two Convent schools, and one school for boys.

129. Are these all largely attended?—I should say so.

130. A good many come from the rural districts?—A great many of them.

131. Now, do you know whether the formation of

MINUTES OF EVIDENCE.

[illegible] electoral division [illegible] the centre of the [illegible]?—I think it goes further in the southerly [illegible] than in the northerly direction.

132. How far does it extend to the south?—About [illegible], or say two and a half.

133. And how far to the north?—[illegible] and a half.

134. And to the west?—About one mile.

135. And to the east?—[illegible] in [illegible] the [illegible] is in the sea.

136. If the electoral division was considered [illegible] as the municipal boundary, in the [illegible] of [illegible], would you say that the persons within [illegible] derive [illegible] advantages from their proximity to the town?—Yes, I should say so, for they come to [illegible] to the [illegible].

137. [illegible] electoral division [illegible] Dungarvan?—Yes.

138. [illegible] keeping up [illegible] works [illegible] by [illegible]?—They are done by the Commissioners. [illegible]; they have a borough surveyor.

139. What salary does he receive?—£50 a year.

140. Do they contract for the [illegible] of the [illegible]?—They do, [illegible] them by the work, and pay them by contract [illegible] they [illegible] the roads, and [illegible] and [illegible] by the yard; but the [illegible] to be paid by the day.

141. Are you able to say whether the cost of keeping up these works [illegible] or less than, when the [illegible] in the Grand Jury?—I don't know what was the cost in the Grand Jury.

142. And you are not in a position to state whether they [illegible]?—I [illegible].

143. Are you [illegible] works are done [illegible] by the Commissioners [illegible]?—I should say they are.

144. So far as you know, [illegible] the public are satisfied with the change which was made, transferring the works, and that it has had a salutary effect [illegible] of that opinion, and others [illegible].

145. What is the general feeling on the subject?—As far as I know, [illegible] the roads are kept in very good order now.

146. Were they kept up formerly?—Well, I don't know exactly.

147. How many miles of road are there comprised in the town?—[illegible] or ten miles, I should say.

148. [illegible]?—I [illegible] tell you [illegible] the [illegible] had [illegible] roads [illegible] was [illegible].

149. In the [illegible] roads and roads?—Yes. In 1869, when the Commissioners took them out of the hands of the [illegible], the cost was £294 1s. [illegible]; in 1870 [illegible] £[illegible]; in 1872 it was £[illegible]; in 1873 it was £[illegible]; in 1874 it was £[illegible]; in 1876 it was £[illegible]; in 1877, £[illegible]; and in 1878, £[illegible]. I have not got the cost in 1879.

150. You mentioned that the [illegible] had been [illegible], and that they gradually [illegible] that [illegible] the last three years they reached the uniform [illegible]?—The Commissioners were greatly [illegible] and they had to pay [illegible] for the special [illegible], and that was charged.

151. Then, it was owing to special expenses, and not to [illegible] the keeping of the roads?—[illegible] they [illegible], and they had to [illegible], which cost £[illegible].

152. When [illegible] that [illegible]?—I think 1871 or 1872; a high tide [illegible] and knocked down the wall.

Mr. JOHN DOYLE examined.

Mr. John Doyle.

153. Mr. O'BRIEN.—You are Clerk of Dungarvan Union?—Yes, sir.

154. How long have you been Clerk?—For ten years.

155. [illegible] the municipal district?—[illegible] area [illegible] 12,[illegible] acres [illegible].

156. What is the valuation?—£[illegible].

157. The townlands have been [illegible] given by Mr. [illegible] agree with him. I think that the total number of townlands in the electoral division [illegible].

158. [illegible] within the borough thirty-one [illegible] within the [illegible] and [illegible].

159. There are forty-two within the [illegible] division, either wholly or in part?—There are nine partly within and partly without, and the [illegible] are wholly [illegible].

160. How many townlands are included in the electoral division?—Eighty-three.

161. What is the area of the electoral division?—[illegible] 2r. [illegible]p.

162. What is the valuation?—£[illegible] 5s.

163. Does the electoral division extend pretty equally from the centre of the town?—No, it runs [illegible].

164. In what direction does it go furthest?—To the north.

165. How far to the north?—About three miles; [illegible].

166. [illegible] electoral [illegible]?—Yes, I think so. About three and a half to [illegible].

167. To the south how far does it extend?—About two and a half miles.

168. And to the [illegible] how far?—About two miles.

169. And to the east?—There is nothing to the east.

170. We have it already stated that the radius of the town is about a mile?—Yes.

171. That is about correct?—Yes.

172. And it extends pretty equally in all directions?—Yes.

173. Would you consider that outside that radius there are many inhabited places, the occupiers of which, in your opinion, derive advantages from being within that proximity to the town?—I do, sir.

174. How far out would the radius of benefit [illegible]?—[illegible] about two and a half miles.

175. You think they derive advantages in that district?—They do.

176. What would be the advantages they derive?—From my own knowledge and experience I know of persons coming to school from a distance of more than two and a half miles.

177. From what direction?—In all directions.

178. Are there any other advantages you consider they derive?—Of course they are near the town for the purpose of markets.

179. Persons living within two and a half miles of the town can derive greater advantages than those living at a greater distance away?—Yes, and [illegible]. They have opportunities of [illegible] and so on.

180. And have the market for the sale of poultry, butter, eggs, and so on?—Yes.

181. And [illegible] what are called [illegible], or accommodation lands, held by persons living in the town?—There are not.

182. Would the inclusion of this boundary for two and a half miles bring in many additional persons [illegible] from [illegible] in the town [illegible]

You will increase the valuation over £4,000 if you enlarged the area to two and a half miles.

183. What would the increased area be?—About 4,389 acres.

184. You are aware that under the Towns Improvement Act arable land, meadow land, market gardens, and lands used for such purposes, are only liable to rates on one-fourth of the valuation?—Yes; I am aware of that.

185. Would that be a fair measure of the advantages they receive?—I think it is only fair that arable land should not be called upon to pay so much, because people living in the town derive more advantages.

186. Do you consider that if the electoral division was adopted, it would be going to far?—I would. I would not be in favour of making the electoral division coterminous with the proposed municipal boundary.

187. Why?—I think it goes too far in a southerly direction.

188. And it would include persons who could not derive advantages?—I don't think they could derive as much as other persons.

189. And you think two and a half miles would not be excessive?—No; and I would be in favour of having the natural boundaries made.

190. What do you call natural boundaries?—Suppose there was a little stream at two or two and a half miles, I would agree to have that fixed as the boundary.

191. Would you agree to have townland boundaries adhered to?—They are not sometimes satisfactory.

192. And you would not lay down a hard and fast rule as to townlands as boundaries?—No.

193. You think townlands might operate inconveniently?—I am not prepared to give an answer as to that question.

194. But you think it is better to have a known denomination to deal with?—Yes.

195. And you don't think it would be desirable to have townlands inflexibly followed?—No.

196. Could you point to any instance where there would be an objection to the adoption of the townland?—Well, at Killongford, in the southerly direction, I find a road passes through the centre of that townland; and if you make that townland the municipal boundary, of course the Commissioners would be responsible for the road, and persons living very close to that road would derive as much advantage as persons living within the boundary.

197. But still a line must be drawn somewhere, and, of course, it would be impossible to draw any line where what you say would not, to some extent, apply?—Of course circumstances must guide you in making the boundary.

198. But don't you think it would facilitate matters if a well known denomination, such as a townland, was followed as a unit of organization?—I do.

199. You are aware that under the Poor Law townlands cannot be divided?—Yes.

200. Are you in a position to know whether local opinion would be favourable to an extension of the boundary?—The opinion appears to be divided on the subject.

201. The Board of Guardians have not entertained the question?—No. Of course, the opinion formed is very much influenced by the way people would be affected by the proposed extension. Those who would be injuriously affected are against it, and those benefited by it are for it. The question is whether more would be improved and benefited than would be injured.

202. Putting aside the question of personal interest and dealing with it as a question of general policy and equity, do you consider that the existing boundary should fairly be extended so as to include a larger number than at present?—I do.

203. Can you state the number of persons in the municipal district who are eligible for the office of town commissioner?—I don't know.

204. Can you say how many electors there are in the municipal district?—I can't say.

205. Or what number would be included if you took a radius of two and half miles?—I cannot give any information on that question.

206. Would you be able to furnish a return containing the information I ask on these points?—I don't think I would, for I think it belongs more to the town clerk's office than mine.

207. He has only the municipal district to deal with?—Well, the outside I would be able to give a return for.

208. Have you got a list of all the townlands I—I have (produces list). I have given the townlands and parts of townlands within the municipal district with the valuation.

Mr. JOHN MAHONY, Chairman, Dungarvan Town Commissioners, examined.

209. Mr. O'BRIEN.—How long have you been chairman of the Commissioners?—Twelve months.

210. And how long have you been a Commissioner?—Twelve months last October.

211. Have you been present at any meeting when the question of the extending or altering the boundary has been under consideration by the Commissioners?—Not exactly under consideration of the Commissioners.

212. It has not been formally taken into consideration?—There was a meeting called for yesterday, and these queries came before the meeting, and the consideration of them fell through.

213. And up to the present the question has not been formally considered?—No, sir.

214. Have you no means of knowing what is the feeling of the Commissioners, whether they are in favour of the extension or otherwise?—I am certain of nine being for it.

215. But as regards the other six?—I don't know.

216. Have you the full complement of fifteen Commissioners at present?—I don't know exactly.

217. Do the Commissioners contemplate holding a meeting for the purpose of considering the question?—Yes. A meeting was called for yesterday, and ten came and three went away, and we did not consider the matter, and it was left to me to do anything I wished; and I knew the mind of those present, and I did not do anything.

218. But the feelings of the nine were against making any change?—Yes.

219. What were the grounds of objection they appeared to entertain?—The chief ground was the additional taxation. We considered we were already heavily taxed.

220. Would it not rather have the effect of lightening taxation?—No; it would bring in twenty-five miles additional roads, and at £43 per annum is what we pay at present per mile, that would be £1,093, and to meet that we could only levy a rate of 8d.

221. But at present you levy the entire rate for the road purposes?—There is a doubt about that.

222. That was one of the points I wished to ascertain. The Towns Improvement Act says it shall be only one-fourth, and I asked whether the scale was one-fourth or the full rate, and the town clerk said the rates were made separately, and that the road rate is made to the full value?—I believe no one knows. It has been assessed on the full value, but it is contested and we are to be brought into a court of law for levying it.

223. You are aware that the road rate has been levied at the full value?—Yes, but it is contested.

224. That has been unavoidable?—You [illegible] got notice about it yesterday.

225. And the question has not been decided yet?—Not yet.

226. According to [illegible] that those [illegible] by pay the full rate, and one-fourth, would the Commissioners then object to the extension of the town?—Not upon the ground of the roads, but they would in case their [illegible] were carried on.

227. Why so?—Because for the use of the [illegible], it would not be levied at the full value.

228. But would not that give you a much larger sum to spend, the expense over?—It would be the larger sum who would have to pay three-fourths of the rate.

229. But won't you have to pay the whole cost [illegible] if there is no extension?—Yes, all that we have ourselves.

230. But, if the valuation was extended, the effect on the inhabitants of the present district, as regards the paying for roads, would be to lighten it by bringing in outsiders to share the burden?—But suppose we [illegible] £1,300, and that the present valuation of the borough is £8,000, we can only borrow on that £1,000 for the additional district, as we can only raise at one-fourth the valuation.

231. But would not the additional land be so much property added?—Yes; but we are unable to pay for their roads; it is too great a burden on us.

232. But would not the burden be lightened by their sharing it?—No; because it would be the means of putting an increased sum on us. We can't borrow more than the amount now in one year.

233. How would the extended valuation increase the burden?—Because it would enable us to borrow money we can't borrow at present.

234. The feeling of the Commissioners is that the roads that would be added [illegible] would increase the burden on the townspeople?—Yes.

235. Then that is the feeling—that it would increase the burden on the rural?—Yes, that it would increase the burden on the town.

236. And they object to it on that ground?—Yes.

237. The present district is about a mile, but don't you consider there are people outside it who derive considerable advantages from their proximity to the town?—Yes, I think there are.

238. How far does the benefit extend?—In what particulars, I would like to know?

239. In the ordinary advantages you have heard referred to—their proximity to the market town?—It is a question of opinion how far it extends.

240. But there can be no doubt that the existence of a market town like this confers advantages on persons within a certain district by giving them a market for supplying their wants, and for the sale of their produce, and so on. The town is also a benefit by supplying schools for children, and affording the people, when they come to the town for various purposes, the advantages of the paving and lighting of the streets. These are advantages that are not shared by persons living at a considerable distance, and how far would you say these advantages could be said to extend?—I would say the town affords all the advantages to those in the neighbourhood.

241. How far, would you say?—About five miles; but as regards National schools, I would not say that, for there is a school within one mile. The benefit of the schools is confined to the richer farmers' children, but I would not consider them much advantage otherwise.

242. Would you say that the inhabitants within two miles derive considerable advantages?—Yes; that is, when they come into town.

243. Admitting lands being only subject to one-fourth of the rate, don't you think that that taxation would be a fair measure of the advantages they derive?—I don't know; I don't know what advantages exactly the dwelling in the town is to them.

244. For instance, if persons living within two miles come much more frequently than persons living at a great distance, isn't it a contribution for them to have flagged footpaths; and if they should be detained in town after dark, isn't it a matter of convenience and comfort to them to have light?—It's of value, of course.

245. Would you consider that the present division would be too wide for the municipal boundary?—Yes, particularly in some directions.

246. Are you able to say whether the maintenance of the roads and bridges, which have been transferred to the Commissioners, is now more favourable or otherwise than when the Grand Jury had control?—I cannot speak as to the expenditure formerly, but at present the [illegible] of road, including those of them that are not attended to at all, [illegible]. I think that is an enormous sum, and the roads along here are especially bad, and many people [illegible] to believe that the roads are [illegible] bad.

247. These are the roads under the Town Commissioners' [illegible]?—Yes.

248. How is that?—Because the work is badly attended to at present. I know the money is laid out, and the work is not done.

249. You don't say it's the [illegible] practice, but the whole thing is done by contract?—[illegible].

250. You have a [illegible] surveyor?—Yes.

251. What salary do you pay him?—£30 a year.

252. Have you reason to find fault with him?—We have frequent complaints; and we have never a meeting but there is something before us.

253. Are the roads worse than formerly?—Yes, much worse. I remember one street particularly that used to get a cart of eight loads of stone, but it is now done with [illegible] except in one that is injured more than benefited.

254. How long have you known the town?—All my life.

255. You don't consider the change of the control from the Grand Jury to the town body a good one?—No, I think I would rather be under the Grand Jury.

256. In the cost more or less [illegible] in stone? I was [illegible]. We are paying £. 8d. between guarantee and the county charge.

257. But the guarantee is for the railway?—Yes; but the cost included must be £. 8d.

258. How much is the guarantee for the railway?—I don't tell; about five years.

259. That was a thing that had to be paid, at all [illegible]?—No.

260. Are you able to say whether the [illegible] is greater or less, putting the guarantee out of the question?—I would not exactly say.

261. But you are quite clear the thing is not so well done?—Yes.

262. There are some sanitary works required—there are sanitary works required?—Yes.

263. Is the circumstance that deters the Commissioners from carrying out the water supply the want of [illegible]?—I think so.

264. It is not from a feeling that it is not required for the town?—No, everybody in for it; but we consider the cost too much.

265. What is the Poor Law rate, Mr. [illegible]?—Two and ten pence within the town altogether.

266. Is there anything else you wish to add, Mr. Mahony?—No, sir.

267. Your opinion is in favour of non-extension?—Yes, sir.

268. You say they are now disputing the assessment of the road rate at the full amount. This Act was passed in 1853—hasn't it been assessed at the full amount every year since?—Yes, sir.

269. It was never disputed until now?—No, sir. These investigations have called attention to this point.

270. Dungarvan is under a local Act; and, of course, you must stand or fall by that—and this, you say, is the first time it has been [illegible]?—Yes.

271. Do the Commissioners intend to have any

Dungarvan. Dec. 16, 1879.

Mr. John Mahony.

more formal consideration of this subject?—I think they do.

273. Will you get a special meeting convened to consider the entire subject, and transmit to the Secretary of the Commissioners a copy of the resolution adopted?—Yes, sir.

Mr. Michael Andrew Anthony.

Mr. Michael Andrew Anthony examined.

274. Mr. O'Brien.—You are one of the Commissioners of Dungarvan?—Yes, sir.

275. And you have been so for many years?—Nearly twenty years, except for a short period.

276. Were you present at a meeting when the Commissioners considered this question as regards an alteration of the municipal boundaries?—Some years since, when I was chairman of the Commissioners, the question was taken up, and the very map before you now was made for this purpose at that time.

277. When was that?—I suppose it was in 1869 or 1870. This map was made at that time by our then county surveyor, Mr. Langley, and the Commissioners as a body, collectively and individually, were in favour of extending the boundary.

278. Was it merely on the general question, or was there any definite boundary?—We went in for it definitely. We went in for the Parliamentary boundary.

279. I believe the present Parliamentary boundary neither corresponds with the electoral division nor the municipal boundary?—Neither.

280. Is it considerably larger than the electoral division?—Yes; half as large again.

281. How many electoral divisions are comprehended wholly or in part within the Parliamentary boundary?—I don't know.

282. It includes more than the electoral division of Dungarvan?—Considerably more than that.

283. Does it include the entire of any other electoral division?—Yes, part of Clonea.

Mr. Boyle.—It includes a great many electoral divisions. It includes the whole of this electoral division, except a small part.

284. Mr. O'Brien.—And how many others does it include part of?—Part of Clonea, and part of two others.

285. What is the area of the Parliamentary borough?—I don't know.

Examination of Mr. M. A. Anthony resumed.

286. What is the valuation of the Parliamentary borough?—£17,000 odd.

287. How far does it extend from the centre of the town?—I should suppose that to the top of Drumlish mountain on the north is close on six miles.

288. And to the south how far does it extend?—About half of that.

289. How far to the west?—About three miles, I think.

290. It has no extent on the east side?—No.

291. On the occasion you refer to the feelings of the Commissioners were in favour of adopting that boundary?—Yes.

292. What was the ground on which they (the Government) considered it objectionable?—At that time it was before the Lord Lieutenant we had to apply, and we were refused.

293. On what ground?—I don't know.

294. You submitted that, and it was not adopted?—Yes.

295. Who submitted the scheme for the present boundary?—The present boundary was in existence some fifteen years prior to that. It was from the smallness of that division that I sought the extension.

296. And the extension was rejected?—Yes.

297. Were any reasons assigned for the rejection?—No, sir, not that I recollect.

298. Your opinion was that that was not an unreasonable proposal?—Well, to some extent; and I think the words of the memorial went to show that we sought the parliamentary boundary, or any such boundary as might be approved of.

299. Do you consider that outside the present municipal boundary, which appears to be a radius of about a mile, there are a good many persons in occupation of lands who derive advantages from the town government without having contributed to any part of the expense?—Most unquestionably.

300. How far would you say the radius should extend?—I would say there would be no objection to a radius of two miles.

301. And you think that if a radius of two miles was taken it would bring in a considerable number to contribute to the rate?—Yes; it would add £4,000 a year to the valuation.

302. And you consider that as the lands are only liable to one-fourth taxation it would be a fair measure of the advantages they derive?—I do; and I think one-fourth of the towns rates, such as our shilling rate, would realise about £70, which, to a small township such as this requiring many things, would considerably tend to its improvement.

303. The extension of the boundary would enlarge very considerably the number of votes for the election of Commissioners?—Yes.

304. And it would also increase the number of persons who are eligible to offer themselves for the office?—Yes; I suppose the valuation necessary is the occupation of a house rated at £12, but my own impression is, that the extension would not bring in more than three or four; I know of three or four who would come in under that extension, but I don't know more.

305. Do you consider it would be an improvement to the constitution of the Board that the rural element should be included?—Yes; and I would say further that if we get an extension of the town we should have a revision of the boundaries of the wards.

306. Is the town divided into wards?—Yes; two—Abbeyside and Dungarvan.

307. There are no wards for poor law purposes?—No.

308. What alteration would you suggest in the wards?—Well, I think with this extension you might have Dungarvan East, if I might so call it, and Dungarvan West.

309. Mr Cotton.—Dungarvan East being exclusive of the town as it at present stands?—Yes. From the present boundary to the contemplated extension should be formed into a third ward.

310. Mr. O'Brien.—And if three wards were formed you think it would be more satisfactory?—Well, it would be only justice to the people brought in to give them a chance of electing representatives of their own choice.

311. You have heard the Chairman express the opinion that the grounds which influenced them in objecting to the extension was, that it would increase the taxation for a road rate and the contemplated scheme for supplying the town with water. Do you concur in that opinion?—I am quite opposed to it. I have gone very minutely into it. The town roads would be eleven miles, and I have gone minutely into the cost in proportion to what is paid now by the county for those roads, and by allowing £16 a mile, which is one shilling per perch, I would leave a margin outside what is paid by the county at present for them.

312. Then as regards the roads, you say the effect of the transfer would be the opposite?—The effect would be to leave a surplus, according to the sum to be taken in on the shilling rate, for road purposes, of about £16 after the expenses of the roads.

313. As regards the water supply, the scheme has been estimated at £10,000?—Well, Mr. Fraser gave it very accurately not at £10,000 but at £8,000; but when we were making the application for the money

[illegible] (which was fully agreed to), apply for £1,000 more than was required, and that we need not draw the money unless it was required, and it would save the trouble of a second application.

314. But assuming the estimate to be correct, what would be the effect as regards the incidence of the cost, on the so-called boundary?—[illegible] it is as simple as can [illegible] the [illegible] the less the taxation.

315. As regards those roads can you say whether the cost of maintaining them was [illegible] under the Grand Jury than now?—Well, I could not exactly say, but taking the cost of maintaining the [illegible] years, I think the Commissioners maintain those roads for very little more than three-fourths of what it cost the Grand Jury to keep those roads.

316. The Commissioners keep them cheaper?—Yes.

317. You have heard the opinion expressed that the work is worse done?—When the Commissioners got up the roads from the county [illegible] the [illegible] roads and the [illegible] were bad. The roads during my time as a Commissioner and under the care of Mr. [illegible] were [illegible] roads, and if the roads have fallen into disrepair for the last four or five years, the [illegible] lies on the Commissioners and not on their surveyor.

318. You don't agree that the roads are badly kept?—No. They are in a very fair condition, and they are improving.

319. And the expense is less?—Very considerably less. The great expense incurred at the beginning was a wall which cost the Commissioners during my time as Chairman a good deal, and in a year or two after our obtaining of that Act, it cost £300 to rebuild a wall, built by the county, as a foundation of sand.

320. That was the sea wall?—Yes, it was knocked away.

321. Is there anything else you wish to mention?—I am a good many [illegible] here, and I would not be an advocate for the extension, if, in the first place, I thought we would not confer on those we were about to bring in advantages, and at the same time, that we were not going to tax them, for I am in a position to show that if they were [illegible] [illegible]

322. That is the parliamentary road?—No, the new mile ending, and if we took the natural boundaries through a great portion of it.

323. Then you don't contemplate following the town-land boundaries?—Well, to a great extent I would follow townland boundaries, but in reference to the [illegible] of the rural portion of the electoral division, which is marked on this map, it might be added to the present town. I am in a position to show the inhabitants of that district that by being connected with the town they would have a [illegible] of [illegible] in the pound. It would be necessary that the [illegible] in figures for [illegible] are [illegible] things. The county cess is [illegible] but suppose those people were in the town what would they have to pay?—[illegible] or a town improvement rate, and [illegible] half [illegible] as the [illegible] [illegible] paid by the occupiers the Grand Jury, making in all [illegible]. Well, [illegible] in the county cess for the [illegible], and [illegible] in the [illegible] for the township of Dungarvan, and that [illegible] in the [illegible] of those who would be brought in, instead of relieving them.

324. According, as a matter of general policy, the principle that where it existed the electoral division ought to be the municipal division also; what would be your view as to the adoption of the electoral division as the boundary of the municipal district?—I would not take the electoral division [illegible], but the [illegible] would be considerably altered, and that is my [illegible] objection to taking in entirely the electoral division. It would add a mile and a half at one side for the [illegible], and if you take those people you would have the same right to go to the other side. As to the [illegible] that [illegible] Mr. [illegible], he told me a good [illegible] as to the £40,000. The [illegible] he could only [illegible], £4,000 a [illegible] half the valuation, but he [illegible] find that, if necessary, instead of borrowing £4,000 we could borrow £10,000.

325. Is there anything further you wish to lay before the Commissioners?—My idea as to the [illegible] on the ratepayers is, that it would be the greatest possible advantage to the ratepayers to have the water supply. They pay so much a cask for it, and if they only paid that for it would amount to more than the water rate.

Mr. THOMAS O'CONNOR examined. Mr. T. O'Connor.

326. Mr. O'BRIEN.—You are a Commissioner of Dungarvan?—Yes, sir.

327. How long have you been so?—For the past six years.

328. I suppose you are acquainted with the town?—Indeed, for my life.

329. You have heard the question under discussion, the proposal to extend, or limit, or otherwise alter the boundary of the town; in short may [illegible] you wish to put forward?—I don't wish to put myself under [illegible] at present, but I wish to ask Mr. Anthony a question. He said it was in 1862 that all the Commissioners recommended the Lord Lieutenant of the time for an extension of the borough and that they were unanimous. I wish to ask him was there a resolution to that effect passed at that meeting where he says they were unanimous?

330. Mr. O'BRIEN.—Can you answer Mr. Anthony whether there was a resolution passed?

Mr. Anthony.—There was, but I am not correct as to the year. I did not say it was 1862.

331. Are you aware that there was a resolution?—Yes, most decidedly.

332. Mr. O'CONNOR.—If there was, it would be well to have that resolution produced and a copy of the memorial presented to the Lord Lieutenant?

Mr. Anthony.—I asked the Town Clerk for the memorial or a copy of it and the Town Clerk referred to the minutes, but there is no record of it.

Mr. O'CONNOR.—That is what I wanted to say, for that shows clearly there was nothing of the sort.

Mr. JOHN [illegible] examined. Mr. J. [illegible]

333. Mr. O'BRIEN.—Are you a Commissioner?—No, sir.

334. You are a ratepayer?—Yes, I am a ratepayer of the borough of Dungarvan and I [illegible] [illegible].

335. You are a resident?—Yes, sir.

336. Is there anything you wish to add to what we have heard up this morning?—I merely wish to ask will the people in the district proposed to be taken in, have an opportunity of coming forward afterwards or [illegible]?

Mr. O'BRIEN.—We have already by advertisement published in every newspaper in Ireland, without exception, intimated that we should be ready and anxious to receive the sheets of anybody who wished to be heard; and if there are any there you wish to submit which you are not prepared without preparation, if you will be kind enough to put them in shape and transmit them to Mr. Robinson, secretary, they will receive every attention. In the first instance we are obliged to visit personally every borough and to explain as far as we can the object of the inquiry, and it is in order we have done that we will have to approach the question.

Dungarvan. Jan. [illegible]. — Mr. John Hunt.

of what our decision is to be. Before that we will be most anxious to have the view of everybody and it shall receive the fullest consideration.

Mr. *Hunt*.—Hitherto all the witnesses examined are inhabitants of the town and of course it is their interest to extend the area, but up to the present there has been no person examined who lives outside the town.

Mr. O'Brien.—If there is anybody here from the outside district we will be ready to hear him, but we cannot compel them to come here. In the towns we have visited they have not attended either, except, in some instances, for example, several outside proprietors attended at Killarney; but we can't do more than give notice, and if anyone desires to tender himself we will be glad to hear him.

Mr. *Hunt*.—Individually I would be one of the persons taken in.

337. Mr. O'Brien.—In what part?—In the townland of Scartore, in the electoral division of [illegible], if the Parliamentary borough is taken in.

338. But would a radius of two miles take you in?—I don't think it would.

339. I think then you may dismiss from your mind, from the discussion of the Parliamentary boundary, any apprehension that the Parliamentary borough will be made the municipal district?—That would suit me.

340. Would the radius of two miles bring you in?—It would very near; it is about two miles.

341. Wouldn't you like to be included?—No, sir.

342. Don't you consider you derive advantages from your proximity to the town which others at a greater distance do not possess?—I think it would be a calamitous thing if the roads were transferred from the Grand Jury to the town.

343. But they have been transferred already?—And I think it would be calamitous if more were transferred.

344. You would not think it would be better for the works that they should be transferred?—No; the works are very badly attended at present in the town.

345. And you would not like to extend the jurisdiction?—No. I have often travelled with the coach from Waterford to this before the railway was completed, and the coachman who has brought the mail from Waterford has frequently complained of the bad state of the roads the moment he came within the municipal boundary; so much so, that he threatened to complain to the Secretary of the Post Office.

346. Do you dispute the proposition that persons within a given radius, say two miles, derive certain advantages from their proximity to the town?—I think the town derives more advantages from them.

347. But they derive advantages from the town?—Very little.

348. But don't persons living within two miles derive more advantages than persons living six or eight miles away?—I don't see that they do.

349. Don't their children attend school here in considerable numbers?—I think not. In my district they have a National school, and from Abbeyside they come out to my school. I don't think there is any advantage.

350. Aren't the lands more valuable?—Certainly they are.

351. And don't they get a ready market, within easy reach, for their different descriptions of produce?—Yes, but I contend that the present area is wide enough.

352. You think the radius of a mile is enough?—Clearly.

353. And that the one-fourth answers the advantages desired?—Yes; and I don't see the object of the extension.

354. You are aware that the Parliamentary Commission have been struck by the fact that at present the areas of the municipal districts appear to be regulated by no definite principle. Some are narrow, and others include outlying districts, and the Committee considered that an anomalous state of things, and that there should be something more definite and uniform about the boundaries?—When the present boundary was formed it was formed by natural boundaries, such as roads and streams. It forms a very natural boundary, if we may call a road a natural boundary. The boundary is very well defined.

355. You expressed a hope that people outside would have an opportunity of being examined. You have heard what some of the gentlemen in the town say, that instead of being a benefit to them, extension, in their opinion, would be an injury?—Yes.

356. Is there anything you wish to add?—I know that the people about to be taken in are unanimously opposed to it.

357. And if you will be kind enough to mention to them that we will be happy to hear them on the question, either through you or through themselves, and any reasons they can urge against being brought in?—Yes, sir.

358. Mr. *Anthony*.—When was it that the roads fell into this fearful state, and were they, prior to that, good roads?

Mr. *Hunt*.—I think this conversation I had with the coachman was a year and a half or two years ago, and the roads are worse now than when he spoke to me about them.

359. Mr. O'Brien.—Is there any other gentleman wishes to give evidence? I can only repeat what I said to Mr. Hunt, that if anyone desires to submit his views he can do so in writing, and we will be happy to consider them.

Mr. *Boyle*.—I have looked into the matter, and I find that the number of persons in the present township qualified to be Town Commissioners is 81, and the number of persons qualified to vote 711. The number of persons in that portion of the Dungarvan electoral division, without the township, who would be entitled to vote, is 100; and the number in that portion of the electoral division who would be qualified to be Commissioners is about three or four.

The inquiry then terminated.

SKIBBEREEN—JANUARY 2ND, 1878.

Before Mr. EXHAM, Q.C.

MR. M'CARTHY DOWNING, M.P., examined.

1. You are the Chairman of the Town Commissioners here?—I am.

2. And have occupied that position for some years?—Yes.

3. What is the present areable area of the township?—1,600 acres and 25 perches.

4. And its present valuation?—£4,335 5s.—the buildings £3,497 10s., and the land £837 15s.

5. Is all the town in the same electoral division?—It is all within the electoral division of Skibbereen.

6. Is it your opinion and that of the Town Commissioners that the boundaries of the town are too small and ought to be extended?—Quite so. We are quite unanimous upon that, and I may add that we originally applied for a much larger township, and, without knowing why it was refused, it was refused, and the present boundary was settled by Sir Richard Griffith.

7. At what time were the present bounds approved of?—In 1861.

8. Was that the time you adopted the provisions of the Towns Improvement Act of 1854?—Yes. The original application would have made it 6,000 acres, and the valuation over £5,000. We also applied that the Board should consist of fifteen Commissioners. That was also refused, and we only got nine, and we very often found it most difficult, in consequence, to form a board. Five is the quorum.

9. To what extent do you and the Commissioners consider that it would be desirable to increase the boundary?—We have considered that very fully, and we have agreed long since that it should be extended to an area comprised within a circle of a two miles radius from the centre of the town, and that wherever that circle touched a townland, that the whole of that townland should be incorporated so as to follow the townland boundary.

10. What would be the areable extent of that?—The areable extent, if it was increased to what we propose, would be 8,699 acres.

11. Would that be in addition to the present?—No. The whole then would be 8,699 acres, and the valuation would be £9,172.

12. How much of that would be lands, and how much buildings?—The buildings would remain as at present—£3,497 10s.—and the remainder would be made up in land.

13. Would the whole of the proposed extension be in the same electoral division?—No, it would not, because our electoral division forms a most irregular and a most extraordinary division.

14. How much of what you propose to take in would be in another electoral division?—There would be out of that in the present Skibbereen electoral Division 4,627 acres; in the Cloughdonnell Electoral Division, 1,016 acres; in the Caheragh Electoral Division (North), 1,376 acres; in the Kilkeenagh Electoral Division, 322 acres; in the Woodfort Electoral Division, 640 acres; in the Aughadown (North) Electoral Division, 68 acres. That shows you how irregular the Electoral Division of Skibbereen is. It runs in one direction four or five miles, and in another part comes within a mile of the town.

16. Do you and the Commissioners think that by confining the extension to the Skibbereen Electoral Division alone that would be sufficient?—We think not, because then you would have portions of the electoral division far more distant from the town paying our tax, whereas a portion of another electoral division much nearer to the town would escape.

17. I presume you are aware that the House of Commons Select Committee have recommended that, as far as possible, all municipal areas should be included in the same electoral division?—Yes.

18. And any warrant directs that we should take special care of that as far as possible?—That is impossible in our case. It has been for many years a suggestion of mine, in which Sir Alfred Power agreed perfectly, and also the Marquis of Hartington, that the unit of taxation ought to be the union division, and not the electoral division, and I think it will come to that hereafter.

19. I presume, Mr. Downing, if we send you one of the Ordnance sheets on the six inch scale, some one down here would mark the present bounds of the town and the boundary you propose by townlands?—Yes. In fact, we can get you the sheet here to-day. Upon this part of the inquiry I would like to satisfy you that this proposed boundary meets not only with the unanimous desire and favourable opinion of all the Commissioners, but with the sanction of the Board of Guardians elected and ex-officio representing all interests. It became necessary to borrow £400 for the purpose of the thorough drainage of the town, the Board of Guardians being the sanitary authority, and on the 18th of June last there was a special meeting of the Guardians, upon notice to meet on that day fortnight, to consider the matter——

20. Was that in June of last year?—No, in June of 1874. A special meeting was accordingly held, and it was largely attended by almost all the ex-officio and elected Guardians, and they considered the matter very maturely, and appointed a committee of five ex-officio and three elected Guardians to meet and consider the question, and report to a full meeting. The Committee consisted of the following gentlemen:—Mr. Robinson, Mr. John Limerick, Col. Somerville, Mr. Newman, Mr. Marmion, and myself, and Mr. Jennings, and Mr. Hennessy, who is present to-day. We made our report, and afterwards, at a very large board meeting, it was proposed by Col. Somerville, and seconded by Mr. John Hennessy, "That the townlands mentioned in the resolution should be the area of taxation for the sewerage of the town of Skibbereen, the same being a radius of two miles from the centre of the town." That resolution was carried unanimously. I am therefore quite justified in saying that you have now the sanction of all parties concerned to this radius of two miles.

21. How many persons would come in as voters in the town under this extended boundary—about how many?—Well, I have considered that, and I think I am probably under it when I say sixty. There are a larger number of holdings, but some very few are under the valuation that would give them a vote, but you may say sixty at least.

22. Would many gentlemen's residences be taken in?—A good many. If you like I will give you the names.

23. That is not necessary. Are they gentlemen of property?—I should say there would be about ten gentlemen's residences taken in.

24. In your opinion, and in the opinion of your brother Commissioners, as far as you know, do the people that are within this extended area as proposed derive exceptional advantages from their proximity to the town, so as that they should be fairly included in the taxation?—In my opinion, the farmers who make this town their market town derive more benefit and more advantage from the proper keeping up and lighting of the town than its own inhabitants. Now, that may appear very extraordinary, but I think I can justify it. Before we had the town, I may say barrel-

M 2

Skibbereen, Jan. 8, 1880.

Mr M'Carthy Downing, M.P.

fully lit, with forty lamps as it is now, the farmers did not come into the town so much, particularly after dark, as they now do. They now come frequently into the town, and particularly in the winter after dark, and do their business, and they are frequently seen in the town at ten and eleven o'clock at night. I therefore think that, as far as the lighting of the town is concerned, they derive more advantage from that than the people living in the town.

25. And have they all the advantage of selling in the town the produce of their farms?—Yes, they have all the advantages of a fair green and market, and before these were established they used to sell their dairy produce, and such like, at a place called the Khyber Pass, it was so narrow. We have a butter market for them now—of course they pay for the weighing of the butter—and it is a great advantage to us, but it is a still greater advantage to them, for they are perfectly safe in having their butter weighed there, and all that kind of thing.

26. In the area you propose how much of the railway would be taken in?—It will go up about to the bridge—about an extra mile of the railway.

27. As far as you know do the inhabitants within this increased district object to be taken in?—I should say that I have given you the strongest proof that they do not, because the ex officio and the elected guardians of those places voted for it.

28. What would be the increase in population by the proposed extension?—Well, I consider that the increase in population would be about 500. Indeed, I think I am under the number in that calculation.

29. What is the population at present?—The population is 3,790 now, but with the increased area it would be about 4,300.

30. Would this proposed boundary bring in the workhouse?—Yes.

31. Is it in it at present?—Not at all. It does not go so far. I could throw a ball from my house, which is in the town, to the workhouse wall, which is not in the town.

32. Have you and the Commissioners considered—if this increased area is approved of—the question of taking up the management of the roads of the town?—Certainly, we have.

33. Would it, in your opinion, be desirable that the Commissioners should get the control of the roads?—In my opinion it would be one of the principal advantages.

34. Is that opinion shared in, so far as you know, by your brother Commissioners?—By everyone of them. It would throw, certainly, a great deal of increased trouble and responsibility on the Commissioners, but they are willing to undertake it.

35. Do you think it would increase the expenditure of the ratepayers?—I think it would save them considerably. I have made a calculation upon that.

36. Would the work be more efficiently done in your opinion?—Beyond all question.

37. In considering the question have you considered the question of the bridges in the town?—I have. My opinion is that if we took up the roads we ought to take our share of what are called "county-at-large" charges. The bridges would be a "county-at-large" charge, because at present for a bridge a barony only pays a fourth of the proportion of the cost of the bridge, and the county pays the remaining three-fourths. I think a great many of the witnesses who appear to have been examined before you and the other Commissioners, as I see their evidence reported in the public papers, have altogether mistaken the bearings of the question, or do not understand how the Grand Jury laws operate. I have made a calculation on the subject, which I am anxious to give you, because I think it is accurate.

38. I shall be very glad to have that, because I regard your views as most valuable?—At present the streets of our town are maintained by the Grand Jury, and the costs of keeping up the roads of the town amounts to £123 a year. 1,056 perches are maintained at a cost of 1s. 8½d. per perch. You will see directly the object I have in giving you the distance. 156 perches are maintained at a cost of 6s. per perch. The reason of the difference is that the 156 perches are a mail-coach road over which the mails are carried, and consequently half of that is paid by the county. There are six main roads coming into the town, and I take it that if we have these six roads to keep up in the increased township that would be twelve miles. I have taken the cost at the present contracts for the keeping up of these roads, and they cost £190 a year. They vary as to the cost per perch, but I have taken the whole. Then there are several small roads—by-roads—and they are maintained at 4d. and 6d. a perch, at a cost in the whole of £110 a year. That would make £300 a year for maintaining the roads that we would have within this two mile radius. Then I take the proportion of the "county-at-large" cess—the very point we are coming to.

39. That includes the gaol, prisons, and everything?—Yes, all "county-at-large" charges. The proportion of the "county-at-large" rates upon the barony in which we are now sitting amount to within a fraction of £1,000. I put it down at £1,000 as it is within a fraction of it. Our valuation within the two-mile radius would be one-fifth of the whole valuation of the barony, and I add that £200 to the £400, and that would be £500 a year. That would be our responsibility in every possible way you could look at it. Then I have taken the county rates that we have paid upon the average of five years. The amounts for maintaining the roads and "county-at-large" charges alone, for I have put malicious injuries and that sort of thing out of the question, to 1s. 10d in the pound. 1s. 10d. in the pound upon a valuation of £9,500, which would be the valuation of our extended township, would be £863, so that there would be very little one way or other, so far as that calculation goes. But I take it for granted that I am quite under the mark when I say that if we had the maintaining of the roads we would do it for at least 20 per cent. less than that work is done for now. I am certain I am not under or over the mark in my calculation. At present there are ten contractors, all of whom have taken the contracts to make money, whereas if we had the work under our control we would try to save every farthing we could, and I take it we could save one-fifth off the £800, and that would reduce it to £640, while a 1s. 6d rate in the pound would make £790, so that we would save 4d. in the pound, according to my calculation, to the ratepayers, and have about £50 a year to the good.

40. In this calculation of yours you have considered the case of persons occupying arable land that would be brought within your proposed area. At present they are paying 1s. 10d. in the pound county cess. Under the 62nd section of the Towns Improvement Act of 1854, arable lands, &c., only pay one-fourth of the improvement rate. What do you propose with regard to that? If they were to pay for keeping the roads in repair on the same scale if they were brought within the proposed area, would they not escape a considerable amount of taxation?—Not at all; for I contemplate their paying the full rate for maintaining the roads, because they would be relieved of the Grand Jury cess.

41. What would be your view with regard to the taxation of the persons occupying the arable land that you propose to bring in?—So far as maintaining the roads in proper condition, I think they should pay what the people occupying houses in the town have to pay at present; and I consider that they should pay to the town the same road rate as they at present pay to the Grand Jury for keeping the roads in repair.

42. I conceive you would save money for them by your proposal, because you save them 4d. in the pound on their county cess, and their share of about £50 a year besides, even though according to your view they should get no benefit, so far as the county cess is concerned, from being brought into the town, but I wish

to know your views with regard to the portion of the Towns Improvement rate they should pay?—That would be quite a different thing. In my opinion that should remain as it is.

43. Is it your view, then, that there should be a differential rate, and, if so, what should that be?—A differential one certainly; but I always considered one-fourth too small a proportion to be paid by the occupiers of arable land, &c., within a township.

44. Is it, then, your opinion that their proximity to the town, and the use they make of it, makes their land so much more valuable that they should fairly pay more than one-fourth of the rates to be levied under the Towns Improvement Act?—Certainly; and there are arable lands outside the town paying £4 an acre, within even a stone's throw of my house.

45. If the same quality of land was three or four miles off, would the tenant pay as much for it?—Certainly not. There is one man in the town who pays the full rate on his house, and on part of his land he only pays one-fourth.

46. I would be very glad if you have considered the matter, to have your opinion as to what would be a fair differential rating to be paid by the persons living within this extended area?—I consider that they should fairly pay one-half the improvement rate, and the full road rate. I am speaking very much against myself, because, as all the gentlemen present know, I have a place called Lovage, on which there is a large house, and another place next to it—they will be all brought in by the extended area. There are others as well as myself in the same position; for instance, Mr. M'Carthy, a Town Commissioner, whose house and yard are in the town, and his land, which is outside it, will be brought within the municipal area, if extended as proposed.

47. I suppose you are aware that by the Public Health Act of last year, so far as arable lands in a township, which is an Urban Sanitary Authority, are concerned, they pay only one-fourth of the sanitary rate, but that if they are outside, in the Rural Sanitary District, that provision does not apply?—No.

48. What would be your view with regard to those within the area—how would you deal with them as regards the sanitary rate?—Do I understand you to say that under the Public Health Act of last year the arable land only pays one-fourth?

49. Yes, where it is within an Urban Sanitary Authority, but not where it is under the Rural Sanitary Authority. I was dealing with this question with regard to your becoming the Urban Sanitary Authority. Probably I should have asked that first. What is your view with regard to that?—I consider it would be desirable that we should become the Urban Sanitary Authority.

50. Suppose you were to become the Urban Sanitary Authority, what would be your view with regard to the sanitary rate which the occupiers of arable land in the increased district should pay; as the law is, they would only pay one-fourth if you were the Urban Sanitary Authority?—In my opinion they should pay for anything done in the town in the same way—that is, a moiety, by way of a differential rate. I think I told you before that I was the person who had towns under 6,000 inhabitants exempted, and I did that after consideration, because I think it would be ruinous to a town like this, as it at present stands, if it were to be obliged to bear all the expenses under the Sanitary Board. It would be utterly ruinous to the inhabitants. Of course, if we got this extended boundary, we would, as a matter of course, become the Urban Sanitary Authority. We would apply for power to do so.

51. You know you have power?—Yes.

52. And would it be your idea, then, that the township would apply for it?—Clearly; and I gave that evidence before, on the former Commission.

53. And that the occupiers of land in the extended district should pay one-half of the sanitary rate instead of one-fourth, under the law as it stands at present?—Yes.

54. It was suggested in other places to my colleagues and myself that if the persons in the outside district were brought in, they would require to get water and light. Is it your opinion that they would ask for those conveniences or should be entitled to them, particularly when you think they should only pay half rates on their valuation?—In my opinion they would not be entitled to them; and as regards water, they have plenty of that in the country; and as regards the lighting, they only want it when they come into the market town on fair days, and that sort of thing. They will never look for them, so far as I know.

55. How many townlands would be taken in by this proposed boundary?—Thirty-seven. They are all in the Skibbereen Union, and the electoral divisions in which they are comprised, and their gross acreage and valuation will be found in the following table:—

Electoral Division.	No. of Townlands.	Area.			Valuation.		
		A.	R.	P.	£	s.	d.
Skibbereen,	[illegible]	[illegible]	[illegible]	[illegible]	[illegible]	[illegible]	[illegible]
Cloughdonnell,	[illegible]	[illegible]	[illegible]	[illegible]	[illegible]	[illegible]	[illegible]
Castle Haven, North,	[illegible]	[illegible]	[illegible]	[illegible]	[illegible]	[illegible]	[illegible]
Killaveenogue,	[illegible]	[illegible]	[illegible]	[illegible]	[illegible]	[illegible]	[illegible]
Woodfort,	[illegible]	[illegible]	[illegible]	[illegible]	[illegible]	[illegible]	[illegible]
Aughadown, North,	[illegible]	[illegible]	[illegible]	[illegible]	[illegible]	[illegible]	[illegible]
Total,		[illegible]	[illegible]	[illegible]	[illegible]	[illegible]	[illegible]

The workhouse is outside the boundary, but the gas company have extended the light there, and for that, of course, they pay. I am very much disappointed that the Local Government Board did not get what we were promised, namely, full power to enable the township to be relieved from the Grand Jury, and to have their own taxation for the roads. I know the Local Government Board have power to do it, but I say that power is to some degree restricted, because they are obliged to make a special report upon it. Up to the present you see how unreasonable the law was. There were four towns that went through all the formalities to enable them to get the management of the roads, and they held meetings and went to expense, and these four towns applied to be released from connexion with the Grand Jury, and when they went before the Grand Juries they all refused their consent.

56. Yes, and I believe the only town in which they succeeded was Wexford?—Yes. At Queenstown they got a special Act. In this township we get from the Grand Jury £[illegible] a year for maintaining the streets, while we pay them £[illegible] a year, and if we apply for a flag that is broken it is a most humiliating to ask for it.

57. In the suggestions you have made about the cost of the roads, have you taken into account the cost of maintaining the roads and the cost of employing an efficient officer to superintend their repair?—I have, certainly. What I regard as to the way in which the roads should be kept is very different from the way in which they are kept now. Mr. [illegible], one of the Commissioners, wishes I should mention that we have had only two rates in five years. The rates of the last five years have been as follows:—

	Municipal.		Poor Law.		County Cess.	
	s.	d.	s.	d.	s.	d.
1874,	1	0	[illegible]	[illegible]	1	[illegible]
1875,	nil		3	0	[illegible]	[illegible]
1876,	nil		[illegible]	0	[illegible]	[illegible]
1877,	1	0	[illegible]	[illegible]	[illegible]	[illegible]
1878,	nil		[illegible]	[illegible]	[illegible]	[illegible]

Mr. [illegible] desires me to mention that if we had the powers of the Grand Jury transferred to us, that is, if we were separated from them, we could and would carry out many improvements which we have a right to, but at present we have to apply to the Presentment Sessions and are often refused, and not only are we refused, but what we have to experience is positively humiliating.

58. In your opinion how many Town Commissioners should there be?—Even as we are the number ought to be at least eleven, but if we are increased it would be fifteen, I take for granted, because we will have a large

SKIBBEREEN. Jan. 1, 1879. Mr. M'Carthy Downing, M.P.

number from the outside who will be eligible, and sometimes it is as well to have a little new blood on the Board. We are often obliged to sit here for an hour to collect in a sufficient number of the Board to form a quorum, in consequence of the small number of members.

59. May I take it that that you are authorized to state to me the opinions of all the other Commissioners?—Yes, all the nine Commissioners, and they are now present. I wish to say that in my calculation, as to the debtor and creditor account in respect of the roads of the town, I have allowed a *fair* margin for the county-at-large charges. A very important thing I wish to add is this: We would be in a position to prevent such a state of things as this. When the government seized upon two occasions refused to allow a sufficient sum for the maintenance of the streets, what was the consequence? There was no contract. The town then became in such a state, that we were obliged to apply to the Post Office, and they sent down and took up the road at double the expense. If anything occurs between one session and another there is no means of rectifying it. As the first time on the there were several holes in the road, and I sent for a contractor and said to him, "At whatever the expense repair the road where necessary, because otherwise there will be an accident," and he did so, and by that means, no doubt, an accident was averted. There is no power between one session and another for anybody to do anything in a case of sudden emergency, except by the giving of a "sudden breach" order, which, I believe, is very often abused.

Mr. Florence M'Carthy.

Mr. FLORENCE M'CARTHY examined.

60. You are a Town Commissioner here?—I am.

61. Do you wish to make any statement?—The only thing I wish to say is that I am one of those who will be brought in under the extension we ask for, and which we hope will be granted.

62. That is as far as your land is concerned?—Yes.

63. So far as your house is concerned, you are in already?—Yes.

64. What quantity of land have you?—Not very much. But there is one significant fact which I would like to put before you. This inquiry has been publicly advertised in the Cork papers, so that there is no person who is not aware of it, and there is not one single person here to oppose it, although there will be ten gentlemen's houses which will be brought in. That is all I wish to say. The butter-market, where all the country butter is sold, pays for the lighting of the town.

The inquiry then terminated.

YOUGHAL. Jan. 2, 1879.

YOUGHAL—JANUARY 2nd, 1879.

Before W. P. O'BRIEN, LL.D., and Mr. C. P. COTTON, C.E.

Mr. J. O'Brien.

Mr. JOHN O'BRIEN examined.

1. You are clerk to the Town Commissioners?—Yes.

2. How long have you been in office?—Since April, 1871.

3. This town is constituted, I believe, under the 9th George IV.?—Yes.

4. How long has it been placed under that Act?—Since the Reform Bill—since '32.

5. Then it has never been sought here to place it under the Towns Improvement Act?—Well, yes, it was brought before the Commissioners, but although the question was often discussed it was never settled by a resolution.

6. What is the municipal area of Youghal?—343 acres.

7. Statute acres?—Yes; 343 acres are within the municipal boundary.

8. And what is the valuation?—£7,418 10s.

9. You say the municipal area comprises 343 acres, and that the valuation is £7,418 10s.?—Well, the valuation is not exactly that—there is a sum of £156 in respect of Commissioners' property, for which the Commissioners charge no taxation, and that reduces it to £7,262.

10. That is the present valuation?—Yes.

11. I think the return I got last year from the Valuation Office for the purpose of my report, gave the valuation as £9,011?—That, sir, is for the Parliamentary boundary.

12. What is the area of the Parliamentary boundary?—The area of the Parliamentary boundary is 564 acres.

13. Then the figures you gave just now are applicable to the municipal boundary?—Yes.

14. Is the town divided into wards?—No; and with reference to the valuation, I wish just to mention that it is divided into three classes. First there are 68 persons valued at £3,564 18s., at 1s. in the pound; secondly, 138 persons, £2,333 5s., at 9d. in the pound; and thirdly, 131 persons, £1,365 10s., at 6d. in the pound.

15. There is, in fact, a graduated scale prescribed by the Act of George IV.?—Yes.

16. Is the town divided into wards for municipal purposes?—No.

17. Nor for Poor Law purposes?—No.

18. What are the purposes to which the Commissioners apply their funds?—The borough tax is applied to cleansing and lighting.

19. How is the lighting provided for—is it done by the Town Commissioners, or is it done by contract?—They manufacture the gas themselves.

20. What is about the annual expenditure at present?—It is, including everything, about £2,500.

21. And the revenue?—About the same.

22. How is your income derived—is it from rates, or is it from any other sources of income?—Yes; we have rent, £461; borough rate, £1,400; harbour dues—last year it was £160, but now the Commissioners have done away with it—the harbour order came into operation on the 1st of October; then there is ferry returns, about £100 a year.

23. What is the total amount of your income?—About £2,500.

24. Now, have the rates been made up to the full extent of your powers?—Yes.

25. And it has been found necessary that that should be so?—Yes.

26. With your other sources of income, have these rates proved sufficient for the purposes the Commissioners had to provide for?—Well, yes; I may say they would, with the exception of this, that perhaps there was a lot of money borrowed, and they have to pay the interest on that. There was £3,300 on which they pay five per cent.

27. Then, may we take it that it has not proved quite sufficient for all purposes?—Well, it would, with the exception I say, and that sometimes they enter into large works.

28. But take say the last five years, have the sums derived as income proved sufficient for all purposes?—Well, yes.

29. In every instance?—Yes.

30. Have you had to leave any works unprovided for by reason of limiting your rate, owing to this limit—have any works been obliged to be left un-

[illegible]

Youghal.
Jan. 2, 1879.
Mr. J. O'Brien.

boundary as defined in answer six to the question?—Yes.

86. Was the question as to whether the Poor Law electoral division would be suitable to be adopted ever under consideration?—No.

87. Does the electoral division run in an unequal line?—Yes, unequal.

88. Then, suppose the electoral division of Youghal were made the municipal district, would that bring in the entire of what is now proposed by the Town Commissioners—would it do so in your opinion?—Yes.

89. And a great deal besides?—Yes, a great deal besides.

90. And would this increased area, over and above what they proposed, be considered as not fairly constituting part of the town. Is that what the Commissioners believed when they limited the radius to what they propose in their replies?—Well, I believe what they intended bringing in at present they have adopted in these replies, and they did not discuss the matter further.

91. Would what they propose to bring in include a great portion of arable land?—Yes.

92. Lands occupied as accommodation land; town-parks used by the people of the town?—I don't think so.

93. Youghal lands would be included?—Portion of it.

94. Has it been considered by the Commissioners that persons within that fully participate in the advantages of the town government?—Yes.

95. Now, in what respect do you consider the portions so proposed to be included, and not included now—in what respect do they enjoy advantages to which they don't contribute any part of the expense?—Well, to the south-west they enjoy the lighting and cleansing.

96. Do they derive advantage from having a market town so close at hand?—Yes, of course they do, and they get land and sea-sand, and enjoy the lighting of the town.

97. Do they also derive advantage from the schools?—Certainly, male and female schools.

98. And can readily sell their rural produce?—Yes.

99. And they resort to the town for various purposes frequently?—Yes.

100. Do you think the proposed area would so extend the radius as to include all the places where those advantages are enjoyed?—I think you might take in a further area, and include people with those advantages.

101. How far would you say—within what radius would you say advantages are derived from proximity to the town?—That would depend upon circumstances. First, if you bring in arable land, the taxes would be only 6d. in the pound, and it is a question whether that would be an advantage to the Commissioners or not.

102. Do you think the Commissioners would prefer not going further?—Yes; but I would be for taking in all the Youghal lands instead of portion of it. I would be inclined to take in all Knockaverry.

103. What you are suggesting now is over and above what the Commissioners propose?—Yes.

104. To what extent would that be?—About half a mile on the west.

105. On what ground would you include them?—They are actually within the town of Youghal; they are all accommodation lands nearly.

106. And this is in addition to what the Commissioners suggest?—Yes.

107. What exactly would you include in addition?—All Knockaverry and all Youghal lands.

108. Did the Commissioners consider the question of including these?—No, as a body they did not.

109. And what was the principle upon which they limited themselves to what was proposed?—Well, the only thing that suggested itself to them at the time they adopted that was that they were anxious to bring up to the railway station.

110. In what direction do the districts you suggest to add lie?—The west.

111. What class of persons occupy those places you suggest to include—are there many inhabited dwellings on them?—No, I think there is only one house.

112. Now, what is the present constituency for municipal purposes?—The number of municipal electors under the Act of 9th Geo. IV. is 329.

113. And how many persons are eligible for the office of Commissioner?—Forty.

114. And there are twenty-nine members on the Board?—Yes.

115. Now, if the proposed extension were obtained, would that increase the number of persons qualified to hold the office of Commissioner?—Well, there is a difficulty in answering that question, for all the houses at the strand are only occupied in summer, and generally belong to people in Cork. I don't think it would add more than one or two.

116. You don't think it would bring in any more than that?—No.

117. In no direction?—In no direction.

118. Are the Commissioners aware that, in the event of the present application being successful for having the sanitary jurisdiction transferred to them, and that they are constituted an urban sanitary authority under the Public Health Act, there is power given to the Local Government Board to transfer certain functions now exercised by the Grand Jury over roads, bridges, and footpaths to the municipal authority?—As a body, I don't think they are aware of it. Some of them are aware of it. There was a discussion here and a memorial in 1868 to Sir Joseph N. M'Kenna, which was sent to him on that very subject.

119. You are not aware if it would be the desire of the Commissioners, in the event of their being constituted urban sanitary authority, to ask also for the transfer of those Grand Jury functions?—I am sure they would wish to have the roads in their own charge.

120. That would be their feeling?—Yes.

121. Are you aware if the Commissioners have formed an opinion about it, as to whether the amount expended for them by the Grand Jury is commensurate with the amount levied off the town?—No; we have scarcely two miles of road. There was £140 or £150 expended on those two roads, but I think the barony and the town of Youghal pays in from £400 to £500 a year.

122. And you think it would be a benefit to have the roads under their own control?—Yes.

123. Do you think the roads would be better provided for?—Yes, for there are other cross-roads, lanes, and so on they have to repair now.

124. Assuming the Grand Jury control were vested in them, do you think they would still desire the extension of the boundary, whether or not the arable lands were to be rated at one-fourth or not?—Yes.

125. You are aware that those arable lands at present contribute in the shape of county cess the full amount?—Yes, but then they have more roads to contribute to.

126. But you think even if they were only to contribute one-fourth they would still desire the extension?—They would. I don't think they would consider it fair to charge arable lands the same rating.

127. How many new roads would be included in the boundary proposed by the Commissioners?—There would be only half a mile—say three-quarters of a mile to the south-west and a quarter of a mile on the main road, there is Williamstown, the high road, and all the Mainstreet.

128. What would be the entire extent?—About a mile and a half of additional roads.

129. Now, you have not exercised any sanitary functions since 1874?—No, not since '74.

130. Are you aware of any special sanitary rate having been struck by the Board of Guardians, as rural sanitary board?—Yes.

131. What was it?—A penny in the pound.

132. For special purposes?—Yes.

133. What was the sanitary purpose?—Suppressing nuisances, and making or repairing sewers.

134. They have not attempted any wide scheme for sewerage or water supply?—No, they attempted to sink wells for the purpose of giving water.

135. Have there been any sanitary schemes of a larger nature under the consideration of your body or the Board of Guardians?—The Board of Guardians had it under their consideration, but the Guardians had not.

136. What was it?—It was a scheme for bringing in water to the town.

137. Is it considered that the water supply is defective?—There is a report to that effect, but the people consider it good.

138. Who expressed a different opinion to that?—The medical doctor—the sanitary medical officer.

139. Has the objection been that there has not been a sufficiently copious supply, or that the water has been defective in quality?—I think there is plenty as far as the supply is concerned, but it is the quality of it that has been objected to.

140. Is the supply of water by means of pumps or wells?—By pumps.

141. Were they subjected to analysis?—Yes.

142. How many of them?—I think about nine of them.

143. When was that?—Years ago. It was by the Town Commissioners, that all the waters were subjected to analysis, and all were pronounced good except one.

144. Where was that?—In Clarke-lane, and that was shut up.

145. Since then has there been any analysis?—There was another since, and some of the water was pronounced not fit for use.

146. When was that?—Twelve months ago.

147. How many pumps were pronounced unfit?—Well, I think the complaint was against them all.

148. And have they been shut up since then?—No, not shut up.

149. Then no action has been taken to carry out the scheme?—No, except to try to make the wells, and not go to the greater expense.

150. Do you know what was the estimate of what would be necessary for the furnishing of a good supply?—I am not aware.

151. Is any sanitary expenditure as to an improved scheme of drainage?—No, there is not.

152. What would you say is the state of the sewerage?—Well, I should say it is defective in some places.

153. Do you mean the main sewers?—Yes, the main sewers.

154. In what respect would you say they are defective—is it in the construction of those sewers?—Yes.

155. In what way are they bad—are they the old flat sewers?—Yes.

156. Would the extension of the boundary, do you consider, in dealing with the water supply or with the question of an improved scheme of sewerage, influence the action of the Commissioners?—I think if the water was brought in the extension would be considered necessary.

157. And as to the drainage, would it, do you think, remove any reluctance of the Commissioners in carrying out the work if the boundary was extended?—If they would not strike a higher rate than 1d. in the pound on arable land, I think they would not like to undertake it.

158. Have the Commissioners considered, with reference to this question, acting under the Act of George IV.—have they considered or do they know that under the Towns Improvement Act there is an acreable graduated scale? Have they considered the expediency of placing themselves under the Towns Improvement Act?—Yes; but after getting sufficient information, they considered that the people would not be able to bear the taxation, that it would come too heavily on portions of them, for it would be a uniform rate, and the parties paying it now would be aggrieved by the change.

159. Are they aware that there was a perfectly well-known Act under the Act of George IV., and that Youghal is one of them?—Well, as a body, I don't think they know it.

160. There has been no move, however, to change the present arrangement?—No.

161. Did the matter ever come before them, do you know?—Yes, but they never came to any conclusion on the matter.

162. And you can't say how it is for municipal purposes?—I am not aware.

163. Is there anything further you desire to add?—No.

164. You have no other statement to make?—No.

165. Mr. John Mahony, J.P.—I would like to know are there any many gentlemen in the town rated for property and paying directly the rate, and who live outside and are thus disqualified to act as Commissioners.

166. Mr. O'BRIEN.—Can you state what amount of property there is inside the town for which people who live outside are rated?—No.

167. Whether they live outside or not they are rated who hold premises within the town?—Yes.

168. Mr. Mahony, J.P.—Do you know that there are such persons, such as myself—Certainly, but to be qualified to be a Commissioner they must be resident.

169. Have you anything more to say, Mr. O'Shea, as to the extending and extending the municipal boundary to the north-west, the inhabitants of that place in [illegible], that would have a revenue of about [illegible] that is in the built-up part, adding in those houses and the adjoining cabins. That is the reason, that one of the Commissioners suggested. We considered the inclusion as it would be too much for any advantage it derived. It was the feeling of the people, unless the lights extended.

170. You have no further observations to make?—No.

171. Mr. Mahony.—Have the Town Commissioners, as a body, any power to enforce property unwisely to the owners of the town which is dilapidated houses, sending one into the streets, condemn buildings, and so on—as the Cork Corporation have?—No.

172. Mr. O'BRIEN.—You have no power to do that?—No.

173. Mr. Mahony.—Do you think it would be well or necessary for the Commissioners to have such power as that?—Yes.

174. Mr. O'BRIEN.—Do you think there is a necessity?—Yes.

175. Mr. Mahony.—Do you think they should have the powers of Wide Street Commissioners to deal with such matters?—I think if this inquiry were made the basis of some legislation hereafter of the kind, it would be well to introduce such powers.

176. Mr. O'BRIEN.—You think increased powers ought to be given?—Mr. O'Shea.—Yes.

Fermoy.
Nov. 4, 1880.
Mr. J. O'Shea.

Youghal. Jan. [illegible]. — Mr. J. H[illegible].

Mr. Jeremiah H[illegible] examined.

177. Mr. O'Brien.—You are Solicitor to the Town Commissioners?—Yes.

178. And have been so for a great number of years, I believe?—Yes.

179. And you are perfectly acquainted with the town of Youghal?—Yes.

180. The town is under the 9th of George IV., we have heard?—Yes.

181. Within your knowledge or experience, have the Commissioners ever been considering the propriety of getting under the more modern Act—the Towns Improvement Act of 1854?—Yes; I am inclined to think they did. I am inclined to think that at one time they passed a resolution to proceed for the substitution of the Towns Improvement Act, but they did not, I believe, persevere.

182. Did not persevere you say?—Yes; no one took the trouble afterwards, I think. I believe that the resolution will be found on the minutes, expressing a desire for the introduction of the Towns Improvement Act.

183. But they carried it no further?—No.

184. And it dropped?—Yes; no one would take the labour and expense on themselves.

185. Then you think it is merely from apathy?—Yes; I think there was no one in the town strongly enough interested to press it forward, and make the necessary movement to effect the change.

186. Are you aware of the grounds (of course it was before your time), but are you aware of the grounds influencing the original decision?—Yes; they are quite patent. The Act of the 9th George IV. was adopted, not, I think, in 1832, as has been stated, but in February, 1830. Youghal was a town corporate at that time, and the Town and Liberties of Youghal extended several miles. The 9th of George IV. was adopted to light the town, and they were obliged to change the boundaries, and they did not consider it prudent to go beyond the limits determined on—the limits that barely required cleansing and lighting. The municipal limits were extended to Kilnatoora and Redbarn, a townland some three miles distant on the sea-side. I remember the Corporation used to ride the bounds at certain times. The boundaries as fixed by the 9th of George IV., were purely for the purpose of lighting; and I may say they were in advance of most towns of Ireland.

187. They were never reformed?—No. The Corporation was dissolved, and the limits remained as they were proposed. The Corporation was transferred to the Commissioners.

188. How are the boundaries described, can you tell us?—Well, there is a definition in the resolution of the first Commissioners—"from Clifton on the south to the end of Tallow-street on the north."

189. Is there a record of that resolution?—Yes. I should think Mr. O'[illegible] would be able to let you have it. It would be a resolution of 1830.

190. Mr. Cotton.—Does it describe the line and course of the boundary?—The map there, which you have before you, is the only one.

191. Yes, the line is on this map, but it is not engraved on it; it is only a line put on by some one.

192. Mr. O'Brien.—Is there any description of the line taken by the boundary?—No; there is no minute description, but there is sufficient to make it clear, and afterwards I drew a description, which was adopted. It was intended to supply any defect of the original description. I don't know if it is forthcoming.

193. You never got a local Act for Youghal?—No, except the 9th of George IV. can be called a local Act.

194. You concur, I suppose, in the views of the Commissioners, that the existing boundaries are quite too limited?—Oh, entirely.

195. And not commensurate with the benefits the town government confers?—No.

196. Do you think the proposed radius includes the portion that may be said to enjoy the benefits of the town government—the benefits it may be said to confer?—No.

197. You don't think it far enough?—No; but I may mention that the Commissioners referred it to me to suggest to them a radius, and my feeling was, on the occasion, to avoid contention, and to make a sort of compromise, for we know that the people outside would strenuously oppose it.

198. You heard the strong opinion expressed by the Parliamentary Committee that sat for three sessions successively—you heard that amongst the things they recommended was, that care should be taken to make the municipal boundaries conterminous with those of poor law electoral divisions. You know the electoral division of Youghal?—Yes.

199. What would be your view—the Committee having expressed that opinion, which cannot be departed from without grave reasons—if the electoral division were selected as the boundary—do you think that that would be judicious?—Well, no; I think that would be too extensive a radius.

200. And would go further than the benefits of the town might be expected to extend?—Yes; the up-side lands and some others. I think it would go too far.

201. And you think that to adopt the electoral division would make people liable who derive no adequate benefits?—Yes, at least no special benefits. There might be, perhaps, half a dozen who could have certain benefits.

202. But you think that within the radius decided on the persons not now included, but who would then be included, do derive substantial advantages, in various ways?—Yes.

203. Such as what?—Such as being within the distance to sell their fresh butter and new milk to the townspeople and the summer visitors, and all that, and the manuring of their lands, and so on.

204. You heard the Town Clerk stating two particular extensions he thought ought to be made—namely, to bring in the entire of Knockaverry and Youghal lands?—Yes.

205. Would it appear to you reasonable to bring them in?—Yes.

206. The boundaries, I presume, as suggested by the Commissioners, are townlands?—Except the street suburb, which, I may say, was the creation of the railway. They have in their reply adopted the Parliamentary borough boundary. The Parliamentary boundary does not include that street at all.

207. Would it appear to you, assuming that in the Poor Law formation the townland is the unit of electoral divisions—do you think, as to these townlands named by the Town Clerk, that there would be much or any objection to include the entire of those portions by townlands in the municipal district?—It would make a [illegible] boundary.

208. Would it, in your opinion, violate any principle of equity?—No.

209. Then there would be no strong objection to make the townland the unit—to introduce the entire of these townlands?—No, I think not.

210. There would be no violation of any principle of equity?—No, I think not.

211. Now, it has been proposed—it appears an application or memorial has been made or addressed to the Local Government Board, praying a transfer of the sanitary authority or jurisdiction from the Board of Guardians to the Town Council?—Yes.

212. Now, do you think that when the jurisdiction shall have been so transferred there will be an increased necessity for a larger area?—I do.

213. To enable them to discharge their duties under those altered circumstances?—At least there should be included the extension proposed. There are many contiguous places that ought to be brought in, so that the town authority would be able to deal with them.

their jurisdictions and powers would be very imperfect otherwise.

214. Making the Town Commissioners the urban sanitary authority might necessarily make the extension needful—might bring the extension with it?—Certainly.

215. That is your belief?—Yes; and I may add that Cork-lane, up to the barracks, it extends to Youghal military barracks, and the present municipal boundary cuts that Cork-lane some place down the lane, and the portion above requires as much attention and sanitary care on the part of the authority as the part below, and the same I may say of Windmill-lane.

216. Now, you know the 70th section of the Act—the Public Health Act—where there is power given, where the Town Commissioners have been constituted the urban sanitary authority, by provisional order to transfer the Grand Jury jurisdiction over roads, bridges, &c., to them. You are aware of the provision to which I refer?—Yes.

217. Are you aware if it would be the feeling of the Town Commissioners to get the transfer of those functions from the Grand Jury to themselves?—I do not think they ever considered it, but I believe their disposition would be to do so—to take the power into their own hands.

218. Now, would they in coming to a conclusion on it, be influenced if the boundaries were more extended—would they be more inclined to come to that conclusion if the extension were made?—The extension might give them more radius than the additional rate would pay for.

219. But if the extension were made, and it were so arranged that the lands had all to contribute equally to the rating instead of a graduated scale?—That would make a considerable difference.

220. You think it would?—Yes. I may say that I think in the contest between Youghal and the Grand Jury, Youghal is the loser. I don't think we ever got fair play from them. Except in the making of the bridge, we never got a fair share of the county expenditure. This town at one time had charge of its own internal works, and that created a sort of feeling that Youghal was able to take care of itself. Besides, we had no gentry here, there was always a town population, no influential representatives on the Grand Juries to stand by us.

221. You think that that operated unfairly?—Yes; and when they gave us this bridge they placed a special portion of the burthen, £4,000, on the town—but the bridge has been a great improvement.

222. Have you any further observations to make?—No, nothing further occurs to me.

223. But you are generally, I take it, in favour of an extension of the existing boundaries?—Oh, yes.

224. You think them decidedly too small at present?—Yes, they are quite absurd, they were never considered to be municipal boundaries.

225. You think the proposal of the Town Commissioners is to some extent a compromise?—Yes.

226. You would not go so far as to bring in the entire electoral division, but would bring in the entire of the townlands named?—Yes, I do think that would be fair and equitable.

227. Mr. Cotton.—Is the building at the strand extending now, or do you think building operations there likely to extend?—Well, I don't think that there is any present disposition in that direction.

228. I notice that the proposed extension ends at the very last house there?—Yes.

229. Would it not be better to go somewhat further?—I think it would be better to go to the end of Clay Castle. I may mention that the Town Commissioners have had the opinion that they had the power of extending the limits—extending the definition of the limits, and they did pass a resolution, and went to expense for the purpose of extending the limits out to the level crossing, beyond the railway station.

230. When was that?—Seven or eight years ago. Here is the map of the extension. [Producing map.] Some of the ratepayers resisted.

231. Mr. O'Brien.—Would that have gone beyond the limits now proposed?—No, it is just the same place.

232. What was the date of that?—It was in 1868—on the 21st of April, 1868.

233. Then the proposal of the Commissioners at that time was the same?—Yes.

234. Entirely?—Yes, as to the southern extension, the object being to light the strand and railway station.

235. Mr. Cotton.—Did the railway company take any action?—The railway company were disposed to have it done, for they wished to get gas to their station.

236. What was the ground upon which it was not done?—It was found that the Commissioners had not power under the Act of Parliament. It was so decided by Mr. Keane, the present Recorder of Cork.

237. Mr. O'Brien.—Can we have the resolution adopted giving the original definition of the boundaries as now constituted?—Mr. O'Shea.—I have the minutes here, and I find it entered:—

"Special meeting of the Town Commissioners held on the 3rd May, pursuant to resolution of 8th of April, 1868. Resolved—that the limits of the town for carrying into effect two of the provisions of this Act—namely, lighting and cleansing, agreeably to the 61st section, be defined as follows, viz.:—On the east by the river, on the south by Clifden and Belleview, on the north by Mr. John Ansell's house at the extremity of Tallow-street, by Cork-hill to the barrack-master's-gate, thence on the west by Raheen-lane, the infirmary, and town walls, to the top of Windmill-lane, along the old mill-course to the west ward of the town, on a line to Mr. Gill's mill."

238. Read that part about the barracks in the resolution of May?—

"On the south by Clifden and Belleview, on the north by John Ansell's house, at the extremity of Tallow-street, up Cork-hill to the barrack-master's-gate, thence on"——

239. That will do—it says the barrack-master's-gate?—Mr. Hallwell.—That was lower down than the barracks themselves.

Thursday, Jan. 2, 1879.

Mr. J. Hallwell.

Mr. John Henry Ronayne examined.

Mr. J. H. Ronayne.

240. Mr. O'Brien.—Mr. Ronayne, you are Clerk of the Union?—Yes.

241. What is the area of this whole municipal district of Youghal—it is included within the electoral division?—Yes.

242. What is the area of the electoral division?—6,685a. 1r. 13p.

243. And what is the Poor Law Valuation?—£16,731 5s.

244. How many townlands are there comprehended in the electoral division of Youghal?—Fifty.

245. Then the electoral division is considerably larger than the municipal district?—Oh, yes.

246. How far does the electoral division—taking, say, the clock-tower as the centre—extend?—I suppose two miles and a half or three.

247. Which is the farthest point?—The farthest point would be Kilcoran.

248. And how far is Kilcoran?—About three miles.

249. Three statute miles?—Yes.

250. That, then, is about the farthest point?—Yes.

251. Is it to the north or south?—The north.

252. What is the farthest point in the south?—It would be about the same.

253. And how far would you say in the west?—About three miles and a half to the west.

YOUGHAL.
Jan. 8, 1880.
Mr. J. R. Brassée.

259. The Board of Guardians, up to the present, since 1874, have acted as Sanitary Authority for the town—is not that so?—Yes.

260. Have you made any sanitary rates this year?—Yes, a special sanitary rate of a penny.

261. In the town?—Yes.

262. Has there been a penny levied each year?—Yes.

263. Was there any other poundage levied during the past five years—commencing with 1874?—Yes; in 1874 there was 2s. 9d.; in 1875, 1s. 6d.; in 1876, 1s. 9d.; in 1877, 2s. 2d.; and in 1878, 2s. 4d. The last included a penny for special sanitary rate.

264. There is a special rate of 4d. for sanitary purposes, too, that is for the current year.

265. It is not included in the 2s. 4d.?—No.

266. Is that for sanitary purposes?—Yes.

267. What are those purposes?—There is a new sewer, and building Willimantown and Clay Castle.

268. Are there any other sanitary schemes under the consideration of the Board of Guardians?—Yes; we tried two or three places to gain water, and that not succeed; and the last thing we tried was outside to the north end of the town for a supply of water.

269. What was the result?—Well, we have not analysed the water there yet. We think a good supply of water, but it has not been analysed; and the guardians don't know whether it will be necessary to improve the supply on a large scale.

270. Have any sanitary reports been furnished to the Board of Guardians making objection to the supply of water?—Yes, several.

271. By whom?—By different inhabitants.

272. Have you had any official report from the Medical Officer of Health?—Yes; we had the water analysed by the Cork Analyst.

273. When was that?—Two years ago.

274. What was the result?—As the result said it was condemned.

275. As bad?—Yes; and then a river or Merchant-lane very good. The water at Green's-quay was not considered the proper thing. The analyst did not consider it safe for the use of the people.

276. How many specimens altogether were sent to him?—Twelve or thirteen.

277. And how many were pronounced by him to be bad, and how many good?—Well, I suppose there were just three or four good.

278. And you are now trying to clear the out-ward—Well, as the people said they knew the water is unfit for drinking, but it could be used for other purposes.

279. Now, have the Guardians been hindered from making improvements in any respects for the improving by reason of the cost it would involve?—Yes, that was the main reason.

280. Are the Board of Guardians aware that the Town Commissioners adopted a memorial praying a transfer of their sanitary jurisdiction to themselves?—Well, we would be glad to get rid of it.

281. Was there any difference between them which would afford any idea of the probable cost of its improved water supply?—It was not sent into the Board of Guardians.

282. Was such an estimate given in any shape?—The County Surveyor, Mr. Kirkby, suggested where the water could be taken from.

283. Where is that?—At a distance a mile and a quarter, on a rock and it holds a very good supply.

284. What would be the estimate of carrying out that?—The engineer said it would cost about £4,000.

285. And the Guardians did not go further with the matter?—No; they thought they would get other schemes and cheaper.

286. And they have not found? At the north end of the town we have a very good supply of water, but we don't know if it be pure or not.

287. Is it a well?—No, it is from a high elevation where there is a quarry. It is very plentiful, and might supply the town.

288. It is abundant in quantity, but has not been tested as to quality?—Yes.

289. Assuming it to be good, do you believe it would be found sufficient to supply the town?—Well, I don't know. I could not say with any certainty.

290. Would it not be easily conducted to all, you the elevation is high enough?

291. But then, would not people have to incur a good expense in it?—But they could have pipes run in order to give thoroughly.

292. You can't give any opinion as to the quality of the water?—No.

293. You can furnish us with a list of the townlands?—Yes.

MR. ISAAC DALTON examined.

Mr. I. Dalton.

299. Mr. O'Hanlon.—You are a Town Commissioner, Mr. Dalton?—Yes.

300. And have been for some time—have you been long a Commissioner?—About twelve months.

301. It appears that at a special meeting of the Commissioners it was agreed by resolution that there was necessity for an increase of boundary, and a resolution in favour of it was passed we have been told?—Yes.

302. How many members were present?—Nine.

303. Were you present?—Yes.

304. And it appears that at that meeting eight were in favour of extension and one dissented?—Yes, only one dissented.

305. And I take it that your opinion is favourable to an extension?—Quite favourable.

306. You have heard the evidence given today and the suggestions, and having heard everything that passed to-day, do you adhere to your opinion as to this particular boundary suggested by the Commissioners—do you think it the best, or do you think any other would be preferable?—I think the suggested boundary a proper and fair one. That is the general view.

307. Mr. O'Shea, the Town Clerk, suggested the introduction of the whole of Youghal-lands and Knockaverry. What would be your opinion as to that?—I think there would be no objection to it.

308. It was suggested as the boundary would cut townlands that these two should be taken whole; would there appear to you to be any objection to introducing those two townlands in their entirety, instead of having one altogether, and the other partially excluded?—No, I do not think it would be objectionable.

309. Another suggestion is to make electoral divisions and divide the town as circumstances will permit; what would you say to the electoral division being taken as the boundary. Mr. Fleming says he thinks it would be too extensive—that it would go a finish too far—and that many persons would thereby be brought in who might not in fairness be asked to contribute to the town advantages?—I think it would be unnecessary.

310. Is your opinion in favour of having the sanitary functions and jurisdiction transferred?—Yes.

311. And if you became the Urban Sanitary Authority would you be in favour of getting the control of the roads, footpaths, and so on?—Undoubtedly.

312. You think the work would be better done?—Yes, and cheaper.

313. And I take it that you think that to enable you to discharge your duties properly the area ought to be extended?—Yes, I think so.

314. You think them too limited at present?—Yes; the present boundaries don't even include portion of the town.

315. Do you think all the persons who would be included by the extension derive advantages from their

proximity to the market town?—Yes, certainly, and ought therefore to contribute.

316. You think it would be only equitable and fair? —Yes.

317. Is there any special suggestion you wish to make?—The only observation I wish to make is that language could not be expressed strong enough as to the pumps and the water.

318. You think the present supply bad?—Yes, decidedly; so much so that the Town Commissioners thought it necessary to prosecute the Board of Guardians for neglecting their duty in reference to the supply of water.

319. The opinion is that it is bad?—Yes.

320. Is it as to quality, or that the supply is not adequate?—Neglect is one of the principal causes.

321. Neglect in what respect?—Neglect in the management of the water, such as it is now. If the water, even as it is, was properly managed—if the pumps were kept clean, I say it would do very well.

322. You think they are unfit to be used?—I do now.

323. And you think their condition is owing to neglect?—Yes.

324. In what respect?—Well, one view is this—if the pump wants repairing or that, a man goes to it with two or three pounds of white lead (a rank poison), and plasters it over the pump; and in one case where a woman took some of the water she came to me and she said, there is a white slime on the top of the water, and I told her on no account to take it, that that was white lead, a poison, and said, come in and I will give you water, for I have a private pump near the public one, and have given water for the past couple of years to thousands of persons daily, to my great inconvenience. On one occasion I brought the sanitary medical officer to inspect the pump, and to show him the white lead, and the man whom I sent down absolutely was startled to find the state in which it was.

325. Do you think neglect of that sort extensively prevails?—Yes; constantly. I protested against it; and, moreover, a pump has been left out of order for three or four days, and thousands were inconvenienced.

326. If you had control of your sanitary arrangements, you think you could do the work better, and improve the water supply without any large outlay?—Yes; we are present, and would see to any officers who would be under our eyes, while at present, perhaps, a guardian lives seven or eight miles away, and knows nothing about the matter, and such a guardian would very often say, "Oh, I know nothing about it," though the matter might be of great interest to the town.

327. Have you anything further you wish to say?—No; I don't know anything else.

Tuesday, Jan. 2, 18[illegible]. Mr. J. Dalton.

Mr. Michael Fleming examined.

Mr. M. Fleming.

328. Mr. O'Brien.—You are a Town Commissioner, Mr Fleming?—Yes.

329. And have been for some time?—Yes, for twenty years, or so.

330. And are familiar with the whole working of the affairs of the town?—Yes.

331. You have heard all that has been said about this question of the extension of the municipal boundary—were you one of the eight gentlemen who were in favour of the proposed extension?—Yes.

332. Then I may assume that you are in favour of it?—Yes.

333. As to this particular scheme, are you still in favour of it—do you adhere to it, or does any other plan suggest itself to you?—No, I think it quite fair.

334. What do you say to the suggestion that, as it severs the boundary line cuts townlands, that the whole five townlands should be included—do you object to that?—Well, yes, I would.

335. Why would you not think it advisable to do so?—Well, dissensions would be created. I agree with what Mr. Hudson said. In my opinion the line proposed is quite large enough for our purpose.

336. And do you think that the area so brought in would justly represent a radius commensurate with the advantages which those places derive from their proximity to the town?—Yes.

337. Do you think the persons brought in would object?—Well, some of them might, but they would be few, I believe.

338. On the ground that they would rather get those benefits for nothing, enjoy those advantages and pay nothing?—Yes.

339. And you think it better and fairer that they should be asked to contribute to the expenses of maintaining those advantages which they enjoy?—Most decidedly.

340. Are you in favour of having the sanitary jurisdiction transferred from the Board of Guardians in the way that has been pointed out?—Yes.

341. You agree with Mr. Dalton as to the water supply?—Yes.

342. You think that it is not so well managed as it would be were it under the control of the Commissioners?—It is not so well managed as it would be.

343. You do not think the Board of Guardians deserve to be prosecuted?—Well, no.

344. You think you would be able to do the work better?—Yes.

345. In the event of such a transfer being effected, would you ask for—would you be inclined to seek the management of the roads, bridges, &c.?—Yes.

346. Have you any special observation you would wish to make?—Well, yes, just with reference to the evidence, I may say, on the point about the Towns Improvement Act, and the feeling of the Commissioners, that, as an old Commissioner, I believe the majority of the Commissioners would be in favour of the adoption of the Towns Improvement Act, and, I may add, the majority of the people, too.

347. Can you account for the fact, bearing in mind that the mode of proceeding is by twenty-one ratepayers sending forward a memorial—can you account for the circumstance that no step was taken?—Well, the fact was, we have been kept very busy; we have had a great deal to do from time to time, and we thought it would entail expense, and we had not very much money.

348. You think if the boundaries were extended that feeling would exist in favour of the adoption of the Towns Improvement Act?—Yes.

349. You are aware that since the passing of the Towns Improvement Act it has been superseding the 9th of Geo. IV., and that you are in a very exceptional position in being under the 9th of Geo. IV.?—Yes.

Mr. William Farrell examined.

Mr. W. Farrell.

350. Mr. O'Brien.—Have you been long a Commissioner?—Only about six months. I am one of the majority who applied for an extension. I am in favour of it still, and think it would be advisable, but I think there ought to be a further extension to Clayworth—to the end of Clayworth.

351. You think that the whole of Clayworth townland ought to be introduced?—Yes.

352. You heard the suggestion that the whole of Tonaghmore and Knockaunmacy ought to be introduced?—Yes, but I think that would be too extensive.

353. Then the only suggestion by way of addition

Youghal.
Jan. 8, 1879.
Mr. W. Farrell.

to the area described by the Town Commissioners in their answers to the queries that you would make would be to take in the whole of Clayquarter?—Yes, and Knockaverry, of course, at the north side, as far as the Mill-road.

352. It appears that five townlands are cut in part by the boundary which you suggest in your answers to the queries. Now, if they were all included would you see any objection to that?—I think there would be reasonable ground for parties to complain if it were so far extended to them.

354. You believe the electoral division would be too wide a radius?—Yes, too wide to be reasonable.

355. Are you in favour of transferring the sanitary jurisdiction?—Yes, I believe the work would then be better done.

356. As a necessary condition for that do you think the boundary ought to be extended?—Yes, to enable the Commissioners to do the work effectively.

357. Would you be in favour then of having jurisdiction over roads, footpaths, &c.?—Yes, that would follow.

358. You heard the suggestion that it would be deemed advisable to place the town under the Towns Improvement Act of '54 instead of under the Act of George IV.?—Yes.

359. And you agree to that?—Yes, I do, and for many reasons, for at present the Commissioners are elected from a very limited body, and it is very often hard to form a quorum here. I think if the selection were widened more an improvement would be effected.

360. You would be for having a larger number of electors and a larger number of qualified persons eligible for election?—Yes, I think it would be better to alter the qualification to bring in not only those who live in the town, but all those who pay rates.

361. No matter where they live?—Yes.

362. That all ratepayers be brought in, irrespective of where they live?—Yes.

363. And be eligible?—Yes; for instance, there is Mr. Ronayne, a very respectable and important member of our community, and a man of business. He would be an instance of what I mean.

364. Where does he live?—Oh, just far out. His actual residence is about two miles, and like him, there are many people who pay more rates than many of the Commissioners.

365. Would there not be some limit to the distance you would suggest that persons might be qualified to vote in?—If persons hold premises in town sufficient to qualify them I think that ought to be enough. Some gentlemen pay rates and live fifteen or twenty miles off.

366. Well, would it be, do you think, an advantage to bring those gentlemen in—they would not be able to attend?—Well, no, perhaps not to attend, but they would to pay the rates.

367. You would be for making them Commissioners irrespective of the question of distance or residence?—Yes.

368. Have any extensive works been undertaken by the Commissioners?—There was some suggestion—I was here when a suggestion was made for certain improvements to be effected, and the only reason I could understand they did not carry out the works was from want of means. It is not fair to judge of the Commissioners by what they did only.

369. Then you believe they did as much as they could with the means at their disposal?—Certainly.

370. Have you any further observation to make?—None.

Mr. Henry Long.

Mr. Henry Long examined.

371. You are an old Commissioner, Mr. Long?—Yes, I was on the Board years ago and have been for a few years lately.

372. You are intimately acquainted with the whole municipal district?—Yes.

373. You are the owner of house property in Youghal?—Yes.

374. Is that house property within or without the municipal district?—Partly within and partly without.

375. I understand you were the dissentient at the Board with reference to the proposed extension?—Yes, but I may tell you that I dissented the case of extension when it was extended before.

376. And on this recent occasion there were, I understand, nine Commissioners present?—That is a mistake that has been made—there was only a quorum of seven.

377. Then I take it that six were of opinion the boundaries should be extended and the seventh dissented?—Yes.

378. May I ask you was notice of the meeting given? I presume it was?—Yes, notice was given to all the Commissioners to attend. The meeting cannot be held without a quorum of seven.

379. Well, Mr. Long, you heard the proposal of the Commissioners? You heard the particular proposal they made?—Yes.

380. And what was the nature of your dissent?—As I understood, they were only to extend the boundary to those building houses or lodges on the strand, which are only occupied three or four months in the year in the summer season, and that by extending the borough to that it would imply that the Commissioners would water and cleanse that district if they took the taxes from it, and that the amount of taxation that must be levied upon the property would not be equivalent to what would be the cost of keeping it in repair.

381. Were you opposed to any extension being made?—No, not to an extension all round the borough. My objection really was to an isolated place being brought in.

382. But the Commissioners proposed a greater extension than that?—Not on that occasion.

383. Well, here is what they propose:—

"An extension of the boundary on the north to the land running into the Cork and Youghal Railway at Clay Castle, including all the lands and premises between the town, between the foot of Knockaverry Hill on the west, and the sea on the east, and an extension in the Knockaverry borough boundary from Knockaverry northward to the northern limit, being the stream which runs on the north side of said stream to [illegible] Castle."

Do you object to that extension?—That only goes north and south.

384. It goes west also—you don't accept that as an extension of the existing boundary to be adopted?—No.

385. Would you say what you consider to be an extension you would approve of?—The boundary may be extended to the lighthouse. I would light up the railway station as a thing out of [illegible], but beyond the boundary on the north or south, or on the west, it is not really necessary for the lighting and cleansing purposes.

386. Then, except to the railway we may say you would not advocate any extension?—No, except under another Act.

387. Yes, but assuming that it was stated that the general feeling was for substituting the Towns Improvement Act for the 9th George IV.—assuming that was stated to-day, and to be done, what would you say?—Yes, but if the Board was for having it here is it that a notice was given—a printed notice—for the purpose of calling together the meeting on the subject, and the matter was deemed so interesting to the public that of twenty-one members only seven appeared.

388. Assuming the Towns Improvement Act were adopted instead of the Act of George IV., do you see

any objection to the extension?—Very great, for it would allow of increased taxation.

389. But give you increased powers and opportunities of doing good for the town. It was suggested by some of the first witnesses that the ground upon which you opposed the extension was chiefly because it would bring in house property of your own?—It would.

390. And make you liable?—Yes.

391. And does that at all influence your opinion?—Indeed, it does.

392. You would consider it a matter of £ s. d.?—Well, I believe there are some thirty-one or thirty-two persons there that would have to bear the whole burthen. If the whole public were brought in to equalise the taxation I would not mind, but I do complain that I would be deriving no interest from it. These houses are of no value in the winter—they are only let for three or four months in the year.

393. Does not the letting value of those three or four months correspond very much with the letting value of other houses for the whole year?—Well, sir, I have several of them, and I purpose letting them for the whole year.

394. Would not municipal improvements generally in the town have the effect of attracting visitors, and of bringing them to those houses of yours—would not that be the natural effect of having the town clean and well lighted, and so on?—Well, as far as my knowledge goes they are fully occupied during the season, and people only want more—I do not think it would improve them.

395. Is there anything else you would wish to say?—As to the pumps, my opinion about the water is that the water is right good, and the supply plentiful, and that the pumps are injured by the sewage.

396. You believe they are injured by defects in the sewage?—Yes.

397. The sewage is bad you think?—Yes; the sewage of Youghal is all open sewers, not pipes, and these are very convenient to the pumps. There is a kind of trap for getting down to the pump, and all the rubbish is thrown across it—the principal pump is down on the quay, but the well of it is in the Main street, and as the main sewer passes by the Main street it must contaminate the pump.

398. Then the drainage of Youghal requires to be overhauled, and a better system introduced, you think?—Yes.

399. That would involve a scheme of some magnitude?—Yes; but the streets run parallel with the sea, and it could be easily done.

400. Now, would it not facilitate the Commissioners in carrying out such a scheme as that, if they had a larger area to assess?—Yes.

401. For instance, if those valuable houses you spoke of were brought in?—Yes, but I don't see how their interests would be affected by the improved sewage of Youghal.

402. Would not the town then become healthy and attract more visitors?—In some places, perhaps.

403. You know bad sewers engender bad and unwholesome air, and the places where they exist become unhealthy and would not that deter people from taking those nice houses, those nice marine residences?—We have had long experience, and nothing of the kind ever occurred.

404. You say the water is contaminated by the sewers?—Yes.

405. Well, there can be no question but that bad water would generate disease?—There can be no argument against the want of sewerage improvement in the town and of its affecting the water.

406. Suppose typhoid fever broke out in Youghal in consequence of this, and that the fact got into the Cork papers and became circulated in June or July, of course it would prevent people coming down to take houses. Would it not be the interest, therefore, of house owners like you to do everything to keep the town in a healthful condition?—I have heard it stated here that there is a discrepancy rate on the town for the sanitary improvement of it.

407. Are you in favour of having the sanitary jurisdiction transferred from the Board of Guardians to you?—I am.

408. And would you be for having the control of the roads, footpaths, and so on?—Yes, I think we are paying four times what we get value for.

Youghal. Jan. 6, 1876.

Mr. Henry Long.

Mr. Samuel Merrick examined.

Mr. S. Merrick.

409. You are a Town Commissioner, Mr. Merrick?—Yes.

410. You have heard the evidence given today?—Yes.

411. You were one of the majority who were in favour of the proposed extension?—Yes. I wish to say that some time ago, when looking for the Harbour Board Bill——

412. You were looking for it?—Yes; we obtained it about a year ago, and it came into operation on the 1st September. We were looking for control over the roads, and we expected we would have got opposition, and the opinion was that we threw it overboard at the time.

413. But it is still the prevailing wish to have control over the roads?—Yes, and has been for a long time.

414. You think the work could be done better and cheaper?—Yes. Some time ago the sewer in the Main street broke down, and the contractor filled it up with stones. We could not do anything with it, because the road belonged to some one else, and there was a complication of authorities.

415. You find that between the Grand Jury, and the Guardians, and the Town Commissioners, with a divided jurisdiction, there is great difficulty?—Yes; the sewers are in a very bad state of repair, and we brought the matter before the Grand Jury, but they threw it out. The streets are at present in a bad state of repair.

416. You don't think the outlay by the Grand Jury is commensurate with the county cess levied?—No, nothing like it. Some time ago £300 was what the Grand Jury allowed for certain work, and we had to supplement it by another £100, otherwise it would not be done.

417. Can you suggest anything else?—Well, extension is very much needed.

418. What extension would you be for?—I would include the five townlands.

419. And you think if these five townlands were included it would meet the case?—Yes. The Town Commissioners were the Sanitary Authority, and the reason they had to throw it up was the area was so limited. The 1d. in the pound did not half pay.

420. You are aware that under the Public Health Act of 1874, in cases where the population did not exceed 6,000 the jurisdiction was transferred?—Well, we were the Sanitary Authority——

421. There was some mistake made about your population?—Yes.

Mr. Hassard.—The mistake arose by the published return being for the Parliamentary Borough.

422. The Guardians, however, became the Sanitary Authority?

Mr. Merrick.—Yes; the radius was so small we could not collect sufficient to pay the expenses.

423. So your view as to the sanitary transfer is to have an extended area?—Yes. In any case we would like to have it for convenience sake.

424. You think the work would be better done?—Yes.

Mr. Hassard.—They are very good men, but too few away for the amount of work involved in attending to the sanitary condition of the town.

YOUGHAL. Jan. 2, 1879. Mr. S. Hosford.

Mr. *Farrell*.—It has been stated that a special sanitary rate was struck for the Strand-houses, but it was for another purpose with reference to the drains and the contributory district, for that was Williamstown, Dysert, and Claycastle.

Mr. John Sampson.

Mr. John Sampson, Chairman of the Town Commissioners, examined.

425. How long have you been chairman?—Going on two years.

426. Were you present at the meeting at which this matter was considered?—Yes, as chairman.

427. You have heard the different statements made by the gentlemen who have given information, is there anything you wish to add?—Well, nothing to what Mr. Hosford has stated to you. He went fully into the matter with the Commissioners. He is Law Agent for the Commissioners, and understands the ups and downs of everything on the subject.

428. You concur generally in his views?—Yes.

429. Are you in favour of transferring the sanitary jurisdiction from the Board of Guardians?—Yes, it would be a very good thing.

430. And you would also wish to have the roads and bridges under your control?—Yes, it would be a good thing.

431. As to the extension, do you adhere to the particular boundary line that has been suggested in your answers to the queries we transmitted you, or would you be disposed to go further?—I think the suggestions of Mr. Hosford are the ones we would wish to adopt. I think it would be too much to bring in the five townlands.

432. But you would bring in Claycastle—the whole of it?—Yes.

433. And Knockaverry?—Yes.

434. And you would not bring in the electoral division as a boundary?—No, that would be too much, I think.

435. Some of the gentlemen were proposing the introduction of the Towns Improvement Act?—I think it would be a good thing if we had that.

The inquiry then terminated.

BANDON. Jan. 3, 1879.

BANDON.—JANUARY 3RD, 1879.

(Before Mr. W. A. Exham, Q.C., Chairman of the Commission.)

Mr. Stewart R. Tresilian.

Mr. Stewart Richard Tresilian examined.

1. You are the Town Clerk here?—Yes.

2. How long have you held the office?—Since the year 1833.

3. I believe the Towns Improvement Act was never adopted here?—No; the town is governed under the 9th of Geo. IV.

4. What is the area of the town at present, and what is the population?—The municipal borough consists of 116¾ acres and 10 perches—taken from the case books—the two divisions in which the town stands. The population is 4,302.

5. And the valuation?—£8,152.

6. The town stands in two electoral divisions already?—Yes.

6. What are they?—Ballymodan and Kilbrogan. The town is divided by the Bandon river.

7. And Kilbrogan is on the north and Ballymodan on the south?—Yes.

8. Have the Commissioners, as a body, met and considered the question as to the extension of the boundaries of the town?—Not as a body.

9. Well, did any of them consider it?—At a committee meeting.

10. A committee of the Town Commissioners?—Yes.

11. Having met for that purpose?—Yes.

12. And have they deputed you, as the Town Clerk, to speak for them?—Yes.

13. Then what is the view with regard to the extension of the boundary here?—They are unanimously in favour of an extension here.

14. The Parliamentary and the municipal boundaries are not coterminous?—They are not.

15. To what extent does the Parliamentary exceed the municipal?—The Parliamentary boundary consists of an area of 395 acres.

16. And what is the valuation, can you tell me?—£8,874.

17. Do you mean of the entire Parliamentary boundary?—Yes.

18. What is the excess of population in the Parliamentary boundary beyond £4,000?—The Parliamentary is £4,131.

19. What is the proposal, then, that you are authorized to make on the part of the Town Commissioners?—The general impression is that a radius of two miles should be the boundary.

20. From the centre of the town?—Yes; taken from some central point.

21. Would that exceed the Parliamentary boundary?—It would.

22. By what extent?—I am not prepared exactly to say to what extent in acres, for there is nothing to guide me, for that radius would cut holdings.

23. That would never do. Can you give me the names of the townlands that you would propose to take in by the extension, and the valuation of each?—I am not prepared to say the points that the two miles radius would extend to.

24. But the proposal is that all townlands within the two mile radius they should be taken in?—Yes.

25. On what principle is it that the Town Commissioners would propose that you should travel beyond the Parliamentary boundary with regard to this town. Are there any institutions, gentlemen's seats, or large buildings that would be taken in by going beyond the Parliamentary boundary?—Yes, there are gentlemen's seats.

26. How many would you say?—Not many. I could almost name them. There is Castle Bernard ——

27. Do you mean Lord Bandon's residence?—Yes.

28. Would that come within the two mile area?—Yes, that would come in the two mile area, and not be in the Parliamentary boundary. Then there is Mr. Sealy's of Richmount. I should say Prospect would be about the limit—that is where Captain Davidson lives; Mr. Hewitt, of Glengrade; Mr. Pope, and Mr. Doherty. Then, on the Kilbrogan side, Mr. Beswick, Mr. Thomas K. Sullivan, and the Rev. Mr. Bache. I think that takes in the western portion. I think that includes all the gentlemen's residences on the western side.

29. Are there any others?—Yes, on the eastern side, about a dozen in addition.

30. In addition to those you have named beyond the Parliamentary boundary, and that would be taken in within that two mile radius, are there any farmers?—There are.

31. About how many within the whole circle—how many of the farming class?—Well, not many; because the greater portion of the ground is held by townspeople. Would you describe them as farmers?

BANDON. Jan. [illegible] Mr. [illegible]

31. Certainly not on [illegible]?—There are a good many.

32. But the people who own these are already rated within the present boundary?—A number of them are.

33. In addition to those rated within the present area, about how many would come on the franchise by the extension—of the franchise class, within the two mile radius and outside the Parliamentary boundary?—I cannot pretend to be strictly accurate in answering that question. I should say, as an estimate, about 150.

34. Beyond the Parliamentary and within the municipal area, as proposed, with a radius of two miles?—I think so.

35. At all events, you think there would be over 100?—I think there would.

36. In the opinion of the Commissioners, do the persons living within the proposed area of two miles derive substantial benefit from their proximity to the town, so as to justify the Commissioners in asking for that extension?—That is the impression of the Commissioners; that is the very thing for their recommending the extension of the area beyond the present limit.

37. That they largely derive benefits from the town from their close residential vicinity to it?—Yes.

38. Can you tell me, without going into the names, about how many gentlemen's seats are there outside the present boundary, and that would be within the Parliamentary boundary?—Within the municipal boundary there are [illegible] gentlemen[illegible].

39. How many voters would there be in the Parliamentary—they would not be as many?—I will give you the buildings.

40. But you don't know the number of electors?—I do not.

41. Can you tell me about how many gentlemen's seats would be between the municipal and the Parliamentary boundary?—I should say about twenty-four gentlemen's seats.

42. Can you tell me, besides the gentlemen's seats, are there any large manufactories and places outside the municipal and within the Parliamentary boundary?—There is one—Allman's distillery.

43. Are there any others?—Yes, there are; [illegible] mills. Those are three.

44. I suppose the valuations of those establishments are very high?—Yes; of two particularly.

45. Now, about what is the valuation of Allman's distillery?—I can tell you in a moment. The distillery buildings will amount to £[illegible].

46. A year?—Yes, sir.

47. Does that include all?—It does. Mr. [illegible] [illegible] will be valued at £[illegible]; that is two. Mr. [illegible] mill and premises is valued at £[illegible].

48. What about [illegible]'s tan-yard. I suppose that is not a large holding?—£[illegible].

49. Are the two railway stations at present within the municipality?—No, sir; neither of them.

50. Is the [illegible] within the present municipal area?—No; the boundary [illegible] about there; it is not within the municipal boundary.

51. I need not ask you if all these premises derive exceptional advantage from the town, particularly Mr. Allman's distillery and the railway?—Certainly, and they derive great benefit from the town, and that is the circumstance which has guided the Commissioners in recommending the extended area.

52. To what length, have you calculated, [illegible] and west, would the railways that are to be taken in be included?—I suppose about a mile and a half on each side of the proposed extension. The radius of two miles takes in a large length of each railway.

53. And they are not to be [illegible] at present?—Not at all, at present.

54. For instance, so far as the West Cork Railway is concerned, that passes through the town, does it not, and is it not valued within the municipal area at present?—Yes.

55. But any of the ground over which it passes in the town?—No.

56. Would any of this proposed extension go beyond the two electoral divisions you have named?—No, they it would be confined to the two electoral divisions.

57. Are your Board of opinion that, with this increased area, becoming as you would then, an Urban Sanitary Authority, the affairs of the town could be better administered by having it all in the hands of the Town Commissioners?—That is the feeling of the Board. They conceive that the [illegible] in the town—that the town being represented by local parties—that they would naturally take a greater interest in the affairs of the town than the Board of Guardians, consisting, as it does, of a few from the town and others from the country.

58. Is it the feeling of your Board that the affairs of the town, including this increased area, would be better managed if you had the administering of the management of the roads and all that is now done by the Grand Jury in the expenditure of the money?—That is the feeling—that there would be more interest taken in the condition of the town if these matters were managed by the Town Commissioners.

59. At present, you are aware, there is no differential rating in the town, although you are under the 9th Geo. IV.?—I am.

60. Of course you know that persons outside the municipal boundary pay county-at-large charges and county rates for the keeping up of the roads. Have the Commissioners considered whether, supposing this extension was to take place, the ratepayers in the extended boundary would be likely to pay more or less than they do at present?—The feeling is, that the rates necessary for the repairs of the streets and roads would be less.

61. So that, even if they paid on the full, they would pay less than they do now?—Yes.

62. Have your Commissioners considered at all this question: Whether, supposing you [illegible] those outlying districts in the extent proposed by them, whether it would be right, in their opinion, that the persons to be brought in in this extended area should pay equal rates or a differential rate with the inhabitants of the town?—The feeling is that they should pay an equal rate with the inhabitants of the town, for they have all the advantages which the townspeople have, both of the public lighting, the markets, and the schools.

63. Of course, they do not to the same extent use the roads?—On the contrary, the impression is that the outsiders use the roads more than the townspeople.

64. Do the Town Commissioners consider that even if the law was to remain as it is at present, under the [illegible] section of the Towns Improvement Act, and that Bandon was put under the Towns Improvement Act, that still it would be of advantage to the town to have this outside property brought in, even though it only paid one-fourth of the rates?—Yes; but they consider that it would be an injustice that they should only pay one-fourth, inasmuch as in the opinion of the Town Commissioners they use the roads and the town even more than the townspeople themselves.

65. What were the rates for the last [illegible] years—municipal, county, and poor law?—I will furnish you with that information.

66. Would the present Parliamentary [illegible] keep you within the two electoral divisions?—It would.

67. But if you go outside, in what [illegible] will take you into [illegible] electoral division?—Yes, it will.

Mr. John [illegible] Callinan examined.

68. You are a merchant, residing in the town?—Yes.

69. And Chairman of the Town Commissioners?—Yes.

70. How long have you presided over the Board?—About four years.

71. As Chairman of the Town Commissioners can you say whether or not there is a feeling amongst the entire body with regard to the extension of the municipal area?—There is a very strong feeling in favour of an extension.

72. Can you say that the ratepayers within the municipality join as well in that feeling?—Yes.

73. To what extent can you say, according to that feeling, the area should be extended?—Well, there are some who speak in favour of the parliamentary boundary, but the majority are in favour of a two mile radius.

74. That is, to take in all townlands as nearly as possible that would be hit by a two-mile radius?—Yes.

75. Can you tell me, in your opinion, and of your own knowledge as an inhabitant of the town, whether the persons living in the extended area derive exceptional benefit from their proximity to the town so as to warrant the townspeople in asking that they should share in the taxation?—I think they are fully entitled to pay their proportion of the taxes, as they derive great benefit from living so near the town.

76. I suppose, so far as the gentry are concerned, they take advantage of the schools, the places of worship, the markets, the railways, and of all these places?—Yes.

77. Have the Commissioners considered whether it would be fair to the people living in the furthest limit of the area, that they should pay a differential rate or the same rate as the people in the town?—Perhaps I should tell you that there is a movement at present to bring the town under the Towns Improvement Act, and we all know that, although there is only a fourth of the rating to be paid by the farmers——

78. A fourth of the improvement rate?—Yes, generally; the Commissioners are of opinion that it should be a great deal more than a fourth; at the same time they are satisfied to take the amount allowed by the Act of Parliament.

79. One-fourth?—Yes.

80. Have the Commissioners considered whether they should pay same, or what sort of moiety they should pay?—The opinion that I have heard expressed is that they should pay one-third.

81. As far as you are aware, has there been any expression of opinion by the gentry outside the present municipal area against owners of property being brought in?—I have not heard of any. A great many of the gentry have offices in the town, and derive a handsome revenue out of them, and so I do not think they should object.

82. Have you considered whether or not, by increasing the area and becoming the Urban Sanitary Authority, that the affairs of the municipality, if extended, would be better managed if everything was under one board?—Yes, everything would be better managed; it would be for the advantage of the town. Everything would be a great deal better managed.

83. For the roads and for sanitary purposes?—Yes.

84. Is it your opinion that the persons in the extended area would not be called upon, if it was under municipal control, to pay more than they do at present?—I don't think they would.

85. And that the roads could be kept cheaper?—Yes; I think they could be better done, and at a less cost.

86. Do you propose to light the extended district?—No, we do not; it does not require it.

87. In your opinion it would not require it?—It would not.

88. Suppose the portion in the Parliamentary area was taken in—is that lit at present?—Not the most of it.

89. Is any portion of it?—A portion of it is.

90. That is beyond the Municipal and within the Parliamentary area?—There is nothing lit beyond the municipal boundary.

91. Supposing those large stores and the railway station are brought in—would you be prepared to light them?—We would go a certain extent in accommodating them.

92. Would you do the same in the Parliamentary boundary that you would do in the Municipal boundary?—Wherever we would see that the thing would be necessary and of public advantage, we would be willing to do so.

93. Then I understand you to say that in such portions of the increased area as would be a thoroughfare you would be prepared to do that, but as to such as would be in the nature of private roads, where houses would be far asunder, there would be no demand for it?—Yes.

94. Even supposing the people outside were only to pay a half, you would be prepared to do that so far as the thoroughfares extend?—Certainly, so far as the thoroughfares extend.

95. Is there anything else that occurs to you as to that?—I may as well mention that there is one thing that I wish to bring under your notice, and that is that the public rate that we derive at present from our boundaries, does not at all meet the cost of the public lighting. The public rate amounts to about £250 a year, and the public lighting costs us about £400 a year, so that we have a loss of £150 a year on the public lighting. I give you that as an argument why we should bring in more taxation.

Mr. William Thomas Sullivan examined.

96. You are one of the Town Commissioners of Bandon?—I am.

97. And have for a long time filled the position?—Yes.

98. And have been long resident here?—Yes. I may state that at the time of the adoption of the 9th of George IV. there was a great deal of difference of opinion with reference to the definition of the boundary. From the time of the adoption of the 9th of George IV., when the boundaries were settled, there has been no alteration since.

99. It is your opinion that the bounds should be extended?—Certainly.

100. And, so far as you know, is it the general opinion?—I am not enabled to say, as I have not had an opportunity of ascertaining the general opinion as yet upon it, but upon the grounds of equity and justice to all parties, I conceive that the boundaries should be extended; and I will give you my reason why. There are two or three very extensive concerns outside the present municipal boundary, which derive all the advantages from the proximity of the town. Under these circumstances, I conceive that it is quite inequitable that they should be free of the taxation of the town.

101. Have you considered the extent to which that extension should go—are you in favour of having the municipal and Parliamentary boundaries the same, or would you go beyond the Parliamentary?—Well, that is a question that I have not certainly given very serious consideration to. I have heard the very elaborate report of the Clerk to the Commissioners, who has entered most fully into everything—the statistics, &c., connected with the affairs of the town—and he certainly has given very strong reasons why the area should be extended beyond the Parliamentary boundary; but, in a financial point of view, I am not enabled to consider, with justice to all parties—to those outside the Parliamentary boundary and those within it—I am not able to form a positive opinion as to whether or not we should extend the area beyond the Parliamentary boundary.

[illegible]

Mr. William J. Sullivan.

102. But at all events to the extent of the Parliamentary boundary, in your opinion, it ought to be increased?—Most decidedly; and for the reason, I think, Mr. Callinan stated, that the present public rate is inadequate to meet the expenses of the town, and, therefore, upon that ground, I think the area of taxation should be extended.

103. Tell me as to the extent of the Parliamentary boundary, what is your view with regard to the payment of the rate—should the persons to the extent of the Parliamentary boundary pay the same rate as those within the municipal?—Unquestionably.

104. Suppose you went beyond the Parliamentary boundary, as suggested by the Commissioners, would you then be in favour of a differential rate for those outside the Parliamentary boundary?—Most decidedly.

105. Have you considered at all with reference to the Towns Improvement Act the question of having a differential rating, and whether they should pay one-half or one-quarter?—One-half should be the fullest extent, and, if possible, it should be under it. I may as well mention with reference to the Towns Improvement Act——

106. I have nothing to say to that.—I only just wish to mention here in reference to this, that we are at this moment paying a county rate in this town, as well as all the other local rates, and the people of the town feel it as a great hardship; whereas, if they were placed under the Towns Improvement Act, they would get rid of a large portion of that rate; and, in a financial point of view, it would be of great importance to the town, as well as giving us ample powers, which we do not possess at present, by the antiquity of the Act from which our powers are derived.

107. In your opinion, it would be for the advantage of the town that there should be one board for all matters—sanitary, roads, and all—is that your opinion?—Well, you have asked me a question which requires some consideration. In the first place, the Board of Guardians are managing the sanitary affairs of the town very fairly in my opinion, and the contracts taken for the streets are fairly carried out. There has to be a competition for those contracts, and there is no advantage, in my opinion, taken in that matter. Of course, I dare say, under one body all those matters may be more economically managed; but I should say where the Commissioners would have such a deep interest in the town, and in everything connected with it, that its interests would be carefully watched by them, and, probably, upon the whole, there would be more or less of a saving.

Mr. Richard W. Doherty.

Mr. Richard W. Doherty examined.

108. I believe you are agent to the Earl of Bandon here?—Yes.

109. What are your views with reference to the proposed extension of the boundary?—As far as my views go, I would be in favour of extending the boundary to the extent of the Parliamentary boundary, and I think that that would be quite ample for all purposes required, and would cause less confusion than what Mr. Sullivan was referring to. If you go farther you must bear a portion of the rates, and all that. For all purposes of lighting, cleansing, and so on, I think the Parliamentary boundary would be ample, and a great deal more.

110. Then, with the Parliamentary boundary should all parties pay the same rate?—I do think so, certainly. I take it, that if extended to that they would get the lighting extended so far. It is right to mention now that there is portion of this town that was originally cut apart for a boundary under the 9th George IV., and the lights were never put up there—up to the quay on the Castle-road. That was the boundary originally agreed upon, and the lights do not extend within 300 or 400 yards of that, and that road is never lighted.

111. Your view, if the Parliamentary area was made the boundary, is that the people within that boundary if made to pay the full rate—that they should get the same advantages as everyone else?—I think so; I think that would be only justice.

112. Is it your opinion that going beyond the Parliamentary boundary the residents outside, to a certain limited extent, at all events, do not, from their proximity to the town, derive exceptional advantages, in respect of which they should contribute something towards the town?—I do not see that they can get much advantage when they are living beyond the limits of lighting.

113. The advantage is this: is not their ground, and are not their places rendered more valuable by their proximity to the town, market, places of worship, schools, &c.?—That won't bring them a bit nearer to the town.

114. But the question is, should they not contribute something towards the keeping up of the town?—That is a matter of opinion.

115. And I want to know your opinion?—I do not see that they would gain anything by it.

116. The question is, do they not gain from their proximity to the town, as a market town, and having a railway terminus here—but you say that they get that whether they are brought in or not?—I do.

117. But you must go with the ear—the question is, should not the rate be increased?—Of course, in any case, land near to a town is more valuable, but I do not think it increases in value to an extent to be affected by taxation in the slightest degree. There are very few residences about here.

118. Is it your opinion that land within a radius of a couple of miles, say, from this point (referring to map), does not derive from its proximity to the town a small advantage?—There is no question but it derives some value, but I do not think that applies to the question of the lighting of the town.

119. But it should contribute to the town which gives it its exceptional value?—Yes; but I cannot see that such property would improve much in value by the change. I am perfectly satisfied that the Parliamentary boundary is the proper one, and the 9th of George IV. is a very good Act.

[illegible]

Mr. David Craig examined.

120. I believe you are acting here for Mr. Barwick, who is agent to the Duke of Devonshire?—Yes, I am the assistant to the agent.

121. Can you tell me, in your opinion, at what—say, from the centre of the town—distance does land derive benefit from its proximity to the town?—I think about two miles. The townparks are let for grazing purposes about two miles out; beyond that it is generally farms. In the Duke's property that is the case.

122. A good deal of the Duke's property consists of townparks?—Yes, a good deal.

123. At all events, you would be of opinion that it would be fair to include the townlands in the Parliamentary boundary, still keeping the municipality within the two electoral divisions?—I think so.

Lord Bandon.—That would be very fair.

Mr. Tuthill.

Mr. Tuthill re-examined.

124. I assume that all the townlands within the present Parliamentary boundary are comprised within these two electoral divisions?—Certainly.

125. Even though portion of a townland may be a little outside the Parliamentary boundary, still every townland within the Parliamentary is within one of the two electoral divisions?—Within the two more electoral divisions.

The Inquiry terminated.

MIDLETON.—JANUARY 3RD, 1879.

Before Mr. C. P. Cotton, C.E.

Mr. [illegible] M'Cormack examined.

1. You are clerk of the Town Commissioners?—Yes.
2. How long have you held that position?—Since the adoption of the Act in 1857.
3. Had the town previously been under the Act of George IV.?—No, sir.
4. Did you on that occasion adopt the Act in its entirety or only in part?—Only in part.
5. What part did you adopt?—All, with the exception of lighting and supplying with water.
6. You subsequently did adopt the Act for those purposes?—No; but we did for lighting.
7. When was that?—On the 12th February, 1877. There is a sealed order of that date.
8. You never adopted the water clauses?—Never at any time.
9. What is the area of the existing municipality of Midleton?—[illegible], 12a. 3p.
10. In the return to me I find it is 98[illegible], but we often find some disparity of that kind. What is the valuation?—In buildings £4,[illegible] 5s.; half annual rents, £116 5s.; lands, £[illegible].
11. Give the total?—Altogether it is £[illegible] 10s.
12. How many townlands or parts of townlands does the municipal district comprise?—There is [illegible] [illegible] and [illegible] lands and townparks, Knockgriffin in the barony of Imokilly, or part of it, part of Knockgriffin, and part of Cahon [illegible].
13. These are also only ones?—Yes.
14. Are all these townlands included in the electoral division of Midleton?—Yes.
15. Now, taking the starting point from the centre of the town, to what distance does the municipal radius extend?—About half a statute mile, at either end due north or south.
16. And to east and west?—Oh, a very narrow strip to the east and west.
17. And about half a mile across to the north and south?—Yes; I consider that the whole length of the town is about a statute mile, according to the scale of the map.
18. Midleton is not an Urban Sanitary District; you are merged in the Rural Sanitary Authority, and since 1874 the sanitary functions, I believe, have been exercised by the Board of Guardians?—Yes, the whole of them.
19. How many **Commissioners constitute the Board**?—Nine.
20. And has the question of the areas, and of extending, limiting, or otherwise altering them, been considered?—Indeed it has.
21. Recently?—Recently and for a long time.
22. Have they recently, since the appointment of this Commission, taken into consideration the question?—Yes.
23. Has any resolution been passed?—Well, not [illegible] resolution.
24. Was any division given to it?—No; there was a committee appointed to take in a certain boundary, and that is on the minutes.
25. Will you kindly read that for me?—Yes. "Valuation of buildings to be included in the proposed extension of the area of the township of Midleton:—Houses in Youghal-road £2 10s.; R. [illegible]'s holdings, house £9, lands £4 5s.; J. C. [illegible]'s house £30, lands £13; R. [illegible] [illegible], house £38 5s., lands £1 5s.; T. R. and R. [illegible], house £45 10s., lands £10; Mrs. [illegible], houses £5 15s., lands £25; [illegible] house £10, no lands; Knockgriffin house £[illegible], lands £[illegible] 5s.; [illegible] Mills, &c., houses £100, lands £4 10s.; quarry and houses, houses £3 5s., land £3; Robert [illegible]'s house £3, lands £4; Park Village, houses £14. **Total houses £387 10s., lands £[illegible] 5s.**"
26. You will supply us the **queries sent to you by this Commission**?—Yes.
27. The Town Commissioners gave you instructions as to the replies?—There was a meeting held and the Commissioners there gave the answers to the printed queries, a copy of which I did not keep.
28. Now is this boundary in the queries which is the area proposed—what has it to do with it?—They did not make any particular [illegible] or news.
29. Was any opinion expressed as to what would be considered a desirable area?—No.
30. You don't think so?—There was not.
31. The Commissioners jointly expressed a general opinion in favour of extension?—Yes.
32. Was there a [illegible] [illegible]?—Yes.
33. Was the subject considered at that meeting?—Yes.
34. How many members were present?—Five or six.
35. Out of nine?—Yes.
36. Were they unanimous?—Yes, I think so.
36. Now are the Commissioners aware that under the Public Health Act of 1878 ample power was given to the Local Government Board, by provisional order, to transfer the sanitary jurisdiction from the Board of Guardians to the Commissioners?—Yes.
37. Has that subject ever been before the Commissioners to your knowledge?—No.
38. You are not aware if they are in favour of it?—No; but from my own observation I don't think so.
39. Are the Commissioners aware that if they were so constituted as the Urban Sanitary Authority they could by further sections of the Public Health Act of 1878 enable the Local Government Board to have power, by provisional order, to transfer the powers of the Grand Jury within the municipal district over roads, footpaths, and bridges, to the town body?—Yes.
40. Were they considering this consideration whether they would take the necessary steps to secure that transfer?—The matter was spoken of.
41. Did no formal resolution pass adopted?—No.
42. Have you any notion of houses being excepted when you return from the municipal area?—No, very and enough portion of them is fully [illegible], and the [illegible].
43. Apart from the poor rates, what income do you derive?—I think about between £15 and £20 a year.
44. From what?—Fairs and the [illegible].
45. What have been the rates for the past few years?—From 6d. to 9d. There have been rates of 6d., 9d., and 1s., and two years there were no rates at all.
46. When was the 1s. rate levied?—Last year.
47. And the year before that?—9d.
48. And the year before that?—6d.; and before that none.
49. What does your annual expenditure amount to?—Last year the expenses amounted to £194.
50. What was it for the year before that?—£190, in or about £100.
51. And the year before that?—About £80.
52. It appears from these figures that the expenditure of last year was vastly in excess of previous years—why was that?—That was occasioned by the exceptional expenses incurred in lighting the town.
53. Is the lighting provided by the Commissioners themselves, or do they contract for the supply?—They have a contract with the gas company for the supply.

54. And it was the expenditure on that that necessitated the increase over the previous year?—Yes; and the getting up of gas lamps and flagging.

55. There was a special expenditure for flagging?—Yes.

56. Have you ever voted rates up to your full maximum powers—up to 1s.?—Yes.

57. What are the objects to which the expenditure is now applied?—Lighting, flagging, and watching the streets.

58. Is there any other purpose for which you tender purchase?—No, except in a very small way.

59. Is there any work connected with your functions which the Commissioners are restricted from carrying out in consequence of the amount of rate it would require?—Well, no.

60. Now, since 1874—since the Board of Guardians assumed the sanitary authority—have any special rates been made for sanitary purposes?—Well, I am not aware.

61. Are you aware if any sanitary works, such as extending the supply of water, or sewerage work, required by the Town Commissioners, have not been supplied by the Board of Guardians?—Well, no.

62. You do not know anything of the rate of sanitary works?—No.

63. You think that there is no doubt the opinion of the Commissioners is, that the present area is too limited?—Yes.

64. Are there any lands, any public lands, at present included in the municipal district?—No; one or two small fields, none of them are considerable lands.

65. Nor any considerable portion?—No, except a couple of fields.

66. What is the present constituency—about how many persons are eligible to vote for Town Commissioners?—About 110.

67. How many persons are there within the town eligible for the office of Commissioner?—Well, I cannot say; there are about sixty persons.

68. Now, if the radius were extended to a mile round the town, would that bring in a considerable extent of agricultural land?—Yes, it would.

69. Would the extension I have mentioned add very largely to the constituency qualified to vote for Commissioners?—No; they are all large farmers.

70. But it would add considerably to the number of persons eligible for the office of Town Commissioner?—Well, no.

71. Do you consider that the persons residing within the radius of a mile derive advantages from their proximity to the town of Midleton—advantages from the cleansing, lighting, and so on, and from the schools in it, and having a market for various produce. Do you consider persons within that radius derive advantages in that way?—I think they do.

72. Is the land owned by these persons more valuable than land at a greater distance from the town?—Yes, being so contiguous to the town, I think so.

73. Their proximity to the town as a market confers advantages?—Yes.

74. Within how far would you consider it might be held these advantages extend to persons outside the town—to what extent would, with any propriety to the town, may be said to confer advantages?—I think within about a mile.

75. Would you say that one English mile would fairly comprise the persons so benefited?—Yes.

76. You are aware that outside lands are, under the "Towns Improvement Act," only rated at one-fourth the valuation?—Yes.

77. Do you think that is a fair measure of the advantages?—Yes.

78. And you think that within a radius of a mile that fairly it would be valid—that those persons should be rated in proportion to the advantages?—Yes.

79. And do you think that the persons within a radius of a mile, and not within the present boundary, would strongly object to be included within that area of a mile circle?—Of course, some of them would.

80. On what ground would they object?—On the ground of the taxation, that is all.

81. Suppose the radius were extended not a mile, but a mile and a half, that would bring in a very considerable number of persons in addition to those included at present?—No, it would not.

82. But it would bring in a good deal of arable land?—Yes.

83. Nor put a large number of inhabited houses?—No.

84. Do you think the advantages of the town might be held to have effect over a radius of a mile and a half?—No, I think that is too much for Midleton.

85. You think a radius of a mile would fairly represent the district within which the advantages of the town are derived?—Yes.

86. You have stated the expenditure of last year that I understood to have been exceptionally high?—Yes.

87. Now that that has been got rid of, will the expenditure of next year be about the same as previous years?—Yes, with the addition of the lighting, of course.

88. What additional cost will that increase to the annual expenditure?—£40 I think; something about that.

89. So that, in point of fact, the expenditure will be about doubled?—Yes.

90. The lighting expenditure is about equal to all the expenditure for other purposes?—Yes.

91. Mr. Cotton.—Is the railway station within the present limits?—Yes.

92. It is not, in this map?—No; the railway station was not indicated on that map, but the ground on which they stand is in it.

93. Is the railway station actually within the boundary?—Yes.

94. Mr. O'Brien.—How much of the line of railway is within the present boundary?—A few perches only.

95. Do you consider it reasonable that the railway should be included?—Yes.

96. If the proposed radius of a mile were adopted would that bring in portion of the railway?—Yes, of the line, about a mile of it.

97. Have you anything further you would wish to add?—No.

[illegible] Mr. [illegible] O'Connell.

Mr. John T. Aitken, C.E., examined.

Mr. John T. Aitken, C.E.

98. Mr. O'Brien.—You are one of the Commissioners?—Yes.

99. How long have you been a Commissioner?—About eight years.

100. And, I presume, you are perfectly acquainted with everything connected with the present area?—Yes.

101. Were you at the meeting yesterday when the question of the area was considered?—Yes.

102. How many Commissioners were present?—Six.

103. That is two-thirds of the entire body?—Yes.

104. What was the conclusion at which the committee arrived yesterday?—They came to the conclusion to adopt a radius of a mile and a quarter.

105. Exactly?—Yes, a mile and a quarter.

106. Now, would that radius of a mile and a quarter—would it not [illegible] considerable [illegible]?

—Yes, it would. [illegible]

107. [illegible]—Yes.

108. [illegible]—[illegible]

109. [illegible]

110. How many whole and how many parts [illegible]

111. [illegible]

112. Are they all in the electoral division of [illegible]—Yes.

113. [illegible]

114. How far [illegible]—[illegible] a mile and a quarter out.

115. [illegible]

116. How much in excess of a mile and a quarter [illegible]

117. In excess of the mile and a quarter [illegible]—Yes.

118. [illegible]

119. About half a mile over the mile and a quarter?—Yes.

120. [illegible]

121. [illegible]

122. [illegible]

123. [illegible]

124. Assuming your proposal were adopted, what would be the new area?—[illegible]

125. [illegible]

126. And do you consider that that would give sufficient margin for [illegible]—Yes.

127. [illegible]

128. [illegible]

129. [illegible]

130. [illegible]—No.

131. [illegible]

132. [illegible]

133. They think it preferable for the Board of Guardians to have the jurisdiction?—Yes.

134. [illegible]

135. [illegible]—Yes.

136. [illegible]

137. Do the Commissioners know that by the Act [illegible]—Yes.

138. If you were constituted the Urban Sanitary Authority, do you think they would ask the [illegible]—Certainly.

139. [illegible]

140. [illegible]

141. [illegible]

142. Do you know about what amount is paid [illegible]

143. [illegible]

144. What would be the cost of [illegible]

145. Mr. Cotton.—[illegible]—Yes.

146. Mr. O'Brien.—[illegible]

147. [illegible]

148. How much per perch would that give?—[illegible]

149. Do you consider the work would be [illegible]

150. Mr. Cotton.—[illegible]

151. Mr. O'Brien.—[illegible]

which are connected with sewering and water supply?—Yes, both of these are much needed.

153. But would it be a necessary demand in your scheme that [illegible] you should have a larger area to charge the expenditure on?—[illegible].

154. What do you estimate would be the probable cost of making as good a thoroughly good system of sewerage and water supply?—We have not made any [illegible] as to the sewerage, but the water supply would cost about £[illegible].

155. In what way would the supply be made?—By pipes from a distance of three miles and a half or so.

156. How much do you contemplate it would cost?—£[illegible]; that has been the estimate made.

157. That would be too large with the present area?—Yes, altogether.

158. Would it be feasible if the new area were adopted?—That I would not like to say. I would not like to answer that, for it is entirely a matter of taxation. Of course it very likely would be adopted if it could be done for a light tax.

159. You know that for sanitary purposes you can get loans from Government, and spread the repayment over a good many years?—Yes.

160. Would it then be feasible, do you think, if there was a larger area?—It is questionable if the ratepayers would adopt it.

161. But you think an improved water supply is needed?—Yes.

162. The present area is too limited to sustain it in its present?—Yes.

163. What would the sewerage expenditure require?—I can't say. There has been no estimate made of it.

164. Would it require a considerable outlay—can you roughly [illegible] think it would; but to say what would make it proper work.

165. What would you be inclined to think?—Well, I should say something between £1,000 and £2,000 to do it thoroughly.

166. There is an undoubted want of good sewerage in the town?—Well, not in the town altogether, but in part of it.

167. You have suggested a radius of a mile and a quarter from the centre of the town, would that bring in a large number of inhabitants' houses?—Not very.

168. A large number of houses in [illegible]?—Not a very large number, but there would be a large proportion of [illegible] eligible for the [illegible] of town than [illegible] who are not [illegible].

169. A larger number in that way than at present?—Yes.

170. Do you consider that the advantages of the town government may fairly be held to extend to that radius that you propose?—No doubt.

171. And I presume you believe the proximity of the [illegible] may be considered to be of value to them?—Yes.

172. In supplying their wants and as a market for them?—Yes.

173. In supplying their wants and in disposing of their agricultural produce?—Yes.

174. And do the majority of persons living outside but within the radius proposed, derive advantage from having the markets in the town?—Yes, and they come each [illegible].

175. But you think a mile and a quarter would be enough—would be as far as desirable to make an extension?—Yes, I think that would be fairly sufficient.

176. You are aware that arable lands pay only one-fourth?—Yes.

177. Do you consider that a fair measure of the advantages they derive?—Those nearer to the town or [illegible] to it derive greater advantages, but on the average I believe it to be a fair measure.

178. You would not go further than a mile and a quarter?—No.

179. Is there any special observation you would wish to make?—No, except that I wish to explain that in the first instance it was proposed to increase the area. There was a complaint from the Town Clerk, and he and, and since your inquiry has been going on, we have seen from the newspapers that several towns have adopted a radius of a mile and a half or two miles, and we thought it better to reconsider the matter; and the Commissioners were entertaining the idea that places within a mile of the town like [illegible] derive advantages from it, and they recommend the matter and [illegible] it [illegible] further, [illegible] in that [illegible] places different [illegible] mentioned. With regard to the [illegible] power—the [illegible] urban sanitary power, and of [illegible] the [illegible]—I may say that in [illegible] we have found a want for a long time of a staff of men to do the work. The reason is, we have been entirely depending on contractors, and, of course, we had power, if the contractor did not do the work satisfactorily, of hiring men and [illegible] him with the expense; but we found that a [illegible] for an [illegible] the [illegible] that [illegible], and take the money out of the pocket of the contractor. We have none at the [illegible] of [illegible] and [illegible]. The people of the town have had [illegible] from [illegible] as to the [illegible] and [illegible] and many things; and for that reason we have been always [illegible] to feel the want of a staff of men of our own whom we could directly appoint. This was impracticable with our present [illegible]. The only chance was to become the urban sanitary authority, and have control over the roads. If it could be managed without heavy taxation, I consider it would be more desirable, but, of course, if the taxes were heavy, people are not in a position to bear heavy taxation at all, and perhaps it is better to leave things as they are. It would depend upon what the rate of taxation would be.

179a. I understand you to suggest, Mr. Riddle, that the views of the Commissioners, as to getting the transfer of the roads, &c., would be contingent on the rate being divided. On that point I may again refer you to the question to which the [illegible] [illegible] considering all the arguments, arrived. Now, assuming the scheme of the Commission should be [illegible] [illegible] for [illegible], then would be part of it, and, I take it the view of the Commissioners as the transfer of the roads would be contingent on that?—Yes.

180. I called attention in the first place [illegible] [illegible] that [illegible] boundary that [illegible] [illegible] as far as possible, [illegible] [illegible] are you aware of the [illegible] of the [illegible] and [illegible] [illegible] of the [illegible] divisions?—No. I may mention that in striking out one boundary there was some proposition to take in the centre of the village of Ballymacarn.

181. Is that in the electoral division in the portion of it is. We finished by taking the boundary that divides the two electoral divisions.

182. But you have not consulted the [illegible] [illegible] divisions?—Yes.

183. And that was the reason you did not take in the whole of Ballymacarn?—Yes.

184. What electoral division is the rest in?—Clogrea.

185. Mr. Cotton.—Ballymacarn is to a great extent almost entirely one long street. Now, what was the point you selected as the centre of the circle or radius you adopted?—The point where Charles street crosses the Main-street.

186. Mr. O'Brien.—Now, as regards the taking of the circle, as Mr. Cotton has pointed out, Ballymacarn is rather peculiar. It consists, as he has said, of one long street, and, therefore, when you take any given radius from the centre, you necessarily include a great deal more rural territory on the east and west than on the north and south.

187. Mr. Riddle.—Well, we have taken that into consideration as far as we could.

188. You were alive to that fact?—Yes.

189. Would there be any difficulty in your getting for us a sketch map, showing the present boundary

Midleton, Jan. 4, 1877.

Mr. John T. Ashlin, C.E.

and marking the proposed extension ?—No, it would not be very difficult.

The *Town Clerk* mentioned that the contemplated extended boundary comprised Castleredmond, Ballyannan (part of), Garryduff, Broomfield East (part of), Broomfield West (part of), Killeagh (part of), Coolcanno, Park North, Park South, Gurranreke (part of), Knockgriffin, in Barrymore, and Knockgriffin, in Imokilly (part of).

Mr. Thomas Coppinger.

Mr. Thomas Coppinger examined.

190. Mr. O'Brien.—You are Chairman of the Midleton Town Commissioners ?—Yes.

191. Were you present at the meeting when the question of the proposed extension of boundary was discussed ?—I was.

192. And you have heard what Mr. Ashlin has stated as to the result of that meeting ?—Yes.

193. Do you concur in what he has stated ?—Yes.

194. And that was the unanimous wish of the Commissioners ?—Yes.

195. Was there any dissentient amongst the Commissioners either at the meeting or who were absent ?—No.

196. You think the feeling is unanimously in favour of extension ?—I do.

197. And would the feeling, if that extension were granted, be also unanimous as to having the functions of the Grand Jury, as to roads, bridges, and footpaths, transferred to the Town Commissioners ?—Yes, in the event mentioned by Mr. Ashlin.

198. In the event of the rating being divided between the landlord and tenant for roadways ?—Yes.

199. And in getting the transfer of the roads, would they be in favour of getting the sanitary functions from the Board of Guardians ?—I think they would seek for the roads.

200. Yes, but they would not ask for the sanitary functions unless they got the roads ?—No.

201. Now, do you know the electoral division of Midleton, how far it extends ?—I think Mr. Reale, the Clerk of the Union, would best be able to tell you.

202. You have not considered would it be desirable to adopt the electoral division as a municipal boundary ?—That would be too large.

203. Do you know how far the remotest part of the electoral division is from the centre of the town ?—Four miles, I should say.

204. And you think that would be too far to take in ?—Yes.

205. You, therefore, would not be in favour of that ?—No.

206. Is there anything you would wish to suggest ?—No, I think Mr. Ashlin has explained everything.

Mr. Timothy Murphy.

Mr. Timothy Murphy examined.

207. Mr. O'Brien.—Have you been long a Commissioner, Mr. Murphy ?—About six years.

208. And are acquainted with all the facts concerning this question ?—Perfectly.

209. Now, as regards the existing area, do you consider it sufficiently extensive ?—Certainly not.

210. You were present at the meeting held yesterday ?—Yes.

211.—You agreed with the other Commissioners ?—Yes, we were quite unanimous.

212. The extension you advocated would be a mile and a quarter ?—Yes.

213. That would comprehend twelve entire townlands, and portions of two others ?—Yes.

214. Assuming that the definition of townlands should be adhered to as the unit of organisation, would you see any objection to including these two ?—I would not.

215. Do you not think that there is advantage in making municipal boundaries include townlands, rather than cutting them, so as to have a well-known and defined boundary ?—I do; and furthermore, being land, and not highly valued, the ratepayer would only have to pay a small proportion of the rates.

216. You would see no objection to including these two then ?—I think not; at the same time owners of land might object to it.

217. Do you consider that one-fourth would fairly represent the advantage they derive ?—I do; at the same time people a little farther off get equal advantages.

218. But you think it necessary to draw the line somewhere ?—Yes.

219. Now, as to the transfer of the jurisdiction of the Poor Law Board of Guardians, do you agree that that would be desirable ?—I have often thought of that. It very frequently happens that the rural Guardians are present and the Town Guardians absent, and then no one takes the least interest in the town affairs. I say that, having been a Guardian and Commissioner.

220. You think that the work would be more efficiently administered by the Town Board ?—Yes; the only objection is that the whole rates would fall on the occupiers.

221. But if the law in that respect were altered—if the rates were divided between the occupiers and owners, that would remove that objection ?—Yes.

222. Assuming you were made the Sanitary Authority, would you consider it desirable to have the control of the roads in the municipal district ?—Yes; because the roads have been getting into an abominable state for years past. People have always been complaining that they are not attended to at all.

223. And you think the amount raised in county cess is in excess of the amount expended ?—Yes.

224. Can you give figures on the point ?—No.

225. You think the present system is defective at least ?—Yes.

226. Now, what are the advantages which you think the persons within the radius of a mile and a quarter derive from their proximity to the town of Midleton ?—They have facilities in the way of a good market, their children come to the town to school, in fact they have nearly all the advantages which the people in the town possess.

227. Do you think the persons outside would object very strongly ?—I know very well they would have no objection if it did not touch their pockets.

228. It would extend the number of persons eligible for the position of Town Councillors ?—Well, not so much as people might imagine.

229. By how much would it increase the number ?—By some seven or eight.

230. Would it not be of advantage to introduce some of the rural element ?—Yes.

231. Is there anything you wish to say further with reference to the subject generally ?—Well, no; Mr. Ashlin has given expression to our opinion, and we were unanimous on all points.

232. I take it that you are all unanimous in the opinion that, as a condition necessary for the transfer of the sanitary functions, and the jurisdiction over roads, all municipal rates should be divided ?—Yes.

233. And you concur in the recommendation of the Parliamentary Commission that the law should be altered in that respect ?—Yes.

[illegible]
[illegible] 1879.
Mr. W. Rorke.

Mr. WILLIAM RORKE examined.

235. *Mr. O'Brien.*—What is the area and valuation of the electoral division, Mr. Rorke? First of all, you are the Clerk of the Union?—Yes.

236. Well, what is the valuation and area of the electoral division of Midleton?—The area is 5,656a. 3r. 8p., and the valuation, £16,752 5s.

237. How many townlands does it comprise?—Thirty-seven.

238. Now, how far does the electoral division extend?—In a northerly direction something over three miles, and to the south about a mile, and in a westerly direction something over four miles, and on the east about three miles.

239. So, that it does not extend uniformly?—No, it is unequal on each side.

240. Of course the electoral divisions were formed with a different consideration than a mere radius—do you consider it would be possible to adopt the electoral division of Midleton as a municipal district?—I think, scarcely.

241. What point was four miles out, did you say?—Well, Ballywalsh is about four miles.

242. That is to the west?—Yes.

243. What other electoral division comes within a mile?—Cloyne immediately joins the townland of Ballynacorra.

244. I take it that if the electoral division of Midleton were taken as the municipal area it would have this effect—that in one direction lands lying four miles from the centre of the town would be included, and in another those one mile or so out would be excluded?—Yes.

245. So that it would not be feasible to adopt it?—No.

246. Having regard to any principle of equity?—No.

247. Is the electoral division of Cloyne large?—Yes.

248. How far is the farthest part of it from the centre of Midleton?—I suppose it is nearly ten miles.

249. We may take it, it would be impracticable to adopt the electoral division of Midleton?—Yes.

250. Would the feeling of the Board of Guardians be in favour of having the sanitary jurisdiction given over to the town body?—I think they would be in favour of it.

251. You think they would rather have the trouble taken off their hands?—Yes, I do.

252. You have been constituted the sanitary authority since 1874?—Yes.

253. Have there been special rates made for sanitary purposes?—Yes.

254. What was the general rate?—1d. in the pound for general expenses, and the last rate was 4d.

255. What was that made for?—For cleaning the sewers—keeping them in order for the last twelve months.

256. Has any proposition been under the consideration of the Board of Guardians for giving improved water supply and sewerage to Midleton?—Well, there was a meeting on the subject, but it fell through.

257. Has any official representation, or any representation of any kind been addressed to the Board of Guardians, urging the necessity of undertaking the works for water supply and sewerage?—Yes; the water supply has been spoken of.

258. I mean from the Medical Sanitary Officers of Health for instance?—Some time ago the water was discussed by the Guardians, and they got all the water in the town analysed.

259. How many pumps or wells are there?—There are a number of wells and pumps.

260. How many were analysed?—Seven.

261. What was the result?—Unfavourable in a great many instances.

262. Unfavourable in any?—Yes; oh, yes.

263. What action was then taken; where they pronounced bad; were they closed?—No; the people were warned and prevented from using them.

264. That is, they were advised not to use them?—Yes.

265. Has there been any representation to the Guardians to get an improved system of water supply?—No; it was discussed several times.

266. But no official representation was made?—No; it was simply discussed several times.

267. What led to the discussion of it?—There was a public meeting of the inhabitants.

268. When was that; about how long ago?—It was about twelve months ago—coming up to twelve months.

269. What was the result of that?—Well, I was not present at it.

270. Did you not hear what was the conclusion arrived at?—Well, at that time they did not consider it advisable to do anything.

Mr. Coppinger.—That was on account of the expense.

271. *Mr. O'Brien.*—Was it admitted that there was a necessity for an improved water supply?

Mr. Rorke.—Well, I think there was some difference of opinion.

272. The main objection was to the great expense?—Yes.

273. Has any question been under consideration for the improvement of the sewers?—No. Whenever they got out of order they were put into repair.

274. Was the question ever discussed?—Yes, at one time.

275. When was that?—It is very nearly twelve months since.

276. Tell me shortly what took place on the matter?—The great defect was the want of a proper system or means of flushing the sewers, the street being so level. An engineer was employed and a map drawn up, and he proposed from the stream at the workhouse to take the water to the top of the street and flush the main sewers, and let it run down to the river. The matter, however, fell through. They put it off until the water supply question would be properly gone into, and if they arranged on that they would have no difficulty in flushing the sewers.

277. So it was allowed to stand over pending the settlement of the water question?—Yes.

278. And that has not been settled, it is allowed to be neglected?—Yes.

279. What was the contract for—what amount?—£5,000.

Mr. Ashlin.—As to the water supply, I may say the meeting was merely a preliminary meeting for the purpose of hearing the present state of the question, and hearing a statement from the different doctors and sanitary officers as to the state of the water in the different wells, the want of proper water, and also of putting before the people the cost of such a water supply and the probable rate it would involve. There were no resolutions proposed. It was merely making a statement of the case, and nothing further was done on the question. There was a good deal of difference of opinion about the matter. Some people were very much against it; some people thought that Midleton was well supplied, and some who thought that then have altered their views. The principal reason that nothing was done was, however, the expense.

280. *Mr. O'Brien.*—If it could be done on moderately reasonable terms it would be done?

Mr. Ashlin.—Yes. I might mention that the plans and estimate were prepared by Mr. Fraser, C.E.

281. Tell me, Mr. Ashlin, how much of Ballynacorra is in Cloyne?—Oh, it is all in it. To bring it in would add to the utility in sanitary matters.

282. *Mr. O'Brien.*—Mr. Rorke, what have been the rates in the electoral division of Midleton for the last five years?—In 1874, 8s. 4d.; in 1875, 1s. 7d.; in

1876, 1s. 7d.; in 1877, 1s. 8d.; and in 1878 the ordinary rate was 2s. 2d., and the sanitary rate 4d.

863. Mr. Aldin.—I wish just to correct one matter. I mentioned that there were portions of two townlands included in the proposed extension. I should have said three. There is Ballyanna Wood in addition to the two I mentioned.

The inquiry then terminated.

MIDLETON—17TH OCTOBER, 1879.

(Second Inquiry.)

Mr. C. P. Cotton, C.E., held the Inquiry.

The Commissioner having explained the tendency of the evidence already given—

Mr. Peterson Fitzgerald was examined.

1. Would you be in favour of having a boundary regulated by townlands or by roads rather than a hard and fast line that would cut through houses?—I communicated with Lord Midleton and I have his views as to what would be advisable, but I don't know exactly what proposal was made on the last occasion. I understand it was suggested to take in Ballyannan, and the entire of the townland of Cahermone, which is purely grass farm. Lord Midleton, I should say, is the owner in fee of the entire town and the whole country that would be taxed.

2. Is he of opinion there should be no extension?—No, I was in England, I may mention, when you were here before, and before I went away I put a proposal before the Commissioners for extension, and it appeared to me that they all agreed to it; but it was totally different from what appears to have been put forward before you in their replies.

3. They have sent forward to our queries, answers in which they merely say that an extension is desirable, but they do not say to what extent. It is only in the evidence that the proposal to extend it a mile and quarter is made?—The principle Lord Midleton wished to be followed was, that all town holdings where business connected with the town is carried on, or accommodation lands, land let as townparks to tradesmen in the town, should be taxed, but nothing outside the town holdings should be fairly taxed for town purposes.

4. How far would that apply out from the town, is it any defined line?—It was all put on paper; as to what they would take in exactly I could not give you it geographically, but it would take in portions of townlands to which town holdings have extended.

5. Could you let us have a map of what Lord Midleton would wish?—I could make it. The only duties the Town Commissioners now undertake are the watering of the streets, and the lighting of the lamps, and flagging the footways. I cannot see what advantage it is to farmers even a quarter of a mile off to have the streets watered in which they drive in it may be a mile and a half.

6. Is it not of advantage to them to have light?—Well, they come in such a long way dark that for the matter they might as well have it so the whole way.

7. Do you not think that the people, say, a mile outside, are sufficiently interested in the town that they might fairly be called on to pay something towards the town for lighting?—No, I think not. I wish it to be understood that Lord Midleton objects to agricultural holdings being taxed. A mile and a quarter extension would take in the wood of Ballyannan where there are no inhabitants except the woodman and his family. I don't know on what principle it is proposed to tax farming land for watering the town.

8. The Towns Improvement Act provides for the payment of one-fourth by arable land, so that it contemplates land being included somehow?—Land held by townspeople as a convenience ought not to be taxed.

Mr. Patrick Michael Moss examined.

9. Do you live within the town?—No, I live within the mile and a quarter radius.

10. And do you object to being brought within the boundary?—Yes, on principle I do.

11. You consider you get no benefit from the lighting of the town, or other advantages?—No, not to such an extent that I ought to be liable for purposes of the taxation, inasmuch as men living seven miles from the town have greater advantage than I would have living close to it. A man living seven miles off may be detained—he comes in bringing his corn to sell in the market and may in all probability not leave till the gas lamps are lighted, but a man living only a mile and a quarter can deliver his goods and be away in time so that the light is of no consequence to him. Well, again, the markets are not of such importance to us that we should be called upon to pay additional tax for it. There is a better market in Cork, and the advantages indeed are nil so far as I am concerned.

12. You think that even the small proportion of one-fourth should not be put on you?—No. There is no advantage to us at all except indeed the advantage we derive of being able to go to Church on Sunday.

13. Do the children come in to school from the outside districts?—Yes, that is an advantage, but at the same time there are disadvantages.

14. Is your land more valuable from being near the town?—No, I consider it is less, for my labour bill is at least one-third more than if I was far away.

15. The labour costs more?—Yes. My reason is this. During portion of the year when farmers do the greatest proportion of their work the town labourers stop at six o'clock. As soon as a man sees the other going off, he goes off. Well the townspeople let them off at six o'clock and cannot employ relays of men to work on continuously in winter.

16. In point of fact it costs you more?—Yes.

17. Is not land more valuable that lies close to the town?—Well, I don't believe land within a mile and a half of the town fetches more than its intrinsic value by the acre.

Mr. Peterson Fitzgerald.—As agent of the estate I can say that land within that distance (one and a-half miles) does not fetch more than its intrinsic value. This is not a consuming town. It is a depot—goods are brought here and sent on. The market is really in Queenstown and Cork.

Examination resumed.

18. Have you any further reasons, Mr. Moss, to urge against the extension?—My impression is that if the area was extended the Commissioners would have lost control of the expenditure of the money and my impression is that if the law were to be extended so that the taxation would bear lightly on the townspeople, you would have more works carried on.

19. What special works do you refer to?—The proposed waterworks. I hold that if human life was in jeopardy or seriously endangered any money should be spent in alleviating the evil, but under the present circumstances I think such works are thoroughly unnecessary. I mean under the circumstances. If they had money it would be well enough, but under the present circumstances it is unnecessary.

Midleton. Oct. 18, 1871

Mr. Patrick Michael Mara.

20. Is it your opinion it is well supplied with water at present?—No, but it could be easily supplied. There are two rivers flowing into the town—one from the north the other from the east. One is the Dungourney river. We sometimes work the steam-engine on the northern river, sometimes on the other, and there is no better way of testing it practically, than by working a steam engine on it a few days, for you can see by the deposit the purity of the water to a certain extent. —There would be after one week's work a great deposit of lime in the Dungourney river—

Mr. *Fitzgerald*.—A plan has been suggested by the engineer.

21. Mr. COTTON.—The only question is, is the water wanted. Mr. Ashlin has expressed a decided opinion that the water supply cannot be got to the present area but that if the area is extended it could be got?

Witness.—But I mean to show that it can be got.

Mr. COTTON.—I would suggest then that you should lay this before the Commissioners.

Mr. *Fitzgerald*.—The Board of Guardians are the sanitary authority.

Mr. Daniel Hutchins examined.

Mr. Daniel Hutchins.

22. Are you in favour of the extension?—No, I don't see any advantage to be derived from it.

23. Where do you reside?—At Park North.

24. Are you outside the present boundary?

25. And you have an objection to be brought in?—Yes, certainly.

26. You don't think you have such an interest in the town being well lighted and so on as that you should pay something towards it?—Certainly not.

Mr. *Fitzgerald*.—The town derives more advantage from the country than the country from the town.

Mr. *Humphries*.—I take Mr. Fitzgerald's view as the correct one, that accommodation lands should be taxed; but there is no advantage derived by the people in my neighbourhood—Broomfield for instance.

27. Can you tell me on what district the sanitary works are charged?—Well, I know the principle has always been to charge them on the townlands benefited.

Mr. Edmund Barry, J.P., examined.

Mr. Edmund Barry, J.P.

28. You live in the town?—Yes. I have not been examined at the previous inquiry. I must say the argument has come very strange to me that these people living outside derive no advantage from their proximity to the town. That is scarcely a thing that can be maintained.

29. What are the advantages you would say a man living a mile from the town derives?—There are many ways in which I say they derive as much benefit from the town as the town people themselves.—The markets and manures, and coming to day by day and indeed in every possible way. They have all the benefits of the lighting and cleansing, every time they come in or send to their children.

Mr. *Fitzgerald*.—As I said before, the town derives more benefit from those country people than they do from the town. Supposing you put down the million every way around Midleton, the town would be swept away but take the town away, the land would not be a bit cheaper.

Mr. *Barry*.—It is a monstrous thing to say gentlemen living within a mile of the town do not derive advantage from it.

Mr. *Fitzgerald*.—I am able to state that a farm within a mile and a quarter of the town will fetch in value reckoning land without a farthing more.

Mr. *Timothy Murphy*. The water of Midleton is admirable; we have not had a fever case here until lately.

Mr. Michael Buckley examined.

Mr. Michael Buckley.

30. Where do you reside?—At Garryduff.

31. Do you object to being brought in?—Yes.

32. You don't consider you derive any benefit from the town?—I think a man living five miles away has as much advantage. Living near the town, we have to pay higher rents than if we were five miles off.

33. Don't you come in here to church?—Yes.

34. And do not the people within a mile and a quarter send in their children to school?—Yes, and so can anyone ten miles from it—they are just as entitled to do so.

Mr. Denis Nolan (Broomfield) examined.

Mr. Denis Nolan.

35. Your land is outside the present boundary?—Yes, I am within half a mile of the town.

36. You would be taken in by the extension of a mile?—Yes.

37. And you would object?—Yes.

38. You don't think you have any interest in the town, or its lighting, and so on, as to justify your being called on to pay some contribution?—No.

39. Do you think all lands, such as accommodation lands, should be taxed?—I don't know.

Mr. William Moore, Knockgriffin, examined.

Mr. William Moore.

40. Do you live inside or outside the boundary?—I am outside the boundary, and I object to being brought in. I derive no benefit from the town, and I don't see why I should be taxed for it.

Mr. *Phillip Cody*.—I object to be town rated. I don't see what advantage I get, in any one spot, from living near Midleton.

Mr. Michael Sandwich, Carrigshane, examined.

Mr. Michael Sandwich.

41. You live outside the town?—Yes, about a mile. I object to the extension to include me, on the grounds that I don't see that I derive any benefit from the town.

42. Do you mean that the town being well lighted or ill lighted, it is a matter of indifference to you?—Yes. I have a farm four or five miles off, and I find that I have to pay more wages and incur more expense near the town.

43. Would you not give more for land near the town than for land of the same quality further off?—No.

Mr. *James Brunt*.—I represent Cork and I represent Captain Smith Barry.

44. What are your reasons, the subject of extension?—Mine is persons living a mile outside, the lights cannot be considered to be of any advantage.

Mr. TIMOTHY [illegible] examined.

45. Do you live within the mile and a half?—Yes.

46. And do you not think you derive such benefit from the town as to warrant your being called on for a rate [illegible]?—No; I would as soon be five miles from the town.

47. It is a matter of indifference to you if the town is lighted or not?—Yes; I don't care whether it is or not. It suits me more to be near the town than if I was four or five miles away.

48. If you were offered two farms of exactly the same value, one near the town and the other four miles off, which would you take?—I would as soon have one as the other.

49. Don't you buy things in Midleton?—I buy and I sell some corn there, but Cork is my only market.

50. But for what you do buy and sell is not the town an advantage to you?—Well, I don't think so. I say people living three miles off derive more advantage than I do, for they supply butter and milk to the workhouse.

Mr. BERNARD M'A[illegible], Main street, Midleton, examined.

51. Have you land outside?—No.

52. What is your opinion as to the proposed extension?—I suppose, if I lived outside, the same as the farmers, I would object to it.

53. Are you a Commissioner?—No.

54. You think there should be an extension?—Yes.

55. How far do you think the area should be enlarged?—I think, myself, that Ballyannan[?] should be taken in, Broomfield and Deer Park.

56. And on what ground do you think they ought to be taken in?—Because I think they derive about the same advantages as the people in the Main-street. All the children are sent in here to school; the people come in to Church and Chapel on Sundays, and in the second place, if they want to come in for a load of grain, or a barrel of beer, they take about half an hour, which, if they were far outside it, would take them hours. It is, I think, of the greatest advantage to farmers living within a mile and a half. One house is as valuable to him as three would be at a distance.

Mr. JOHN [illegible] (Broomfield) examined.

57. How far is your place from the town?—About an English mile. I am within a mile and a half radius.

58. Do you object to being taken in?—Yes.

59. On what ground—is it that you do not like to be taxed?—I don't see any interest to me in being brought in.

60. You have no interest in the town being lighted; you don't care whether it is lighted or not?—Not a button; we went there when it was without flagging and light, and we were better able to walk then now. As to the water we have the finest water in Ireland.

Mr. DAVID [illegible] examined.

61. You have heard the evidence?—Yes.

62. Do you reside at Broomfield?—Yes. The lighting and watering and flagging of the town are no use to me.

63. You wish to record the fact that you object to the extension?—Yes.

Mr. DANIEL [illegible] examined.

64. Where do you live?—At [illegible].

65. How far is it from the town?—It is about two miles from the town.

66. You object to being brought in?—Yes.

67. You object to being asked to pay any [illegible]?—Yes, I [illegible] the [illegible] in my [illegible].

68. You have no interest in the town being lighted?—No.

69. Do you come into the town on Sundays?—Yes.

70. Do your children come in to school?—Yes.

71. Is it no interest to the people whose children come in to school that the town should be lighted and well kept?—No; for they are home before dark and require no light.

Mr. DANIEL [illegible] examined.

72. Where do you live?—Near the last witness.

73. Do you agree with his evidence?—Yes.

Mr. MICHAEL [illegible] examined.

74. You heard what the other witnesses have said?—Yes.

75. And do you agree with them as to not being interested in the town being lighted?—Yes.

76. You have nothing to add to their evidence?—No.

Mr. WILLIAM COGAN[?], P.L.G.[?], examined.

77. How long have you been a member of the Town Board?—Three or four years.

78. Do you think the present boundary ought to be extended?—Yes.

79. Why?—I think those adjoining derive advantages from the town, and should contribute towards it.

80. How far do you think those advantages extend?—About a mile and a quarter in [illegible].

81. And you think the imposition of the one-fourth rate would not be troubling them, unduly?—No; I am sure not. I myself will be brought in under it.

Mr. WILLIAM M'CARTHY[?], P.G.[?], examined.

82. Do you agree with the opinion expressed that there ought to be an extension?—I think there ought to be—the area is too small. It would lessen the rate.

83. You would extend into the country in order to lessen the rates in the town?—Yes.

84. Do you think the advantages of the town extend to the people a mile off?—Yes.

85. And is it fair to ask them to pay 3d. in the pound?—Yes; buildings would be taxed the full, and land one-fourth. I think it is a great matter to those

people to have the lights at night, and many of them complain that the Commissioners do not light them after eleven o'clock.

66. Who are the people who complain?—Well, some of the townspeople say they ought to be lighted all night.

Mr. Fitzgerald.—The bulk of the farmers come in at a very early hour, and from very long distances.

The inquiry terminated.

Hamilton. Oct. 8, 1878.

Mr. William M'Carthy, &c.

FERMOY.—JANUARY 4TH, 1879.

Fermoy. Jan. 4, 1879.

Before Mr. O'Brien, and Mr. [illegible].

Mr. J. W. Healy examined.

Mr. J. W. Healy.

1. Mr. O'Brien.—You are Clerk of the Town Commissioners?—Yes.

2. Fermoy is constituted a Municipal Town under the Towns Improvement Act?—Yes.

3. When was it placed under that Act?—In 18[illegible].

4. What is the area of the town in statute acres?—[illegible] 2a. 1r.

5. What is the valuation?—£[illegible].

6. Now, does it consist of entire townlands, or how many, and how many parts of townlands?—There are parts of [illegible] townlands, and [illegible] of any.

7. What are the names of the townlands, parts of which are included?—They are Fermoy, [illegible], [illegible], [illegible], and [illegible]. These are the [illegible] townlands, parts of which are included.

8. Then every townland is cut?—There is no entire one in the Municipal District?—No.

9. Now, in what electoral division is the Municipal District?—Fermoy.

10. Entirely?—Yes.

11. Now, what is the radius of the Municipal District, taking the most central point to start with [illegible] [illegible] [illegible] beyond this Court-house?

12. Well, on the west, how far?—About a mile and a quarter.

13. From the centre of the town?—Yes.

14. I am speaking of the Municipal District—what is the radius of the Municipal District from the centre of the town?—About a quarter of a mile. It takes in [illegible] of Mr. [illegible]'s place.

15. Well, on the north?—Three-quarters of a mile.

16. From the centre of the town?—Yes; [illegible] the railway station.

17. Is the railway station included?—Yes.

18. How far does it extend on the south?—About half a mile—between a quarter and half a mile [illegible] in [illegible]. It is less than a half, and more than a quarter of a mile. To the east it extends just to the [illegible].

19. All those measurements are from the centre of the town?—Yes.

20. Now, take the electoral division of Fermoy, how many townlands are there—just that will show what is the area of that?—5,610a. 3r. 24p.

21. And the valuation?—£18,005.

22. Does the electoral division of Fermoy radiate equally, or in its irregular manner?—I think, taking the radius, it is, say, two and a quarter miles to the north, and east, two miles to the south, and to the west side a mile, or something more.

23. Then how many townlands are included in it?—Thirty-four townlands.

24. If the Fermoy electoral division were taken as the boundary of the Municipal town, it would therefore be open to this objection, that while lands two and a quarter miles from the centre of the town would be included in the township, lands a little more than a mile in another direction would be excluded?—Yes.

25. Now, have the Town Commissioners of Fermoy considered the question of extending, limiting, or otherwise altering the boundary?—Yes; they have.

26. How many members are there on the Board?—Fifteen.

27. Was there a special meeting convened to consider this question?—Yes.

28. How many members attended at that meeting?—Eleven.

29. Did they come to any unanimous conclusion on the subject?—Yes.

30. What was that conclusion—have you got the resolution on record?—Yes; it was last night they resolved to adopt the resolution as drafted by Mr. Daly. The decision was come to late last night, and expressed the unanimous opinion of the Commissioners.

31. Will you kindly read it?—It was as follows:—

"Proposed extension of the township of Fermoy, unanimously adopted at a special meeting of the Town Commissioners, held on Friday, 3rd of January, 1879.—Northern Boundary, commencing at the bridge over the river Blackwater at Mount Rivers; on by the road leading to [illegible], as far as the end of the high wall at [illegible] Park [illegible]; thence north by said road to the north of the mill-stream road, from Fermoy to Kilworth, where said road [illegible] by [illegible] to [illegible] Cross, and thence east to [illegible] Cross and the Army."

That is the North Boundary. The West Boundary is not—

"The road leading from [illegible] Cross to the highroad leading from Fermoy to [illegible] across said road, and on by the [illegible] to the rear of [illegible] demesne, across the river Blackwater to the road to [illegible] south by said road to [illegible] Bridge, formerly [illegible]; thence by the [illegible] road to [illegible], on the [illegible] road; then by said road to the [illegible] to the [illegible] pages, on by said road across [illegible], to the road leading to [illegible]."

The Southern Boundary suggested is:—

"The [illegible] road, south of [illegible], to the [illegible] from [illegible] to Fermoy, [illegible] at the [illegible]; then [illegible], across the line, to the [illegible] of the [illegible] wood, on the [illegible] road, [illegible] to the [illegible] of [illegible], [illegible] to [illegible]; and thence to the [illegible] by [illegible], to the west of [illegible]."

We are all acquainted with those localities. The Eastern Boundary is:—

"The [illegible], or [illegible], leading from the [illegible] road, under the [illegible], to the [illegible], and [illegible] the said [illegible]-road, to the river Blackwater, on by the [illegible] of [illegible] lands, across the Blackwater, to [illegible]-road; on by the [illegible] road, [illegible], to the bridge over the river [illegible], at Mount Rivers."

32. Now, Mr. Healy, is [illegible] was adopted in favour of this [illegible] or boundary suggested by Mr. Daly?—Yes.

33. What area are you in a position to say, would this give [illegible]?—I am not sufficiently familiar [illegible] to be able to state [illegible].

34. Can you state what [illegible] townlands, and how many [illegible] it would, because the scheme was considered irrespective of townlands.

35. You cannot say how many?—No. It was done so recently I did not go into it in detail.

36. Now, the Town Commissioners of Fermoy act as [illegible] sanitary authority?—Yes.

37. What [illegible] source of income have the Town Commissioners of Fermoy. Have they anything except the rates?—Yes, tolls and fines from the

Commissioners' Court, and presentments from the Grand Jury, and payments from Government in lieu of rates.

38. They have no property?—No. There is the dog tax, too.

39. They have no tolls or customs?—No.

40. Now, has the "Towns Improvement Act" been adopted for all purposes?—Yes.

41. What have been the rates made during each year—in '74, '75, '76, '77, and '78?—In '74, the rate was 11*d.*; in '75, 10*d.*; in '76, 8*d.*; in '77, 8*d.*, and no rate was struck in '78.

42. Why was that?—They had a sufficiency of money in hand, and intended to postpone it till May next.

43. What is your annual expenditure for municipal purposes?—£460, about.

44. And how much is comprehended in the sanitary expenditure?—Very little.

45. You have had no special rates?—No.

46. Now, are there any important sanitary works considered advisable that the Commissioners have been restrained from carrying out in consequence of the small area of the township?—Except the water supply.

47. The water supply—is it considered to be deficient or imperfect?—Yes.

48. Has anything been done in reference to it?—A requisition has been sent out for a special meeting for Tuesday next, for the purpose of considering the question as to an improved supply of water.

49. Has any scheme been under consideration on the subject?—Yes, I believe so, and I believe an estimate was taken.

50. Have you any knowledge of any estimate having been made?—I believe I am accurate in saying that Mr. Burke got an estimate from Mr. Lyons, the County Surveyor.

51. Are you in a position to state what the estimate was?—No, I am not.

52. Are the Town Commissioners aware that under the 20th Section of the "Public Health Act of last Session, there is now a power to transfer to the urban sanitary authority certain functions hitherto exercised by the Grand Jury over roads, bridges, and footpaths?—Yes.

53. Have they had under their consideration the propriety of making application for such transfer?—Yes, and passed a resolution unanimously to apply for a separation from the Grand Jury.

54. Is it the opinion of the Commissioners at present that the expenditure is not commensurate with the amount levied?—Yes.

55. What is that amount?—£900, and they only give benefit to the extent of £450.

56. What is the amount of county cess raised?—£900.

57. What is the valuation of the township?—£9,836.

58. And the average rate?—About 1*s.* 8*d.*—that is between £800 and £900 a year, and the expenditure on the roads would be covered by £500.

59. Then the Commissioners, you say, would be in favour of it?—Yes, and the feeling has been so for a long time. It has been considered that being separated from the Grand Jury we would have all the powers of rating, and would not be restricted to one-fourth.

60. That was the view of the Commissioners?—Yes.

61. Do they consider that the works are not properly or sufficiently executed at present?—Yes; they have great difficulty in getting presentments—a great many have been thrown out. So many presentments for new works had been thrown out that at length they ceased to apply; there was great dissatisfaction, and I don't know if I am right in saying that they felt humiliated in coming before the Grand Jury.

62. Mr. *Healy* (a Commissioner).—I would like to ask you, Mr. Healy, do you know within how many years did we get anything from them?

Mr. *Healy*.—The last sum we got from them was in spring, '77, when we got £40; that was at the Spring Assizes, and we got nothing since.

63. Mr. O'BRIEN.—What was that for?—That was for reforming a footpath at the Cork-road. The presentment obtained before that was in the summer of 1875, when we got £40 for flagging a footway from King-street to the chapel. That was a total of £80 for the past three years.

Mr. *Burke*.—In the meantime we continued to apply to the Road Sessions, and our applications were thrown out.

64. Mr. O'BRIEN.—Now, Mr. Healy, if the municipal district were extended, would it take in the whole of the electoral division?—Yes.

Mr. *Barry* (Commissioner).—At all events that proposition was made irrespective of electoral boundaries.

65. Would it take in Cool and Castle Hyde?—Yes, parts of Cool and Castle Hyde, and if Mr. Sheriff's amendment or proposition were adopted it would take in the whole of Leitrim.

66. Then it would take in nearly the whole of Fermoy, Cool, Castle Hyde, and Leitrim?

Mr. *Barry*.—Not Leitrim.

67. What has been the percentage of the sanitary expenditure for the past five years?—There has been no sanitary expenditure except for scavenging the town.

Mr. JOHN BARRY, Chairman of the Town Commissioners, examined.

68. Mr. O'BRIEN.—You have been a member of the Town Commissioners since the commencement?—Yes.

69. You were charged lately, I understand, with the duty of preparing a scheme to meet the requirements of the town regarding extension of the boundaries?—Yes; I was asked by Mr. Burke to prepare the scheme for the new boundary. I was asked by Mr. Burke and others.

70. And did you accordingly prepare the scheme now given in evidence?—Yes.

71. And which was adopted by the Commissioners?—Yes; I prepared the draft of it, and it was finally settled at a meeting of the Commissioners.

72. And unanimously adopted?—Yes. I may say for myself that when the town was under the old Fermoy Police Act—a local Act procured by Mr. Anderson, the late proprietor—and when the townspeople thought it advisable to get rid of that Act and adopt the Towns Commissioners Act we are under now—the Towns Improvement Act—it became necessary to fix a boundary, and Mr. Thomas Rice and I, of our own motion, sketched out a boundary and made it very limited, so as to prevent opposition—for peace sake. It was purely a town one. Since then the law has changed very much, and various functions, sanitary and other, have been placed in the hands of the Commissioners. Since then it was thought advisable to take the first opportunity to extend the boundaries, which are considered far too small in extent.

73. Has the limited nature of the existing area operated so as to restrain the Commissioners undertaking works of great utility to the town, and which are considered necessary?—I don't know that it had that effect, but it struck me and others that it was unfair to put up so limited an area the whole taxation of the town, where persons outside were deriving undoubted benefit and advantages, and that it would be

more just and equitable to extend the boundary, so that these people, deriving such advantages, might contribute towards the expenditure.

74. Has it not been under consideration to give an extended water supply?—Yes.

75. An improved water supply?—Yes.

76. Would not such a scheme as that involve a considerable expenditure?—Assuredly.

77. Do you consider that the advantages that would be derivable from that would extend much beyond the existing area?—I consider that any advantage done to the town by the supply of water, gas, or otherwise would be a direct advantage to very many persons outside the area, certainly to those within the proposed area of taxation.

78. Do persons living in the neighbourhood of Fermoy derive benefits from the schools? Do they send their children in to the schools?—Yes.

79. And I presume that proximity to a large garrison and market town like Fermoy increases the value of agricultural land?—Yes. I may mention that the water project was taken up chiefly with the view of satisfying the parties in London headquarters with reference to the supply to the barracks. It was thought possible that we would even lose the garrison altogether, and it therefore became a matter of necessity to see what could be done to supply good water.

80. Are the military authorities dissatisfied?—Yes.

81. With the supply of water?—Yes.

82. So that to secure to Fermoy the advantages of the garrison it becomes necessary that there should be something done to improve the supply of water?—Yes.

83. Is any drainage of an improved character required?—No, I do not know that there is. I may tell you, however, that several of the pumps in the barracks have been condemned on analysis, and it is really a matter of urgent necessity.

84. Within what distance or radius would you say do the people outside derive advantages from the town government in the shape of lighting, cleansing, flagging, and so forth, and having schools for their children, a market for their produce, and supplying their lands with manure—within what distance would such advantages extend in an exceptional degree over those from a greater distance?—I should say from two miles to two miles and a half.

85. What was the principle that guided you in your selection of a boundary?—I thought principally that those persons who have property outside in the neighbourhood of Fermoy, who come in here and use the town, who attend the monthly fairs, and have here a good market for their goods, and who get such facilities and advantages from the town in every way, were fairly bound to contribute.

86. But it appears that you did not follow up exactly equal radius; in some places it is two miles and in some two and a half miles?—Yes, we took in the property of some gentlemen here, landed proprietors, whose tenants and themselves enjoy the advantages of and are benefited by the town of Fermoy.

87. Why did you leave out some people in other directions who are within two and a half miles?—Well, because there was no property outside of any consequence commensurate with our doing so—with our taking it in. There was some rough mountain land, and we wanted to have a well-defined boundary.

88. Your boundary would not follow townlands?—No.

89. Don't you think where you have a well-known denomination, such as a townland, it is better to follow it?—Well, I think if you have a boundary well defined, it is then a mere question of valuation to allocate it.

90. But the townland being the unit of taxation for poor law purposes, would it not, where feasible, be well to follow it?—I think if we don't get the proposed extension it would be well to get the electoral division.

91. There are several townlands, it appears, comprised in your scheme. Now, wherever a townland comes into the municipal boundary, would you see any objection to taking in the whole of those townlands now part of your scheme?—No, I see no objection.

92. Wherever it cut a townland to bring that townland in?—Yes.

93. That would be better than adopting the electoral division?—Yes.

94. Do you think it would be impossible on any principle of equity to take in the electoral division of Castlehyde and Coul?—Oh, yes.

95. How far would Castlehyde and Coul extend?—Coul would extend four or five miles.

96. And that would not be feasible?—No.

97. And you think, therefore, that it could not be in fairness attempted?—Yes; and as to the electoral division being adopted, I think it would be a mistake in this case.

98. Now, you have heard me alluding to the section of the Act empowering the Local Government Board by Provisional Order to transfer the Grand Jury functions to the town body in respect of roads; now, it is stated that the unanimous feeling of the Commissioners is in favour of that transfer?—Yes.

99. What would be the advantage of such a transfer, in your opinion?—Very great, indeed. First of all it has been ascertained on calculation that we are paying £400 or £500 to the Grand Jury in taxes in excess of money expended on the township by them. We also find that on some occasions Mr. Barke and others got presentments from them for flagging, but never without a great struggle in the most niggardly and grudging way. The Grand Jury seemed, in fact, determined upon never granting presentments to us, and the consequence is that works deemed necessary have been left unexecuted.

100. Works have thus been left in that way unexecuted?—Certainly.

101. And works that would be executed by yourselves if you had control of the matter?—Assuredly.

102. And do you think that you would be able had you the matter in your own hands, more reasonably than the Grand Jury?—Yes.

103. How many miles would be comprised in the municipal area proposed by you—how many miles of roads?—I have not looked into that.

104. Have you considered what the cost of maintenance would be?—No, except this, the cost of maintenance would be more than thirty per cent. less under us than under the Grand Jury.

105. You would do the work cheaper?—No doubt.

106. Mr. Cotton.—How would you account for it?—Well, there is some difficulty exactly in explaining. Road contractors are a class of people in themselves. We would have nothing to say to them, but would get the work done under our own eyes, and a great deal of money would be saved in that way.

107. Now, you are aware that under the Towns Improvement Act arable land is liable to be rated at one-fourth of the valuation?—Yes.

108. Do the Commissioners contemplate in the event of the transfer that the Grand Jury works shall be charged on the full amount?—Yes, I think so.

109. The whole of the Grand Jury cess to be paid by the occupiers?—Yes.

110. Are the Commissioners aware of the fact that the Parliamentary Committee expressed an opinion in their report to Parliament that the law in that respect ought to be changed, and that in future the expenditure ought to be divided equally between the occupiers and landlords?—Yes, we are aware of that recommendation, and are quite prepared to accept it.

111. You are aware the Committee expressed themselves to this effect—

"Your Committee have given very careful consideration to the arguments on both sides of this question, and have decided to recommend the proposed division of rates and representation. In addition to the arguments already stated, they believe it may be fairly argued that such a measure could not fail to exercise a most beneficial influence in

Fermoy. Jan. 4, 1878. — Mr. J. Barry.

greatly diminishing those divisions between the different classes in Ireland, which are the most serious impediment to its happiness and prosperity. It would bring the representatives of different classes together for the common interest in a common field of activity from which the great subjects of controversy would be mostly excluded."

The Commissioners would concur in that?—Certainly.

112. How many electors are there in the present district, do you know?—The total number of voters is 294.

113. And how many persons are eligible to hold the office of Commissioner?—140 are eligible.

114. Would the proposed extension increase the constituency, the number of persons who would be entitled to vote?—It would.

115. Now, Mr. Barry, do you think it is the feeling of the Commissioners that it would be of advantage to the public to have a number of persons brought in and included in those who would be likely to take an interest in the affairs of the town?—Yes.

116. And that the introduction of the rural element, which this extension would affect, would be favourable?—Yes, I think it would be favourable.

117. There are a great many occupied houses that would be brought in?—Yes, a good many.

118. Do you think the people outside who would be introduced by your scheme would entertain any very strong objection?—Well, I think as a rule people object to be taxed at all.

119. But you don't think they have any reasonable objection—any reasonable grounds of objection to it? —No. I am not single in this. The Commissioners are unanimous in thinking that this alteration would be a most proper proceeding, and that the first one was a mistake.

120. You have heard no very strong objection to it?—No.

121. Now, is there anything special that you would like to add to what you have already been good enough to give as your evidence?—No, nothing.

122. Mr. *Burke*.—Would you kindly say, Mr. Barry, what was the amount during the past three or four years we have got from the Grand Jury?

Mr. *Barry*.—Out of £400 we have got altogether about £135.

123. Mr. O'Brien.—If the Commissioners got charge of the roads and bridges, would it be necessary to give you increased rating power over the present limit? —Yes. That would be a general measure to enable us, if necessary, to increase the taxation.

124. You will be able, Mr. Barry, to send us a map with the proposed and the existing boundaries marked on it?—Yes.

Mr. M. Burke.

Mr. Michael Burke, Town Commissioner, examined.

125. You are a member of the Town Commissioners? —Yes.

126. And also agent for Sir Robert Abercromby, owner of Fermoy?—Yes.

127. You have heard the statements made by Mr. Barry?—Yes.

128. Do you concur in them?—Yes. He has told you there was a special meeting, and that the opinion was unanimous. I was at that meeting.

129. Is there anything you would like to add to what he has said?—No; nothing particular.

130. Are you aware, Mr. Burke, that there is great necessity for a water supply?—Yes.

131. Was any estimate of the cost been made—any estimate of what the water supply would cost?—Yes; the landlord, Sir Robert Abercromby, has, at his own expense, taken measures and employed the county surveyor of the East Riding, Mr. Lyons, and he has made a map and estimate for us, and taken great pains, and has made a report, and is perfectly satisfied of the desirability of the work in every way for the town, and for the people.

132. And what is the estimated cost?—It is calculated at about £12,000.

133. That, I take it, would be too great a sum for the existing area to undertake—it would be, I presume, too great a burthen on the people of the present area? —Yes.

134. It would be, in fact, impracticable?—Yes.

135. So that the maintaining of the present area would shut the door upon the provision of a proper water supply?—Yes.

136. And it is a fact, I understand, that the military authorities have threatened to withdraw from the barracks?—Yes; they have been thoroughly dissatisfied with the water supply, and we have reason to believe that by the proposed scheme the town will have the advantage of an improved supply as well as the barracks.

137. Now, assuming the bad and defective supply of water led to the withdrawal of the garrison from Fermoy, would that inflict not only a serious injury upon the inhabitants but upon those living within the proposed extended area?—Most serious.

138. You think their withdrawal would be a serious injury?—Decidedly, in every way.

139. And the injury would extend beyond the present municipal district?—Yes; the landed proprietors not only within the proposed district, but much farther away, would suffer serious injury by it. It would affect the markets and everything.

140. Now, as to the transfer of the Grand Jury functions, you agree in that; you concur as to the advisability of the transfer?—Yes.

141. And you think the work would be better done? —Yes; I hold the work is not by any means satisfactorily done.

142. You consider that it could be more efficiently done by the town body?—Yes, more satisfactorily in every way. We think it a great hardship that a sum of £400 should be going out from us without any commensurate return, and what we do get from the Presentment Sessions is given most reluctantly.

143. I presume you would not ask for any transfer of these functions unless you got an increased boundary? —We look upon an increased boundary as essential. In point of fact the original boundary was done in a hurry. There was not sufficient consideration for it.

Mr. *Barry*.—It was done for peace sake.

144. Mr. O'Brien.—Do you consider that the rate for these purposes ought to be divided as the Parliamentary Committee suggest?—Yes. I may mention to you that I myself would be brought in under the proposed extension.

Mr. Michael J. Maguire.

Mr. Michael J. Maguire, Town Commissioner, examined.

145. Mr. O'Brien.—Have you any remarks you would like to make, Mr. Maguire, in addition to what we have heard?—I have heard Mr. Barry and Mr. Burke, and I entirely concur in the remarks of both gentlemen.

146. You are a landed proprietor?—Yes.

147. Would lands of yours be brought in?—Yes.

148. So that to some extent you would be a loser? —Yes.

149. Have you heard any objections urged to the proposed extension?—No, not up to the present.

Mr. Cornelius Dennehy, Town Commissioner, examined.

Fermoy, [illegible] 1879. Mr Cornelius Dennehy.

150. Mr. O'Brien.—Were you at the meeting of the Commissioners, Mr. Dennehy?—No, I had not the pleasure of being there, but I have listened to Mr. Barry's lucid explanation, and also to Mr. Burke, and I may say that I quite concur in what they have said, though I myself will be a considerable sufferer by the extension.

151. You don't think it would be inequitable to taking persons within the boundary?—No.

152. You think they ought to share in the expenditure as they enjoy the advantages of proximity to the town?—Yes.

153. And you think that people holding lands outside would suffer serious loss, if owing to the bad supply of water the garrison were to be withdrawn?—Yes, but I don't like to enter into the question as we are to have a meeting on that subject.

154. But you think if the garrison was withdrawn injury would be inflicted?—Oh, yes. Fermoy would be nothing without the military.

155. Mr. Cotton.—How much of the railway would you take in, Mr Barry?

Mr. Barry.—We would take in some of the Fermoy and Lismore Railway, about a mile and a half of it, and about a mile and a half in the other direction, the Mallow and Fermoy.

Mr. William Smith, examined.

Mr. W. Smith.

156. Mr. O'Brien.—You are a Town Commissioner?—Yes.

157. I understand that at one point you differ with the other Commissioners as to the boundary?—Yes.

158. That was as to the eastern boundary?—Yes.

159. What was your suggestion?

Mr. Barry.—Perhaps, sir, it would be better that we should be unanimous, and Mr. Smith does not press his proposition.

160. Mr. O'Brien.—Do you concur generally, Mr. Smith, in the views that have been expressed [illegible].

161. Do you think, Mr. [illegible] [illegible] to be desirable, as recommended, [illegible] being the [illegible] for [illegible] purposes, should be [illegible] the boundary [illegible]; do you see any great objection to taking in all these [illegible]?—No. I think there would be no objection.

Colonel Lucas examined.

Colonel Lucas.

162. Would you be brought in under the proposed extension, Colonel Lucas?—Yes, I believe so.

163. You would have no objection?—Well, I do not benefit by the gas or water.

164. Except what you [illegible]. [Mr. O'Brien explained to Colonel Lucas the [illegible].] You derive advantages from your proximity to the town.

Colonel Lucas.—I [illegible] in [illegible] taken as the [illegible].

165. Mr. O'Brien.—[illegible] Don't you think the boundary of Fermoy ought to be extended?—I think a radius of a mile would be sufficient. It would be a very proper limit, a [illegible] from the bridge.

166. A radius circle?—Yes.

167. You think that would be going far enough?—Yes.

168. And would you bring in the townlands it would cut?—Yes.

169. Would you have any objection to take in, say, two miles?—Well no; that would bring in a very considerable [illegible].

170. Would you have any objection to the transfer of the jurisdiction of the Grand Jury over roads and bridges to the Town Commissioners?—I think it would be [illegible] for the [illegible] of the town to have them managed by the county surveyor.

171. Would it be desirable, do you think, that they should have it in their hands, that the Commissioners should have the control and payment of these works instead of being dependent on the Grand Jury?—I don't know as to that.

172. Would it be desirable, fair, or reasonable?—Well, I would not say that.

173. You are yourself a member of the Grand Jury?—Well, I would say that things are going on [illegible], and the town has got a great deal.

174. Do you consider that it would be desirable or equitable that the taxation for the maintenance of roads should be divided equally between [illegible] and [illegible]?—I think that under the present Land Act at present——

175. What I want to know is whether you approve of that as a general principle that the [illegible] should be divided equally between [illegible] and [illegible]?—[illegible].

176. You are aware that the Parliamentary Committee expressed a strong opinion in favour of the adoption of such a principle?—Oh yes, but how is it to be managed?

177. This is the recommendation of the Committee. [Reads recommendation of Select Committee [illegible].] That is a strong expression of opinion?—Undoubtedly.

178. I take it you would be brought in under the proposed extension?—Yes.

179. And you are a member of the Grand Jury body?—Yes.

FERMOY—OCTOBER 15th, 1879.

(Before Mr. C. P. Cotton, C.E.)

Fermoy, October 15, 1879.

1. The Commissioner.—I think it desirable that I should briefly mention the circumstances under which I began to hold this inquiry again. The Municipal Boundaries Commission have received a great many letters from different gentlemen living in the vicinity of Fermoy, some of which stated that the writers were unaware of the holding of the former inquiry, and others expressing [illegible] the proposition which was made by the Town Commissioners. Mr. [illegible] and the other Commissioners, however, [illegible] that it would be better to give the gentlemen who wrote these letters an opportunity of putting their evidence upon the record, so that it might be [illegible], and also with the view of enabling the Town Commissioners to [illegible] the gentlemen who [illegible] come forward to oppose the proposition of the municipal body.

2. Mr. [illegible].—The Commissioners [illegible] to do anything [illegible] the [illegible] was [illegible]. [illegible]

Fermoy. [illegible]

you is this: that the Commissioners were only here before in a corporate capacity, and not as individuals—merely as a Corporation—and they only made suggestions to you; but they didn't put forward their views in any other way than as suggestions, which could be passed upon or ignored in the discretion of the Boundary Commissioners.

3. Mr. Cotton.—Do you wish to add anything to your former evidence?—Nothing. The Commissioners have put their case forward, and, in my opinion, it is only right that those who are opposed to their views should also be heard. If I were to venture an opinion, I would take a different view from those gentlemen, as, I think, instead of opposing any suggestion, if they were to argue the point with me in a boundary point of view, I would show that they are quite wrong.

Colonel Charles Deane.

Colonel Charles Deane examined.

4. Mr. Cotton.—Where do you live, Colonel Deane?—At Crowane.

5. Then you reside about two English miles from the town?—Yes, a little over two English miles, which is the nearest part of my land.

6. And you are included in the proposed extension?—Yes.

7. You are aware of the nature of the extension proposed by the Town Commissioners?—I am.

8. And, may I ask, what is your opinion of it?—I think it is one of the most unfair propositions that any body of public men could put forward.

9. What are your reasons for coming to that conclusion?—My reasons are that, in some cases, the Commissioners propose to extend four miles, and in other directions, only one and a-half miles, and evidently taking in what I consider pet proprietors—for instance, Mr. Montgomery's; and, as an engineer, you will see by a reference to the map, how irregular is the line of boundary they propose.

10. They extend out a long distance on one side to take in Mr. Montgomery's property, and take in your property a long way off on the other?—Quite so.

11. And do you object to the distance of two miles, or that everyone within the two miles is not taken in?—I think a radius of two miles ought to be the outside of the benefit that the town should derive. I do not think you should go beyond two miles; but whatever distance you go from the centre of the town of Fermoy, I think you should take a fair radius. A fair circle.

12. Would you object to a two-mile circle?—No, I would not. I think a two-mile circle would be fair; but not beyond it.

13. Do you think that the people living within a two-mile radius have a certain advantage—a certain interest—in the town being properly kept?—I do; a certain interest, but not in the same ratio, of course, as the people living in the town.

14. But you are aware that all arable land that would be taken in, would only be rated at one-fourth?—I thought it was one-fifth.

15. Have you anything to say upon the question, as to whether the Town Commissioners should become the road authorities in case they did get an extension—that all the fiscal powers of the Grand Jury should be transferred to them?—I would prefer that they should remain with the Grand Jury.

16. I thought the opinion you expressed when you wrote to us, was that the radius should be only one mile?—What I wrote was, according to my recollection, that in most cases where I had seen reports in the newspapers of inquiries held by the Municipal Boundaries Commission, I observed that it was one mile that was proposed.

17. The principal thing that you contend for is that whatever it is, it should be a circle?—Yes, a fair circle.

18. Or as near it as possible?—Yes, as near it as possibly the circumstances will allow; but to take in property in the way the Town Commissioners have suggested—going out in some cases four miles, and others only a mile and a half, is most unfair.

19. Is there anything else that you would wish to have recorded?—No; I would never wish to do anything that was not perfectly fair.

Mr. G. Montgomery.

Mr. G. Montgomery examined.

20. Mr. Cotton.—You live at Careysville?—Yes.

21. And the whole of Careysville would be included in the proposed extension?—No, the proposed extension is even worse than that. They have included it to the very furthest limits. It is over four miles to the end of my demesne; but on the other side—on the north side of the Blackwater—they divide the townland of Ballinaclashet, which is my property, into two parts, and I need hardly draw your attention now to the inconveniences that would occur in that way, for my tenants who hold the townland of Ballinaclashet, would have their farms divided into two.

22. So that part of the farm would pay town rates and the other part would not?—Part of the farms would be included in the municipal boundary and portions included in the county.

23. Do you think if there was an extension, that as a general rule it would be better to make the townland boundaries the boundaries?—I certainly think so. I mean to state that I think that considerable inconvenience would occur to everyone, to have the tenants in this way; for instance, to have 100 acres paying rates to the town of Fermoy, and thirty acres paying the Grand Jury cess—collected probably in different ways.

24. If the Grand Jury powers were not transferred, he would pay the cess the same upon all, and he would pay just one-fourth of the rate upon the portion of his land in the town?—That I don't know. I am not conversant with that. The only thing is that I say the farms would be split by this division, and I think it would be better that the farms should not be divided. Another thing is that I object very strongly to the distance—that it would be four miles in one direction, and a short distance in other parts.

25. Do you think that a distance of two miles from the centre of the town of Fermoy is too far for an extension?—I don't like to speak of other people's property, but my reason for saying that four miles is too far is because I know that my tenants do not sell their produce in the town, but it is sold in Tallow, which is twelve miles away.

26. How far is Clondulane station from you?—It is close to the demesne. I know that corn is always sent by road to Tallow, which is twelve miles off in an easterly direction.

27. And what about coal—how do you get that?—There is a vast trade in coal beginning now from Wales, via Waterford, and it is brought on to Clondulane, and does not come into Fermoy at all, and the people are getting it at their prices.

28. They get it at Clondulane at the same price as the people get it landed in Cork?—Yes; so that a man living that distance would probably never get any coal in Fermoy.

29. You don't need into town for coal from Careysville?—I have done so hitherto, but I do not intend to do so for the future.

Fermoy. Oct. 16, 18[illegible]

Mr. G. Montgomery.

30. Do you wish to say anything on the question of the road authority?—I certainly think, from my experience as a magistrate attending the road sessions, and from my knowledge as a ratepayer, and from my knowledge of road structure in general—which is a good deal, living, as I have always lived, in the country—I should have no [illegible] whatever in the [illegible] of the present Town Commissioners, with a few exceptions, over road [illegible], particularly in the present state of things. It is of the greatest [illegible] to the [illegible] of carrying on roads, a good attendance of the local magistrates, who, in many cases, know the [illegible] and what [illegible] the road contractors have, and it is perfectly impossible to believe that [illegible] in Fermoy would know that so well.

31. Would not the effect of an extension be to bring in a good many resident gentlemen?—It possibly might, but I think that they would possibly find themselves in a very different position from that they occupy at the road sessions. I may mention that I [illegible] in Mr. Barry's evidence at the last inquiry, he is asked, "[illegible] that you do not fully [illegible] [illegible] of the [illegible]." I merely wish to say, with regard to my [illegible], [illegible], [illegible], that [illegible] [illegible], and almost all that part of the country is sold at Glanworth. [illegible] it would be [illegible] to [illegible] contribute towards the municipal expenses of Fermoy. There is a fair [illegible] at Glanworth, which is two and a half miles from Fermoy. The [illegible] at Tallow—that is, the main [illegible] in that part of the country. The [illegible] goes to Tallow also; and, as for drawing [illegible] to my certain knowledge I never knew any instance of [illegible] to draw [illegible] from Fermoy. These are the advantages which my [illegible] gain from being brought into this scheme of extension. I have found, from the evidence given on the occasion of the former inquiry that complaints are made that the town of Fermoy does not get its proportion, as the road expenses of the county, to which the people who were examined [illegible] to think they were entitled. Well, I can only say, with an experience, that certainly is not very long, of eight or nine years, but as far as I have seen, Fermoy has got considerably more than its share of the [illegible] [illegible], [illegible] complaints from [illegible] of Mitchelstown and Kilworth.

32. Then you think that Fermoy has got its fair share of the county cess?—Yes; and I think anyone who walks through Fermoy and notices the way in which the streets are flagged, and the roads generally, must say that it is better off than a great many towns in the United Kingdom.

33. It was stated that the town paid £900 to the county yearly, whereas only about £400 was spent upon it?—That may be, but anyone of us here may be in the same position. I pay £[illegible] or £[illegible] a year in rates, and I may say I have not had anything spent for that. Of course we cannot all get an equal expenditure for what we pay.

34. The roads are maintained through your property?—Yes; but we pay the roads here. For instance, I will only give one instance. In Cork you walk up to the Queenstown Railway Terminus, it is one of the principal places in Cork, and the pavement is gravel, but here the whole place has been flagged right up to the barracks.

35. Has all the flagging been done by the county?—I am not prepared to say; I believe it has. Of course we have to consider the requirements of Mitchelstown and other places, and have not only to get the flagging done, but the sewers, and everything else.

36. Colonel Deane.—If there is £900 collected for Fermoy, there are other charges beside the road charges.

37. Mr. Cotton.—May I ask you, Mr. Barke, has any step been taken to obtain the control of the roads since we held the former inquiry here?—Nothing whatever has been done. There was a feeling in favour of trying to get this town separated from the control of the county, but I, and one or two others, set our faces against it. It is all a matter of opinion whether such a change would be advantageous or not. We don't think we get our fair share, and those who don't think so are anxious to separate.

38. I want to know has anything been done since we were here before, as the Town Commissioners then expressed their wish in favour of separation?—You may take it, as a matter of fact, that nothing has since been done.

39. Mr. Montgomery.—There is another matter that I wish to direct attention to. It has been stated that the cost of the maintenance of the roads would be 30 per cent. less, if they were under the control of the Town Commissioners, than is the case under the Grand Jury. I take leave utterly to deny that assertion, and, as far as I am concerned, my impression is that it would be exactly the opposite.

40. Colonel Deane.—I think so too, it would cost double.

41. Mr. Barke.—I am of the same opinion.

42. Mr. Montgomery.—I object, as Colonel Deane has done, to the unfair way in which the radius has been mapped out. Personally, so far as regards my own property, I object to the townland being divided, and also to the distance out that the Town Commissioners propose to go.

43. Would a two mile radius take in some of your property?—I fancy so. I am pretty sure it would.

44. It would go beyond Bellview?—It is adjacent to Bellview.

45. Have you considered the operation of a two mile radius at all?—No, sir; but, I may add that I certainly think that the present boundary is too small.

46. And do you think that the people living outside the present boundary, but near the town, are so interested in it that it is fair that they should contribute towards its support?—I certainly think that if a gentleman has large business premises in the town and lives quite close to it, it is fair that he should contribute towards it.

47. Would Colonel Lucas's property be brought in if the area was extended?—If the area was extended Colonel Lucas's property would be included. I am representing him and a quantity of agricultural tenants who do not derive any benefit from the town.

48. And who do not come into Fermoy every day?—Quite so.

49. And who sell their produce at Tallow?—Yes.

Mr. Dunscombe examined. Mr. Dunscombe

50. Mr. Cotton.—I think we had a letter from you objecting to Castle Hyde being annexed?—Yes.

51. Do you wish to say anything on behalf of the party objecting to the extension suggested by the Commissioners?—I have. From what I have read of what has taken place and from what I have since heard, I have no reason to know that the present boundary is objected to by the people generally.

52. The present boundary is, you may say, confined to the buildings of the town—it does not extend into the country at all?—It has existed for a considerable period and the taxation is not very heavy in it, and I never heard of any complaints with regard to it. As far as I know, and I have spoken to several Commissioners, who tell me that they do not see that there would be any great advantage in extending it, either to them or to the people who would be taken in.

53. Your principal objection is to Castle Hyde being taken in at all?—Quite so; and I do not speak for tenants, for there are no tenants on it. We are not connected with the town in the slightest degree, we have no property in it and I do not see that we should derive the slightest advantage from the additional taxation that we would have to pay.

Q 2

54. Do you think you are not sufficiently interested in it to have the town kept clean or anything of that sort that is necessary for the public—are not the public interested in that?—Yes, and we pay our proportion of the cost of it.

55. How?—We don't pay for the lighting certainly, but we pay towards the roads.

56. Colonel [illegible].—And that is the only value we get out of it.

57. Mr. Cotton.—Is there anything, Mr. Beecher, that you wish to mention except what you have already said, that you object to Castle Hyde being taken in?—I see no reason for any change being made in the present radius and I have heard of no complaints with regard to it; and as to being separated from the county, I should look upon it as a great grievance, I should dislike it very much.

58. Would you think that the roads would not be kept so well as at present?—I could not form an opinion about a new body managing the roads. I do not know anything about that.

Mr. Beecher re-examined.

59. Colonel [illegible].—Do you object as a [illegible] to the way in which the roads are kept at present?—I think I would not object.

60. Could they be kept better?—I think they are kept very well indeed.

Mr. Timothy Hallinan examined.

61. Mr. Cotton.—You own the mills at Clondulane?—Yes.

62. How far is your place from Fermoy?—A little over two miles.

63. You would be included within the proposed boundary?—Yes.

64. And you object to being so included?—Yes.

65. Upon what grounds?—I derive no immediate benefit from Fermoy. My place is my market place. There are a few little houses there; it is a small village, and everything is bought and sold there. The wheat is brought into my market from the east side, and not at all from the west, because the people on that side have their markets there for their commodities, and they sell them in Fermoy. I am isolated from Fermoy.

66. Do you send your horses and carts into Fermoy?—I do.

67. Much?—A fair share.

68. And are you not interested in the streets being properly lighted and scavenged?—Not particularly. I would like to see the place kept up nicely, but I do not see that that would be of such great importance to me. All the stuff I get down from Cork—all the raw material is brought down by rail, and I merely draw it from Clondulane, down to the mill. It is only a small amount of stuff I manufacture to send into Fermoy, and that I send in by road. That is, however, a very small item in the quantity I send out in the year. Any stuff sent to any other part of the country is sent by rail, except that which is for Fermoy alone, and of course that is not very much.

69. Do you think the roads would be better kept by the Grand Jury, than by the Town Commissioners?—I fancy they would, and I fancy we would get them done cheaper. I have no reason to complain of the way in which the roads are kept from my place into Fermoy.

70. But you don't think that you have such an interest in the town that you should be taxed for keeping it up?—Certainly not.

71. Do you express any opinion as to whether the boundary should be extended at all or not?—I don't know. I am rather a new comer into the place, and I don't know much about it one way or the other, and I have not spoken to any person on the subject.

72. Did you ever hear the shopkeepers complaining of the rates being too high or anything of that sort?—I never did.

Mr. John W. Hallen, Town Clerk, examined.

73. Mr. Cotton.—What is the valuation of Fermoy—kindly give me the buildings and land separate?—The land is £344, and the valuation of the houses amounts to £9,314.

74. And what is the rate that has been struck since we were here last?—One of 6d. in the pound.

75. There was no rate in 1878?—There was not.

76. What was the reason no rate was struck?—There was a sufficiency of funds, and they did not like to strike a rate until 1879.

77. The proposed extension would go into six new electoral divisions?—Yes, additional electoral divisions or parts of them. Their names are—Castle Hyde, Rathcormac, Castletown, Coole, Leitrim, and Kilworth, and of course, Fermoy. It is, at present, in Fermoy. It would include twenty-eight whole new townlands, and parts of fourteen townlands.

78. Mr. Cotton.—(To Mr. *Montgomery*.)—In the evidence you have given, you have expressed the views of Mr. Devonshire as well as your own?—I have.

79. Where is Mr. Devonshire's property?—Mr. Devonshire owns a place called Brook Lodge.

80. Is it within the proposed extension?—Yes.

81. Mr. Cotton.—(To Mr. *Beecher*.)—You are aware, Mr. Beecher, that the land would be only rated at one-fourth?—Yes, I am.

Examination of Town Clerk resumed.

82. Witness.—The total valuation of the property that would be taken in by the proposed extension would be £9,832.

83. Do you know the additional amount of acreage that would be taken in?—I didn't take that down.

84. I mean in addition to the present valuation?—Yes. It is very large—almost the same amount again—double the present. The number of additional voters that would be taken in would be 110.

85. Is there anything you think it necessary to add to your evidence?—I don't think there is.

The inquiry then closed.

KINSALE.—JANUARY 6th, 1879.

Before Mr. O'Brien, Local Government Inspector.

Mr. Michael [illegible] examined.

1. You are clerk of the Town Commissioners?—Yes.

2. And also of the Poor Law Guardians?—Yes.

3. How long have you been clerk to the Town Commissioners?—Since June last.

4. This town has been constituted under the Towns Improvement Act of 1854?—Yes.

5. Since when has it been so constituted?—Since 1854.

6. And was it adopted then in its entirety, or only for particular purposes?—In its entirety for cleansing, lighting, and watering.

7. What is the area of the existing municipality?—[illegible]

8. And what is the valuation?—£5,173 [illegible]s.

9. How many townlands or parts of townlands are

comprised within the municipal area?—Fifteen townlands in all, wholly or partially comprised within it.

10. How many wholly, and how many partly?—Three wholly and twelve partially.

11. And taking the centre of the town as a standing point, how far does it extend on all sides?—Not a [illegible] of a mile, or of half a mile, with the exception of the south.

12. How far does it extend on the north?—Not a quarter of half a mile.

13. And how far does it extend on the south?—Not far on that side, the village of Scilly is included.

14. Then, with the exception of the southern side, it extends pretty equally in a radius of about half a mile?—Yes.

15. From the centre of the town?—Yes.

16. How far is Scilly?—About half a mile by the road.

17. And on the line direct what is it?—About an eighth of a mile.

18. In what electoral division is the municipal district of Kinsale?—All in the electoral division of Kinsale.

19. I presume the electoral division of Kinsale comprehends a good deal more than the municipal district?—Yes.

20. What is the acreage of the electoral division?—The area of the electoral division is 12,313 acres.

21. And the valuation?—£10,830. 10s.

22. How many townlands does it comprise?—Ninety-seven in all.

23. Does Kinsale extend pretty equally in all directions from the centre of the town?—Well about from three to three and a half miles.

24. Pretty equally at all points?—Except the south at the sea, it is pretty equal.

25. Between three and three and a half miles?—Yes.

26. What is the remotest point?—About three and a half miles.

27. I believe the Town Commissioners of Kinsale are also the Urban Sanitary Authority; the population exceeding 6,000?—Yes.

28. You never got any Local Act for Kinsale?—Not that I am aware of.

29. There is a Harbour Act?—Yes.

30. This is a distinct body, and the duties are administered by them separately?—Yes.

31. Is Kinsale divided into wards for municipal or other purposes?—No.

32. How many members constitute the municipal body?—Fifteen.

33. What is the constituency; how many voters are there?—About 180.

34. And how many are qualified to fill the office of Town Commissioners?—Fifty-one.

35. Have the Town Commissioners any source of income except the sanitary rate under the Act?—Yes; they have the Corporation property rents.

36. What is the annual value of that?—Last year it amounted to £158 5s. 8d.

37. Have you any other incomes?—Yes; we have the sanitary and the improvement rate.

38. First give me the income apart from the rate?—Well, Corporation rents £158 5s. 8d.; rent of [illegible] £83 9s. 1d.; market tolls £26 15s.; Petty Sessions fees £12 11s. 3d.; Grand Jury Presentments £63 0d.

39. These are for the [illegible]?—Yes.

40. What else?—Grants from the Treasury in lieu of rates £13 3s.; Local Government Board grant for sanitary purposes £6 10s. 0d.; loan from Treasury £[illegible]; sale of manure £36 3s. 6d.; incidental receipts £5 11s. 7d.; dog tax £14 9s. 8d.; total altogether £526 5s. 7d.

41. But you levy rates?—Yes.

42. What was the amount of the rate?—The improvement rate was 1s. in the pound, and the sanitary rate 1s. 6d. in the pound, making £183 13s. 4d.

43. What was the total income?—In round numbers it was £800.

44. What was your corresponding expenditure for the entire year?—£806.

45. £806?—Yes.

46. Your income and your expenditure, therefore, were nearly balanced?—Yes.

47. Was any portion of your expenditure for sanitary purposes, and what were they?—There was scavenging and cleansing.

48. How much for sanitary purposes?—£50, I should say, for scavenging and so forth.

49. Did you undertake any important works, such as a water supply, or a large scheme for sewerage of the town?—No; but it is in contemplation, and £1,500 has been applied to supplement the water supply.

50. This subject has been under consideration?—Yes; in fact the project is afloat.

51. Was it agreed to yet?—The **Parliamentary** notice has been served.

52. How was it contemplated to get the supply of water?—By pipes from the western side of the town.

53. From what distance?—Half a mile.

54. Has it been estimated how much it would cost?—Yes; about £1,500.

55. And such a supply would be much required?—Yes.

56. Has it been under consideration to improve the drainage of the town—to introduce a new system of sewerage?—No.

57. Is there any necessity felt to exist for such an improved system of drainage?—No; not that I know. The water supply is the main thing.

58. That is the main project at present?—Yes.

59. Now, Kinsale is a considerable residential town?—Yes.

60. Inside the radius?—Yes, **within the municipality**.

61. Are there a considerable number of people residing within a radius of, say a mile to a mile and a half, outside the municipal area?—No, except in the little village of Scilly and Cove.

62. Taking the centre of the town as a starting point, and describing a radius of about two miles, would a great many persons between that and the existing boundary—if the area were extended, say two miles—be included who are now excluded?—There would be a considerable number.

63. Are a great many persons resident, and occupying farmhouses there?—Yes, farmhouses generally.

64. Are there any [illegible] lands held by persons resident in the town?—No, I know of none.

65. And do persons within that radius of two miles derive advantage from their proximity to the market town, and from other causes?—Undoubtedly. This is one of the most important market towns in the fishing season.

66. What time of the year is that?—In March and from March to the end of June. There are an extremely large number of persons engaged in the fishing trade who come here.

67. And a considerable sum **of money is spent here**?—Certainly.

68. Do the advantages that follow from this trade, and from the presence of so many people, extend to a radius of two miles?—I should say the persons living within that radius derive much material benefit from it during that time.

69. The lands bring a higher rent in the vicinity of the town than those farther removed from it?—Yes, so far as my experience goes.

70. Do children resort to town for school purposes?—They do; there are convent schools, and they avail themselves of them.

71. Is Kinsale lighted with gas?—Yes.

72. During the whole year?—During eight months of the year.

73. And, I presume, persons living within a radius of two miles of the town come into it for the purpose of transacting business more frequently than those at a distance?—Yes.

KINSALE. Sept. 4, 18[illegible]. Mr. [illegible]

KINSALE. Jan. 8, 1879. Mr. Michael Hegarty.

74. And do these persons resorting to the town for the transaction of their business derive advantages from the cleansing, lighting, and watering of the town?—Well, they do, of course, for if they come to market they have the benefit of gas, and have the advantages you mention at fairs, and so on.

75. How far would you say these advantages extend—the advantages provided by the town government?—I should say about two miles.

76. Are you aware that, under the 62nd section of the Towns Improvement Act, arable land is only rateable at one-fourth the valuation?—Yes.

77. Is that, in your opinion, a fair measure of the advantages they derive—do you think one-fourth enough?—I think so.

78. If the radius of two miles were adopted as the boundary would it take in land outside the electoral division of Kinsale?—No, it would be within it still.

79. Would a radius of two miles cut townlands?—I am certain it would, for they are numerous and small.

80. They are small, you say?—Yes; one holding, in fact, sometimes.

81. Would you think, in determining the municipal area—if an area of two miles, say, were decided on—would it be better to adhere to townland boundaries, if possible, they being well known denominations, or do you think it would be better to divide them?—I think the townlands would, in this case, be the best.

82. Being a well-known denomination, and on the ground of general convenience, would you say?—Yes.

83. Would you say that in extending the area to a two-mile radius, wherever that line, drawn on that basis, were to cut a townland, that townland should be included?—Yes, I think that would be the proper thing; I may say, the question——

84. First, I want your own opinion. Have the Town Commissioners had under consideration this question of extending the boundaries since the appointment of this Commission?—Yes, they had, at their last meeting.

85. When was that?—The last meeting was on the 9th of December.

86. How many members were present on that occasion?—There were eleven members present.

87. Were they unanimous in the opinion or conclusion they arrived at?—Yes.

88. What was the conclusion at which they arrived?—Well, they did not adopt any formal conclusion; they merely recorded their opinion.

89. What was that record?—Merely this:—"Circular from the Municipal Boundaries Commissioners, received and submitted, containing queries to which replies were ordered to be forwarded."

90. What was the general tendency of the opinion—for instance, I take Query 6—"Are the present municipal boundaries regarded with dissatisfaction by the ratepayers generally, or by a section of them?"—That was negatived.

91. Then Query 7 was similarly answered, I presume, for it is, "If so, what is the objection?"—Yes.

92. Then there is Query 8—"What is the opinion of the Commissioners on the subject?—The answer to that was, "That no change be made."

93. Query 9, of course, was similarly answered?—Yes.

94. Are you aware of the grounds upon which it was deemed advisable that no change should be made?—Well, no, I am not in a position to give the particular grounds.

95. You said the municipal rate last year was 1s.?—Yes, the improvement rate, and sanitary rate 1d.

96. That was in '78?—Yes.

97. What was it the year before that—in '77?—I think it was the same.

98. And for '76?—The same.

99. And for '75?—About the same.

100. And for '74?—It was the same; but they were different a couple of years before that. There was a 6d. gas rate and a 6d. sanitary rate, but fault was found with it, and it was said they had not a right to strike a gas rate, and it became improvement rate during the past five years.

101. During the past five years it has been practically the same?—Yes, 1s. for general purposes and 1d. for sanitary.

102. What do you calculate will be the number of years that it would take to pay off this loan for a water supply if carried out?—I should think fifty years.

103. Assuming it to be fifty years, and repayable in instalments, what rate will that involve the first year?—I did not go into that.

104. Can you make a rough calculation what it will be on the existing municipal valuation?—I am sure it would be very small, because when we had a loan of £650 the rate was only 3d.

105. I asked you if there was any necessity for an improved system of drainage—is there any consideration of the expenditure it would entail involved in the matter?—No; there has been no complaint as to the drainage.

106. No complaint?—No.

107. Is it in a satisfactory state?—I have heard no complaint.

108. The military officers made no complaint?—No, not about the sewerage; I believe there is a good system of sewerage.

109. The workhouse is within the municipal district?—Partly; a little bit of the land is.

110. Only that?—Yes.

111. And the railway station—is that within the municipal district?—Yes, the goods store is, but the station is not.

112. Is any part of the Kinsale railway liable to municipal rates—the line of railway itself?—A very small portion of it is.

113. Now, would a radius of two miles, assuming it to be adopted, take in the workhouse?—Yes.

114. And the railway station?—Yes.

115. This is a large garrison town?—Yes.

116. What would you say the strength ordinarily is of the military?—I suppose about 600, or up to 1,000.

117. What is the number in recent years generally stationed here?—About 800, between the barracks here and the fort.

118. Is the barrack within the municipal district?—Yes.

119. Would you say the presence here of a large military force is of advantage to the town and its surroundings?—Yes.

120. And does not the advantage of the presence of such a force extend beyond the municipal area?—Yes.

121. Those outside the municipal area, then, I take it, derive advantages from the presence of the military, and, as you have said, from the dealing?—Yes; the military are sometimes supplied from Cork.

122. And you consider it reasonable that persons so situated, and deriving exceptional advantages, should take some share in contributing to the expenditure?—Yes.

Dr. J. Carey Hogan.

Dr. J. CAREY HOGAN examined.

123. Mr. O'Brien.—You are Chairman of the Town Commissioners?—Yes.

124. Have you been long so?—For three years.

125. Have you been long a Commissioner?—Several years.

126. And I presume you are intimately acquainted with the locality?—Yes.

127. Did you preside at the meeting the Clerk has referred to, in December, at which the question of the boundaries was considered?—Yes.

128. You were chairman of that meeting?—Yes.

129. I am correct in saying that the opinion of the Commissioners was that no change in the existing boundaries was required?—Yes.

130. No change of any kind?—Yes; except in the [illegible] the contract for the roads and the keeping of them in repair, and the leaving them in one own [illegible].

131. Were the Commissioners aware, when considering the question, that under the Public Health Act of [illegible], by section [illegible], there is power vested in the Local Government Board, by what is called a provisional order, to transfer from the Grand Jury of the county in which the municipal district is situated to the sanitary authority powers of by road bonds, bridges, and [illegible]?—I don't think they were fully aware of it, but I am aware of it.

132. If the Commissioners were aware of that provision, do you think that they would desire to have control over the roads and bridges now presented by the Grand Jury?—We would prefer to have it under our own authority.

133. You think they would be in favour of having it?—You can ask the others.

134. But that is your own opinion?—Yes.

135. Do you consider the amount raised in the shape of Grand Jury cess from the municipal district is not commensurate with the amount expended on county works?—Quite so, I should say, for the good they are doing it is enough.

136. Do you consider you get value in the shape of the works done by the Grand Jury for the money raised?—At present I think we do, but we want greater improvement; we want more in the future.

137. Do you consider if these works were transferred to your jurisdiction from the Grand Jury, that you would do the work more economically and more [illegible], and more particularly than the Grand Jury?—Yes, I think so; we would [illegible] it.

138. Assuming the functions of the Grand Jury were transferred, would that alter your view on the question of the boundaries being extended [illegible]?

139. You would still wish them to [illegible] as they are?—Yes.

140. Don't you consider that persons living outside your present limited radius, and who occupy houses and lands outside, derive [illegible] advantages from their proximity to the town of Kinsale?—Some of them do, but we would not derive any advantage from adding them in. We would not derive any advantage from taking in Scilly.

141. What portion is Scilly in?—It is a townland itself, it is in the electoral division of Kinsale.

142. Now, I take it the reason you would object to including Scilly is that if you were to light it and supply it with water, it would cost you more than you would derive from a good deal more.

143. But if the area were enlarged, so as to include not only Scilly, but a considerable quantity of land besides, which would contribute rates without being sent to the expansion of Scilly, would you then, and in the event of the radius of two miles from the centre of the town being adopted, object to the proposed extension?—Well, I really cannot give a decided answer, for I have not considered it.

144. Don't you think, Dr. Neal, there are a great many persons now outside the existing boundary who derive great advantages from Kinsale from the expenditure of money involved in the presence of a large military force, of a large number of [illegible], the [illegible] of trade, the increased value of land, the advantages of schools for children to resort to, and so on?—Yes.

145. And would you say these advantages may be fairly considered as extending to a radius of two miles?—I would say more; I would say as far as Charles Fort and Cove.

146. How far are they?—Two miles, or two miles and a half.

147. If the two mile radius would take in Scilly, Charlesfort, and Cove, you would be satisfied?—Yes.

148. You would say those are the only places you think that specially require to be taken in?—Yes.

149. Are those villages?—Yes, Cove is [illegible] to a military station.

150. There is a barrack there?—Yes.

151. You think the persons living within that radius of two miles should be considered as deriving advantages?—Yes. They are [illegible], and [illegible] is [illegible] to get inside the municipal area.

152. You are aware that within the Town Improvements Act there are certain classes of property rated at one-fourth?—Yes.

153. Do you think, as regards those lands and property of that description in the neighbourhood of the town, that considerable [illegible] augments the condition that they should pay?—I think it would be too little.

154. What would you say they ought to contribute?—I should think more than one-half.

155. You think one-fourth would be too little?—Yes.

156. It appears that a radius of two miles would bring in the railway, and it derives advantage from the town?—Yes; I would bring that in.

157. Don't you think one-fourth too small a proportion for the railway to pay?—I really could not give a decided answer.

158. You are quite clear that you would manage the Grand Jury work yourselves?—Yes.

159. You are a medical gentleman, practising in Kinsale?—Yes.

160. You have heard about the water supply—do you think that there has not got a good water supply?—Yes.

161. Are the works necessary to provide a good water supply be accomplished for £[illegible] [illegible]?—I could not say what it would cost.

162. Do you believe, as far as you can judge, that [illegible] would be sufficient?—I think myself it would require more, but I really cannot say.

163. You are not in a position to say?—No.

164. Is there, in your opinion, a necessity in the town for an improved system of drainage?—Yes, I believe there is a good deal required in the way of sewerage arrangements.

165. Have you been restrained, as sanitary authority, from undertaking a scheme of improved sewerage, by reason of the limited area, and the comparatively limited amount of rates?—No.

166. Do you think an improved system of sewerage required?—Yes.

167. Can you make a rough estimate of what would be required to carry out the works?—That would depend upon what was done.

168. Can you, as a medical man, give any idea of what would be required to carry out such a scheme as would be necessary for the purposes of the public health?—I think it is an engineer should give an opinion as to that.

169. Is there any other description of sanitary work that requires to be done?—Yes, there are the water works.

170. Any other works you think require to be attended?—Yes, there are a lot of old houses that ought to be knocked down, and taken away.

171. Do you consider, on this question of extension, that the persons living outside the existing municipal boundary would object, on the ground of taxation, to be brought in to contribute?—I think there would be a few objecting to it, but the general people would not, especially the villagers. There are a few of the farming classes will object.

172. That is, they object to pay taxes?—Yes.

173. They object as a general rule?—Yes.

174. Is there anything special you would like to add to what you have told us, for we are anxious to obtain as much information as possible?—No.

175. You have nothing further to add?—I believe I considered about taking up the roads.

176. You are strongly of that opinion?—Yes.

177. You have not made any application on the subject?—Yes, we did, to the road sessions.

178. Under this section of the Act you could only get control within the municipal limits?—We applied, and could not.

179. To whom did you apply?—To the road

[illegible] Jan. 6, [illegible]. Dr. J. Casey [illegible].

members of the Grand Jury; that was the only application.

180. Did they refuse to give it?—No; but we should take in four miles outside.

181. But you could not do it?—We would not accept of it.

182. The way the matter stands is this:—Heretofore, under the Local Government Act of 1871, the transfer of the control over works within the municipal district could only be obtained—could only be given by provisional order, but it was required that the consent of the Grand Jury to the change should be had. There were instances in which application was made for that sanction, but with the solitary exception of Wexford, the Grand Juries threw out the presentment, and the result was that it ceased to be applied for. Now, it was felt that the Grand Juries would not give assent, and the municipal bodies ceased to apply, so that the law has been changed or modified by the Public Health Act of last session. Did they make application to the Grand Jury?—They did; to the road sessions first.

183. And they refused their assent?—They refused to give the control of the part we wanted. That we should take three or four miles of country roads which we would not do.

184. Having failed to obtain the assent of the Presentment Sessions you took no further steps?—No.

185. Were the Commissioners aware that notwithstanding the refusal of the Presentment Sessions or the Grand Jury to grant the transference, they could get it from the Local Government Board on special application?—No, I don't think they were.

186. You are aware that while all the expenditure under the Towns Improvement Act is only charged upon arable land, at I explained, at one-fourth of the value, you are aware that all expenditure for Grand Jury purposes is charged equally upon all descriptions of property?—Yes.

187. Assuming these works were transferred to the Commissioners do they contemplate that these should be charged for at an equal rate on all descriptions of property or not?—I don't know.

188. Are they aware of the fact that all municipal rates are paid by the occupiers at present?—Yes.

189. And that the Parliamentary Committee of the House of Commons, under whose Report this Commission is sitting, have expressed a strong opinion in favour of having the municipal rates divided between the owners and occupiers?—I am aware of it.

190. Would the opinion of the Board be in favour of it?—I think so.

191. If the area were extended, say two miles, it would bring so many voters and persons eligible for the office of Commissioner?—I was just considering whether it would bring in the Eastern Bridge, I don't think it would.

192. Do you think that ought to be brought in?—Yes.

193. Would the extension of the present municipal boundary to a radius of two miles introduce a considerable number of new voters—electors entitled to vote for Town Commissioners?—Yes.

194. And also qualify a large number more for the office of Town Commissioner?—Yes.

195. Don't you think it would be an advantage to the body to be elected from a wider area of election?—I don't think there would really be much change.

196. Have you any further observations you would wish to make on the subject of the extension of the municipal area?—No, nothing more.

Dr. George N. Dowse.

Dr. George Newman Dowse, examined.

197. Mr. O'Brien.—You are a Town Commissioner?—Yes.

198. And have been for some time?—Yes.

199. Several years?—Yes.

200. Do you hold any public medical appointment?—No.

201. You are intimately acquainted with the town of Kinsale?—Yes.

202. Were you present at the meeting in December when the subject of the extension of the municipal boundaries was discussed?—Yes.

203. And the feeling at that meeting was adverse to any change?—Yes.

204. You hold with Dr. Neng, I presume, that the opinion of the Commissioners would be in favour of the control over the roads, bridges, and footpaths being transferred from the Grand Jury?—Yes.

205. Is the opinion of the Commissioners in favour of that transfer within the municipal district?—Well, it would be a most perilous thing.

206. I understand you to say you would be in favour of it?—Only in favour of having the control over such portions as are within the present municipal district. I think Dr. Neng was under a slight mistake in the matter.

207. The Commissioners, I understand you to say, are in favour of a transfer as regards roads, bridges, and footpaths within the present municipal district?—Yes.

208. But not of a control over any wider district?—Certainly not.

209. You would not, yourself, be in favour of a more extended control?—No.

210. On what ground do you base your opinion as to that?—It would embrace two very important structures, one an iron bridge that cost upwards of £1,000, and another that cost upwards of £1,500—the first is the Eastern bridge, and the other the Western.

211. Are these both constructed?—One of them is; the other is in course of construction.

212. By the county?—Yes.

213. What is the expenditure involved in their construction?—One is upwards of £1,000, and the other is to be upwards of £1,600.

214. Are they charged on the county at large?—They are, in a great measure.

215. What radius would bring these within the municipal district?—Two miles would bring them in.

216. You would object to any radius which brought in these two bridges?—Yes.

217. What townland are these bridges in?—I could not tell you.

218. Are they in the electoral division of Kinsale?—Yes.

219. Now, you would be opposed to taking charge of these bridges from the county?—Yes.

220. But if these were not included, would you see any objection to extending the area, and of having a transfer of the control of the works?—The point I think would be gain to us would be keeping the roads in repair; in other respects I don't think we would have any advantage.

221. You don't think you would do the work better than the Grand Jury?—We would, so far as the roads are concerned.

222. The roads, bridges, and footpaths. Now, if the bridges were excluded, would you be in favour of having the roads and footpaths under your control?—Within the present district, certainly.

223. Assuming the radius was extended to, say, two miles of an area, would you be in favour—if the bridges were excluded—of making the transfer of control over the roads, footpaths, and other public works?—No. The extension of the boundary would simply include villages which we could not benefit. We could not give them gas and water. When the people come in to Kinsale they use the water for drinking, otherwise there is no benefit they derive, and the only thing else is that they get an increased value for their produce.

224. Don't you think all the persons living within

a radius of two miles derive advantages from their proximity to the town?—I do not. I do not think they derive any more advantages than those residing four miles away.

225. You must surely draw the line somewhere?—I think our present boundary is a good one.

226. Don't you think the fair principle would be to place the rating proportionate with the benefit?—Yes, if you could see that the benefit existed.

227. Don't you think the advantages extend beyond a half a mile of the town?—No.

228. Don't you think it is an advantage to the people outside to have a market like that afforded by Kinsale?—I do. That is the only advantage derivable, and that is equally derived by persons four miles away.

229. Do you think persons living four or six miles off would be as frequently able to sell their produce as well as those one mile outside?—Yes.

230. Then do you think the same thing would apply to those living twelve miles away?—No.

231. You don't go so far as that?—No, but it would be unfair to extend the taxation to two miles and not further.

232. You are aware that arable lands only contribute in the proportion of one-fourth?—Yes.

233. Don't you think that is a pretty fair measure of the advantages derived at a distance of a mile and a half?—I think they should pay somewhat more.

234. How much would you say?—Between one-quarter and one-third.

235. When you say you would wish to get control of the footpaths, roads, and public works of the existing municipal division, do you contemplate that the charge of that should be by a rate equally made on all descriptions of property, or should it be adjusted to a graduated rate as made like that under the Towns Improvement Act—would you say an equal charge on house property, or only one-fourth on lands?—I think the existing system is fair.

236. You would consider that if you got the roads?—Yes.

237. The electoral division, I presume, you would consider entirely too large?—Yes.

238. And could not be adopted?—No; I think the line is very sharply defined between town and country, the moment you go outside the limits of the town you are as much in the country as if you were miles into it. I also think there must be the number of people within the two mile radius you think, but it would be quite in the country.

239. It would bring in a considerable amount of property?—Yes, it would do that.

240. You heard Dr. Nason express an opinion that there was not only a necessity for an improved water supply, but for an improved scheme of drainage?—Yes.

241. Do you agree with that?—Yes as to the necessity, but I cannot see the possibility of its being done. The tide is our destruction, it accumulates filth and dirt where the sewers debouch; it does not bring it away, and we cannot well bring into deep water without entailing an enormous expenditure.

242. That is the impediment to the adoption of an improved drainage scheme in the town?—Well, the situation of the town.

243. And the consequent large outlay the scheme would involve?—Yes.

244. Don't you think that by being able to carry it out, the town would be improved?—Yes.

245. Even if you made a moderate improvement on the present system, it would take a large sum?—Yes.

246. Would it not be an advantage in undertaking such a work to have a larger area on which to charge it?—Yes.

247. Don't you think if the health of the town were improved that the fact would be of advantage to those who resort to it constantly in their daily business. If, on the other hand, an epidemic broke out, would it not be attended with disadvantage not only to the residents, but to those outside who come in?—I suppose that is to be considered.

248. If people outside derive advantage in that way, don't you think that some contribution would be fairly expected from those persons who, in a modified degree, share the advantages of the town government?—I think it would be very small.

249. Now, don't the children of parents outside resort to Kinsale for their educational purposes?—Yes.

250. That is an advantage?—Certainly it is.

251. They share in the advantages of the watering and cleansing?—They do.

252. You light the town with gas?—Yes.

253. When farmers come here and are detained at night, is it not of advantage to them to have the gas lighting?—Yes.

254. There is a good public supply—the people who come in get good water?—Yes.

Kinsale. [illegible]

Mr. Richard Knowles examined.

Mr. Richard Knowles.

255. Mr. O'Brien.—You are a Town Commissioner and a very old Poor Law Guardian?—I am.

256. Are you an *ex officio* Poor Law Guardian?—No; elected.

257. How many years have you been a member of the Town Commissioners?—Only a few months.

258. You have heard the questions that have been put and answered to-day?—Yes.

259. And may I ask what your views are on the subject of extension of the municipal boundary?—I am inclined to agree with Dr. Nason, that if it was decided to extend the radius by two miles, it would be a great advantage.

260. And do you think it would be of advantage to get control over the roads and footpaths?—Yes, within the limits of the municipal district.

261. Assuming the radius of two miles were adopted, would you consider it of advantage that all the roads and footpaths within that should be vested in the control of the Town Commissioners?—I think it would be too much for them.

262. You think it would only be of advantage to have the transfer as regards the limits of the present area?—Precisely.

263. You think if the boundary were extended it would be too much for the Town Commissioners to undertake the charge of the roads within the limits of that extension?—Yes.

264. Don't you think a body meeting constantly, acquainted with the district, able to make arrangements, supervise the works, would do the work more economically and efficiently than the Grand Jury?—I merely form my opinion from the difficulty we have at present.

265. But at present you have not charge of them?—We have charge of some of the streets—that is cleansing, paving, and lighting.

266. And you would not be in favour of taking a greater responsibility?—No.

267. But as far as the present municipal district you would be inclined to take the control of that?—Yes.

268. But if you comprehended in your area the rural district you would not think it advisable?—No.

269. Don't you think that persons within a radius of two miles derive substantial advantages from their proximity to the town?—I do, decidedly.

270. Having a large fishing population during the year, a large military force, and a large population in the town, it is a good market for their produce, and so on?—Yes, I have property myself, and I know that.

271. Is that property within the district?—No, outside.

272. Would you object to that being brought in?—Well——

273. What radius would bring you in?—About five at least.

KINSALE. Jan. 4, 1879. — Mr. Richard Knowles.

274. But it has been enhanced in value?—No doubt.

275. Would a two-mile radius bring you in?—No.

276. You are aware that arable lands, and so forth, should be liable to be rated only at one-fourth?—Yes.

277. Do you consider that a fair representation of the advantages that outside lands may be considered to derive?—I should rather say one-third.

278. Assuming the transfer of the Grand Jury powers, do you think it should be charged as at present on all descriptions of property, or that there should be a graduated scale of rating, such as that under the Towns Improvement Act?—A graduated scale, I think.

279. You would charge for Grand Jury works a graduated scale?—Yes.

280. Do you consider there is a necessity for an improved water supply?—I do.

281. And that it would be of advantage to the public health of Kinsale if there was a better system of sewage?—I would not like to give an opinion on that. It would be very expensive.

282. You would not like the town to undertake the charge of these two bridges?—Certainly not.

283. Is there any special suggestion you would like to make?—No.

Mr. C. Bawn.

Mr. CHARLES BAWN examined.

284. Mr. O'BRIEN.—You are a Town Commissioner?—Yes.

285. And also rate collector, I believe?—Yes.

286. What rates do you collect?—Poor rate for the electoral division of Kinsale.

287. Do you collect Grand Jury rate?—No.

288. You are intimately acquainted with the whole circle of the town?—I am.

289. Do you consider the existing boundary too limited?—I don't think it is. I would be in favour of leaving it as it is.

290. Do you consider that persons living outside the present boundaries derive advantages from being within two miles of a market town like Kinsale, for the sale of their produce?—No doubt.

291. Don't they derive advantages in the way of having their schools in Kinsale to send their children to?—Well, I would not say that.

292. Within what radius of the town do you think advantages are bona fide enjoyed by ratepayers?—Do you mean outside?

293. Yes, outside the present area?—From two to three miles.

294. Then would you consider it inequitable that persons deriving these advantages in that way should pay some contribution towards the town expenditure?—I would have no objection to their paying something, but I fear it would involve our giving them something in return.

295. Such as what?—Why gas, water, or anything of that sort.

296. If it were not contemplated you were to give gas to the fullest extent, or water, don't you consider they should pay a contribution to the advantages they derive from intercourse with the town?—Yes.

297. You are aware that arable land, and property of that description, contribute only one-fourth, don't you think that one-fourth is a fair measure of the advantages they would derive?—I should say one-half would be fairer.

298. You would not consider it inequitable that persons living within a radius of two miles should pay to our rates one-third?—No.

299. You agree that there is a necessity for an improved water supply?—There is.

300. And of having the control now exercised by the Grand Jury over roads and footpaths?—Yes; within the present municipal area.

301. And you would not be in favour of taking charge of these bridges?—No.

302. If the radius were extended to two miles, you would not take up the charge of all these roads and footpaths comprised within that area?—No.

303. Why so?—We could never accomplish it.

304. Why could not the Town Commissioners manage it as well as the Grand Jury?—Their system is more one of organization than any that we have.

305. Would there be any difficulty in your effecting the organization necessary?—I agree with what Mr. Knowles said on that point.

306. Are you aware that several places have obtained, by legislation, control over these roads from the Grand Juries?—No.

307. Would it alter your opinion as to the practicability of it, if you heard that a considerable number of towns have obtained for themselves, by local legislation, control over the works?—No.

308. Do you consider an improved scheme of sewerage is necessary?—I would not like to give an opinion as to that.

309. Assuming a competent medical opinion was obtained to the effect that it was necessary, and that considerable cost would be incurred, I presume you are of opinion that that outlay would confer undoubted advantages, not only upon the town, but on the neighbourhood; that it would improve the place generally, further its repute, and make it or keep it free from disease?—Yes; certainly.

310. Don't you think that persons daily receiving advantages from resorting here should pay their contribution to the town expenses?—Yes; if it were practicable at all I would go in for thoroughly improving the sewage.

311. What are the poor rates in the electoral division?—1s. 4d.; 1s. last year; 10d. the year before.

312. The Grand Jury Rate—what is that?—This year, 1s. 4d. twice a year.

313. That is 2s. 8d. in the year?—Yes.

314. Is that exceptionally high?—Yes; in consequence of this bridge.

315. Is it likely to continue?—No; only for a short time.

316. Taking the normal condition of things, what is it?—10d. or 11d.

317. Each half year?—Yes.

318. 1s. 8d. or 1s. 10d.?—Yes.

319. So there is an increase of 10d.?—Yes.

320. How long will it continue?—Six years.

327. And you think they ought to contribute?—Yes.

328. Is your opinion in favour of the transfer of the functions of the Grand Jury for roads and footpaths?—Yes; within the present boundary.

329. But if it were extended to two miles, would you be for the transfer?—No; for the Grand Jury have the county surveyors, and so on, and we have not the same advantages.

330. Assuming you got the transfer of any functions, would the outlay be made up by a rate assessed equally on all descriptions of property, or would you make it varying?—A varying one.

331. And you would raise the one-fourth to one-half, and apply it to all works?—Yes.

332. Have you any further evidence to give?—No.

Mr. JAMES HURLEY examined.

333. Mr. O'BRIEN.—You are not a Town Commissioner?—No.

334. Where do you reside?—On the boundary, but within the borough boundary.

335. You are a ratepayer within the boundary?—Yes.

336. Is all the property you hold within the [illegible] area?—No.

337. You are rated in the boundary, I understand?—Yes.

338. Have you property outside?—Yes.

339. How much?—About 105 acres.

340. And how much within the boundary?—About five.

341. So that you are chiefly outside?—Yes.

342. What [illegible] would bring you in?—About three-quarters of a mile.

343. Are you desirous of being brought in?—No.

344. Would you not wish to be eligible for the office of Town Commissioner?—No; I would not desire it.

345. Are you opposed to having the area extended so as to bring in your holdings?—Yes.

346. On what ground?—That I derive no advantage from the light from the gas or water.

347. Don't you resort here for the disposal of your produce?—Well, we have to send it to Cork.

348. Do you dispose of [illegible] produce in Kinsale?—Yes.

349. What do you dispose of?—[illegible].

350. Anything else?—Sometimes a little milk.

351. Don't you consider it an advantage to have a market here by so near?—Yes.

352. Are there not a good many persons who dispose of buttermilk, and so on, who come into the town?—Yes.

353. Do they not derive advantage in living adjacent to such a town, in selling their produce, and milk, in Kinsale?—Yes.

354. And don't many persons living outside send in their children to school at Kinsale?—A few of them do.

355. These from outside derive undoubted advantages?—Yes.

356. These persons have to resort to the town frequently?—Yes.

357. Is it not of advantage to those if they are obliged to [illegible] to have the town well lighted with gas?—They don't complain of that.

358.—Well, if the town, by an outlay of money, obtained a good and plentiful supply of water, and the drainage was improved, would not the advantages of the [illegible] of the town be shared in by those who come into it, as well as by the residents?—Yes.

359. By the town being made free from disease?—Yes.

360. Besides those being only [illegible] under the present state of the law to contribute one-fourth, don't you think that if the town rate is so, that one-fourth is but a reasonable amount of the advantages they derive?—You would not get them to pay anything like it.

361. The objection, I take it, is to pay anything in the way of taxes?—Yes.

362. The objection is not that they consider the advantages they derive, but an objection to pay any taxes?—Yes.

The inquiry terminated.

CLONAKILTY.—JANUARY 8th, 1879.

(Before Mr. W. A. EXHAM, Q.C., Chairman of the Commission.)

Mr. DANIEL O'LEARY examined.

1. You are the Chairman of the Town Commissioners?—Yes.

2. How long have you filled that position?—About three years ago I was first elected.

3. Have you been a long time a Town Commissioner?—About thirteen years.

4. When were the boundaries of the Town of Clonakilty first fixed?—In 1857, I think.

5. Was that the time when you adopted the Towns Improvement Act?—I believe the Lord Lieutenant was memorialised for the adoption of the Act then in 1856. I was not a Town Commissioner then. The boundary then was larger. The Commissioners were then acting under the 9th of George IV., and applied in 1856 for the Towns Improvement Act; they memorialised the Lord Lieutenant, and there was a good deal of opposition given by the landlords, who were very much afraid of taxation; and a great deal of confusion arose afterwards inasmuch as the Lord Lieutenant did not then grant the Towns Improvement Act, so that they worked then under the 9th of George IV., to 1858 when the Lord Lieutenant was again memorialised to grant the adoption of the Towns Improvement Act and it was then granted and the boundaries are fixed by Griffith. That was the first occasion, as far as I can learn, which they were altered.

6. Were they altered in 1869?—Yes, and fixed in 1869.

7. Are they smaller than those under the 9th of George IV.?—Yes; I think the boundary at present does not extend more than half a mile—a little over half a mile. It is a radius of half a mile in some directions and then of one mile as the crow flies at the end of the town.

8. What is the acreage of the present boundary?—About 1,000 acres. We have made it up rather more accurately since the quantity was furnished to you in the answer to your queries.

9. What is the valuation?—About £4,845.

10. In the answer to the queries we sent you, you give the valuation £4,815?—That was an old valuation of the present borough that you have in the answer to the query and I think everything was wrong in that. You cannot take those statements as accurate. We have, however, gone over the union books with the clerk's book and have got everything here now as accurately as possible.

11. Then what is the present valuation?—The present area is 1,000 acres, and the valuation is £4,845. The replies to the queries are not accurate, but this return is very accurate.

12. What is the population of the present town?—3,645.

13. Is the town at present all in one electoral division?—Yes, the electoral division of Clonakilty.

14. I understand from the answers to the queries that the ratepayers of the town and the Town Commissioners think that the present bounds are too small, is that so?—Yes.

15. Is that the unanimous opinion of the Town Commissioners as far as you can learn?—Yes.

[illegible]. Jan. 8, 187[illegible].
——
Mr. Daniel O'Leary.

16. And of the ratepayers of the township generally? —Yes; as far as I can learn.

17. To what extent, according to the opinion of the Town Commissioners, should the boundaries be changed?—To a little over a mile radius if the different townlands proposed, and shown on the map could be taken in.

18. You propose a radius of about a mile from the centre of the town?—We should get a radius of a mile to a mile and three quarters to take in the townlands, but bear in mind that that radius would take in a good deal of land adjoining the town where the tide ebbs and flows.

19. Have you placed on the map before me the boundary that you propose?—You will see on the map the boundary where the tide ebbs and flows.

20. Which is the present boundary on the map before me?—The red dotted line is the present boundary; it is marked on the Ordnance map.

21. To what extent have you put down on this map the altered boundary as you now propose it?—We have not put it down exactly on the map. We do not want to extend the boundary to the west; we want to extend it to the east, and our reason for extending it so far to the east is so as to take in the [illegible]

22. I wish to know if you are authorised to speak for the Commissioners as a body?—Yes.

23. What is the extension that they, as a body, propose?—You can see on the map what is intended to be taken in. The present boundary, I may say, was through four townlands. We propose to take in the whole of the townlands of Youghal, both north and south. We want to take in Cappagh—a small portion consisting of, I think, about 50 acres.

24. Where is that?—It is not within the present boundary, but lies between Tawnies Upper and Temple Brian South. We want to straighten the boundary at that critical point.

25. You want the whole of the townland of Youghal South down to the sea?—Yes, and that is bounded to the south by the sea.

26. Do you want to go down to the bay so far as that townland is concerned?—Yes. We want the townlands of Youghal North and South, and the whole of Clohane. We also want Knockaverry taken in; then we take in the portion of the Millst, which is not at present included in the existing boundary.

27. How do you then propose to go from the northward corner of Clohane?—We propose to follow the townland boundary between Millst and Ballydaniel.

28. Do you propose to take in the Tawnies?—Yes, both north and south.

29. Is it proposed to take in Kilgarriff Church?—No. We do not want to meddle with Kilgarriff. The boundary is a straight line along the Tawnies Lower, bounding Kilgarriff Church and the Tawnies Upper, along to the north, and if you take in Cappagh it forms a straight boundary to Templebrian South.

30. So far as dividing any townlands it is objectionable, of course; but if you have a well-defined boundary, such as a road, it may not be objectionable?—The boundary as described by me is well-defined, because it follows townland boundaries which are the same as the river up to Templebrian.

31. And you want to carry on the townland boundary up to Cappagh?—Yes, we include that to square the boundary. Then we take in Gallanes, Cahergall, East and West, Ashgrove, and taking in the workhouse and the whole of Dunmore, and that is only partly in at present.

32. Do you propose to take in Curraghgrancing and Curraghgrannamore?—Yes.

33. Where does the electoral division of Clonakilty come?—At Dunmore, to the east.

34. Does the new division come in then?—Yes, the division of Templeomalus.

35. In the line you propose there would be a portion of the extended boundary of the electoral division of Clonakilty?—Yes, at Templeomalus, but that is a special case.

36. Are you now authorised, on the part of the Commissioners, to propose to take in only the townlands mentioned in the answers to the questions sent down to you, or to take in those that are mentioned above?—At the time of the meeting to consider the answers to be sent to your queries, they would not include South Templebrian, Gallanes, both Cahergall, Ashgrove, Curraghgrancing, and Curraghgrannamore, but now we are agreed to ask to have these and all the rest included.

37. When you get down to Curraghgrannamore, what do you propose?—First of all we have Curraghgrancing.

38. Do you propose the whole of Curraghgrancing down as far as Knockaloge and Seven?—Yes, and then to take a straight line from the southern boundary of the pier to the northern extremity of the causeway from the island to South Youghal.

39. Have, on the part of the Commissioners, have you stated your entire proposal?—Yes, sir.

40. What would be the area of the new boundary? —I am not in a position to say in consequence of these townlands being added to our original proposal, but we will send you that information, and also the valuation of the extended area.

42. How many gentlemen's seats will be taken in in the proposed boundary?—Only two, I believe, Mr. Newman's and Major O'Leary's.

43. About how many farmers' buildings will be taken in?—I cannot tell you that now, but we will send you the information as to that.

44. How many voters would be brought in by the extension?—We will be able to send you information as to that also.

45. Are you able to say, of your own knowledge, whether or not the lands you propose to take in derive exceptional value from their proximity to the town?—They derive considerable benefit.

46. Do you know whether or not the persons who would be taken in would object to it, collectively or individually?—I do not think they would; and as far as I know, I think they would be in favour of it.

47. Are the Commissioners aware that under the Towns Improvement Act the arable land to be taken in will only pay rates on one-fourth of its valuation? —They are quite aware of what you say.

48. Do the Town Commissioners think that the one-fourth would be a fair proportion for the occupier of that land to pay?—They don't think it would. They think and propose that the occupier should pay one-half of the improvement rate, the same as he is to pay for the sanitary rate, under the Public Health Act of last year, and that he should deduct the half of what he pays from the landlord.

49. Have the Commissioners considered the question—supposing the proposed increased area is taken into the township—of taking up the management of the roads in that area?—We think to do so would be a source of special advantage to the ratepayers of the town, and also to those in the increased area.

50. Have they considered whether or not they would derive benefit having regard to the sanitary work if you were to increase the urban sanitary authority?—Decidedly so; and since the guardians became the rural sanitary authority, the ratepayers have felt it considerably.

51. How long have they been the rural sanitary authority?—About two years.

52. What is the poor rate?—The sanitary rate was only 1d. in the pound, whereas, if the Town Commissioners were the urban sanitary authority, they would not have to pay that rate at all; besides, they would look after waterworks in the town, which the Guardians have neglected to do.

53. In view of the extension you propose, would there be any difficulty because the occupiers of the arable land who would be brought in under the present state of the law would only pay one-fourth?—I think they should pay a half.

54. You think that would be a fair ratio—that whatever the townspeople pay the others should pay one-half?—Exactly so.

Q. Who manages the pier at present?—It is managed by the Grand Jury.

Q. Then it is public property?—Yes.

57. Are the Grand Jury the persons who were authorised to build and maintain it by Grand Jury presentment?—I believe so. No, it was owing to the [illegible] of Railway Commissioners it was built.

58. I wish to know what advantage do you think the Town Commissioners would derive from getting the management of the pier into their hands, if it is [illegible] from time to time as they are thrown up there? Have they considered that?—They have, and consider it would be a great boon to the ratepayers if the Commissioners had the management and control of the pier in their own hands, inasmuch as they would [illegible] the approaches to the pier, and the pier itself, which [illegible] under their supervision. Some one or two years ago, the [illegible] the [illegible] pier [illegible], and [illegible] from time to time about it, against the pier, so that it was not accessible even to small vessels, which were unable then to come to the upper pier. A farmer living next to the lower pier had a private pier of his own, and the vessels coming up were obliged to land at his pier, for which he [illegible] the [illegible], and in addition, every ratepayer and every person having goods within the town at that time was obliged to pay [illegible] a ton cartage from the lower to the upper pier.

59. Have you considered the expense that would be entailed on the ratepayers if they take the management of the pier, and keep it up?—Yes; and when it is properly kept, and vessels can discharge and load there, I see some there, it is a large revenue to be derived from it.

60. In your opinion, would the revenue to be derived from the pier be sufficient to compensate the Town Commissioners for any outlay they may necessarily expend—they would have to make in keeping up the pier from time to time?—I should think so.

61. Are the Town Commissioners willing to undertake the management and keeping up of the pier if it is brought within the boundary?—Quite so.

62. Is that opinion shared in by the Town Commissioners and the public, to your own knowledge?—It is shared in by every ratepayer of the town, so far as I know. There was even a private subscription raised to pay for the clearing away of the obstructions which prevented vessels from getting to the upper pier.

63. Were any applications made to the Presentment Sessions for the purpose of clearing away those obstructions?—Yes.

64. Is the opinion you have expressed with regard to the pier the general opinion of the Town Commissioners?—Certainly. I wish to mention, with reference to another matter, that their opinion, also, is that if the management of the roads within the township were in their own hands it would be the greatest boon to the ratepayers; we have made frequent applications for the sewerage and lighting of the town, but they were very often refused, and the ratepayers were [illegible] in fact.

65. Is it your opinion and that of the Town Commissioners that the farmers and those that would be brought within the township by the proposed extension of area would be benefited by the change, supposing the payments for the roads was made to the Town Commissioners instead of the Grand Jury, and that they paid besides a proportion of the improvement and lighting rate?—It is, and I think they would save the [illegible] the rates they would now have to pay; and as far as the sanitary rate is concerned they will have some small [illegible] if we increase the urban sanitary authority.

Mr. [illegible] R. Wright examined.

66. You have resided a long time in Clonakilty?—Yes.

67. And were chairman of the Town Commissioners for a long time?—Yes; and I was chairman of the Town Commissioners, I believe, when we sought to be brought under the Towns Improvement Act. At that time we intended a very extensive area, larger than we could avail ourselves [illegible]. Opposition did, however, arise, owing to some [illegible] that it is our boundary for the [illegible] to [illegible] in, and owing to that opposition being of a rather violent character our application was refused. The town was subsequently brought under the Towns Improvement Act, and it is now under that Act. As an inhabitant of the town, and knowing its wants, I desire to state that I think the present area is entirely too limited. If you will kindly look, sir, you will see the pencil lines drawn round the map. One is about a mile-and-a-half wide, and the other a [illegible] from the centre of the town. I certainly, having given the question a great deal of consideration, and I would, if you could accommodate the circumstances, be for the mile-and-a-half one.

68. That is to follow as closely as possible townland boundaries?—Yes.

69. Then you would go by the townland boundaries, keeping as closely as possible to the mile-and-a-half radius?—Yes; and I come to that conclusion regarding the welfare of the town first. That is the first and primary concern, regarding also the welfare of those who are within that area, irrespective of rank or position—whether they are gentlemen or farmers, shopkeepers, traders, or artisans, [illegible] or position, if that boundary be followed, as nearly as possible under the Act, I have no doubt, I am sure, [illegible] it would be for the benefit of all parties.

70. Is it your opinion that the people within that area from their proximity to the town derive such advantages as should compensate them for any additional rate put on them?—Yes, decidedly.

71. I would like to know your view with regard to the amount of rate they should be levied. Apparently, under the Towns Improvement Act, you are aware that the lands within the township only pay a rate on one-fourth of its value. Have you considered that matter?—I have considered that, and I really think, from the benefits they derive, that they should be made to pay a moiety.

72. Of whatever the town rate is?—I think the people living in the vicinity should be assessed [illegible] with the people living in the town. Somewhere in [illegible]. I could not enumerate, I am sure, the advantages which the people living in the vicinity of the town possess.

73. Have you considered whether it would be advisable, if the boundary were extended as you propose, that the management of the roads should be taken up by the Commissioners?—I certainly think that then they would have proper management. If they take the advantages, they should take the liabilities as well. I do not think it is fair to take and cull and say, "We will take this townland because there are no roads; and we won't take other townlands because there are roads." I would take the advantages and liabilities, and I think the advantages would compensate for more than the liabilities.

74. You think that if the township had the management of the roads, the expense of them would not be greater than they are at present?—I am not sure that [illegible] would not, but the advantages would more than compensate them for the extra liabilities.

75. Would they be able to keep the town accounts and would not the [illegible] be of great advantage to those living outside?—Yes; and the [illegible] they pay [illegible] be [illegible] as [illegible] and [illegible] is much less than they are paying at present.

76. Have you considered the question of the pier?—I have; and since I came into this room I have been shaken in my opinions; and I have seen some [illegible] here who know the interest of the town at heart.

CLONAKILTY, Jan. 8, 1879.

Mr. Thomas R. Wright.

and who have considered the question of the pier more than I have considered it; and when I came in I was afraid of incurring the liability, because, unfortunately for myself, I saw that pier when it was being built. I think it was built badly; I think it was constructed badly, and I think it will ultimately come down, and I think the expense, if thrown on the township, would be very heavy. I think it would be a pity to exclude it, and I also think it may be a very hazardous thing to do; but on the whole I concur with Mr. O'Leary and others that it would be the safer thing at present to take the pier with all its infirmities, and it is especially necessary to do so for reasons that it is not necessary for me to mention here now.

77. Of course it must be a great advantage to the town to have a pier there?—Yes; what has made me change my opinion is that I think the mercantile men who have an interest in the trade will see that it is always kept in proper order; and in that way the town will derive considerable benefit from it. At present they have been considerably hampered by the way in which it has been kept. Perhaps you may not be aware of it, so I may mention the fact that we have men here who are very largely engaged in the corn trade, some of whom I see around me now, so that the interest on that pier and the traffic on it to merchants are really very considerable.

78. At present it is in the hands of the Grand Jury?—Yes; and very badly managed it is—that is about the worst, I should say. You will please take me as being of opinion that it would be of advantage to the town if the pier was included in the boundary, so I have changed my opinion on the subject.

Mr. W. B. Leslie.

Mr. W. B. Leslie examined.

79. You are an old inhabitant of the town?—I am.

80. Is it your opinion that the present municipal boundary is too limited?—I think it would be beneficial to the district to have more of the land embraced within the boundary.

81. Allow me to show you on the map what the Commissioners propose. (Having pointed out, on the map the boundary as proposed)—Are you in favour of that?—I do not see the slightest objection to that. The impression of the people is that in the way of trade we are very young, and that we do not quite understand the importance of economy. When we have a larger area the people think we will be less economical; but I hope we are outgrowing that, and that we will learn in time that economy is money.

82. In your opinion, would it be for the advantage of the town to have the area included in the way I have shown you on the map?—I think it would.

83. Is it your opinion that the town should have the pier, and that the town should have the management of the pier and the roads, &c.?—Yes; and I think the island should also be included.

Mr. Thomas R. Wright.

Mr. Wright re-examined.

84. I believe you wish to add something to your evidence?—Yes; I wish to say that I gave that question of the island very anxious consideration. We actually derive enormous advantages from it. It is the depot of sand for the whole country round, and though we have paid, and pay, something for the roads to it, they are made for our advantage, and for that of the people living in Dunmanway, Ballineen, and Enniskeen, and the country in that direction; so that we derive enormous benefits from it; and as to including it because we would have to consider the question of taxation for it, I am perfectly satisfied that if there is not the greatest mismanagement the taxation will always be nil. I am sure of that, unless there is the greatest perversion of and the greatest prodigacy in the use of public money.

85. Do you then consider that the island should be taken in and comprised within the municipal area?—No.

Mr. Daniel O'Leary.

Mr. O'Leary re-examined.

86. Do the Town Commissioners desire to have the island in the municipal area?—No.

87. The Commissioner.—Is there any other gentleman who would wish to give me his views of the matter?—

88. Mr. Wright.—I think now, sir, you have the opinion of the Commissioners as well as the public.

QUEENSTOWN—JANUARY 9TH, 1879.

Before Messrs. Exham, Q.C. (Chairman), and O'Brien.

Mr. James Wm. Scott, Chairman of the Town Commissioners, examined.

Mr. James W. Scott.

1. How long have you been a member of the Board?—Six years, I think.

2. What is the present area of the township?—[illegible]

3. And what is the valuation?—£20,539.

4. And the number of tenements or ratepayers [illegible] valued at £50?

5. You are under a special Act of your own?—Yes.

6. Are you under the Towns Improvement Act?—Yes, we have the Queenstown Improvement Act of 1862, which incorporates the Towns Improvement Act as well. We have an Act which enables us to [illegible] the Grand Jury powers to ourselves.

7. Mr. O'Brien.—What is the title of that Act?—The Queenstown Improvement Act of 1862.

8. Chairman.—Within that, how much outside land is there?—I mean as distinguished from houses within the entire municipal area?—Within the township?

9. Yes; outside land as distinguished from houses?—There is outside land to the value of only £500.

10. Is the outside land under your Acts, or do you tax that at only one-fourth of the valuation?—Yes.

11. Mr. O'Brien.—That is for the purposes of the Towns Improvement Act?—Yes.

12. But do you tax it to the full amount for the road cess?—Yes.

13. You see the Act says this in the 6th section:—

"It shall be lawful for the Commissioners in addition to the rates which by law they are authorised to make, to levy an [illegible] rate, which shall be called the Queenstown road rate"?

Yes.

14. And the 9th section goes on to say:—

"The said road rate shall, in all respects, be assessed, levied, or recovered, and be subject to the same liabilities, exemptions, remedies, and appeal, and otherwise, as the [illegible] which the Commissioners now levy under the provisions of the Act of 1854"?

Yes.

15. You use the expression rural rating as distinguished from a rating of suburbs?—The whole thing only amounts to a valuation of £500, and it is a very small item. We did not alter the rating when we got our Act.

16. Chairman.—It seems that the Town Commissioners did not think it expedient to have any alteration in the existing boundary?—That was the feeling of the Commissioners.

17. How far do the present boundaries extend on the whole?—If you have the map there you will see—from [illegible] to Monkstown Ferry, including [illegible].

18. Now, looking at this map—do you not think that the houses that are to the north, that is, out by Belgrave House, Hawthorn Cottage, and Ross Cottage, derive great advantages from their proximity to the town?—Yes, I do.

19. Do they not very largely use the roads of the township?—Yes.

20. And the markets, churches, schools, and in fact everything in the town?—Yes.

21. And tell me, then, on what principle you think the line should be—should it be so drawn as to take in [illegible] on the west, and leave out such a place as Hawthorn Cottage, and not go up as far as Carrigaloe?—Personally, I am of opinion that it would be of advantage to the Commissioners to take in the piece of land there adjoining our present boundary, and go up to Carrigaloe.

22. Would you say from the top of [illegible], or immediately beyond Ross Cottage?—I would take in all these. From the townland of [illegible] I would take from Mr. Hardy's house, and go by a line beyond the works that Mr. Cummins has erected there to Carrigaloe.

23. Why would you stop there—do not the Carrigaloe people derive substantial advantages from the town?—Yes; but the taking in of Carrigaloe would put us to much cost, and it would not confer much benefit on the town, but would add to the expenses considerably.

24. Mr. O'Brien.—How far does it extend east and west from the centre of the town?—Little more than a mile at each side.

25. And to the north how much does the area extend?—About a third of a mile; hardly a third.

26. Now, are there not a large number of inhabited houses, and a large quantity of land, within a radius of a mile, extending northward, as well as east and west?—No, not much; very few houses. There are only about six houses built there within the last twenty years.

27. Supposing the radius were extended a mile north from the centre of the town, can you give how many inhabited houses would be within it?—About forty.

28. Are these generally farm houses?—All but six.

29. Do not the occupiers of all those houses derive considerable advantages, and are not their lands enhanced in value by the fact that they have a market town like Queenstown in their vicinity?—Well, I don't think so.

30. Do they not dispose of their produce in Queenstown?—Well, yes, they do partly; but anything but what is sent to the Midleton and Cork markets.

31. Do they send their butter and corn and other produce to Cork and Midleton?—Yes.

32. But they do dispose of some produce here?—Yes.

33. And when they come here for the disposing of that produce, they derive certain advantages from the [illegible] and so on?—Yes.

34. And at present they contribute nothing to it?—No.

35. Does the present boundary cut townlands?—Yes, it does.

36. How many townlands, and parts of townlands, are divided by the municipal boundary?—They are all cut.

37. Chairman.—How many townlands have you, or parts of townlands?—Six.

38. Are they all in the electoral division?—Yes.

39. What is the area of the electoral division of Queenstown?—I do not know.

40. Do you know how many townlands are in it?—No.

41. How far does it extend?—It comprehends the whole island.

42. And how far would you take the smallest part of the electoral division to be from the centre of the town?—About two miles or more.

43. In what direction?—Due north.

44. And how far to the east?—About five miles.

45. And to the west?—About two and a half miles each way.

46. Would you consider the electoral division of Queenstown would constitute a fair municipal district?—I think it would be too large; it is the whole island.

47. Would you be prepared to say what would be a fair radius or area to adopt?—I should say that "The road" would be a very good one. From our eastern boundary it comes in rather a circular road till it comes to the west, and it includes those houses that have been spoken of.

QUEENSTOWN.
Jan. 8, 1880.
—
Mr. Angus W. Scott.

48. That would comprehend a radius from the centre of the town of about a mile?—Yes.

49. CHAIRMAN.—But if you wanted to take in Carrigaloe, it would be left out by that boundary?—Yes; but there are few houses there.

50. Mr. O'BRIEN.—Is there not a village there?—There are only very few little houses.

51. CHAIRMAN.—There is Anne Brook up there?—Yes.

52. Whose place is that?—Mr. Rumyon's.

53. And is not that a fine place?—Yes, it is.

54. Well, does not that house derive a very great deal of advantage from its position in regard to the town?—Yes.

55. And there is Ballydaniel House?—Yes.

56. Does not that derive advantages from its position in respect of the town and the road?—Yes.

57. Mr. O'BRIEN.—The "Ten" line you mention would not absorb the whole electoral division?—No, nor half of it.

58. What is the valuation of the electoral division?—It is £28,000.

59. And of the township itself?—The township is £19,000 of that.

60. And what is the area of it?—I do not exactly know.

61. Now, do the children of parents residing there within that "Ten" line, or outside it, and not at present included in the municipal district, derive advantage from the schools of the town, and so on?—Yes; they do come to school in the town.

62. Now, above the "Ten" line, immediately north of it, are there not inhabited houses that derive advantages from their proximity to the town, and having its schools, and so on?—Well, there are not many.

63. But the electoral division would not in any direction carry you a radius of much more than two and a half miles?—No.

64. CHAIRMAN.—But just outside that "Ten" line, when you go beyond only a quarter of a mile, are there not several houses?—Yes.

65. And don't the gentlemen who live in these houses derive enormous benefit from the town of Queenstown?—They do derive benefit.

66. Mr. O'BRIEN.—The Parliamentary Committee expressed a decided opinion in favour of having municipal areas and electoral divisions conterminous, and wherever the Commissioners find that they have to recommend anything at variance with that, strong reasons must be shown for doing so. I therefore wish to know from you, to state your view as to whether there is any valid objection to adopt here the electoral division in its entirety?—The objection we would have is this, that it would bring in an enormously increased responsibility. What I mean is this. The township is valued at £19,000, and the entire rest of the electoral division at only £9,000; and there is an enormous amount of roads to be kept in order, and besides that, by the Act of Parliament, we would have to light and watch these places. Even with the "Ten" line, that would appear to be the natural boundary, running through the centre of the Island; even with that line, we have been making up a rough estimate that it would bring in six miles of roads there, and the result, if we were obliged to light and watch it, in even the most economical manner possible, as we have been able to make it out, there would be a loss of about £150 a year, by our taking that as the boundary. I am expressing my individual opinion that I would be glad to take in the western boundary, not as far as Carrigaloe, but taking in Mr. Gummer's place.

67. Would you do the same as to the east, taking in Cuskinny and the gentlemen's houses and seats just on the borders of the harbour?—No; I think that would be very costly.

68. The lighting would be costly?—Yes, and the roads, keeping them in repair.

69. CHAIRMAN.—Have you considered the question in this light—supposing you are not right in your reading of the Act of Parliament—that an "equal rate" means one-fourth, but that you are authorised to charge them the full rate, so far as roads and all are concerned, would that alter your view?—No; I don't think it would. With reference to the western end, I may tell you that at the present moment plans are being prepared for a road, to take a lower level than the present, which is on a tremendous hill; and if we were to take that into our township it would throw a tremendous onus on the town in the shape of compensation.

70. Mr. O'BRIEN.—But if you had the control transferred to you, would you not have the power to do the work more economically, or at least more economically, if you had the power to assess arable lands at the full amount instead of one-fourth?—Yes, so far as the money is concerned, but we could not have the same radius to tax. For instance, the bridges would have to be made by us, which are paid by cess-thirds of the county at large.

71. In speaking of this extension, do you assume that it is necessary to extend the lamps and lights in the direction mentioned?—Yes.

72. But if it were understood you were not to be bound to the lamps in every point?—That would, of course, be a different thing, but then there is the making of the roads.

73. Now, except that extension to Mr. Frend's, could not all the roads within the "Ten" boundary be maintained as efficiently by the town body as the Grand Jury?—Yes.

74. It was in '63 that you obtained the transfer of the roads from the county?—Yes.

75. CHAIRMAN.—Has your experience been favourable in getting the work done more economically than under the old system?—It is more costly, but I think the roads are better kept than originally.

76. You do more work?—Yes.

77. You are the sanitary authority?—Yes.

78. What are the rates at present—the municipal rates?—Two ten penny rates in the year, one an improvement, the other a road rate.

79. They are levied separately?—Yes.

80. Have you any source of income but these rates?—We have the dog tax, £10 a year; Government property, £18; Petty Sessions Fines, £25; and out of the market there is a profit of about £30 a year.

81. What do the rates produce?—£1,600.

82. And what does your annual expenditure average?—Well, it averages more than that, because we had to borrow money; we have made wonderful improvements in the town—we flagged and sewered it.

83. Was that in recent years?—Yes.

84. What does your expenditure amount to?—We have just got two new loans; we have not felt the burthen of our interest.

85. Will the rates be enough for all?—We hope not to require to increase the rates.

86. Your rates go up to 1s.?—Yes.

87. What were the works—were they all drainage?—The sewers are nearly completed, and we flagged and put down permanent improvements, and contemplate spending £3,000 more.

88. What was the cost of the drainage scheme altogether?—£3,000 has already been expended.

89. Mr. O'BRIEN.—Is there any additional sanitary work to be executed?

90. Have you a scheme of water supply under consideration?—Yes.

91. And is it much needed in Queenstown?—We consider that it is.

92. Have you had estimates prepared as to the cost of such a scheme?—Yes.

93. And what is the cost estimated to be?—The rough estimate, including compensation (passing through property for a distance of eight miles), is £23,000—that was the estimate, but the Local Government Board in writing to us considered it would cost a great deal more, that that figure was very much under what the actual cost would be.

[illegible] What sum is it [illegible] likely to [illegible]?—Well, I would think it will be more likely to reach £20,000; but you must only take my opinion as an individual expression.

[illegible] That will throw a considerable charge on the township?—Yes.

[illegible] [illegible] the advantages will extend in a greater or less degree to beyond the existing area?—I don't know that they would.

[illegible] [illegible]

[illegible]

101. Would it not very much improve the sanitary condition of the town?—Yes, it would.

102. And would not the effects of any such improvement in the sanitary condition of [illegible] [illegible] by [illegible] the town [illegible] of epidemics, by an improved sewage system and water supply?—Well, yes; the town being built upon the side of a hill, the sewage is as good as any in the world; as good as in the United Kingdom as far as the sanitary condition is concerned. The sewage is [illegible] complete.

[illegible] This improved water supply—would it not enable you to keep the town in a good sanitary condition?—Yes.

[illegible] And would not that good sanitary condition confer advantages upon those who would [illegible] in the town?—Yes.

103. Would it not form a heavy charge upon the existing township?—Yes.

104. Under the Towns Improvement Act, owners of [illegible] land, as you are aware, only [illegible] one-fourth of the valuation—do you think that is a fair representation of the advantages they derive?—Well, their valuation is so very small.

105. Yes, but do you consider that paying one-fourth [illegible] owners of houses in the town pay 1s. and they pay [illegible] is fair?—No, I do not think it is enough. I think one-third would be more fair.

106. Would you consider it not unreasonable in view of the outlay and the advantages which the improvements to the space will extend to those outside—that an extension should be made such as that comprehended in the "Tee" line?—I don't think that would be unreasonable, but the value of what you would get is would be very small.

107. What would you get in?—The valuation of that portion of the district south of the "Tee" line as [illegible] [illegible] would be £1,303 [illegible], and 1,0[illegible] acreage.

108. CHAIRMAN.—That would not have much [illegible]?—Yes.

109. Mr. O'BRIEN.—But if you brought in the [illegible] [illegible], what would be the addition in the valuation?—That would be only £2,000 more than the present.

110. CHAIRMAN.—How many miles of road would that give you?—Twenty or thirty miles of road.

111. And the area brought in by the "Tee" road?—There would be brought in six miles of road; that would cost [illegible] a year to keep in order, and if lamps are put there, £105 more, or a total of £335.

112. But as regards the whole electoral division, taking in the whole district, would you consider that too large for the municipal district?—I consider that it would [illegible].

113. That is assuming you were expected to light it all [illegible] and keep the roads in order.

114. You think it would be [illegible] to have even the roads?—I do. I think it would be decidedly disadvantageous.

115. Would you not keep them as economically as [illegible] the Grand Jury?—Well, the people are not satisfied with the way the roads are kept at present, and they would expect us to do more for them. The [illegible] we would have to [illegible] in the [illegible] [illegible].

116. CHAIRMAN.—Are you not of opinion that it should be [illegible] to one [illegible]?—They are [illegible].

117. I know that; I see they are, but one thing that we see is [illegible] to do in these localities, is to [illegible] as possible. Would it not be possible, taking say a radius of a mile, or a mile more, from the centre of the town to the [illegible] would it not be possible going about a mile on the east, or a mile and a half, and a mile and a half on the west, just a mile or a little more on the north and not dealing with [illegible], but to follow [illegible] boundaries, that would take in [illegible], [illegible], Ballybeely [illegible], and so on?—The six miles of road taken in by the "Tee" road would involve an expenditure to keep them in order of £230.

118. [illegible] they are kept by the county at [illegible]?—They are not kept up at all. One path alone would cost an enormous sum.

119. Mr. O'BRIEN.—Then the county has not done what is required to be done?—No.

120. So that from that view of it you would get works to do which are not now done, and which are required?—Yes.

121. And those [illegible] the public stand in need of?—Yes.

122. In what [illegible] is the place you were particularly [illegible]?—In Ballymena.

123. CHAIRMAN.—Now, passing from that proposed line, could you not obtain such a boundary bringing in, say a quarter of a mile more on the north, extending it round the margin of the harbour a couple of miles to the west and to the east, and taking in those gentlemen's seats which really derive advantages from the town?—Yes, but the roads would be in place [illegible] increased amount of cost on the township. We would have fences, and, especially to the eastward, with the [illegible] improvements there, it would [illegible] with or without them place an increased expense on the township and on the inhabitants of the town.

124. On what [illegible] then do you carry the [illegible] to the westward?—Because there is very valuable building ground there, and it would [illegible] [illegible] as it already, and there is a [illegible] [illegible], and every house would pay for the lighting.

125. Why not take in [illegible]?—Well, the [illegible] of [illegible] would be enormous. We [illegible] [illegible] with [illegible] and [illegible] to the west, so we have [illegible].

126. What is the county cess?—It is 1s. 9d. in the pound. That is 9d. in the county at large charges.

127. Your opinion, I take it, is that you would not possibly take in the roads in any district to be brought in except at a loss?—Yes.

128. As a board is that the opinion entertained by the Commissioners?—Well, we are against extending the bounds; as a board we consider it would be an injustice to take them in—that in fact they would cost more than we receive.

129. Mr. O'BRIEN.—And you prefer remaining as you are?—Yes.

130. And the only change you would be in favour of making would be to go a little further to the west, I think?—Yes, that is my individual opinion.

131. And you think if the entire electoral division were taken it would be [illegible] for you to undertake?—Oh, yes.

132. You don't form so strong an objection to the "Tee" line as to the electoral division?—Well, no, but it would impose an increased burden of £150 a year on us, and if you take all the lighting of £50.

133. Well, assuming you were not expected to extend the lighting to all the rural territory; would you be in favour of the adoption of that "Tee" boundary?—

Ardrossan [illegible] [illegible], 1883.

Mr. James W. [illegible].

Queenstown. Jan. 8, 1879. Mr. James W. Scott.

Well, even taking off the lighting, it would be, as I say, an increase of £50.

134. Well, as that calculation do you assume the work would be better done?—Yes.

135. And would not the advantage be commensurate with the increased expense?—Yes, that is very true, but we would be the people who would have to pay for it, and hence the change would be no great advantage to us.

136. How many Town Commissioners are there in Queenstown on the Board?—Fifteen.

137. And how many persons eligible for the office?—One hundred and fifty.

138. If the "Tea" line were adopted as a boundary, would it add very much to the number of persons who would be eligible?—No.

139. CHAIRMAN.—In fact, it seems to me that you would want to take in what will bring you in money, without laying out a shilling?—That is precisely the feeling. We only want to take in what will pay its way, and we do not want to swamp ourselves with the cost of country roads.

140. Mr. O'BRIEN.—How many Commissioners were present at the meeting of the Commissioners at which the subject was discussed?—Thirteen out of fifteen.

141. Were they unanimous?—Yes.

142. If you increase the boundary at one side, it seems somewhat absurd not to do so at the other?—That is one of the reasons the Commissioners, after weighing all the facts, came to the conclusion that it would be better for them to remain as they were.

143. Is the Fever Hospital outside the present boundary?—Yes.

Mr. EDMUND FARRELL examined.

Mr. E. Farrell.

144. CHAIRMAN.—You are a member of the Town Commissioners?—I am.

145. What is your view with regard to the extension of the town boundary?—Well, I go for the whole island. I am for taking in the whole electoral division of Queenstown, provided we are not to watch and light it. My first reason for holding this is, that the whole island outside the present municipal boundary derives advantages from being near so good a market as Queenstown, so much so, indeed, that in some cases the landlords want to double the rents—my landlord wishes to double mine.

146. Mr. O'BRIEN.—Are you willing to give it?—No, I object. My second reason is, that all the guardians of this division are within the township, and I need not tell you that their interests are, and will be, more in the town than outside. The third reason is, that the cesspayers who are elected every half year are principally from the town, and seldom or never attend, inasmuch as they have no interest outside the town; therefore, the badness of the roads was a question they don't go much on at all into; it does not affect or interest them much. The County Surveyor, I understand, goes about twice a year over the roads, but seldom more. Another reason is, I have taken from some of the returns of the Grand Jury information regarding the quantity of roads, and what we pay at present for them, outside the present limits particularly. I have taken about one-half of these roads, or about eight miles, and, assuming the rest to be similarly circumstanced, the cost at present, outside the town bounds, is £150 a year, and the amount levied on it is about 1s. 6d. in the pound—6d. for the quarry-stone and 1s. for the barony, which would amount to £450, leaving a clear profit of £300 to pay for the improvement of the roads and footpaths and everything else, assuming we only paid the present rates.

147. CHAIRMAN.—That is of the portion at present excluded?—Yes. It has been stated that the cost of keeping the roads and footpaths would be more in the town than in the county. I admit it would be, but I have here a return of the cost of the different years, and I say that from the time that our Town Improvement Act was obtained in '53 the cost of the roads in the returns there was just a little under £4,000. It was, in point of fact, £3,949, and if we take the present year, or the data at which this was got, the same amount would be £4,030, showing clearly that, as there was no increase then, we would have no increase now. I may tell you I would be very sorry, having the interest of the town at heart, to take in the whole electoral division, if we were to light it and watch it.

148. Mr. O'BRIEN.—And you don't consider there is a necessity for lighting and watching?—No.

149. CHAIRMAN.—Well, there would be just this difficulty—the roads outside at present pay the full 1s. in the pound?—Yes.

150. Then, suppose they are brought in, the owners of the agricultural land, who pay on their valuation 1s. towards the rates, would, if brought into the borough, only pay one-fourth?—The road rate, I think, should be the same, and the improvement rate pay the one-fourth.

151. And that being so, what do you say as to the roads within the borough—do you think the owners of agricultural land should get off by paying only one-fourth?—I do not.

152. Would you say the lands outside should pay the same proportion of improvement rate as those inside?—Yes, because the difference—that is, the increase of one to the other—is a matter of nothing.

153. Mr. O'BRIEN.—And as to their not getting light, is not the fact of their only paying one-fourth a fair answer to that objection?—Yes.

154. They can't get all the advantages when they only pay one-fourth?—Yes.

155. Do you think one-fourth represents fairly the indirect advantages they derive from their proximity to the town?—Yes, I think so, if they paid their full share of the road rate.

156. And as regards the others, you don't think there should be any change in the one-fourth, believing it is a fair arrangement?—Yes.

157. You would not have to light it—you told that you should not be asked to do that?—Yes.

158. But without that, and as compensation for any indirect advantages derived, you think one-fourth fair?—Yes.

159. According to the computation you have made, there would be, if the roads were placed under the control of the Commissioners, a profit of £300 a year?—Yes, to benefit the town and island.

160. You have heard the suggestion as to the "Tea" line—do you consider the entire electoral division would be preferable?—I do.

161. You heard what the Chairman said about the practical difficulty about the extension to Cuskinny? He says, in effect, that if that were comprehended, the effect would be to include about £21,000 in making this road, which would otherwise be provided for by the Grand Jury out of county rate?—I think he may make his mind easy as to that, for the outside gentlemen would never grant that amount. I know that very well, for I was looking for £80 for improvement, and could not get it.

162. I understand this £20,000 was compensation that would be asked for?—No, that is a mistake; no gentleman asked for compensation. That was with reference to the supply of water.

163. Mr. O'BRIEN.—What is the length of the road that would cost this money?—Six or eight miles.

Mr. Scott.—There are two schemes—the one passing Cuskinny is to adopt the present road. The estimate for that will not cost more than £4,000; but the £20,000 is to make a concrete wall down to Rush Ferry.

164. Do you think, Mr. Farrell, that the sanitary arrangements would be better by having the extension to the whole of the electoral division?—I do.

165. And more economically?—Yes. I happen to

[illegible] question, and [illegible] experience. I [illegible] that the [illegible] Board [illegible] the principal portion of the [illegible] and [illegible] whole [illegible] [illegible]

169. Then I suppose, at present, the [illegible] of the [illegible] is in the hands of the [illegible] Board?—Yes.

170. Mr. O'Brien.—Do you think the Town Commissioners would [illegible] the [illegible] of the [illegible] [illegible] Grand Jury?—[illegible] economically, [illegible]

[illegible]. Now, do you consider that the inhabitants of the [illegible] would object to the change?—Not if the [illegible] were properly [illegible] out to them, and if they saw that their interests were not being [illegible]

[illegible]. Would it not interfere with their interests to the extent of one-fourth or 2d. in the pound?—Quite possibly.

[illegible]. Mr. O'Brien.—That would not [illegible] objection to [illegible]?—Yes, I am one of them myself.

[illegible]. Chairman.—You think, as between the [illegible] and the inhabitants of the town, it would be [illegible]?—Yes.

[illegible]. Mr. O'Brien.—Do [illegible] of land outside the municipal boundary [illegible] [illegible] in [illegible] the [illegible] of having a good market [illegible]—Yes, there is not a [illegible] [illegible]

[illegible]. And butter and eggs, I suppose?—Yes, and [illegible]

[illegible]. Chairman.—And I suppose they come to [illegible] the [illegible] they [illegible]?—Yes.

[illegible]. And their children come in to attend the schools here?—Yes, they do, but there are also schools in the country.

[illegible]. But the chief [illegible] in the town?—Yes.

[illegible]. And they come in to the chapel?—Yes, the children [illegible] a long distance to attend the schools.

[illegible]. Is there a Roman Catholic church on the island, except at [illegible]?—Yes, there is one at [illegible]. It would be my opinion [illegible] for the Town Commissioners to have the roads under them, they are [illegible] kept.

[illegible]. Mr. O'Brien.—Do you think the [illegible] of the [illegible] would be [illegible]?—It would not be the slightest harm. There are [illegible] should be [illegible]

[illegible]. Do you, in point of fact, think the majority of the rural [illegible] on the Board would have a [illegible] [illegible] of [illegible]?—Yes.

[illegible]. Chairman.—Have you any idea how many would be included by the [illegible] you propose?—There would be about 3,000.

[illegible]. And the number of [illegible] could you say?—I don't know; probably one-fourth.

[illegible]. Would you say there would be a [redacted] [illegible]?—Yes.

[illegible]. As I understand your proposal, you would [illegible] to the present bounds of the town as to lighting, and cleansing, and watering [illegible]?—Yes.

[illegible]. And then that the outlying district should get the roads kept up as they ought to be kept by the Commissioners, but no more—no lighting or watering?—No.

[illegible]. Mr. O'Brien.—And no graduated scale of rating [illegible]?—No.

[illegible]. Chairman.—And you would, for sanitary purposes, give them the [illegible] they get from the [illegible] Board?—Yes.

[illegible]. And you think, so far as the town is concerned, that having the one body to act in sanitary matters would make a [illegible] and [illegible] authority for the town and country?—Yes, I do.

[illegible]. Have you any further suggestion to make?—Nothing further.

Mr. [illegible] G. Doran examined.

159. You are a Commissioner, Mr. Doran?—I am. The principal thing I want to refer to is to the Chairman's statement as to the water supply. He says it would cost about £25,000. Now, that statement is only his own individual opinion. We have had the estimates for the work made by two competent engineers, with the authorisation of the Local Government Board, and those gentlemen have reported, allowing a fair sum for everything, that the cost would be £31,[illegible] for introducing a water supply.

[illegible]. Chairman (to Mr. Farrell).—Suppose this new water scheme were introduced, would you think it right to make the inhabitants of the [illegible] outside the present boundary liable to pay any, and what proportion, of what it costs to supply the town with water. At present you say they should pay one-fourth [illegible] [illegible], which, at the [illegible], [illegible] more than [illegible]—there must be [illegible] for the water, and I would like to know your view as to what proportion you would ask them to pay when you don't propose to give them water outside?

Mr. Farrell.—I would propose to give them water everywhere by sinking wells, and I would let them pay a small proportion for the benefit of the town, for the [illegible] down of [illegible] would indirectly be of advantage to those who use the town.

[illegible]. Then you would ask the inhabitants of the [illegible], as well as themselves, to pay for the sinking of the wells?—Yes.

[illegible]. And you would make them pay a proportion of the water rate of the town?—Yes.

[illegible]. And you hold that to keep the town well cleansed, and so on, would be for their benefit?—Yes.

Witness.—I made an estimate—happening to be personally engaged in that way—at the time, and I added 20 per cent. to their estimate—to the estimate of the engineers—and that would bring it to £27,000. That would cover all.

[illegible]. Chairman.—£27,000 would cover everything?—Yes. I thought the question was of importance. I was asked by people what would be the advantage people would derive from the water supply. Well, the advantages would be a constant supply of water for [illegible] the streets, and it would do away with the present expensive [illegible], and there would be an unlimited supply for [illegible] then, as well as drinking fountains. But the question which your inquiry will have the most important effect on, is as to the boundaries. Now, my feeling on the matter is that we ought not to include the rural [illegible] for the [illegible]—that if they are not prepared to receive [illegible] the same advantages from the rating, and be rated in a similar proportion, we ought to have nothing to say to them—for if we take up their roads and maintain them, we will have imposed upon us a great deal of trouble, and no return for it except, if there was a deficiency in their rates we could supplement it.

[illegible]. What you say is you would not be for taking up the roads, because you get no advantage. Mr. Farrell says yes, and proposes to take in the whole [illegible] division, and says—"Let the Town Commissioners take up the management of the roads, the people outside paying the same, and what I will give the town for their trouble is to impose on all people in the island the obligation of paying one-fourth of the existing rate."

[illegible]. Mr. O'Brien.—You are aware that the Grand Jury authorities, so far from making the transfer of

Queenstown. Jan. [illegible]. [illegible]
Mr. Charles O'[illegible]

their jurisdiction to the town bodies, have in almost every instance opposed it?—Yes, I am aware of it. I consider these people whom it is proposed to bring in ought to be left as they are, if they are satisfied with their condition. I don't think they would apply to be annexed if they considered, especially, that they had to pay for that annexation without deriving any advantage.

197. CHAIRMAN.—You must remember that as one is applying one way so the other. We sit in pursuance of the recommendation of the Parliamentary Committee—it is neither the Town Commissioners nor any other body that applied for the inquiry. We are to see whatever lands and gentlemen's residences in the immediate vicinity of the town—within a mile or a mile and a half—do not derive exceptional advantages from their proximity, from having a good market town close to them to buy and sell, from having churches and schools, and so on?—Yes, but there is reciprocity, for people in the town like to go out into the country to breathe the new-mown hay, to be sentimental.

198. Do you think the people outside should not contribute?—If the boundary was to be increased I would be for no exceptional legislation, but would have equal rates.

199. Mr. O'BRIEN.—An exception exists at present. Under the Towns Improvement Act there is a special clause that arable lands are only liable to one-fourth?—We are obliged to look after them for that fourth.

200. CHAIRMAN.—We must go with the times. Everywhere you go you hear people saying the land next the town gets exceptional advantages, the landlord better rents, the tenant has advantages that are presented by a market where ready sale is had for produce, and where the cleansing and lighting are of benefit to those who resort there?—That is on the same principle that where the tenant improves the land the landlord increases the rent. As soon as the district is improved the persons who contribute to that improvement are to be further taxed, but without getting any further advantage. Now, as to the bridges that have been mentioned. There are two, one would be a mere nominal expense—the only improvement with regard to it, with regard to carrying it out would be this. The military authorities refuse permission to pass through their grounds, and a difference of [illegible] feet would be what is wanted. There is another thing. If the Cushkinny-road were carried out there would be a great deal of building on it; that is the only direction in which extension of building will take place.

Mr. R. O'Driscoll.

Mr. ROBERT O'DRISCOLL examined.

201. You are a member of the Town Commission?—Yes.

202. Have you been so for long?—Yes.

203. What is your view on the subject of the extension of the boundary?—Well, as some of the gentlemen around me have stated the Commissioners had several times gone into statistics on the subject, and they find that it would be a great loss to the town, the maintaining of the roads for the sake of the little benefit it would confer, and would be a great burthen on the ratepayers, and the Commissioners unanimously came to the conclusion not to extend the boundary. In fact when we were looking over the present boundary they found that it would be a loss, and so they left it as it is for the present boundary for town purposes.

204. CHAIRMAN.—Then you are against any extension?—Yes.

205. Well have you, when you state that, considered the cost of roads outside your present boundary is about £150 a year. Mr. Farrell says take the taxation—take the valuation of the land at its usual rate which is the proportion for road rate, and it amounts to £450 a year, the roads cost at present about £150 a year, so that that leaves a margin of £300 a year which you would have to lavish towards those roads. In fact take what is paid at present, £450; they cost the Grand Jury £150, so that the Grand Jury is making for the rest of the barony £300 a year?—Yes, I heard Mr. Farrell giving his evidence. He is a very old Commissioner and should know. If these roads, however, were under the control of the Town Commissioners they would have every week more or less people applying for portions of roads to do that which they don't ask about now.

206. Mr. O'BRIEN.—But you would not be obliged to do it?—No.

207. CHAIRMAN.—Am I right in thinking that you believed if you took in these roads, you would only be able to tax these people for one-fourth instead of the whole?—Yes.

208. Supposing the law were modified—were so regulated that in future all expenditure on the roads, when transferred from the Grand Jury to the town body, were chargeable equally on all descriptions of property—would that modify your view?—Yes, it would.

209. I understand, Mr. Farrell, you have obtained your figures from the surveyor?—Yes, I got them from the surveyor's office.

210. Mr. *O'Driscoll*, T.C.—I see no objection to the present boundary, and if it were put to the vote I would vote to have it continue as it is.

Mr. Joseph Fitzgerald.

Mr. JOSEPH FITZGERALD examined.

211. You are one of the Commissioners?—Yes.

212. Have you been long a Commissioner?—Twenty-seven years.

213. What is your view with regard to alteration of the boundaries?—Well, on the general subject of Mr. Farrell's figures I would go in pretty with his statements on the subject, that is, if the taxes levied on country districts will pay the expenses connected therewith.

214. Do you think then that the persons outside from their proximity to the town and the advantages they derive ought to pay something?—Yes.

215. To what extent?—To a considerable extent.

216. Would you say to the extent of one-fourth or one-half?—One-half I should say, but I would not tax these people without their consent. The country people would not like it.

217. All the people inside the boundary pay it?—Yes, and some of them very reluctantly.

218. Equitably you would say these people outside very largely use the town?—Yes.

219. And you think they should pay something?—Yes.

220. Mr. *O'Driscoll*.—As to bringing the road to Cushkinny, the necessity for doing so existed from time immemorial. It was a clear bar to the interests of the island. If that road were carried out the value of property would be enlarged 500 per cent.

Mr. Jeremiah Healy examined.

QUEENSTOWN. Jan. 8, 1879. Mr. J. Healy.

281. Are you a ratepayer?—I am a ratepayer within and without the present boundary. As to Mr. [illegible]'s evidence, though I agree with some of what he has said, I don't see why the rural people should be [illegible] to pay for the advantages they derive by the improvements of Queenstown. It is stated by Mr. [illegible] that they sell a great deal of produce in the town, but Mr. [illegible] knows that there is very little produce sold here. It is sent to Cork and Midleton and other market towns. The farmers have very small holdings of land, and they grow a limited quantity of potatoes; as much as would do the [illegible] [illegible]. They don't bring them to market here, and I don't think the roads are much used in bringing in produce.

282. Mr. O'Brien.—Where do they dispose of their milk, butter, poultry, and eggs?—The supply of milk is brought in on donkey's carts.

283. Do you mean to say the consumption of milk is small, considering the population, the military, and [illegible]?—Yes; there is a lot of it brought in on the heads of women.

284. What price do they get for milk?—[illegible] a gallon, or 1s.

285. What do the householders pay?—[illegible] a quart, [illegible] a gallon; it is as high as 4d. and as low as 3d.

286. And that is a great deal more than they would get in the country, by selling it from house to house, or if they had to turn it into butter?—Oh, yes, double. Well, milk is the only advantage.

287. And butter—have they not a great advantage in having a close market for the sale of that?—No; none at all.

289. Nor eggs?—No; the farmers, as I say, have very small holdings.

290. Mr. [illegible].—There is £4,000 worth of milk sold in the town in the year.

291. Mr. [illegible].—That is brought in on donkey carts, or on the heads of the women.

292. Chairman.—It is not that they must be dependent on the town, but that there is a market brought to the door of the inhabitants of the outlying district; and if they derive advantage from their proximity to that market, should they not contribute something towards the expenses of the town?—There is nothing else, I may say, that they sell; even they send to Cork and Midleton.

293. [illegible] everywhere I have been—in Mallow, [illegible], Kilkenny, [illegible], Clonmel, and [illegible], all the [illegible] examined, or nearly all, and the people who gave evidence, say that within an area of about two miles from the town, the landlords and tenants derive exceptional advantages from their proximity to the town—do you agree with that?—Well in some way I must agree with it; but Cork is too contiguous to Queenstown; if it were four or five miles away it would be far better for us.

298. Mr. [illegible].—As to the roads, I may also say that you would have to employ a new staff, and there would be an increased expenditure. If the roads were once enlarged to enable you to walk cleanly on them, it would cost what is called a surplus by Mr. [illegible]. The road to the graveyard [illegible] is in a bad state; and if it costs £100 a year to keep it up [illegible], it would absorb more than the surplus to keep them properly.

The inquiry then terminated.

ENNISCORTHY.—FEBRUARY 7th, 1879.

ENNISCORTHY. Feb. 7, 1879.

Before Messrs. O'Brien, [illegible], and Cotton.

Mr. Thomas Wilkinson examined.

Mr. Thomas Wilkinson.

1. You are Clerk to the Town Commissioners?—Yes.

2. How long have you been Town Clerk?—Since the Cleansing and Lighting Act was adopted, in 1851.

3. That is the Act of George IV?—Yes.

4. At what time was the Towns Improvement Act adopted by you?—In 1858.

5. So that you were Town Clerk under both Acts?—Yes.

6. Was the Towns Improvement Act adopted in [illegible] in its entirety or in part?—In its entirety.

7. So that you have the full rating powers which the Act of '54 contains?—Yes.

8. What is the area of the present municipal district?—[illegible] [illegible] [illegible].

9. Is that the entire area of the existing township?—Yes.

10. What is the valuation of it?—£6,148 10s.

11. Now, how many townlands or parts of townlands are there in the township?—Parts of three in the present township.

12. And not the entire of any one?—No.

13. Mention their names?—Enniscorthy, Templeshannon, and Killagoley.

14. In what electoral division are they?—All in Enniscorthy electoral division.

15. Taking the central point in the town, how far does the municipal district extend to the north, south, east, and west.

16. Well, taking the market-house as the centre, I could only give an idea.

17. Give us then an approximation as you can—the distance in each direction?—Not more than half a mile—an English mile—in any direction.

18. Does it go half an English mile in each direction?—I think it would go to the south and west, and perhaps to the north, about half a mile, and perhaps in the west then goes up to the south-east, a mile fully; that is what I think.

19. Well, now, the electoral division of Enniscorthy is very much larger than the town?—Oh, yes.

20. Can you say what the area and valuation are?—No, I am not aware; the Clerk of the Union will be able to tell you.

21. Are you able to say how far the electoral division extends—or does it extend equally in every direction?—I think it does; I think it is a fair circle.

22. Are you aware, taking the centre of the town, what is about the radius of the electoral division of Enniscorthy?—From two to three miles.

23. Would you say it was three statute miles?—In parts; indeed, I think it very nearly is all round.

24. The electoral division is not divided into wards, I believe?—No.

25. The rates, I find, according to the return furnished to us, are as follows, for the past five years:—For 1878, 6d.; for 1877, 7d.; for 1876, 7d.; for 1875, 7d.; for 1874, 8d. These are the rates made for municipal purposes?—Yes.

26. Then, these are about the average rates you have been in the habit of making?—Yes; since 1858 the average has been 7d.

27. You have not been, I believe, the Sanitary Authority since 1874?—No; it was taken from us.

28. You have not, as a matter of fact, been the Sanitary Authority for the town?—No; it was taken from us; we are not the Sanitary Authority.

29. Did these rates I have mentioned, 6d., 7d., and so on, constitute the entire income you had, or were there any other sources of income but those rates?—Well, in some years [illegible].

30. For last year, for instance, what income did you

Enniscorthy. [illegible]

Mr. Thomas [illegible]

[illegible] beyond the rates?—There would be, say, £13 7s. 6d., or from that to £20, for the dog-tax. It varies.

33. What other sources of revenue have you?—Earl Portsmouth makes a grant of £15 for lighting in districts too poor for taxation. He makes that grant for lamps.

34. To enable you to light poor portions of the town?—Yes.

35. Is there any other source of income?—Yes; there are some fines, but they are very precarious. They are fines from the petty sessions.

36. What would be about the average?—The average would be about £10, in or about that.

37. Have you any other source of income?—No; we have no property of any kind.

38. What is your annual expenditure—your total expenditure for last year?—It would be about £170.

39. And with the exceptions you have named, all that sum is supplied by the rates?—Yes.

40. What are the purposes to which that expenditure has been most applied?—Lighting the town.

41. Tell me first, do the Commissioners light the town, or is there a gas company who supply the gas?—There is a gas company, a company formed by private persons in the town, and the Commissioners contract with them, and it comes to about £124 a year, or £130.

42. To what other purpose is the money applied?—To cleansing the town; at least it used to be, but we are not doing that now; it cost from £20 to £30.

43. What other expenses had you?—Well, there is salary, printing, stationery, paying the Local Government Auditor and the Officer, that would all come to £60, or to between £60 and £70.

44. You have had no outlay at any time in respect of providing water for the town?—Well, the Earl of Portsmouth has constructed water works in the town, and when he completed them, at great expense, he presented them to the town. He gave the Town Commissioners power of attorney to carry out the work for the benefit of the town. There are public fountains through the town, and the inhabitants are enabled to take the water into their premises at a certain stipulated rate.

45. The Commissioners never were under the necessity of going to the full limit of your rating power for the water supply?—No; the water rents will be quite able, after very little time, we hope, to pay the expenses of the supply.

46. Then, you never found it necessary to go to your full rating limit?—No.

47. Were any works deemed to be necessary for the benefit of the town, but which have been left unprovided for, in apprehension that the rate would be too high for the people?—No; I think not.

48. Now, the Commissioners, I think—is it not a matter of fact—have, since the passing of the Public Health Act of last session, applied to the Local Government Board for a provisional order, to transfer their jurisdiction as Sanitary Authority from the Board of Guardians to the Town Commissioners? Is that not so?—Yes.

49. And a provisional order has been made?—Yes.

50. But it has not been confirmed by Act of Parliament?—No; but it is in progress.

51. And when that becomes law, will there be, do you anticipate, a considerable outlay in connexion with the carrying out of those functions?—There will be some.

52. In addition to the present?—Yes.

53. Can you form any idea as to what will be the addition for sanitary purposes?—Well, except there are some new rules laid by the Local Government Board on us, I don't apprehend there will be very much.

54. Is there any want of improved sewerage?—No; the town is very well supplied with main drains.

55. Then there is no necessity for either sewerage or watering?—No.

56. And do you anticipate there will be a very serious addition, when the transfer is effected?—No.

57. Are the Town Commissioners aware that when they are made the Urban Sanitary Authority, that under another section of the Public Health Act, the 206th section, there is also power given to the Local Government Board to transfer to the Commissioners, if they think fit, the jurisdiction of the Grand Jury, in relation to roads, bridges, footpaths, and other public works?—I did not know that it was under the Public Health Act, but the Commissioners are aware of the provision you speak of.

58. Well, is it their intention, in seeking to become the Urban Sanitary Authority, to seek for a transfer of the Grand Jury power over those public works?—I think it would depend on circumstances. They have not, up to the present, sought such transfer. It has been done in Wexford, and we want to see how it works there.

59. They have not taken it formally into consideration yet?—No.

60. Is it the opinion, so far as you are aware, of the Town Commissioners, that the amount raised in the shape of Grand Jury cess, that the expenditure of the Grand Jury within the municipal district, is not commensurate with the amount levied?—Yes, for it takes about £100 to keep the streets in repair, and there is £400 raised.

61. And if they got the control of these works, are you able to say would the work be more efficiently and more economically carried out by them?—Well, I would not like to say that, but if I might venture on a general opinion, I would say it could be done.

62. You say the present radius of the town is about half a mile?—Yes.

63. Now outside that is there a district lying pretty thickly inhabited?—Well, not so thickly inhabited as in the case of the suburbs of larger towns.

64. Within the radius of say a mile or so, outside the half mile area, would you say there are a good many inhabited houses?—There are a good many.

65. What class of people inhabit them as a rule?—I would say, generally speaking, gentlemen.

67. Are there a good many farmers?—No, not so many.

68. Would you say the inhabitants of a district such as this, lying outside the existing boundary, derive special advantages by reason of their proximity to the town of Enniscorthy?—Yes, those living close to it do.

69. Do you know do persons living outside find a market here for their produce?—Certainly.

70. They resort constantly for various purposes to the town?—Yes.

71. And, I presume, when they so resort, the town being properly lighted and cleansed and supplied with water, is of advantage to them?—

72. Do children come to school to Enniscorthy from the outlying district?—Yes.

73. And are the lands outside the town better let, do they derive higher rents from the fact that they are near the town?—Yes.

74. Higher rents are paid than for lands a greater distance away?—Yes.

75. How far would you be inclined to say do the exceptional advantages of the town extend outside the present boundary?—I should say for a mile from the town. I should mention that under the old Lighting and Cleansing Act the radius was a mile from the market house.

76. And that was reduced under the Towns Improvement Act?—Yes.

77. What was the ground of that?—They did not think that a circular boundary was a proper boundary at all.

78. If you adopted, say a boundary of a mile radius, would that all still be in the electoral division of Enniscorthy?—Yes.

79. And it would cut townlands—it would not be conterminous with townlands?—No, it would not

80. Would portions of a good many townlands be introduced if the boundary were extended a mile?—If the boundary were extended a mile, it would embrace, perhaps, seven townlands partly.

81. And would it include the centre of some?—Yes, I think it would take in some.

82. How many Town Commissioners have you?—Fifteen.

83. Were the answers to the queries sent you by the Municipal Boundaries Commissioners agreed to?—Yes.

84. How many members were present when the question was discussed?—I cannot say exactly at the present moment.

85. Can you say generally?—About eleven.

85. What was the date of the meeting?—The 3rd of December.

86. In answer to query 6, asking are the present municipal boundaries regarded with dissatisfaction by the ratepayers, the answer given is "By some"?—Yes.

87. And to query 7, asking what are the objections to the boundaries, the reply is, "They are too limited as an area of taxation." The next query is, "What is the opinion of the municipal body on the subject," and the reply is the same as that to query 7, namely, "They are too limited as an area of taxation"?

88. Were they unanimously of opinion that the area was too limited?—Yes.

89. And so far as you could collect, what area appeared to recommend itself?—A meeting was held subsequently to that, and they agreed to the boundary marked out on that map.

90. Well, what area does it represent?—It represents five townlands and parts of two townlands.

91. You say there was a subsequent meeting of the Commissioners held?—Yes.

92. When was that?—On Monday.

93. Was that a meeting summoned specially to consider this subject?—Yes.

94. How many members were present?—About ten.

95. Did they agree among themselves as a particular extension?—Yes.

96. What was it?—They recommended taking in Ballintemple, Templebreaghan (whole of), Killingaley (the whole of), Rathcourtky (part Cherry Orchard), part of Carrigtohill, and part of Clashavin, about 100 acres, and part of St. John's, about 150 acres.

97. What would be about the acreage comprised in the whole?—About 2,041 acres.

98. How many entire townlands?—Four entire townlands and four parts of townlands.

99. And what would be the valuation?—The valuation would be about £2,084 10s., that is the old valuation as supplied.

100. Now, does that area as proposed there, does it radiate pretty equally from the centre of the town?—Yes.

101. Now, how far does it extend, what is the radius of it, taking the centre of the town as the starting point?—I think it would take in very nearly an English mile, or more in some places.

102. You would say at the minimum an English mile, and in some places more?—Yes.

103. You have mentioned certain townlands, some entirely included, and others only in part taken in; now, what was the objection to taking in the entire of the townlands part only of which have been taken?—Well, Cherry Orchard is a little slip of land lying between a mill stream and the original stream, and I may say Carrigtohill is the same, and it was just to get the stream as a boundary.

104. There were two others you mentioned?—Yes, part of Clashavin and part of St. John's.

105. And what was the objection to include the whole of these?—Well, St. John's is a long way out; its farthest point extends away nearly three miles from the town.

106. And the other one?—That would take the boundary away more than two miles, and I think there would be a good boundary of Clashavin by the road.

107. They consider that to take the entire in would be going out too far?—Yes.

108. Then the proposed area would as nearly as possible be a radius of a statute mile?—Yes.

109. As near as you can estimate it?—Yes.

110. Now, so far as you know, would those proposed to be included entertain a strong objection to it?—I think if it was merely to get them to contribute to the lighting and cleansing of the town they would; but I would not say that if the Commissioners were to take over hereafter the duties of the Grand Jury over streets, roads, &c.

111. The Town Commissioners are aware that under the Towns Improvement Act, arable lands and such like are only assessed at one fourth?—Yes.

112. Do you consider that there would be any strong objection by the people outside to an extension?—Well, as I say, if there was to be nothing done for them but receiving the benefits and advantages they now receive, I believe they would object.

113. But you think that if a further extension of their functions took place—if the powers of the Grand Jury were transferred to them, they would not object?—I do.

114. I take it that you assume they would be only rated at one fourth, instead of the whole amount?—Whether or not, I believe the rates to be raised for general purposes like that, would be less in the aggregate.

115. Have you any special suggestions to make?—No.

116. Mr Cotton.—Do you, in the extension suggested, go beyond Mr. Hill's house?—Yes; there is a straight line on the asylum road, and we took that line to cut off Mr. Hill.

117. It includes him?—Yes.

118. How far does it go in Clashavin?—To what is called the "New road" of Clashavin.

119. Is that beyond Mr. Edwards's?—Yes.

120. Now, as regards the water supply, it appears the water supply was established for the town by Lord Portsmouth, at his own expense?—Yes.

121. You spoke of the supply being self-supporting; in what way are there any expenses connected with it?—Well, there are incidental expenses of one sort or another. I may mention that we derive a revenue from the houses that take the water in for domestic purposes. The rate in that way amounts to £70 a year.

122. The public supply, of course, is all free?—Yes.

123. You mentioned the grant by Lord Portsmouth of £25 a year for lighting, was that to be devoted to lighting any particular or specified portion of the town?—No.

124. Is it a perpetual grant?—We have it since 1855.

125. You get it year by year since then?—Yes; but it is a mere gratuity. He gets nothing from the Commissioners in return.

Mr. PATRICK WILLIAM CAMP examined.

ENNISCORTHY.
Feb. 1, 1877.
Mr. Patrick W. Camp.

126. You are one of the Town Commissioners?—I am.

127. How long have you been a Town Commissioner?—For twelve or fourteen years.

128. You have been chairman?—Yes.

129. Were you a member of the Commissioners body under the Act 9th, George IV.—what is called the Lighting and Cleansing Act?—I think not.—No.

130. Then your experience is altogether under the Towns' Improvement Act?—Yes.

131. Were you at the meeting where they agreed to recommend the increase of area described?—Yes, I think it was my proposition.

132. The increased area which your body suggested would be, we have heard, about an English mile?—Yes, that was the intention.

133. Did you think an extension of a mile would fairly represent the advantages derived by persons living outside?—Yes; we thought it a uniform extension.

134. And fairly represented the extent to which the benefits of the town might be said to have extended?—Yes.

135. And I presume your own opinion is, that within that district the residents derive advantages?—Certainly.

136. In what respect would you say?—They benefit by all the improvements of the town, being so nearly connected with it.

139. They have, I presume, a good market for their produce?—Yes.

140. And you think they should contribute towards the expenses of the town?—We think they ought at least to contribute some proportion towards the expenses.

141. You look forward to becoming the Sanitary Authority?—Yes.

142. And you think the sanitary work will be better done by you?—Yes, we really do, because the Guardians are an outside body altogether.

143. Do you think anything done to improve the sanitary state of the town is an improvement and an advantage to the outlying district, and a benefit to those who come into the town?—Certainly.

144. Are the Commissioners aware that once you become Urban Sanitary Authority under the Public Health Act of last session, there is power to transfer to the Commissioners certain control at present exercised by the Grand Jury?—Yes, we anticipate getting that.

146. That object being in contemplation, does it increase your desire to extend the area of the municipal boundary?—Yes, we consider the people we introduce will be contributory to the benefit as well.

147. You are aware, of course, that at present the Grand Jury rate is assessed equally on all descriptions of property?—Yes.

148. Do the Commissioners anticipate if the Grand Jury works were transferred—if the jurisdiction over these works was transferred to the Town Commissioners—do they contemplate that those works should be charged on arable lands at the full amount or onefourth?—We calculate that the town rate and the county cess rate given to us combined would be less than the two together as they are now.

151. Do you contemplate assessing the arable lands in the county parts at onefourth?—We have not considered that.

152. But irrespective of how that point would be settled, you would be willing, you think, to have the boundary extended?—Yes.

153. And the control of those works transferred to you?—Yes.

154. Is it considered that the amount raised in Grand Jury cess greatly exceeds the amount expended?—Oh, yes.

155. Do you think you could administer your own affairs, in the event of a transfer, more efficiently and more economically?—Yes.

156. Do you consider a mile would be about as far as it would be reasonable or fair to carry the municipal boundary?—Our wish was to make it within a mile, and at the same time we inclined towards [illegible] a natural boundary wherever practicable. I may say it was suggested that Upper Blackstoops should be omitted.

157. Are the Commissioners aware that in the recommendations of the Parliamentary Committee one of the recommendations was that, as far as practicable, municipal boundaries and Poor Law electoral divisions should be conterminous?—I believe so.

158. Now, do you think that it would be practicable to adopt the electoral division as the municipal boundary?—No.

159. In the first place, does the electoral division radiate pretty equally, or is it unequal—does it represent an unequal radius from the centre of the town?—It would be entirely too large; we could not attempt to adopt it as the municipal boundary.

160. How far does the electoral division extend?—Some parts of the electoral division of Enniscorthy extend three miles.

161. Are there parts of it even more than that?—I think there would be.

162. And you think it would be unreasonable as a boundary?—Yes.

163. And the people outside would object?—I think it very probable they would.

164. As regards the radius you propose, do you think the people who would be brought in if your suggestion were adopted would object?—Well, I don't think they would, if we got control of the county works in [illegible] of the effect of that extension.

165. When you say that, do you mean that they contemplate they would only pay onefourth of the amount expended?—Well, I cannot say.

166. Do you think the Commissioners are unanimous as to the proposed extension?—Yes; I believe they all have the same feeling on it.

167. And as to taking over the Grand Jury power of roads, &c.—Yes.

168. I presume when they entertain that opinion, they are aware, from personal experience, of the working of a similar system in Wexford?—Well, I don't know if they take that into consideration; they have their own experience here, and that is what has actuated them.

169. Mr. *George Roberts*.—In the suggested boundary, I would ask why Greenville was excluded, and Clonhaston, which extends further, taken in?

170. Mr. *Camp*.—The same question Mr. Roberts asks now I put at the meeting.

171. Mr. *Wilkinson*.—I may explain. There is no person living at Greenville. The road leading to it terminates there; it does not go through it, and it would not derive the same advantages the other places do.

172. Mr. *Roberts*.—Well, there is Mr. Leary, who lives at Greenville, and he derives just the same advantages as Mr. Edwards, who resides at Clonhaston. On general principles I just put it that if we bring in Clonhaston we should bring in Greenville.

173. Mr. *Camp*.—Certainly, if there was a public road through it.

174. Mr. *O'Brien*.—The gentleman who resides at Greenville has access to the town by road?—Certainly.

175. And so far as proximity is concerned, he may be said to be in as good a position as the person living at Clonhaston?—Oh, yes.

176. Mr. *Cotton*.—Can you send us a copy of the map, showing us exactly what is proposed as the extended boundary?—Yes.

177. Mr. *O'Brien*.—There are schools in Enniscorthy?—Yes.

178. And these schools, I presume, are attended by children from the rural districts?—Yes.

179. From how far do the inhabitants derive

Enniscorthy, Feb 1, 18[illegible].

Mr. Patrick W. Carey.

towards in sending their children to the schools at Enniscorthy?—They send their children from four or five miles outside.

180. But you think the radius of a mile fairly enough represents the benefits derived from proximity to the town?—Yes; I think it is fair.

181. Have you any suggestion to make?—No; except this—at any cost that may accrue to us, if we get the charge of the sanitary work, there is one thing in reference to the sanitary work, in reference to the making of a sewer at the Pound Field. It is a costly undertaking, and either by the Board of Guardians or the Town Commissioners, it will have to be done.

182. That will entail a considerable expenditure?—Yes [illegible] couple of hundred pounds, I am sure.

183. And it is a necessary work?—Certainly, most necessary.

184. And will the benefits derived from the carrying out of that work extend beyond the limits of the town?—Certainly, for it is at the back of the Presentation Convent schools, where a number of children from the rural districts come in to school. It is at the back of the priest's house.

185. And you think it would be only equitable that the area of taxing that should be extended beyond the present boundary?—Yes.

186. Are the townlands—the three townlands mentioned—rated for sanitary purposes?—Yes; Enniscorthy, Templeshannon, and Killagoely, are rated for sanitary and poor law purposes.

Mr. Daniel Kelleher.

Mr. Daniel Kelleher examined.

187. You are the Clerk of the Union?—Yes.

188. What is the acreage of the electoral division of Enniscorthy?—10,302a. 1r. 3p.

189. And what is the valuation?—£16,159.

190. How many townlands are included in the electoral division?—Thirty-nine.

191. Does the electoral division extend pretty equally in a circle from the centre of the town, or does it extend unequally in different directions?—It is not equal in every direction.

192. Take the different points of the compass, and tell me how far does it extend to the north, south, east, and west?—It does not go very far north.

193. How far would you say?—Not much farther than an English mile.

194. How far to the south?—About two miles perhaps. I should say about two miles.

195. And how far to the east and west?—To the east about a mile; not more than a mile, I should say.

196. And to the west?—To the west it goes out farther in some parts. I should say about three miles.

197. So that, in point of fact the electoral division extends very unequally?—Yes.

198. Do you consider that the electoral division could be adopted as the municipal boundary?—No; it could not be entertained for a moment.

199. The Board of Guardians have been the Sanitary Authority from 1874 to the present?—Yes.

200. And steps have been taken to alter that?—Yes.

201. And with the concurrence of the Guardians, I understand?—Yes; they raised no opposition.

202. During the time the Guardians were Sanitary Authority have any special rates been struck?—Yes.

203. What for?—For what is called the Enniscorthy area cleansing, and sewers.

204. What was the amount?—It was rather trifling.

205. Have the Guardians had under consideration at any time the necessity for constructing the sewer, to which allusion has already been made by Mr. Carey?—Yes, they have.

206. And was the outlay which that would involve considered too large?—Well, it was, that was the principal reason the Guardians fixed for the area of that the electoral division of Enniscorthy. The Local Government Board were not satisfied with that—taking so large an area—and confined it to the area originally fixed by them for the sewerage work.

207. The Guardians did not then go on with it?—No.

208. Was it considered that the advantages of that scheme, if carried out, would extend beyond the limits of the town?—Yes. It was meant to benefit the Roman Catholic clergymen, and being near the convent it was thought that an area larger than the town derived advantage from it. No objection was raised to that.

209. It would not, however, be the opinion that the electoral division would be a proper one to adopt for a municipal boundary?—No.

210. What was the area on which the sanitary rate for the sewers was assessed?—Three townlands—Enniscorthy, Killagoely, and Killishanler.

211. Have you anything to add to what you have already said?—No.

Mr. Matthew Furlong.

Mr. Matthew Furlong examined.

212. You are a member of the Town Council?—Yes.

213. And have been for some time?—Yes, since the passing of the Act.

214. You have heard the evidence given by Mr. Wilkinson, and by Mr. Carey—do you agree in their views on the subject of the extension of the boundary?—Yes, perfectly.

215. And is there anything you would like to add?—Well, no, there is nothing that I can say to supplement their evidence.

216. Were you at the meeting of the Council where this question was considered?—I was.

217. When they agreed to recommend this increase of area?—Yes.

218. And do you think that that proposed increase fairly represents the advantages derived by those who reside outside of the present boundary?—Yes.

219. That is a mile radius?—Yes.

220. About an English mile?—Yes.

221. Are you of opinion it would be of advantage to the town if the control of the works now executed by the Grand Jury were transferred to the Commissioners?—I could not say.

222. You have not considered the question?—No.

223. Do you consider that you would be able to do these works, if the control were transferred to you, more efficiently and economically than the Grand Jury?—Yes, I do.

224. Do you think the town at present gets a full equivalent for the amount levied by county cess?—No.

225. And you think if you had it in your own hands you would manage it better?—Yes.

Mr. George C. Roberts examined.

WEXFORD. Jan. 7, 1880. Mr. George C. Roberts.

226. Mr. O'Brien.—You are agent for Lord Waterford?—I am resident agent.

227. You have been a member of the Town Commissioners and of the Board of Guardians?—Yes.

228. You are not now a Town Commissioner?—No.

229. But you continue a member of the Board of Guardians?—Yes.

230. You heard the views expressed to-day as to the extension of the boundary, do you consider that the radius of about a mile would be a fair extension, and would include the persons who derive advantage from their proximity to the town?—I think it is only fair that those residing in the immediate neighbourhood should contribute. I myself am perfectly willing [illegible] I am not contributing at present, being outside the boundary.

231. What radius would bring you in?—The proposed radius would include me. I think Mr. Wilkinson said a large number of residents were inside the proposed extended area, but I do not concur with him. I don't think, of itself, that the number would be very large. Perhaps there would be twelve or fifteen or so. However, I do think that many of these would willingly contribute to the rates of the town provided they derived some profit therefrom. So far as the lighting is concerned they do derive benefit from it, but there is no advantage from the water, that is confined to the town.

232. But do they not derive advantage from it when they visit the town?—Well, it is not exactly water they drink when they come into the town. I may say that I was not aware of the extension proposed by the Town Commissioners till I examined the map, and looking at it here, it struck me forcibly that it was unfair to exclude Greenville when you take in the greater portion of Clonhasten, and when it is almost three portions of Clonhasten, and closer than portions of St. John's. Mr. Leary has a good farm at Greenville, and Ballyhealy in his market town; Mr. Hill has a very extensive farm at St. John's, and he resides in a very large house in St. John's, and though his advantages from the town are undoubtedly greater than those derived by Mr. O'Leary, still I think Mr. O'Leary may be considered to derive, and to be likely to derive in future, substantial advantages from proximity to the town.

233. Then, Mr. Roberts, I understand you to say that in addition to the boundary suggested by the Town Commissioners, you would suggest the taking in of the whole of Greenville?—Yes. The reason I mention this is that when Mr. Wilkinson was giving his evidence he defined the boundary but did not mention Greenville was excluded; when I got the map and looked at it, I found the word "out" written on it. I don't like to set myself to suggest that Greenville should be included, but I throw out the suggestion just as it occurred to me.

234. From your intimate local knowledge, Mr. Roberts, I would ask you do you think there is any other place that ought to be taken in, or have you any observation to make as to the boundary decided?—I think what the Town Commissioners suggest is a very fair extension.

235. The way you think there are only some twelve or fourteen or fifteen residents would be brought in within the present boundary and the proposed area?—Yes, about that; I am not, of course, quite positive.

236. Are there lands held by a good many people living in the town?—Yes.

237. And you think it reasonable that they should contribute something considering the advantages derived?—Certainly.

238. Having regard to the fact that arable lands are liable only to one-fourth?—Yes. One gentleman asked me whether his house would be valued at the full extent, and I was unable to answer him. The [illegible] is that land only will be. The suggestion is to take in Bleachgreen.

239. Is there any general suggestion you would like to make?—No. The only thing I would like to say would be this; before the Town Commissioners would think of taking up the county roads—taking into their own hands the repairs of the streets and roads immediately adjoining the town, it would be well to ascertain whether Wexford has derived much benefit from it or not. My own impression is that the town of Enniscorthy never received from the county its legitimate right.

240. You are aware that at present the Grand Jury rate is assessed equally on all descriptions of property, that there is no graduated scale?—No. I am aware of that.

241. Well, if the control of these bridges, roads, &c., were transferred to the Town Council, do you advocate that these works should be charged on arable land on the full amount, or only be subject to the same scale of rating they are subject to under the Towns Improvement Act—one-fourth?—That is a difficult question to answer, for this reason, the footpaths and streets would give the first advantage to the townspeople; those residing some distance away would not derive so much benefit as the householders and gentlemen in the town—business men, and so on. Therefore it would require some little consideration to arrive at a just conclusion on the subject of the rating.

243. But at the present moment they do all pay to the Grand Jury the full amount—is not that so?—Yes, but that extends to the entire county.

244. You are not prepared to say as to whether or not, in the event of the control over the roads within the municipal district being transferred to the Town Commissioners, the charge for that particular class of work should be as at present on the full amount, or on the reduced amount of one-fourth or any reduced amount?—It is a subject that I think would require some further consideration.

245. Mr. Carey.—I think even if we got this extended boundary, we would be entitled to charge the full rating, for we would have to keep up the expenses of the roads. I don't anticipate that the footpaths would be much more. What we wish would be to charge the full amount.

246. Mr. Roberts.—The town would have to contribute, as in Wexford, to the general cess. A good deal would depend on the way in which the Town Council would insist on the work being done. In Wexford it is done, and well done. I am sorry to say the county work here is wretchedly done.

247. Mr. Carey.—If we had it in our own hands it would be much better done.

248. Mr. O'Brien.—As I understand you, Mr. Carey, you think the works, in case of their being transferred to you, should be charged on the full amount?—As at present.

249. Mr. Roberts.—In conversation with some people who live outside, the opinion of those living outside the present boundary—living at a comparatively remote distance from the town—is, that if the Town Council are allowed to levy the rate as at present, the town itself would take the lion's share of that.

250. Mr. Carey.—The boundary would be clearly defined.

251. Mr. O'Brien.—Mr. Roberts thinks you would lay it out chiefly on the portion you are most interested in. Can you tell me, Mr. Wilkinson, what is the present constituency—the municipal constituency or number of voters?—I cannot say for certain.

252. Mr. Carey.—It is 250 or 260.

253. Mr. O'Brien.—And how many persons are eligible for the office of Town Commissioner?—

254. Mr. Wilkinson.—About forty.

255. Mr. O'Brien.—How many Commissioners are there?—Fifteen.

256. If the radius suggested by the Town Commissioners were adopted, about how many would it

add to the number of electors?—It would make up about fifty, I think, and bring it up to 300.

257. And add how many to the number eligible as Town Commissioners?—About one.

258. Do you not think that the persons outside it would be as eligible to be made eligible for the honour and dignity of holding the position of Town Commissioner?—Well, judging from this point, I should say not. I would wish to see a greater interest in these matters taken; but as a matter of fact, most of the people with the largest interest in the town, keep away from the Town Council.

Ennisc[illegible]. [illegible] Mr. George E. [illegible].

Mr. Thomas Furlong examined.

Mr. T. Furlong.

259. Mr. O'Brien.—You live outside the present boundary?—Yes.

260. And would you be included in the proposed extension?—Yes.

261. In what townland do you reside?—In [illegible].

262. How far are you from the town?—About an English mile.

263. Are you in favour of the extension?—I am not in favour of being taxed any way. I have two farms on two leases.

264. Do you not derive advantages from the town?—Yes.

265. You are aware that arable lands are only liable to be assessed at one-fourth of the net valuation?—Yes.

266. Do you consider that fair?—Yes; but my house would be rated in full.

267. Houses in connexion with land are not valued as high as houses in the town?—No.

268. Don't you consider that this fourth assessment on land would fairly represent the contribution towards the expenses?—If they assessed at one-fourth, it would be perfectly satisfied.

269. Are you in favour of having the money, the present influence exercised by the Grand Jury, being transferred to the Commissioners?—Well, I never thought about it.

270. But you think in any case that the charge should not be more than one-fourth?—Yes.

The inquiry then terminated.

WEXFORD.—FEBRUARY 8th, 1878.

Before Messrs. Exham, Q.C., O'Brien, and Cotton, C.E.

Wexford. Feb. 8, 1878.

Mr. Thomas O'Leary examined.

Mr. Thomas O'Leary.

1. You are the Town Clerk?—I am, since 1859.

2. The town is divided into three wards?—It is.

3. For municipal purposes?—Yes.

4. Are there the same wards for Poor Law purposes?—No, they are all the same.

5. Are there separate wards for Poor Law purposes, for the election of Guardians, and Guardians elected for these three wards?—No.

6. They are not elected for wards at all?—No.

7. There is no Poor Law ward?—No.

8. Chairman.—Can you give me first the valuation and population of the town?—The population is 12,077.

9. And the acreage now?—[illegible].

10. And the valuation?—£[illegible] of the borough.

11. That is the total valuation of the borough?—Yes.

12. Could you give me separately the valuation of those three wards? First of all, what are their names?—St. Selskar's, St. Mary's, and St. Iberius.

13. And the number of municipal electors?—[illegible]; in St. Selskar's there are [illegible] electors; in St. Iberius [illegible], and in St. Mary's [illegible].

14. Are the limits of the Parliamentary and municipal boundaries the same?—Yes.

15. Do you know the acreage of the municipal boundaries?—I can tell you in a moment.

16. How many representatives on the Council are there for each ward?—Eight—two Aldermen and six Councillors.

17. Are the Parliamentary and municipal boundaries equal now?—Yes, they are.

18. Now, could you tell me the number of voters at present here, and how many for each ward?—For municipal purposes, [illegible] voters altogether.

19. And can you say are they pretty equal for each ward?—No, St. Mary's is the smallest number, a great deal.

20. How many Parliamentary voters are there?—[illegible].

21. Now, with regard to the present wards, are the Corporation or Town Commissioners satisfied with the present arrangement of the wards?—I never heard them complain about them.

22. Is it thought advisable that they should be altered in any respect?—I never heard any complaint about the wards. St. Mary's is considered small—the number of burgesses is small.

23. And can you say whether it would be advisable, in your opinion, that any change should be made, so as to equalize the number?—Well, I think myself that if the town were divided into two wards it might be better.

24. And can you say is that, or has it been, the opinion of the Town Commissioners as a body?—No, I never heard them say it.

25. But that would be your own opinion?—It would.

26. Well, the town at present is all in the electoral division of Wexford?—Yes.

27. And that extends largely out?—Yes.

28. What is the acreage?—[illegible] acres.

29. I suppose, then, knowing, as we do, that it is bounded by the sea on one side, the electoral division may be said to extend about [illegible] miles from the town in every direction?—Oh, more than that, I should say.

30. At all events, it extends a couple of miles, that is certain?—Yes, a long way.

31. Would any extension of the borough that has ever been made, or suggested to be made, be still within the electoral division?—Certainly.

32. Now, the next question I shall ask you is as to the roads. First of all, the roads here are under the management of the borough?—Yes.

33. How long have they been so?—Since 1873.

34. You obtained a provisional order, transferring to you the control of these roads, previously exercised by the Grand Jury?—Yes; it was confirmed by Act of Parliament in that year.

35. What year?—In 1873.

36. Will you be able to give me a copy of that?—Yes.

37. I shall have the rates that have been made for the past five years, dividing them in columns, municipal, poor law, and county:—

	Municipal.		Poor Law.		County.	
	s.	d.	s.	d.	s.	d.
1873,	0	[illegible]	[illegible]	0	1	10
1874,	0	10	[illegible]	0	1	[illegible]
1875,	[illegible]	[illegible]	[illegible]	0	1	0
1876,	[illegible]	[illegible]	4	0	[illegible]	[illegible]
1877,	[illegible]	[illegible]	4	[illegible]	1	[illegible]

Are these correct?—Yes.

WEXFORD. Feb. 4, 1880. — Mr. Thomas O'Leary.

39. The last one was the first after the provisional order?—Yes.

40. The county rate mentioned there is what you are entitled to charge under the provisional order?—Yes.

41. Not exceeding two shillings in the pound?

42. Now, does that include the proportion of county at large charges?—Yes.

43. The entire?—Yes.

44. Can you tell me was that about the amount of county rate that was levied in former times—in the year preceding 1874 was it more or less?—It is less.

45. This is less?—Yes.

46. On the average, as far as you know, for four or five years before you got the provisional order, what was the county cess?—I think it was generally 1s. 8d.—that is 10d. each half year.

47. But you say it is less since 1874?—I think the county cess has increased since 1874.

48. Since you got the provisional order do you mean?—Yes, it has increased partly in consequence of the change.

49. In the five years since the passing of the Act the county cess has been heavier?—Yes.

50. Heavier than it was before?—Yes.

51. Including the county-at-large charges?—Yes.

52. But since the passing of that Act the lands in the town have only been paying rate on one-fourth of the valuation?—Yes; but they are very trifling.

53. I was confining myself to county cess which, as I understand, since the passing of the provisional order is payable by the barony?—By the barony of Forth.

54. Is not the county cess payable by the inhabitants of the barony of Wexford since the passing of the provisional order?—No, it is the county cess payable by the barony of Forth. Wexford, before the provisional order passed, paid its proportion the same as all the rest of the barony of Forth. The rural part of the barony of Forth pays more than it did before.

55. Comparing what was paid prior to 1873 and what was paid since, which is the largest?—Since we got the provisional order?

56. Yes?—The county cess has been heavier.

57. The *Mayor*.—We pay less.

58. Mr. O'Brien.—You said there were two temporary rates, that would be 1s. 6d., but the figures just read would show more than that?—It could be largely increased, but that the surplus is expended on the improvement of the town.

59. Chairman.—You have given me here what is struck in the county for the last five years in lieu of old county cess. Now, take five years before that, and what I want to know is whether was the county cess more or less for those five years, as payable, mind you, by the inhabitants of the borough?—I am not prepared to answer the question.

60. I want to know if the cash payments were less by the people of the borough before or since the passing of this Act. Now, according to your experience and judgment, have the roads been better kept by the Commissioners since the Grand Jury powers were transferred to them than before?—Well, I can't exactly say, but I believe they are certainly better kept.

61. This town is under the Towns Improvement Act?—It is, for that purpose; but it is under the Municipal Act both.

62. But so far as the improvement rate is concerned, it is under the Towns Improvement Act?—Yes.

63. Arable lands, and so on, are only liable to be rated at one-fourth the net annual valuation?—Yes.

64. Have you, since the passing of the Provisional Order Act, levied the road rate, or county cess in lieu of it, only on one-fourth of the valuation of arable land?—That was all.

65. And they, in point of fact, have only paid one-fourth of the county-at-large charges, and one-fourth of what it cost for keeping the roads in repair?—That is all.

66. Then by the passing of the provisional order, the owners or occupiers of the arable lands, calculated under the 63rd section of the Towns Improvement Act, have derived great advantage by it?—Yes.

67. In fact, for the past five years, they only paid one-fourth of the county cess, in place of what they paid before?—Yes.

68. And that applies to the county at large charges, as I understand you?—Yes.

69. Mr. O'Brien.—The Grand Jury do not pay within the borough now at all?—No.

70. Then I presume you levy it and pay the consolidation?—Yes.

71. Have the works executed in connexion with those roads, previously under the control of the Grand Jury, been of a more extensive character than before—have the Grand Jury or you done more work?—We have; in fact we commenced to spend £400 a year.

72. Do you now more work done?—Yes.

73. And the increased work, you say, is represented by £400 a year?—Yes. In fact they gave nothing almost; nothing at all I may say for some years.

74. So that, I presume, the proportionate rates of the last five years, and the proportionate rates of the five years before, would not be a fair criterion of what the effect was, without having regard to the work done; for you have done more work within the last five years than was done before?—Yes.

75. That increase you say is represented by about £400?—Yes; more than 6d. in the pound.

76. How is your payment to the Grand Jury calculated in lieu of county-at-large charges?—By a warrant of the Grand Jury each assizes to the Corporation to pay the proportion of Grand Jury charges, and that is estimated on the relative value—the proportionate value.

77. Chairman.—In estimating that do the Grand Jury give credit for the arable land in the borough paying only one-fourth?—They do now.

78. So that, in point of fact, the town, or persons, pays the county-at-large charges the same as they did before?—Yes.

79. And the occupiers of the town, that is such as are holders of house property, pay the whole part?—Yes.

80. They have to make up the three-fourths and pay it over to the Grand Jury in favour of the men who hold land that is exempted up to three-fourths under the 63rd section of the Act?—Yes; there is that disadvantage.

81. Mr. Cotton.—What proportion of the town is arable land?—Oh, I don't suppose there is more than, perhaps, some ten acres.

82. Your total valuation, you said, is £13,727—now, how much of that is represented by arable land?—Only about £20 a year.

83. I mean how much of the valuation of £13,727 is arable land, only to be assessed at one-fourth, I understand. Perhaps about £20 a year.

84. £20 a year valuation only?—That is all.

85. Chairman.—With reference to the roads, Mr. O'Leary, you tell me that from your own knowledge the roads have been much better kept since you got them under your own control than before you had them?—They have.

86. And have they been kept at a greater or less expenditure than before?—At less expense—by the perch.

87. Mr. Cotton.—Are your roads kept now by contract?—No; by a staff employed for the purpose.

88. By your own staff?—Yes; we found it less than by contract, and so we decided upon having it done by a proper staff.

89. You have your own town surveyor?—Yes.

90. Chairman.—You have your own officers to keep the roads, footways, and so on in repair?—Yes.

91. And you say you can do it much better and at a less cost than the Grand Jury did when they had it under their control?—Yes.

93. And the footways are kept in order, too?—They are. The footways are vastly improved within the last few years. There are concrete footpaths made; and the sewerage, which was in a very bad state, is now drawing to completion.

94. Well, was the expenditure in regard to sewerage paid for out of what you levy in lieu of county rate?—Yes.

95. And not by a sewer rate?—Quite so.

96. You spoke of a certain amount saved during the past four or five years—a certain sum representing the advantage derived under the new system—can you say how much, of your own knowledge, was saved?—£300 or £400 on the average for the past four or five years we have saved.

97. Mr. O'Brien.—Would the Corporation, having now had four or five years experience of the working of the present system—would they have desire to revert to the old system—to the original arrangement?—I am very sure they would not. I may say there was a good deal of difference of opinion as to the effect of the altered system before, but there is none now. Everyone is quite satisfied with it.

98. Chairman.—Are you able to speak on the part of the Town Commissioners as to whether they think the existing boundary too narrow—the existing boundary of the borough?—Well, as I believe you have seen from the answers to the queries you forwarded, there is a difference of opinion on that subject.

99. The matter has been discussed by the Town Commissioners?—Yes.

100. And there was a divided opinion amongst them on the subject?—Yes, and estimates have been made by three or four at the meetings as to the effects that would follow from extension.

101. Mr. O'Brien.—Does the objection of those who resisted any extension rest on the supposition that lands brought in would be only rated at one-fourth?—Certainly.

102. And that, you say, influenced those who were unfavourable to an extension of the boundary?—Yes, that is the chief point influencing them.

103. But suppose a different arrangement were made—suppose the county expenditure were to be charged, as it was previously, uniformly on all descriptions of property, would the feeling then be in favour of extension?—I think so.

104. Chairman.—Suppose the owners of land outside the present boundary—say for a mile—suppose they were brought in within the boundary, paying even the present proportion of improvement rate—one-fourth—but left liable to the same county cess, do you think the people inside would oppose that, or be in favour of such an extension?—That is just the point on which the difference of opinion arises.

105. Would there be unanimity among the members of the Town Commissioners if the land to be brought in were only made liable to one-fourth of the improvement rate, but still remained liable to pay rate equal in amount to the present county cess?—I don't understand what you mean by saying improvement rate and county cess.

106. Improvement rate is under the Towns Improvement Act, lands liable to one-fourth. Now, suppose the lands outside were to be brought in liable to pay one-fourth only, and liable at the same time to the same county rate to which they are liable now, would that produce a unanimity of feeling?—Well, if they paid that to the town, it would be of advantage to the town, no doubt.

107. Understand me. Suppose the occupiers of land outside—say, for an area of a mile—suppose they were brought in, paying one-fourth of the improvement rate, and remained liable to pay the full proportion of the road rate, instead of to the Grand Jury, would the Town Commissioners be unanimous in bringing them in?—I must say I am still somewhat at a loss to understand the proposition exactly.

108. The object would be this—the town would get three-fourths more of the road rate—the entire of the road rate—and one-fourth of the improvement rate?—Would the road rate and the improvement rate the same.

Wexford.
Feb. 3, 1877.

Mr. Thomas O'Leary.

109. I am talking of the improvement rate proportion that you are empowered to levy under the 62nd section of the Towns Improvement Act of 1854. Under that section of the Act you are entitled to strike an improvement rate not exceeding 1s. in the pound. You are of course aware that by the 62nd section of that Act arable land is only liable to be rated at one-fourth the net annual value?—Yes.

110. Still those arable lands remained up to the time you got your Provisional Act liable to pay the entire of the county cess. Suppose that arable lands outside the present boundary were brought in, in precisely the same way liable to pay one-fourth of the improvement rate, one-fourth of that shilling, and to pay to the town instead of to the Grand Jury the whole county cess, would the people of the town be unanimous in bringing them in?—I think so; but I may mention that the improvement rate you speak of under the Towns Improvement Act, there never has been a rate struck for that in Wexford.

111. I thought you said you adopted the Towns Improvement Act in its entirety?—But we never struck the rate. We strike a rate under the Municipal Act.

113. Then, under the Municipal Act of 1840, how comes it that the arable lands pay only one-fourth?—This is the way it is—under the provisional order of 1876 all rates levied under that shall be levied, calculated as under the Towns Improvements Act of 1854.

114. But, in point of fact, the owners of arable land still continue to pay the whole?—The whole of the borough rate—the ordinary rate.

115. Well, now, with regard to the people outside, is there any feeling, as far as you know, amongst the people outside the borough boundary in favour of their being brought in?—I know some of them that would not like it, but I have been told by some that they would wish for it.

116. In other words, there is a difference of opinion on the subject; some would like it, and others would not?—Yes.

117. And I suppose it is really a question of terms more than anything else?—Yes.

118. Mr. O'Brien.—Taking the centre of the town, what is the radius of the present municipal boundary?—About a mile.

119. An English mile?—Yes.

120. The Mayor.—An English mile would be from the Bullring. It is about half an English mile north-west or north-west, and about a mile on the south-east.

121. Mr. O'Brien.—Take a radius of two miles, are there lands, within a radius of two miles, not included in the present boundary, that derive advantages from their proximity to the town of Wexford?—Certainly; no doubt of it.

122. And are many of those lands occupied by inhabited houses within that radius?—Yes, there are some; they are not very numerous.

123. Would the radius of two miles increase very much the number of ratepayers within the municipal district?—It would bring in occupiers and owners of land.

124. And within that radius of two miles you say they all derive exceptional advantages from their proximity to the town?—Yes, there is the great advantage of being so near the market.

125. Do the children of those people living outside resort to the town for school purposes?—Yes.

126. Chairman.—Is the railway station within the borough?—It is; the borough is extended out beyond the bridge.

127. Now, what is the largest extension you have heard discussed, favoured, I may say?—Well, when the matter was brought before the Corporation, what received most favour was a small alteration bringing in as many houses and as little land as they could.

128. Mr. O'Brien.—But the whole of this, as I

understand, proceeded on the supposition that lands were only to be rated at one-fourth; is not that so?—Yes; decidedly.

129. But the case would assume an entirely different aspect if the law were altered, and they were to be assessed at the full amount?—Yes.

130. CHAIRMAN.—Now, suppose there was a two-mile radius adopted as an extension, how many gentlemen's seats would it bring in, would you say, supposing you were to take an extension of two miles from the centre of the town?—About twenty residences, I would say.

131. *The Mayor.*—That would take in Ferrycarrig townland.

132. CHAIRMAN.—How many townlands, or parts of townlands, are included in the present municipal district?—There are a great number of small ones.

133. Does it cut townlands—does it cut townland boundaries?—It does.

134. Does it cut fields?—It does.

135. *The Mayor.*—I may mention that it even goes round fields, or rather goes round houses, and leaves out houses, and takes in the land.

136. CHAIRMAN.—Would it be feasible so as to limit or alter the boundary that it would comprise entire townlands?—I could not tell that.

137. MR. O'BRIEN.—Don't you think that in practice it would be of advantage, and a convenience, if the municipal boundary were made coterminous with townlands, that being a known denomination?—It would be some, but it is not of material consequence, I think.

138. CHAIRMAN.—Do you know how many, in point of population, and then how many voters would be brought in by a radius of two miles from the centre of the town being adopted?—Well, comparatively, I should say, a very small number; for, of course, the outlying districts are mostly land, and, in some cases, land held by persons residing in the town.

139. Who have already votes residing in the town?—Yes; some of them. I don't suppose it would add a very large number. I think it is my duty as Town Clerk to mention that one difficulty would arise as to an extension, and that is that the land lies very high. Now, suppose in the case of supplying these people with water, from the new waterworks, it would make a difference, the land lying so high.

140. Suppose in the case of an extension being agreed upon, has the Corporation considered the question of giving the benefit of lighting and water, to the extent of this district?—Of course they have the power of doing it.

141. Yes; but have they considered the question as to whether they would propose to do it or not?—They have made a calculation as to what would be the effect even on the one-fourth valuation, and they have calculated for the number of lamps, and the water, and so on.

142. And have they considered it irrespective of giving water and light to those districts?—No; it was calculated on the basis of giving water and light.

MR. JOHN J. WALSH, Mayor of Wexford, examined.

143. Can you give us the valuation of the three wards?—St. Iberius' is £3,316 5s.; St. Mary's is (with the smallest number of voters) £4,887 5s.; and St. Selskar's £4,891 15s.

144. I would ask as to the statement of the Town Clerk, to the effect that in his opinion it would be better if there were two wards only; have you ever heard that view expressed?—No; I never heard the question mooted till to-day.

145. Do you think it would be better to have any change made, as to the arrangement of the wards?—Well, considering how it has worked up to the present, and for such a lengthened period, I don't think so. I would not be for making any change in the wards, for I really don't think they could be better than at present.

146. You have heard me asking the question as to the alteration in the town since you got possession of the roads in 1874; is it your opinion that the roads have been better kept, and more economically than before—better kept than when they were under the control of the Grand Jury?—The way it was is this—Previous to the separation of the barony we had to go to the county for anything—any little improvements we wanted—when we were made a separate barony. The county were in the habit of allowing £100 a year for flagging. After a little the county cess payers stopped that, and if we wanted anything, we had to go begging for it. Then we got this provisional order; since then our rating is about the same as we would be paying otherwise, maybe a penny per year more, and we have £400 a year to spare to spend on the improvement of the town.

147. That is £400 a year more than was spent under the old system?—Yes; the town of Wexford pays from £700 to £800 a year for county-at-large charges, if not more, and while on that I may say there is another thing I think is a great hardship here. If a fire occurs within the town, or malicious injury, we have no representation at the presentment sessions, and we are assessed for it, and made pay for it, if it is brought in a malicious injury or otherwise. We have, as I say, no representation on the baronial sessions.

148. CHAIRMAN.—Do you mean for a burning in the town itself?—Yes; they assess us. £100 being claimed the rural gentlemen come in, and find it to be malicious injury, and strike it on us.

149. And in that case had you to pay the whole of it?—Yes.

150. Then, it appears to me to be an enormous sum that you have to pay towards the county-at-large charges. It appears to be 1s. 1d. in the pound about, for county-at-large charges; in other places it is only 7d. or 8d. in the pound. It is a wonder to me why it is so much more in Wexford than elsewhere.

151. MR. O'BRIEN.—Your assessment for county-at-large charges is precisely what it would have been if the change had not been made under the provisional order at all. It made no change at all?

MR. Walsh.—No.

152. CHAIRMAN.—It is 1s. 1d. in the pound for county-at-large charges out of 2s., and in other places, as I have said, we found it was 7d. or 8d. in the pound. I was wondering why it was so much larger.

154. MR. *Henry Wynne.*—The expense of maintaining the District Lunatic Asylum probably makes the difference.

155. *Witness.*—I may mention that before we obtained the provisional order, I believe (I am not quite clear, however, about this) we formerly had the main street, perhaps a mile and a half through, for which the county-at-large paid half the cost for keeping it in repair, because it is the mail-coach road. Now, however, we have to pay the whole of it, and there is no allowance made for it.

156. CHAIRMAN.—Yes, but you say that, after keeping your streets in repair, and so on, you are £400 a year to the good?—After keeping the streets in repair we have about £400 a year to lay out on flagging and sewering.

157. And the roads you are able to keep in good order?—Yes.

158. Taking the general result, now, do you think you would be inclined to revert to the former system?—No, I don't think anyone would broach such a proposition, as to go back to the old system.

159. I suppose you had some persuasive power exercised on the Grand Jury?—The Grand Jury agreed to the separation unanimously. We gave them

WEXFORD. Feb. 5, 18[illegible]. Mr. John J. Walsh.

saving on the outside. You have a surveyor, a [illegible] man, and so on, and would you not be able to add on those extra roads so as to make a much larger saving in proportion even than you do in the town?—Well, I would rather not give an opinion on that.

188. At all events, you ought to [illegible] proportionately with the way in which you do the town work?—Yes, no doubt, according to what has occurred, and judging solely by that. But I have a doubtful objection to extend our operations too much, as I have said they would not be carried on so well as they would be under our own eye.

189. At all events, I understand the trend of your opinion is this, that if the people outside were made liable to one-fourth of the present improvement rate, which cannot be more than one shilling in the pound, and the same county cess, would be fair?—Yes; yes there would give more advantages. We would be able to give lighting, for instance, further than at present.

190. But in the event of no more watering or lighting than at present were given, you would consider the one-fourth fair rating?—Yes.

191. These outsiders, as they may be called, are under the rural sanitary authority?—Yes.

192. You are aware that under the Sanitary Act of last session, as far as the rural sanitary district is concerned, they pay the whole, and deduct one-half from the landlord, and in the urban sanitary districts these people would pay only one-fourth, and deduct nothing?—I think it ought to be divided equally between the landlord and tenant if the rural districts are to be brought in. The landlord derives as much advantage as the tenant.

193. Mr. O'Brien.—You are aware that the Parliamentary Committee recommend that in their report?—Yes; I may mention in passing that it would affect me, for I have about 40 or 50 acres on the verge of the boundary.

195. That would apply to the sanitary rate?—Yes.

196. Chairman.—But not to the county cess?—No, not any share of the county cess, for that was existing at the time of getting the provisional order. The lands inside the present boundary were attached knowing it, and when you were taking them or making them you knew what you were to charge.

197. Well, now, bearing that in view, how far would you say it would be reasonable or fair to extend the boundary? At one side, of course, you have the sea?—We would not like to take in the new bridge. It would not be a direct boundary. I would strike the boundary at a place called [illegible]—that would be about two English miles.

198. Mr. O'Brien.—From the centre of the town?—Yes, a mile and a half Irish from the Bull-ring. It would leave [illegible] out.

199. Mr. Cotton.—That would be to the north-west.

200. Mr. O'Brien.—And to the south?—To a place called the Washing Pond.

201. How far is that from the centre of the town?—About a mile and a quarter.

202. [illegible]?—Yes. On the west I would follow the boundary of the river to [illegible], then by [illegible] I would take in the whole of the townland of Ballyboggan, half of the townland of [illegible], the townland boundary of Ballyboggan, to the place where it joins the lane dividing the townland of [illegible], then by the parish boundary to the townland, and taking in Prospect House, keeping to the west of Prospect House, along the western townland of [illegible], and thence to the Washing Pond by as straight a line as possible, taking in [illegible] House.

203. Chairman.—That is the boundary most available to follow?—Yes.

204. And that is based on this, that the owners of land within that district should continue to pay the same rate of county cess, and one-fourth of the other rate charged between landlord and tenant?—Yes.

205. Would you think the one-fourth rating fair?—Yes, that is if we gave them an advantage.

206. Mr. O'Brien.—You are aware that by the most recent legislation on the subject—the 62nd section of the Towns Improvement Act—it is provided that where any such rate shall be made by any Commissioners or Corporation, or persons becoming urban sanitary authorities after the passing of that Act, all lands used as meadow lands, market gardens, nursery lands, &c., "shall be assessed and liable in proportion of one-fourth only of the net annual value of such lands." Is that a fair principle to apply, generally speaking, to lands of that description?—I do, but except as to town [illegible].

208. And as regards Grand Jury cess, but in all other respects?—Yes.

209. Mr. Cotton.—In contributions from the town to the county-at-large charges are there any exemptions, such as county officers' salaries. Do you, for instance, pay a share of the County Surveyor's salary?—We do pay our share, and we have, of course, to [illegible] from that. We have a surveyor of our own.

211. If there was an extension made, on what principle would you allocate that extension among the wards?—Well, if there is an extension on the west, if that is ever carried out, there will have to be a redistribution of the wards altogether.

212. Could you tell us off-hand what is your view as to that?—Well, St. Mary's Ward is very unequally situated as regards the others.

213. Mr. O'Brien.—What general principle would you apply?—You would not add by the increase, if it were ever carried out, 48 electors to the municipal body. I would divide the wards equally as to the number of electors.

214. Have you considered the question in any way as to putting the outlying district altogether in one ward?—No.

215. Do you think that such a plan as that would be likely to work well?—No, certainly not; for if you did you would leave the representation in a few. I would divide the wards as to numbers.

216. Mr. Cotton.—That would apply to any other class?—Yes. I would divide it as to numbers, and only have three wards.

217. Mr. O'Brien.—You would class them as to the number of voters?—Yes.

Mr. John Greene, J.P., examined.

Mr. John Greene, J.P.

218. You are an Alderman of Wexford?—Yes.

219. And I understand you have been some time Mayor?—Yes. I was instrumental in procuring the charter of incorporation, and am the only original member.

220. When was the original boundary fixed, do you know?—At the time of the charter, in 1846.

221. The old boundaries, were they larger or smaller than the present?—They were considerably larger.

222. About how far did they extend at that time?—I think better than two miles.

223. And there has been no change of the boundary since 1846?—No.

224. Is it the same as the Parliamentary boundary?—Yes.

225. Now, Mr. Greene, I want to ask you do you know the lands in the neighbourhood of the town of Wexford?—I suppose you do?—I have listened to the evidence, and I am decidedly in favour of an extension of the boundary.

227. You are of opinion that those persons who live outside the existing bounds derive special advantages from their proximity to the town?—Yes; there is no doubt of it.

228. And the occupiers of the land outside use the town of Wexford very extensively?—Yes; and I may

[illegible] some of those [illegible] and expressed a hope that they might be taken in—that the extension would be made.

229. To bring them in?—Yes.

230. When you say "many," you mean of the better class?—Yes.

231. Are there many of the small farmers there that would be brought in?—Not very many. Of course I may say that some of those, they [illegible]—they have [illegible] a natural [illegible] to [illegible].

232. Mr. O'Brien.—But they have not given the matter very much consideration?—No.

233. Would they not value the privilege of being [illegible] electors, or of being eligible for the office of Town Commissioners?—Well, perhaps there might be some. On abstract principles I am in favour of extending the boundary, for I think it would be of great advantage. I think at one time a great portion of our township was formerly under water; it is now swept [illegible], and comprises many very fine buildings. I think the town [illegible] to extend.

234. And there is portions of this land outside that you think is likely to become building ground hereafter?—Yes.

235. Now, to what extent would you say the boundaries ought to be extended?—I am quite in accord with what the Mayor has said on the subject.

236. About the radius of two miles?—Yes.

237. And you would follow the boundaries he laid down?—Yes.

238. You think that would be fair?—Yes, I believe that would be a fair adjustment.

239. Now, with regard to giving light and water to the district taken in, do you think if the extension were carried out that the district should be lighted?—Not to the extent of two miles.

240. And therefore some of those should not pay the same rating—the same improvement rating?—Yes; but some of them will derive the benefit of the water.

241. You do not consider, then, that lands lying outside should pay the same as you?—No.

242. Do you think the terms of the [illegible] [illegible] that I have read are fair?—Yes.

243. Chairman.—That is this [illegible]—outside lands—that would be brought in by the extension, being lands, and therefore not standing light and water as much as houses, that the fair share would be for them to pay one-[illegible]?—Yes.

244. They derive advantages, you believe, from their proximity to the town?—Yes. The fact that they are [illegible] higher [illegible] than.

245. In other places we have been told the views of the people, amongst others, of Mr McCarthy Downing, the lands outside, in his opinion, should pay one-third, and that they ought to get benefits to the extent of one-half. What would be your view of it?—Well, if I was living myself outside, I would not complain of that tax. It is hard to give evidence on the point, for people have a repugnance to have taxes imposed on them. I was the original promoter of the water scheme. I fought the question for twenty-five years. The people rendered it up in [illegible].

246. We may take it, however, that you believe they derive advantages, the people outside, to the extent of one-third, at least?—Certainly.

247. That, from the exceptional advantages they derive from the town as a market town, and its having an opportunity of daily selling their produce, and using the town in that way, they derive decided advantages to the extent of one-third?—Yes. So far as the county cess, including the county at large charges, I would have them pay it, as at present, to the Town Commissioners instead of to the Grand Jury.

248. What I understand is this, that so far as what we call Grand Jury cess, including the county-at-large charges, you would make them pay that to the Town Commissioners instead of to the Grand Jury?—Yes.

249. Just as it is paid?—Yes.

250. But as regards the improvement rate, one-third?—Yes.

251. Now, of course, from your knowledge of the place, you are able to say have the roads been long kept?—Considerably.

252. And a large saving effected?—Yes, a large saving. It was in consequence of the [illegible] of the survey, for we were part of the county, the [illegible] of the town proposed to give [illegible] for the [illegible] of the boundary. [illegible] in the [illegible]. [illegible] point, [illegible] I was [illegible] by the separation, but being connected with the town I advocated the separation.

253. You suffer by it, then?—Yes, though I advocated it.

254. Now, Mr. Greene, bearing in mind that there has been very much [illegible] in keeping up the roads within your jurisdiction, you think that [illegible] saving would be effected with regard to the [illegible] to be taken in and [illegible] the extension?—Certainly; we would have the same staff.

255. Would you give the benefit of your [illegible] [illegible] to the town, to apply it to the outskirts?—Well, the savings would be very trifling; the [illegible] of roads that would be added would be very little.

256. You are only saying you would get would be [illegible] to the length of the roads.

257. Mr. O'Brien.—In point of fact, practically, the [illegible] of changing the jurisdiction [illegible] [illegible] [illegible] but the [illegible] you get nothing and now you are getting something?—Yes. I may [illegible] that the Grand Jury were unanimously in favour of the change.

258. Chairman.—In fact, the Grand Jury [illegible] went to the Grand Jury went to the change, and is now in the town?—It was an [illegible] [illegible] change. I have had [illegible] [illegible] and Dundalk on the subject, and I encouraged them to seek the separation, for the benefit of those towns.

259. Is it your opinion that all [illegible] land brought in ought to be made to pay its [illegible] share [illegible] and [illegible]?—Yes.

260. Mr. O'Brien.—You apply that to all outside land?—Yes; if you extend the boundary you cannot make an exception.

261. Chairman.—Mr. [illegible] has been telling us that there would be twelve or fifteen miles of road brought in by the proposed extended area; [illegible] it, I understand, that the Corporation [illegible] take over the management of those twelve or fifteen miles, and do it cheaper than the Grand Jury?—I think so; we would have the machinery.

262. Now, about the wards—what is your opinion on that subject?—I think the three wards should be, if possible, [illegible].

263. Mr. O'Brien.—The Mayor suggested that they should be [illegible], and [illegible] as nearly as possible according to the number of voters?—I don't see how that could be done.

264. But as nearly as possible?—Yes; I think they should be [illegible] according to numbers. I think it is a [illegible] to have [illegible] men electing eight representatives under the Government. A ward may have 200 voters and its valuation, and a ward valued at only £[illegible] has 100 voters, and the [illegible] may [illegible] as many as the [illegible]. There are difficulties that cannot be got over, but, as far as practicable we should combine population with property.

265. Mr. O'Brien.—Do you think, then, that there should be a cumulative system of voting?—I do, sir.

266. How would you, Mr. Green, suppose the extension [illegible] by the Mayor were carried out—how would you suggest the voters living in the area so taken in should be divided among the existing wards?—I can hardly say that.

267. Would you adopt, or be in favour of the same system as the Mayor suggested—he would [illegible] those according to the number of voters—he would have the number of voters the same?—That requires more consideration.

268. Chairman.—There would be a large district brought in by the boundary as suggested by the Mayor

Wexford. [illegible]
Mr. John Greene, J.P.

—would you try and divide that into the three different wards—I mean divide it into thirds, and add one-third to each ward?—Oh, suppose you throw the voting power into Mary's ward, it would hardly bring it up.

270. Mr. O'Brien.—What is the general principle you would apply—what would you be guided by—is it by numbers?—By property and voters. That was endeavoured to be adjusted at first. We found great difficulty in adjusting Mary's ward.

271. Chairman.—I am told there would be forty or fifty voters brought in by this extension—now, could you give us any idea as to what the valuation of that extended area would be?—No.

272. At any rate, would it be an addition to throw these forty voters into Mary's ward?—Yes; that would give a fair representation. The three wards would, in voters, be almost equal. But I think it would be better to rearrange them.

273. Mr. Cotton.—Is the railway station in the town?—It is.

274. Is it rated to the town?—Yes.

275. Because it is made on the place that was slob, when the town boundaries were settled?—Yes.

276. Now, with regard to the water supply, would it be of advantage to have the boundaries extended?—Yes.

277. An advantage to the town to have the area extended and enlarged?—Yes.

278. Chairman.—Is there any scarcity of water in this extended district?—Yes.

279. Of water?—Yes; it was in consequence of that that exertions were made for nearly a quarter of a century.

280. Is the Corporation prepared to supply water to this district?—I would not say that. Those who would get it would be glad to pay for it.

281. Would the Corporation give it to those two miles out?—No; they would not give it.

282. Those places, however, that you can supply you will?—Yes.

283. And they should pay the full rate in your opinion?—Yes.

284. And those who cannot, the one-fourth?—Yes.

285. Mr. Cotton.—In fact, then there would be two boundaries, so far as the water supply, at least, is concerned?—There would be exceptions, according to liability.

286. Chairman.—Where they can be supplied, they will be charged in the full measure, and where they cannot, it will be one-fourth?—Yes.

287. But then the people, in any extension outside the town, won't know whether they are to get the water or not?—So far as practicable, we will give them the water.

288. But how are we to tell how far it is practicable?—So far as the elevation will allow of it.

289. He means that they will lay mains as far as they can, and they will pay the full domestic, and one-fourth of the public, rate. So far as the natural elevation will permit you will lay the mains?—Yes.

290. Do you propose to go to the contemplated extent of the new boundary, if the elevation would permit?—Oh, no; they have plenty of water outside.

291. That is, I suppose, they have wells, and so on?—Yes; plenty. It is the people in the immediate vicinity who want the supply.

292. Mr. Cotton.—What do you mean by the word practicable. Is it every one who can pay you for the supply?—First of all, I mean the question of our mains, their capacity; and secondly, the elevation.

293. But the man outside might claim to have the water if he had a low level?—The Corporation might think it would not pay. He might want it, no doubt.

294. He might think it would pay, and the Corporation think otherwise?—The Corporation would not do it; it would cost us several hundreds of pounds.

295. How are you to define where "outsiders" begin?

296. The Witness.—They will very easily adjust themselves.

297. Mr. Cotton.—I really do not see how that is to be managed, unless you have two boundaries.

298. Chairman.—All within the present municipal area pay the full amount—the full public water rate (except the lands)—all, whether lands or houses, outside the present municipal area, so far as it may be brought in, pay one-fourth of the public water rate; and any of those able to pay the domestic water rate, pay the full domestic water rate. That is how it stands.

299. Mr. Cotton.—And then the Corporation will not supply it unless they like.

Mr. William Stephens.

Mr. William Stephens examined.

300. You are a member of the Town Council?—Yes.

301. Representing what ward?—St. [illegible].

302. Have you been long living in Wexford?—Since my birth.

303. Now, does the land, say within two miles outside the town, to your knowledge, derive exceptional value in the market from its proximity to the town, and is the town used by the people outside as a market for their produce?—Yes; certainly.

304. To a great extent, I suppose?—To a large extent.

305. To what extent. Now, if you were to take land, say three miles or four, and compare it with land within an area of two miles, how much per acre would the land more contiguous to the town be likely to bring?—The land immediately close to the town goes on an average from £3 10s. or £4 there to £5 an acre; it varies in that way, and goes less as you go out, till it goes to 30s. or 20s. an acre.

306. For the same quality of land?—Yes.

307. The difference, in your opinion, is caused by the occupiers of the land closer to the town being able to pay this higher rent, from using the town as a market place?—Certainly.

308. Then I may ask you, in your opinion, do they use the town largely?—Yes; they do.

309. More than those living further off?—Yes; decidedly.

310. Do they use it daily in travelling with their produce?—Yes.

311. Is it your opinion—and is it an opinion shared in by the inhabitants, to your knowledge, that they should pay something towards keeping up the town?—Yes, I think so; but I may say it was a question never discussed or spoken of—never discussed by the Council, or by the inhabitants generally; but I am certain it would be the opinion of many of the Council and of the townspeople.

312. Is it your opinion that they should?—Yes; but I should say in proportion to the rents they already pay. The amount should not be so large if the rents are small. It would not be fair to make the man living near, who is charged a higher rent, pay the same as the man living further out, and paying a smaller rent.

313. Yes, but he pays a larger rent—the man living near the town—and is able to pay that larger rent better than the man living away, because of his proximity to the town. How much do you think he ought to pay towards the rates of the town, for the advantage he derives of having a market town well cleansed, watered, and sewered, and well lighted?—Well, I hold, possibly, a different opinion from the other members of the Council.

314. What I want to know is—never mind what they would have to pay to the improvement rate—is your opinion if they are brought in to the present

[illegible] should pay any portion of the county [illegible]

[illegible]

316. Mr. O'Brien.—[illegible]

[illegible] the Grand Jury [illegible]

317. [illegible] Grand Jury, and [illegible] the Municipal Council [illegible]

318. [illegible] Corporation [illegible]

319. Under the Towns Improvement Act, which [illegible]

320. Would it be fair, in your opinion—would it fairly represent the advantages derived?—Yes, it would be.

321. Chairman.—Would you think it fair to apply [illegible]

322. [illegible]

323. [illegible]

324. [illegible]

325. [illegible]

326. [illegible]

327. Mr. O'Brien.—[illegible]

328. [illegible]

329. [illegible]

330. [illegible]

331. Mr. O'Brien.—[illegible]

332. Chairman.—[illegible]

333. [illegible]

334. [illegible] the Grand Jury [illegible] Wexford. [illegible]

335. Mr. O'Brien.—[illegible]

336. [illegible]

337. Mr. Curran.—[illegible] Grand Jury [illegible]

338. Chairman.—[illegible]

339. Mr. Curran.—[illegible] the Grand Jury.

340. Chairman.—[illegible]

341. [illegible]

342. The Town Clerk.—[illegible] Wexford.

343. [illegible]

344. [illegible] Commissioners, and the Mayor [illegible] Corporation.

345. [illegible]

346. [illegible]

347. [illegible]

348. [illegible]

349. What would you propose to do with the north-west boundary?

350. I would take the water as the boundary, and I would follow the water's edge as far as Park.

351. Mr. COTTON.—Do I understand you to say you would take in the whole of the Townland of Park?—No, portion of it. I would go as far as Alma.

352. Would you be satisfied with "No. 2" as it stands?—Yes, I would leave it so. The reason of that is because of the advantage it would be in sanitary purposes, and the giving of lamps to that district. We propose giving lamps on the road of that district, to the number of 12 or 13.

353. CHAIRMAN.—And water?—Yes.

354. Do you differ from those who say if the people are to get lamps or water—do you propose, I should rather ask you, that the lands brought are only to pay one-fourth for the lamps?—Well, the extent of roads taken in would cost £55 a year to keep in repair.

355. Do you mean £55 a year representing the roads between the existing boundary and "No. 2"?—Yes.

356. And what is the valuation of that district?—You may say about £1,000.

357. Then at the present rating that would give £100 a year?—Yes.

358. And the county at large charges would be how much?—£30 about. I made the calculation on the existing rates to be a total amount that would be receivable on that valuation to be as £150.

359. Your view, as I understand it, would be that if the Corporation go beyond No. 2—the boundary as suggested by you—they could not undertake it?—No, I think not. If we got the rate in aid, we would have the £50 a year, and that in addition to what we could spare from the town for sanitary arrangements. My object would be to give them all the advantages without loss to the town.

360. If they get all the advantages, would you not say they should have all the liability?—Yes.

361. How many of the members of the Town Council are in favour of extension No. 2?—Eight or nine or ten went out that day, and were in favour of that extension more than any other. They considered the extension suggested by the Town Clerk too great.

362. Is it your opinion that whatever they would have to pay, the borough rate and the water rate should be shared by the landlord as well as the occupier?—Of course that would be a question.

363. Is it your opinion that the land should be made to pay one-fourth, no matter who pays it, or is it too little?—One-fourth, and the landlord to pay the major portion of it.

364. Taking in that district, it would take in some twenty voters; what is your opinion as to the wards are they satisfactory at present; are they right, or would you suggest any alteration?—Well, I would be inclined to say they are all right at present, but—

365. Suppose the extension were to be made, do you think the wards at present satisfactory?—There was no any expression of opinion or of dissatisfaction at least.

366. I understand from the Mayor that St. Mary's was too small, and that something ought to be added to it?—There are a number of gentlemen in St. Mary's ward who vote out of St. Iberius, and the same say as to St. Selskar's, who vote for another.

367. Then suppose an extension of boundary was made—suppose "No 2" extension were carried out in the way you propose, what would you say as to the wards?—I would leave them as they are, and enclose them out where the extension would be made.

368. That is, add on to the present wards the additional portion brought in, making the wards large in accordance with that extension?—Just so.

369. Mr. COTTON.—What is the qualification of a voter?—£10.

370. Mr. O'LEARY.—re-examined. What is the area and valuation of the Poor Law Electoral Division?—3709A. 1R. 23P.

371. And the valuation?—£20,711 10s.

372. How many townlands are included in it?—Thirty.

373. Including the three wards of the town of Wexford?—Yes.

374. Thirty townlands?—Yes.

375. And in the municipal district?—Only the three.

376. What are the names?—The three wards.

377. These are not townlands?—They are reputed townlands in the valuation book.

378. Well, now, according to the Mayor's extension, can you tell how many townlands would be brought in?—I think there would be portions of townlands brought in—townlands either wholly or partly.

379. That is not exactly what I asked—tell us what is the furthest point of the electoral division; do you know?—I don't know.

380. CHAIRMAN.—Can you tell from the books what it cost you for doing the roads the same as the Grand Jury did them?—In 1877, it cost £222 18s. 8d., repairs of the streets alone and other works, £870 7s. 11d.

381. That is for the whole town entire?—Yes.

382. Mr. COTTON.—And before you did them—before you took them up from the Grand Jury—they used to do the work and get your £100?—Formerly, but latterly they refused to give anything.

Mr. NICHOLAS MACDONNELL, examined.

383. You are the Town Surveyor?—Yes.

384. And have charge of all the roads?—Yes.

385. Could you, may I ask, keep those twelve or fourteen miles, if the extension were made as proposed by the Mayor, in as good order at the same cost as the Grand Jury at present?—Yes.

386. And save money?—Yes, I think so.

387. Would there be any difficulty in doing it by increasing your own staff or by contract?—Either, but there would be no difficulty about it whatever.

388. You are aware that there has been a considerable saving effected by the town taking up the portions they have done?—Yes.

389. Mr. O'BRIEN.—The effect of the Mayor's statement is that the expenditure is pretty much the same, but that the work was formerly not done?—That is exactly it.

390. You get value for your money now?—Yes.

391. The Town Clerk.—Not only that, but the fact in comparing the cost now with what it was, that it is a deal cheaper.

392. Mr. O'BRIEN.—And you, Mr. Macdonnell, think that that being so you would be able to do as well in the extended district?—Yes, I am certain of it.

393. And keep the roads in better order?—Yes.

394. And do you think—do you complain that the property be charged only at one-fourth, or the full rate, if placed under the Corporation?—I don't think that would be enough.

395. CHAIRMAN.—But supposing they paid to the Town Council the same they pay to the Grand Jury at present, the Town Council or Commissioners would be, you believe, better able to do the work?—Yes.

396. You are aware that the outside lands only pay one-fourth?—Yes.

397. If the extension were made, you would contemplate that that should be changed, and that they should pay the full amount?—Yes.

398. I suppose, Mr. Macdonnell, from your position you are able to say whether the roads are not cut up very much and injured by the country people coming in to the town?—Certainly.

399. And they cause the trouble of cleaning and repairing them to be increased?—Yes, as far as watering is concerned at least.

400. And Wexford being a shipping port, I presume the roads are largely used for carting to the country districts?—Yes.

401. In fact, the country people contribute more than the townspeople to the wear and tear of the roads?—Yes.

The inquiry then terminated.

BAGNALSTOWN.—FEBRUARY 11th, 1879.

Before Messrs. W. P. O'Brien and C. P. Cotton, C.E.

[illegible]

[illegible]

Bagenalstown. [illegible]

ings; do they provide for it a new body?—Nothing known.

57. You have nothing to do with any of the functions connected with the keeping of the town clean, or any thing of that sort?—No, sir; that is done by a committee.

58. You say the Town Commissioners are not anxious to regain the control of the sanitary affairs of the town—they prefer having them remain as they are now in the Board of Guardians?—That was their inclination when the matter was brought before them.

59. How many Commissioners were present on that occasion?—Nine.

60. How many persons are there within the municipality entitled to be elected Town Commissioners?—I could not say offhand, but I could get you the information from the books.

61. Can you not tell us, from your experience of Town Councils, in the number of electors, what the number of voters is?—I do not know.

62. The Commissioners have had under their consideration the queries as addressed to the different municipal bodies upon the various points connected with the municipal rates, &c. Did they take these queries into consideration at a special meeting?—No; at an ordinary meeting.

63. How many members were present at that meeting?—Nine.

64. Were the other members of the Board aware that the questions mentioned in the queries would be considered?—They were.

65. Your answers to these queries have not reached us here. What was your answer to query 4?—"Are the municipal bounds regarded with dissatisfaction generally by the ratepayers or by any section of them?"—That they were not; that they were satisfied with the present boundary.

66. And as regards another query—"What objections are entertained to them?"—They replied that they were not dissatisfied.

67. And as regards number eight—"What is the opinion of the municipal body on the subject?" Was it their opinion that they would be quite right—that they were satisfied with the present boundary?—Yes.

68. Bagenalstown is a considerable market town?—It is, sir.

69. Have you weekly markets here?—Yes, on Saturdays.

70. Have you fairs here?—Yes.

71. How often?—Monthly.

72. And the town is a very thriving, good, business town of its size?—Yes; it is improving in its valuation.

73. Are the lands lying immediately outside the existing boundary—say within a radius of a mile of the town—occupied by agricultural tenants?—Principally; nearly all of them.

74. If you take a circle of the radius of a mile around from the centre of the town, [illegible] it and the existing boundary is small. Many persons living there who are now entirely outside the town district, still [illegible] their municipal buildings; and there a great many inhabited dwellings there?—There are.

75. Do the occupiers of these houses and lands derive considerable advantage from being so close to a good market town such as Bagenalstown in the way of having a market for the easy sale of their produce, such as butter, eggs, poultry, and other articles of small produce—do they derive advantages from being so close to a good market?—I think considerably so.

76. Are there schools in Bagenalstown?—There are.

77. Do the children of the parishes living within the circle I have suggested come to Bagenalstown for educational purposes?—They do avail themselves of the school.

78. I presume the lands within that circle are more valuable, by reason of their close proximity to the town, than lands lying at a much greater distance in the County.

79. Do the Town Commissioners, notwithstanding the fact that these lands possess all these advantages, think it should not be desirable that the lands lying within that radius should contribute anything to the municipal taxation and expenditure of the town?—I could not answer that.

80. Who is the Chairman of the Town Commissioners?—Mr. Pierce Maguire.

81. In what year was the district so formed?—In 1854.

82. Had it been previously under an old Act—the Act of 9th George IV.?—I don't know; I think not.

83. Mr. Cotton.—Have you any description of the boundary in your books?—No.

84. No details?—No.

85. Is that the first meeting of the Commissioners in the book?—Yes, sir. (Book handed to Mr. Cotton.)

86. [illegible]—[illegible].

87. There is such a discrepancy between the [illegible] that I should like to see the boundary fixed by the Lord Lieutenant at the time of the formation of the municipality.—I daresay [illegible] you would get that.

Mr. Pierce Maguire.

Mr. Pierce Maguire examined.

88. Mr. O'Brien.—You are the Chairman of the Town Commissioners?—Yes.

89. How long have you been Chairman?—Three or four months.

90. Have you been long a member of the Town Commissioners body?—Yes.

91. For how many years?—Ten or twelve.

92. Were you present at that meeting at which the Commissioners considered the answers to the queries sent them by the Municipal Boundaries Commissioners?—I was.

93. Were all the members present unanimous in thinking it desirable that there should not be any alteration made?—They were all unanimous.

94. You concurred yourself in that opinion, I presume?—Yes.

95. You have heard the clerk state the existing distances to which the town extends to the north, to the south, to the east, and to the west?—Yes.

96. Do you not consider that outside that boundary there are lands and inhabited dwellings the occupiers of which derive considerable advantage by being so close to the town?—I have heard a good many speak to the contrary.

97. You have a good market town, and do they not dispose of their produce in your town?—Yes; they do.

98. And sell their eggs, butter, milk, and so on?—Yes; they do.

99. Therefore, must it not be of advantage to persons living within a mile of the town—to persons living so close to a town like this—to have a ready market at a small expense of time; don't you think they derive advantage from that?—I am sure they do.

100. At present they contribute nothing towards the municipal expenditure?—That is so.

101. You are aware that under the Towns Improvement Act, arable lands are only liable to be rated for municipal purposes on one-fourth of the valuation?—I am.

102. Bearing that in mind, would you consider that, within a radius of a mile, extending out equally in all directions, a fourth of the valuation would be a fair measure of contribution for lands situated within that distance—that they should pay for the municipal ex-

[illegible]

148. Don't you think that portion derives greater advantage from its position than the portion north of the railway?—I don't think it does.

150. But it has a road straight to the town, and the other has not?—Yes.

151. Surely it has not less advantage at any rate?—I don't think it has.

152. Do you know the townland of Kilcurrig?—Yes.

153. Do you know the portion that lies south of the railway?—Yes.

154. Does not that derive far greater advantage than the portion of Kiltra north of the railway?—It is closer—that is true.

155. Yes, and it is full of roads?—Yes.

Mr. Philip Newton, examined.

156. Mr. O'Brien.—You are a member of the Town Commission?—I am.

157. Have you long been a member?—Always.

158. Do you live within the municipal district?—I live outside the municipal district; but I hold a good deal of property in the town.

159. How far do you reside outside the town from where we are now sitting?—A few hundred yards outside the town; not more than 600 yards.

160. Are you not the owner of the entire town?—I am not; Mr. Regnal owns a good portion of it—about half of it.

161. Were you present at the meeting of the Commissioners when the question of the boundaries was under consideration?—I was.

162. Do you concur in the opinion expressed in the replies to the queries we sent you?—Yes.

163. That it would not be desirable to make any change in the boundaries?—I do not think it would be fair, because the great advantage which the town derives from being put under the Act is the lighting, and I consider that the people living outside would derive no benefit whatever from the lighting. Our whole rate goes for the gas almost, and I may say it is entirely a question of lighting.

164. But when the people living outside the town attend the markets and fairs, do they not derive some advantage from the lighting?—Well, the fairs are usual fairs.

165. In your opinion it would not be fair to tax the outlying land for any advantage it derives from proximity to the town, when the advantage it derives comprehends only lighting?—I think so; lighting is the only thing.

166. If your functions were larger, and provided for the paving, cleansing, watering, and sewering, you would not then consider it inequitable that persons within a reasonable distance should make some contribution to the municipal expenditure?—But we do not undertake those duties, because they would not pay at all. I think we performed the duty of the sanitary authority better than it's done now; but I think it would be too great a burden to impose on the ratepayers. The area is too small to undertake work which might cost a great deal.

167. You are aware that under the Act the sanitary expenditure is made a special charge, and can be assessed on any denomination, no matter how minute, so that the burden would be as light as it could possibly be made?—Anything that has been done in this town in the way of sanitary improvements has been assessed on the entire electoral division.

168. That was done, I presume, on the ground that the people outside the town do derive advantages?—I don't know; I suppose so; but there has not been much done in the sanitary way.

169. You do not dispute the fact that the occupier of land, living within a radius of a mile from the centre of the town, does derive advantages?—They derive no more now than when the town was put under the Towns Improvement Act, for they had a market always.

170. Do they derive any advantages as compared with lands lying at a greater distance?—Yes.

171. In repairing to the market, and in the sale of milk, butter, and other produce in such proximity to them?—Yes.

172. They use the town for schooling purposes also?—Of course they do.

173. Assuming that your functions were wider, you would not consider it inequitable that they should contribute some proportion towards the town expenditure, if you were vested with the sanitary functions, and with the other functions to which I have alluded?—I think if any of the rates that they would have to pay were devoted to any special purpose that would give them advantages, it would be fair; but as all the rates go for the purpose of lighting the town, I think it would be unfair to make them pay for that.

174. Is it not the case at present that, for all sanitary works, the expenditure is assessed on the whole electoral division?—But it has been something very slight.

175. For general purposes; you have had no special rate for sanitary works?—We have had some expenditure.

176. Is the water supply good?—There is a great abundance of water of good quality.

177. Is the sewerage of the town in a satisfactory condition?—There may be one or two sewers bad, but there is no large scheme of sewerage required.

178. Is the population of the town increasing?—Yes.

179. Do you happen to know how far the electoral division extends in each direction?—It extends a long way; it is a very large electoral division.

180. Speaking roughly, do you happen to know what the farthest point of the electoral division is?—I think about three miles.

181. I suppose you are aware that the Parliamentary Committee have expressed the opinion that, where feasible, the municipal boundary should be made coterminous with those of poor law electoral divisions—would that be desirable in this case?—I think it would be absurd. I think it would be a monstrous thing to do.

182. Is there anything else that occurs to you, or any suggestion you would desire to lay before us?—I have nothing to add. Just let us alone, that is all; and don't make any alteration in our boundary.

183. If you were made the sanitary authority, would it be conducive to your interests to have those works, now executed by the Grand Jury, within the municipal district, such as the roads, footpaths, &c., transferred to your jurisdiction?—I am afraid not.

184. You think they would be done better by the Grand Jury?—There is no complaint of the way in which they are done. The Grand Jury do not object to give anything that is reasonable.

185. You have no idea how many persons are eligible for the office of Town Commissioner at present?—I have not the slightest idea. I do not think a great many. I don't think there are more than fifteen or sixteen altogether.

186. Do not you think that rather a narrow limit out of which to select nine representatives?—I think, of course, that it is.

187. Don't you think that if the boundaries were extended, it would be of advantage, both to the constituency, and to the number of persons eligible to take office as Town Commissioners; would it not conduce to a more healthy system of municipal government?—I think when it is so difficult to get the attendance of Town Commissioners who reside within only a few yards of this place, how much more difficult will it be to get men to come who live at a distance.

188. You do not think those people are ambitious

of taking a part in municipal affairs?—I don't think so; I think the people who do the work of the Town Commissioners merely do it from a sense of duty.

152. Would the people living in the outlying districts take an interest in municipal affairs?—I am sure they would refuse to do it. Take a radius of three-quarters of a mile, and there would be scarcely one who would do it.

153. Did you take a part in the original introduction of the Act, and what was the guiding principle you kept in view?—Our object in putting the town under the provisions of the Act was merely to get it lit, and the people were brought within the area by the natural bounds of the suburbs, the river, and one road.

154. You were essentially a lighting body?—Yes; that is all.

The inquiry then terminated.

[illegible] Feb. 11, 1879. [illegible]

NEW ROSS.—FEBRUARY 10TH, 1879.

New Ross. Feb. 10, 1879.

Before Messrs. W. P. O'Brien and C. P. Cotton, C.E.

Mr. John Tobin, examined.

Mr. John Tobin.

1. You are the Town Clerk of New Ross?—Yes.

2. How long have you held your office?—For fourteen years, last October.

3. And the town is constituted under the Towns Improvement Act of 1854?—It is.

4. When was the town placed under that Act?—In September, 1858.

5. Had it been previously placed by the Commissioners under any other Act?—Yes; under the 9th of George IV.

6. How many Commissioners constitute the present municipal body?—Fifteen.

7. And is the town divided into wards?—Yes, it is divided into two wards.

8. And what are they called?—One is the New Ross ward, situated in the county Wexford, and the other is called the Rosbercon ward, and is situated in the county Kilkenny.

9. What is the area of the entire municipality, as at present constituted?—440 acres, 3 roods, and 33 perches.

10. Is that the full extent of the area, because in the return, that I received from the Valuation Office, in 1877, it is given as 456 acres; what is the valuation of the municipal district?—The gross valuation is £7,844 14s.

11. Well then, that evidently refers to the same thing, because that amount corresponds with the amount in the return given to me, so I presume there has been some waste?—Yes.

12. Was the act here adopted in its entirety or only for a special purpose?—It was adopted in its entirety, with the exception of the provisions respecting a water supply.

13. This is, I believe, an urban sanitary district?—Yes; since the Act of 1874.

14. There has been no transfer to your body of the Grand Jury powers as to the roads, bridges, footpaths, &c., in the municipal district?—No, sir; the matter was some time under consideration, but no steps have actually been taken to bring about such a transfer.

15. Are the Commissioners aware that under the Public Health Act of last Session, there is a power to transfer the jurisdiction of the Grand Jury in relation to those works, from the Grand Jury to the Urban Sanitary Authority?—They are, sir; for they instructed their borough member to support that proposition.

16. So that they are quite aware of it, but have not taken any steps to obtain such a transfer?—No.

17. Is it in contemplation to take any steps of that nature, so far as you are aware?—The question was considered from time to time, but no important steps taken.

18. The Commissioners recently received a form from the Municipal Boundaries Commissioners containing a series of queries to which replies were required from the Town Commissioners; did they not?—Yes.

19. Have you got them there?—Yes.

20. When was this taken into consideration by the Town Commissioners?—Only last week; on last Thursday night the subject was finally considered.

21. These answers were agreed to at a meeting held on Thursday night last?—Yes.

22. How many Town Commissioners were present at that meeting?—Six.

23. And were they unanimous in coming to the conclusions at which they arrived, and in the answers furnished to the queries submitted to them?—They were.

24. There are no wards for poor law purposes here?—No.

25. Are these wards situated in the same electoral divisions, or in different electoral divisions?—In different electoral divisions.

26. In what electoral division is the New Ross ward?—It is situated in the electoral division of New Ross.

27. And in what electoral division is the Rosbercon ward situated?—In the electoral division of Rosbercon.

28. I presume that neither ward comprehends the entire of either of those electoral divisions?—No.

29. Take first the New Ross Ward—the Wexford portion of the municipality—how many whole townlands and parts of townlands does that comprehend?—There are fourteen townlands, sir, and five out of that number are wholly included within the borough.

30. Can you give me the valuation of these in bulk?—The gross valuation of these is £7,533 10s.

31. And what is the area?—321a. 2r. 31p.

32. Now, take the Rosbercon Ward—how many townlands or parts of townlands are comprehended in that?—There are parts of four townlands, and not the entire of any one townland.

33. What is the central point of the town of New Ross?—The Tholsel.

34. Now, taking the Tholsel as the starting point, how far does the town extend in each direction of the municipal district?—About half a mile on an average.

35. Equally in all directions?—Very nearly.

36. Have you within the municipal boundary much property that would be brought under section 63 of the Towns Improvement Act, and only liable to be rated at the reduced scale of one fourth?

[Mr. O'Brien read section 63 of the Towns Improvement Act.]

37. Have you much property coming under that provision?—Yes.

37. What is the valuation of the property coming under those heads?—£215 18s.

38. Outside the existing boundary, and within a radius of say one English mile from the centre of the town, are there many lands which are occupied by inhabited houses?—I believe, sir, that the ground you refer to is almost as thinly inhabited as any you would find in any town in Ireland.

39. How are the lands between the existing limits and a radius of a mile, generally speaking, occupied?—I believe generally by tenants who till them.

40. Where do those tenants reside?—Some of them are townspeople.

41. Are these accommodation lands held by residents of the town?—A good part of them are.

41. Could you form an idea as to about how many inhabited houses would be found between the existing limit and a radius of an English mile, to which I have already referred?—I fear I could not answer that question.

42. Could you form an estimate as to the number—if you are not able to give me any estimate of it, say so?—I am not in a position to give you even an estimate such as you ask.

43. Are there a good many inhabited houses within the circle I have mentioned?—I believe they are rather few in number.

44. But there are some?—Yes, sir.

45. Do you consider that those lands within that distance derive exceptional advantages for their proximity to such a market town as New Ross?—Yes, I do.

46. And that accordingly their value is enhanced?—Yes.

47. I presume also that the products of those lands are disposed of at great advantage in the town of New Ross?—I believe that the lands in the proximity of the town are, far and away, higher in value.

48. Are the agricultural produce of those lands sold at an advantage in the town of New Ross?—I believe they are, sir; through the town's proximity.

49. What are the agricultural products that are brought into the town from those lands?—Corn, butter, vegetables, milk, eggs, poultry—all agricultural produce.

50. And those who dispose of those products in the town of New Ross do so at great advantage by their proximity to that town?—Half the town believe that.

51. How far would you consider that exceptional advantages are enjoyed, derived from proximity to the town?—I believe at the least a mile.

52. Do you consider that a mile fairly and fully represents about the area within which exceptional advantages are derived from the proximity of the town?—Well, I must acknowledge that I have not sufficient knowledge to give an opinion.

53. Is this town lighted with gas?—Yes.

54. Have you a water supply?—We have.

55. Was that provided in recent times or is it of long standing?—It was done progressively from time to time. In 1824 the present water tanks that supply the town were made. There have been a few little additions since.

56. Was there any large outlay in regard to the construction of sewers, or any sanitary work of that description?—There was not at any particular period, but the work was done continuously as required.

57. But no large scheme of sewerage has been carried out?—No large scheme has been carried out at any particular time.

58. Is the sewerage of the town in a satisfactory condition?—It is middling fair. There is one great defect which I believe will, in the course of some time, be very detrimental to the effectual working of the present system. Below at the river side the place appears to be silting up, and the sewers closing, and I am afraid from the level of the town there will be a great deal of matter silted up with the down currents, which will also carry up gravel and sand. There is no free outlet from the river at all, and I am afraid that in the course of some time our sewers will become much impaired in their effectiveness.

59. Mr. Cotton.—Does that apply to the outlets along the quay—does it apply the whole way or in only one particular portion of the quay?—It applies to the greater number of outlets. There might be some sewers whose outlets are full of mud, but as a general rule I am afraid the outlets will give us some trouble and expense after a time.

60. Mr. O'Brien.—I find, Mr. Tobin, your rates are returned as being, in 1878, 6d.; in 1877, 6d.; in 1876, no rate; in 1875, 1s.; and in 1874, 10d.?—Yes, sir.

61. The average taking for the five years being then here 7½d.?—Yes, sir.

62. Have you any sources of income in the municipality, except what you derive from the levying of the rates?—Yes.

63. Have you corporate property?—We have.

64. What sort of property is it—house property or land?—Some houses; but, generally, land.

65. What is the amount of the corporate property?—On an average £360 a year, less £30 allowed by rates.

66. What is the amount available?—About £330.

67. Beyond that corporate property, have you any other source of income to supplement the rates?—There is the pipe-water, averaging about £30 a year, for water conveyed from the tanks I have already mentioned.

68. Is that for domestic use?—Yes, sir; for pipe-water rent, but not as rate.

69. About £30 a year?—Yes.

70. That is £360 between those two sources?—Yes.

71. Is there any other source?—Yes, the sale of manure.

72. You collect the manure and sell it?—Yes.

73. And what does that realize on an average?—About £70.

74. What profits have you on the manure?—I do not think there is any profit from the sale of the manure.

75. Have you any other source of income?—Yes; there are the rents from the Town Hall, the occasional letting of a large room below stairs for entertainments, &c.—that averages about £8 a year.

76. Is there any other source?—Then there is the dog tax; we get from the Government about £20.

77. Is there any other source of income?—There are the fines under the Towns Improvement Act, and under the Drunkenness Act.

78. What do they yield?—On last year's audit they came to £40.

79. Is there any other source of income that you possess, but have not mentioned?—The only other source of income I see is the contribution towards the salaries of the sanitary officials, the half salaries.

80. As a grant from the Government?—Yes, "half salaries, £34 6s. 6d."

81. What was your total income for the past year?—£828 1s.

82. How much was made up from rates?—£141.

83. And the rest from other sources?—Yes, from the miscellaneous sources I have mentioned.

84. What was the expenditure for the year?—The expenditure was £780 6s. 6d. for the past year.

85. Did that give you a credit balance at the end of the year?—It did, sir; it gave us a credit balance of £47 13s. 6d.

86. Did that expenditure fully represent the requirements of the town, or was any work left unexecuted in consequence of its not being considered that the funds were sufficient for the purpose?—Not that I can recollect at present.

87. Did that income fully provide for the wants of the town?—It did, for the past year. There might be some things which I could not recollect, and as to which it might be safer to take the average of former years.

88. In reply to the question in the queries as to whether the municipal boundary is regarded with dissatisfaction by the ratepayers of the town, or any section of them—the Commissioners' reply is to this effect—"So far as we can learn the subject has not engrossed the attention of the ratepayers." Then it appears that the matter has not been very particularly considered by the town?—It was late when it came before the Town Commissioners. This is a copy of a report which I sent to Dublin, as soon as I could, and which embraces the opinions of the Commissioners as to why they are not prepared with evidence to-day.

89. In number eight of the queries, they are asked

—"What is the opinion of the municipal body on the subject?" and in reply to that they say: "We beg to submit for the information of the Municipal Boundary Commissioners the report of the Committee who investigated the subject." That is the report now before you?—Yes.

90. Was it adopted by the Commissioners?—It was, sir.

91. Kindly read that report for me?—I will, sir. The report is as follows:—

"Municipal Boundaries Commission.

"Report of the Committee appointed to consider the question of curtailing, limiting, or extending the present boundary of the borough.

"Regretting that the time at our command has not permitted us to give the question adequate consideration. It appears that in November last, the Municipal Boundaries Commissioners issued for the guidance of witnesses of [illegible] and boroughs [illegible] a sheet of numbered queries, [illegible] copy to the town clerk, [illegible] and that the copy now before you came to hand only a few days since; so that, not having had earlier notice, we [illegible] detailed information on the various branches of the inquiry.

"Without anticipating the views of the ratepayers on the subject generally, it [illegible], we think, be admitted that the area of the borough is [illegible] the smallest possible [illegible], and that an extension of the boundary would be desirable, as [illegible] the importance and influence of the borough, and affording increased scope for the exercise of the powers vested in the Town Commissioners. Still, we regret that, for the following reasons, we cannot recommend you to apply for an extension.

"1. Because the subject has not engaged the attention of the ratepayers.

"2. Those persons outside the borough, who enjoy the advantages derivable from proximity to the town, markets, &c., without contributing to its taxation, and who might be affected by an extension of the existing boundary, have not had an opportunity of expressing their opinions on the matter.

"3. Taking the difference between the present area and a larger one, for instance, that of the New Ross Poor Law [illegible] on this side of the river and counting [illegible] [illegible] one-fourth rate, the amount payable on the added [illegible] would not be more than £[illegible]. An enlargement of the area would necessarily involve an addition to the working staff, and increased expenditure under the several heads of the lighting, cleansing, and sanitary purposes. An extension of the other side of the river would not materially affect our calculations, and, on the whole, we do not consider that the increased income would meet these considerations the increased expenditure. We may remark, that this present state would [illegible] the Commissioners from undertaking new responsibilities, and an enlarged sphere of usefulness, when other circumstances favourable; but, from the information now available, we can, merely recommend to your body, while giving no approval to the present boundary, to lay the facts as set forth in the query sheet before the Government Commissioners, without adopting active measures for obtaining an altered boundary.

"New Ross, Feb. 6th, 1879.

"P. A. Pope.
"David Murphy.
"Patrick Kelly."

92. How many persons are there within the municipal district, who are qualified to fill the office of Town Commissioner?—There are 60 persons that the buildings they reside in would qualify them, but I believe that half the number would not be available as candidates.

93. But if an extension to a radius of a mile took place, would not that extend both the number of electors and of the persons who would be qualified to act as Town Commissioners?—It would increase the number of persons eligible to be elected Commissioners, in all probability more than it would extend the number of electors.

94. Are there suburbs to the town of New Ross that are connected by the continuation of [illegible], in the adjoining districts?—Yes, sir, there are.

95. Within what distance would you say the [illegible] are on the [illegible] from the [illegible]?—[illegible] I should say about a mile.

96. Do they occur in as large numbers?—I should not be able to say that, sir; it would depend upon the proximity or otherwise of [illegible] residents.

97. Is the electoral division of [illegible] and New Ross pretty equally in all directions from the town, or is it in an unequal [illegible]?—I believe it extends pretty equally in all directions.

98. You say that the Commissioners have not made [illegible] the question of applying to [illegible] to themselves of the jurisdiction over roads, bridges, &c.?—I [illegible] in any way—yes, sir.

99. The county rates for the last five years stand thus—£[illegible]. for 1875?—Yes, sir.

100. [illegible] for 1876; [illegible] for 1877; [illegible] for 1878; and [illegible] for 1879?—Yes.

101. Each [illegible] bridge rate?—Yes.

102. What is the poundage for the bridge rate?—[illegible] the rate [illegible].

103. The Commissioners were considering this question [illegible] the subject of applying for the transfer of the Grand Jury functions over the roads, bridges, and footpaths within the town; did they [illegible], in considering the question, that they could claim [illegible] if they got the transfer, to be raised at one-fourth only, or did they intend that the rate should be at same as the whole valuation as for the county rate?—I do not think they have considered that point particularly; the chief point they considered was this—that though they applied for, sake of utility, repairs of roads, &c., they were met by a vexatious and unnecessary opposition; and they thought it would be for the advantage and [illegible] of the town to have those matters under their own control.

104. How long have the Commissioners considered this matter?—About three years.

105. Are they aware that under the Public Health Act of last session the Local Government Board have power to [illegible] them such a transfer [illegible] [illegible] [illegible] though the Grand Jury may not consent to it?—They are; [illegible] and they have [illegible] their [illegible] to suggest that legal provision.

106. Can you explain why it is then, that being the feeling of the Commissioners, no practical steps have been taken to carry out the object they have in view?—I could not say.

107. Mr. Cronin.—Is the boundary of the town the same as the Parliamentary boundary?—Yes, they are coterminous.

108. I don't think you gave us the areas of the wards separately?—The New Ross Ward is 323a. 3r. 21p., and the Rosbercon Ward 112a. 0r. 12p.

109. Making a total of—436a. 0r. 33p.

110. Mr. O'Brien.—Now give us the valuation?—The gross valuation of the New Ross Ward is £7,753 10s., and of the Rosbercon Ward £[illegible] 5s.—making a total of £[illegible] 15s.

Mr. James E. Galavan examined.

111. You are Chairman of the Town Commissioners of New Ross?—Yes.

112. How long have you held that position?—Since last June.

113. Have you considered this question with sufficient [illegible] to enable you to form a definite opinion on it?—I would not at present, at all events.

114. The Clerk of the Town Commissioners has intimated that the radius of the present municipal boundary is about half a statute mile from the centre of the town. Is that about correct?—I think in an easterly direction it extends nearly a mile. In the southerly and westerly directions—

115. Take it from the four points, and state the

X 2

New Ross. Feb. 18, 1879. — Mr. James E. Galgey.

extent to which the municipal boundary reaches in each. Taking the Tholsel as the centre of the town, how far does it extend to the north?—About half a mile.

116. How far to the south?—Half a mile.

117. To the east?—More than half a mile.

118. How far then?—Nearly a mile—about three quarters of a mile.

119. Taking that to represent the existing area, from your knowledge of the surrounding district and of the lands outside that area, are there many inhabited houses and lands occupied by inhabited houses that are within a radius of a mile, that are not included within the present municipal district?—There are, a great many.

120. Would you say that the property that lies between the radius of half a mile and the radius of a mile—would you say that that property derives advantages in various respects by reason of the proximity of the town of New Ross?—Most decidedly, in every respect.

121. Would you mention the advantages which it derives in your opinion?—Having such an advantageous market for the sale of its products—eggs, butter, milk, vegetables, and so forth.

122. Do the children from that district resort to the town of New Ross for schooling purposes?—A great many within a mile of the town.

123. Would you say that a mile represents the distance from which children do come into the town for the purpose of availing themselves of the schooling accommodation which it affords?—I do, more than a mile.

124. How often do the occupiers of those outlying lands resort here to your weekly markets?—There is a Saturday market, and then in the busier season there is a Tuesday market in addition; of course there are several market days in the corn season.

125. You have got a good water supply?—Very fair, of course it is defective at times.

126. And the town is lighted with gas?—Yes, it is.

127. And are the footways flagged and well kept?—Yes, the streets are well flagged; certainly.

128. Those who resort frequently to the town participate more or less in the advantages it affords?—Certainly.

129. Of course they do not derive the same measure of advantage as the people actually living in the town?—Of course they do not.

130. Do you consider that the advantages derived by the townlands in the proximity of the town, but not strictly within the present area, are fairly enough, measured by that provision of the 62nd section of the Towns Improvement Act which makes them liable to be rated at one-fourth of the valuation—would you take that as fairly representing the amount of contribution which they should give towards the expenditure?—That would be a very serious question to answer.

131. I am merely asking your own estimate. Of course, it would be very hard to say positively; but viewing the proposal for an increased area of taxation, and taking it on the principle of equity and sound public policy, would you consider the basis the legislature adopted in the Towns Improvement Act, making arable lands and property of that description only liable to be assessed for municipal purposes at one-fourth—would it appear to be a fair enough measure of the advantages they derive?—I could not say.

132. You would not say whether it was too much or too little to contribute, but you do think that persons living within a mile of the town do derive advantages although they contribute nothing towards the town expenditure?—Unquestionable advantages.

133. Would you consider that it would be fair that they should contribute something towards the town expenditure?—I think they should contribute something at all events.

134. Would you consider the radius of a mile a fair one, and that those exceptional advantages do not extend beyond that, or would you propose a still wider radius than a mile?—I would not.

135. You think that a mile would fairly enough represent the extent to which the exceptional advantages are enjoyed?—I think a mile fair, because if you go beyond that they become less and less.

136. You have not any means of knowing whether the proposed extension of the municipal area would be received with favour by the ratepayers, or whether they would be opposed to it?—I have not any means of knowing.

137. There has been no meeting on their part to consider the question?—No, it has not engaged their attention.

138. It appears that the queries sent by us to you, to get information from you on various points relating to this inquiry, did not reach you?—They did not reach me; I never knew anything about this inquiry until Thursday last.

139. I asked the Town Clerk one or two questions bearing on the subject of the transferring of a certain jurisdiction from the county to the municipal body. has not the subject specially engaged the consideration and attention of the Town Commissioners—that of seeking to obtain a transfer of those powers?—Not as far as I know.

140. Are they satisfied, and do you believe it is the opinion of the Town Commissioners that the amount expended by the Grand Jury on the municipal district corresponds with the amount levied off you in county cess?—Not at all, we contribute £300 or £400 and only get in return about £200, and then the Commissioners have to run by contracts and otherwise.

141. Then you are not satisfied with the amount you get, and you do not consider that it is a fair return for the county cess?—We do not consider it is a fair return.

142. Assuming that you were to-morrow to seek, and successfully seek, to obtain this transfer, and get the control now exercised by the Grand Jury over the roads, bridges, and footpaths, do you consider that the equity of the case would be that in the case of arable lands, and so forth, they should contribute the full amount, as they do now to the Grand Jury, or be only rated one-fourth for municipal purposes?—I could not say.

143. You are not in a position to say?—Quite so; in fact I never heard that part of the subject until this morning.

144. Would the Town Commissioners like to give this entire subject of the municipal boundaries, and the arrangements to be made in connexion with any extension of them, or a transfer of the Grand Jury powers, further consideration, and would they desire to transmit to the Municipal Boundaries Commissioners in Dublin their views with regard to these matters in writing?—As far as I know, I believe they would wish that the subject could be opened again, and that they could give it further consideration.

145. And if I inform you that the Boundary Commissioners will be most happy to receive and consider any statement which you forward to them, may we expect that you will do so?—I think that will meet the views of the Commissioners.

146. Perhaps you will be good enough, in considering this question, to take into consideration also this other question; whether you will seek to obtain a provisional order transferring to the Commissioners the Grand Jury jurisdiction, and if so, upon what basis you think the transfer should be made; whether you think that if that transfer were made, arable lands which are now only liable to one-fourth for the municipal expenditure—that whether those lands, with regard to the expenditure on county works, should be assessed to the full value as now, or come in at the reduced scale, as they do for other purposes, because that is a material point. You are aware that a good many towns have obtained the transfer, but that Wexford is the only one that has obtained it by provisional order,

and in the other towns where that transfer has been obtained, it has been by special Act of Parliament; the practice is not the same in all these towns; in some the Grand Jury works are provided for on the full assessment, and in some the arable lands are only charged a fourth of that;—It will be a question that it would be well that you should keep in mind when you come to consider the subject.—We shall take care and keep those points in view when we consider the questions you have referred to.

New Ross, Feb. 10, 1880. Mr. Joseph R. Graves.

Mr. Thomas Boyd, examined.

Mr. Thomas Boyd.

147. You have been a long time residing in New Ross?—I have.

148. Are you well acquainted with the town and its circumstances?—Yes, I am.

149. You know the existing municipal district?—Oh, well; and I am agent for the principal proprietor here.

150. You are agent for Mr. Tottenham?—Yes.

152. From your knowledge of the town, do you consider that the existing area is too limited, or do you consider that it is large enough?—I would be rather inclined to leave it as it is.

153. On what ground?—Because I think it is quite large enough. I do not see what advantage could be gained by any change.

154. I suppose we may take it as correct, that the radius is half-a-mile?—Yes.

155. Taking it in that, do you consider that the lands lying within a radius of a mile do not derive special advantages by reason of that proximity?—I do not think they do, commensurate with the valuation.

156. Do you not think that those lands [illegible] for the owners a higher rent by reason of that proximity?—Of course they do, they would do that under any circumstances, in consequence of their proximity to the town.

157. Have not the occupiers of those lands, too, an advantage in having up close to their doors a market for their various agricultural products. Would not advantages, special advantages, be derived by persons residing at one, two, or three miles?—Of course the closer to the market the better.

158. Don't you consider that enjoying those advantages, that by resorting so frequently to the town, that persons who make it the place for the transaction of their business, and the sale of their products—do you think it would be unreasonable as a return for those advantages, that they should in some modified form contribute towards the general expenditure of the town?—I think that would be a very hard thing to do. I do not think they derive anything from the lighting.

159. Are not the persons who live outside, when they come into the town for the transaction of their business and the sale of their produce, and to supply their own wants here, are they not often delayed here until an advanced hour of the evening, and do they not in that way derive benefit from the lighting?—They may be delayed, but they should not be delayed. The same observation might be applied to any person going into a town, stopping for a few hours on any occasion.

160. What I am asking you is—is it not a fact that persons living within a mile of the town much more frequently resort to it, those persons having it as a greater [illegible]?—That may be; but I do not think there would be the slightest advantage, commensurate with the taxation, in persons being taxed, because of their being close to the town.

161. Have you contemplated what the taxation of such land should be, supposing it was comprehended with the municipal area?—One-fourth, and the same as [illegible].

162. Have you considered the question of the desirableness or otherwise of the town body getting control over the works executed by the Grand Jury?—I have not, but I think there is a good deal of just complaint on the part of the Commissioners that they do not get enough of the county cess.

163. Do you think that if the jurisdiction was transferred to the municipal body that the work would be better executed and at a cheaper cost?—I am not prepared to say. That might involve a considerable outlay in the way of an extra staff, and so on.

164. Now, if that transfer did take place, do you consider that, for the purposes now provided for out of the county cess, arable lands should be rated for the municipal expenditure at the full amount, or at one-fourth of the full amount?—I would not have any hesitation in saying that.

165. Do you think they would object if they were to be charged to the full amount for Grand Jury purposes, and only one-fourth for municipal purposes?—I do think they would.

166. But would they not become eligible to serve as Town Commissioners?—They would not consider that an advantage. It is very hard to get the body filled up, even as it is.

167. Would not they consider it an advantage to become entitled to vote for Town Commissioners?—I do not think they would. I think a great many would be glad to be without votes.

168. The Boundary Commissioners will be glad if, when you have time, you will understand from the [illegible] what the points are upon which we desire information, if you will be good enough to forward to our secretary a statement of any facts or views which you think ought to be presented for our consideration. I shall be very happy to receive and investigate such a statement from you?—I shall consider your suggestion.

169. Mr. Graves.—How long since the bridge was [illegible]?—About eighteen years from the time it first started. I think we have paid to the toll nineteen years. It will close now in a comparatively short time; but I cannot pledge myself as to the perfect accuracy of any of my statements to-day.

170. Mr. O'Brien.—You had previously to pay a toll every time you crossed that bridge?

171. And without any permanent outlay you get rid of that toll, at all events?—Yes; the exact time the tax has to run can be easily ascertained. I would not like to be bound by any opinion I have expressed to you, for I might change them all.

Mr. Peter Aloysius Furr, examined.

Mr. Peter A. Furr.

172. You are one of the Town Commissioners of New Ross?—I am, but only a very short time. I am the junior member of the Board.

173. You are well acquainted with the town?—I am.

174. You know the municipal boundary?—Yes.

175. What is your opinion about that—is it that the boundaries are large enough, or do you think that the boundaries should be extended?—I think, speaking generally, that the municipal area is rather too limited.

176. Do you think, as the municipal district is at present determined, that lands are excluded which derive advantages from the proximity to a town to which they contribute nothing?—In my opinion they do, but I have not heard anything said about it.

177. Do you think it just, equitable and fair that

they should give their contribution, in return for those advantages?—I think it would be most equitable.

177. What do you consider should, in the contribution, they should make for those advantages—do you think it is fairly enough measured by the limit laid down in the Clauses of the Town Improvement Act, that would limit should contribute one-third of the valuation?—Well, in the immediate vicinity of the town, I think that is a rather small contribution. If there could be a graduated scale I think it would be made more desirable.

178. What would you recommend?—I think that within a radius of a mile they should pay one-half. Of course they have the advantage of the proximity of the market.

179. Have you considered the question of the transfer of the county jurisdiction for county works to the municipal authority?—Generally. I have considered it generally here on any other person.

180. Is your opinion favourable to making a transfer, or are you anxious in the making of such a change?—There are some points which the Commissioners feel some doubt about, as also do the ratepayers generally, and that is as to the liabilities. Of course we do not know what our responsibilities would be as regards the bridge. It was a very costly work, and if anything happened to it, and New Ross was constituted a borough by this proceeding, we do not know what liabilities might be incurred by it. We therefore do not know whether it would be of advantage that the transfer should take place or not.

182. If that point about your liability for the bridge in case of accident was settled to your satisfaction, would your opinion be favourable to the transfer?—It would be favourable.

183. You think the work would be better done, and at a cheaper rate if that change was effected?—Well, we pay £800 or £900, and only get in return £200, for which we have to take contracts.

184. In advocating the transfer do you contemplate that those arable lands for county works should pay on the full amount of the valuation or only one-fourth?—I think they should pay as at present.

185. On the full amount?—Certainly.

186. Is there any other suggestion you would wish to make?—I wish to add that if those who are at present outside the boundary, would be affected injuriously under the Land Act, by being included within the boundary, we would not enter into the question at all.

Mr. Galavan, re-examined.

188. You have heard what Mr Pope has just said as to the Land Act—are your views the same as his on that point?—Yes.

189. And are those the views of the whole body of Town Commissioners?—I think so.

Mr. [illegible] Clark, examined.

190. You are the Clerk of the New Ross Union?—Yes.

191. Taking the radius of the New Ross Electoral Division, how many townlands does it comprise?—Thirty-nine.

192. What is the area of it, and what is the valuation of it?—The area of it is 4,[illegible] acres 3 roods and 4 perches.

193. And what is the valuation of that?—£13,[illegible].

194. Now take the Rosbercon Electoral Division—how many townlands are in that division?—The valuation is £5,[illegible].

195. And what is the area?—I cannot tell you that now, as I have not the book here; but I will send you the information as to that.

196. Do the two electoral divisions extend pretty equally in all directions?—They extend pretty equally.

197. Taking the centre of the town as the starting point—how far does the Electoral Division of New Ross extend in each direction?—About a mile and a half, as nearly as possible.

198. How far does the Rosbercon Division extend from the centre of the town in each direction?—About the same distance. It is nearly a circle.

199. Would you consider that it would be practicable to adopt the electoral division boundaries of New Ross and Rosbercon as the municipal boundary?—I think there would be nothing fairer.

200. You think the advantages derived from the proximity of the town extend as far as those boundaries—you would not think they would go too far?—I would not think it would go too far; I would only object on the Rosbercon side.

201. You think it would go too far on that side?—I do.

202. Do you think those advantages extend too far on the Wexford side?—I do not.

203. Do you think the people would object to be included within the municipal district?—I dare say they would object.

204. Do you think those advantages are the whole of the electoral division of New Ross?—I do.

205. And that the inhabitants derive exceptional advantages from their proximity to the town?—Yes, I am the farthest myself, and I think that therefore I should be in a position to speak of the advantages they derive.

206. You don't think it would be acceptable that they would be included?—I don't think so.

207. If the whole of the electoral division of New Ross were included, would it be necessary to bring in the other electoral division?—Decidedly not. No.

208. Then, on the other side, the Electoral Division would extend too far—but did I not understand you to say that they extend pretty equally?—Yes, but the people have not the same advantages as those on the other side. The people in this case are very poor, and besides the ground is hilly on the Rosbercon side.

209. You don't think that the advantages are enjoyed to the same extent, then, on the Kilkenny side as they are on the Wexford side?—Yes.

210. At the Rosbercon side what distance would you consider it equitable that the boundary should extend?—I think about half a mile would be quite enough.

211. You think an extension of an equal character would be fair for the people on the Rosbercon side?—Certainly not.

212. The people living on that side are a very poor class of people?—Yes, and they do not derive the advantages which the people on the other side possess.

213. Do they only sell their produce?—Most decidedly, they sell all they have to dispose of.

214. And therefore don't they derive advantages from the proximity of the town?—But the advantages they derive are very small.

215. You don't think the advantages on the Kilkenny side are all the same as those on the Wexford side?—That is my opinion.

216. Do you concur with the view of the Parliamentary Commissioners that, as far as possible, poor law and municipal boundaries should be made conterminous?—If you extend the boundary at all, you should extend it to the whole electoral division, or not do it at all.

217. On the Kilkenny side you would draw a line about half a mile from the centre of the town—in that you would adhere to the existing boundary without making any alteration at all?—Yes.

218. Is there any suggestion you would make as to the municipal boundary?—I would say that if you

extend the boundaries at all you should extend it to the whole division.

219. Have the Board of Guardians considered the question?—They have never considered it.

220. Do you consider that the outsiders would be opposed to the extension of the boundary?—Of course they would not like it, but I have been speaking to a good many, and they do not seem to care whether the extension is made or not.

221. Don't you think that, in addition to having the municipal vote, they would like to have the power of becoming members of the Town Commission?—I don't think they would care much about that. Most of them would like to have a Parliamentary vote in the borough, but they would not walk across the street for the municipal vote.

New Ross. [illegible]

Mr. [illegible]

Mr. Patrick Kenny, examined.

Mr. [illegible]

222. You are a Town Commissioner?—I am.

223. For how long?—About fifteen or sixteen years.

224. Were you present at the meeting when the question of the municipal boundaries was considered?—I was.

225. And your name is amongst the signatures to the report that has already been referred to?—Yes.

226. And you concur, I presume, in the views expressed by the Chairman and Mr. Kenny?—I do.

227. You have not been able to give the subject as much consideration as you would like?—Not as much as one would wish.

228. And you would desire to consider it at a future time?—Yes.

229. Speaking generally, does it appear to you that the present boundary is too limited?—Well, yes, I would consider that the present boundary is too limited.

230. Don't you consider that a great many of the persons occupying houses and lands outside the municipal district, as at present constituted, derive a great deal of advantage from the proximity of the town?—Certainly.

231. And you don't think it would be inequitable that they should be made to contribute towards the town expenditure for those advantages?—Yes; one-fourth, I think.

232. Do you think that one-fourth would be a fair basis?—It would be, in my opinion, scarcely enough.

233. Supposing there was a change in the law, would you advocate an increase in the amount of their contribution?—Yes, I think it should be about half [illegible] a mile or limit.

234. How far would you consider that the boundary should be extended so as to bring in the lands deriving exceptional advantages, would you consider that a mile would be a fair average to extend it to?—Yes, I would.

235. Mr. [illegible] thinks that the whole of the electoral division derives these advantages. Do you think that the electoral division of New Ross might be fairly taken into the municipal boundary?—It would do for a boundary [illegible], but [illegible] going so far.

236. Do you think the advantages arising from the proximity of the town are really enjoyed over the whole of the electoral division?—I do not think they are.

237. You think that the electoral division would go too far?—Yes, I think so.

238. What radius would it seem to you would be a fair one?—I think about a mile would be sufficient.

239. Would you go a mile on each side of the river, or would you take it from one side more than the other?—I would take a mile all round.

240. Did you ever give any consideration to the question of making the transfer of the Grand Jury control over the roads, bridges, and footpaths?—It was only when considered in this body.

241. And are you in favour of seeing that transfer?—I am.

242. Assuming it was effected, would you consider that arable lands included within the district should be charged the full rate for these works or that they should only pay a fourth?—I think they should be charged the full rate for county cess.

243. There should be no distinction made on arable lands?—No.

244. Is there anything else you would like to add to your evidence?—Nothing.

Mr. David Murphy examined.

Mr. David Murphy.

245. You are a Town Commissioner?—I am, sir.

246. Were you present at the meeting when the Commissioners considered the question of the municipal boundaries lately?—I was.

247. Are you of opinion that the existing boundary is too limited, or do you consider that it is large enough?—I am of opinion that it should be larger.

248. It has been given to us in evidence that the existing radius is about half a statute mile, and do you consider that the advantages derivable from the proximity of the town extend a good deal beyond that?—I do.

249. How far do you think these advantages extend?—I would go nearly an English mile from the centre of the town.

250. You think that taking in a statute mile would be fair?—Yes.

251. You are aware that under the Towns Improvement Act arable lands within the municipal district are only liable to be rated on a quarter of the valuation. Do you think that that is a fair basis?—I think not. I think it should be more.

252. How much more would you say?—I think it should be about half.

253. Have you ever considered the question of making a transfer of the Grand Jury control over roads, bridges, and footpaths in the municipal district?—I have not given it much consideration as yet.

254. Have you formed any opinion on the subject?—Yes.

255. Do you consider that in the town you get a fair value and a fair return for the amount you pay for Grand Jury cess?—I do not.

256. Do you think you pay more than you get value for?—I do.

257. And you think that if it was in the hands of the Town Commissioners you would do the work better and on better terms?—That is my belief.

258. Assuming that you were to get control over the roads, bridges, footpaths, &c., transferred to you, would you consider that the arable lands should pay for Grand Jury purposes on the full amount of the valuation, or only one-fourth?—I think for Grand Jury purposes they should pay the full amount—just as they do now.

ATHY—FEBRUARY 19TH, 1879.

Before Mr. W. P. O'Brien.

John Glover examined.

1. You are Clerk of the Town Commissioners of Athy?—Yes.

2. How long have you been so?—About four years.

3. The town of Athy is constituted under the Towns Improvement Act of 1854?—Yes.

4. And it was placed under that Act in 1856?—Yes.

5. It had previously been several years under the 9th of George IV.?—I believe so.

6. Have you a copy of the boundaries as defined when the Towns Improvement Act was adopted?—Yes.

["Commencing on the bank of the river Barrow at the boundary between the townlands of Townparks and Cardington Demesne; (1) thence westward along the river Barrow to the northern boundary of James Anthony's holding in the townland of [illegible]; (2) thence north-east along said boundary to the [illegible] road; (3) thence southward along said road to the northern boundary of the townland of [illegible]; (4) thence eastward along said boundary to the eastern angle of the townland of [illegible]; (5) thence eastward, southward, and eastward, along the boundary between the holding of James Anthony, in the townland of Tonard, and the holdings of Patrick Cummins and John Peppard to the same townland by the Carlow Railway; (6) thence eastward along the old road between the holdings of Thomas Peppard and John Peppard, and southward along the boundary between John Peppard's holding and Patrick Cummins' field on the stream, which is the boundary between the townlands of Tonard and [illegible]; (7) thence southward along said boundary stream, and along the eastern boundary of the townland of [illegible] to the Kildare-road; (8) and along the boundary between Townparks and [illegible] to the Dublin-road; (9) thence westward along said road about 80 yards, and southward along the eastern boundary of Patrick Murphy's holding to a [illegible], about 350 yards from the Dublin road; (10) thence southward across Patrick Murphy's field in a straight line to the east end of his [illegible] house at the boundary of [illegible]; (11) thence southward by [illegible] through [illegible] to the boundary of [illegible] West; (12) thence westward along the southern boundary of Chanterlands, across the Carlow Railway to an old by-road; (13) thence southward along said road about 170 yards; (14) thence westward along the boundary between the fields of Mark Cross and Andrew Malone in the townland of [illegible] to the northern boundary of the townland of [illegible]; (15) thence westward along said boundary to the Carlow road; (16) thence southward along said road about 220 yards; (17) thence westward along the southern boundary of John Lamb[illegible] [illegible], crossing the canal to the river Barrow; (18) thence southward along said river to the boundary of the townland of [illegible]; (19) thence southward and westward along the boundary between the townlands of [illegible], Woods, and [illegible]; (20) thence westward along said road to the northern boundary of the townland of [illegible]; (21) thence westward along said boundary to the western boundary of [illegible] holding in the said townland; (22) thence southward along said boundary to the Kilkenny road; (23) thence in a north-west direction in a straight line to a point in the boundary between the holdings of the Rev. Leo [illegible] and Patrick [illegible] in the townland of Woodstock South, about 40 yards north of the Kilkenny road; (24) thence northward along the eastern boundary of the Rev. Leo [illegible]'s holding to the southern boundary of John [illegible]'s holding; (25) thence eastward along said boundary about 6 yards, and northward along a continuous line of fences through the holdings of John [illegible] and Patrick Cummins, and across [illegible] through Henry [illegible]'s holding to the road between the townlands of Woodstock North and Woodstock South; (26) thence eastward along said road to the Grand Canal; (27) thence northward along the canal to the northern boundary of Townparks at the fever hospital; (28) thence eastward along said boundary to the river Barrow at the point first described."]

7. What is the area of the present municipal district of Athy?—379 acres, 2 roods, 18 perches.

8. What is the valuation?—£1,063 10s. is the value of the land.

9. What is the total valuation?—£4,760 10s.

10. In the return from the Valuation Office it is given as £5,392. Was there any reduction made in the valuation; did any property disappear?—There was a lot of old houses fell down and new ones built.

11. Has the valuation reduced within the last couple of years?—I believe it has.

12. What have been your rates?—We have had no rate for the last four years.

13. £4,760 is the total valuation. You are clear as to that?—I am.

14. The boundaries of the municipal district are at present as they were set forth in the notice published at the time the Act was adopted?—Yes.

15. And those boundaries were adopted without alteration?—Yes, sir.

16. How many townlands or parts of townlands are comprehended within the municipal district?—I would not distinguish which are wholly within it and which partly only.

17. How many townlands altogether are there included within the municipal boundary?—Nineteen.

18. There are nineteen townlands either wholly or in part within the municipal district?—Yes, wholly or partly.

19. How many are within the municipal district wholly, and how many in part within it?—I don't know.

20. In what electoral division are those nineteen townlands situated?—In the electoral division of Athy.

21. What is taken as the centre of the town of Athy?—The market square is the centre.

22. How far does the municipal district extend in each direction, taking the market square as the centre of the town?—I think about half a mile in each direction.

23. Does the municipal district extend pretty equally in each direction from the centre of the town?—I think it does.

24. And you take the extent of the municipal area to be about half a mile in each direction?—I think about a half a mile.

25. When you say in each direction, you mean east and west, but not north and south?—I think it extends in each direction about half a mile, as far as I am able to judge.

26. Does the municipal boundary include much arable lands that are rated at only one-fourth?—The value of the land inside the municipal area is £1,063.

27. That is taking the land as valued at one-fourth?—Yes, sir, at one-fourth the valuation.

28. Has the Act been adopted in Athy for all purposes, or for limited purposes only?—All purposes.

29. Including the supply of water?—That was taken from us, owing to our not having a large enough population.

30. You are not the sanitary authority now?—No; because our population is only about 4,700.

31. And you are merged in the Board of Guardians as the Sanitary Authority for the district?—Yes.

32. Do you know have the town Commissioners of Athy had under consideration the question whether it would be desirable to extend, limit, or otherwise alter the existing boundaries of the township?—They had the matter under consideration, but I can't speak of that; the Chairman can.

33. The Chairman will be able to explain that matter better than you can?—Yes, sir.

33. But they had the question under consideration?—Yes.

34. And was the matter discussed at a meeting of the Commissioners specially convened for that purpose?—Yes.

35. When was that meeting held?—It was held last Monday.

36. How many Commissioners were present?—I don't know, I was not present and I can't say.

37. How many members constitute the board?—Five members form a quorum.

38. And how many Commissioners are there on the board altogether?—There are fifteen members.

39. There were no answers returned to our queries by the Commissioners?—No.

40. Why were the questions not answered; was there any special reason for not answering?—At the meetings when the matter was brought before them, the Commissioners said they did not care to have any alteration in the boundaries.

41. Are the Commissioners aware that there is a provision in the Public Health Act of last session enabling the Town Commissioners of any town to apply to the Local Government Board for a provisional order to transfer the Sanitary jurisdiction from the Board of Guardians to themselves?—I believe the Commissioners are aware of that provision of the Act to which you refer.

42. Have they had under consideration the feasibility of availing themselves of that provision?—To the best of my knowledge they have.

43. What was the result of their consideration?—They did not care to have it.

44. They did not care to take any action upon it?—No.

Athy, July 13, 1875. John Glover.

Mr. Edward Lord examined.

Mr. Edward Lord.

45. You are Chairman of the Town Commissioners of Athy?—Yes.

46. Have you been long a member of the municipal body?—Three years.

47. Have you been chairman all that time?—No; this is my second year as chairman.

48. Did you preside at the special meeting held to consider the question?—Yes, having heard that you would be here, I convened a special meeting to consider the question on Monday last.

49. How many of the Commissioners were present at that meeting?—I think seven or eight Commissioners.

50. Were they unanimous in the view they took of the matter?—No; having informed them what the meeting was for, a brother commissioner, Mr. Lawler, who is very much interested in the town because he has property in it, urged on the meeting strongly the necessity and the great advantage of extending the area, that their taxes would be more equally divided. It is true we have had no rate struck for several years, but in the event of having to strike a rate it would be very hard on the town particularly, as the town is improving, and the area is very small considering the extent of the town itself. If you look at the map you will find that the boundary only goes round the town itself, and doesn't go outside it, so as to bring in those who live around it.

51. There is only a very small portion of rural territory included within the municipal boundary?—Very little, and Mr. Lawler urged these things, and on the other side it was equally urged by a gentleman who has a large interest in the town, and property in it, that is Mr. Duncan. He was against extension of the boundary, and he put forward what was the advantage to be gained by the change. Resolutions were about to be proposed and seconded, and I suggested, as chairman, that each party interested who wished to give their views should attend here today and give their views to you, instead of passing any resolution, as the Board was not unanimous, and they adopted the suggestion of the chairman, and hence we are here to give all the information we can.

52. Are there any sources of income possessed by the municipal body of Athy besides rates?—Yes; we have one court, provided over by Mr. Lawler.

53. What does that produce?—It varies very much, but the Town Clerk could tell the amount exactly.

John Glover, Town Clerk, recalled.

John Glover.

54. Would you have the kindness to tell me what are the sources of income of the Town Commissioners of Athy?—I have them here. They are tolls at public scales for the past year ending 1st May, 1875, £132 11s. Dogs licence duty, £13 5s. 1d. Fines in Town Commissioner's Court, £41 5s. 2d. Petty Sessions Court, £16 5s. Manure sold, £30 15s. Interest for treasury, 6s. 5d. County presentment towards repairs flagging and crossings, £30.

55. Had you no rate?—No.

56. How long is it since you had a rate?—Four years.

57. Then these sources came to how much?—£253 1s. 8d.

58. What was your expenditure for the year?—Salaries of officers—town clerk, inspector, weighmaster, £63 10s.

59. How is the lighting provided: is it by contract with the gas company?—Yes, by contract with the company, £59 15s. 7d. Then there is lamplighters' wages, £4, repairs of lamps, £2 18s. 3d., repairs of gutters and fire engine, &c., footpaths, £30 5s. 5d. We get a presentment of £30 from the county towards that, and that is expended. Watering the streets, £46 17s.; new water-cart, £37 11s. 6d.; printing and advertising, £17 13s. 10d.; men employed at fairs, £4 10s. That is to each quarter of the town we keep a man to see after the fairs.

60. How often have you fairs?—Once a month.

61. How often have you markets?—Once a week. Then there are expenses for removing a wall in Meeting-lane to widen the street or passage, £5, surveying boundary railings, incidental expenses, &c., making a total of £283 5s. 3d., and leaving a balance of £26 11s. 10d. in the treasurer's hands.

62. Then the sources you have described have for the last four years provided quite a sufficient sum to meet your expenses, and to leave a balance, and you have had no rate?—Yes.

63. What was the amount of the rate struck before that time?—Six pence on buildings and three halfpence in the £ on land.

Edward Lord, Chairman, Township Commissioners, recalled.

Ardee
Jan. 12, 1880
Edward Lord.

54. You have mentioned that the Commissioners are not all of one view on this question of extension. What is your own view regarding it?—My own view is certainly in favour of extension.

55. The existing radius has been described as half a statute mile, and I understand that that doesn't comprehend much arable land?—It is simply the town boundary.

56. You know this town very well?—I belong to it.

57. Taking a radius of a statute mile from the centre of the town, would you say that between the present boundary of half a mile and the proposed boundary of one mile there are many lands and occupied houses the owners of which derive, in your opinion, substantial advantages by reason of their proximity to the town, as a place of resort, and as a market where they can buy and sell with facility?—If you say a mile and a half, I would say there are.

58. Then, if you take a radius of a mile and a half from the centre of the town, you say there are between the existing boundary and that proposed boundary, lands and occupied houses the owners and occupiers of which derive substantial benefit from their proximity to the town?—Yes.

59. What are the advantages you think those people in that position derive by reason of their proximity to the town?—Well, as an instance of the advantages they derive there is Mr. Duncan, whom I see here, he has a very handsome house very little outside the town, a mile radius would certainly bring him in. If any one could derive more advantage than another it is Mr. Duncan, for he has his house in the country and his splendid business in the town, and he has all the advantage of coming into a clean town, where we occupy our time in cleaning and lighting the streets which he uses. Mr. Duncan has a very handsome place, also about a mile outside the town. I am afraid a mile would not bring him in, but a mile and a half would. Mr. Lobby would be brought in by a mile, or a little over it.

60. Besides the gentlemen you have mentioned there are a great many farmers and occupiers of land who derive advantage by having a market so close, where they can dispose of their produce, and buy anything they want?—Immediately outside there is Mr. Lynch, who has a large business in the town, his farm immediately outside the town; a mile radius would take him in.

61. Are there many residents in the town who have corresponding lands outside the boundary?—Yes, there is a good deal of accommodation land; I am one of the holders myself.

62. Within what radius would these be included?—About a mile.

63. This is a very good market town?—Yes indeed.

64. You have a weekly market?—Yes.

65. And that, I suppose, is a market for all sorts of produce?—Yes.

66. I presume the persons living within a radius of a mile and a half find advantage in the existence of that market—they obtain better prices and find a ready sale?—Yes.

67. What description of produce do they dispose of chiefly?—Corn, principally; they sell butter, and milk, and eggs, and poultry, and we are going to supply Dublin [illegible].

68. Do the children within that radius resort to the town for school purposes?—Yes.

69. Are the schools availed of to a large degree?—To a very large degree, for we have very large schools in the town; we have the Model School and the Christian Brothers' School.

70. And the persons residing in the town have the advantage of having the town lighted and kept clean, and the use of footpaths, &c.?—Yes, and so they have the advantages we should have the radius increased to a mile and a half.

71. How many are now qualified to vote in the election of Commissioners, and how many would be qualified in the entire district, which it is proposed to bring in?—We never have such a thing as voting here.

72. You are not the sanitary authority, and you have no control over the roads and bridges?—We have nothing of that kind.

73. You are aware that up to 1871 the Town Commissioners were the sanitary authority, and that by the Act then passed all towns with populations under 6,000 became merged in the Board of Guardians as the sanitary authority?—Yes.

74. You are aware, also, that under the Public Health Act of last year a modification has been made in the law, and that while the general law remains the same as in 1874 there is a power given under the 7th Section of the Act whereby on the petition of the Township Commissioners, the Local Government Board can, by provisional order, constitute them the sanitary authority?—Yes.

75. Are the Commissioners generally aware of that provision in the Act?—They are.

76. Have they ever taken into consideration the expediency of availing themselves of it?—The matter has frequently come before the Board by way of desultory discussion, about having the control of the sanitary matters especially, and many said they could do them much better because they live in the town, and because we know much better than the Poor Law Guardians, who live at a distance of five or six miles away. I think they would be unanimous in getting back the power but for one reason, and that is, that the rate would not come upon the landlord.

77. That is, that half would not be put upon the landlord, that the onus would be on you?—Yes.

78. You are aware that upon the lessee it would only fall in the proportion of one-fourth?—Yes.

79. Assuming that the rural district was brought in, would that one-fourth fairly represent the proportion they should pay?—I think so.

80. You think the fact of the rate falling entirely on the occupiers would influence them in wishing for the change?—Yes.

81. Are the Commissioners aware, that amongst the other points with which the Parliamentary Committee has dealt is that question of the division of the rate?—Yes.

82. Perhaps you are not aware of the recommendation they have made?—No.

83. This is the recommendation (Reads paragraph from Report). You were not aware of that?—No.

84. If that division of the rate between the owner and the occupier were made part of the law would it alter the view of the Commissioners regarding the expediency of getting a change?—That is my impression. I think it would be more popular with the people; here, at least, we are always getting on well together, that the people would like the Commissioners to have the power.

85. You think that a body representing the town interests merely would be better able to deal with questions affecting the sanitary arrangements of the town, than a body of gentlemen coming from a far distance?—No question about it; they are the more competent parties to do it.

86. They have, you think, more interest in it, and would look after it better?—They have; because they are owners of property that would be affected.

87. You think the impediment which presents itself would be entirely obviated if the law was altered in that respect?—Yes.

88. You are aware that under the Poor Law the landlord pays half, and in the town the occupier pays the entire?—Yes.

89. Assuming that change to be made, are you aware that under the same Act there is a further power now to obtain a transfer also of the functions

exercised at present by the Grand Jury over the roads and bridges within the municipal district?—They are aware of that.

90. That the sanitary authority may obtain, by provisional order, a transfer of the control over the roads and bridges? —Yes, that was one view Mr. Lawlor put. He mentioned the fact of having control over the roads and bridges.

91. Do you think that if you were made the sanitary authority you would be in favour of having a transfer of the jurisdiction in respect to roads and bridges?—My own opinion is strongly in favour of it, because local people have more interest in those matters than people who live miles off.

92. Under the 62nd section of the Towns Improvement Act arable lands are now rated at one-fourth of the valuation?—Yes.

93. At present, any expenditure incurred by the Grand Jury on those works is charged equally on all descriptions of property. Assuming that the transfer was to be made, is it your opinion that arable lands included within the town should be charged on the one-fourth scale, or on the full scale as at present? What would be your view of the equity? Don't you think that the owners of the lands should pay the full amount as at present?—Yes; as far as roads and bridges are concerned; but as regards anything in the town, they should not pay the full amount. As far as roads and bridges, they should pay the full rate.

94. I wish to ascertain whether you make a distinction between the classes of work which the legislature has already laid down they are to pay one-fourth for; or whether, in the event of the transfer of authority, you would continue to charge them at the full amount?—I would have them pay the full amount so far as the roads and bridges are concerned.

95. I understood you to say that one-fourth, as regards the class of expenditure for which a different charge should be made, is a fair charge?—Yes.

96. As regards lands lying within a mile and a half, do you apprehend that the persons interested there would object to be introduced, or would they be glad of it?—I have had no conversation with them.

97. Do you think they would be anxious to have a share in the municipal government of the town, being entitled to vote at the elections, and qualified to become commissioners?—I think they would.

98. Do you think yourself it would have a healthy effect on the administration of affairs in the town to have this new area introduced into it?—Yes. But for people like me, who have already to pay in the town, and who would then have to pay on the land outside, it would be heavier.

99. But if people outside having different tastes and interests were brought in, and mixed with the town people, would it not have a good effect in the administration of town affairs?—Yes, if it was only to get their suggestions.

100. Mr. *Palmer*.—I want to ask Mr. Lord why does he make a distinction between the taxation for roads and bridges and other taxation?—Because the roads and bridges are outside the town.

101. Assuming that there was an extension of the boundary, why should the taxation for roads and bridges be put on a different footing from the taxation for other purposes?—Because the people in the town have more or less more advantages from works done in the town than people living a mile and a half out.

102. You don't apprehend the meaning of my question. Mr. O'Brien says one-fourth would be charged on the land that would be brought in: now why should you make a distinction between the charges for roads and bridges, and charge on the full amount all lands outside, instead of one-fourth the valuation of the lands brought within the increased municipal boundary? How would you draw the distinction between paving and sewerage?—The people outside use more of the roads.

103. Mr. O'Brien.—This is a question on which a good deal of difference of opinion exists; and even where the thing has been accomplished already by local Acts the practice is not uniform. In some towns they are charging one-fourth, and in others the full amount. They charge the full amount in some places because it is merely a substitution, they say, for the amount they pay at present; and in the other because it is merely a contribution by those who don't derive all the advantages, but derive certain advantages, which are met by the one-fourth taxation. Those are the grounds put forward, generally speaking.

104. Mr. *Palmer*.—I confess I don't see the force of it.

105. Mr. O'Brien.—Do you contemplate, if you got that area of a mile and a half, extending the benefits of lighting and watering to the increased district?—I don't see any necessity for it.

106. How does Athy stand as regards water supply?—We have too much water.

107. Are the houses supplied by pumps or pipes?—We have an excellent supply, and within a few yards of where you are now we have a great piece of engineering work carried on by the Duke of Leinster, the water is brought up 300 or 400 yards from a well, to the centre of the town, and there is plenty of water.

108. Then you won't require any more outlay for water purposes?—No.

109. How do you stand as to sewerage?—I think that subject is so very difficult.

110. Is there a want of sewer scheme at present; is it in an unsatisfactory condition?—I think not, it requires to be constantly looked after.

111. Is there a want of main drainage?—There are very large drains, whether they want to be flushed or not I can't say.

112. Are they the old sewers?—Yes.

113. Not pipe sewers?—No.

114. The sanitary state of this town has not been satisfactory of late; have you been able to trace anything to the sewerage of the town?—We have, from one epidemic to another.

115. Do you consider an outlay for sewerage purposes would be a necessity?—I think it would be very well expended money.

116. If you were to put this town into a proper condition as to sewerage, would it involve a considerable cost?—No doubt of it.

117. Would that expenditure confer advantages not only on the inhabitants of the town, but on the people in the neighbourhood, by making it a more healthy resort?—By all means.

118. And you think, therefore, that they should in some way contribute to the expense?—That is my view.

119. Have the Board of Guardians been restrained from undertaking any works of the kind by reason of the taxation it would involve?—I don't know.

120. Is there anything else you would like to suggest bearing on the subject of the inquiry?—No.

ATHY, Jan. 15, 18[illegible]

Edward Lord.

ALEXANDER DUNCAN examined.

Alexander Duncan.

121. You are a member of the Town Commissioners?—Yes.

122. Have you been long so?—Over thirty years.

123. Do you reside within the municipal district?—No.

124. You have business premises in the town?—Yes.

125. Where does your residence lie from the centre of the town?—About an Irish mile; about a statute mile and a quarter.

126. Then you would not be brought in unless there was a radius of a mile and a half?—I think not.

127. Are you in favour of having the existing

APRIL 25, 1877.
—
Alexander Duncan.

municipal district extended or not?—Apart from any personal interest that might be involved by my residence, I am not in favour of extending the area of taxation at present, unless we get duties added, for our present duties are very limited, we have only lighting and scavenging practically to do, and these can be done as you have seen, almost without levying taxes at all; therefore for the purposes of taxation there is no need of extension, but if we get what I, as a deputation from this board, waited on Sir Michael Beach and other Members of Parliament in London for the purpose of getting, namely, the sanitary authority, then it would be desirable to have the area of taxation extended, for it would be both desirable and fair; on the grounds of equity, I admit it would be wrong under our present taxation, and with our present duties to extend the area, for we have nothing to give those outside, they don't want our light, or their roads or grounds, and some of the men living outside must already be paying heavy taxation in the town, for instance, Mr. Byrne is already paying heavily in the town, and to tax them in the town and then to tax them outside, it would be double taxation, that would be the case with at least several people who live out of the town. If we became the sanitary body, and if we undertook the care of the roads and bridges, which are things we had earnestly discussed in former years, but which we could not see our way to undertaking, as we could not discharge the duties as economically as the Grand Jury, then I say, by all means, when we undertake the roads and bridges, and become the sanitary authority, extend the area, with our present duty it would seem to be a most foolish thing to extend the area of taxation.

128. As to the sanitary jurisdiction, is your opinion in favour of having the sanitary jurisdiction transferred to the Commissioners, or are you adverse to such a change?—That was a change which I waited on Sir Michael Beach, with representatives from other towns, for the purpose of having accomplished, provided a little portion of the taxation was allowed us, but otherwise it would not be at all practicable or desirable to undertake the sanitary business.

129. You have heard that Sir Michael Beach's Committee appear to have adopted the same view as you have adopted, and have recommended that where practicable there should be one body for the discharge of the several duties?—Yes.

130. If that difficulty was got over, and the municipal taxation was divided between the occupier and the owners, would you be in favour of transferring the sanitary jurisdiction to the town body?—Decidedly.

131. You think it would be a duty you would be able to perform better, and more qualified to discharge it than the Board of Guardians?—Yes; I should say so. In the past when we were the Sanitary Authority we got exceedingly valuable and liberal help from the Grand Jury in the county at large, portions of the work that was done under our directions and auspices, in the way of main sewers. We got considerable help from the county, in fact, the work though done by us was done through county presentments. We had not the resources ourselves. If, however, we could draw on the wider area, I believe we could do the work as reasonably and more skilfully than the Board of Guardians.

132. Assuming that you got the sanitary jurisdiction and that your boundary was extended, to what radius would you consider it equitable to extend it?—If we undertook the roads and bridges as well?

133. Do I understand you to advocate, that if you became the Sanitary Authority you should seek a transfer of the other authority?—Yes; I think it is only with that work, and with a proper area, of a mile and a half that we could get on well, for there are many things connected with the roads and bridges that could be practically carried out under the sanitary sections of the Act.

134. You consider a mile and a half a reasonable radius in the event of your being constituted the Sanitary Authority, and getting control over the roads and bridges?—Yes; I think so.

135. And you think that fairly represents the extent to which lands, and the occupiers of land adjoining to the town may be said to fairly derive advantage from their proximity to the town?—Of course there are advantages derived by persons beyond that, but that is as wide a district as we should undertake.

136. Are you clearly of opinion that persons within a mile and a half do derive advantages from having a market so close to them, and that they would be ready to take a share in the town work?—Of course, I believe they derive advantages, but I don't think there is one person outside the present boundary who cares one jot to interfere with our business, or who would take the trouble of becoming a Commissioner.

137. Do you think that if the area was extended a mile and a half, the persons brought in would be glad to have participated in the municipal government?—Assuming the other works to be added?

138. Assuming you had got all the authority, don't you think there would be ambition on the part of those outside, to come in and take a share in the management?—I believe there would be not only from public interests, but from smaller aims and interests, for it would be their interest to have persons put in here, and many persons seeking their own personal ends would accomplish that, and the only question is whether we would have strength and power as a Board to resist the personal interest used in order to get jobs under our direction. I believe, the Grand Jury has done its duty exceedingly well as far as I know of it. At present all the men who form it are placed far beyond the influence which we as a Board would be subject to, and that they would be able to resist personal influences. It is on that ground, I believe, the persons within a mile and a half would be very anxious to come in to join our Board.

139. Assuming that the arrangements were carried out, and that you had the sanitary jurisdiction, and the control over the roads and bridges, which do you contemplate that the arable lands as regards the expenditure of the works transferred from the Grand Jury should pay the full amount or one-fourth?—If we got control of the roads and bridges they should pay the full amount.

140. If you had that control you think they should pay the full amount?—Yes; may I ask a question? This inquiry doesn't bind the Board of Commissioners to a present alteration.

141. This is only one element in an inquiry of a very general and comprehensive scope, it is merely that before the Government undertook to legislate in pursuance of the report they considered it necessary that there should be a local inquiry, and when they receive the result of that, they will not be bound by it, and whenever they adopt their views it will be for Parliament to ratify them or not afterwards?—This intended legislation as regards bodies such as this would be very foolish indeed unless we were placed under the Local Government Board or some other controlling Board.

142. There are certain things which at present require the sanction of the Local Government Board; to what extent would you suggest that this controlling power should exist?—To the same extent under the Local Government Board as the Poor Law Guardians are now; not one jot less.

143. You think such a control would have a good effect?—Yes; for there are questions arise where personal matters come in and there must be a central authority to control.

144. Is there anything else you would like to suggest on any matter connected with the inquiry?—No, except with reference to the Board who sat here on Monday to consider this subject. There were some of us in persons present, and the majority were against. I withdrew my motion against extension of the area, believing we could come and see you and state our own views, but the majority were decidedly against the thing within our present duties.

Alexander [illegible]

145. The Chairman of [illegible] body has [illegible] mentioned that if the sanitary jurisdiction were to be transferred to you, he was of opinion that the rate should be divided as it is, for poor law purposes, between the owner and the occupier. Do you think the rate ought to be paid by the occupier as at present, or [illegible] divided as it is [illegible] would [illegible] the town [illegible]?

146. What is your own individual opinion as to dividing the rate between the owner and occupier?—Between landlord and tenant certainly.

147. You think that the municipal rate ought to be divided between the landlord and tenant?—Yes, and for two reasons in equity and because it would give the landlord influence and interest.

148. Does that opinion extend to all the rates for sanitary and grand jury purposes?—Yes.

149. You believe it would have a good effect for the landlord to pay half?—Yes.

Michael Lawler

MICHAEL LAWLER examined.

150. You are a Town Commissioner of Athy?—Yes.

151. How long have you been so?—Since 18[illegible].

152. You are also a magistrate for the county?—Yes.

153. And you are well acquainted with the town?—Yes.

154. You have heard the views suggested by the Chairman and by Mr. Duncan; which proposition are you in favour of; are you an advocate of extension of the boundaries?—By all means.

155. Do you contemplate [illegible] on that arrangement that you should get sanitary jurisdiction?—Yes, and I say we would do the sanitary duty much better than it is done at present.

156. And when you advocate extension it is with the view of getting sanitary jurisdiction?—Yes.

157. You think you would do it much better than at present?—Yes, and much cheaper.

158. Do you contemplate also getting the grand jury control over roads and bridges?—I have not made my mind up on that matter [illegible]; I think we should undergo a good deal of trouble. We went to a good deal of trouble and got a great deal of satisfaction about [illegible] years ago, and we then found that, owing to the liberality of the Grand Jury towards us in public works here, that when we came to have a proper [illegible] to undertake the works such as Mr. [illegible], the County Surveyor, that expense would be considerable to us, and that while we [illegible] liberally dealt with by the Grand Jury it would be better leave that department as at present.

159. Are you of opinion that in the amount expended by the Grand Jury within the municipal district in the various works for which they provide they give you a fair equivalent for the value they take from you?—I think they do. Some people may take exception to that, but I think they do.

160. You think the amount they give is commensurate with what they receive?—Yes, I do. For instance, these roads [illegible] town was greatly worn by the great traffic, and the Grand Jury put two feet six inches of broken stone all through the town, and improved the roads greatly.

161. And you have no complaint to make against the Grand Jury?—No.

162. And your mind is not at all made up about the transfer of that duty?—No.

163. But you are quite in favour of a transfer of the sanitary duty?—Decidedly.

164. What radius would be fair as representing the extent to which advantages derived from proximity to the town extend?—Less than a mile and a half would not be sufficient.

165. And you think that within a mile and a half the owners and occupiers of land derive advantage from the town?—Decidedly.

166. And land within that distance sets at a greater value?—Yes, [illegible] always do.

167. And the occupiers have an available market where they have a ready sale for their produce?—It is one of the best markets.

168. And [illegible] children resort to the town for school purposes from [illegible] around the town?—Yes, from [illegible] distance, and as far out as three miles, but particularly from a mile and a half.

169. You have not been in a healthy state here recently. Are you of opinion there is an existing necessity for a considerable outlay to improve the sanitary arrangements of the town, especially the sewerage?—It is.

170. Do you consider that it would take a large sum of money to effect these improvements?—I should say it would. There is a great deal to be done still in the town.

171. Would the expense of the works in which you either fall on the existing municipality as a very heavy burden?—Undoubtedly there should be at least a shilling rate [illegible] on the town.

172. Do you think that that improvement in the sanitary state of Athy would, to some extent, be an advantage to those in the neighbourhood of the town?—I do.

173. And it would be reasonable that they should make some contribution in respect of that?—Yes.

174. Under the Towns Improvement Act the sense of the legislature appears to have been that certain lands should be rated at only one-fourth. Does that appear to you to be a sound basis to take in making a distinction between the residents in the town who derive all the advantages, and the occupiers outside who enjoy those advantages in a modified degree. Do you consider it an equitable and fair division for the advantages derived by both?—Yes, I do. That is what we always [illegible].

175. It is your opinion that those who own land, and those who occupy land within a mile and a half would object to be included in the town boundary, a good many would object.

176. On what ground do you think they would object to be included?—That they don't want further taxation.

177. Don't you think they would be ambitious of being able to take part in the municipal government?—I think they would so far as that.

178. Do you think it would have a healthy effect if you widened the area of municipal government, and introduced a new class of ratepayers?—I think it would. I think we are not [illegible] at present. Half an English mile from the market is not at all sufficient.

Walter B. [illegible]

WALTER B. D[illegible] examined.

179. You are magistrate in the neighbourhood?—Yes.

180. And you have lived in Athy?—I have lived here a great number of years.

181. You have no property in the municipal district?—I have none.

182. How far is your residence outside the municipal boundary?—The house is about a mile and a half English.

183. Assuming that a radius of a mile and a half were adopted, would that take in your place?—I could not answer that; it may be a few yards inside or outside, but it would be very close to the mark.

184. Assuming that the radius of a mile and a hal

ATHY.
Dec. 13, 1879.
Walter E. Bodkin.

would bring you in, would you consider it objectionable that you should be included?—It is a principle on which I have always expressed a very decided opinion that those living in the immediate vicinity to a town like this, certainly derive advantages from it, and that they should not be unwilling to pay for those advantages.

185. Would you consider that in laying down the basis of what they should contribute; one fourth which is the basis prescribed by the Towns Improvement Act is a fair proportion?—I think, taking the rates that have been struck here it would be fair and not oppressive.

186. I am aware you have acted as a member of the Board of Guardians?—Yes, when I am here.

187. You have had experience of the way the sanitary work is usually transacted by the Board of Guardians. Do you think the sanitary affairs of the town could be best provided for by the town body or by such a body as the Board of Guardians, comprehending gentlemen from rural districts?—Of course in answering a question like that I should prefer confining myself to the actual case before me of Athy, and my answer might possibly be different if I had to consider other circumstances; but considering the constitution of the Board of Guardians of Athy, the attendance there is there, and the exceptional intelligence there is as far as I know amongst the Town Commissioners of Athy, I think the Commissioners of Athy would be by far the more competent body to carry out sanitary arrangements. I think they would do it less expensively and much better. More than that, the great element that is wanting in the present sanitary laws is what I am convinced will be ultimately supplied. In my opinion, and I have had considerable experience of it, I go so far as to say there is an absolute necessity for effectual local supervision. Under the present Act and the late Act, I don't think the omission is sufficiently supplied. The sanitary laws are likely to be productive of enormous expense with very little result, and any body like the Town Commissioners here, where they have men competent to supervise these things on the spot, I think can carry out these things much better than a Board of Guardians, who don't know the localities, and have a great many other things to attend to and without speaking very harshly of them, are utterly ignorant of the whole thing as a body.

188. Would it in your opinion have a healthy effect, if those who are at present outside the town, within the radius of a mile and a half, were added to the constituency, and thus enabled to take part in the affairs of the town, and be incorporated with the electors and with those eligible to be Commissioners?—Yes, I think it is desirable to have a mixture of classes, if possible. I need not tell you it is popularly supposed that gentlemen have intelligence commensurate with their education.

189. Assuming that the area was extended and that the functions of the Board of Guardians were transferred, do you think it would be desirable to have the control of the roads and bridges, also transferred to the town body?—I think that question stands on a different basis altogether. I am afraid in a place like Athy the taxation for roads and bridges would be enormously heavy if we took the whole charge of them, for instance the bridging of Athy alone has cost hundreds, and the municipal taxation would be utterly unable to provide for it.

190. You think the expenditure would be increased and that it would fall heavily on the town?—Yes, so heavily that I think it would be a bar to any improvement and it would be found sufficient for them to keep the roads and bridges without thinking of improvements of any sort.

191. You think the grand jury gives an equivalent for whatever they receive?—I do, and I think it is fairly and economically expended.

192. Generally speaking the allegation by town bodies is that while the grand jury receive large sums the town people find it impossible to get anything done, and at Wexford they said there was £800 paid to the county grand jury of which £500 went to the county at large, and that of the £400 balance they got no equivalent but that since they managed things themselves they have been able to do all for themselves?—Athy is quite different, and I know the place for a long time.

193. You found no unwillingness on the part of the grand jury to do what was asked?—No; they have on the contrary been always willing on all occasions to meet the views of the inhabitants provided there was any sort of equity.

194. Suppose the legislature did transfer to towns the jurisdiction over roads and bridges, do you consider that the arable lands contributing within the municipal district should pay one fourth or the whole amount?—I have not considered the subject, but primâ facie, I don't see the grounds on which the distinction is made.

195. You think all should come under the same rule?—Yes, I don't see why there should be a distinction.

196. Is there anything else you would like to suggest on the subject of this inquiry?—Nothing except that I thoroughly agree with Mr. Dunne's recommendation as to having a controlling power vested in some superior authority.

197. As regards the division of the municipal rate, what is your view; that it should be divided between the landlord and tenant or paid by the occupier?—It is a matter of the most perfect indifference by whom it is paid, but for the sake of satisfying the ratepayers I would say divide it.

198. You would do that to satisfy them although it makes no difference who pays?—I think substantially it makes no difference.

199. Is there anything else you wish to add?—No. Except that the municipal accounts have to be audited by the Local Government auditor.

200. You are in favour of that?—I am.

Richard T. Levret.

RICHARD T. LEVRET examined.

201. You don't live within the municipal boundary? —No.

202. Have you any property within it?—No.

203. How does your residence stand as regards the centre of the town?—I think it is about a mile and a half out.

204. Would a radius of a mile and a half include or exclude you?—I think it would about take me in.

205. What is your feeling on the subject, are you in favour of extension of the boundary or otherwise? —I have not given the subject any thought, but I don't see any objection to our being included because no doubt we derive benefit from the town.

206. You are a member of the Board of Guardians? —Yes.

206. Would you consider that the sanitary affairs of the town would be best looked after by the Board of Guardians or by the Commissioners?—I never had a doubt on the subject, I think the Commissioners are the better body.

207. And you consider also that if they had the power over sanitary matters and looked after them instead it would be reasonable that those living within a certain distance should pay a contribution towards the expenses of the town?—Certainly.

208. Does it appear to you that the basis laid down of one fourth is fair?—Yes, I think so.

209. And you would not individually object to that? —No.

210. What would be your view with regard to the

proposal to transfer the jurisdiction over roads and bridges, from the grand jury to the town body?—I would not be in favour of that; I think the grand jury would do it better than the town body.

211. As regards the division of the rate, what would be your view? would you be in favour of dividing it between the landlord and tenant, or otherwise?—I don't think that will make much difference any way.

212. Assuming there was a general popular feeling that it should be divided, would it be generally [illegible] between the landlord and the tenant who is to pay, and it makes no difference any way.

213. You don't see anything [illegible] in it?—No.

214. You think they do practically divide it at present?—I do.

215. And if the general feeling was in favour of dividing it, you would have no objection?—No, I would have no objection on my part.

MATHEW MAGRATH, Clerk of the Athy Union, examined.

216. How many townlands are there in the electoral division of Athy?—Thirty-two townlands.

217. What is the area of the electoral division?—[illegible] acres.

218. And the valuation?—[illegible].

219. Are you aware whether the electoral division extends equally in all directions from the town or unequally?—Unequally.

220. What is the farthest point in any direction to which the electoral division extends?—The farthest point from the town would be about four and a half or three miles.

221. In what direction would that be?—Towards Churchtown, which is to the north.

222. That is about the most remote point?—Yes, I think under three miles.

223. To the south?—To the south-west, at [illegible].

224. How far does it extend to the south?—A mile and a half.

225. How far to the east?—About three miles.

226. How far to the west?—Two miles.

227. So that it doesn't extend equally?—No, sir.

228. Have you had any special rates for sewerage purposes?—Yes, sir, every year.

229. What is the amount of the special sanitary rate?—Two pence in the pound.

230. What was the nature of the work for which the rate was assessed?—For sewers in Athy, cleaning and repairing them, and some new [illegible].

231. Not large works executed?—No, sir.

232. Then, the Guardians have not undertaken any extensive scheme of sewerage?—No, sir.

233. Have they had under consideration any general scheme of drainage?—Not that I am aware of.

234. Have the Guardians ever been considering the question, whether it would be desirable that the sanitary jurisdiction should be transferred from the Guardians to the Commissioners?—No, sir.

235. Are you aware, whether the feeling of the Guardians would be adverse to such a measure, or in favour of it?—I am not aware. It was never spoken of.

Mr. LUCAS, Chairman Town Commissioners, recalled.

236. The Parliamentary Committee made one recommendation which, in a great many instances in the [illegible], would be utterly impracticable; namely, that municipal boundaries should be made coterminous with electoral divisions. Would it be practicable in this case to adopt the electoral division as the municipal boundary?—That would be going outside what we were proposing.

237. You don't consider it would be feasible?—No.

238. Do you see any advantage that would be gained by adopting the electoral division as the municipal boundary?—No.

239. You think it would be bringing in people who don't derive much advantage?—Yes.

240. Mr. DICKSON.—With regard to the sanitary question, you asked one of the questions that led me to believe that you were anxious to know whether the Board of Guardians had ever considered any scheme of drainage for Athy. I was Chairman of a Committee appointed by the Guardians to carry out the Sanitary Act, and many instances. I pointed out the [illegible] of allowing the sewage of Athy to run into the river, which is strongly forbidden by an Act of Parliament, and at my request two schemes were considered, one to convey all the sewage into a large reservoir, and to treat it in the way it has been treated in several towns in England and elsewhere, more particularly in Kilkenny county, at Castlecomer. That was only intended to get rid of the solid matter, and let the water run off; and another scheme was to bring the sewage down about a mile and a half away from the town into low-lying lands, and there distribute it as it came from the sewers, but the expense was so very considerable that the Guardians were, I think, frightened. My own individual opinion is, that sooner or later some such scheme will have to be adopted.

241. Such a scheme would involve very considerable outlay?—I think it would cost from £3,000 to £5,000.

242. Would you consider it equitable and fair that those outlying lands within a mile and a half should contribute to that work?—Certainly, and I go a great deal further, for I think a mile and a half would scarcely include the advantages derived from such a town as Athy.

243. But will you not go so far as to extend the boundary beyond that for all purposes you would not be extending it for some purposes only?—I would be inclined to extend it beyond that for all purposes; I look upon such a market town as Athy as of immense benefit and advantage to the country.

244. Would you consider the electoral division a fair municipal district?—I think it would be very fair for certain purposes.

245. But not for all purposes?—No.

246. For instance, such a matter as sewerage?—Or lighting.

247. For such a scheme as that sewerage scheme you think that a fair district?—Yes, for such a scheme where there is a wide scheme the advantages would be more extended. I am entirely against making the occupiers in the 20s or 30s [illegible] in the more than the [illegible] a little [illegible] for the people who live near it.

248. Mr. DUNNE.—For the equalization of taxation it might be a great object to have the electoral division coterminous with the municipal boundary for roads, bridges, and sanitary affairs for taxation.

249. Mr. O'BRIEN.—Yes, but a town must be a town wherever it is, and were you to adopt a boundary it might be for all purposes—for the purpose of light, what we have to do is very [illegible].

250. Mr. O'BRIEN.—Then, there are certain purposes for which you would not consider the electoral division too large as a municipal district?—No, if we understood all those purposes.

251. Mr. O'BRIEN.—For military purposes you would not consider it too large?—No.

Athy. Feb. 15, 1879. Mr. Reid.

252. Mr. O'Brien.—Rate for lighting you do?—Yes.

253. Mr. O'Brien.—And for all other purposes you would not object to the electoral division to the municipal boundary?—No, but I think the people within it would not object if we took in all these districts.

254. That would give about three miles, speaking roughly?—Yes, the holders of fairs and markets [illegible] of great distances to the people near a town, and within the electoral division, and the people would have for a return their vote, and they would be able to take part in the regulation of the fairs and markets, one of the matters that has caused us most trouble is the matter of fairs, especially pig fairs, and horse fairs, and it would be well the country people should have a voice in the regulation of the fairs and markets, and it would be an essential service for the country, that they should have power to see what was being done in the town.

Mr. Glover.

Mr. Glover, Clerk to the Town Commissioners, recalled.

255. There are in the township, 175 persons qualified to vote, and 56 qualified to be Commissioners.

The inquiry then closed.

Gorey. Feb. 24, 1879.

GOREY—MONDAY, 24th FEBRUARY, 1879.

Before Messrs. Exham, Q.C., and Cotton, C.E.

Mr. *O'Dempsey*, solicitor, asked leave to appear professionally for a number of persons who objected to any alteration in the boundaries of the town.

John O'Neill.

John O'Neill examined.

1. Chairman.—You are Town Clerk of Gorey?—Yes.

2. For how long have you been Town Clerk?—Since November, 1868.

3. The town is under the Towns Improvement Act?—Yes.

4. When was it adopted here?—In 1859.

5. Were the boundaries fixed then?—They were.

6. And have the boundaries as then fixed continued the same ever since?—They have.

7. Has there been any alteration or change in them?—No.

8. What is the population of the town of Gorey?—In the year 1871, the population was 2,639.

9. Has the population increased since that or not?—I think it has decreased.

10. What is the area of the town at present?—The present area is 631a. 1r. 1p.

11. I believe you were good enough to mark on the Ordnance Sheet the present boundaries?—Yes.

12. Mr. Cotton.—Are they taken from any map you have, or how did you get them?—The only thing I had was a little map in the office.

13. It was from that you marked it?—Yes.

14. Have you a copy of the Gazette in which the boundaries are described?—No; I have a copy of the order from the Lord Lieutenant.

15. Describing the boundaries?—Yes.

16. What is the date of the Gazette?—The 2nd September, 1859, is the date.

17. What is the entire valuation?—The entire valuation is £3,899 10s.

18. How much of that is land, and how much buildings?—Buildings £3,436 16s., and land £423 15s.

19. What are the rates that have been struck for the last five years; improvement rate, poor rate, and county cess?—The town rate in 1874 was 6d. in the £; in 1875 it was 6d. in the £; in 1876 and 1877 there was no town rate struck, and in 1878 it was 6d. in the £.

20. What is it this year?—We have struck no rate this year yet.

21. Will you require a rate?—Yes.

22. I suppose it will not be greater than in the preceding years?—No; it will not be greater at all events, it might be less.

23. What are the poor rates you have been paying?—In 1874 the poor rate was 2s. 10d. in the £, and there was no sanitary rate; in 1875 the poor rate was 1s. 8d. in the £, with one penny sanitary rate; in 1876 the poor rate was 1s. 8d. in the £, with one penny sanitary rate; in 1877 the poor rate was 1s. 8d. in the £, and one penny sanitary rate, and in 1878 the poor rate was 1s. 7d. in the £, and the sanitary rate two pence.

24. What has been the county cess during the same years?—The county cess in 1874 (paid in two instalments) was 2s. 8d. in the £; in 1875 it was 1s. 11d. nearly; in 1876 1s. 5½d. nearly; in 1877 1s. 7d., and in 1878 1s. 4½d. That is, you will see, it has been decreasing since 1874.

25. Was that increase in 1874 owing to anything the Grand Jury did for the town?—No, I don't think it was.

26. Because I observe there has been a great deal of flagging done in this town?—That was done from the year 1875.

27. Were the town Commissioners able to do that, or was the work done with help from the Grand Jury?—It was done in this way. The town Commissioners applied to the associated cess-payers for a grant.

28. When was that?—In 1875. That was in the first commencement of the flagging, and they got a grant of £40 10s.

29. We don't want the figures, but did the cess-payers from time to time contribute from the funds of the Barony at large, towards the flagging of the town of Gorey?—Yes; they have contributed largely.

30. And then I suppose you have added to that contribution out of the rates or by private contribution?—It has been done in this way: first, the grant of the Grand Jury, and then the shop-keepers, in front of whose premises the street has been flagged, have been charged with the kerbing, and the deficiency was made good by the rates.

31. We sent out queries to be considered by your Board—have they been considered?—At the time in November when the queries arrived they did not consider them.

32. Have they considered them at all?—They have, in this way: when the queries came down they asked me what were the present boundaries of the township and I could not tell them, and they asked me were they an English mile.

33. I believe the Town Commissioners are not unanimous as a body in their opinion as to whether the boundaries should be extended or not?—No.

34. Did they pass any resolution on the subject?—They called a meeting of the ratepayers to consider it.

35. But, as a body, the Commissioners did not pass any resolution on the subject?—No, sir.

36. Then you are not authorised on the part of the Commissioners, as a body, to offer any opinion on their

part as to the extension of the boundary or otherwise?—Yes, sir.

35. Of course you live in the town?—I do.

36. Are you in business in the town?—I am.

37. Having lived here for some time, do you, as a matter of fact, know whether lands in the immediate vicinity of the town are more valuable, and bring more to the landlord in consequence of their proximity to the town, than lands further off?—They do, of course.

38. Do the people who hold these lands use the town of Gorey largely?—They do.

39. I suppose they send in their produce daily to the market, such things as butter and eggs, and poultry, and so on?—Yes, sir.

40. Could you say to what extent that exceptional value extends; does it extend a mile all round from the centre of the town, or two miles, or only a half mile?—I could not say exactly—I think the lands in the immediate vicinity are valued higher than at a distance.

41. That may arise from other causes, but could you say whether land in the immediate vicinity within a certain distance does derive from its proximity to the town a higher value than land of a similar quality, that is further off?—I could not say, I don't understand the question.

42. Suppose that the town was extended a mile and a half from the centre of the town, could you tell me how many voters could be brought in, and to what extent there would be an increase in the constituency?—The clerk of the Union would be better able to tell that.

43. Could you tell me how many voters are there at present rated in the town?—About 115 within the township.

44. How many are qualified to be Town Commissioners?—I think there are about forty.

45. How many qualified to be Town Commissioners would be brought in by adopting the radius of a mile and a half?—It would increase the number by about forty or fifty.

46. Of those qualified to be Commissioners?—Yes; that is, houses of £10 and £12 and upwards, I don't think there would be so many. I think the number qualified would be raised to about fifty altogether within the whole increased area.

47. The township boundary is only in two electoral divisions, namely, Gorey and Courtown?—Yes, sir, Gorey and Courtown.

48. It is entirely included within those two electoral divisions?—Yes.

49. To what distance should you go from the town at the nearest point to include any other electoral division?—Huntington is a mile on the Gorey hill side.

50. How far is the nearest point of Huntington from the centre of the town?—About an Irish mile, or a mile and a quarter from the centre.

51. Mr. Cotton.—How is the town supplied with gas?—By the Gas and Water Company.

52. There is one Company for water and gas?—Yes, it is a Gas and Water Company.

53. And the Commissioners pay rent to them?—Yes, they pay £3 a lamp for the public lamps. There are sixteen public lamps in the town.

54. How do the private parties get gas?—By agreement with the Gas Company.

55. Chairman.—Are the people here, so far as you know, satisfied with the way the roads are kept by the Grand Jury?—I think they are satisfied enough.

56. And also with the way the sanitary affairs are carried out by the rural sanitary authority?—Yes, I think so.

57. Mr. Cotton.—Have the Commissioners ever considered the advisability of becoming the sanitary authority themselves?—They have been speaking of it.

58. But no resolution was arrived at on the subject?—No, I was directed to write to other towns to inquire how the sanitary work was being done.

59. The sanitary rate you mentioned as being one penny?—Yes.

60. What was that for?—For the water supply.

61. On what district was it struck?—On the contributory district.

62. Chairman.—To the eighth query we sent you, the reply is, "The Commissioners are of opinion that it would be of advantage to extend the boundary, if it would not interfere with the rights of land holders under the Land Act; if so, the Commissioners would object to any alteration being made in the present boundary; secondly, that the extension of the boundary would lessen the town rate by affording a larger area," and there were present, concurring in that, six of the Town Commissioners?—That was adopted, not at a formal meeting, but they came to that conclusion for the purpose of aiding me.

63. That was the opinion of six of the Commissioners?—Yes.

64. And there are nine of them altogether?—Yes.

Cross-examined (by Chairman, at request of Mr. O'Dempsey.)

65. I believe you told us you did not represent the majority of the Commissioners, do you represent even a considerable minority of them?—I am not authorized to speak for any one.

66. Are you aware that two meetings were held, at which this proposal for extending the boundary was unanimously condemned?—Yes, I think I sent up the resolutions of the public meeting to the Boundaries Commissioners in Dublin.

67. A resolution was passed at a public meeting on the 31st January, 1879, to this effect, "That any extension of the existing boundary is wholly unnecessary and uncalled for"?—Yes.

68. I believe, according to the rates struck, they amount to about 3d. in the pound annually?—Yes.

69. What is the rating power of the Commissioners?—Up to one shilling.

70. But you have never been obliged to go higher than 3d.?—Yes, a great deal higher.

71. Doesn't the irregularity of the boundary conform to the geographical formation of the town, which I believe is one long street?—Yes.

72. And of course the boundary is necessarily oblong to a certain extent?—Yes.

73. What is the class of people who occupy the land about the town?—Principally gentlemen who have dwelling houses outside, and persons in the town who have land round it.

74. Doesn't it principally consist of rate payers in the town who have small holdings of land about it?—Yes.

75. Which are not at present within the boundary?—No, of course not.

76. And I believe they pay an increased rent in respect of those lands outside?—They do.

Gorey.
Feb. 28, 1881.
John O'Neill.

William Miller Kirke, examined.

William M. Kirke.

77. Chairman.—You are Chairman of the Town Commissioners of Gorey?—Yes.

78. You reside at the park?—Yes.

79. Is it your opinion that the boundary of the town should be extended?—Decidedly.

80. I believe you have a quantity of land that will be brought in by any proposed extension?—Yes.

81. That is at present outside the boundary?—Yes.

82. Are you aware from your own knowledge whether lands within a certain distance acquire an additional value, owing to their proximity to the town?—I am, because I receive an increased rent for them.

83. We have marked on the map before us the present boundaries of the town; to what extent do the

Z

Sept. 7. Feb 25, 1879.

William H. Gale.

lands around the town derive exceptional value from it?—They vary according to the character of the land. I myself get from £3 to £5 an acre.

84. Within what distance from the centre of the town is that?—I should say half a mile in.

85. Do you receive a higher rent from the lands that are just outside than from those inside, or as high?—Almost the same rent; I have lands let within the boundary at present very low, and I have lands within the boundary with a considerable increase of rent since I bought the property in 1870; there are other lands outside let, which are not higher than inside, and some also let higher, and it is right to add that a feeling has got up in the town, that this is a job of mine for the purpose of raising the rents, and that it is for the purpose of enhancing the value of those lands that are outside.

86. Have you considered to what extent you, as an individual ratepayer, and as Chairman of the Commissioners, think the area should be increased?—No; I leave that entirely to the hands of the Commissioners, and whether they make it half a mile, or a mile, or two miles, it is perfectly immaterial to me, all I want is some regularity in the boundary.

87. Do you consider that, following the townland boundaries as far as possible, within an area of one mile, the lands derive exceptional value from their proximity to the town?—I am perfectly satisfied they do.

88. You are aware there is a circle drawn on this map of a minute scale?—Yes, and I believe the reason the Commissioners advocated that in the first instance was, that they heard, and had the evidence which Mr. O'Neill told you about, that he had corresponded with a great many other towns, and that was what they wanted.

89. They varied in their views, but, at all events, your opinion is that, to the extent of the one mile circle, and adopting the townlands as near as possible, lands do derive exceptional benefit from the town?—Decidedly.

90. Are there a number of gentlemen's seats that would be included within that area?—No, not many, somewhere about five.

91. I observe there is a place called Woodlands, for instance?—Yes; and the Cottage, Knockanrallen House, Ramsgate House, and there is General Gale's (Mr. Walrond's), the Deanery, Corkslin Cottage, Millmount, Westmount, and Ramsgate Cottage.

92. I observe that by a circle of a mile a great deal of your demesne and park would be taken in?—Yes.

93. But following the townland boundary it would not come up to your house?—No.

94. And if we followed the townland boundary which would go half a mile below your house, you would not object to that?—Not at all. I look upon it in this light, not as a matter of a few pence more or less, but what would be the benefit. The rates I paid last year, which were for three years, I look upon in this broad sense, £3 7s. 7½d. was what I paid, and I find the valuation I am under at present would amount to £101, and if a bigger area is brought in and my neighbours are included, instead of having to pay 5d. rate in three years, I will have to pay 6d., and that, even on the increased area, will result in my being absolutely nothing more out of pocket, for my neighbours will be brought in to share the burden.

95. But your neighbours will be brought in to a less extent than you?—No matter.

96. Do the Commissioners supply light to the present boundary?—They pay for it.

97. With regard to the proposed increased area, what would be your view in reference to the Commissioners supplying it with light?—I believe we would have to do so, and thereby incur additional expense, but I go on the broad principle that if we get an increase of taxation we are bound to give value for it.

98. Do you think you would be able to do that, having regard to the fact that lands only pay one-fourth. As far as lands are concerned, you would not light them, but if the streets were increased you would propose that any continuously inhabited portion of the district should be supplied with light, and that as to water they would have to supply themselves?—No, I believe the Gas Company would do that also.

99. You are aware of the exception in the 62nd section of the Towns Improvement Act, by which lands only pay one-fourth?—Yes.

100. Is it your opinion that the land introduced should continue to pay one-fourth, or be increased?—No; I think the contribution is very well and properly adjusted. Those people living in houses outside, and visiting the town, would get the greatest value.

101. You are aware that under the Public Health Act of last year those lands are only to pay sanitary rate on one-fourth?—Yes.

102. Is it your opinion they should continue to pay that if they are brought within the boundary of the town?—As far as that is concerned we are determined we shall separate from the guardians, and that we will make the provisions of the Act of Parliament, and go back to things as they were before.

103. That is, become the urban sanitary authority?—Yes, because I don't see the sense of giving over to my fellow-citizens to the amount of £15 a year, when we can get the work done as well for £7. I will put money in my pocket by so doing, and so will every inhabitant of the town.

104. If you become the urban sanitary authority the lands would have to pay the whole of the sanitary rate?—Yes; and when I talk of £15 and £7, I speak of absolute figures. We are under salaries to the amount of £30, and we would get half of that from the Consolidated Fund, and I don't see the slightest use in our taxing ourselves for £15, when we could get the work as well done for £7.

105. The lands to be brought in would be differently circumstanced, would you think it right there should be no alteration in the rate they pay?—No, because if you bring in lands there is no occasion to be incurred.

106. Then, at present, so far as the lands are in a rural sanitary district, the tenant gets half the rate from the landlord?—Yes.

107. Do you think the rate should be divided?—Yes.

108. Do you say the same with regard to the improvement rate?—Yes.

109. Then you are saying that your own tenants should have power to deduct half the rate from you, as landlord?—Yes; I think we are all bound up in the one bundle.

110. What do you mean by speaking of £15 sanitary rate?—I think the sanitary officer costs us somewhat about £30 a year. There is a sanitary officer and sub-sanitary officer. The present sanitary arrangements are more expensive than under the old régime.

111. Have you taken any steps to get the sanitary authority transferred to you?—We are going, as soon as the boundaries are settled, to seek to get back the sanitary management of the town.

112. Are you satisfied with the way the roads are kept at present?—Yes, on the whole we are, and they are improving.

113. Have the Commissioners considered whether they will try to become the authority over the roads?—Not finally, but it was under discussion, and for the present we are not going to seek the power, for we have the experience of other towns where it was not successful, and we believe under the new Grand Jury Laws we can get the work done properly, and we are prepared to wait, for we don't know what the new Grand Jury Law will do for us.

114. Can you tell us whether your opinion as to the extension is shared by any number of the Commissioners?—Yes.

115. Then you are authorised to speak for yourself, and how many of them?—I would rather not state the number, but it is shared in by a great many.

116. But you say it is absurd to be [illegible] [illegible]?—I can't say.

117. Do you know it is adjacent to the gentleman whose fields would be taken in?—Yes, they would object to it.

118. Then you are only giving so far as possible your own individual views only?—Yes, and in my capacity as chairman of the Commissioners; and I believe I am not far wrong in saying they are pretty unanimous.

119. Following the townland boundary within this red line, how much of your land would be taken in?—I could not tell how much.

120. But it would take in a very considerable proportion?—Yes, very nearly as much more as what is in it now. The total amount of acres I hold is 1227.

121. How much of that 1227 acres is in the proposed area?—I could not tell.

122. Independent of the gentlemen's lands to be taken in by the proposed extension of a mile or a mile and a half, are there many houses which would be taken in?—Not many; it is principally people in the town who hold those accommodation lands, and they are the people who would be brought in, and then their rate would be only three halfpence in the pound.

123. Do they use those lands largely for grazing?—Certainly.

124. Do they supply from those lands produce for the town?—No, I think they principally use the produce for their own purposes, and any surplus they have they sell of course.

125. Mr. Curran.—You know the electoral divisions of Gorey and Courtown?—Yes.

126. I presume we may take it that it would be absurd to think of them as a townland?—Yes. There is only a very little portion of Courtown in the borough, and it runs away to the sea three miles from this.

127. The improvement rate of one-fourth would be payable by those owners of land outside, in your opinion, but it should be borne by the landlord?—Yes.

128. And would you apply the same principle to lands at present within the town?—Yes.

129. And the military rate the same?—Yes.

Cross-examined.

130. Mr. O'Connor.—Do you say this opinion of yours was shared by unanimously?—No, not largely.

131. Upon what is your opinion formed that this extension would benefit the town?—That it would relieve the [illegible] to a certain extent in certain parts, and bring in others who are equally enjoying the privileges and not paying anything.

132. How many would it bring in?—About a dozen or fifteen.

133. Have you counted them?—No, but I thought out eight or ten.

134. Is that all the areas?—No.

135. How many is the constituency?—I don't know.

136. What benefit would extension bestow on the ten who would be taken in?—It would bestow very considerable benefits. Up to the present time the inhabitants of the town, as you have been informed, have fought it and stemmed it, and everything of that sort, and I myself and the gentlemen living around enjoy those privileges without paying for any of them.

137. What advantage would it confer on those people within a mile and a half, more than on Lady Ramsdale, say?—Yes, a great deal more, for every time she comes into the town those people come a dozen times, and the same answer applies to the whole of them, and I am sure General Chain comes in twenty times for every time Lady Ramsdale comes in.

138. Are there any other advantages?—Yes, they would get their letters and telegrams delivered free. Lady Ramsdale does not. It is well known what benefits people living near a town get as opposed to persons living four or five miles away.

139. I believe persons living three miles away get their letters by leaving a bag at the Post Office?—Yes; and they have to pay for it.

140. You will deliver that fine to Mr. Hamilton, for instance?—Yes.

141. Do you think would this extension be any benefit to you?—Perhaps it would, and perhaps it would not; but as far as I am concerned, if the Commissioners fix the boundary at a mile or a mile and a half, I am quite satisfied with their decision.

142. Do you think it would confer any additional rights on you in respect of your tenants?—I don't believe it would.

143. Assuming that it would make these holdings brought within it townparks, would it confer any benefit?—It would, and it would not.

144. Isn't it a fact that since you got this up you have damaged the roads?—No, not at all.

145. Well, injured it?—That is a different question.

146. Isn't it a fact that in one instance at least in which I have specific instructions you included the road within the boundary, and you left untouched the land in the same man's possession outside the boundary?—I did for the present.

147. There is no such thing in Gorey as a suburb where people live who carry on business in the town?—No, except two or three.

148. It is strictly a rural area?—Yes. I believe there are only two who live outside and have business in this town.

149. Chairman.—You know several other towns well; is your opinion that it apply to them, all that land is within a certain distance derive exceptional benefit from their proximity to the town?—Yes.

150. Is there anything in the circumstances of Gorey to make it different from any other town?—No, not the slightest. In the Rocky case, which my father brought in 1858, and which you will have an opportunity of inspecting presently, you will find that which is the case there is the same here. I say the lands derive exceptional value. You will find it so.

150. Mr. O'Neill told us it was the Grand Jury did the paving?—No, it is done partly by them, and partly by the people who have flags opposite their houses.

151. General Chain.—There is one thing that I would like to put to Mr. Kirke with respect to his evidence, and that is that he should define something of the advantages which he says will result from extension of the boundaries. His reason for extending the boundary is, that it would give a regular boundary. What do you mean by a regular boundary; and what advantage does it give?—If you take a statute mile or an Irish mile round from the market house, that gives a regular boundary.

152. What advantage does that give?—It gives a definite thing. Some of it at present is within less than a quarter of a mile from the market house, and other parts of the boundary are a mile and a quarter away.

153. What advantage would that give?—It puts every one on an equal footing, because I can't see the fair play or common sense of having a town going out a quarter of a mile in one direction, and a mile and a quarter in another direction.

153. But that is owing to the shape of the town?—Yes; and a radius of a mile will bring it in.

154. But is there any specific reason why that extension would confer especial advantage?—It is just to bring every person within a certain fixed distance of a given point in the town within the radius, and to make them to pay.

Michael J. Redmond, examined.

155. Chairman.—Are you a Commissioner?—I was Chairman of the Commissioners before Mr. Kirke, and I wish to give my evidence, subject to the condition that any alteration of the boundary will not cause tenants to lose their tenant right.

156. You are a Town Commissioner at present?—Yes.

157. And you have been Chairman?—Yes.

158. And you own land outside the town?—Yes.

159. Do the owners of land receive greater rent out

Gorey. Feb. 12, [illegible]. Richard J. [illegible].

of their land owing to its proximity to the town? Of course any land in the immediate vicinity of the town is rented at a great deal higher than land outside.

160. Then, as I understand you, you are in favour of extension, but that is on the understanding that such extension shall not interfere with any rights that exist at present, in favour of the occupiers of those outside lands under the Land Act, or with any privileges they have?—Yes. I am a very large contributor.

161. Have you considered the extent to which this extension should go, bearing in mind that we are to take care to keep the townlands boundaries as the boundaries of the town?—No; I could not suggest any particular extension.

162. How far would you say that lands derive from the present borough that exceptional advantage?—That is a very difficult question. Some parts of the townland derive more advantage than in other directions.

163. But, as a general question, within what radius would you say the land derives this advantage?—I would rather not decide any particular distance.

164. But we must depend to a great extent on the distance to which the land derives additional advantage?—I would extend the boundary considerably in some directions.

165. Why in some directions more than others?—Because I would make the township more regular; it extends more in one direction than another.

166. Would you extend it more north or south or east or west?—I am not able to answer that question.

167. Taking a circle of a mile from the centre of the town would bring in the railway, and they pay no rates at present?—It would be very desirable to bring them into the township.

168. If you were to extend the boundary to the northeast and to take in the railway, would it not be duty to extend the boundary correspondingly round other portions of the town?—I don't feel competent to give an opinion on that.

169. But at all events you are of opinion it should be extended some distance beyond the present boundaries?—Yes. Of course, subject to the condition I have mentioned as to the Land Act.

170. Have you formed any opinion as to the rating of these lands that would be brought in, and whether they should continue to pay one-fourth?—Yes; I think they should pay one-fourth.

171. Have you considered the question, whether if they are brought within the borough half of the rate should be paid by the landlord?—I think it should.

172. Have you considered, with regard to the lands to be brought in, and that would only have to pay one-fourth of the improvement rate as at present, whether the whole of the district to be brought in should get the benefit of light from the municipal Commissioners, or would you consider it would be enough to give light in any continuously inhabited district?—That is all we could be expected to do. The mere land would not want light.

Cross-examined.

173. Mr. *O'Dempsey*.—Are there any houses wanted at all?—There are dozens wanted if we could afford to put them up.

174. Have you formed no opinion at all as to what advantages would be derived by the persons to be brought in?—No.

175. You have not formed any opinion on the subject?—No; but I think they have a perfect right to pay for the accommodation of having the town convenient, having such a place to resort to for different purposes.

176. Can you point to any special advantage they have?—No.

177. Would the fact of their being near the town, within a mile, for instance, give them in your opinion any additional advantages over the people who were say three miles from the town?—No; only they use the town often.

178. The farmer living a mile from the town is he likely to use the town oftener than the farmer who is several miles away?—Not so much the farmers as the gentry.

179. Are there more than two or three to whom that would allude?—Oh yes, seven or eight.

180. The great majority of the lands are occupied by farmers who use the lands for their maintenance?—Yes, and it is an advantage to them to have a market near them where they can dispose of their articles.

181. Is it any advantage more than if it was three miles from them?—It is very small, but it is an advantage to them.

182. Do you know of any of the Commissioners who are in support of the extension?—I don't mention names, but I think they are all in favour of it. I was the only one who objected to it.

183. But they did not propose any resolution?—No.

William Graham.

WILLIAM GRAHAM, examined.

184. CHAIRMAN.—You are one of the Town Commissioners?—I am one of the oldest members on the Board.

185. Have you any land outside the boundary?—Yes.

186. I may take it that your evidence is given on the supposition that the land outside to be brought in would not lose any rights under the Land Act?—That is what I understand, otherwise I would not be in favour of extension.

187. Giving your views on that supposition, what is your view, do you think that the land to a certain distance around the town does acquire exceptional advantage from its proximity to the town as a market town?—I don't know that. I am not for extension at all. I am well satisfied with the boundary as at present.

188. Do you think that the land within a mile of the town pays more rent than if it was three miles off?—Some does and more does not.

189. Is it your view as a rule that the lands close to a market town derive benefit from their proximity to the town?—They do sometimes, it is convenient to people to have a market to come into.

190. Do you think that Gorey affords that advantage?—For some places.

191. You know the present boundary of the town?—Yes; I do, well.

192. Do you mean there is no portion of the land outside the boundary of Gorey that derives advantage from its proximity to the town, that the tenant is not able to pay a higher rent, and that the landlord is not able to get a higher price for the land on account of its being close to the town?—What I understand by that is town parks. Some of them are paid for at exorbitant rates.

193. Do the lands outside pay more rent?—Some of them do, and more do not.

194. Then the landlords who get this larger rent, get it because as these fields are in the nature of town fields?—Yes, quite right.

195. Is it your opinion that anyone ought to pay for that any portion of the rates?—I don't know; it is immaterial to me one way or the other.

196. The landlord at all events gets a large rent?—Yes.

197. And isn't the tenant able to pay the larger rent?—I don't know about that.

198. How many acres do you hold yourself outside the present boundaries?—Six acres twenty perches.

199. Where is that?—Ramstown, lower.

200. What is the valuation of that?—The poor law valuation is £5 a year.

201. According to the present rating, if you were brought in, your rate would have been only 5*d*. for the last three years, and on the three years you would pay a penny farthing, and if you got half back from your landlord, why it would not be more than a halfpenny one-eighth in the three years—would you object

to pay that?—I would rather have the boundary where it is.

202. Would you suggest that Mr. White should not be brought in, or do you think he should pay anything towards the town?—If he [illegible] thought it he should pay, but I don't think he has any right to pay at all.

203. Then you would not increase the boundary at all?—No; I would not be for the extension at all; I think things are very well as they are.

204. Would you suggest that the boundaries should be lessened?—I would leave them as they are.

William Graham.

WILLIAM WHITE, examined.

William White.

205. CHAIRMAN.—Are you living in the town?—I am.

206. How long have you been living there?—More than twenty years.

207. Do you know the present municipal boundary?—I do, pretty well.

208. Is it your opinion that the lands outside derive [illegible] advantages from their proximity to the town?—I believe they derive some benefit.

209. That is, I suppose, that the occupiers are able to buy their goods and sell their produce at the market in the town?—Yes, and draw their manure from the town. It doesn't take them so long to come into the town as to the [illegible].

210. Where do the people about draw coal that [illegible] from?—They draw it from the railway, and from Courtown Harbour, and Ballymoney.

211. Do people up at the [illegible] take their produce through the town?—They do, to a great extent, anyone living outside the town has to come through it to get coal.

212. At all events they have to use the town in winter nights when it is dark?—Yes, of course.

213. And do you think it is advantageous to them to have the town lighted?—Yes, I think it is a great benefit to them on market days and fair days.

214. Have you formed any opinion as to extension; do you think the present boundary ought to be extended?—I do, to a certain limit.

215. What would be your view of the limit?—About a mile.

216. Following the townland boundaries as far as possible?—Yes, on the condition that the rights would not be interfered with under the Land Act, or any other Act.

217. It is your wish that they should have to pay one-fourth of the town rate whatever that may be?—I think it is very fair.

218. Do you think they derive, as compared with the man in the town, benefit to the extent of one-fourth?—I think the people outside derive nearly as much benefit as I do.

219. Have you thought at all whether the rate should be divided between the landlord and tenant?—Yes, that the tenant should get half from his landlord. I think he is entitled to it.

220. Does the landlord get a larger rent on account of the land being close to the town?—He does.

Cross-examined.

221. Mr. O'[illegible].—You have no land yourself?—No; there are not many farmers within a mile of the town; there are a great many gentlemen there who derive benefit.

222. What benefit does the man who lives a mile away derive over the man who lives three miles away?—In the first place he has not so far to come to the town.

223. Is that the only thing?—No, he has other things. If a man lives three miles away he would not come in at all if there is a wet day, but the day only clear up and he can then come in if he lives near the town; then there is the extra wear and tear on his cart, and the extra time employed in coming in and going out.

224. How do you arrive at the estimate that one-fourth is a proper charge?—I think the land is already charged one-fourth, and that I think is fair.

225. Do I understand you, that you would have a different estimate of the amount a man should pay according to the distance he is from the town?—The man outside doesn't pay anything at present.

226. You say that your rates as an occupier in the town are necessarily increased by the use the people outside make of your roads, and they should pay accordingly?—Yes, and we have been obliged to keep up the roads for them up to the present time.

227. Might you not as well take in the county?—No, because we would then have to have a third cemetery and all that.

228. I believe there are a good many outside against extension?—There are a good many outside who are owners of land, and are in favour of extension, only they are afraid their rights will be taken away under the Land Act.

229. General [illegible].—As to the disadvantage to the town by reason of their coal being obliged to go through the town, I should like to ask how many of those who will be brought in under the extension will be likely to use much of the lighting of the town in bringing in coal, because it seems to me that people and a great many who would be brought in, don't derive any such advantage.

Richard [illegible].

RICHARD [illegible], examined.

230. CHAIRMAN.—You are clerk of the Gorey Union?—Yes.

231. You live in the borough at present?—I do.

232. Are you a tenant occupier?—Yes.

233. How much land do you hold outside the boundary?—About twenty-four statute acres.

234. What is the valuation of the twenty-four acres?—Upwards of £30 a year.

235. Do you pay a higher rent for that on account of your proximity to the town?—I am very doubtful on the point, I hardly think I do; my land is considered a farm, and has always been considered such, and not a town park.

236. Don't you pay more for the same quality of land having regard to its being so close to the town, than you would pay for the same quality of land out in the country?—Not myself, as I have admitted.

237. But suppose that land was in the market, and that you were not tenant of it at all; don't you think that the landlord would get more rent for that than on account of its being so close to the town than if it was three miles away?—Not as a farm; if it was cut up and let in small lots it would be the case.

238. But suppose it was put up for sale in the market, don't you think it would bring more on account of its proximity to Gorey?—No, I don't think it would. Land has been sold in the immediate neighbourhood of Gorey, at Mr. [illegible]'s sale, for less than land three or four miles away.

239. Do you think that land within a mile of the town does derive advantage from its proximity to the market?—That will depend on the town. In Enniscorthy and Wexford there are suburbs, and there is a tremendously large population, but there is really no market in Gorey for market produce. People there either can get the same prices for their potatoes at [illegible] the town, and there is no difference except the distance.

240. Do they frequent the town as a market town?—Yes.

241. Do they frequent the town after night?—Yes, on market days as much as the town people.

242. And isn't that a benefit to them?—Not more

them to the people living three or four miles off, and when Lord Courtown is at home, or Lady Esmonde, they make as much use of the town as General Owen or Mr. Hamilton or Mr. Kirke. The boundaries of the townlands are all irregular, and unless you cut houses and land you will have to take the townland boundaries. There are only a few acres of Gorey Corporation lands outside the boundary.

243. Mr. Cotton.—Why did they do that with the Gorey Corporation land?—I could not tell you. I think it was a mistake in making it so. Gorey is an old Corporation, and under the Irish Parliament it sent a member to Parliament, and I think these boundaries were fixed then.

244. Chairman.—Do the people living outside supply milk and butter to the town?—No, the people living in the town have nearly all fields of their own, the greater part of them are within the town at present.

245. Do they buy milk?—Yes, from shopkeepers.

246. Where do the shopkeepers get it from?—From the fields outside.

247. And don't they derive advantage in that way?—It is very trifling.

248. But there is a very large acreage to be brought in?—Take for instance the articles of butter and milk, there are people coming in for three miles and selling it for the same price as the shopkeepers, and they get no greater advantage than the man a mile off.

249. That admits they get some advantage?—Yes, they save half-an-hour in the transit, and they must have some one to send in with it and a horse and cart, but the people in the town must have the same. I would like to disabuse your mind about the sanitary act. Mr. Kirke made a great mistake about the sanitary act. There is no such thing as £12 saving at all. There is no sanitary expense here except the water rate, which is one penny in the pound on the average. It is twopence this year.

250. Mr. Cotton.—On what district is that one penny sanitary rate struck?—It is on eight townlands of the electoral division in the town, and two outside it.

251. What are the names of those?—Ballyminaun, Ramsfort Park, Clonattin, Lower, Creagh Demesne, Gorey Corporation lands within and without the town, Gorey-hill, Knocknasillogue, Ramstown, Lower, Gorey-bridge, and Mill Lands.

252. That rate was for the water supply?—Yes.

253. Water is not supplied outside the present boundary?—No, sir; I think water is supplied to one case outside the boundary. There is a fountain.

254. And many of these townlands though rated for the water are not supplied with water?—They are not.

255. Did the guardians fixed that rating?—Yes. With regard to the sanitary rate, if the Commissioners take the sanitary rate it will be altogether a new and additional expense. The cost of the staff in the union is at present less than one farthing in the pound. The Town Commissioners will have to pay a sanitary staff. They will have to pay three or perhaps four officials, and that will be an additional expense on the town rates just in the same way as county officers would have to be paid if they took up the Grand Jury rate. I suppose there is no use in my entering my protest against my rights being taken away.

256. Are you against extension of the boundary irrespective of that question?—I am.

257. Suppose there was an extension of a mile, what would be the increase in the population within the district?—It would be very little. It is very slightly populated.

258. Would there be many farmers brought in who are resident on small farms outside the present boundary?—There would.

259. That is persons not living in the town?—Yes.

260. About how many?—Fifteen about.

261. And there would be about eight or ten gentlemen's places brought in?—Yes.

General Owen examined.

262. Chairman.—You live outside the town?—Yes.

263. You know the present boundaries?—I have a sort of vague idea of them; they are not very strongly defined; they went on the fact of townlands.

264. And we are directed still to keep as near townland boundaries as possible; is it your opinion there should be any extension?—I can't see the least reason for it. If any reason can be shown, I will be prepared to consider it, but I can't see any reason for it.

265. Take any market town in Ireland; is it your opinion that the lands within a mile or so of the centre of the town don't derive some exceptional benefit from their proximity to the town?—That depends on circumstances. I can well understand that in Enniscorthy for instance they are getting a benefit from the town, in the sale of produce to the people in the town, but here it is different, and I can't see the benefit exactly.

266. With regard to your own residence, don't you use the town yourself?—I never use the town excepting it is for the benefit of the town. For instance, I come in to petty sessions once a fortnight, and I come to the post-office, and I use the church in the same way as if I lived in one of these rural places; but I don't see what exceptional benefit arises from that point, for I would use the church the same if it was not in the town at all.

267. Do you use Gorey as a market town?—Well, there are markets all round; there is a market at Glenageary hill, and according to that view you should go there and extend the bounds too. Mr. Creighton has corroborated the view I hold, that there is no increase of value given by the proximity of the lands to the town. I certainly don't think there is, and I certainly don't use this town much at night—I can answer for that.

268. Don't you use Gorey as a town for buying your marketing?—Very little, and whatever use I do make of it is because I wish to assist the people in the town, and it is only for that reason I come to it at all. I could get the articles in many cases cheaper down from Dublin, so that it is only for the purpose of assisting the people in the town, that I deal in it. One likes to help one's neighbour when he can, and I think it is right that I should assist the town whenever I can; but in some cases I find the difference is so great it is better to get the goods from Dublin.

269. Have you much land yourself?—No. I don't attempt tillage; I have only about twenty-four Irish acres.

270. What is your valuation?—I believe it is £44.

271. Don't you think you derive advantage to the extent of half one-fourth the rate?—Well, that is very small, but what is there to stop this rate, or to keep it at that infinitesimal value? Suppose a Rural Town Council came in and began all sorts of improvements, where would the rate be then and what could we do?

272. According to their present power they can only go up to one shilling and not beyond it?—Well, I would not like to see it at one shilling.

Cross-examined.

273. Mr. O'Donoghue.—You have your own residence and a number of houses on your land?—I have my own house.

274. And under this scheme any house taken in would be rated at the full amount?—Yes.

275. And not one-fourth?—No, and as to the [illegible] some of us out there come under that objection. There might be something in the objection if it concerned us

Cavan. Feb. 14, 18[illegible].

Michael Kelly.

MICHAEL KELLY, examined.

276. CHAIRMAN.—You are a ratepayer in the town of Cavan?—Yes, sir.

277. Have you land outside the boundary?—No.

278. What is your valuation?—I don't [illegible].

279. Is it your opinion the boundary should be extended?—I think in a small place like this it doesn't require it. It is a very small little market town; it is not like a large place.

280. Do you think the people having farms round the town and living outside the boundary don't get advantage from the lighting of this town, and don't use it?—I don't think they get much advantage.

281. Do you think they get any advantage?—They might get a little, but I don't think it would be any great advantage to them.

282. Do you know of your own knowledge whether any of those farmers come to the town and sell and barter?—Yes; and they sell it four or five miles away as well.

283. But the people near the town sell them?—Yes, and the people far out sell them too.

284. But the people far out don't get the same advantage?—Yes, to a great extent; [illegible] are not so [illegible], and they have more time to come in.

285. Doesn't it take more time, for instance, for the man who lives several miles away to come into the town than the man who lives outside it?—Of course it does.

286. And the man whose time is occupied must be paid?—Of course, but the difference is nothing.

287. Is it your opinion that the fact of bringing in anybody would lessen your rate, and do you still believe, after what you have heard, that they should not be brought in?—I am quite willing to pay the rates I am paying in the town.

288. Do you think those people outside should not pay something to help you with the rates?—I think what they would pay would not make a great difference.

289. But no matter whether it only made a difference of £1 or £1 a year?—I don't think they get much benefit from it. There is not one here after night.

290. Having heard the matter explained, are you still of opinion that this extension is not necessary?—Yes.

291. And that the people around derive no substantial advantage from the town?—No.

292. General [illegible].—We have to pay for the light we use, and as to flagging, it appears to have been half paid by the county, and we are satisfied, therefore, to half of the flagging, but the town is getting the extra value out of it, yet they only paid half of it.

William Reynolds.

WILLIAM REYNOLDS, examined.

293. CHAIRMAN.—Are you living in the town?—Yes.

294. Are you a rated occupier?—Yes.

295. Have you land outside the present boundary?—Some.

296. How much have you outside the present boundary?—Three and a half acres in one place, and [illegible] in another.

297. Would the land be brought in by the new extension?—One part of it would, and the other would not.

298. What is the part that would be within the extension valued at?—£4 10s., and I pay £3 for it.

299. Am I right in thinking you pay that larger rent because the land is so close to the town?—I think it is on that account, or rather the improvements I have made on the land.

300. Would that land be as valuable suppose it was three miles from the town?—No, not quite.

301. Then it derives some advantage by being near the town?—Yes.

302. And it is more valuable to the landlord because he gets the larger rent for it?—He gets a larger rent.

303. And it is more valuable to you because it is so close to the town?—It is not so very close, but it is within a mile.

304. Do you sell anything?—No.

305. You use that for your family purposes?—Yes.

306. Is it your opinion that there should be an extension or not?—I believe it would be injurious to the whole inhabitants of the town to have any extension.

307. Do you mean that, as applied to the ratepayers who have no land, or to those who have land?—I have heard a great deal about reduction in the rates; they are small now, and I think that instead of a reduction they would be increased by the increasing of the boundaries.

308. Why do you think so?—Because there would be a staff of officials employed that is not now employed, and then their salaries would come out of our taxes.

309. What staff do you allude to?—The sanitary town inspector, and all that.

310. At present, taking in a mile, or whatever you would take in, would not make you the urban sanitary authority?—No, nor give power to take in the roads.

311. But they may have power over the roads if they apply for it?—Then there would be [illegible] the whole of the road about the town to be repaired by us.

312. At present they have not the roads, nor can they get them without what is called an Act of Parliament?—I think they intend to look for the sanitary points.

313. With regard to the existing state of things, what is your opinion as to extension, leaving the other questions about roads and sanitary matters out of sight for the present?—My opinion is it would be injurious to the inhabitants; they would suffer from it.

314. That is, that in the future they would suffer?—Yes.

315. You are, I believe, one of the largest business men in the town?—I have a large business in the town; my poor law valuation is £[illegible].

316. Is this land a mile away more valuable than land two miles off?—What the difference there is is nothing worth bringing in a cow.

317. It would cost you more if it was two miles off?—Yes.

Thomas Mullahan.

THOMAS MULLAHAN examined.

318. CHAIRMAN.—You are a rated occupier in the town?—Yes.

319. And have land outside the town?—Yes; about 170 acres.

320. Would it all be within a mile from the town?—Yes. I have some within the township boundary; about two and a half acres.

321. Do you think this land you have round the town is not more valuable than if it was three miles off?—Well, I have made it valuable to myself. I have land far away that was more valuable. It was no value to me until I made it valuable.

322. How did you do that?—By my own labour and manure. I have a farm some two miles away, and I could have made it valuable nearly as cheap as this.

323. Take the land you have at present within the

Gorey.
Feb. [illegible]
Thomas Mulligan.

township boundary. Does it cost you less to manure that than land farther off?—Well, the two and a half acres within the boundary, I had no way of getting manure to it unless on a man's back, until I cut away four and a half feet of rock.

324. In reclaiming land can you not reclaim land close to the town for less than land farther off?—No; because I can get labour cheaper out there than near the town.

325. But you can draw manure easier to the place that is close to the town?—But I could keep a horse cheaper out there than in the town.

326. Then you have no advantage. Is it your opinion that your two and a half acres should be taken off the town?—I paid only £6 for that when I got it, and now I pay £13 for it, and that is all owing to my own labour on it improving it.

327. Is it your opinion that we should put the field you have in the town outside the boundary?—It doesn't matter where you put it; but I know it would be a great injury to the people of the town to have the boundary extended.

328. That is that it would be injurious to the people in the town who have land outside?—We would lose our protection of our rights. My opinion, and, as far as I know, the opinion of all persons outside would be against being taken in on any terms if they are to lose the benefit of the Land Act. I have lost my right under the Land Act in respect to this small bit of land.

Bernard Flood.

BERNARD FLOOD, examined.

329. CHAIRMAN.—Are you a ratepayer in the town of Gorey?—I am.

330. And you have land outside the town?—Yes, and inside also, and I have about five landlords.

331. Are you for or against any extension of the boundary of the town?—I am against any extension; no matter how it goes I am against it.

332. How much land have you outside the boundary of the town?—About thirty-eight acres, and I am afraid they might lay the claw on it too.

333. What is your valuation?—£30 a year.

334. Don't you think you pay more for it because it is near the town?—I don't know.

335. Where is the land that is outside the boundary?—It is a good distance off.

336. Then, except what you have in the town, your land is a mile and a half away?—Yes.

337. Is there any of it within a mile?—No.

338. Do you think this extension would be any substantial benefit to the town?—No; I think it would be more harm than good.

339. Suppose any gentleman in the neighbourhood was to make the town a present of £25 a year in aid of the rates, would that be any benefit?—I don't think it would. He would want something in return for it.

James Doyle.

JAMES DOYLE, examined.

340. CHAIRMAN.—Are you a ratepayer in the town?—I am.

341. And have you land outside the town also?—Yes.

342. Within the mile radius?—Yes.

343. How much land have you outside the town boundary?—About three acres within a mile of the town.

344. What is the rent of that land?—£3 17s. 6d. a year.

345. Do you think it is more valuable by reason of its being close to the town?—It is more for accommodation than anything else we have it. I have a house in the town, but I don't live in it; I live within three miles of it.

346. Don't you send your produce from this three acres into the town?—I never got 4d. out of it these three years, only what I brought into it.

347. What is the value of the three acres?—£1 10s. or thereabouts. I think it is better to leave as it we are.

John Doyle.

JOHN DOYLE, examined.

348. CHAIRMAN.—Do you live in the town of Gorey?—I do.

349. Are you rated in the town?—My father is, but he is not able to attend here to-day.

350. Has he any land outside the boundary?—Yes.

351. Within a mile of the town?—Yes, and outside a mile.

352. Within a mile of the town how much land has he?—About 20 acres.

353. Does he pay more rent for that 20 acres of land because it is so close to the town?—He has to pay for it on account of improvements he made in it himself. It was worth nothing when he got it.

354. But suppose your father had liberty to assign it or to sell it?—He has not liberty.

355. Is it more valuable to the landlord through being so close to the town?—To the landlord it is, but to the tenant it is not.

356. Don't you think if your father was out of that farm, and the landlord wanted to set it, he could get more from a good tenant for it?—He could not have better than my father.

357. But isn't it more valuable by reason of its proximity to the town?—No, it is more value farther off. The land near the town is bad on account of vermin of all sorts.

358. The land farther off is better?—Yes. There is some of my father's land inside the town, and what was inside was raised from £20 to £18, and the land outside was not raised at all.

359. The outside land was not raised?—No, what was inside the corporation was raised, and what was outside was left as it was.

360. Your opinion is that at all events taking one a mile radius round the town the land is not more valuable in the market than land three miles off?—I think it is as valuable outside the town.

361. But is it more valuable?—I can't exactly say. I know we have land three miles from the town, and it is more valuable than land that is inside the town, and as to the milk, if it was as dear as whiskey it would not pay the rent.

362. Mr. COTTON.—Would you be in favour of having the boundary increased?—I think everyone is satisfied with it as it is, gentry, farmers, and shopkeepers.

363. And you don't want anybody to come in to help the town?—No, the town is very well satisfied to pay their rates, and I think the farmers who are coming into the town have rates enough on them outside the mile—more than they are able to pay.

Mr. Cliff Owen, examined.

[illegible] Cliff Owen.

364. Chairman.—Are you at present within the town boundary?—No, I am outside it. I live at Knockmullen.

365. Would you be brought in by the mile radius?—Yes. I am about an eighth of a mile outside the town.

366. How much land have you?—I have a very old leasehold on it. A great deal of money has been spent, and it is very cheap.

367. Suppose that land was in the market would it bring more on account of its proximity to the town, than if it was three miles off?—It might, at villa residences, but I don't think the land would be anything more.

368. For instance would not the farmer have facilities for getting manure from the town?—He would, but two or three miles off he would have the same facilities. There is no daily market, it is only a weekly market.

369. But the man who is close to the town saves time, and he must have similar advantages in other respects?—I think the advantages extend to a certain area for those who use Gorey, and I think these people improve the town, and if they did not come in the shopkeepers would not be able to live.

370. Both they use the town and the shopkeepers get the advantage from their coming in?—Yes.

371. And you also have the advantage of having close at your door the opportunity of buying under more advantageous terms than if you were three or four miles off?—Not sufficient to cause us to be brought in to the boundary.

372. Do you think you ought to pay anything, be it the smallest coin you can imagine, towards the lighting and keeping up of the town?—My idea is that that argument would just as well apply to an area of three or four miles, and to all the people who use the town.

373. Yes, but it would be very hard to increase the town out to that distance?—I think the circular line has attracted a good many people; it looks a compact and nice boundary. If the boundary was extended a mile it would be so irregular, for it would go by townland boundaries.

374. Mr. Cowper.—You think that in the extension of any town it would be advisable to keep to townland boundaries as much as possible?—I think it would be much more convenient for the collection of taxes. I am a tax collector myself, and I know it is very inconvenient when townlands run into one another.

375. It would be an advantage to adhere to the townland boundaries?—Yes, I think the boundaries should be the same; it would facilitate the collection of rates if the town boundaries and the townland boundaries were the same. We have no guarantee that we will not be contracted out of the Land Act, and as to the railway, it benefits as much by the town as the town by the railway; if I was owner of Knockmullen in fee, I would vote for the extension of the boundary to Knockmullen.

376. What would be your reason for that?—I would get more for it if let to a tenant, but there would be a chance of doing away with the goodwill of it, if the boundary was extended, at present; I have a certain good will of the lands, and if they were brought in I would be jeopardising that.

377. But suppose you were absolutely protected against anything of that kind, would you be for extension, particularly if you would only have to pay one-fourth of the valuation, and half of it should be paid by the landlord?—It would be for my own good, but it would not be for the good of the town?

378. Why do you think it would not be for the good of the town?—Because I don't think there is any reason brought forward why these boundaries should be altered.

379. Except that these outlying districts would have to pay something to the town?—I think the town has got sufficient property to tax, for they have a valuation of £4,000, and why do they want another £1,000?

380. Because if you give the other £1,000, you give that in aid of the present rates, and you are relieving the ratepayers in the town, and throwing that amount of responsibility on the country, which it is said gets some little advantage from its proximity to the town?—Who are the townspeople who have said so? There was only one resident of the town examined here in favour of it, and I have heard a great many townspeople who were against it; it is not like a daily market, if you send in produce here on ordinary days, the chances are you will not be able to sell it; it is not like Wexford, where you can send in garden produce daily, but here you are in the same position as the person living four or five miles off, and in fact I am not certain it is legal to send in farm produce, except on market days, however, if you do send it in, the chances are it will go back to you unsold.

381. Is there not any appreciable advantage to the man within a mile, as against the man within three miles?—He must save in the time occupied in coming into the town—that is the only advantage.

382. Mr. Cowper.—If there were two farms, one within a mile, and the other within three miles, would there be any difference in the letting value of the farms?—I could not tell; I am not sufficiently acquainted with land to know that.

383. Do you think the advantage would be infinitesimal?—I don't think it is sufficiently large to alter the present boundary.

Mr. John Redmond, continued.

John Redmond.

384. Chairman.—Are you a ratepayer in the town?—I am.

385. Have you land inside?—Yes, and outside too.

386. Outside how much have you?—Three acres inside, three acres outside, and five acres besides.

387. Are the five acres within the mile?—No.

388. You have three acres within the mile?—Yes.

389. What is the value of the three acres within the mile?—£5 10s.

390. What makes you pay more for that land than the other, is it because it is close to the town?—No, it is because I made it more valuable myself.

391. Take it as it is now, suppose it was to be let in the market, do you think it would bring more on account of its being so close to the town?—I think it is bringing plenty as it is.

392. If you had three acres of land of the same quality three miles from the town, would it be valued as high?—I can't say.

393. How far from the town is the five acres?—About a mile and a half.

394. Is that of the same value?—I am paying more for that, than what is near the town.

395. What is the valuation of that?—The Government valuation is £3 10s., and I pay £12 for it.

396. Is it as good land as the three acres?—No; I don't think it is, for I made that better. I think the whole thing is unnecessary; you would not get a farmer within a mile, or a mile and a quarter of Gorey, who has land, and would be in favour of extension; every gentleman round here has land up to three miles from the town, and as I don't see what advantage it would be to them to have taxation put upon them, as they are satisfied to remain as they are.

397. Nearly all the people outside, within a certain distance, are ratepayers already, you say?—Yes.

398. And therefore you say it is no advantage to them to have any alteration?—Yes.

399. Because what they would have to pay on one land would be lightened on the other?—Yes.

400. Do you apply that to Mr. Elrick's land?—It is suited to all the people round here, except what he holds himself.

401. Do you not think he should pay for what he holds himself?—What he holds himself goes away out too far.

The inquiry then closed.

WATERFORD.—MARCH 7TH, 1870.

Before Mr. Exham, Q.C., and Mr. Cotton, C.E.

Mr. Joseph Howard, Town Clerk, examined.

1. Chairman.—You are the Town Clerk of Waterford?—Yes.

2. And have been so for a long time?—Yes, several years.

3. What is the extent in acres of the municipal area of Waterford?—479 acres 2 roods 16 perches.

4. And the population?—About 2[illegible],000 inhabitants.

5. And the present valuation?—£56,738 5s.

6. I believe there has been a little increase in the population?—Well, nothing material. We are just under the figures that would entitle us to take advantage of the provisions of the Artisans' Dwellings Act.

7. How many wards is Waterford divided into?—Five.

8. And are these the same for poor law purposes?—They are not coterminous, but they have all the same names except one. What we call the Centre Ward in the municipal district is called St. Patrick's in the poor law; the other four are the same.

9. Can you give the valuation of these wards for municipal and poor law purposes?—Only in the city. For the Centre Ward for municipal purposes the total area is 60a. 2r. 6p., and for poor law purposes it is 54a. 3r. 23p.

10. What is the valuation of the Centre Ward?—For civic purposes £8,011 10s., and for poor law purposes £6,776 10s. The area of the Custom House Ward for civic purposes is 85a. 1r. 8p.; for poor law purposes 63a. 0r. 37p.; valuation for civic purposes £9,833, and for poor law purposes £8,110 10s. The South Ward area for civic purposes 116a. 1r. 39p., for poor law purposes 103a. 1r. 16p.; valuation for civic purposes £6,868, for poor law purposes £6,010 10s. Tower Ward, civic area 180a. 1r. 6p., and the same for poor law purposes; valuation for civic purposes and poor law purposes £9,740 15s.; and West Ward 166a. 3r. 37p.; for poor law purposes area 88a. 0r. 33p.; valuation for civic purposes £11,186, and for poor law purposes £10,040 5s. West Ward comprised £3,600, the tolls of the Waterford bridge. Although there seems to be an apparent difference in the areas, that is only an error in calculation.

11. Can you tell the number of burgesses in each ward?—In Centre Ward the number of burgesses is 128.

12. How many are qualified for the office of town councillor?—I could not say exactly. Our lists only give the name and description of the property they are rated for. But by going over the names and from the rate book I could get it. It is hard, for this reason, that there are two qualifications for town councillors, that is to be rated at £25, or to be a burgess at any rating, and to be worth £1,000; therefore I could not tell except by repute. I can only give you the rating of those at £25 and upwards. In Centre Ward there are 128 burgesses, 61 being qualified by rating; in Custom House Ward 168, 80 qualified by rating; in the South Ward 161, 7 qualified; in the Tower 177, 48 qualified; and in the West 186, 86 qualified.

13. Each of the wards has two aldermen and six councillors?—Yes.

14. That is 40 altogether?—Yes.

15. And how many guardians are returned for each ward?—Two guardians.

16. Is the whole of the municipal area within the one electoral division?—Yes.

17. And that electoral division extends much beyond the municipal district?—Yes, as shown on the map before you.

18. Well, the Parliamentary boundary, I think we have it, is larger than the municipal?—Yes.

19. How much actually does the Parliamentary boundary contain in acres?—9,1[illegible] acres, and the population is 29,1[illegible].

20. And the electoral division?—It contains 7,[illegible] acres, and the population is 2[illegible],[illegible].

21. Do you know what is the registrar's district for the registration of births, deaths, and marriages?—It is 17,[illegible] acres, and has a population of 30,[illegible].

22. And we have it that the municipal and poor law wards are not coterminous?—No, the wards for municipal purposes are not coterminous with the others.

23. Is the entire area within the five wards for poor law purposes in the aggregate the same as the municipal?—They include the municipal, but they contain a larger extent of land.

24. Then they are not coterminous?—No. Take the Centre Ward in the municipal area, it is included in St. Patrick's Ward in the electoral division.

25. Mr. Cotton.—Take the Custom House (municipal) Ward does it go to the north side of the river at all?—No, not for municipal purposes.

26. Then, in point of fact, they are not the same?—No, except in the case of the Lower Ward, which is the same for municipal and poor law purposes.

27. At present you are under the Municipal Corporation Act of 1840?—Yes, the 3rd and 4th Victoria, chapter 108.

28. Have you adopted the Towns Improvement Act at all?—Only one or two clauses.

29. Which are they?—Those with reference to hackney cars, and some very trifling things.

30. Now, as to the rates, you have never levied in Waterford any municipal rate?—No, never. We did formerly, the old lamp tax, which was under an old local Act called the Waterford Police Act, but that has been discontinued; but we have the power of levying it still. It has been discontinued, however, for some time.

31. Then there are no municipal rates at present?—None at present.

32. Now, as to the poor law rates, can you give us the poor law rating for the past two or three years?—I am afraid not from memory, but I can get it.

33. Can you give the county cess, the city grand jury cess?—Yes, I can give the average—from 1s. to 13d. in the £; it averages about 2s. 1d. in the year. The cess levied is about that.

34. The cess levied in lieu of grand jury cess has averaged about 1s. 1d. each half year, or about 2s. 2d. in the year. Then the only other rate that would be levied here is the water rate?—Yes. There is no water rate, however, at present. There is a water rate collector, but no rate levied.

35. What is it contemplated the water rate would be?—It is limited by Act of Parliament to 3d. in the pound.

36. Then the lighting—how is that paid for?—It is paid by the Corporation out of the borough fund.

37. Not the borough fund, for there is no borough rate?—Out of their property.

38. What are the debts of the Corporation at present?—Well, the water debt, that is about £36,000.

39. I thought it was only £25,000?—Oh, there was a mistake in the report in the printing, perhaps, of the report of the Committee of the House of Commons, in which it was put down at £30,000. The original amount was £30,000 borrowed from the Board of Works, and that sum has been expended.

40. The whole of it?—Yes, and at present an application is pending before the Local Government Board for a further loan of £15,000, to complete the works, and distribute the water through the city. We are informed by the Secretary of the Local Government

[illegible], that the provisional order has been prepared. I should say that the other side of the river has been exempted. It has been exempted from the operation of the local act, and won't have to pay any water rate.

42. Is it the opinion that any alteration ought to be made in the present wards, or is it believed that they are fairly divided. Is there, in fact, any feeling expressed with reference to the subject?—I have not heard much feeling expressed with reference to the matter, or as to any alteration, but there is no doubt the area of the wards is very unequal.

43. Here is the Centre Ward with only twenty acres, and the Custom House with twenty-five acres, whilst the others are six times that—seven times that, in fact?—Yes, but those two are the most densely populated of the city.

44. Yes, but would the property be more valuable in proportion?—Yes, much more, for they are situated just in the very heart of the city.

45. I see the smallest number of burgesses is in the Centre Ward, 123, and the largest is in the Tower Ward, 177, could there be any better or more desirable division made than at present, in your opinion?—Well, I could not suggest anything that would be an improvement.

46. Was it discussed at all, to your knowledge?—Well, the division of the wards was not. The extension of the boundaries was, but the division or alteration of the wards was not discussed by the Town Council.

47. In the bill proposed by the Corporation a few years ago here, was there any suggestion about the alteration of the wards?—No, not that I remember.

48. With reference to the queries we forwarded to you, the question was asked whether or not the present municipal boundaries were regarded with dissatisfaction by the ratepayers generally, or by any section of them?—Yes, that matter was considered by a Committee in charge of the matter, and they thought the ratepayers were indifferent whether the extension took place or not.

49. Has the matter been considered by the Town Council here, in consequence of the queries we sent to them?—Yes.

50. And was the consideration of it referred to a Committee?—Yes, to the Finance Committee of the Corporation.

51. To report on it?—Yes.

52. When was it referred to them, about what date?—It was first referred to the Finance Committee, as far back as when we first received your queries, that was last November, or about that time.

53. The Finance Committee then, I take it, considered the matter?—Yes.

54. Was that at a full meeting of the Finance Committee?—Yes.

55. How many were present?—Well, there were ten members of the Committee, and when first it was considered, I think there were five members present.

56. Did they afterwards come to any formal decision, or make any report on the subject?—Merely to the conclusion that it would be desirable to extend the boundary in accordance with this map (produced), following the black line you see marked on it.

57. That is, they considered it would be desirable to extend the boundary to the extent proposed by the Parliamentary Committee, the Committee of the House of Commons?—Yes, one is marked.

58. Mr. Cowvot.—Could you let us have a copy of the Parliamentary plans lodged?—Yes. In 1875 the Corporation proposed a bill by which they sought amongst other things for an extension of the municipal area, and making it coterminous with the electoral division. That bill was opposed in Parliament, and a compromise was offered by the Corporation to have the boundary extended to the line shown, but in consequence of further opposition that was not accepted by the Committee. The Finance Committee then adopted an intermediate area between these two, and which is also shown on the map, and this was submitted to the Council. That is how the matter stood.

59. What was done by the Finance Committee [illegible] brought before the Corporation?—It was [illegible] back to the Committee for further report.

60. When was that?—On the 28th of February. The resolution referring it to the Finance Committee on the 20th December was as follows:—

"Resolved,—That the letter of the [illegible] Commissioners, dated 18th November, 1876, be referred to the Finance and Law Committee to prepare a draft report."

And their further report was as follows:—

"Council Chamber, Town Hall,

"Waterford, 3rd March, 1877.

"Finance and Law Committee.

"As to the extension of the Borough Boundary, we beg to submit for the information of the Council the valuation of the additional area proposed to be included, the municipal rates thereof, the estimated cost of repairs of the roads, and the cost of lighting said roads.

"Borough Boundary. Valuation of Additional Area.

	£	s.	d.
Tower Ward, ...	[illegible]	[illegible]	[illegible]
Custom House Ward, ...	[illegible]	[illegible]	[illegible]
Centre Ward, ...	[illegible]	[illegible]	[illegible]
West Ward, ...	[illegible]	[illegible]	[illegible]
South Ward, ...	[illegible]	[illegible]	[illegible]
	[illegible]	[illegible]	0

	£	s.	d.
Value of Electoral Division outside Borough Boundary, . . .	[illegible]	[illegible]	[illegible]

	A.	R.	P.
Area of Electoral Division outside Borough, ...	[illegible]	1	[illegible]

"Borough Extension—Additional Area and Roads.

	A.	R.	P.
Tower Ward, ...	[illegible]	[illegible]	[illegible]
Custom House Ward, ...	[illegible]	[illegible]	[illegible]
Centre Ward, ...	[illegible]	[illegible]	[illegible]
West Ward, ...	[illegible]	[illegible]	[illegible]
South Ward, ...	[illegible]	[illegible]	[illegible]
Total, . . .	[illegible]	1	[illegible]

"Roads.

	s.	d.		£	s.	d.
[illegible] perches at	[illegible]	0.	. .	[illegible]	[illegible]	[illegible]
[illegible] "	[illegible]	[illegible]	. .	[illegible]	[illegible]	[illegible]
[illegible] "	1	[illegible]	. .	[illegible]	[illegible]	[illegible]
[illegible] "	1	9.	. .	11	[illegible]	7
				[illegible]	[illegible]	[illegible]

"Additional Roads for Lighting Borough Extension.

"[illegible] miles and [illegible] yards—18 lamps to each mile equal to [illegible] lamps at [illegible] per lamp—£[illegible].

"Sanitary Expenses.

"About £100 per cent. per annum additional."

62. Now, what action did the Town Council take upon that?—On the 4th of March they held a meeting, and the question came up for discussion, when the following resolution was agreed to:—

"That, believing the extension of the Borough Boundary would entail additional expenditure on the Borough without any corresponding benefit, we consider that no extension should be made."

63. Mr. Cowvot.—Was that adopted unanimously?—Well, there was no division, but I don't think Mr. Fisher agreed to it, and perhaps there were one or two others who agreed with him.

64. Did the Finance Committee consider anything about the ward boundaries?—No, they did not go into that subject at all.

65. How far does the county of the city of Waterford extend?—For Parliamentary purposes it extends five miles.

66. I mean how far does the county of the city extend for taxing purposes under the Grand Jury?—It is equal to the municipal boundary.

67. This proposed extended district is under the county Grand Jury?—Yes, under the county Grand Jury.

68. Can you tell me what the cess outside the borough is at present?—About the same as the city Grand Jury cess. The cess is about the same; there might be a penny in the £ difference, but practically it is the same.

69. CHAIRMAN.—In what baronies are the proposed extended lands situate?—In Kilculliheen, Gaultier, and Middlethird.

70. What was the Grand Jury cess for these three?—Well, the average would be, taking last year, about 1s. 6d. There was for Kilculliheen 1s. 6d., Gaultier 1s. 5½d., Middlethird 1s. 6½d.

71. That is for the half year?—Yes, I have taken it from the July Assizes of last year.

72. I see then that the inhabitants of the district proposed to be taken from the county and added to the city are paying about 6d. in the £ or 7d. in the £ more than the people in the municipal district?—Yes.

73. They would appear to pay more than the people in the municipal part?—Yes.

74. But at present they are getting no lighting?—No.

75. And they would not have to pay public water rate at present?—No, it is not levied, and they do not pay any public water rate.

76. That is in the municipal area?—Yes.

77. They gain 6d. on the one hand, and it would be an actual saving of 3d. about?—Yes.

78. But at present they have no lighting?—No, and they derive all the benefits of the city—of using it.

79. Then, if they were brought in and had no lighting to pay for, the city would make money on bringing them in, in fact, and they would save about 3d. in the £?—Yes.

80. They would get one-eighth of their threepence towards the public water rate?—Yes.

81. And the roads would cost them about the same?—In the estimate we have given in we only give it for repairs of the roads, we have not taken anything into account for sweeping.

82. But you add on about £100 for sanitary expenses?—Yes, but we don't mean sweeping of the streets, that is kept separate.

83. Would you not be able, for say about 2s. 1d. in the year, to keep the roads of the city, if your Grand Jury cess in the city is sufficient to enable you to repair, water, and scavenge the streets?—Yes, but there is a misapprehension—the Grand Jury does not do anything about the roads in the city. The Corporation does the entire thing with the Corporation finances. The Grand Jury does not use a penny on that, with the exception perhaps of £12 or £20 a year on the roads.

84. What then?—On the Lunatic Asylum salaries, what we call "imperatives"—all the streets within the municipality are done by the Corporation, but the Grand Jury have nothing to do with the repairs of the streets or roads, except the boundary road around the city, one half of which is kept in repair by the county and the other half by the city.

85. MR. COTTON.—But it is all within Waterford?—Yes, the county and the borough of Waterford keep that road between them, and that is the only road the Grand Jury has anything to do with. All the streets are kept in repair, scavenged, and so on, out of the Corporation finances. The boundary wall is kept by the Grand Jury of the county and the Grand Jury of the county of the city. The Corporation attends to everything else.

86. Why does not the municipal body instead of the county of the city Grand Jury keep up that one-half road?—By the Improvement Bill of '73 we tried to transfer the fiscal powers of the Grand Jury to the Corporation; but that bill failed.

87. CHAIRMAN.—What are the other fiscal powers of the Grand Jury?—They present, they contribute towards the support of the lunatic asylum, till recently they paid their quota for the maintenance of jails, a number of officers, they are charged with the payment of reformatory schools, weights and measures, and, in fact, very little else.

88. There is, in fact, what is called the county at large charges?—Yes. There is a guarantee of which we have to pay our proportion—that is a sum of about £1,200 a year. Here is the only road I see here in the Spring Assizes of '78. It is recorded there is a sum of £11 11s. paid to Thomas Powry for repairing it—for half-year's contract for keeping in repair for [illegible] years 780 perches of road from Waterford to Portlaw, including 180 perches of the footpath between the borough boundary at Poulsberry and the borough boundary at Summerland.

89. Out of what is that £11 paid?—Out of Grand Jury cess, and this cess goes to pay the County Grand Jury charges. If you take in Kilculliheen, portion of which we propose to take in, the valuation of that barony is £3,536; the barony charge on that is £165, and the proportion of the county charge is £62. In Gaultier now the county charges would be about £497 on a valuation of £28,638; and in Middlethird the county at large charges would be £704 on a valuation of £40,450. Therefore, if we are correct in our estimate of the valuation of the proposed extension, you can readily see what the county at large charges on the whole would be. The total amount of the charge on the county makes about 4½d. in the pound on the total valuation of the county. Therefore, 4½d. on £3,744 gives the amount of the county at large charges which would be thrown into the city. We have made a calculation of £306 as being what it would probably cost the city for the repair and maintenance of these roads, £306 6s. 3d.

90. £306, and say £100 for sanitary purposes?—Yes.

91. It would thus cost you £400 a year?—Yes.

92. Additional expense?—Yes.

93. And the taxation you would get then would be what?—The taxation would be, say, 2s. 6d. on £3,396, it would be about £400. That would be exclusive of lighting, and it would be about the same to the outside people—they would neither lose nor gain by it; indeed they would get a profit. Take the average of the cess here—2s. 2d. in the pound, Grand Jury cess at present, we would only ask them to pay 1s. 9d., and by the addition of the 3d. water rate it would be 2s. 0d., so that there would be a gain. They would gain that 2d. in the pound.

94. Yes, they would gain that 2d., and be better off on the score of lighting?—They would have a better chance.

95. I believe it is a fact here that the municipal boundary is right through the centre of some of the streets?—Yes.

96. That is, portion within and portion without the boundary?—Yes; in some places one-half is in the county, and the other half in the city.

97. Well, now, don't you think it would be desirable, at all events, that the houses on one side of the road or street should be brought into the city?—Most decidedly.

98. So that taking this boundary road you will have to lay the water pipes along it?—Yes, we have done so.

99. So that the people on one side are paying water rate, and those on the other side are not?—Yes. In one of the most populous districts part is in the city and part is in the county—that is in Barrack-street. One side, or half, of Barrack-street is in the city, and the other half outside it.

100. And the pipes are laid up to the extremity of the boundary?—Yes. I may add that one of the barracks—the Artillery—is outside the boundary,

and the Infantry, which is just a few yards further out, is inside.

101. Mr. Cotton.—Do you think that if the effect of extending the boundary was to bring the population over the 25,000 necessary for the purpose, the Artisans' Dwellings Act would be put in force?—Yes, I do.

102. And it would be a great public advantage?—Yes.

103. Chairman.—Independently of the point you have mentioned of the boundary going through the centre of some streets, is there any of it, and, if so, any large portion of the district proposed to be brought in by the Finance Committee of the character that you would call an urban district?—Yes, a large portion of it is immediately adjacent to the city. Not only a large number of small houses, but large public buildings, the Lunatic Asylum, St. John's College, the Poor Law Workhouse, the Presentation Convent, the Ursuline Convent, several private dwelling-houses, like Mr. Harvey's, "John's Hill," Newtown House, would be included, and, in fact, a large number of places which are practically in and form portions of the city, though nominally they are not in it.

104. And are there rows or terraces of small houses?—Yes.

105. And what would be the valuation of these?—Well, the greater number of the houses are small.

106. And they would be below the burgesses' qualification?—Yes.

107. But have you made any calculation of the number that would be added to the burgess roll by the extension suggested by the finance committee?—Well, we have not made any calculation of that, for I did not believe that the number would be very much. A large number of these have the franchise from their premises elsewhere.

108. At present that district is under the rural sanitary authority?—Yes.

109. Do you think it would be an advantage to those people living in that district outside, and to the present inhabitants of the municipal district, that they should be brought in to you as the urban sanitary authority?—Yes, for I think the urban sanitary authority has greater facilities for working the Public Health Act than the Board of Guardians, for we have a staff—a larger staff, and so on. We have the executive sanitary officer, the sanitary officer, the consulting medical officer, and eight sub-sanitary officers within the municipal boundary.

110. And would that be sufficient to work the district you would bring in?—We calculate that it would be necessary to have two additional officers.

111. About £100 a year more?—Yes.

112. At present do they contribute that £100 a year to the rural sanitary board?—I may say they do, under the poor rate.

113. Then it would cost them no more, and for them and for you it would be better that they should be attached to you as the sanitary authority?—Yes.

114. Is there a sanitary rate levied on the city?—No, we don't levy any sanitary rate under the Public Health Act.

115. Then you say that if you levy £100 a year on them, it would be no more than they pay at present?—Very little, I should say.

116. And that would amply compensate you for the increased advantages conferred?—Yes.

117. Mr. *Delandre*, Solicitor.—There is the public water rate of 3d. which would be levied. There is the domestic water rate of 7d., "not exceeding 1s. in the pound," that is a further liability that has not been mentioned yet.

118. Chairman.—Yes, but I understand it is not the intention to extend the water beyond the municipal boundary.

119. Mr. *Delandre*.—I would ask Mr. Howard is it not the fact that the Corporation are in extreme pecuniary difficulties at present?—No.

120. Is it not a fact that they have had a writ served on them for a large sum of money?—Yes, a writ for a debt of £807 [illegible].

WATERFORD. Nov. 7, 1878. Mr. Joseph Howard.

121. Is it not a fact that the sum of £24,000, if granted, will not be sufficient for the purposes required by the Corporation?—No, it is not.

122. Is it not a fact that the income derived from this water rate, in whatever way it may be levied, will be insufficient to pay the interest on the loan, amounting in the gross to £30,000?—No, if we levy a sufficient tax.

123. You will be obliged to have recourse to the borough rate?—No, not necessarily, the valuation of the present borough is £[illegible] &c.; of course that is not all available for the purpose of water tax. In round numbers the amount that would be subject to water rate would be £35,000, nearly £37,000, £33,000 for the domestic water rate. That would be about £1,800 a year.

124. I understand in any loan at present, it is to be repaid by annual instalments of about £[illegible]?—Yes.

125. Then there would be a deficiency?—The deficiency would be £200 a year, but we have to take into account the large sum we would receive for the sale of water.

126. Mr. Cotton.—Have you any water salaries?—Yes, we have a paid superintendent at £150 a year, Kennelly, as secretary, £50 a year, and there are besides that two men in charge of the reservoirs at £1 a week each, labourers required to keep other the [illegible], &c.

127. Taking all that together, and also the interest on the loan, what would be the deficiency after a full supply, the domestic and public water supply, and the supply [illegible]?—Do you mean supposing we got the £[illegible]?

128. Yes?—Well, the charge on the whole cost would be, on £35,000, would be estimated at about £[illegible], or £3,100 a year, the tax at 1s. 3d. would be in round numbers about £2,000, that would leave £1,100 to be made up; there would be a charge of about £100 a year for expenses of maintenance; that would be £1,000 a year; well, at least from sales of water we anticipate from £500 to £1,000 a year to commence with—possibly it would go to much more than that.

129. Chairman.—Then if you only got that it would leave a deficiency of £700 a year?—Well, under the Water Act we have power to levy the whole water rate. It is not anticipated it will be required, but it could be done.

130. Mr. Delandre.—What I want to know is, why people outside who don't require water would incur liability to this water tax?—It was never proposed by the Finance Committee that the domestic water rate should be levied on the additional area, unless the people asked for and obtained the water supplied to them.

131. Is it not a fact that the £[illegible] you have applied for will not be sufficient?—I think it will.

132. Have you not shown that the [illegible] outlay to carry the matter out would be more than the £[illegible] would cover?—Yes, £37,000 odd.

133. Then there is that deficiency?—Besides that was on prices calculated as they were at the time, but since then they have gone down.

134. There would be a deficiency at any rate, as has been shown, of about £[illegible]?—Yes.

135. And how do you propose to make that up?—We have power under the pound additional water rate would make that up.

136. Then in order to make up that deficiency you would impose a greater chargeability on the outlying districts?—No.

137. Chairman.—As I understand it, the outside district is only to be made liable for the public water rate, and not for the domestic?—Mr. Howard says we don't propose to carry the pipes further than the existing boundary, except to the barracks, which are outside, and who will pay for it specially; we don't propose to charge domestic water rate upon the county, but we think they should pay the public water rate of the city, because they make as much use of the city and of the public water when they come in, for their

WATERFORD.
[illegible]
Mr. Joseph [illegible].

houses, &c., and they have the [illegible] [illegible], and desire in fact as many advantages in that way as the inhabitants themselves, and therefore they should pay 3d. in the pound." That is what they say, and what I understand is this: there is no suggestion that if any adjoining district is to be brought in it should be charged with domestic water rate at all, nor have put on it the burthen of this £55,000.

140. Mr. Delmedge.—Is not this £75,000 a charge on the borough rate?—Yes, if there was such a thing. The first charge on the Corporation property is £15,000, that is the debt of the old Corporation, and some more borrowed since. That is charged on the Corporation property, and a borough rate is levied. The £55,000 is further charged on the Corporation property, and on the rates to be levied under the water rate.

141. That £75,000 is **exclusive of course of the** £55,000?—Yes.

142. And I take it the intended district would be liable for that £55,000?—Yes.

143. Well, they have no liability whatever now?—I don't understand. The Corporation property is liable, that is how it stands.

144. Mr. Cotton.—Is the property of the Corporation fully acquired?—It is.

145. Then, I presume, the persons brought in, though they partake of the liabilities, partake also of the assets?—Yes.

146. What do the Corporation **assets amount to?** —To over £10,000 a year.

147. Is not part of the **borough excluded from** water rate?—Yes.

148. Would there not be the power of getting this part exempted?—Yes, the legislature will have the power.

149. That is the proposed extended part?—Yes.

150. But if it was brought in, and no exemption made by the legislature, would not the Local Government Board have the same power as they had with reference to Ferrybank?—Yes.

151. It was never contemplated to put the water rate on them at all?—Yes, like Ferrybank.

152. Mr. Delmedge.—There is great difficulty, is there not, in getting through the Corporation business?—Well, I get through a great deal of it from time to time.

153. Is it not a fact, beyond doubt, that a great many roads within the municipal boundary have been for the past four or five years in a wretched condition?—It is not.

154. Do you know the road up to the Lunatic Hospital from [illegible] street?—I do.

155. Was it not in a very wretched condition?—No, I don't think so. I [illegible] over it for four or five years.

156. Was it not full of ruts?—There were ruts in it, but it was not full of ruts.

157. Are not the county roads better taken care of?—No, there is not the same amount of traffic on them as in the city, and therefore they don't require the same amount of repairs.

158. Chairman.—I suppose the roads outside the boundary get a great deal of hard usage from the people outside?—Yes, a great deal. The farmers do more damage to our roads than we do; we spend about £3,600 a year on them.

159. Was there damage done by the road engines? —Yes.

160. And does not all the traffic from the railway go along your roads?—Yes.

161. Mr. Delmedge.—I certainly know of one road within the municipality which is, as I say, full of ruts, or was so, and it was certainly within the last four or five months that they got down stones, and did something to improve its condition. It was impossible to travel it. There is, and was, however, a marked change for the better when you get outside the boundary.

162. Mr. Fisher.—Did you receive a return from the Government about the burial ground, Mr. Howard? —Yes.

163. The Corporation do make the burial grounds.—Yes.

164. What burial grounds are there?—There is the Friary, Ballybricken, and the French Church burial ground, close off the Quay, where there is not a burial once in five years.

165. Do you know of any site within the city limits suitable for a burial ground for the Corporation?—No, there is not a single place in the city that could be made available.

166. And we can appoint the burial board, without the chance of getting a burial ground within the city?—Yes.

167. Are there burial grounds outside the city limits?—There is Ballynaneashagh.

168. Would that come within the proposed extension?—No.

169. How far is that out?—It is outside the proposed extension, it is about a quarter, or from that to half a mile, outside the proposed extension.

170. Mr. Hopkins.—Would it be within the electoral division of Waterford?—Yes.

171. Is it largely filled by [illegible], is it much used by them?—No, there has sprung up a prejudice against it, on account of the interment of paupers. It was intended to be the burial ground for the county of the city of Waterford.

172. With whose money was it made?—Waterford at large—the county of the city of Waterford. They spent £1,500 on it, and the Board of Guardians were made Trustees, and they made it a paupers' burial ground. In the proposed extension, we take in the Protestant cemetery.

173. Mr. Fisher.—We are only paying £40 a year for auxiliary alliance?—Yes. I should like the large district to be taken in two additional alliance would be enough. I think that in a large district like this would be even more expensive than in the city.

174. If this district were brought in would it be incumbent on to continue the Grand Jury cess on it? —No.

175. Would it be a hardship on those people brought in to ask them to contribute the same rate as they do at present?—No.

176. Mr. Barrett.—You; let them be subjected to the same liability, but would it be fair to add the public water rate; 3d., if you wish, "Give them credit for the 3d. out of the whole 1s. 3d., and let them pay 1s. 0d.?" You would be granting the benefit of that.

177. Mr. Fisher.—I am asking Mr. Howard whether, in his opinion, considering the advantages derived by the people outside, it is unreasonable or unfair to ask them to pay the 3d. in the pound— whether he would consider that an unfair thing?—Yes.

178. Mr. Cotton.—What is the [illegible] in respect of the [illegible], in the [illegible] of Chairman, and [illegible] in this city.

179. For how many years?—Thirty-five years.

180. From the present date?—From August last —from the time the loan was repaid.

181. Mr. Fisher.—As to the water rate, you used to have the opinion that we can levy more than 1s. in the pound?—Yes.

182. Are you aware that Mr. Purcell says we cannot?—No.

183. I can produce his opinion?—Well, perhaps Mr. [illegible] would advise otherwise.

184. Mr. Barrett.—Is there anything special in the Act enabling you to levy it?—The public water rate is limited to 3d. in the pound, but the Act also provides that the Corporation shall have power to levy a domestic water rate of 1s. in the pound (under section [illegible] Act).

185. Mr. Cotton.—Suppose an extension was made, do you think there would be any advantage derivable from having it guided by natural boundaries, instead of a straight line through fields and

[illegible]

Mr. Thomas [illegible], examined.

[illegible]

WATERFORD, Jan. 7, 18[illegible].

Mr. Thomas S. Harvey.

the city magistrates who commit an offence there?—No.

221. Would it not be a great advantage to persons who have to frequent those stations and other public places that any offence committed at those places could be tried by the magistrates here, and not brought to petty sessions to a place some miles off, perhaps?—Decidedly.

222. Now, Mr. Harvey, do you know of your own knowledge is there any objection amongst the people outside to the extension proposed by the Finance Committee?—No, I heard of none. My father and several friends live within the boundary that would be annexed. So far as the jurors' question is concerned, I think it would be a great advantage. Some of the persons now summoned in the town would be exempt, and the number altogether available would be increased.

Mr. THOMAS SMITH HARVEY, examined.

Mr. Thomas S. Harvey.

223. CHAIRMAN.—Mr. Harvey, do you reside within the present municipal boundary?—No. I reside within what is called the old boundary, virtually in the county.

224. Is it your opinion that the present municipal boundary should be extended?—Most decidedly it is. The present boundaries of the city are most irregular and unsatisfactory. Although almost trespassing on the city, I am quite willing to submit to extra taxation, because I will get the benefit of it in being included. In other parts of the city I am agent for a good many houses, a good deal of house property. In some places I have the city on one side and the county on the other, and it is the source of great expense and annoyance to me to look after it under the present state of things.

225. Do I understand that in some streets where you have, or are agent for, house property, you have the city on one side and on the other the county?—Yes.

226. Do they light up that road or street where that happens?—Not at all.

227. Don't the Corporation light it?—No; there is not a single lamp in the Lane, one-half of which is city, and one-half county. Where I live myself several of us pay. We individually subscribe for a lamp to make the road decent.

228. Mr. Fisher.—But that is outside the boundary?—Yes. We pay for a lamp specially there amongst us. My argument is that for whatever small taxation there is put on those who are brought into the boundary under the extension they will get value for. The property will become more valuable, and building will be more readily carried on. It is far better to be within the municipal district than to be outside and on the edge of the county, and I consider it far better for any city to have room to extend itself, and not be cramped.

229. As I understand it, there is no means by which the present municipality can acquire a burial ground within the city?—No, there is not.

230. Nearly all the burial grounds in the city are closed up?—I believe so; except the Society of Friends' and the French.

231. So that if a person dies his friends have to bring him for burial outside the city, although the Corporation are the burial board, because they have no burial ground?—Yes. There is a burial ground outside the city, and there is a burial ground that is private property to a certain extent—every person choosing to pay for a grave there can get it for a pound or so.

232. But at present it is under the control of the rural sanitary board?—No; it is private property, vested in a number of trustees.

233. Do you, with others, suffer inconvenience from the hackney cars in consequence of the municipal boundaries being as they are?—Yes.

234. That is from their being outside of the control of the magistrates here when they bring you a certain distance?—Yes.

235. Would it be desirable, in your opinion, for that purpose that the boundaries should be extended?—Yes, I have no hesitation in saying so.

236. You think it would be more convenient that offences committed within a short distance of the boundary should be decided or adjudicated on in the town instead of waiting and going to the Petty Sessions?—Yes. We have sessions in the city every week, and only every three weeks outside. In every point, no matter how I look at it, I think it would be of great advantage, and for the public good, to have the boundaries extended.

237. Do you think that those outside the borough would object to the taxation if the bounds were extended, and they would be taken in?—Certainly not any one I am concerned for, or that I know of.

238. Mr. Delahunty.—I am concerned for persons outside, and I certainly do object, and everyone consulted on the subject objected. The difference can be very, very little.

239. CHAIRMAN.—Mr. Harvey, do you find any difference from the way the county Grand Jury keep the roads, and the way they are done in the city?—I think our road is very well kept—rather better than the city.

240. I suppose the traffic over the city roads is ten times greater?—Yes; our road is not a great thoroughfare.

241. Do you think the sanitary arrangements would be better in the hands of the Corporation as the urban sanitary authority than in the hands of boards of guardians?—Yes; I would rather have it in the city a great deal. I have no doubt the work would be better done—certainly better attended to.

242. Do you know of your own knowledge that other ratepayers situated as you are would prefer being in the city—do you know that from speaking the matter over with them?—Well, I did not. I have not been able to take much trouble in it, but I may say I have heard different opinions.

243. I suppose the persons who are opposed to it are opposed to it on the ground that there might be increased taxation?—Yes; I don't think they go into it generally.

Mr. THOMAS F. DELAHUNTY, Solicitor, examined.

Mr. Thomas F. Delahunty.

244. CHAIRMAN.—I am residing at the verge of the city bounds, and am rated for it, and I am concerned for some property a short distance out. I consider that the taxation would be very much increased—that it would be rendered liable to the city improvement, to the borough rate, a domestic water rate, unless exempted by provisional order, and to that rate of 3d. in the pound. I can say that the state of repair of the different streets and roads within the city is far worse than the county. I traverse the city streets in different vehicles every day of my life, and I also travel a deal about the country, and I speak, therefore, from my own knowledge of the facts. I have seen accidents occur through holes and ruts in the streets of the city. A serious accident occurred no later than Saturday through want of repair of the city streets. I believe the city affairs to be badly conducted. I am aware from conversations from outside ratepayers, several of them within the district proposed to be brought in, that they are strongly opposed to it.

244. On what grounds are they adverse to it?—On the ground, firstly, of the increased taxation it would entail. They are particularly satisfied with the management of the Grand Jury, and they do not wish to be under the control of the Corporation. I was present when the Improvement Bill of '73 came before the Committee of the House of Commons. I heard the various reasons advanced in favour of an extension. I heard also the reasons against it. I heard the [illegible] and arguments raised by the Grand Jury of the county of Waterford, supported as they were by, I believe, the feeling and general opinion of the county. All were opposed to the extension, even in the [illegible] district, as I may call it. And for the reasons then given, the Committee refused to extend the boundary, and they passed a bill limiting extension to the city only within the present limits.

245. Well, but were there any reasons given, as far as you know, by the Committee for refusing to extend the boundary?—I am afraid there were. The report, if I may so term it, presented by the Corporation was such as not to induce the Committee to interfere there with further or extended powers.

247. Were you there yourself?—Yes, I opposed the bill.

248. Was the fact presented to the Select Committee that the municipal boards were in the middle of [illegible] as has been described?—Yes, it was. I was present when the alleged [illegible] was made, and when that step was initiated by the County Surveyor. That was, I believe, done without authority, and I may here state it was afterwards not upheld by the Grand Jury. I may mention, too, that it was proved before the Local Government Inspector that the [illegible] scheme under the water rate would be insufficient to meet the charges, and that recourse should be had to the borough rate, and also that, in addition to a sum of £15,000 borrowed, a further sum would be necessary; in fact, that in order to complete the works, and render them valuable at all, a further sum of £5,000 or £3,500 would be required. I have also to state that the condition of the lighting of the streets is defective to the extreme. Going through the streets at night at any time after nightfall, in fact, they are rather a [illegible] than an advantage.

249. In the [illegible]?—Yes.

250. Then I see the two objections you and your friends have to the proposed extension are: firstly, fear of taxation, and, secondly, the mismanagement of the Corporation. Is that so?—Yes.

251. Mr. Fisher.—Are you aware the [illegible] ... be levied on the borough rate?—Well, you see that is opening up a whole lot of questions.

252. Are you aware there is no express provision against it in the Act?—I believe there is, but what is to be done.

253. Chairman.—Do you not think houses so very close, the Artillery barracks, for instance, should not pay its rates towards the town, the Infantry barracks being in the borough, and the Artillery barracks outside?—I would certainly think it fair that the Artillery should pay a contribution.

254. Then you think there should be some extension?—Yes, in some parts I do think so. But at the same time—

255. We have the fact, however, as I understand it, that you do think there might be some extension?—I am very averse to going under the Corporation, but if you hold that buildings adjoining the town should be brought in, of course the Artillery barracks ought to be included.

256. But what about buildings in a street, one-half of which is in the city, and one-half in the county?—The Artillery barracks is a very strong case.

257. The boundary is where there is a street between the Infantry barracks and the Artillery barracks in Ballybricken, I believe that is the name of it. Now, do you think that such a state of things as that is right or proper?—Well, as an interested person, I will answer you in this way:—As an interested person, I object to the extension on the grounds I have mentioned, but looking at it in another capacity I do think that a slight alteration should be made.

258. Yes, but your objection would appear to be only to the mismanagement of affairs by the Corporation; for it would be fair that the portion brought in should pay some taxation?—I think the ratepayers have proposed an very fit change, if developed.

259. Mr. Cotton.—Which a change do you refer to?—The Poor Law [illegible].

260. Chairman.—Do you think that in such a large city as Waterford, the lands, as in the case of other large places, the lands close to the city are exceptionally valuable from their proximity, and that the larger the city and the greater the business there the more valuable that land is?—Of course it is, but that would continue in the [illegible].

261. Yes, but you must stop somewhere. In some places a mile or a mile and a half was suggested. In Kilkenny, two miles, I think?—Well, I am aware that the rents of some of the land just outside the city are much larger than on lands far outside. They are simply pasture grounds.

262. Do not the people holding those pasture lands supply the town with butter and milk, and so on, and are they not more valuable to them on account of that?—Well, the distance is so small between the Poor Law Commission's report and their [illegible], there is really a difference. Taking that into view, I think I, on the part of my clients, assented to an extension.

263. Mr. Cotton.—To the proposed extension?—No. I opposed the extension, but thought it inexpedient not to include the portion towards the west of the ornamental district, but considered it advisable to include the portion of the district at the Kilkenny side of the river.

264. What were your reasons for that?—Well, I did not consider it advisable to include the western portion, but I considered it advisable to run the boundary up to the goods terminus of the railway, and then that it should cross the river from the [illegible] ... including Dobbyn's Park, Gracedieu, Bowling Green, the Artillery barracks or Infantry barracks. These, on the municipal boundary, and that there was no objection to alter the municipal boundary to that.

265. Mr. Fisher.—Are you aware that the present county surveyor is also city surveyor?—I am.

266. Are you not aware that roads proposed to be taken in are under the care of that surveyor?—Yes.

267. And as city surveyor that they would still remain under his care as one road? ... the roads in the city are under his care.

268. But they are at present the extra-municipal roads are under his care?—Yes.

269. And he is paid as city surveyor?—Yes.

270. Now do you think, and, if so, on what grounds, that these roads would be taken from under his care as he stood managed than they are now?—Well, they would come under the same management as the city roads are now.

271. They would be managed under the Grand Jury, as has been stated in the evidence, and the surveyor is paid, as you know, as city surveyor.

272. Mr. Cotton.—That is, he is surveyor in the county of the city, and not surveyor to the Corporation?—He is paid as surveyor to the city.

273. What I wish to know is, what are his duties as surveyor in the county of the city?

Mr. Fisher.—I wish to convey that until the Grand Jury of the city is abolished, if this addition takes place, the roads would be under the care of the Grand Jury of the city, and not of the Corporation.

274. Mr. Cotton.—What has he to do, what has the city surveyor to do if he is paid as city surveyor, and, as I understand, the roads and streets are looked after by the Corporation?

Witness.—He looks after the one road, round the city, part of which is in the city and part out of it.

275. Chairman.—And what is the maintenance of that road?

Waterford. Jan. 4, 1879. Mr. Thomas F. Delandre.

Mr. *Howard*.—£11 a year.

276. And how much does the City Surveyor get for superintending this work?—£10.

277. So that he gets £10 a year for looking after the expenditure of £11?

Mr. *Fisher*.—Yes; and in addition to that there is the city court-house which is the principal thing. The objection of Mr. Delandre that the roads would deteriorate by the extension is wholly unfounded.

278. What Mr. Delandre says is this, "I don't want to come into the city, because of the Corporation management, for we have no confidence in them."

Witness.—Quite so. You asked me my opinion generally, and I think the boundary I stated there would embrace fairly what should be taken in.

279. Would it take in the convents and other large buildings?—No.

280. Mr. *Fisher*.—Do you not appear for Mr. Morris?—Yes.

281. Did you not appear for him at the Parliamentary Committee?—Yes; I appeared for the barony of Kilculliheen, and he is there.

282. Did not all assent to the extension proposed but Mr. Morris?—No.

283. For the compensation?—No.

284. Did not Mr. Rosenfield initial the change proposed?—He did initial it, but if he did so it was afterwards repudiated by the county.

285. He is a ratepayer?—Yes.

286. And he got up a meeting, did he not?—Yes.

287. And took the chair?—Yes.

288. And he initialed the change proposed on behalf of both parties?—No; only on the part of the county, and his authority was repudiated.

289. CHAIRMAN.—Suppose the legislature were to say we will take care that none of the existing debt is thrown on the portion brought in, would you say then that the people outside should not be brought in to contribute something to the city. Do you think that the people outside for a given distance should pay something towards the public water rate of the city?—No, for they pay in the town very largely.

290. Yes, but suppose there were gentlemen living outside not having places of business in the city, should they not contribute something in case of the city towards the public water-rate which is a thing for the public benefit. It is not well that Waterford should be kept as healthy a place as possible, the streets to be kept well watered, and so on; don't you think that for this, the people outside who derive the benefit of it should contribute something towards it. They come into the town, get the advantages of the water supply; now, suppose there was a Corporation here with which you were satisfied then considering that these people derive the benefits of having the city properly watered, and kept in a healthy state, of being enabled to send their children into schools in the town, attending places of worship there, having the railway and all that, should they not contribute something towards the gas, the lighting of the town the sanitary arrangements and the water?—Well, estimating those advantages to be derived by them they do.

291. Do they not derive those advantages I have mentioned?—No, for in the first place treating of sanitary matters, go into the town and you will find it disgusting, wretched sanitary arrangements. That is not so in the county. The portions adjoining the city are much better kept than the streets and places in the charge of the Corporation. I believe the Corporation duties are very carelessly discharged. A case within the last six months occurred in which through the neglect of the Corporation officials or employés, a wall belonging to the Corporation was allowed to fall into such a bad state of repair that an unfortunate man was killed, and a summons was issued against the Corporation officials but it was found impossible to fix them with liability. That is encouraging to anyone who would wish to entrust them with further powers.

293. As I understand from your evidence you would agree to an extension, but you believe the extension proposed is too large?—Far too large.

294. Mr. *Fisher*.—It would be unfair if Mr. Delandre's statement about the accident and the Corporation should go unexplained. I may be allowed to state that with regard to the old house in question, the Urban Sanitary Authority issued a summons on the party for having the wall in a dangerous condition and the law officer of the council advised that the Corporation as Urban Sanitary Authority have no power with reference to these dangerous walls, that we were put out of court with regard to that matter under the Act.

295. CHAIRMAN.—What I understand Mr. Delandre to convey was that the Corporation allowed this wall their own property to fall into such a state of disrepair that a man was killed by it, and that therefore it cannot be expected that people outside would be anxious to give them further powers when they cannot keep their own property in proper repair.

Witness.—Whether rightly or wrongly the matter was the subject of magisterial investigation.

296. Mr. *Fisher*.—And the magistrates dismissed the case as against the Corporation officers and if they were not to blame, how can it be said that the Corporation were to blame?—I only say that it was in consequence of neglect the thing occurred, some officer should have been appointed who was lost or some neglect decidedly existed.

Mr. Joseph Fisher, j.p.

Mr. JOSEPH FISHER, J.P., examined.

297. *Witness*.—My opinion, as to extension goes a great deal further than the Corporation of which I am a member. In support of my opinion I would refer to the bill of 1873, and state that it was adopted unanimously by the Corporation at that time.

298. CHAIRMAN.—The boundaries at that time were adopted unanimously?—I think the division was twenty-nine to four.

299. But there was a large majority at all events?—Yes. I was one of the committee appointed to go over to London about it. I never assented on the part of the Corporation to the diminished boundary.

300. Did the Corporation by a large majority seek for an extension?—Yes.

301. And the committee of the house did not give it?—Yes, but if you are taking the reasons of others it is fair for me to state that if a limited extension is taken we will take the roads on which there is the largest amount of traffic and the greatest expense, whereas if we take the largest one we take roads where the traffic is small and a tax being levied on the district at 2s. 6d. in the pound. If you were to take the roads that come near the city and tax the townlands in which it is these taxes would probably be 1s. 6d. instead of 2s. 6d. for that is arrived at being the charge for the whole barony. The evidence of Mr. Howard is that that is the average of the whole barony.

302. Are you in favour of an extension?—Yes, of one that will take in the whole of the electoral division of Waterford. I would take in the whole of the electoral division of Waterford and I base that on this ground that from the reign of Charles I., down to 1846 the civic authority of Waterford administered the whole of this district and the additional part shown on this map. The area they administered was 8,100 acres, and the area I propose to be taken in is 7,304 acres.

303. Then that area that you propose to take in comprises the entire of the electoral division?—Yes. The charter of Charles I., describes the boundary

WATERFORD. Jan. 8, 1878.

Mr. James Fisher, J.P.

of the county of the city of Waterford—which district will form what is called the Parliamentary borough of Waterford. It comprises an area of 9,348 acres, and has at present a population of 29,979 persons. It formed the county of the city of Waterford for Fiscal and for Grand Jury purposes. The principal roads, bridges, and footways therein were made by the city Grand Jury and it was recognised as the county of the city of Waterford by the Grand Jury Act of 1836, and was curtailed in its extent by the Corporate Reform Act, which was intended to deal solely with municipal matters, but which effected important changes in Grand Jury and fiscal arrangements.

305. Do I understand you to say the area you propose taking in is 7,000 and odd acres?—Yes, that is what I propose. The electoral division in fact.

306. If the whole electoral division may taken in that way—that would not include all these townlands?—I will show you. I will take first Gracedieu. It will take from the barony of Gaultiere to the value of £4,203; it will take from Middlethird £52,995, and it will take the whole of the barony of Kilculliheen, or a valuation of £3,836.

306. Then the total valuation that would be taken in would be £15,174 about?—Yes. It would make the total valuation about £61,912.

307. And the population?—The population would be about 25,000, which would bring it under the operation of the Artisans' Dwellings Act.

308. I find the baronial charge, taking the charge for the whole barony, for Gaultiere is £608 13s. 2d.?—The baronial charge on the portion of Gracedieu which we would take would be £163 15s. 9d.

309. That is on a valuation of £4,000 and odd?—Yes.

310. Middlethird—how much?—£663 7s. 2d.

311. Kilculliheen?—£209 11s. 5d., being a total from the outlying district of £719 14s. 2d. Taking the expenditure of the city from the [illegible] respectively I find the sum of £1,129 7s. 2d., which added to the former sum would give the Grand Jury cess for the year £1,829 1s. 11d., which would be levied upon the whole district for the half year.

312. There is another charge which in the county is a large charge, that is £1,4[illegible]. I don't know if the county would allow this towards their county at large charges, or whether it would go into the city, and as to the question of the repairs of the roads my view was that the present proportionate portion would go on for the repairs of those roads that are called municipal.

313. That is the Grand Jury?—Yes, until it becomes the pleasure of Parliament to transfer to the city those functions. The presentments would have to be [illegible] in the ordinary way, they would pass through possibly the same [illegible], and it would work so that those people outside would not be made liable for any purely municipal tax. The county of the city of Waterford was authorised by the 25th George III., cap. 93, to close up the burial grounds within the inhabited parts of the city of Waterford and to purchase a burial ground in the extra-mural portion, and a piece of land was purchased at Ballynaneashagh under that Act and was enclosed. The Corporate Reform Act divided the county of the city into two districts, some parishes are wholly within the city, some are partly within and partly without the city, and some wholly without it. This has required special legislation in the Burial Board Act, 1856, and in the Public Health Act of 1878. The latter makes the Corporation the Burial Board for the city of Waterford, and hands over to it some burial grounds closed by order of the Lord Lieutenant and Privy Council, but leaves the burial ground purchased by the city and cess of the Grand Jury in the hands of the board of guardians. Now an extension of the boundaries of the county of the city would give the burial ground to its rightful owners, and would vest it in the council returned by the citizens who purchased it.

314. With reference to the water supply, your plan is not that the Corporation should be obliged to extend pipes to all the added districts?—No, but that they may simply be at liberty to do so whenever an agreement or arrangement is made for the purpose. My idea was not to make them liable to any lamp tax or water tax but to leave the lighting and watering to be done by arrangement with those who would want the accommodation. The gentlemen who got frightened about the taxation did so from not calculating the exact amount they would pay; it would give 3s. 6d. at the present rate of taxation where they only calculated on getting £600 from it. I don't know that it is necessary to say anything about sanitary matters, but I think it would be better managed by the Corporation.

315. Your idea is that there would be better sanitary arrangements made and that the work would be better done by the Corporation as the urban sanitary authority than by the rural sanitary authority?—Decidedly better. I may say that upon the passing of the Poor Law Act, 1 & 2 Vic., cap. 56, the Poor Law Commissioners proceeded to define the electoral division of Waterford, and, for a considerable portion of the circumference adopted the boundaries of the then county of the city of Waterford, but included a small portion not within those boundaries and excluded a portion which was part of the county of the city of Waterford. The electoral division comprises an area of 7,369 acres and a population of 28,954, being about 2,000 acres less than the former county of the city of Waterford, but having a population of only 1,026 less than that of the Parliamentary borough. The electoral division was divided into five wards, the area and valuation of which has been stated by Mr. Hammond. Each ward elects two guardians, but there is a provision in the Public Health Act enabling the Local Government Board to divide the extra-mural portion into other wards for the purposes of that Act. The electoral division is divided into two dispensary districts, with separate physicians, but the entire under the Medical Charities Act is controlled by one committee, which meets at the dispensary, in Lady-lane, in the city of Waterford. These physicians are sanitary officers under the Act, and their salaries as sanitary officers are partly paid by the intra-mural portion of the electoral division and partly by the extra-mural portion. The Corporate Reform Act, which was made to remedy municipal abuses, formed the municipal borough out of the Parliamentary borough. The boundary lines were chosen in an arbitrary manner, running in some cases in the middle of streets, and by a strange regulation it altered the Grand Jury lines and made the municipal borough so formed the county of the city of Waterford for judicial, fiscal and Grand Jury purposes. That portion of the county of the city which lies at the north of the river Suir was formed into a new barony in the county of Kilkenny, and is called the barony of Kilculliheen; it contains only 2,152 acres, and is valued at £3,836, yet the expenses of one of the arterial roads approaching the city is thrown upon it. This district is essentially suburban and ought to be under the control of the City Grand Jury or the Corporation. The other portion of the county of the city which was excluded from the existing county of the city was added to the baronies of Gaultiere and Middlethird. The effect of this has been to necessitate the holding of a county petty sessions, called St. Patrick's Well sessions, the inhabitants thus excluded from civic rights; and as the portion thus transferred from the city to the county is mainly urban, and the residents are only half [illegible], considerable inconvenience has arisen. Such buildings as the lunatic asylum, the railway stations, the [illegible], the proposed dry docks, and other public buildings, are outside the civic bounds. There is no legal provision for lighting these roads, nor does the Harbour Act apply.

316. You consider that considerable inconvenience arises from the fact that, when you drive out [illegible] to any of those places, the drivers are only bound [illegible] outside the city jurisdiction?—Decidedly; there are many instances of that; take the cost of wages, if a dispute as to wages arises, in which you [illegible]

2 H 2

the old tenant has to discharge; they are outside of the boundary, and a delay follows of three weeks, till the windows smash or the vessel goes away. There is in fact no summary jurisdiction in cases of the kind. If it was in the city the case would be disposed of without difficulty, and with expedition at the Police Courts which sit every day. I observe that the two mile and two mile and a half area has been discussed, and it has been, I take, considered a reasonable area. Following the electoral division, if a circle were struck with a two mile radius, all that would be left outside it would be portions of Kilbarry, and needless to say, the whole of that property up there is corporate property.

317. So that any portion that would be outside two miles would be corporate property?—Yes, the corporation property runs up for five English miles, with regard to the electoral divisions, there is this community of purpose between the whole of them; we all pay the same poor rate, and my idea would be, that there would be an equality of taxation over, it would probably increase on the city 1*d.* in the pound, if we made an equal rating over the whole; Waterford stands different from other places in that way. In the addition we propose we don't want to saddle the outsiders with any taxation, and the reason Waterford citizens are averse to an extension, is, because they fear that portion of the taxation on outlying districts will be thrown on them.

318. That so far from their deriving any benefit from it, they will be worse off?—Yes, that is what they apprehend.

319. Can you say whether amongst the people you propose to take in, is there a difference of opinion on the question?—The only way after all we have of testing it is this; at the time the Improvement Bill was proposed there was a great outcry against taxation got up by the barony of Kilculliheen, and a meeting was held.

320. Can you say is there a difference of opinion entertained?—Yes, the feeling out of doors is this, you may take it that both parties are apprehensive of an increase of taxation being the result of any increase of boundary.

321. Then, opinions are divided within the city boundaries and without?—Yes. You were asking about the boundaries of wards. I was about to mention that I have gone through the list. Now, the average valuation for each voter in Centre Ward is £34; for the Custom House Ward, £28; for the South Ward, £48; for the Tower Ward, £43; and for the West Ward, £44. Now, in any change that would take place the Centre one is the one that wants to be increased, and the way is to diminish the Tower Ward, add to the Custom House, and diminish the Custom House by adding to the Centre Ward.

322. In your opinion would there be any difficulty in adopting the Poor Law Wards as wards for municipal purposes?—None whatever; I think it would be a great convenience. If the Poor Law boundaries were adopted it would be a great convenience to the Commissioners of Valuation.

323. Have you any idea how it would affect the constituency in each ward?—The average number of burgesses in the South Ward is 151; in the Tower Ward, 177; in the West Ward, 136; in the Centre Ward, 178; and in the Custom House, 146. I think you would add to the West and Centre Wards, but the Tower Ward would remain the same.

324. Mr. Delandre says that to a great extent at present the town is not lighted at all; that there are several roads in which there are no lights at all?—Well, I could not say; of course there must be places where there are no lights, but, as a matter of fact, I think the town is as well lighted as any town I ever was in. He might be right speaking, perhaps, of a short time ago, for at the north side of the city it was not lighted until within the last month or two. The new lamps have been erected at Ferrybank. Under the old Act people beyond a hundred yards from a lamp were exempted from payment, and the Corporation at that time only put up a lamp where they would get sufficient to pay for it. Since then, however, they have been extending them. It is a preposterous thing to run the boundaries in the middle of a road as they do now. If the proposed extension took place I have no doubt the populous places would be lighted. Mr. Delandre has spoken about the Corporation finances. It is right to say that the general debt of the Corporation has been within a few years reduced very considerably. I may mention that they spent over £1,300 in widening two new streets.

325. Is there any probability of an increase to the Corporate property by leases falling in?—No, not any immediate prospect. The principal increase has fallen in, and there will not be any great increase until 1924. Since the year 1870 we had an increase of about £2,000 or £2,300 a year.

327. There will be an increase of at least £20,000 a year, and probably it will be worth a great deal more in the year 1921.

Mr. Howard recalled.

328. Chairman.—It appears we cannot get the members of the Corporation to come here to express their views on this subject, but Mr. Fisher says what would simplify matters entirely would be to bring in the whole electoral division, and he says that in other places the proposal has been made to extend the boundaries from a mile to two miles, or two miles and a half. He says that in this particular case to adopt the boundary he proposes it would only in one spot be beyond two miles or so, and in that part it would be Corporation property. What do you say to that?—Well, I don't go so far as Mr. Fisher, but my own individual opinion is that an extension ought to take place.

329. But what about the electoral division?—It is a moot point if we should go for the whole electoral division.

330. In asking you your opinion I do not ask you to speak as town clerk, but simply to give your own private opinion as to whether you agree with Mr. Fisher?—I would go very near agreeing with him. One great advantage is regulating the boundary by townlands.

331. Suppose we adopted the poor law divisions of the wards, how many burgesses would be in each, and how many would be qualified for the office of town councillor?—I could not say. The clerk of the union might be able to tell you that.

332. Mr. *Fisher*.—It would be of great further utility to define the bounds in such a way that the terms, the County of the City, the Parliamentary Borough, the Electoral Division, and the Registrar's District, should mean and convey the same idea.

Mr. Joseph Cassidy, examined.

Waterford, Mar. 1, 1879. Mr. Joseph Cassidy.

333. I am a member of the Town Council, and of three of the standing Committees. I am opposed to any extension. At the last general meeting of the council, I moved a resolution which was carried with one dissentient, to the effect that an extension was necessary. I did it on the ground that it would cost the town, at present, at least, £600 a year extra, if they did not light the district proposed by the Finance Committee, and £800 a year extra if they did light it. I could see no commensurate advantage to make up for that additional outlay by bringing in the people of the district proposed to be brought in. I am, myself, strongly opposed to any extension. This place is not like Dublin, because there are no new buildings here, and I may say there have not been any new building operations for the past fifty years. In that way it is unlike Dublin and other places. I do not see any reason on account of the boundary running along roads or across public streets for enlarging the boundaries. On one side of the places mentioned, the road is in charge of the county, and in the other, of the city, and Mr. Dufin, the County Surveyor (who is here), takes charge of those parts of the city of Waterford.

334. Are you aware that all that is paid by the city towards the road that is partly in the city and partly in the county, is only £11 each half year, and that Mr. Dufin gets £10 a year for looking after the expenditure of that?—That is a question for the Grand Jury to see after. If the Grand Jury are fit to give it, in the present way, one man, while another gentleman might do it equally efficiently for the, that is the fault of the Grand Jury, if they continue such an abuse.

335. There is a street called Barrack-street, and it appears that the Infantry barracks and the Artillery barracks are in that street, and that the infantry are in the municipal boundary, and the artillery outside it?—Yes, that is the case.

336. Now on what principle is it that the entire of that street—one continuous street—should not be within the municipal boundary?—I believe, if you wanted to extend the municipal franchise, you would not get two persons outside the city qualified to be burgesses of the city of Waterford, who live contiguous to the Artillery barracks. With reference to the borough rate—there is no borough rate. Now we find that ones with an income of £16,000 or £15,000 a year, we cannot get on without contracting by our expenditure, considering the £1,000, our present income. Our present income won't do, and we must go in for a borough rate. In fact, it is at present contemplated to have a borough rate. There is, in fact, notice given to levy a borough rate for lamp tax; to levy lamp tax in the shape of borough rate. We have a 2s. rate, and we are looking forward to a 3s. water rate.

337. Mr. Curran.—What is the lamp tax?—In the pound. It will be for them to consider if it is to be levied.

338. Chairman.—Suppose it is struck, and the inhabitants think that the rate to be paid unfairly to be one-fourth?—I think it would be very unfair to charge anybody, to make them pay one-fourth or one-eighth of what they don't derive any benefit.

339. Take the gentry outside, do they not derive great benefit from the lamps in the town driving to the railway stations, coming into places of worship, using the streets of the city, and the lights in the winter evenings and so on. Do they not in fact derive great advantages in every way from the town?—They do not. In the first place they have all their parish churches outside.

340. But suppose, they come in to the Cathedral, suppose they come to the theatre, and to the railway, and so on?—Well, if people come for their amusement and pleasure, or convenience, I do not see why their poor neighbours and tenants should be rendered to pay for it.

341. According to present principles, if this town was under the Towns Improvement Act, it is only land, market gardens, and so forth, that the legislature has considered that would pay one-fourth, owners of houses would pay the full amount. Do you think, that any extension of the borough boundary—do you think that any further impost would be imposed on the farmers than at present?—I can well, you all know the state of the country at present, as a landlord and tenant, I know from experience of tenants who do not live very far from Waterford, that some of them cannot pay their rent. To impose additional taxes upon those people, no matter what the advantages, would be a hardship. Our trade is depressed, and under all the circumstances it would be hard to saddle on those people additional liabilities when they really cannot meet their demands.

342. There would be the railway station, and the artillery barracks, and those would be those large good people's houses?—Well, as to the railway station, with trucks, and waggons, and all sorts of vehicles cutting up the roads, what benefit we would derive from them would not pay one-fourth of what we would have to pay for them.

343. That are, are there not market gardens in the neighbourhood of the town lands, their lands about the town is not one bit more valuable in that respect. We have not a garden round. One pint, 6d., when then they do not milk away.

344. Where is all the supply of milk, that is daily used by the people of Waterford—where is the supply of milk and eggs got for all these 22,000 people?—Just as it comes in any other place from the country.

345. Does it not come from the district just outside the boundary?—I can tell you, the price of milk, we have a very large contract to day of 140 gallons, and the present price for new milk as we took it at the poor-house is 6d. a gallon.

346. Mr. Fisher.—If the boundaries were extended, would not building operations go on around the city?—I do not believe it. There is not a demand for houses in Waterford. In fact, I think the consequences of extending the boundaries would rather have the effect of preventing building going on. There would then be the anticipation of taxation to impede it.

347. Chairman.—Were you in the Town Council in 1878?—Yes.

348. And on what principle did you approve then of the proposed extension of the municipal area?—I opposed it then and now, because I believe it to be an imposition on the city. I was only one of five. I may mention here, that there was incurred a sum of £2,[illegible] costs, and in order to cover that, as a sop, they took the course to regulate the bridge matters, to get that £1,[illegible] to be put on the city of Waterford. I may also mention, that gentleman who proposed or aided this movement, the Mr. [illegible] M.P., became afterwards its most strenuous opponent.

349. You are aware that the population at present is about 22,000, and that that is just 1,000 below the limit for application of the Artisans' Dwellings Act, would you not think it of advantage to be able to put that measure in force?—I think we have all the powers we require.

350. You cannot put the Artisans' Dwellings Act in force?—Well, one gentleman seemed to give it as a reason for extension that it was a miserable thing to have the population of Waterford only 22,000 or 24,000; "and for the sake of making it 30,000," I said to him, "would you go merely for figures, and for the sake of figures saddle the city with £600 or £800."

351. Mr. Fisher.—But it would not saddle the city with that, on the contrary, it would lessen the taxation.

352. Mr. Curran.—Supposing the population, by the extension, is increased beyond 25,000 would the

Waterford. Jan. 7, 1879. — Mr. Joseph Grubb[?].

Artisans' Dwellings Act be used?—I am quite sure it would not.

353. CHAIRMAN.—Is there ample room for the poor people now?—There is. There are plenty of small houses idle. I have some idle myself. There are a couple of hundred of small houses. I have some, and I can't let them, ranging in rent from 2s. 6d. to 3s. a week.

354. Where are they?—In Castle-street.

355. Mr. *Fisher*.—Are you not the owner of houses set in tenements?—Yes, large houses rented up to £20 a year, and houses from £4 to £14, and houses from 2s. to 4s. a week idle.

357. CHAIRMAN.—When I was here before I remember Mr. Hamilton brought me down to the manure depot—to Willey's marsh—and he showed me houses, places built upon the very walls. I was horrified to see them. I understood him to say that the poor people had no other place to live.

358. Mr. *Fisher*.—They are living in filthy dens in the city.

359. WITNESS.—All I can say is that these people would prefer living there.

360. CHAIRMAN.—In 1875 the Corporation went forward with this bill. There were only four dissentients then, of which you were one, but all the rest were in favour of the extension proposed. I wanted some of the gentlemen to come here and tell us what was the reason they changed their minds. You are the only one to come and give any single reason. You are consistent, for you say—I did not go in for an extension then and I do not go in for it now. Mr. Delahunty says:—"I am opposed to extension, to the extension proposed, but I certainly think there should be some extension, a considerable extension, but not the one proposed by the Finance Committee." There were five members, according to Mr. Hamilton, of the Finance Committee recommending an extension of these boundaries. The Corporation then referred it back to the Finance Committee, to see what was suggested. They prepare their figures, and the moment their report goes back it is all but unanimously thrown out. So that four years ago we have the Corporation, with thirty-six or thirty-four members, going forward for this extension, and now we have them, with thirty-nine against it, asking that there should be no extension. Now, what we would like to know is what made the thirty-six who were for it before go round and say, no, we won't have any extension. These thirty-six gentlemen are found going to Parliament, to the expense of that bill; and if it goes to the House of Commons every one of these men being against the extension now, what claim would they have, is being represented to the Committee of the House of Commons that these gentlemen were for it, with only four dissentients out of forty, whilst now twenty-five actually voted against five. Now, as to the burial-ground question, at present you have not any burial-ground in the city of Waterford. There is the Society of Friends' and the French burial-ground. We know the tendency of the law is to close up every intra-mural burial-ground. It is now stated to us that there is not a bit of ground in the city that you can get, and yet you are the burial board. Would you not think it advisable to extend the boundary a short bit in order to get a piece of ground for the purpose?—When the graveyard here was closed, the Protestants went outside and bought a burial-ground. There is no necessity for a burial-ground. There was one splendid one paid for—several acres were paid for out of the rates.

361. Mr. *Fisher*.—And it was turned into a paupers' burial-ground.

362. WITNESS.—The guardians reduced the charge, but it is very extensively used.

363. CHAIRMAN.—Do you think now that it would not be desirable—with reference to the regulation of hackney carriages and police arrangements at the railway station and elsewhere—that the boundary be extended in order that the Corporation have the management of the hackney cars?—We have that.

364. Only within the municipal boundaries; but, as has been said, why should a man not have the benefit of the police regulations up to his hall door? Why should not the police regulations be enforceable, why not applicable to, say, the artillery barracks? And, as to the fare, you must give him 6d. to the borough boundary, and 6d. to, say, the workhouse?—But that might apply if you extended the boundary to three miles.

365. In the one street, if there were two shebeens, one in one spot and the other in another, the one man may be as careful and as circumspect as he likes, and may say to me bring me up to petty sessions in three weeks if you like—would it not be better to extend the boundary so three miles than to have that state of things?—But would not that apply if you extended it three miles?

366. Of course, but we must have regard to the suburbs and places that have a community of houses?—My argument is that if you were to Kilmeadan the same thing would apply.

Alderman Ryan. ALDERMAN RYAN examined.

367. CHAIRMAN.—You were on this Finance Committee, I understand?—Yes, and I suggested that boundary.

368. And do you abide by it still?—When we went on the Finance Committee we considered that anything we would take in, would be more or less lost to the city, and we determined on taking in nothing but what ought really to be brought in as part of the city. My view of the extension is that whatever addition we take in ought to be treated just like others as the city at present, as regards water and sanitary works, and that we should not keep a special account at all. The streets at present are repaired out of the Borough fund, and I would have the new streets or roads paid out of the rates. This and sanitary expenses would amount to about £400, giving credit for amounts we would receive out of the Public Water rate, and the saving that would be effected in our Grand Jury cess both amounting to £795—it would leave a loss of about £300 per annum. As I would treat the extended districts as part of the city any borough rate to be levied, I would levy on all. The council, however, did not see their way to approving of the proposed extension. I made out the Grand Jury cess, the present Grand Jury cess payable by the city of Waterford at present is £4,235, which is equal to 2s. 9d. in the pound, that is on the valuation of £38,000, with the proposed increase the valuation of the city would come to £43,000 that is by adding the proposed increase of £5,000 to the £38,000. The additional charges to be put on the present Grand Jury cess would be 8½d. for the railway guarantee which would be equal to £212 10s., and collection, &c., £20, bringing it up to £4,467 10s. That would then be the gross presentments. Now the effect would be if you spread that £4,467 10s. over the £43,000 to reduce the Grand Jury to 2s. in the pound, and that would be a saving of 9d. per pound, so that if the proposal of extension of £5,000 valuation were agreed to, and that the only charges are the only additional charges on the Grand Jury cess were the railway guarantee of 8½d. per pound, and collecting additional cess it would effect the saving I have mentioned of 2d. in the pound on present city cess, and that would be equal to £325. The public water rate of 3d. in the pound would be £75, and that with the £325 would amount to £400; but the loss would be in this way. Cost estimated of maintaining the roads of proposed extension payable as existing streets are

out of the borough fund £506. Sanitary expenses £100—total expenditure £606 from which abstract the £400 and you have the net loss of £200 exclusive of lighting.

369. The view you took then was this, that in justice and fairness, and having regard to the proximity to the town of these outlying parts they ought to be a portion of the town, but at the same time you thought it would be a money loss to you and a gain to them?—Yes.

370. In your opinion is it right that a line should be drawn across Barrack-street dividing the boundary?—No, it is absurd.

371. The railway station should be taken in if for nothing else than police purposes?—We could not take in any less than the black line on the map.

372. Supposing there is any extension, or even if things were left as they are, do you consider that it would be better to have the poor law division and the Municipal wards alike?—Most decidedly.

373. Whatever extension be made?—Yes.

374. And even if no extension were made?—Yes.

375. Do you think even if there was no extension that the Municipal and Poor Law wards should be the same?—No, I see no objection, I mean quite unprepared.

376. You think that the Artisans' Dwellings Act should be put in force?—Certainly. The reason the poor people live in the places they do, is because there is a scarcity of small houses. You will see where the Corporation are building the cottages the poor people are leaving their tenement houses and going to the cottages.

377. The advantages of the Artisans' Dwellings Act will not apply unless there is an extension, and consequent increase in the number of the inhabitants?—We built a certain number of labourers' cottages, and we owe the contractor something like £200, and that contractor was compelled to serve a writ on Mr. Howard who has to borrow the money from private individuals to pay that £200.

The inquiry then terminated.

Wexford. Mar. 1, 1879. Alderman Ryan.

MARYBOROUGH.—MARCH 8th, 1879.

Before Mr. C. P. Cotton, C.E.

Mr. Patrick O'Brien, examined.

Maryborough. March 8, 1879. Mr. Patrick O'Brien.

1. Mr. Cotton.—You are the Town Clerk?—Yes.

2. Maryborough, I understand, is under the Towns Improvement Act?—Yes.

3. When was it put under it?—In December, 1854, shortly after the Act was passed.

4. Is Maryborough under the Towns Improvement Act for all purposes?—Yes, I think so.

5. It includes lighting?—Yes, lighting and watering.

6. You received the form of queries from us?—Yes.

7. But you did not send us the replies back to those queries?—No. I did not.

8. Can you fill them in now?—Well, the Commissioners have not approved of them, and I would not like to take on myself to give the answers.

9. What is the population of Maryborough?—2,761.

10. What is the area of the municipal district?—The area is a radius of one half an English mile.

11. And the acreage?—The acreage of that is 503 acres, but that includes the town and acreage under assessment—the acreage liable to assessment is 450.

12. That is the area given in the rate book?—Yes.

13. And the other fifty acres?—That is that portion which is not included in the assessment, the part not occupied by houses.

14. What is the valuation?—The entire valuation is £3,076.

15. You have no wards?—No wards.

16. Is the town entirely included in one electoral division?—It is.

17. How far does that electoral division extend north, south, east, and west?—It would average about a statute mile—in some directions it would exceed a mile.

18. Have you a map of the town showing the boundary of the town itself?—Yes, I have; and I have made a circle showing what a radius of half a mile would extend to.

19. Where is the town itself marked on this map?—Within this circle (indicating circle marked red on the map).

20. Surely the boundary of the town is not a circle?—Yes, it is, and it is a radius of half a mile.

21. Where do you get this, what is your authority for saying it is half a mile radius, this town boundary?—That is what the Town Commissioners adopted when they were adopting the Act.

22. Have you got the resolution adopting that?—I have not, but I have seen it.

23. Have you the [illegible]?—No; I [illegible] it, and I have not got it.

24. Is it not entered in the records of the first proceedings of the Town Commissioners?—[illegible] been cut that book.

25. I [illegible] [illegible] [illegible]

26. What is the [illegible]—[illegible] in the old [illegible] of [illegible].

27. Is that [illegible] on the [illegible]?—[illegible]

28. How many Town Commissioners have you?—[illegible].

29. How many people are on the [illegible] eligible [illegible] of Town Commissioners?—About sixty.

30. [illegible] pounds qualification?—Yes.

31. And how many are qualified to vote in the town?—[illegible] 187.

32. What are your receipts during the past?—At [illegible] shilling rate the [illegible] £1 [illegible].

33. [illegible] [illegible] [illegible]

34. [illegible] [illegible] the public [illegible].

35. Can you give the amount [illegible] [illegible] [illegible] [illegible] [illegible] Town Commissioners [illegible].

36. You have no landed property?—No.

37. Can you tell me in '78 what your income and expenditure was?—I could not tell for 1878 from recollection. I have the accounts of it, of course.

38. You can give it to us afterwards?—Certainly.

39. Can you tell me what the [illegible] rate was the [illegible] five years?—In '74 the poor rate was, I think, [illegible] in '75 [illegible] in '76 [illegible] in '77 [illegible] in '78 [illegible]. I think that is it.

40. If you like [illegible] [illegible] [illegible] [illegible] there. What was the [illegible] in '78?—[illegible].

41. Was any portion of that sanitary rate?—Yes.

42. How much?—[illegible].

43. What was that raised for?—[illegible] through the town.

Bally-shannon. Nov. 6, 1877.

Mr. Joseph O'Hagan.

44. And on what district was that rate raised?—It was raised on the townland adjoining the town.

45. Can you give the names?—Belleek.

46. What I want is the number of townlands that were subjected to the sanitary rate of 1s. 1d.?—Well, I don't know if Belleek was subjected to the sanitary rate, but it is within the boundary of the town.

47. You don't know then on what district the sanitary rate was struck?—No.

48. Is there any debt on the town—do the Town Commissioners owe anything?—No.

49. Have the Board considered this question of the extension at all as a body?—Well, they have, it was before them.

50. Have they come to any resolution?—No; they thought it would be better to leave it as it is.

51. Well, that is a resolution—did they come to that resolution?—They did not come to that resolution, but that I consider to be the feeling.

52. All the sanitary works in the town now are under the control of the Board of Guardians?—Yes.

53. Have the Commissioners ever considered the question, whether they would wish to be formed into the Urban Sanitary Authority, so as to restore the sanitary powers to themselves?—The matter was under consideration, but no resolution was passed on the subject.

54. They have not passed any resolution?—No, but the feeling that I could gather or glean from them was that they thought the area of taxation being more extensive under the Poor Law Board than with us, we had better leave it so.

55. That is that the Local Government Board had the power of putting the sanitary rate on a larger area?—Yes.

56. Is there any expenditure for sanitary works required in the town?—I could not answer that question. I believe the Commissioners think there have been sanitary works enough done.

57. You have placed on that map, I see, some larger circle—what is that?—That would be supposing the boundary were extended another half mile.

58. If it were so extended, would it take in many gentlemen's places?—It would not.

59. Would it add much to the number of voters?—It would not.

60. Would it add to the number of gentlemen qualified to be Town Commissioners?—One more or two; I am not quite certain about two more, that is all.

61. You don't know how many voters it would add.

62. What are the lands, what class of lands lie between the present boundary and the additional half mile—are they townparks?—Not exactly townparks, they are average middling fair lands.

63. Would it take in any public buildings at present outside the municipal boundary?—No; only the lunatic asylum and jail. They are exempt.

64. I suppose all the land within that mile radius you have there derives great benefit from the town, on account of its proximity to the town?—Yes. There is no doubt of it.

66. As regards markets, those lands are exceptionally well off?—Yes; and as regards the value of land.

67. Having facilities for disposing of their produce is a great advantage?—Yes.

68. Are there schools in the town to which children come from that distance?—Yes; and outside that.

69. How far beyond that half mile extension would you say the benefit of having the town adjacent extends as making an increase in the value of the land?—Well, I don't think the Commissioners would be inclined to extend it much beyond half a mile further.

70. Do you then mean that the Board are in favour of extension at all?—Well, my impression is that they are not.

71. Do they intend to come to any resolution about it, is any meeting to be held to give expression to an opinion about it?—No meeting is fixed.

72. What is the opinion, do you know, of the people living within that half mile circle—what is their opinion, do you happen to be aware?—If it decreased the rates they would be very glad it would be taken in.

73. Who would be in favour of it?—The people of the town.

74. What is the opinion of the people within the extended half mile?—I don't know that. I have not consulted any of them.

75. Of course, as you have never considered the question of being Urban Sanitary Authority, you never considered the question of whether the Town Commissioners should take up the roads—the maintenance of the roads—instead of the Grand Jury?—Yes, some of them have expressed a feeling to that effect, that is, they have become contractors for some of the roads within the town for the Grand Jury.

76. You are aware that they cannot become the authority over roads and bridges, except they first become an Urban Sanitary Authority, and take up the sanitary work?—I am aware. They have become private contractors for those roads.

77. But they have not come to any resolution about any of these matters as a Board?—No. We presented a petition to the Grand Jury on one occasion under the Local Government Act for the privilege, and we were refused it.

78. The Grand Jury refused it?—Yes.

79. Well, are you aware that if you became the Urban Sanitary Authority, the Local Government Board could give you a Provisional Order to take the roads and bridges, whether the Grand Jury consented or not?—Yes.

80. But you have not done anything?—No.

81. What is your own private opinion as to this question of the boundaries; do you think it would be better for the town to be extended or not?—I think if they became the Urban Sanitary Authority it would not benefit them at all.

82. It would not benefit them, you think?—No; provided they take up the management of the roads and bridges.

83. Why would it not?—Because the additional income would not be equal to the outlay.

84. Do you think not, if they had the power, and got the same rights the Grand Jury now possess for the same purpose?—Oh, if they had that power it would be different.

85. Well, suppose they had that power?—That would make a great difference; I did not calculate it in that light. I think it would do very well if they had that power. I was calculating for the one-fourth.

86. If they were made the Urban Sanitary Authority to take up the powers of the Grand Jury, they could settle the rates to be paid; it would be left to the Local Government Board to determine. Have you any observations you would like to make?—Nothing further.

Mr. William Fitzgerald.

Mr. William Fitzgerald, Solicitor, examined.

87. Mr. Gotto.—Can you tell us, Mr. Fitzgerald, what the feeling of the Commissioners is regarding an extension of boundaries?—No; I don't think there has been any meeting on the subject. There has been, in fact, no exhibition of their feeling on the subject. They don't really understand it at all.

88. Are you a Town Commissioner yourself?—Yes.

89. You are aware, perhaps, what is the general feeling amongst them?—Well, my own impression of their feeling is, that there is a feeling of doubt as to what would be the result of an extension.

90. In what way?—For my own part I should say that we don't know, supposing the boundary is extended, we don't know what sanitary work the town may be

raised on as may be, which the town rates may be [illegible] in paying. At present there has been a very large outlay from a sanitary point of view in the town, and I doubt if the town rates would afford, within the proposed boundary, any additional outlay. For instance, if additional drainage were required within that half mile radius, I doubt if the town could afford it, as the ratepayers would be prepared to assent to it. As I understand that half mile extension proposed that is my view.

91. But that half mile radius, as it appears to me, does not take in [illegible] many buildings at all. In that case, therefore, what sanitary work—what drainage would there be?—I think the feeling is that we are rather groping in the dark, taking a leap without knowing exactly what we were doing—what we were to get—what compensation we were to get for the extension, for the liability.

92. Well, suppose you have not made any application to become the Urban Sanitary Authority, or taken any steps to take up the roads, suppose you simply remain Town Commissioners as you are, would it not be an advantage to you to have the area extended?—Well, we have taken steps to take up the roads within the present municipal boundary—we have become, in fact, private contractors.

93. But that is not taking steps as a Board?—Not as a Board, but it has the same effect. Steps have been taken by members of the Board to take up the matter within the minute, and I doubt if the boundaries were extended and the same state of things would apply. I don't think the extended district of roads would enable the Commissioners to do it with any profit, or satisfactorily at all.

94. Whatever you may agree to do as private contractors you know would not apply or be obligatory upon you to perform if the area were extended—you would not be obliged to do the same thing outside?—Well, there would be no necessity for taking up the roads outside; it was simply for the convenience of the town that the Commissioners took it up at all.

95. Would it not be an advantage to this town to have an additional area of taxation contributing to the lighting and cleansing of the roads?—Well, I would be personally inclined to doubt, if the new rates to be obtained by the additional radius would compensate for the additional expenditure on the extended radius. MARYBOROUGH. Aug. [illegible] Mr. William [illegible]

96. But suppose you don't touch the roads at all, you have no power at all, you know?—Except as private contractors.

97. But keeping the roads within, altogether, would it not be an advantage to have an extra sum contributing to the paving, cleansing, and lighting?—Well, putting it on the principle that there were extra ratepayers, it would. If I were making the compensation, [illegible] would not put the Commissioners to the [illegible] I would say "yes" [illegible]. But we have not discussed [illegible] the extent of the ratepayers [illegible].

98. [illegible] I would say it would be very desirable. I am informed by [illegible], and I believe it to be the fact, that the ratepayers of the town held to a very large extent the lands proposed to be comprised in the new area.

99. Yes, so that the increased taxation would fall upon residents in the town to a great extent?—Yes.

100. How is the town lit?—At present by gas. There is a gas company that supplies us.

101. Is there any water supply?—No, not any waterworks.

102. There are wells?—Yes; plenty of wells, but no possibility of a supply being laid down. The town lies on the flat, and from the circumstances it would be impossible to bring water to the town.

103. Can you tell me what would be the feeling of the residents within this proposed extension of say half a mile, sketched out by Mr. O'Brien, the feeling at the [illegible] within that district?—I cannot; for the reason I told you; no means of finding of the ratepayers has been taken. I am sorry there have been no steps taken. Mr. Teague is here, and he can give you more information than I can.

Mr. GEORGE V[illegible], examined. [illegible]

104. Mr. COTTON.—Are you a Town Commissioner yourself?—No, not now.

105. But you were, I understand?—Yes, for six years.

106. So then you are intimately acquainted with the feeling of the town?—Yes.

107. And can let us know [illegible] information?—Yes.

108. Well, give your opinion as to the advantages or disadvantages to be derived from an extension of the boundary?—My opinion is—and I believe I have spoken to a great many people on the subject—

109. Give your own opinion?—My opinion is that the electoral division of Maryborough as it stands would be best to adopt for a radius. On the north side you could reach about three quarters of a mile (Irish); on the south it would be about a quarter of a mile, on the west on the [illegible] road, about three quarters, that is the Mountrath road, and on the north west three quarters of a mile. On the north east it would reach about a mile and a quarter, and on the south east about a mile and a quarter.

110. Can you tell me what the area of the electoral division is?—I could not tell you; I have not asked the [illegible] of that [illegible].

111. I asked already, you may remember, with reference to the raising of [illegible] 1878, [illegible] over what district was it levied?—Borris, Little, Clonminam, and [illegible] and Maryborough; I was one of the parties who struck out that rate myself. It was a [illegible].

112. That I understand was for the purpose of [illegible]?—Yes.

113. And this was considered a fair district?—Yes.

114. Have you any further observation you would wish to make?—Another point I wish to bring before you is this—[illegible] the town, [illegible] and I have heard the [illegible] as to whether it ought to [illegible] I don't quite know, but we have three very large public institutions, an asylum, a gaol, and an infirmary, and there are the persons of those institutions, who [illegible] the benefit of the lighting of the town, and so on, and if these institutions could be rated it would I think be a very useful and proper thing. I don't know if I am right in bringing this before you?

115. Well, it is out of the limits of our inquiry; it would need the subject of legislation, and is beyond the scope of our inquiry.

116. There are a great many parties in our town who would like to have them brought in if it could be done. The Government at present gives us portion of the rates in respect of the barracks.

117. [illegible] Government [illegible]?—Mr. O'BRIEN.—The valuation is [illegible], and Government gives us whatever the amount of the rating we make.

118. Mr. COTTON.—Do you think the advantages of being in the neighbourhood of a large market town extends to the limits of the electoral division you have suggested as a boundary line?

119. Mr. TEAGUE.—It does, decidedly, and beyond it, for the farmers come in and take their [illegible] out of the [illegible] and employ them. [illegible] in that way, that they have got to [illegible] but must [illegible] get the labour they want.

120. And they derive a [illegible] from the streets being lighted, when they come in [illegible] at night in the [illegible]

2 C

winter mornings, or evenings?—Yes, certainly they do. I may say that some of the people consider object to pass.

121. They object to having any additional rate put upon them?—Yes, I have spoken to a number of them.

122. You are not a guardian at present, are you?—Not at present, but I will be one. I had been for a number of years, but I had to resign on taking up the clerkship.

123. What would be the feeling of the guardians as to your becoming the Urban Sanitary Authority?—I have an idea that they would, at least a section of them would, like to keep the rates in their own hands.

124. Is there anything else you wish to add?—Well, I think the county roads, looking at them in one sense, it would be perhaps as well to be left as they are, for we have a very efficient county surveyor who is doing his best to save in a great many ways. We might improve our footways, but not our roadways much.

125. Do you think if the Town Commissioners had as much money at their disposal as the county has, they would be able to do the work better, living as they do on the spot and meeting once a week to look after it?—Well, I don't think they would. They might do it perhaps, but I scarcely believe it. They would have to get a regular staff to work them up, and you have a staff in the county.

126. Do you think the county contributes towards the roads in the town a fair amount of work for the money they get?—Yes, for the past four or five years they have contributed very liberally.

127. Have you any other observation to make?—I agree with Mr. [illegible] about the water—you would have no way of bringing in water except you brought it from four miles. The Sanitary Authority is giving them a fair supply of pumps now and a very large supply of water.

128. By pumps?—Yes, by pumps.

Mr. Thomas Turpin, examined.

129. What is your opinion as to the extension, Mr. Turpin?—I am clearly of opinion that the area ought to be increased. I have always been of opinion that the people in the suburbs derive nearly as much benefit from the town as the people in the town themselves.

130. In having markets for the sale of produce, and from lighting, watering, &c.?—Yes; they send in all their butter every Thursday, an immense quantity of them. They sell their produce here on Thursday; they bring in their potatoes, and they get a deal of corn, and sell it, and the land from the bogs around the town every day of the week is [illegible].

131. Well now, how far from the centre of the town would you say it would be fair to ask the people to contribute?—Well, I think Clonkeen ought to be taken in, the greater part of [illegible] from [illegible]. I think the boundary should certainly take in Clonkeen.

132. Tell me are you aware what the general extent of the electoral division is?—No, I am not. I think the poor rate collector would be able to tell you.

133. Would you say the people who derive exceptional advantages from the town live more than a mile from the town?—Not much.

134. You would consider a mile a fair limit?—Yes; there was an old charter, [illegible] of Elizabeth, and [illegible] the town extended from the [illegible]—the old borough—a boundary of [illegible] yards, and that is a mile and a half. That was exactly the boundary under the charter of Elizabeth.

135. You think then that a mile would be a fair distance?—Yes; I think so, Irish mile.

136. The Town Clerk.—It would require two miles English to take in Clonkeen.

137. Mr. Turpin.—My impression is that it ought to extend to that. It is right for me to say this, that when we established this Commission, we were under the impression that we had made a mistake in not applying to have it further extended in the first instance. I think there was a technical error. It was confined there. But we wanted to extend it.

138. Under what Act was the town before that?

139. Mr. O'Regan.—It was not under any Act previously before that.

140. Mr. Turpin.—It was a borough originally; Maryborough returned two members of Parliament, and a large track of land was attached to it. In [illegible] the corporation divided it into three parts, one part for the Sovereign, one part for the burgesses, and another part for [illegible], and they made leases for themselves for 999 years.

The inquiry then terminated.

KILLARNEY.—DECEMBER 28, 1876.

Before Mr. Kernan, Q.C.

Mr. Henry Downing examined.

1. You are the Chairman of the Town Commissioners of Killarney?—I am.

2. Has the boundary, marked on the map before me, always been the boundary of the town?—I am not very certain, that is so, I do not know if it was the same as that when the town was under the old Commissioners, that is, up to three years ago. Up to that the Commissioners were appointed, and acting under the Act of the 9th George IV. c. 82, and in December, 1874, the town adopted the provisions of the Towns Improvement Act of 1854.

3. Since I was here before in September, 1876, have you had a new set of Commissioners?—Yes, there have been some who have gone out by rotation, and others elected.

4. Are you in working order now?—Yes.

5. How was the present boundary as marked on this map fixed?—Mr. Downing who is our Solicitor drew up and prepared a map, to go before the Local Government Board, in order to get their sanction to the boundary.

6. Did they sanction this as the bounds?—Yes they did in 1874. They were approved of by Mr. Hamley of the Local Government Board, who was sent down to inquire into the matter, and he approved of them. All that time we were under the impression that we could not travel outside of the parish here, and there were some few townlands, such as Cloghy, which is very close to the town; that was omitted; Gortroe was also omitted, on the ground that we could not travel outside the parish.

7. Is the present boundary all in one electoral division?—Yes it is, the electoral division of Killarney.

8. How far does that electoral division extend?—It extends in some directions four miles from the town, and in others only one mile.

9. Did you answer the queries which were sent to the Town Commissioners here from our office in Dublin?—Yes, on last Friday week.

10. Do the Commissioners of the town think it desirable to extend the present area of the town?—

KILLARNEY. Sept. [illegible]

Mr. Henry Downe.

They considered the question, but not as to the full extent of the extension, I think that they consider it would be desirable to extend the boundary of the town, but they are not agreed as to the extent.

11. Do all agree that there should be some extension?—Yes, but some propose an extension, which would bring in some townlands, that I myself, and I think several others are of the same opinion, consider should not be taken in. A good many are of opinion that if you take a radius of two miles from the centre of the town, that would be a reasonable boundary.

12. What is the present valuation of the town?—£7,148 10s.

13. And its acreage?—1,736 acres, 2 roods, and 19 perches.

14. What addition to the acreage and valuation would an extension to a radius of two miles give?—I don't know but I would be able to get that information for you. It would be only mere guess work on my part if I gave it to you now.

15. Is it your opinion that the lands outside the town—to the extent at all events of a two mile radius, derive exceptional value and benefit from its proximity to the town?—I think so; I certainly think so.

16. To that extent at the least?—Yes.

17. Do the occupiers of the land within that radius use the town for all purposes that they require, such as coming and going to the train and as a market town, and attending their places of worship?—Yes; the present township in some places extends two miles, and in other places—and that is a great cause of complaint—not half a mile from the centre of the town, to the east and west the town at present extends about a mile and a half, while to the north and south it does not exceed more than half or three quarters of a mile.

18. How many gentlemen's residences would be taken in by the proposed boundary, supposing it was about two miles?—About ten or twelve in addition to those within the present boundary.

19. Are there any of the small farming classes, valued at £4 and upwards—that would be taken in by the proposed boundary?—Very few, the people who would be taken in are mostly gentlemen or substantial farmers.

20. How many substantial farmers would be comprised within the proposed area?—About twelve substantial farmers in addition to the gentlemen's residences.

21. Would the proposed extension take in any of the hotels near the lakes?—The only hotel it would take in would be the Lake Hotel.

22. Would it be considered reasonable to take in the other hotels towards Muckross?—They are three miles away.

23. Then this proposed boundary would not take in any part of Muckross?—No, it would not.

24. What is the meaning of the blue line that is on the Ordnance map now before me?—In entering back the queries the answer had reference to the blue line on this map and that was the proposed boundary.

25. Is the two-mile boundary that is proposed shown by the whole of the blue line boundary on this map?—That was not the unanimous conclusion that was come to. It was merely that some were for extending the boundary so much further than others.

26. I ask you as Chairman of the Town Commissioners is it your opinion merely, or are you expressing it as the opinion of a good many other Commissioners, that the boundary should not be extended more than two miles?—That is the opinion of a good many—my own and others.

27. Can you say anything as to the feeling of the town people on the subject of the proposed extension of the boundary?—They would be willing to have as large an increase as possible.

28. The larger boundary as shown on this map would only take in Lord Headley—that would be the only one?—Yes.

29. Taking the point at Killeenagh[illegible], and the townland boundary then up to the road, and then following the townland boundary again on to the road at Aghadoe Round Tower—would that be as you consider the best boundary on the western side?—Yes.

30. As far as you know, within the boundary that you now suggest, are there any residents outside the town, and in that boundary, that so far as you know would object to the extension?—I believe there are two of those residents at present here before you, Mr. Coltsmann, and Mr. O'Riordan.

31. The only ones you know of that would have any objection are Mr. Coltsmann, and Mr. O'Riordan?—Yes.

32. Can you tell me how many electoral divisions it will take in, the proposed two-mile boundary?—I think it will be all in the electoral division of Killarney, with the exception of a small portion of Muckross.

33. One of the recommendations of the Select Committee of the House of Commons that we are desired to follow, is to take care that towns shall so far as is at all practicable be coterminous with electoral divisions, therefore if there was only a very small bit, that would come in of the electoral division of Muckross, I do not think we could put that in. We wish to keep all the town as much as possible within the electoral division of Killarney?—Yes. There are parties who use the town very much in the portion of the boundary that would be in the Muckross electoral division, that is a portion from which people use the town most largely on account of the tourists frequenting the Lake Hotel.

34. There are other hotels also in the same locality, and it would be very easy to make lines that would take in those other hotels if we think it right to go outside the electoral division. How many hotels could be brought in besides the Lake Hotel supposing you went down to Muckross?—Two others.

35. Are there any other houses that could be included, because my recollection is that there are houses there?—Nothing to speak of.

36. Are these two hotels both on the same side of the road?—They are adjoining each other, in fact joined to each other.

37. Is there any boundary between them, and the Muckross demesne wall?—The public road divides them.

38. Supposing you drew a line, bounding the road on one side, and taking in these two hotels, or the townland boundary on which they stand—how do you think that would answer?—They both stand on the townland of Dromyrourk.

39. Is that a large townland?—A very poor and small one. The only thing in reference to the suggestion you make is that it would almost stand like an island, because you leave a lot on the Killarney side that you do not take in. The only reason you could use, and that would be urged for bringing in that property is, that the people who go there do invariably use the town much more than a good many people who live in the town.

Mr. SAMUEL MURRAY HUSSEY examined.

Mr. Samuel M. Hussey.

40. You are agent to Lord Kenmare here?—Yes.

41. And I believe about nine-tenths of the area sought, to be added to the municipal boundary, is his Lordship's property?—Yes.

42. And that would be taken in by the proposed new boundary?—Yes.

43. Do you approve of the proposed boundary, taking in townlands as nearly as possible and with a radius of two miles from the centre of the town?—I do.

44. Would you be in favour of, as nearly as possible, following the townland boundaries for the municipal boundary as a rule?—Yes.

45. Lord Kenmare would have no objection to that?—No.

Killarney. Dec. 22, 1879.

Mr. Daniel Conyers.

Mr. Daniel Conyers examined.

46. The proposed boundary would take in part of your property?—It would; the distance to my place by road, either way is over two miles and a half to my house, and as the crow would fly it is a mile and a half exactly, but that is going by the river boundary which no man could pass, and my demesne runs out a long way, and a distant part of it is three miles and a half from the town.

47. Do they propose to take in the whole of your demesne?—If they go by townlands they should do it, and that is the reason I object, because I am three miles from the town.

48. As far as you are concerned, would you object to the boundary going out to the proposed extent of two miles, in your direction?—I would not object to that; but it is nearly three and a half miles by road, by any road you take, to the distant part of my demesne.

49. Taking it in all the other directions, you think that that would be a fair boundary, following the townlands as nearly as possible?—Yes; I certainly think that the Lake Hotel ought to be taken in. It is only a mile from the town—an Irish mile, as the distance has been measured.

Mr. Thomas H. Dowling.

Mr. Thomas Henry Dowling examined.

50. What is your opinion with regard to the proposed boundary?—I think it is almost the unanimous feeling of the town that the proposed two-mile boundary would be a fair and equitable one.

51. And do you think the people to be taken in would object to it?—I do not think any person could possibly object to it; they may if they are to pay a little of the rates, but [illegible] I think those ought to be included within the boundary, as much benefit from the town as the townspeople do themselves.

52. Do you think that the Lake Hotel should be taken in notwithstanding the fact that it is in a different electoral division?—Yes, I do, because they get [illegible] as much benefit from the town as anyone who lives in the town.

Mr. Edward Carey.

Mr. Edward Carey examined.

53. You are one of the Town Commissioners?—I am.

54. The gentlemen who have been examined before me up to the present all appear to think that an extension of the boundary to two miles would be enough?—I think that would be fair. I would like to go further, but I think the two-mile extension would be very fair.

55. On this map before me it is proposed to go out further?—Yes; I was one of the parties who proposed that.

56. Do you now still propose that?—Yes, I do.

57. Why would you suggest that you should go that distance out?—I would suggest it for the purpose of relieving the ratepayers of the town, of getting an increase to the rates, of getting more money, of course, for the relief of the town, for the cleansing and lighting of the town, and for the expenses which the Commissioners have to go to for all those things.

58. There is no gentleman's place, as I understand it, except Lord Headley's, that would be taken in by the immense extension of the boundary that you suggest?—No; I think not. Lord Headley's place is not more than two miles, I think.

59. You will see Ma[illegible] is on the Ordnance map, and you will find that it will be over three miles?—But I was taking it from the nearest point of the town to Lord Headley's.

CASHEL.—11th MARCH, 1879.

Before Mr. Exham, Q.C.

Cashel. Mar. 11, 1879.

Mr. Cornelius Hanley, Agent for the Corporate property of Cashel, examined.

Mr. Cornelius Hanley.

1. What is the area of the town at present?—About 250 acres.

2. What is the valuation of it?—We don't know the valuation in consequence of [illegible].

3. Is it all in one electoral division?—Yes; the electoral division of Cashel.

4. When was the Towns Improvement Act adopted?—It was in 1858.

5. And I believe the Act was adopted for all purposes?—Yes; the whole Act was adopted.

6. Do the Town Commissioners think it would be desirable to have any alteration in the boundaries?—The Town Commissioners held a special meeting convened for the purpose, and they unanimously agreed it would be no benefit to the town to have any extension of the municipal boundary.

7. Are there any villa residences at all outside the present municipal boundary?—Only very few.

8. Are any gentlemen's places?—There is only one outside within a radius of half a mile.

9. I believe the Commissioners manage the roads, and that they take the contract from the Grand Jury themselves?—Yes; that is only within the last four or five years.

10. And they think an extension would be of any benefit?—They think it the prevailing opinion with the Commissioners, and a great many of the townspeople, that it would be no benefit to the town.

11. You are not the urban sanitary authority?—No; but we will be. The necessary proceedings have been taken to have us made the urban sanitary authority.

12. That is you have applied to the Local Government Board?—Yes.

13. What is the population of Cashel?—At the last census it was 4,[illegible], but I think it has decreased since. The staff of the militia was there [illegible], which with men, women and children numbered about [illegible], so that the population is about 4,[illegible].

14. Would it be desirable for sanitary purposes to take in any of the outlying districts, or do you prefer to leave them with the rural sanitary authority?—I don't think it would be the least use to us. There is a small river running in the middle part of the town, and there is nothing to hinder us from letting [illegible] the river which is a couple of miles away.

15. Then neither the people inside nor the people outside wish to have any extension?—I don't know about the people outside.

Mr. John Davis White examined.

John Davis White.

16. You are one of the Town Commissioners?—Yes.

17. You are living in the town?—Yes; about thirty-seven years. The Chairman of the Commissioners would be present but for a death in his family, and he asked me to speak for him.

18. In your opinion would it be desirable there should be any alteration in the boundary?—My private opinion is that for sanitary reasons there might be an extension, but it is not the opinion of the townspeople. It is possible if the boundary was enlarged we might get a [illegible] of the franchise.

19. But as far as the municipal matters are concerned, you do think it is desirable, as do the Commissioners, that there should be any increase or diminution in the area?—No, except this. That there are two gentlemen at present who have property in the town who are resident within six miles or so of Cashel, and as outside of that distance they are not qualified to become councillors.

20. You would not extend the boundaries six miles?—No; but if there was any remedy in a case like that.

21. You are about to get the management of the sanitary matters?—Yes; but it requires an Act of Parliament, I believe.

22. You have the management of the roads at present?—Yes.

23. You contract for the roads under the Grand Jury, and you are able to effect a saving?—Yes; so I am informed, and it is well done.

24. Would you think it desirable to go in for getting the management of the roads entirely in your own hands?—No; because we get money from the county.

25. Have you considered at all with the view of increasing the voting power the advisability of bringing in the Commons lands?—That was my idea; my own opinion was that every man in the electoral division of Cashel ought to be within the bounds of the town—everyone who is helping us to pay the rate. We are paying very heavy poor rate in Cashel, and every man who is helping us ought to have the privileges we have.

26. How far does the electoral division extend?—It extends about three miles with a valuation of about £11,[illegible].

27. What is the poor rate in Cashel?—It is 2s. 6d. It is at present 2s. 6d., and the average is 2s. 6d. It has been 3s. 6d., and in the bad times it was 5s. 6d. in the pound.

28. Then the whole electoral division helps you?—Yes; the whole of the electoral division helps us, and I think the electoral division has a right to some of the privileges.

29. They have power to vote for the Poor Law Guardians?—But I think if our number was extended so as, they should have a right to vote for the Parliamentary representative. We are a very small constituency, and that is one of my reasons for it.

30. There are no roads here?—No.

31. The ratepayers of the entire electoral division elect the guardians?—Yes.

32. That is, that they both are represented on the Poor Law Board?—Yes; town and country alike. There are twenty-eight persons eligible to be Commissioners, but there are eighteen Commissioners.

33. The only question is whether you would have a larger constituency by extending the boundary, and whether it is desirable to have it extended?—You would get Mr. Ryan of Hore Abbey. Mr. [illegible] has property in the town, and he wishes to become a Commissioner, and Mr. [illegible], as where he would be resident is Deerpark, and Mr. [illegible] the resident magistrate. There are not five houses within a mile of Cashel that are valued at £12.

34. In every good house within the boundary at present?—Then you would not get those houses qualified unless you went six miles out of the town.

35. You never had a sanitary rate?—No.

36. And when you become urban sanitary authority you will not have to strike a rate?—No, we have too much money.

The inquiry then closed.

KILLINEY AND BALLYBRACK. April 22, 1879.

KILLINEY AND BALLYBRACK.—22ND APRIL, 1879.

Before Mr. C. P. Cotton, C.E.

Mr. Andrew O'Brien.

Mr. Andrew O'Brien, examined.

1. Mr. Cotton.—You are the Town Clerk of Killiney and Ballybrack?—I am.

2. How long have you filled that office?—Since May 1872.

3. Killiney and Ballybrack are under the Towns Improvement Act of 1854?—Yes.

4. At what time was that Act adopted?—In July 1866.

5. Was it adopted altogether or only in part?—In part, at that time.

6. Was it afterwards adopted for water?—Yes, in 1870. For water and lighting in 1870.

7. In 1874 your sanitary powers all went to the guardians?—Yes; the guardians of the Rathdown Union.

8. And in fact your work is now restricted to lighting only?—Yes, to the lighting only.

9. What is the population of the township?—According to the last census 2,290.

10. Do you know whether it is increasing or diminishing?—I cannot exactly say.

11. What is the area and valuation of the township?—The area is 1,006 acres, and the valuation, £9,753 15s.

12. What is the number of Commissioners?—Twelve.

13. How many of the householders in the township are entitled to vote for Commissioners—do you know?—I don't exactly know.

14. Have you ever had an election at which you have had reason to know that?—We have had no opposed elections.

15. Do you know how many would be qualified to sit, if they were elected as Commissioners?—I do not know.

16. Could you make out a return of that number also?—Yes, I could.

17. In the queries submitted to you from the office of the Municipal Boundaries Commission, you have given a return of the rates. You have had no rate since 1874?—No municipal rate since then.

18. And then a rate of 1s. 6d. in the pound was struck?—Yes.

19. Will you give me the Poor Law rates in each year—take 1874—the Poor Law rate in 1874?—13d. in the pound.

20. What was it in 1875?—12d. in the pound, with a special sanitary rate of 6d., and a general or burial rate of 1d. In 1876 the Poor Law rate was 13d. in the pound, with a special sanitary rate of 1s. 6d., and a burial rate of 1d. In 1877 the Poor Law rate was 10d., and the special sanitary rate 18d., and there was in that year no general rate. In 1878 the Poor Law rate was 11d., and the special sanitary rate 10d.

21. With regard to these special sanitary rates, can you tell me what district they were struck on?—On the township of Killiney and Ballybrack, which was taken in with the contributory district marked on this map.

22. And it was the same contributory district each year?—Yes.

23. Can you describe that district, and give the names of the townlands?—Yes, the names of the townlands are, Ballinclea (part of), Rochestown (part of), Rochestown (part of), [illegible] (part of), Ballybrack (part of), Killiney (part of), Rathmichael (part of), Killiney (part of)—these are all in the electoral division of Killiney—Loughlinstown (part of), Loughlinstown (Commons), and Shanganagh (part of), and the last named are in the Rathmichael electoral division.

24. As these replies to the queries have been signed since they were sent to us, I may consider them accurate?—Certainly, yes.

25. The township of Killiney and Ballybrack extends into two electoral divisions?—Yes. Killiney and Rathmichael.

26. Do you know, at all, how far the boundaries of the township are conterminous with those of either electoral division?—They are not conterminous at all, I think.

27. Do either of the electoral divisions extend very much beyond the boundary of the township?—They do, very much.

28. Are they pretty equally divided, or is there much more—say of the electoral division of Killiney in the township than of the other?—I cannot exactly say.

29. You don't know the boundaries of the electoral divisions?—I do not.

30. They are not marked on the map?—They are not.

31. How is the township supplied with gas—do you contract?—It is from the Alliance and Gas Consumers Company.

32. You have a yearly contract?—Yes.

33. How much do you pay per lamp?—They charge at the rate of 5s. a thousand cubic feet.

34. You pay by meter?—Yes, the same as ordinary consumers, by meter.

35. Can you tell me what these special sanitary rates in the different years were for?—They were struck by the Poor Law Guardians, I dare say for the purpose of carrying out the sanitary arrangements.

36. What were the special ones for—sewerage?—No, for water.

37. How is the supply of water to the township regulated now?—The supply is taken from the Rathmichael reservoir as formerly, and was paid for by a water rate.

38. And that water rate was portion of this special sanitary rate?—Yes.

39. How much does the rate amount to?—The water rate that the Corporation charges is 6d. in the pound on the valuation of the township.

40. Well, as regards the rest—what does the special sanitary rate come to?—I don't exactly know.

41. Have the Commissioners ever considered, as a body, the question of whether they would like to have the powers and the control of the sanitary matters restored to them?—They have; but at present they have decided not to apply for the restoration of those powers.

42. Is there any resolution on the minute book to that effect?—The question is only in abeyance pending this inquiry.

43. The township has no debt connected with it at present?—None.

Mr. Robert Warren, D.L.

Mr. Robert Warren, D.L., examined.

44. You are the chairman of the Commissioners of the township of Killiney and Ballybrack?—I am. I wish at once to say with reference to the reservoir which Mr. O'Brien referred to in his evidence—he said that we got our water from the Rathmichael reservoir—I wish to mention, with a view to a further inquiry which I have in my mind; and it is very important that you should be aware that we are the only township that gets water from the Rathmichael reservoir, and we got it from that place on application to the Corporation, on the ground that it would be utterly impossible for us to get it anywhere else, on account of the high levels of different places in the township; the reservoir commands a supply 240 feet above high-

water mark, but in the highest portion of the township here, the high level excludes them from the benefit of the water supply, but we are able to supply the water to almost all the other portions of the township, and any interference with that supply would be very injurious to Killiney. My observations are now made in reference to any attempt, in the future, at annexation.

45. I suppose you are aware that in reference to Dalkey, it is stated to be the wish of the Commissioners there to seek to include the whole of Killiney and Ballybrack within their township, and, of course, if you like to give evidence now, as to why that should not be done, you are quite at liberty to do so; but it would be a question for you to consider whether it would not be better for you to reserve any evidence you may have to give on that point, until the Dalkey inquiry is held?—Well, sir, I am desirous of reserving any evidence I may have to offer on that subject, until a future time, as you suggest.

46. With regard to this extension, I understand it is the wish of the Commissioners now, that there should be no extension whatever?—They have passed a resolution this day, to the effect, that there shall be no alteration whatsoever in the existing boundaries of Killiney and Ballybrack.

47. I cannot help telling you that when I read the answers to the queries you sent us, and looked at the map, that I could not see any reason for not taking in a portion of Scalpwilliam. We are naturally looking forward now, in defining the boundaries, to make them as much townland boundaries as possible, and it strikes me that that portion of Scalpwilliam to which I refer, should be included within your boundary—but perhaps you would not wish to say anything as regards that now?—I had some objection in the original formation of the township to that—as to not taking it in. I objected as strenuously as I could, and I am of the same opinion that it should be in Killiney. The reason I put before my brother Commissioners for not seeking for it now was, that it was so small, and that we would be involved in litigation with Dalkey, consequent upon our applying for it now, inasmuch as Dalkey is under a special Act of Parliament. That is, under their powers, and under their Act of Parliament. We are under the Towns Improvement Act of 1854. We have taken advantage of that lower road (referring to the map) that divides that small portion there, and that is in the parish of Dalkey, and I am not sure that the Grand Jury would not oppose any seeking to have it placed upon the Grand Jury accounts, and in the face of these two oppositions, we thought it more prudent for the present, seeing that Dalkey was looking for power to annex Killiney, not to take any steps, if you think it right to recommend the annexation. Therefore, I have some hesitation in pressing it on you; but it would be a matter of great benefit to two or three of us if it was taken in, but we don't wish to go to any expense in the matter. It is not only a townland boundary, but it is also a parish boundary.

48. As we are on this subject—do you know also, whether it is the boundary of the electoral division?—I think that is the electoral division of Killiney.

49. The boundary of it?—Yes.

50. Is the whole of that road in the Dalkey township?—The whole of it is in Dalkey. It is all repaired by Dalkey. The Grand Jury repudiate any connection with it at all, and I think it is included within the Dalkey Act, but I am not sure of it. The road is kept in very bad repair; that is one reason why we are anxious to have it under the Grand Jury again. We have no power, under the Act of 1854, over roads.

51. Do you know whether the Grand Jury pay half of that?—I don't know whether they do or not.

52. Up to the present the Commissioners have taken no steps to become an Urban Sanitary Authority?—Not yet; but I have no doubt we will as soon as your inquiry is over.

53. Supposing you became an Urban Sanitary Authority, have you considered the question whether you would wish to go further, and would wish to have the control of the roads—to take over the control of the roads from the Grand Jury, as if you were under a special Act?—We have not actually come to any conclusion on the subject yet.

54. You are aware, I suppose, that you can get the power?—I am perfectly aware of that, and I think, perhaps, that opinion is divided upon it. I have not formed my own opinion on it yet, to tell you the truth.

55. With reference to these queries, is it a thing that the Commissioners have come to a unanimous conclusion on the point, I may say, I suppose, that the conclusion they have arrived at is that they seek for no alteration whatever?—Yes, they seek for no alteration whatever.

56. That resolution was passed at a meeting of the Commissioners—consisting of how many?—Seven, and two absent, whose consent I have—Mr. Green and Mr. Jameson. It is only Mr. Bahan who is not present.

57. I had better place it on our notes that the resolution adopted by the Commissioners wishing to include a portion of Scalpwilliam, and the Glebe house and ground of Killiney Church, and the house belonging to Captain Shiddham, and the portion of Scalpwilliam that lies in the township of Dalkey that they wished to include—that that resolution was rescinded by the one just referred to and passed today?—Yes, quite so.

Mr. O'Brien, Town Clerk, re-examined.

58. Have you the accounts—the expenditure and receipts—for 1878 made up. I don't want the items; I merely want the amount of the expenditure and receipts—what was the amount of the receipts?—£305 13s. 6d.

59. What do these receipts come from?—From—balance on foot of account, 15th of October, 1877, in Treasurer's hands £47 5s. 9d., from balance in Clerk's hands £3 8s. 6d., and from cash on deposit, £150.

60. That cash on deposit is cash that is the balance of the former rate that was struck, I suppose?—Yes.

61. What was the expenditure in 1878?—The total expenditure was £168 11s. 1d.

62. Leaving a balance of £37 2s. 5d.?—Yes.

63. Has any rate been struck for 1878?—No, sir. The Commissioners have struck no rate since 1876.

64. I presume a rate will be necessary in 1879?—Yes, it will.

65. Have you considered what it will be?—A rate of three pence in the pound will defray the expense of lighting, and the other expenses attendant upon it in the township at present.

The Rev. Robert Staveley examined.

66. I believe you wish to tender some evidence?—Yes. It was with regard to the sanitary arrangements of Killiney and Ballybrack. I have, perhaps, made myself a little officious on the subject accidentally, but both in my personal capacity as a ratepayer and also as a clergyman I must say the subject of sanitation comes very much under my own eye and I have very grievous reason to complain of the way in which sanitary matters are carried on under the Board of Guardians. The Board of Guardians, you are aware are the sanitary authority now and they are a very large body and they have a great deal to do indeed, and the result

DALKEY AND BALLYBRACK. April [illegible].

Rev. Robert Staveley.

is that the sanitary work I have no hesitation in saying is a mere farce in this neighbourhood. I have lately written to one of the Guardians complaining of a nuisance as I don't think it appears to be the business of the paid sanitary officers to attend to such communications. I have a fear that the danger and disagreeableness of the present state of things will increase and my belief is, that so long as the Board of Guardians are the sanitary authority, I do not think we can look for decent sanitary supervision. They are too large a body and they have too much to do.

67. You think it would be a benefit to the township if the Town Commissioners were to resume the sanitary authority?—I am most decidedly of that opinion. I am of opinion that no one will have any safety or comfort in Killiney or Ballybrack until they resume their sanitary authority. I don't know how they are to do it, but it seems to me that if they could extend their boundaries so as perhaps to get in a greater area of taxation and to make it more worth while levying a rate—I think if that could be done it would be a matter of great benefit, but as things are at present, I have no hesitation in saying that the Act is a perfect farce, the way it is carried on.

68. As regards the boundary, do you think that they have got a sufficient area of taxation to enable them to take up the sanitary business if they became an urban sanitary authority?—I speak with considerable hesitation on that point, but I have reason to think that if they became the urban sanitary authority the taxation might press unduly upon the present township of Ballybrack and Killiney, but I am not quite sure on that point. I think, however, that our area is at present rather limited considering that the population is not numerous and that there are no such places as there are in Dalkey such as streets and terraces—and here we are a rather limited body.

69. I may tell you as a matter of fact that the area is very much larger than in most other townships. It is probably the largest in Ireland?—Yes, very likely. I speak, as I said before, with regard to the extension of the boundary. There is another district that contributes to the so-called sanitary rate. There is a large district that does not get any benefit now from the water and yet it has to pay for the water. I am quite at liberty to be corrected by Mr. Deane and Mr. Wilkinson who understand the matter much better than I do. But I do not understand why if there was an extension of the township it should in any way injure the sanitary prospects.

70. Well, with reference to the extension of the township—you think the township should be extended for the purpose of bringing in more means to enable the sanitary work to be carried out in a more satisfactory manner than at present, but you don't know whether they would have sufficient over the present area?—I do not.

71. Because that would be at the foundation of the question?—Yes. My principal object is simply to bring forward what I know to be facts and that is as to the scandalous condition in which the sanitary arrangements are at present.

72. In fact so far as it bears upon this present inquiry your opinion is that it would be desirable in the interest of the township that the Commissioners should become the sanitary authority again?—Yes, certainly.

73. And as a matter of course they would do their business if they undertook it?—Yes, they would. They are all on the spot, they would have a narrower area to look after than the Board of Guardians, and they have a strong personal interest in the matter.

74. You are not prepared to point out any other ground of complaint?—I am not.

Mr. George Wilkinson.

Mr. GEORGE WILKINSON examined.

75. You are a Town Commissioner of Killiney and Ballybrack?—I am. I wish to remark that with reference to what Mr. Staveley has said as to the extension of the township, that I think it would be a mistake with regard to the matter of our finances.

76. For you to take in any extension?—Yes.

77. To expand the boundary all round?—Yes, what Mr. Staveley alludes to is this. At present there are two portions that join us—they are made into a sanitary district with us. They pay, perhaps with a great deal of injustice, a water rate, and get no benefit for it, but if they were brought in and made part of our township, we would have a very small valuation for a very large area, we would incur a large cost to supply the waterworks to those which they would be entitled to, and we would be put to great expense.

78. I don't know why they should be more satisfied than now, as they are paying to a contributory district?—But they get no water.

79. Would they be more satisfied if they became included in the township?—Yes; the Board of Guardians levy a sanitary rate only, and not a township rate.

80. You only receive water as a sanitary district?—We get it by contract—by special contract with the Corporation for which we pay 4d. in the pound over a defined area, and we cannot go outside that without breaking the contract. We have had a great deal of difficulty in supplying the clergyman's house at Ballybrack.

81. You don't think it would strengthen the authority and powers of the Commissioners if they had included within the township this sanitary district?—It would saddle us with increased cost without a more efficient control, I think.

82. What is the valuation of that additional sanitary district?—£1,378—that is, the district outside our union formed into a sanitary district.

The Rev. [illegible] examined.

[illegible]

Mr. J. [illegible], examined.

[illegible]

The Rev. Mr. [illegible] examined.

[illegible]

The Rev. [illegible] examined.

[illegible]

The Inquiry then terminated.

THURLES. Mar. 18, 1879.

THURLES.—MARCH 18TH, 1879.

Before Mr. C. P. COTTON, C.E.

John [illegible].

Mr. JOHN [illegible] examined.

1. How long have you been Town Clerk of Thurles?—Since 1861.

2. Thurles is under the Towns Improvement Act of 1854?—It is.

3. When was it put under that Act?—On the 19th March, 1861.

4. That is when you were appointed clerk?—Yes.

5. Was the town under any previous Act?—No.

6. How many Commissioners are appointed under that Act?—Twelve.

7. That map which you produce contains the boundaries of the town?—Yes, we got that (map produced) at the time, and we have also a newspaper with the details of the boundary.

8. The description of the boundary is in the Gazette?—The Gazette does not describe the boundary, it only contains the order giving the Commissioners a standing.

9. It must have been described in a previous Gazette?—I saw this newspaper (produced) at the time, and, as it contained a description of the boundaries, I preserved it since.

10. Have you not got on the minutes of the first meeting of the Commissioners a description of the boundaries?—No.

11. Was that map furnished to you by the Valuation Office in Dublin?—Yes.

12. You received queries from our office?—Yes.

13. And you filled up the replies?—Yes.

14. What is the population of Thurles; you say about 6,000?—5,908 is the population.

15. Has the population decreased since that census was taken?—It has increased since.

16. The area of the town you have not given in your replies?—I did not know it at the time. I could only take it from the map.

17. What is the area given at the end of the rate book?—1,269 acres 3 roods 33 perches.

18. That is the area of the town?—Yes.

19. And what is the present valuation?—£9,938 7s.

20. In what electoral division is Thurles?—In Thurles.

21. The Commissioners don't wish for any alteration?—No.

22. Has the subject been considered by them, as a body, at a regular meeting?—Yes, it was last week. They were talking over it, and I showed them the circular, and told them they should make up their minds if they wanted any change, and they considered the present boundary satisfactory.

23. Was that that there should be no alteration, and was that recorded by a regular resolution?—Not a regular resolution, but it was the opinion of the meeting.

24. The opinion of the majority?—Yes, of all who were here—five or six.

25. How many attended that meeting?—Six.

26. There were six present, and their opinion was that there should be no alteration of the boundary?—Yes.

27. Do you happen to know the opinion of those who were not here?—No, but they were invited here.

28. Purposely to discuss that question?—Yes, and I never heard anything to the contrary.

29. But there was no formal resolution?—No formal resolution.

30. The boundary extends about three quarters of a mile from the town in every direction?—It does.

31. That is from the centre of the town?—Yes.

32. Do you know the statistics of the electoral division of Thurles—its size and valuation?—I don't know it.

33. What are the receipts of the township and the sources of income?—This year there was £234 for town rates at 1s.; last year it was 10d. in the pound, but it is likely to be kept up at 1s., which would give £234.

34. What other sources of income are there?—We have the fines which, at the average of the last five years, are £36.

35. And the dog tax is how much?—It is £13 [illegible]

36. Have you any property?—No.

37. What was the expenditure in 1878?—For the year ending 30th April, 1878, the total expenditure was £273, but there is something to come off that because we had some flagging for which we are to be allowed £45 by the county. There is flagging and paving £73 6s., but that is larger than it should be, for the county gives us £45 for that, which will leave about £228.

38. That is the normal expenditure?—Yes. The average expenditure is about the amount of the rates.

39. Then we will take the average expenditure to be £218 a year?—Yes.

40. The rate in 1871 you have given as 1s.?—Yes, I believe so.

41. And in 1878 what was it?—It was 10d.

42. And in 1876?—Up to the 18th April, 1877, it was 10d.; April, 1878, and up to April, 1879, (the present year) 1s.

43. Can you give me the poor rates and the county cess for the same years?—The county cess, I believe, averaged 1s. 6d. in the pound for the maintenance of the roads.

44. What year was that for?—Taking it for the last three years.

45. You can't give it for each year?—No, I have not got it.

46. Have you got the poor rates?—No.

47. You did not fill up the rates column?—No.

48. Was the Act adopted entirely or only in part?—In part; they did not adopt the water clauses.

49. How is the town lighted?—With gas.

50. By a company?—No, a private individual.

51. The works don't belong to the Commissioners?—No.

52. You contract with the owner?—Yes, we contract with him for the lighting of the street lamps.

53. What do you pay him?—£3 each for thirty-four lamps for eight months in the year.

54. What do you bargain for in the way of time for light?—From dark until two o'clock for eight months.

55. And do you except it on moonlight nights?—Yes, but during the time of the moonlight if it becomes dark he must light the lamps.

56. How is the town supplied with water?—There are plenty of pumps and wells.

57. And good water?—Yes, good water.

58. There are no complaints about the water?—There are some complaints, but arising partly from neglect of the people themselves.

59. How is the town off in the matter of drainage and sewerage?—Well, it is very well off at present. I have kept as good an account as I could for some years past, and I find the Commissioners have laid out about £1,100 in opening new sewers and repairing old ones.

60. That was before the Guardians became the Sanitary Authority?—Yes, and they do not bestow so much attention on it.

61. Is the town supposed to be as well lighted as it is required to be?—Well, indeed it is.

62. There are no complaints about the lighting?—No; sometimes there are complaints that the lighting is not as good as it should be, but it is generally improved when we look after it. On the whole it is very well lighted.

63. How many qualified voters are there in the township?—I could not immediately say.

64. Approximately how many are there?—I could not say. We had no contests here for fifteen years.

and, therefore, my attention was not called to the matter.

65. How many are there in the town qualified to act as Commissioners?—I suppose there would be from thirty to forty qualified to sit.

66. Have the Commissioners ever considered the question of becoming the Urban Sanitary Authority and taking up the sanitary works from the Guardians again?—Well yes, they petitioned for it last week; they considered whether the shilling rate would be able to keep the town in order, should they get rid of the penny that is added to the poor rates for that purpose.

67. Then their memorial is before the Local Government Board now?—Yes.

68. Have the Commissioners ever considered whether when they became the Urban Authority (supposing they do) they would also take up the charge of the roads from the Grand Jury?—No, there is a good deal of talk about that latterly as some of the Commissioners are very much inclined to take them up. There is a road by the river which has become a nuisance—the road from the Castle round by the Mall—and the county surveyor seems to be able to do what he likes, and in five years this road was once with a contractor but there was a limit of a shilling a perch and of course no one would take it up for that and he did not trouble himself for the five years.

69. How much does the town pay to the Grand Jury?—£536.

70. Is it the opinion of the Commissioners they get a fair return from the Grand Jury for the money they contribute?—It is the opinion of the Commissioners they do not, and the way the roads are attended to is rather unsatisfactory. The contractor takes as much out of them as he can and one road was neglected altogether for five years and now it is impassable.

71. Has application been made at presentment sessions or elsewhere for works which have been refused?—Only for flagging the footways. It is very hard to drag anything out of them.

72. You say the Commissioners have been considering the question of taking up these works?—Yes.

73. But they have come to no resolution about it?—No, they could not see their way. They were talking about it and Mr. Cowcross said he would make inquiry about the matter.

74. But if they saw they could financially work it they would desire to have charge of those works?—Yes, they consider they would keep the town in better trim.

75. Being on the spot and having an interest in looking after it?—Yes, and I don't think it would require so much to do it, if we were in a position once to take charge of it.

76. Are you aware of the feeling of the people around the town. I don't suppose any of those living around would wish to be included in the town?—I don't think they would, there would not be much advantage. It is generally land you would get and there would not be any residences added worth while. It is chiefly small farmers who would be brought in and it would not be worth while.

77. There is only one-fourth charged on land for improvement purposes?—Yes, and when you go further out into the country there is nothing but land.

78. Supposing that there was an extension of half a mile any around the present boundary would it take in any gentlemen's places?—Well it would take in Turtulla House.

79. Half a mile extension would take in Turtulla House, are there any others it would take in?—I don't think there are any more. Our present boundary takes in the glebe and all from that part up, it takes in the pay-houses and the railways.

80. Half a mile extension all round your present boundary would take in no gentleman's residence except Turtulla House?—No.

81. Then it would not add to any extent to the number of people qualified to be Commissioners?—I believe not much and they would not come in and would not be present.

Mr. MICHAEL C[illegible] examined.

82. You are Chairman of the Town Commissioners?—Yes, sir.

83. How long have you been so?—About six months.

84. Have you been long a Commissioner?—For nine years.

85. The feeling of the Board as far as you know it is unanimous against having any alteration in the boundary of the town?—Yes.

86. Either by increasing or decreasing it?—Yes.

87. You were not in the body when they were formed?—No, I was not.

88. Do you know the opinion of any of the immediate outsiders—whether they wish to be brought in or not?—No, I do not.

89. With regard to becoming the sanitary authority you have made application so that you are anxious to get it?—Yes, we think it would be better vested in ourselves, the only difference is that we of course only have power over the bye streets and lanes while the public streets are kept in a very bad and dirty state.

90. What works have the Guardians done of late years since they became the sanitary authority in 1874?—They have done nothing except a few passages they have looked after.

91. Do you happen to know how much of the poor rate of 1876 was for sanitary purposes if any?—A penny was charged extra on us.

92. That was for sanitary purposes?—Yes.

93. What district was that charged on?—On the township.

94. On the township only?—I believe so.

95. Have you ever asked the Guardians to do work which they have declined to do?—We have.

96. What kind of work?—Several nuisances that turned up round the locality. We applied to the Local Government Board first and the application was sent to the Board of Guardians, and they passed the matter over and gave us little or no satisfaction, and we also applied in reference to some nuisances that existed in the river and some that were smelling badly round the town and they did not look after them.

97. These are matters which you think you would have looked after if you were the sanitary authority?—Yes.

98. Do you consider that if you got the care of the town yourselves you would be able to do it with the shilling rate?—I think we would. We would be sure to do it better than they do it now.

99. You do not consider you want any extension of the municipality for the purpose of increasing the rates for sanitary purposes?—Some of the sewers are in very bad order, and I think it would take something to put them into proper order again.

100. Suppose you became the sanitary authority, how do you propose to get the money for that purpose?—I don't think we would require a great deal more than we have for that.

101. Of course that will be a question to be considered into where your township is being considered?—Yes; we did it always when we had the sanitary work in our own hands with the present rate.

102. Did you do more while you were the sanitary authority than the guardians have done since 1874?—Certainly; a great deal. We have plenty of sewerage if it was kept clean. It is the opinion of the Commissioners or a great many of them discussing the matter over here, and of a great many of the public round the town, that if we had a separation from the county altogether it would be better for ourselves seeing that we paid the county such an amount as over £500 a

Thurles.
Mar. 13, 1877.
John Bergin.

Michael C[illegible].

Thurles. Nov. 14, 18[illegible]. — Michael [illegible].

year, and that really we don't get more than £200 a year out of them.

103. You consider that if you got the same amount of money into your hands as the county draw from the town, you could keep the town and all the roads in better order?—Yes; and with a great saving in the rates to ourselves, about half the amount would do, and I have calculated it.

104. Have you gone into figures on the subject?—I have calculated the amount received by the contractors round the town, and I find the average cost would not be more than half what they are receiving—that is about £120 or £140.

105. I suppose there are several road contracts within the boundary?—Only three altogether.

106. Do you remember the names of the contractors?—James Hayes is one.

107. Which road has Mr. Hayes charge of?—The Main-street and the principal roads in the town. Mr. Ahearn has another contract, he is deputy surveyor under the county, and there is no contractor but himself on the Turalla road.

108. Has he only that road?—He has got some other bye-roads.

109. Who is the third contractor?—James Hartney.

110. He has the Johnstown road?—Yes.

111. You think that if you got all the county cess you would be able to keep the roads much better?—Yes.

112. You make that statement from your [illegible] and [illegible]?—Yes; I am certain the town would be kept in far better order if it was vested in the town board.

113. But the Commissioners have made no regular resolution on the subject?—Yes, they did. There are five or six of the Commissioners I have been speaking to; we had a public chat on the matter, and they did not all understand it, and did not [illegible] we could get a resolution, but it is [illegible] the [illegible] you have been making that application at [illegible] from [illegible], and I think it would be better we should apply. A good many of the Commissioners agree with me.

114. Is there anything else you would like to add respecting the subject of this inquiry?—At the present time we are expending a lot of our own rates on county works.

115. What is [illegible]?—No, not exactly, but keeping some of the wall and public walks round the town. We go out as far as Turalla-bridge, and that belongs to the county, and up towards the railway we put in gravel on the piece that belongs to the county. In fact we are expending our private money on the county works. There is a [illegible] up to the [illegible]-road, but so neglected are they that the Commissioners have been obliged to spend money on it, and the same way with the Turalla-road. We are obliged to spend money there too.

117. I see that the township of Thurles with the exception of one or two places consists of whole townlands, would there be any objection to dividing in the case of those townlands that are not at present wholly included so as to make it a township of complete townlands?—I could not answer this. We have not made any inquiries about that.

118. There is no particular local objection to taking in the rest of the townland near Turalla, for instance?—I know at the time the boundaries were being made in order to avoid a great deal of trouble, and to obviate any difficulty in carrying on the township, because they left out some people who really should be included.

119. That was done to obviate any trouble about the measure?—Yes.

120. Would there be any working difficulty in having the boundaries of these townlands known?—No, I don't think there would be.

121. Mr. Bergin (Town Clerk).—The reason they confined the boundary so much then was to avoid opposition. The opposition of those excluded would be to the taxation connected with it. Most of the trouble came from outsiders who hold bits of land. These people came in and said—"We want to be liable to taxation or otherwise, do what you like with the town, but don't bring us under taxation," and the cry was "If you bring us in we will always be taxed."

122. Take that townland opposite Turalla bank, portion is included in the present township, but more than half is outside the township. Is there any objection of a local nature to putting the whole of that townland into the township?—Except what objection the persons in occupation would give. I am sure they would not consent.

123. But there is no other objection?—No; I think not.

124. To Witness.—Do all these people derive considerable benefit from being so close to the township, for markets and schools for their children, and so on?—Yes.

125. How far do you think does that advantage extend into a country like this?—I think it would be little or no advantage to us.

126. But the people within a certain distance of the town derive advantage from the markets and schools in the town, and so on?—They derive advantages within two miles, great advantages.

127. And the land lets at a higher rate on account of being so close to the town?—Much higher, it would go once and a half the value it is outside that distance.

128. Have you anything to add?—No, except that, I agree with all that has been said with regard to the town.

129. You told me that the railway and other buildings were increasing very much?—Yes.

130. Would there be any chance of the railway buildings on property beyond the present township?—No I think not. The new railway will come in by the side of the present workshop.

131. Then there is no chance of any of the new buildings extending in any direction beyond the present town?—I think not. The only thing I was going to add was, that if we could compel the county to do the work required for the benefit of the town, as they receive such a sum from it.

132. You would rather not have the authority if you could compel them to do the work?—Yes; at the present time, when we are putting in presentments we don't get any adequate amount. There are often complaints about the roads in the town. There is only one well in the town, and that would be in a very bad state, although it is supplying the whole of the town. The wells in the other parts of the town are very bad, and the water is bad, so that there is not a good drop of water in the town, except in the one well I refer to.

133. Where is that well?—In Quarry street.

134. That is removed a long way from the centre of the town?—Yes; I have to keep an animal purposely to carry water to my house from that well.

135. Do the people get drinking water from the river at all?—The water of the river has been analysed by a gentleman in Cork, Mr. O'Keeffe. It has been analysed for the convent, and they have been getting up some works to enable them to use it as it is far better than any other public water in the town.

136. Have any waterworks ever been projected here?—No; never.

137. Is it due to the fault of the Board of Guardians that the other pumps are not kept in good order?—It is, that is one of the faults, but I really think the water is bad in any case, although we have a plentiful supply.

Mr. [illegible], (Town Clerk) re-examined.

Thurles, Aug. 12, 1878. — Mr. [illegible].

138. The pump in the street is not good for drinking purposes?—It is not sweet enough, there is no lift so that the water runs back always.

139. It is the duty of the guardians to keep these pumps in order?—Yes. I have searched the rate-book, and I find the number of qualified voters is 301.

140. How many are qualified to sit as Commissioners, if they chose to be candidates for the office?—About thirty. I look to their intelligence as much as anything else, for there are some who are qualified and who would not be fit to act.

141. Does the twelve Commissioners include the Chairman?—Yes, but the number in the Chairman's report, namely, eleven, might be in consequence of a vacancy. There are about seventy occupiers who would be entitled to act as Commissioners, of which number about thirty or forty could act as Commissioners.

Mr. Thomas Everitt examined.

Thomas Everitt.

142. You are one of the Commissioners of the town?—Yes.

143. How long have you been a Commissioner?—About nine months.

144. You agree with the other Commissioners, that an extension is needed in the present township boundaries of Thurles?—Yes.

145. You also agree that it would be desirable to get this auxiliary power?—Yes, I am quite satisfied with that.

146. Have you anything further to add?—No, except that I quite agree with every thing that has been said with regard to the town.

The inquiry terminated.

ARDEE.—14TH MAY, 1879.

Before Mr. C. P. Cotton, C.E.

Ardee, May 14, 187[illegible].

Mr. Peter Shekey examined.

Peter Shekey.

1. You are Chairman of the Ardee Town Commissioners?—Yes, sir.

2. For how long have you held this post?—This is the second year of the second term. I was chairman from 1855 to 1857 on the first occasion, and from 1878 to the present year.

3. You were a Commissioner for a number of years?—For thirty-six years. We were first under the 9th of George IV.

4. At present the town is under the Towns Improvement Act of 1854?—Yes.

5. When was it placed under that Act?—In February, 1855.

6. Previous to that it was under the 9th of George IV.?—Yes.

7. How many Commissioners are there?—Nine under the Towns Improvement Act. The number under the 9th George IV. was fifteen.

8. The Town Clerk has returned the population at 2,973?—That is correct.

9. What is the area of the town?—1,285 acres.

10. And the valuation?—£5,975.

11. The Town Clerk has given it at £6,000?—I think that is right.

12. The town is not divided into wards?—No.

13. It is altogether in the electoral division of Ardee?—Yes.

14. Are you acquainted with the electoral division boundary?—I could not describe it.

15. You could not tell me how far the electoral division extends from the centre of the town?—I could not. I should say it would average three miles from the centre of the town. I was chairman of the Commissioners in 1855, when they considered the question of extending the boundaries. The old boundaries were very circumscribed, and they then memorialed the Lord Lieutenant, Lord St. Germans, I think, for an extension. They wanted a very large extension in 1855, and they got the present boundary then. This was in 1856 or 1857; but they asked for a far larger extension than the present boundary, which is marked out on the map, and which was fixed by Lord St. Germans in 1857. They asked for the boundary marked in black on that map (produced).

16. That was a circle of about a mile and a half?—Yes.

17. In 1857 the Commissioners applied for an extension of the boundary by a mile and a half, and they got an extension up to the present boundary?—Yes, the old boundary was very circumscribed.

18. On what ground, do you remember, did they ask for the extension at that time?—Whatever it was it is here (produces book). It says here in the memorial:— "That the boundaries of the borough being so very limited, as exhibited in the map sent to your Excellency like the twelve months, memorialists were obliged to tax to the highest rate of 1s. in the pound to meet the expenses of [illegible] a water supply."

19. The lowest rate was [illegible] and they asked for an extension in order to get a larger area?—Yes.

20. They applied in 1857 for an extension, on the ground that they had not money enough to carry out the [illegible]?—Yes.

21. And then the present boundary was fixed?—Yes.

22. Do the Commissioners now wish for any further extension?—Well, I think so.

23. Has the question been regularly brought before any meetings of the Commissioners?—I think so.

24. Do you remember any meeting at which it was brought forward?—At the last meeting a meeting at which it was brought forward and regularly discussed.

25. Who authorised the Town Clerk to fill up the replies to my queries, for he says they wish the area extended in order to get their present income increased? —We were just talking of it at the meeting, and he was instructed by the Commissioners to fill up the replies.

26. From your knowledge of the Board as chairman, what do you think is the general feeling of the Commissioners?—I think the general feeling is for extension.

27. Excepting that, have you any particular extension in view; you have an area at present of an area of 1,285 acres?—Well, no; I merely want this boundary as it was in the memorial a good many years ago.

28. Would you propose as an extension the one applied for in 1857?—I think it would be rather large.

29. Do you think yourself it would be advisable to adopt it as the boundary?—It looks very large, and I think it would be much better to fix upon some distance from the market house. I consider the boundary then proposed looks on the large side.

30. Then you have no definite idea of what the extension should be when you propose extension, except that there is something wanted?—Yes.

31. How far does the town extend from the centre? —It is more than half a mile to the north side.

32. If the boundary was extended half a mile all round would it take in much property that is not agricultural land?—No. I think the present boundary is half a mile or more.

Ardee.
May 14, 1877.
Peter Hickey.

33. But if the boundary was extended half a mile, a mile beyond the present boundary, would that take in much land that is agricultural and many gentlemen's residences?—No; not many.

34. Have you any idea how many voters there are in Ardee qualified to be Town Commissioners?—Seventy-four I think.

35. Have you any idea how many are qualified to sit if they were elected Commissioners?—There are seventy qualified to sit.

36. Surely all the voters are not qualified to sit?—I was surprised to see it.

37. Then there are seventy-four entitled to vote?—Yes.

38. Of those how many are qualified to sit at the Board?—Seventy qualified. The number rated at £12 and upwards is seventy; the number rated at £4 and under twelve is seventy-four.

39. That is, 144 qualified to vote, and seventy to sit as Commissioners?—Yes.

40. Can you tell me, suppose there was an extension of half a mile all round the present boundary, would it add many to the voters who are rated over £4?—I don't think it would. I don't think it would change the numbers much.

41. It would not add many?—No.

42. Then the land about must be all agricultural?—Yes; it is mostly agricultural land.

43. Is it principally held by people living on it or by town people?—The land at that distance outside is held by people living on it.

44. Do the children of those people come into the schools in Ardee?—Yes, I think so.

45. And they use Ardee as a market town?—Yes.

46. There are fairs held here?—Yes; thirteen fairs in the year; one fair monthly, and one at Christmas.

47. From how far, do you think, do the children come into Ardee to attend school?—Some of them come nearly two miles.

48. What were the rates for the last five years in the town?—They did not exceed one shilling; they were always one shilling.

49. Do you know what were the poor rates during those years?—For the present year it is 1s. 5d. in the pound.

50. Is that for 1876?—No; that is for 1875.

51. Do you know what was the poor rate the year before that?—I do not.

52. What was the county cess in 1876?—I think it was 11d. in the pound.

53. That is for the half year?—Yes; that is one cess.

54. There is in 1s. 10d. in the year?—Not so much as that—1s. 8d., I think.

55. How is Ardee supplied with gas?—By a gas company.

56. You contract with the gas company?—Yes.

57. How many lamps have you, and at what cost are they supplied with gas?—Fifteen lamps at £3 5s. each. They are lighted from the middle of September until the middle of April; they are not lighted during the summer months.

58. And they are not lighted during moonlight nights?—No; not on the two nights next before and the two nights next after full moon.

59. What do the gas company charge private consumers?—They charge very high; it is 8s. 4d.

60. How is the town supplied with water?—By pumps.

61. These pumps are repaired and looked after by the guardians as the sanitary authority?—Yes.

62. With regard to the sewage how does the town stand?—We are a long time about that, and it is only now active steps are being taken to make a main drain.

63. By the guardians?—Yes; by the sanitary authority. The Commissioners tried and they got plans from the county surveyor eight or nine years ago, but it was rejected by the rate-payers. Then we began to press it on the Local Government Board, but it is only now anything is about to be done. There is no town in Ireland looks cleaner, but the yards of the houses are in an awful state.

64. There is no main drainage whatever?—No; and it is impossible to carry out any sanitary arrangements, but by pressing it on the Local Government Board we have at last got the sanitary board to take it up in earnest. The reason for not taking sooner in the matter was, they said that the ratepayers were so badly off they would not go on with the work. I was speaking to Mr. Neville on last Monday week, and he tells me the work of making the main drain will be in full operation before the 1st of July.

65. Have the Commissioners considered whether they would desire to become the urban sanitary authority?—They have; and they do not wish to become sanitary authority, they would rather leave it in the hands of the guardians. The guardians made them an offer to transfer the sanitary work to them, but they would not accept it.

66. The guardians offered to consent to the Commissioners being made the urban sanitary authority?—They did, and the Commissioners wouldn't.

67. Have the guardians of late years spent any money in sanitary matters in the town, and have they struck any special sanitary rate in addition to the ordinary poor rate?—I really don't know. It must be a small rate they use for whitewashing the lanes in summer, 1d. or 2d.; but I am not certain.

68. What were the receipts of the Commissioners for the year 1876?—The rate at 1s. in the pound produced £130; there was £70 for rents.

69. From what?—From lands that the old Corporation held by charter, and which fell to the new Commissioners. The moiety of the dog tax about £8, and the fines for drunkenness £15.

70. Had they any other receipts?—No, sir.

71. How is it that the rates only come to £180; shouldn't they have been £200 or more?—£180 is the sum stated. Our financial year ends on the 25th April.

72. Then the accounts have not been audited for the present year?—No, not yet.

73. Can you tell me the opinion of the ratepayers of the town generally who are not Commissioners as to whether there ought to be extension of the boundaries or not?—I think they are in favour of extension.

74. But they have not considered any particular extension?—No, sir.

75. Have you ever heard any expression of opinion from the people living immediately outside the present boundary who would be taken in by any extension either for or against extension?—I have not.

76. Although they did not come to any particular resolution when they had the matter before them, yet in considering the question of extension in order to get increased income, have the Commissioners considered what particular increase of income they wanted?—They have not.

77. What is the increased income wanted for?—I was just going to remark a few minutes ago that there were sanitary arrangements wanted; that main drain for instance. We don't know yet on what area the sanitary authority will put the cost of that.

78. But if you don't wish to become the sanitary authority yourselves that matter is completely out of your power?—I know that, but if we had extended area it would be well to have it to meet the cost of that main drain.

79. The Local Government Board must decide what district is to pay for that main drain?—But if we had an increased area of taxation to meet that it would be well.

80. Do I understand you, that if you had an increased area you would then wish to become the sanitary authority?—I don't know that.

81. Your present income is about £180 a year, and you have not in your mind any particular increase of income that is necessary for your purposes—it is only that some increase is necessary?—I think some increase is necessary. We have not half the requisite number of lamps; we require as many more lamps.

ARDEE. May 14, 1878. Peter Hickey.

82. Is there anything else besides lighting, putting sanitary matters out of sight altogether, that you require more money for?—There is. We had it in contemplation here some years ago to get a fire engine. The town is completely at the mercy of fire at present, and if we had the engine we would require a supply of water for it, and I have my eye on a place where we could get a supply of water; about a mile or less than a mile away we could get a very good supply of water. Dr. Hore, the medical officer, agrees with me as to getting a supply of water for that purpose from that source, and supplying the town with it too if it required it.

83. Would there be any objection to the Town Commissioners coming to a distinct resolution as to whether they do wish for this extension, and what extension, because this information you are giving is your own opinion, and it is very indefinite?—Yes, it is.

84. You neither give us an idea of what extension you wish for in area, nor what increase in income you want, but the two purposes for which you want an increased income are the fire engine and the extension of the gas lamps?—The supply of water for the fire engine would be the first thing.

85. Have you had any fires in Ardee?—Not lately, but there was a string of fires here five years ago, and not for twenty years before.

86. You have no fire engine of any sort?—No.

87. Do you think that the Commissioners would care to give definite information on the subject?—I think they would.

88. Do you think, from your own knowledge of the electoral division, whether it would be too large to adopt as the boundary of the town?—It would be too large.

89. Is there anything else you wish to give as your opinion on the subject of the extension or alteration of the boundaries in any way?—I think not.

Mr. THOMAS DOLAN examined. Thomas Dolan.

90. You are a Town Commissioner also?—I am.

91. And have been for some time?—For long.

92. What is your opinion as regards the present boundaries of the town?—I think it would be a very pleasant thing to have them enlarged, so as to give us a greater area for taxation, but I don't see on what grounds we could get it, for all that would be taken in would be altogether agricultural, and would not add money to the revenue [illegible]—I would suppose some [illegible] or two of them.

93. And look to the number qualified to act as Commissioners?—Yes.

94. Would the Commissioners as a body desire extension if it involved any additional obligation, such as lighting further out?—I think they would scarcely like to undertake the responsibility of lighting further out.

95. In that case the income you think would not balance the expenditure?—No; because I believe we would only get one-fourth of the rate on the land.

96. What is your opinion about the Commissioners becoming the sanitary authority instead of the guardians?—The Commissioners were unanimous in [illegible] it, because there is a big sum to be put on us now. The Commissioners would like to have the sanitary management if there was sufficient income to bear the expense, but under its present powers the chief sanitary officer the consideration of a water supply, which will cost £3,000 or £4,000; and that will put 4s. or 5s. on the town for the next thirty or forty years.

97. You think if that was left to the guardians it would be distributed over a larger area?—Yes.

98. And except for that special work you would wish to be the sanitary authority?—Yes; and, I believe, that would be the wish of the Commissioners.

99. Have the guardians made any outlay in the [illegible] the last few years?—There is one pump erected here.

100. That is distributed over the whole electoral division?—Yes; 1s. 4d., and 1d. are the rates for 1878.

101. But the question of what district the cost for this [illegible] would [illegible] to be [illegible] has not been decided?—Yes; some of the guardians wanted to put it on the township, and I don't know whether they have not argued it the other way, for the guardians are all from the country.

102. Suppose the rate was put on the town would the Commissioners wish to be the authority in carrying it out?—No, but I think they would wish to be the sanitary authority after the work's done; because it may cost more than at first estimated.

103. Again there was the question of the obligation to light all the extended district, but have not considered any particular extension?—No; in fact for my part I was not for extension, but the Chairman argued against that, that extension would be desirable, and that such a thing was done before.

104. The extension proposed before would be a single [illegible]?—We could do nothing for the people out there except we put lamps on the roads.

105. How is the town off for water?—We get up a very good system of pumps in the town, just before the change came in the law. Our taxation is pretty light, and it leaves us very bare.

106. The maintenance of the roads is altogether in the hands of the Grand Jury?—Yes.

107. And you have never considered the question of taking up the roads?—No, we get a great quantity from the Grand Jury for the streets.

108. Do you do anything in the way of keeping in order the Grand Jury?—No; we don't undertake, but we get some paving done by the Grand Jury sometimes. When there is a large job to be done we apply to the Grand Jury, and get a presentment.

109. Do you contribute to that work as a body?—No; but the water channels for footways along the streets are kept by us.

110. Your expenditure, you say, runs your income pretty tight?—Yes, we have not nearly more than half the required number of lamps, through our inability to pay for them.

111. Is there anything else you wish to add bearing on the subject of extension?—I am afraid we have no case to make, although it would be very pleasant to get something larger to tax.

112. Don't you think the Commissioners would give us something more definite than the general answer, that they wish for extension in order to get a larger sum of money?—If they could not, I don't think they should get it.

The inquiry then closed.

NEWBRIDGE.—MARCH 17TH, 1879.

Before Mr. COTTON, C.E.

Mr. PATRICK DOYLE, examined.

1. You are Chairman of the Town Commissioners?—Yes.

2. How long have you been a Commissioner?—Some ten or twelve years.

3. The town of Newbridge is under the Towns' Improvement Act?—Yes.

4. Do you remember about what time it was put under the Act?—It was before '66.

5. Was the Towns' Improvement Act adopted in its entirety for cleansing, lighting, and watering?—Yes, all at the one time.

6. Was there any power for striking a rate for water?—No.

7. Your rate is limited to 1s.?—Yes, 1s. for houses, and 3d. for lands.

8. What is the population?—3,254.

9. And the area?—620 acres.

10. You take that from the rate book?—Yes. I have here a book from which it appears that in 1863 the town was put under the Towns' Improvement Act. In May—May 29th—the meeting of the ratepayers was held to elect the first Town Commissioners.

11. What is the valuation?—£4,037 10s.

12. You have no wards, of course?—No.

13. In what electoral division is the town situated?—In Great Connell and Morristown Biller.

14. Is it pretty equally divided—or is there more in one division than in the other?—It is pretty equal.

15. Have you a map?—No, we never had a map showing the township. I think the division is pretty equal.

16. The Municipal and Poor Law boundaries, are they the same, do you know, in the town?—Half the town is in one division, and half in another.

17. Do you know what are the rates that have been struck during the past four or five years?—1s. in the pound every year.

18. Since '73 have you exercised the full rating power?—Yes; we had a great deal to do in the way of flagging the streets. We have lodged, these two years or so, with the treasurer of the county, £200 for flagging.

19. £200 from your rates to the County Grand Jury?—Yes, and they gave us a grant of as much more to help us in the flagging.

20. They gave £200 conditional upon your contributing?—Yes.

21. And they do the work?—Yes, they reserve to themselves that the County Surveyor will inspect the work.

22. In fact, it is done by the county, you contributing?—Yes, done under the supervision of the County Surveyor.

23. What were the poor rates during the same time?—I cannot say at this moment.

24. How far does the town of Newbridge extend from the centre of the town—in the north direction towards the railway?—Something near a mile.

25. It goes out a mile?—Yes.

26. And on the south?—Scarcely so much as that, only about half a mile on the south, and on the east about half a mile, I think.

27. And the west?—About the same thing.

28. Then it is rather more to the north?—Yes.

29. Have the Town Commissioners, as a body, considered the question of whether an extension should be made or not?—Yes; when I got your note or queries they all were unanimous in favour of leaving the boundaries as they are.

30. They do not wish to have them extended?—No.

31. Or contracted?—No. They wish for no alteration whatever.

32. Was any formal resolution to that effect adopted?—Well, no. The subject was entertained at the next meeting after I got the queries.

33. How many Commissioners were present?—Nine, in the number we have altogether.

34. How many attended that meeting?—Five, I think.

35. And do you know the feeling of those who did not attend?—They are all of the same opinion; they won't make any change, they think it better to remain as they are.

36. Do you know the feeling of any of the people who live immediately outside the township boundary?—Yes.

37. Do they wish to be brought in?—No.

38. Do you know what the receipts and expenditure during the past five years have been?—Yes.

39. Take the receipts first, tell me the different items from which they come?—Would the abstracts do?

40. Yes—have you printed abstracts?—Yes.

41. How much have you, during the past year, received from rates?—£130. We received also about £60 from Government contribution to rates; fees, £31; dog licenses, £11; from cars, £30; letting of the Town Hall for concerts, &c., £5, receipts from the same, £16; weighing machines, £80; rent of Sessions house, £10.

42. The Sessions house is the property of the Commissioners, is it not?—Yes.

43. And is let for holding Petty Sessions?—Yes.

44. That altogether is about £360?—Yes.

45. Now as to the expenditure—what did it amount to last year?—To £310, including £250 contributed to the Grand Jury.

46. Is the railway station within the limit of the township?—Yes, but we have no power to go further than outside their gate.

47. You have control over the cars plying to the railway station?—Yes.

48. Your regulations for the car drivers go as far as the township boundaries, of course?—Yes.

49. Of the 3,254 people composing the population, how many are in the barracks?—I could not say, for it varies.

50. This is the population of all together?—Yes, there are generally from 1,200 to 1,400 in the barracks.

51. This return of the population is that given on 3rd April, 1871?—Yes.

52. And that included the military?—Yes.

53. How many persons are there in Newbridge qualified to vote for the election of Town Commissioners?—About 103 altogether.

54. How many of those are qualified to be Commissioners, how many are rated at £12 and upwards?—About one half; mostly all are town people.

55. Yes, but are they sufficiently highly rated to become Commissioners?—Yes, about one half.

56. You know the country immediately surrounding the boundaries?—Yes.

57. If the boundaries were extended to a radius of a mile or a mile and a half in every direction would it add more to the number of voters?—No, they are all farmers around nearly.

58. Where do they live?—On the farms.

59. Would it add anything to the number of persons eligible to be elected Commissioners?—Yes, I dare say all the farmers outside would be eligible.

60. Would it add a dozen?—I dare say it would add about ten.

61. Don't you think that the people who live within a mile from the centre of a town like Newbridge derive very considerable advantages from their proximity to

Newbridge. Mar. [illegible] Mr. [illegible]

the town by reason of the markets and so forth?—Yes.

63. Don't they all sell their produce here?—Yes, to a certain extent, but we are very disadvantageously situated here; we have two very well established markets—[illegible] and [illegible].

64. But take the people living within say a mile, wouldn't these people sell most of their produce in Newbridge?—They do certainly sell milk.

65. Have they not got schools here to which they send their children?—Yes, there is the National school and the Convent.

66. The people come in for mass within a mile, I should think?—Yes.

67. Don't the people within that district derive advantages for which they ought to pay something towards keeping the town in order?—I think they might, but the markets at these two markets they don't derive so much advantage as they otherwise would. Those two markets are attended principally.

68. Do you think there would be anything unfair in asking these people who live within a mile from the town in which they sell their produce, and to which they send their children to school, to contribute something towards the lighting, watering, and so on of the town and not levy it all on the people of the town?—I do, I think it would be fair.

69. Then if it is fair why would you object to an extension of the area?—Well, I know that most of the people outside would object to it.

70. But I want to get at the reason. We generally find there is a tendency or wish to bring the people outside within the boundary. It is thought generally to be unfair to keep up the lighting, watering, and cleansing of the town for the benefit of the people outside who pay no rates towards it. Is there any other reason against it except that some people would object?—I think not. The principal reason would be that there are mostly all large farms outside. There are not many people on them.

71. Yes, but they are the farms. They come into it and derive the benefits of it. Now would there be anything in your opinion unreasonable in their paying a small contribution towards those advantages?

72. No, certainly not. Nothing unfair; it would be very fair.

73. And the land being only liable for such works as that at one-fourth rating, it would be a very small thing on them?—Yes.

74. How is the town lighted?—By gas.

75. Do you mean that it is supplied by a gas company?—It was owned by a gas company but was sold to a private person for so much a lamp.

76. How much do you pay in the year?—About £90.

77. How many lamps are lighted for that?—Fourteen, [illegible] lamps.

78. About £3 a piece?—Yes.

79. How is the town supplied with water?—That is all taken from the Commissioners.

80. There is nothing but pumps?—No.

81. Is the drainage well managed?—Yes. [illegible] many years. We went to great expense to drain the town.

82. Was that previous to the sanitary work being taken up from you?—Yes.

83. Is the general feeling of the Commissioners that they would wish to recover their sanitary powers?—Yes.

84. Have they made any motion towards it?—No, but they asked me to represent it to you.

85. Well, you know it does not rest with us. If you ask the Local Government Board by memorial when the sanitary powers restored, under provisional order, then the Local Government Board would inquire and then issue a provisional order if it was so advisable to restore the urban sanitary authority. They have not taken any steps, you say?—No; and I would ask you, sir, suppose they got back the sanitary authority, would it not be on the same terms as before?

86. Certainly?—That is, we will not have to contribute more.

87. You will have to get your own [illegible] for any sanitary works you may engage in. You will have power of employing a man; you will have the power, and you will be the executive to do it. Do you think the Guardians have not done the sanitary work satisfactorily?—No.

88. Have they refused to do things you brought under their attention as necessary?—No, I cannot say that, but the process has been so slow as to be almost useless. They only meet once a week.

89. You think the Town Commissioners being on the spot would be better able to attend to sanitary matters than the Guardians?—Yes, the time we had the jurisdiction we used to go around with the sanitary inspector in the hot summer months with the police and inspect all the yards. Since then however it has all been taken out of our hands, and the town is in a bad way.

90. If you became the urban sanitary authority and [illegible] it would be open to you to make application to the Local Government Board to get control of the roads and bridges from the Grand Jury, would that be likely to be looked for by the Commissioners?—No, they would not want that.

91. Are there any works connected with the town you would do if you had a larger income?—In the first place we would have a better supply of water.

92. But as Town Commissioners?—Well, there is nothing we would do if we had [illegible].

93. What I mean is, with your present powers, if you had a larger income, is there any necessary work you would require to do?—No.

94. No work that is left undone from want of funds?—No, the flagging of streets is in course of being done.

95. That is done by the Grand Jury, you contributing?—Yes.

96. Can you tell me about the electoral division, how far they extend from Newbridge?—I could not tell exactly. I think they extend about a mile.

97. At any rate the electoral division would be far larger than the boundary of the town?—Yes, certainly.

98. What sanitary works have been done by the Guardians—you say in the union of Naas?—Yes, they have not done anything except to keep the pumps in order.

99. Not any drainage works?—No.

100. Have they struck any special sanitary rate?—They have, 1d. in the pound. The last rate paid was 1d. in the pound.

101. Was that in 1878?—Yes.

102. Anything since they got their authority in 1874?—I think there was a special rate of 1s. 3d. in the pound.

103. But the sanitary rate in 1878 was 1d. in the pound?—Yes.

104. What was it for?—For the electoral division, for the whole union.

105. It was spread over the whole union?—Yes.

106. What portion was it struck on—for a special sanitary rate to strike on a particular district are necessary any division or union?—I think it was the union at large. I am not quite sure.

107. What fairs have you in the town?—Twelve fairs—one every month.

108. At the time of the discussion as to whether there should be an extension of the boundaries [illegible], did the question of the applicability of the Land Act raise the question at all?—No, sir.

109. Then independently altogether of the Land Act the Commissioners were of opinion it was better to leave the boundaries as they were?—Yes.

110. Is there anything more to you that you would like to say?—Well, the Commissioners told me to bring before you the bad way the sanitary work is done—that is that the machinery is too cumbersome. There is a very long time taken up in going through the necessary forms.

111. Supposing you got back the sanitary authority, would it be an advantage or not in your opinion to have

a larger area than at present on which to strike a rate—to strike sanitary rates?

112. I think it is sufficient—they all think so.

113. Would the Guardians object to your taking the necessary steps to obtain the provisional order constituting you the sanitary authority in their stead?—No. I don't think so, they have quite enough to do without it.

114. The town drains straight into the river?—Yes, and so does the barracks, but they filter the sewage.

115. Through charcoal?—No, through gravel. I think it costs £300 or £400.

Mr. John Leahy examined.

116. Mr. Cotton.—You know the town boundary?—I do.

117. Take this house as a centre. How far does it extend generally speaking all round?—I think it is about half a mile all round.

118. It is a little more in one direction than in another?—Yes.

119. However you have no map of it?—There should be a map here.

120. You know the electoral divisions?—Yes, there are three—Great Connell, Marydown [illegible], and Newbridge.

121. Great Connell, how far does it extend from the centre of the town?—It is I think a mile and a half. Newbridge electoral division extends about two miles.

122. Do you know a place called [illegible]?—Yes.

123. It is in the Newbridge electoral division?—Yes.

124. But it goes about a mile beyond it?—Yes.

The inquiry then terminated.

MOUNTMELLICK.—MARCH 14TH, 1879.

Before Mr. C. P. Cotton, C.E.

[illegible]

1. You are Town Clerk of this town?—Yes.

2. How long have you held that office?—Since shortly after the town was placed under the Towns Improvement Act in October, 1858.

3. Was it under any Act of Parliament previously?—No.

4. Was the Act only adopted in part?—Only as far as cleansing and lighting.

5. [illegible] in [illegible]?—[illegible]. Here are the minutes of the original time it was entered into. (Produces copy of extract from the minutes.)

6. This is a description of the boundary as it was [illegible] by the Lord Lieutenant?—Yes.

7. What is the population of the town?—Within the municipal boundary it is [illegible].

8. What is the area of the municipality?—[illegible] acres.

9. The town is not divided into wards?—No.

10. In what electoral division is it?—In the [illegible] and Mountmellick electoral divisions.

11. Are the municipal and the poor law boundaries coterminous?—No.

12. Can you give me the rates for the years [illegible], [illegible], 1876, 1877, and 1878?—In [illegible] there was no rate; in [illegible] it was [illegible], in 1876 the same, in 1877 it was [illegible], and in 1878 it was [illegible].

13. Do you know the poor law rate in the same years?—Yes; [illegible] vary in the electoral divisions.

14. In the electoral divisions of [illegible] and Mountmellick?—Yes. In [illegible] in 1874 the poor rate was [illegible], in 1875 it was [illegible] for poor law purposes and [illegible] for special improvement or sanitary rate, in 1876 [illegible], in 1877 [illegible], and in 1878 [illegible]. In Mountmellick the poor rate in 1874 was [illegible], in 1875 [illegible], in 1876 [illegible], in 1877 [illegible], and in 1878 [illegible].

15. Do you know the county cess for the same years?—Not exactly; but it is about [illegible] each half year on the average.

16. Are the present municipal boundaries regarded with dissatisfaction by the ratepayers or any section of them?—No, I think not.

17. Were our queries put before a regular meeting of the Commissioners?—Yes, and before the ratepayers; we called a special meeting.

18. Did the Commissioners come to any special resolution regarding revision of the boundary?—Yes.

19. How many Commissioners have you altogether?—Nine—Six attended that meeting.

20. Have you [illegible] of the Town Commissioners to consider the replies?—No; they [illegible] public notice to [illegible], and then this meeting was held, [illegible] partly of ratepayers and partly of Commissioners, and this was the resolution come to (Reads):—

"The [illegible] queries having been carefully gone into and considered, it is proposed by [illegible], seconded by Mr. [illegible], and unanimously resolved, That this meeting are quite satisfied with the present boundary of the town, and do not wish that it be changed either by curtailing or extending it."

21. How many ratepayers were there present?—There were a good many here, and I put down the names of the principal ones present.

22. Roughly, what was their number?—I suppose there were fifteen, about.

23. Ratepayers of the municipality?—Some outside the boundaries—most of them outside; some of them had land inside and outside the boundary.

24. And the feeling of the meeting was unanimous?—It was, no one dissented.

25. The ratepayers outside don't want to be brought in?—No; and the Commissioners were not anxious to have the boundaries extended.

26. Are there any general observations bearing on the subject of the inquiry which you wish to add?—No; that was the answer we sent to your query to this office.

27. What were the receipts and expenditure this year?—I can tell you since [illegible] if you like; in 1874 the receipts were £[illegible]; in 1875, £[illegible]; in 1876, £[illegible]; in 1877, £[illegible]; and in 1878, £[illegible].

28. How is the income in 1878 so small, when you had so [illegible] rate?—It was not all collected in that year.

29. Those are the net receipts?—Yes.

30. Generally what amount do the Commissioners [illegible] from besides the rates?—From fairs.

31. What do they average?—On an average the [illegible] come to £[illegible], and the [illegible] £[illegible], and the dog tax £[illegible].

32. There are no property or any other kind?—No.

33. How many qualified voters have you in the municipality?—We had 173 on last year's list.

34. And how many are qualified to act as Commissioners?—About twenty-five.

35. And your number is nine?—Yes.

36. How far does the boundary of the town extend in the different directions from the centre of the town?—It runs in a zigzag direction.

37. You take the Market square as a centre?—Yes.

38. How far does it extend to the north?—I suppose about half a mile.

39. How far to the south?—[illegible] the same.

40. To the east how far?—A little over half a mile.

41. And to the west how far?—Three quarters of a mile, or [illegible] seven-eighths of a mile.

42. Have you considered the question at all, if there

MOUNTMELLICK. Nov. 14, 1878. Mr. Robert [illegible].

was an extension to a certain distance, say a mile, round that central point, what the effect would be in bringing in voters or persons qualified to be Commissioners?—I did not go into that question at all.

42. You did not consider the question of any extension as the effect it would have?—No.

43. I thought from asking these times as the rate you had considered that question?—It was for business purposes I put them in.

44. How much of the electoral division of Dungans is in the town?—There is a very small part. About half of the townland of Dungans is in it. Dungans extends a long way.

45. Of the acres of 256 acres how much is in Dungans?—I do not know. There are about 3,000 acres in Dungans, and there is of Dungans in the township 200 a. [illegible], and of Mountmellick town parks 291a. 1r. 30p.

46. They are very nearly equal?—Yes, but the value of one part is more than double the other—nearly three times.

47. Can you give me the valuation of the part of Dungans in the town and also of the other electoral division?—Yes; Dungans 200 acres valued at £3,[illegible] [illegible], and Mountmellick 293 acres valued at £2,91[illegible] 10s.

48. How far does the electoral division of Mountmellick extend away from the town?—I think the extreme point is about a mile and a half.

49. Is that to the north?—It is north west.

50. How far does the furthest point of Dungans extend from the centre of the town?—Four miles, or three and three quarters.

51. The sanitary authority for Mountmellick are the Board of Guardians?—Yes.

52. Have the Commissioners ever considered the question of becoming the sanitary authority instead of the Guardians?—I have never heard.

53. You are aware they have power under a recent Act?—Yes.

54. They have not made any application?—No; the question was never raised at all.

55. That being so, they have never considered the question of taking up the roads and bridges from the Grand Jury?—No.

56. Of the poor rates in 1878, how much was a special sanitary rate?—4d.

57. Out of 3s. 1d.?—Yes; 3d. in the pound.

58. What work was that for?—For drainage and pumps in the town for water supply.

59. That applies to each division?—Yes.

60. What was the contributory district on which that was struck?—The townland of [illegible], and the townland of Town Parks in Mountmellick.

61. Does that nearly comprise the entire municipality?—It more than comprises the municipality.

62. What was the sanitary rate for?—For drainage and pumps.

63. That was considered a fair district by the Local Government Board, on which to strike that rate?—Yes; they declared that by sealed order.

64. Any other sanitary rates which have been struck on the same area?—Yes, and all for the same purposes.

65. How much was it in 1877?—5d., and in 1876 nothing, and in 1878, 4d.

66. How is the town lighted?—With gas; there are thirty-seven public lamps which are lit by contract.

67. Is the contract with a private gas company?—Yes, the Mountmellick gas company.

68. How much do the Commissioners pay?—£3 per lamp.

69. They don't light on moonlight nights?—No.

70. How is the water supplied?—We have plenty of pumps, and good water in the town. There are one or two exceptions, but the town is very well watered.

71. There is no project for any water works?—No, they are not required at all, rivers surround the town.

72. What is the state of the drainage of the town?—It is in a very miserable state, it requires a good drain in one direction, and it requires [illegible], a main drain of about 150 yards would do.

73. Are there any works required which the Commissioners have not been able to do for the want of funds, and which they would be inclined to do if they had further receipts?—None that I am aware of.

74. Have you anything you wish to give us the benefit of your opinion about?—I have not.

Mr. John M'Manus examined. Mr. John M'Manus.

76. You are Chairman of the Town Commissioners of Mountmellick?—I am.

77. Have you been long in that position?—Only a few months.

78. Have you been long a Commissioner?—Very short time.

79. You were at this combined meeting of the ratepayers and Commissioners?—I was.

80. And the feeling of the meeting was unanimous, as the Town Clerk has told us, against any alteration at all?—Yes.

81. Is that your individual opinion?—At first, I thought it would be a good thing to have the boundaries extended, but, then, when I heard it explained that it would take in some of the farmers, and make town parks of their farms, so that they would lose the advantage, whatever it be, of the Land Act, I would not join it at all, and I find the feeling of the community against it.

82. The feeling of that meeting was grounded on the supposition that the land brought in would be affected under the Land Act?—Yes.

83. I don't think there is any use in asking you what would be the opinion of that meeting if the law was otherwise, but what would be your own opinion if the land would not be affected?—I would be of opinion we would then have them extended.

84. And on what grounds would you extend the boundaries?—To enlarge the area for taxation, or any sanitary purpose.

85. And increase your resources?—Yes, that was my idea at first.

86. Have you considered what would be the increase in the number of voters by that extension?—No, so have given it little thought at all. When first the report came down I spoke to some of the farmers, and one said it would be very little use to them to have the land taken in; and others said the same thing, and finding them all opposed to it I left it so.

87. I asked the Town Clerk if in his opinion there were more works than required and that would be done if you had increased resources, and he said, no?—I am not aware of anything; we have a great deal of drainage done.

88. Do you think the people within a mile derive great advantage from being near a market town?—They do, certainly. I dare say their land is somewhat higher, and I think the [illegible] takes a view of that in letting the land.

89. Independent of the lands, don't those people derive great advantage from having the town lighted, and kept clean?—Certainly.

90. Do you think that within a certain distance, say a mile, it would be fair to ask the people who, from that distance, use the town so much, to contribute something towards keeping it in order?—That was my idea in the beginning.

91. I ask you on the supposition that any land brought in will not be affected by the change?—Like those who are to be brought in, I think they will be.

92. But suppose it was settled there should be no alteration in regard to land, would it be fair they should contribute something to the town, suppose there was no Land Act at all?—In reference to land alone, which I would be very slow to give an opinion, but it would not be [illegible].

93. But suppose they are brought in so suddenly [illegible] a great many farms they will be sold, since they are [illegible]

MOUNTMELLICK.
Apr. 15, 1879.
Mr. John M'Mahon.

affected whatever under the Land Act by being so brought in, would it be fair they should pay some small thing to the town?—I was always of opinion they should.

94. On the supposition that the Land Act doesn't affect them at all?—Yes, on that supposition, and if the Land Act did affect them I should be sorry to bring them in.

95. It is the feeling of the Commissioners that it is better to leave the sanitary matters in the hands of the Guardians?—Decidedly.

96. That they do what you want in a satisfactory way and at a fair rate?—Yes; I think so, and it would not be better managed, I don't think it would. We get anything done pretty fairly, and with regard to taking charge of the roads and streets out of the hands of the Grand Jury, I would not like to do that because we should keep a staff, and we could scarcely expect to get such a staff as the Grand Jury have. These excellent County Surveyor and contractors give very good value for their pay.

97. You think the lighting and water supply satisfactory?—I do.

98. Is there anything you would like to put on record regarding the boundaries?—Nothing beyond what I have already stated.

Mr. James Millar.

Mr. James Millar examined.

99. You are one of the Town Commissioners here?—Yes.

100. How long have you been a Commissioner?—Since the establishment of the Town Commissioners here in 1855.

101. Perhaps you can tell us what guided them originally in the selection of the area now acted upon?—I am not prepared to say that. I think there was a recommendation came down from the Government.

102. Mr. *Goodbody* (Town Clerk).—They proposed to have a circular area of a mile, and they at first recommended that to the Lord Lieutenant, and he sent down to them to change it, and this is the area as fixed by the Lord Lieutenant. (*Produces document describing boundary of the town.*)

103. Are there any portions of the road running outside the present boundary continuously built upon?—I think very little. No, I think all the houses are taken in by the present boundaries. Here is the Roman Catholic Chapel (*indicating place on the map*), and the boundary is within 100 yards of the chapel, and all the houses leading down to it are included. All the continuously built upon portions are included.

104. Mr. *Millar*.—As regards the supply of water for the new fire engine, I would suggest that some steps should be taken to have a supply provided.

Mr. Anthony Pim.

Mr. Anthony Pim examined.

105. I also think there is not a sufficient supply of water in case of fire.

106. Is there any way you would suggest for improving the supply?—Yes, by metal pumps over the bridges.

107. Is that to be done by the Guardians or the Commissioners?—I think the Guardians.

108. Mr. *M'Mahon* (Chairman, Town Commissioners).—I think the Guardians ought to do that.

109. Mr. *Goodbody* (Clerk).—I don't think it could be done by the Commissioners, as they are not the Urban Sanitary Authority.

Mr. Millar.

Mr. Millar re-examined.

110. The Commissioners have provided a fire-engine?—Yes.

111. And they have not provided the means of procuring water for it?—Not sufficient means. We suggested about getting pumps put down at the different bridges, which was not fully considered.

112. Do you think that would be beyond the power of the Commissioners?—I don't know.

113. Mr. *Goodbody*.—It was suggested that these pumps could be used also for sanitary purposes, and that then the Guardians would put them up.

114. Mr. Cotton.—You are of opinion, Mr. Millar, that the boundaries should be left as they are?

Mr. *Millar*.—Yes.

115. Is that opinion based on the fact that the lands included might be affected by the Land Act?—No; I can't say it is.

Mr. Humphrey Smith.

Mr. Humphrey Smith examined.

116. You are one of the Town Commissioners of Mountmellick?—I am.

117. How long have you been a Commissioner?—A great many years—fully twelve or fourteen years.

118. Are you of the opinion, which seems to be the unanimous opinion of the Commissioners, that there should be no alteration in the boundary?—Yes; we were all quite unanimous about that.

119. It is based on the fact that the Land Act would apply to any extension brought in?—That was portion of our belief.

120. What was your individual opinion?—That was one partial reason, but we don't think the people outside get any benefit from our lighting, that they should pay taxes for.

121. Do people within a mile, who come in to market late and early in winter, derive no benefit from the town being lighted?—No, they are out of town before the lamps are lighted.

122. In winter days is that so?—Well, in a general way they are; the markets are very early.

123. Do they derive no interest from the streets being kept clean?—A little.

124. Do the people within a mile, or a mile and a half, derive no advantage from the schools in the town?—There are schools outside the town to which the children are sent.

125. Do the children from a mile and a half come into town, as a rule, for school?—Beyond a mile and a half, or at a mile and a half they go to other schools.

126. There are schools within a mile and a half to which they go?—There is a school on one side which is a mile off, and on the other there is a school [illegible] miles off.

127. I suppose I am right in saying that a great many children from a mile do come in to schools in the town?—Yes, and beyond that.

128. Still you think the advantages they derive within a mile would not entitle them to be asked to pay anything?—I don't think they should be asked to pay anything.

129. Wholly irrespective of the Land Act?—Yes, although I say that it is to my own disadvantage, they should not be rated in the town, for I am nearly the largest rate-payer in it.

130. As far as you know, that is the general feeling of the Commissioners and rate-payers?—Yes, decidedly.

131. Do you think there would be any advantage in the working of the town body, if the number of Commissioners was increased?—I don't think there would be. Everything goes on very quietly and peaceably here.

132. You get a good working quorum out of the nine Commissioners?—Yes.

Mr. [illegible]

Mr. Andrew Mahon examined.

Mr. Andrew Mahon.

133. Where do you live?—In Graigue.

134. How far is that from the town?—About a mile.

135. From where we are now?—About a mile and a half from where we are now.

136. What is your own opinion?—My own opinion is that we have taxes enough to pay without paying any more.

137. Do you and the ratepayers about you use the town as a market?—We do.

138. Do the children from about you come into school here?—They do.

139. Don't you frequent the town in winter during the dark of the morning and evening?—Yes, but generally, the people who live within a mile of the town are [illegible] a great deal nearer than the people who live seven miles away.

140. But do you not derive some advantage from the fact that the Commissioners have to light the town?—I think we have not derived any benefit at all by the light.

141. Would it suit your purpose quite as well to have it dark?—Better, for if we are in the light here, and get outside, the night appears darker.

The inquiry then terminated.

RATHKEALE.—MARCH 19TH, 1879.

Before C. P. Cotton, Esq., C.E.

Rathkeale. Mar. 19, 1879.

Mr. Stephen Casey examined.

Mr. Stephen Casey.

1. You are the Town Clerk of Rathkeale?—I have been Town Clerk for the past ten years. I succeeded my father.

2. Was this subject of the extension of the boundaries considered at a special meeting of the Commissioners?—Yes, at a special meeting of the Commissioners.

3. How many of the Commissioners attended at that meeting?—Five.

4. How many Commissioners are there in Rathkeale?—Fifteen.

5. And they desired you to fill up the replies that are given here?—Yes.

6. Were they unanimous on that?—Yes, unanimous.

7. Five were present, and, at all events, the other ten got notice of the meeting?—Yes, all got notice.

8. You put down the population at 3,000, how do you make that out?—2,721 in the town proper, and the remainder outside.

9. What do you mean by outside?—There are 2,721 in the town proper.

10. But isn't it all in the municipal district?—No, it is not.

11. What is the number in the census return?—2721.

12. The area you put down as 1,482 acres 3 roods 39 perches, what is your authority for that?—The valuation book.

13. In the return given by Mr. O'Brien, it is only 1,380 acres—there are no wards in the town?—No.

14. In what electoral division is it?—Rathkeale, and a small portion of Ballyallinan.

15. To the west of the town there are 35 acres 1 rood 1 perch in another electoral division?—Yes.

16. When was the town put under the Towns' Improvement Act?—In 1854.

17. Was there any municipal body before that?—No.

18. Have you got a description of the original boundary?—Nothing only this map (produced). This is a map showing the present boundary in red.

19. What is the yellow line?—That was the original boundary in 1854.

20. When was the alteration made?—About ten years later on.

21. How far does the town extend in the different directions from a central point?—About half a mile.

22. Half a mile to the north?—Yes.

23. And half a mile to the south?—Yes, taking an average.

24. And nearly a mile east and west?—I should say so; the town is one straggling street.

25. What were the rates that were struck during the last five years?—In 1874 the municipal rate was [illegible]; in 1875, [illegible]; in 1876, [illegible]; in 1877, [illegible]; and in 1878, [illegible].

26. And the poor rate for the same periods?—In 1874 the poor rate was [illegible]; in 1875, [illegible]; in 1876, [illegible]; in 1877, [illegible]; and in 1878, [illegible].

27. And the county cess in the same periods was how much?—In 1874 the county cess was [illegible]; in 1875, [illegible]; in 1876, [illegible]; in 1877, [illegible]; and in 1878, [illegible].

28. You say in reply to one question that the present municipal boundaries are regarded with dissatisfaction by the ratepayers of the township?—Yes.

29. Has any definite boundary been proposed by the Commissioners who approve of extension?—Yes, there is. At a meeting held on the 22nd November, it was resolved to get certain townlands included in, and on the 3rd March, 1879, the description of townlands, with the list attached, and their valuation was unanimously adopted.

30. What are the names of the townlands proposed to be added?—[illegible], and the portion of Rathkeale not at present within the boundary, containing 3,[illegible] acres [illegible] rood 32 perches, with a valuation of £[illegible].

31. To what extent would the proposed additions go from the centre of the town?—Something over two miles.

32. I see that the area the proposed extension would add would be [illegible] acres 1 rood 32 perches, and the valuation £[illegible]?—Yes.

33. Then altogether that would make about 5,000 acres in the township?—About 5,000 acres.

34. The valuation of the proposed additions would be £[illegible]?—Yes.

35. Would that extension go into any other electoral division but the one you have named?—It would, three others.

36. What are their names?—[illegible], Croagh, and

RATHKEALE. Nov. 12, 1878. — Mr. Stephen Casey.

Dromard, and the original one of Ballyallinan, and all of Rathkeale, only portion of which is in the township at present.

37. Were you clerk to the Commissioners when this extension, marked in red on the map, was made?—No, my father was.

38. Do you happen to know the grounds on which it was applied for?—No. It was applied for nothing more than on the formal belief that it was considered the area was too small and not sufficient for the working of the Commission, that there was not sufficient area for taxation.

39. What is the size of the Rathkeale Electoral Division?—3,863 acres 1 rood 23 perches.

40. Would it be entirely taken in by the proposed extension?—Yes.

41. The whole of it?—Yes, all.

42. And portion of three others?—Yes.

43. Of the poor rates you have mentioned as having been struck in the last five years, is 6d. in for the year 1878. Does that include any portion of the sanitary rate?—Yes, it includes all.

44. How much is sanitary rate?—I am not aware.

45. What are the receipts of the Town Commissioners of Rathkeale?—They have nothing more than the rates.

46. But besides the rates what have they?—Merely a moiety of the fines of the Town Court and dog licenses; but they only amount to a few pounds, £7 or £8 in the year.

47. And the fines from the Town Court would be only £5 or £6 more?—Yes.

48. And the expenditure in the town is about the same as the receipts?—Yes.

49. Was the Towns' Improvement Act adopted altogether, or only in part?—Only in part.

50. It was not adopted for water purposes?—It was not for water. It was adopted for sanitary purposes first, but in 1874 the sanitary powers were withdrawn.

51. And you can't rate beyond a shilling?—No.

52. And you have not rated up to that in 1878?—No, not in 1878, but in all the others we have.

53. How is the cleansing of the streets looked after?—The road contractor has to do it.

54. The road contractor under the Grand Jury?—Yes.

55. Are all the streets of the town under one contract?—Yes, but the branch streets are not. The Main-street is under one contract, but there are several other contracts for the streets that branch off the Main-street.

56. The Guardians are the Sanitary Authority of the town?—Yes, they are at present.

57. Have any works been executed by them of late years?—Yes; they have made a main sewer through the town, and other minor sewers through the streets.

58. Then portion of that is. 6d. for 1878 was a sanitary rate for works of that kind for the town?—Yes.

59. On what district was that sanitary rate struck?—On the entire division of Rathkeale.

60. Was any portion of it levied off the other electoral divisions?—No, sir; it was separate in this division.

61. How is the town lighted?—By gas. There is a Gas Company here, and the Commissioners contract with the company for the lighting of the town.

62. Is it well lighted?—It is pretty well lighted. It is very well lighted at present.

63. And the Commissioners desire to make a further extension of the town?—If they had the means at their disposal they would extend the lighting of the town further than at present.

64. But I see they have not exercised their full powers in that respect?—They were not able to light the town as they wished, and that being the case they only left the old lamps standing.

65. They did not consider it worth while to raise the other 6d. for lighting purposes?—No; as they had not a larger area.

66. Have the Commissioners ever considered whether it would not be better for them to become the sanitary authority instead of the Board of Guardians?—Yes, but in the way the law stands at present they would not wish it—until the landlord has to pay half.

67. They would not wish to become the sanitary authority now?—No; not until there is further legislation to make the landlord pay half the rate.

68. Then they have not made any application for any change?—No; by-and-by I think the feeling of the Commissioners is for a change if there is an extension of the boundary.

70. What is contemplated to be the effect of the proposed extension as regards the income and expenditure and working of the town?—The further extension of the lighting of the town, and other improvements that may arise by-and-by. They would also raise a sum of money for the improvement of the market if they had an extension.

71. It is not intended even with this proposed extension to take up the sanitary work?—No, not at present in consequence of the landlord now paying half the rates, whereas if the Commissioners were constituted the sanitary authority the occupier would have to pay the entire rate. Until there is some change in that I don't think the Commissioners would care to become the sanitary authority.

72. Of course, then, if they have not considered that they have not considered the question whether it would be better for them to take up the charge of the roads from the Grand Jury?—The funds at their disposal would not be adequate to the maintenance of the roads—the valuation of the place is too small to think of that.

73. Of that 1,444 acres how much is arable land that would be liable to only one-fourth rating?—The most of it is, unless what are houses.

74. What is the nature of the arable land included in the town—is it town parks?—No, it is ordinary arable land.

75. What is it proposed to do in the way of extending the lighting—if this proposed extension is taken in how far do they intend to extend the lighting of the town?—As far as the town is extended—as far as the buildings go and a little further on, the approaches to the town and all round, which are not lighted at present; up to the railway and beyond that.

76. Have you any means of knowing the feeling of the people outside who would be brought into the town by this proposed extension?—No.

77. We shall be glad to hear any opinion you like to give yourself, as to whether the one-fourth would be a fair charge upon the people who would be taken in for the advantages they get from the town?—I think it would, for they profit very much from the town, and they have a right to be taxed. These improvements are very heavy on the town, and these people outside share in them.

78. They have the advantage of this being a market town?—Yes, and it enhances the value of land around very much, and when coming in to make their purchases very late they have the advantage of the light. To such an extent is land round the town affected that it is valued at twice as much as land further away.

79. Does that apply to the whole of the extension?—Yes, no doubt of it.

80. Are there schools in the town to which children are sent in from that district?—There are very good schools in the town.

81. I suppose this extension is based on the supposition of the area brought in being liable to the one-fourth limited as such it will only mean £24 difference.

82. You think one-fourth is not too much for the benefits they get?—No.

83. Would there be any townlands cut in your proposed extension?—No; I took in all the townlands—there is no portion of townlands taken in. The Commissioners would go further on one side but the river forms the boundary there, but it would be a consideration by-and-by whether they should not take in more on that side.

84. In addition to the extension you have already

[illegible]—Yes, to take part off one side, and add it to the more on the opposite side.

[illegible]. How many people, if the present boundary are [illegible] to [illegible] the [illegible] of Commissioners?—About 100.

[illegible]. And how many are eligible to be Commissioners?—Thirty-three.

[illegible]. How many people would be brought in by the proposed extension who would be eligible to vote?—There would be a considerable number.

[illegible]. Could you give a rough idea of the number?—About as many more; about 100.

[illegible]. And how many would be brought in who would be eligible to be Commissioners?—Forty or fifty more.

[illegible]. Would it make in any [illegible] [illegible]—Yes.

[illegible]. [illegible]—[illegible]. [illegible] was obtained. If the Commissioners are [illegible] the military authority the [illegible] of the [illegible] would fall [illegible] the [illegible], and the Commissioners [illegible] that do not wish to [illegible] the military authority.

[illegible]

[illegible]

Mr. [illegible] examined.

Mr. [illegible]

[illegible]. You are Chairman of the Town Commissioners of [illegible]?—Yes, sir.

[illegible]. How long have you been Chairman of the Commissioners?—This is my third year.

[illegible]. How long have you been a Commissioner?—It is a long time; ever since the formation of the body.

[illegible]. There was a special meeting of the Commissioners held to consider the matter to [illegible]?—Yes, and it was only [illegible] by five out of [illegible]—[illegible].

[illegible]. The Commissioners who [illegible] that day were unanimous in recommending this extension then. [illegible] may be given [illegible]?—Yes.

[illegible]. How can you explain the apathy of the others not [illegible]?—I [illegible] for it; they got notice of the meeting.

[illegible]. Have you got any idea of the feeling of the others [illegible]?—In the [illegible] [illegible] they appeared to be in favour of extension.

[illegible]. Then you think the extension is in favour with the Commissioners as well as with those who were present?—Yes.

[illegible]. Were you a Commissioner at the time the former [illegible] was got?—I was.

[illegible]. Do you remember the grounds on which it was asked for?—They did not consider the [illegible] sufficient to meet the expenses of [illegible] on the Commission.

[illegible]. I don't know whether you are aware that [illegible] [illegible] of the largest [illegible] in the population of any town in Ireland; it has [illegible] [illegible] [illegible]?—But the value of the property in [illegible] may not be the same as in other places.

[illegible]. Have you any means of knowing, or have you heard the opinions of the inhabitants now outside, who would be taken in by this proposed extension?—I did not hear them saying anything about it.

[illegible]. Do you consider that those people who live within [illegible] of the town, [illegible] the present boundary, have such advantages from the town and the [illegible] and schools and everything, that they would [illegible] to contribute something to the keeping of the town in proper [illegible]?—I think it is a great advantage to those [illegible] to live so convenient to the [illegible] for markets and fairs, and to have their [illegible] properly attended to.

[illegible]. They have the advantage from the [illegible] [illegible] [illegible] they come into town [illegible] [illegible]?—No doubt, it is a great advantage.

[illegible]. Mr. [illegible] stated, I [illegible], in saying that the wish of the Commissioners is not to take up the [illegible] [illegible] of the [illegible], but [illegible] [illegible] [illegible]?—Yes; that question was considered, but they decided not to take it up.

[illegible]. On what grounds?—Well, it would be [illegible] [illegible] that the [illegible] would be too heavy, in fact [illegible] [illegible] would be [illegible] sufficient to pay the expenses of keeping the roads in repair. The same thing applies to [illegible] works.

[illegible]. But the Commissioners may [illegible] [illegible]?—They did not consider it that way, for we thought we were bound by the [illegible] rate, and then the [illegible] would not carry out what is required.

[illegible]. In [illegible] [illegible] work required?—There is a great deal done, but a good deal more to be required.

[illegible]. Under what heads?—Under the head of [illegible].

[illegible]. Is the flagging of the town well done?—There is [illegible] [illegible] to be flagged, and a great deal has been done.

[illegible]. But the sewerage is the principal thing that is wanted?—Yes; there is some portion of that not done yet.

[illegible]. Suppose there was an alteration in the law by which half the rate was to be paid by the landlord and half by the tenant, would that make any change in the views of the Commissioners?—Yes.

[illegible]. Would they then wish to take up the sanitary works?—Yes.

[illegible]. Would they then wish to have authority over the roads?—That is a matter I can't say.

[illegible]. Do you consider that [illegible] gets a full share from the county, considering what it contributes to the [illegible] of county cess?—Yes; the roads are pretty fairly kept [illegible] [illegible], they are kept the same as the roads in any other part of the county.

[illegible]. Would there be an improvement in the roads then, if the Commissioners took charge of them?—I don't know. I can't say that the county have not discharged their duty fairly. The [illegible] of the Commissioners would not be equal to the [illegible] [illegible].

[illegible]. Suppose you got charge of the roads, and you got the same money as the county now puts for the maintenance of them?—It would not be adequate [illegible] [illegible] for the [illegible], to keep the roads [illegible], for the [illegible] of the town is very [illegible]. There are the [illegible] [illegible] [illegible] other towns. The maintenance of a [illegible] [illegible] of the road [illegible] [illegible] [illegible] a year, and the [illegible] would take £[illegible] a year, and we never could grapple with that in [illegible] with the [illegible].

[illegible]. [illegible] at the time the former inquiry was held, evidence was given that the streets were in a very bad state for a long time, and the Commissioners had no [illegible] of cleaning them?—The [illegible] is [illegible] [illegible], and he is obliged to clean them. The [illegible] [illegible] all things has been remedied in a great [illegible].

[illegible]. Is there anything else that occurs to you that you would like to mention bearing on the subject of this inquiry?—I think the clerk has answered all the questions [illegible].

[illegible]. Is [illegible] increasing in business or population?—It is holding its place pretty well. The town has very much improved for some years past. Trade is, generally speaking, very bad now, in [illegible], we cannot [illegible], but, on the whole, the town has improved for some years past, and there have been considerably improved. There are the largest fairs in [illegible] [illegible], and very important, and a great number of persons attend them. We have a pig market, the day before the fair, and a large number come from all parts of Ireland, and from England to it. The largest buyers come to attend the fairs. We have [illegible] [illegible] [illegible], and sixteen pig markets, and [illegible] of them [illegible] [illegible] [illegible] and they are improving rapidly, and very probably they will be as large as the others in a very short time.

Mr. JOSEPH CAREY, examined.

122. You are a member of the Town Commissioners of Rathkeale?—I am.

123. How long have you been a Commissioner?—Since the adoption of the Act.

124. Do you remember the reasons for seeking this former extension in 1861?—It was just as our chairman has stated; by reason of our contracted area we were not able to discharge the duties expected from us, or give any benefit to the people in lighting the town.

125. It appears the area was not large enough?—No. I was going to observe that the vitality of this town depends on its fairs and markets. We have sixteen cattle fairs, and sixteen pig fairs the day previous to the cattle fairs. I am telling you this to show the desirability of having our neighbours brought in, and the justice of our neighbours taking their share in the expenditure for their own accommodation.

126. You mean by neighbours the people living immediately round the present town and outside it?—Yes. On the subject of the extension you asked what would be their feelings, and whether it would be fair and just to bring them in, and that is what I am endeavouring to answer.

127. Then what is their feeling on the subject?—I have good reason to know, because, in addition to being Town Commissioner, I have the honour to represent the electoral division of Rathkeale, which is far and away larger than the township. I am the Guardian for the last twenty years for the Rathkeale electoral division.

128. Then is Mr. Carey correct in saying, that in this proposed extension the entire electoral division of Rathkeale would be taken in?—Yes, entirely correct.

129. What is the feeling of your constituents outside regarding this extension?—They feel fairly and justly towards the extension.

130. That it would not be too much to ask them to pay one-fourth rates for the advantages they get from the town?—No, I think, taking them as a whole, for, as representative of the electoral division, I never met anyone opposed to the doing of it. As I remarked, we have, on the day before the cattle fair, a pig fair, and we have crowds of people from the country, for buyers come at a distance from Waterford, and they come up here early for the fairs, and they make the day previous to the pig fair another fair. Country people come in here, and come up at night and in the early morning, and in the winter time, if the streets were not well lighted and cleaned carefully, they would subject themselves to great abuse, both themselves and their cattle. These people come the night before for both fairs, and they spend the greater part of the night in the town. Our fair is opened at daybreak, and business people come in from great distances; trains are arranged to suit the carriage of stock. Where the fairs are very early it is the greatest possible convenience to the people to have the town well lighted, and there is nothing dark or gloomy about this town.

131. How is the lighting done?—It is by contract with the Gas Company.

132. It is a separate company?—Entirely separate.

133. They have a contract per lamp?—Yes.

134. How much is it?—£3 10s. for each lamp for six months.

135. And there are certain hours stated?—Yes; these lamps are the public light.

136. And the lighting of the town could be further extended with advantage?—It would be further extended, and the lights would be put closer together.

137. Does the lighting go as far as the buildings go at present?—In a fair way it does. Not in the by-streets; in the extremes of the town they are not so well lighted as we ought to have them, if we could afford it.

138. Mr. Carey (Town Clerk).—The lamps have to be extinguished early in the night in consequence of not having sufficient revenue.

139. Witness.—I have nothing additional to add to what has been stated. Under our sanitary circumstances the sanitary duty would be better done by the Guardians, if the half of the rate was paid by the landlord.

140. Suppose you got this extension and that the landlord was to pay half the rates, then you would be inclined to take up the work?—Our body would do it far better then.

141. Your opinion is they would do it a great deal better then?—Yes, and feel a greater interest in it. I know the feelings of the two bodies, and I can speak confidently.

Mr. JAMES BLACKWELL, examined.

142. You are one of the Town Commissioners of Rathkeale?—I am.

143. What is the feeling of the outsiders who would be affected by this proposed extension?—They are in favour of it. The town is old and is not rated as high as other towns with a smaller area. Of course, if it was a modern town it would be rated higher.

144. I don't think you can say Rathkeale has a low valuation for its size?—We have a good many landlords and the places are not improved. They are like the day in the summer.

145. I understood you to say that Rathkeale had a low valuation considering the inhabitants?—I think it has.

146. Have you any other town you would compare it with?—Newcastle West, for instance; the houses that rate for £15 in Rathkeale would bring £16 in Newcastle West.

147. Rathkeale has 3,000 inhabitants and it is valued at £4,000, have you any reason to believe that a low valuation, for it doesn't appear from other towns to be low?—I think if it was a modern town it would be higher. We would have better houses built, and the rate would be higher. On the whole, I think it is valued high enough at present.

148. You have heard the evidence given by the Chairman and Mr. Carey, have you anything to add about this extension or any alteration?—No. I think there is nothing to add except that it is very fair, and that the people living round seem all very favourably disposed to the town. They are all nearly aware of this meeting to-day, and none of them have attended to give any opposition to it.

149. Is there anyone present who is not a Commissioner?—No.

150. Are the ratepayers aware of this meeting?—Yes, several of the people outside are aware of the meeting, and they have not come in.

151. You have all the Commissioners here to-day except one.

152. You say that this extension would take in the entire of Rathkeale division and portions of three others?—Yes.

153. How much of the other three would be taken in?—Rathkeale is 3,090 odd acres, and there is a difference outside the town of about 2,374 acres, but these others are only skirts or small little portions of the divisions.

154. Is it four or five electoral divisions that would be concerned in the extension?—Four and Rathkeale.

155. That is five altogether?—Yes.

The inquiry then terminated.

BANBRIDGE—SEPTEMBER 10, 1879.

(Before the CHAIRMAN.)

MR. WILLIAM M'CORMACK examined.

1. CHAIRMAN.—You are the Town Clerk of Banbridge?—I am.

2. Banbridge is under the Towns Improvement Act of 1854?—Yes.

3. When was that Act adopted?—In 1866; for all the purposes of the Act.

4. Was the boundary fixed then?—Yes.

5. Was the usual Gazette notice given?—Yes.

6. Have the boundaries remained the same ever since?—Yes.

7. I see by your return that the area is 763a. 0r. 33p.?—Yes.

8. What is the valuation?—£12,517 15s. at the last revision.

9. How much of that is land and how much buildings?—Buildings are £11,091; land, £1,071 10s.; and half the annual rents, £353 5s.

10. Has it been a gradually increasing valuation here?—Yes.

11. What was the population at the last census?—5,600. With reference to that, I should say that I do not believe the returns sent forward were correct, and I will state my reasons. I have heard from competent authority that in the taking of the census of the town some streets were omitted from the return sent forward, viz., half of Bridge-street, Law's row, Doctor's-lane, and Friars' lane. These four streets were not included in the returns. I should say the population is now upwards of 6,500.

12. Is the town divided into wards for municipal purposes?—Yes; into two—the eastern and western wards. They return five Commissioners for the eastern ward and ten for the western ward.

13. What is the valuation of the two wards?—I cannot tell you that.

14. Are they fairly represented—that is, do they get representation according to the valuation, as five is to ten?—I think they are fairly represented.

15. Is there any feeling, on the part of the Town Commissioners or the ratepayers, that the wards should be altered?—I have not heard of any.

16. Is the town in one electoral division?—Yes, in the Banbridge electoral division.

17. Does that extend much beyond the present boundaries of the town?—Yes, I should say so.

18. How far would you say?—I cannot say.

19. Have you any map showing your own boundary at present?—We have.

20. Are the municipal and the Poor Law boundaries conterminous?—They are not. There are three townlands that are severed by the boundaries.

21. Would the outside boundary, marked on this map with a blue line, be conterminous with townlands (referring to map produced)?—It would not cut through several townlands, and I think only one or two fields would be cut through by that boundary.

22. I want the rates from 1874 up to 1878, inclusive—the municipal, Poor Law, and county rates?—

	Municipal.		Poor Law.		County		
	s.	d.	s.	d.	s.	d.	
1874, .	0	8	0	8	1	6	
1875, .	0	10	1	3	1	10	
1876, .	0	10	—		1	11	
1877, .	1	0	0	8	1	10	
1878, .	0	8	1	5	0	7	for the one half-year.

We have not yet struck a rate for this year.

24. How much was the county cess for the second half of last year?—10d. was the amount.

25. Did you find 8d. a sufficient municipal rate for 1878 for all your wants?—Yes, because we lost the sanitary powers; they are now vested in the guardians.

26. But, if you were over 6,000 in population, you should be the Urban Sanitary Authority?—We were not over 6,000 in population according to the census of 1871, although we would have been if the census had been properly taken.

27. However, you have ample power, if you petitioned the Local Government Board?—We did petition and they would not grant it.

28. When was that?—About five months ago.

29. Was it represented to them that you were over 6,000 in population?—I should say it was. I believe the difficulty was that the population was returned as under 6,000 at the time the census was taken, and we could not go beyond that, according to the Public Health Act. On the faith of the real census, we imagined we would be able to take the sanitary powers into our own hands, but there was an objection raised by a certain number of ratepayers to the transfer.

30. On what grounds did they do that? Would the work be as well done by the Town Commissioners as by the guardians?—I think the principal reason of the opposition was that several Town Commissioners were in favour of having a public cemetery for the town, and the people did not want to be taxed for that purpose. I believe that was the reason.

31. Do the guardians, according to the opinion of the townspeople, look after the sanitary works properly?—Well, some people are satisfied and some are not.

32. Is there any water supply here?—No; there is a dreadfully bad water supply, and several pumps have been condemned on analysis.

33. Is the supply entirely by pumps?—Yes.

34. Have the guardians ever started any plan for supplying a high pressure supply of water?—No.

35. Are the present boundaries regarded with dissatisfaction generally by the ratepayers or by any section of them?—Some of the Town Commissioners consider that an extension of the boundary would be desirable, while some do not; and then there was a meeting called, and there was a resolution passed that they would not go in for an extension.

36. Was that resolution unanimous or carried by a majority?—By a majority, because there was a portion of the body opposed to it.

37. As far as you know the feeling of the Commissioners, are they evenly divided, or is there a large majority against extension?—I really think they did not go in for an expression of opinion on the subject, as they, perhaps, might have done.

38. Have the ratepayers generally expressed an opinion that the boundary should be extended?—I believe there are many who think so.

39. Has there been any public meeting called on the subject?—None.

40. To what extent do those in favour of extension wish to have the town extended—is it to the blue line marked by the Town Surveyor on this map?—Yes. The Town Surveyor was instructed by a committee appointed by the Town Commissioners to take this matter into consideration; and he was appointed to draw out the proposed extension, and this is what he has drawn out.

41. When the report came from the Town Surveyor what was done?—As I tell you, a committee was appointed, and they were to report, and the matter dropped. They did not report.

42. You say there has been a good deal of building going on in Banbridge. At present is there much building in progress?—Not very much at present; but I can tell you that since 1831 the number has increased largely. In 1831 there were 446 houses

2 F

[illegible]
Sept. [illegible], 1879.
Mr. William [illegible].

then built, in 1841 there were 578, in 1851 there were 618, in 1861 there were 777, and in 1871 there were 1,100.

43. So that in nearly forty years the number has nearly doubled?—Yes.

44. Is there much more good building ground within the present area, or are there better sites within the boundary as marked out by the Town Surveyor?—There are some good building sites within the present township boundary; but I should say there would be many better within the proposed extended boundary.

45. Are there many gentlemen's seats outside the present boundary, and within the line suggested by the Town Surveyor?—There are.

46. How many would you say—about how many?—There are certainly twelve; and besides there is a very large factory at [illegible], the village of [illegible], and a large [illegible] at [illegible]. The proposed township boundary also takes [illegible] in, a place that had [illegible] inhabitants at the last census.

47. Is the town very largely used by the gentlemen living in that extended district, and other people living within the proposed extension?—Yes.

48. Are you able to say, of your own knowledge, that the property within the area marked out by the Town Surveyor derives great benefit from its proximity to the town?—I should certainly say so.

49. Is it more valuable on that account?—Yes, certainly. I believe that with an extended boundary we would have an equalization of the rates; and if we had an extended boundary, we would eventually have an increased population, and a commercial more influence. We would be taking due credit for the amount of business done, as exhibited by our traffic. We would place ourselves in a better position to command the attention of Parliament for measures which may be introduced. We would be in a better position to take charge of the sanitary affairs of the town.

50. Would [illegible], where there are 400 inhabitants, require extensive looking after in sanitary matters?—Certainly; and if they came into the township we would be obliged to, and would look after them.

51. Would it be an advantage to them, in your opinion, to be joined to the town, and if the town were made the urban sanitary authority?—Certainly. It would increase the value of their property very much.

52. Would it facilitate you in getting a water supply, having the boundary extended?—It would.

53. How long have you been Town Clerk?—Twelve years.

54. You know the district well, I suppose?—Yes. If the extension were granted, we would have a larger area for town and court [illegible], and dog-tax; and if we could get a separation from the county, one board could manage the affairs better than several boards and several sets of officers.

55. With reference to taking charge of the roads, do you think it would be fair, if the town got the management of the roads, to get from those people the same county cess as they pay at present to the Grand Jury?—Yes; and if it has been successful in other towns, I do not see why it should not be successful here.

56. From your knowledge of the town, do you think you could manage those roads as cheaply and as well as they are at present managed under the Grand Jury?—I believe we could.

57. Is it your opinion you could manage the roads of your own town better than the Grand Jury?—I do not say better, but quite as well.

58. And as cheaply too?—Yes; I believe so. As parties living within the proposed extension enjoy nearly all the advantages and privileges that are afforded to those living within the present circumscribed boundary, I think it would be fair that they should contribute for that which they enjoy, in so far as they reap the advantages of the markets, shopping, attending public worship, and lighting of the town. They largely use and wear our streets and sidewalks, being passengers by our railways, and having in our town the heavy traffic peculiar to manufacturing centres, and they consequently have everything enjoyed by those already taxed.

59. Do you light the township?—Yes, the whole of it.

60. What would be your proposal with regard to these matters—would you extend the benefit of lighting to the entire district you suggest to be brought in, and then make it pay the same rate; or would you leave the lighting as it is at present, and bring them in at a differential rate?—If the lighting remains as at present, it would be better to have a differential rate.

61. If you gave them exactly the same advantages as you have in the town, why should they not pay the same rates; I suppose you are aware that land—arable land—pays only one-fourth; and under these circumstances do you think it would pay you to light them, or that it would be better to let them stay as they are as regards lighting, and bring them in at a differential rate?—That is a question I could hardly answer. If the Town Commissioners succeeded in buying the gas-works, at a reasonable rate, from the Gas Company, perhaps they might be able to light the entire township properly.

62. Can you say that the opinions you have expressed are shared by some of the Town Commissioners?—Yes.

63. Can you say that they are shared in by any considerable portion of the ratepayers within the present boundary?—I have not spoken to them very much. Some are in favour of the proposed extension, but I question very much whether, if the matter was put before them at a public meeting, they would be likely to go in for it.

64. On what grounds, have you heard, are others of the Town Commissioners averse to the extension—what grounds have they put forward against it?—They never stated their reasons particularly.

65. With reference to the persons outside the present boundary, what is their feeling on the subject?—Well, I think, after all, no matter how circumscribed the boundary might be, people do not like to be put into an extended boundary, because of being taxed.

66. Is it a question of taxation with them?—I think that would be the great question.

67. Has there been notice given of this inquiry?—I gave notice myself, and I saw another notice in to-day's paper.

68. We published it in the local paper?—I also published it.

69. Was it published last week?—Yes, in Saturday's paper, and in this morning's paper.

70. What is the area of the extended district?—The difference between the present, and what is proposed is 1477A. 0R. 38P., making the total 2240A. 1R. 19P., and the difference would be 1477A. 0R. 38P.

71. What is the valuation of that?—I cannot tell you that.

72. Would there be a very considerable increase in the valuation?—Yes, I should say there would be an increase of £16,000 or £20,000.

73. How would you propose that the extended district should be added to the wards. Would you make the outside district a separate ward from that comprised in the present boundary?—I would have an addition made to the two existing wards, both eastern and western.

74. Having regard to the increased valuation would it not be better to have one ward more, and to allow the town wards to stand as they are, and to lessen the number of representatives in those two wards—that is, if you took off two representatives from the smaller ward and three from the other ward, that would be five, which could be given to the new ward, and then the total number of representatives would remain as at present?—I think that would be very fair.

75. And then you would have as large a ratepaying

only be one as in the other?—But you would have a larger valuation.

77. But you would have fewer electors?—Yes, that is true.

78. Have you any idea how many ratepayers would be brought in by this proposed extension, occupiers of £5 and upwards?—I cannot answer that question. There is another matter I would like to mention with regard to transferring the sanitary powers. We have been placed in an awkward position with regard to the markets. The Town Commissioners have for the last ten years been anxious to get the control of the markets of the town.

79. Who do they belong to at present?—To the trustees of Lord Downshire. The Commissioners have spent a considerable sum of money in trying to get by-laws passed, and to get the control of the markets; but not being the Urban Sanitary Authority they consider the Public Health Act interferes with them in that respect, and that they cannot take advantage of the markets, as it prevents them doing so. I am sure the trustees of Lord Downshire are willing to treat the Commissioners liberally with reference to the markets, and will hand them over their patent rights to a certain extent, and give them the tolls for a certain rental, and the Town Commissioners would be very glad to accept the offer if they were in a position to take the markets over, and I think that militates very much against the progress of the town.

[illegible]. Sept. [illegible]. Mr. William M'Cammon.

Mr. Hugh Glass examined.

Mr. Hugh Glass.

80. You are a Town Commissioner?—I am.

81. You have heard the evidence of the Town Clerk?—I have.

82. Do you agree generally with the views he has expressed?—I do indeed.

83. And that it would be desirable to extend the boundary to the line pointed out by the surveyor on this map?—I think that is a very fair line.

84. Of your own knowledge, does all the ground within that area derive exceptional benefit and advantage from its proximity to the town?—I think there is no doubt of that.

85. Do the owners and occupiers of houses within that area derive the same advantage, and make the same use of the town as the ratepayers?—Certainly.

86. Is it on that ground you think it would be fair to have them brought in?—Yes.

87. Do you think it would be desirable to bring them in, giving them the benefit of the lighting, on equal taxation to that which the townspeople are at present paying or not to light the district, and bring them in on a differential rating?—I would say the latter would be better, because otherwise we would have a great many miles of road to light, and I don't think we could do it in any other way.

88. In every way you then agree with the evidence the Town Clerk has given?—I do. I think he has given his evidence most fairly.

89. As far as you know do the people living within this proposed boundary object to the extension, or is their objection confined solely to the matter of taxation?—I believe solely to the matter of taxation. I am outside the boundary myself, and I would be a severe sufferer in that respect, if the extension were carried out.

90. You will have to pay more taxation?—Considerably more.

91. And, notwithstanding that, you are in favour of the extension?—I will tell you how it is. My valuation in the town is £83 10s., and if the boundary be extended my valuation would be £315 10s.

92. And yet you are in favour of the extension?—Certainly.

93. Of course, then, you think it desirable you should become the Urban Sanitary Authority?—Yes, certainly.

94. And also get the control of the roads?—Yes. I am not so certain about the roads. I do not know that we could manage the roads much cheaper than the county at present.

95. But are not divided Boards very much more expensive?—Yes, that is true.

96. If you were the Urban Sanitary Authority, then scavenging the roads would come cheaper, and keeping them up cheaper, because you would have a certain amount over that you could use for other purposes?—Certainly.

97. You said you were in favour of a differential rate. In your opinion should it be thrown on the occupier and the landlord. At present, under the Public Health Act of last year, the sanitary and poor-rate is divided, in the rural sanitary district, between the landlord and the tenant?—An opinion has been expressed in other places, that the same thing should be done with the rates in the extended district?—I think that would be an equitable way of doing it.

98. Is that your opinion? You are aware that under the Towns Improvement Act, arable land pays only one-fourth of the valuation. Is it your opinion that that is too low? In several places what has been stated is this—that in the case of all land within a township, the really fair thing would be to make it pay half of all rates, and divide them between the landlord and tenant, but that this should not apply to the county cess or land rates. It is said so far as the land is concerned at all events, the landlord gets an increased rent for his land in and near a town, and the tenant is able to pay a higher rent from the advantages he gets from that land, and that therefore it is not fair that it should pay only one-fourth, and that by the tenant?—Indeed I think one-half would not be too much, and payable as you suggested.

99. Would you think that would be a fair way of dealing with land in the borough, and also land outside the borough, that would be brought in?—I think there is no doubt that it would, and that the enhanced value of all that land would be equal to the additional taxation.

100. Do you think that the value of the land would be increased in that area if brought in?—Certainly.

101. Are you able to say that the land in that area brings a higher rent than land of a similar quality further off?—I have no doubt about it.

102. Are you able to say to what extent?—I know that land immediately adjoining the town, lets for £5 or £6 an acre for grazing purposes.

103. What would the same land if two miles further off let for?—£2 or £3 an acre. I think it would be unfair if the landlord did not pay his portion of the tax on the land, whether inside or outside the present borough.

104. Is there any other Town Commissioner in favour of the extension?—I believe we are unanimous that the extension would be desirable for the town.

105. Do you feel yourself authorized to say under the conditions I have stated, that the Town Commissioners would be in favour of it?—I believe if we had a meeting to-morrow, there would be a unanimous opinion in favour of the proposed extension on the terms you have suggested.

109. With reference to the question of voting, supposing this extension was granted, would you make the extended district into one ward?—I think I would.

110. Taking two representatives from one ward and three from the other, that would make five, to be given to the rural district altogether?—Inasmuch as my own opinion is that there should be a differential rating, then I think that would be quite right.

111. You are aware that they would only pay at present one-fourth valuation in the case of land?—Yes.

112. Would your suggestion be to make them pay one-half?—I would be in favor of charging land in the extended boundary the same rate as land is now charged in the immediate township. But I would make all land pay one-half rate, divided between landlord and tenant.

113. What would you think of the alteration of the wards as follows—to give four to the smaller ward, seven to the large ward, and then four to the new district to be brought in?—I think that would be an equitable distribution of the representation.

Dr. Dowden.

Dr. Dowden, re-examined.

114. What would you think of that?—I do not think that would be an unfair representation. There is one thing due to my constituents that I should state. I do not think I fully represent their views in saying the extension boundary is universally viewed by them as being necessary. Still I think it is by most of them.

115. One would think the ratepayers inside the present boundary would not object to the extension if they thought they would get some little increase to the funds to be paid by people who use largely and avail themselves of the advantages of the town. It would not increase, but would be likely to lessen the taxation?—There is something about putting in the thin edge of the wedge, which crops up in this matter. That is about getting up a new cemetery. I know that, speaking on behalf of the Catholics, they are very much opposed to that, because they have provided one for themselves, and they do not wish to be taxed for another. I think it is only fair that I should tell you that.

116. Does not that question crop up whether the boundary is extended or not?—I cannot understand what the extension of the boundary has to do with it. If the rural sanitary authority think that the town requires a cemetery, they have power to promote it, being the burial board, just as much as any other?—It is supposed by the majority of the Catholics here that, if the Town Commissioners get the powers vested in them, as the urban sanitary authority, they would then construct a cemetery at the public expense.

117. The *Town Clerk*.—I may say for the Town Commissioners that they, as a body, never went in for providing a public cemetery.

118. Chairman.—To promote it or to prevent it?

The *Town Clerk*.—Yes.

Mr. Samuel Hill.

Mr. Samuel Hill examined.

119. What are your views on the subject of the proposed extension?—I am opposed to the extension. I think you should be prepared, if you tax the people, to give them something commensurate with their taxation. I believe that if the extension was granted we would not be in a position to supply these people—who would require gas, for instance—or anything else commensurate with the taxation.

120. Would not the occupiers have something commensurate for their taxation by the advantages they derive from the town; and has not the landlord great advantages who gets a much higher rent for his ground on account of its being so close to the town? If so, why should they not both be made pay something towards keeping up the town which gives them these advantages? If you give them these benefits, why should you give them to them at the expense of the townspeople?—I cannot say that I am opposed to the measure being carried into effect, but that was one of my principal reasons. I may say I forego my opposition to the measure, if it is the wish of the majority of the Town Council.

Mr. Robert M'Clelland.

Mr. Robert M'Clelland, Chairman of the Town Commissioners, examined.

121. Will you state your views with regard to the question of the proposed extension?—I hold the same opinion that Mr. Hill has expressed, that we could not give them sufficient compensation for the extra taxation we would impose.

122. Do you think that the occupiers of the ground outside the present boundary, and the houses outside it, derive advantages from their proximity to the town?—I think they do.

123. Do they use the town largely?—Yes. They benefit the town as well. I am not speaking in a selfish manner, because all my places are in the township at present, so that I am not likely to be further taxed by the extension of the boundary.

124. Mr. *Glenn*.—Do you think it is an honourable feeling that the Commissioners have on the subject in proposing the extension?—I think it is an equitable feeling in their minds.

125. Chairman.—Suppose a recommendation was made by us to extend the boundary as proposed by the Town Surveyor, on this principle, that whatever the town rates were the outside persons should only pay one-half until they got the same benefits as the townspeople, what would be your opinion?—I think that would be very fair.

Mr. *Hill*.—I think, also, that would be very fair; and it would lessen the rate on the people in the town.

[The inquiry then closed.]

BALLYMENA.—SEPTEMBER 23RD, 1879.

[Before Mr. Exham, Q.C., and Mr. H. A. Robinson.]

Mr. Frederick Mathews examined.

1. Chairman.—What is the present area of Ballymena?—Four hundred and sixty six acres.

2. Is it under the Towns Improvement Act?—Yes.

3. When was that Act adopted?—Immediately after the passing of the Act. It was the first town that came under that Act.

4. That was in 1854?—Yes.

5. Were the boundaries fixed then?—Yes, but they were enlarged about ten years ago, long before my time as town clerk.

6. Have they remained the same ever since?—Yes.

7. Was the Act adopted for all the purposes?—No, only for lighting and cleansing. The water clauses were never adopted.

8. Was the town previously under the 9th of George IV.?—I could not answer that question.

9. What is the valuation?—£20,331 10s., made up of £825 15s. for land, and £18,848 for buildings, and £575 15s. for half annual rents.

10. What was the population at the last census?—7,856.

11. Is it an increasing population?—I should say so, considerably.

12. How many new houses have been built within the last six years?—Two hundred and ninety-four houses have been built and rebuilt within the last six years, and 180 of them have been rebuilt since 1876, the time of the appointment of our present surveyor.

13. In what electoral division is the town?—Ballymena.

14. I am aware that the Commissioners propose an extension of the boundary—would the extension proposed by the Commissioners still be in the electoral division of Ballymena?—Yes.

15. What is the area and valuation of the electoral division?—The area is 2,535 acres and 3 roods, and the valuation is £24,581.

16. How far to the north does the electoral division extend from the centre of the town?—About three miles. Certainly over two.

17. What have your rates been for the last five years?—The improvement has been, at all events, 1s. in the pound, and a burial rate varying from 2d. to 3d. The poor rate in 1874 was 1s. 3d.; 1875, 1s. 4d.; 1876, 1s. 1d.; 1877, 1s. 1½d.; 1878, 1s. 6½d.; this year it will be 1s. 2d., that will be struck next month.

18. What has been the county rate for that time?—For 1874, 2s. 1d.; 1875, 1s. 11d.; 1876, 1s. 7d.; 1877, 1s. 8d.; 1878, 1s. 10d.; 1879, 1s. 6d.

19. Do the Grand Jury manage the roads?—Yes, and the Town Commissioners cleanse the streets.

20. Have you got a town surveyor here?—Yes, since February, 1876.

21. Are you able to do your work properly with a rate of 1s. in the pound?—Not quite; no.

22. Have you any water supply here?—No high pressure water supply. There are a few public pumps.

23. You have been making some sewers through the town. Have you struck a special sewer rate for making them?—No, they were paid for out of the improvement rate.

24. Is the town at present properly sewered?—Not at all; very far from it.

25. Is the sanitary condition as good as it should be?—Not at all.

26. You said that the Town Commissioners have not struck a sanitary rate or a sewer rate which they might have done beyond the improvement rate—do you know why they have not done so?—I cannot answer that question; it is only two years since I was appointed, and there has not been any money spent, nothing worthy of notice, since my time.

27. The streets appear to be remarkably well kerbed, and the footways are in fair order?—Yes.

28. Have the Grand Jury done that, or have you done the kerbing out of the improvement rate?—The Grand Jury, within the last few years, has given a moiety towards the expense of flagging, but not of kerbing. In reference to the flagging, the county gave half, or gave what was supposed to be half, at the time the contract was taken.

29. Have the Town Commissioners ever tried to get the management of the roads, as do they think it desirable?—There is a movement going on at present to obtain a separation from the county.

30. Do the Town Commissioners consider there would be a saving?—They conceive that they would save 6d. in the pound per year out of the county cess.

31. Is that taking the county cess as low as it is this year?—It was taken on the average of the past six years.

32. Have the Town Commissioners, as a body, ever considered this question of the extension of the boundary?—Yes.

33. Are there any wards here?—No.

34. What is their opinion as to the boundary—are they unanimous on the point?—They were unanimous in sending the boundary as marked on that map. There was some difference of opinion at first.

35. We may take it that the boundary of the town, as it is at present, is the red line, and that the proposed boundary is the black line?—Yes.

36. Does the existing boundary include the whole of townlands, or divide them?—Well, in the existing boundary there is part of the townland of Ballymena, and the rest is all the townland of Townparks, and part of Ballykeeghan and Brocklamont.

37. Only portions of them?—Yes; portions of them.

38. Will the proposed new boundary include the whole of those townlands?—No; it is drawn without reference to townlands.

39. How have you determined about the proposed boundary?—The Commissioners, as a body, went round the town and inspected it, and on that map they marked those parts they thought it desirable to have brought in.

40. Have they adopted a well defined boundary?—I think they have.

41. How many acres would there be in the proposed extension?—344; and the approximate valuation would be about £781 on the land, and £1,010 on the houses; making about £22,008 in all.

42. What would you say to taking in the whole of the electoral division and making it coterminous with the town itself?—I think that would not do at all.

43. You see that there is only £2,000 of the valuation left out—you gave us the valuation of the electoral division as £24,581?—If that was done it would extend the supervision of the Town Commissioners over a very large area.

44. It would; but you say the Town Commissioners would be able to save 6d. in the pound on the roads in the present boundary, and if so, they ought to be able to save more than 6d. on the entire electoral division, because the roads in the area outside would be less costly to keep up than those in the town; while our warrant directs us, as far as possible, to make towns coterminous with electoral divisions. This is a town in which you say the electoral division goes a very little further outside the proposed area, so

[illegible]

outside. Some are now building residences outside the town.

78. Are they villa residences?—Some being built now too.

79. Is there any special reason for building outside the town, or is it for the purpose of avoiding the town taxes?—I think not. I think no such idea entered into their minds at all.

80. Are there any improvements required for the roads, which you would carry out if you had an increased income?—Nothing that any increase like that suggested would give the Town Commissioners the means of carrying out.

81. If you carried out any improvements would they be a benefit to the people you propose to bring in?—Certainly, they would.

82. Do you think they would be an advantage to persons residing within the electoral division?—I would not go so far as to say that.

83. Do your markets take place late in the day?—The Saturday market does.

84. So that the people who come into the markets have the advantage of the lights in your town?—Yes, at the season besides particularly, for it is long after the lamps are lit when they leave the town.

85. What is the nearest market town to Ballymena?—Antrim.

86. How many miles away is that?—Eight Irish miles.

Cross-examined by Mr. M'Mullen, solicitor, on behalf of the owners of the Leckanmore Bleach Works.

87. You say that the reason that the Town Commissioners give for taking in the Leckanmore Bleach Works into the proposed extension is for the purpose of getting control of the [illegible]?—No; it was the Chairman of the Town Commissioners said that; I did not say it.

88. What benefit do the Town Commissioners propose to confer upon the Leckanmore people?—The usual benefit that is conferred upon all people coming within the area of a township.

89. Do you mean to say that you would give them the benefit of the lighting?—I think so, along the Galgorm-road.

90. Would you go as quick as them with your lighting than the Galgorm-road?—I would not tell you. I don't think they would go nearer than the Galgorm-road. I am only speaking from my recollection of the place.

91. Would you only give them lighting—you would not give them sewerage?—That would come into the sewerage scheme.

92. Has the sewerage scheme not been approved of?—I know that.

93. You say that the intended increase, or at least the proposed increase in the valuation of the land would be £101?—Yes.

94. And of houses £1,[illegible]?—Yes.

95. How much of that increase would the Leckanmore people contribute if they were brought in?—The present valuation of the Leckanmore Works is £150, and £[illegible] on forty-five acres of land.

96. And in return for what they would pay on that you would only give them lighting upon the Galgorm road?—And any other advantages they would derive from their junction with the town.

97. What other advantages?—I could not say.

98. Mr. Robinson.—Would you ask them for the advantages they now enjoy?—That would be a very material item. They enjoy all the advantages of the town from being close to the town.

99. Mr. M'Mullen.—How do they enjoy any advantages? Don't you think the proximity of the [illegible] to the town confers greater advantages upon the town than the town confers upon it?—I cannot see how that would be.

100. Do you think that the same land, if occupied for building purposes, would be as valuable, or if occupied for bleach green purposes it would be as valuable?—[illegible]

101. To anyone?—The owner would get more money for it for building purposes, I should say.

102. Would you be surprised to find the land three times more valuable for bleach green purposes?—If you say so, I would not be surprised; I know nothing about it.

103. Is the land let for building on the Galgorm-road at £8 an acre?—Yes, I know one case, at six guineas, that was £8.

104. Has not some land been let in close proximity to the bleach works on the Galgorm-road?—Yes.

105. Did you ever hear how much it was let for?—No.

106. Is it above £10?—I have not the least idea.

107. If you had the control over the lower portion of the ground, shall it drain towards the site of the proposed sewerage works, would that be your general purpose in annexing it?—How do you mean "for any general purposes"?

108. Do you want the control over the sewage works?—I don't know what you mean about wanting any "control." The Town Commissioners want to extend the boundaries in order to make the area of taxation larger.

109. If you take in the Leckanmore Works, for what reason, do you take them in, and exclude the buildings and houses on the south side of the road?—I cannot answer that question.

Mr. Robert Simpson examined.

110. Chairman.—Are you the Chairman of the Town Commissioners?—Yes, for about three years.

111. Have you considered the question of the extension of the boundary?—We have.

112. Do you and the Town Commissioners consider it desirable that the boundary should be extended?—Yes.

113. Can you say whether or not it is the feeling of the ratepayers of the town, as well as the Town Commissioners, that some extension is desirable?—Any of those that I met with agree with us.

114. Do you approve of the boundaries, as marked on this map with the black line?—Yes.

115. Have you considered, supposing the boundary was extended so as to take in the whole of the electoral division, whether it would be fair and right to bring in the persons outside the present boundary on a differential rate, and not to give them the benefit of the lighting for the present—I mean until you would be able to light them?—I am in favour of that supposing we got separated from the county; so that we would be able to give the people in the electoral division, outside the present boundary, equal terms to what they are at present getting from the county.

116. Are you in favour of having the present boundary and the proposed boundary put under the management of the Town Commissioners, and taken away from the county?—Yes.

117. Would a saving be effected by that?—Yes, we think so.

118. Are you of opinion that a saving would be effected even supposing there would be no alteration of the boundary?—Yes.

119. Is it then your opinion that if you were taken away from the county the boundary should be increased to the whole of the electoral division, and that you should not, for the present, be required to light the roads outside the present boundary, and that the people in the outside district should not be required to pay the same improvement rate as the town people?—I would be in favour of the scheme that they should pay half the improvement rate, and the whole county

Ballymena, Sept. [illegible]

Mr. Robert Simpson.

this, supposing that half the present improvement rate would not increase their present taxation. My reason for answering in that way is, that I don't know that the outside portion of the electoral division would be much benefited—they might be slightly—by their connexion with the town.

120. Can you say if the land in the furthest corner of the electoral division is more valuable than land of similar quality three miles away from the town?—I believe that farms close to the town bring more money than farms further off.

121. Is that from their proximity to the town?—Yes.

122. Then that is an advantage both to the landlord and the tenant?—Yes, to both.

123. Do you consider it fair then that both the landlord and the tenant should contribute something towards keeping up the town which makes their land more valuable?—I think they should, where the land is in close proximity to the town.

124. Is the land within the whole of the electoral division more exceptionally valuable in your opinion from its proximity to the town?—Yes.

125. Suppose you brought that land in at half the improvement rate, which would be putting at the minimum the expense upon the valuation, and that the expense was divided between the landlord and tenant, do you think it would be fair to make them pay the expense between them, when their land derives exceptional value from their proximity to the town?—I don't know that I can answer that question. I think they should be brought in, but only on the terms that we get a separation from the county.

126. Suppose you do not get that separation, would you think it fair to make a landlord, who derives such exceptional benefit for his land from its proximity to the town, pay something in the pound in the rates of that town, and also to make the tenant pay the same?—I don't know that the land on the outside of the electoral division, except where it is in close proximity to a town, such as Ballymena, is of such value, as that the landlord and tenant should come in and pay expenses.

127. Within the electoral division does the land derive exceptional benefit, and does it bring an increased market value?—I think it is of more value.

128. Is it to the extent of sixpence in the pound on the valuation?—I think, if I had a farm within two miles from Ballymena, and a farm five or six miles out, or some five or five miles away, I would rather pay sixpence in the pound on the farm near, than have a farm of equal value that distance away.

129. Can you say from your knowledge of Ballymena, what is the value of the land in the electoral division, as compared with the same quality of land further away?—I could not answer that question.

130. Mr. ROBINSON.—Do you consider that the fact of land being more valuable owing to its proximity to the town, is of advantage to the tenant or whom the municipal rates are assessed, as the law at present stands?—Yes, I do.

131. What advantage does the tenant derive from the land being more valuable?—He gets a better price for his crops when he is near the market, and has the market at his door.

132. But he has to pay a higher rent?—Yes, he pays a higher rent for town parks.

133. CHAIRMAN.—As the law stands at present he would pay a fourth of it in the township, and that is considered too little by many people. If half of that was thrown on the landlord, and half on the tenant, they would each only pay three halfpence in the pound?—I think they would each pay very much value for that taxation, added to which we would be able to earn for them sixpence in the pound on the roads, if we got the management of them.

134. The sixpence they would thus save would more than pay for their rates, even if they had to pay the halfpenny, so that they would not be a loser, but, in fact, better off?—That would be so if our calculations

were correct; but those calculations cannot be regarded as perfectly correct without knowing what the actual expenditure for keeping up the roads would be.

135. From your knowledge of this district, and taking the case of gentlemen residing in that district, do they derive benefit to the extent of sixpence in the pound from their proximity to the town?—I think they do, by getting the town properly cleaned and lighted, and coming in to make their purchases.

136. Do they derive, in your opinion, the same benefit as the people of the town themselves?—They do.

137. Do you see any objection to taking in the whole of the electoral division?—In drawing this line for the present boundary, we kept in view probable building ground.

138. I understand that was taken in view of keeping building-ground the full rate; but we put the question as to a differential rate. Suppose that there was a differential rate, and you were not obliged to light the districts, because as first you might not be able, on account of the expenditure you would put upon them, to carry the cost of the mains, would there be any objection to the Town Commissioners including the entire district, and would you think it right that they should pay half the rate?—I don't think they would be, and I don't think that would be fair.

139. If you get the roads over all the electoral division would you not be able, with the half rate, to manage them, always, and save the ratepayers in the outside districts at least sixpence in the pound?—Yes, but I think that the ratepayers residing in the outside portions of the electoral division would object to be brought in except we can show them that they would lose nothing by being brought in.

140. There has been a strong feeling that the people close to the town have no right to put on the ratepayers of the town altogether the cost of keeping up that town which they so largely use, and derive so much benefit from, from day to day; and it is said, why should they not pay something towards keeping the town up? Do you agree in that opinion?—I do.

141. Mr. ROBINSON.—Are you in favour of including accessible land within the town?—Yes.

142. Would you give the owners of that land any extra benefit beyond what they now enjoy?—I would bring them in for the general improvement of the town.

143. Does the town need improvement to which you would apply this increased income?—The present rate is scarcely sufficient to keep up the town.

144. Do not those people, coming into the town, confer advantages on the town?—They do.

145. Do not the proceeds of the sale of their agricultural produce find their way into the pockets of the ratepayers, and help to support the town to a certain extent?—We are an agricultural community here to a great extent, so that the merchants are more or less supported by the people outside.

146. Is the town properly assessed according to your view?—Yes.

147. CHAIRMAN.—Would it be an advantage, at all events, for the country immediately outside the town, that the town should be properly sewered?—Yes.

148. And that all the sanitary arrangements should be made better?—Yes, it would.

149. Then would it be right, in your opinion, that they should contribute something towards the sewerage and sanitary arrangements of the town?—I consider that they should.

150. Mr. ROBINSON.—Do you consider that the improvement of the town would be an advantage to the people outside?—I do.

151. Does your proposed boundary, as represented on the map, include any property of the farming class who have not got property in the town?—It does not.

152. CHAIRMAN.—Do you mean that there are no farmers in the district besides those who have residences or property in the town?—No.

153. Mr. ROBINSON.—Within the proposed boundary

[illegible] the proposed boundary [illegible] the town, as [illegible].

[illegible]

155. Then you consider it of importance that this place should be included?—Yes, I do; that is, if they carry out the sewerage scheme.

156. Where will the sewerage go to?—It is to be drawn away after being purified.

157. Could you not carry out the scheme without that?—It could not be done so cheaply. I believe it would be a great saving of money to put it there and carry it away. It would save making a new road.

158. I see you have taken in one portion of the boundary on the west where there is a railway; what railway is that?—The Cookstown Railway.

Mr. W. A. [illegible] examined.

159. [illegible]

160. Do you think that if the town was extended [illegible]

161. What would you say to [illegible]

162. Suppose the rate was one-half, and then was divided between the landlord and tenant, [illegible]

163. [illegible] Town Commissioners [illegible]

164. [illegible]

165. Where are the nearest [illegible] of Ballymena.

Mr. [illegible] examined.

166. Mr. M'[illegible].—[illegible] proposed boundary [illegible] with the view of [illegible] building ground [illegible]

167. I suppose that [illegible]

168. Is the north side of the Galgorm road more occupied with buildings, and more likely to be [illegible]

169. In your present extension you have left [illegible] the Galgorm road, and the buildings on it [illegible]

170. Do you think the Leighinmohr property on the southern side of the Galgorm road, [illegible] building ground as the land on the northern side?—I do, up to that point.

171. And you think that [illegible] of the Leighinmohr Bleach Works will be building ground [illegible]

172. I presume you would say that the land occupied at present by the Leighinmohr Bleach Works [illegible] than the lands further away?—I think so.

173. So then, that primary ground would not apply to the lower portion of the grounds of the Leighinmohr Bleach Works?—It would not at present.

174. Have you any other object in bringing in the lower portion of the Leighinmohr Works, than the one you have already mentioned?—They want them taking in the Leighinmohr property within the boundary, because they should, in my opinion, pay their fair share of the rates, where they receive such benefits from the town.

175. And because they have a high valuation they would contribute a large amount?—In point of fact, in drawing out the boundary we were influenced [illegible] was inside or what outside of it. We were anxious to get a defined boundary.

176. Don't you know that the land used for bleaching purposes is more valuable than land used for building purposes?—If you asked my judgment as representing the Commissioners, I could not answer the question; but if I was asked my own opinion, I would say that building ground would be more valuable. That is my opinion.

177. Would you be surprised to learn that the lands on [illegible] Leighinmohr are bringing in [illegible] building ground in the [illegible]?—I don't know indeed. Will that land be bringing a rent as much as the building ground?

178. [illegible] With regard to the lighting, would you propose to light the Leighinmohr property any further than the Galgorm road?—I think not.

179. By an extension of the lighting along the Galgorm road, would you confer a benefit upon the Leighinmohr Works greater than what they now receive?—Yes. People going to the works would have the benefit of the lighting.

180. Don't you know that the lighting goes as far as the railway station, at present, which is quite close to the entrance to the Leighinmohr Works?—I don't know how near it is.

181. Probably the Commissioners think they have extended that length quite long enough?—Yes, that is what one would think.

182. Would you make them pay for the lighting of part of the Galgorm road, although it is a considerable distance from their works?—I would not make them pay for it.

183. But if you brought them in you would?—I think if they are brought in they should have to pay their fair portion of the rates the same as the others.

184. The full amount?—Yes; the same as the others, from their situation.

185. You think that if they were brought in they should be rated the same as business houses in the middle of the town?—Yes, such a valuable property as you say it is.

Ballymena, Sept. [illegible]

Mr. Simpson.

185. Do you think it confers a greater benefit upon the town than the town upon the bleach-works?—I think the benefit is mutual. I think it is. There is benefit derived from the bleach-works by the town, and benefit by the bleach-works from the town.

186. Could they not exist if there was no town there at all?—They would require some place for their people to live in.

187. Could not they live without the town at all?—I don't know how I could answer that question. They are the better of getting their supplies from Ballymena.

Mr. Young.—I wish to say that Lachenmore [illegible] within the line of boundary that we marked out, but there are other places nearly as valuable as Lachenmore that come in within that boundary. There is my own house that comes in.

188. Mr. Robinson.—Then you propose to tax yourself?—Yes; because it comes fairly within the boundary. I would be very glad to do so.

189. Do you own it in fee or are you subject to rent?—I am the owner in fee. At present I enjoy the benefit of the town and pay very little taxes.

Mr. Alexander Caruth.

Mr. Alexander Caruth examined.

190. Chairman.—How long have you been a Town Commissioner?—For nearly twenty years.

191. Was there much addition made at the time of the extension of the original bounds?—Not very much.

192. From your knowledge of the town for the last twenty years, do you think it would be desirable that there should be now an increase of the boundary?—Yes, but to what extent is a question.

193. Are you aware of the value of land in the vicinity of the town?—I should say so, for I am a solicitor practising here for the last twenty-five years.

194. What is the value of land at the northern portion of the electoral division as compared with land of a similar quality three or four miles off?—Do you mean as rent or as purchase.

195. As rent?—Where people living in the town send their cattle to townparks within a radius of a mile of Ballymena, they would let at one-third more rent than land which is three or four miles away.

196. Have you seen the boundary that is proposed by the Town Commissioners, that black line on the map?—I have not examined it, but I know pretty accurately what it is intended to be.

197. Would you say that that would be a fair extension?—I think that in one direction they scarcely go far enough. I would be rather disposed to go a little farther.

198. In which direction?—I think upon the Galgorm-road; in that direction the line that they have taken may be an accurate one, but I would have gone farther.

199. The difficulty we are under is, that except there is some overwhelming reason we ought not to propose an extension in that direction beyond the present electoral division. What is your opinion of the proposal to make land pay half the town rates, and to divide that half between the landlord and tenant, that is on the principle that they both derive exceptional benefit from having the land used as a market garden, and townparks, so near the town, and that the landlord who gets a high rent should contribute something towards the keeping up of the town which enables the tenant to pay that rent, and that the tenant should pay half also, because he has the market at his door, and has a greater profit than he would have elsewhere? —There is not much of that sort of thing here, market gardens, and so on. The outside land is principally townparks. In the direction of the electoral division the land does become valuable as building-ground, undoubtedly.

200. If the landlord gets a third more rent on account of the land being townparks, it would appear not unreasonable to say that he should pay one-third of the town rate for keeping up the town. Besides that, would you think it desirable to have the place under one undivided management?—I don't like the boundary of the electoral division exactly.

201. If possible we would like to follow the boundary of the electoral division?—If it is to be that way I don't see any great objection to including this portion of the electoral division, because, undoubtedly, the land is valuable for building purposes. At Brookmount, I built my own house there, and there is some building-ground outside there.

202. Supposing the electoral division boundary is followed up there, would you see any objection to take the electoral division boundary in the other place?—No, in the view you have put I would see no objection, particularly by carrying out the scheme that the management of the roads should be in the hands of the Town Commissioners, if we could get a separation.

203. Do you think that desirable?—Yes. If the Town Commissioners do not have to light the whole of those roads.

204. No one would dream of saying that they should light the whole of the roads out to the end of the electoral division, because it would not pay them?—Yes.

205. They are lit up to a certain distance, and when they get out into the country roads they would not require lights?—Yes.

206. Would you consider it desirable to have the electoral division included in order to have one scheme for the sewerage of the town and district?—If that boundary is found most suitable of course it would be most desirable to have it, and in the carrying out of any sewerage scheme wherever the works connected with the sewerage are they should be within the municipal boundary, because it would afford facilities for taking the land which they cannot take outside the boundary without going to extra expense, and, therefore, to have all the land they would require for such a purpose inside the boundary would be a saving of expense.

207. If the electoral division boundary was adopted there would be no practical difficulty in the way, the only question might be the making a road which would cost a little more if it was made within the electoral division instead of outside it?

Mr. Young.—That would be a considerable cost. There is a difference of opinion as to where the outfall should be. We want it here (pointing to map), the Local Government Board want it here at Tyescullo-town.

Mr. Mathews.

Mr. Mathews re-examined.

208. Chairman.—What is the quantity of land in the portion of Ballyaing that you propose to take in—what townland is it in?—Ballee, and the extent is 750 acres.

Mr. Samuel M'Kay.

Mr. Samuel M'Kay examined.

209. Are you in favour of the proposed extension?—I am. There are a great many houses just adjoining the present boundary which they are leaving out. They are only a few perches from the present boundary, and they derive all the benefit of the town, of the lighting, and cleansing of it, and they have the post office, and transact their business in the town the same as we do who live in it.

Ballymena. 4 Jan. 1878. Mr. Samuel M'Kay.

210. In the proposed extension by the Town Commissioners would these houses be included?—They would not, but by taking in the electoral division they would.

211. Are you in favour of taking in the electoral division?—I am; for instance, on the Ballymoney line seven years ago there was ground let at the rate of 2½d., and at present that ground is letting at 2s. a foot as building ground.

212. Would that ground be taken in?—Yes, and the houses built upon it, and a small portion of the railway would be, but not far enough.

213. Do you think it would be fair to bring in the whole of the electoral division?—I do.

214. Would the town lands and arable land which are benefited by the town be taken in?—Yes; I have one myself of 11 or 12 acres.

215. Would you object to be taken in, and pay your portion?—I would not.

216. Is the land more valuable on account of its proximity to the town?—Yes; it realizes £3 an acre at townparks.

217. At all events it is more valuable than if it were two or three miles off?—Lord Waveney is letting such land at the present moment at £7 10s. an acre, so far as I can learn, and he would not get that if the land was farther off. I think he is only getting about 10s. an acre about three miles off. There is another point—though, perhaps, it is not within the scope of your inquiry to consider—and that is with regard to the county cess here. If a house is vacant we are bound to pay county cess for it. I think while it is non-productive we have a right to get it off.

218. Would you be in favour of taking over from the county the management of the roads?—I certainly would. As we are now situated the Commissioners expend portion of the rate in cleansing the streets, whereas the Act of 1854 states that nothing shall be taken off the county in that way unless by agreement. Therefore we pay a local rate for cleansing the streets, and we pay county cess also. I think the roads adjoining the town are kept in better order and cleaner than some of our streets are. I do not think we should pay for the one work twice.

Mr. Joseph Gilmore examined.

Mr. Joseph Gilmore.

219. You are one of the partners in this company of the [illegible] Works?—Yes.

220. How many hands have you at work there?—About seventy.

221. Do they live in the town, or elsewhere?—They live in various places—some in the town, some in Harryville, some at [illegible]; and some at other places.

222. Is not Harryville in the boundary?—Yes, it is part of Ballymena.

223. Do you object to being brought within the town boundary?—I object, if it is going to be made so small as to [illegible].

224. Would you object if the whole electoral division is taken in?—I would not.

225. Do you think an extension of the town is desirable?—I cannot say. It is not at all desirable to us. We are [illegible] very well without it. We derive no benefit whatever.

226. Chairman.—From being close to the town?—Not the slightest. We have our railway to bring in the stuff to us, and to take it away again.

227. Don't your work-people use the town largely?—Yes, but I think our wages are spent in the town.

228. To get to the railway station must you not use a portion of the town?—No, sir.

229. You must, because the railway station is some little distance from the town?—We go by the [illegible] road to go to the station—up the [illegible].

230. If you had not the town of Ballymena you would not probably have a railway there at all, or the railway there, if you push the matter a little further?—I think there is something in that.

231. Would you be satisfied if the whole of the electoral division is brought in?—Yes. There are a few who should be brought in. I have not a list of them. Mr. Montgomery should be brought in.

232. Mr. Montgomery is in another electoral division which we cannot touch?—I hear that Mr. [illegible] and Messrs. [illegible] are also in the other electoral divisions.

233. Would you think it fair to the people of Ballymena that the town should be extended so as to comprise the whole of the electoral division?—I don't know about the fairness of it; they might [illegible] it will make their rates cheaper.

234. Suppose there is this difference that the rate on arable land, that is one-half, and that that half is divided between the landlord and tenant?—I think that would be fair.

235. Would you consider it of advantage to your place if the sanitary condition of Ballymena was improved, and proper sewerage made?—It would.

236. Would it, in your opinion, be much better to have it all under one management—that of the Urban Sanitary Authority, and that they should have the management of the roads of the entire district, and the management of the town?—I think so.

237. Mr. M'Fadden.—To the present proposed extension would you offer any objection?—Yes, we do not like it.

238. On what grounds? Do you consider that it would confer any benefit upon you for the money they would receive annually out of you in rates?—I do not know of any.

239. I believe the lighting would not be brought nearer than at present?—No, it would not be of any use to us.

240. What benefit will it confer on the [illegible] Works unless they take away the sewage which at present flows into the water?—That would be a very great deal of loss. They [illegible] our water [illegible], and it is [illegible] in a filthy state, and we have to re-wash the cloth again.

241. I understand it is the intention of the Commissioners to [illegible] your [illegible]?—I think that is only theory.

242. I understand that the plans are actually before the Local Government Board, and all they want is that they shall carry away the outfall further?—And that is all we want them [illegible].

243. Would not that confer great benefit?—Yes, taking the sewage out of our river.

244. In conjunction with the proposed scheme suppose they [illegible] as where they did, [illegible] the sewage from your [illegible] if they create a nuisance [illegible], what will be done then.

245. They cannot do that, because if they attempt to create a nuisance you know the means of preventing them.

Mr. Young.—If we throw the sewage into the mill-race it will do no harm.

246. Chairman.—In reference to the present sewerage scheme, Mr. Gilmore, the one object merely is the outfall of it?—Yes.

247. That would it would be a benefit if it did not pollute your water?—Yes.

248. If a proper sewerage scheme were carried out would it be a great benefit to you?—We would want drains through the town.

249. If any extension is desirable, is it your opinion so a [illegible]—that any scheme should be brought in as well—that there should be an extension to bring in the whole of the electoral division?—Certainly; and we will come in and be satisfied.

The inquiry then closed.

BALLINA.—SEPTEMBER 4TH, 1879.

[Before Mr. COTTON and Mr. ROBINSON.]

Mr. JOHN CARDLAY examined.

1. Mr. COTTON.—You are Town Clerk of Ballina?—Yes.

2. How long have you held that post?—For over twenty years.

3. Under what Act is the town governed?—The Towns Improvement Act was adopted 10th December, 1855.

4. Was it previously under any Act?—No.

5. What is the population of the town?—5,881 in 1871.

6. Do you know whether it is increasing since that?—I believe it is.

7. That includes both sides of the river?—Yes. I took the number from some document the constabulary had at the time.

8. Mr. ROBINSON.—Was the Act adopted for all purposes?—Yes.

9. Mr. COTTON.—Has the population increased since 1871?—I think it has considerably.

10. You don't know as a matter of fact, whether it is over 6,000?—Except to offer an opinion, I believe it is.

11. Do you think the census of 1881 will show a population of 6,000?—I think it will.

12. Is building going on to any extent in the town?—To some extent, not very much.

13. What is the area of the town at present?—1,056 acres 16 perches.

14. And the valuation?—£8,298 7s. in 1874.

15. Has the valuation been increasing of late years?—Yes.

16. On how much is the full rate struck, and how much one-fourth?—Full rate is struck on £7,005, and one-fourth on the lands.

17. There are two wards in the town?—Yes.

18. That is the two sides of the river?—Yes.

19. Do you know the separate area of each?—I do. The Ballina ward has an area of 654 acres 1 rood, and Ardnaree ward 401 acres 3 roods 16 perches. The valuation of Ballina ward is £6,845, and of Ardnaree, £1,358. The fishery is valued at £980. There are two electoral divisions in the town.

20. They are also separated by the river?—Yes.

21. Can you give me the rates struck since 1874?—Yes. In 1874 municipal rate was 1s. 6d. and 6d.

22. What was the 6d. for?—For water; that was before the transfer of sanitary jurisdiction to the Guardians.

23. In 1875 what was the rate?—1s.

24. In 1876?—1s.

25. In 1877?—1s.

26. In 1878?—1s.

27. Have you struck a rate for 1879?—Yes, 1s. also.

28. What was the poor-rate in the Ballina ward in 1874 and succeeding years?—In 1874 it was 1s. 10d.

29. In 1875?—1s. 11d.

30. In 1876?—1s. 6d.

31. In 1877?—1s. 6d.

32. In 1878?—1s. 6d.

33. What is it this year?—I do not know, the rate has not been struck yet.

34. Give me the poor-rate in Ardnaree ward for the same years?—In 1874 it was 1s. 10d.; in 1875, 1s. 10d.; in 1876, 2s.; in 1877, 1s. 6d.; and in 1878, 1s. 6d.

35. Does that 1s. 6d. include any sanitary rate?—The Clerk of the Union can tell.

36. What was the county cess in Mayo for 1874 and following years?—In 1874 it was 2s. 1½d.; in 1875 it was 2s. 0½d.; in 1876, 2s. 2½d.; in 1877, 1s. 11½d.; and in 1878, 1s. 10½d.

37. What was the county cess in Sligo for the same years?—In 1874 it was 2s. 1½d.; in 1875 it was 2s. 1½d.; in 1876, 1s. 11d.; in 1877, 1s. 10½d.; in 1878, 1s. 10d.

38. How many Commissioners are there?—Fourteen.

39. How many municipal voters are there in Ballina ward?—196.

40. And in Ardnaree ward?—Forty-one.

41. Do you know of that number how many are qualified to be Commissioners, if elected?—Seventy in Ballina, and eight in Ardnaree.

42. How is the town lighted?—With gas.

43. Under contract with the gas company?—Yes.

44. For how many lamps?—Fifty-six.

45. At what rate?—Last year's contract was £10 [illegible] the lamp for lighting and extinguishing. This year it is £80. The contractor also undertook to leave six of the lamps lighted during the entire night, from the railway down to the bridge.

46. And the other lamps are lighted until when?—They are put out at twelve. They are lit from an hour after sunset until twelve, from September until April.

47. No exception for moonlight?—Yes, three days before and three after full moon. We had a new project for lighting the town by rock oil, but it was considered too late in the season.

48. You have no project before the Commissioners to acquire the gas works?—Yes, we were the promoters of a Bill in 1874 for that purpose. The boundary proposed would increase the valuation by £4,818 and the area by 7,000 acres.

49. At present you have no project in hands as to the gas works?—No.

50. How is the town supplied with water?—Very badly from wells.

51. Is there any project on foot for a water scheme?—The guardians tried something in that way in 1875; I think it was a pumping scheme.

52. However, it is not under the control of the Commissioners at present?—No.

53. How is the town drained?—Pretty well, indeed. The guardians expended some money on it lately; something like £1,000.

54. Mr. M'ANDREW.—How many years had the Town Commissioners charge of the town before the sanitary authority?—From 1855 to 1874.

55. Did the Commissioners during that time divide the town into sewage districts?—No.

56. Did they ever lay out a farthing on the sewage of the town?—No, but I will give you a reason. The reason is, that in consequence of the town having to pay county cess the Commissioners thought it would be a hardship to divide the town into districts, and impose additional taxation, but we made application to the government engineer for plans.

57. Mr. COTTON.—Have the Commissioners had before them any queries?—Yes.

58. Did they come to any resolution whether extension or alteration of any kind was desirable?—They did not come to any formal resolution, but the majority of the Commissioners decided not to extend the boundary.

59. Is that resolution on the books?—Yes.

60. What is the date of it?—10th February, 1879.

61. How many Commissioners attended on that occasion?—Six.

62. What is the quorum?—Five. It was before them at two meetings before that.

63. But that was the one at which the Commissioners adopted the resolution?—The Commissioners decided not to suggest any changes in the town boundaries at present.

64. Was that carried to a division?—It was.

65. How many voted for it, and how many against it?—Four for and two against it.

66. Do you know whether that resolution represented the views of more than four of the Commissioners?—I don't know.

67. Was the question whether any rearrangement of wards was necessary before the Commissioners?—No.

68. Have the Commissioners ever applied to become the urban authority?—Yes.

69. When?—Last November.

70. What was the result of the application?—The result was, it was opposed at the time, and the Local Government Board said they would not proceed with the provisional order.

71. They refused to issue the provisional order?—Yes; on account of the opposition of course.

72. Why did they wish to be the urban authority—was it because they were dissatisfied with the way the sanitary work was carried out?—No.

73. Are they satisfied with the way the guardians carry out the work?—I would rather leave that to the guardians themselves.

74. I take it, you sought to be the urban authority for the purpose of acquiring control of the roads?—Quite so.

75. And the provisional order was not granted?—No.

76. There has been no alteration as to the boundaries since 1853?—No.

BALLINA. Sept. 6, 1879.

Mr. John Carolan.

Mr. Bernard Ryan examined.

Mr. Bernard Ryan.

77. You are a Town Commissioner?—Yes.

78. How long have you been a Town Commissioner?—About six or seven years.

79. Were you one of the Commissioners attending this meeting?—Yes.

80. At which it was decided not to extend the boundaries?—Yes.

81. Do you know the feeling of the Commissioners who were not present?—Well, I do not.

82. Were you for or against extension?—I was against it.

83. On what ground?—On financial grounds. I don't remember the grounds on which I opposed extension.

84. What extension was proposed?—A two-mile radius.

85. You were against that extension on what ground?—On the ground first that that would create opposition.

86. Do you think the two-mile extension would be desirable, putting opposition out of the question altogether?—I do not think it would.

87. Why?—From a financial point of view, in my opinion, it would not be a benefit to the town.

88. How so?—The expenditure would not be in proportion to the rates.

89. What would be the expenditure?—I forget the figures, but I went into it at the time.

90. Did you consider it simply a question of bringing a two-mile radius under the control of the Commissioners, as they are, or with the future possibility of their being the road authority?—With the possibility of their being the road authority. We thought that by-and-by the county cess would be transferred to the Commissioners, and the control of a great many of the roads converging on the town, and we thought the income accruing from extension would be not equal to the expenditure, if we had got these roads. We believe we would be in a better position by leaving the boundary as it is.

91. Did you consider the question of contracting the present boundary?—Certainly not; we were rather in favour of some slight modification in the present boundary—there might be some little extension.

92. Does any extension occur to you as being desirable?—I would be in favour of the mile and a half radius.

93. On what ground?—I cannot very well define it, but if I had the figures before me on which I founded my opinion before, I could define it. It struck me that mile and a half would be more beneficial to the Commissioners than the two mile extension—that two miles would be rather too far.

94. Did you consider it at all from the point of view that the people to be brought in should be contributory to the town?—We thought that to have a two-mile extension would be too great, but that those living within a mile and a half do benefit very much from any improvement we have in Ballina, from lights, markets, and schools; but we thought it would not be fair to extend the boundary to two miles.

95. You think that two miles away the people don't derive sufficient benefit?—No.

96. But you do consider that the people within a mile and a half are so interested?—Yes, an English statute mile and a half.

97. That is your private opinion?—Yes.

98. But the only question before the Commissioners that day was the hard and fast line of two miles extension?—Yes.

99. You did not consider the question of an intermediate extension between two miles and the present boundary?—No; it was the hard and fast line between two miles and the present boundary.

100. I am taking it as your own opinion?—Yes; that a mile and a half would be very fair.

101. That you think those living within that mile and a half have considerable benefit from their proximity to the town?—They frequent the town more than those living at a greater distance.

102. Have you considered how many people would be taken in by that boundary of a mile and a half?—No.

103. Nor the valuation of it?—No.

Mr. Carolan recalled.

Mr. Carolan.

104. What is the present radius—from the centre to the north?—Three-quarters of an English mile.

105. And to the west?—An English mile exactly at one point.

106. And to the south?—About seven-eighths of a mile.

107. And to the east?—The same.

108. Then in fact it is roughly a circle of seven-eighths of a mile?—Yes.

109. What do you consider the central point of the town?—I took the cross.

110. That is the cross at Knox-street, and Bridge-street?—Yes.

111. How many electoral divisions would the two miles radius go into?—Into two and the angle of a third.

112. How many beyond Ballina and Ardnaree?—Into two; Ardnaree north and Ardnaree south.

113. What others?—None others.

114. I thought it went into four?—Yes, it goes into Carrowmore.

115. Then it would go into Ballina, Ardnaree north, Ardnaree south and Carrowmore?—Yes.

116. What is the valuation of the part beyond the present boundary within that radius?—£4,316 15s. That was obtained in 1870 when extension was first spoken of.

BALLINA. Sept. 4, 1879. Mr. Gordon.

117. The line between the two boundaries has that valuation ?—Yes.

118. Mr. Exham.—I suppose if you were to adopt that two miles radius it would bring the population over 6,000 ?—Oh yes, considerably, and the number of rates brought in would be about the same as that in the town.

119. Mr. Cotton.—Do the guardians perform their sanitary duties to the satisfaction of the townspeople ?—I believe they do. They are doing nothing at present, but they have done a great deal for the town and have done it satisfactorily.

120. And as far as the sanitary matters are concerned you would not care to become the sanitary authority yourselves ?—Not particularly; the Commissioners could do the duty no better so far as they have gone. I happened to be a Poor Law Guardian myself at the time the arrangement was come to as to sanitary matters; the Chairman and Vice-Chairman of that Board are members of the Poor Law Board. Those people expressed themselves in favour of having the sanitary authority vested in the Commissioners.

121. I want to get your own opinion ?—Well as far as the sanitary laws are concerned they could not be better executed by the Commissioners than they have been, and are being executed by the Poor Law Board so far as they have gone.

122. Do you know what sanitary rates have been struck of late years ?—I do not. Of course there is this in it; the townspeople complain of having so many rates to pay, and the Poor Law Board have their sanitary officers, and the Town Commissioners have their sanitary officers, and they are all paid out of the rates, and the people have to pay for them all. Sometimes they clash rather than otherwise and they don't pull well together.

123. What sanitary officers ?—The town inspector to look after scavenging, and the Poor Law Board have a similar officer.

124. They don't look after the scavenging ?—No, we have the supervision of the work.

125. Are the streets cleaned by the Commissioners or the road contractors ?—By the Commissioners.

126. Mr. Robinson.—Are there any improvements required in the town which the Commissioners would carry out if they had an increased income ?—Yes.

127. What is the nature of them ?—Water supply. They had a Bill before Parliament for it, and for [illegible] The question is this—the Poor Law Board have quite the ability, and the capacity to do all these things for the town if they only applied themselves, but a great many of the traders complain that the guardians have no personal interest in the town; the Commissioners would have a greater personal interest in the matter.

128. Sir Charles Knox Gore.—As chairman of the board of guardians I may say the board have always got their financial arrangements in the best order; we have spent about £8,000 since the Act passed which is not long ago, and we propose according as our finances permit to carry out any project necessary for the benefit of the district, but until we see our way to do so, and the finances for the purpose we don't intend to proceed.

129. The guardians have no scheme before them for water for the town ?—The subject has been brought forward, but we consider we have no funds to do it; it would raise the rates to such a pitch that there was a strong feeling against it. There was a strong feeling against going to the expense in the town.

130. They have not considered the question of raising a loan for the purpose ?—They don't consider it desirable to do so. The matter was discussed before the board as well as the question of sewerage, but we can see no scheme for doing it at anything like a moderate cost.

131. Mr. Egan.—The feeling as to the water supply is this; we have to pay cess to the county Sligo and to Mayo; with the town rate and the poor rate, and all the rates if amalgamated we believe would enable us to have a fair amount of water for the same rate as the people are paying at present.

132. Mr. Cotton.—That amounts to this, that if you had in your own hands the difference between the county cess you pay and what is spent on the town you would be able to improve the town ?

Mr. Egan.—Yes; and that the water would be brought into the town for the same as the ratepayers pay at present.

133. You have not gone into any figures on the subject ?—I have; we pay more than we receive.

Mr. Gordon.

Mr. Gordon further examined.

134. What is the amount of the county cess ?—£[illegible] a year.

135. How much of that is for county-at-large charges ?—Less than a half.

136. And how much of the £[illegible] is expended in the town ?—£[illegible] a year is expended, and the remainder goes into the coffers of the Grand Jury. The entire county cess at Dr. [illegible] to [illegible] 18[illegible]. The county-at-large charges, as ascertained in 18[illegible], before Dr. Hougham, amount to £[illegible]. That was the average for that period, and that leaves £[illegible] 10s. for the maintenance of the roads and footpaths within the town; £[illegible] 18s. 7d. was spent, and that leaves £[illegible] [illegible] to be spent on the town.

137. The inquiry by Dr. Hougham was when you sought the provisional order for separation from the Grand Jury ?—Yes.

Sir Charles Knox Gore.—The Mayo Grand Jury opposed it.

Mr. Egan.—The money the people pay in the town is expended in other parts of the county. The town is paying more to the county than they receive to the extent of about £[illegible], and if that was kept in the town it would relieve the townspeople of a considerable amount of taxation.

Mr. Owen Kavanagh.

Mr. Owen Kavanagh examined.

138. You are a Commissioner ?—Yes.

139. Are you of opinion there should be any alteration in the boundaries ?—I think the majority of the Commissioners agreed there should be.

140. What is your own opinion ?—I think there should be.

141. To what extent ?—A mile and a half or two miles.

142. On what ground do you think extension should be made ?—The revenue to be derived would be brought in for the benefit of the town.

143. That would be an advantage to the Commissioners ?—Yes.

144. Should the people within two miles fairly be expected to contribute ?—I think so; they have the advantage of the town.

145. And you would fix the limit of that extension at two miles ?—About a mile and a half.

146. You don't know what additional income the mile and a half would bring in ?—No.

147. Mr. Robinson.—Would the mile and a half cut into four electoral divisions ?

Mr. Gordon.—No; it would all be within Ballina and Ardnaree, South.

Mr. Kenyon recalled.

Ballina.
No. Boundary.

148. You said an increase of a mile and a half would bring in additional money to the Commissioners: what do they require it for?—At present they are in debt, and if they had more money they would be able to make greater improvements in the town.

149. It is not properly cleansed at present?—Yes, but it might be done better if they had more means to clean the lanes and other parts of the town.

150. Mr. Robinson.—Would they apply that money to the improvement of the markets?—They would.

151. And are they in a bad state at present?—They are. The fairs are held on the streets. There is no fair green; there is a small patch of a place, and it is not half sufficient for the purpose.

Mr. Cotton.—I find that a mile and a half boundary would cut into three electoral divisions.

Mr. Thomas C. Perkins examined.

Mr. T. C. Perkins.

152. You are a Commissioner?—Yes.

153. Do you agree in the evidence given by the Commissioners?—I never applied myself to the question of the boundaries, but what struck me was we were very badly off for water, and the sanitary condition of the town is not good.

154. Do you think the guardians attend to their duties properly as regards sanitary matters?—I think they do remarkably well, but they have not gone to the extent they should. They have only covered the sewers—the connexions to the houses are made in very few instances.

155. Generally, do you think it would be an advantage that the Commissioners should be the sanitary authority?—I do not think it would, for then the occupiers would have to pay all the rates, and, on the contrary, I think I would let the landlord pay portion of it. I think we want water and connexions with the houses very badly. I do not believe there is a town of the same extent in Ireland so badly off for water. There are two or three wells. There is a hole in a certain part of the town which was exposed to the surface water, but since the guardians became the sanitary authority they have built a little wall about it.

156. What is it?—A well, and it is open at the top, and anyone could dip any vessel into it, no matter how filthy. The whole supply depends on two pumps, and the people in portions of the town must come at least a quarter of a mile for their water. If the guardians would give water, and make connexions from the houses into the main sewers, cleanse the lanes, and send their sanitary officers up Ardnaree and get those houses cleansed, it would be well. The lanes are in a most filthy condition. There are no public privies.

157. Sir Charles Knox Gore.—I don't think, as chairman of the Board of Guardians, I can allow this to pass without observation. In a large town like this cleansing is a matter of time. We are doing all the best means of doing, and doing it in the way government would suggest—by degrees. We must work by degrees.

158. Mr. Cotton.—If the town was larger, and the Commissioners were the urban authority?

Sir C. Knox Gore.—Yes, it would bear very much on that question, for they would have additional money to carry out these works; but they have no urban authority, and apparently will not for some time. At the time the Commissioners had control I am not aware that the matter was much better. I have spoken to a great many in the town, and their answer is that, as things stand, they would incur greater responsibility than the income would meet, and they think it would be better to leave things as they are.

159. Mr. Cotton.—What kind of responsibility?

Sir C. Knox Gore.—For instance, they would have to undertake these roads.

160. Mr. Cotton.—I suppose, for the moment, that the Commissioners are to be the urban authority, and not to be the road authority; would there be any object, then, in extending or diminishing the present area?

Sir Charles Knox Gore.—I cannot see any advantage.

161. In the first place, it would bring in some additional money to the Commissioners?—I suppose so.

162. Suppose the boundary was extended to a mile and a half, do you think the people within that area would be fairly asked to contribute to the town?—I think in some respects it would be very unfair.

163. They are too far away?—That they are deriving benefits not at all in comparison with others.

164. That applies to the question whether portions of the present area should not be shut out because they are over a mile from the town?—The intention in enlarging the boundaries from time to time was that, originally, a limit was fixed to a town actually comprising the town; but according as the town improved, as Ballina has, it extended itself in different directions, and then arises the question whether those districts built upon, may not fairly be included; but to extend it to anything like a mile and a half or two miles, then running into the open country, is not compatible with common sense. I think you will also agree with me that, by placing one leg of the compass in the centre of the town, and drawing a hard and fast line with the other leg, you will comprise the town.

Mr. Thomas M'Andrew examined.

Mr. Thomas M'Andrew.

165. You are a ratepayer?—Yes.

166. You think the present boundary ought not to be extended?—Certainly.

167. You think it should be curtailed?—I think it is very proper as it is.

168. Do you think an extension of a mile and a half would bring in people who should not be asked to pay?—Yes; and, if a poundage rate be put on, I will probably have to pay 1s. 6d., while the man in the country will only have to pay one-fourth.

169. That is owing to your having house property?—Yes. If you go to clean the streets for a mile and a half into the country, you will have to pay more money.

170. Do I understand that the present Commissioners clean the roads out to the boundaries of the town?—They are bound to do it.

Mr. Egan.—Certainly not; it is the duty of the road contractor.

Mr. M'Andrew's examination continued.

171. You think they are bound to clean the roads for a mile out of the town?—I think they are bound by law. They may think that by cleaning the principal street they do enough; but, if they are to cleanse the town, it means the whole area. If it is increased they will have to pay more, and of that sum I will have to pay more than the man in the country.

172. Taking that view of the matter, don't you think the boundary should be curtailed?—I would rather submit to increased taxation than curtail it, for I think the present are the natural boundaries of the town, which should be adhered to.

Sir Charles Knox Gore.—I never heard any question about curtailing the boundaries.

173. Mr. Cotton.—I take it as a matter of fact, the Commissioners do not clean the roads out to the boundary of the municipality?

Mr. Carolan.—No.

The inquiry then terminated.

Bangor, June 18, 1879.

BANGOR.—JUNE 18TH, 1879.

(Before Mr. C. P. Cotton, C.E.)

Mr. Francis Pollock examined.

Mr. Francis Pollock.

1. Mr. Cotton.—You are the Town Clerk of Bangor?—Yes.

2. How long have you filled the post?—Since the town has been put under the Act of 1854—in 1864.

3. The town is under the Towns Improvement Act?—Yes.

4. As far as you know, had the town been previously under any other Act?—No, sir.

5. What is the area of the township?—614a. 3r. 17p.

6. And the date when it was put under the Act?—The 21st of December, 1864.

7. What is the population of Bangor?—About 3,600 at present.

8. What was it last census?—In 1871 it was 2,560.

9. And do you mean to say that it has only increased 100 since then?—Yes, sir; it was the police gave us the number as 3,600.

10. Well, in the census of 1871 it was 3,260?—Yes.

11. Has it been increasing since that time?—Yes, I think so.

12. What was the last valuation?—£9,176 5s.

13. There are no wards in the town?—No, sir.

14. In what union is it?—In Newtownards.

15. What electoral division?—In Bangor.

16. Do you know yourself anything about the size of the electoral division of Bangor—how far it extends?—It is in the parish of Bangor.

17. Does the electoral division extend more than two miles all round the town?—Yes, it does.

18. There is a recommendation of the Committee of the House of Commons that electoral divisions should be made the municipal boundaries. Is the electoral division of Bangor too large to be made the municipal boundary?—Yes, quite too large.

19. Will you now give me the rates for the last five years?—In 1874 it was 6d.; in 1875, 6d.; in 1876, 6d.; in 1877, 6d.; in 1878, 6d.; and in 1879, 6d.

20. Have the Commissioners any property?—No, sir.

21. You have got the dog tax, and you have half the dogs?—Yes, sir.

22. Have you any other source of income?—Our tonnage.

23. Have you bye-laws?—We have, sir.

24. Regulating the case?—Yes, sir.

25. What was the poor rate in these same years?—The poor rate in 1874 was 8d.; in 1875, 8d.; 1876, 10d.; 1877, 1s.; 1878, 1s. 2d.; and in 1879 no rate has been struck.

26. You are not the urban sanitary authority?—No.

27. But you have petitioned to be one?—Yes.

28. And the Local Government Board have approved of your application, but it has not yet been confirmed by Parliament, I think?—No.

29. It is in course of confirmation?—Yes.

30. And of the poor rate struck in 1878, was any portion of that a sanitary rate?—In 1878—no, I believe not.

31. Has any sanitary rate been struck since 1874 by the Guardians?—No.

32. What has been the county cess for those years?—In 1874 the county cess—the two rates—amounted to 1s. 7d.; in 1875 it was 1s. 11½d.; in 1876 it was 1s. 9d.; in 1877, 1s. 10d.; 1878, 1s. 11d.; and 1879, 1s. 8d.

33. What is the number of your Commissioners?—Nine.

34. What is the number of voters in the municipality?—274 was the number on the last roll.

35. How many are qualified to sit as Commissioners if elected?—Ninety-one.

36. Have the Commissioners considered the question as to the desirability or otherwise of any extension of the municipal boundary?—They have.

37. Was it considered at a regular meeting of the Commissioners?—It was.

38. When was that meeting held?—It was held on the 4th of November, 1878.

39. How many Commissioners were present at the meeting?—Five.

40. Did they come to any resolution on the subject?—They did. I will read the resolution for you:—

"Proposed by Mr. Harvey, seconded by Mr. M'Kenzie—That Mr. Dixon be consulted respecting the enlargement of the present boundary by adding Ballyholme to it, and that the chairman and Dr. Bell be deputed to wait on Mr. Dixon concerning same."

41. Is there any further resolution?—No. There is a resolution here:—

"Proposed by Mr. Harvey, and seconded by Mr. M'Murray—That Mr. Russell, chairman, and Dr. Bell and Mr. Pollock be appointed a committee to answer the queries submitted by the Municipal Boundary Commissioners."

42. Were the five Commissioners unanimous about that?—Quite so.

43. What was the feeling of the Commissioners about what extension they desired?—They came to an understanding that they would like the boundary extended to the old Corporation, with Ballyholme added to it.

44. What do you mean by the old Corporation?—I have traced this map before you with a blue line. That indicates the boundary of the old Corporation.

45. Then on this map the red line represents the present boundary?—Yes.

46. The blue extension, plus Ballyholme, represents what you would wish to take in?—Yes.

47. And the blue line represents the old Corporation?—Yes.

48. Very well; that shows us what you wish for, at any rate. Have the Commissioners considered what additional area that would give?—No. We have had no means of ascertaining that.

49. Did you not estimate the number of people that would be brought in by this extension?—No.

50. I mean the Commissioners had not that before them?—They had not.

51. Had you not a valuation made of the additional land?—I made inquiries.

52. Can you give me any idea of it?—About £1,200.

53. That will be the additional valuation?—Yes, of Ballyholme, but not of the whole boundary.

54. But of the old Corporation, you have not ascertained that?—We have no means of ascertaining that.

55. Have you any idea how many additional voters it would bring in?—No, I cannot say that.

56. Can you form an opinion?—I cannot.

57. On what ground is the extension of the old Corporation boundary desired, or are you able to speak to that?—No, I am not; perhaps the chairman can.

58. How is the town lighted?—By gas.

59. How many lamps have you?—Fifty lamps.

60. A contract with the Gas Company I suppose?—Yes, sir; by the 1,000 cubic feet.

61. And how much per 1,000?—7s. 6d. was the last contract. With an abatement of £16 off.

62. What is the abatement?—£16 for the man that lights the town.

63. How is the town supplied with water?—By pumps.

64. How many pumps?—Fourteen.

65. You are not in charge of the pumps yet?—No, sir, not yet.

66. Do you know what the inhabitants think about

that—do they think that the supply is good or fair? —Yes. I have had no complaints about it.

67. Either in quantity or quality?—Well there have been some complaints as to the quality. Dr. Bolton, had some samples analysed, and the analysis was very satisfactory.

68. However you will be the Urban Sanitary Authority in a few months?—Yes, we expect so.

69. How is the town drained?—There is no scheme of drainage.

70. Is there any drainage at all in it—any main drains through the streets?—Yes, through the main streets.

71. From the railway down to the sea?—Not yet from the railway; from the head of the main street.

72. The railway drains into the river I suppose?—Yes.

73. Has there been any system of sewerage prepared hitherto?—Yes, there was, by the Board of Guardians.

74. Do you know anything about the evidence of it?—I do not.

Mr. Robert Richards, examined.

75. Mr. [illegible].—You are the Chairman of the Town Commissioners?—[illegible].

76. How long have you occupied the position?—About one year.

77. And you were a Commissioner before that?—I was.

78. Were you a Commissioner at the time the Towns Improvement Act was adopted?—I was not, sir.

79. The Commissioners have come to the conclusion that they would wish for an extension—[illegible] extension, because they are two different things, [illegible]

80. What was the object to be gained by this addition?—[illegible]

81. In what way?—[illegible]

82. In what way?—For instance, [illegible]

83. In computing the municipal rate?—Not the municipal, but the poor rate.

84. I do not clearly understand you; just explain?—[illegible]

85. [illegible]

86. [illegible]

87. [illegible]

88. Is there any other reason that presents itself to you that you would wish for this large increase, because it is a large increase?—[illegible]

89. On what roads are new buildings likely to be built?—There is [illegible] leading to Dundonald running along the railway.

90. Are there any buildings going on there?—[illegible]

91. Are there any buildings likely to be erected within your present boundary?—Yes.

92. [illegible]

93. [illegible]

94. On the [illegible] there any buildings on there?—No, sir.

95. [illegible]

96. Have you any reason for bringing in these [illegible]

97. [illegible]

98. [illegible]

99. It will be in your jurisdiction?—[illegible] town in this proposed extension.

100. That seems to me a very slight reason for going in for an extension of [illegible]

101. What building is there in that?—We think we should derive rates from the whole of it.

102. Then it would be more in the long run?—Yes, of course; but there would not be much, except on the land as we only charge one-fourth on the land.

103. But that is a very large area?—Yes.

104. You don't know the valuation, but I suppose it would be something like [illegible]

105. Take the Ballyholme direction—what is the reason this extension brings it so much in that direction?—The principal desire is to get as [illegible]

BANGOR, June 26, 19[illegible]. — Mr. Robert Russell.

106. There is a good deal of room yet?—The bulk is built on, and there is building there every year. At present there are buildings going on there, and we find that in that place they have no system of sewerage whatever, and the parties building houses are using tanks for holding sewage.

107. Cesspools?—Yes, and sometimes these things are not attended to, and complaints have been made.

108. The Guardians are perfectly competent to deal with that?—Yes.

109. And to deal with it now?—Yes, of course they are.

110. So that that is hardly a reason for taking them in. Is there any other reason why they should contribute to the town?—I might say in addition to that reason that we would like to embrace them in one sewerage scheme because we will complete one if we can get it.

111. But it strikes me—I don't know whether you have considered it properly—it strikes me there would be some difficulty in bringing all that into one drainage scheme. I don't see how it could be done at first sight?—We have not consulted our engineer with reference to this question. It has only suggested itself to us.

112. Is there any other reason?—Another reason is that these houses are occupied by people coming to and from Belfast, and they are fast becoming permanent residents, and they are a very short distance from the railway, and they have no light along there, and, as we propose to buy the gas works, we would light that place with lamps all the way, and light the houses with gas.

113. You propose to extend the lighting all through Ballyholme?—Yes; all through Ballyholme.

114. Have the people living in Ballyholme the advantage of the town of Bangor as a market?—Yes; and they are obliged to pass through it to the train and boat from here to Belfast.

115. Do they market in Bangor or do they get their things from Belfast?—They do a great deal in Bangor.

116. What is the number of houses in Ballyholme?—There are upwards of fifty.

117. And the buildings are going on at present?—Yes, buildings are going on at present, and high-class buildings. There is another reason why we would like to embrace Ballyholme. In the matter of bathing great complaints have been made from time to time as regards these Ballyholme people. People come into Bangor and make complaints of parties bathing along the strand without any regard to decency. There is no provision for a gentleman's bathing place, and those who cannot swim take the shallow water where the ladies bathe.

118. Would that come within your bye-laws?—Yes; we have bye-laws under which we would confine ladies and gentlemen to two different places when bathing, and make the gentlemen wear bathing dresses.

119. Have you any idea how many people would be brought in by the extension as voters and ratepayers?—We have not gone into that.

120. In Ballyholme how many additional voters would be brought in by the addition of that district?—They would be every one voters, because all the houses are above the valuation.

121. Are they all in such occupation as would give votes? If they are only taken for a few months in the year there might be only one vote out of a whole terrace—if it is owned by one man, and he only rated for it?—I know the district well. There would be about thirty voters out of fifty houses.

122. Thirty occupiers who are on the rate books?—Yes.

123. How many of those would be qualified to act as Commissioners if elected?—All them, thirty, because all the houses are above the valuation of £12.

124. Have you considered the question—supposing such a suburb as Ballyholme was added to Bangor—of whether there should be any division of the township into wards?—Well, that has never been entertained. I brought it before the Commissioners as I thought it a wise thing to do, but they did not seem to take that view.

125. Have you any view yourself on the subject?—I think it would be better to do so, because if the town was divided into wards it would make the Commissioners, who represented a particular ward, enquire more closely into the carrying out of the business.

126. Supposing there was a division into wards what would you suggest?—I have not gone into that.

127. Ballyholme is increasing every year?—Yes; increasing every year in the number of buildings.

128. Have you any idea of how many of the fifty houses were built last year?—Four houses.

129. I see there has been a good deal of expense on the new road at Ballyholme. Who is doing that?—The county. However, Mr. Lyle, the owner of the property at Ballyholme, has done a great deal too.

130. Is there much building going on on the other side of Bangor?—Within the township?

131. Yes?—There are a great number of houses being built.

132. But not outside the town?—No, sir.

133. The Town Clerk gave me an estimate of the valuation that would be added by the Ballyholme extension as about £1,800, is that correct?—That is quite correct; it is taken from the county cess collector.

134. And every house built would add to that?—It would, sir.

135. Do you know what the ratepayers think of the proposed extension—what opinion they have formed concerning it?—No; except beyond that it is their opinion, that they were in favour of having this extension. We consider Ballyholme as a portion of Bangor.

136. Have you heard any opinion expressed by the Ballyholme people?—I have, sir, and some of them are opposed——

137. They are aware of the fact that you are intending to take them in?—They thought this inquiry would take place before the guardians. On one occasion when I was before them I saw three gentlemen present as a deputation to oppose it.

138. Do you know the feeling of the people in the Corporation extension?—No, sir.

139. How do you happen to know that it is the old Corporation boundary?—The clerk has taken it from the map.

140. Have you got the map?—Yes.

[Map produced.]

141. When was this map prepared?—This was prepared at the time the town was put under the Act of 1854.

142. Was Bangor an old Corporation?—Yes, sir, very old.

143. When did it cease to be a Corporation?—Indeed I could not tell you, not in my time. I could not speak safely as to that.

144. Because there were a great number ceased to be Corporations in 1837?—Yes. We had a Seneschal Court here at one time.

145. Is there anything else you would wish to add to your evidence?—No.

Dr. Henry Bell examined.

146. You have heard what the Chairman has said?—Yes.

147. Do you agree with the way in which he has expressed the opinions of the Commissioners?—Yes.

148. Do you think it represents the feeling of the rest of the Commissioners?—Yes.

149. With reference to your opinion, Dr. Bell, as to the extension which has been proposed—there are two extensions, I may say, indeed, and the other the Ballyholme extension?—Well, as far as the inland extension is concerned, I must confess I don't know anything of it. I don't see any particular reason for that, except for what the Chairman has stated, that is, that we might require to draw water from some of those districts, and it might be prudent in time to have the control of the district; but as far as the extension to the old boundary is concerned, I do not see any reason why that should be done.

150. Apart from the possibility of having to go to some portion of that district for water, and for having drainage control over it, you don't see any other reason?—I do not.

151. And as regards the Ballyholme extension?—I consider that that would be both for the benefit of Ballyholme and Bangor.

152. How for the benefit of Ballyholme?—Well, it would be under proper control.

153. Under your by-laws?—Yes; under our by-laws.

154. And do you propose to extend the gas?—We propose to light it, and we propose to embrace it under the sewerage scheme that we propose for Bangor.

155. The drainage scheme?—Yes; but should we not do so, because I do not consider perhaps that the two are likely to work together——

156. Would you form a separate system for Ballyholme?—Yes.

157. And you would undertake the drainage?—Most decidedly, and I look upon it as a most important matter, because Ballyholme being at the present time a newly built place is likely to contaminate the water; it would not be long before it would be contaminated.

158. How are the Ballyholme houses supplied with water?—By pumps. At the present time there is no system of sewerage, and, therefore, in the end the water taken from those would be contaminated.

159. Generally speaking, you would look after the drainage of Ballyholme, and so benefit the inhabitants there?—Yes.

160. In what way would the taking in of Ballyholme be of advantage to the town of Bangor?—I did not say it would be of any advantage.

161. I thought you said there would be a reciprocal advantage?—It would be an advantage in the shape of the rates of the property it would embrace.

162. Have you gone into any calculation as to whether the rates you would receive would in your time supply the cost of gas and drainage?—I have not, but I think it would be of advantage to the people down in Ballyholme to have gas.

163. And that your by-laws should apply there?—Yes. At the present time we light to within, I suppose, 400 yards of Ballyholme.

164. You do not light beyond your own boundary?—No; but we light up within 400 yards of Ballyholme.

165. Do you light up to your own boundary at Ballyholme?—We do.

166. Along the present road to Ballyholme how far do the town lights go?—Merely to the end of the town; merely to the end of the street.

167. Why you would, in fact, have to light nearly a mile and a half of additional road?—No sir; not a mile and a half; it would not embrace that. The whole distance would not cover more than three quarters of a mile at the farthest.

168. To the end of Ballyholme from the end of the street?—No, sir; not more than that at the very outside. I think half a mile would embrace the whole of Ballyholme.

169. It would be fully a mile more to the end of Ballyholme?—Yes.

170. And the proposition is—the intention is to light it and drain it in exchange for the rates?—Yes; that is one of the principal reasons for asking for Ballyholme to be included.

171. Of course in the case of the Ballyholme people their access to the rail and steamer is through the town of Bangor?—Yes, sir; and it is very dangerous on dark nights driving from the train to Ballyholme. Some of the Ballyholme people would be delighted that we should have the control of their district.

172. When you talk of the Ballyholme people, Dr. Bell, do you mean the present occupiers or the owners of property there?—Mainly the present occupiers.

173. They would not be the ratepayers?—No, sir; but we have to study their comforts. The actual rateable [illegible] of the [illegible] be drawn from those people; and in the first place to satisfy the people that they draw the [illegible] [illegible], and I think it necessary that they should be satisfied.

174. But it is this way; do you think that Ballyholme will, when lit and drained by you—that that would raise the rents of the houses?—How do you mean?

175. The rents of the houses. That people would be willing to pay higher rents for a house?—I don't know that it would. I would not say that.

176. How is the drainage of Bangor itself?—Well it is not in a condition that I consider satisfactory.

177. How is it drained?—We have one main drain running from, you may say, the market house to the bridge at the foot of Main-street, and we have another drain.——

178. The main drain running down Main-street; and are the houses connected with that main drain?—Only some. There is a different outlet for the sewage as well as that main drain.

179. What is the other outlet?—The outlet is something similar to, but has no connection with, that main drain.

180. Where does it [illegible]?—It runs at the back of the houses in Main-street.

181. Does that go along the new road towards the rail?—No, it is in a different direction.

182. There is one at the bottom of the railway?—There is a good system of sewerage about there.

183. There is an open drain?—No, it is not open now. It is covered by a culvert.

184. That takes the drainage of the [illegible]?—That takes the drainage of that district.

185. Then how are the houses drained that are up at the west side of the bay—up on the hill?—They have no main drainage.

186. At all. There are new houses?—We made drains. They have cesspools, and the cesspools are connected, and, with the surface water, the sewage passes into the sea.

187. The surface water goes to sea and the sewage of the houses into the cesspools?—Into the cesspools. They are merely receptacles for solid matter.

188. You don't consider that a good state of things?—Well, I don't consider it the best. It is fair generally.

189. It is one you would alter under a drainage scheme?—Decidedly. I would allow no surface water to pass into the bay.

190. And Ballymagee-street, Fisher's-hill, and Quay-street, have any they drained?—Ballymagee-street is only semi-drained.

191. What do you mean by that?—A drain running half-way up, and merely attached to one side of the street.

192. Are the houses connected with it, or is it merely a road drain?—I don't think there are more than six houses in the street attached to it.

Belfast, 29th Jan. 1878.

Dr. Henry Bell.

Bangor. June 13, 18[illegible].

Dr. Henry Bell.

193. The houses in the other part of that street, how are they?—The other part of the houses have dry water-closets.

194. Privies; and the stuff, is it removed to the land?—Yes.

195. Now about the water supply, what do you think of that? Do you think [illegible] pumps sufficient?—Anything but sufficient.

196. Has there ever been any scheme for a high pressure water supply to the town from any distance?—No; there has been talk about it, but nothing more than talk.

197. Do you consider the town fairly lit now?—Well, yes; I consider the town fairly lit.

198. Were you a Commissioner at the time of the adoption of the Act?—No, sir. I don't know whether I mentioned about Ballyholme being under any control at and. That is one of my reasons. For instance the bathers——

199. I asked you whether the application of your by-laws was one of the things that Ballyholme should be included for?—Yes.

200. With regard to the bathers; and is there anything else that the by-laws would specially apply to?—They would apply to cars and car-drivers.

201. You would have control over the cars plying from the railway station to Ballyholme?—Yes. At present when they go beyond your boundary you have no control over them.

Mr. James Pollock.

Mr. James Pollock examined.

202. You have heard what the Chairman and Dr. Bell have stated?—Yes.

203. Do you coincide with them?—I do, in regard to Ballyholme, but I do not go in for taking much of Ballyvarnet.

204. It adds in a good deal of the Corporation area, but the proposition before me here does not take in any more of Ballyvarnet than is at present in the town?—There is a little, some twelve acres. I have seen a difficulty arising at the Newtownards Board of Guardians about that very piece of land.

205. About that twelve acres?—Yes; the Guardians had no power to assess anything but the whole area of the townland of Ballyvarnet, and I saw there was a difficulty arose at different times. I think there is now a law empowering to assess part of a townland. There are many matters connected with this town lying over for this purpose, and the Guardians don't want to do anything with the sanitary state of affairs of Bangor.

206. You don't think there is any occasion to take in any land on Ballyvarnet way?—None. The Guardians thought it would not be fair to [illegible] outside these for the sanitary affairs of Bangor. [illegible] in the [illegible] in Bangor.

207. What is your opinion about the extension to Ballyholme?—I think it would be for the benefit of Ballyholme. I think the Ballyholme people would receive great benefit by it, both in lighting and in sanitary matters.

208. You would be prepared to fairly light [illegible]. Certainly. I would go in for lighting, and not that they are not forgotten. I think it would encourage building to go on there.

Mr. David M'Keown.

Mr. David M'Keown examined.

209. You are a Town Commissioner?—Yes.

210. How long have you been a Commissioner?—Three years.

211. You know the extension to Ballyholme that is proposed?—I do.

212. Would you kindly give me your views as to that?—My views coincide perfectly with those expressed by the Chairman and the other Commissioners examined regarding Ballyholme, and I was labouring under considerable misapprehension with regard to the extension of the boundary to the fields at Ballyvarnet, and I am satisfied that the boundary there should be as it is.

213. But you would not go further out than you would not go further.

214. Do you know a place called [illegible] in [illegible]?

215. The proposed extension goes more than a quarter of a mile beyond that, out along that road? Do you think that should be not [illegible]?—I think it would be quite [illegible]. [illegible] would be [illegible], and it would be no expense to take lamps, or any other sanitary arrangement so far as that, going up a hill.

Mr. David Harvey.

Mr. David Harvey examined.

216. What are your views on the question of the proposed extension?—I agree with what Mr. M'Keown has said, both with regard to Ballyvarnet and Ballyholme. I wish to state nothing further than that.

Mr. John Johnston.

Mr. John Johnston examined.

217. Are you in favour of the proposed extension?—On behalf of the portion of Ballyholme that is held under Lord Dufferin, I oppose this extension.

218. The portion that is proposed to be taken in, at least that the Commissioners wish to be taken in, is represented by the blue line on the map. The eastern half of the Ballyholme district is the one that you are interested in?—Yes.

219. Do you own the property?—I own portion of the property.

220. There is a good deal of building going on upon your property?—There is no building but one double house at the present time.

221. Then you don't own the front?—I own portion of the Dufferin Villa property.

222. Are there any buildings along the eastern portion of Ballyholme?—There are five villas at the eastern end of Ballyholme.

223. Are you interested in these?—I am interested in two of them—two blocks.

224. How many houses are there in that terrace altogether?—There are included in the Dufferin Villa property eight houses walled round, and with a complete sewerage scheme.

225. There are eight houses there?—There are.

226. And they have a sewerage scheme of their own?—Yes.

227. What is that scheme, just describe it?—There is a main drain running in front of these houses; behind them there are large cesspools, and each house empties the sewage into the cesspools, and the overflow from the cesspools goes into the bay.

228. From each house [illegible], one pipe conveys the overflow from the houses.

229. There is one cesspool for the eight houses?—Yes, a large cesspool.

[illegible]

Mr. Robert Murray examined.

[illegible]

Mr. James Gaw examined.

[illegible]

[illegible]. *James M'Donald*, *John Patterson*, and *John Hamilton*, stated they were all opposed to the proposed extension.

[illegible]. Mr. Murray.—There are other owners of property in Ballyholme who are opposed to the extension, but they could not attend today.

[illegible]. Mr. Patterson.—I don't know any resident or owner of property that is not opposed in the very strongest manner to anything of the kind.

The Inquiry then terminated.

BALBRIGGAN.—MAY 13th, 1879.

(Before Mr. C. P. Cotton, C.E.)

Mr. Daniel [illegible] examined.

1. You are clerk of the Town Commissioners of Balbriggan?—Yes.

2. For how long have you been so?—Three and a half years.

3. Under what Act is the town?—The Towns Improvement Act, 1854.

4. When was it put under that Act?—The Act was adopted so far as lighting is concerned, on the 23rd April, 1860, but on the [illegible] July, 1874, it was adopted for all purposes.

5. Including water supply?—Yes. There are no water works but the Act was adopted for all purposes.

6. Was the town previously under any body of Commissioners?—No. That was the first time any Act was adopted, and they had no other power except that of lighting.

7. What is the area of the town?—Five hundred and twenty-eight acres one rood and twenty-one perches.

8. What is the population of the town?—Two thousand three hundred and eight.

9. That was in 1871?—Yes. That return is taken from Thom's Almanac.

10. What is the valuation of Balbriggan?—Three thousand eight hundred and ninety pounds fifteen shillings.

11. That is the last valuation?—The last valuation, as certified by the clerk of the union.

12. You know the shape of the town—does it extend equally in all directions from where we now are?—I think on the average the town extends about a quarter of a mile from the centre of the town.

13. Are there whole townlands comprised within the town or only parts of townlands?—Whole townlands. They are the townlands of Balbriggan and the townland of Tankardstown. There are three.

14. That comprises the entire town?—Yes, sir.

15. There are no wards?—No wards.

16. In what electoral division is the town?—It is in the electoral division of Balbriggan.

17. Do you yourself know the size of the electoral division?—No; but as far as I heard it is something about two and a half English miles from the court-house all round except to the sea-coast.

18. How many Commissioners are there?—There are nine Commissioners.

19. How many voters are there?—There are ninety-three ratepayers qualified to vote.

20. And how many of them are qualified to sit as Commissioners if elected?—Twenty-seven are eligible to be elected.

21. Have the Town Commissioners had under their consideration the question sent down to them by us?—Yes, sir.

22. Have they come to any resolution on the subject?—Yes.

23. Were they unanimous in their decision?—Yes, sir.

24. What resolution did they come to?—"The Commissioners as a body considered the question of the boundaries and they were unanimously in favour of leaving them as they are, inasmuch as any extension of the boundaries would merely have the effect of putting additional taxation on those who already have the principal part of it."

25. That is that the owners of land outside, are already ratepayers inside?—No. The Town Commissioners were unanimously opposed to any extension of the boundaries and were satisfied with the present boundaries, that is what they said, and I wrote this out myself.

26. What were the grounds on which they came to this resolution?—On the ground that the land is so thinly populated outside the boundary, and that if you added half a mile to the boundary the land brought in would only pay one-fourth; and if the Commissioners had to supply that district with gas the revenue derived would not pay for the lighting, and there are a great many of the Commissioners owners of house property, and they pay nearly all the rates themselves.

27. That is on the supposition that the lands would contribute only one-fourth, and that the Commissioners would be bound to give light and other facilities to the extended area?—Yes, sir, and all they could recover would be one-fourth, which would not pay for the additional expenses.

28. Do you know the country round well enough to say if there was an extension of half a mile how many people would probably be brought in?—No. I think there would not be many within half a mile. There would be Hampton and Bush Hall.

29. That would be only two places?—Yes, sir. There might be a few farmers brought in.

30. How far is Balrothery from this?—It is a mile or more.

31. What size is Balrothery?—It is a small place. The population of it is about [illegible].

32. The Commissioners never considered the question of bringing in Balrothery?—No, sir. The houses there are nearly all cabins, and there would not be much derived from them; they are all poor people living there.

33. You have not got a valuation of it?—No, sir.

34. What rates have been struck in the town of Balbriggan since 1874?—For 1874 the town rate was 10d. in the £.

35. For 1875 what was it?—For 1875, 8d. in the pound.

36. For 1876?—It was 7d. in the pound.

37. For 1877 how much?—6d. in the pound.

38. For 1878?—It was 7d. in the pound.

39. You have not struck a rate this year yet?—Not as yet.

40. Can you tell me the poor-rate for those years since 1874?—Yes, sir; in 1874 the poor-rate was 1s. 6d. in the pound; in 1875 it was 10d.; in 1876 it was 1s. 2d.; in 1877 it was 1s. 8d.; and in 1878 it was 1s. 6d. also. That includes 2d. sanitary rate.

41. In what year?—That is in 1878.

42. That is included in the 10d. rate for that year?—Yes, sir, 2d. sanitary rate in 1877 also, and 2d. in 1878.

43. What was that sanitary rate for?—That rate was for sewers. There was a main sewer made through the town, and there was £300 borrowed for it.

44. Was this sanitary rate all for this sewer?—Yes. In 1874 the Commissioners were the sanitary authority, and the £300 was borrowed in about September of that year, but the passing of the Public Health Act then took the authority from them and the guardians became the sanitary authority. The Commissioners then handed over the £300 to the guardians, and this 2d. rate was made for the purpose of redeeming that loan, paying interest and redeeming part of the principal.

45. Do you know how much has been repaid of that loan?—£16 is paid of the principal every year, and 5 per cent. interest on the balance.

46. Did that 2d. rate cover anything else—was there any other sanitary work undertaken by the guardians?—No, sir. There is part of the rate to pay the executive sanitary officer. I don't think it would take the whole of the 2d. rate to pay the interest and part of the principal.

47. But there were no other works done?—No.

48. On what district was that 2d. rate struck?—On the town of Balbriggan.

49. That is on the municipal area?—Yes. It is

BALBRIGGAN. May 24, 1880. Mr. Daniel Synnott.

enough money to do their ordinary work within their present powers with the 1s. rate?—Yes, sir.

92. Would they have enough with the 1s. rate to carry out whatever they would want for sanitary works in case they became the urban authority?—I think so; the rate never exceeded 10d. in the pound.

93. And with the 10d. they did what they wanted?—Yes, and there was more laid out then than now, for there were more improvements made.

94. And they don't want any special rate for any other purpose?—No, sir.

95. Is there any other information you wish to give regarding the subject?—No.

96. The commissioners have considered the question as to the transfer of the management of the roads?—The commissioners decline for the present to give any opinion as to it.

97. They don't wish to become the authority for the maintenance of the roads within the district?—At the present time they don't, but hereafter they may change their minds on the subject.

98. What fairs are there held in Balbriggan?—Four fairs, I think.

99. Are they large fairs?—They are. They are held on the 29th April, 29th September, and second Monday in December, and first Monday in February—four in the year.

100. There are markets held here?—Yes; on Mondays.

101. Are there any schools in Balbriggan?—Yes, a National school.

102. From how far round do you think the children come to that school?—I think they are nearly all from the town.

103. There are no farmers' children from outside attending them?—No.

104. Are there any schools outside the town?—Yes; one at Balrothery.

105. A National school?—Yes; a National school.

106. Do you know whether the people living on the present township boundaries wish to be included in the town or not?—Speaking with some of them I think they would have an objection.

107. Has the fact that we were going to sit here been notified in any way?—Yes, sir; it was posted outside the police barrack.

Mr. TERENCE O'NEILL examined.

Mr. Terence O'Neill.

108. You are a town commissioner of Balbriggan?—Yes.

109. How long have you been a commissioner?—For 14 years.

110. And a resident in the town?—Yes, sir.

111. You have heard Mr. Synnott say the commissioners were unanimously in favour of leaving the boundaries as they are?—Yes.

112. They wish to become the urban authority for sanitary matters in the district?—They do. For, as Mr. Synnott stated, it is a slow sort of system at present. The dispensary committee under the Board of Guardians meet here once a month, and if any nuisance occurred within that time, and particularly in summer, the pumps very often get out of order, there will be delay in setting the matter right. I recollect on one occasion the attention of the Board of Guardians was called to the fact that the pumps were out of order, and we were left at least three months without water; one body reported to the other—the dispensary committee reported to the Board of Guardians, and the Board of Guardians sent back the report, and then it seemed the work could not be carried out by the dispensary committee, and we were left without water.

113. We have nothing to do with the transfer of authority, and the only question is whether you consider the present township, with its present power of rating, is sufficient to enable the commissioners to carry out the sanitary arrangements if they became the sanitary authority?—Yes; I think so.

114. And they would not want the help of any additional rates for sanitary matters?—Certainly not. I think we would find we could do with less rate.

115. Your rates have never come up to the shilling yet?—No.

116. Has there been any proposition for a supply of water from any other source than at present?—No; the people are quite content with the supply.

117. There is no complaint as to the quality of the water?—No, sir; but there is some complaint of negligence in keeping the pumps in order.

118. But the quality of the water is good?—Excellent.

119. That opinion of the Commissioners was shared in by the other Commissioners?—There were eight Commissioners at the meeting. There was only one absent Commissioner.

120. Is there anything else you wish to add regarding this question of the boundaries?—No, sir.

121. Do you know the feeling of the ratepayers immediately inside or outside the present boundary?—I think the feeling outside would be against extension, for this reason principally—they are farmers, and they imagine if they were annexed they would forfeit their right under the Land Act.

122. Independent of that, do you know of any objection to the extension?—I don't think there would be any objection.

123. Would there be any objection if they knew they would have to pay something more in the way of taxes?—I think so.

124. Something small?—They might. It is principally land, and it pays only one-fourth.

125. Are the holders of land within, say, a distance of a mile from the centre of the town, but outside the present boundary, residents in the town?—No, they are not.

126. Then the adjoining lands are not in the nature of townparks?—No, they are not.

127. These people outside live on their own land?—Yes.

128. Do you know where the children go to school who live, say, a distance of a mile and a half from Balbriggan?—I do.

129. Do they come into Balbriggan?—No; two English miles from Clonard—they come into Balbriggan, but there are schools all round.

130. I suppose the farmers use Balbriggan as a market town?—They do; and respectable farmers send their children into the Convent schools here.

131. The people who live within a certain distance, say, a mile derive advantage from having the town properly kept?—Yes.

132. And their land is of higher value on account of being near the town?—No doubt they derive greater value, if it was for no other purpose than that of gathering manure.

133. But that is because the town happens to be on the seashore?—Just so. Of course as Balbriggan is improved it would benefit the neighbourhood around, as it would become a better market.

134. How far into the country do you think any special benefit accrues to the residents and farmers?—I would say two and a half miles north, west, and south, or I would say about three miles, as this is the principal market place to those people resident out there.

135. I see that Balrothery is a small village within a short distance of Balbriggan—has the question of including it been considered?—It never has, but it would not come under the same category as other places, for there are very few people there except the parish priest and the rector, and a few people like that, who would pay taxes.

136. The union workhouse is in Balrothery?—It is about a mile beyond Balrothery.

137. In which parish is the workhouse situated?—In Balrothery.

138. Is there anything else you wish to state in reference to this question?—No. The Commissioners held a special meeting with the view of considering this subject, and they instructed Mr. Synnott to answer any questions, and he has [illegible] their general opinions on all the subjects on which he has given evidence.

139. Mr. Synnott.—The electoral division, I think, extends on the sea Balbriggan [illegible] that is about one and a half miles to the north, and it extends to the south—A very short distance.

Mr. O'Neill recalled.

Balbriggan, May 1, 1879. Mr. Thomas O'Neill.

140. You know the extent of the electoral division?—Yes, I do.

141. It has been one of the recommendations of the Select Committee which gave rise to this inquiry, that where it was feasible the boundaries of towns should be made coterminous with electoral division boundaries; in your opinion, would it be wise at this question to make the boundaries of the town of Balbriggan coterminous with the boundaries of the electoral division?—Quite out of the question.

142. On account of the immense distance to which the electoral division extends?—Yes, and bringing nothing in but land.

Mr. Synnott recalled.

Mr. Synnott.

143. Is Balbriggan increasing in population?—There are a great many improvements in regard to building houses and the population is not decreasing.

144. The valuation has slightly increased within the last few years?—Yes, and I think next year it will be further increased, for a good many houses have been built, and have not yet been inserted in the rate-books. They will add a good deal to the rate.

145. Business houses?—No, sir, private houses.

146. Is the business of the port increasing?—I don't know, I am not long enough here to say.

147. Mr. O'Neill.—It is very much decreasing.

148. Mr. Synnott.—The electoral division extends on this side to the sea, and on this side to a place called Whitestown, and on the south to a place called Dovrie, and to the north to Balrothery.

149. How far are these?—They are about two and a half miles distant.

The inquiry then closed.

BRAY.—MAY 2nd, 1879.

Bray, May 2, 1879.

Before Messrs. W. A. Exham, q.c., Chairman, and C. P. Cotton, c.e.

1. Mr. Edward Dennis, Chairman of the Town Commissioners.—It is my duty, as Chairman of the Town Commissioners, to remove a misapprehension that appears to have prevailed, and to say a few words. The Town Commissioners, when the question was sent to them, were perfectly ignorant of the holding of the Commission and for in fact were themselves surprised; and as to what were the requirements. The impression that has gone abroad is that this inquiry emanated from the Town Commissioners. They, however, knew nothing about it until they received these papers, and the inquiry is purely a Government one as I understand it. The Town Commissioners have made up their minds after carefully and minutely going into the question to have nothing to do with an extension. It would be totally out of the question to bring in a district to pay rates only as one-fourth of their valuation. After seriously considering the matter the Town Commissioners decided not to have an extension. They think their own funds are not quite sufficient, even now, to carry out all the improvements that are required, and would not be at all adequate to the increased responsibility and burthen.

2. Chairman.—It is, of course, a misapprehension to suppose that the Town Commissioners have in any way originated or promoted this inquiry. It is held in pursuance of a recommendation of a Select Committee of the House of Commons contained in the report before me, and the warrant issued by His Grace the Lord Lieutenant under which we act. [Mr. Exham read portion of the warrant.] There was no suggestion of statement made this [illegible] morning, in answer only to obtain an [illegible] of all the town. The amount of complaint now may merely come to the county for keeping up the roads and county at large charges, and I did not hear anyone say that, because they were taken in they were to get the benefit of paying only one-fourth of the county rates. The [illegible] which, in point of fact, so far as that matter was concerned, make no difference to them, for it would be only the land that portion that is changed. We are suggested that by being brought in they were to be relieved of the responsibility of the entire county rate.

3. Mr. George Keogh, Solicitor for the Dublin, Wicklow, and Wexford Railway Company.—What guarantee have the ratepayers that the legislature hereafter will give effect to your recommendation, and they not then be found in that the present [illegible] with the obligations will that [illegible] extended with additional obligations, and without any additional [illegible] advantages. A recommendation may be of itself very equitable, but where different parts of the country have taken different views as to what that recommendation should be, it is hard for us to be quite content that it will not affect us unfavourably.

4. Chairman.—Whatever are the county-at-large charges, we cannot alter those, and in any [illegible] that is proposed by us it will be practically only the land that portion that will be charged so far as this rating is concerned.

Mr. Edward Devereux examined.

Mr. Edward Devereux.

5. Chairman.—You are the Town Clerk of Bray?—Yes.

6. What is the area of the town at present?—1,044 acres 13 perches.

7. What is the entire valuation?—£29,304 10s. made up of £1,530 10s. for land, and £26,763 15s. for houses; and the balance, £999 15s., is for railways, water and gas works, and toll roads, &c.

8. What is the population?—In 1861 it was 3,156; in 1871, 6,000; the 6th September, 1876, it was 6,733.

9. When was it taken in 1871?—In the 2nd of April.

10. At all events we may assume that the population is increasing?—Yes.

11. Is there a good deal of building going on?—Yes. The valuation since last year alone has increased by £700.

BRAY.
July 5, 1878.
—
Mr. Edward Dempsey.

12. What was the valuation in 1871?—£20,169, and at present it is £23,804 15s.

13. What were the rates for the three last years?—Since 1874, 3s. 6d., except 1877 when they were 3s. 3d.

14. Was that the maximum for the last five years?—Yes.

15. Did you strike any separate sanitary rate?—No. The improvement rate covers all.

16. Then 3s. 6d. is the maximum?—Yes; that includes 1s. 4d. improvement rate, 6d. water rate, 7d. special rate for the sinking fund, and 2d. under the special Act.

17. What debts do you owe?—The present debt amounts to £8,103 6s. 1d., that includes the two Government loans of £1,800, and £1,100 borrowed for sanitary purposes in 1870 and 1872; there is, I should say, £3,003 6s. 1d. due on these.

18. Are they being paid off by sinking fund?—By annuity.

19. How much a year do the annuities amount to?—£114 9s. annually on the £1,800, and £46 6s. 6d. on the £1,100.

20. What are the other debts made up of?—£4,700 private mortgages in sums of £2,000, £800, £1,100, £600, and £100.

21. What is the interest?—Five per cent.

22. Are you applying any sinking fund to that?—Yes; we have in New Three per Cents £1,431 11s. 4d.

23. How much is the sinking fund each year?—£157—the thirtieth portion of it.

24. Is that £4,700 all in one loan?—No, I have mentioned the separate sums.

25. Who manages the roads in the town?—We do.

26. Under your Act?—Yes.

27. Is the cost paid out of the rates?—Yes; the improvement rate.

28. How do you manage the county at-large charges?—They average about £600 a year. The Wicklow Grand Jury send in a warrant for its amount, and we pay it out of the general rate, and also about £30 a year to the county Dublin Grand Jury.

29. What is the county cess payable immediately outside the boundary?—From 1s. 6d. to 1s. 9d. on an average.

30. Are you the urban sanitary authority?—We are.

31. What are the poor rates in the township?—The rate for the present year is 10d., but it averages 1s. to 1s. 3d.

32. Will there be a sanitary rate?—Not on the township.

33. What is the poor rate outside?—About 1s. to 1s. 6d.

34. How much is the sanitary rate outside?

Sir George Hodson.—Two pence.

35. CHAIRMAN.—Have the Commissioners, as a body, considered the question of extension of the boundaries of the town?

Mr. *Dempsey.*—They have not.

36. Have the people in the town expressed any opinion on it?—So far as I have been able to learn, the opinion of the people of the township is opposed to any alteration, except a very small one.

37. Mr. COTTON.—Have the Commissioners ever applied for an extension?—Well, Mr. Brett's report was under the consideration of the Board some years ago, but it was strongly opposed.

38. *Sir George Hodson.*—I did not think it would apply at all.

39. CHAIRMAN.—Is Little Bray included in the present township?—It is.

40. Does the present boundary follow townland boundaries?—Yes.

41. Is the present boundary in one electoral division?—No; it is in two.

42. Would an extension of any one mile bring it into another electoral division?—No.

43. Has there been any meeting here, so far as you know, of ratepayers to consider it?—No.

44. Mr. COTTON.—How many wards are there?—East, West, and Little Bray.

45. Can you give the area and population of these?—The area of Little Bray is 167a. 1r. 30p., and of East and West wards jointly 918a. 0r. 0p.

46. Cannot you separate them and give the valuation of each?—No.

47. Can you give the number of voters?—Yes; 154 in East ward, 89 in West ward, and Little Bray 50; total 303.

48. Can you separate the valuation?—No.

49. Can you tell, out of these voters, how many are qualified to sit as Commissioners?

50. I find there are about 350 ratings at £7 and up to £20, and 270 ratings at £20 and upwards. A large number of those who are so rated are females.

51. How many Commissioners are there?—Fifteen; nine for East ward, three each for Little Bray and West ward.

52. Mr. COTTON.—Have the Commissioners ever discussed the question of the alteration of the ward boundaries?—When the question were sent here it was referred from one meeting to another, but no definite decision was come to on the matter.

53. Mr. *Bewley.*—They did not come to any decision on the matter, but the last time the Commissioners discussed it, there was a unanimous opinion that we could not attempt to take in any additional district.

54. How is the town supplied with gas?—We pay 5s. per thousand cubic feet to the Alliance Gas Company. We have 116 gas lamps, and twenty-two matrix lamps; the average cost for four years was £170 (cost of gas) £35 for wages, and £30 to £35 for repairs.

55. Do you supply water by arrangement with the Corporation of Dublin?—Yes.

56. CHAIRMAN.—What was the balance on the last yearly account to the credit of the township?—We had a balance to our credit at the end of the year 1877 of £723 17s. 4d.

57. What were your receipts?—Car licenses, £23 1s. 9d.; rent and tolls, &c., £34 0s.; fines, £71 0s. 1d.; dog licenses, £17 17s. 1d.; miscellaneous, £83 7s. 9d.; £23 6s. 8d. Government contribution in lieu of sanitary officers' salaries. That is for 1877.

58. How did you stand last year—you borrowed no money?—Last year the balance due to the treasurer of the Hibernian Bank, at the end of the year, was £1,183; and for the year ending 31st December, 1878, the receipts were—rates, £3,667 14s. 10d.; car licenses, £29 11s. 6d.; rent and tolls, £40 6s. 3d.; fines, £108 3s. 10d.; dog licenses, £15 18s. 7d.; miscellaneous receipts, £103 16s. 1d.; which includes £44 10s. 1d. of Government contributions for salaries and rates on Government property.

59. You owed that?—Yes. The Grand Jury charge for the year was £1,163 19s. 8d.; there were law and parliamentary expenses £485 13s. 10d. that was all paid in 1878.

60. How much was it the year before for the Grand Jury?—£571 8s. 1d.

61. How could it have increased so much?—First there was £380 compensation for the value of ground taken for a road, and we had to pay three warrants that year to the county of Wicklow Grand Jury. Before that the warrants were not collected so quickly, but we had to pay all we owed that year.

62. At the time you owed the balance last year what rates were in arrear?—£2,785 1s. 6d.

63. Outstanding?—Yes.

64. Were these good rates?—Yes, except some small sums.

65. Up to what time was the balance sheet for last year made out?—Up to the last day of December.

66. When was the warrant for these rates?—In August some time.

67. What was the entire amount of the warrant?—About £4,000.

68. And how came there to be some £2,000 due?

[illegible] all, the collection was put before as quickly as it ought to have been.

69. Mr. Curzon.—What rate is the rateable value [illegible] generally speaking?—

70. Is there any land for building purposes?—Yes. The rate [illegible] £1,600 [illegible] £1,700, which I understand [illegible].

71. Chairman.—Were they entirely for grass then—Yes.

72. Mr. Edward Brodie.—From the views and [illegible] statement you have made, Mr. Chairman, anything is greatly changed, and I would be in favour of an extension of the boundary. For instance, I would be inclined to do what would develop the road [illegible]. There is the Old Connaught-avenue to Shankhill-bridge. I would take from the Old Connaught-road to Shankhill-bridge.

73. Chairman.—That is where the Old Connaught-road passes under the railway bridge?—Yes, I would ask you to take the right and left of that road; there are about twenty-three gentlemen's residences, and there is only that straight line of road, no [illegible] road at all. I think that to take this in would enhance the township, and be more beneficial to the district. It will be borne in mind that there is a very poor population in Little Bray, between 800 and 900, and they are very badly off for water. The water, in fact, has been supplied by the last summer, to be of a very [illegible] character. Now I would not go in for taking the land, except where the houses stand on, such as in the case of those detached houses. I have no doubt they [illegible] would [illegible] and [illegible] by lighting and watering. The lighting and watering is really wanted, and is sought for by several gentlemen residing along there, who are anxious to get water. They called a meeting of the Rathdown Union to [illegible] the necessity of meeting the great want of pure water.

74. Mr. Curzon.—With regard to land, would you exempt arable land altogether?—Yes, except where houses stand on.

75. You don't mean to say you would run a line around the houses?—I would take a straight line right down by the railway, down to Judge Lawson's.

76. Mr. Brodie.—What breadth of land would you take in?—I would go to the sea, and I would go to Shankhill-bridge. I would take a radius of the town, from Ravenswell. There is Lord Plunket's place, that is a large place, and I would take that in.

77. Chairman.—You go say a mile from the centre of the town, to take in Old Connaught?—Yes.

78. Are there a good number of gentlemen's seats around there within a radius of say two miles from the Post Office?—Yes.

79. Is it your opinion that these gentlemen, being adjacent to the town of Bray, derive exceptional advantages from the town, having it as a town to come to and use for the purpose of marketing, going to the railway, &c.?—Yes. You have hit upon a tender point, the market. A market is a thing wanted badly, for it takes place here at three, four in the morning.

80. Do they derive the benefit of having their places of worship in the town, and of sending their children to schools in the town?—Yes, most decidedly, and they have the full benefit of the lighting, cleansing, and so on.

81. Do you think that the occupiers of land, and the owners of land, derive exceptional advantages from their proximity to the town?—I do, most decidedly. For instance, there is Mr. Langfield, who has light to his own gate.

82. Does the land near the town pay a higher rent, say within a radius of two miles, than land farther off?—Yes, from my experience that is decidedly the case, sometimes £6 an acre.

83. In almost every place we have been, it is admitted that land within a short distance of the town derives exceptional advantages and benefit; and higher rents are paid?

Mr George Whitaker.—Not one for a radius of two miles from the town.

84. Chairman.—To what extent, Mr. Brodie, would you say the owners and occupiers of land derive exceptional advantages from their proximity to the town of Bray?—I know land at Shankhill which belongs to me at one time, and it is now [illegible] would now bring about £8.

85. Chairman.—Does the occupier make a profit out of it by having a market town so close?—Yes.

86. Mr George Whitaker.—That does not affect any [illegible] at all.

87. Mr. Brodie.—Land within a mile of the town goes up to £8 an acre. I was offered, by a [illegible] [illegible], £8 for every acre I have at [illegible]; and about a mile beyond that the land decreases in value.

88. With what distance would you say gentlemen's seats, or the owners of those places derive exceptional benefit from the town; how far would you go?—Well, I would go as far as the Glen of the Downs. Everywhere gentlemen's seats are, they derive exceptional benefit from the town of Bray. I am giving this evidence, as it were, in favour of an extension from the information I have drawn from your information. You have explained, so far as I could understand it, that the proposal is that the Town Commissioners should [illegible], if the boundaries were enlarged, the same rate as the county rate is.

89. Chairman.—I may tell you what is said elsewhere. It is not [illegible] they are brought into a municipality that entitles us I call them, are to get the benefit of all the advantages whatever it may be that are enjoyed by the present body. Am I to understand that your proposition or suggestion, would be to take in up to Shankhill and Judge Lawson's place, and that you would give them light and water?—Yes, if they required it, and they should pay for it.

90. That is if they paid the same taxes altogether that anybody living in the town does, you would give them light and water?—Yes.

91. Chairman.—It would only be the duty of the Commissioners to lay the [illegible]; it is for those who want the supply to put in the branches?—That is so.

92. Now take it this way; if there was an extension, of say a mile, or a mile and a half outside the town, would this be your view, having considered it since what I said, that the persons living in that district, within the boundary so extended, should only pay a proportion of the rates payable in the town, that is for merely lighting, watching, and cleansing the town, but that they should pay the main rates, and then, with that addition, should they choose to pay all the rates (the share of the inhabitants of the town) they should get all the advantages enjoyed by the townspeople?—Most decidedly; and that would enable the rates to be considerably reduced each year if proper management were exercised, and the Commissioners elected for the added districts would be able and in a position to look after the affairs of their respective constituencies. Good Commissioners, gentlemen of position and intelligence, would be selected.

93. The further question then would be, if you had an extension outside, and if you got from these people brought in, under it, what they pay at present, would you be able to keep them as cheaply as the County Grand Jury?—That would greatly, as far as a certain extent depend on the branch roads; that is more a question for Mr. Brodie. I think myself, to give my own personal knowledge of the roads, there is scarcely enough to keep the main roads in as proper order as one might wish to have them in.

94. Take a radius of a mile and a half, and looking this way, are there many gentlemen's residences that would be taken in?—Well, except the ground in the the Dargle, I have not considered it; but I may here mention that another great advantage it would have, would be to give the Commissioners power over all the commons, so as to establish certain rules, and to

that way to a great extent tend to develop the bounties of the place. We have no power at present beyond four miles of the post office.

95. CHAIRMAN.—Oh, well, as that would extend it beyond that.

96. Mr. Breslin.—It is a great pity there would not be some extended control over them.

97. CHAIRMAN.—Is not the boundary of Bray rather exceptional and curious?—Yes, it is extremely irregular. It goes considerably over a mile to the east and south-east.

98. And takes in a large portion of Bray Head?—I am sorry to say not a large portion, except Mr. Breslin's place. It goes about a mile and a half; at the northern side it does not go a quarter of a mile. What I would suggest is this:—I would recommend that we should go to the north of Bray Head and take in round Bray Head, coming round to Windgates, taking the whole of that, and on the north side of Bray Head out to a certain point and have a compact boundary, for I may mention that Kilruddery is overcrowded, indeed nearly all the building ground there are overcrowded, except Kilruddery.

99. Then you would, as I understand you, take in Kilruddery demesne?—Part of it. Lord Meath has been advised to take in the whole of Kilruddery. The road around Bray Head is badly kept, and it would be a great thing to have it properly kept and improvements effected. If it was in another country it would be a second Switzerland for beauty and attraction.

100. CHAIRMAN.—Is it in the hands of any one at present?—No.

101. Mr. COTTON.—Your suggestion would be to take in Bray Head or some of it near the sea, and not extend towards Kilruddery, would you extend inland at all?—There is a piece of land between the county and Bray, a piece belonging to no one, it is just between the two counties, and I would go as far as Mr. Doyle's or the Dargle gate.

102. Mr. COTTON.—You were a member of the Board in 1873?—Yes.

103. Do you remember instructions being given to Mr. Brett to prepare a report on the subject of extension of the boundaries?—Yes, that was chiefly at the instance of Lord Meath.

104. Was Mr. Brett given instructions on the subject?—Yes.

105. In the report indicated by the line marked yellow on the map?—Yes.

106. Was Mr. Brett's report, as prepared in conformity with instructions sent to him?—Yes.

107. Was any application made to the Lord Lieutenant?—No. The suggestions made were opposed by a great many.

108. Were the Commissioners unanimous on the subject?—Well, not unanimous.

109. Was any resolution adopted on the report, or what was done in it?—Yes. The Town Clerk will be able to tell you from the minutes.

110. The Town Clerk.—On the receipt of the report, I find a resolution of December 2, 1873, was passed at a meeting, Lord Meath in the chair. At that meeting the report from the Surveyor, Mr. Brett, was read on the subject of extension, and on the motion of Mr. M'Cormick, seconded by Mr. M'Neill, it was resolved—

"That Mr. Brett's report on the increase of the Bray township, just submitted by him to this Board, be printed and circulated among the ratepayers."

And at the last meeting that year it was proposed—

"That a Committee be appointed, consisting of Messrs. Breslin, [illegible], O'Neill, and [illegible], to consult with and obtain the opinions of the proprietors of the lands proposed to be added to the township of Bray, and to report upon the steps necessary to be taken for such enlargement, with the instruction that the maximum taxation shall not exceed in amount the Grand Jury cess paid at the same time by the proprietors, and that the proprietors shall not be charged for water, gas, or for sewerage, unless upon their requisition to be supplied with them. All further motion on this resolution is postponed until after the consideration of the report."

111. Mr. COTTON.—If that proposed extension was adopted, what was contemplated with regard to a subdivision or other arrangement of wards?

Mr. Breslin.—I do not recollect. As far as I remember concerning Mr. Brett's proposed extension, on making inquiries we found that a large majority of the land owners were very much opposed to it.

112. Mr. COTTON.—Has there been at any time since then any meeting of ratepayers generally?—No.

113. But they knew of it?—Yes.

114. To your own knowledge do these gentlemen occupying seats outside and their families use the town of Bray largely?—Yes, decidedly.

115. Do they drive in and go through the town to the railway and so on?—Yes, constantly. Mr. Verner now has gas and water to his very gate.

116. Mr. Wingfield.—He has not gas or water.

117. Mr. Brett.—Mr. Verner applied to us for water, and we could not give it to him. If the Commissioners were made aware of what Mr. Brett has stated they would not be opposed to the extension. What I advocate on the north side would have a large surplus. The value of the houses and out-offices along that road is large, and even getting confined on the land and full valuation of the houses, mansions and out-offices we would have a margin. We went into a calculation to show that.

118. Mr. Wingfield.—If we pay county cess, will we not, if taken in, have to pay 10d. besides?

119. CHAIRMAN.—Yes.

120. Mr. Wingfield.—And get nothing for it?

121. CHAIRMAN.—No, you get the light of the town, which is so largely used by you.

122. Mr. Wingfield.—Well, all I can say is, that so far from considering it to be of advantage, this proximity to the town that has been spoken of, I think it does not tend by any means to our benefit to be near it. It is a disadvantage instead of any advantage. We have a lot of idle people, loafers and vagabonds, running riot about the place, everything is stolen from us, and we can't trust a single man. It is nothing but robbery and dishonesty. We who are the occupiers have to pay higher for our land than if we were not near, that is the only advantage, if you can call it an advantage, to be near thieves and vagabonds. We have the whole of this dreadful population of Bray (worse than is in the world) prowling around and stealing what they can put their hands on.

123. CHAIRMAN.—I should mention to you, Mr. Wingfield, that there is a very strong opinion expressed by the Parliamentary Committee, that the rates should be distributed between the landlord and the tenant, and then the 10d. or 10½d. you pay would be only 5d. The question comes to this, ought not the people living within a certain distance of a municipal town enjoying the lighting, cleansing, keeping of the streets clean, and other advantages of the kind which they use largely, pay a share of the expenses attending them because they enjoy?—But we don't enjoy them, we would rather be without them.

124. Mr. Griffin.—I derive more advantage from Dublin than Bray, and more from London than either.

125. Mr. Verner.—I don't see the advantage of living near a place where you have to be watching every individual who comes near your house, and as to the market or cattle, why I should like to know what is the great advantage you derive from shopping here, everything is so dreadfully expensive. Indeed so expensive is it that I deal for my bread and mutton in the Queen's County.

126. CHAIRMAN.—But if you do you have to have it brought by train, and then carried along the roads to your house?—Well, yes, but then that would apply to any other part of the country.

127. Mr. COTTON.—I intended to ask you, Mr.

Breslin, are the ratepayers, as a rule, satisfied with the arrangement of the wards ?—I have not heard any objection to the contrary.

128. Do you know the number of voters in East ward ?—One hundred and eighty-seven. There has been an increase of property in East and West wards and Little Bray of £350 in last year.

BRAY. Sep. 3, 1878. Mr. Edward Dempsey.

Mr. JOHN BRUEN examined.

Mr. John Bruen.

129. CHAIRMAN.—You are a Town Commissioner of Bray ?—Yes, for fourteen or fifteen years.

130. Do you yourself own any land outside the present boundary ?—Yes, and in it.

131. Does the land outside the present town, say for a mile and a half or a mile, pay more rent in consequence of being so close to town ?—Yes, I pay £6 an acre for land.

132. Is that inside or outside the present boundary ?—Inside the boundary.

133. Have you any outside ?—Yes.

134. What is that paying ?—From £4 to £6 an acre.

135. What would land of the same quality bring were it farther off, say a mile or between that and two miles ?—About £3.

136. Is the tenant to pay that increased rent from having a market close at hand, at his very door ?—Well, yes ; from the advantages of the position of his land.

137. Does the landlord also get an advantage by being paid a larger rent by his tenant ?—Yes, quite so. Manure is near at hand, and the cows' milk is sent in and sold.

138. Does the traffic, occasioned by the persons who send in their produce in that way to the town of Bray, and bring out manure and so on, tend to injure and dirty the roads ?—Yes.

139. In your opinion should they, in justice, contribute something towards it ?—Yes.

140. What would you consider a fair rate to be put on the land ?—I would put very little on the land now.

141. But, Mr. Bruen, supposing there was a revaluation of the land, we are to suppose that whoever would do that would do it fairly and in accordance with the [illegible], would your think [illegible] the [illegible], [illegible] ought to be [illegible] ?—I think one-fourth would be enough.

142. Do you think those rates ought to be [illegible] between landlord and tenant ?—Yes.

143. Now with regard to this extended district, would you say they should continue to pay still the same road rate ?—Yes.

144. Would you add an [illegible] for the benefit they get from the town ?—Yes.

145. You heard Mr. Breslin's suggestion to go up to Judge Lawson's, and [illegible] the road that goes to the back of Old Connaught ?—I would not go much to the west at all.

146. Mr. Breslin.—I would take in Kilmurrin, and all the [illegible] there.

147. CHAIRMAN.—That is the road between Shankhill Castle and Kilmurrin ?—Yes. It is all studded with houses.

148. Suppose the lighting is not extended beyond the present town ; but, in having regard to the advantages derived by those people, what would you say to the extension running to the back of Old Connaught and those people brought in only to pay one-third, the one-fourth to be divided between the landlord and tenant, what would you say to that ?

Mr. Bruen.—I would be in favour of that.

149. Would it be your view, Mr. Bruen, to extend the boundary as suggested by Mr. Breslin ?—Yes ; and take in [illegible] Edward [illegible].

150. CHAIRMAN.—Mr. Bruen, do you know [illegible] and [illegible] Cottage ?—Yes.

151. Do you think the extension [illegible] should take in them ?—It would be too much I think.

152. Do you know Killarney Cottage ?—Yes ; that is a very small extension from the present line.

Mr. HENRY BRETT, C.E., examined.

Mr. Henry Brett, C.E.

153. CHAIRMAN.—You are county surveyor of Wicklow ?—Yes ; and the surveyor of the township.

154. Have you made any calculation as to the cost of the roads, outside the present boundary, if extended as Mr. Breslin suggested ?—No ; not beyond what is suggested in my report (produced).

155. Could the roads, as mentioned in your report, be kept by the Commissioners as cheaply as by the Grand Jury ?—Certainly.

156. Could they be kept for the county rate ?—No doubt about it ; and probably there might be some saving ?

157. Mr. COTTON.—You prepared a report, Mr. Brett, in 1873 ?—Yes.

158. What were the instructions you received when you defined that yellow boundary ?—Lord Meath and the Commissioners went over the map, and the line as marked in the map (marked yellow) was what appeared to be what the general approval seemed to point to.

159. Do you know any principle they worked upon ?—No. It was chiefly advocated by Lord Meath, who was anxious to bring in his demesne.

160. Was there any reason given why they did not go further off to the north ?—No ; but they seemed to think that by taking in the portions marked on the map they would be doing what was of advantage to the whole. It was entirely carried by Lord Meath's desire.

161. At the time they were considering it did they discuss how they should distribute the wards ?—No ; they did not enter into details at all ; the thing was allowed to drop as not being generally favourably received.

162. Suppose it was increased, as suggested by Mr. Breslin, towards Judge Lawson's, following the road to Old Connaught, could the roads be kept for the same amount ?—Yes ; there would be a considerable margin for the township.

163. Mr. GEORGE KNIGHT.—Do the Grand Jury at present make more than is requisite for the roads ?

Mr. Brett.—No.

164. Mr. Knight.—How then if the Grand Jury, as I presume they do, only strike sufficient for the roads and county-at-large charges—how do you make out that there is a margin, or that there would be a margin if it was taken away from the Grand Jury ?—I mean the Grand Jury of the county of Dublin.

165. Taking in Wicklow 1s. 9d., or 1s. 6d. to be amply and simply sufficient for the maintenance of the roads and the county-at-large charges, how do you make out that if you take away the Grand Jury and substitute the Commissioners there will be a saving and a large margin of profit to the Commissioners ?—Because the proportion of the valuation in this portion of the township is larger than the rural portion of the barony. The valuation of the part of the county proposed to be added on the Wicklow side is £4,775, the county cess payable out of which at 1s. 9d. in the pound, £398, and the road charge applicable thereto, £174, and county-at-large proportion about £110 (£224). There is a clear gain of £110 to the township

BRAY.
May 5, 1879.
Mr. Henry Brett, C.E.

in this way; this district which is highly valued and has but a limited road charge has to pay for the roads in the distant parts of the barony, where the valuation is small and the road charge large; the same rule applies to the Dublin side where we propose to add in a district, the value of which is about £9,000, and the county cess payable at present is about £700 per annum, the road charge thereout would be about £200, and charge on county-at-large about £150, making a total outlay of £350 and showing a clear gain to the township of an equal sum, and this is caused by the like circumstance as on the Wicklow side, namely, that the highly valued lands near Bray have to pay for the remote districts of the barony of Rathdown.

166. But once you go outside the present boundary does it not then become just the same as the rest of the rural district?—No; for the first mile or so the value is increased, and then it decreases until you go to the extreme end of the county.

167. Mr. *Keogh*.—How much an acre is the land valued at between the present boundary—half way between the present boundary and Sir George Hodson's demesne and the land of Mr. Le Touche?—As a general rule the land within a mile of the town is valued at double what it is at Delgany.

168. Could you tell us what the value is per acre above Mr. Wingfield's and Sir George Hodson's?—No. I could give you general results.

169. Mr. *Keogh*.—Well now Mr. Brett, has the township had funds to light even the roads within the township—at the present moment are they all lighted?—They have not sufficient funds to make all the improvements that might be deemed necessary or advisable.

170. Take one matter, take lighting, is there a single lamp beyond the Herbert Road—is the Herbert Road all lighted in fact?—No.

171. Well now take the portion between my gate and Mr. Wingfield's—the township boundary comes to the corner of Mr. Wingfield's land—is there a lamp in that place?—No. I think there ought to be a lamp there.

172. There are none on the Herbert Road?—No. There are none as far as it is built on.

173. Mr. *Breslin*.—The reason we did not do this was because it was only this month we got the money.

174. Mr. *Wingfield*.—Mr. Keogh might go further and ask as to the lamps near ————?

175. Mr. *Brett*.—I may mention that the object of that report was to enable the Commissioners to procure larger funds and distribute them over a larger area.

176. Mr. *Keogh*.—Is it not a fact that the chief object municipal corporations and commissioners are created for is to give municipal benefits, is not that so?—Yes, and when there is a small or limited area of jurisdiction, you cannot carry out all that is required except gradually. It would be different if you had a large rated area like Kingstown, but here where there is a limited area it is different.

177. CHAIRMAN.—What you mean by limited is as to funds?—Yes.

178. Mr. *Keogh*.—Well what municipal object would there be secured by taking in a number of square miles—if you are unable to do to your satisfaction the work required by the existing area—except to become road makers?—There would be advantages such as lighting great county roads, jurisdiction over nuisances and so on.

179. Mr. *Keogh*.—Jurisdiction over nuisances; they have that as far as they are likely to get it, and as for lighting, if the extension were made to say Shankhill would you contemplate having a row of lamps like Sackville-street?—No, certainly not like Sackville-street.

180. Would the 10*d*. pay for painting the lamps alone to say nothing of anything else?—Yes, for the gas company would be glad to lay the mains and contribute to portion of the expenses.

181. Was there not a good deal of difficulty in getting them to lay down the mains, because there was not enough of custom except in respect of the street lamps. On the road in the direction of Mr. Wingfield's, I believe there is no one takes the gas except myself, they all refuse?—I am not aware of that, but I suppose it is because the gas company asked them to contribute towards the mains.

182. Mr. *Wingfield*.—There was a proposal some time ago made, that each person should take a certain quantity of gas, but although it was laid before the gas company, so little did they think about it that they did not even answer the letter.

183. Mr. *Keogh*.—The gas company told me there was no one to take the gas.

184. Mr. *Brett*.—I would not recommend an extension, unless funds were given to those brought in.

185. Mr. CORRIGAN.—Is the lighting perfect now to the boundary of the township?—No.

186. Is that because of not having rates sufficient for the purpose?—Yes.

187. If there was additional money and funds to complete the lighting, and if it was continued and perfected to the limits of the boundary, would not the people outside be benefited and interested in it, even if the lighting was not continued beyond the limits of the existing boundary?—Yes.

188. Mr. *Keogh*.—Do you not consider, that the people living outside and who come into the town of Bray and make purchases there, confer benefit upon the shopkeepers?

Mr. *Brett*.—The town benefits the people outside, and the people outside to a certain extent may be said to benefit the town.

189. Mr. *Keogh*.—Is not one a fair set-off against the other?—There is certainly what might be called a mutuality of interest.

190. CHAIRMAN.—Should there not also be some mutuality of contribution? Now take this case Mr. Keogh, you are situated close to Mr. Wingfield's place, you are taxed for keeping up the township and so on, now suppose (instance) of Mr. Wingfield's being a couple of hundred yards from the boundary, he was put at it on the other side of the road, would you then think it right or fair that he should not contribute?—My answer to that is this; I think the question might go on ad infinitum. There must be some one who just adjoins the place that is within the boundary.

191. Yes, and that appears to be the very thing which led the Select Committee to see the great necessity for some revision of the existing boundaries, and of having this inquiry. The existing condition of affairs pointed to the necessity of a general inquiry into the question. In many towns the recommendation and resolution of the Commissioners was that there should be an extension of two miles, or a mile and a half or a mile radius and so on; the reason for that was stated to be that the land around derived exceptional benefit from its proximity to the town; that the occupier was able to pay a higher rent having a ready market at hand and facilities for procuring manure and other advantages, and that the landlord had a large benefit because he derived perhaps double the rent he would get if his land similar in quality was three or four miles off.

192. Mr. *Keogh*.—All I can say is that the town of Bray ought not to be extended, no matter what the Select Committee thinks. The Commissioners have not money to light within the township, and it would be wrong to give them a larger area and without any more money to work it.

Bray. May 1, 18[illegible]. — Mr. Charles Dufresne.

Mr. Charles Dufresne examined.

193. How long have you been a Town Commissioner?—Since 1871.

194. Are you a large ratepayer in the town?—Yes.

195. What is your view as to extension?—That land to be brought in should only pay one-fourth of the improvement rate, and the same county rate, the land remaining, as you have expressed it, only being changed. I believe as to gas and water being supplied to the districts to be added to the town, that it would ruin the township if it were made compulsory on the Commissioners to do so. There is an immense deal that could be done in the way of improvement to the district; in fact, Bray could well be made, and ought to be made, the first watering place in the country, if not in the kingdom. A nice walk could be made around Bray Head. This place is frequented by strangers, tourists, and a great number of "cheap trippers," as they are called, and everything ought to be done to develop the natural beauties of the district.

196. Chairman.—Is it your opinion that for a distance of say a mile or mile and a half outside the town the owners of land and houses derive exceptional benefit?—It is my opinion.

197. Is the letting value greater on account of being near to the town?—Yes.

198. You would not think of bringing in these places outside at one-fourth and supplying them with gas?—No.

199. But do you think they should fairly pay something even though they did not get anything more than they have at present?—I think it would be only fair that they should pay something considering the benefits they even now receive, and that the roads would probably be kept in better order than at present.

200. What is your idea of the rates to be paid—would you put one half on the landlord?—Yes.

201. Mr. Cotton.—I want to ask the Town Clerk was Bray under the Towns Improvement Act?—Yes; the first meeting was on the 5th of November, 1867.

202. Mr. De Fresne, were you a Town Commissioner when Mr. Brett was instructed to prepare his report?—Yes; that was in 1872.

203. Were you opposed to the extension then proposed?—I was, and for this reason it would have entailed great expense, we would have had to go for a new Act of Parliament, at a cost of £3,000, and we were not prepared to pay that. I was very much opposed on the ground of expense.

Mr. Joseph Burke.

Mr. Joseph Burke examined.

204. Chairman.—How long have you been a Town Commissioner?—Since the commencement.

205. You heard Mr. Brodie's observations?—No; unfortunately I did not.

206. Do you think the boundary ought to be extended at all?—I do think there ought to be an extension to take in the north side and join Ballybrack. I would have it to join Ballybrack township.

207. Do you know the road at Old Connaught?—Yes.

208. Mr. Brodie suggested to have that road as a boundary?—Yes.

209. Would that be advisable do you think?—Yes, I think it would be very well to take that.

210. Do you know the neighbourhood of Bray well?—Yes.

211. Now, for a distance of say a mile and a half round the town, in your opinion is land more valuable because of its being so close to the town?—Well, not more than in the town.

212. Yes, but it is more valuable than land would be two or three miles off?—Yes.

213. From being so close to the town?—Yes.

214. Do people keep dairy cattle, and so on, and bring in milk and butter to Bray?—Yes.

215. And take manure away and get it more easily?—Yes.

216. Do the landlords get a larger rent?—Yes.

217. Do they get more than they would if the land were three miles away?—Yes, considerably more.

218. With regard to taxes, would it be fair to make them pay, at all events, one fourth towards cleansing and lighting, and so on?—I think it would not be too much.

219. Mr. Wingfield.—Mr. Burke, do you think it of advantage that in addition to paying more rent for the land you should be charged another 10d. in the pound for the advantage of being asked to pay a high rent?—I don't understand.

220. You pay a higher rent because you are near the town?—Yes.

221. And is that any reason why there should be additional taxation put on the person who pays that. If I pay a higher rent for my land, is that any reason why I should pay a higher taxation?—No, unless you get some consideration for it.

Mr. Columba Dunne.

Mr. Columba Dunne examined.

222. Chairman.—Where do you live?—On the Old Dargle-road. I would like to get out of the boundary.

223. You are in the boundary then?—Yes.

224. Would you prefer that the borough was made smaller?—Yes, because they are really doing nothing, and you are in danger of your life in walking on the footpath. There is no gas or sewerage, there are some houses on it built two feet or so over the road, and they are in a terrible state from the bad drainage.

225. Mr. Brodie.—Did you send in a report to the Commissioners?—I complained to the Inspector of Nuisances.

226. The Town Clerk.—The sewerage is now provided for.

227. Mr. Dunne.—I would not come before them with complaints because they had not the money; but now they have the money, and there is nothing done [illegible].

228. Chairman.—Well, suppose they do all that you require and bring out the gas, what is your notion about extending the boundary?—I am not well made up on it, but I heard tradesmen say they would be very sorry there was an extension. There are not many gentry's places about, and the shopkeepers receive as much benefit from the gentlemen around as they do from the town.

229. Chairman.—Mr. Brodie says he would go as far as Judge Lawson's—he is anxious to be brought in.

230. Mr. Ryall.—Why should other people pay for that?

231. Chairman.—Mr. Brett says, "we can keep the roads and make money of them—we will keep these roads better than at present;" he says that from his experience he will be able to do that, and do it at less expense than it costs the Grand Jury at present, and the difference will come in aid of the town.

232. Mr. Ryall.—I don't see why an existing tax should be raised to give a bonus to the town which the landowners outside will have to pay.

233. Chairman.—The saving which would take place according to Mr. Brett, would, of course, go to

Bray. May 8, 18[illegible]. Mr. Colum[illegible] Pearse.

the general rates. The parties to be brought in would be getting the benefit of the surplus. In fact as the rates would be reduced the outsiders would be getting the benefit of it.

234. Mr. *Wingfield*.—But would they do that—would the Commissioners do that?

235. CHAIRMAN.—Certainly, if there was a surplus.

236. Mr. *Ryall*.—They would spend as much as they could.

237. CHAIRMAN.—Well, they cannot spend more than 5s. 6d. as the law now stands.

Mr. R. B. Wingfield, J.P.

Mr. R. B. WINGFIELD, J.P., examined.

238. CHAIRMAN.—You think the boundaries ought not to be extended?—I think they ought not. I don't think the business of the township has been so well managed as to make it at all desirable that the people outside should be brought in.

239. But if you were to extend the town in the way it has been suggested, would you not get a great number of very wealthy gentlemen to come in as Commissioners and take their seats here?—I quite disagree with you. There are very few outside who would be Commissioners, who would be able to find time for the duties; and with the present franchise under the 13th section of the Bray Act, you will never get any gentlemen appointed. You can't do it. You will never have any different class of Commissioners from what there are at present.

240. Mr. *Brodie*.—Surely if your ward is formed it is your own party would vote you in, then the other wards would have nothing to do with it. You would be sure to be taken in.

241. CHAIRMAN.—Suppose there was an extension would you form the new district into separate wards?—It would greatly depend upon what the new district is. The extension to the north should be a separate ward, but any extension to the south would not be enough. It has been shown that East ward returns nine representatives, Little Bray, three, and West ward, three?—Yes.

242. Now what would you say to this arrangement of the wards. Suppose this extension towards the north and whatever was taken in there was formed into one separate ward, and if there were still to be fifteen town councillors, then the East ward could be reduced by three, the new ward would have three, and Little Bray and West ward three.

243. That would be an advantage?—I think, however, there are very few of the gentry who would have time to join the Commissioners' body. Down by the sea in that East ward there are a number of gentlemen, who would be very good Commissioners, but not one of them would have the time to spare to devote to the duties.

244. Well, I hope you would be able to get gentlemen who would take sufficient interest in the district. In Rathmines the Commissioners meet regularly at nine o'clock, and yet they are all business men.

245. Mr. *Wingfield*.—But there are the difference of time in getting in, you must allow for that. No doubt there are gentlemen who might meet if they chose to do so. When there is an election of Commissioners, very few of them take any trouble about voting or anything connected with it.

246. Mr. *Brodie*.—The men you speak of are gentlemen who just come down here to live here in the summer.

247. Mr. *Wingfield*.—Yes, but they have their houses permanently.

248. Mr. *Brodie*.—In the rural districts you will find plenty of gentlemen to come as Commissioners to keep down the rates, and it would infuse new blood into the Council, and bring the Board to the state it ought to have.

249. CHAIRMAN.—You know, Mr. Wingfield, that the boundary goes at present to the north, to Oak Abbey?—Yes.

250. Does not the owner of Oak Abbey get great benefit from the light of the lamps up there?—Well, I don't know that he does—he might perhaps if he was going in and out constantly to Bray, but I think the people there have very little communication with Bray.

251. Mr. *Brodie*.—Take the case of Sir John Ribton's place, where they are anxious to get the water up.

252. CHAIRMAN.—Take the case of Wilford House and Palermo, would not a larger rent be got for these places from being near Bray?—Yes.

253. Should they not, in your opinion, contribute something towards keeping up Bray?—Well, I think perhaps the owners might, but I don't see that because a man hires a house there and pays a higher rent for it from its being near to Bray, it is any advantage to him. The only advantage to him is from being near to Dublin.

254. He goes to the station at Bray, and uses the streets of the town?—No, he would probably go to Shankhill.

255. Mr. O[illegible].—May I ask you, Mr. Brodie, does your agreement with the Corporation of Dublin enable you to compel them to supply an extended area?—No, we cannot supply anyone with water except with their assent. We have got the water on very reasonable terms from the Corporation, and they are willing and anxious to extend their mains wherever it is required. I believe Mr. Ryall has the supply.

256. Mr. *Wingfield*.—They allow you to tap the main on its way.

257. Mr. *Dufresne*.—The gentlemen who would be elected would be most certainly anxious to come to see that their interests are preserved and properly represented. They would be greatly interested with regard to the roads, and would manage the work well, besides being vitally interested in keeping down the rates.

Sir George Hodson.

Sir GEORGE HODSON examined.

258. I live a good deal outside, and have a small property inside, and wanted to mention to you that that property has been acquired in the Landed Estates Court. As it stood then under the Grand Jury, my payments under the Grand Jury system were £3 5s. to £4, including all. Since then I have got Vartry water and light, both very defective. As to the Vartry the supply is very irregular, we sometimes have the water and sometimes not—not always. In the summer before last things went to such a pitch that I was required by the tenant to put in a force pump in order to secure a supply. That cost £40. The difference to which I wished to call your attention was the rise from paying £3 15s. to £4 under the old system to paying £21 4s., and on one occasion £13 [illegible] under the present system. You can't, under these circumstances, be surprised at my wish not to be included in the proposed area.

259. CHAIRMAN.—But, Sir George, this property of yours, to which you refer, is in the township as I am informed?—Yes.

260. Do you then suggest that the boundaries be altered by curtailing them?—I don't do that, for that is out of the question, but I would not like to have the taxation on my own property increased, for it is vastly in excess of what it was under the old system. My valuation is £75.

261. Mr. *Brett*.—You have improved it very much.

[illegible]

[illegible]

The inquiry terminated.

Carrick-on-Suir. March 10, 1879. Mr. William Harding.

CARRICK-ON-SUIR, MARCH 10TH, 1879.

(Before Mr. EXHAM, Q.C.)

Mr. WILLIAM HARDING, Clerk to the Town Commissioners, examined.

1. The town is under the Town Improvement Act?—Yes, since the year 1855.

2. Was it adopted then for everything?—Yes.

3. How were your boundaries settled then, was it by an order published in the *Gazette*, and have you got a copy of it?—I am sure we got it, but I was not Town Clerk then.

4. What is the area of the town?—It is 2,160A. 2R. 16P.

5. How many townlands are in that?—Between townlands and parts of townlands, fourteen, and there is a separate valuation made for the telegraph wires, which extend over several townlands.

6. How many of these townlands are partly in and out of the town?—There are seven townlands entirely in, and the rest are partly in.

7. What is the farthest extent of the boundary from the centre of the town?—From the Butter market, the farthest extent is about two statute miles to the east; about one statute mile to the west; and to the north and south, it is within a stone's-throw, I might almost say, for the boundary does not extend at all out of the town, either to the north or south; on the south, the boundary is about 600 yards from the river, which runs through the town. There are about 320 statute acres of the town in the county Waterford.

8. What is the population?—In 1871 it was 7,792.

9. Are there wards in the town?—Yes, two wards—Carrick-on-Suir in Tipperary and Carrickbeg ward in Waterford.

10. What is the valuation of each ward?—Carrick-on-Suir is £7,305 1s., and Carrickbeg is £1,541 1s.

11. Is the whole town in one electoral division?—No. It is in three electoral divisions—one, Carrick-on-Suir, on the Carrick-on-Suir side; two electoral divisions—Carrickbeg and Fenough—on the Carrickbeg side.

12. How much of the municipal area is in each electoral division?—163 acres in Carrickbeg electoral division, and 103 acres in Fenough.

13. What is the valuation of each of them?—£873 17s. in Carrickbeg, and £115 5s. in Fenough.

14. How many Commissioners are there in the town?—Twelve for Carrick-on-Suir and three for Carrickbeg.

15. Are there poor law wards here?—No.

16. Are the guardians elected off the entire electoral division?—Yes.

17. And the same way in Carrickbeg?—Yes.

18. Are the wards here considered satisfactory, or is it suggested there should be any alteration in them?—Not in the wards, but as regards extension of the area, alteration is suggested.

19. As regards extension of the area, have the Commissioners met to consider the subject?—They did meet on one occasion specially on the subject.

20. Was that when our queries were sent down?—Yes. On the 15th January there was a special meeting convened to consider them, and they came to a resolution that it was not desirable to have any extension; but when I received an intimation from you that you intended to sit here, there was another resolution passed to convene a meeting last Friday.

21. Was that a meeting of the Town Commissioners only or of the people as well?—Of the Commissioners only at both meetings. They came to this resolution at the last meeting:—"Resolved that the resolution of the 15th January last about the boundary be and it is hereby rescinded. And that our clerk be directed to convey to the Boundary Commissioners, on Monday next, that we are desirous to have a rectification of our present optic[illegible] limits, but to what extent we leave it to the Boundary Commissioners after any [illegible] or other manner to recommend as they may think proper."

22. Was that an unanimous resolution?—Yes.

23. How many Commissioners were present at the meeting?—Six, and when the resolution of the 15th January was passed there were seven Commissioners present. The resolution of the 15th January was as follows:—

"That in reply to the queries of the Municipal Boundaries Commissioners they be informed that we do not consider it desirable to make any alteration in the present municipal boundary."

24. Do you know to what extent the Commissioners recommend there should be an alteration?—I do not. At the first meeting they had a map, and the land surveyor attended, and he pointed out the two electoral divisions of Carrick-on-Suir and Carrickbeg, and then they pointed out another boundary more limited, but the resolution they arrived at, on looking at both boundaries submitted to them, apart from the present municipal boundary, was that resolution of the 15th January last. They then thought it was not desirable to alter the boundary. What I mean to convey is that on the 15th January there was a special meeting convened and the two electoral divisions of Carrick-on-Suir and Carrickbeg were submitted to them for consideration as to whether they would recommend an extension, or not to take in the whole of those electoral divisions.

25. Mr. *Richard O'Donnell* (Chairman of the Town Commissioners).—The object of the meeting was to inquire whether we should have any extension or not.

26. Do you mean to include the whole of the electoral divisions of Carrick-on-Suir and Carrickbeg?—Yes.

27. Mr. *William Harding* (Town Clerk).—The meeting, after seeing the boundaries submitted through these maps, came to the resolution of the 15th January that it was not desirable to have any alteration.

28. When they came to the conclusion the other day that there should be extension, did they say to what extent?—No; they left it to the Commissioners.

29. Mr. *O'Donnell*.—The original resolution was passed on this basis. We got the surveyor to make an estimate of the valuation of the two electoral divisions, and also of what the additional taxation would be on the valuation of the outlying districts within the electoral division, and we found upon a calculation of the acreage and the Poor Law valuation that the income we could gain by the extension would be £90 a year, inasmuch as there are no houses or villas, and all we could gain would be whatever we could get at the rate of 1s. in the pound on the extreme valuation, but we knew nothing of the extra charges that might be on the extension, and we came to the general conclusion that it was better to leave matters as they were. At the same time there is an irregularity in the present boundary. We gain nothing by the extension, and we were under the impression we might be at expense, which would more than counteract the benefit to be obtained, and one of the Commissioners came here afterwards and seemed rather angry that such a thing should have been passed behind his back, and he moved that the resolution be rescinded. I objected to that except by notice, and then there was notice given for an adjourned meeting, to have the resolution rescinded, and there were five or six here, and they passed the resolution. That is the whole history of the matter.

30. To what extent does the electoral division of Carrick-on-Suir extend beyond the present municipal boundary?—It contains 5,185A. 2R. 21P. Carrickbeg

[illegible] Mar. 20, 1878. Mr. O'Donnell.

contains 1,039A. 0R. 39P., and [illegible] contains 1,673A. 0R. 35P.

31. Do these electoral divisions extend in some places four or five miles from the town?—Yes. Very nearly four Irish miles.

32. When you speak of rectifying the boundary, would you think of taking some of it off?—No. The boundaries took a turn and [illegible] my place in. In about two years after we came under the operation of the Towns Improvement Act; there was a memorial sent to the Government for the purpose of having the area extended, but they refused to entertain it.

33. On what grounds?—They gave no grounds, but simply refused to entertain it.

34. Do you consider the boundary towards the north and the east a fair one?—The east is [illegible] in comparison to the west. We derive no benefit from extending the boundary. What we wanted was to have an official boundary on the Ordnance map which would bring in the two electoral divisions.

35. But you don't mean to bring in the whole of the electoral divisions?—Yes; that was what was proposed, making altogether about 19,300 acres instead of 2,300, which we have at present.

36. Surely you would not be in favour of that?—I would not favour that at all. On the 9th April, 1858, the Commissioners proposed to extend the boundaries, but not so much, and the Government at that time refused. On the 14th May, 1858, a letter was written from the *Chief Secretary's* office that the Lord Lieutenant did not approve of the extension of the boundary, and then it was resolved—

"That the clerk be directed to write to the Chief Secretary to express the disappointment of the Commissioners at the conclusion the Lord Lieutenant had come to of not altering the boundaries, and they are satisfied that it will give great dissatisfaction to the ratepayers generally if the present boundaries be not altered, as it appears there was a mistake made in the survey of the present boundaries and the measure would not originally have been carried out even within the present boundaries but that the professional gentleman engaged for the old Commissioners, and who was also conducting the arrangements for the adoption of the new Act, pledged himself publicly in open court that the boundaries would be so extended, and then he was [illegible] so to act by a large number of the ratepayers, as also by many of the parties who have since been elected to that office, upon which pledge all opposition to the introduction of the measure was withdrawn."

37. Then the boundary has continued the same ever since?—Yes.

38. What was the boundary then proposed?—There was a map attached to the memorial which is not here. They are now indifferent on the subject here and they don't care what is done.

39. Was it ever considered that if you became the urban sanitary authority you should take up the management of the roads?—No; we refused to do anything of the kind. What we wish to do is to let well enough alone. We don't want to increase any burden upon us, for our taxes are very trifling.

40. What is your rate?—1s. in the pound improvement rate.

41. And the sanitary rate?—Nothing, we have done away with that for the present.

42. You have a tax of 1d. for keeping up the Green?—Yes; the tax for the Park is 1d.; our sanitary rate is 3d., and our general purposes 8d.

43. You keep within the shilling?—Yes. It is a poor district and a poor town, and we can't afford it. We must keep within it. We are trying as well as we can to keep out of debt and to nurse our little funds; and the only question would be whether it would be desirable to increase it to any extent and to bring in those lands to pay one-fourth; but the area is so large, it would be about 10,000 acres, and if any subsequent legislation should bring those places within our compass here it is hard to know where it would end, if we are to supply officers and inspection and all that.

44. You are the urban sanitary authority at present?—Not for those districts at present.

45. But within the boundary you are?—Yes; and if we had that increased district it would be a very serious thing.

46. Those districts now pay the full sanitary rate, and half is deducted from the landlord, and if they come into the town they only pay one-fourth so that it would be better for them to come in?—We don't want to be burdened with them at all—we don't know where it would end. What we would rather do is to get something that would give us an income quite irrespective of that. We are anxious to get up a better market here, which would be of vital importance to us, as it would give us an additional income of about £300 a year.

47. I would like to know whether you could suggest what the increase would be?—These gentlemen do not suggest any increase, though they thought rectification would be desirable and they left it to the Commissioners.

48. But rectification might mean decreasing the boundary and not increasing?—Yes.

49. Did any of them, as far as you know, go in for diminution of the boundary anywhere?—No.

50. Then it was a rectification by increasing?

51. Mr. *Hewitson* (Town Clerk).—What I gleaned from them would be something like this, to increase the boundary all round to its present extreme limit, so that it should be the same distance in each way.

52. Mr. *O'Donnell*.—You see how indifferent these gentlemen are on the subject, for not one of them came here to-day. These valuable pasture lands, the grass of which is set for £5 an acre, don't extend more than a mile round the town.

53. Do they extend a mile to the north and a mile to the south?—No; some lands are far inferior. Only part of [illegible] would produce that, because the hill intervenes, and there is bad land; but on the [illegible] side the land about the town will set for £5 an acre.

54. They are in the town at present?—Yes.

55. Is it your opinion that land outside the town is of exceptional value?—Certainly. There are lands outside the town which, if they were two miles further off, would not be worth more than half what they are paying at present.

56. Is that from their proximity to the town as a market town?—Yes.

57. Do you think they should pay something towards the keeping up of the town?—No doubt about it. They derive more benefit than the townspeople themselves, for they have the benefit when they come in, and they have a market here, and the closer the market is the less the expense of bringing the produce in, so that they have the advantage of being within a quarter of a mile or half an hour of the market.

58. Do you think, in view of that, that you might safely take in an area of two miles round the town?—I think that would be too far.

59. Would you say a mile and a half?—I think you might fairly go to that distance taking the matter in that point of view.

60. Whether they paid half or one-fourth, would you make the landlord pay half of that?—I would not say how much, but I think they should pay something. My impression is that the landlord derives more benefit from the proximity of his lands to the town than the occupier does.

61. The same thing has been said everywhere, namely, that the person who gets the greatest benefit is the landlord. Do you agree in that opinion?—Yes.

62. If that is so, is it your opinion that he should pay for all that?—I would not venture to say that, but I go upon the principle that he should pay something. I think you should examine Mr. Harding on that question as a land agent, and not merely as one of our officers.

63. Suppose the area was extended to the extent you

CARRICK-ON-SUIR. Mar. 15, 1879. Mr. O'Donnell.

suggest, would there be any difficulty in the Town Commissioners managing the sanitary portion of the work?—That is the difficulty I see all through, that it would involve us in expense which our present funds would not enable us to carry out, but if we got an increase it would be different.

64. With regard to the expense of any sanitary works, you have power to strike an additional sanitary rate?—Yes; but we have a very poor district, and unless we got the help of the landlord, we would not be able to do it, and any addition from extension of the area would be no use to us if we had corresponding liabilities.

65. Certainly not, but would not the sanitary management be very little?—You would have to pay additional to your medical officers, and inspectors, and sub-sanitary officers.

66. Yes, but the ratepayers in the extended district would have to pay that?—Yes, certainly, but we are obliged to regulate our funds very economically. They are very small, and up to the present we have kept out of debt. There is scarcely a little community in Ireland that has so well kept itself clear of liabilities with the little means we have.

67. Of course, I understand that it is not proposed to give these outlying districts any benefit of lighting which you have at present, and that is the reason you propose to make them pay one-fourth or one-half?—Yes, but how would they be affected as regards cleansing.

68. As regards that I suppose unless you took up the roads there would be no cleansing other than for sanitary purposes?—Suppose we got this increased area into our charge and that we taxed it, would we be liable to be called upon by any person in that area to keep the roads clean?

69. That is for the legislature afterwards, and at present we could not say as to that?—I apprehend we might be called upon by any person outside the present boundary who might be brought in, to keep these roads clean notwithstanding that we are not severed from the county. That is a very serious thing for a small community.

70. I take your view to be that if they are brought in they should be brought in paying a portion, whether a fourth or a half, and that they should not get light?—My individual opinion is that if we are to supply them with equal benefits to the town they should be equally taxed.

71. I was putting it in the same way. You could not light these outlying districts for it would cost too much, and they don't want it, and your view is that if they are brought in on a differential rate, it is to be on the understanding that they are not to get the benefit of lighting, and that you are not to be bound to clean these roads outside the present district, but that they should remain with the county as at present for cleansing purposes?—Yes. We object—this is my own individual opinion, and, I believe, the opinion of the other Commissioners also—we object to be separated from the county.

72. You want to remain attached to the county for all road and county purposes?—Yes; but we ought to have the management of our internal affairs. That is what we complain of most. A man may charge by weight or measurement, or whatever he likes, and we have no control whatever.

73. Do you consider it would be more important to get the management of the market than to obtain this extension?—Yes. We would sooner have the management of the market than any extension.

74. Who has the management of the market here?—There is no control over the butter market at all.

75. Who keeps it?—A man named Boyd, who was appointed by the assistant barrister about twelve or fourteen years ago.

76. What does he do with the tolls?—He pockets them, and we want the butter market to be put under our control, and we want to have sworn tasters and weighers. There is no confidence in the market, and £10,000 or £15,000 a year of the butter goes away to the Waterford market. If that butter was sold here it would be better for the town.

77. Would you get the toll on it if it was sold here?—Yes. We would get threepence in the pound to the benefit of the town.

Mr. HARKNESS, Town Clerk, examined.

78. Are you a land agent?—Yes, to some extent.

79. Do you know the value of land near the town?—Yes.

80. Can you say whether land within an area of two statute miles from the centre of the town is more valuable and pays a higher rent than land three miles off?—Yes, it does.

81. To what extent would you say?—I say that land within the two miles area is well worth £4 an acre, and land similar in quality if three miles off is only worth from 30s. an acre to £2.

82. For the same quality of land?—Yes, and the grazing land would be worth £5 an acre. The people within that district use the town largely for selling their produce and buying goods, and getting manure and everything in that way. They also use the schools for their children, and come in to attend their places of worship, and in many other ways they enjoy the town just the same as the people in it.

83. Do they take the advantage of lighting in that way?—I can't say that, because it doesn't extend much.

84. During the winter months, when it is dark here in the evenings, do they get the benefit of the lighting as far as it goes?—Certainly.

85. Suppose you gave them nothing except the benefit they derive themselves from their proximity to the town, how much do you think they should pay towards the keeping of the town—would you say one-fourth, or one-third, or one-half?—At present my land is—it pays only one-fourth.

86. Is that too little for them to pay to the town?—I think they should pay at least half.

87. Do you think that the half of that should be paid by the landlord?—Certainly.

88. So you would make them pay half, and if the landlord paid half of that, they would only have one-fourth to pay?—Yes.

89. Because if it is a fact that the landlord gets £5 an acre for land for which he would only get £3 if it was further off, he has the benefit to the extent of £2 by reason of his proximity to the town, and the landlord should pay something?—Certainly.

90. Following out that principle, would you think it fair that, within an area of about two statute miles of the town, the boundary ought to be extended, keeping to townland boundaries as near as possible?—I do.

91. Would that go beyond the present electoral division boundary?—No.

92. Mr. *O'Donnell*.—Perhaps that would be too far, some of the Carrickbeg land is not worth more than £1 an acre.

93. If it is only worth £1 an acre it is only valued at that amount, and if it is to pay on the valuation it only pays its proportion according to its value?—I am speaking of the benefits derived by the landlord.

94. Well, that man whose land is only valued at £1 would have to pay threepence, whereas the man whose land is valued at £4 would have to pay a shilling?—But throughout Ireland we find the bad land is valued too high, and the good land too low.

95. Mr. Howard's view is that within that area they should pay half. Is it your view that they should pay one-fourth, but that in either case the landlord should contribute half?—Yes.

Mr. John [illegible] examined.

Carrick-on-Suir. Jan. 16, 18— Mr. John [illegible].

96. I am under agent to Lord Bessborough, and I [illegible] outside the town.

97. Would a good deal of Lord Bessborough's land be affected by this?—No.

98. Do you know the town well?—Yes, I am here every Saturday.

99. Do you think it would be fair that the owners of property and occupiers within a certain district should contribute?—I don't think the county derives much benefit from the town. There are not many advantages to be got in this town. I don't see any advantage to our part of the county except coming in to an odd market. For business the best market is Waterford. I am outside the two miles; and I have nothing to say to the matter.

Mr. Hargrave, Town Clerk, recalled.

Mr. Harding.

100. Suppose there is an extension, what would you say as to the wards?—I suppose any extension on the Carrickbeg side should go to the Carrickbeg ward, and the same way with the other ward.—I suppose so.

101. Would there be any further modification of the wards necessary?—No.

102. How many people would be brought in as voters by the proposed extension?—Not many, because it would be principally land that would be brought in.

Mr. James Wallace examined.

Mr. James Wallace.

103. I am one of the Town Commissioners of Carrick-on-Suir. The boundaries of the town are in my opinion too limited and irregular, and they require extension. I would be for going for an extension of about two miles from the centre of the town, keeping to the townland boundaries as near as possible. The land within that area is much dearer than land of the same quality about three miles out. The persons holding land within that area use the town very extensively for buying and selling, and they are enabled in that way to pay a higher rent for the land than they otherwise would. The landlord gets the benefit too, and I think it would be fair that the people holding that land should pay one-half the taxation that the town-people pay, even without getting any benefit from the lighting of the town or watering. In my opinion the taxes which they should pay should be further divided, and paid half by the landlord and half by the tenant. I think that if the town is extended the extension at the Tipperary side should be added to the Carrick-on-Suir ward, and the extension at the Waterford side should be added to the Carrickbeg ward. I would be brought in for land I hold, but I would not object on that ground as I think it is fair. I do not think it would be any advantage that the Town Commissioners should acquire the management of the roads from the Grand Jury. We are satisfied with the way the roads are kept, and I don't think we could keep them so economically. Whatever district is added should be apportioned to the two existing wards. No further alteration of the wards is desirable or necessary.

Mr. Thomas J. [illegible] examined.

Mr. Thomas J. [illegible].

104. I am one of the Commissioners of Carrick-on-Suir. I think the boundaries are too contracted, and very irregular; they require to be extended, and I think they should be extended to the extent of two miles from the centre of the town, following townland boundaries as near as possible. I know of my own knowledge that land within that area pays a considerably higher rent than lands about three miles further from the town, though they are of the same quality. The increased value is caused by their proximity to the town. The tenants who occupy those lands make as much use of the town as those who live in the town; they buy manure in the town, and everything, in fact, they want; they sell their produce daily, to a large amount, in the town, and derive considerable profit from it; and they are thereby enabled to pay a larger rent than they would otherwise do. They also have the benefit of the lighting of the town, and of its arrangements. I think, in fairness, they should pay one half of the improvement rate in the town, and that what they then pay should be divided between the landlord and tenant, as the landlord derives a much higher rent from their lands than he otherwise would. I don't think it would be any advantage to give the Commissioners the management of the roads, which are now in the hands of the Grand Jury; we are satisfied with the way the roads are kept and I don't think we could keep them so economically. Whatever district is added should be apportioned to the two existing wards. I don't think any further alteration of the wards is desirable or necessary.

Mr. Denis Howley examined.

Mr. Denis Howley.

105. I am a shopkeeper in the town. I have business in the town. I know of my own knowledge that lands within a circle of two miles from the centre of the town pay a considerably higher rent than lands of an equal value a little further off. The occupiers of those lands are able to pay, in consequence of the advantages they derive by buying and selling in the town; they make use of the town largely for buying and selling produce, and they get the advantage of the lighting of the town and the cleansing of the streets. I think it would be fair that they should pay one-half of the improvement rate payable by the people in the town, and that should be paid in respect of the advantages they derive from the town. That half, I think, should be divided between the landlord and tenant, inasmuch as the landlord derives a higher rent from the land than he otherwise would. I do not think it would be advisable for the Town Commissioners to obtain the management of the roads from the Grand Jury, for I don't think they could be so cheaply kept by the Town Commissioners; neither do I think it is necessary or desirable to make any alteration in the existing wards. The land to be brought in, if there is to be any extension of the boundary, should be added to those existing wards.

The inquiry then terminated.

CARRICKFERGUS.—SEPTEMBER 24TH, 1879.

[Before Mr. Exham, Chairman, and Mr. Robinson.]

Mr. T. Dance Jones examined.

1. Chairman.—You are the Town Clerk of Carrickfergus?—Yes. Carrickfergus has a form of government of its own.

2. You are the only town under the 3rd and 4th of Victoria, chapter 108, and the 6th and 7th of Victoria, chapter [illegible]?—Yes.

3. Has your municipal boundary always been the same?—Yes, ever since the charter granted by James I. The limitation was then fixed by the charter, and by it the borough and county of the town were made coterminous.

4. Have the Municipal Commissioners met and considered the question of the extension or alteration of the municipal boundaries?—Yes, they had a special meeting yesterday, for the purpose of considering the question, knowing that you were going to sit today. They passed the following resolution:—

"That seeing the borough and county of the town of Carrickfergus as at present constituted has been the area of local taxation and jurisdiction from a very remote antiquity with the general satisfaction and contentment of all the inhabitants thereof, that the Municipal Commissioners are the owners in fee of the entire property, that there is no area better fitted for municipal purposes within this district, and that the Municipal Commissioners are also the Harbour Commissioners and owners of the entire foreshore of the county and borough: Resolved—that it is inexpedient to extend, limit, or otherwise alter the existing boundaries of the borough of Carrickfergus."

5. As far as you know, from the inhabitants of the town, is there any desire to [illegible] or extend the limits of the municipal boundary?—None whatever.

6. Is there any outside district, the residents of which would wish to be brought in?—Certainly not.

7. Is the county of the town and the town of Carrickfergus coterminous with the Poor Law Electoral Division?—It is.

8. How far does the electoral division extend on all sides from the town of Carrickfergus?—How many miles?—About four or five miles. It is very irregular on the west side.

9. What was the poor rate for the past five years?—In 1874, 1s. 6d.; 1875, 1s. 4d.; 1876, 1s.; 1877, 1s.; 1878, 1s.

10. Do you manage your roads yourself?—The Grand Jury of the county of the town of Carrickfergus manage the roads entirely. It is a separate county and has a separate Grand Jury, and they levy a separate county cess.

11. Have you considered whether it would be better to get a transfer of the Grand Jury powers to the Municipal Commissioners so that you would be enabled to manage your own roads?—The Town Commissioners have got enough to do with their own business, and they don't want to interfere with the Grand Jury.

12. Do you think that there would be any benefit derived from it?—I don't think so.

Mr. James Lepper examined.

13. Chairman.—You are one of the Municipal Commissioners of Carrickfergus?—Yes, I wish to remark that there has been some talk about the town contributing more than it gets, and I have made some inquiries on the subject.

14. Do you consider there would be a saving effected if you had the roads under the control of the Municipal Commissioners?—I believe the Commissioners would have things in a better state for the amount of money that the town contributes. The county people are disinclined to do anything for the town. They say, "What right have we to contribute towards the work of the town?"

15. Do you consider that you could do this work cheaper and better, and that it would be for the benefit of persons within the municipal area if you got control of the roads and got the county cess?—We have not considered the matter. The valuation of the town is about £11,000, and the average charge is 1s. in the pound, about that every half-year, which makes about £500 a year paid for roads by the town.

16. Do you think you could keep your roads much cheaper if you got that £500 a year, and the Municipal Commissioners had the laying out of it?—Most decidedly.

Mr. Jones re-examined.

17. Chairman.—Then in that view it would be of advantage if you got the Grand Jury powers transferred to you?—There had been no suggestion made in reference to the matter.

18. Under the Act of last session—the Public Health Act—what can be done, and no vote of the Grand Jury can prevent its being done if the Local Government Board approve of it?—We have nothing to do with it at present.

19. In Wexford they have saved enormously by it?—Very likely so.

Mr. Lepper.—I have no doubt the town would save £400 or £700 by it.

20. Mr. Robinson.—You don't think you get value out of the cess you are compulsorily paying, a quota to the rest of the barony?—Yes.

21. You are the urban sanitary authority, aren't you?—No; we are not the sanitary authority. The Guardians of Larne are the sanitary authority.

22. The population is 9,000?—Nevertheless we are not the sanitary authority, and the Municipal Commissioners took counsel's opinion on the subject.

23. Do you think it would be desirable that the Town Commissioners should be the sanitary authority, and have the management of the roads, and of the sewerage, and all that?—I do think so.

Mr. M. R. Dalway, M.P., examined.

24. Chairman.—What are your views on the subject of this inquiry?—As Chairman of the Municipal Commissioners here, I may mention that I consider that there should not be any alteration of the boundaries, and further that it would be desirable in my opinion that we were made the urban sanitary authority, and that we had control of the roads within the present district, and that the district should not be altered.

Mr. Jones.—If the whole of the county cess of the county of the town of Carrickfergus is devoted to

Carrickmacross. Feb. 1st, 1879. Mr. M. H. [illegible]

Carrickmacross it would make no difference to the town except to give some trouble to the Municipal Commissioners?

Mr. Lordan.—I don't consider that there is very much in it, only that sometimes the country people say—"these are town improvements that we should not pay for."

35. Chairman.—You think, Mr. Dobbyn, there would be no good in passing this power to the Grand Jury?—I do. There are no complaints about the Grand Jury that I ever heard of, and if any change was allowed the Municipal Commissioners would have to employ a surveyor and pay him the same as the Grand Jury.

36. It would probably cost them the same?

Mr. Dobbyn.—It would cost them just the same.

Mr. Lordan.—I think the same objection applies to any alteration in existing matters. If that power was changed the Municipal Commissioners would have to appoint a staff.

37. Chairman.—Do you think, Mr. Lordan, it would be desirable that the Town Commissioners should have in their own hands the existing arrangements of the town, and not have to be going over to Lorrha to get the Board of Guardians to look after them?—I would most decidedly object to that alteration at the present time, because I think it would incur expense to a considerable extent, and in a variety of ways that the Municipal Commissioners should not incur at present. That is my opinion.

38. Do you think it would not be desirable that you should increase the urban sanitary authority beyond the present time? I think not. It may be so further on, in two or three years hence. I think matters have gone on pretty satisfactorily. As to satisfaction with the conduct of the Grand Jury, I may truly say that I have had good reason to be dissatisfied with their conduct in one or two cases. I had a fighting case which cost me a lot of money.

39. Well, we cannot interfere about that?—Yes; but I do not think it is out of place, when a statement is made as to the satisfactory conduct of the Grand Jury, that it should be contradicted. I may state decidedly that there was great ground of dissatisfaction in connexion with their conduct.

The inquiry then closed.

CARLOW.—FEBRUARY 19th, 1879.

Carlow. Feb. 19, 1879.

(Before Mr. W. A. Exham, Q.C., Chairman, and Mr. W. P. O'Brien.)

Mr. James Kelly examined.

Mr. James Kelly.

1. Chairman.—You are the Town Clerk of Carlow?—Yes, about five years.

2. I see that the present boundaries of the town were fixed by an Order in Council of the 2nd of January, 1856?—Yes.

3. That was the time the Towns Improvement Act was adopted in Carlow?—Yes.

4. Have the boundaries remained the same ever since?—Yes.

5. And the municipal and parliamentary boundaries are the same still?—They are.

6. The town is divided into two wards?—Yes, Carlow and Graigue.

7. Are Carlow and Graigue their two wards also?—Yes.

8. Mr. O'Brien.—Are they wards for Poor Law purposes?—Yes.

9. Chairman.—Are the wards the same for municipal and Poor Law purposes?—Yes.

10. Is the town in two electoral divisions also?—Yes, Carlow and Graigue.

11. What is the population?—7,842 in 1871.

12. Is it an increasing or decreasing population?—Decreasing.

13. What is it supposed to be now?—About 7,000.

14. What is the acreable area of the town?—[illegible]

15. Mr. O'Brien.—According to the returns of the Valuation Office it is given as 480 acres?—The total I have given you is taken from the books of the Clerk of the Union, 540 acres.

16. Is that for the two wards?—Yes.

17. What is the valuation?—About £8,400 for Carlow.

18. Are there any waste lands included in that sum?—I do not know. The valuation of Graigue would be £2,485 5s.

19. What is the total valuation?—£10,885 5s.

20. It is quite clear that the missing (land) given by the Valuation Office refers to the same thing, because the valuation given in that return is £10,885, so that there must be some waste land included?—Probably so.

21. Chairman.—Will you give me the rates which have been struck here for the last five years?—Yes, they are as follows:—

	Municipal.	Poor Law.	County.
	s. d.	s. d.	s. d.
1874,	1 0	2 11	1 4½
1875,	1 0	2 3	1 10
1876,	0 11	1 7	1 9½
1877,	0 10	1 11	2 1
1878,	0 10	2 7	1 9

22. Have the Commissioners considered the question as to the extension of the boundaries?—Yes.

23. Have they expressed a unanimous opinion on it?—Yes.

24. Are you authorized to state what that opinion is?—I think so.

25. Mr. O'Brien.—How many Commissioners are there?—Eighteen, fifteen for Carlow and three for Graigue. Seven members were present at the meeting at which this question of the extension of the boundaries was considered.

26. Was it a specially convened meeting?—Yes; all the members got notice of it.

27. Chairman.—What is the opinion of the body according to the view taken at that meeting?—The record on the minute book of the Commissioners is—

"At a meeting held on the 30th of December, 1878, seven members present, it was agreed that the borough boundary be extended to a radius of one mile from the centre of the town—the market cross."

28. What is the present radius from the centre of the town?—Half a mile.

29. In each direction?—Yes, in each direction.

30. Is it uniform in every direction?—Yes, except in one direction, which is three-quarters of a mile from the centre of the town.

31. Would the proposal of the Commissioners carry the bounds outside the Carlow and Graigue electoral divisions?—I think it would, but I cannot tell exactly.

32. How many townlands would this proposal take in?—I cannot say. Mr. Jameson could tell you that.

33. How many townlands are included in the present limits, or part of townlands?—Two, Carlow and Graigue.

34. No parts of townlands?—No, the whole of them.

35. Can you tell me whether the proposed boundary would go beyond the electoral divisions of Carlow and Graigue?—I think it would. It would go beyond the electoral division of Carlow, but not beyond that of Graigue.

36. How many electoral divisions will it take in on the Carlow side?—I don't know the exact number.

37. Will you tell me what would be the extent of the increase, how many acres?—I cannot tell you.

38. Nor the valuation?—No.

39. Do the Commissioners propose a hard-and-fast line of two miles of a radius without reference to townland boundaries or anything of that kind?—Yes.

40. What would be the increased valuation of this two-mile radius?—I cannot tell you, but I can tell you the acreage of the two electoral divisions outside the borough. In the Carlow electoral division outside the borough there are 5,419A. 2R. 13P., and in the Graigue there are 4,241A. 3R. 20P.

41. 646 acres is the entire borough at present?—Yes.

42. How much of that is in Carlow and how much in Graigue?—512A. 2R. 20P. in Carlow, and 133A. 3R. 31P. in Graigue.

43. Then how much do you propose to take in?—4,311 acres of Carlow.

44. And how much beyond that, because you say you are to go into another electoral division?—I cannot tell; I do not know the area outside the electoral division.

45. On what grounds do the Commissioners consider the extension of the present boundaries desirable?—They think it would be a general improvement and advantage both to the town and its neighbourhood in every respect, for instance, in lighting.

46. In what do the advantages consist?—They think it would have the effect of lightening the rates on the townspeople inside the borough.

47. Do they consider that lands in the immediate vicinity of the town are more valuable by having the town to resort to as a market town?—They do.

48. Is it a fact, and do you know that lands near the town, and within the two-mile radius, are let in the market at a higher rate owing to their proximity to the town?—Yes.

49. That is a fact?—Yes.

50. How much more rent would lands near the town bring than lands three or four miles off?—From £1 to 30s. an acre, at least.

51. Is the entire of the town within the municipal boundary lighted?—Yes.

52. With oil or gas?—There are seventy-eight lamps lighted with oil.

53. Have you found that more economical than gas?—A great deal more. For three years we have used oil.

54. Are there many gentlemen's seats that would be brought in by this proposed extension?—I would say about a dozen.

55. How many of the farmer class would be brought in?—A very large number.

56. Occupying farms of what size?—From 10 to 100 and 150 acres.

57. Could you give us about the number?—I am sure there would be 200 ratepayers.

58. Would it bring in persons who would be qualified to fill the office of Town Commissioner?—Yes; a good many. I could not say the exact number.

59. How many persons are eligible at present for that office?—About seventy I should say. Over £12 and under £20 there are seventy-six, and over £20, eighty-two—that is 158.

60. Do the persons living between the existing limit and the two mile-radius dispose of their produce in this town?—Yes.

61. What articles do they so dispose of?—Corn, butter, potatoes and milk, eggs, vegetables, and poultry.

62. Do the persons having a town like Carlow in such close proximity to their land enjoy exceptional advantages over and above persons living at a distance?—Yes.

63. Do they use the town coming to the railway?—Yes.

64. Are the schools in Carlow resorted to by the children of these people?—Yes; they have very good educational advantages also.

65. Have the Town Commissioners considered the terms upon which they should be brought in; have they considered whether the people living in the proposed extended district should pay an equal rate with those in the town?—Yes.

66. Are you aware that under the sixty-second section of the Towns Improvement Act, the owners or occupiers of land within a township pay a rate only on one-fourth of their valuation?—That is 2½d. in the pound here where it is a 10d. rate.

67. Is it the proposal of the Commissioners that it should remain the same?—Yes.

68. Do the Commissioners propose to light all that extended district?—They could not light the whole length of it I am sure.

69. Was that considered by the Commissioners?—Partly; I am sure they would extend the lighting a good way.

70. Was the question of the rate considered?—Yes; the quarter rate on the land.

71. Did the Commissioners consider that under the Sanitary Act of last year—so far as sanitary matters are concerned, they would be only liable to pay one-fourth?—Yes.

72. Would they be satisfied with that?—Yes.

73. Are they satisfied to bring them in on those terms?—Yes.

74. Have the Commissioners considered the queries submitted to them by us?—Yes.

75. In answering the queries did they consider the question of taking up of the roads?—No.

76. Do the Commissioners propose that the roads should remain still in the hands of the Grand Jury?—Yes.

77. Mr. O'Brien.—Are they aware of the powers given under the Public Health Act enabling them to get possession of the roads?—They are, but they prefer leaving them in the hands of the Grand Jury.

78. Do they get a good equivalent for the money expended on the town?—Yes.

79. Chairman.—When I last sat here, I remember, there was a great complaint made about the conduct of the Grand Jury in relation to Graigue, that nothing was done for Graigue?—That is the Queen's County Grand Jury.

80. Do you want now to extend the boundary in the Graigue district?—Yes.

81. What do you propose?—It is that the extended part of Graigue should remain as it is, and that nothing should be done with regard to the roads of it, of which such complaints were made before. We propose to leave it still in the hands of the Queen's County Grand Jury.

82. Although they do nothing?—Yes.

83. Do the complaints still continue?—There were no complaints for the last two years.

84. Have they maintained the roads properly since then?—They have; it was the sewers that were complained of at the time you speak of.

85. Mr. O'Brien.—Is the town pretty well regulated both as regards sewerage or water supply?—Yes.

86. Is there any necessity for a large scheme?—No. There is not any water supply; it is all done by pumps.

87. Is there a good water supply in the town?—Yes, there are sixteen public pumps and very good water.

88. Chairman.—Are you satisfied with the way the Grand Jury keep the roads cleansed in the town?—The Commissioners manage the scavenging, but the Grand Jury repair the roads, streets, footpaths, water-tables, and sewerage in the town.

89. If you take in the roads in the extended district

do you propose to scavenge them for the one-fourth [illegible]?—It could not be done to the full extent.

90. What do you propose to do for the men living at the farthest extent of the two miles in return for the 3s. in the pound; do you propose to do anything?—They will extend the lighting and the water supply, but not to the extent of two miles.

91. To what extent do you propose to extend these advantages?—I should say about half a mile further than at present.

92. Then for a mile you propose to do nothing?—I say that those advantages to which I have referred would not be carried out farther by the Commissioners.

93. Have the Commissioners considered the question of taking up the roads, so that there should be one sanitary authority, and that you would have one body looking after the lighting, water, scavenging, and cleaning of the roads, and the sanitary arrangements of the town also?—They would propose to take the repairs of the roads out of the hands of the Grand Jury.

94. Have the Commissioners considered this question with regard to those people outside that are at present in the rural district, that while in the rural sanitary district they pay the full sanitary rate, and have a right to deduct half from the landlords, while if those persons are brought into the town, they will only have to pay one-fourth of the sanitary rate with no deduction from the landlord, except the law be changed?—I am almost sure the Commissioners have considered all that.

95. Will you be able if you receive only one-fourth from them to make all necessary sanitary arrangements?—Yes, but no sewers; they are made by the Grand Jury.

96. The Grand Jury only make surface drains; I am talking of sewers. Suppose the Commissioners become the Sanitary Authority, have they considered what would be necessary for drainage and other purposes?—I think with the present borough rate they could not do that work without striking a special sanitary rate for that purpose.

97. If that were done by the Local Authority, the people would have to pay the full sanitary rate and deduct one-half from the landlord, but the moment you take them in, and strike a sanitary rate, then they will only pay one-fourth to the town without any deduction. If you are obliged to strike a sanitary rate for the purpose of [illegible] [illegible] they will only pay one-fourth, whereas the people in the borough pay the full rate, and they will have to pay no [illegible] of the sanitary rate of the people of the outside district. Have they considered that?—They have.

98. Are they prepared to do it?—Yes.

99. You say there would be an advantage to the ratepayers of the town in having these places brought in, but if the people living within this [illegible] were brought in, and you are obliged to strike a sanitary rate on the whole of the district, the people in the town will have to pay the full sanitary rate for the outside district you bring in, while the people of that district when brought in will only pay one-fourth of that?—Yes.

100. What advantage will it be for the ratepayers of the town, supposing you strike a 1s. sanitary rate. The people outside will only pay 3d., and the townspeople will not only have to pay 1s. for themselves, but 9d. for those outside; they will pay three [illegible] more beyond the people outside the present district. What advantage will that be to the people of the town?—They consider that it would be an advantage, as it would reduce the taxation of the people inside the boundary.

101. How will it reduce their taxation?—In the light in which you have explained the matter I don't see how it would. The Commissioners must not have considered that question fully.

102. Did they consider the question with reference to the Public Health Act of last year, and that, as the law now is, all this land, if brought in, is only to pay one-fourth of the sanitary rate and the improvement rate?—They were aware that all lands only paid one-fourth of the rate.

103. Are you prepared to say that you are ready to undertake to scavenge all the roads over that two miles of an area, and that the people outside the present boundary are only to pay one-fourth of the cost of doing that, while the townspeople pay the full amount of the rate?—They were aware of that, but I am sure they could not scavenge that two-mile area. They could not go beyond the present boundary, so that the expenditure would not be much heavier for scavenging.

104. Then what do you propose to do; are you to leave the roads of the proposed added district unscavenged, if I may use the expression?—In the case of the country roads, the road contractor would do that.

105. The road contractors only keep the roads in repair?—Before repairing them they always clean them.

106. Are they to leave them from one [illegible] to another?—I am almost sure they would, but not from one section to another, because they could not carry them out that distance.

107. What are the amounts of the contracts for the repairs of the roads within the town?—I cannot say; we have no control over them.

108. Any one could see from the contracts what it cost the Grand Jury to keep the roads in repair for the town for the last year—what they paid their contractors—then we know what they got from you, or we could see easily whether you would lose money by taking up the roads from them?—I cannot say; I will make out a list for you in a few minutes.

109. Was that considered?—It was, very often, as to the taking up and repair of roads and streets.

110. You are paying the Grand Jury something more than £1,000 a year, and the county-at-large charges would be about £800. The question then is what is the expenditure?—Yes, but I don't know what they pay for the roads.

111. Have you any surveyor here?—We have a town surveyor.

112. Have you any map of the town here as prescribed under the Acts of Parliament?—No map except the one you have before you.

113. But that is not a map at all?—Well it is the only one we have.

114. By the 12th section of the 10th and 11th of Victoria, chapter 34 you ought to have a map of your district, giving its limits and showing the sewerage and so on, accessible to the public, with the proper levels marked on it?—I was not aware of that.

115. Have the people you propose to bring in any objection to be brought in?—I am sure they will oppose the proposition of the Commissioners.

116. Even though they should pay only one-fourth of the rates?—I believe they will object even to that.

117. Mr. O'Brien.—Then they prefer to remain as they are?—Yes.

118. I presume they contemplate that the sanitary expenditure will be much heavier on the town than on the rural district?—Yes.

119. Chairman.—Are the sanitary arrangements in the town satisfactory?—Very unsatisfactory.

120. Then you don't want any outlay?—I think not, at any rate not anything in the town worth speaking of.

121. Then if there was any sanitary rate it would be for the benefit of the outside district to be brought in?—Yes; for sewers and drains.

122. Are you able to speak for the Commissioners or the urban sanitary authority with regard to the sanitary arrangements within the town at present, and are you in a position to say whether or not the outside district that you propose to bring in would require sewerage and sanitary arrangements to be made for it?—In several districts I am sure it would be required.

123. Don't you know you would have to do that work if you brought them in?—Yes.

2 L

[illegible]
[illegible]
Mr. James Kelly

CARLOW Jan. 13, 1879. Mr. James Kelly.

124. How far do the electoral divisions of Graigue and Carlow extend?—I cannot say.

125. Have you a scavenging staff at present for the town?—Yes, we have.

126. Utilising that staff for the purpose of the roads, if you had them in your own hands—what reason is there—if any outside district is brought in, why there should not be one undivided authority in the town to look after the roads and all?—I don't know; I think they were always in favour of leaving the roads in the hands of the Grand Juries.

127. The sum paid by the Grand Jury to the road contractor for Carlow is £333 6s. 8d.?—Yes.

128. Does that include all the lanes and everything?—All; inside the present boundary.

Mr. DARBY HENDRICK COOPER examined.

Mr. Darby Hendrick Cooper.

129. CHAIRMAN.—How long, Mr. Cooper, have you been Chairman of the Carlow Town Commissioners?—For a good many years.

130. Were you one of the seven Town Commissioners who met to consider the question of the extension of the municipal boundary?—I was.

131. Is it your opinion and that of your brother Commissioners as far as you know, that there should be an extension of the boundaries of the town?—Yes, but not to the same extent as we stated in our answers to the queries you submitted to us—two miles. After we got your notice we had a meeting to consult over the matter, and to see had anyone considered what had been done in other places, and that if there was a good suggestion from the course pursued by any other place we could take it into our consideration and perhaps do the same thing, but we had no grounds to go upon, and we then mentioned two miles. Since that time, however, we have changed our opinion very much, and we think that one mile would be sufficient for what we want. There is a question that we were ignorant as to up to this and remain so still, and it is whether supposing this mile that we now seek an extension to was granted the people holding land in that extension would be liable to lose the advantages of the Land Act or not?

132. That is a matter outside our jurisdiction?—If we thought any injury might accrue to the farmers immediately about the town by an extension we should call attention to it in our report.

133. Mr. O'BRIEN.—That is that you would not advocate an extension of the boundary if the Land Act was to operate in such a way as to prevent the farmers to whom you refer getting compensation?—As a farmer I would not like to do that and I do not think the Commissioners would either.

134. Therefore in recommending an extension you do so on the supposition that it is to have no effect whatever as regards the operation of the Land Act?—That is my idea and I dare say—though I have not spoken to them on the subject—it is the idea of many of the Commissioners. I don't think they would recommend any extension if they thought it would injure the farmers about us.

135. CHAIRMAN.—You say you are in favour of one mile extension; would that be within the two electoral divisions?—Yes; Graigue is a different thing entirely. The Grand Jury of the Queen's county regulate all matters with regard to Graigue, except sewerage. I mentioned at the former inquiry that they were doing nothing for us; that they made us pay very heavy county cess, and yet did nothing for us. It is a continual source of annoyance, that there is no sewerage. We cannot do anything with them. I believe in many of the houses there is no outfall for the sewage.

136. Have the Grand Jury improved since?—No, they have never done anything and will not. If our boundary was enlarged to Graigue, we would be able to strike a sanitary rate to do that work which the Grand Jury will not do.

137. Mr. O'BRIEN.—Would the extension to the mile radius bring in as much of the Queen's County portion as you think necessary?—I think it would bring in a fair, but a small portion.

138. But the Grand Jury there, might ask what you required the sanitary work for, while you pay county cess to them, and they might prevent you striking any sanitary rate on that district?—If we had to extend that sanitary rate to Carlow, it would be a great hardship on the people here. We have everything done in this town that is needful to be done by the Grand Jury. There are only one or two [illegible]—badly built ones I may say—in a bad way now.

139. What you propose to do would be to amend the Graigue portion and then to get a sanitary rate for that district alone?—That is the very thing we want to do. The position of Graigue is this, it is composed of a great many poor houses, and very few of them are valued at £4 a year, and therefore it would be very hard to say who it would fall on, but the rate I suppose would fall on the landlords.

140. With regard to those under £4 a year, the rate would fall on the landlord and as to all over £4 it would stand in this way—the district you would bring in, the extended district, would only have to pay under the present law one-fourth of the rate?—I dare say.

141. Would not that be a great hardship on the landlords of the houses under £4, and too great boon to the occupiers of the houses over £4? But how are you to drain the place? How are you to do it?—It cannot be done without raising money. We have often thought of that, and we find it very difficult to know what to do.

142. The district you propose to bring in at the Carlow side in the Carlow Electoral Division—would that require sanitary work?—We want I may say nothing; there is only one small street or two of newly built houses there that want a drain put to them. Everything is done in the town to keep up a system of proper drainage by the Grand Jury. I am a member of the Grand Jury myself, and have been so for many years, and I am in a position to say, because I know it, that they are very anxious to do everything that is right. The reason why we did not at the time of the last Commission take that question much into our consideration, was that we were engaged with our fairs and markets. At the same time should we see that after a time we could serve the ratepayers of the town by taking up the roads, and the county roads, of course we will avail ourselves of the law, but at present we do not see any reason for that, because we calculate that as we have a County Surveyor who superintends everything, if we took up those county roads we would have to pay a man to do all that and almost one-half goes to pay the county-at-large charges. I think if there is not something more—some few things put on us—on the county-at-large charges than the other half there would be hardly anything to be made out of it. I think £300 odd is the contract for the streets.

143. Is that for the whole of the streets including Graigue?—Graigue is different. There is no record of anything relating to Graigue in this office, it being under the Queen's County Grand Jury.

144. If you had the entire of the roads under your charge, and that you got from the people the same money as they pay to the Grand Jury at present, would you be able to manage them?—That is a question we have never considered. We were aware that we had the power of taking the county roads belonging to the Borough, but we never entered into the question minutely.

145. You would just as the law stands at present if you had those roads now, the owners of land, &c., would only have to pay in effect one-fourth

of the cost of keeping them up under the [illegible] section of the Act?—Yes.

146. But suppose you got the same amount from the owners of the land that they pay to the Grand Jury, and out of that you paid the contingent charges, and kept the roads [illegible], would you be able to keep up the roads if they were put under your management and care?—But we would have to do something to supplement [illegible] out of that money. It is a question we have not considered, and therefore could not answer it definitely, but it is my impression that the cost of supervising the money would be as much as it is at present. We pay our County Surveyor £100 a year, besides having a Clerk and offices. Then we would have to calculate what it would be if we took up the money and then had to pay, which we would have to pay, a proper person for superintending the work.

147. Do you propose to give the people residing in the extended area the benefit of lighting?—Not for such extension; but we would have more lights on the outskirts of the town than there are at present. At present the outskirts are badly lit. I have a good deal of land in the Queen's County and here myself; and I think it would be of advantage, and desirable, to have better lighting at the outskirts of the town. There is no doubt it enhances the value of the land to be so very near a town, and also so near a good market.

148. Have the people been paid for out of the improvement rates?—Yes; we are very peculiarly situated with regard to water. We have the Barrow running through the town on one side, and the Burren in another direction.

149. Do you propose to water the extended district?—If it wanted it we should, and would do so.

150. Even if they only paid one-fourth rates?—I think we would be bound to do it. We should give them something for their money.

151. Do the lands, from your own knowledge of the district around, derive exceptional value in the market from their proximity to the town?—There is no doubt about it that they do. There is a very good price given for land about the town. Town parks and accommodation are let at £5 and £6 an acre.

152. What would that land be worth as land two or three miles further off?—I think about 40s. an acre. I think the same quality of land [illegible] would double immediately about the town.

153. Do the people living in the locality largely use the town as a market town?—Of course they do; they send in for everything they want, and when we have our markets and fairs properly established we will be even more prosperous than now. It will have very great advantages, indeed, in their own [illegible] respect, [illegible] they could not be worse than now, but I hope we shall get through it in the course of some time; but at the same time I don't think any of the Commissioners, as far as I know them, would advocate an increase, or think of increasing the borough boundary if they thought they would injure the farmers [illegible] about town.

154. Mr. O'Brien.—We will take it that all rights they have to property are to be preserved to them under the Local Act?—Yes.

155. Chairman.—We are anxious to know the views of the people living in and about Carlow; as to this question, of taking up the management of the roads, because in other places that we have been to, the general idea has been, that the Grand Jury are making money out of the towns in that way, and that if the towns took up the roads they would be able to have a larger saving, and keep them in better order, and devote the saving to the benefit of the town?—Any way we can save money we will take it.

156. At Wexford they got their privilege in 1874, and the witnesses examined there on Saturday stated that they were able to save, and have saved about £400 a year for the last four years, which has been expended for the good of the town; and besides they were able to flag the town, and do other things which they never could get the Grand Jury to do before?—I know, myself, with regard to the flagging, that it is a very heavy expense, and we are in a very unfortunate position at present, because we must have flags of a particular description, and of a particular thickness, and the county surveyor would pass no other; and it is a [illegible] quarry, and they say it will take three years to get good flags again. The Grand Jury are anxious to do their duty. I could not give you an opinion on that subject, because we never discussed it, we never consulted about the taking up of the roads, and getting the money ourselves.

CARLOW.
Jan. 13, 18[illegible].
Mr. [illegible]
[illegible]

157. You have [illegible] in the town independent of the road contractor. Would you propose in this extended district the same way as the town?—The road contractor may do it himself. He would be glad to get, when it comes to be managed by the town; but [illegible] of the Commissioners would rather have their own surveyor.

158. The question is would you be able to manage this extended district of a mile beside?—I suppose we would.

159. But the people in that district would only pay one-fourth of that surveying, and the townspeople would have to make up the other three-fourths out of the rates?—As I told you the contractor would rather do it himself, because when his men go out scraping the roads, they do it so carelessly, and do not remove or take up the stones, whereas if we sent out men they would clear away, and not mind or care what harm they would do in leaving the stones, and therefore the contractor would rather do it himself.

160. But he would not do it unless he was paid for it?—I think he would rather do it himself than lose by it, but this is a matter which we did not discuss, because we were taken up so much with our fairs and markets.

161. As the urban sanitary authority would you consider it desirable to take up the management of the roads within the present and the extended area, so as to have one body managing all?—As I said before this is a matter that we did not discuss, but of course if we saw our way and thought we would be able to save anything to the ratepayers we would undertake it, and I dare say we will do it when we get out of our present difficulties.

162. You are in Carlow able you would want extension sanitary work?—We would.

163. Do you think it would be fair to put the sanitary rate on Graigue district alone?—Certainly.

164. Is there any portion of the Carlow district in this mile radius that would require sewerage?—I think only one—that is in the present boundary—and I intend to try to get that done by the Grand Jury.

165. But it is not with reference to what is within your district at present as the Urban Sanitary Authority that I am asking, but with regard to the district that you propose to bring in, would that require sewerage?—I think not, I don't know of any place that would, and I know it pretty well.

166. Then in point of fact the [illegible] sanitary rate payable by that district would exclusively be for the benefit of the town?—Yes.

167. Have you any sources of income except what you derive from the rates?—No.

168. Have you no property?—No. We were very much in debt some years ago, but we are pretty [illegible] now. We have only struck a 10d. rate, and when we get our fairs and markets we will be able to do it with less.

169. Are the existing powers sufficient for all purposes?—Yes.

170. Are you obliged to leave any sanitary works unexecuted in consequence of the limit of your rating powers?—No, nothing of that kind. The only thing that had to be done was to run a sewer through a street, and that was the only thing there was any difficulty in; everything else has been done. The bridges and all those improvements have been done by the Grand Jury, and we are paying a loan every year to the Board of Works that we borrowed from them; so

Carlow. Feb. 12, 1879. Mr. Dudley Hervey Cooper.

that if you add that to the expense of keeping the roads, and also a surveyor's salary, I don't think we would make anything by taking up the roads from the Grand Jury. That is my present view without going very closely into the matter.

171. Are there any persons living within this extended district who would be eligible as Town Commissioners?—Not many; but there are some.

172. What is the reason you have changed your view with regard to the mile instead of the two-mile radius?—We changed our view with regard to that when we saw it would take in too large a district.

173. But if the land within the two-mile radius is as valuable as the land within the one-mile radius, why should it not be brought in?—Well, I don't think it is. The land within the one-mile radius is very valuable. I have land that I could get a very large rent for; but when you go beyond that it is not of the same value. When you go to the two-mile radius I should say that the land has its regular letting value, and is not enhanced by proximity to the town. From a mile to two miles the land would let at about one-third beyond the value, but within a mile the land is of great value. There are people living in the town who would like to get a bit of land outside for cows and so on, and they would pay a high price for that land.

174. Mr. O'Brien.—Is there any general suggestion you would like to offer?—There is nothing further than what I have said before, that I would not wish by any act to injure any of the farmers.

175. Chairman.—Then I understand that your proposal, as the Chairman of the Town Commissioners, is to extend the boundaries to as nearly as possible within a mile from the centre of the town, the Market-cross, and not to have the roads transferred to you at all events for the present, and to take in that external district on the terms even of their having to pay only a fourth?—That is so.

176. May the evidence given by the Town Clerk and yourself be taken to represent the views of the Town Commissioners?—Yes; but there are several here.

177. Is there anything they would add?—I don't know, they may have something to add.

178. Are there any other Commissioners present who desire to give evidence in favour of or against extension, because if not we will take the Chairman's views as those of the Commissioners?

Mr. O'Brien.—Unless some other members desire to add to or dissent from the views put forward by the Chairman we will not go into further evidence of the Commissioners personally.

179. Mr. *John B. Mulhall*, Solicitor.—I appear here on behalf of a great many rural gentlemen outside. They object entirely to an extension, first, on the ground that when they took their places, and some of them purchased very recently, they would be deprived of the Land Act compensation if that extension was made.

180. Chairman.—As far as that is concerned we understand that all evidence given with a view of taking in any outside district or land is on the assumption that all land brought in shall enjoy all the privileges that it has at present under the existing law.

Mr. *Mulhall*.—That is the principal matter with which my clients' objection has to do.

181. Mr. O'Brien.—If that was got over would they object?

Mr. *Mulhall*.—They would not; and they have very little more to say if that be the case.

182. Supposing that is got over would they object to be brought in on the ground of increase of taxation?

Mr. *Mulhall*.—They think now it is not worth while to talk about that.

183. Chairman.—If they are brought in now, as the law stands, they would only have to pay a fourth of the improvement and sanitary rate, and they would not get any deduction from their landlord for their sanitary rate. At present they pay the whole of the sanitary rate, and they have the power of deducting half of that from their landlord. That being so would they rather come in or not?

Mr. *Mulhall*.—In that view they would rather not come in; they would rather have things exactly as they are.

Mr. Charles Carey.

Mr. Charles Carey examined.

184. Chairman.—Where do you reside?—About a mile from the Market-cross.

185. How far are you from the nearest point of the municipal boundary in your direction?—About sixty yards, but I think the boundary extends almost a mile in an eastern direction, and I do not think that the advantages which have been stated by the Chairman are such as on my part would induce me to wish for any change in the boundary. I do not think the lighting comes within a reasonable distance, and the water is at present so close, that in the eastern district at least I do not think we would derive any advantage from being taken into the borough.

186. Do you agree with those that say that lands within a short distance of the town derive exceptional value from their proximity to the town?—That is quite true; all the land contiguous to the town brings a rent of about £5 an acre, whereas the same quality of land further out would not be worth half the price.

187. Do the people holding those lands use the town largely?—Of course they do.

188. Don't you think they should therefore contribute something towards the taxation of the town?—I have no desire to be brought into the town, or within the borough, because I do not take advantage of the town; but I think that farmers who raise stock and grow vegetables and so forth, and make use of the town for the sale of their produce, derive positive benefit from it, and that such if brought in and only asked to pay a fourth, should be made to contribute.

189. That is the law at present, but I cannot say what may be done afterwards?—No.

190. Mr. O'Brien.—That is the law as defined by the Towns Improvement Act, section 62, that arable land and property of that description is only liable to pay a fourth?—Yes, and you have already stated that any change to be made would be subject to the existing law as regards the Land Act.

191. Chairman.—Mr. Cooper's proposition on the part of the Town Commissioners is, that any change that is made should be made subject to the existing law, and that the parties should have the benefit of it; but under the 62nd section of the Act the words are, "Any rate to be levied under this Act shall be only one-fourth," and so on. Don't you see the people outside would derive great advantage so far as any sanitary rate is concerned?—There can be no doubt about that.

192. And the landlords would get a benefit because they would not have to pay anything?—Yes; as to improved scavenging, I do not think the area brought in would derive much benefit from it, because the Commissioners could not do it at all, and in the present mile area I do not think we would expect any work from them.

193. Would you think it unfair that persons having land within a mile of the cross should pay something towards the keeping up of the town, if they derive exceptional benefit from it?—You must remember that they pay for the exceptional value of the land which they rent. They already pay £5 instead of £3 10s.

194. That is a benefit the landlord has, and that they are able to pay that rent by the increased value of their land?—They are, by their proximity to the town; there is no doubt about that.

193. Mr. O'Brien.—Then except for a question that they derive considerable advantages?—Certainly.

194. Chairman.—Do you think then for such exceptional benefits they should pay something, and that the landlord should pay something for the benefits he derives?—Yes.

195. Mr. O'Brien.—Don't you think that the system in municipal government should be extended as far as possible—don't you think the effect would be a healthy one, instead of limiting the municipal government to the town limits, that it should include the population immediately around it, introducing additional element in the constitution of the voting bodies and the electorate of the voting bodies?—That is a speculative opinion purely political and purely social. The town clerk mentioned that there were good many to vote and sit on the Town Commissioners' Board.

196. Don't you think that giving a wider constituency interested in the good government of the town might have a healthy effect?—It ought to have; I have no doubt in saying that. The parishes are qualified for Commissioners.

198. Chairman.—Suppose the district were extended as proposed, have you considered whether it would be advisable for the Town Commissioners here to get control over everything in the town?—Yes.

199. To have the management of every single thing?—Yes, especially after the illustration of Wexford that you have named.

201. Mr. O'Brien.—I asked at Wexford if they would like to revert to the original arrangement, but not a single member of the Board wished that he [illegible] back to the old arrangement.—I am not [illegible] at all surprised at that.

202. Are you aware that there are twenty instances in Ireland where the jurisdiction through has not always remained the same where the control of the Grand Jury has been vested in municipal boards, in numerous cases by special Acts of Parliament, and in the instance of Wexford, by provisional order?—I was not aware of that, but it is interesting to know it.

203. Chairman.—Supposing the impositions were conducted in a town, and then the management of everything within the borough was vested in the Town Commissioners, and then they got the full cess, the same thing as is paid to the Grand Jury at present—would you think it desirable?—I would, and I think the work would be better managed.

204. And as economically?—Yes.

205. The Town Commissioners out of that would pay their proportion of the county-at-large charges, and keep the rest for the maintenance of the roads of the town. Then you would have the same body looking after the water, the lighting, the sanitary arrangements, the scavenging and the repairs of the roads in the town?—Yes.

206. Perhaps Mr. Mulhall would like to express his views with regard to this question. Would his mission be towards having rather under the old system or under the Town Commissioners?

Mr. Mulhall.—They would rather remain as they are.

Mr. George Pascoe examined.

207. Chairman.—Is your property within outside the present boundary?—It is partly outside and partly inside the present boundary.

208. Would you be taken in by this extension?—The whole of my land would be taken in by it.

209. Do you object to any extension?—I don't see what advantage it would be to us in any one way.

210. Do you, or do you not consider that by reason of its proximity to the town the land near the town is more valuable both to the landlord and to the tenant?—Most decidedly. I have to pay more for it than if it was ten miles from the town.

211. On these sides?—Yes; on those sides. I think so, however, that I receive the advantage of that. I think it is my landlord who gets them, because he gets an increased rent.

212. Are you not able to pay that rent better by having a market at your door?—If I may use the expression?—Most decidedly, it is no advantage to me. I hold my lands three miles from the town, and it is the same to me to drive my cattle three miles as one mile.

213. Do you not dispose of your produce in the town?—No; my land is all grass and tillage. I have just as good a market for my land at three miles away from the town as I would if I were within a mile of it, and I think there are several others here who would say the same.

214. What makes the land so much more valuable to the landlord?—There is something in that, because if I didn't hold it other people in the town would have it.

215. From its proximity to the town?—Yes.

216. Then the question comes to this—should not the owner and occupier settle between them in some way the means and extent to which it should be done, but should they not between them contribute towards the keeping up of the town which makes the land so much sought after?—Most decidedly. I should say that the landlord should pay it and not the tenant. By this new arrangement the landlord who gets all the advantage will not pay anything, and the tenant will have to pay it all.

217. The way the matter stands at present is, that with regard to the new sanitary rate you would deduct half from the landlord?—But the landlord would not pay anything the other way.

218. It was very much considered by the Royal Commission whether there should not be a division of the rates between the landlord and the occupier. At present you would have to pay if there sanitary works to be done in the district, the whole sanitary rate and deduct one-half from the landlord, whereas if you came into the town you would only have to pay one-fourth and deduct nothing. So that you see by the present law it would be of advantage to come into the town?—Quite so. As to lighting, I am sure they could not light out so far, and as to its being an advantage it would, in my opinion, be a disadvantage, for with the present lighting it is easier for a man to drive without lights than with them.

219. Supposing any portion of the district was taken in as you say on fair terms, and that the landlord should contribute something towards the expense, in your opinion would it be better that the Commissioners should take up the roads and have everything under one undivided authority?—Most decidedly. I agree with Mr. Carey that it would be better for the Commissioners to have the management of the whole thing. I see that every day. I should however be totally opposed to any extension of the municipal boundary as it would be a great disadvantage to farmers to have their farms taken into the municipal area, and made town parks under the Land Act.

220. There is no proposition on the part of the Town Commissioners here to deprive those of any benefit they are entitled to under the Land Act at present. How much of the railway would be taken in by the proposed extension?—A good deal; it runs parallel with the town and on both sides a good deal would be taken in. I don't know exactly how far down the line the boundary goes.

221. Is it then your opinion that the taxation should be paid similarly by the landlord and tenant?—Yes. I don't see, however, what advantage the tenant farmers outside the town would derive from the proposed extension. I am sure the Town Commission-

dingers are not going to give them any additional advantages.

222. Mr. Cooper says they would extend the lighting some distance?—I am sure the people outside the town would rather not have the lights. I am always very much embarrassed with them when driving out, I am almost blinded by them—with one here and another a great distance off.

Mr. *Cooper*.—That is the very thing we want to remedy.

223. CHAIRMAN (to witness).—As you go to the town for shopping and purchasing your necessaries and all that sort of thing, the question is whether you should not contribute something towards it too?—But the townspeople use our country roads; there is scarcely a day they are not driving upon them.

224. But they pay for them?—Well we pay for them too.

Mr. WILLIAM BYRNE examined.

225. CHAIRMAN.—Do you live within the two-mile radius and outside of the one-mile?—I am afraid I would be inside the two-mile radius.

226. Upon what point do you wish to give evidence?—I am of opinion that the roads would be better and more cheaply kept by the Town Commissioners than by the Grand Jury.

227. With reference to the extension to two miles do you think that the land is more valuable by reason of its proximity to the town?—I am not aware that it is—not to the extent of two miles. Townparks about half a mile around the town of course bring more rent, but I think that the land two miles away is not of a bit more value than if it was ten, eight, or six miles off.

228. Everywhere else where we have been there appears to have been unanimity in opinion that to the extent of, at all events two miles from a town, the land is more valuable—that if it was in the market you would get plenty of people inclined to give a much larger rent where they have an opportunity of sending in their milk, butter, poultry, eggs, and those sorts of things daily to the town, and I should like to know if you think there is any difference in the case of Carlow as compared with other places?—I cannot say; in fact I have often found that land two miles away from the town is of less value, because you have a great deal more annoyance. You have a great many people from the town on Sundays and holydays, and other times coming out and going over the land, and often a great deal of harm is done. I cannot see any good it does. Certainly if there is a good house on the land you will have to pay more for it, but I don't see any other way in which it is more valuable.

229. Would you not think that to the small class of farmers it would be more valuable. Perhaps it is not to the large farmers who would not be sending in milk and butter to the town?—May be land does go to a higher price, especially small bits such as townparks, but you could send in produce just as easy from a two miles or so out. The land fetches a higher price, but I think the landlord has all the advantage.

230. Is the land dearer in the market?—The land is dearer in the market and the tenant has more to pay for it. Of course it is more value to the landlord, but not to the tenant—that is what I mean.

231. Could the tenant afford to pay that increased rent only for its proximity to the town?—No.

232. Then he is made to pay it; but you say the land is of no more value to him on account of the high rent he has to pay for it, and that it is the landlord who gets the real benefit?—Just so, so.

233. Is it your opinion that the taxation should be put exclusively on the landlord and tenant?—It is. There is no doubt about it he certainly has the advantage because he gets a higher rent. Even at two miles he gets a higher rent—considerably more rent than he would if the land was six or seven miles off, and I cannot see that the land is of any more use to the tenant than it is within six or seven miles, although he has to pay more for it, and is more heavily taxed.

234. He saves time in sending in his produce—in that way he gets some advantage?—Yes that is so, he can bring in two loads, in place of one.

235. At present that outside district is under the control of the rural sanitary authority. For any sanitary work that has to be done at present the tenant has to pay the full sanitary rate, getting half back from the landlord. If it is brought into the town the tenant would only pay a fourth, and then not get anything back from the landlord. Which do you think would be most advantageous to the tenant—to pay the whole of the sanitary rate, getting back half, or be brought into the town, and pay one-fourth and not get back anything?—I cannot say, really I cannot myself see the advantage of his being brought into the town.

The inquiry then terminated.

CARRICKMACROSS.—SEPTEMBER 17TH, 1879.

(Before Mr. H. A. ROBINSON).

Mr. EDWARD M'NALLY examined.

1. You are clerk to the Town Commissioners?—Yes.

2. How long have you been so?—About ten years.

3. When was Carrickmacross constituted under the Towns Improvement Act?—In 1859.

4. Was it for all purposes?—No, for lighting only.

5. Was the present area then adopted?—Yes, there has been no change since.

6. Does the present area include whole townlands or portions of townlands?—Portions.

7. No entire townlands?—No.

8. Give me the names of the townlands of which portions are included?—Kilmacrenna, Magheross, Mullinally, Drumanibreta, Lurgans, and Drumcondra.

9. Can you tell me the valuation of those portions within the boundary?—I can't tell the exact valuation.

10. How far does the boundary extend from the centre of the town to the north?—About a quarter of a mile I should say.

11. To the south?—About the same.

12. Would you say a quarter of a mile all round?—Somewhat about that.

13. Excepting the north-west which appears to extend somewhat more?—Yes.

14. On how much of the valuation is the full rate assessed and how much the quarter rate?—I am not able to tell exactly; the full rate is levied on almost the entire, there are very few arable lands coming within it, and in the townland of Drumanibreta the landlord allowed the full rate to be charged.

15. But what did the tenant who paid the rate say to that arrangement?—I don't know.

16. Would the Town Commissioners have any objection to include the whole of these townlands a part of which are now included?—I could scarcely say that.

17. What is the population of Carrickmacross?—2,017 according to Thom.

411—2,043.
that the census of 1881 will
ase?—There will I think be

a town that you would say
a thriving certainly up to a
ink it is still.
operations going on to any
within a few years past.
?—Above the centre of the

easy to extend without the

ly within the electoral divi-
-Yes.
a from the centre of the town
a new boundary would it
electoral division?—I should

Islown would it cut?—Bally-
al Donaghmoine.
ion of the electoral division?

are?—No.
the municipal rate for the
In 1875, 1s.; in 1874, 10d.;
erage for the past ten years

town your rate for the past
the pound for the last few

what is the average for the

missioners ever expressed any
y functions of the guardians
think they are inclined to

assed any resolution to that
there are for it and some

as a general rule, that they
mate with the money they
tary works?—I never heard
the sanitary authority, the
ver complained against the

provements in a sanitary way
Not that I am aware of.
provements which the Com-
ld carry out if they had any
m not aware of any.
ent money for paving and
y have sufficient money for

well lighted?—Yes.

ntract for the lighting?—
e are twenty-five lamps, they
t.
d to the borders of the exten-

town is lighted?—Not exactly
to the borders.
mers pay their share of the

ands of the Commissioners
e town.
the Act for cleansing?—No;

in the town?—Yes.
on.
t town?—Yes.
uld late in the day?—It de-
the year.
me in from the outlying dis-
produce here?—Yes.
hat the people in the entire
ound out of those markets?—

st town to Carrickmacross?—

Well Castleblayney is near, but Dundalk is, perhaps, the nearest town of importance, but no one thinks of going to Castleblayney; they do go to Dundalk sometimes being a seaport town. CARRICKMACROSS. Sept. 17, 1878. Mr. Edward M'Kelly.

53. This is, however, their principal market town?—Yes.

54. Are there any what you would call villa residences near Carrickmacross, where people carrying on business in the town go to live?—No. There is one merchant in the town who has a residence outside.

55. And he pays rates for the town?—Yes.

56. If you were to include say a radius of half a mile from the centre of the boundary, it would be altogether land liable to the one-fourth taxation that you would take in?—Yes; there would be very few houses.

57. Now those queries which were submitted to you from Dublin—were they laid before your Board?—Yes.

58. And did they pass any resolution on the subject?—No; nothing more than that a reply should be sent to the questions.

59. Replies to the questions were given?—Yes.

60. What was the nature of the replies?—As far as I recollect, that no extension of the boundary was required.

61. Were they unanimous?—Yes.

62. Did you take any steps to ascertain the feeling of the ratepayers on the subject?—No.

63. Have the Commissioners ever considered the question of adopting the electoral division as the boundary of the town?—No; it never came before them.

64. You are aware that when the Select Committee appointed this commission they wished as to make the towns coterminous with the electoral divisions as far as possible; do you think the recommendation can be applied fairly to Carrickmacross?—No.

65. Are the Commissioners aware of that recommendation?—I do not think that they are.

66. But they would be opposed to the electoral division boundary?—Yes.

67. Do you think that the population of the electoral division would object to pay their quota of the taxation of the town considering the advantages the town confers on them?—I think they would have a feeling against it.

68. I suppose they allow the town confers advantage on them?—Hardly.

69. Is not the land about the town more valuable from its proximity to the town?—It is chiefly owned by people in the town.

70. But it is let at a higher rate in consequence of its proximity?—Yes.

71. You think they get advantage as manure, and so on?—Yes.

72. But you think they would object to pay for it?—Well I think so, those who hold townparks would object.

73. Do you think the farmers would think that if they had to pay one quarter of the municipal taxation it would be a hardship?—Yes.

74. And do you think it is a hardship?—Well I think so, I don't see that they have any advantage.

75. But do you not consider the town itself is an advantage which ought to be paid for?—I should say not.

76. Have you any property outside the town yourself?—No.

77. You don't think the people outside have any advantage from the town?—I believe the advantage of the townspeople and those outside is identical.

78. And you think the people outside have an advantage?—Well it is mutual, but not to such an extent that they would like to pay a quarter rate.

79. They avail themselves of the light of the town?—Yes, they do.

80. Is it not an advantage to them to have the

town well kept, and well lighted?—Well, I would rather not express an opinion on it.

81. Have you formed an opinion yourself as to the advisability or otherwise of an extension?—Yes.

82. You have lived a long time in the town?—Yes.

83. And is there any necessity for an extension?—I think not.

84. Is there sufficient land within the municipal limits for building for some time to come?—Yes, I should say so.

85. Is there facility for getting building leases?—I fear not.

86. So that if any building operations were to take place it should be outside?—There is sufficient land inside, but I don't think the landlords would be inclined to give leases.

87. Would there be better opportunities for getting leases outside?—I should say not.

88. How long have you lived in the town?—About thirty-one years.

89. Do you notice any great difference in the character of the town now and what you first remember it to have been?—Yes, the houses are better.

90. Are there more of them?—The population is less now than it was then. I don't think there are more houses now, but they are of a better class. There are some parts of the town where houses were thickly built and these are gone there now.

Mr. Bernard M'Cabe examined.

91. You are clerk of the Union?—Yes.

92. You are acquainted with the electoral division?—Yes.

93. How far does it extend?—About three miles on the north.

94. And on the south?—Not so much.

95. And on the east?—It is close to the town on the east.

96. And on the west?—Nearly three Irish miles.

97. What is the valuation of the electoral division?—Something about £8,000.

98. Do you remember the acreage?—No.

99. How many townlands are there in it?—Thirty.

100. What were the poor rates for the last four or five years?—The lowest was 1s. 4d. and they varied from 1s. 4d. to 1s. 6d.

101. Do they include any rate for sanitary purposes?—Yes.

102. What was the contributory district on which it was charged?—Drumsradrain and Drumcondra.

103. Do portions of those extend outside the town?—Yes.

104. For what purpose was this special sanitary rate struck?—For the drainage of Carrickmacross.

105. Would the electoral division be too large to select for a boundary?—It would be quite out of the way altogether.

106. Do the people in it derive advantage from the town?—Very little, except at night when of course they have the light coming in or out of the town.

107. Altogether we may say that the question of selecting the electoral division as a boundary as regards Carrickmacross is not practicable?—It is not.

108. Are you a ratepayer yourself?—Yes.

109. Have you got any property outside?—Yes.

110. And you don't think an extension of the boundary would be required?—I think not.

111. Is there land available for building within the town for any time to come?—There is not much inside.

112. If any building operations were to take place would they have to go outside for land?—Yes, building operations to any extent.

113. Is it a thriving town?—Yes.

114. Are there good markets in it?—Yes.

Mr. Thomas Phelan, examined.

115. Mr. *Phelan*, T.C., handed in a letter from the Chairman of the Town Commissioners, and requested to have it entered in the notes. The letter was as follows:—

Carrickmacross, September, 17th, 1879.

Mr. T. Phelan,

My Dear Sir,—I greatly regret that owing to indisposition I will not be able (as I had intended) to be present at the inquiry to be held this day at the Court-house here, relative to the extension of the town boundary.

As you informed me at the last meeting of the Town Commissioners you expected to attend at the inquiry, I think you might (if you approve of the suggestion and be allowed by the Commissioners to do so) when stating your opinion and that of the Town Commissioners, *i.e.*, that under existing circumstances there is no necessity for extending the town boundary, allude to the present very unsatisfactory state of the law under which the management of the affairs of the town (the lighting alone excepted) is placed in the hands of the Board of Guardians of the Union, the majority of whom being rural guardians, have no interest whatever in the welfare of the town, more especially when the matter of taxing themselves or the divisions they represent, is in question, as was witnessed in a late occasion when they met to decide upon the area of taxation for the keeping in repair of Mahernagh cemetery, the expense of which they decided to throw upon the division of Carrickmacross and two small outlying divisions—when that expense should in all reason and justice have been fairly divided over the whole Union, as the graveyard is one in which persons from all parts of the Union have been, as all times, and are still interred.

I am of opinion that all power for the control and management of the town should be exclusively in the hands of the Town Commissioners, the members of which being persons living in and having direct interest in promoting the welfare of the town, would be the best guardians thereof, and would prevent the ratepayers thereof from such injustice as heretofore considered to have occurred in the case of the Mahernagh graveyard business. This is only one of the many reasons why the Town Commissioners should be allowed to control the affairs of the town. I could address many others, which you are as well (if not better) acquainted with than I am, but from "you have the many."

Yours &c.,

Thomas M. Fleming, Chairman,
Carrickmacross Town Commissioners.

116. You have been a Town Commissioner for a length of time?—About six years.

117. And you have lived in Carrickmacross before that?—Yes.

118. You take an interest in the town?—Yes.

119. Were you present when the question of the extension of the boundaries was discussed?—Yes.

120. Were you one of the gentlemen who voted against any extension?—Yes.

121. And your reason was that the boundary was sufficiently large already?—Yes.

122. And that the people who paid for the town were the people who most directly derived advantage from it.

123. You have heard of the suggestion of the select committee that an extension to the electoral division was advisable when possible?—Yes, but it would not be practicable in this town.

124. It would be too far?—Yes.

125. Have you ever considered the question of becoming the urban sanitary authority?—I agree with the opinion expressed by the chairman.

126. And you think that whole management of the town ought to be under the one authority?—Yes.

127. And that that authority should be the Town Commissioners?—Yes.

128. And as to the roads, do you think that they should also be under the management of the Commissioners?—Yes, all matters relating to the management of the town should be.

129. You are aware that under the Public Health Act of last session, section 7, you can get a provisional order from the Local Government Board giving you jurisdiction over the sanitary matters?—I am.

130. Have the Commissioners discussed that ?—No, it was considered was not discussed.

131. You are aware that under the 20th section of the Act you can obtain a repayment from the Grand Jury for the maintenance of the roads, but that is only to obtain that you must first become the Urban Sanitary Authority ?—Yes, but it has not been discussed to any extent.

132. Is it the view of the Commissioners generally that it would be better to have the town under one body ?—I think it is the feeling of the entire body, although the clerk said that some were opposed to it.

Mr. M'Neilly (Town Clerk).—Yes, that is my opinion.

133. Examination resumed.—You never heard an objection ?—No.

134. You yourself are in favour of it ?—Yes.

135. Do you think that you get from the Grand Jury what is commensurate with what you pay in county cess ?—I never went minutely into it, but I think that we do not.

136. If you became the Sanitary Authority, and had control of the roads, would you not be in favour of having a larger area of taxation ?—The land adjoining the town in the possession of those residing in the town should pay its proportion.

137. That is one-fourth ?—Yes.

138. If you were the Sanitary Authority would you be of opinion that the whole of the townlands now partly included should be included, without extending any hardship on the people ?—I would hardly, in the entire distance of the townlands. Taking Ballymoney, those in that townland are farmers, and if their close proximity to the town is an advantage to them, their lands are at a higher rent, and the advantages of their proximity is paid by their rents.

139. And do you consider their proximity to the town is a greater advantage to the landlord than it is to the tenant ?—Fully as much.

140. The tenant has the advantage of a good market, and the landlord is enabled to strike a higher rent on that account ?—Yes.

141. Would it be better a broad and fair line, a circle, in defining the boundary ?—No.

142. The great objection to that is, of course, that it cuts through a man's holding, it might cut through a man's house, or lawn ?—I don't think that would do.

143. You think all the accommodation lands where people can hardly ought to pay their quota ?—Yes.

144. Is that your own opinion, or the opinion of your Board ?—It is my own opinion.

145. Have you ever discussed it at your Board ?—Yes.

146. And was the opinion divided ?—It was never put to the vote. My opinion is that there is a difference of opinion. At all events the Commissioners agreed not to go for an extension of the boundary.

147. Do you think if the Commissioners had the control of all the powers relating to the town they would not desire a larger area of taxation ?—I rather think not.

148. Have you any idea, if your look in portions of those townlands now outside, how many people you would bring in qualified as such ?—To what distance.

149. Say three town parks ?—Not many.

150. If you took in portions of the townlands now partly included, how many would there be brought in ? —Very few.

151. What is the population of the electoral division ?—I forget it.

152. Are you a Poor Law Guardian ?—Yes.

153. You consider you could do the sanitary business better in the town ?—I should think all town business could be best administered by the Town Commissioners.

154. Are you of opinion that the landlord ought to pay half the rates ?—Yes.

155. You believe that if a town is clean and well kept it adds to the value ?—Yes.

156. And if it is clean and well kept it is not to the advantage of the people living outside ?—It is an indirect advantage to all having those personal connexions with the town.

Mr. John Thomas Holland examined.

157. You are agent to Mr. Shirley ?—Yes.

158. He is the landlord of great part of the soil ?—Yes. [Witness pointed out on a map the portions of the town owned by Mr. Shirley and the portion held by the Marquis of Bath.]

159. Do I understand that Mr. Shirley is altogether against an extension of the boundaries ?—Certainly. I don't know anyone in favour of it.

160. Would Mr. Shirley be opposed to adopting the electoral division as the boundary ?—Certainly. It was very unfairly made out under the Poor Law ; they took in about thirty-one townlands, and the proper electoral division would have been a circle around the town.

161. From your knowledge of the town, you know fairly made any building operations in it ?—Mr. Shirley has built a good deal lately in it ; he has built a street in one part.

162. Would you say the present house is improving ? —Old ones are being thrown down and good ones are being put up.

163. All within the municipal limits ?—Yes. I don't think there will be any building outside the many years to come.

164. And you yourself think that no extension is required ?—Yes, I do.

The inquiry then terminated.

COLERAINE.—JULY 14th, 1879.

Before Mr. Cotton, C.E.

Mr. William Eccles examined.

1. You are Town Clerk of Coleraine ?—Yes.

2. How long have you been so ?—For 14 years.

3. The town was originally under the 9th George IV. ?—Yes.

4. It was put under the Towns Improvement Act, in January, 1840 ?—Yes.

5. Have you a copy of the Gazette of that date ?—No ; but I have the record of the minutes of the proceedings at the time.

6. Has there been put upon the minutes the boundary that was then fixed ?—The boundaries then fixed were the same as existed under the previous Act.

7. And it is just described as being the previous boundary ?—Yes.

8. The last alteration was in 1861, and the present boundary of the town is shown upon this map ?—Yes.

9. What is the area of the town ?—397 acres.

10. And the population ?—6,[illegible] according to the Census of 1871.

11. Do you know anything about the population now—whether it has increased or diminished since ?—I think it is much about the same. I don't think there would be any increase.

12. That is within the present boundary ?—Yes.

13. Do you remember Mr. Corbett's inquiry here ?—Yes, I was present, and the number of the population was then stated at 6,[illegible], but perhaps that was the parliamentary boundary.

COLERAINE.
Aug. 14, 1878.
—
Mr. William Logan.

14. But 6,082 is the population within the boundary?—Yes, within the municipal area, according to the Census of 1871.

15. What is the valuation?—£12,312 2s.

16. What is the number of Commissioners?—Eighteen.

17. Is that the full body?—Yes.

18. How many municipal voters are there within the town boundary qualified to vote at the last election?—481.

19. How many qualified to be Commissioners if elected?—176.

20. Can you give the municipal rates for the last four years, taking 1874 first?—There has been a rate levied since 1874, under the Bann Navigation Act, of 6d. in the pound.

21. What was the municipal rate in 1874?—In 1874 it was 1s.; in 1875 the same.

22. That is the maximum?—Yes.

23. In 1876?—1s.

24. In 1877?—1s. 3d.

25. What is the 3d. for?—For sanitary purposes.

26. And what was it in 1878?—1s. 6d., that is 6d. more, which includes 6d. of an additional rate inasmuch as waterworks were erected that year.

27. Was there any rate struck for sewers?—No, not yet.

28. Are there any wards in the town?—No.

29. What electoral division is the town in?—The electoral division of Coleraine.

30. Altogether in the Coleraine electoral division?—Yes.

31. Do you know the size of the electoral division?—It is pretty extensive.

32. Do you know how far it extends in the different directions?—I cannot say. It varies.

33. How is the town lighted?—The Commissioners are the proprietors of the gas works.

34. How many lamps have you?—124.

35. How are they lighted, and what rules are there for lighting them and extinguishing them?—They are not lighted from 12th May to 1st September, and during the months from 1st September to 12th May they are fully lighted, except about five days at each full moon. That varies.

36. And that is in the judgment of some officer?—Yes. The manager of the works.

37. Are they lighted after 12 o'clock?—Yes.

38. With regard to the supply of water you have said something about waterworks—have they been constructed?—The water is turned on at present, but the contract has not been given over to the Commissioners.

39. But it is all settled?—Yes.

40. With regard to the sewage question has there been anything done of late years?—Yes, there have been works in that respect.

41. What money has been expended in sewers, in 1877 and 1878?—I could not tell.

42. Was there any special sewer rate struck?—Yes; there was 6d. in the pound, which is included in that 1s. 6d. Eight pence was the ordinary town rate, 6d. for water, and 3d. for sanitary purposes.

43. Has there been any large project for the drainage of the town under any main drainage scheme?—No. The main drainage I think is fairly good.

44. Have you any drainage works on hands?—Not just now.

45. The guardians have nothing to say to you in these matters?—No, except we gave them sanction to [illegible] sewers.

46. You are the urban authority?—Yes.

47. Have the Commissioners ever considered the question of taking up the control of the roads within their jurisdiction?—Yes. We are rather anxious for a separation from the Grand Jury.

48. But have they taken any steps?—No.

49. They are aware they can memorialize the Local Government Board to have a separation?—Yes; but it appears it requires the consent of the Grand Jury, except under certain conditions that they think inapplicable.

50. The Local Government Board may make a separation whether the Grand Jury wish it or not—they were not aware of that before?—I think in part they were, but they had considerable work in hands during the last twelve months, and they did not want to take up the other question.

51. But I want to know whether they were aware that the Local Government Board had power to grant them that separation, whether the Grand Jury consented or not?—Yes.

52. In the queries that we sent down, there was a question asked, whether the Commissioners wished for any alteration in the boundaries—what was the answer?—The reply was that they were anxious for extension.

53. Was there any special resolution on the subject?—Yes. There was a resolution passed some time ago. The board have had the matter under consideration for a long time.

54. And is there any resolution on the books that embodies their present views?—In June of the present year, there was a resolution passed to meet the present inquiry. It was on the 18th of June, and was as follows:—

"That the Board are desirous of extension of the present municipal boundary, and approve of the extended [illegible] coloured yellow on the map prepared by Mr. Gibbon."

55. This coloured yellow on the map is what is referred to in that resolution?—Yes.

56. How many Commissioners were present at that meeting?—Twelve.

57. Were they unanimous?—Yes.

58. Do you know what additional area that extension would bring in?—About 550 acres.

59. Do you know what additional number of voters it would bring in?—I am not quite sure.

60. Or the valuation?—Something under £3,000.

61. Are there many gentlemen's places taken in by it?—Yes. The recent improvements in buildings have been almost altogether confined to the coloured area.

62. Buildings are extending more in one direction than another?—Yes.

63. In what direction is that?—On the Portrush road. There is a good deal of building beyond the railway crossings, and on this side of the road there is a very fine terrace.

64. Is there building going on beyond the present boundaries in any other direction?—Yes, in the Ballymoney direction.

65. There is building going on beyond your present boundary out there?—Yes.

66. Is there building going on anywhere else?—Yes; at Killowen, beyond the railway station, and there is some additional building on the [illegible] road.

67. Is there any building going on on the other side of the river?—Yes; there is a good deal of building beyond the present boundary on this road (pointing to map).

68. Beyond the National District Model School?—Yes.

69. Do the lamps of the town at present go beyond your boundaries?—No.

70. Have the Commissioners considered the question—whether they would afford gas and water to the entire area they propose to take in, or what the expense would be in that way?—No; there was no estimate of the expense prepared.

71. Did they consider that they would be obliged to supply lights to the extended area?—They thought that lighting and cleansing should be carried out the same as within the present township.

72. Along all those roads to the full extent of the new area, or only as far as built on?—As far as built on, I think, but that if the building extended they would be prepared to extend the lighting and cleansing.

73. Getting additional rates for that purpose from the buildings in question?—Yes.

74. Of course they are aware that for town improvement purposes they would only get a quarter of the rating from agricultural land?—Yes.

75. Does your increased [illegible] go beyond the boundary?—No; we don't [illegible] the public lamps beyond it, but there is a private contract for gas outside.

76. In your gas account those lamps are not brought in, but the gas company [illegible] for each lamp [illegible].

77. The present supply of gas outside the boundary is only for [illegible] purposes?—Yes.

78. What has been your gas rate for the last few years?—In 1874, 1s. [illegible]; 1875, 1s. [illegible]; 1876, 1s. 10d.; 1877, 1s. [illegible]; 1878, 1s.

79. Can you give me the county cess for the same period?—The county cess for the two baronies in [illegible]—1874, 2s. [illegible]; 1875, 2s. [illegible]; 1876, 3s. [illegible]; 1877, 2s. [illegible]; 1878, 2s. [illegible]

80. What was the last levy?—One shilling.

81. That is for the half year?—Yes.

82. What is the county cess for the half barony?—[illegible]

83. What is the [illegible] valuation [illegible] of the town?—The town and liberties, £10,030 [illegible]; and the half barony, £1,073 [illegible].

84. An application was made to the Local Government Board for an extension some years ago; do you know anything about that?—No.

85. That application does not [illegible] any reason?—No; but the matter had been under consideration for a length of time.

86. Could you tell me what were the reasons?—It was felt that the present area was very confined, and that the building had been almost entirely confined to the district immediately outside the present boundary limits, and there was felt a necessity for extending further the public lamps. The ratepayers outside had been making applications to the Commissioners to extend the lamps, and the Commissioners had been forced to extend them to the very utmost limit. There was building going on outside, and the ratepayers of the town who resided outside the limit wished to have lights.

87. Not according to the present boundary?—Yes.

88. On all the roads?—Yes.

89. There is a necessity for extending that too?—Yes; the sanitary works, and water works, and public [illegible] in the town had become available to the ratepayers immediately adjoining, and they have all the advantages of the town in fact. At [illegible] it is a continuous row of houses with the [illegible] right through there.

90. You have not [illegible] boundaries outside the boundary?—No; but the ratepayers outside are [illegible], and the [illegible] would be very [illegible] for building purposes, and [illegible] purposes. The [illegible] have [illegible] to make [illegible] accommodation outside the present limits, but when they do so they will make available the works which the Commissioners have recently completed.

91. They have been [illegible] with a view to their extension beyond the boundary?—Yes; the sewers have been so constructed.

92. In each direction as far as this new proposed boundary, do you think, the people are so interested in those matters of [illegible] that they would be [illegible] to pay for them?—The matter has been under consideration for a long time, and there are very few persons who have expressed dissent, but a great number have expressed their willingness to come under taxation.

93. Are you talking of outsiders?—Yes; there are a number of those [illegible] persons who would be qualified, but for the want of residence, but who at present are not qualified [illegible] interest [illegible] in the town.

94. You are able to tell me the number?—There are a good many on the [illegible] list who would be qualified as Commissioners, but are disqualified by non-residence.

95. How many do you think?—About twelve.

96. That is the qualification on which they are shut out. They are rated within the limits, but they are not living inside, and they are disqualified thereby. You don't know the number of voters the extension would add to the list?—No.

97. Would you say 100?—No.

98. Less than 100?—Yes. A cemetery has recently been provided for this town, and provision made for the interment [illegible] the poor. The Guardians had made a provision in that respect, but the poor people objected to be buried in that cemetery, and they preferred to be buried in the cemetery attached to the town, and the extended area would meet with more [illegible] from them in that respect.

99. The ratepayers inside have not expressed any opinion?—Not formally by meeting, but they have almost unanimously through their representatives.

100. Do you know whether this extension would run into any other electoral division?—No; it would not.

[illegible] Mr. William [illegible].

Mr. Hugh A[illegible] examined.

Mr. Hugh A[illegible].

101. You are Chairman of the Town Commissioners?—Yes; only for a short time—about a month.

102. Have you been long a Commissioner?—I have been for about nine years.

103. You heard the town clerk's statement that there was a resolution come to that this extension marked with the yellow line should be sought for?—Yes. I was not present at that meeting—Mr. [illegible] was then chairman.

104. What was the opinion of the Commissioners not present, did they coincide with the others?—I believe they are quite unanimous as to the desirability of extension.

105. On what grounds were the particular boundaries laid down on this map, for I see they run through some fields, and don't adhere to the townland boundaries or anything of that kind?—I think in most cases they are with the boundaries of fields, but in other cases, perhaps it is where a little stream runs through a field, or some little natural boundary of that kind.

106. Can you tell me in this case, in the extension to the [illegible] beyond the workhouse, why should you not extend it so as to take in the parliamentary boundary there?—It is purely agricultural and it never can be available for building purposes. It is an entirely agricultural district.

107. And it was entirely with regard to how building would run along the roads that the boundary was laid down?—To a large extent.

108. The boundary at present includes a large extent of agricultural land?—It does, but it was extended in such a direction as would be likely to be occupied chiefly with buildings.

109. But you did not confine yourselves to stripes where buildings would be likely to go—for instance you have taken a large stripe at the back of the workhouse where it would not be likely to be built upon?—There is no reason why, if the town was extended this ground should not be interspersed with roads.

110. Is there any other reason except that the ground brought in was likely to be built on?—No.

111. Do you know what would be the valuation of the district proposed to be taken in?—No. That map was made before my term of office. I cannot say.

112. Were you a Commissioner at the time the memorial was presented to the Local Government Board?—I was.

[illegible]

113. Do you remember the particulars of it?—No, but Mr. [illegible] our solicitor can tell you.

114. Do you know what are the feelings of the residents outside who would be taken in by this extension?—I believe they are almost unanimous. There may be some exceptions, but by a very large majority they would prefer being included in the municipal boundary.

115. They understand the way in which they would be brought in, with full rates on houses and one-fourth on land?—Yes.

116. Have the Commissioners discussed the question of taking up the charge of the roads?—We have had it frequently before us; but we did not understand exactly how to go about it, and we rather looked upon it as a hopeless task to attempt so long as we would be obliged to have the sanction of the Grand Jury.

117. The Parliamentary Committee have expressed a strong opinion that everything within a municipality should be under the control of one body, and that the tendency is to throw the roads into the hands of the Commissioners. Well, the report of the Committee is strongly in favour of giving the control?—We are all in favour of that.

118. Did you consider the mileage of the roads that would be thrown upon you in case you got this extension?—I am not aware there was an accurate calculation made.

119. Have you a borough surveyor?—No.

120. In case you became the road authority you would have to have a regular staff—have you considered that, and the expense it would entail?—I am not sure whether the matter has been gone into.

121. Who is the superintendent of the drainage?—Our town officer looks after it.

122. Does he lay out new drains?—No, we have to employ a surveyor.

123. But you have no permanent officer?—No.

124. Have you got a drainage map?—Not completed, I believe. There is a map in preparation.

125. You know of course there is one required?—Yes; but recently the drainage has all been carefully laid down, and there is a large map with the drainage of the town being prepared. We have had some difficulty in ascertaining the site of the old drains; no record was kept of them.

126. Do you consider yourself that this extension is large enough?—Yes; I think it would be large enough, but perhaps our late chairman would say something as to that.

Mr. Joseph [illegible] examined.

127. You have been chairman?—Yes; I was chairman in 1876, and for five years before that.

128. Did you take any active part in designating this area?—Yes; I think it was about the time I was in the chair it was fixed upon.

129. Mr. Anderson has told us that one thing that guided the Commissioners in making this area was the probability of buildings extending along the roads—was there any other reason?—That was the chief reason—almost the sole reason.

130. There seems to be a very large amount of agricultural land taken in at the north-west corner that would be very unlikely ever to be built upon?—There are buildings at present there, and there is no reason why these fields, which are well situated for villa sites, should not be taken for building.

131. You consider it likely to be built upon?—Yes; it may not be built upon for some time, but a great deal of it will I think.

132. It appears that that corner is much further away from the town than other places of the town where there are buildings—why is the chapel field left out?—There is a story about, and it is not likely there would be buildings there.

133. It has been a question of building in every case?—Nearly every case. We took into account the probability of any building being carried out on the ground.

134. Don't you think the people living in the chapel field are as much interested in having the town drained as the people in the north-west corner?—Perhaps so.

135. And why should not they contribute to the rates?—I think if you were on the ground the reason would strike you.

136. I am not talking of new buildings, but about those people who are within that distance of the town, contributing something to the rates?—There are no buildings there except the chapel field, and it is not of much consequence. There are only a few small houses. It is only in some districts that building leases can be got.

137. I want to know why you should leave out a place that is so near the town, and that appears to derive as much advantage from the town being lighted and cleansed, as the people you do take in?—There are residences there.

138. Why not take in [illegible]?—We went as far as we thought necessary. There is no likelihood of building beyond [illegible] Cottage, which is only a small house.

139. I want to know your reasons, if you have gone so very carefully into it?—One reason that guided us very much is that it would not pay us to extend the limits beyond a certain point.

140. Why?—Because if we were obliged to take the sewerage works, and the watering of the district there would be a serious loss to the town.

141. Did you, in defining this boundary, consider that you would have to supply light and water and drainage to the outside limits along the roads, whether the roads were built upon or not?—What we thought was that if at the extreme limit there were a few houses erected, even two or three, we would be obliged, as the sanitary authority, to provide sewerage works for those houses, and that that could not be done without a system of sewerage that would actually embrace the whole district.

142. On the north side of the townland there is a small area of fourteen acres or so that you have left out, on the [illegible]-road—is there any special reason why it should not be taken in, for it is evident it would be desirable, if there is no reason against it, to make the boundary coterminous with the townland boundary?—That is on the opposite side of the railway. The railway is there, and a high embankment.

143. Is it a building question still?—Yes. That could not be occupied by buildings.

144. Then, except building, there is no other reason?—No.

145. Then the same applies to the small portion left out on the east?—Yes.

146. Down to the south there are 20 acres left out that would complete the townland—what about it?—That would not be used for building. It is not situated.

147. There would be no objection to take it in so far as the town is concerned?—No; but the Commissioners thought it would not be desirable to take into the boundary what would not be likely to be occupied with houses—in fact that it would be rather an unfair thing to be taxing agricultural land.

148. That land is within half a mile of the centre of the town?—Well, it is more.

149. Take the other land that is here—the portion along the [illegible] road is not half a mile from the town?—I think the town may be extended with advantage in that direction.

150. Don't you think that the owner of that twenty acres is as much interested in the town, and that he is as much interested in its being well kept as the others that he might pay some small rate towards it?—He might not like to pay it, but he would be entitled to pay it.

151. Don't you think that every person living outside a town, and using it for a market for selling and buying may be expected to contribute something?—I think it is only just, within a reasonable limit.

152. And what would you put as a reasonable limit, considering that they would only have to pay one-fourth on agricultural land?—I think a radius of a mile; I think in a town like this a mile would be sufficient.

153. I suppose the schools are situated in the town?—The Model school is outside and the Academical Institution outside, but it would be brought in by the proposed extension; and the workhouse is outside the present boundary.

154. Did you take any part in suggesting the area before when the memorial was presented to the Local Government Board?—Yes. We fixed this area at that time as the most natural. The time the memorial was presented was in February, 1877.

155. Was it this yellow area that was then suggested?—Yes. The map of that boundary was sent to the Local Government Board.

156. Mr. Lawlor's report says the extension proposed would be 1,000 acres?—I don't think it was very accurately gone into. At the time they were here we were just changing our Town Clerk, and it was merely a guess.

157. Mr. [illegible] (Town Clerk).—Five hundred and fifty acres is exclusive of the roads for the extended area; with the roads it would be about 630 acres—for the extension of the present boundary altogether.

Mr. [illegible] examination continued.

158. Would you be in favour of taking up the roads from the grand jury?—Yes, it is most important, for this reason; there is a [illegible] between the grand jury and the town [illegible] about making the [illegible], and the county cess is £1,[illegible] a year.

159. And of that how much is expended in the town?—For a number of years there was almost nothing spent except the mere maintenance of the roads. We have lately been agitating with the grand jury to get a fair share for the town.

160. Have you made applications for presentments and they were thrown out?—They have lately refused to pay anything towards flagging, but lately they have [illegible]; but it was always with the greatest difficulty we have got some presentments [illegible].

161. How much is the county-at-large charge out of the £1,[illegible]?—I could not say.

162. The county-at-large charge you would have to pay still?—About £[illegible] would meet the county charges.

163. How much did the grand jury expend here in 1877 and 1878?—They expended more in 1877 and 1878 than they ever did before.

164. Have they expended £1,[illegible]?—No, not anything approaching it. About £[illegible] in the [illegible]. Any presentments for footpaths were smaller than the [illegible], and we had to supplement it. We had a [illegible], and we had to make a [illegible] specially to get it passed.

165. Is there anything else you wish to state?—There is just another point as to the sewerage works, and the margin outside the town; that is called the [illegible] of [illegible].

166. That is outside the present boundary?—Yes.

167. On the eastern side of the river?—Yes. The [illegible] there is a row of houses called [illegible] on the [illegible] road. They required sewerage, and the residents there might up the guardians to the [illegible] sanitary authority to get sewerage for those houses, and the guardians agreed to make sewerage, and [illegible] to [illegible] the [illegible].

168. What did they do for that sewer?—They made arrangements with the [illegible] of the houses into the [illegible]. It only [illegible] these [illegible], and the guardians [illegible] who should pay for that sewerage. The Local Government Board [illegible] the guardians to [illegible] it on the [illegible] of outside—this very [illegible] round the whole area.

169. Excluding the municipality?—Yes.

170. They would not [illegible] it on the municipality?—No.

171. [illegible] they [illegible] it on the [illegible] of the [illegible] of [illegible]?—Yes; and the valuation of that [illegible] is only £[illegible] a year; it was levied off in a single year.

172. Then do those [illegible] people living down beyond the workhouse had to pay a rate for that sewerage?—Yes. I [illegible] the [illegible], that is not a [illegible] of use to [illegible], and [illegible] had to pay 1[illegible] or 1[illegible]d. for it.

173. If [illegible] was [illegible] taken in, as you propose, this [illegible] would have [illegible] on the whole town and the [illegible]?—Yes. And it would have been [illegible], but it [illegible] a very unjust tax on the small [illegible]. On this the Lodge road or Ballymoney road the sewerage works are at present in operation. The Commissioners carried sewerage works to the very verge of the boundary there, and they are being carried on by the guardians up to very near the parliamentary boundary, and I understand that the guardians are going to levy on the same principle as before.

174. Surely the guardians must have had the contributory district settled before they began any works?—The contributory district is the same, and a number of [illegible] who are [illegible] to benefit [illegible] from those sewerage works are now objecting before the Local Government Board to the guardians taking this area in [illegible] and [illegible] it [illegible] so.

175. They have commenced the works, and the rate must have been [illegible] that?—I don't think it is [illegible] yet.

176. You are not a member of the board of guardians?—No; but of course it is a very [illegible] thing to have that ring round the town.

177. In the course that you have been seeking you have had [illegible] advice?—Yes.

178. They are [illegible] out on to take in these [illegible] places?—Yes; we always [illegible] we would have [illegible] [illegible] in that [illegible].

179. And the [illegible] would be the [illegible]?—Yes.

180. You don't think that the sewerage works would extend beyond the yellow boundary?—Not for some considerable time, and as to the borough surveyor, there is no other [illegible] wanted.

181. It is the only town of this [illegible] that has not got [illegible]?—I am informed by Mr. [illegible]. I suppose it must have been before [illegible] there was some difficulty about the Local Government fixing the salary, and that was the cause of his not being appointed. It has been a difficulty that was all along. We employed a surveyor for each individual work.

182. And that is really an economical?—We have found it so.

Mr. David [illegible] examined.

183. You are a Commissioner of the town?—Yes.

184. Have you been long a Commissioner?—A number of years.

185. You know this suggestion before us now about taking in the yellow area—does that meet with your approval?—It hardly goes far enough to please me.

186. In which direction?—Generally.

187. On what ground; is it that the people have such an interest that they should contribute further on?—Yes.

188. Where would you put that limit?—I would go about a mile out each way.

189. You would not go far outside the present boundary with a mile?—I think it would be a considerable deal out in some directions.

190. You think that, within a mile, people should contribute something?—Yes, the fields within that distance are town parks, and they have more advantages than people at a greater distance.

191. And they would be only taxed one-fourth?—Yes.

192. Would you be in favour of taking up the roads?—Yes.

193. And getting a regular borough surveyor and staff?—Yes. It would be a great improvement, and we could get improvements made. It is a difficult matter to get anything done now at all.

194. Do you think you would be able to save money by it?—We would be able to make a great many improvements, and to have sewers where they are very much needed.

195. You own property outside?—Yes.

196. And it would come within the proposed extension?—Yes.

197. And you consent to this proposal as a proprietor?—Yes.

198. What is the feeling of your neighbours outside?—The feeling of most of them is that they would like the advantages other people have in the way of water, sewerage, light, and cleansing.

199. And are willing to pay for it?—Yes.

200. What is the feeling of the ratepayers of the town?—They are generally in favour of the extension; there are very few object to it: they think it very much wanted.

201. Is the town increasing?—Very slightly.

202. There are a good many new buildings dotted round—is the population increasing?—I don't think the population is increasing very much; but the buildings are increasing outside. The boundary should be extended down towards the Cranagh.

Mr. John M'Lachlan examined.

203. You are a Commissioner?—Yes.

204. Were you one of the Commissioners that considered this question?—No.

205. You know what is proposed?—Yes. I have a local knowledge of it.

206. Do you think it desirable?—I do.

207. Do you think it goes far enough?—I think it does. My reason for saying so is, there is great anxiety on the part of the town to get the management of the roads from the county, and we would wish to be disconnected from them; and if we extended the area further, we would be losing instead of gaining. I think it would be impolitic to extend the boundary too far.

208. On the supposition, that you would be obliged to supply it with water and gas to the extremities?—Yes.

209. Though you were only bound to supply where the roads are continuously built upon?—Yes; but there are house-owners who would be taxed, and who would insist on having those privileges, and my opinion is we should not go too far. We would be incurring expense that might not be right.

210. It appears the yellow area has been sketched out, having in view how far the buildings would be likely to go on the different roads?—That was the leading reason.

211. And so far as continuous building goes it ought to be taken in?—Yes. I think so. The general feelings of the Commissioners and of the town are that they should have the management and the expenditure of our own county cess.

212. That is the portion of it excluding the county-at-large charges?—Yes. We have great difficulty in getting the county to do anything. At the last Presentment Sessions I was the applicant for two footpaths within the present boundary, and I got only one, with great difficulty, and it is in a street that is in a very wretched state; and if we had control of the county cess, we could improve the town very much by putting footpaths and streets in very much better order, and I know that the town is very anxious to have it.

213. Does the county do anything in the way of cleansing the streets, or is that done entirely by the Commissioners?—Entirely by the Commissioners. They do that entirely at their own expense, and there is the expense of looking after the gratings at the various sewers, although they should be done by the road contractor. In fact, we have the general management and care of the footpaths, and, till very lately, we got no money from the county, and what we get is what would make the ordinary roadway and path, and we supplement it to make a street footpath, and, from my knowledge of the proposed extension, I think it far enough.

214. The yellow area includes all the portions of the roads running out of Coleraine that have been built upon?—Yes, my own residence is just at the verge of the yellow boundary. Cartball is my residence, and it extends a very short distance beyond it. And there is a range of private residences along that hill. It is considered a favourable locality for building. My house is almost the extreme boundary.

215. And beyond you there is no great building?—And there is no chance of building beyond it. I would not have any objection to extend it a little beyond one, but I don't think it would pay. The sole object we had in view was, looking at the land would it pay, and would the ground be favourably situated for building.

216. But you did not extend the area for the purpose of getting more funds than it would cost you?—No; not with the view of getting more funds, except whether it would pay, and my reason for not extending it further is, that it would not be desirable to do so. The Town Commissioners own five acres with a net rental of £450.

Mr. Thomas Hume, examined.

217. You are a Commissioner?—Yes.

218. You know what extension is proposed?—Yes, generally, I do.

219. Do you think it desirable, and do you think it sufficient?—I think it is, generally speaking. There is one road on which, I think, it is not sufficient. That is the Portstewart-road. I think there is one side of it that should be included, but the map was made before some of the buildings were erected.

220. Up towards Ballysally?—Possibly not so far as Ballysally. There is a stream that runs there that should be the boundary.

221. You think it should be extended to the stream to the south-east of Ballysally?—Yes. That map was made in the time of the late clerk, and there would be some alterations in it if made now. There are other buildings which should be included in it. It would take in the entire townland of Millburn and Crosshill. I live in Clifton-terrace, and I, of course, quite approve of the extension.

222. And your neighbours?—I think they all do, because we get the benefits of light, and so on, out there.

223. You have heard what the other Commissioners have stated?—Yes.

224. Have you anything to add to it?—No; but I approve of it.

Mr. Thomas G. Greer, Solicitor to the Town Commissioners, examined.

Coleraine. July 26, 1878. Mr. Thomas G. Greer.

225. When was this memorandum to the Local Government Board presented?—In February, 1877.

226. Do you remember when the Local Government Commissioners were here?—I was not before them.

227. Was it before or after their visit?—I could not say. There was only one memorandum on this subject, and that was in February, 1877.

228. What was the gist of it?—I have got a rough draft of it:—

"To His Grace the Duke of Marlborough, Lord Lieutenant General and General Governor of Ireland.

"The Memorial of the Town Commissioners of the Borough of Coleraine

"Respectfully showeth:—

"That the town of Coleraine has been under the provisions of the Towns Improvement (Ireland) Act, 1854, since February, 1869, when the provisions of that Act were duly adopted under the direction of the then Lord Lieutenant of Ireland.

"That neither at the period of the adoption of the said Act, nor at any former period, of which any record can be discovered, were the ancient borough boundaries of the town of Coleraine ascertained, verified, or altered.

"That of late years, owing to the steady prosperity of the locality, and the desire of merchants and others carrying on business in the town to reside in the suburbs, and from other causes the real inhabitants of the town have extended beyond their ancient limits, and your memorialists have, for a length of time, felt that an extension of the original boundaries of the borough should be made. The occupiers of the districts beyond the limits and precincts of the town [illegible] advantages which an extension of the boundaries would give them, and the [illegible] has, in one case, been [illegible] by the rural sanitary authority, and the expense levied off a county district in no way connected or benefited by the improvements. The assessment amounting to [illegible] per pound of the Government valuation of the country district affected, [illegible] memorialists desire that the boundaries should be extended so as to embrace a further area, and admit such area to the advantages enjoyed by the rest of the town as well as to an equitable contribution by the cess thereto.

"That your memorialists have considered the new boundaries which should, in their opinion, be adopted, and have had a map prepared on a sheet of the Ordnance Survey of Ireland showing, firstly, by the colour red, the ancient boundaries of the borough, and, by the colour yellow, the boundaries which your memorialists desire, by the consent and approval of your Grace, to adopt in lieu of the said ancient boundaries. A copy of this map is sent herewith, and to it your memorialists beg to refer.

"That your memorialists are providing new waterworks for the use of the borough, and are also promoting other public improvements, and are anxious that the said extension of the boundaries should go hand in hand with the other works.

"Your memorialists accordingly pray that your Grace will be pleased to give your consent (under the 17th and 18th Vic., c. 103, sec. 5) to the extension by your memorialists of the boundaries of the town of Coleraine from the said ancient boundaries set forth upon said map herewith sent, and thereon coloured yellow."

229. What action was taken upon that?—That was transmitted to the Lord Lieutenant, and on the 26th February, 1877, I received a reply acknowledging it, and stating that business of this kind had now been transferred to the Local Government Board, and that the papers had been transferred to the Local Government Board for their attention; and then there was a letter from the Local Government Board addressed to me, dated 20th June, 1877, in which they referred to the memorandum as having been transmitted to them by the Lord Lieutenant, and pointing out that they would not act under the Towns Improvement Act for the purpose of extending the boundary, that the Towns Improvement Act gives the Lord Lieutenant authority by mere order to extend the boundaries, and to point out that they would not act under that; but that they consider it is superseded by the Public Health Act, and although it is not formally repealed, they consider the Public Health Act is the one under which they should go, and they declined to entertain it except under the Public Health Act, and the Commissioners found it required considerable inquiry, considerable expense, and a Provisional Order turned into an Act of Parliament, and they were rather frightened at it, and having large undertakings of other kinds on their minds—the waterworks and the [illegible], and the Bann navigation—it was allowed to rest for a time, but there was never any intention of abandoning it.

230. Nor was there any inquiry, and refusal?—No; the matter just rested.

231. I may say [illegible] that the Local Government Board have power to separate a town from a county without the consent of the grand jury.—We were not aware of that, although I believe that was an improvement in the law since [illegible]; but we were quite ignorant of what view the Local Government Board might take of that, not seeing what they thought on the subject we were afraid, till some preliminary steps [illegible], to incur the large expense, but we would like very much to have extension. About seven years ago, not acting in any way professionally, but just as an individual here, I went into the thing with very great interest myself, and examined it to the very best of my ability, and I came to the conclusion that the county levied a cess of £1,200 a year nearly out of the town, and that very little over £300 a year was spent in it. Taking the road contracts merely, I took the warrant and I ascertained what was laid out for everything, and I found it came very close upon it; it was about £1,100 a year, and they laid out under £400.

232. How much would be the county at large charges?—I had no data to make estimates, but there is no doubt the town is a great loser by its connection with the county, and we found what we thought was considerable difficulty in getting contributions; but since then I am happy to say more liberal views are taken by the road sessions and the grand jury, and we are now getting more contributions towards our flagging, to an [illegible].

233. Has this altered your opinion about having charge of the roads?—It has, as to the necessity of it, but not as to the desirability of it.

234. Do you happen to know on the other side of the river there, is that expenditure by the grand jury, whether it was thrown on a presentment district [illegible] the town?—I don't know as to that. There is a sewer being made now up towards the Model School.

235. Mr. Anderson, Chairman of the Town Commissioners.—The grand jury have never expended anything in that direction. We have to drain it in that direction as far as our present boundary goes.

236. Mr. Greer.—In my opinion the yellow line is pretty nearly as much as the extension should be. There might be some little additions if you went into it nicely, but I agree with Mr. M'Laughlin, then a very great extension would not be an advantage.

237. You think it would not pay?—I think it would not be fair to the people to be added—to put burdens on people merely because they lived within a mile of the town. It would not be right according to my idea. Those who would be included in that new area would have the benefit of some roads that we keep [illegible], and I was about to point out that already a good part of what is included in the [illegible] is [illegible] building ground.

238. Part of the townland of Waterside in the north of the present town is all mapped out as building ground?—Yes; it is now the property of Sir Harvey Bruce.

239. This northern portion of the townland of Waterside?—Yes. And it is all laid out for building ground, and some parts of it already taken.

240. It is north of Cashel?—Yes.

DANIEL TAYLOR, esq., M.P., examined.

241. You live within the area proposed to be taken in?—Yes. I live at Millburn, which is within the yellow area.

242. And you are consenting to the extension?—I am.

243. You think it goes far enough?—I think the thing has been very fairly done. Knowing all the lands that are taken in and what are excluded, I think no one who is thoroughly acquainted with the town would fix any other boundary than that; and that portion that you speak of as being left out, Chapel Field, is not a district likely ever to be taken up as building ground. There is an approach to it which you could not drive up at all, and to get to it by another road would take you away a mile, so that it is altogether excluded. There might be extension in the direction of Ballysally. These are all sites which are sure to be built upon.

244. That place as far as the stream on the south side of Ballysally?—Yes. This is my brother's house at Ballysally. I don't object that you should take it in there.

245. There is one reason for not taking in Ballysally, and that is, that it is not in the electoral division of Coleraine?—No, Ferrerah. There are four or five fields running down to the stream that are sure to be occupied with buildings, and on the other side Mr. *Henry* is building very fine houses.

246. That is towards Cavehill?—Yes.

247. Do you think in the other direction the yellow area is sufficient?—I do. There has been a tendency for a number of years of people who formerly lived within the present boundary to look out for a house outside, still convenient; and although a man pays £400 or £500 a year for his business premises within the boundary, if he lives outside he is disqualified as a commissioner, and that has been felt as one grievance.

248. Do you agree in the estimate made by Mr. Kenlen of there being twelve such cases?—Well, I think there are more. With regard to the number of electors added on account of people who live outside now, but are ratepayers already, I think that in most cases where fine houses have been built—Mr. Anderson is a ratepayer, Mr. Gibson, Mr. M'Laughlin, and Mr. Henry, and all the people who live in Clifton-terrace, where there are a dozen houses—eight or nine in a row, and several detached houses—I don't know almost a fine house outside that are not ratepayers within, so that it is just a feeling of joint interest in having the town extended.

249. You are not a Commissioner?—Not now. I was from 1849 to 1874.

250. What would you think about taking up the roads?—I am quite with the Commissioners. I have always felt that it would be an immense advantage to the town, and I feel very strongly that the town that is called upon to pay heavy rates in addition to the county-cess has a fair claim to be excluded.

251. And have charge of its own roads?—Yes. Because there is no question the amount they contribute to the county is somewhere about nearly double. It is at least one-third more than all it would cost them to carry on their improvements and pay their proportion of the county-at-large charges. And I think the town has a clear right to be excluded from that considering that those outside portions are free from all the town rates, and that they get very large advantages when they come to visit Coleraine. I advised the town people here and they were unanimous in going before the Grand Jury, and I advised them not to go, knowing the feeling of some of the Grand Jurors, that it would not be at all successful. The town has been undertaking some very important works such as waterworks and the improvement of the river, and it was on account of the cost of these works that some proceedings were not taken before. We have really had enough in hands.

252. Don't you think the taking up of the roads will pay itself?—I think it would be a great saving, but the Commissioners had plenty to do, and we have successfully, I am glad to say, carried out the other undertakings, and now their hands are clear for taking up this subject, which is most important for them. It is most valuable for a town like this to have £650 coming in to aid the rates, and the outsiders who participate in that would immediately become part owners of this estate which now exclusively belongs to the ratepayers within the municipal boundary. This extension would not be anything at all like the extension of the Parliamentary borough, which was fixed in a very peculiar way apparently—at least it looks so now. And I suppose the interests that existed at the time of the fixing of the borough boundary. I don't wish to find any fault with it, but it is very peculiar.

Mr. JOHN [illegible], examined.

253. You are not living in the town at present?—No, I live on the Portstewart road.

254. You would be taken in by the proposed extension?—Yes.

255. And you are a large ratepayer in the town?—Yes.

256. What is your feeling?—I think it should be extended for the benefit of all—for instance we have been trying to get the water up there; it would be worth all the difference.

257. How are you supplied with water at present?—Wells and open spouts, which are supposed to be sometimes slightly contaminated with sewage.

258. Do you think this extension goes far enough?—I think it goes far enough. My idea is that for many years this would include all the buildings around. Beyond it is agricultural ground, and my view was that the Commissioners wished to avoid all unnecessary expense as far as possible, and at the same time to give service to all.

259. They wish to accommodate all land built upon, or likely to be built on?—Yes. As to the population, in 1861 it was a little under 6,000; in 1871 it was a little over 6,000. I think there is an increase of close on 600 in the ten years.

260. Do you think there is any increase since?—I think it has gone on since then.

261. Do you think the other gentlemen living at Clifton-terrace would agree with you?—Yes, they all agree.

262. You are the owner of property in the town and outside, both?—Yes, I never heard anyone express themselves against it.

263. You are not a Commissioner?—No.

264. Mr. COTTON.—Will we have no evidence by the Irish Society?—

Mr. *Daniel Taylor*, M.P.—I saw the Governor of the Society, a few days ago, as to the extension of the town and he said they had no objection—that it was a matter entirely for the people living within the area that was to be included. Whatever their wish was, the Society were perfectly satisfied with, of course the rates are all paid by the tenants, and the property is held in perpetuity, so that the Society would not be touched.

The inquiry then terminated.

ARMAGH.—JULY 25th, 1879.

[Before Mr. C. P. Cotton and Mr. H. A. Robinson.]

Armagh. July 25, 1879.

Mr. Thomas Graham Peel, examined.

Mr. T. G. Peel.

1. Mr. Cotton.—You are the Town Clerk of Armagh?—I am.

2. How long have you filled the position?—Since the 7th of April last.

3. The town is under the 9th of George IV., chap. 82?—It is, sir.

4. When was it placed under the Act?—In the year 1833.

5. What is the area of the town?—There are 360 acres within the municipal boundary.

6. And what is the population?—9,000.

7. That is according to the census of 1871?—Yes.

8. Do you know whether the population has been increasing or diminishing since then, can you put the increase at any definite figure, would you say it has been 1,000?—Should say there has been about an increase of 300 from the number of houses built, giving five to each house, which is a fair average.

9. What is the valuation?—The valuation that we last upon is £13,712.

10. Is that increasing year by year?—It is increasing with the number of houses gradually, but very slightly unless within the last two years.

11. I see the valuation in 1876 is put down in Mr. O'Brien's report as £17,000, so that it has gone down very much, how is that?—That must include townlands of the Corporation, which we don't include in the municipal boundary. The Parliamentary boundary is larger than the municipal in certain places. Mr. O'Brien has taken his report from the Clerk of the Union and not from us. We don't go beyond the streets.

12. Oh, yes, but is the £13,712 the valuation of the portion upon which you strike rates?—The portion upon which we struck the last rate.

13. It has as would appear from this return gone down £3,300 since?—Not at all; it has increased.

14. It has increased something?—Yes; our revenue has increased; therefore it must have increased.

15. Mr. O'Brien has also got the population, 8,946?—Well that is a mistake.

16. And the area, 1,092?—That includes the townland of Corporation. There is 730 acres of the townland of Corporation that is not in the municipality.

17. You have no wards?—No.

18. In what electoral division is the town?—In the Armagh electoral division.

19. Entirely?—Entirely, sir.

20. Will you give me the rates struck for the last five years, at 6d. 9d. and 1s., of course you always have these rates?—Yes, sir.

21. But give me the maximum rate?—The maximum rate in 1874—we strike three rates on three valuations.

22. And 1s. is the highest?—Yes.

23. Has it been 1s. always?—Yes; except last year when we had only a portion of the year—it was then these 9d., but that was as I have said for a portion of the year.

24. Wait until I understand that. In 1878 was it?—Yes.

25. You have given in the reply here?—In 1879 it should be, it is for 1878–9. We are now striking for 1879 on the first Monday in August.

26. Then it is last year. Has there been a lower rate than 1s.?—The rate that we should have struck last August we were not able to strike in consequence of a municipal disturbance in the town. The Corporation disputed the validity of an election, and they didn't strike a rate until March, and then they struck a 9d. rate for the 1s., because they didn't want the whole of the funds.

27. And that 9d. rate was sufficient up to this August?—Yes, sir, sufficient.

28. Besides that 1s. have you any sanitary rate?—We have a 1d. rate and always have had from the time of the passing of the Act of 1874.

29. That is up to 1874 or since 1874?—Since 1874.

30. You have had a sanitary rate of 1d. in addition to the 1s.?—Yes.

31. What was that used for, what was that expended on?—Sanitary purposes; the payment of the salaries of the sanitary staff—the sanitary medical officer, the sub-sanitary officer, the executive sanitary officer, and the other expenses connected with the working of the Sanitary Acts.

32. Yes, but that is not enough to do any extensive works of drainage or water works?—No, sir; it only amounted to a sum of £36.

33. Would you now kindly give me the poor rate?—The poor rate in 1878 was 1s.; in 1877, 10d.; in 1876, 9d.; in 1875, 10d., and in 1874, 1s.

34. And what was the county cess?—In 1878 it was 1s. 7d., the two levies of the county cess.

35. Yes, I wish you to give me the gross amount of the two levies?—Well, in 1878 the gross amount of the two levies was 1s. 7d.; in 1877, it was 1s. 6d.; in 1876, it was 1s. 7d.; in 1875 1s. 7d.; and in 1874 1s. 5d.

36. How many Commissioners have you?—21.

37. How many voters have you on your municipal list?—375 on the municipal list.

38. Of those how many are qualified to sit as Commissioners if elected?—About fifty. We have more than that in the parliamentary.

39. I don't want the parliamentary at all, I have nothing to say to it. How is the town lighted?—We have 230 lamps through the town.

40. It is lit by contract with the gas company?—We pay them by the thousand, by meter.

41. How many lamps are there that each have a meter?—20 lamps; we have the meters situated in different parts of the town—the low and high parts of the town, and the average of those meters is taken.

42. You have twenty meters, and how many lamps also?—230 altogether.

43. How much per thousand feet are you charged?—Last year it was 5s.

44. And what is the current price?—It is the same. They charge us less than they do the townspeople.

45. Would you kindly tell me what are the two prices?—I don't know exactly the town price, as I don't burn gas myself. 5s. 6d., I believe, is the town price.

46. 5s. is your price, at any rate?—Yes.

47. And are the lamps always lighted?—They are lighted for seven months during the winter—for seven months, beginning in September.

48. That is, they are lighted during September, October, November——?—They are lighted then from September on for seven months, except those nights on which there are full moons.

49. For what length of time are they kept lighted generally, when are they put out?—From sunset to sunrise—continuously burning the whole night.

50. How is the town supplied with water?—We have a reservoir called Lowry's Lake, about two and a half miles from the town.

51. Does that give a full supply?—It gives us a very large supply. We have lately extended it nearly

ARMAGH.
July 26, 1879.
Mr. T. D. Pope.

six acres, at a cost of over £1,000 in the purchase of land, and the works which the Commissioners have executed.

52. The Commissioners are Water Commissioners under another Act?—Yes, they are Water Commissioners under two other Acts.

53. Can you give me the names and the titles of those Acts?—Yes, I can; the 29th of George III., chap. 42.

54. In what year was that Act passed?—1789.

55. That is the first Water Act?—Yes.

56. And, now, what is the title of the succeeding Act?—The 34th of George III., chap. 9, passed in the year 1794.

57. And it is under those two Acts that the water has been supplied and charged for?—Under these two Acts they raised the money originally; and there were several sums of money contributed by the members of Parliament and by Lady Primrose. Lady Primrose, I believe, gave £1,000 towards it, and the late Lord Primate Beresford gave a large sum, and also gave ground free of rent to the Commissioners, that he had under the See, and we represent the old Commissioners.

58. Do you strike a special water rate?—We strike no tax, but a rate; that is, it is a private contract rather than a tax.

59. How is that?—A number of houses that do not take the water are not taxed.

60. I see; it is optional with a man to take the water, but if he does he pays the tax?—Yes.

61. What public supply have you?—Fountains through the town; but the Commissioners complain that they have not the power of taxing and making people take the water who should take it. A number of respectable houses do not take the water.

62. A number of respectable houses do not pay for having it taken into the house?—Parties in the town take water from their neighbours, and don't pay us the water tax, and we are left defrauded by this means of what we have a right to get for the use of the water.

63. What is the rate you charge the people who take the water?—For houses the sum we charge is £1 5s.

64. Per annum?—Yes.

65. How do you estimate the charge?—For houses valued at £20 and upwards the Commissioners charge £1 5s.

66. That is under the Act?—Yes.

67. And what are the other rates?—And for houses under £20—a shilling in the £—5 per cent. on the valuation.

68. Is the supply sufficient?—Abundant.

69. Is it high pressure?—The pressure is good, but it might be better.

70. Does it supply the highest parts of the town?—It supplies the highest part of the town—nearly to the top of the cathedral—that is the highest part of the town. I have a map here showing it.

71. Kindly allow me to see it?—Certainly. [The witness then pointed out the plan of the water supply to the Commissioners.] This map shows the situation of the reservoir and water works. This (pointing) is Lowry's Lake. It is the course of the canal that conveys it; it is not pipes. This is a river until it comes to this point, and then it is a mill-race which we have to convey our water through, and then—this is the mill. It passes through the mill-race along a special course that we have made for it, passing over a large water trough into our special conveniences, and then it goes on up and falls into two—basins we call them.

72. And then this map shows the distributing pipes from that?—This map shows the distributing pipes from the reservoir through the town. It is a nine-inch pipe from that reservoir down to this, and until it comes to the corner of Ballynasaran. Will you allow me to mention that the Commissioners complained, and do complain, of the position they are placed in by the analysis of the water. The military authorities to whom we give water had samples analysed, and the analysis made by the chemists at Netley gives a not very favourable report of the character of our water.

73. When was that analysis made?—In March, 1878. Now we complain that we have no control of those courses which are outside our boundary, but are outside the boundary of the rural sanitary authority, which is the Board of Guardians. Along these courses there are a number of houses, and the residents allow their manure, liquid manure, and other matters to go into the river, especially here at the point (referring to the map), in the townland of Drumbee and Terramoyle.

74. And in those outlying places you say the water is polluted, and you have no control?—Yes, it is seriously polluted, and we have no control. We have been endeavouring for years to try to get it done, and we cannot.

75. How?—Pressing the people and the guardians to get this matter remedied.

76. Surely the guardians must act! Have you applied to them?—I have corresponded with them myself, and I was a member of the Board, as well as a Town Commissioner before I became Town Clerk. I was a member from 1863 until appointed Town Clerk, and I brought the matter before the Board, but they would not go to the expense. The economy principle was paramount, and they would not go to the expense, and they have not done anything since.

77. Have you asked, or have the Commissioners asked the guardians to stop the pollution?—We have, sir, repeatedly.

78. How lately?—Well, sir, I suppose this year. Mr. Wm. Best and I went out and inspected the places. I made a report, and then an agreement was come to that £30 should be given.

79. Who was this agreement by?—By the Water Commissioners; who sent out a committee with me to inspect the places, complaints having been made of its being polluted—of very dirty pollution from manure, and then an agreement was made that this reservoir should be made at one place.

80. Do you mean to say that the public Water Commissioners agreed to give money for the improvement?—They agreed to pay half. They offered to pay half if the guardians paid the other half, and that has not been done.

81. Has that offer been officially sent to the guardians?—It was officially notified to the guardians.

82. And the guardians have taken no action?—No, sir.

83. Was it under the Public Health Act you asked them to pay?—It was; we were the urban sanitary authority.

84. And they were the authority for the rural district?—They were the rural sanitary authority, and we applied to them to remedy this, and it has been going on since 1874. Previously we had no authority at all to look after sanitary matters.

85. However, as a matter of fact, they have not removed the nuisance?—They have not. I don't make any complaint against the Board, and I merely mention the matter for the purpose of having the nuisance remedied.

86. You say that the pollution is going on still?—Yes it is, and very bad it is, sir.

87. Mr. Rotheram.—The people of the town are aware of the pollution?—Yes, most of them are. It has been discussed at the Town Commissioners' meetings time after time. What we proposed was—and I have got a letter in my hand on the subject—that they should join us under the Act of 1874, and make us an united district, for the purpose of obtaining a proper public water supply.

88. And was that proposed to the guardians?—It was.

89. Mr. Cotton.—And what did the guardians say?—I have not got the reply they made.

90. Mr. [illegible].—Is it still under their consideration?—It is.

91. Mr. Corrance.—Did the guardians apply to the Local Government Board to be made a united district?—They sent a report—[illegible] the Town Clerk of the Commissioners then—they sent a copy of their [illegible].

92. Did they apply to be made a special district?—They did not officially. They objected to the guardians [illegible], and when they didn't agree, we [illegible] the [illegible].

93. I don't think so. [The Commissioner then referred to the Act of Parliament.] It appears to me that [illegible] may apply to the Local Government Board to form them into a special district, or [illegible] or not?—I dare say. Here is a resolution relating to [illegible] passed in 1875, and if you read it you will find that it is on the same subject. It [illegible] the [illegible] I have before me.

94. The Commissioner read the resolution:—

"At the [illegible] 1876, the following resolution was passed:—Resolved—That in the opinion of this Board the Poor Law Guardians of Armagh Union should discharge the duty devolving upon that Board as a [illegible] authority, and [illegible] Armagh, but [illegible] the Urban Sanitary Board of Armagh [illegible] Keady, Market Hill, Richhill, and Armagh, [illegible] and the attention of the Local Government Board is again called to the existence of the nuisances which are yet unremoved."

That is not an application to the Local Government Board to be formed into a united district?—Well, sir, there's the resolution, and here is another resolution passed at the meeting of the Armagh Town Commissioners, held on the 7th of September, 1876:—

"Resolved—That the clerk of the Commissioners be directed to communicate with the Board of Guardians of the Armagh Union, also to communicate with the Local Government Board, regarding the formation of a sanitary district of [illegible] Armagh [illegible] sanitary purposes; the Town Commissioners being of opinion that [illegible] it is desirable for the proper carrying out of the existing laws for the Town Commissioners to have control over the adjoining townlands."

95. Was application then made to the Local Government Board?—I cannot say exactly whether a copy of that resolution was sent to the Local Government Board, but I believe it was sent. As it appears it is on the minutes of the Board of Guardians, a copy of which they got once a week.

96. It appears to me that if the Board of Commissioners applied to be made a united district with the guardians for this surrounding district, the Local Government Board would entertain the question whether the guardians agreed to it or not?—We have had no communication with the Local Government Board on the matter.

97. You wanted to make the drainage division the sanitary district?—We did.

98. Lonsdale's Lane, and where those [illegible] are situated appear to you to be outside the [illegible] district?—Not all.

99. Describe the portion that lies outside?—A portion of Ballinahonemore.

100. Is that Ballinahonemore the only exception?—It is not in the drainage division.

101. One great source of contamination was close beside Lonsdale's Lane?—That is the chief cause of complaint.

102. Mr. Hemersley.—And that would be outside your jurisdiction if you adopt this division you suggest?—It would.

103. Mr. Corrance.—Would it not be better to take in the whole district where the contamination comes from?—We think it would be too far, for that extends out two and a half miles.

104. I do not see that by taking in the district you now propose you would stop the evil you now complain of?—We would stop part of the evil, [illegible] there is a portion of that through there that we have to [illegible], and we don't want to allow the water [illegible] pipe.

105. Mr. Hemersley.—What do the people [illegible]?—[illegible]. We have a scheme for [illegible], and we want £3,000 to complete improvements at the [illegible], and the [illegible] near the [illegible], and we got a contract for £800 for doing the work, and we had everything ready to go on with the works here, until the [illegible] last winter caused a tremendous amount of [illegible] pipes and caused a large expenditure of money, and the money we had for the [illegible] we had a large expenditure in the purchase of pipes, and the laying down of new pipes from the [illegible], and to get money from the Board of Works for the purposes of the [illegible] the completion of the new works [illegible] the Board of Works will not give any money to pay off a debt, and that [illegible] in that position.

106. Mr. Corrance.—What were the later improvements that you were going to make?—We took in [illegible] to give a larger quantity, and we took away some bad [illegible], and we had to build up a large quantity of [illegible] and buildings, and that cost [illegible] £600.

107. The works were begun when you applied for the money to the Board of Works?—The work was begun and we were getting on with it, when we had to purchase pipes and lay them down in place of broken pipes in consequence of frost. I think we have power to compel the Board of Guardians by [illegible] to make them do their work; but we don't want to go to that extremity.

108. You never took proceedings?—We did not. I wrote to them the other day, calling their attention to the works in which they should do their duty. That letter is dated May 29th, 1876.

109. You wrote [illegible] their attention, and telling them that they would be compelled to do it?—Yes; compelled to do certain work and not this alone.

110. Besides the pollution of the supply of water is there anything else for which a [illegible] sanitary district would be desirable?—Yes; for sanitary purposes generally. We have a large quantity of [illegible] which a large quantity of sewage [illegible] and these drains were not [illegible] considerable time.

111. Have you any map showing the drains of the town?—No, sir; we have no maps of the outside portions of the town.

112. Have you no map showing the sewers inside the municipal boundary?—We have a large map that we got made within the last twelve months.

113. Does it show each of the drains?—Yes; each drain within our boundary.

114. Can you describe the general system of drainage and where the drains run to?—There are a number of drains down each street.

115. Where do they run to?—This is English-street (pointing to the map)—this portion of the city.

116. Is that north, south, east, or west?—It is east and north.

117. The east and north parts of the town?—Yes; and a portion of the west.

118. These portions drain into the river?—Yes; they drain into the river. That is called the [illegible] River, and it goes along past the Courthouse into the Callan.

119. Is that a running stream?—Yes; and it carries away a quantity of the sewage of that part of the town, but not all.

120. Where does the rest go?—The rest goes in the [illegible] direction.

END

121. Is that to the north?—More in the direction of the north; it goes into two or three old wide sewers—open sewers.

122. Where do they run to?—They don't run anywhere; the sewage matter consolidates there, but the surface water finds its way to the Callan river, but the solid matter is left there still.

123. Are these wide ditches in fields?—Yes.

124. In fact they are long cesspools?—Yes; they are long cesspools.

125. Are they within the municipal boundary?—No, sir; they are outside it.

126. Is it for the purpose of gaining control over these among other things that you would wish to have a united district?—Yes; that is what we proposed in our resolutions.

127. Did you ever ask the guardians to do anything with that part of their drainage?—We have asked them to clean them out.

128. And what did they do?—They said that if we would pay half they would pay the other half.

129. What was done with the stuff?—The stuff was given to the parties owning the fields around the ditches.

130. Supposing you were a joint district, and you should have a voice in the matter, what would you do yourself if you had the control?—I think they should be cleaned out every three months—these drains. The gases arising from fermentation during the summer months are the chief cause of complaint with us.

131. Are these fields beyond the railway?—No; they are this side of the railway.

132. Between the railway and the college?—No; they are not; they are quite north.

133. They cannot be more north; it is more west. (Referring to the map.) I see a lane running down—you know the bridge carrying the railway over the Callan river?—Yes.

134. Are the fields near that at all?—If you allow me I will show you where they are. (Pointing to map.) You will see that between the infirmary and the convent there are several of these open stagnant drains into which the sewage of that portion of the city runs.

135. And it has no outlet?—None, except when the water rises to a certain level it runs into the Callan river. The drains are very bad and foul there. (Pointing to map.)

136. Where is that—is it outside the municipal boundary?—It is, sir. It is in the field adjoining, and to the south of the Charter school, where there are more of these drains.

137. Is that within the limits of the boundary?—No, sir; that is outside our boundary.

138. Are there any other places where similar bad drains exist?—In that direction. That is all we have. We have the sewage matter of a large portion of Irish-street, Ogle-street, Dobbyn-street, and it runs down the boundary of the Palace Demesne, and inside the Palace Demesne, until it comes in at the rere of Dobbyn-street—at the rere of the Royal Hotel.

139. Where does it go then?—Along and across Scotch-street, down to the Mall, and goes on down here to the end of the court-house.

140. Where does it run to then?—That is what I have been describing; it runs on down into the Callan—in fact, it runs nearly round the town.

141. The drainage of the part of the town about Irish-street runs by Gallows Hill towards the demesne?—It rises at the foot of Gallows Hill.

142. It runs by Gallows Hill, to the demesne at the inside of the demesne wall, in a partly covered and partly open sewer. Is that right?—Yes; but before you go into the demesne wall there is a serious nuisance in one of these open drains—in the orchard of Mrs. M'Cann.

143. In the orchard it is open, and then it enters the demesne, and goes a partly covered and partly open sewer, until it goes to the rere of the Royal school?—Yes.

144. Then it is covered in the Mall to the end of the Court-house?—Yes.

145. And then it goes round by the pavilion and past the pavilion. Is that covered?—No, it is open.

146. Is it open at the pavilion?—As far as the house goes it is covered.

147. And then from that it goes down by the lunatic asylum?—Through the grounds of the asylum. It does not go near the asylum.

148. Is it open?—No; it is covered there, nearly all covered, very little open.

149. It is open from the pavilion to the railway?—It is.

150. And from the railway to the lunatic asylum it is covered?—No, it is not; for it passes Mr. M'Crum's Mill at Callan, and he avails himself of the water for machinery purposes.

151. Is it between the two railways that the mill is?—It is not between both railways, it is between the lunatic asylum and the manse-house.

152. And it is fed by the water of the sewer?—Fed by the water carried away, fed by the water of the sewer.

153. The water that supplies the mill in the townland Ballinahonemore?—No sir, it does not go there at all. That is another mill.

154. Is it near the railway?—It is, sir.

155. And that is outside your jurisdiction?—Yes, it is.

156. You have no control over that, and you would desire to be a joint board for the purpose of having control over that?—Yes, sir; if we had authority we would get the work done.

157. In replying to one of the queries we submitted to you, you say the Town Commissioners would recommend an extension of the boundary?—Yes.

158. Is there any resolution of the Commissioners on the subject?—They passed no formal resolution.

159. And you are enabled to speak to what you believe to be the feeling of the Commissioners?—Yes. From what I know after consulting them.

160. What extension do they consider would be a proper one?—They consider it would be most desirable if they could have their area extended to the electoral division, except the two townlands of Ballyrea and Ballymath.

161. Any other?—No, sir.

162. On what grounds was it that they wished for that extension?—They desire it, first, on account of the sanitary arrangements of the town; they want to get control over these drains in several portions of the sanitary district. Then there are a number of houses outside our present boundary, but immediately in the town, I may say, and they get all the advantages of the town and pay no town taxes.

163. Mr. Robinson.—What class of houses are they?—Very good houses; generally good houses. Some of them are middling.

164. Will you let me see any resolution defining the boundary?—There is no resolution defining the present boundary. We tax as far as we light, watch, and cleanse.

165. You must have had a limit originally, surely. Have you the first minute book of the Commissioners?—Yes, I have the first minute book here.

166. Is there any resolution in it defining the limits?—Nothing defining the limits of the town, only so far as they light, watch, and cleanse.

167. What is the document you have in your hand?—This is a copy of a resolution indicating those townlands, Ballinahonemore and all those townlands.

168. Let me read it.—(Resolution handed to Mr. Cotton who read it.)

169. Mr. Robinson.—Has there been any alteration of the boundary since then?—Yes, there has.

170. Mr. Cotton.—The thing is as clear as possible; you have done it in the most complete way. On the 9th of December, 1833, it was unanimously resolved:—

"That the Commissioners do determine the limits of the city and suburbs, and particulars thereof respectively, to

[illegible] Mr. T. G. [illegible]

which the purposes of the Act shall extend, to be as follows ——"

And then the limits are exactly defined. Surely that is defining the limits?—Yes, but they had to withdraw that and get counsel's opinion, as it is further on stated in the book.

171. And will you tell me why they had to withdraw it?—They had no power under the 9th George IV., chapter 82, to levy a rate or exercise any authority beyond where they lighted and cleansed, and they declined to take the responsibility of lighting and cleansing it more than in those places.

172. Once they defined their limits I do not see how they had any power to alter them. Where was counsel's opinion taken? I have got [illegible] of it?—I have not, but it is in that book. It is a very long opinion.

[Witness handed in a copy of a resolution limiting the boundaries from the minutes of the Commissioners of December 9th, 1853.]

173. This resolution is to the effect that the Commissioners cannot strike a rate where they do not do any work?—Yes.

174. You have certain limits defined by the resolution of December, 1853, and there is a certain boundary, and when the town extended out in that direction you would extend the lighting and cleansing in that direction, and then rate them?—Yes.

175. And if the town extended out beyond the limits laid down here you would put all these, even if they extended?—That is so. When we put up lamps beyond the entrance to the new houses or in the future, then we bring those houses within the municipal boundary and tax them.

176. It is not within the municipal boundary you bring them, but within the rating district. They are within the municipal boundary before that or you would not do it. Don't you see that the limits in which the Acts apply are defined, on the first meeting of the Commissioners' meeting, and if there is no building going on within that district, and you provide them with gas, water, and so on you can tax them; but where that, for any building outside that limit, where if you gave them water you could not tax them?—We are under the Act that only applies to water. That is for the water.

177. I am talking of lighting and cleansing. The application of the 9th of George IV. applies to the whole boundary, provided there are buildings. Of course, you cannot tax people under the 9th of George IV. except you give them lighting and cleansing?—We have followed that practice.

178. Is that the boundary shown upon this map—do you know?—Yes.

179. The brown boundary?—Yes.

180. Why do the Town Commissioners want to have that extended?—They thought they could extend it to take in the portion of the electoral division that was not included. That they thought was fair.

181. And the places you showed me where those drains were—are they within the present limits of the municipal boundary?—They are if we had any houses built there—if the premises extended so far, but they do not.

182. Our extending the boundary would not give you any power more than you have at present?—Your extending the boundary would give us authority over those fields over which we have no authority at present.

183. You have just as much authority over them now as we could give you, because they are within your boundary?—They are inside the boundary of the rural sanitary authority for sanitary purposes. We don't tax them for that.

184. I think there is something wrong about the whole thing, because they are decidedly within your limits?—Our limits are defined by the Act of 9th George IV. to where we light, watch and cleanse.

185. Your limits for striking a rate are, but not your municipal limits—your municipal limits are limits defined in this document here—whatever rights are conferred upon you are conferred by that upon it?—They don't confer any power, not for sanitary purposes.

186. If we extended it we could only give you the same powers; our extending it won't give you any other powers than you have?—If we had power as the urban sanitary authority outside the outskirts of the city, we could tax them or summon them for a nuisance if it existed, and take all the proceedings you would take in the city. The Town Commissioners are under the impression that they cannot do that.

187. I am not a lawyer and I am very unwilling to give any legal opinion, but my impression is that whatever powers you would have within that boundary line at this present moment—whatever powers you have are conferred by the resolution of the 9th of December, 1853.

188. Mr. [illegible].—Are the Commissioners carrying on any works within the municipal limits as defined by the brown line?—They contribute towards the cleansing of those drains. I got the work done and they contributed a portion of the expenses.

189. Mr. [illegible].—But they don't give you any aid for any sanitary works within the town?—No, we never ask them.

190. I don't see why they should give you any aid for carrying on works within that brown line?—(No answer.)

191. It is an entirely legal question. The fact is you are the urban sanitary authority for the entire area of your town?—Yes.

192. And the area you have defined in December, 1853, as the limits of your town is that which is shown by the brown line upon this map?—Yes; that was done when the Commissioners had been appointed.

193. Exactly. It appears to me that you are urban sanitary authority over the entire of that area, and neither did the Commissioners should have defined their boundary by advertisement at the time they announced the holding of the meeting.

194. That is what they have to do for the Towns Improvement Act?—Oh, no.

195. Under the 9th of George IV. it is that after the town is put under the Act, the Commissioners define the limits. Under the Towns Improvement Act, before you got the Improvement Act you have to define the limits?—Yes, I see.

196. Would the Commissioners consider the area within that brown line sufficient for their purposes?—I think they would. It gives them control over those drains.

197. But then you know it would be very much less than the electoral division?—Yes, sir.

198. It would leave out the village of Ballinahown's townland?—Ballinahownmore is a little village outside the town, and a great number of people live in it. Mr. [illegible] has a mill there (pointing to map) that would be taxed.

199. Would the Town Commissioners in taking in such a large area as this be prepared to supply the people they taxed with gas?—We don't supply them with gas. It is a private company as we do not manufacture gas. I think they would light the street along that way.

200. Would they light any portion of Ballinahown?—Yes, it is quite convenient to the town.

201. How far do the Commissioners' lamps go out upon the road leading to Moate?—They extend up to the end of Long-lane upon the Ordnance map.

202. They go to the end of [illegible]-row?—They go a little beyond the end of [illegible]-row.

203. Now out at Barrack-hill how far do they go?—They go to beyond the new houses that are built on the top of the hill. The half of the row of new houses.

204. Do they go beyond the mill pond?—They don't reach the mill pond.

205. Do they go beyond the military barracks?—They go beyond the military hospital—that is beyond the military barracks again.

206. By the workhouse here [illegible] the [illegible]?—They go to the end of Victoria-street by the workhouse.

207. Do they go up to the cross roads at [illegible] bridge?—They do not.

208. I see a lot of houses down on that road running south of the workhouse?—That is the village we are speaking of.

209. Is that lit?—No, there are no lights, but there are [illegible] laid upon this road [illegible] to [illegible].

210. Which road is that?—Not by the Bridge, but by Victoria-street.

211. And how far are they laid down in Victoria-street?—Down as far as this point here (referring to map).

212. That is opposite to the workhouse?—Yes.

213. To the east of the workhouse?—Yes.

214. Then is that there [illegible] from the boundary of your rating district at present?—They do, sir; except [illegible].

215. Which is [illegible]?—Those cottages.

216. Why do they not [illegible] when they are in the boundary of Drogheda?—The law [illegible].

217. But some of those houses [illegible] unoccupied now?—Yes.

218. Did you amend the district upon which you struck rates [illegible]?—Not since the passing of the last [illegible] Bill; we didn't extend them then.

219. When was that?—In 18[illegible].

220. Has there ever been any motion made towards adopting the Towns Improvement Act instead of the 9th of George IV.?—Yes, we had two motions, and on both occasions people objected to the proposition to adopt the Towns Improvement Act.

221. Mr. Robinson.—Do you rate the palace?—We do, sir, for municipal purposes.

222. Mr. Cutts.—You rate **the palace?—Yes, sir.**

223. Is the whole [illegible] within the town?—No, sir. There is, I think, [illegible] outside that are not in the town. [illegible] is in the town.

224. Mr. Robinson.—Do you or the guardians carry out the sanitary work for the [illegible]?—The guardians perform that duty in a portion of the township, and we do it in the other portion. They have more than half; we have less than half.

225. Then you rate the palace for municipal purposes?—We rate the palace for all [illegible] for municipal purposes.

226. If the Town Commissioners adopted the electoral division as the boundary, would they carry out [illegible] a [illegible]?—Yes.

227. What power would they have?—They would have power to enter and inspect premises, power to levy a rate, and to carry out necessary works.

228. Mr. Cutts.—It appears to me that they would have the power then of doing all those works to the extent of the electoral division; they certainly have the power as to their [illegible] to the extent of the boundary line on this map, and that includes all the [illegible] you have spoken of. I don't think we can go further than we can light, watch and cleanse.

229. You would light, watch and cleanse the whole of the electoral division?—Not if the county rate is applied to that purpose.

230. Whatever powers you would have **in the** electoral division, you have now over the houses **[illegible]**?—Yes.

231. Then, if you would have sanitary powers over the electoral division if we extended you to it, you now have it over all this area. We can't create any new powers?—The Commissioners don't agree with you there.

232. All we have any power to do is to extend or diminish a boundary?—Well, we don't look upon that as our boundary. In fact the resolution of the Commissioners afterwards relinquished that boundary.

233. What resolution?—A resolution by which they agreed not to tax.

234. Show me the other boundary if you can.—There is no other boundary that I can find [illegible].

235. No, because once you adopted this, you had no power to alter it?—They relinquished the existing boundary on counsel's opinion.

236. They could not do that?—For what purpose would they hold a boundary except the ratepayers' houses were built upon it that would tax them [illegible]?

237. For what purpose?—Beyond that we cannot do a single thing except lighting upon it and [illegible] extending it.

238. You would extend the [illegible] rural area?—We can exercise no authority beyond where we build.

239. If you can do nothing now over this boundary, you [illegible] do nothing over this area, we could give you?—Not unless power was given to exercise within us, and powers and authority to do those things.

240. Do you mean that Parliament would give you power under the Towns Improvement Act?—I understood the whole would be submitted to Parliament, and according to the recommendations of the Commissioners that the boundary would be extended for the purpose of enabling us to do those things outside the boundary that we could do inside the boundary under the [illegible] Act of 18[illegible].

241. Mr. Robinson.—Is that the view of the Board?—Yes.

242. Mr. Cutts.—You don't understand, this is your boundary, the boundary of your municipality; is the larger than the area you tax on?—We are aware of that.

243. In what way then do you want to apply the Act—your rating powers are confined to the district to which you do the work?—The Commissioners consider that, [illegible] other powers are confined within the limits of their lighting and watching and cleansing.

244. Then, if we were to extend the boundary all round, we could not give you any advantage, because we cannot extend your powers?—Then what would be the use of extending at all?

245. I don't agree with you that you have no power as a sanitary authority. Your powers as a sanitary authority are perfectly different from **your** powers under the 9th of George IV.?—Yes.

246. Do you consider that the guardians are the authority within your district?—We do, sir.

247. And they are doing the work?—Not within our city district, but between the lights and the boundary, as shown on the map. The guardians are the sanitary authority in the district existing between the outside limit of the lights and the boundary, as shown on the map.

248. You consider that it is the duty of the rural sanitary authority and not of the urban sanitary authority?—Yes.

249. Mr. Robinson.—And are the guardians accepting that duty?—They are.

250. Mr. Cutts.—That, **however, is an entirely** legal question.

251. It is only with the view of getting the benefit of further sanitary powers that the Commissioners, you say, desire an extension?—Only with the view of getting rid of sanitary nuisances [illegible] caused, in fact, by ourselves, and we want to get the power of removing them. The Act of Parliament says:—

"For the purposes of this Act, Ireland shall be divided into urban and rural sanitary districts. The urban sanitary districts shall consist of places in that behalf mentioned in the first column."

And then it goes on:—

"Towns, the population of which exceed 6,000, and have Commissioners by virtue of an Act made in the 9th year of the reign of George IV......"

and so on. Then the question is—What is a town? Is the town the area within the limits fixed by the

Commissioners, or is it the area within the lights?—We consider that it is the area within the lights, and the other portion has been looked upon by the county valuator, and he has dealt with it in dividing the city lands. They call them townparks.

353. It is quite clear that you put no additional [illegible] on it; you don't want any additional [illegible]?—We don't put any additional charges—we don't put any additional sanitary powers, we don't want any extension.

354. Do you want to tax this suburban area for anything but sanitary purposes?—Nothing but sanitary purposes.

355. You don't want to tax them for the cleansing of the streets?—Not at all, except those houses which adjoin or are immediately within the area of the Corporation.

356. You want to strike this 1d. sanitary rate over this district?—Yes, and there are some houses there we have not yet reached and we believe they are inside the Corporation.

356. You don't want an extension to touch them?—We think they should contribute towards the cleaning expenses of the city, for they derive all the advantages of the city, though left outside the municipal boundary.

357. Do you mean outside the lights?—Yes.

358. But your municipal boundary is half a mile outside the lights all round?—Yes.

359. There is no question about that—that is the boundary of your town?—Yes.

360. I think I understood, when the Commissioners were with [illegible] to-day, [illegible] you [illegible] by taking [illegible] in?—Nothing that I know of, except that we [illegible] the [illegible] of the Act of George IV. [illegible] those [illegible] of rating upon [illegible] should be [illegible] in the Towns Improvement Act.

361. And, if so, why not adopt the Towns Improvement Act?—The people won't do that.

362. Do you think it should be adopted?—Yes, I think we have good authority for adopting it.

363. Besides the [illegible] of the [illegible] in the adoption of the Towns Improvement Act?—Yes; it does all [illegible] with the present [illegible].

364. What are the feelings of the Commissioners, as a body, about adopting the Towns Improvement Act?—I could not say; there would be a division of opinion with regard to it.

Mr. JAMES BEST examined. Mr. James Best.

365. The brown line upon this map represents the limits fixed by the Commissioners in 1853, and do you consider that that area would be sufficient?—I think it would.

366. And you would not extend the area to the other electoral division?—I would not, and I will give you the reason for it: people who live at a distance—in the country as it is called—have no right to be taxed for the advantage of the town.

367. What tax would you put upon them, except the sanitary tax?—I would only tax them for sanitary works.

Mr. WILLIAM BEST, examined. Mr. William Best.

368. Mr. CULLEN.—You are a Town Commissioner?—I am.

369. What is your view in reference to an extension of the boundary?—I think there are some buildings which should be taken in in Ballynahonemore. I would take in Ballynahonemore village.

370. By the way I may tell you that Ballynahonemore village is outside the present limits, so that that is an extension?—The next place I would take in would be the workhouse.

371. You would take in the union workhouse?—Yes; and then the Shiels' Institution, which is adjoining the workhouse and near it. The next would be the Deanery grounds to the north of the Shiels' Institution again; and the Royal College I would take in again.

372. That is in?—The observatory is exempt by law.

373. Is it within the lights?—It is. Then Mr. M'Kenna's mill, that is beyond the railway—just adjoining the railway. And the next would be a large field—I think it is called Cherry's field, that would join Dr. M'Gettigan's.

374. Is that beside the railway station?—It is.

375. A large field in Abbey park?—Yes, that would join Dr. M'Gettigan's—the Seminary.

376. What else would you take in?—Murphy's mills—that is just adjoining the large field I have mentioned. I think that would cross then into the [illegible] school and then go into the Palace ground. All the other houses of the Palace are [illegible]. There we don't tax. We only tax the palace and portion of the ground round the palace.

377. And the farm offices of the palace are not taxed?—The farm offices, garden, and the houses that the gate keeper live in are not taxed. There is a separate entity and they are outside of our lights.

378. Is there any other place you would suggest should be brought in?—No; that line would go round in where the commencement of Ballynahonemore, taking in the Crump-hill and the parade ground for the soldiers.

Mr. PEEL.—It is not on the map by that name. It is just behind the military barracks.

379. Mr. ROBINSON.—The Crump hill is just beside the county gaol?—Yes.

380. Mr. CULLEN.—You would take in Crump hill there, it is to [illegible] already?—Yes, I would.

381. Mr. ROBINSON.—What are your reasons for taking in these places, Mr. Best?—Because there are a great many buildings, and they derive a great deal of benefit from the town.

382. And the people living in these buildings come in and make use of the town every day?—Yes.

383. Mr. CULLEN.—What would be the use of including them if you have no power of taxing them?—It might be no use.

384. With reference to the extension of the boundary, would you be of the same opinion—in favour of no extension of the boundary—if what I have stated would be the result?—If you could not give up the power of taxing, it would be no [illegible] to extend the boundary. At present the Poor Law Guardians do tax that [illegible] portion of it.

385. For sanitary purposes?—Yes; they do all the works.

Armagh. Aug. 24, 1880. Mr. T. G. Peel.

ARMAGH, July 24, 1877.

Dr. Gray.

Dr. Gray examined.

256. Mr. Cotton.—I presume you consider the boundary defined by the lights?—Outside the lights I send in reports of sanitary works to the Guardians, and inside the lights to the Town Commissioners.

257. As the Urban Sanitary Authority?—Yes.

258. I cannot say definitely but it appears to me that the limits of the town are the limits defined in that book, which are very far outside the limits of the lighting all round. However, it is purely a legal question?—I act in the way I have stated.

Mr. James Best.

Mr. James Best re-examined.

289. Mr. Cotton.—Is there anything else you wish to add?—I may mention that the Guardians don't seem to think they should do the work that the Town Commissioners should do. Whatever is the work of the Guardians they are very willing to do it. Another matter I wish to refer to is that, Mr. Peel forgot one thing; the Guardians did order an investigation and directed the medical officer to examine the pollution at Lowry's lake, and he did so, and declined to give a certificate that it was pollution. That was about four years ago—and the medical officer was Doctor Pratt—and although I visited the place and would say it, and so would anyone else, that it was pollution, and we have endeavoured and I think probably we will get it remedied. What I want to set right is that the Guardians did their duty and sent their sanitary officer.

290. If their sanitary officer said it was no nuisance, their duty was at an end?—Yes.

291. Mr. Robinson.—And have the Guardians disclaimed doing certain sanitary work. You said there was certain works that the Guardians were asked to do and it was the work of the Town Commissioners. Can you tell me some of those places where such work should be done?—At present there is work round by the Foundry, and I impressed upon the Guardians that it was part of their work, and I think they are agreeable to do half of it.

292. Mr. Cotton.—And is the Foundry within the lights?—It is.

293. How would you make it the duty of the Guardians to touch anything there?—It is outside the Foundry. The Guardians are often put into a difficulty to know what their portion of the work is, and they are very willing to do it, if they know it; but they are very unwilling to pay anything more than they have a fair right to pay.

294. Do the guardians levy a sanitary rate within the town's boundary?—They levy all their sanitary rate as a poor rate.

295. And any works they do come out of the poor rate?—Yes; and if they tax it is for poor rate.

296. Mr. Robinson.—There has never been any special sanitary rate struck by the guardians?—I think not.

297. Mr. Cotton.—I don't think that we can, by extending the boundary, confer any additional powers whatever. It would be merely extending their boundary with the same powers they have at present?—Then we don't want an extension.

298. Then, as you think, they have no powers beyond their lights whatever?—None, sir.

299. They would not have any additional powers if we extended the boundary, for it appears to me that they are the urban sanitary authority for the district named by the resolution of December, 1833?—That is where the difference of opinion arises.

Mr. Alexander Blane.

Mr. Alexander Blane examined.

300. Mr. Cotton.—Did you send us a communication about dividing the town into wards?—I did, sir.

301. Do you now wish to give us any evidence upon that point?—I do.

302. I think it seems doubtful whether we have any power to entertain the question at all, by the terms of our warrant. I will read for you the terms of our warrant. (The Commissioners then read the warrant.) I don't think it says anything about making wards where they do not already exist; but for fear I might be wrong I will hear anything you wish to say on the subject for the consideration of Mr. Robinson. Are you a Town Commissioner?—I am not; I am only a ratepayer.

303. And do you consider that it would be for the benefit of ratepayers if wards were created in Armagh?—Certainly.

304. And how many wards would you suggest?—Well, were I to make a suggestion I would say four. That would leave upwards of 2,000 in each ward, or about that.

305. On what grounds do you think that that is desirable?—On these grounds, that the present Commissioners are all nominated by one person—that is Mr. Peel. He nominated the twenty-one Commissioners now sitting, and they nominated Mr. Peel in turn. All the Commissioners reside within a certain district of the town.

306. How do you mean Mr. Peel—as the Town Clerk?—He was not then Town Clerk—he was one of the Commissioners at that time.

307. I don't catch the reason that the present system requires change?—My reasons are, that the Commissioners all reside within a certain district of the town, and of course they take very good care that those portions of the town in which they reside are properly watched, cleansed, and lighted. But there are other portions of the town that are not so well watched, cleansed, and lighted. I know Ogle-street to be badly lighted during the past winter. I know that Ogle-street, Charter School-lane, Primrose-hill, and also Irish-street have been for a long series of years in a very filthy state, by reason of not being properly cleansed by the Town Commissioners, though they struck a rate upon that district.

308. Do you say they are now in a bad condition?—I do say they are in a bad condition at the present time.

309. Compared with other parts of the city?—Yes.

310. And do you say that that is in consequence of not having wards?—If the town was divided into wards we should have all the representation spread over the taxation, and we would have the resident gentlemen in that end of the town who would see to its affairs, and who would reside there and take an interest in it that gentlemen residing a quarter of a mile away would not take any interest in.

311. Your object for desiring the town to be divided into wards is to localise representation all over the town instead of in one quarter?—To spread it over the greatest area of taxation, because at the present time the representation on the taxation is very unsatisfactory.

312. And you say you would make four wards of about 2,000 each?—Yes.

313. How would you divide it into four wards. There are 373 ratepayers that have an interest in the town under the 9th of George IV.?—We consider

that every inhabitant in the city should have an interest.

314. They would have no vote?—Irrespective of their having a vote they have an interest in sanitary affairs.

315. What I want to know is whether you would divide those 572 voters by four into the wards—would you make the wards with 143 voters each?—No, sir, I would not; I would make it on geometric lines, and allow the taxation——

316. Upon what? The result of that would be that you would have 2,000 inhabitants with perhaps only twenty voters?—But those 2,000 inhabitants would have a representation in the Town Commissioners.

317. By means of twenty voters?—Yes; I would expect so.

318. Would you make the wards depend on the absolute population, and not on the number of ratepayers over £5 within that district?—Certainly not.

319. Would you look to the valuation of the wards in dividing them—the absolute valuation of property? —That is to give its representation an interest?

320. Yes?—I think so; I think that would be only reasonable.

321. Therefore in dividing the wards you would have regard both to valuation and population?—Yes; having regard to both the objects would be to give representation to taxation, and to have the Commissioners representing the whole population at large. A section of the ratepayers put forward, I think, about six or seven gentlemen as candidates last time, but there was no use in their going to the poll, simply because the town was not divided into wards, and they would have been defeated by a majority. They have no representation in the taxation, although they pay the taxes.

322. I think your letter to us was to the same effect?—Yes; there is, I may mention, an open sewer there, that is represented as coming from Lower Irish-street, and it passes by the demesne wall to the rear of Ogle-street. It is in a filthy condition.

323. Yes?—And the inhabitants of that portion of the city are not represented in the Town Commissioners, and consequently they cannot bring pressure to bear upon the Town Commissioners to abate any nuisance that they would bring under their notice.

ARMAGH. July 26, 1877. Mr. Alexander Blane.

324. Are you aware that they applied to the Commissioners complaining of the nuisance. Can you state that of your own knowledge?—I think I can.

325. And to what Commissioner did they complain? —Well, I cannot exactly say just now.

326. You think if the town was divided into wards and each district represented, that the sanitary matters would be better attended to?—Certainly. Gentlemen would be elected to the Town Council who reside in those portions of the city, and they would have an interest in keeping the streets clean and attending to the sewerage, and that sort of thing; whereas, at the present time, it is optional with the Commissioners whether they do or do not.

327. Are you aware that there is provision made under the Act of 1848, of which any ratepayer can avail himself and oblige the Commissioners to do the sanitary work that you say is optional?—It is optional with the Commissioners to do it or not.

328. You can compel them to do their duty?—Probably so. I think it proper to mention, that from 1873 to 1876 there were no Commissioners in the city of Armagh, simply and solely, because a number of gentlemen came together and without regard to the Act of Parliament or anything else one nominated the other, and proposed the other, and so on.

329. But there are Commissioners now?—Well, it was with a great deal of difficulty they were got.

330. All you wish now to represent is the desirability of the creation of wards?—Yes; if we had wards in the city this nuisance that is represented as being at the back of the infirmary and the convent would not exist.

331. You would have five representatives from that district—one-fourth of the twenty-one?—I think not. I would have——

332. If there were wards the number should be changed to twenty?—Well, I would say so—I would not make any suggestion as to that. My only object in speaking now would be to extend the representation over the largest area of taxation.

Mr. James Best re-examined.

Mr. James Best.

333. Mr. Cotton.—Now that the question of wards has been started, would you like Mr. Best to say anything upon that subject?—No, sir; except this, that I think it would be quite unnecessary. There is no Town Commissioner that is not trying to do his duty, and there are Town Commissioners in the very district Mr. Blane speaks of. Mr. Hillock lives in that district, and also Mr. Thomas Marshall.

Mr. *Blane*.—There is no Commissioner living in Irish-street at all.

Mr. *Peel*.—Mr. Blane has complained of the lights being bad. The reason of that was, that the lights were only burned half time last winter.

334. Mr. Cotton.—And do you mean to say that that was common to the entire town?—Common to the entire town.

335. It would not apply to a particular district?—No. In consequence of a petition lodged by Mr. Blane himself against the return of the then Commissioners, the Commissioners didn't order the lighting of the town, and didn't care to undertake the expense until the Court of Common Pleas determined the validity of their election, and the Gas Company volunteered to light the town half time and run the risk of getting the money, and that was the reason, as Mr. Blane must know, that the town was badly lighted.

336. Mr. Cotton (*to Mr. Blane*).—Do you say, Mr. Blane, that a particular portion of the town was worse lit than the others during the last winter?

Mr. *Blane*.—I do, sir. Since the Commissioners got power, Ogle-street was worse lighted than other parts of the city.

Mr. *Peel*.—With regard to the expenditure of money by the Commissioners, I wish to say that Irish-street on one side has been completely re-flagged within the last few years. All Irish-street on one side, and portion of the other; and the drain that Mr. Blane complains of not being done—as to that the complaints come from his direction. They came from the direction of other parties, coming through the present Commissioners. No complaint ever came from his direction or from Mr. Blane, or to any of the Commissioners. At the present time I have two men, jointly paid by the Guardians and the Commissioners, working at that sewer.

337. Is that the sewer from Lower Irish-street to the Demesne?—Yes. It has been cleaned out. I paid the men £2 5s. to clean it out. At the present time they are taking the cover off other portions of it, and doing the cleansing. As regards Charter-lane not being swept, if the Commissioners could now see it, they would find it a clean street. No such matter ever influenced the Commissioners of the town. It has been cleaned properly ever since I came into office, and that remark applies to any part of the town.

Mr. Cotton.—The question is not so much whether the Commissioners are doing their duty or not, but whether, under any circumstances, it would be desirable to have wards.

338. Mr. Robinson.—What is your opinion as to wards?—I think the town is very well managed.

Mr. Cotton.—I don't think, as I said before, that

Ardee. July [illegible], 1879. Mr. James Bell.

we have any power to create wards in a town where there are no wards originally; but we have power to go into the question of remitting wards. However, Mr. Bleas, your evidence will be submitted to Mr. Exham, the Chairman of the Commission.

Mr. Bleas.—There is this open sewer at the rere of the Infirmary. It is very offensive. I know that if the town was divided into wards the people there would have a certain pressure to bring to bear on the Town Commissioners.

239. Mr. Cotton.—Upon what portion of the Town Commissioners?—They would be represented in the Town Council, and they could bring those matters forcibly before that body.

240. I understand your argument?—The Commissioners levy a rate, and the town is in the same condition as regards some of those sewers then existed.

Mr. *Peel.*—If the town was divided into wards, as Mr. Bleas suggests, his party would be represented.

Mr. *Bleas.*—Certainly.

Mr. *Peel.*—And I don't think he would be in a bit better position.

Mr. Cotton.—If the town is divided into wards, the ward that is on that side of the town must have its representative out of it.

Mr. Bleas.—What we complain of is that portion of the town outvote other portions by a small majority.

Mr. James Bell.—I don't think there is anyone in there who would agree to that opinion.

The inquiry then terminated.

Dundalk. July 28, 1879. Mr. Neville, C.E.

DUNDALK.—JULY 28th, 1879.

Before Messrs. Cotton and Robinson.

Mr. John Neville, C.E., examined.

1. Mr. Cotton.—Are the roads maintained by the county?—Not now. At present they are maintained under an Act of Parliament (or are about to be maintained) by the Town Commissioners.

2. Is it an Act of Parliament now?—Yes. In some cases the boundary between the town and the barony runs along the centre of the road. (Map produced.)

3. The red line is the boundary of the municipality?—Yes; in some parts the boundary line runs along the centre of the road, and in others the whole of the road is in the town.

4. That happened in other cases?—Yes; the road is divided in that way between two authorities, the Commissioners and the barony. I think it is right that each should do its own portion, but it would be impossible to do so with any harmony, and work side by side with each other. Therefore, I have considered the subject of the alteration in the boundary, and what I propose is this:—That wherever the boundary of the township at present runs along the centre of the road for one-half its length, it should be changed, so that one-half of the length of the road should be given to the one authority, and one-half to the other, for it is impossible for the county to repair half the width of the road, and leave the other half undone.

5. You are aware it is often done by agreement, so that one authority repairs the whole road and divides the expenses?—I am afraid in this case it would be much better if the alteration is made. We wish to make it more workable, and to have one-half completely in the county, and the other in the town.

6. The only object is to have a more harmonious working?—Yes; and that there may be no possibility of disagreement, and that was the only matter I wish to mention.

Mr. Edward Farrell.

Mr. Edward Farrell examined.

7. Mr. Cotton.—You are Clerk of the Town Commissioners of Dundalk?—Yes; since 1864, nearly fifteen years.

8. What Act is the township under?—The Towns Improvement Act of 1854.

9. When was it adopted?—In 1855.

10. Was it under any Act previous to that?—Yes; the 9th George IV.

11. Have you any description of the boundaries as adopted in 1855?—They are the existing boundaries.

12. What is the area?—We compute it at about 1,[illegible] acres.

13. Mr. Cotton.—What is the population?—We may fairly say 12,000 now, for in 1871 it was 11,377.

14. It is increasing?—The valuation is certainly increasing.

15. Are there additions being made to the buildings?—Certainly, every year.

16. What was your last valuation?—Our valuation for 1878 was £20,197. That was what we struck our last rate on.

17. What was it in the four years preceding 1878?—In 1877 it was £20,153; in 1876, £19,[illegible]; in 1875, £19,440; and in 1874, £19,461. I might mention of the sum I gave you first for 1878, that £2,144 10s. comprises land and railway, which is treated as land, and it is valued at only one-fourth valuation for rate purposes.

18. Can you distribute that valuation of £20,197 between the wards?—I could not do that, but it certainly might be done; just as Mr. Neville told you the boundaries in some cases are on one side of the road only, so it is with our streets. The right hand of a street may be in one ward, and the left hand side in another ward, and even Wellington-place, which is a small place, comprises three wards alone.

19. Surely your books give you the valuation of the wards?—It could be ascertained.

20. The rate-book is not made up in wards?—No; it would take half a day to make out the return you ask for.

21. Mr. Robinson.—Are the wards the same as the poor law wards?—Quite different.

22. How many wards are there?—Four; namely the Middle ward, Seatown ward, North ward, and South ward; Mr. Murray will furnish the area of each ward.

23. Mr. Cotton.—Can you tell me the number of voters in each ward?—Yes; in the list prepared for the last municipal purposes the Middle ward had [illegible] voters; Seatown ward, 231; North ward, 150; and South ward; 144.

24. Do you know how many of those in each ward are qualified to be Commissioners?—Not in each ward. The register of Parliamentary voters only deals with the borough as a unit and not in wards. The wards are exclusively for municipal purposes. The total number of persons rated, and the amount necessary for a commissionership is 177.

25. Could you divide the number amongst the wards?—That could be done.

26. How many Commissioners have you altogether?

—We had eighteen, but there are only seventeen at present.

27. How are they distributed amongst the wards?—The present number in the middle ward is three—it is one short.

28. It should have been six?—Yes. Northern ward has six; North ward, eight; and South ward, three.

29. Can you give us the rates for the last five years commencing in 1874?—Yes; they were as follows:—

	Municipal.	Poor Rate.	County Cess.
	s. d.	s. d.	s. d.
1874,	1 6	1 9	2 0
1875,	1 6	1 7	2 6
1876,	1 4	1 8	1 11
1877,	1 0	1 8	2 1
1878,	1 0	2 0	1 11

30. Of that 1s. 6d. rate for 1874 was there any special rate, or was it altogether the improvement rate?—There is one penny every year of an improvement rate, which might be called foreign.

31. What is that?—It is a library rate of one penny all through.

32. Is there any other special rate?—That is for sanitary purposes, and there is a shilling rate for the ordinary purposes of the Act.

33. Was there a sanitary rate in the previous years?—No; but there is in this present year of '78. In '77, '76, '75 and '74, the rates above a shilling consist of the mortgage rate and the library rate. The mortgage rate is to pay for the liquidation of the building, &c. as in debt—the town hall.

34. Is that paid off?—There is still £3,000 due. It was originally £4,000.

35. There was no mortgage rate this year?—No; there was a question as to the legality of it, and now we are charging the mortgage rate on the shilling. We charge the sum requisite for the liquidation of the debt on the general shilling rate.

36. You include it in the shilling rate?—Yes.

37. Have the Commissioners had these inquiries under their notice before them?—Yes.

38. Did they come to any resolution on the subject?—Yes; they held a special meeting for the purpose.

39. On what date?—The 5th December last.

40. And what was the resolution come to?—A special meeting was given at the meeting for that very purpose. We had ten Commissioners present including the Chairman. This is the entry:—

"Special meeting held in accordance with the Board order, to consider your answer to be given to the Commissioners' inquiry on the subject of the municipal boundaries. The question being submitted, on the motion of Mr. Charles, it was decided that the boundaries should not be enlarged, and it was suggested by the Chairman that they should remain as they are at present."

The boundaries were considered fair and such as satisfied the general public. It was deemed unnecessary to increase the taxation of a few people who might not be common. The surveyor was desired to remit to this report of the area within the municipal boundary, and the town clerk to give replies to the remaining questions.

41. Were the Commissioners unanimous?—I think they were; there was no division.

42. Has the question been before the Commissioners since?—I merely submitted your notice last Wednesday, when we had a meeting.

43. Has there been any meeting of the ratepayers on the subject?—On the question of the boundaries, none.

44. Have you got control of the main roads?—It is pending an Act of Parliament. I cannot well say. We have them now, though I have not seen the Act. What happened is—we have a bill which gives us control of the roads, but the particular day on which we are to get control is not given.

45. You applied to get control of the roads?—Yes. We applied for a provisional order. It was granted, and it is now going through the House of Commons—it has it not got the Royal assent. I have never got a copy of the Act. I wrote long ago to Mr. Sullivan, who says that the Act, in its form as an Act, is printed to-day, and will not be for a few days. "I had I send you the bill, which, I believe, is word for word with the Act?" That is from our member, and the Secretary of the Grand Jury has written to the Local Government Board for it, and he has not got it yet.

46. How is the town lighted?—There are 125 public lamps at the present time.

47. Do you contract with the Gas Company for the The price for gas is £2 15s. from the 1st August to the 1st June, the contract.

48. From what hour are they lighted?—Three days before full moon they are not lighted at all, likewise on the nights of full moon, and after full moon three nights they are lighted up to eleven o'clock, and then they are extinguished.

49. They are then all put out?—Yes; the moon is supposed to shine from about eleven o'clock.

50. And what about the other nights?—They are lighted from forty-five minutes after sunset until forty-five minutes before sunrise.

51. Is there any complaint of the light being insufficient?—No, sir; I cannot say there is.

52. How is the town supplied with water?—We have twenty pumps, but the supply is very deficient.

53. Are there complaints about the deficiency?—I cannot say the complaints are very loud.

54. However, you think it is deficient?—There is a committee appointed on the subject.

55. Is there any scheme before you for a water supply?—There is a committee appointed only very lately, to investigate water works. They have been in communication with two towns, and have got important communications, both from Newry and Banbridge, and I have called a meeting of the committee for this week.

56. But you have no definite scheme before you?—No; we have no definite scheme or estimate prepared as yet.

57. Twenty pumps seem a very small allowance for such a town as this?—It is very deficient.

58. Is there any complaint about the quality?—I think the health of the town is remarkably good, and I think the health of the town would show the quality of the water if it was really bad. There was an analysis made in Dublin, but I have very little faith in analyses. In dry seasons the water might be deficient in quality, but there is nothing else against.

59. The question of the water supply is under consideration?—Yes, decidedly.

60. What is the state of the drainage?—It is quite unfinished. It could hardly be considered as extending to more than quarter of the town.

61. Have the Commissioners been expending any money recently on sewerage?—We have not made any important main sewers to any extent.

62. How much money have you been spending for the last two or three years on sewerage?—£230 within the last year and a half but the principal thing is the main drainage of the town which was practically county work.

63. How do you mean county work?—Inasmuch as the roads were under the control of the County Grand Jury.

64. But the drainage of a town of 13,000 is a work for the Commissioners and not for the County Grand Jury?—But there is a great nuisance immediately in connexion with the jail of the county, the sewage of which discharges itself into Lord Baden's demesne and we always considered we had a claim on the county and a very substantial one, and in point of fact we had submitted a presentment from the sessions, but at the last moment it was rejected by the Grand Jury although it was passed by the associated cesspayers. It was rejected some years since and ever since that we have applied to the cesspayers and Grand Jury to grant a presentment, and it was lost in some way or other.

65. What would be the amount of it?—It was always disputed and we put so much on the county or so much on the municipal charge. It was something about £1,500.

Dundalk, July 23, 1879. — Mr. Edward Powell.

66. For the one nuisance arising from the one sewer?—That nuisance could not be properly removed without extensions, of which we had the plans prepared by Mr. Murray our surveyor, and to make things complete it would require £1,500 for the main drainage of that part of the town.

67. That is for one particular district?—Yes, any main drainage for the town has been by presentment on the county or barony-at-large.

68. Do you mean the Commissioners don't extend the mains themselves?—We had no money except by raising the sanitary rate.

69. Would you have power to strike a sanitary rate for the purpose?—Now we have the right.

70. You have had that power for some years?—Yes, we always thought we had a primary claim on the Grand Jury inasmuch as we have never received any money for the flagging of these streets, as they do in the south of Ireland.

71. But that does not excuse you from doing your duty?—In sanitary matters our taxes are thought to be high enough.

72. Have you got a proper scheme of drainage and what that would cost?—It might be done at from £3,000 to £4,000, but we have no formal report. The completion of our drainage would certainly cost about that.

73. Have the Commissioners ever considered the matter at all as a body?—We thought we had a primary claim on the Grand Jury.

74. And the Commissioners deferred thinking of it until they could get money out of the Grand Jury?—Yes, until we could get it out of the Grand Jury as we now hope to do.

75. Did you consider you were quite free from any claim on the Grand Jury now that you have got control of the roads?—I think, I have said, we have still a very fair ground for a claim against the Grand Jury for the county-at-large. The nuisance from their overflow drainage into the Roden demesne in the proximity of the National schools I think gives us a claim, although we are separated at [illegible] boundary.

76. Independent of that isn't there a very large amount wanting to make the drainage good—the rest of it?—Surely there is a couple of thousands wanted.

77. The main drainage of the town has been suspended for want of funds?—That is fairly the case.

78. Is there any other improvement that is in abeyance for want of funds?—The water scheme is one.

79. Do you think there would have been a water scheme if you had more funds?—There would certainly have been more disposition to take up that project. The encumbrance of the debt of this building has been a drawback in the way of increased taxation. This hall cost £3,000 or £4,000, although it originally cost the proprietors £10,000 or £8,000, and ever since the purchase of it, it has been an incumbrance on the rates of the town of £200 or £300 a year. There is a revenue of £150 from the corn market, but it is totally inadequate to pay the debentures and interest.

80. You have no sinking fund?—We have debentures collateral with our mortgage.

81. Terminable debentures?—No, sir, they are numbered and become due in rotation. When they were originally in the hands of the bank, there was no fixed rate of interest, but the current rate of interest, which sometimes ran up as high as ten per cent.; but since then private persons fortunately have stepped in and taken up the debentures, and we are limited to the payment of a five per cent. interest, instead of a variable rate; but it never went below five.

82. Do you know the feelings of the ratepayers as to whether they think it advisable to have an extension or not?—I don't know the public feeling, but I think it would be a great injustice to the Commissioners, having regard to this Act of Parliament, to extend the boundaries, and I don't know how we could bear the expenditure.

83. Just explain that. Do you think if the boundaries were extended it would be unfair?—It would be particularly unfair to the Commissioners and, as far as the outside people go they should be very happy to come in.

84. Why?—My reason for saying so is this. The county cess is levied alike on house property and on land, at the rate of two shillings in the pound. Under the Act of Parliament, if my construction of it is right, the additional rate which we have power to levy under this new bill, will only be assessable in the quarter proportion on land, while on house property it remains at the full rate of two shillings.

85. You mean for the road rate, so that the provisional order rate will be distributed in the same way as the improvement rate is?—It appears to me to by the reading of the Act, but, perhaps, my construction of it is utterly wrong.

86. Then you think if any additional land was taken in outside the present boundary, you would have to maintain their roads and only receive one-fourth of the rates?—We would receive more than one-fourth.

87. One-fourth of the additional improvement, and one-fourth of the road rate, but you think that that would not pay for the additional expenditure on the extended roads?—I think not.

88. What did you pay to the county before you became the road authority?—Three shillings, but on a valuation, £20,000.

89. How much did the county spend on the town?—I made up a return in connection with the inquiry held by the Local Government Inspector, and in a period of two years we were £3,046 on the wrong side, we were at a loss to that amount.

90. You paid more than was expended?—Yes, to that extent, and the surplus went to the benefit of the barony outside the boundary.

91. Did you take out the county-at-large expenses?—Yes; Dr. Brougham's report which he made out in his own way is substantially correct.

92. You have now to pay the county-at-large charges?—Yes.

93. And have you to pay a share of the county surveyor's charges?—We will have to pay all county-at-large charges as before.

94. No exemptions?—No.

95. But when you say you were in certain years at a loss of about £3,000, do you mean that the county expended £300 a year less on the town than they received?—Quite so, and that the surplus went to the works in the barony outside the municipal boundary.

96. You have considered all that question, and consider it advisable to become the road authority?—Yes, we thought that a very great grievance.

97. It is a smaller disproportion than some other towns?—It is so, but £300 is more than 3d. in the pound on our taxation.

98. Did you calculate at all what the additional expense would be?—We did not go into that question at all.

99. Or whether you would be able to do it for the same?—No, we looked upon it as imperative on us to take up the control of the roads, provided only the Local Government Board and the Grand Jury would sanction it.

100. You think it imperative independent of the saving of money?—Yes, we thought that the thing had come to a dead lock, owing to the contention that existed as to the duty of cleansing the streets. It was always thought that that was an inseparable portion of their maintenance.

101. Do you mean of the road contractors?—It was provided in the specification that the contractor should scrape and cart away all mud. The Commissioners were always anxious and willing to do the scavenging, but wished the road authorities to remove the mud—I mean scrape and remove the mud.

102. That is different from scavenging. The Commissioners were always willing to do the scavenging, but they wished the road authorities to remove the mud?—Yes, the mud caused by the broken stones and [illegible] of the town.

103. This has all come to a conclusion now?—Yes, and we have maintenance [illegible] repairs and lighting, and the expense [illegible] £3,712 [illegible].

104. What do you think?—That is the estimated expenditure for general purposes 4d. for sanitary purposes, and 1d. for library rate.

105. That is the total?—Yes, that is the government of the [illegible] and [illegible] with [illegible] a few pounds [illegible] £20.

106. Mr. Robinson.—In which direction is the building extending?—There are, [illegible], new buildings in [illegible]. Mr. Wilkinson is making some new buildings there, and there are some buildings going on in [illegible].

107. Is the land suitable for building land?—Williamson's [illegible] is let on building lease. The difficulty is to get land [illegible] for building land.

108. Are there any villa residences outside whose people go to this [illegible] in the town?—No, there are a few.

109. Do you know the electoral divisions?—Yes.

110. Is it good land [illegible] round the town [illegible] is nearly rural.

111. But the electoral division is all very valuable land in proximity to Dundalk?—Yes.

112. Dundalk is the market town of everybody living within the division?—Yes.

113. Mr. Cherry.—Would you consider the electoral division too large to be the boundary of the town?—I think I am right in my recollection of the Act. We would be swamped altogether by taking it in.

114. Which is the most convenient?—Yes.

115. Mr. Robinson.—Has any meeting of the ratepayers been convened to consider this question?—No, nothing beyond our annual meeting.

116. Have they had notice of the meeting here?—I saw it advertised in some of the local papers. Of course I reported it at the meeting on Wednesday that there was an inquiry would take place to-day.

117. Do you know the poor law wards?—Yes; but we have no dealing with them. They are, Upper, Lower, South, and North.

118. Mr. Cherry.—How many townlands are there in the division?—Twenty-five in all.

[illegible] July [illegible], 18[illegible]. Mr. Edward Farrell.

Mr. E. H. M'[illegible] examined.

Mr. E. H. M'[illegible].

119. Mr. Cherry.—You are Chairman of the Town Commissioners?—Yes.

120. How long have you been so?—Twenty years, I think.

121. Have you considered the question of extending the present boundaries?—I have given it my best consideration, and I think the boundaries should be left as they are.

122. Were you a Commissioner when the Act was adopted in 18[illegible]?—Oh, yes, I think I was.

123. Do you remember what guided you in fixing the present limits which you have adopted?—Well, I think we took, as near as I can recollect, a circle from the centre of the town.

124. Are the only residential [illegible] within the town?—Yes. The railway is the boundary through the [illegible].

125. Why should the other portions not be included?—Because [illegible] being within the limit of the circle. The railway through the demesne is not half [illegible] from the centre of the town on the other side, and beyond taking the railway as a convenient boundary there, I know of no other.

126. Do you think it desirable to take in the rest of the demesne?—I don't think so; the portion that is not there [illegible] is a [illegible] and the [illegible] being [illegible].

127. The Town Clerk has told us the great reason [illegible] extension is that under the present circumstances you would be obliged to [illegible] the roads, [illegible]. Was that the reason?—Yes, that was the [illegible] reason urged against [illegible] should any the town [illegible].

128. How long is it since you began discussing the question of [illegible] the road authority?—It must be at least four years.

129. Beyond that was there any talk of extension of the town?—No, there was not.

130. Do you consider drainage is in a bad way in Dundalk?—I do.

131. The Town Clerk said it is causing [illegible] the Commissioners?—Yes. I consider it is considerably. A portion of my land is completely inundated for want of drainage.

132. And is that drainage that you describe the drainage of the lands or of the town proper?—It is the drainage of the whole, and I live outside the boundary.

133. Is it want of funds that prevented you entering on the question of drainage before this?—Certainly.

134. With regard to the water supply of the town, is that in the same way?—To a large extent it is, in the same way.

135. If you had means would you want a better supply?—We have no [illegible] supply in some places, but the quality is not as good as it might be.

136. Are you agreeing on the question of a better supply?—Yes.

137. And you would have done it before but for want of funds?—Yes.

138. Mr. Robinson.—Do you think any [illegible] is necessary or desirable?—I don't think so. I think they are very fairly divided.

139. Do you think they should be [illegible] for poor-law purposes?—[illegible].

140. You have nothing to add to what the Town Clerk has mentioned?—No.

[illegible]
July [illegible]
Mr. Edward [illegible]

difficulty is, that the water lying towards the seaside is invariably bad and the water at the other end always good.

144. Do you consider twenty pumps sufficient for the town?—Up to the present it is, in this way. There is scarcely a public establishment in the town or large premises but have pumps, and the people are allowed free access to those pumps. Hotel yards and all have pumps, and, except in very dry seasons, there is no complaint as to quantity, but the difficulty that has arisen at any time is as to its quality.

145. Has any scheme of water supply on a large scale been before the Commissioners?—Yes. It is the want of funds and the necessity of putting on additional taxation, while the burden of the town hall lay on the Commissioners, that prevented the Commissioners taking up the matter in a practical form, but the Government have intimated that they would contribute to the waterworks in order that the barracks might have a good supply, and the thing has taken a practical form now, and we expect the Government will be prepared to go further, as we are prepared to supply the county prison which has now become Government property.

146. What is the provision in regard to fires?—We are very well provided in that way. The military barracks has an engine, and not only do the engines turn out but large bodies of soldiers in cases of fire.

147. But when that military engine goes to a fire, where does it get a water supply?—Every house has a pump, and in very few instances has the water supply failed. We have the barrack engine, the distillery engine, and the foundry engine.

148. Do you mean in case of fire the pumps provided sufficient water?—Sometimes the river has been used, and of course there has been some trouble, but, as a rule, the water has always been found sufficient for the three engines. If there was a fire of any great magnitude our water supply would not be available, but it is owing to the fact that there is such assistance rendered by those three engines and by the military that there is no case recently where the fire obtained any height before it was suppressed.

149. If it were not for this question of the roads and the additional expense the barracks would bring the town, would you have extended the boundaries?—No; the feeling, on the contrary, is rather in favour of contracting the boundary in a small way.

150. Why?—There were four persons who suffered grievance by the present boundaries. The Rev. Mr. Black, whose place is marked on the Dublin-road; Mr. Robinson; Mrs. Dickie; and Mr. Roche.

151. You think, in the case of these people, there is a hardship?—Yes. Those four residents have a grievance; for, while they are paying town rates, they are getting no benefit in the way of water and light; and, in the way of light, it is not in the power of the Commissioners to assist them, as the gas company would not extend their mains in that way. Their water-supply they get from pumps, and they, besides, remained without water for several years, and the Commissioners felt that they were quite right in equity. However, at the meeting, when the matter was discussed, it was considered that although it was a grievance to these four people, if Mr. Exham's contention is right as to land only paying one-fourth, it would be better for them to remain within the boundary; because instead of paying 5s. cess, as they would be liable for in the county, if they came into the borough they would only have to pay a fourth of that.

152. What Mr. Exham said was not with that provision before him at all?—Of course, the question is whether we should deal with that 5s. as with the cess, or as really part of the general consolidated rate. If we deal with it as a cess, we can put 5s. on those lands.

153. Was that not d[illegible]
visional order was sought
to carry out the provisi[illegible]
the time we refused to ca[illegible]
with no desire to keep the
but we believed that, b[illegible]
boundaries, they would b[illegible]
under. It all depends on
—as county cess or part [illegible]

154. Don't you think
that distance of the town
in the town being kept
urged that point on the [illegible]
not see it.

155. But don't you
within three-quarters of
greater interest in the
miles away?—Yes, cert[illegible]
feel they have a grievanc[illegible]
persons aggrieved, the li[illegible]
laying the boundary co[illegible]
grievance; but they tho[illegible]
probably would be be[illegible]
less.

156. Can you tell m[illegible]
are not extended as far
No; except in this way:
as you may see from the
of building-ground availa[illegible]
any that would do for
town is built in the fo[illegible]
back and front of each f[illegible]
vast quantity of building
of, owing to the late [illegible]
limited. But once this
building, there is ample
the boundary. That is
not desired to extend [illegible]
boundaries, as there is a[illegible]
ing is likely to be made.

157. Have you ever c[illegible]
boundaries of the wards
able to lay my hand o[illegible]
ago of the population [illegible]
wards; but the two b[illegible]
Middle ward—were £[illegible]
the other two wards wer[illegible]
valuation each. From
division was well consid[illegible]

158. And then you c[illegible]
Yes. You observe that
representation. It is as
could make. As regard[illegible]
additional burden which
out of the Harbour Com[illegible]

159. Are the quays
Harbour Commissioners
private property; they a[illegible]
Harbour Board by a sp[illegible]
forgot an important item
I saw you observed th[illegible]
pence in one year. Tha[illegible]
for the construction of a[illegible]
laid out on the portion
Halson-quay, where it fi[illegible]

160. Six hundred po[illegible]
—Yes, but the London [illegible]
made a contribution of
necessity for portion of [illegible]
was laid out by the Com[illegible]

161. When was that [illegible]
1876. It was made in [illegible]
we are quite unable to [illegible]
ago.

Mr. John Murray examined.

Mr. John Murray.

163. You are borough surveyor?—Yes.

164. Can you give us the size of the different wards?—Yes, the North ward is 209 acres; South, 3?0 acres; Seatown, 330 acres; Middle, 130 acres.

165. Do you know anything about the population?—No.

165. Have you formed any estimate of it?—No.

166. What is the mileage of the streets and roads you will now have to maintain?—I have not got the return here.

167. Do you know what the maintenance of the roads would be outside the present boundary per mile?—Not accurately.

168. Then you could not tell what the additional expense would be if there was an extension of two miles?—Not correctly at present.

169. Are they anything more than the ordinary roads, is there any special traffic?—No, nothing more than the ordinary traffic coming into a little town like Dundalk. There is more traffic on the Ardee and Carrickmacross roads.

170. And these have been heavier contracts?—Yes.

171. Have you any map of the roads?—No, it is with the Grand Jury.

172. *Town Clerk.*—We have no map; the map is in reality the property of the town and paid for by them, but it is in the custody of the secretary of the Grand Jury.

173. Mr. Cotton.—Are you aware of the provisions of the Public Health Act on the subject?

Town Clerk.—All we would have to do would be to appoint a deputation to wait on the Grand Jury at their next meeting and get the map.

Examination of Mr. Murray continued.

174. Can you tell me what the drainage of the town is like?—It is by ordinary sewers, [illegible].

175. Is the town divided into districts?—No, it all [illegible] towards the [illegible]. There is a main which was made [illegible] by the Grand Jury. The main [illegible] Castle road, [illegible] Clanbrassil street, [illegible] Park street, and [illegible].

176. Have you any other drainage?—No, except the ordinary surface drainage.

177. Have you any other outfalls?—Yes, by Park street, [illegible] in the direction of [illegible], and there is [illegible] at the wharf.

178. Then there will be a further extension [illegible] in the direction of the bridges?—That is what we now require.

179. What do you suppose that will cost?—It will cost [illegible]. I brought a presentment on three or four occasions before the Grand Jury for the extension of the sewerage and it was thrown out.

180. Have you formed any opinion of your own as to the boundaries?—I did not [illegible] as the [illegible] portion of [illegible] Lord Roden's demesne.

181. Do you think it ought to be extended in that direction?—I think so. It would involve no expense, as there are no roads whatever in that division, and it would be a great advantage. Having control of the [illegible] we will be able to [illegible] them. It was a [illegible] at the same time.

Rev. Robert [illegible] examined.

Rev. Robert Black.

182. The only thing I wish to say in this regard is the sewerage of the town, is that in my part of it the sewerage is exceedingly bad. I may say there is none at all.

183. That is on the south?—Yes, [illegible] the [illegible]. The whole sewerage of the district comes into an open ditch, [illegible], and the [illegible] goes through the whole district.

184. Is there no main?—No, but there should be a main; I am far more anxious about that than about the boundary.

185. You think that money ought to be expended on the drainage to improve it?—Of course, but a very small expense would [illegible]. The drainage is not only defective, but is [illegible]. The [illegible]. With regard to the water, I have heard complaints that it is not good; of course, there is [illegible]. There are no waterworks. There were pumps before the Commissioners got the management into their hands. There have been a few sunk since, and in some parts the water is bad, [illegible] where I have to [illegible]. I had to sink a well in my own place in order to get water, and very good water it is. If [illegible] I should have been very anxious that the boundaries would have been extended so as to [illegible] for I could then get [illegible] water, [illegible] lighting. I [illegible] the Commissioners [illegible] lighting that road.

186. You think if the boundary was to remain the same, [illegible] it should not be extended in other directions?—Yes, I think it is a most suitable boundary. I think it is [illegible] to go out to Fair Hill or Mrs. [illegible]'s place and leave the [illegible].

187. That is speaking comparatively; but do you think if all the other places of the same distance were taken in Fair Hill should be taken in also?—Yes.

188. That is about a mile from the town?—It is about a mile and a quarter.

189. Do you think that every person within a mile and a quarter like this ought to pay something towards the town being kept in good condition?—For my own part I would have no objection if all were treated in the same way, but I don't think the town boundary is at all a fair boundary.

190. But if all others were treated in the same way would you have any objection?—Not any [illegible] myself, but [illegible] I think Fair Hill and my own place should be [illegible] the boundary [illegible]. And there is one other matter I [illegible] to mention. It is [illegible] within the range of the [illegible] that something should be done with regard to the [illegible]. It is a [illegible] to the [illegible].

191. We have nothing to say as to whether the Commissioners do their duty; we have only to go into the question of [illegible] them in [illegible] giving them more taxable property [illegible].

192. Mr. [illegible].—That is really a grievance that [illegible]. There [illegible] large establishments [illegible] from this [illegible], and it seems when [illegible] they [illegible] of water to flow [illegible], and I have told people that the only way is to [illegible] a petition against those people, [illegible] the Town Commissioners [illegible] a sanitary nuisance.

193. Mr. [illegible].—It is a sanitary matter.

194. Mr. [illegible].—I am a ratepayer, but I [illegible] and chiefly [illegible], but as representing [illegible]. They [illegible] Mr. Russell has alluded [illegible]. He said some objection might be made by [illegible]. Those [illegible] not content with the existing boundary, [illegible] the boundary should be

DUNDALK. July 25, 1879. Rev. Robert Black.

not extended but contracted. The chief objections were laid before you in the memorial that was sent to the then secretary of your commission on the 15th November, 1878. It was sent by Mr. Black, who has already given his evidence, and the other signatories are Mrs. Dickie, Fair Hill; Captain Caddell, who lives at Brighton Villa. Of course I don't appear for Mr Black, as he is here himself, but there are other parties on the Shore Road, who are not signatories, whom I also represent, and their objections are mainly these: They consider that the boundary should be restricted for the reason that while subject to all the other rates to which the ratepayers in the town are subject, they get no advantage whatever from those rates, except the same advantage that would be derived by any person at a distance of six or seven miles coming into market in Dundalk. Take the case of Mrs. Dickie. She lives at Fair Hill, which is a mile and a quarter away. Her objections are that she gets no water, and that she gets no gas. She gets no advantage from the proximity of the Post-office, letters not being delivered out there, so that she does not derive from the town the advantages other persons derive living in it.

195. Mr. Cotton.—The Commissioners have no control as to the letters.

196. Mr. Black.—No; but the grievance would, at the same time, be removed if she was relieved from the burden of the payment of rates which falls on the persons living in the town. She has no cleansing whatever. She has no benefit from that or paving, or water, or footpaths out as far as her residence.

197. Mr. Cotton.—Do you maintain that the owner of Fairy Hill has no more interest in the streets being kept clean than the man living four miles away?—I maintain that a person living at Fairy Hill may not have any further advantage from the water, lighting, and cleansing of the town than any other from any distance who chose to make Dundalk his market town. I presume that any person coming into the town, as a market town, has some little interest in having the streets kept clean.

198. Do you think a person living a mile and a quarter away would not use the town more frequently than persons living at a greater distance?—I presume they probably would, but those are the main objections on Mrs. Dickie's part.

199. Will she object to pay that rate if everyone at the same distance away from the centre of the town also paid, or is it that she is further away than other people?—I think she is further away than other people. I don't think she would be selfish enough to say she would pay if other people would pay, but she says I am obliged to pay although I get no advantage from the rates, and I can see no stronger existing objection to the boundaries than that on her part. On the part of other persons there is a feeling that the small area for the Commissioners is better for those outside and those inside; for those outside, because they would be subject to some other authority than the Commissioners' and to those inside, because the Commissioners, by devoting their time to the smaller area, would attend to it in a more satisfactory way. The objections on the part of Mr. Caddell are exactly the same. He gets no advantage. Fair Hill is half a mile from the nearest gas lamp. It has been mentioned as an answer, but it is no answer, that the gas works are in the hands of the Gas Company, and not of the Commissioners, that the Commissioners could not force the Gas Company. The answer to that is that there is nothing in the world to prevent the Commissioners taking the gas into their own hands.

200. Captain Caddell's place seems to be nearer town?—Yes, but at the same time it is nearly a quarter of a mile from the nearest gas lamp, and I am informed that the nearest gas lamp is never lighted. The Post Office refuses to deliver letters so far as that, and these ladies and gentlemen have to send to their boy to the Post Office. With regard to some parties, whom I represent on the Shore road, which is called the Boundary-road, the objections there are the same. There is no light, there is no water, and the letters are not delivered, and the footpath there is in the most dreadful condition. It is not only in such a state that you cannot walk, without running the risk of breaking your neck, but there is never anything done to it, and although it is recognised as part of the town, they receive no benefit whatever from the rates of the town. It has been suggested by these parties that in order to remedy this thing you will see that two of these places, Fair-hill and the other place, are at a considerable distance from the town, and between these and the outlying villas of the town there are no other villas. I could easily understand, if the suburbs were densely crowded the boundary running out to the farthest villa, but the boundary here seems to have twisted out to catch these two or three villas which lie at a great distance, while between these and the town there is no appreciable number of houses. It does not, therefore, appear what principle they adopted in laying down the boundary, or they would not have taken in Fair-hill and leave out other places.

201. Mr. Carleton.—It is quite incorrect to say there is nothing done in the way of cleansing the footpaths. The road is not only cleansed at the expense of the county, and the footpaths kept in order, but there is a private road extending up to Mrs. Dickie's residence, and it is perfectly absurd to say she is not provided with cleansing, because the Main road is the road the county have control over.

202. Mr. Leech.—None of my remarks apply to the private road. This private road is kept in much better order than the public road there.

203. Mr. Carleton.—The Commissioners have had nothing to do with the public road up to the present. The road has invariably been well kept by the county, and the footpath too. At the same time the Commissioners would have been glad, if it would not entail trouble and expense, knowing of Mrs. Dickie's grievance, to meet her views, but the number being small it would not be worth while, and we know that under the changed circumstances Mrs. Dickie may be benefited.

204. Mr. Leech.—You say if there was such a decision as to leave out Mrs. Dickie, the Commissioners would not feel aggrieved?—Not the least.

205. Mr. Black.—I applied to the Commissioners to leave out my place and Mrs. Dickie's, and they came to a resolution saying, if it would not entail expense they would do it, so they wrote to Dublin and were told there would be no expense, and then they receded from the position they took up. That is years ago.

206. Mr. Carleton.—It was recognised that there was a grievance, but it was found that some one must suffer, and you cannot make any boundary under which some ratepayer will not suffer, and it was felt that the number being so few it would be better not to disturb existing arrangements.

207. Mr. Black.—It is quite clear from the map that the boundary was fixed not with regard to the general interests of the town, but ran in a zigzag way in and out in every direction to catch one in and not another. I think there should be some uniform boundary taking only in those who should be in.

208. Mr. Cotton.—You think the boundary ought to be altered so as to treat every one in the same way?—Yes. The way these boundaries were formed was by leaving out people who objected to the formation of the town.

209. Mr. Carleton.—To this the Commissioners have no objection, but at the last meeting it was considered that those people would be benefited.

210. Mr. Farrell.—The late Mr. Pa[illegible] was Mrs. Dickie's predecessor in the very premises under consideration, and if he was not Chairman of the Town Commissioners at the time the boundary was fixed, he was certainly one of the body, and he never raised his voice against the boundary.

311. Mr. Lamb.—I understand that since he was put off the board he declined to pay rates. That is a very strong opinion as to the benefit of it.

312. Mr. Ferrall.—No; he was allowed to sit on the Board and fight his battle as best he could.

313. Mr. Carleton.—If the Boundaries Commissioners make a recommendation to omit those people we will have no objection; but it was simply because we thought they would be benefited.

314. Mr. Lamb.—There is one point more, and it is as a ratepayer I speak, with regard to water. I live at one part of the town and I have now tried all the pumps in the town, and in order to get drinkable water that won't poison myself and my family I have sent nearly three-quarters of a mile, and it is only just fit for use.

315. Mr. Cotton. You mean in the interests of the town there should be some scheme for a water supply?—It is one of the most important things.

316. Mr. Carleton.—That is what struck the Commissioners in the first. We believe certainly that the water such as it is, would be preferred, and that there would be the greatest objection to take water from waterworks—that they would be satisfied with the water without having abundance of it rather than take water from the waterworks.

[The inquiry then terminated.]

[illegible] July [illegible], 1878. Rev. [illegible]

LARNE.—JUNE 11TH, 1879.

(Before Messrs. C. P. Cotton, C.E., and H. A. Robinson.)

Mr. John M. [illegible] examined.

Larne. June 11, 1879. Mr. John M. [illegible]

1. You are clerk to the Town Commissioners of Larne?—I am.

2. How long have you held that office?—For about [illegible] years.

3. Under what Act is the township of Larne?—Under the Towns Improvement Act, 1854.

4. When was the town put under the operation of that Act?—In April, 1856.

5. Had it been under any previous Act?—It was under the 9th of George the Fourth.

6. Was the Act of 1854 adopted wholly or in part?—Only in part.

7. What were the portions of the Act omitted?—Sewage, paving, and watching.

8. You have power to levy a rate for water?—Yes.

9. What is the population of the town?—I am sure I don't know what it is.

10. What was it in 1871?—[illegible] I think.

11. Was it [illegible] or thereabouts?—Yes; very much on the increase.

12. Do you know what the population is at present?—I don't know the exact number, but I daresay it is beyond [illegible].

13. What is the size of the township?—It is very irregular.

14. But what is the number of acres?—I can't tell.

15. Won't the rate-book tell it?—No; we never enter any land; it is simply house property.

15. The area is returned on Mr. O'Brien's return as 216 acres, and he must have got that from somewhere?—Perhaps he got it from the Valuation Office, but he did not get it from us.

16. Don't you get a rate-book sent down by the Valuation Department, and shouldn't that show what the area was?—We take our rate from the valuation supplied to the Board of Guardians.

17. And what is the area included in that book?—We don't copy anything but the house property.

18. Have you any lands within the municipal boundary from which you levy the agricultural rating?—No.

19. What is the valuation of the town?—The valuation for the half-year ended 15th May, 1878 was £3,[illegible] [illegible].

20. You have no wards in the town?—No.

21. In what electoral division is the town of Larne?—In the electoral division of Larne.

22. You have given me three electoral divisions in your return?—Yes, because the boundary is partly in three electoral divisions; that is our old boundary.

23. That is your present boundary now?—Yes.

24. It is in three electoral divisions?—Yes.

25. Are you quite sure of that?—Well I think so. There are the electoral divisions of [illegible], Larne, and [illegible].

26. Is this a map of the town?—Yes. (Produces map.)

27. That is altogether in the electoral division of Larne, and doesn't go into any other electoral division?—It is in an electoral division.

28. No, it is only a townland?—This includes Larne.

29. What are the rates that have been struck within the last five years, beginning at 1874?—It was 12d. in the pound in the year 1874.

30. That is the municipal rate?—Yes, what we call the town rate.

31. And in 1875?—8d. in the pound.

32. In 1876?—It was 6d. also.

33. In 1877?—7d. in the pound.

34. And in 1878?—It was 6d. in the pound.

35. Have you struck no rate this year?—No, not yet.

36. Give me the poor rate for the same years?—In 1874 it was 1s. 6d. in the pound; 1875, 1s. 3d.; 1876, 1s. 9d.; 1877, 1s. 6d., and 1878 1s. 6d. in the pound.

37. Can you tell me whether any part of that rate, since 1874, was for special sanitary purposes?—I am not aware of that.

38. What is the county cess for the same years?—In 1874 it was 11d.; in 1875, 12d.; in 1876, 13d.; in 1877, 11½d.; and in 1878, 13d. in the pound.

39. How many Commissioners are there in the town?—Nine.

40. How many voters are there within the municipality?—I can't exactly say.

41. Can you say how many of the voters are qualified to sit as Commissioners, if elected?—I can make out a return of both from the books here and I will send it in.

42. Have the Commissioners had before them the question of altering the boundaries?—We have talked it over a little.

43. They have come to no resolution?—I think the general feeling is that the boundary should be extended.

44. Have you no resolution on your books on the subject?—No.

45. But that is the Commissioners' view of the question?—Yes.

46. Is there any particular way in which they wish to have the town extended?—Yes.

47. How is the town of Larne lighted?—By lamps.

48. How many lamps are there?—There are forty-eight at present.

49. Do the Commissioners own the gas works?—No; there is a gas company by whom the gas is supplied.

50. And they contract with the gas company?—Yes.

51. What are the terms of the contract?—For the last year it was £1 13s. per lamp, and under the contract there is a scale of hours, commencing on the 1st September ending 1st May, and the light is uniformly extinguished at twelve o'clock. The scale of hours, of course, will be longer the shorter the day, and the longer the day the less light to be burnt.

52. How is the town provided with water?—With

LARNE. June 12, 1879.

Mr. John R. Gawn.

there have been fountains erected for supplying the town with water.

53. How is the town supplied and where does the water come from?—From various points. We have water from a reservoir at Greenland—a spring reservoir.

54. That is led down by pipes?—Yes, it comes past the poorhouse to the town. Then we have water from another source called the Coldwell. The town is partly supplied from that source.

55. Is the supply as much as is wanted?—Not always.

56. Has it been in contemplation to improve the supply?—Yes, [illegible]. We have not been able to come to any definite conclusion as to how it is to be supplied as yet, but the thing is before the mind of the Commissioners, and they are endeavouring to have a supply sufficient for the wants of the town.

57. But they have no definite scheme fixed?—Not yet.

58. Is the town well drained?—I think it is pretty well drained, a great many parts of it, but I am not so well acquainted with that, inasmuch as the Commissioners did not take anything to do with the drainage since 1874 nor before it. That was one of the things they did not enter upon at the time the Act was adopted.

59. Have the Town Commissioners ever had under their consideration the question of their becoming the sanitary authority?—Frequently.

60. Have they petitioned to be made the authority?—No.

61. Are they going to petition with that view?—I think so.

62. But they have come to no resolution upon it?—No.

63. Are there any schools in the town?—Oh yes, a great many schools.

64. And I suppose the farmers' children come in from a long distance to attend the schools?—Yes.

65. How far would you say?—Well, some at least come in three miles, but there are schools within three miles of the town.

66. How far does the present boundary extend from this hall here?—It is very irregular.

67. To the north how far does it go?—Well, it goes, shall I say, about half a mile, Mr. Chairman.

68. Mr. *John Crawford* (chairman Township Commissioners).—No; about a quarter of a mile.

69. Mr. COTTON.—And to the west how far does it extend?

Mr. *Crawford*.—It extends nearly a mile to the west.

70. Mr. COTTON.—And to the south and east how far?

Mr. *Gawn* (Town Clerk).—There we are bounded by the sea, and the town only extends a few perches.

71. Has there been any meeting of the ratepayers to consider this question of the alteration of the boundaries, or has it been discussed by them at all?—There was no meeting of the ratepayers on the subject.

72. Are you aware of the feelings of the ratepayers on the question?—I have conversed with a great many, and the general feeling is there should be an increase of the boundaries.

73. In any definite direction?—The town is extending in a northeasterly direction—to what we call the Curran—and they have fixed their minds upon that as one of the boundaries.

74. Have the buildings extended beyond the town?—Very considerably. For the last few years the principal buildings have been beyond the limits of the town.

75. What are your receipts for the last year?—From every source.

76. What sources have you?—We have rates and petty customs' dues.

77. How much from dues?—£16 11s. 4d.

98. How much from dog tax?—£3 11s. 10d., and besides that we had a ninepenny rate.

99. Are there any things required to be done in the town that the Commissioners would do if they had more money at their command?—I don't know of anything. Of course if they were the Urban Sanitary Authority they would do things they don't do now.

100. Do the guardians attend to the sanitary work of the town in a satisfactory way?—Not always. There have been a great many complaints.

101. Of what kind?—That the streets are not properly kept, and that the sewers are not kept in good order. The fact is, the Board of Guardians, so far as I could understand them, look upon this as a burden put upon them which they have neither the inclination nor the facility for performing.

102. Have any specific complaints been made to them of things they have not attended to?—I can't say.

103. Have they spent any money upon sanitary works in the town of late years?—Not that I am aware of.

104. What should you say were the questions for which this extension is desired? To bring in part of the town that is now outside it?—That is the principal reason.

105. Is there any other reason?—Yes, so that they would be able to light and cleanse those outside parts the same as those within the present boundary.

Mr. John Crawford.

MR. JOHN CRAWFORD examined.

106. You are Chairman of the Town Commissioners of Larne?—I am.

107. Has this question of the extension or alteration of the boundaries been brought before the Commissioners of the town?—Several times.

108. Have they come to any definite resolution?—No, but they have simply [illegible] a kind of form of boundary which they suppose might come very near the boundary that is wanted. This boundary commences at the railway bridge.

109. Has it been put down upon any map?—No, this has not been put upon any map, but I think we [illegible] the railway bridge at Fergustown, and from thence in a line [illegible] to road leading to Glenoe from Larne, thence by said road north to the new [illegible], thence by said road to the west end of Mr. [illegible]'s garden, and thence in a line north to a stream [illegible] on the [illegible]-road, thence in a line to the [illegible], and by said [illegible] to the [illegible] to the [illegible] south of Patrick [illegible]'s house, thence by said [illegible] to south side of James Alexander's house, from thence to bridge at north of new [illegible] [illegible] (if not by straight line to high water-mark), thence by Drumalis burn to Old Waterloo-road, by said road passing south end of Mrs. Campbell's house to high water-mark, thence by high water-mark to north-east wall of Mr. Malcolm M'Neill's garden at Curran; and then the question comes in, of which the Commissioners know nothing, namely, whether Mr. Chaine would wish them to take in the wharf, and that was left until to-day to see what arrangement was come to; but supposing the wharf was not to be taken in, then the boundary would be, "thence by Drumalis burn to Old Waterloo-road, by said road passing south end of Mrs. Campbell's house to high water-mark, thence by high water-mark to north-east wall of Mr. Malcolm M'Neill's garden at Curran, thence by road passing east of Olderfleet Hotel and Mr. Nelson's house, thence by high water-mark east of coastguard station, including Curran Point, thence from Olderfleet Castle in a line to Fergustown bridge."

110. On what principle was that boundary struck out?—The principle was that it takes in pretty well all the new buildings that are going on.

111. Would it provide for any probable extension of those buildings?—It would in some cases.

112. It includes places where you think buildings

will be extended?—Many fine buildings, as Pringsteinia buildings, are going on, and are being finished there.

113. Can you give any idea how much additional area that extension would give to the town?—I could not give the number of acres, but I can tell the valuation.

114. What additional valuation would it bring into the town?—About £1,222, but that would not be including the Curran property.

115. Would it include much agricultural land?—Yes, it would include a good bit of land.

116. Would it bring in many additional voters for the election of Commissioners?—Oh, yes; it would bring in a good many.

117. Would it bring in many gentlemen who would be qualified to act as Commissioners, if elected?—No doubt it would.

118. You could not say how many?—No; I took no note of it.

119. Would it bring in many villas or gentlemen's residences not in the town now?—Yes, the houses that are outside within these would be brought in.

120. How far would it extend?—About a mile in one part, that is to the Curran; but on every other point it would be hardly so far. The line there about would be about a mile, and it would be about three quarters of a mile on the north side.

121. Do you know what the boundaries of the electoral division of Larne are?—No, I don't exactly know, but the Clerk of the Union will be here and he can tell that.

122. Can you give any idea how far it extends?—No, not exactly, I could not give a definite answer to that question.

123. You know, however, that the electoral division would be too large a boundary to adopt for municipal purposes?—Oh; yes; it would be too large altogether for this.

124. The reason I ask the question is that we were directed to see whether it would be possible to make the electoral division, including the boundary of the municipality coterminous?—The electoral division would be quite too far; it would be far too large.

125. Then you think the electoral division boundaries are too large to think of adopting them as the municipal boundaries?—Yes; in some cases under the Poor Law Board they run fully a mile out of the town for poor law purposes.

126. Do you know whether any special sanitary rate has been struck by the guardians of late years?—Oh, yes.

127. For what purposes?—Sanitary purposes—sewerage.

128. Sewerage in the town?—Yes, in the town.

129. On what district do you know was this special sanitary rate struck?—I don't know the amount of it, but it was all struck in the boundary, and outside the boundary a long distance in a great many cases. It is generally fed by the guard.

130. What is the feeling of the ratepayers as to extension?—I know for years they have been at me to see if I would try to get extended, and, I said, no; it was a thing I would never move in, for I knew we had a great deal of trouble getting it settled before.

131. What is the feeling of the residents outside on this question?—I really don't know. I believe the change would be rather beneficial than otherwise.

132. Have you considered the question of becoming the urban sanitary authority at all?—Well, we have thought it over sometimes, but we found great difficulty in the main question, and I was decidedly against going in for the urban sanitary authority.

133. You are afraid of being obliged to go to a great deal of expense?—Yes, and a great deal of difficulty in getting it.

134. But you have not applied at all would?—No; certainly not; but the guardians have applied for us to do the sweeping of the town, and we thought it up to them.

135. How many people do you think would the extension you have mentioned include?—It would include more than 1,000; well, perhaps, nearly 1,000.

136. It would make your population up to 6,000? —No. I think it would not at present but very soon it will.

137. Then you will become the urban authority?—Yes.

138. Is there anything else you would like to put upon our notes, as your opinion about extension of the boundaries?—No; nothing particular. I never had a decided opinion on the matter. I knew it would require to be extended, and it was a question altogether for the ratepayers, and how far, and in what direction, they wish the town to be extended. I don't think there could be a better line than what is marked out; that is, taking in nearly equal distances; provided we want to take in the property on the Curran. Then the question I mentioned before arises—about the wharf. A great many believe it should be included; but I differ from them on the question.

139. What wharf is this?—Mr. Chaine's wharf at the Curran. I think there would be interests there that might clash. The valuation of the wharf is £300.

140. That is at the terminus of the railway?—Yes; exactly at the end of the railway.

141. What do you say about these wharfs?—I may own I know nothing about them, but that the interests of Mr. Chaine and the Commissioners might clash, and there would be great difficulty about them.

142. Your own opinion is that they ought not to be taken in?—It is my own opinion at present, if I gave an opinion on the matter at all.

Examined by Mr. MacNeill, solicitor (who said he appeared merely as a ratepayer, and not as representing any one).

143. Are these wharfs all built out below low-water mark?—Yes; they are extended out into the sea. The valuation of them is £300. The tolls are not included in the valuation.

144. Don't you know they were built altogether nearly at Mr. Chaine's expense?—Yes.

145. And the roads too?—You mean the road past the hotel.

146. No; but the road from Larne down to the Curran?—It is made at the expense of the county. Mr. Chaine gave the land, and did something towards it.

147. And all the county was asked to pay was £300, while the road went outside that out of Mr. Chaine's property?—This needless they gave £400 previous to giving that.

148. Don't you know there are lamps down that Curran-road?—Yes.

149. And they are outside the boundary of the town?—Yes.

150. Were not these lamps built by Mr. Chaine?—I suppose so.

151. Out of his own pocket?—I suppose so.

152. Are not they kept lighting all night, while the lamps in the town are out?—I could not tell, for I have not been on the road after Midsummer.

153. Who pays for the lighting of them?—It is Mr. Chaine pays for them.

154. And you know very well that the Curran-road is properly covered?—I do not know.

155. What more do the Commissioners want with it—why do they want to drag it into the town?—Because, you know, the buildings are all going out in that direction.

156. Are the people out there deriving any benefit from the town?—I think they are deriving as much benefit as I am, living in town.

157. As for the cleansing of the streets, don't you know that there are heaps of dung in the streets for days and days?—I know there is nothing of the kind now.

158. I know a friend of mine who, within the last fortnight, nearly fell over a heap of muck which was left in the street. The muck is left in places, just waiting to remove. The gentleman I refer to is Mr. Boyd. I know they are bound to take away the muck the day it is swept.

Larne, June 11, 18[illegible].

Mr. John Crawford.

159. I want to know what benefit it would be to the people of the Curran to be brought within the town—they have better lamps; they are not put out until daylight in the morning; whereas the lamps here are lit at dusk, and put out at twelve o'clock at night when they are wanted; there are stones at the corners of the streets just sufficient to knock down a horse when there's no light to see them—so that the people on the Curran are better off than the people of Larne. I want you, therefore, to show me how they would be benefited by being brought into the town. I speak as an individual, and not on behalf of anybody else at all?—I am not expressing any wish, or saying we have any anxiety to have the boundary extended to them, but I believe it would be a great benefit to them.

160. As regards the increase in the number of voters, don't you know that there are a great many people living in Curran who also have residences in Larne?—No; there may be, but it's for want of houses they come to Larne.

161. Doesn't Mr. M'Meekan, for instance, live in one of the new houses at the Curran?—Yes.

162. And hasn't he a house in Larne also?—Yes, he has his saddlers' shop.

163. Mr. Nairn lives at the Curran, and hasn't he a place in Larne?—Yes.

164. And aren't you aware that the houses there are held by people who come to the Curran for three months of the year?—They are birds of passage.

165. Mr. Cotton.—Do you think an extension of the boundaries in the way Mr. Crawford suggests would not increase the number of voters to any considerable extent?——

Mr. M'Neill.—No.

166. Mr. Crawford.—It is not just or fair that the ratepayers on the west, living nearly a mile from the Town Hall, should be paying rates, while on the east side, those who live only a few perches away escape them.

Mr. Francis Wilson examined.

167. You are one of the Town Commissioners of Larne?—Yes.

168. How long have you been so?—For three or four years.

169. You have heard the evidence of the chairman of your board?—I have.

170. And that represents the opinion of the Commissioners that there ought to be extension of some kind?—Yes.

171. You heard the extension he read out?—I did.

172. Do you agree in what he stated?—I do, perfectly.

173. Is there anything else you wish to add of your own opinion?—I heard a question asked of the Chairman, would there be any more voters brought in, and I say there would be.

174. Voters who have not votes at present?—Who have not votes at present in the election of Town Commissioners.

175. Would many be voters who would be eligible to sit as Commissioners, if elected?—They would.

176. How many?—A couple of dozen I suppose.

Mr. Crawford. (Chairman of Town Commissioners.)—In striking the town boundary at first we included Inver, which is the only place we could get property that would lighten the tax upon us, and on the east, next the Curran, there were no houses except two, and we never thought of extending the boundary any further to the east at that time, but it is quite different now.

177. Mr. Wilson.—As to the new line of road going to the Curran, though Mr. Chaine encouraged that road and gave a large sum of money towards it and the ground and bottom of it and all these things, yet that might be partly for his own interest; and then the road was handed over to the county and if so Mr. Chaine has no more claim to that road than I have. If you make a road and hand it over to the county it then belongs to the county. I know if I set back my house in the street and the public used the space I cleared, the Commissioners claim it. I don't care who owns it.

178. Mr. M'Neill.—Will the Commissioners pay Mr. Chaine for the lamps he has put up and the sewers he has made?—They will put up lamps for themselves if that district is brought into the town, and we will be bound to light the Curran the same as we light the town, independent altogether of Mr. Chaine's lamps. I was present when this was struck as the boundary in accordance with the wish of the Commissioners.

179. Mr. Chaine.—I don't wish to appear here as opposing this project, but, as I said at first, the thing has taken me very much by surprise. What we came here for was to get a quiet discussion of the matter and to see the pros and cons of the question. My property may be benefited by it, or it may not, as the case may be, but I hope you will make an inspection of the ground before you arrive at any decision on the matter.

180. Mr. Cotton.—Certainly, and I may add that this inquiry is not held under the direction of an Act of Parliament, and the fact of its being closed here leaves it open to any one to give us further information at any time hereafter.

181. Mr. Chaine.—It may be that the Town Commissioners will confer great advantage on this property, but it appears at a glance that we will be put under heavy taxation for things we have done already, such as lamps. There may be ultimate benefit to the matter, but what we want now is to have a quiet discussion of the question.

182. Mr. Cotton.—Could you give us your own opinion whether the town should be extended?—I cannot at this moment give my own opinion on it, but recently the railway has done much towards the building. They give free tickets to persons building outside the town, but they would not give these free tickets if the buildings were within the town. That has always been a rule of the Board.

183. They would not give free tickets if the buildings were within the boundary?—No.

184. On what ground do they make that distinction?—I cannot say, but they do, and, on the other hand, there are gentlemen here, who have built upon that property outside the town, who, if they had thought they would be brought under the Town Commissioners, would not have built upon it at all. I did not know, until I saw the proposal of the Commissioners, what they proposed to do, but it seems to me that what they are doing is premature. No doubt what they propose will have to come sometime or other, but I think for the moment it would check the building that is going on.

185. The building is going on towards the Curran?—Yes.

186. Mr. Crawford.—With regard to the checking of building I believe the Commissioners would have nothing to do with anything that would check the building that is going on. I have a quite different opinion on the subject, for I think it would have the very opposite effect.

187. Mr. Cotton.—Is your opinion, Mr. Chaine, formed on account of the supposed additional taxation?—Yes, and the withdrawal of the railway free passes.

188. I presume the Secretary of the railway company will be able to give us some information about those passes.

189. Mr. Frederick Rew, Manager, Larne and Ballymena Railway Company.—I know the arrangement that exists. It is to encourage building of villa residences outside the town. These tickets are given for a period of ten years.

Larne. June 13, 1878.

Mr. Francis Wiles.

190. Mr. Cotton.—Would these tickets be taken away if the buildings were put under the Town Commissioners?—That is a matter for the Boards of the two railways that I would not like to answer, but if they granted tickets to houses in the town anyone in Larne might claim the same privilege.

191. But on that ground does it affect the question of the extension of the buildings whether a house is within the boundary or outside it?—The object is to encourage the building of villas near the shore, and thus to encourage people to come down to visit people living here.

192. Mr. M'Neill.—The visitors pay railway fares?—Yes.

193. Mr. Cotton.—I can understand their encouraging building, but how can they draw the distinction between the new houses built in the town and those built outside?

Mr. M'Neill.—They believe that if they granted passes to the people in the town they must grant them to all.

194. Mr. Crawford.—I think the reason they made the difference was that there were no efforts being made to bring people from other parts to live in Larne; there was no ground for building houses upon in the town and the railway directors very properly said we will try and encourage people to build outside the town; I may say as a railway director it would have no influence whatever in the withdrawal of free tickets if the boundary is extended; of course the railway company will look to their own interest and of course wherever there is extension they will stretch the right hand of fellowship to it.

195. Mr. Wiles.—As to the number of houses that would be brought in on the Curran road, there would be [illegible] in one direction—to the north-east.

196. Mr. Cotton.—How many of the owners would be eligible to sit as commissioners if elected?—I don't know.

197. Mr. Chaine.—I want to say a word about Mr. Wiles' evidence; he says that a good number of those houses would have votes; of course they would be voters provided you made this extension, but if you make it, you are certainly making it through private property; for that road through the Curran to the Coastguard station is distinctly private property; the county have never paid a shilling for it, and I can close it any day I think proper. Although we may be brought into the town it would be a clear case of confiscation of property if you do anything of the kind.

198. Mr. Cotton.—I don't see how including any property in the town can affect its title in any way; if it is private property it will remain private?—But then you will ask us to pay taxes for the cleansing and lighting of it. If it is private they would be taxing it.

199. In the same way as a man's own private house is taxed. Surely you don't hold that the resident a quarter of a mile out of Larne has no interest in the town being kept clean?—But this is a mile away.

200. Well it is more than half a mile?—I say that most of the people who live on the Curran-road never see the town of Larne.

201. They never come into the town of Larne?—No, they all go through Larne by train, and that is why I would like you to see the place and the ground.

202. Mr. Crawford.—I suppose there are few roads in the county that are occupied more in the summer than that road to the Curran.

203. Mr. Wiles.—Mr. Chaine says he made that private road; granted he did, it is on his own ground, he says he built those houses, granted that he did, but he lets these houses and receives rent for them from tenants and the tenants have the benefit of the town. There is no shop at all there and they must come to Larne for their goods except what they bring by rail.

Mr. William Hamilton Burke examined.

Mr. William H. Burke.

204. I have only come to live in Larne six weeks ago, but I was an old resident, and have returned again. I was Chairman of the Town Commissioners and a Commissioner for some years, but I am merely a resident now and a ratepayer. I merely want to make a remark, not that I have any interest in the matter one way or the other, as to Mr. Chaine. For the last five years I was living in High Hollywood, and I paid £3 [illegible] rent for those years, and we had neither water, light, nor sewerage. That was because we were private property. The water was supplied by gravitation. There was never a sweeper on the road, and the landlord sent a man once a week to sweep the place.

205. But if you choose to keep the road private you must be subject to that inconvenience?—We did not keep it private, but the Commissioners considered it private. There is a county town near this, and eighteen months ago they formed Stranmillis into a town, and they marked a boundary, and that did not stop the Railway Company giving passes. The villas they would give their tickets to, and not to houses in the town. That is a question for the railway, and it is merely to bring grist to their own mill that they do so. They are just like anybody else. They wish to make as much money as they can, and they think they will do it in this way.

Mr. William Wallace M'Neill examined.

Mr. William W. M'Neill.

206. You wish to give your view of this proposed alteration of the boundary?—Yes, and as an inhabitant of the town and as a ratepayer, I condemn the whole thing [illegible]. The town is neglected as it is. The other day I saw a young man in one of the streets there almost turn head over heels over a heap of mud that had been left there. We can't get a drop of water in our houses. We are in a bad state.

207. Is it your opinion that the boundaries should be extended or altered in any way?—Decidedly not extended.

208. Well, do you think they should be diminished?—Abolished entirely.

209. On what ground would you abolish the township?—Simply because I know the town was better where the Act was introduced.

210. Which Act?—The Act of 1854.

211. It was better when it was under the 9th of George IV.?—I knew it before we had Commissioners or anything of the sort, and I prefer it then to what it has been since.

212. How long ago is that?—It was in 1854.

213. Before that it was under the 9th of George IV.?—For a few years only.

214. You knew it before that Act was adopted?—Yes; the town was much better as it was before the introduction of either of the Acts.

215. I presume the town was very much smaller then?—No, indeed. In 1841 it was above 3,000 in population, and I would like anyone to tell me what the population is now.

216. In 1841 it was 3,345?—Exactly, and what is it now?

217. 3,288?—Just so. A great many of the people have skedaddled. We have lost about 200 of our inhabitants under the Town Improvement Act.

218. Is there anything else you wish to have put upon our notes?—With regard to the water supply, there is a shocking bad supply.

219. In quality or quantity?—Both; it can't be got in the private houses, I understand.

220. Surely, you know it yourself, as a matter of fact?—Well, I have had it in my own house, and it just rises, I am told, sufficiently high to fill the boiler in the kitchen, but as to taking water up through the house that can't be done. Other people have applied for water, and they can't get it. Then, as to cleansing the streets, I have seen mud heaps.

221. They have nothing to say to that now?—But during the time the Commissioners had charge of the streets, the mud heaps, with all sorts of stuff, were, as a rule, piled up beside people's houses, and mud would have been piled against my place too, but I told the fellow I would send a man long step to scatter it over the street again.

222. What this all leads to is, that you would be happier without Commissioners at all?—Yes; Mr. Crawford says he does not agree with me at all, but we had example of that the other day, when Dr. Miller fell in the street owing to their bad condition.

223. What do you wish to infer from that?—That the paving of the side-paths is bad.

224. But the Commissioners have nothing to say to that?—No; they keep clear of that.

225. And what do you wish to infer from that?—That they were afraid to touch them. Then, again, the lamps are lighted about dusk, and they are popped out about half-past eleven o'clock, just at the time a fellow might require them. If you are in Ballymena or Belfast, and are coming home late, you where [illegible] by M'Master's farm, and there is a trap eighteen inches deep, and there is another that would turn over a caravan. I think the Commissioners have something to do with keeping the traps.

226. Would that be improved if the Commissioners were abolished altogether?—Very likely; Mr. [illegible], the county surveyor, would cast his eye on these things.

227. Doesn't he repair the roads as it is?—Yes; he [illegible] part of the work, and the others throw it over on him. I did not come here prepared to give evidence, and what I state is only my own opinion. I merely wished to see what was going on.

228. Mr. Crawford.—Are you aware we are supposed to have the best water in the county Antrim as far as the quantity is concerned?—I don't know. Don't you get the surplus water from the mine?

Mr. Crawford.—No.

MALCOLM M'NEILL, Esq., J.P., examined.

229. You are a ratepayer of Larne?—Yes.

230. What is your opinion as to the question of the extension of the boundary of the town?—I ought to preface what I have got to say by saying I live, myself, at the Curran, one of the parts proposed to be taken in, and if it was considered for the good of the community in general to have the boundary increased, I, as a ratepayer, would not object on account of paying a higher rate, but I think it would be a very imprudent thing to tax the Curran, which has been the cause of all the improvement in Larne. I think the time may come when it may have to pay tax, but at present it should not be taxed.

231. You think it would check improvement?—I think, certainly, it would.

232. Is there anything else you wish to state?—No; that is shortly my view of the case, that all the improvement that has gone on in Larne—there has been considerable increase in buildings—is entirely consequent on the increase of trade at the Curran.

233. And it has all been in that direction?—There has been considerable increase in buildings within the boundaries also; but the whole impetus has been given from the Curran, and I think it would be an injudicious movement, the moment a thing goes ahead to cramp it. The works are only in their infancy and it is entirely in consequence of what Mr. Chaine has done that there is this impetus at all.

234. And you don't think that district would derive corresponding advantages from being included in the town?—I don't see that it would derive any benefit; I don't know what benefit it could derive. Probably the time may come when it would be necessary to increase the boundaries and perhaps in the Curran direction; if including it in Larne would be the best way which is a question I don't give any opinion on, but for the present it would certainly be premature. I have no possible feeling in the matter, and if it is for the benefit of the public that the boundary should be extended to the Curran I have no objection to pay the extra taxation, but looking upon it as a public question it would be a great mistake as far as I can judge.

235. Then you can give no opinion about the extension of the town in any other direction?—I don't know anything of that. It is merely with regard to the extension Curran-wards that I speak and I think it premature upon those grounds I have stated.

MR. JOHN NAPIER examined.

236. Do you reside outside or inside the town of Larne?—I live outside the town.

237. Would you be included in the proposed extension?—I would.

238. And what are your views on the subject of extension of the boundaries?—I built a number of houses at the Curran and the reason why I chose the Curran as my place of operation was that it was free from taxation. I have built my nine houses, and I have laid out a good deal of money on them, I have since [illegible] fully as many more, and of course I look forward to the time when possibly I would be erecting houses on this waste ground, and as a matter of course if the ground is included in the boundary I would hesitate before doing so.

239. What would be the valuation of those houses you have built there?—The valuation would be about £3½ each.

240. And the prospect of a tax of 1s. in the pound would make you hesitate before building any more?—I would not do it. I would prefer to seek another place. Not because I wish to make any further outlay in the way of building. I should tell you that those houses of mine are nearly solely let to people who take them by the month.

241. That is in the season?—Yes, and as a matter of course they are mere birds of passage; they stay a month and then go away again and they would not be entitled to any vote. I think myself it would be very bad taste towards Mr. Chaine who has done so much for the place; when he has done a good thing for Larne to think of putting an embargo on the remainder of his property and preventing it from being let. He has still a large tract of ground there for building purposes, and I believe if his ground is included in the town people will prefer seeking other places for building. The Curran is as it were under way, if let alone, and it would not be fair to Mr. Chaine or to those who have laid out money on it up to the present to make any change in the position of the place which would have the effect of checking improvement.

242. That is your own feeling?—Yes.

243. Mr. W. W. M'Neill.—Do the people living

there derive any advantage from the town of Larne? —No. The bulk of my tenants are from Belfast, and not from the town.

243. Mr. Cotton.—Where do they get their supply of milk from?—Of course they get their supply from the town, but some of them get their supplies of groceries, and butter, and all that from Belfast.

244. Do they, as a matter of fact, come into the town here to purchase anything?—They do; but I would not say they purchase all their requirements here; by no means, for they look naturally upon a place like Larne as inferior to Belfast, and a place not likely to supply their wants, on as good terms as the larger place.

245. But they come into market here?—Occasionally they do.

246. Mr. M'Neill.—It is generally in the summer season these houses are occupied?—Yes.

247. During the summer is Larne lit with gas?—No, I don't think so.

248. Mr. Cotton.—Is the town fairly lit when gas is wanted?—I should say it is not. They study economy a good deal, and when people are dining out late they have not very good light on the subject. As regards water, we don't require any further; at the Curran. You have only to sink about four feet and then you get an abundant supply. I have erected two pumps, and they are quite sufficient to meet the wants of my tenants, and if there were as many more people there the supply would be abundant.

249. Mr. M'Neill.—Isn't the Curran supply lighted up?—Yes.

250. And at Mr. Chaine's expense?—Yes.

251. Mr. Cotton.—Is there anything else you wish to tell us?—No; except as to these railway free tickets. It was, I believe, simply from the circumstance of these houses being erected at a good distance from the town, that I was enabled to secure free tickets for them on the railway.

252. These free tickets were given to encourage building?—Yes, and very wisely given too.

253. Do you think if the town boundaries are extended so as to include these houses, the free tickets would be taken away?—No; but they will not be given to others, as they are most particular about the tickets.

254. You have unbuilt-upon ground in the same locality?—Yes.

255. And you hope to get tickets for each of the new houses you build there?—I do.

256. And would the fact of their being within the town prevent your getting the tickets?—It would prevent me altogether from getting them.

Larne, [illegible] — Mr. John [illegible].

Mr. [illegible] examined.

Mr. [illegible]

257. All I have [illegible] [illegible], is a person who has [illegible] a [illegible] houses at [illegible], to not being brought into the town. I would be subject to a taxation of [illegible] per year, and I would not get any benefit whatever.

258. [illegible] to you whether the town is kept in a good condition or not?—[illegible] I would be glad to see the town kept in a good condition.

259. Don't you derive any benefit from its being kept in a good condition?—Well, the benefit that every person derives from their neighbours keeping their places clean.

260. Don't you come into the town now and again? —Yes.

261. And isn't it an advantage to you to have it kept clean?—Yes, if I have to walk it; but I don't see that I should be obliged to pay £5 10s. a year, or [illegible], and get almost no benefit whatever. I have had to take gas up myself; of course the Gas Company have [illegible] to a certain [illegible], but it has cost me a considerable deal more than they gave. [illegible] [illegible], and I would be forced to [illegible] like to [illegible] the [illegible], and to get nothing for it.

262. How far outside the boundary do you live?— It would be half a mile from this.

263. Mr. Crawford.—Would you be receiving no benefit if the gas were put up to your [illegible] gate? —None, whatever; you must light the gas in the [illegible]. I [illegible] it. It is very natural you should wish to have the boundary extended to tax [illegible], but I don't think it would be fair to me.

264. Mr. M'Neill.—But you get the use of all [illegible] [illegible] people as you [illegible] [illegible] [illegible], and they [illegible].

Mr. Daniel M'Donald examined.

Mr. Daniel M'Donald.

265. Mr. Cotton.—Do you live outside or inside the town at present?—Outside.

266. What is your opinion as to extension of the town boundary?—As a ratepayer I think I would be getting no benefit, and I should object to pay extra tax.

267. How far do you live from the town?—About a mile.

268. Do you not derive any advantage from the town being kept clean and well lighted?—No, I can't say I do.

269. It would make no difference to you if there were no gas in Larne at all?—No difference at all to me.

270. Or to your neighbours?—I can't answer for them, but it would make no difference to myself.

271. Do you think there would be any advantage to the town from having the limits made [illegible]?—I could not answer that question.

Colonel [illegible], [illegible] examined.

Col. [illegible].

272. Mr. Cotton.—Do you live inside or outside the town?—[illegible] my place has always been included, from the first.

273. You heard the idea of extension that was sketched out?—Yes, I have heard it [illegible]; I [illegible] [illegible].

274. It is proposed to have extensions in different directions all round the town, and what is your opinion of the [illegible] that is taking in the Curran?—I think in [illegible] the Curran should be taken in; I am in favour of taking it in for that reason.

275. On what grounds?—Because it derives very great benefit from the town of Larne. There are [illegible] [illegible] on the very limits of the present boundary. The last witness but one has built a very handsome house within a very short distance in a [illegible] line with the [illegible] boundary. He is similarly situated with myself, that is to say, he derives no benefit from lighting or cleansing. I suppose that I would be as far from any lamp as his house would be, and I derive no benefit from the water either, or from the town's improvement, except that the streets are kept clean and sufficiently lighted.

276. Is the lighting of the town fairly done?—I consider it is not sufficiently done; it may be fairly in one sense, but not fairly in the sense of sufficiency.

277. Mr. Crawford.—That is altogether in the hands of the [illegible]. If they wish to have the lamps

Larne. June 11, 1878. Col. Solomon Dawson, &c.

lighted for longer hours, could they have it done?—I should think so.

278. Mr. Cotton.—Has any complaint been made to the Commissioners as to the lighting, or any request to extend the hours of lighting?—I am not aware, as I have not attended the meetings of the Commissioners.

279. Is there anything else you wish to state?—It was said as to the houses at the Curran, that there was a possibility of the Railway Company withdrawing the privilege of a free ticket hitherto granted to them, but I apprehend they could not do that to those they have already granted.

280. But the question was would the Railway Company make any difference in granting tickets to houses out at the Curran, if the place was brought within the town boundary?—That is a question I could not answer.

281. Mr. M'Neill.—Are the houses at the Curran all newly built?—They are all nearly newly built or added to.

282. Don't you think it is rather soon to run them into the town?—It must be done some time, and if the building goes on you may make the same observation with respect to the houses built in the future.

283. But at present isn't it too soon?—I say the answer applies to all time. If they go on building new houses you might go on saying, "It's too soon."

284. But don't you think it premature to bring in the Curran district?—No, I do not.

285. Have you any knowledge of the people who live in the houses out there, or what class of people they are?—Yes, I know one gentleman who gave evidence here.

286. Taking Mr. Nairn's house, how are the people living there permanently?—I should apprehend not.

287. On whom then would the tax fall?—These are all inferences. Of course it would fall on Mr. Nairn.

Mr. Frederick Rew.

Mr. Frederick Rew examined.

288. I am resident at the Curran, about a mile from Larne, and I object to being brought into the town, and taxed, on the ground that I would derive no benefit for it.

289. Do you market in Larne?—No, principally in Belfast; nearly all.

290. Do you derive anything from Larne?—Occasionally. Very seldom.

291. Of what kind?—Sometimes I buy some groceries in the town, but that's all.

292. Do you mean to say you derive no benefit and have no interest in the question whether the town is properly kept?—I have an interest, that I would like to see it properly kept, and in the same way with Belfast or any other town I go to.

293. Do you object to pay for it?—I object to pay, and I believe that it would affect the building on the property brought in.

294. Inasmuch as the additional tax would tend to stop building?—It would to a great extent.

295. But you cannot tell us anything authoritatively as to what the Railway Company would do in case the Curran was brought in?—No further than that I know there may be twenty or thirty people in Larne who would ask free tickets and they would demand them if the Curran was brought in, and tickets were given to people there.

296. But the Railway Company need not give the tickets except where they like?—The Company would derive no benefit from them.

297. But the Company have made no hard-and-fast rule on the subject?—No, but I believe they would not grant tickets to houses in the town.

298. Though they would grant tickets to the same houses if they were built outside the town?—Yes.

299. Surely they derive the same benefit from a house in the town as from a house in the country?—No; the parties at the shore would have a number of friends coming down from Belfast to visit them.

300. If a new house is built away from the town, how does it affect the railway company whether the house is in town or not?—A large number would come down to visit the people living in houses away from the town and on the sea shore.

301. But if such a house was within the town boundary, why should the railway company refuse to give a ticket?—They would feel bound to give tickets to every one in Larne if they did that and then they would stop the system altogether.

302. The same thing would apply if there were no Commissioners in Larne at all?—As it is we are giving tickets outside to all houses of a certain class.

303. And they have given no free tickets to build [illegible] anywhere within the municipality?—No.

Mr. William Hayes.

Mr. William Hayes examined.

304. Mr. Cotton.—You are Clerk of the Larne Union?—I am.

305. In what electoral division is it?—In the electoral division of Larne.

306. What is the extent of the electoral division?—3,984 acres.

307. And there is no other electoral division affecting the municipality?—None whatever.

308. Have you the area of the town in your books?—Not of the town, but I have of the Townparks.

309. And not of the town of Larne?—No.

310. Has there been any sanitary rate struck in the last year or two?—There has.

311. For what purpose was it struck?—For water and sewerage purposes.

312. On what district was that sanitary rate struck?—On the townlands of Townparks and Inver.

313. Only?—Yes, only.

314. When was that rate struck?—Last year, on the 30th of October there was a rate of two pence in the pound struck on the townlands of Townparks and Inver for sanitary purposes.

315. Was there any previous rate of the same kind?—Yes, three pence.

316. On the same townlands?—Yes.

317. And for the same purposes?—Yes.

318. Have the guardians ever been asked to do any sanitary works in the town which they have refused to do?—There have been recommendations laid before them that they have not carried out.

319. Through the Commissioners?—No, but through parties making complaints about different matters.

320. About sanitary matters?—Yes, about the sanitary state of the town principally.

321. Is there anything in particular of which complaint has been made?—Yes, the covering in of a stream called the Maggie Burn.

322. Upon what grounds was that sought to be done?—It is an open sewer, and it is a nuisance.

323. It is running through the town?—Yes.

324. You have not got any got the area of the town itself?—No.

325. Do you know yourself how far the electoral division extends?—I do.

326. How far would you say it goes to the north of the town?—It goes I suppose to the north nearly a distance of two English miles.

327. And to the south how far?—It goes to the water beyond Henry M'Neill's, a distance of nearly two English miles.

328. And how far to the west?—To Ballyboley nearly two English miles.

329. Mr. Gibbons, M.P.—Mr. Nairn has also houses

at the Curran rated at £30 apiece, yet he only gets one vote for that £270.

330. Mr. Cotton.—I am aware of that.

331. Mr. Chaine.—Then there is a hotel there rated at £30 and it would not get a vote at all.

332. Mr. Cotton.—No, under the present law it would only have one vote.

333. Mr. Chaine.—So you see we would be rather handicapped there as regards voting.

Larne. June 23, 1879. Mr. William Hayes.

Mr. Alexander Fleming, T.C., examined.

Mr. Alexander Fleming, T.C.

334. Mr. Cotton.—You are a ratepayer of the town?—I am.

335. Do you live inside the town?—I do.

336. What is your opinion about extension?—I am one of these unfortunate Commissioners of whom you have heard, and I wish to speak of what I heard some of the gentlemen from the Curran district state—that they get no benefit from the town; our streets are kept pretty neat and tidy; their children and nurses with perambulators come down into the town, and they have every accommodation they require, and I don't know why they should wish to cast so much slur on the Commissioners.

337. Do you think the boundary should be extended towards the Curran?—I would not exactly say, but I think we came to the conclusion that the boundary should be extended, and we went as near the thing as we could possibly go.

338. That is the boundary sketched out by the Chairman?—Yes.

339. And that includes the entire of the townland of Curran?—Yes, the entire of the townland of Curran, not interfering with Mr. Chaine's quay.

340. You think the works at the quay ought not to be included?—No, we think they should remain in Mr. Chaine's own hands as at present.

341. That is the opinion of the Commissioners as a body?—I think so.

342. Mr. M'Neill.—Is it your opinion that the town is deriving any benefit from the Curran?—Undoubtedly it is, but then you see, as Mr. Nairn has stated, all his tenants are monthly tenants, who don't get much goods out of the town of Larne.

343. Since the wharfs were completed at the Curran, and since the narrow gauge railway ran down to the Curran, have you noticed any new houses being built there?—Yes.

344. Have you noticed any difference in the rents of the houses in the town of Larne?—I can't say I have.

345. Do you know of any houses being built lately in the town of Larne?—Yes.

346. Are you aware what are the rents they are let at?—I know they are not letting at as good rent as they did some time ago.

347. Tell me one house that has gone down in rent?—I know there are more houses empty than there used to be.

348. Colonel Dawson.—Mr. M'Neill asked you whether there were any houses lately built in the town of Larne?—Yes, there were.

349. And these were built notwithstanding that there was no privilege given by the railway company?—Yes.

350. The inference is that they would still continue to build at the Curran, though there would be no privileges given by the railway company?—There is no benefit from building in the town of Larne.

351. The Station-road is being built upon?—There is a new street being laid off there, which is within the boundary.

352. Mr. M'Neill.—That is on the road leading to the station for the purpose of opening up shops. Isn't that leading down to the Larne Markets Company?—Yes.

353. Where there are four markets held weekly?—There is only one market in the week in the summer, and in the winter there are two days for wheat.

354. These markets are frequented by the people from the country all around, who bring produce into them?—Yes.

355. People from all directions round?—Yes.

Mr. George Bain examined.

Mr. George Bain.

356. Mr. Cotton.—You are one of the Town Commissioners of the town?—I am.

357. You know the extension that is proposed?—Yes.

358. What is your opinion about it?—I am certainly of opinion the extension should go as far as the Curran.

359. As far as and including the Curran?—Yes; and there are several reasons why I say so. It would add considerably to our number of voters.

360. How many voters do you think it would add?—I could not exactly say; but Larne is actually removing down to the Curran.

361. The extension is in that direction?—Yes; and out of the voters who would be brought in a great many would be qualified to act as Commissioners, for the houses there are of a good class.

362. And you think it would be an advantage to increase the number of persons who would be qualified to sit as Commissioners?—Yes; I am somewhat surprised at these people living towards the Curran seeming to throw so much objection in the way of including the Curran; they are all people who have very good taste, and when they find the streets of Larne dirty, they make great complaints about it. Well by extending the boundary out to the Curran, we would get a great number of them in as ratepayers and Commissioners, and so they could manage to keep the places cleaner than they are.

363. And it would be the interest of the people outside to be represented on the Commissioners?—I think so. At the present state of things they complain greatly against the acts of the Commissioners, and the Commissioners require money to improve these things, and by including these houses towards the Curran, the Commissioners would be better able to do this cleansing.

364. The Commissioners require more money?—They require money to carry out other things.

365. They have not struck their full rate?—These people would come in for part of the expenses.

366. They enjoy a good deal of the work of the Commissioners, though they live at the Curran, and you think they should pay something for that?—Yes. In reference to the water question I am sure if the inhabitants had known that any evidence would be taken as to it, this hall would not have held them.

367. What is the prevailing opinion on that question?—We are most miserably situated as to water.

368. And has any scheme ever been before the Commissioners for improving the supply?—I am not aware. There have been applications time after time, but the proper source has never been struck on yet. As far as I know of the ratepayers, they would be quite willing to pay anything fair to get a good supply of water.

369. Would you advocate that the Commissioners should become the sanitary authority, and take charge of the sanitary matters of the town?—I don't know; but they know more of the wants of the town than the guardians do.

370. Do you think the guardians do not attend to the complaints made about the sanitary condition of the town?—Not always. With regard to the question of railway tickets, I think that the principal point considered in giving tickets is the kind of house that was built, not exactly where it is. If it was a very fine house there could be a ticket got for it nearly any place. I would just like to know how many tickets these new houses have got, that have been built from Barnhill to the Curran. There is a great number of

LARNE. [illegible] Mr. George [illegible]

houses, and I would be curious to know how many free tickets are amongst them. My idea is there are very few tickets to all these houses that have been built there lately.

371. Do you think if the tickets were not given it would affect the building?—I don't think so. There are other localities where building has been going on just as extensively certainly as towards the Curran, that is, towards the north.

372. Colonel Dover.—Being vice-chairman of the board of guardians, I may say it is the general feeling of the guardians that they would be glad if the sanitary matters were handed over to the Commissioners. They have at present agreed, both the Commissioners and the guardians, to hand over the cleansing of the town for a period to the Town Commissioners, and I can say, on the part of the guardians, they are very much obliged to the Commissioners for having acceded to that request, and taken the trouble upon themselves. The guardians would wish to hand over all these matters to the Commissioners, feeling certain they would have more control living on the spot, and that they would attend to the work much better. The board of guardians have such an immense quantity of business to attend to they are not able to attend to every complaint made as to things in the town.

373. Mr. Chaine, M.P.—You say the addition of the Curran would add greatly to the number of voters. Could you say how many would be added?—At the present time there would be eight or ten, I suppose.

374. Certainly not more?—Perhaps more.

375. I think the exact number is six?—I am not looking exactly to the number that is there to-day, but the houses are going up at the rate of three or four every two or three months.

376. Do you know anything personally of the water supply in the Curran?—No. I only referred to the water supply in the town of Larne.

377. You don't know anything of the water supply in the Curran?—No.

378. Don't you know it is very well supplied with water?—I don't know anything at all about it.

379. You go in for this extensive supply for the town, but I suppose the Curran is not to pay for that?—I don't know.

380. By this scheme the places supplied with water already would be brought in and taxed for supplying water to the town?—I don't know anything about that, but I know I have to provide water in my place. There have been days when I could not get it.

381. Mr. M'Neill.—You own some house in Larne?—Yes.

382. Do you think the extension of the town down to the Curran would lighten the taxes on the town?—I don't know.

383. Have you never formed any idea about it?—No.

384. Is not that your impression?—No.

385. Mr. Cotton (at the request of a ratepayer).—You state that if the boundary was extended it would not prevent building?—I have been asked for my opinion, and I have simply given my opinion.

Mr. William M'Mechan(?)

Mr. William M'Mechan(?) examined.

386. Mr. Cotton.—What is your view as to this question of extension?—I know that ground has been taken for building beside me, just outside the boundary towards the Curran, and that if that gentleman who took that thought he would not get tickets for the houses he was about to build he would not have taken the ground at all.

387. You think the question of giving free tickets by the railway will affect the building?—It will certainly. All the gentlemen here know that if we were inside the boundary no ticket would be granted, and I know Mr. Hayes has built a very nice villa, and he did not ask for a ticket, for the simple reason that he would not get it.

388. Mr. Crawford.—I don't believe it and I speak as a railway director.

389. Mr. [illegible] (to Witness).—How far do you live from the boundary of the town?—Not very far, I am outside the boundary.

390. Do you get any benefit from the lighting of the town?—I know the Commissioners have given no benefit in the place I live. Mr. Chaine has made the road and lighted it and made all the improvements, and you desire to come in now and derive all the benefits of what has been done.

391. You derive no benefit from Larne although your workshop is up here?—I know that very well.

392. How far is our boundary from your house?—It is not very far from it.

393. And yet you get no benefit?—I did not say I got no benefit, but I can show that to extend the boundary would stop building.

394. That is your opinion?—It is my opinion which I know to be perfectly true.

395. Mr. M'Neill.—Aren't you building houses yourself?—Yes.

396. And would it stop you if the ground was brought within the town?—Yes.

397. Mr. Cotton.—You would not build in the town at the present time?—Not at the present time if I could get land outside it for the purpose of building.

398. Mr. Crawford.—If you could get tenants would you not get as much for the house in the town as if it was outside the boundary?—Yes; but there would be more taxes to pay.

Mr. Robert Howard.

Mr. Robert Howard examined.

399. Mr. Cotton.—You are a ratepayer of the town?—Yes; and I have a shop in Larne; but it is not with regard to that I wish to speak, it is with regard to the extension of the boundary.

400. What are your views as to that?—I have some property outside the boundary to the south of Larne and I would like the boundary to include that.

401. You would like the boundary of the town extended so as to include that?—Yes.

402. On what grounds?—On the grounds that I would derive what benefits the Commissioners have to bestow; such as water, lighting and cleansing.

403. You wish to have the gas extended to that point?—Yes.

404. And you are willing to pay the tax for it?—Yes.

405. What is the feeling of your neighbours out in that direction?—I can't speak for them, but I think they are in favour of the extension; any I have spoken to are in favour of it.

406. How far do you live from where we are now?—About half a mile, but I don't live there; I have a small property there.

407. The ground you are speaking of is half a mile away?—Yes; but it is not more than three or four perches from the town boundary.

408. It is just outside the town boundary?—Yes.

409. Mr. Chaine.—You have not got water or gas there now?—We have water abundant.

410. Mr. Cotton.—But you have not got gas along the road to that?—No.

411. Mr. M'Neill.—Have you any water fountains, or does the water run to you in pipes?—No.

412. How many houses have you?—I have built eight on the property I speak of.

413. And are you now building more?—Yes; I have sites for four times as many more.

414. And would the fact of bringing that ground inside the boundary have the effect of causing you to cease building?—No; it would cause me to build more rapidly.

415. It would not interfere with your rent?—No. I think, if anything, it would add to it.

The inquiry then terminated.

DOWNPATRICK.—JUNE 13TH, 1878.

(Before C. P. COTTON, Esq., C.E.)

SAMUEL CHARD NELSON examined.

Mr. S. C. Nelson.

1. Are you acting for the Town Clerk now?—Yes; Mr. Clarke and I are acting for Mr. John Marshall the Town Clerk who is ill.

2. Under what Act is the town regulated?—Under the 9th of George the IV.

3. Have you any map of the town?—Yes, my chairman has a map (produced.)

4. How many Commissioners are there?—There are nineteen.

5. How many voters are there in the town, entitled to vote in the election of Commissioners?—I cannot tell.

6. You will be able to find out the number and also the number of those who are qualified to act as Commissioners if elected?—Yes.

7. Can you tell me the population of the town?—The population in 1871 was 3,621.

8. Has it increased or diminished?—Rather increased.

9. What is the area of the town?—1,420 statute acres.

10. And the valuation?—£6,887 [illegible]

11. You have no wards?—No.

12. Is it entirely in the electoral division of Downpatrick?—Altogether.

13. *Edward Gardiner*, Chairman Town Commissioners.—The valuation is a little more than that. There is some little difficulty about our valuation. The valuation for rates is about £6,800 according to the last valuation, but in addition to that there are a number of small houses of less than £3 valuation that are not rated.

14. It is the rateable valuation I would take?—Well the rateable valuation according to the last return of the Commissioners was about £6,896.

Examination of Mr. NELSON resumed.

15. The poor law boundaries and the town boundaries are not conterminous?—No.

16. Could you give me the municipal rates for the last five years, beginning in 1874?—Yes; in 1874 the rates 11½d., 8d. and 6d.

17. There are three rates in the year?—Yes.

18. What were the rates in 1875?—6d., 6d. and 4d.

19. In 1876?—11d., 8d. and 7d.

20. In 1877?—8d., 6d. and 4d.

21. In 1878?—6d., 4d. and 8d.

22. Have you struck any rate for this year?—I believe not.

23. Mr. Gardiner (Chairman Town Commissioners.)—Yes, we have and it is being collected, 10½d., 7½d. and 8d.

24. Mr. *Nelson*.—Yes, I have found it in the books 10½d., 7½d. and 8d. for this year.

25. That is from the 31st July, 1878, that is your year?—Yes.

26. What was the poor rates in those years?—The poor rate in 1874 was 1s. 8d.; in 1875, 1s. 1d.; in 1876, 8d., and 1d. for sanitary purposes; in 1877 it was the same, 8d., and 1d. for sanitary rate; and in 1878 it was 10d. and 4d.

27. What was the 4d. for?—That is for education.

28. Do you know what those sanitary rates were for?—Chiefly for abating nuisances.

29. In the town?—Yes, in the electoral division.

30. Was that sanitary rate struck on the whole electoral division?—Yes, the whole electoral division is subject to any sanitary rate.

31. Was the 4d. rate last year struck on the whole electoral division, or only on the contributory district?—On the contributory district.

32. You don't know what that 4d. rate is exactly?—It is a sanitary rate; it is called a sanitary rate.

33. On what district was it struck?—Only the townparks.

34. Do you mean the townland of the demesne of Down?—Yes.

35. It was struck on the whole of the townland and a portion of it?—No, on the whole of it. The borough is conterminous with the townland and it was on the borough it was struck.

36. Could you give me the county cess for the last five years?—Yes; in 1874 it was 7½d. at the spring, and 8½d. at the summer assizes; in 1875 it was 9d. and 8½d.; in 1876, 7d. and 9d.; in 1877, 8d. and 10½d.; and in 1878, 11d. and 9d.

37. And this spring assizes it was what?—11d. for spring and 9d. for summer.

38. Have the Commissioners had under consideration the question of extending the boundaries of the town?—Yes, we have considered it, and only wish for extension of the boundaries, not diminution.

39. Your purpose was to increase the area, but to what it is extended?—Yes.

40. Was there any resolution of the Board on the question?—Yes, there was a resolution of the Town Commissioners on the subject.

41. When did they come to that resolution?—I think the first time it was mooted was in September, it is upwards of two years ago since it was first brought forward; it was the 4th December, 1876.

42. They came to a resolution in 1876?—Yes.

43. Had the Board since then any recent consideration of the subject?—Yes, we had it under consideration again last night.

44. Did you come to any resolution?—Yes, we came to a resolution approving of what we had contemplated in 1876.

45. Adopting the same resolution?—Yes, at the same time we thought it desirable before coming to a final conclusion to have a special meeting called, which will probably be done next week.

46. But at present the opinion of the Commissioners is that the 1876 scheme should be adopted?—Yes.

47. Have you a map showing that boundary, or is it on this map?—Yes, that copy will show it.

48. Mr. Gardiner.—It is a scheme adopting the Towns Improvement Act and laying down that improved boundary.

49. Mr. Cotton.—Do you mean that the alteration of the boundary would be contingent only on the adoption of the Towns Improvement Act?—Yes, that was our view, as the town stands at present there is really no boundary laid down under the 9th of George IV., the boundary is limited by the lighting.

50. Mr. Cotton.—Surely under the 9th of George IV., you are bound to have a boundary laid down?—Yes, but we don't tax the houses on the outskirts of the town, where there are no lamps placed.

51. Mr. Cotton.—But one of the first things required by the Act is to fix the boundary?—Yes, there is no boundary necessary under that Act. That is the last thing to be done under the Towns Improvement Act.

52. Mr. Cotton.—But, I think the Commissioners are first to describe the boundaries of the town.

53. Mr. James Marshall, (Solicitor to the Grand Jury).—The Commissioners merely tax where they can for lighting; and then they only tax where they place lamps. We must have a limit within a certain distance of the lamp posts.

54. Mr. Nelson.—There are a number of small tenements on the outskirts, which are not taxed, because there are no lamps placed there.

55. Mr. Cotton.—What you do in the way of taxing is another thing.

Downpatrick. June 13, 18[illegible]. Mr. [illegible] C. Nelson.

57. Mr. Gardiner.—I think the boundary is left to the Commissioners under the 9th of George IV., that is which the [illegible] provision, and we define it by the lamps.

58. Mr. Carton.—When was it put under the 9th of George IV.?—About 1834, I think, or 1833. Our books go back to that but we have not got a copy of them here.

59. The very first meeting of the Commissioners defined the boundary as they should have done?—Yes, and we have that in the books.

60. Mr. Morland.—They can only tax houses and the only way they define the boundary is to put a [illegible] upon the different portions.

61. Mr. Curran.—How do you get at the area of the town?—We take the Ordnance and [illegible] taking any houses beyond the lamps.

62. You have given me the area of the town as 1,[illegible] acres, being the area of the townland of the Demesne of Down?—Yes, that is the parliamentary borough, and I know the municipal borough is coterminous with the parliamentary borough.

63. Mr. Gardiner.—No.

64. Mr. Curran.—I find Mr. O'Brien in his report has given the area as 278 acres. There must have been some foundation for getting at that?

Mr. Morland.—That is the area of Downpatrick proper.

65. Mr. Curran.—That is the town over which the Commissioners have control, at any rate you cannot give the information as to the exact boundary over which the Commissioners have control?—No, but they don't tax beyond the lamps. When we had sanitary powers we did extend them over the entire of the townland demesne.

66. You called the entire townland of the Demesne?—They have power to tax over the whole parliamentary borough if they desire to extend the [illegible] so far. What they do is that so far as they give light or confer benefit, they make a register of the householders though they have never acted within the powers of the section of the Act.

67. Mr. O'Brien says they have limited the boundary to 278 acres, he must have found that somewhere or he could not have put it into his report?—The way they have always done here is, that so far as they confer benefit on the parties they included the houses within that district, whether they are within the district or not.

68. Could not you refer to the first minute which will show what was done?—Yes, I am quite satisfied there never was any line laid down.

69. Could you suggest anything that put 278 acres into Mr. O'Brien's head?—No, unless he got it from the Commissioner of Valuation.

70. Mr. Curran.—And where did the Commissioner of Valuation get it?—He would get it exactly from the valuation book. He keeps our valuation of this town to pass.

71. He must give it upon the limits you originally supplied?—He only gives the valuation of the houses.

72. Suppose a new house is built, have you any means of knowing whether it is within or without your limits?—No; except the lamps.

73. Mr. Morland.—They have power where they make their benefits. The borough must be the limit of their taxation.

74. Mr. Curran.—If they desire it to be so, they could make it smaller.

75. Mr. Gardiner.—The Commissioners have power at any time under the 91st section to extend the borough on their own motion.

76. Mr. Curran.—It would suit my purpose perfectly if I could only get out what is the boundary of the town. Have you any resolution extending the borough?

Mr. Nelson.—We have from time to time put lamps beyond where they were previously, and then we taxed the houses.

77. Mr. Morland.—I think it is lawful for them to extend the borough from time to time.

78. Mr. Curran.—But if they are going to tax things they must come to a resolution on it and that resolution must be on the books. Whatever was done here before, the limits were defined. That was the very thing that was done. It is done in the case of towns under the Towns Improvement Act, before they come to [illegible]. The Valuation Office must have some authority for making up their valuation?—They [illegible] to the Commissioners the rateable valuation of each house within the municipal boundary; they keep a register of all the houses they tax and if they [illegible] within the [illegible] of them, because they are only receiving the [illegible].

79. Suppose a new house is built outside?—The thing comes in [illegible] unless they extend light so far that it is within the borough.

80. Whose opinion is it on the borough?—Suppose they have power to do so under the Act, but we can't go beyond the borough.

81. The municipal Commissioners have power to keep a register of the houses that are to be taxed. What is the meaning of [illegible] the limits?—The end of the municipal borough is the house last taxed.

82. The boundary of the borough is so elastic that it would go as far as houses are built?—That is if they chose to extend the lighting.

83. Mr. Nelson.—We extend the limits to include the [illegible] of the Roman Catholic clergyman, which had not been in before.

84. Mr. Morland.—When the late Mr. Watson was a Commissioner he had a fight about it. The question was whether he should be taxed at all or not. The town of Downpatrick is the borough of Down.

85. Mr. Curran.—The map from the Ordnance people [illegible] the municipality to be much smaller than the borough.

86. Mr. Morland.—That is because that is the only part taxed by the Commissioners. This is just exactly the town; it is what they propose to adopt now.

87. Mr. Curran.—This is a map of the [illegible] Court and it is prepared for other [illegible].

88. Mr. Gardiner.—I see by the old minute book there was a direction given at one of the meetings to prepare a map. This minute book shows also the memorial to the Lord Lieutenant in 18[illegible].

89. Mr. Curran.—Haven't you that memorial in the books?—Yes; it says in it—

"Your memorialists are resident householders inhabitants of Downpatrick, and occupy dwelling-houses of £20 and upwards; they are desirous that the Act passed last session should be put into operation for lighting, watching, cleansing, and paving, which the town has not yet [illegible] under any other Act of Parliament."

And they pray:—

"May it therefore please your Excellency to authorise the carrying of the Act into operation in the said town."

Then there were two or three meetings held and the provisions for lighting the town were eventually adopted. The Commissioners were duly elected and the oath taken on the 6th March, 18[illegible], and on the same day it was resolved that Mr. William Dwyer, land surveyor, be appointed to make a survey of the town and estimate the value to the full and annual valuation of the houses "situate within our jurisdiction." On the [illegible] April, 18[illegible], he submitted a sketch map. I suppose the minutes would show further on, that a regular map was prepared, but I don't know what has become of that map. He gave in his valuation on the 10th May, and I assume he gave in the map at the same time. There is no doubt the map was made.

90. Mr. Morland.—I never saw a map of the town proper, but all this was based upon this estimate and valuation.

91. Mr. Nelson.—The minutes speak of a map being made by Mr. Dwyer, father of the present Mr. Dwyer, Civil Engineer.

92. Mr. Curran.—I must only ask Mr. John [illegible] what authority he had for giving Mr. O'Brien 278 acres as the area of the town.

93. Mr. Gardiner.—He took it from the valuation.

94. Mr. Curran.—Where did the Ordnance people

out the patch of brown, for that is called the town of Down?—That is called Down, but it has no concern with the Town Commissioners at all.

95. Can you tell me what is the wish of the Commissioners now as to the extension of the boundaries?—Our wish is to adopt a boundary such as that laid down by the coloured tracings on the map before you.

96. Mr. Cowan.—Is that boundary marked on this map?

Mr. Gardiner.—Yes; it is the boundary marked by blue on this map.

97. Mr. Cowan.—Do you know anything about the extent of that?

Mr. Nelson.—It is not much different from our present extent.

98. Mr. Cowan.—But it is very different from the extent of the borough?—It is less than the borough, we have it distinctly defined what houses and lands are included in it.

99. Roughly, Mr. Nelson, the land included within the blue boundary is about 300 acres, and the borough is 1,600 acres, so that there is a considerable difference?—It is considerably less than the parliamentary borough.

100. Mr. Cowan.—What do you mean by saying we don't propose to increase the area; don't you tell me they only propose to alter and not to increase it?—I think it is not much increased beyond what we tax at present.

101. What you mean is that you won't tax much more than at present, but the area will be quite different?—There is a small increase in the area.

102. Would it bring in houses that are not taxed now?—It would.

103. How many?—It would bring in four or five good houses of upwards of £20 valuation.

104. Mr. Gardiner.—You will see a street to the north? The starch works from that to the fork of the road we propose to include.

106. Mr. Cowan.—From the starch works up to the letter K?—Yes.

107. That is not taxed now?—No.

108. Tell me how it is that that is not taxed, because that is within the borough?—Because we have not placed lamps there, and the people derive no benefit from us.

109. If you placed lamps there could you tax it?—Surely.

110. Then it would not be extending your area?—It would be slightly extending it in some directions; for instance, at Mount Pleasant, which you see there to the east or north-east there is a good house there that is not included at present, and that we would include.

111. I don't understand what you mean by saying it is not included at present; it is within the borough, and if the borough is your limits then it is within your limits already?—No we limit our taxes to those who are deriving benefit from the rates.

112. If you give benefit to that house at present can't you tax it?—We could of course.

113. Then it is not extending your powers, but to the limits you are going to do?—I suppose that is so.

114. I don't understand your proposition to increase the area; to extend the land over which you have jurisdiction, for you have that jurisdiction at present at Mount Pleasant, but you don't tax it?—Because it is not lighted.

115. The only question I have to deal with is the boundary—the area over which you have jurisdiction.

116. Mr. Morland.—I have discovered what you inquired in the minutes; I had a recollection that there was this entry in the minutes, signed by Mr. Wallace. Reads from minute book.)—

"Resolved that the provisions of the Act under which the Commissioners have been appointed, shall extend to and throughout the borough of Downpatrick."

Therefore what they only wish to do is to tax as far as they give benefits.

117. Mr. Cowan.—Then what the Commissioners wish to do is to adopt this blue line as a boundary?—Yes.

118. And to restrict their powers to 300 acres, instead of 1,600 acres?—Yes.

119. Is it the wish of the Commissioners now to adopt this blue line?—It is their wish.

120. That will restrict your powers from 1,600 acres to 300 acres, or thereabouts?—Yes.

121. Mr. Morland.—Do you understand exactly what the effect of this is. It doesn't help you in the slightest degree, and hereafter you could not go beyond that and tax the people, though you may confer benefits. As a ratepayer I know I would be very much opposed to it. They have power to go and tax as far as they confer benefits, but this will prevent them doing that after a certain point, and I don't think they understand it.

122. Mr. Cowan.—You admit they can't go beyond the borough?—Clearly, and I said so at first.

123. But I did not attach the same importance to it at one, for the borough boundary has been fixed now as the municipal boundary.

124. Mr. Morland.—The first thing the Commissioners are to do is to have an estimate and valuation. The great thing is the estimate and valuation for the purposes of taxation, and in that is given the names of the occupiers; the houses they occupy with the house for which each is assessed. That is in full force for the first year, and they can only do that to the extent necessary for carrying on the lighting and cleansing of the town.

125. Mr. Cowan.—Not exceeding the limit of the borough?—Yes.

126. Don't you think the map prepared for them should have been a map of the entire borough?—What Mr. Boyd prepared, was simply a sort of tracing of what there existed of the town.

127. Was it as much of the borough as they had rated at the time?—As much as they had lighted.

128. But they did not commence lighting until they had got Mr. Boyd's map?—Yes.

129. And then he prepared a map of what they were going to light?—Yes; they can go to the whole extent of the borough, and may carry out lighting as far as they please. They have power every year to extend the lighting, provided they don't go beyond the borough.

130. But I want to draw the distinction—they may extend their lighting and taxing powers, but they can't extend the area?—Yes, but they were right in taking new houses in. I am sure they did not understand this question.

131. If the Commissioners wish to consider the question again, they can do so. If this blue line is put forward as your wish, the effect would be to restrict their powers in case of the extension of the town houses beyond that line, so that while they conferred benefits they could not tax the houses.

132. Mr. Gardiner.—The Commissioners must consider the question in this new light that has been thrown upon it.

133. Mr Cowan.—Think over it, and we will hear you afterwards.

134. Mr. Gardiner.—Our object in laying down that boundary was to confine the taxation to where we proposed to give benefit.

135. Mr. Morland.—But you have power to do that at present, and you don't wish your area of taxation to be restricted.

136. Mr. Cowan.—When the Commissioners fixed upon this blue line, it was under an erroneous impression.

Mr. Gardiner.—Yes, that is so.

Examination of Mr. Nelson, resumed.

137. Do you know the extent of the electoral division yourself?—No; I don't know the area of it.

138. Do you know how far it extends in the different directions and the townlands it includes, for it is part of the recommendation of the Committee that, where it is possible, the boundary of the electoral division should be the boundary of the municipality, and I wish to put it on

Downpatrick, June 25, 18[illegible]. Mr. R. C. Nelson.

pursued whether that is out of the question?—Quite so; quite out of the question.

139. Do you know the electoral division sufficiently well to say it would be impossible to make it the boundary of the town?—Utterly impossible.

140. You are not the urban authority?—No. We were at one time—before the Act of 1866.

141. Have the Commissioners considered the question whether they would wish to become the urban authority?—Yes; we would not.

142. Have they come to that resolution?—We don't wish to become the urban authority.

143. For what reason, or have you any definite reason?—The principal reason is the rating.

144. The sanitary rate at present is struck upon the one townland which is the borough?—Yes.

145. And if you became the urban authority, you would have a right to strike that rate?—But we don't wish to tax the people higher than at present.

146. Mr. *Gardiner*. The landlord pays half the rate, while the guardians are the sanitary authority; and if we became the sanitary authority the tenant would have to pay the whole of the sanitary rate.

147. And that is the reason why you don't wish to become the urban authority?—(Mr. Duane.)—Quite so.

148. How is the town lighted now?—By gas.

149. Are the gas works the property of the Commissioners?—No there is a gas company in the town and we have a contract with them.

150. In what way?—We contract with them each year.

151. At so much a lamp?—So much a lamp.

152. How many lamps; at what rate, and under what terms, as regards light?—There are 65 lamps at 50s. a lamp; sometimes it is higher and sometimes lower.

153. And what are the terms of lighting?—From September until May.

154. On dark nights only?—No; during the full moon, and for two or three nights during that time they are not lighted.

155. Otherwise they are lighted for the entire night and not put out at 12 o'clock?—No.

156. How is the town supplied with water?—not well.

157. I see that in 1876 you had a water scheme prepared?—Yes, we have been working at it for three years.

158. In what state is it now?—There is a bill approved by the Local Government Board, and just recently passed by Parliament.

159. That is approved of by the Local Government Board in the form of a provisional order?—Yes.

160. For what is that provisional order?—For bringing the water a distance of eight miles.

161. At what expense is that to be done?—£12,000 is the estimate. At one time it was resolved by the guardians as the sanitary authority that we should not go beyond £10,000, but it is extended now to £12,000.

162. How is the town off in the matter of drainage—are there complaints made about the sewerage?—There are occasional complaints. The fact is, we never can have this town drained thoroughly until we have the marshes drained, for when there is a flood in the marshes, which is often the case, the filthy sewage is thrown back up the sewers. Until that is put right we can't have proper sewerage for the town.

163. Is there any scheme proposed for the improvement of the drainage?—We have been improving the drainage repeatedly for the last five and twenty years. There was not very much done of late as there was only one penny sanitary rate.

164. What has been done during the last four years?—Not much—only making branch sewers; but nothing has been done to remedy the main sewer, which is in a bad state when there are floods.

165. No scheme has been proposed to remedy that?—There have been schemes suggested.

166. But approved of by the guardians?—I don't know.

167. As the Commissioners never wished to become the urban authority, they have never considered whether they wish to have the control of the roads?—No we never contemplated that.

168. Is it contemplated to put the town under the Towns Improvement Act?—Yes; it is desired by the Commissioners and the greater number of the inhabitants.

169. Have they ever held any meeting about it or taken any legal steps to have the Act adopted?—Yes, we had a meeting, at which we requested a number of these landlords of small houses to attend, as they might be unwilling to pay for the small houses, but now taxable; a number of them attended, and they almost all signified their approval of the adoption of the Act.

170. But you have not taken any statutory steps?—No; but on two former occasions we did take steps, and through one cause or another the matter fell through. At the last town meeting we had it was almost unanimously approved of, with only one or two dissenting voices: and we had a memorial prepared and signed by the greater number of the inhabitants, but that memorial was by some means lost. We feel obliged to you for the suggestion you made with regard to the blue line as a boundary.

171. This is not an inquiry which closes when we leave Downpatrick; it is open to the Commissioners, in any case, to give us their views at any time hereafter?—We will be able then to reconsider the matter in the new light in which you have put it.

Mr. Edward Gardiner examined.

172. You are chairman of the Town Commissioners of Downpatrick?—Yes.

173. For how long have you held that office?—This is the third year.

174. I was going to ask you, had the Commissioners considered the question of the extension of the boundary. What is your view now on the subject?—It is hard to say; we are rather in a difficulty on the subject. Of course we would be anxious to confine our taxes to the area to be benefited.

175. We find that at present, under the old law the way the thing stands is, that the area of the town is the area of the borough—that is 1,400 acres; and the question is do you wish that altered in any way, or do you wish to have that area still preserved?—We are anxious, for many reasons, to adopt some of the provisions of the Towns Improvement Act for we think it is an Act which would benefit us and that it would press more lightly on some of the ratepayers and bring in a class of houses to pay rates that are not paying rates at the present time.

176. That is not exactly the question we have to deal with here, but I might ask you the question, supposing you were to take proceedings to come under the Towns Improvement Act, you should define an exact line for the operation of that Act; what limit would you adopt?—I cannot answer that question in view of what has been discovered to-day. We would have adopted the blue line but for what we have heard.

177. If you think well of it, if you think the Commissioners would like another opportunity of considering the question, we can come here some other day in August and you can consider the whole question over again?—Yes, or we can send our views to you.

178. The only thing is that if you come to any definite conclusion as to any fixed boundary, the ratepayers might wish to be heard too?—The ratepayers might object to the present boundary.

179. Of course I need not say that the Commissioners know the town to all intents thoroughly well, and so their views would have great weight, but we are not bound to coincide with them at all?—Of course.

180. Mr. *Macleod*.—We are all agreed upon keeping the present boundary and the jurisdiction the Commissioners have, and if they adopt the Towns Improvement Act the whole townspeople will agree amicably upon a boundary. It must come to that in the end unless they go on agreeing.

181. Mr. Carson.—I don't know that there is any question of boundary.

182. Mr. *Macleod*.—But when they make up their minds to apply the Towns Improvement Act they can come to an agreement as to their own boundary, and they will give all the ratepayers an opportunity of discussing it at a meeting called for the purpose.

183. Mr. Carson.—Is the railway station rated?—(*Witness*.)—It is and beyond it.

184. Mr. *Macleod*.—It is only the railway station building.

185. Mr. Carson.—On this evidence may the railway station is just outside the boundaries of the town.

186. Mr. *Nelson*.—The railway station was not built then.

187. Mr. *Macleod*.—It is all within the borough, and it is rated.

Examination of Mr. Gardner resumed.

188. Do you agree in the view that it would be desirable to have the guardians the sanitary authority?—I do upon the question of taxation, and it is upon that question, I think, it should be made optional with the town to determine the urban authority on application to the Local Government Board, as it desires.

Mr. Edward [illegible].

189. That is the present law?—But the landlords should follow at being able to decide the rate between the landlord and tenant.

190. As the law stands at present you would see difficulty in removing the urban authority on that ground?—No, sir.

191. Then I take it that a great portion of the borough; that is the portion that is [illegible] distant from here, is just the same as if it was not within the town at all?—Just so.

192. You don't exercise any jurisdiction beyond the limits of the town, and you are not likely to extend the limits a mile outside the town?—No.

193. I want to see why you adopt the borough as a boundary?—(Mr. *Macleod*.)—The reason was, just to give the Commissioners control of taxation, according as it was necessary to increase the benefits and extend them.

194. According to the houses extended?—(*Witness*.) Yes.

195. Is there anything else you wish to state?—No, sir.

196. Then I may take it you don't wish to bring any alteration in the boundaries, so long as you are acting under the 9th George IV.?—No, sir; no change.

197. I think it would be well we should send you down a [illegible] of questions, and then you should answer them in that effect?—Yes.

John Richard M'Connell examined.

Mr. John R. M'Connell.

198. You are one of the Town Commissioners of Downpatrick?—I am.

199. And you think, as long as you are acting under the 9th George IV. the boundaries of the town should be left as they are?—I do. At present the present adopted boundaries were that where a house was built, and where the Commissioners thought it would pay, for that is the sole [illegible] of it, they would light the lamps and tax it for doing so. Of course the houses outside the limits were not lighted and they did not come under taxation.

200. You do not want any alteration in your limits to suit the new state of things?—No.

201. The present boundary is so large that you are not likely to have any new buildings extending beyond it?—It is.

202. And the circumstances of the town, as to the houses are such that the town, as the town proper, stands almost in the middle of the demesne land, so that if they extended a mile on one side they would not be outside the demesne of Down?—Yes.

203. So that extension beyond the parliamentary boundary is very unlikely?—Yes.

204. The only place is Jordan's Acre?—Precisely.

205. You think there would be no advantage in having it brought within the township?—No, but there would be considerable advantage in including Audley's acre. For lighting purposes it would not pay at present.

206. Do you think it likely there is any future time the Commissioners would wish to exercise their jurisdiction over Audley's acre or Jordan's acre?—I think the time is too far distant to give an opinion.

207. It appears to me it would not make the slightest difference one way or the other, whether it was included or not, so long as you did not exercise your powers over it?—Quite so. In that case it would be an advantage to include both, for it would make it a more distinct boundary. It would not at all interfere with the inhabitants at present.

208. Is the Ardglass-road one on which building is likely to arise?—It is possible. There is one new large [illegible] which is outside the limits of taxation at present. The asylum is out there.

209. Mr. *Nelson*.—The asylum supply their own gas, otherwise we might wish to include them.

210. What rood is the asylum on?—On the Ardglass-road. And it includes the whole of Russell's quarter?—That is a townland in itself; it is a small one.

James Kemp examined.

Mr. James Kemp.

211. You are a Commissioner too?—I am, only going to confirm what has been stated.

212. You have heard the observations of the Chairman?—Yes; I agree with them.

213. Have you anything to add?—No; I don't see that any advantage would be gained by altering the boundaries; the chances are so small of any increase of the town in that direction which extension might become necessary if the town was extended.

214. And you have not considered the question what boundary you would define if you were going to adopt the Towns Improvement Act?—I believe the boundary would be very suitable.

215. If you came under the Towns Improvement Act, and were bound to tax the agricultural land one-fourth, you would like to restrict the area?—I think it would be judicious to keep the whole of the demesne of Down, if agricultural land was only taxed one-fourth.

216. That is all it would have to pay under the Towns Improvement Act?—Then I don't see why it should not all be kept in, for they derive direct benefit.

217. They have an interest in the town being kept clean?—Yes.

218. And on account of its being used as a market, and the schools being attended by their children, they have an interest in the place?—Yes; they use it as a place for selling produce.

219. And you think these advantages extend as far as the whole parliamentary borough?—Yes, I quite believe so.

Dungarvan. April 22, 1879.

Mr. Edward M'Loskey.

EDWARD M'LOSKEY examined.

220. You are a Commissioner of the town?—I am.

221. Do you agree with the last witness?—Yes.

222. And you have nothing that you would like to add to what he has stated?—No.

223. Mr. Cotton.—We are ready to hear any ratepayer who is not a Commissioner, either in favour of or against extension.

224. *Robert Whiteside*.—It has been suggested that Audley's acre, which I own, is not likely to be built upon, except where I am building. I would not like to be included. It is a townland, but it is only four acres. There is an old road in it, entirely disused by the county; it runs at the back. It was originally the road, but now there is a road that runs along the asylum wall; the boundary between Russell's quarter and Audley's acre, and that is the road used now.

225. Do you think it is probable they will ever extend the lighting out to you?—I don't think so. As regards sanitary matters, I would not benefit by it, for I live at the other side of the hill. *If you run a lamp* past my gate, I have not the slightest objection to your bringing it in.

226. If you get the benefit you have not the slightest objection to pay the tax?—Not the slightest.

227. Mr. *Gardiner*.—I would like to confirm the opinion of Mr. Kerr, that it would be quite fair that a larger area than is actually embraced in the bounds should be liable to taxation, such as the demesne of Down. They derive considerable advantages from the town, and they should contribute something towards its expenses.

228. You think the borough boundary is one that fairly represents the district that derives benefit?—I think it does.

229. Mr. Cotton.—The first thing to be done is to repeal the 9th George IV. That must be done before you can tax the land. Do you wish to convey that if the Towns Improvement Act was applied, the borough would be about what you would think the fair boundary?—I think so. If we could adopt the Towns Improvement Act, and take in the whole parliamentary borough—the whole of the demesne—I think it would be the most satisfactory area we could adopt. Of course we could not propose to light the whole of that area.

230. Mr. *M'Connell*.—That blue line was adopted by the Commissioners as the boundary under the Towns Improvement Act, supposing it was adopted.

231. Mr. Cotton.—Then I am not to take it as the boundary you ask us to fix now, and whatever boundary you have fixed, it is for the Commissioners acting under the 9th Geo. IV., and not under the Towns Improvement Act?—Take it only as having reference to the 9th Geo IV.

232. Mr. *Moreland*.—As a ratepayer I am not going to say I would approve entirely of that. I say it would be wrong to leave the entire of the borough in the boundary. That is a matter for grave consideration upon which the town ought to be consulted. We have had a great deal of consultation amongst the entire ratepayers about this, and I don't think it would be prudent to suggest anything to be put upon your minutes as a boundary until we have had a meeting to consider it. As a ratepayer I would not like to be bound by an opinion given by individuals upon a subject of that kind. I only want to keep myself right afterwards, and not to have it said I heard those opinions and might be taken as consenting to them. I don't dissent or assent, for I have not considered them.

233. Mr. Cotton.—The question of adopting the Towns Improvement Act has been discussed?—Yes.

234. Has it been discussed by people who own property in the far-off portion of the borough?—I don't think it has. I think it was the people in the town proper and the owners of property in the town who discussed it, and there was a great deal of difficulty how we would fix the boundary in case we went on. The matter would be hardly pertinent to this inquiry, and I merely wish to protect myself afterwards. I am not going to express an opinion one way or the other.

235. Mr. *M'Connell*.—I might mention that being to a certain extent connected with Mr. Mulholland (who is the owner of all the land in the demesne of Down, a great bulk of the people being his tenants from year to year, and the other persons paying a head-rent or ground-rent), that as to the outside persons having been consulted as to the adoption of the Towns Improvement Act, I would say they have not. I have reason to know that. I might also state, although it is not necessary to your present inquiry, that the reason why the Commissioners, by the resolution on their books, adopted the confined line, namely the blue line, was to prevent opposition to the adoption of the Towns Improvement Act.

236. Not to bring in opposition from the outsiders?—Precisely. It was with a view to facilitate the adoption of the Act, because all those persons outside, when they found we were going to adopt boundaries, might come in to oppose us; they do not of course wish to pay, for they get no advantage, and my recollection is that the people who hold land would have to pay whether they received benefit or not.

237. Certainly?—Very well, then, take a mile out in the country where the borough boundary extends, the people living out there and holding land would pay taxes and derive no advantage, and hence their opposition.

238. Do you mean derive no additional advantage?—No additional advantages, no lighting, and they would have to pay rates.

239. But don't you consider that the people living within a certain distance are interested in the town being properly kept?—True; but that doesn't prevent their opposing the Act.

240. But isn't their reason for objecting that they would have to pay?—Yes. I quite agree that that is the reason. There are several lands we would like to bring in but it would bring in opposition also, and then the Act would not be adopted at all.

The inquiry then closed.

Wicklow. April 5, 1879.

Mr. Robert Halpin.

WICKLOW.—5TH APRIL, 1879.

Before Mr. Exham, Q.C.

Mr. Robert Halpin examined.

1. You are the Town Clerk here?—Yes.

2. And have been for a great number of years?—Yes, thirty years.

3. The population, I believe is 3,164?—Yes exactly, it was that by the last census.

4. That is in 1871?—Yes.

5. Has it increased?—It decreased by some 300 odd from what it was in 1861 when it was 3,446.

6. Can you say if it has decreased since 1871?—No.

7. How many acres are there within the town?—763 acres.

8. And what is the valuation?—£[illegible].

9. How much of that is land?—Not quite one-third.

10. Is there not a large quantity of that land owned by the Corporation?—Yes.

11. About how much?—I should say the Corporation own about 130 acres.

12. There are no wards here?—No.

13. The whole of the borough is in the one electoral division of Wicklow?—Yes.

14. And the municipal boundary and the poor law electoral division are not the same?—No. The electoral division extends for miles around.

14. You have not heard it necessary to strike a rate for your [illegible]?

15. What was this poor rate for the past five years?—In 1875 1s. 4d.; in 1877 1s. [illegible]; 1878 1s. [illegible]; in 1879 1s. 4d.; in 1874 1s. 4d.

17. The average of your county cess is about 1s. 6d. in the pound in the year?—Yes, sometimes much half year.

18. Is there any feeling or wish on the part of the ratepayers to have the boundaries extended?—No sir, there is no wish to have them changed.

19. Have the municipal authorities been consulted [illegible] [illegible]?—Yes.

20. Have they expressed, or authorised you to express an opinion on the subject?—Yes.

21. And what is that opinion?—It is that they don't think it necessary to change them at all.

22. Neither to curtail nor enlarge the boundaries in any way?—No.

23. What is the present income of the Corporation?—About £1,[illegible] a year.

24. And how is that expended?—There is £[illegible] for interest in respect of the loan—the harbour loan. The balance goes towards keeping up the town and its [illegible]. We pay something like £[illegible] a year for lighting, that is the largest item we have.

25. Are there any of the Corporation lands that are outside the boundary?—None outside the boundary. We have, in the midst of the Corporation lands, and [illegible] other property. But there is no Corporation property outside the bounds.

27. Are there any gentlemen's residences outside the boundary except Marlston House?—That is within the boundary.

28. It is nearer from the road to [illegible] outside the boundary?—Well, the grounds are inside.

29. Is Marlston House a large one?—It is a good one.

30. Who owns it?—Dr. [illegible]. I always understood Marlston House was within the boundary. It would be a pity if [illegible] [illegible] [illegible] it within our jurisdiction.

Witness [illegible] [illegible] [illegible] Halpin.

Mr. John Chapman examined.

Mr. John Chapman.

31. You are the agent of the Corporation property here?—Yes.

32. Have you marked out the present boundary on the map?—Yes.

33. Can you tell me how that boundary was first ascertained?—Yes; the old Corporation had this boundary. They used to walk over the municipal area—or what was called "riding the franchise"—every Michaelmas Day. The practice had been neglected for some years before I became a Town Commissioner.

34. Then the town went under the Towns Improvement Act?—No; the 9th of George IV. Shortly after that I became a Town Commissioner and they elected me Chairman. That was in 1831 and I got them to walk the boundaries on the following Michaelmas Day which they did. I was anxious to have the boundary [illegible] and it was known at that time and they all walked it with the Town Sergeant of that day, John [illegible].

35. And the boundaries are now the same as the old Corporation had?—Identically.

36. When they adopted the 9th George IV. they adopted the old bounds?—Yes.

37. And it continues up to the present?—Yes.

38. I see you follow townland boundaries almost in every place except at Ballarney and from Ballarney north you turn to the sea?—Yes; because that adopts the old boundary. The old Town Sergeant guided us the whole way. The present boundary includes the whole of five townlands and part of four other townlands, the extreme extent from the north to the south is two miles in length and about three quarters in Irish miles in breadth, but varying in its distance from the sea.

39. Having regard to the fact that there are no taxes here, and that you would not get any increase in income by extending the boundary do you think it would be desirable to extend it in any way?—No.

40. As far as you know, the people in the town don't ask for it?—No. I never heard any one ask it, or being anxious to have it done.

41. Have you ever heard any of the residents outside expressing a wish to have themselves brought in?—No, never.

42. How far is Rathcarn?—An Irish mile and a half—about two English miles.

43. From the centre of the town?—Yes, from the Town Hall.

44. Are there many persons residing there?—It is a commons with very poor people living there—there are only four good houses there.

45. And in point of fact within a distance of two miles say or a mile and a half from the Town hall, there are no gentlemen's seats except Marlston?—Yes, there is Mr. [illegible]'s of [illegible]. There is Mr. Magee of Parkhill, I heard him complain of being in it when there was a tax going to be put on for sanitary purposes he wished to be left out.

46. But he is in at present?—Yes he is.

47. Well, with regard to your sanitary arrangements, are the Guardians the rural sanitary authority?—Yes but we are waiting for the provisional order of the Local Government Board to be confirmed transferring it to us.

48. You will then be the urban sanitary authority?—Yes.

49. Have you considered at all the question of taking over the management of the roads?

50. Mr. *Halpin*.—I don't think we would take that out of the hands of the county.

51. Mr. *Chapman*.—The Grand Jury act fairly and liberally with us and sanction every presentment applied for by the inhabitants, and I think the roads and streets could not be better done than they are by the county.

52. You would not then consider it judicious to get the control of the roads into your own hands?—No. As to the extension of the boundary if there were taxes it is a question that perhaps we might go into but I don't see what good object any change could serve.

Mr. Henry M'Phail Chairman of the Town Commissioners, examined.

Mr. Henry M'Phail.

53. I believe you have heard all you wish here Mr. M'Phail?—Yes.

54. And of course you know the place well?—Yes; I fully concur in the observations of Mr. Halpin and in the answers he has given.

55. There would be no use in any change?—No. [illegible] [illegible] I don't think it [illegible] to see the opinion prevailing is that the boundaries are just what we require and no more. If they were extended we would have to extend the advantages of lighting to an enormous distance without any return.

56. Is there any building going on now, or likely to go on?—Very little.

The inquiry then terminated.

DUNGANNON—JULY 24TH, 1879.

(Before Chas. P. Cotton, Esq., C.E.)

Mr. [illegible], examined.

1. How long have you been Clerk of the Dungannon Union?—Ten or fifteen years.

2. The town is under the 9th of Geo. IV.?—Yes.

3. When did it come under that Act?—In the year 1834, as you will see by the minute in that book; in October, 1834.

4. Can you tell me the population?—At the last Census it was nearly 4,000, but I believe it has been considerably increased since.

5. Could you say to what extent?—I should say by 1,000.

6. Is it up to 5,000 now, do you think?—No.

7. What is the area?—The area of rateable property is 229a. 1r. 8p.

8. Is that the same as the Parliamentary area?—It is; the two are coterminous.

9. What is your valuation?—£7,794.

10. What is the date of the return of that valuation?—June, 1879; £6,291 is the valuation on which we collect the rates; there is a rateable valuation of £7,794, but there is £1,500 representing small house property which we can get no rates on.

11. You have no wards?—No.

12. What electoral division is Dungannon in?—In Dungannon.

13. What were the municipal rates struck for the last five years?—In 1874, 1s.; in 1875, 8d.; in 1876, 8d.; in 1877, 8d.; in 1878, 8d.

14. And the poor rates for the same period?—In 1874, 1s. 4d.; in 1875, 1s. 8d.; in 1876, 1s. 6d.; in 1877, 1s. 8d.; and 1878, 2s. 4d.

15. And the county-cess?—In 1874, 2s. 4½d.; in 1875, 2s. 1½d.; in 1876, 2s. 3½d.; in 1877, 2s. 0½d.; in 1878, 2s. 3½d.

16. Do you know what the municipal rate was for 1879?—The same as last year, I think.

17. And what is the poor-rate now?—Two shillings and four pence.

18. Have the Commissioners considered the question of extension?—Some years ago they considered it desirable.

19. Have they had our queries before them?—No, they had none of these queries before them.

20. I see that you answer our communication. You say that the Town Commissioners and the principal inhabitants "are of opinion that the boundary should be extended so as to include general business premises and dwellings lying in close proximity to the present boundary, but the opinion of the present Master of the Rolls was that it could not be done?—Yes.

21. Was that opinion expressed some years ago?—Yes.

22. In what year?—In 1851.

23. And have the Commissioners not considered it since?—Not since then.

24. Because your answer reads as if it was the opinion given by the Commissioners now?—Well, I followed that in the terms you read. They took the opinion of the present Master of the Rolls, and some of them have been talking individually about the matter since.

25. Why did you not submit the queries to them?—I spoke to the Commissioners and put my views on paper and they approved of them.

26. Do you mean to say it is the opinion of the Commissioners now that an extension should take place?—Yes, the same opinion prevails now as then.

27. What extension was desired?—There is a resolution on the books expressing the opinion that the municipal boundary should be enlarged.

28. Give me an idea of the particular extension desired?—They specified Ranfurly in the townland of Ballymaggart; an extension was desired up to the "crossroads" to include all the buildings in that direction, and the spinning mill and linen factory were to be included, and so much of Dungannon park, house, and pleasure-grounds as lay on the Dungannon side of the park lake, to include Northland House, and so much of the demesne up to the lake and up to the public road.

29. Was it intended to include Killyman?—No, it was not mentioned. It was also resolved that the clerk call on the solicitor to the Board, and lay before him the necessary instructions of the Committee to carry out the matter.

30. You were town clerk at the time?—Yes.

31. Did you know the valuation of what they intended to bring in?—No.

32. What is the number of Commissioners?—Twenty-one.

33. How many voters are there?—Three hundred and one.

34. How many of these are qualified to be Commissioners?—Fifty-six.

35. Can you tell how many additional voters would be brought in by the adoption of the extension proposed by the Commissioners?—It would be, roughly speaking, under ten.

36. And how many of these would be qualified to sit as Commissioners if elected?—At least five.

37. The workhouse is not included in the boundary?—No, nor the almshouses.

38. Was there ever a proposition to change the town so as to constitute it under the Towns Improvement Act?—No.

39. How is the town lighted?—By contract with the gas company.

40. How many lamps are there?—Seventy-nine.

41. At what rate?—£1 13s. 6d. per lamp.

42. During what term are they lighted?—From 1st October till the 1st of April.

43. What hours?—All are lighted before dusk, and half of them are put out at ten o'clock and the other half at six o'clock.

44. In the morning?—Yes. There are seven nights—at full moon—that they are not lighted at all.

45. What is the price at which the gas is supplied to the town generally?—Seven shillings and six pence per 1,000 feet.

46. How is the town supplied with water?—At present they are making a reservoir under a provisional order. They have all the land purchased and the contract entered into. One reservoir indeed is completed and the other is in progress, and the whole will be done in a few months.

47. That is all under the guardians?—Yes.

48. What about the sewerage of the town?—It is done in the same way; they have got a new system within the last twelve months, carried out under Mr. Dickinson.

49. What is the special sanitary rate?—1s. is the poor rate, and 6d. for drainage, and 1s. for water. That is what I understand.

50. On what district is that water rate and sewage rate struck?—It includes the principal townparks around the town.

51. You cannot give it more definitely than that?—No; it is not under my cognizance. Mr. Kelly is solicitor for the guardians.

52. Mr. Kelly.—There was an order made fixing the area for that purpose.

53. I suppose the same area for water as for the drainage?

Dungannon, July 24, 1878.

Mr. John Ewing.

Mr. Kirby.—No; I think the main area is represented here.

Witness.—Yes, the drainage is similar, because they only drain part of the town—the water goes further.

54. Were the Commissioners ever discussed the question of becoming the urban sanitary authority?—Yes; Mr. Anderson, of Hollymount, would have brought it to the end, the Chairman of the Commissioners, and the matter was talked over.

55. They were satisfied with the way the guardians acted?—Well, I won't exactly say that, but they would prefer the guardians having those powers, and a considerable amount of money to be levied there by the Commissioners. He (Mr. Anderson) said a memorial to be signed, but the Commissioners refused to allow it to be signed.

56. Then I suppose they never discussed the question whether they would like to be the sanitary authority?—We considered we got a fair share of the money, and that we might leave it alone.

57. When building operations are going on, are they extensive?—Yes; there are five or six fine villa houses being erected in the direction of the Royal School; and a few years ago, there, at the Washington road, in the direction of Moygashel, there were buildings.

58. All those were within your boundary?—Yes; and those in the rectory to be built just outside the boundary.

59. Have many buildings been going on down beyond the railway station, out beyond the boundary?—No; not many. There is Murdoch's factory, and all belonging to it. Buildings dependent on the gas made towards the Donaghmore road.

60. Is not that within your boundary?—No.

61. Do you supply gas out to the very edge of your boundary in all directions?—No; it does not go to the limits, but nearly.

62. You have not gas outside your boundary?—No; but we supply gas to private consumers.

63. The whole town is within the one townland?—Yes; Drumcoo.

64. Would these extensions you speak of go into any electoral division but Dungannon?—Yes; I think portions would be in Donaghmore. In the opinion of some of the Commissioners there should be a different extension, which they will explain to you. It is only instead of.

Mr. Dickson Patterson examined.

Mr. Dickson Patterson.

65. You are chairman of the Town Commissioners?—I am.

66. How long have you been so?—Within two months of two years.

67. You were a Commissioner before?—Yes; I have been for twenty-seven years.

68. Can you tell me the feeling of the Commissioners—I understand they have not come to any definite resolution on the subject of extension?—I have been speaking to a good many individually, and to rate-payers of the town, and the prevailing opinion is in favour of an extension.

69. Can you give me, in any way, an indication of the extension they desire?—Towards Dernalecky and Northland Manse farm.

70. And not any further?—No; not any further than Mr. Ewing pointed out.

71. On what grounds is the extension proposed?—To enable us to get more funds towards our rates.

72. Have you any idea how much that would bring in?—No; I have not. I never made any calculation; but it would be considerable, I think.

73. If you extend in one direction, why not extend in another; I see, for instance, a house here—Edenmeel—why not take in that, which is about the same distance as Northland Manse?—Well, I don't see that there is any valid reason against it.

74. But, with the exception of these two, there seem to be no gentlemen's places within a mile of the town all round?—No.

75. And you are now speaking your own opinion, as well as that of the Commissioners?—Yes; as well as most of the Commissioners I have been speaking to, and the ratepayers. I don't think there will be much building outside the present boundary.

76. Do you think the boundary should at least be extended to take in the existing or prospective buildings?—Yes; existing buildings, at least.

77. Do you not think that people living within half a mile in every direction should contribute something towards the town?—Well, I don't think they can be said to derive any benefit from the lighting.

78. Don't they get advantage from the lighting coming in during the dark mornings of winter, or going out late at night?—No doubt, to that extent.

79. It is generally alleged that people living within a certain distance of a town should pay something towards it, when they use it for markets, sending their children to the schools, and so on?—Well, all the people who use it at present, and who derive advantage from the lighting, are rated.

80. Do you mean that all people who have property within any three quarters of a mile of the town—being the centre of the town—live in the town and pay rates?—Yes.

81. Would there be any advantage in bringing in the union workhouse?—Well, I don't think it would be any advantage to the Commissioners; as to the gas, it is now within the boundary.

82. It is your opinion that the sanitary matters would be better left in the hands of the guardians than placed in the hands of the Commissioners?—No, it is not my opinion. I think the Commissioners know their own wants best, and I would say that the sanitary authority should be the Board of Commissioners.

83. But that is not the opinion of the majority of the Commissioners I take it?—It is the opinion of a good many of them I think. We would know how to lay out our own money better than strange gentlemen coming from three or four miles away.

84. The drainage works are in progress I understand?—Yes, it is all but finished.

85. You think that fully provides for the requirements of Dungannon?—I do.

86. The water supply is of course a good one?—We hope when we get the water it will be.

87. It is in progress?—Yes.

88. Where is the water taken from?—A distance, about eight miles from this.

89. It is an expensive piece of work?—Yes, the ratepayers will know that, but it is very desirable.

90. Well, you would wish the Commissioners to be the sanitary authority?—Yes, and I have spoken to a good many gentlemen who are of the same opinion.

91. If you were the urban sanitary authority would you wish to have the sole control of the roads?—Well, we are not dissatisfied with what we get from the county, compared with what we pay.

92. How much is contributed by the town in county cess?—2s. 4d. on £7,000.

93. How much is expended by the Grand Jury on the town?—I don't know, but I am satisfied we get good value. We get the footpaths flagged and the town cleansed, which many don't.

94. This is always been so?—It is ten or fifteen years since they took up the cleansing. They have expended I should say £4,000 towards the streets.

95. You think, in fact, that the Grand Jury do whatever can be fairly expected of them?—Yes, we ask them and they freely grant.

96. Mr. *John Simmons*, Solicitor.—I appear for ratepayers, and on their behalf, and for myself, I must say that we are quite in favour of an extension, even

Dungarvan. July [illegible], 187[illegible]. Mr. [illegible] Fitzgerald [illegible].

larger than that proposed by Mr. Ewing, or [illegible] by him as having been agreed to by the Commissioners. I would be for enlarging the boundary to Ballynagarry [illegible] where I reside, myself, and of including [illegible] Ringphuca, so far as the [illegible] marked here on the map "Fish Ponds."

97. Mr. Cotton.—You live outside and are willing to be brought within the boundary?—Yes. We think not only that, but that a larger extension than has been suggested in they should be made.

98. Can you indicate in [illegible] what way?—Yes. If we begin at the extreme northern point [illegible] Carraiglea[illegible], viz., in the [illegible] point of the present boundary. I think that should be extended in the southern direction, so as to include also "Spring[illegible] hill," [illegible] close to the boundary wall, and also to include [illegible] called "Windmill [illegible]."

99. You would not go north of "Windmill [illegible]"?—No, but I would include it, and then [illegible] a [illegible] line up to the corner of the boundary, immediately beyond the [illegible] of the Railway, I would not go beyond that.

100. You would not extend the boundary to the [illegible]?—No. Looking at that point the present boundary should be slightly diverted [illegible] so as to include Fairview House. It should go more to the [illegible] of Fairview House.

101. In what direction?—I would proceed in a right line, so as to include the Union Workhouse.

102. Would you go up to some quarries, I see marked?—Yes. They are private quarries. I would include the Workhouse, and also include the Almshouse immediately to the right of the Workhouse, and keeping that right, line include Killyvall House, and then [illegible] the boundary just immediately [illegible] of that at [illegible], the [illegible] boundary, and then by the "Fish Ponds."

103. Would you go beyond the "Fish Ponds"?—The Fish Ponds would be the proper boundary.

104. Do you know the electoral division?—Yes.

105. Now taking the electoral division marked by the blue line, would you say it would be too much?—I think it would be a better boundary still, and for this reason, it would do no injustice to the people in the agricultural rank of life, and for this reason: There are very few farm holders situated within the electoral division—that is very few people who live by farming alone. I think there would not be more than perhaps half a dozen.

106. And do I understand that they are owned chiefly by residents of the town?—Yes, in the way of town parks by the residents in the town, and as accommodation lands, and therefore I think that the electoral division would be a better boundary still. One other reason I think would operate in that direction, and that is that it is the area in which the water rate and sewer rate are charged.

107. Are you sure about that?—Well, I think so.

108. [illegible] Mr. Ewing gave me to understand that the sewerage rate was not charged on a large area as the water rate?—I went for information to the workhouse, and I was informed by the Clerk of the Union that there was the same rate in both cases.

109. At any rate, if I may infer it, it is the electoral division on which the sewerage and water rate is struck, it would be an additional reason for [illegible] in the [illegible] boundary?—Yes, I am aware of the [illegible], and so are my clients. Buildings will be springing up in the direction of the Almshouse and in other directions. The town is, I think, in a [illegible] condition than in former years, and it would be only right and proper that these buildings should be included within the municipal boundary. They derive all the advantages of being in the neighbourhood of the town, and they should, therefore, contribute towards the expenses of it. The electoral division [illegible] contains 1,329 acres in round numbers, but I see by "Thom's Directory" that the present boundary contained 888 acres. For some reason, at some period—[illegible] I think—the boundary was narrowed down to the dimensions it is at present.

110. Well, after all that bears very little on the present question, because the reasons that guided the original boundary would, doubtless, be different from those that would apply now?—[illegible].

111. As a ratepayer, would you think it desirable that the Commissioners should be the sanitary authority, or that it should be the Board of Guardians?—My opinion is, that as the sanitary authority is much more immediately connected with the town and the immediate locality, that it places the power in the hands of those who know more thoroughly the requirements of the town as [illegible] would be desirable. The guardians are elected from a very wide area, and cannot possibly have such an intimate knowledge of the requirements of the town as the Town Commissioners.

112. Do you know are the Guardians asked to do any sanitary work which they neglect?—I think not. I think—as far as I know—that they perform their duties, and have done so. They have put in force the provisions of the Act with great [illegible] and with moderation, where moderation was necessary.

113. You think, however, that the Commissioners residing immediately on the spot would be better judges of what was required?—Yes, that would be the only reason I could give.

114. Have you formed any idea yourself as to the advisability or otherwise of taking up the roads—to the Grand Jury [illegible] in that respect?—Well, I think there is no reasonable ground of complaint as to the roads in the immediate neighbourhood of the town and the public streets.

Mr. Thomas H. Aiken.

Mr. Thomas H. Aiken examined.

115. Mr. Henry A. Kelly, solicitor.—You have heard Mr. [illegible] evidence—do you agree with it [illegible]; only I would not extend in the direction of [illegible], but with that exception I agree with it. I would not go to the extent of taking in the entire electoral division. I would include Windmill Hill.

Mr. Ewing.

Mr. Ewing recalled and examined.

116. Mr. Kelly, solicitor.—There are buildings in the direction of [illegible]?—Yes.

117. And it is your idea to enlarge in that direction?—Yes, and I would not extend so far.

118. You never heard any complaint of the way the guardians carried out the sanitary work?—No, I never heard any complaints. I heard persons saying they might have done things better, and so on.

119. Mr. [illegible].—The only thing I ever heard exception taken to as regards the Guardians was their [illegible] the water, and opinion in the town was a good deal divided as to that.

120. Mr. Kelly.—And that is remedied now, for they are getting in a good supply of water. If the Town Commissioners were the sanitary authority we would not have the water at present. I would now say a few words on behalf of my clients.

120. Mr. Cotton.—For whom do you appear?

121. Mr. Kelly.—I attend partly as solicitor for Lord Dunkerley. It was only a day or two ago I heard you were going to hold this inquiry here, and I have not had an opportunity of consulting with Lord Dunkerley or ascertaining his views.

122. Mr. Cotton.—We are open to receive any communication from you at any time.

[illegible]

Mr. George Moss, T.C., examined.

196. I understand you are one of the Town Commissioners?—Yes, I am a long time a member of the board.

197. What do you think on the question of altering the boundaries?—Well, I think, so far as I can see, I would make the electoral division the boundary, with the exception of a place they call [illegible].

198. You mean the whole townland of [illegible]?—Yes; [illegible]

[illegible]

[The inquiry terminated.]

CLONES—JULY 21st, 1880.

(Before Mr. W. A. Exham, Q.C.)

Clones. July 21, 1879.

Mr. J. Galway, Town Clerk, examined.

Mr. J. Galway.

1. The township is under the Towns Improvement Act of 1854. The area is 162 acres, and the valuation is £3,466 5s. The population in 1871 was 2,170 which has not increased. The boundaries have not been altered since they were first fixed. There has been some slight building going on within the last few years, but it has been within the township boundary. There is not, and has not been any new building within any short distance of the new boundary. The township is all in the electoral division of Clones, which extends for a very considerable distance in every direction beyond the present boundary. There are not any gentlemen's residences or houses within a mile of the present boundary. The following have been the rates made for the last six years:—

	Municipal.	Poor Law.
	d.	d.
1874, . .	12	12
1875, . .	6	9
1876, . .	6	10
1877, . .	6	10 and 6d. Sanitary Rate.
1878, . .	6	16 and 6d. Sanitary Rate.
1879, . .	6	6

The municipal rates have been sufficient to pay for the due and proper lighting of the township with gas and for its scavenging, and the Commissioners consider that they will be able to do the same work in the future for the same rates as the last few years. The County Cess has usually been up to the present about 1s. 6d. in the pound in the year. There are at least 100 acres of land outside on within the present township, which is used almost exclusively as accommodation land for the township. This land is consequently valuable on that account, and pays much higher rent than similar land would pay if two miles from the boundary. Sir Thomas Lennard is the owner of all the land within the present boundary. He expends considerable sums of money in keeping up a proper water supply, and subscribing to the town rates. What he thus gives is more than he would have to pay if he, as landlord, had to pay any share of the municipal rate, even if that was thrown to one-half on the valuation. The Commissioners do not consider that they could advantageously take up the management of the roads within the present boundary. They are also unanimously of opinion that it is not desirable to have any increase or other alteration of the present boundary. The ratepayers also do not wish for it, and there are not any persons residing outside the boundary who desire it.

Three or four of the Commissioners also attended the inquiry, and stated that the evidence of the Town Clerk was accurate in all respects.

(The inquiry then terminated.)

GALWAY.
July 8, 1879.

GALWAY.—JULY 8TH, 1879.

(Before Mr. EXHAM, Q.C., Mr. COTTON, C.E., and Mr. H. A. ROBINSON.)

Mr. John Redington examined.

Mr. John Redington.

1. CHAIRMAN.—You are Secretary to the Town Commissioners?—Yes.

2. What is the present area and valuation of the municipal boundary?—24,133 acres; the valuation is £26,133. And the population at last Census 13,135. There has been a decrease within the past twenty years.

3. Since 1871 has there been a decrease?—No, I don't think so.

4. Is the borough in the Galway electoral division?—The electoral division is larger.

5. What is the valuation of the portion of the electoral division outside the borough?—£2,864 17s. The county of the city comprises the entire of the Galway electoral division, part of Ballinacourty, the entire of Barna and portion of Carrowbrowne.

6. What are the rates that have been struck here for some years past?—The municipal rates were in 1874, 1s. 3d.; in 1875, 1s. 11d.; in 1876, 1s. 11d.; in 1877, 2s. 6d.; in 1878, 2s. 6d. That municipal rate includes the maintenance of the roads, and also a three-penny public water-rate.

7. Have you high pressure water here?—Yes.

8. That rate has nothing to say to lighting. We got a Provisional Order to levy a rate for the maintenance of the roads, the tolls not being sufficient to keep the roads in repair. There is a receiver over the tolls for a debt due to the Gas Company, and we got a Provisional Order to levy a rate not exceeding 2s. in the pound for the borough.

9. For the roads in the borough?—Yes.

10. How is the town lighted—is it out of the tolls?—Yes, tolls and customs.

11. Are they sufficient for the purpose?—Yes.

12. What was the poor rate for the same period?—In 1874, 2s.; in 1875, 2s. 6d.; in 1876, 2s. 6d.; in 1877, 2s. 6d.; in 1878, 3s.

13. The same rate is payable over the entire electoral division?—Yes.

14. Is there any county cess payable by the borough?—Yes, for imperative presentments.

15. Is the portion you pay in the borough the same as is paid in the county of the town?—No; it is much heavier outside because they have to maintain the roads outside.

16. When did you get power to strike the improvement rate?—In 1875.

17. What was the county cess?—In 1874, 2s. 7d.; in 1875, 1s. 3½d.; in 1876, 1s. 7d.; in 1877, 1s. 2d.; and in 1878, 10½d.

18. Did the difference between 2s. 7d. in 1874, and 10½d. in 1878, pay for the roads which are now paid out of the improvement rate?—Yes.

19. Will the county-at-large charges be less?—Yes. At present the county cess is 10½d. and will be less, when we knock off the establishment charges.

20. Then in fact the taxation in 1878 including poor rate and county cess is about 6s. 3½d.?—Yes.

21. Mr. COTTON.—What was the date of the Provisional Order about the roads?—1874 or 1875.

22. Before the Provisional Order who repaired the roads?—The Grand Jury maintained the roads. But it was found that, under our local Act—the Galway Town's Improvement Act, 1853—we were obliged to maintain the roads inside, and not the Grand Jury—out of the tolls and customs, and then it was we asked for a Provisional Order to give power to levy a rate, the other source not being sufficient for the purpose.

23. CHAIRMAN.—Then in 1874 the county of the city Grand Jury did not repair the roads?—They did.

24. You were bound to do it?—Yes, but we did not do it, and for the last twenty or thirty years they have been maintained by the Grand Jury.

25. What were the rates in 1878, the county cess in the portion outside the municipal boundary and in the hands of the city grand jury—the portion outside the municipal boundary and inside the county of the town?—Three shillings and sixpence farthing county cess, that is for the maintenance of the roads and imperative presentments. The Commissioners wish to draw attention to how unduly it presses on the tenants outside. They have to pay 3s. 6¼d. for the maintenance of the roads outside, imperative presentments, and that is entirely payable by the tenants.

26. What was the amount for other years?—It was about the same. The estimated cost of the roads outside to the confines of the county is about £700, between the borough and the extremity of the county of the town. This £700, if levied off a valuation of say £8,814 (that is the valuation of the outside ring), would require a rate of 2s. 3d. to cover it, while, if amalgamated with the inside portion, it would only take 1s. 3d. to cover the entire.

27. Is the surveyor's salary included in the £700?—No, the salary is £100, and the £700 is the contract for the roads.

28. Does the borough pay anything towards that?—Merely for the maintenance of the courthouse, but nothing towards the salary of the surveyor.

29. How do you make out the 1s. 3d. you speak of if there was an amalgamation?—If you amalgamate this £700 with the cost of the roads inside, and take it upon the total valuation of £32,800, it will only cost 1s. 3d. if you spread it over that large area.

30. Would it not increase the road rate inside the borough?—No.

31. What will 1s. 3d. produce on the valuation of the outside "ring"?—The valuation of the outside ring is £8,814, and then will take 2s. 3d. to produce the £700.

32. One shilling and threepence would produce £460 upon the valuation of the "ring" between the two, and that will leave £240 to be raised by the borough in addition?—Yes; but if you take it upon the valuation of both inside and outside, 1s. 3d. will produce £2,000 which will cover entire expenses of road.

33. Does arable land in the borough pay the full rate?—Yes.

34. Mr. COTTON. If you calculate the maintenance of the roads outside the borough and inside the county of the town, you must add something, I think, to the rate of the borough?—Why.

35. If you put 1s. 3d. on the outside it won't produce £700, and you must raise £240 somewhere else?—Yes; but I have already shown you that 1s. 3d. on the entire rating will cover all expenses of roads.

36. CHAIRMAN.—According to the Provisional Order you got giving you power over the roads, is the entire of the rate chargeable on the land?—It is divided between the landlord and tenant.

37. Is the entire rate imposed on the land or does arable land pay only one-fourth?—The entire.

38. Is the £2,000 raised for roads inside charged half on the landlord and half on the tenant?—There is only £1,800 required for the roads inside, and the rate is divisible between landlord and tenant.

39. Do you propose if the "outer ring" is taken in, [illegible]

that it should be divided in the same way ?—Yes; the persons outside the township rather pay 2s. 6½d., whereas, if it is amalgamated with the town they would pay very much less and it would be divided between the landlord and the tenant.

40. Mr. Cotton.—Then, I presume, the tenants are in favour of it, and the landlords are not ?—Some of the landlords are.

41. How far does the county of the town extend from the centre of the town ?—About four Irish miles.

42. Chairman.—Are the county-at-large charges heavier in what you call the "ring" than the town ?—With the exception of the salary of the county surveyor, they are not. In fact, they are spread equally over the entire, with that one exception.

43. Mr. Cotton.—I suppose you would have a corresponding charge in respect of surveyor's salary and additional staff, if you took over the work ?—The same staff already employed by the Commissioners would suffice——

44. Chairman.—Have you a surveyor inside the boundary ?—Yes.

45. Would he do all the roads as cheaply and well ?—Well, he ought to be able.

46. Would you not have to increase his salary ?—I don't know that; and besides that, by-and-by these establishment charges would drop off.

47. Is there building going on outside the borough ?—No.

48. Are there many gentlemen's seats outside ?—Yes. Under the Galway Town Improvement Act we have power to levy a rate, and divide it between the landlord and tenant.

49. Does that apply to the road rate ?—Yes.

50. If the boundaries were extended the same principle would apply ?—Yes.

51. Is the town rate payable in full on the agricultural land ?—Yes.

51. Are the municipal and poor law wards coterminous ?—No; the poor law wards are larger.

52. Within the borough are the boundaries ?—Yes; but the poor law wards extend further.

53. Chairman.—How many voters are there in Barna ?—One hundred and ten parliamentary; forty in Ballybrit-temple; and fifty in Carraghmore.

54. Does the county of the city boundary follow townlands ?—Yes.

55. Mr. Cotton.—In the proposition to take in that area up to the county of the town boundary, have you considered what would you do with reference to the wards—would you create new wards or extend the present ones ?—I would extend the present ones, to save any confusion.

56. Mr. Robinson.—They would be the same so far as the electoral division of Galway is concerned; but would you extend them beyond that electoral division into others ?—I don't see any difficulty. At the present moment they are not what you can call disfranchised; and, if we take in the entire county of the town, it would be only fair and right to the ratepayers who pay the rates that they should have some representation here at the board.

57. But, if you did not give them outside an independent ward, would not the voters in the present wards swamp them ?—Well, yes, that might be so.

58. Chairman.—What is the difference in the valuation of the electoral division boundary and the municipal ?—The electoral division exceeds the municipal by £9,554 17s.

59. If you extend West ward by adding to it all the county of the town that lies to the west of it, the number of voters in that country district would be small compared with those residing in West ward ?—Yes.

60. Would that give any representation to outsiders ?—Very slight.

61. It would not give them anything like the same as they would have if you gave them an independent ward ?—You would then, likely, give them too much power. My view would be to have the four wards, and extend them wherever you extend the boundary.

62. How would it interfere with the "ring," if you left out the portions of Ballybrit-temple and Carraghbrown ?—And merely took in the electoral division of Galway ?

63. Yes, and the entire of Barna electoral division —could you show us on the map how that would run ?—

[Witness marked on the map the line indicated by the Chairman.]

Witness.—If you drew the line the way you wish to draw it, you only take off £1,600 of the valuation of the entire county of the town.

64. If we did that, adopting the Galway electoral division and the Barna electoral division, you could have a separate ward for Barna ?—Yes, but you should then extend the other wards on the other side.

65. Yes, you could throw in whatever portion of Galway electoral division runs round the city wards, making in that way the poor law and city wards coterminous, and leaving Barna as a separate ward to itself ?—That is very feasible.

66. What is the number of the Town Council ?—Twenty-four, that is, six for each ward.

67. Would you propose to increase the number ?—I think twenty-four is sufficient.

68. Then you could do this. You could have five wards, and if you increase the number of municipal representatives to twenty-five, it will enable you to have five for each of the existing wards and five for Barna, and in that way you can give it separate representation ?—Yes.

69. The only difficulty then is with reference to Carraghbrown and Ballybrit-temple, and the proper thing would be to so arrange it that the portions of Ballybrit-temple and Carraghbrown that might be remaining outside the municipal boundary might be attached to the county—no longer belonging to the town ?—Yes, that could be done.

70. Barna is differently situated—that is an electoral division—and there is a complete boundary that can be turned into a complete ward. I am not sure that I asked you in general terms the grounds on which this extension of the boundary is considered advisable ?—They consider that the mode of transacting the fiscal business in the borough and county of the town is imperfect and anomalous, as there are at present two sets of officers employed in discharging these duties, one of which would suffice, and the Commissioners are favourable to an extension, and have sent a memorial to the Local Government Board praying for it, because of the advantages of having uniform local administration, which would eventually diminish considerably the cost of establishment charges, and likewise more equitably divide the cost of maintenance of roads between landlord and tenant in the portion of the county of the town not included in the municipal boundary.

71. What would you say to this proposition—that the borough of Galway be extended to the electoral division, and that all outside then belong to the county of Galway, and no longer to the county of the town of Galway ?—I know there would be a strong objection to that. In the first place we have two members of Parliament, and if you go and lessen the number of voters we have, we will likely lose by-and-by one of our members.

72. Mr. Cotton.—There can be no difficulty about that—in leaving the old boundary as regards voters.

73. Chairman.—If you look at this map you will see there cannot be many voters in Carraghbrown.

74. Witness.—It would be detrimental to us to take away portion of the county of the town, and throw it into the county.

75. The tendency has been to get rid of counties of cities as far as I can see, and to throw into the hands of the municipal authorities as the governing body the management of all the wards ?—There is no doubt that

GALWAY. July 5, 1876. Mr. John Redington.

it is very objectionable to have the two separate bodies of officers.

76. It would be desirable to have such a boundary outside. There should not be three authorities inside the electoral division—the municipal, then the grand jury of the county of the town of Galway, and then the grand jury of the county. It would be better to have it arranged as in Cork.

77. Mr. Ferdinand, T.C.—We have a large rural population.

78. CHAIRMAN.—What arrangement do you contemplate as to the majority of which to remove distance?

Mr. Redington.—The people living, say, three miles away would be entitled to it, if the majority was [illegible] on the quay.

79. Mr. Ferdinand.—We have not water yet to [illegible].

80. Mr. Redington.—The capital [illegible] as to the Galway electoral division, and also the Barna electoral division.

81. Mr. Cooper.—Have you the area of the Barna electoral division?—Well, the valuation is £2,[illegible]. The county get rid of the [illegible] by throwing portion into the county.

82. What is the special object of taking in Barna?—It gives the Town Commissioners greater valuation for rating purposes, and it lessens the rate for that portion, as already shown.

83. CHAIRMAN.—The electoral division is bounded by the [illegible] and the little town of Barna is close to the sea?—Yes.

84. Was there any resolution passed at the meeting to include the county of the town?—Yes.

Mr. Ferdinand.—Yes, and at the Grand Jury.

85. Did the Commissioners approve of it?—Yes, at an ordinary meeting. On the motion of Mr. Davis, seconded by Mr. Gill, it was resolved that arrangement No. 3 referred to in the report of the Commission, was agreed to by a majority of nine to one, and the Chairman was authorised, on behalf of the Commissioners, to give evidence before the Local Taxation (Ireland) Commission, sitting in [illegible]. That was on the 16th of June 1876. Arrangement No. 3, referred to, was as follows:—

"To abolish the county of the Town Grand Jury, both as to the criminal as well as the fiscal jurisdiction, and to extend the four wards of the present municipal area, to the limits of the borough, or three mile radius from the Church of St. Nicholas; and similarly, to extend the jurisdiction of the Town Commissioners for all purposes, except the criminal business for judges of assize, which could be taken up by the Grand Jury of the county with facility & very more trouble, and with much saving to the ratepayers of the borough. By this, as regards taxation, the ratepayers of the outer circle would contribute to all borough taxes, the rateable valuation of which is £[illegible]—by sum of maintenance of roads, £1,[illegible]; imperative presentments, £[illegible], sewerage work, £[illegible]; annual charges, total, £1,[illegible]. This £1,[illegible] on the valuation would be equivalent at present to a rate of about [illegible] in the pound for all purposes, but would be reduced on the falling-in of the superannuation allowances, consequent on the abolition of the Grand Jury officers, namely about £[illegible], equivalent to a rate of [illegible] in the pound. There would then be a road rate of [illegible], imperative presentment rate, [illegible]; sewerage rate, [illegible], or about [illegible] for the whole year for all purposes—a considerable reduction on present rates, in which ratepayers of the outer two miles would participate. Occupiers would under this arrangement be relieved of half the rate, as a rating for relief of poor—a change which will naturally be opposed by owners of property who have let their lands without anticipating or taking into consideration the rates at which their lands are let, such a radical alteration and who may not, on other grounds desire to see such wide and extended powers given to the Commissioners."

That is the arrangement adopted by the Commissioners after discussion.

86. Was there any resolution after that?—Yes; a resolution passed by the Grand Jury by eleven to three. It was on the motion of Captain O'Hara, seconded by James Campbell—

"Resolved, that we having before us a memorial of the Town Commissioners praying that the town wards for the present municipal area be extended to the county of the town of Galway, are of opinion that the arrangement proposed would prove a saving in expenditure in maintenance of the roads, and therefore meets our approval,—it being distinctly understood that the outer radius be exempted from all rating for waterworks or sewerage."

And Sir V. Blake proposed, and Mr. John Gill seconded as an amendment—

"That in our opinion the outside radius ought to be added to the adjoining baronies for fiscal purposes."

This amendment was rejected.

87. Who is to look after the waterworks and sewerage in the outside district.

Mr. Ferdinand, T.C.—We are after borrowing £[illegible],000 for a complete system of sewerage. The rate for that was not to extend to the outer radius.

88. At present the outside district is in the hands of the rural sanitary authority—the Poor Law Guardians. Suppose it is brought into the municipality, who is to look after the sewerage of that district?—The Commissioners are willing to take charge of the sanitary affairs in the outer district, provided the sewerage rate is extended over it.

Mr. Robert Stephens.

Mr Robert Stephens, Secretary to the City Grand Jury, examined.

89. CHAIRMAN.—You hear, Mr. Stephens, what the proposition of the Town Commissioners is—to take in the whole of the county of the town and bring it into the city?—Yes, my own opinion with regard to that is that it would be very unfair to charge the outer district with sewerage and water rate, because they derive no benefit whatever from one or the other, and it would likely increase their taxation.

90. Mr. Redington makes out that even putting all taxation on them you can reduce their taxation by at least 17d. or 18d. in the pound?—I know the rate on the county of the town of Galway at the present moment is 1s. 7d. for the half-year.

91. 3s. 6½d. he gives it for the whole of last year?—Yes, I dare say about that.

92. Then he says if you are brought into the city that all you would pay is 3s. 3d.?—I don't know how you make out that.

93. He says that for the last year 3s. 6d. was the municipal tax and the county at large charges were 10½d.; that makes it 3s. 3½d.; then he says that you are paying 3s. 6½d.; so there would be a saving of 3d. But he goes further and says that the whole thing could be done for less than 3s. 2½d. if you had an undivided authority, as you would not have to pay county surveyor and county officers' salaries—all could be done by one staff. He says the outside people would get advantage from this amalgamation?—No doubt, the outside tenant would be better off, but the landlord would have to pay for it. The occupying tenant in the outer district would have the taxation lessened by the enlargement, but the landlord would have to pay additional taxation he does not pay now. I am speaking on the old lettings; as for the new lettings it does not matter, for the landlord has the power of making his own arrangements, but in the case of existing leases there would unquestionably be an undue and unexpected onus thrown on the landlords, not existing at present.

94. One of the things we have to consider is what is called the incidence of taxation, and suppose any portion of this district was brought in, existing contracts might be preserved.

Witness.—It is certainly strange to have the Grand

Jury exercising authority over part of the town, and the Town Commissioners exercising a similar jurisdiction.

95. Mr. *Redington*.—That is what we want to do away with.

96. What would you say to extending the municipal boundary to the electoral division—because the Select Committee of the House of Commons has expressed an opinion that towns should, as far as possible, be made coterminous with electoral divisions?—I would say that in that case the outside district should have separate representation on the municipal council.

97. Mr. *Redington*.—I would, at all events, take in Barna Electoral Division, for we don't lose many voters by doing that. The Town Commissioners are anxious to extend the area, to lessen the taxation if they can.

98. CHAIRMAN.—What would be your view, Mr. Stephens?—I would be sorry to recommend the curtailment of the county of the town. What I would say is this, give to the Town Council the jurisdiction of the Grand Jury in fiscal business——

99. What would you keep the Grand Jury for?—I would not keep them at all.

Mr. *Redington* read the proposal of the Commissioners, described as "Arrangement No. 2."

100. CHAIRMAN.—Is there any reason you suggest why the county of the town should be preserved at all? —It is the wish of the inhabitants of the county of the town, that it should be preserved as heretofore.

101. But suppose we were to propose the extension suggested and approved of by the Town Commissioners —an extension to the entire county of the town,—you would not keep up the municipal authority, then that of the Grand Jury of county of the town—over one and the same area.

102. Mr. *Redington*.—What the Commissioners wish is to get the extension as far as the county of the town, and the Grand Jury would cease for fiscal purposes. Vested rights could be preserved, and eventually we get the benefit of that.

103. Then you would not want to have the county of the city, as in the case of the county of the city of Dublin, which is nothing at all except in name?—Yes.

104. Mr. *Stephens*.—My idea was this: the Town Commissioners should have the same jurisdiction as the Grand Jury in Dublin have with the Justices' veto on the presentments, and they should be governed by same laws, such as the Grand Jury laws at present.

105. CHAIRMAN.—In Cork the Recorder wields them.

106. Mr. *Stephens*.—I would like to have some governing body over the Town Commissioners, so that if any one complained with reference to any particular presentment there would be control over them.

107. Mr. *Redington*.—The only control is the auditor.

108. Mr. *Stephens*.—Yes, and the auditor cannot go into certain matters over which there ought to be control. I have known cases before the Town Board in which roads have been disallowed, and afterwards, without any notice to individual members of the Town Board, the contractors have been paid for those roads. No such thing could occur before the Grand Jury.

108. CHAIRMAN.—I understand you will soon have a cemetery rate?—Yes, it is the pound—there is power of levying that.

109. Would you think it right that the people of Ballintemple, Barna, and Oranmore should pay that?—They have to pay it; it has been settled for Oranmore, Ballintemple, and Galway.

110. Does it take in the whole of Oranmore, Barna, and Galway?—I know it has been already settled. I would like to know have you the power of recommending that payments made for roads hitherto by the Grand Jury should be brought before the judge, and fiated by him as in Dublin.

111. The way we could do it is by suggesting that in any alteration of the boundary, and where the Town Commissioners were to take over the functions of the Grand Jury, it should be on the principle adopted in Cork or Dublin.

112. Mr. *Stephens*.—That certainly would be a very reasonable solution of the question—for without that I would be slow to recommend the functions of the Grand Jury being handed over to the Town Commissioners—for otherwise there would be no check.

113. What would you say to the municipal body taking over the management, and becoming the Urban Sanitary Authority for that district, looking after the sewerage, disinfection, and sanitary arrangements generally, and bringing in the centre of Barna, Ballintemple, and Oranmore, within the survey of the town, would the municipal body be capable of performing all these duties?—As capable as the Grand Jury.

114. Or the rural guardians?—Yes, I believe so, with a proper and sufficient check.

115. Mr. *Redington*.—They ought to be able to do the work better, for they meet more frequently.

116. Mr *Stephens*.—The only thing against it is that there is no means of compelling them, by contract, to do the works—it is handed over to their own officers.

117. Mr. *Redington*.—As far as they can they put the roads under contract, and the streets being opened up for sewerage works, that would be under contract.

118. CHAIRMAN.—If this district were brought in, on what principle would you say they should not pay sewerage rate?

Mr. *Stephens*.—Well, sewerage is different from cleansing—sewerage is a work done for the benefit of the houses about the town, and they would have no benefit from that.

119. But if you annex this district, it would be surely for the advantage of the district so annexed, to have the town well sewered, and consequently in a more healthy condition?

120. Mr. *Redington*.—The same argument would apply to two miles beyond.

121. Mr. *Stephens*.—What about the water—there is a separate water rate for houses.

122. Mr *Redington*.—Only for domestic purposes —the 3d. rate is spread equally over the entire.

123. Mr. *Stephens*. The sewerage works are for domestic purposes, and it would be unfair to charge the outer district for a work now done, and for which they certainly have no benefit.

124. CHAIRMAN.—What would you say to making them pay a differential rate, one-half or so, on general sewerage and water?

125. Mr. *Stephens*.—I think that would be more just.

126. And divided between landlord and tenant?—Yes.

127. Mr. *Redington*.—It should not be forgotten that the parties inside pay more—pay a larger proportion of tolls than those outside. There is a tax on the parties in town if they get goods from the railway, and in fact they pay heavy tolls, that the persons outside do not.

128. CHAIRMAN.—Yes; but these goods are sold outside, and the person who pays the tolls gets the benefit of it.—I can understand that sewerage is, strictly speaking, for the use of the town, as distinguished from other works—the sewerage works are no doubt for the use and immediate benefit of the town; but the advantage of having a healthy town well watered, sewered, and scavenged, is evident, and the question arises, do not those who daily frequent the town partake of these advantages to such an extent, as to make it reasonable that they should be expected to pay, not the full rate, perhaps, but a fair proportion.

Mr. *Stephens*.—Make him pay the 3d. rate—there are two rates you know—he should not pay the domestic rate.

129. CHAIRMAN.—Should he pay the public water rate?—Yes.

Captain O'Hara, Chairman of the Town Commissioners examined.

130. Chairman.—You are in favour of an extension of the boundary?—Yes. I may say, that as chairman I did not express any opinion. I only formed an opinion that a change should be made, as the imaginary line of the boundary was unsatisfactory, and should at least be altered.

131. We may take for granted that in your opinion the imaginary line of a circle should be altered?—Yes.

132. The only question then will be whether to restrict or enlarge the area. I don't very well see how we can restrict it—or what line you could draw to curtail it. Therefore we must recommend an enlargement? Exactly; the question is, to what extent should that enlargement be carried.

133. We would like to have your views as to that. The best arrangement would be to make the boundaries coterminous with the electoral division.

134. Do you mean the electoral division of Galway?—Yes.

135. Do you suggest to have everything within the electoral division under the control of the Town Commissioners and everything outside of it under the control of the County Grand Jury?—Yes.

136. Do you think you would get rid of all difficulty by having the municipality of Galway the sole managers of all within the electoral division, and the county Grand Jury of all outside that?—Yes.

137. Would you get rid of the county of the town altogether?—Yes.

138. Mr. Rathington.—May I ask you, Mr. Rahim, whether you can go into or consider the question as regards Parliamentary values?

139. Chairman.—We have nothing to do with that question.

140. Captain O'Hara.—I think, on consideration, and as an arrangement best for all parties, that an extension to the electoral division of Galway would be the best course to adopt.

141. In view of that, what would you suggest about the wards. At present we know there are four wards, would you add on the additional district to each ward?—Yes, I would. I would, so to speak, draw the wards out and extend them to catch the electoral division.

142. Mr. Rathington.—In fact you would make them coterminous with the poor law wards?—Yes. And I may add that we would then get a better election body for the Town Commissioners, and have every prospect of having our board represented by men of influence; and there would be a better electing class.

143. Do you think that everything within the electoral division should be brought in on the same terms as the present municipality?—Yes.

144. Whereas if you extended the boundary four or five miles you would have to get into this question of differential rate?—Yes; and I would not be in favour of that at all. I think the great thing would be to secure a boundary coterminous with some other recognised boundary; and so I would extend the wards outside to meet the electoral division.

Major Lynch, J.P., examined.

145. I would take the liberty of reading a letter I wrote to Captain O'Hara:—

"[illegible], 14th February, 1876.

"My dear O'Hara,—I have carefully read over the memorial to the Local Government Board (Ireland), which is to be considered by the Town Commissioners at their meeting to-day, and am of opinion it would not be for the advantage of either the owner or occupier of property in the county of the town, that it should be placed under the control and jurisdiction of the Town Commissioners.

"I quite agree that the [illegible] [illegible] at present [illegible], are [illegible] and [illegible], but I consider that [illegible] be [illegible] removed, by [illegible] to [illegible] the county of the town [illegible] into the county, and [illegible] portion of the [illegible] of [illegible], [illegible], and [illegible]. That would [illegible] [illegible] the [illegible] in the [illegible] [illegible] of which they at present complain.

"As a large occupier and ratepayer in the county of the town, [illegible] [illegible] [illegible] [illegible] from the memorial, as at present framed, [illegible] by your stating my views to the Board. [illegible] [illegible] [illegible] [illegible].

"Very truly yours,

"[illegible] Lynch.

"To Captain O'Hara, Chairman of Town Commissioners, Galway."

146. Chairman.—Do you see any reason since then to change your mind?—No.

147. Would you recommend an inclusion to the electoral division?—No; I would not like to see any extension from what the boundaries are at present.

148. Mr. Cotton.—Would you like to see things diminished?—Yes; if possible. The taxation is increasing every day through the action of the present Town Commissioners, and it affects occupiers of [illegible] [illegible] inside and outside the [illegible], to a considerable extent. This taxation will be still further increased by the [illegible] —— [illegible]

149. Mr. Rathington.—That is levied by the Grand Jury.

150. Major Lynch.—Those [illegible] outside the present jurisdiction of the Town Commissioners to whom I have spoken, would decidedly not wish to be put under that body—they [illegible] property [illegible] of [illegible].

151. Mr. Cotton.—Would they object to being put into the county at large?—No; I don't think so. I [illegible] [illegible] the rates for 1876 for three baronies [illegible]:—[illegible], [illegible]; [illegible], [illegible]; and [illegible] [illegible]. I was [illegible] of [illegible] who [illegible] in the minority on the Town Board, and at the Grand Jury, against the resolution. I could give instances in my own case [illegible] [illegible] [illegible] [illegible] how the jurisdiction of the Town Commissioners [illegible] and how they [illegible] the [illegible] [illegible] on them.

152. Chairman.—Bearing in mind that we would think of having a circle like that, which now exists, as the boundary, and having regard to the difficulty of getting a satisfactory and well-defined boundary, what would you say to an inclusion of the electoral division of Galway?—I would not have it.

153. What alteration then would you suggest?—There is a [illegible] [illegible] of [illegible] [illegible] [illegible]. [illegible] would be [illegible] the Town Commissioners of so much power as possible. I may give [illegible] of the way they act. [illegible] [illegible] were [illegible] by the Local Government. [illegible] [illegible], [illegible] [illegible], I would [illegible] [illegible] [illegible] to [illegible], Mr. Doherty [illegible] an estimate and tender [illegible] was considered by the town engineer [illegible] to [illegible] [illegible] works, as a fair estimate. [illegible] there was another contractor who [illegible] [illegible] [illegible], but he was not a man bearing the same high [illegible]. We [illegible] [illegible] [illegible] that he should not get the contract, but the Town Commissioners [illegible] the well [illegible] portion of their body, and the result was that they [illegible] "[illegible]" for a contractor who offered an [illegible] which our legal advisers told us [illegible] [illegible]. This contractor took [illegible] of the work, did the lightest part, and when it came to the [illegible] part of it he threw it up, and we are [illegible] in a law suit.

154. Chairman.—What was the difference between the two estimates, Mr. Doherty's and the other?—£1,[illegible] I think.

155. Mr. Ferdinand.—It is right to state that there was only a majority of one against Mr. [illegible].

156. Chairman.—How much of your property is within the two mile radius at present?—If the boundary was extended to the new area, I would be all inside, at present half is in and half out. These [illegible] would [illegible] under the Town Commissioners. They say their salaries are [illegible] and [illegible] of the efficiency of the officials. There is a lavish expenditure prevailing.

157. Captain O'Hara says that if the boundary were extended to the present electoral division of Galway you would be likely to get in a class of municipal representatives that would improve the town. More [illegible] we felt it incumbent on us to get rid of that circular line, and I may tell you we would like to get some [illegible] or well defined boundary and not an imaginary line, could you suggest a better [illegible] defining it. The ratepayers know the present two miles to a inch. It is a [illegible] boundary so far as that is concerned. It has been working for years in Galway. The original boundary was one mile, and in '53 it was increased to two miles.

158. How was it defined originally?—By an imaginary line of one mile.

159. Was it not under the Municipal Corporation Act of 1840?—No, a special Act. It was one mile up to '53, and it was only two years ago that it was pointed out we had no right to leave the town Grand Jury for local purposes, and it was only recently that two miles have been under the town Grand Jury.

160. Suppose we felt obliged to go on all outside the present boundary, what would you say to the electoral division?—It would be a great injustice in my opinion. The proposition is to take in the entire county of the town.

161. As far as the electoral division of Galway is concerned if there is to be any extension, would that [illegible] he did [illegible] would be sorry to see it included, I would have it thrown into the county. The ratepayers would be all [illegible] if the extension took place, and we would be [illegible]. The county Grand Jury will keep the expenditure down to a minimum. They will look very sharply after their county surveyor. They dismissed one county surveyor under a sealed order, and they have another now.

162. Bearing in mind, that according to the express opinion of the Select Committees municipal towns should be made coterminous with electoral divisions, what objection would you see in taking in the electoral division of Galway if there is to be any extension?—I hope you won't do it. I hope I won't see the day when it is done.

163. Mr. Ferdinand.—He has no confidence in the administration of the Town Commissioners.

164. Chairman.—It is that we could recommend that there be a check upon them as suggested, if they are to be under the Grand Jury.

165. Mr. [illegible].—Don't you think your property outside derives advantage from its proximity to the town?—Well, indeed, as a matter of fact, I often wished it to be four miles outside. I can only repeat that the greatest possible dissatisfaction would arise from giving an extended jurisdiction to the Town Commissioners.

166. Captain O'Hara.—I wish to say a word as to the Town Commissioners. I have been Chairman for some time and have been here for a great many years a member of the Town Board, and I object to hear the statements made by a gentleman in Major Lynch's position about that Board. He is a member of the Board and there are other gentlemen of his position on it, and if they attended the meetings, it would in all probability infuse a better spirit into it. But I regret to say, that though I as Chairman attend those meetings, Major Lynch and those other gentlemen to whom I allude do not come there and give me that support to which I am entitled as Chairman.

Galway.
[illegible]
[illegible]

Mr. Lewis L. Ferdinand examined.

Mr. Lewis L. Ferdinand.

167. Chairman.—Are you a member of the Town Commissioners?—Yes.

168. What is your view on the question of extension?—My view is in favour of it. I voted for it at the Grand Jury and at the meeting of the Town Commissioners. I was of opinion that the county of the town should be coterminous with the municipal boundary. It would go in for a differential rating. I would not charge the persons outside two miles the same rate as within them. It became a question of dispute, what area would be included under the jurisdiction of the burial board for the expenditure of the £8,000 for the new cemetery. It became a question of debate at the Board of Guardians what area should be included for the purposes of taxation. The most influential members of the board decided by a large majority that the electoral divisions of Barna, [illegible], Ballinacourty, and Galway should constitute the district to be taxed for the construction of this cemetery, involving an expenditure of £8,000. Well that will continue the [illegible], for the Local Government Order has the effect of an Act of Parliament. If you do include the portion of Ballinacourty and [illegible], so as to make the burial board area the municipal area, and have uniformity of taxation, it is only four miles and a half (Irish) from St. Nicholas's. That arrangement agrees with the recommendation of the Town Commissioners and the county of the town Grand Jury, and also of the Board of Guardians in deciding the area of taxation for the new burial board.

169. Is that four and a half miles outside the present boundary?—No; Mr. Somerville tells me the [illegible] [illegible] to the limit of [illegible] and Ballinacourty is only four miles and a half. That is the second [illegible] of the question.

170. What will the landlords say to it?—I don't know. I think they are very well off. There are very good landlords there. If a certain district is suitable for burial purposes, I think it ought to be regarded as satisfactory for municipal. Major Lynch, at the Board of Guardians, voted for those [illegible] being included, and he refused, for a time, as Chairman of the Board of Guardians, to sign a [illegible], which would relieve Barna from being included in the district.

171. **Major Lynch.—That is simply for burial purposes.**

172. Chairman.—The question is how to give that district the benefit of sewerage, and so on.

173. Mr. Ferdinand.—They have the benefit of it [illegible] the people within the proposed boundary derive advantage—considerable advantage—from their proximity to the town of Galway. The sewerage works may be considered for the town proper, and that sewerage runs only about within two miles.

174. Would you make them pay the public water rate?—That is [illegible] in this way. If any district convenient to Galway could show there was a [illegible] of 10 per cent., it would get the supply [illegible] as they do at [illegible]. In my opinion, the larger the area the more important the municipality, and that I think is an important consideration in this matter. I think the [illegible] of the Grand Jury is [illegible].

175. Why would you [illegible] the management of the main drainage, and not get these people under the liability of paying their share of keeping up the lamps—lighting and [illegible] and domestic water supply, and so on?—In some towns that would be right, but there are occasional [illegible] for lighting purposes. The water [illegible] to where it will pay 10 per cent.

176. Do not the people outside derive material advantage from having in their proximity, and constantly using, a healthy town?—Yes, they do, no doubt. A resolution was deliberately passed by the

Grand Jury, and I would adhere to that, that the county of the town, this ring or outside circle, should be included within the municipal area, and be subject to the Town Commissioners. They adopted at that time a resolution that those taxes should not extend beyond the present municipal area. I would keep faith to that.

177. Yes, but it would be very simple to have a differential rate over that extended area?—Well, as to taxation, I would leave that to yourselves.

178. Mr. *Bellington*.—Mr. *Ferdinand* is aware that if you extend the rating to four miles say, you lessen the present taxes?

179. Mr. *Ferdinand*. Yes, you confer a benefit on the tenant farmers, and that is the object of the legislature. I am only saying I would keep to what I voted for. As it appears to be the instructions of the Parliamentary Committee to this Commission to have the municipal and electoral boundaries coterminous, I would recommend that the entire electoral divisions of Galway, Barna, Cloughlowera, and Ballintemple, should be included within the municipal area. Already the Barna electoral division is entirely within the county of the town. A portion of Cloughlowera and a portion of Ballintemple are also within the Parliamentary borough. Including the areas of these electoral divisions within the municipal area would slightly increase the boundaries of the Parliamentary borough, and would satisfy the resolutions of the Town Commissioners and the Grand Jury. My suggestion as to the extension of the municipal area meets exactly the suggestion of the Parliamentary Committee. It is simply suggested that, as far as possible, electoral divisions and municipal areas should be coterminous, as has been explained, and my suggestion would have the advantage of complying with the resolutions of the Grand Jury and the Town Board. It would be an advantage to the tenantry in the rural districts, as the landlords will have to pay half the Grand Jury cess, and it would preserve for us what we consider of very great moment—the importance of our Parliamentary borough. Galway is the second largest county in Ireland, and it would not matter very much to take such a small slice of it to add to the county of the town.

180. CHAIRMAN.—That would be pushing the municipal area to a distance of six miles from the centre of the town?—No, it would be only extending the municipal area four miles, and already it extends two miles, and includes a large rural population. It would not matter much to make a slight increase, and it would add to the importance of the municipality. The Town Council would then be the Grand Jury, and the separate jurisdiction of the borough for judicial and legal purposes would be maintained. I hope you will adopt these suggestions or something similar, as it is the only change that fully and fairly would meet the case, and be satisfactory to all parties.

181. Mr. *James Davis*, T.C.—I wish just to say one word with reference to an observation of Major Lynch. I am sorry he is not here now, but he charges the Town Commissioners with doubling salaries, reckless expenditure, and so on. Now, as to doubling the salaries of officers there is absolutely no instance of that except in the case of the county surveyor.

182. CHAIRMAN.—How much had he when his salary was increased?—£50, and at that time he had nothing to do with looking after the roads. The Grand Jury at that time kept the roads in order, and when they were deprived of that he got it to do, and his salary was increased.

183. What do you say on the general question of extension?—I would agree with Captain O'Hara.

184. That is you would be in favour of adopting the electoral division?—Yes.

Mr. RICHARD N. SOMERVILLE, T.C., examined.

185. CHAIRMAN.—What is your view regarding the extension?—I must say, with reference to what has been said here by Major Lynch, that I don't at all agree with an opinion of what is said by those gentlemen who run down the Commissioners. There are gentlemen who attend constantly and carefully to the affairs of the town, and it is hardly fair that they should be so spoken of by gentlemen who rarely attend. I may say that no more conscientious men could be found than those who discharge the business of the Commissioners. They are a large majority of the Grand Jury. They came to the resolution that it would be advisable to extend the area to the county of the town. It was considered if the limits were continued within the present borough we would lose one of our members. We found there was to be a readjustment of the county generally. It was then agreed by the Town Board to extend the area to the county of the town. It would considerably relieve the ratepayers of the county of the town.

186. Would you make them pay the same rate as the people in the heart of the town?—I think it was suggested they should be relieved of the lower rate, and I think something else which would not amount to a very large sum. Whatever the Town Board agreed to, I would adhere to.

187. Would you say that contiguity to the town makes those places more valuable?—Yes.

188. Mr. *Bellington*.—And we lessen their taxation by extending the boundary.

189. In no part of Ireland are we asked to extend the boundary more than two miles or two miles and a half—is there anything exceptional in the case of Galway to induce you to say we should go from six to twelve miles?—Well, the county of the town now forms a distinct body, and they are charged with heavy expenses which they would be ultimately relieved of.

[The inquiry terminated.]

FETHARD.—AUGUST 15TH, 1879.

(Before Mr. H. A. ROBINSON.)

Mr. MICHAEL MURPHY examined.

1. What position do you hold in Fethard?—I am Town Clerk.

2. How long have you been Town Clerk?—For seven years.

3. Under what Act is the town?—The 9th Geo IV., cap. 82.

4. Have you ever entertained any idea of adopting the Towns Improvement Act, 1854?—No.

5. When was the town constituted?—On the 27th October, 1840.

6. Have the boundaries since been altered or amended in any way?—No.

7. Does the boundary include whole townlands or does it cut townlands?—In some instances it cuts them.

8. How many townlands are wholly and how many in part included?—It cuts [illegible], [illegible] and Fethard.

9. But no townland is wholly included?—No, except the Liberties.

10. What is the population of the town?—2,105.

11. Did the population in 1871 show any increase on the population of 1861?—No.

12. Do you anticipate that the population of 1881 will show an increase?—Yes.

13. Can you give me the area of the municipal boundary?—I could not define it, on account of the way it runs.

14. Give me the total valuation?—For municipal purposes, £[illegible].

15. Is the town wholly within the Fethard electoral division?—Yes.

16. Can you tell me how far the north of that electoral division extends?—To [illegible].

17. How far is that?—About an English mile and a quarter. The electoral division extends about two miles on the south, from the centre of the town; a mile and a quarter on the [illegible]; about three miles west; and a mile and a quarter east.

18. Would the municipal boundary, taking the centre of the town, give you a radius of half a mile all round?—Yes.

19. Which is the most remote point of the boundary on the north?—The [illegible], which is about half a mile; on the south-west to [illegible] Bridge, about the same distance; on the east it only extends to the limits of the [illegible] at [illegible] Bridge; and on the west it extends a little under a quarter of a mile.

20. That is from the main street?—Yes.

21. You marked the boundary on the map I have here?—Yes.

22. What authority had you for marking this boundary?—I got the information from the old books. This is a copy of the resolution adopted in 1840, and these are the boundaries which exist now. (reads resolution)—

"Moved by Mr. [illegible], seconded by Mr. William [illegible], that the provisions of the Act, 9 Geo IV., Cap 82, be [illegible] the limits and boundaries of said town or borough be extended as far as [illegible] Bridge on the [illegible] road, [illegible] to William [illegible] on the [illegible] road, to the [illegible] on the [illegible] road, to the [illegible] house on the [illegible], and to the [illegible] as far as [illegible] Bridge; and from [illegible] Dowling's kiln, on the [illegible], to Patrick Dempsey's forge, from the bridge [illegible] gate to the house of [illegible], including Main-street, [illegible] and Abbey-street. Carried unanimously."

23. There are no rates for municipal purposes?—No.

24. How many [illegible] have you?—Thirteen.

25. You have never made any rate?—No.

26. You have property vested in you?—Yes.

27. How did you acquire it?—We have it for hundreds of years.

28. What income does it bring in?—About £140, [illegible].

29. What is the nature of it?—Tolls and customs, and houses, and lands.

30. Tolls and customs in the market house?—Yes.

31. As far as you can see there is no likelihood of your ever being obliged to strike a municipal rate?—No.

32. You have sufficient funds for all purposes?—Yes.

33. Are there any improvements you are prevented from carrying out through want of funds?—No.

34. Have the Commissioners considered the question of extending the [illegible] authority?—No.

35. Is the sanitary work of the town carried on by the [illegible] and the Commissioners?—Things are slowly done. If you report a thing it would be done two years afterwards.

36. When these notices were sent down were they considered at a special meeting of the Commissioners, or were they considered at an ordinary meeting?—There was no meeting at all.

37. You considered the question yourself?—Yes.

38. And they were not submitted to the Board?—No. The clerk was ill, and I answered them.

39. And it is the opinion of your Board no extension is required?—Yes.

40. And the principal reason that prompted you to come to that conclusion is, that if you brought in any body they would be getting all the advantage of the town property, and be paying no rates towards the expenditure?—Yes.

41. Have you ever heard any desire on the part of those outside to be included in the boundary?—No.

Fethard, Aug. [illegible], 18[illegible].

Mr. Michael Murphy.

Mr. John M'[illegible] examined.

Mr. John M'[illegible].

41. You are a Commissioner?—I am.

42. And have been for how long?—For something like twenty-five years.

43. How long have you been Chairman of the board?—I am not Chairman at present, but I have been Chairman off and on three times.

44. You are well acquainted with the town?—Yes.

45. And you think under the peculiar circumstances under which the town is situated there would be no advantage derived from having a larger area for taxation?—None whatever. We have £[illegible] a year to our credit over all our expenses.

46. Are you acquainted with the electoral division of Fethard?—I am.

47. Do you know how far it extends out from the town?—I do not, but it goes a long way.

48. The Parliamentary Committee have recommended that, wherever it is possible, the municipal and electoral division boundaries should be made coterminous—I suppose I may take it, that, in your opinion, that recommendation would not apply to Fethard?—It would not.

49. You would be bringing in a large arable district and giving them no advantages?—No advantage.

50. This is a market town?—No; we have only the monthly fair.

51. And the people from the centre of the electoral division come in and make use of the town for all purposes?—Yes.

52. It is of considerable advantage to them that the town should be well kept by the Commissioners?—Yes.

53. But inasmuch as there is no rate they would have to pay nothing towards the town expenses and improvements?—No.

54. And [illegible]?—No.

55. Would the Commissioners desire to have the sanitary jurisdiction transferred to them?—I think it might be well, I am a guardian myself.

56. Do you attend the Board meetings?—I do occasionally. I and the sanitary officer have charge of the pumps and other such nuisances that have to be remedied, and if the work was under the Commissioners they would have more power to have it quickly done.

57. Previous to the passing of the Sanitary Acts is it your opinion that the Commissioners managed the work better themselves?—Yes. But it is a benefit to the Commissioners to have it under the Poor Law Guardians because the division has to pay for the repair of our pumps and the cleansing of the streams, whereas if it was otherwise, and the works were in the hands of the Commissioners, we would have to pay for the repairs of our pumps, and so on. In that way it has saved a good deal of money to the corporation.

58. The rate when struck by the Poor Law Guardians is half on the tenant and half on the landlord, but if any outside district is brought into the municipality, the rate would fall entirely on the tenant?—Yes.

FETHARD.
Aug. 15, 1879.
Mr. John M'Carthy.

59. Would that influence your opinion in any way?—Yes.

60. Do you think the roads would be better managed by you than by the Grand Jury?—We have nothing whatever to do with the roads.

61. But if you got a transfer of the powers from the Grand Jury, do you think would you manage the roads better yourselves?—I think we would be better off as we are.

62. It is your opinion that the entire of the administration would be better managed in your own hands?—I say as far as the roads are concerned it would be better to leave it to the Grand Jury.

63. Do you think the work would be better done under an undivided authority?—I think it would be. If we had control of the streets ourselves it would be better, in some parts they are very badly attended to. If we had the power to get the roads repaired, we would have them better done. However that might bring additional tax upon us.

64. Do you foresee any likelihood of any municipal rate being struck?—No.

65. Is the property increasing in value?—I think it is rather diminishing—I am sorry to say so.

66. Has it decreased to such an extent that in future you will be obliged, in order to carry on the work of the town, to strike a rate?—No; because we have a standing property, which we have for ever, worth £130 a year. Then we have tolls and customs, which bring in £35 or £40 a year. This income from the tolls and customs pays our officers and the lighting as well as our town sergeant. We light our town very well in the winter time.

67. What is the expenditure of the town?—The gross expenditure was about £70 or £80 a year; but sometimes our expenditure has been more than at other times.

68. What is your income?—Our income is about £140 a year on the average, and after payment of the collectors' fees, the expense of lighting, and all the other town works, we generally have about £20 a year to spare.

69. However I may take it you are in affluent circumstances?—Yes.

Mr. Laurence Byrne.

Mr. Laurence Byrne continued.

70. You are Chairman of the Town Commissioners?—Yes.

71. And have been since when?—Since July.

72. You are a resident in Fethard?—Yes; and have been resident here for sometime.

73. Are you one of the Commissioners since 1840?—Yes; and I became Chairman in July last. I was once Chairman before.

74. What had the Commissioners in view when they adopted the present boundary?—I could not say.

75. They put the matter into the hands of the surveyor and he defined the boundary?—Yes.

76. Is the town well lighted?—Yes.

77. And have you a good water supply?—Yes.

78. Do the people from the adjoining districts come in here to attend school?—Yes.

79. Does the town in any direction extend outside the municipal boundary?—No.

81. Is there a tendency shown to extend the town more in one direction than another?—No.

82. Are there buildings going on in any part of the town?—No.

83. The town is at a stand still?—Yes.

84. But you think it has an increasing population?—Yes.

85. And, so far as you see, there is no probability of the Commissioners being obliged to strike a rate?—No. I don't think we will ever have occasion to strike a rate.

86. Are you acquainted with the electoral division?—I am.

87. Do you coincide with the last witness that it would be impossible to adopt the electoral division as the municipal boundary?—I do.

88. You have sufficient funds at present for all purposes?—Yes.

89. And if you had a larger income there are no improvements to which you would specially apply it?—If we had a larger income we could make a good many improvements in the town.

90. Has the advisability of levying a rate for that purpose ever struck you?—Yes. I said we would be better if we had some provision for recreation—some nice walks, and something in that way.

91. And if you were to strike such a rate would it be desirable to have a larger area over which to spread it?—Yes, if we had to strike it.

92. Would you in that event see any objection to including the entire of the townlands of Fethard, Moneypark, and Spitalfields?—I would include them if we had to strike a rate.

93. Is the town lit up to the cottage limits?—Yes.

94. With gas?—No; paraffin.

95. Does it give good light?—Yes; we have twenty-seven lamps.

96. You take them down in the summer time?—Yes.

97. Do you think it would be desirable to have the sanitary jurisdiction in your own hands?—It would be more satisfactorily carried out.

98. You are on the spot; the guardians are eight miles away?—Yes; and if there was a pump to be repaired there is delay and water is the first thing we should look to for the public good. Very often the pumps are long out of order before we can get them done. Mr. M'Carthy is very good and does what he can for us, and but for him there would be more delay.

99. You think these matters would be more efficiently carried out by yourselves?—Yes.

100. Do you think would the roads be better managed?—I don't know.

101. Do you consider the Grand Jury give full value accommodation with the rates you pay?—They do; that is my opinion.

102. And have they better appliances for carrying out the work than you have yourselves?—I think so.

103. Are you in favour of the broad principle that the entire jurisdiction should be vested in one undivided authority?—It is my opinion it would be better to have the work carried on under one body.

104. The entire area of those townlands which you would include is 40 acres for Moneypark, and 51 acres for Spitalfields, and there is only a very small portion of them at present in the boundary?—Yes very small.

105. How many acres of each of those townlands are in the town?—I think there are only about 4. There is no house on them.

106. If you were to bring in the entire of those two townlands, and the portion of Fethard that is outside the town boundary, it would give an increased area of about 280 acres?—Yes; and if there was any necessity for striking a rate in future that would be the increase.

Mr. Murphy, Town Clerk, recalled.

Fethard, Aug. 1879. Mr. Murphy.

107. The poor rate in 1874 was 1s. 8d. and the county cess 10½d.; in 1875 the poor rate was 2s. 3d., and the county cess 10½d.; in 1876 the poor rate was 2s. 3d., and the county cess 11d.; in 1877 the poor rate was 2s., and the county cess 10½d., and in 1878 the poor rate was 2s. 2d., and the county cess 10½d. The poor rate mentioned is for each year, but the county cess mentioned is for half a year.

108. Of this poor rate how much was for sanitary purposes—was there any special rate?—Yes; 6d. in the pound.

109. When was that?—I don't remember. It is about 4 years ago. It was on account of sewers in the town.

110. What division was it struck on?—On the electoral division of Fethard.

111. On the entire district?—Yes.

112. Was there any other special rate?—Yes; 1d.

113. And that was assessed on the entire electoral division also?—Yes.

Mr. Patrick Hogan examined.

Mr. Patrick Hogan.

114. Are you a Town Commissioner?—Yes.

115. And have been so for some time?—Only for a short time.

116. You have heard the evidence of the Chairman and Mr. M'Carthy?—Yes.

117. And you coincide with them that there is no advantage in having the boundary extended much?—I do.

118. If you had an extended area the land brought in would be entirely arable?—Yes.

119. You think also that the town would be better managed under one undivided authority?—I think so.

120. Would the work the Grand Jury and the Poor Law Guardians now do be better managed?—Yes; I think so.

121. Do you foresee any likelihood of there being any necessity for levying a municipal rate?—I don't think so.

122. At present, does the diminution in the tolls arise from the bad state of the country?—I can't say, for I have only come in as a new Commissioner.

123. Mr. Byrne (Chairman, Town Commissioners).—I think the tolls and customs are paying as much now as four or five years ago, but they were higher eight or ten years ago. They are about stationary now.

124. Do you let those tolls out?—Yes; we let them yearly.

125. Who is the present lessee?—A man named Patrick Dunney.

126. Do you exercise supervision over them in any way?—The Commissioners do; if there is a complaint made we see after it.

Mr. James Tierney examined.

Mr. James Tierney.

127. You are Receiver for the Town Commissioners?—Yes; and have been for thirty-one years.

128. I hear that you are of opinion that if the sanitary matters were transferred to the Commissioners, there would be no possibility of their recovering rates for the work?—I know I could not. I have interest enough to collect from the people there, and only for me it is very little rates would be got from some of them; but I have an influence over them.

129. If the sanitary work was transferred to the Commissioners, you think there would be no advantage gained?—We would have no chance if the sanitary work was in our hands. Who have it at present? Isn't it the dispensary?

Mr. Murphy.—Yes.

Witness.—Then let them keep it.

The inquiry closed.

KEADY.—SEPTEMBER 9TH, 1879.

(Before Mr. Exham, Q.C., Chairman.)

Mr. Edward Quinn examined.

Keady, Sept. 9, 1879. Mr. Edward Quinn.

1. Chairman.—You are the Town Clerk of Keady?—I am.

2. It is under the Towns Improvement Act of 1854 since the 5th of January, 1863?—Yes.

3. Were all the clauses of the Act adopted?—I believe so.

4. Were the boundaries fixed then?—Yes. That is the date of the Lord Lieutenant's approval of the boundary.

5. Has the boundary been changed since?—No.

6. What is the area within the present boundary?—I cannot give you that. I cannot tell the number of acres inside the boundary, but the valuation of land inside the boundary is £2,596 5s. made up of £204 15s. for the land inside the boundary, and the rest for buildings.

7. What is the population?—1,815 according to the last census of 1871.

8. Is it increasing or not?—Well, I should say it was increasing up to the last year or so, but I don't think it has been increasing since. Dulness of trade and such things has prevented that.

9. There are no wards here?—No.

10. How many Town Commissioners are there?—Nine.

11. In what electoral division is the town of Keady?—Keady and Crossmore.

12. The town of Keady embraces parts of five townlands?—Yes. Two in Crossmore and three in Keady.

13. I see your municipal rates for the last five years have been up to their maximum?—Yes, sir.

14. Your poor rate has been 7d. in the pound for the last three years and 6d. in the pound for the two previous years?—Yes, with the addition last year of a special water rate of 1d. added to the 6d. in Keady and Crossmore electoral divisions—at least in the parts assessed for the water tax.

15. And your county rate has been increasing very much?—No, sir; there was a little error made in the last two years. In the year 1878 it was 1s. 9d.; in 1877 1s. 8d.; in 1876 1s. 7d.; in 1875 1s. 6½d.; and 1874 1s. 4½d. These are the correct figures. The county cess for this year 1879 is 1s. 6d.—1s. last March and 6d. the July one—making 1s. 6d.—it was twice increased.

16. When did you get a water supply here?—About three or four years ago.

17. Because it was last year your first rate was struck?—But then there were a few years preparatory to the getting of it.

19. What debts do you owe here?—The Commissioners owed last year to the Northern Bank about £35.

20. I don't mean the balance due to the bank, but what debts do the Commissioners owe—for instance, you must have borrowed money for the water supply?—We are not the sanitary authority. I wish we were, for then we would not have water at the price we have to pay for it.

21. Was there a meeting of the Town Commissioners to consider this question of the extension of the boundary?—There was; and here is a copy of the Commissioners' order, calling a public meeting, which was held on the 21st of last February, and here are the minutes recorded in the Commissioners' books as the result of that meeting.

22. Let me have the resolution passed at that meeting. Was it a meeting numerously attended?—There were nearly 300 ratepayers present, who live both inside and outside the boundary—persons threatened to be affected both inside and outside the boundary. At that meeting the following resolution was unanimously passed:—

"That it is the opinion of this meeting that the town boundary should not be extended."

23. Are you able to say that the Commissioners as a body are unanimously of the same opinion?—They are unanimously against any extension.

24. Within a mile of your present boundary are there any gentlemen's seats, or any houses of importance?—Well, I should say not, with the exception of old Mr. Kirk's house and Mr. M'Keown's who is represented here. That house is in the boundary. Within a mile outside the boundary there is no house, I think.

25. Are there any small farmers' houses within that distance?—Yes; there is an extension of the Annvale Works outside, just at the end of our boundary here. There are a good many small houses on the land that is just outside, but not many farmhouses.

26. What description of houses are those close on the boundary?—Very good; built by the late Mr. Kirk. Some of them very good for labouring men, set at about 1s. 6d. a week, and some a little better than that. They are not within the boundary.

27. If they were brought within the boundary would they be valued high enough to be ratepayers?—I do not think there are more than five or six that would get a rate. Something about £3 10s. is the valuation of most of them. There are three or four on the other side of the road of £5 valuation.

28. Can you say whether land close to the town, and within a mile of the present boundary, is of exceptionally high value on account of its proximity to the town?—I don't think it is here.

29. You don't think it brings more than a mile further off?—I should say it would yield a little better rent convenient to the town. I am only judging that from the land in the town and that a little farther out, but convenient to the boundary at present. You might get 10s. an acre more for land convenient to the boundary than you would if it was further out. What way other land would be affected I cannot say.

30. Is there any, and if so, what increase in the value of the land for any distance outside the present boundary, on account of its proximity to the town of Keady—what would you say?—Well, you know it is as near it now as it ever was, and I don't think if you were to bring it into the boundary that that would increase its value; it would, in my opinion, instead of increasing its value rather deteriorate it.

31. But is it to the landlord and tenant more valuable on account of being so close to the town—taking the rent and value of land within a mile of the town and land two miles off?—I don't think it is, because at the same time they would have to pay higher rates than they would in the country. I don't think it is a bit more valuable.

32. Do you mean to say that if it was let tomorrow that it would not bring more rent, being so close to the town, than land four or five miles off—taking the same quality of land exactly?—I cannot give an opinion on that; I have never considered it.

33. I see you are at the maximum taxation, and you owe some money to the bank? Yes.

34. The question is, if the land outside is a little more valuable, as it appears to be in all the small towns in Ireland, whether the people who use the town so much, and get from the town certain advantages, should not contribute something towards the taxation of that town?—I think so far as that is concerned that if they had to pay, the Town Commissioners could not give them any value for the money they would pay; and I think it would be unjust to them at the present moment. We are only too happy to see them coming into the town to make use of the market and to use, as they do considerably, the town shops. We don't want them to go to Armagh, and as a proof of that the Town Commissioners have reduced the rates to 10d. We are quite prepared, and only too happy, as I said before, to see them come here, and we give them every accommodation to bring in their butter and dispose of it at our market. The reason we were at our maximum rate for the last two years is this, we spent within the last five or six years £519 17s. 11d. for the flagging of the town. We have flagged nearly nine-tenths of the town, and out of the sum I have named we received half from the Grand Jury, £273 15s., leaving the Commissioners to expend out of the rates the sum of £273 15s., which in six years was an average of £45 15s., which was nearly half of their income devoted to that one purpose alone. That is the cause of our rates being so high, and now that we have our debt reduced, I don't mind a small balance due to the bank, the Town Commissioners are taking advantage of that reduction to levy this year a 10d. rate, and by so doing to aid those who have been sorely taxed for water, and to reduce our rates, so that the ratepayers may meet the extraordinary expenditure of the water rate.

35. Is the letting value of land near the town more than the same quality of land two or three miles off?—Really there is very little of it let on account of its being occupied by humble farmers, and there are very few instances where occasions have arisen that we could see the value of it. It is nearly all occupied by small farmers and people working about the mills, and as there are only slight changes of occupancy from year to year, we have not many chances of knowing the value.

35. Do the people living outside the town wish to be brought in?—Certainly not. The Town Commissioners and ratepayers here are anxious to pay for everything, and to afford accommodation in markets and everything of that sort out of the rates under the Act, and they want no extra taxation, or taking power of extending the boundary; for they think they have sufficient to look after.

36. Do the people use the markets here?—Yes, and they pay the usual tolls. There is an arrangement by which we have the markets from the representatives of the late Mr. Kirk, and we pay the rent for them to Mr. M'Keown, and we let them again to two crane-masters who levy the tolls on hay, straw, and all such things as are liable to the dues, and I may add that the amount we derive from that arrangement just pays itself, it is neither an injury of a shilling to the rates, nor a benefit. It is nearly equal; what we get from all sources just pays Mr. M'Keown his rent and we have not a margin of five shillings when all is settled.

37. Do you light the town with gas?—Yes, sir.

38. Is that paid for too?—Yes, out of our rate. We get it from the gas company.

39. Is there any building going on outside the town?—No.

40. Have the Town Commissioners authorised you as their Town Clerk to express their unanimous opinion as you have done?—Yes, they are all of opinion that an extension would be undesirable—unanimously so.

Mr. William M'Kean examined.

Armagh. 26th June 1877. Mr. William M'Kean.

40. You are the agent for the Kenly estate?—I am. The Kenly estate extends from [illegible] and a half to two miles around the town.

41. Are the Kirk family owners of the land there?—Yes, and they hold it under Trinity College; and it is all set, or very nearly all, in grants of perpetuity.

42. In the land immediately outside the present boundary set in the same way?—Yes. There are only two farms, I think, here in Drumminanagh, which is the road to Tynan side away, that are not granted.

43. Speaking for the owners of the estate, do you think there would be any advantage to the town or the people outside by having this [illegible] extended?—I don't think there would, and I don't think that any one wishes for it.

44. Is there, in your opinion, any greater value in the land within a mile of the town as contradistinguished from land two and three miles away?—To be sure, all land near towns is more valuable than that further off. The nearer the boundary is, the better; but by increasing the boundary that would not increase the value of it.

45. It would not increase the value of it, it is true, but the thing is whether land increased more while the town being close to the town should not pay something towards keeping the town up, that is the principle on which it is sought in all the towns in this act?—If the extension had been made before the waterwork was started, it would have been for the benefit of all parties, but these are standards set all very long, and there are people living nearly two miles off who pay water rate, but get no advantage from it in the slightest degree.

46. Is everyone within a certain distance of the boundary of the town made to pay for the water?—Yes, because these are [illegible] are obliged to pay; but they are all widows and are living [illegible].

47. I have nothing to say to that, however. The principle is stated. In most towns, as far as my knowledge is, to be, that it tends to [illegible] and [illegible] or any other value [illegible] from their proximity to the town, the owners and occupiers of the land should contribute something to the expenses of the town, because where the land is made more valuable by having the town so [illegible], and where the occupiers travel [illegible] through the streets and roads of the town, the occupiers of the lands have a [illegible] to contribute towards the rates?—Well, yes, but the increase would be very little on the land. They now only pay one-fourth.

48. Under the 63rd section of the Towns Improvement Act, arable land is only rated at one-fourth, and these lands, if they were brought in, would only pay according to the law [illegible] of [illegible] one-fourth on the valuation towards the town rate. Then the proportion in that that again should be divided—half being paid on the landlord and half on the tenant, because the former gets a higher rent from the land on account of its proximity to the town, and the tenant, in respect of his occupation of the land, gets the use of the streets and roads of the town, so that you see if the maximum rate was 1s. on the town, then it would be 3d. on the land, one-half of that would come from the tenant, and half from the landlord. It would be very little on the [illegible], while the town would get the benefit, whatever it would be of the valuation of the [illegible] area of a mile around the town?—We didn't know that it was proposed the landlord would have to pay half.

49. What would your view be if an extension was carried out under the circumstances I have described?—If it was done so fairly, and that arrangement carried out, it would be very wise to do so.

50. You think it would be a wise thing to do if that was carried out?—I think it would.

Mr. Edward Quinn, Town Clerk, re-examined.

Mr. Edward Quinn.

51. Chairman.—Have the Commissioners considered the question in the light in which I have just put it?—They have considered it in the [illegible] point of [illegible], and they would object to the parties outside paying even a farthing.

52. What is their reason for coming to that view?—They think that if the taxation would only be 1½d. in the pound, it would be unjust to charge them more. What would they have to give them as an equivalent?

53. They give them the town well lighted, well [illegible], and having all the advantages of the things here while the shopkeepers are obliged to pay all the taxation for that?—They have already got that, and the ratepayers are quite content to give it to them still. We are quite alive to Armagh, and we want our market-houses full of butter, oats, and so on, and [illegible] that should be brought to Armagh, and, therefore, we don't want them to pay a farthing.

54. If they were anxious to save their carts and horses, and to save themselves going into Armagh, and if they got the same prices for their produce here, it would go a long way to make up for the 1½d. or [illegible] they would have to pay?—The Commissioners notwithstanding all this, do not want them to pay a farthing. We will give them the advantages, and we hope that they will avail themselves more of them. We hope we will have to put down more [illegible], and that Mr. M'Kean will have to build a bigger market-house. We think that they are [illegible] taxed at present for the water, and we don't want them to pay a halfpenny for things that they do not derive any value from.

55. This tax is only for [illegible]?—There is already it [illegible] on the farmers in the county who contributed partly by county cess to [illegible] the town of Kandy. The Commissioners only paid half, and the Grand Jury contributed the rest. I think the prosperity of this town of Armagh would be the means of inducing farmers to take their produce of butter, oats, flax, pork and so on there—while we have a very large and [illegible] pork market at present; and we are satisfied that if they got good prices they would go to Armagh, if they had more taxation put upon them here.

HOLYWOOD.—24th NOVEMBER, 1879.

Before Mr. Exham, Q.C., and Mr. Robinson.

Mr. Exham.—We are here to-day to inquire as to whether any change is desirable in the present boundary of the municipality of Holywood. We adopted the same course here as we did in other places—sent requisition to the Town Commissioners to obtain their opinion as to whether there should be any alteration. I find by the answer that it was then the opinion of the Town Commissioners that there should not be any extension of the municipal boundary. However, I understand that there is now an opinion that there should be an alteration, but I don't know what the proposal is at present, but we will hear the Town Clerk, and any of the Commissioners and other parties, who wish to be examined on the subject.

[illegible] Watters examined.

1. Mr. Exham.—You are the Town Clerk of Holywood?—I am.

2. When did the town adopt the Towns Improvement Act, and was it adopted then for all the purposes?—In January, '65.

3. Did you adopt it for all the purposes of the Act?—I am not in a position to say, I was not Town Clerk then.

4. Were the boundaries fixed then?—Yes.

5. Has there been any change in them since?—None.

6. Is the present township all in one electoral division?—It is—the electoral division of Holywood.

7. What is the present area?—363 acres.

8. And its valuation I see was in '75, £11,871—do you know what it was in '79?—£11,983 10s. Some of the houses since 1875 have been revalued, that is made up of £11,763 on houses, and £574 on land.

9. How many townlands are included in the municipal boundary?—One.

10. Mr. Robinson.—I think there are portions of two, Ballykeel House is in one?—Yes, there are two.

11. Mr. Exham.—The population was in '71, 2,573?—Yes.

12. Has that population increased since that?—I believe it has slightly increased.

13. There are not any wards here?—No.

14. Has there been much increase in building within the last few years?—Not within the last two or three years, but for five or six years before, there was.

15. Mr. Robinson.—Was that outside the municipal limits?—Outside the town.

16. Mr. Exham.—Have you struck a uniform rate since '74 of 1s.?—Yes.

17. What is the water supply?—There has been nothing done about water, it was in contemplation at one time to form water-works but it was not carried out.

18. The electoral division of Holywood extends greatly beyond the present boundary?—Six or seven miles.

Mr. Robinson.—Nothing of the kind, about two miles; you are thinking of the poor law union, the electoral division only extends two miles, it extends to Craigavad, that is not six miles, I think.

Mr. *James M'Lean.*—About 2½ miles.

Mr. Robinson.—At the northern portion of it.

19. Mr. Exham.—What is the area of the electoral division?—4,985 acres, 3 roods, 1 perches, and the valuation £24,979 10s. A good many buildings have been erected in the direction of Cultra outside the boundary.

Mr. *James M'Lean.*—In fact for the past few years the building has been outside, but there is a good deal of land inside available for building.

20. Mr. Exham.—There are eight townlands in the entire electoral division?—Yes.

21. What was the county cess?—In '75, 1s. 11½d.; in '76, 2s.; in '77, 2s.; in '78, 1s. 10d.; and in '79, 1s. 10d.

22. What were the poor rates during the same period?—They have varied from 1s. 1d. to 1s. 8d.; they are 1s. 7d. this year.

23. Mr. Robinson.—Did that include any special rate for sanitary purposes?—Yes, there was 6d. last year for a sewerage rate.

24. What was the contributory district upon which that was assessed?—I cannot say.

25. Mr. Exham.—At the time our question was sent to the Commissioners, did they meet and consider them?—They did.

26. At that time they were not in favour of extending the township?—No.

27. Has the matter been reconsidered by the Commissioners?—It has, recently.

28. Have they come to a unanimous decision or a decision by a majority?—They came to a unanimous decision, the resolution passed on the occasion did

Mr. M'Lean.—The resolution has been passed, we simply rejected the resolution previously passed, but evidently we have changed our minds.

The Clerk.—There is no official record of it.

29. Mr. Exham.—How many members were present at that meeting?—Seven.

30. How many town Commissioners are there?—Nine.

Mr. *John Anderson* (Chairman Town Commissioners).—There were then two vacancies.

Mr. *James M'Lean.*—Not at the time the first resolution was passed.

Mr. *Anderson.*—No, but at the last meeting.

The Clerk.—There were six members present.

31. Mr. Exham.—What was the change approved by the Commissioners then?—They determined then to extend the boundary considerably over what it is and have it laid down on the Ordnance map according to the dotted line (map produced); a large portion of this land is suitable for building purposes, and [illegible] on two roads.

32. Are building operations going on?—Yes.

33. Do they propose to extend the advantage of lighting along the public road?—Yes.

34. Do the Commissioners propose to get sewerage from the country?—That is, I think, a question.

35. Do you know if the feeling of the ratepayers in the proposed township is that there should be an extension?—There is a difference of opinion about it, some think yes, and some think no.

36. With regard to the district proposed to be brought in, is there a feeling on the part of the inhabitants against being brought in?—Nothing beyond a remark, more any they might not and appear to feel it much.

37. Did the Commissioners in recommending that this district should be brought in, consider whether it should be brought in on differential terms over the extended district?—No, they simply intend to ask the extension now, and as the district improved to raise it in by degrees, the resolution is to give them power to take it in afterwards.

38. Mr. Robinson.—Can you tell me the increased revenue to the town funds if this extension was granted?—I can not, the Chairman will.

39. Do you know what the valuation of it is?—I do not, I have no means of knowing these things.

Mr. John Anderson, J.P., examined.

40. Mr. Exham.—You are Chairman of the Town Commissioners?—I am, and I have been Chairman continuously for over twelve years, and I was a Commissioner previously for several years.

41. The town adopted the Towns Improvement Act in 1861?—It did, having been previously under the 9th George IV., and I was Chairman under the old Act as well as now.

42. We will be glad now to hear your views.—One of the questions you raised was, did we adopt the Act in its entirety in '61, the answer to that is, yes, we did. As to the enlarging of the district the Board would not [illegible]. The two townlands that are now partially included are Ballykeel and Holywood. Some years ago and the first year they [illegible] the sewerage rate on this district, there was a [illegible] rate for two years. There was an attempt made to get water works by the [illegible], the Commissioners previously having gone a large length in securing ground, water rights, and so on. The Public Act of '78 transferred the power to the Board of Guardians. Since then nothing has been done, except the expenditure of a large sum of money, perhaps £1,000 or £1,500, without anything to show for it, by the Guardians. On this map the red lines give the present boundary, the blue lines and green give what is proposed to be added to it.

43. Is that the present proposal?—Yes. The lines also here indicate what will be taken in at once and [illegible], and this [illegible] of it is proposed to take in and put under a much diminished rate, perhaps a third or a fourth. I have written out a description of the ground proposed to be taken in, which I will just read to you.

Mr. Exham.—If you hand it in the shorthand writer [illegible] take it down on the notes:

The description was then handed in and was as follows:—Proposed boundary of the town of Holywood (county Down) by the Town Commissioners.—On the North—the sea at high-water mark, from a point on the Railway Embankment at western extremity of the [illegible] to a point on the sea wall in Ballycultra, opposite the western side of the road forming the [illegible] boundary of Mr. [illegible]'s grounds at [illegible], including all piers, landing stages, bathing places, boathouses, or erections, that are or may be made on the foreshore abutting on or leading to or from the beach.

On the East.—The eastern side of said road, and at the eastern extremity [illegible]-road and the road leading past the Culloden Railway Station and over the railway to the Holywood and Bangor county-road.

On the South.—The southern side of said county-road to a point opposite the western side of the [illegible] county-road, again, on the north along the western side of [illegible] county-road to a point opposite the southern side of the road leading to William Ferguson's house in Ballymenoch, again on the north, right across to and along the northern side of [illegible] road and the county-road in continuation from Newtownards to Holywood, then, right across said county-road and across by lower part of Ballymenoch and Ballykeel [illegible] to the Ballykeel stream, then down same till it meets the present southern boundary of the town, the present southern boundary to be continued, the boundary, and to be extended skirting the [illegible] till it meets the drive in Captain [illegible]'s house, [illegible].

On the West.—Down the eastern side of said drive and the eastern side of the county-road to [illegible] and right across the Belfast and Holywood-road and the Railway Embankment, and lastly on the south along the northern side of said Railway Embankment till it meets the first-mentioned point at or opposite the western extremity of the [illegible] at high-water mark as shown on accompanying map, coloured red, blue, and green.

44. Mr. Robinson.—Is there any special reason for going out of the electoral division as Mr. [illegible]'s being, the Select Committee say it is undesirable that that should be done? There is a county-road running up here, and would it not be a better boundary?—I don't think the Commissioners knew it was in another electoral division.

45. Would there be any objection to leave it out?—I think not.

Mr. M'Kean.—That is a place likely to be built upon and the people there derive all the advantages from the buildings of the town.

Mr. Anderson.—It was thought it would mark the division better; that place that you indicate goes through fields.

Dr. Mackay.—There is only part of Holywood in Knocknagoney; part of it is also in Holywood.

Captain Harrison.—It is out of the division altogether.

46. Mr. Robinson.—The Select Committee are of opinion that towns should, as far as possible, be in one electoral division. It is very little matter about excluding this other portion when without it you have the electoral division, unless there is some good reason for bringing it in.

Mr. Anderson.—There is a large house there which derives all the advantages from the town, I think they would be without sufficient.

Dr. [illegible].—And the ground about it is available for building ground, and is advertised as such, and those people have all the advantages of the town without paying anything for it.

47. Mr. Exham.—Does all the rest of the ground that you recommend to be brought in within that area, fairly come under the head of building ground or land which derives exceptional benefit from its proximity to the town, so that it should pay some portion of the taxation of it?—Yes, that is the opinion of the Commissioners, and my opinion too. They have all the advantages of the town since they have the use of the Town Hall here and the large room above it, the meetings and openings of the same, the Petty Sessions Court for the district, and library and reading-room, and, as you will see, the school-house there.

48. Practically they have the same advantages as the people of the town?—They have, the children come from all round to the school; even the [illegible] supplies are considerably below the point that we suggest to be taken in.

49. Independently of that, is the ground marked out at present for building ground?—Yes, a great deal of it, and has been advertised as such. Cultra and Ballymenoch—some of it has been laid out in roads and. I don't know anything that Holywood has suffered from so much as a want of supervision in its earlier days, from want of main and sanitary arrangements.

50. Are there public sewers through Holywood?—Yes, through the streets. There has been £1,700 expended upon it, and there is not a better sewered town in the three kingdoms, but I spoke of the mistakes made originally.

51. Have the houses within one hundred feet of those public sewers made connecting drains with the sewers?—Yes. I speak now of the part along the terraces. I am speaking of new Holywood altogether, houses being brought under control and the difficulty of dealing with it now, so that I think there ought to be supervision about and over this part proposed to be taken in, for there is a want of supervision, and this Act gives us power.

52. Mr. Robinson.—The property to bring in is a quantity of arable land.

53. Witness.—This place is a market for a good deal of their produce, and butter and those sort of things, and they take out manure, and they have labourers and gardeners living here who go out to them—these are all advantages.

54. Do the people who keep arable land close to the town, supply the town with milk, butter, vegetables, &c.?—Yes.

55. Mr. Exham.—Does the landlord get an increased rent for this land from its proximity to the town?—Certainly.

56. Is there any of it laid out in private roads?—

HOLYWOOD. Dec. 24, 1879. Sir John Anderson

There is a good deal of it, and some of it is advertised for building.

Dr. Dunlop.—What the Commissioners want to know is—is the proposed portion sought to be taken in arable or building land, I say it is all building ground or will be building ground within a limited period, the only portion that is not available is Ballymenoch, and that is depending upon a life that is now 75.

Captain *Harrison*.—No, no.

56. Mr. Exham.—What is your idea about the taxation of this district, under the Towns Improvement Act any land that is arable land only pays one-fourth, while houses and buildings pay the full rate—is it your idea that that should be the case here?—It is the opinion of the Commissioners that there should be a smaller rate put on the part that does not receive full benefits, that is, a lower rate than is paid in the general township.

57. That is going to another matter—do you propose to extend lighting, watching, and scavenging, over the proposed area?—Not over the full extent of what would be taken in.

58. Well, to the extent that you propose to take in at present, would you propose to make them pay the same rate as similarly circumstanced property in the township pays?—Yes.

59. And the other?—The opinion is about one-fourth, or something more, until they get the full benefits.

60. You must bear this in mind that the opinion of the Committee of the House of Commons is, that taxation should be divided between landlord and tenant. Now this land to be brought in at present would only pay the fourth; if that one-fourth was divided between landlord and tenant, it would be only putting three-halfpence in the pound on the tenant, and three-halfpence on the landlord—it could hardly go below that. The proposal in other places is to make the land pay one-half what the houses pay within the area, and divide that half on the landlords and half on the tenants, and then put the extra taxation on the landlords, leaving the tenants to pay as they are, for it is said that the landlord is really the person who obtains the benefit, because for his land he gets double or treble what he would get for the same quality of land if it were some distance from a market town, and that therefore he should contribute towards keeping the market town up. that appears to be the view also of the Select Committee of the House of Commons, what would your view be?—

Mr. Anderson.—We have not gone into that.

Mr. M'Lean.—So far as that explanation goes I think it fair and reasonable.

Mr. Exham suggested an improvement in the boundary of the proposed extension by taking in as much of the road as goes up by the corner of the wood.

61. Mr. Robinson.—Can you give us any statistics as to the ground you propose to take in?

Mr. Anderson.—It includes 880 acres on the east, and 185 and 181 on the west. These would be added to that the distance between Cultra station and the townland boundary of Craigavad and Ballygrainey, and also the little bit that would be included to the north of the gate lodge.

62. Mr. Exham.—What is the valuation of that district?

Mr. Anderson.—The portion on the western side is valued at £759—£337 for the land, and £423 for the houses. On the eastern side, Cultra and Ballymenoch, the valuation for houses is £2,928, and £663 for land. From that down to the townland boundary the valuation of houses is £673, and of land £77. There are some of those houses and land taken down where there is land surrounding the houses and where there is not a separate valuation, or not given separately.

63. Did you calculate what the increase to the town funds would be?—I did not.

64. Do you not think it would be advantageous to make the new boundary the townland boundary above Woodside-bridge, and strike in to the top of Bryan's-hill there to meet the point proposed—do you think that would be desirable?—I agree that the boundary as it is put on the map is an awkward one.

65. To follow the continuation of the northern side of the road to Woodside-bridge, and then take the townland boundary to the sea?—I think that would be very desirable.

Dr. Dunlop.—I think that would be a much better line; there would be no difficulty in taking the line across the fields.

66. Mr. Exham.—I would ask the Chairman this, if the boundary should be extended and all the land that is in that, made pay only half rates on the valuation, that half to be divided between landlord and tenant, and the houses to pay half valuation as long as they were not lighted or watched, but the moment they were lighted and watched, then to pay the full—how would that do?—Certainly I think that would be very fair and proper.

67. Mr. Robinson.—Is there any improvement in the town of Holywood which the Commissioners are unable to carry out through want of funds?—No, except water works.

68. Mr. Exham.—At your northern boundary, do you propose high or low water mark at ordinary spring tides?—High water mark.

69. Would you propose an extension to the low water tide for the purpose of giving you control over the foreshore for sanitary purposes?—We prefer the high water mark and leaving the rest to the owners, whoever they may be, but with the power to tax all piers or landing stages, or bathing machines extending between high and low water marks.

70. Mr. Robinson.—I suppose Holywood derives its support from people living outside the town who spend money in it?—Yes, nearly all the roads are supplied from here.

71. But so far as provisions, and shopping, and clothing, &c., for families are concerned?—A great many of them go to Belfast for those things.

72. Mr. *M'Lean.*—A great many of them.

Mr. Anderson.—But a good many purchase in Holywood.

73. Mr. Exham.—Have you considered whether you could keep up the roads for a rate the same as the county rate?—I have gone into that question, and I can give you statistics. I believe we would save. I believe if we had the supervision of our own roads there would be a saving of twopence in the pound.

74. Dr. *Dunlop.*—There is no place in the north of Ireland where there are such complaints about the state of the roads. They are a disgrace to the county, and the County Surveyor will take no notice whatever of the matter.

Mr. Anderson.—It is many years since this matter was before the Commissioners, and at that time on their request the County Surveyor in the application sheet separated all the county-roads passing through the town from the other roads in the barony, so that the Commissioners might become contractors under the Grand Jury, if so disposed, for the maintenance of their own roads, so to speak, and the Commissioners afterwards acting as such contractors know exactly the amount expended on these roads by the county, which they could not have known but for this separation. They also see by the grand warrants of the county the proportion which the town is obliged to pay for county at-large charges—opposite these two separate roads the county cess levied off the town. The valuation of the town is in round numbers £13,020, which at 1s. 11d., being the average county cess for the last five years, amounts to £1,163, deduct from this £347, the amount expended on the roads, which I take from the grand warrants, summer 1878, and spring 1879, which is equivalent to a saving of 6d. in the pound sterling, also £387, being equivalent to a further saving of 7½d., being the proportion of county-at-large expenses assessed on the town (the valuation of the county being £744,818, and the requirements for the summer of 1878, which I take from these warrants, is £12,188, and for the spring of 1879, £10,317), these deductions together, £834, being the entire amount actually expended for the town taken from £1,163, the amount of county cess levied in round numbers off the town, leaves £329 as the annual loss which the town suffers by the connexion with the Grand Jury of the county. In other words, while a rating of [illegible] is levied off the county by the Grand Jury, a rate of [illegible] would seem to be sufficient for all purposes, according to [illegible] showing. Of course I [illegible] am responsible for this calculation, I give the figures, &c., [illegible] are the documents to speak for themselves, and I shall be very glad indeed to be set right, if I am wrong, and I [illegible] those who [illegible] the other side to test my accuracy.

77. Would there not be a larger saving on the portion outside because there is not so much traffic on them as on the inside portion?—I think so. There is a matter I want to mention—about the divided rate—the divided rate won't touch the roads at all. I am speaking of the sanitary rate. In those small towns of Ireland as long as they remain under the Guardians, the sanitary rate is a divided rate, the same as the poor rate, but if they are the Urban Sanitary Authority it is thrown on the tenants and occupiers. There was an attempt made to get this right when the Bill was passed, but the deputation were not successful in getting it accomplished.

78. That is the Public Health Act of last year?—Yes, the thing is a kind of grievance for small towns as they are under the Towns Improvement Act [illegible] they get the half rate, but the moment they go into them [illegible] not. If you take that, and help these small towns to get this divided rate continued, it would be a good matter. We have got nearly all the landlords to agree to treat the sanitary rate, when this matter is transferred to the Town Commissioners, as though it were a divided rate. This is the agreement with the landlords to meet this difficulty here (document handed in), consequent on the transfer of Holywood to the Sanitary Authority. Continue to run, and to carry out and show their idea, they came to this agreement—"As the rates levied by the Poor Law Guardians for sanitary purposes are payable with and form part of the poor rate, and as the tenants paying the same have the right to take a portion of the same from their landlord out of the amount payable to such landlords, we, the undersigned landlords, believing that if the Sanitary Authority is transferred to the Town Commissioners of Holywood there will be a [illegible] [illegible] hardship, [illegible] transfer to the Local Authority take place, to allow the proportion of such rate as if it had been levied as poor rate." That is signed by [illegible] landlords. Mr. Harrison also wrote to the following effect—"If Holywood is made an Urban Sanitary Authority I am willing to pay my proportion of the sanitary rate, same as I now do under the Belfast Board of Guardians, on condition that the majority of the other landlords holding property in Holywood do the same. J. Harrison."

Mr. *Anderson* continued.—This may help to get it done. Nearly everyone we asked of any importance agreed with us. Perhaps you would think it of importance to note what we propose here we suggested it to Sir Michael Hicks-Beach, but he had objections to creating a new Voting Board, their policy, he said, was to lessen them in number. There is another matter which I wish to mention, the population of Holywood was [illegible].

79. Is that a rising population?—It has not increased much since 1871, but there are new electors and the most of them, more than half of them, occupy houses between £4 and £12, and some of us, and I myself, have an idea that the voting should be on the same principle as for the Poor Law Guardians.

Mr. *Exham*.—We will take down that as a suggestion from you. That is one of the things, however, which were considered by the Select Committee, and with which we have nothing to do. Have you calculated what would be the increase in the constituency by the extension you propose, about how many?—It would take in nearly 100 houses, that is what is proposed without going farther.

80. And farther, taking in down to the townland boundary would add how many more to it?—Somewhere about seven or eight.

81. Would they be all of the higher class of valuation?—They would.

82. What distance will the western extension you propose leave intervening between it and the eastern extension proposed at Sydenham, how much space will intervene there at what you call the Strandtown District?—Nearly two miles, I think.

Dr. *Dunlop*.—It would not be more than a mile.

Captain *Harrison*.—It is as high as mile and a half.

83. Mr. *Exham*.—The reason I ask about it is that I have heard it stated that there is a nuisance complained of at that foreshore, and I heard something with that, you were anxious to get an extension, so as to get some authority to deal with the foreshore, and that nuisance on it [illegible], but we think it better for the town that it should be in the hands of the Guardians. We don't wish to be burdened by it.

Dr. *Dunlop*.—We have no power at all [illegible] the place, because it is outside our boundary.

Mr. *Exham*.—It would be a very silly thing if there is an injury done to Holywood, that there should not be some power to remove the nuisance.

Dr. *Dunlop*.—If that nuisance is not removed the township will be depopulated. The nuisance extends from below Cultra, and the whole thing arises from the way in which the foreshore has been closed up. The drainage from the large town of Belfast with such matter as becomes incorporated with it, comes down and is deposited on the banks, and becomes decomposed, so that it is perfectly intolerable. The owners of this foreshore must be made to attend to it.

Mr. *Exham*.—It doesn't seem to be very offensive. I saw several carts of it taken away, and it appears to be good stuff for manure.

Dr. *Dunlop*.—You don't know what we have suffered.

Rev. Mr. *O'Donnelly*, P.P.—There is absolutely no person to remove the dead animals, the dead dogs and cats which lie along the foreshore, particularly about Ballymenoch and Cultra, and which are most offensive as well to the sight as to the smell.

Dr. *Dunlop*.—The foundation is the most prejudicial matter to health imaginable, decaying seaweed, and sewage, and drainage matter.

Mr. *Anderson*.—When the farmers had the privilege of taking it away there was no nuisance sufficient there to become a nuisance.

Captain *Harrison*.—Nobody interferes with them now.

Dr. *Dunlop*.—I beg your pardon; except at certain times at Cultra, neither do [illegible] with persons attempting to take seaweed on the foreshore.

Captain *Harrison*.—I hold a lease for 21 years from the Woods and Forests, and I can say no one has been prosecuted by me for taking seaweed. Of late years there has not been so good a way of removing it, as it had to be thrown up, but within the last year there has been a convenient place made for taking it away. As we all know there has been an extraordinary quantity of seaweed thrown on the foreshore this past winter. Never in my memory, and I can recollect for thirty years has there been such an extraordinary quantity as this year, and if you had kept sight of the time, going the whole season they would not have drawn all the quantity that came in here. No doubt it was most injurious to have it lying there, but I don't see that I can be taken, for that is not a nuisance created by me.

Dr. *Dunlop*.—If a nuisance exists on any man's ground he ordinarily removes it by the Sanitary Authority, and let him then find out who is liable for it.

Mr. *Exham*.—Mr. *Harrison* speaks to the extraordinary quantity of seaweed thrown up this winter. There appears to be something very much the same at Sandymount, near Dublin.

Dr. *Dunlop*.—It is only within the last year that Captain Harrison has permitted the seaweed to be taken away. Before that there was a price put on it and everyone was interfered with.

Captain *Harrison*.—It has been stated that a charge has been put on seaweed and I must say that I never received a charge for it in my life since '61.

Dr. *Dunlop*.—I can produce evidence in this very room that his bailiff most offensively interfered with parties.

Holywood. May [illegible], 18[illegible] — Mr. John A. Anderson.

Captain *Harrison*.—Neither I nor my agent have ever received one halfpenny as a charge for seaweed.

Mr *M'Lean*.—I knew a man who was taking some seaweed and he put in some small shells with it and he was compelled to throw out the shells or drop the entire load. I don't think conduct like that is to be tolerated.

83. Mr. Rankin.—Where does the sewage of Holywood go to now?

Mr. *Anderson*.—It goes into the sea. There are four sewers that empty on the foreshore.

84. Does not that create a nuisance?—I don't think so. In going along there I have not perceived any smell of any great consequence, that is where they discharge themselves, the tide comes in twice in the twenty-four hours.

85. If these sewers discharge on the high water mark then as the tide recedes must they not discharge on the empty foreshore?—I think if there is any deposit on the foreshore it is from Belfast.

86. Mr. Crawford.—Did you read Dr. Dunlop's and Dr. Reid's reports that the sewage was the principal cause of the offensive smell and that it was neglect of the Town Commissioners not carrying their sewers out to low water mark.

Mr. *Anderson*.—I could not read in paper what was said in it.

Dr. *Dunlop*.—I beg your pardon, at Cultra, a mile from the place the smell was simply intolerable, and one little bay on this side of Cultra pier, was as bad as any place along the shore.

Mr. *Crawford*.—Caused by Holywood.

Mr. *Anderson*.—It is not.

Rev. Mr. *O'Laverty*.—No one can go in to draw seaweed from that.

Dr. *Dunlop*.—The whole shore is a close boundary, and if these men will have the benefit of it they must keep it clear, the stench in that little bay was intolerable, you could not unless you were there know anything about it.

Mr. *Anderson*.—If we get this extension there should be an increase in the number of Commissioners we think.

87. Do you think it desirable to increase them; how many are there now?—The present number is nine.

88. As it has been always thought desirable to have an odd number, would you suggest eleven or thirteen, or would fifteen be too many?

Mr. *M'Lean*.—Twelve would be enough, and give the chairman a casting vote.

89. Mr. Rankin.—Would you think it desirable to have wards?

Mr. *Anderson*.—I think there should be three wards, if we get this extension, that is my own opinion; you see we have 550 electors at present and there would be 100 added, that would be 650.

90. You would then have wards of only 200 or 150 each, would there be any inconvenience in voting at one place?—It would be very troublesome to separate the town so.

Mr. *M'Lean*.—In a town like this it is not necessary to have wards.

91. Mr. *Charles H. Ward*, Solicitor.—I appear for the owners of scattered villas outside this township, and for a number of parties who feel an interest in it, and who are opposed to the proposed extension; now, Mr. Anderson, you are Chairman of the Town Commissioners?—Yes.

92. What benefit do the Town Commissioners propose to give those who are out of the township in exchange for their paying town taxes?—Better supervision in the way of buildings; that is, looking after the buildings to see if there were proper bends for sewage arrangements and matters of that sort.

93. Have you any legal power at present in the township with regard to buildings?—Oh, yes.

94. I was not aware of it?—The Commissioners are at present framing by-laws that the Act empowers them to do with regard to supervision of buildings.

95. But up to the present have you any power to regulate buildings in Holywood?—Not very much, but this Act gives us the power, this new Health Act gives us additional powers.

96. The Act of last year?—Yes.

97. It gives you power to frame by-laws, but you have not framed them yet?—Oh, no.

98. Any powers you have under that provisional order from the Local Government Board is confined to the township of Holywood?—Yes.

99. Outside of Holywood, the district that you propose to take in, consists of farm houses and villas that gentlemen built according to their own taste and on their own property?—Yes, and houses to let.

100. Can you tell how many houses have been built within the last sixteen years in the Marino direction from the limits of the township, up to Mr. Robinson's house?—I cannot tell exactly.

101. Would you be surprised to learn that it was at the rate of one a year, sixteen in all?—I would.

102. I thought so, how many of these are vacant now?—I cannot tell you.

103. Now, what do you propose to do for all these people outside the township in return for their paying town taxes, provided they were willing to come in, which they are not?—I have told you, the supervision.

104. What kind of supervision?—Well, with regard to sewerage and cesspools, and having proper sanitary arrangements, these are some of the things.

105. Don't you know the owners of the villas have made their own sanitary arrangements, the owners of villas are more particular about them than any sanitary authorities?—I know some of them have made bad arrangements with regard to cesspools emptying into streams.

106. Can you point out any stream outside the town that is polluted by cesspools from any of those houses?—There is one marked on the Ordnance map called the "Stinking Burn," between Holywood and Ballymenoch.

107. Doesn't that separate it from the adjoining townland, and is not that caused by the sewage of Holywood polluting it?—No.

108. Are not the poor law guardians the sanitary authorities outside your district?—They are.

109. And don't they exercise sanitary authority outside?—I don't think it.

110. Is it not owing to their efforts that the foreshore has been cleared of all the sea-wrack, within the past three weeks?—It is within their jurisdiction, they are only doing their duty.

111. Supposing you extended the township boundary, would you like to exercise authority over the foreshore?—Yes.

112. Can you point out any place in the district you propose to annex, that requires any sanitary attention whatever, in the direction of Marino, I take it for granted, you cannot?—I have not been over it very much.

113. It is a great luxury to examine a magistrate you often placed before, and I am sure I will get the truth out of Mr. Anderson. I suppose you propose to give us water, sir, if you extend the township?—If it is wanted.

114. Where will you get pure water to give us?—Well, the engineer that the Board of Guardians had employed suggested that the water should be taken down as far as Craigavad.

115. Don't you know that all these owners of villas have water, pure and uncontaminated, without getting sewage water up from the Stinking Burn?—I don't know that.

116. All these hills are full of water, for example, at Rockport and Marino. Are the Commissioners themselves united about this extension of the township?—So far as I know, they are.

117. Was there not a resolution passed at which it was decided not to extend the township?

118. Mr. Rankin.—Yes, we have that. It was passed last November.

119. Mr. *Ward*.—Have they a second resolution at which they decided to extend it?

120. Mr. *Anderson*.—They have a note on the minutes, I think, not a resolution, but an unanimous agreement.

121. Mr. Rankin.—Six out of the nine Commissioners met and approved of the extension.

121. Mr. Ward.—Six out of nine, so that you are divided amongst yourselves?

122. Mr. Anderson.—Six for, and there were two neutrals.

123. Mr. Ward.—So that you propose to take these people in without giving them any benefit whatever?

124. Mr. Barr.—You are assuming that they are not getting any benefit. Is it not a benefit for a man to have the police of this township [illegible] for him on his road to the train and [illegible] through with his family?

125. Mr. Ward.—But at night, we are in [illegible] people, and we are very little out after night. There is a late train to Holywood, but none to my district.

127. That is the reason, if you had a train down to Culture you would not want it.

128. Mr. Dargan.—We have one up to half past 10 o'clock.

129. Mr. Ward.—Have you the valuation of Holywood?

130. Mr. Barr.—We have; it was £11,971 last year, and this year it is £11,938. We have it on land and buildings.

Holywood. July 24, 1878. Mr. John Anderson.

Mr. James M'Lean examined.

Mr. James M'Lean.

131. Mr. Barr.—Are you in favour of this extension?—I am in favour of an extension, provided we can have that extension as we wish it. I was one of the [illegible] that assisted in [illegible] this resolution that has been spoken of by Mr. Ward, on the 2nd June, 1878. And that resolution was carried by a small majority, the minute is "The boundary question having been fully considered, it was moved by Mr. Gray, seconded by Mr. M'Lean, and passed, that the existing boundaries should not be altered or extended." [illegible] Municipal Commissioners." Now, what induced me to second that resolution, and to take an active part in having it passed, was this, two members of the Board made calculations, and I think, said that to extend the boundary a certain distance raised by [illegible] would put the town to a certain loss, and I [illegible] I thought my duty was to save the money of the ratepayers, not to take money out of their pockets, and until the parties sought to be brought in would be self-supporting I would not support any extension [illegible]. I say now I would be in favour of extending the boundary, provided it would be done without expense, that the Town Commissioners would not be compelled to light up any portion of the extended district until they would consider that that portion was self-supporting; my own impression is, I may be wrong, I have not looked at it closely, that if we looked a little at any person in the extended district, and they were not lighted and taken care of, the money would be [illegible] so [illegible] if [illegible] the [illegible] of extending [illegible] the [illegible] that we can extend the boundary but not light it until the extended districts were self-supporting.

132. Mr. Barr.—What would you take them in for?

133. Mr. M'Lean.—I don't mean to say, I would not tax them. The parties would all derive certain advantages from the lighting of Holywood at present, and they ought to pay something towards it.

134. Mr. Barr.—In other words, what you say is this, that this district should be brought in on a differential rate; that is what is proposed everywhere, that in taking them in and making them a part of the family, that if you make them pay full taxation, it follows, to be reasonable, that you should give them the same benefits as the people living in the centre of the town. The proposal in such cases elsewhere has been to make them pay half rates.

135. Mr. M'Lean.—I am only speaking of the law as it now stands, and I am sure the Queen's Bench would make us light them if we tax them fully.

136. Mr. Barr.—It has not been proposed anywhere that the parties outside should pay full rates until they get the full advantage. They should pay half their rate which makes up [illegible]. It is only the [illegible] which would require it that would be different. The sanitary rates are the same, and then the only thing is, with regard to the [illegible] improvement rate, under the Act of 1854. It is said that the people in the district living round the town which benefit so largely by the [illegible] of the town, should contribute something to the expenses of the town. It may be a question, too, if you take the roads and bridges, in towns in which there are bridges, whether the county should not contribute something towards their maintenance, because they are, also, largely, particularly [illegible]. For instance in the town of [illegible] there is a bridge that has been frequently swept away by floods, and it is said that the Grand Jury should contribute towards its future maintenance, otherwise [illegible] it would be a hardship for [illegible] township to have to keep up bridges and roads which, it might be [illegible] the advantages of the township.

137. Mr. M'Lean.—The principal road in Holywood goes to Bangor, and [illegible], and [illegible], and it is kept by the county at large. If we now take the roads from the county within our district, the county should provide a proportion of the expense.

138. Mr. Barr.—Taking any one [illegible] boundary proposed, would you be in favour of carrying it down to the [illegible] boundary [illegible]?

139. Would you be in favour of taking it along the road, on [illegible] the road, as we were suggesting?—I don't see the advantage of taking it at a place where there would be no likelihood of building.

140. Would you be in favour of taking the boundary the proposed line of the townland boundary, and [illegible] down by [illegible], and up to the townland boundary. You would thus get the main [illegible] road into your own hands from the point of [illegible]?—I have no objection to that; the roads are kept in a very bad condition at the present time.

141. Do you think you could keep the roads in [illegible] order and at less cost?—I think so.

142. Mr. Barr.—Do you see any advantage in keeping the boundary there, as Mr. [illegible] suggests?—Well, I have no objection to it.

143. Mr. Barr.—It would be unwise for you to take it at the right side of the road. Are you able to say, of your own knowledge, that the land and houses in the district you propose to bring in are rendered exceptionally valuable by their proximity to the town of Holywood?—I should say so.

144. In your opinion, do they derive advantages from the town?—Yes.

145. Would you be in favour of dividing that rate, half on the occupier and half on the landlord?—I think it would be a very fair arrangement. I wish to draw attention to the way in which the roads are kept in Holywood. We don't derive any advantage from the county having charge of them; some of them are [illegible]. There is a road leading up to my own house which is in a disgraceful state; there were two accidents on it in which I was thrown out. I will ask you to look at that road and see the condition in which it is. It is in High Holywood and [illegible] the boundary.

146. That appears to be a regular [illegible] road [illegible] a certain point in a certain place it is high in the centre with a fall to each side of two and a half feet. [illegible] you run the danger of having your neck broken.

147. Mr. Davison.—I know the road.—I passed it.

148. Mr. M'Lean.—Had your attention been directed to it you would have seen it [illegible]. I wrote to the County Surveyor on the 15th [illegible], saying that the Presentment Sessions had twice passed a presentment

Downpatrick, Nov. 21, 1878.

Mr. James M'Lean.

and the Grand Jury had with them thrown it out. I wrote as follows. I have a copy of the letter here:—

"[illegible], Belfast,
"12th October, 1878.

"Thomas Stevens, Esq., County Surveyor,
"Downpatrick.

"Dear Sir,—A portion of the road lying between Mr. [illegible] and Mr. [illegible] is [illegible] state. [illegible] Grand Jury [illegible] you [illegible] whether the road is considered good enough for use either by you or the Grand Jury.

"Yours faithfully,
"James M'Lean."

To that I got this answer from him :—

"County Surveyor's Office, Downpatrick,
"15th October, 1878.

"Dear Sir,—In reply to your letter of the 12th, I will direct my assistant to have an application put forward at the next Presentment Sessions for the improvement of the road you refer to.

"Truly yours,
"H. Stevens."

For years it has been in this state, and when I draw his attention to it he will send his own man to put a presentment forward. That is an admission that it is in a bad state, otherwise he would not get his own man to do it. Holywood would derive all the advantages in the world if we had control of the roads ourselves.

149. Mr. Exham.—Do you think there would be any use in extending the boundary to the low-water-mark to bring in the foreshore ?

150. Mr. M'Lean.—It is a serious question. I would not be inclined to take it in to low-water-mark. We would have a limited area of taxation, and we might have great expenditure there. I think I would be inclined to agree with Dr. Dunlop that it is the duty of a man when a nuisance is on his property to remove it.

151. Mr. Exham.—There is a little danger at home when you start that proposition. You discharge a portion of the sewerage on the foreshore ?—We may not, and that there is not a town in Ireland so well sewered as Holywood. There is no solid matter discharged into it at all. There is a great fall in these sewers.

152. The solid matter must go somewhere ?—The force of the flood breaks it up, and it goes away with the flood.

153. Does it not come back with it again ?—It may, but I have never seen it.

154. A considerable portion of sewage matter at any rate must discharge itself on the foreshore. The moment the tide recedes from the high-water-mark this sewage spreads out a long distance from the foreshore of the shore. Then all that comes down during the ebb is spread all over the foreshore and washed back again by the flood tide ?—Well, I am not prepared to say that the Commissioners might make some kind of tanks which would enable it to be carried away. As a Commissioner I would not be inclined to take the responsibility. I have heard a suggestion which I consider the most absurd I have ever heard—to build a sewer out in the sea—to build a sewer in sand.

155. Mr. Ward.—Is it your opinion that no sewage pollutes the foreshore in Holywood ?—It is not. It is my opinion that some sewage pollutes it less or more.

156. Had you an opportunity of reading Dr. Reid's report the other day ?—I glanced at it.

157. Did you see where he certified that he found sewage matter between parts of the seaweed ?—I cannot say I saw that, but if you say he wrote it it's all right, but I don't care about Dr. Reid's or any other person's opinion.

158. Don't you know that Dr. Reid is the Public Officer of Health, that he is Consulting Sanitary Officer under the Poor Law Board ?—Yes.

159. And don't you know that Dr. Dunlop is the Local Sanitary Officer ?—Yes.

160. And do you happen to know that these two eminent authorities have certified that there is sewage from Holywood polluting the foreshore ?—Suppose there is ?

161. Did you hear the Chairman of the Town Commissioners speak of the Stinking Burn ?—Yes.

162. It is polluted by sewage matter from the town of Holywood ?—I am not aware.

163. Perhaps you have not examined the matter for yourself ?—I keep as far as possible away from all things stinking.

164. Now, your first opinion was that it would never pay the town to extend the district as proposed ?—Yes, that it would never pay the town—that it would be a losing matter. I thought it would be a losing matter to the ratepayers if we would be compelled to light the district before it was self-supporting.

165. If you were not compelled to light, you would like to tax before we got value ?—I think you get advantages from the lights in Holywood, and having the supervision of the Town Commissioners.

166. Do you happen to know that these parties outside have two stations to get out at, without passing through Holywood, Marino, and Craigavad ?—Some of the trains don't get the length. You get out at Holywood, and walk home.

167. What time do you put out the lamps in Holywood ?—When every decent man ought to be in bed.

168. At 10 o'clock ?—No.

169. Half-past 10 o'clock ?—After the last train arrives. I think you can answer that as well as I can.

170. What benefit are they likely to receive from lighting, when the lamps are put out in Holywood at half-past 10 o'clock ?—That's only the time when drunken fellows are going home. I am told by the clerk that they commence to put out the lamps at half-past 10 o'clock.

171. Mr. George Murray.—An hour before the last train arrives—A quarter past 11 o'clock.

172. Mr. Ward.—Have you never, before half-past 10 o'clock, seen the lamps out ?—Very frequently. Will you allow me to explain ? that is at the time that the lamps are not lighted—in the summer months, for instance.

173. Does it never occur in the winter ?—I think not. Except on very clear nights I have not observed the lamps put out before half-past 10 o'clock. If the night is very clear there is no occasion to have the lamps lit. The clerk tells me that they are not lighted during the time we have a moon.

174. It's important to note that. How many months in the year have you the lamps lighted ? I am told by Dr. Dunlop that there are some lighted all night ?—Some are, I suppose.

175. Why did you alter your original opinion about the extension of the district being a tax on the inhabitants of Holywood ?—For the reasons I have given. If we can extend the district, without being compelled or compellable to light the extended district—if we can do so upon the principle of taxing at a smaller rate those outside, we ought to have the extension. The people of Holywood should not bear all the expense of lighting Holywood, for the benefit of those outside it.

176. What would you give in exchange for the small rate ? What advantage would you give to the parties outside for that small rate ?—I would give the advantages I have already told you. Amongst others, having Holywood lighted for the advantage of those who go a mile beyond it.

177. Lighted for the benefit of those going to Marino ?—Yes, if they pass through it.

178. How much would it cost to erect lamp posts, and light lamps from the present limits on the Bangor road to Woodchurch, three miles away ?

Dr. Dunlop.—One mile and a half.

179. Mr. Ward.—How far do you say it is ?

Mr. M'Lean.—I don't know ; I never made a calculation, but when the time comes when the lamps are required I will make the calculation or attend to it.

180. Assuming that the scheme did not pay and that there was a large deficit, would it fall on the inhabitants of Holywood ?—It would fall on the outsider according

to you, for you are fighting for the outsiders. If there is any deficit it will not fall entirely on the insiders.

181. Is there any advantage you can give except that of lighting?—They will have the supervision of the Commissioners and their officers, who will see that houses are properly built; they will have regard to sanitary construction, the making of roads and seeing that they are properly formed and all that sort of thing. It's a pity that we had not had the power years ago.

182. They will look after sanitary arrangements already made, villas already built, and give light to those who don't want it?—If you view it in that way you can do so. I am speaking of the creation of future buildings, and also of the supervision we would have over present buildings, to see if the sanitary arrangements are what they ought to be.

183. Having regard to the fact that for 15 years there was one house built every year, you would give yourself a lot of trouble for nothing?—That's not true. Probably the houses might average one in every year, but I know of my own knowledge four built in one year.

184. You would not take the jurisdiction over the foreshore, although you would take it over villas?—I never heard of villas on the foreshore either at high or low water-mark.

185. I mean along the shore; although you would wish to take them in, you don't propose to deal with the foreshore in the way of removing nuisances or otherwise?—No, we don't want anything to do with the foreshore; but we do wish respect to any nuisance coming from the villas.

186. What do you mean, then, by saying you will give supervision in sanitary matters?—The man who has bungalow villas built on the foreshore can't [illegible] anything. It is with the villas not on the foreshore as all that we will deal.

187. In other words what you want to do, and I think it is apparent to the Commissioners, is to have the power to tax the people outside the township, and to do nothing in return?—We wish to prevent their discharging any nuisance on the foreshore.

188. Talking about your own nuisance, how do you propose to deal with the Holywood nuisance discharging on the foreshore—will you deal with that?—Yes; that I will leave to the engineer.

189. Everything is to be left to the engineer. Suppose you get possession of this district for taxation purposes, when do you propose to light it?—When it is self-supporting, or that the taxation for it won't fall principally on the parties within the borough.

190. In the meantime will you tax it?—In proportion to the benefit they will receive.

191. In the future or the Greek Kalends, or at Tibb's Eve, you will light the district outside?—When, as I have said, it is self-supporting.

192. Have you made any calculation as to when, in your opinion, it will be self-supporting?—Whenever there will be a sufficient number of houses built there.

193. That may be in a half century or so?—That again it might be in less than a quarter of a century. We cannot see far enough into the future.

Holywood. Dec. [illegible]

Mr. James [illegible]

194. Do you know where Holywood House is?—Yes.

195. Do you know Mr. Richard Harrison who resides there—would you take him in?—I would, I don't see any reason why he should not be taken in.

196. Do you know that he farms 200 or 300 acres of land there?—I don't know. At all events he grows a large quantity.

197. Do you propose to light his farm—what do you propose to give him in exchange for taxation?—Only a portion, and when we take the light out to his gate-house we will tax him; and all the Harrisons, and all his family, servants, &c., will have the benefit of it.

198. What will be the individual benefit they will receive?—The same benefit that you or I receive.

199. There can't be much when you have put out the lamps at half-past 10 o'clock. The use of light would be to have it at night?—Then take a lamp with you. Our object is to make the rates in the town as light as possible. We think Holywood is a place that people would like to come to but won't in consequence of the high taxes, and we want to keep the taxation as low as possible to induce people to come here.

200. Are you not in debt at present?—I suppose we are.

201. How much is rental now here?—That is more than I can tell you; it was contracted before my time.

202. Do you propose to put any portion of the debt on this outlying district?—I don't know; we have not taken that into consideration yet.

203. It appears to me to be a very rare proposal altogether.

204. Dr. *Dunlop*.—The area of taxation is fixed. It would not affect any place that the Poor Law Guardians do not at present charge for. You ought to know that, Mr. Ward, as the representative of the Poor Law Guardians.

205. If they get these outlying districts is there anything to prevent them getting a provisional order to make them contribute?—There is no debt, strictly speaking, by the Commissioners on the rates; there is the sewerage rate.

206. Dr. *Dunlop*.—There is the sewerage rate and water rate.

207. Mr. *Ward*.—Doesn't it amount to this—that you wish to extend the district for the purpose of collecting funds or taxes from a larger area without giving any corresponding advantage?—No, it does not; if you had been listening to my evidence you would have known that.

208. We think here that you would tax us, and yet you cannot tell whether you will light us in a quarter or a half a century?—I have told you that we propose to light you when you are self-supporting.

209. Will you fix that interesting date when we will be lighted for your purposes?—I could not.

Dr. Dunlop examined.

Dr. Dunlop.

208. Mr. Ennis.—You are a Town Commissioner?—I was a Town Commissioner for a great many years, but seeing in this place being mismanaged [illegible] I was obliged to resign.

209. You have been a Commissioner, you are a ratepayer and know a great deal about it, are you in favour of this proposed extension?—I am.

210. And down to the point I indicated to take in this townland boundary and the upper road above the road [illegible]?

211. From your own knowledge can you say that the inhabitants, whether farmers or gentlemen, living in this extended district derive exceptional advantage from their proximity to the town of Holywood?—I know they do.

212. Do they use it largely?—Yes; their children go to school here, and they attend churches in the town. I believe they should pay something for all the advantages they receive. The way in which you explain that division of rating would be perfectly satisfactory to me, and I believe it would be very advantageous in so far as these people are concerned, and every effort should be made to get, if possible, the roads in charge of the Town Commissioners. The roads down along there are extremely bad; nothing could have been worse than the road from Holywood to Craigavad and down this district last year. It was almost neglected; part of the way it was almost impassable. Mr. Ward says no advantages would be derived from taking in this district. Why, to get those roads under the control of the Commissioners would be a marked advantage in itself, for the road down to Mr. Ward's own house is an ugly rough, narrow and ill-constructed, [illegible] at certain points along the road.

213. Is it not a county road?—No; the only other available road down along there runs past the [illegible]

Holywood. Nov. [illegible] Dr. Dunlop.

Guard Station and is kept in such order by the proprietors of Cultra that it is simply impassable. I have to get off my vehicle to go down to the houses there, I cannot drive down, I have to walk down.

314. Mr. Ross.—Which road is that?—Fort Farm Hill. It is kept in the most frightful condition, no person could at all believe it.

315. Mr. Exham.—There will be great difficulty in keeping them up and in order. You can have private roads in a township, and until they are given up to the township the Commissioners do not take charge of them.

Dr. Dunlop.—Those roads would be in the boundary.

316. Mr. Exham.—Yes; but you would not be bound to keep them up if they were private roads?

Dr. Dunlop.—I have no doubt that if we had charge of those roads we would save as much money as would keep them in order. And I think we should have the power to erect gasworks for ourselves, and instead of paying an enormously high rate that we do at present for the gas, we should get it at a much lower figure. The reason why we have to put out the gas at night is that the prices charged for it are so great that we cannot afford to keep them lighted longer than we do. The shorter time we keep the lamps lighted, the less the people have to pay. We should really have the power to erect gasworks ourselves, or to purchase them. I think if we had that, and also the roads, it would cause a lessened taxation.

317. You should know the feelings of the people in the township; is their opinion in favour of extension?—It is; and on the ground that they think the people outside who get advantages should pay something for them, while the people outside object because they are asked to pay for the advantages.

318. Mr. George Murray.—You have spoken of the price of gas in Holywood; can you tell me what is the price on the opposite side of the shore?—I don't know.

319. You have stated that the gas is very expensive here?—Yes; five shillings a thousand. What is it in Belfast?

Mr. Murray.—That's not a fair comparison; as a gas director I should like to be able to give it as cheap as in Belfast, but that, of course, is impossible.

Dr. Dunlop.—What has made the gas so very expensive here is the way in which they have expended their money, and the foolish way in which they laid an extra piping in down the road—the idea of a gas company piping along a railway! all the pipes had to be taken up again, and the town of Holywood had to pay for it.

Mr. Exham.—The gas all goes from Kingstown down the line of railway to Killiney, and they charge no[illegible] five shillings a thousand for it.

Mr. Murray.—On the opposite side of the shore they charge seven shillings and sixpence per 1,000 for it; in Holywood it is five shillings. The gas directors here, it is said, charge an enormous price; the dividend paid to the shareholders shows whether they charge enormously or not.

Dr. Dunlop.—That arises from bad construction; look at the expense they went to.

Mr. George Murray.

Mr. George Murray examined by

Mr. Exham.—I would suggest that the present boundary should be extended to the road passing the palace ground, held by Bishop Knox, and carried straight to Ardtullagh avenue. I don't want to bring in the Bishop's palace, but by the road that adjoins the palace. The present boundary is at the extreme end of the town; I would bring it up to the gate lodge; I would go straight up that road to the side of the Bishop's demesne and, as I have said, to Ardtullagh gate, where Captain Harrison resides, to the foot of his avenue; I would then continue along the King's-road straight on towards Mr. Gregg's of Ballymenoch, then on a straight line to the sea, adjoining Mr. Gregg's field; I would not go towards Belfast further than the Bishop's palace; I propose to leave Ballymenoch out.

320. Mr. Ross.—What advantage does Holywood House derive that Ballymenoch does not?

Dr. Dunlop.—They are precisely situated alike.

Mr. Murray.—I would take in Palatine cottage, value £40 a year; I would take five houses at Belview, value £65; Holywood House, value £110; Miss Ireland's, value £130. I would go in a straight line from that to the Croft, then I would take in Mr. Smith's house, £70; Mr. Prenter's, £60; Mr. Patterson's, £34; Mr. Maxwell's, £40, and the house adjoining, £40; Reverend Mr. M'Alister's house, £41, and two other houses £30; Mr. Bell's, £71; Mr. Anderson's hotel; Mr. Bar's house, £40; Mr. Moreland's manor, £60; then six houses at Seapark, towards the foreshore, £36, and another house close to the railway, £30. These are the valuations in the extension I would propose.

321. Would you stop there then?—I would; I would not go farther towards Marino than that. The total valuation I propose is £1,136 on houses, £246 on lands.

322. Dr. Dunlop.—You would give Ballymenoch all the advantages and charge them nothing for them?

Mr. Murray.—It would not pay to take it in.

323. Dr. Dunlop.—I don't see why you exclude Ballymenoch?

Mr. Murray.—For the reason I state that it would not pay, the reason I would extend towards Holywood House and that direction is, that the ground is now marked to let and houses will be built upon it; this ground of Mr. Gregg's is not so marked, nor is it likely to be let.

323. Captain Harrison.—Do you take in the whole of the Ballymenoch?—Yes, to the foreshore so far as it goes on a line to the Bishop's palace.

Captain Harrison.—That is a low flat of ground, and I think it would be a hardship to bring it into the town. Holywood House is in the same position as Mr. Gregg's; if you take it in you might as well take in Ballymenoch.

Mr. Crawford.—There is not a house on the way but Mr. Gregg's own, and the only portion that could be lighted would be the county-road. There is Marino station here, and Cultra station is the next one, and Marino and Cultra are the stations used for those lands along here; the people who live here occupying four acres, and so on go to Marino or Cultra, and go to Belfast daily for their different requirements, and don't go near Holywood.

324. Mr. Anderson.—You know this field of Mr. Gregg's down at the shore, don't you know that this is laid out in roads formed for building?

Mr. Murray.—I believe it is, but I am not sure.

Rev. Mr. O'Laverty.—And "barked" at present.

Mr. Murray.—About the town. I believe that the town is well sewered and paved, badly lighted, although Mr. M'Lean says it is well lighted; the lamps are put out at half-past ten o'clock; the burner he uses is the very smallest made.

Dr. Dunlop.—Some of the lamps are burning all night.

Mr. Murray.—The cost of the lamps is 16s. for the season, when in other towns it varies from £2 10s. to £3.

Mr. M'Lean.—Yes, burning all night.

Mr. Murray.—The Commissioners are only charged what they consume, as they pay by meter. The supply of water to the town is very bad; the supply should be brought from the hills above the town; at present it is only obtainable by pumps. I have not got anything further to say if the reporter has got down the valuation of the boundary proposed—£1,136 for houses, and £246 for lands.

325. Rev. Mr. O'Laverty.—You must still adhere to the opinion, after hearing about the differential rate, that the Town Commissioners should not have jurisdiction the length of the townland of Cultra?—I think what I have proposed would be fair.

Holywood you say is well paved, well sewered, but badly lighted and watered. Hundreds in the neighbourhood are benefited by it, the farmers can sell their

Holywood, [illegible] 1883. Mr. George Kilpatrick.

produce here, and there are schools kept up in the town in which these children can come, and they have other advantages in a great many ways.

Mr. Murray.—I think they should pay a small differential rate, but it should be a small one.

226. Do you think the landlord should pay something?—The landlord will be benefited as well as the tenant.

227. Mr. Rankin.—Doesn't he get a great deal higher rent for the land?—He does.

My suggestion was, that instead of paying a fourth, as at present under the Towns Improvement Act, the tenant or occupier should pay half, and that this half should be divided between landlord and tenant, thus letting the tenant only as he is and making the landlord pay one-fourth for the advantage he derives in getting his increased rent for his land.

228. Mr. Jamison.—Where a person is his own landlord what rates do you put on the house?

Mr. Rankin.—That is a question. They might probably be asked to pay the full rate, if they get the full advantages.

Mr. Murray.—At the time I made out the arrangement, I thought that all the places that would be taken in would be obliged to pay the shilling rating.

Rev. Mr. O'Laverty, P.P., examined by

Rev. Mr. O'Laverty, P.P.

Mr. Rankin.—My opinion is that there is an immense jealousy existing on the part of the ratepayers here that they have to keep the town lighted, build churches, schools, and the like for the convenience of the neighbourhood, whereby that neighbourhood is in a great measure in every respect and yet pays nothing; for instance, Holywood is the only place where churches for the neighbourhood are situated. Every church in Holywood has its services on Sundays and also sundry meetings on week-day evenings, while the parishioners of these districts attend, the members in the rural district also attend, and we are very jealous that here we have to keep lights for the convenience of those people to come to their churches and at the same time that we bear the expense of those lights, and those people pay nothing. It is well known that the approaches to the churches and the lights towards the churches are in every way better taken care of than in other districts simply for the convenience of so many of the ratepayers and parties outside the township going to those churches, and we unanimously think that the people residing at Cultra should pay a proportion of this rate.

229. You are one of the resident clergy here?—I am parish priest.

230. Is your place of worship largely frequented by people in the district proposed to be brought in by the municipality?—It is the only place in the whole parish of Holywood which extends a great distance round where they can come to.

231. What applies to your church applies, I suppose, to the others also?—Much more so. I was going to remark that what is everybody's business is nobody's business in this case. Now it is known that the foreshore at the Cultra end is in a disgraceful state; there are dead dogs and animals thrown up there which are never removed; nobody knows who should remove them; and it would be a decided advantage that the corporate body should have a jurisdiction over those things. Every person feels aggrieved at present and yet no one takes action. Very frequently filthy things are lying on the beach, and yet Mr. Ward and others take no trouble, and sometimes you can scarcely pass by from the smell of matter lying on the foreshore; and if we had a corporate body having jurisdiction over the locality, that body would take action to have the nuisance removed.

232. In your opinion are the sanitary wants of the people and the district better attended to by the urban sanitary authority than the Board of Guardians?—Yes; the Board are too far from around the local people would be more easily approached.

233. I would like to know your opinion, as being the parish priest, who is always moving about amongst the people, have you looked at this proposed extension?—I have.

234. From your knowledge of the situation of Holywood and the surrounding district, do you think that the extension now proposed, and with the addition I have suggested would be a fair line of boundary?—I think it would. We propose to carry it to the road that passes Mrs. Ireland's property, and I think it would be unfair to make that boundary without making four hundred feet beyond it the boundary for the people, and the other side would derive all the advantages from it, and we would have to pay for everything and they would enjoy the advantages. For instance in the Cruft we have our lamps so arranged that they shine down the Cruft, and rich people living there in palaces don't pay one farthing.

235. How far would you propose to take it at the north beyond the gate of the Bishop's palace?—I think 300 feet beyond it would be a fair boundary. Most of the rivers in Holywood have been polluted by sewage matter. I remember a case brought here before the Magistrates; it was brought by Mr. Barry against a Mr. O'Neill, for letting sewage matter run into the little river as it is called; and every other person is complaining in the same way.

236. Mr. Rankin.—If the Commissioners became the Urban Sanitary Authority over the proposed district, do you think the sanitary arrangements would be improved?—Very much improved.

237. Have you heard my suggestion about the extended district and the differential rate?—Yes.

238. Do you think one-half would be the sum for those people to pay for all these advantages?—Perhaps there should be a second division, a district extending down to Cultra Station or some place in that division, which naturally should pay a very large proportion of what we are paying in the town, and beyond that they should pay less.

239. Up to the present, the tenant has paid only one-fourth the rate on the valuation of his land; now it is proposed to make the landlord pay his proportion, do you think it would be fair to make the landlord pay one-fourth, and the tenant a fourth, thus making a half?—I think not, when we in this country have to pay Americans for bread stuffs; if a gentleman who has fifty acres of land, instead of turning it into tillage produce, keeps it under grass and in beautiful groves, it is fair that he should pay to the general public a proportion. It is his own business whether he has it the one way or the other.

240. What is the advantage to land in the immediate vicinity of a town in comparison to land that is a distance removed?—It is let from £20 to £30 an acre for building purposes.

241. What is paid for gardens, &c.?—I believe the farmers pay from £4 to £5 an acre for land that is turned into grazing ground, and the town of Holywood is in a state of starvation at present, for what is turned into grazing ground which the poor formerly worked on the potato system, and while the potatoes they grew they could pay their debts, that is all turned into grazing, and in the meantime, the people of Holywood are starving; what I want to show is that those places go for £4 or £5 an acre an acre, and if they were not near Holywood, they would be worth only about 35s. an acre.

242. Mr. Ward.—Dr. Dunlop, you referred to two roads in the neighbourhood of Marino that you thought the Commissioners should deal with, would you be surprised to learn that these roads are a closed-on right of way to the inhabitants of the village at Marino and neighbourhood, and no one else has a right to put a foot on them?

Dr. Dunlop.—I don't think that by any possibility such would be the case.

243. Why not?—Because I don't believe it is.

2 U 2

Holywood. Jan. 18, 1879.

Rev. Mr. O'Laverty, P.P.

243. Do you know where my gate is—did you ever see a gate across the road at Mr. Barbour's lodge?—I did. Is not that gate removed?

Mr. Ward.—No; and I mean to keep it there.

Dr. Dunlop.—There is no gate on the other road.

Mr. Ward.—I agree with you that the other road is a bad road.

Dr. Dunlop.—And so is yours.

244. Mr. Ward.—No; it is a nice road. Do you know that the other road is reserved by the owner of the Cultra estate, for the use of the farmers drawing seaweed from the foreshore?—I know it is an almost impassable road; I have to get down off my car and walk down it.

245. You refer to the road at Barbour's house?—It is the only entrance to Farm Hill and the Coastguard Station, and used by the public.

246. And used by the Coastguard and public?—It is used by the public, and I never heard of any one being stopped there.

247. Is there not a footpath for the use of the people in Farm Hill and the Coastguard Station?—It may be according to your ideas a well-kept road, but it seems to me extraordinarily bad.

Mr. Ward.—My object is to show that they are private roads.

Mr. Rynam.—Then the Commissioners would have nothing to do with them.

Mr. Ward.—No person has a right on these roads except——

Mr. Crawford.—It is enough to assume that they are private roads.

Mr. Ward.—Then the Grand Jury have nothing to do with them.

Mr. Rynam.—Some people in this country have queer notions as to what are roads.

248. Mr. Ward.—You say that the feeling of the people here is, that there should be an extension of the boundary?

Rev. Mr. O'Laverty.—Certainly.

249. How was that feeling ascertained, by public meeting or otherwise?—In passing through amongst the people no person could know better than I do their opinions, and I know that the general feeling is in favour of the extension.

250. As regards these people getting certain advantages and benefits for which they contribute nothing, do you remember that it was proposed to extend the area of taxation for water purposes; do you remember Captain Harrison proposed it at a public meeting, and a vote was carried against any extension?—I do, but you must remember that that meeting was largely composed of the people outside, and that it was the outside people that swamped the town.

Mr. M'Lean.—It was a packed meeting.

Mr. Ward.—It was called by public advertisement so that all had a right to attend.

Dr. Dunlop.—And the people of Holywood did not attend in the numbers that they attended from the outside district, and the vote was given against it. It was shown that they would have a good supply of water, and the Cultra people said they were about creating a reservoir down at Cultra to supply the village there: what was the fact?—That the reservoir was not sufficient for the one house it was created for.

251. Has there been any public meeting of the inhabitants of Holywood called by the Town Commissioners to ascertain whether or not the inhabitants were in favour of the proposed extension?—Dr. Dunlop, there has been no public meeting convened, because the Commissioners are the representatives of the people, and are the mouthpieces of the public, and none of the ratepayers came to object.

252. Was there any public notice whatever given to the parties residing outside the township of Holywood of this proposed extension?—Yes, by public notice in the papers, and by placards.

253. Posted where?—Along the roads.

254. Has any notice whatever been given by the Town Commissioners of Holywood to the inhabitants of these outlying districts of their intention to annex them?—It was not necessary. This Commission came down here to find out what should be done.

255. How can you, in your individual person, speak for the feelings of the people of Holywood?—I have explained it.

256. Mr. Rynam.—I asked him this question—from your knowledge of the people from going about amongst them, can you say there is a feeling in favour of the extension? He answered, he could say that there was. Then we have the parish priest, and he is a good authority, stating the same thing. If the people outside knew what the proposition now is, I think it very likely you would have a meeting to-morrow, and they would be desirous of coming in. They are, according to Mr. Anderson paying 1s. 10d. for county cess, but he says "we can do the work for 10d."; therefore there will be a saving of 1s. in every £1 within the boundary, in respect of the county rate. Then the proposal is to make them pay in lieu of the improvement rate sixpence; and to divide even that between landlord and tenant. If this was done they would benefit to the extent of 9d. in the £1 on the whole, and if the people knew this, you would have them saying, "Oh, if that is the case, bring us in by all means." So that you see it comes to the question of taxation.

256. Mr. Ward.—Now, Mr. O'Laverty, I think you based your opinion that there should be an extension on the fact that there are churches in Holywood?—Yes, that amongst others.

257. You think it a great hardship to have these churches lighted in the evenings for people who come from outside?—Yes.

258. And on that account you would like to tax the parties outside. Now, don't you think those parties are sufficiently taxed when they support their own clergy?—They are paying so much, but when coming to the church they are going through Holywood, deriving advantage from the light.

259. Don't you think that is more a matter for each congregation to do? What will you do with those who don't go to church, and I know some who cannot smell it more than once a fortnight?—The churches are there for them.

260. Now, you spoke of Marino foreshore—did you ever see a [illegible] foreshore in your life?—I was past it the other day and there was a dead animal lying there, and from the seaweed there was a fearful stench. I said when I went down why doesn't some one see to this sort of thing, but nobody does and I suppose nobody will.

[illegible] drainage and well attended to, and if you did [illegible] that it was the duty of the rural sanitary authority, [illegible] up to [illegible] the [illegible] it will be the duty of the Town Commissioners to compel you to do this with every single house you have.

That has been already done [illegible] at private expense.

Witness.—The [illegible] improvement rate.

Mr. Exham.—[illegible] have nothing whatever to [illegible] the improvement rate. The improvement rate is for other purposes.

Witness.—Is there to be no compelling then?

Mr. Exham.—Then you ought to compel the [illegible] to have it done.

Witness.—My houses are better [illegible] than any in the town. I want to know if the Commissioners or any other body have the right to send the whole of the [illegible] from this [illegible] down at [illegible], and [illegible] all the [illegible] in the town. They [illegible] within a few yards of [illegible] of the [illegible].

Mr. Exham.—I am not at liberty to give an opinion, [illegible] you [illegible] there.

Witness.—Oh, [illegible] it in any impartial tribunal that the great source of the [illegible] is that [illegible] of the [illegible] from the town; when it blows from the south west and the north-east, we get it both ways.

265. Mr. Exham.—What do you think about extending the district?—I think if it was [illegible] and [illegible] that it would be well; but, if they attempt to do with the people outside as they have done with us inside, I would call it [illegible].

James Emmerson.—I am a large ratepayer.

HOLYWOOD, Nov. 24, 1879.

Mr. William Woodside.

266. Mr. Exham.—Have you considered the question of the extension of the boundary here?—I have.

267. Is it fair and just that the boundary should be extended?—Very just; a great many people are deriving benefit from the [illegible] of Holywood who contribute nothing to it.

268. Do the people in this extended district make use of the town largely?—Those people use the town daily, and the Town Hall [illegible] for their own private accommodation.

269. Do you think it would be fair that those parties outside should be made to pay half the rate, [illegible] divided between landlord and tenant as long as they do not get all the advantages of those inside?—I think if the outlying parties paid a differential rate of one-third, divided between landlord and tenant equally, it would do. I think Mr. Anderson makes remarks [illegible], I would not like to [illegible] his way of speaking.

269. Captain Harrison.—Are you more [illegible] for [illegible]?—Yes.

270. Mr. Ward.—Where there was no landlord what would become of your theory?—He would be a happy man who had no landlord. He should just pay the whole.

271. And you would like him to pay it without corresponding advantage?—I would [illegible] like to use the [illegible] as he liked, and also, the Town Hall for private parties, and all that sort of thing.

272. I dare say they paid for the Town Hall?—We support the Hall.

Mr. [illegible].—Are you not aware that the outside people contributed towards [illegible] subscribed, and my brother subscribed £50.

Mr. [illegible] Legg[illegible].

Mr. George M'Cann examined.

Mr. George M'Cann.

I would approve of the extension of the boundary.

273. Mr. Exham.—Do you know the proposal to take in Miss [illegible]'s and Captain Harrison's in the [illegible] boundary, on the [illegible] side; would you think that a reasonable extension?—I do. I have had an opportunity of speaking to the people of Holywood on this subject, and I have never heard any objection except from those outside. I think, on the grounds of justice that there should be an extension. The people [illegible] very largely for [illegible], and as a [illegible] consequence the land [illegible] higher than Holywood than if it were further away.

274. Mr. Ward.—Would you go up to the mountain, where Captain Harrison lives?—I don't think there is a reasonable limit.

275. Would you not like to go and take in Mr. Black and Mr. Valentine?

Mr. Exham.—Mr. Black wants to be taken into Belfast.

Mr. M'Cann.—I would not go further than Captain Harrison's.

276. Now tell the Commissioners what advantage they will make [illegible]?—If it cost more, I would suffer the rate, if I was an outsider.

277. And for the pleasure of being in it?

Witness.—Yes, and I would like to be lighted.

Mr. Robert [illegible].—I am a ratepayer, and I am in favour of the extension as proposed, on the grounds spoken of by the other witnesses.

Mr. James [illegible].—I would approve of the extension also. I am a ratepayer and owner of house property in the town; and I think there is not one of the outsiders that would not derive as much benefit as I do, although I pay the full rate. I have not a footpath up to my own door.

Mr. James [illegible].—I am in favour of an extension, but only as far as suggested by others. I would stop at [illegible], but I would not go down to the [illegible] boundary [illegible]. I have to keep up my own roads myself. Holywood can give me no benefit in the wide world, except sending a lot of idle vagabonds every Sunday trespassing over the place, so that we have to keep a man to keep them off.

The Commissioners then adjourned till the next day.

HOLYWOOD.—NOVEMBER 25, 1879.

HOLYWOOD, Nov. 25, 1879.

277. Mr. Exham, Q.C., said he had just been over the road alluded to on the previous day by Mr. M'Lean, and he must confess he would be afraid to go up it on a dark night.

278. Mr. M'Lean.—It has been left there in that state for two years. The road is in good order, so far as the surface goes, but it is the making and formation of the road that is to be complained of.

279. Mr. Exham.—This is not a matter of keeping the road up, it is a matter of the original construction. The footway is, at least, two feet under the centre of the road, the road coming out down sharp towards it.

280. Mr. Anderson.—I want to explain the [illegible] [illegible] on the [illegible] that I gave yesterday. I brought down here the [illegible] of the Grand Jury [illegible] for the [illegible] of 1879, and the spring of 1879. The valuation of Holywood is £12,000 [illegible], and the [illegible]. [illegible] [illegible] 1s. 10d. and 2s. and the [illegible] paid by the town was £1,[illegible]. I [illegible] [illegible] for what is not [illegible] £[illegible] or £[illegible], but in round numbers the [illegible] £1,[illegible]. There [illegible] [illegible]

HOLYWOOD. [illegible]

townships in roads and crossings, and so forth, somewhere about £220 a year; according to those warrants it amounts to £223, and I would be happy for any gentleman to correct me for I want to be set right. The county-at-large expenses for these two half-years has been £23,833. Our proportion would be a 7¼d. rate all over, and £223 that we pay for roads would be a 4¼d. rate, so that these two added together makes our annual expenditure—7¼d. and 4¼d. that is 11½d.

281. Mr. Kehan.—It would appear from that that except the roads outside the district proposed to be brought in would cost more than those inside, which is contrary to the experience I have had elsewhere. There would be a practical saving to the people outside of 10d. in the pound.

282. Mr. *Anderson*.—I wish also to say the valuation of the whole of this eastern part that is proposed to be taken in by the Town Commissioners, for houses and lands is £8,363, and I am the owner of one-twelfth part of the whole of it, and I am quite favourable to its being taken in.

283. Mr. *Crawford*.—You don't consider yourself to be the owner of one-twelfth of the area.

284. Mr. *Anderson*.—I am, of property which will pay one-twelfth of the rate that will come out of it.

285. Rev. Mr. *O'Laverty*.—I find from conversation with several persons, yesterday evening and this morning, that they think the boundary should go westward towards Belfast, about the same distance as eastward. They believe that it would be a bad inconvenience to have a portion lying there between the two towns under the Grand Jury. Of course Belfast is certain to extend, and I believe Holywood will be a sort of county in itself; and consequently Holywood district should be extended about the same distance westward as eastward, namely about Connsrville, to which Belfast would come up.

286. Mr. Kehan.—The proposal in Belfast is to take in down to the Sydenham station—would your proposal be to go as far as Sydenham?—Rev. Mr. *O'Laverty*.—Yes.

287. Mr. Kehan.—So that there should be no hiatus?—Rev. Mr. *O'Laverty*.—It is the general opinion that that should be the natural boundary between the two peoples.

288. Mr. Kehan.—You say the opinion is that the whole shore is likely to be largely built upon. If so, in your opinion, would it be judicious to have a gap which would probably be no man's land?—I think not.

289. What would be the actual difference from the present western boundary up to Sydenham?—Captain Harrison—about one mile and a half. From the present boundary.

290. Mr. *Richard Patterson*.—I was unable to be here yesterday, but reading in the papers that it was stated the Town Commissioners were unanimous in agreeing about the extension of a certain boundary towards Cultra, I think it right to put myself in a proper light. I was present at the meeting referred to. I did not agree with my brother Commissioners and I think it is necessary, it having been stated that we were unanimous, that I should come down here and contradict that statement.

291. Mr. Kehan.—What is your idea with regard to the extension?—

292. Mr. *Patterson*.—There was a scheme originally drawn out by our Chairman, Mr. Anderson—I don't know whether he submitted that scheme or not—but towards Cultra side we came down by Ballymenoch bridge—that scheme I heartily approved of. On the western side we went down to the shore past Mr. Gray's house; on the Belfast side I would go by the road that lies between Miss Ireland's house and the Bishop's property. I would run up to Captain Harrison's house, not taking in his avenue or house, until we came to our own boundary at the top.

293. Mr. Kehan.—Then you are not for taking in Marino or Cultra, or for going down to the town land boundary by Craigavad?—

294. Mr. *Patterson*.—I don't object to going any distance provided you don't ask the people to pay for any portion of it. It would be unreasonable if you went [illegible] down the line and asked the people to contribute any portion of our rates, who are only two or three times in Holywood in the year. If you are looking forward to future extension or getting any extension from the county there would be a different [illegible].

295. Dr. *Dunlop*.—That's the very thing we are considering and the very thing we want.

296. Mr. *Patterson*.—There is an exceptional circumstance in the [illegible] line, a line of railway. We have a station at Marino and if the people don't come to Holywood and don't make use of our town [illegible] why should they pay for it.

297. Mr. Kehan.—The Parish Priest has yesterday stated that within the district proposed to be brought in there are congregations of Roman Catholics who all [illegible] to Holywood to attend their place of worship [illegible] the [illegible] [illegible] Protestant [illegible], they come to Holywood to their place of worship—their place of worship being all concentrated in Holywood. They have their schools here also; they come for amusement; many of them come in to go to the market, and use the town in that way. It is said it is for their advantage that they should have the lamps in use, but that they should not have it lighted [illegible] keep [illegible] for [illegible] altogether by the ratepayers in the town. That is the argument put forward in every other place. The people have the lights and they use the lights, and it is [illegible] their [illegible] that the [illegible] should be [illegible] and cleaned and the town should be improved so as to keep it as healthy as possible—that is all the [illegible] benefit and they accept it, but they say "don't ask us to pay for it; we will be glad to accept the [illegible] but we won't take any weight upon our own shoulders in payment." That's not the view [illegible] the legislature [illegible] [illegible] the [illegible] to make a new [illegible] for Queenstown, nor for [illegible], nor for Ballymena, nor for Clondalkin—would not be likely, we must [illegible] on some general principle, and the general principle seems to me, so far as I can see, to be whatever [illegible] [illegible] to be [illegible] valuable [illegible] of [illegible] to a town, and especially if it [illegible] building districts, whether it should not be brought in at least on a differential rate. And then comes another question, whether in these townships it would be advisable, as the Commissioners of the Howard Commission did, to have an individual authority managing the affairs of the townships, and further, that no town with less than 3,000 inhabitants should have the privilege of being a township at all.

298. Mr. *Patterson*.—My statement refers only to this town here. You have laid great stress on the advantage the farmers in the immediate neighbourhood have, of disposing of their produce in Holywood. My experience is, I have bought farm produce, hay, straw, and oats, and I find I can buy those things cheaper in the Belfast market, and cart them down, than I can in Holywood.

299. Mr. Kehan.—That is in the case of farm produce, but take the case of market gardeners, who sell vegetables at your doors, as well as milk and butter and poultry and all those small things—you would not get your milk every morning and evening from Belfast.

300. Dr. *Dunlop*.—Mr. Patterson is exceptionally situated; he has milk himself and he keeps his horse.

301. Mr. *Patterson*.—With regard to the lighting, it is little matter when a man is driving in his car, whether he is lighted half a mile or two miles through the darkness. If we go to Belfast they don't ask us to pay for their lights.

302. Mr. Kehan.—One of the arguments in Dublin about the townships is that they are Dublin citizens outside.

303. Mr. *M'Kenna*.—Mr. Patterson is one of the largest ratepayers in Belfast—very much more than we [illegible] they are—I am a ratepayer in Belfast and the majority of the people that I know going there by the train are ratepayers in Belfast.

304. Mr. *Patterson*.—There are a large number of

people who don't pay rates in Belfast living in Holywood.

305. Mr. M'Lean.—They don't go up to town then?

306. Mr. Patterson.—They do.

307. Mr. Exham.—Suppose that you were satisfied there would be a saving to those people if the roads were taken up, and the management put under one undivided authority, what would be your view?—[illegible] except there is some great mistake in Mr. Anderson's figures, it comes to this—at present the people there, both the occupiers of land and houses, are paying county cess at 3s. [illegible] in the pound on the average each year. The same work that is done by the county cess, Mr. Anderson says, be done by the Town Commissioners for [illegible]; so that there would be a saving of [illegible] to the people, if brought in, and if the Town Commissioners took up the roads. The highest rate, by the law as it stands, could be put on the people, the [illegible] the differential rate, and bringing them in, would be [illegible] for improvement rate, so that there is a saving of [illegible] to every ratepayer and occupier in that district, and a further saving of [illegible] in the pound to the occupier if the landlord is made liable for the half of that [illegible] would that alter your view?

308. Mr. Patterson.—I am sure all the residents would be glad to come in if you reduce this taxation.

309. Mr. Exham.—It is a question altogether of taxation. The residents want to bring them in and the outsiders don't want to be brought in if the taxation is increased. In every place this said, "if there is a saving being made, and if not, don't," so that it comes to a question of figures.

310. Mr. Ward.—Mr. Patterson, was that scheme that you approved of, the one the Commissioners approved of themselves, stopping at Ballymenoch?

311. Mr. Patterson.—It was Mr. Anderson's scheme.

312. Have they, by resolution, approved of the proposed scheme that they now submit?—There was no [illegible] at all; we were divided in opinion, and before we separated it was more or less [illegible] than debate.

313. Mr. Exham.—We have the minutes [illegible] the [illegible] here. It is as follows. This is the adjourned monthly meeting of the Commissioners:—

"After a lengthened discussion regarding the propriety of extending the boundary of the town, with its [illegible] map of the district [illegible] them, it was finally agreed to unanimously, that the Town Commissioners should recommend, at the forthcoming visit of the Boundary Commissioners, an extension of the boundary westward, to include the whole of the [illegible], the Holywood Rock [illegible] which the road to [illegible] and [illegible] [illegible] up to the wind, [illegible] [illegible] the present boundary, and on the eastern side to include those portions of [illegible] including [illegible] Mr. [illegible]'s and Mr. Gregg's to the [illegible] on [illegible], then along [illegible] to the Holywood and [illegible] road, and along [illegible] to the road leading to [illegible] station, and thence [illegible] the Harbour Commissioners to the sea, as shown more particularly on map."

314. Mr. Patterson.—Those minutes have not yet been confirmed, and I wish also to state that these [illegible] was written after the Commissioners had left the room.

315. Mr. Exham.—It appears there were only five present.

316. Mr. Anderson.—There were two vacancies and one absent. Mr. Chairman, I must say this, that I [illegible] upon Mr. Patterson's objection as a very [illegible] one. He did not say, "I don't agree with this," or make any [illegible], he merely said, "Well, I don't think it would be right to go so far," some objection of that kind, and there was not at all an [illegible] objection.

317. Mr. Exham.—If there was such an impression as that the proposition was adopted unanimously, it is corrected now. Mr. Patterson does not approve of the further extension.

318. Mr. Crawford.—With regard to Ballymenoch demesne, you will see where the Commissioners are talking about taking it in.

319. Mr. Exham.—There is nothing in our warrant enabling us to recommend that a certain portion should be taken in now, with power to the Commissioners to take in more afterwards at their pleasure.

320. Mr. Crawford.—Quite so. Mr. Hanson is here, who is agent for Mr. Gregg, and if you please we will deal with Ballymenoch first.

Mr. John Hanson examined.

Mr. John Hanson.

321. I don't know what advantage can be derived by Ballymenoch, unless what light would be emitted from three or four lamps up the road. There is one portion laid off for building purposes, and I have no objection that that should be included, but I should and do object very strongly to the whole demesne being taken in. It is a private residence, and taxing it to the amount of expense would bring it up to £23, £24, or £25.

322. Mr. Crawford.—Are these adjoining lands used for market gardens?

323. Mr. Hanson.—No.

324. And they don't sell produce in Holywood?—No.

325. Mr. Exham.—Does Mr. Gregg own the portion towards the east, as well as the demesne lands?—Yes.

326. Has he all that in his own hands?—Yes, he has 140 acres in his occupation.

327. What is the value of the agricultural land outside the demesne?—£3 an acre.

328. Mr. M'Lean.—Is there any of it let?

329. Mr. Hanson.—A portion down at the shore.

330. Mr. Crawford.—A part behind the demesne is let. If you want to test the agricultural value of it—the ground at the back of the demesne is in the hands of tenants of Mr. Gregg, who holds the townland of Ballymenoch, 320 odd acres, 140 of which he keeps in his own hands—if you want to know the agricultural value of the land, what the tenants are paying for what they hold as tenant farmers is a fair test.

331. Mr. Hanson.—It is let for £3 an acre. Mr. Gregg is not a resident in this house; he has it let to Mr. Crawford.

332. Mr. Exham.—Is this portion here (indicated on map) let out for building ground?

333. Mr. Crawford.—It is let to the railway company.

334. Mr. Hanson.—I may say I agree with the plan proposed at first by Mr. Anderson and agreed to by Mr. Patterson, and that it should be carried out.

335. Mr. Exham.—Do you think it an advantage to Ballymenoch to have lights up to the gate lodge?

336. Mr. Hanson.—Well, if the light of four or five lamps be worth £25 a year it is. Marino is the nearest road for the house.

337. Mr. M'Lean.—It is not used as much as Holywood.

338. Mr. Exham.—Suppose he had a splendid house where the gate house is, would you think he would derive advantage from having lights up to the very door of that house?

339. Mr. Hanson.—I do, that's the only advantage.

340. Don't you think it a great advantage to him when driving in to have this town swept and properly cleaned and kept a clean town and not dirty.

341. Mr. Ward.—Mr. Crawford travels in by Marino, never by Holywood.

342. Mr. M'Lean.—I meet Mr. Crawford every morning at Holywood.

343. Mr. Ward.—Yes; in the train; he gets in at Marino.

344. Mr. M'Lean.—No; I see him at the station getting in.

Belfast. Dec. [illegible]

Mr. John Hanson.

344. Mr. Ward.—I travel with him every morning.

345. Mr. Hanson.—If the lights of a few lamps is an equivalent for a tax of 6d. on £100, I am satisfied.

346. Mr. Kirwan.—Suppose it were a tax on a valuation of £[illegible] a year?

347. Mr. Hanson.—That is supposing a case, that is not a reality.

348. Mr. Crawford.—The Holywood railway is the means of access to Belfast.

349. Mr. Hanson.—Yes; it is.

350. And several stations along that railway are the points at which parties get in and out?—Yes.

351. Is there a station at Marino?—There is.

352. That is the nearest point to Mr. Gregg's gate?—It is.

353. Mr. Crawford.—What I want to show is that there are stations along here, and that the value of the land is affected by its situation and suitability for villa residences, and by its vicinity to Great Belfast, and not by the fact of Holywood being a town in the neighbourhood. The lands are benefited in value owing to their proximity to the stations only and not to Holywood, and the railway is the means of communication with Belfast, and they take their special value from being in the vicinity of Belfast and not Holywood.

354. Mr. Kirwan.—Then, according to your idea all these villa residences require as much of self government?—Not at the present time.

355. If it is let out as building ground is it your idea that the owners are to be left itself as until the houses become so numerous that they might self government?—At the present time the Commissioners don't propose to take them.

356. They must bring them in now or not at all, as far as our Report is concerned.

357. Mr. Crawford.—What Mr. Hanson says is this—if they bring in the lower portion of the road and prepare the roads, and light and discharge the other duties of Commissioners he has no objection to being brought in, but if they are brought in and get an corresponding benefit, he does object.

358. Mr. Kirwan.—These stations, you say, are forming the centres round which the buildings are going on?

359. Mr. Crawford.—Yes.

360. Is it then your opinion that there should be no authority watching the erection of these buildings? nothing provided that for sanitary purposes they have a sanitary protection at the present time.

361. In what?—In the Board of Guardians. These parties would not object to being brought under the same sanitary district as Holywood or to extend the township if the thing was to be done beneficially and not partially; they object to being charged a half rate for the imaginary benefit they get at the present time. Now with regard to the situation of the land, I think it would be desirable if we should have some evidence to show that along the shores of the Belfast Lough to Bangor is built of the same character, a long strip of land. Mr. Hanson, is this land bounded by the Belfast Lough, on the north; and does it rise in a southerly direction?

362. Mr. Hanson.—Yes.

363. Mr. Crawford.—Is that the character of the land from Belfast to Bangor?—Yes.

364. And the sewerage of Ballymenoch and the other districts from Holywood to Bangor have no connexion with and derive no special benefit from Holywood sewerage?—No. It is quite independent and distinct sewerage.

365. Is there any necessity or want of a water supply in connexion with Ballymenoch, Culloden, and so on?—I think not.

366. Could Holywood supply water to these adjoining lands?—Certainly not.

367. Are the lands of Ballymenoch, Culloden, and so on, occupied as market gardens for Holywood?—No; I am not aware of it, so far as I know it.

368. Are their lands where they are laid out used as villa residences?—Yes.

369. Not as Crown with agricultural produce?—No.

370. Then, in your opinion, is it necessary for these people to go to Holywood at all in connexion with their daily business, or is it their ordinary custom to go to Holywood?—Unless those who go for religious purposes on Sunday.

371. But on week days are they in the habit of going to Belfast?—Belfast is the principal market town, unless for eggs, or butter, or milk.

372. Mr. Hanson.—Is there any system of sewerage about these houses except the natural drainage? There is a gentleman in court who will answer that question.

373. Where does the sewage of Mr. Gregg's property go to?—In the sewage from Ballymenoch conducted in the sea in an open drain?—It is.

374. Do you think it is right that the sanitary authority should allow that—drain that drain pass close to inhabited houses there?—Within a few yards.

375. How far are the houses from the drain?—The nearest house is above the drain but so fifteen feet.

376. Why are Mr. Gregg allowed the sewage to be discharged that way? (No answer).

Mr. Crawford.—Is there a drain?—Not that I am aware of. There is a large culvert down from the house to the sea.

377. Mr. Kirwan.—Is all the sewage from that discharged into an open drain which passes so close to inhabited houses, and have the sanitary authorities permitted them to go on unmolested with it?—It is the greatest mistake in the world to call it a nuisance.

378. How many houses are there on Mr. Gregg's property?—None, except his own.

379. What is the quantity of building ground you say is built on there?—Twenty or twenty-two acres. It is between Ballymenoch House and the sea.

380. What is the rent asked for it?—£[illegible] an acre.

381. If Mr. Gregg were to throw open this portion of the demesne (building in this way), would it be taken for building?

Mr. Hanson.—That's not very likely.

382. Mr. Crawford.—Has there been any complaint as to this drain?—I never heard of any.

383. Is it offensive to the inhabitants?—No.

384. Mr. Kirwan.—If a sewage drain passes the door of any man there must be some nuisance. You say you don't see why Mr. Gregg should pay £[illegible] odd towards taxation towards the lighting up of Holywood. Suppose Mr. Gregg were saved £[illegible] by being brought in, would you say bring him in?—Yes, if there was a guarantee.

385. You were here yesterday, and you heard Mr. Anderson's figures, and from the books it is as clear as the daylight. If those figures are true and the County Grand Jury rate remained the same, Mr. Gregg would save [illegible] in every £1 he now pays—such a case would you object to his being brought in?—I would not.

386. Then it comes to this, that the only thing is a question of money?—I have found figures on paper very deceptive.

387. Can you point out the slightest fallacy in Mr. Anderson's figures. There is the return taken from the public books of the Grand Jury of the county of Down for the spring and summer assizes of last year?—I have no doubt of its accuracy. Are the Commissioners bound to take the roads under their charge. If roads were made on this building ground, are they bound to take those roads over?

388. If the owners made those public they would be bound to keep them if they were within the township.

389. Mr. M'Lean.—Is this house of Mr. Gregg's occupied by Mr. Crawford?

Mr. Hanson.—Yes, it is.

390. Has Mr. Crawford the ground as well as the house?—He has the lawn and a portion of the farm besides.

Belfast. [illegible]

Mr. John Hanson.

391. And the other portion is kept in Mr. Gregg's own hand?—Yes.

392. Are you aware that there is a garden in connexion with that house and that not only the fruit but the vegetables are sold in Holywood?—I am not aware that they are sold. I am not aware that Mr. Crawford sells.

393. Have not you a man there yourself?—Yes, a caretaker, but he has nothing to do with it.

394. Does he sell the vegetables?—They were sold at the time the house was vacant, but I don't know now.

395. Are you aware that Mr. Crawford uses the Holywood station to travel to Belfast?—I don't know that I ever met him.

396. Mr. M'Lean.—Then I meet him every morning. Mr. Crawford does go to town daily?

Mr. Hanson.—He goes frequently.

397. Was the late Mr. Russell the law agent?—He was.

398. Were you present at the inquiry before Mr. Boyd with regard to the value of Mr. Gregg's land?—I was.

399. Did you yourself swear that the land was worth more than £20 an acre?—I swear nearly that it was worth more than £20, I am not certain that I swore that.

400. You heard Mr. Russell swear that he refused £20 an acre for it?—I did.

401. Was there any reason for not granting leases to parties?—I am not aware of it.

402. Was Mr. Gregg unable to lease the property on account of being a minor?—Mr. Crawford can answer that. During the last two or three years I have let several portions in perpetuity.

403. Have you taken any means to prevent the discharge of those houses being objectionable to the village in the neighbourhood?—

404. Mr. Crawford.—It is objectionable. That is the last thing.

405. Mr. M'Lean.—Have you passed it on yourself, Mr. Hanson?—Sometimes I have.

406. Have you ever felt a stench from it?—Sometimes I have on a summer day.

407. Has Mr. Gregg taken any means to prevent that stench being injured by the discharge of this sewage matter from it?—No; but if Mr. Gregg had heard any complaint he would have obviated it.

408. Didn't you, as Mr. Gregg's agent, discover this stench?—I have.

409. Why not, as his agent, take precautions to prevent the public suffering from it?—It was a matter of such trifling inconvenience or annoyance that I did not think anyone complained.

410. Were you passing on the public road at the time you perceived it?—Yes, I was.

411. Mr. Brown.—Did you ever hear it said the Sanitary Acts; the only question is not, whether a nuisance is existing or great but whether a nuisance exists?

412. Mr. M'Lean.—Are you aware that the public lamps are taken, at present, almost out to Mr. Gregg's place?

Mr. Hanson.—I am not sure. I think they go to Mr. [illegible]'s gate.

413. Then you derive all the advantage of it you want, in town?—That is the only advantage I know of at present.

414. Mr. Brown.—That is all you can have at present.

415. Mr. M'Lean.—This house derives all the advantages from lighting that a house in town derives from it.

416. Mr. M'Lean.—And you know it that we are obliged to economise as much as possible from want of funds, and we put it out at 10-30 p.m.

417. Mr. Robert Gordon.—Mr. Hanson, how much do you receive from Mr. Crawford for the land you have sublet to him?—It is a lump sum.

418. How much?—The rent is £60.

419. And the field on the other side of the road?—Yes, I think it is £30 a year.

420. How much per acre?—I don't know.

421. Do you know it is at the rate of £5 an acre?

422. Mr. Brown.—How much is in it?—There is more than four acres in it. He does not pay £5 an acre.

423. Could you give me the valuation of that ground you say is worth £20 an acre?—I think it is £200. I think about that.

424. What are you paid at present for this land that you say is laid out as building ground?—It is let to a man named Boyd. He pays £45.

425. How many acres are in it?—I could not give you the exact quantity. I suppose there might be eleven or twelve acres.

426. Mr. Dundas.—It is usual for parties to supply Holywood with milk. Mr. Boyd realises a large sum by it. There are, I believe, no less than eleven cows on it.

427. Mr. Brown.—It is valued at £2 an acre.

428. Mr. Wood.—I appear to say there is an extraordinary desire on the part of the Holywood Town Commissioners to take charge of the gentlemen who are here to oppose any extension of the township. Now I scarcely know what is at the bottom of the eagerness exhibited by the Commissioners themselves, and their friends, to take us into the township whether we will or not. I don't know whether it is that they know our own business better than we do ourselves, and that they are better able to judge what would benefit us than we are ourselves. Probably they do, probably they do not, but it does appear to me to be an extraordinary claim that they propound. If the scheme adverted to yesterday by Mr. George M'Lean, which was the original scheme of Mr. Pattison, and I presume, of the Commissioners also, has been carried out, as they resolved upon, there never would have been probably any sense of complaint. Mr. Pattison, one of the Commissioners themselves, who has given, I dare say, the clearest and best evidence we have yet heard since this Commission opened, assures us in the Minutes, that it would not go further than the lights they have pointed out upon the map to him. Now it appears, as I have heard the original intention of the Commissioners themselves, that they would not further extend the boundary, and although it was apprehended yesterday that this extended boundary had the countenance of the Commissioners themselves, we find that, though in putting upon their feelings enough a short interval, and then actually these schemes have come into the world; and Mr. Pattison tells us a most extraordinary thing, that it was not until after all the Commissioners had left that that scheme was sprung out. I could very well understand the Commissioners, if they said to the parties residing outside the present township, "We propose to tax you, but at the same time we also propose to give you some advantages for the taxation, which we will presently explain to you." When I pressed Mr. M'Lean in cross-examination, he said, "We propose to light you." "When?" "When the district is sufficiently strong," was the cautious answer. "And when may that interesting period arrive; will it be within one hundred or within fifty years?" "Probably," he said, "within a period of [illegible] years." When do you propose to supply us with water? I don't know whether that's in the scheme or not, but it would be part of their duty, for it is incumbent upon them to supply the inhabitants with water, otherwise the Court of Queen's Bench might have something to say in the matter. Do they propose taking charge of us from a sanitary point of view? No; although you pressed them strongly, sir, what was the answer they gave?—"We will have nothing to do with the drainage, we won't light you or water you, we will do nothing for you until it pleases us; the kind assistance, however, to you we have, which we will have great pleasure in drawing out of your pockets, without giving you anything in return." That's the scheme and a more [illegible] one never was propounded. It's like Dutch reciprocity, all on one side. They urge that the inhabitants

benefits from Holywood in the shape of churches and schools. I presume those who attend our several churches pay all that is necessary to support their clergy, and if there be lights in the churches, I apprehend the congregations pay for them, and if any of them send their children to the schools, excellent schools they are too, the best in the country, they pay for them. But are we to be taxed outside the borough? Mr. Crawford in the most admirable way, when examining Mr. Hanson, demonstrated clearly that so far from those adjoining lands being improved by their proximity to Holywood, the advantages which they enjoy, they derive from proximity to Belfast and the railway stations. The parties who have reared the magnificent villas that adorn the district, which the Commissioners propose to annex, have built those villas there for the express purpose of getting away from towns and taxation, and being in a pleasant place where they can live with their families, without having anything to say to the nuisance of corporations or the pleas of Town Commissioners. It is to get rid of all that we come to the country—for the purpose of getting home happiness and retirement when we go there. You were good enough, sir, to refer to Banbridge. There is no analogy between Holywood and Banbridge. Banbridge is a borough and parliamentary town and a market town. Holywood is not a market town. Why the farmers from the surrounding districts are obliged to go into town with their buttermilk, preferring Belfast. There is no open market here. If a weekly tenant is sought to be ejected they must go to Newtownards, because it is not a market town, and because the law of small tenements does not apply to Holywood, and that is the best proof I could give you, that it is not a market town. Beyond all question, parties can buy cheaper in Belfast than in Holywood. Then is it not a cool proposition, to say the least of it, that the Commissioners propose to go a mile or two miles out on the east and west, take in parties who don't want any supply of water from them, because they have made all the necessary arrangements to supply pure water for themselves, and who don't want any supervision as to sanitary matters, because, as far as that is concerned, they have made their own sanitary arrangements. All the Commissioners practically say is "Keep the county cess, pour money into our pockets, and perhaps in a century or a half century we will condescend to light you, and perhaps if you are not civil we will clap the maximum rate of one shilling on you, and not light you at all." There are two parties to a contract. Whether this scheme is recommended or not recommended there will be more heard of it, because it cannot be allowed to you when it is at present. I won't say more, because the proposition is so monstrous that there is no gentleman here can fail to see that the greatest injustice would be done to the inhabitants living outside this district if they were to be taxed, and obliged to pay taxes, without getting any corresponding benefit whatever.

429. Mr Kernan.—With regard to the unreasonable nature of the proposition I could name to you several towns in Ireland in which the inhabitants of villas within a certain distance of the town have begged to get in provided they got in on half terms.

430. Mr. Ford.—Those are exceptional cases. I now hand in this memorial to you (memorial produced) signed by twenty-two of the residents of Cultra and Marino. (See Appendix, No. 3).

Mr. William Francis Durand examined.

431. Mr. Ford.—Where do you reside?—At Woodleigh, Marino.

432. How long have you resided there?—Upwards of sixteen years.

433. Do you know the district very well that the Town Commissioners propose to take into the township?—I do.

434. Will you state, since you went to reside there sixteen years ago, how many houses have been built in the district?—In the district first proposed by the Commissioners—that is up to the arch at Cultra station, there have been sixteen houses during that time.

435. Can you say whether, in your opinion, the district derives any advantage from being near Holywood?—I consider it derives no advantage whatever; as far as I am personally concerned I don't care if Holywood was wiped off altogether. It would not cost me a moment's inconvenience.

436. Do you go to church there?—I do not, I go in another direction.

437. Would not you think it rather hard to be annexed to the Holywood township and taxed for it because you went to church in Holywood?—I would think it very hard.

438. Are these houses principally villas in the district proposed to be annexed?—They are entirely villa residences.

439. With the exception of some few cottages at Cultra?—Yes, and a coastguard station.

440. So far as you are aware, are these villas, or most of them, supplied with water?—I believe they are all supplied with water as far as I have ever heard of them.

441. The landlord makes his own sanitary arrangements in connexion with them?—As far as I am aware.

442. Do you use Holywood as a market, or go there for marketing purposes?—I deal with Belfast as cheaper and more convenient.

443. I suppose you are anxious to avoid town taxation—that is your object in living in the country?—Partly, and partly for the health of my family.

444. Did you hear Mr. M'Lean's evidence yesterday, that although we might be taxed at this differential rate they did not propose to light the district until it was self-supporting?—Yes.

445. Did you also hear him say, that it might be twenty-five years before that they would light it, although they will tax it?—I think he admitted that.

446. What is your opinion about that proposition?—I think, in the meantime, it would be unfair to ask us to pay the half of the Holywood rate.

447. Have you anything more to add?—I have nothing more to add.

448. Mr. Kernan.—You know this ground of Mr. Gregg's, between Ballymenoch House and the shore, which Mr. Russell stated the value of to be £20 an acre—do you think that is caused by the proximity of that land to Holywood?—No; the proximity of Belfast, and the accommodation of the railway.

449. Do you think it desirable that this district should be put under any form of government?—It requires none at present that I am aware of.

450. Is every man allowed to make his own sanitary arrangements?—As regards sanitary supervision, I believe there should be a sanitary authority of some sort to prevent wilful injury or injury through ignorance.

451. Do you know this drain into which Ballymenoch House discharges itself?—Yes.

452. Does it pass close to your house?—It does not.

453. Mr. Harrison adapts for much in it?—I have felt it too. I think that might be improved, and ought to be.

454. You don't deny the justice of the Sanitary Act; do you call that a nuisance?—It is.

455. Don't you know that since 1844 that nuisance has been going on there?—There never was any objection to it.

456. You say the tenants make their own sanitary arrangements, and you are satisfied to allow a nuisance to exist for several years a short distance up from your own house—do you know how these houses drain at

[illegible] there, or do they know any public sewer?—No; they drain into cesspools, so far as I am aware.

457. What becomes of the overflow from the cesspools?—I believe the overflow goes [illegible] the cesspools on their land.

458. Mr. Anderson.—Are the Holywood [illegible] [illegible], Mr. Hanna?—Partly, I understand generally by Marino.

459. Mr. Ward.—Mr. Crawford generally travels from Marino, doesn't he?—He does.

460. Dr. [illegible].—Is it not a fact that you generally come by Holywood?

Mr. Hanna.—Sometimes.

461. Is it not invariably?—No.

462. Mr. M'Lean.—As you have [illegible] my [illegible], how far [illegible] how often this [illegible] Mr. Crawford travelled from Marino station?—Three or five days out of the week.

463. Are you prepared to say he travelled four days out of the six from Marino station?—As far as I could judge.

464. What do you mean by saying that "public lighting, which is the only feasible benefit within the power of the Commissioners, the inhabitants don't consider necessary, as then it would materially add to their taxation." What do you mean by "public lighting, which is the only feasible benefit attainable"?

Mr. Dunwoody.—I mean that the Commissioners can do nothing more for us [illegible] than [illegible] to the public road and we don't want these.

465. You ignore the fact that they would have a sanitary [illegible] over you? If you read the memorial you will see about that.

466. Mr. Ward.—They have a Sanitary Board at present—the Poor Law Board.

467. Mr. M'Lean.—Tell me do you know anything about the sanitary condition of Mr. [illegible] house?—No.

468. Of Mr. [illegible] house?—Yes.

469. Has he cesspools?—No.

470. Where do the [illegible] discharge before the Holywood Town Commissioners, on the beach?

471. You consider that a proper thing to do?—I do not.

472. Do you know anything about Mr. [illegible] house?—I know nothing about the sanitary condition of his house.

473. I see Mr. Kennedy of [illegible] has signed. Do you know anything of his house?—I do not.

474. Of Mr. [illegible]?—Yes.

475. Has he cesspools?—He has.

476. Where does the overflow go?—I think into drain.

477. Do you know that of a fact?—I cannot speak positively.

478. Do you know anything about the sanitary arrangements of Mr. [illegible] house?—No.

479. Do you know of any others in this memorial?—I know Mr. [illegible] have houses and [illegible] cesspools.

480. You have said [illegible] about [illegible]

Mr. Dunwoody.—I know they fall into cesspools.

481. Is it an open drain?—Yes, I think so; if there is an overflow at all.

482. Mr. Hanna.—How many houses drain into this open drain, from Ballymenoch House?—I think there is only Ballymenoch House.

483. For the sixteen years you have been there, has any officer from the Poor Law Guardians come down to inspect those houses?—The sanitary officer is here, and can answer that.

484. Do you know that he ever went there?—I leave at an early hour in the morning, and come home late in the evening, and consequently I don't know.

485. Did he ever come to inspect your own house?—I don't believe he did.

486. And when you say they are drained, is the Commissioners' area drained on the foreshore; should not the local sanitary officers have complained?—They should.

487. But did they do it?—I don't know.

488. Mr. M'Lean.—Do you know anything about Marino House?—I do not.

489. Don't you know that it drains into that very open drain on Mr. [illegible] demesne?—They were connected long before I went there.

490. Would you think it right that that district should be properly drained, and sewered having regard to the sanitary [illegible] of the present day?—Yes, wherever the drainage is defective.

491. Would you think it right that some authority should examine them to see if they are defective?—Certainly.

492. Suppose it were found defective, then it would have to be remedied, and it would cost money whether done by the Commissioners or by the Guardians?—I suppose the Commissioners could as easily remedy [illegible] nuisance as the Guardians.

493. Well, having regard to that district, do you think that some body should take charge of sanitary arrangements, looking that for sixteen years this open drain has run from Ballymenoch House, and [illegible] [illegible] [illegible] into it [illegible] do you say?

Mr. Ward.—That's not proved.

Mr. Hanna.—I object to the expression that can [illegible] done.

494. Mr. Hanna.—Mr. Dunwoody admits it is a nuisance, and if so, it could very easily be remedied to [illegible] that nuisance [illegible] [illegible] certainly think the Sanitary Act should be carried out all over Ireland.

495. What Sanitary Act?—The Public Health Act of last year.

496. The same powers were in existence since 1866, as regards the abatement of nuisances, and the Act of 1878 only made it more stringent; but for sixteen years the Board of Guardians, who were the parties to abate the nuisances, don't appear to have taken one single step towards doing so. That is the reason why I asked you was that a nuisance, and you say it is?—I presume, because it was not brought to their notice.

497. Mr. M'Lean.—For the sixteen years that you have lived there, Mr. Dunwoody, was that drain opened and cleaned out?—Yes.

498. You said you came here for the health of your family, and to save taxation, is not that the reason why you oppose this plan?—No.

499. Mr. Ferris.—Do you see any fallacy, or could you point out any fallacy in the figures of Mr. Anderson about the rental?—I daresay Mr. Anderson has taken accurately the figures and various items out of the valuation, but I doubt that the Commissioners would stick to the figures that he states has been set [illegible] on them, and I am very doubtful whether we would find it profitable to be under the Commissioners as regards our roads.

500. On what do you base that, do you think that they would not keep the roads as clean as at present?—I don't see that Holywood is kept so exceedingly clean. Our county roads are kept, on the average, nearly as clean as Holywood. Unless on the crossings, I would get my boots soiled as well crossing the streets as crossing the roads.

501. Have you been in other towns in Ireland?—I have been in a good many.

502. Do you know of any town kept in a better state than Holywood?—I don't think we can say much for the sanitary arrangements of Holywood.

503. Do you say that Holywood is in a bad sanitary state?—I do.

504. Mr. Ward says you have as good a Poor Law Board as any in Ireland, it that is the case, what is the sanitary condition of Holywood and the surrounding district to us but as your agent, of what are those sanitary [illegible] about?—I don't think the Board have done their duty there.

505. Mr. Ward.—With regard to the Board, the question is this, the following [illegible], if he discovers a nuisance, reports it to the medical officer for the district, and he [illegible] whether this nuisance is injurious to health, and the Board is [illegible] its medium.

Holywood, 1st [illegible]
Mr. William S. Dunwoody.

HOLYWOOD. Jan. 22, 1879.

Mr. William F. Dugand.

506. Mr. *Dugand*.—My objection to the sanitary condition of Holywood is, that I think it very injurious to have four outlets for the sewage of a town like Holywood at high water-mark, as it is washed backwards and forwards by the tide and not swept out to sea. This has been the cause of the dreadful smell we have been suffering from the last year, and no wonder that has the sanitary arrangements in that state is in a satisfactory state.

507. Mr. KEHAN.—Who is responsible for that—is it this compulsory Board of Guardians, they could have made proper sewers, and could have formed a contributory district for paying the expenses of making them.

508. Mr. *M'Lean*.—Was not Sir Thomas M'Clure anxious to get Sydenham brought into the Holywood township?—I never heard that.

509. You never heard that he wanted us to extend our Act to embrace *Sydenham*?—I don't say that he did not, but I am not aware of it, but what you are leading to I suppose is that he would have preferred having it under the Holywood township, as the sanitary authority, than under the Board of Guardians for they neglected their duty.

510. He preferred being under Holywood to Belfast?—Yes, he would, as he would have smaller taxation.

511. Mr. KEHAN.—Would you approve of having undivided management in a town like this, one Board for everything?—I think it would be an advantage, but I would not extend the area until there was a necessity arising from the multiplication of houses and population.

512. Your idea then would be that you are to wait until the houses spring up, and not to get control over the builders beforehand?—I don't see that the Act gives them any supervision over the building ground.

513. What Act?—The Act of 1878.

514. It gives supervising powers over all sanitary arrangements and plans for houses, and so on. No man can be permitted to build houses, except he has submitted them to the Town Surveyor, and now is it your idea that a district laid out for building ground, and according to you it is all building ground all the way down to Bangor, should not be under supervision?—Not further than the sanitary authority which exists everywhere.

515. Would you leave them under a Board of Guardians, that you say has neglected its duty and done nothing?—I admit they have not done their duty.

516. Very well; would you leave them under that Board?—I have no objection to the Town Commissioners as the sanitary authority.

517. Suppose the district was extended as proposed by the Commissioners here, and that they took the management of the roads into their own hands, and that these figures of Mr. Anderson are right, what would you say—suppose the owners of the land and houses were able to save threepence or sixpence in the pound in taxation, would you prefer to stay as you are?—I would prefer to stay where I am with the certainty of knowing what expenses I have been at, rather than to be brought in with the uncertainty and vague hope of saving.

518. There is no uncertainty; there is no person allowed to levy unlimited taxation?—Yes, but there are other rates that are prospective, for instance, the water rate.

519. The Act of Parliament will settle that, if that is your idea; there is a limit to all rating. If they fix a sewer rate they must show a necessity for it, they cannot say two shillings for making sewers, ten shillings for supplying water. The water rate would be a fixed rate; in any provisional order the rate would be fixed. There is no town that I know where a rate can be levied at the Commissioners like.

520. *Witness*.—Taking the supply of water to a sanitary measure is it not practically unlimited.

521. Mr. KEHAN.—To this extent; you must get a provisional order from the Local Government Board, authorising you to carry out the scheme, they cannot do it themselves but they estimate what it will be, the interest on the borrowed money, and so on.

522. *Witness*.—What would happen were I in want of water, and did not want to be brought in at this rate?

523. Mr. KEHAN.—There are lots of people who want to make their own sanitary arrangements; they won't do it properly but the Act of Parliament compels them.

Mr. THOMAS GARRETT examined.

Mr. Thomas Garrett.

521. Mr. *Ward*.—You live in Craigavad?—Yes.

522. Are you landlord of the house in which Mr. Dugand lives?—I am, with my brother.

523. How many houses have you there?—Three houses.

524. Would you state what the sanitary arrangements are?—For the three houses there is a cesspool into which the water-closets empty.

525. Do you find that cesspool answer the purpose?—Yes; so far there has never been any complaint.

526. Do you have it cleaned out at stated periods?—Several times a year.

527. You know this district that the Commissioners propose to take in?—Yes.

528. You would prefer to remain as you are, paying county cess, than to be brought in?—Certainly. Supposing they bring in the water rate here we will be liable to 2s. cut there.

529. Mr. KEHAN.—Don't you know that water brought into Holywood would probably be put upon a contributory district of which you would have to pay your fair proportion? (No answer.)

530. Mr. *M'Lean*.—Is there any overflow pipe from that tank?—No; there is no place for it to overflow to. It is cleaned out.

531. What is the size of the cesspool?—In the houses there are three water-closets and privies; they are all separate.

532. What is the size of the cesspool?—I don't know.

533. About what size?—I can't say.

534. Mr. KEHAN.—Do you know the drain coming down from Ballymenoch House?—I do not, I think my houses are a quarter of a mile from it.

535. Mr. *Robert Carlisle*.—How many feet is that cesspool from the edge of the county road?—I don't know.

536. Mr. *Carlisle*.—I am in a position to say it is not more than fifteen or sixteen feet from the county road, and that it is lying open with a few boards over it.

537. Mr. KEHAN.—Is that so?

Witness.—It was covered in with boards at one time, but perhaps they have rotted away.

Mr. KEHAN.—It must be covered in.

Mr. *James Moore*.—I have passed it often, and it is covered over almost.

Mr. KEHAN.—It should be covered over entirely.

Mr. SAMUEL TRIMBLE examined.

Mr. Samuel Trimble.

538. Mr. *Ward*.—You reside in Ballycultra?—Yes.

539. Have you recently built some houses there?—I have three, one small cottage, a larger cottage, and a house. The poor law valuation is £113 a year.

540. Are they all tenanted yet?—They are.

541. Mr. KEHAN.—What ground rent do you pay?—£9 an acre for the first five, and £8 an acre for the remaining four—£87 odd in the year.

542. Mr. *Ward*.—Is it your opinion that your property would be improved if brought within the Holywood township?—I think not.

543. Would you prefer to remain paying the county

... without being included in the town lands of Holywood?—I certainly would.

544. Mr. [illegible].—What is your objection?—[illegible] objection in supposing I were building, as I intend to do, other houses, I would have the trouble and annoyance of submitting plans to the Commissioners and then [illegible] would be inclined to dictate, whereas, at present, I can use my own discretion.

545. You are wrong, in that respect, you would go to the Commissioners and get their [illegible]?

Witness.—My plan is for my own sake, and for the sake of the parties living there, to get all things right.

546. The Legislature does not leave people a discretion there.

Witness.—I know. I am anxious to have everything as complete as possible.

547. What other objection would you have to coming into the township?—At present I know exactly what money I will have to pay in the shape of taxes; supposing the Town Commissioners were to put the place into their own hands, I don't know what I would have to pay.

548. Only what the law permitted?—But supposing the taxation by the Commissioners amounted to more than I at present pay, were I building those houses I have built, the taxes would have to be deducted from the rent and the houses would not bring in [illegible].

549. But supposing the taxation was lowered it would bring [illegible]?—Yes; but I have given [illegible].

550. Those are the figures?—I believe the figures are right, but I don't understand their anxiety to get us in to give me this advantage.

551. They say that for every 10s. you pay, everyone in the town will have it also.

Witness.—With regard to water, I have a [illegible] and [illegible] for rain water, and besides all these I get water from the hills, a [illegible] pipe down to my own place, and [illegible] I think the only [illegible] I should be taxed for water. I have sufficient water for all the houses I may build on the place.

552. What are the sanitary arrangements you have made?—The sewerage is [illegible]. It is enclosed, and I have given instructions for a larger tank to be made.

553. Mr. Ward.—In point of fact, would it not depreciate the value of your property, if it was known as in the Holywood township, subject to town taxes?—It would, just the very [illegible] of the thing.

554. Mr. [illegible].—Have you any tanks at present?—I have one, [illegible].

555. Where do they drain to?—Into the sea.

556. Will it drain into the river and thence to the sea?—From the tank, and from the tank into the sea.—[illegible].

557. Take care whether you will be allowed to do that?—The grounds were all laid out by an architect.

558. Mr. Ward.—What station do you use and your tenants?—Sometimes Cultra, and sometimes Craigavad.

559. Do you derive any advantage from Holywood?—I do not; I am not in it at all, except [illegible].

560. Mr. [illegible].—Suppose [illegible] you [illegible], and if [illegible], would you still [illegible] to pay [illegible], and not be brought under the township?—I would. They are considered more [illegible] than if connected with the town. Villas let better the further you go down towards Bangor, on account of being [illegible] further down and nearer to Bangor.

561. Mr. Anderson.—Your property is beyond Dalchoolin?—Dalchoolin is my boundary.

562. [illegible] boundary between the two townlands?—There is just a field between the two.

563. Who has been building beside you in your locality?—Mr. Ross is the only gentleman.

564. Are you aware of what buildings he has put up?—A cottage.

[illegible]. Mr. [illegible].—In the ground laid out for building [illegible]?—The [illegible] laid out for that purpose.

Mr. [illegible]: Mr. Henry Campbell said that [illegible] to the Town to prevent their building there.

Mr. [illegible].—I believe that was his object.

Holywood. Jan. [illegible]

Mr. Samuel [illegible].

Mr. JAMES HARKNESS examined.

Mr. James Harkness.

565. Mr. Ward.—How many houses have you here?—Three villa houses.

566. Are they all properly drained?—Yes.

567. Describe what sanitary arrangements you have made?—I have two cesspools for two houses and one for my own, and a third cesspool into which all these fall, whence the sewage flows through a pipe to the sea. The late agent of Mr. Kennedy took every precaution to have all tanks properly trapped and made secure from overflowing or doing any harm.

568. The Cultra tenants are all bound to have proper appliances for that purpose?—Yes.

569. Are you opposed to the extension of the Holywood township?—I am.

570. What station do you use?—Cultra.

571. Do you derive any benefit from Holywood?—[illegible].

572. Don't you think that Holywood derives considerable benefit from you and other gentlemen residing along there?—I think it does. We derive what is only an injury in the way of beggars and tramps going about who live in Holywood.

573. Mr. Anderson.—Is not Cultra ground laid out in roads?—There is one road, and one circular road there—two roads.

574. For building?—It is intended for building.

575. I see an advertisement in yesterday's paper: "Cultra—several building sites possessing varied and extensive views, combined with sea-bathing, &c., apply to George M'Auliffe." Do you know of these sites?—It is on Mr. O'Connell's property.

576. Mr. M'Lean.—Is there an open drain from the stableyard at Cultra?—I think not, I have never seen one. I presume, Mr. M'Lean, you mean the stableyard of Cultra House, I think there is no sewerage from it at all. I wish to add with regard to the lighting that we never go to a place of worship in the evening at all, so that we don't use the lighting.

577. Mr. M'Lean.—You go in the daytime?—Yes.

Mr. WILLIAM A. ROSS examined.

Mr. William A. Ross.

578. Mr. Ward.—You live at [illegible]?—Yes.

579. What station do you use in travelling?—Craigavad station.

580. I believe you have built a residence there?—I have built a cottage.

581. Are you one of the unfortunate persons that go to church in Holywood?—I go to Glencraig.

582. What are your sanitary arrangements?—Eleven-inch pipes all the way to the cesspool, and the water is to be filtered; there is a cistern in my house that the water is to be [illegible].

583. Are you opposed to the proposed extension?—I am.

584. Have you built your house to your own taste, and made all your sanitary arrangements, and do you even want water?—I have an ample supply of filtered water from the mountain.

585. You don't want now, I suppose, to be disturbed in the happy arrangements you have made to accommodate yourself?—I do not.

586. Mr. Carlile.—Have you a vegetable garden, and do you sell the produce in Holywood?—I do not.

587. I see your cattle in every day.

Mr. Ross.—I say it is not correct.

Holywood. Nov. 25, 18[illegible].

Mr. Richard Gallagher.

Mr. Richard Gallagher examined.

588. To Mr. *Crawford*.—I have been for the last nine years assistant to Mr. Lyle on Mr. Kennedy's property.

589. In the arrangements you make with your tenants, do you bind them to make proper sanitary arrangements?—We do, by special clauses in their leases.

590. Is there a station on these lands?—There are two stations on the part proposed to be included by the Commissioners—Marino and Cultra.

591. Do the tenants of these lands make use of these stations for the purpose of going to Belfast?—They do.

592. Is their principal object in going to Belfast for business?—It is.

593. Are they in the habit of going daily to Holywood on business?—Not that I am aware of.

594. At present, tell us how the land is occupied, is it not actually let to tenants?—It is all under grass I may say.

595. Is that grass let?—It is.

596. Who to?—Partly to the owners of villas, they have all fields as accommodation for their cows to supply themselves with milk; the other part of the estate is let in grazing for cattle and horses.

597. And do they come from all parts of the county?—Yes.

598. Is there any difference in the rates these cattle pay per day?—No.

599. They come from Bangor and Craigavad, and Lisburn?—We don't care where they come from. They are all milch cows, yearlings and young horses.

600. From the old Cultra entrance over to the Craigavad boundary on the southern side of the road, that is where the rough ground on the hill is—is that very steep land?—Very steep.

601. And is it suitable or desirable at present for building purposes?—There are two good sites on it, but it will not be let for twenty years to come; the one half is wood, and it is very rough.

602. Mr. *Kenah*.—What is the valuation of it?—The Poor Law valuation is about £2 per acre on the lower side. We have no special valuation of that particular part.

603. Would that land be valued at more than £1 an acre? What use is made of this?—Part of it we get about £6 a year from for the grass, and the other portion is used for the grazing.

604. And have you the whole of the area that is below the road to the railway, or the greater portion of it still available for building purposes?—We have a large portion of it.

605. What rent do you get for this portion let out for building?—The average would be about £10 the acre.

606. And that which is valued as land at £2 is let for £10 an acre?

607. Mr. *Crawford*.—Is that owing to its proximity to the station?

Witness.—It is, and having good sea-bathing and other attractions.

608. Is there ample water on the hills to supply all these houses?—There is, at a height of 300 feet.

609. Have you made any calculation of the area of Cultra that would be taken in?—It would include 188 acres, exclusive of roads.

610. What would be the additional area, supposing it went along the top of the rough road?—About 20 additional acres.

611. That would be 208 acres at Cultra alone of Mr. Kennedy's property, exclusive of the roads—208 acres of that is averaging £10 an acre?—No, the land below the road would average £10.

612. Mr. *Crawford*.—As regards the past few years, has there been any rapid increase of building on this ground?—None.

613. Are all the houses occupied on it?—No, there are a number empty.

614. How many houses have been built there within the past number of years?—Since 1863 about seventeen have been built on the place proposed to be taken in—up to Cultra station to Craigavad boundary there have been four additional.

615. Are you at present constructing a road down past Mr. Ross's house to the shore?—We are.

616. And are you in process of constructing a street down to the sea?—We are.

617. Is that to open that up as building-ground?—It is.

618. Have you on the far side of that ground leased the land to Mr. Mitchell?—To the east of the Craigavad boundary is leased to Mr. Mitchell.

619. Mr. *Kenah*.—Why do you object to bring this under the Commissioners?—On account of the taxation, that is one reason, and the other is that it would be depreciated. People don't like to take ground that is liable to rates. I believe it will affect our letting the ground there for building purposes.

620. Is it because people would not like to be under the surveillance of the Commissioners as to their plans?—People there take five or ten or thirty acres of ground to have villas and land round it, and people like to please themselves. We bind them as to the sanitary arrangements that must be made, and there are no streams there to be polluted.

621. Are you in favour, as far as the eastern portion is concerned, of having it extended?—Yes.

Captain Harrison.

Captain Harrison examined.

622. Mr. *Kenah*.—What would you say if we took in the public road, and took you in here?—I think it would be very absurd.

623. Well, what would you say to taking in the Bishop's place?—I think it would be a ridiculous thing.

624. Doesn't he derive immense advantage from Holywood?—None whatever.

625. Mr. *Ward*.—Mr. Harrison has a large farm there simply used for agricultural purposes—he doesn't require that lighted or watched?—No, the present boundary in that direction is quite sufficiently far to go.

Mr. *M'Lean*.—This is a large farm with probably 100 cows on it; but he supplies the town of Holywood with milk, morning and evening, his milk cart goes through every street, lane, and alley in the town, and these cows are driven along the roads within the present boundary to other ground belonging to Mr. Harrison, and they are more injured by the cows in one day than I would injure them in forty years.

Mr. *Kenah*.—He also derives a large revenue from them. All parties agree to an extension on the east, if there is to be any extension there is no earthly reason why Mr. Harrison should not be brought in.

Captain *Harrison*.—I consider Mr. Gregg's and Holywood House exactly parallel cases, if one is taken in the other should be taken in also.

Mr. *Samuel Patton*.—Provided they extend to the east as far as to the west, I am quite prepared to fall in with it.

Mr. *Wentworth*.—After the explanation I have heard, I am decidedly for the extension. The reason of my doubt yesterday was, that I hold a few acres that will be taken in, and from the explanation I have since heard, I believe it will be to my advantage to be taken in.

The inquiry terminated.

LONDONDERRY—JULY 11TH, 1879.

Before Messrs. Exham, Q.C.; C. P. Cotton, C.E.; and Henry A. Robinson.

Londonderry. July 11, 1879.

The Mayor examined.

The Mayor.

1. Chairman.—You are the Mayor of Londonderry?—Yes.

2. We understand that you had a change of the boundaries effected in 1864?—Yes.

3. Were they then enlarged considerably?—Yes.

4. Has the Corporation considered the question of a further area taken?—Yes.

5. What decision have they come to?—That the present boundary embraces as much as we require for many years to come.

6. Have you already within your boundary all land built on, or likely to be built on, for a number of years? For the purpose of roads, sanitary matters or otherwise, could there be any beneficial change made?—We think not.

7. Is that the feeling of the Corporation?—Yes.

8. Do you speak as the head of the Corporation on their behalf?—Yes.

9. We were not aware there had been any extension in 1864?—There was, and to a very large extent. There was a very large quantity of land taken in, sufficient for our purposes for the next fifty years.

10. How many wards are there?—Three.

11. Is there any change considered desirable in these wards?—I would say not. I think they are arranged satisfactorily.

12. Are the wards here the same for municipal and poor law purposes. Are there the same number of voters in the wards for municipal and poor law purposes?—Well, I am not prepared to answer that for there are different rating.

13. Are there three wards for poor law purposes?—No.

14. Are you able to say, of your own knowledge, and independently of the Corporation, whether there is any outside district the inhabitants of which, wish to be brought in?—No application has ever been made to us on the subject, and in any case the Corporation consider that no extension is necessary or will be necessary for a number of years.

Mr. William James Robinson examined.

Mr. William J. Robinson.

15. Chairman.—What was the area of Londonderry before 1864?—I could not say, I was not surveyor at the time.

16. What is it now?—A mile exactly from the Corporation Hall.

17. What is the population?—About 30,000, but it is increasing.

18. Have you any map here showing exactly the present boundary?—There can be no difficulty about it, for it is shown on the deposited plan.

19. What are the rates here now?—4s. in the pound.

20. What have they been for the past five years?—The same. That is for buildings within 100 yards of a public lamp, outside of that they pay one-third rate.

21. Does the boundary now cut through townlands?—It does.

22. Has the Corporation the management of the roads under their own Act?—Yes.

Mr. Robert A. Chaldecott, Town Clerk, examined.

Mr. Robert A. Chaldecott.

23. Mr. Robinson.—How long have you been Town Clerk?—Since the 14th April, 1879.

24. What Acts is Londonderry administered under?—The Towns Improvement Acts of 1848, 1856, and 1864.

25. Did the Londonderry Improvement Act of 1864 extend the boundaries very considerably?—Yes.

26. Are you aware to what extent?—No.

27. Did they alter the parliamentary boundary under the Act of 1864?—No.

28. Has the parliamentary boundary been since extended?—It has. It is the same as the municipal boundary.

29. Do you know by what authority it was then extended?—No.

30. How many electoral divisions does it include?—Three or four.

31. Does it include them wholly or in part?—It includes the [illegible] of them I think, and portion of one.

32. There were some [illegible] to you when this Commission began?—Yes; but I have only been informed of that this morning (in consequence of the death of the late Town Clerk who, I believe, replied to them). I have no record of the reply, but I believe he did answer them.

33. Do you know if that reply was submitted to the Corporation?—I believe it was, [illegible], and received their approval.

34. It was to the effect that no extension of the boundary was desirable?—I believe so.

35. Was there a special meeting of the Council convened to consider that?—It might have been the ordinary meeting of the Police and [illegible] Committee of the Council.

36. How many representatives have you for each ward?—Eight—six councillors and two aldermen.

37. Is the valuation pretty much the same in each ward?—Yes.

38. Chairman.—Could you give us the number of burgesses, and the valuation of each ward?

Mr. William Stafford, Assistant Town Clerk.—The East ward contains 309 burgesses, and the valuation is £[illegible], including government buildings and all; the North ward, 310 burgesses, and its valuation, £[illegible]; the South ward, 171 burgesses, and the valuation is £17,[illegible].

39. Is the full rate struck on all houses that are not more than 100 yards from a lamp?—Yes.

40. If the houses are more than 100 yards from lamp?—Then one-third rate is payable.

41. Is it the same on land?—Yes.

42. Chairman.—Under the Act of 1864?—Not since then. It is also under the Acts of 1848 and 1856.

43. Mr. Robinson.—Have you had sufficient experience to enable you to form an opinion as to the desirability of a redistribution of those wards, or do you think they are fairly balanced, as far as the valuation is concerned. Do you know the opinion of the Council on this point?—It has not been discussed before the Council during my time.

44. Could Mr. Stafford give us the map showing the new boundary under the Improvement Act of 1864?—Yes. (Map produced by Mr. Stafford.)

45. Could you tell us on how much of the valuation is the full rate payable; and on how much the one-third?—The collector's books would tell that.

46. Mr. Stafford.—About £[illegible] is the valuation of the property on which the one-third is payable. The total valuation of the city, on which the full rate is struck, is £[illegible]. I should say rather that £[illegible] is the amount on which a full rate is struck. The difference is principally caused by government buildings, the gaol, lunatic asylum, workhouse, and so on. The area of the East ward is [illegible]a. [illegible]r.; North ward, [illegible]a. 3r. [illegible]p.; and the South ward [illegible]a. [illegible]r. [illegible]p.

47. What is the total?—[illegible]a. [illegible]r. [illegible]p.

48. And that is the same as the parliamentary boundary?—Yes.

LONDONDERRY. July 11, 18[illegible]. Mr. William J. Robinson.

Mr. William J. Robinson, City Surveyor, re-examined.

49. Mr. Robinson.—Can you give me the area comprised within the old municipal boundary?—660 acres.

50. Do you know the area within the old parliamentary boundary?—No.

51. Do you know if the old parliamentary boundary was the same as the old municipal?—I do not.

52. What is the area within the present municipal boundary?—It is, exclusive of water, 3,187 acres. The water covers 257 acres, or a total of 3,444 acres.

53. How many townlands does the present boundary cut?—Four.

54. Give their names?—Creggan, Ballymagowan, Coleraine, and Termonbacca.

55. What is the area?—625 acres outside the boundary, divided in this way, Creggan, 150 acres; Ballymagowan, 80 acres; Coleraine, 89 acres, and Termonbacca, 303 acres.

56. Are the present boundaries regarded with satisfaction by the ratepayers?—I think they are, and also by the Corporation.

57. Do you think the boundary is too large in any direction?—I think it is fully large enough. That is the opinion I have heard expressed.

58. Did you ever hear it insisted by any one that limitation of the boundary would be desirable in any way?—I do not know that I did. The people are quite content that it should remain as it is.

Mr. John T. Russell.

Mr. John T. Russell examined.

59. Mr. Robinson.—You are Clerk of the Londonderry Poor Law Union?—Yes.

60. How many electoral divisions does the boundary cut?—The borough of Londonderry, for parliamentary and municipal purposes, is composed of the entire electoral division of the city and suburbs and portions of the Waterside, Upper Liberties division. The city division is valued at £86,142, and the Waterside £13,861, of which there is within the borough the townland of Clooney, valued at £7,252.

61. So that the only townland of that electoral division within the borough?—Yes; and then there is part of Coleraine, £2,034; and part of Termonbacca, £36; making a total of £9,402. The total valuations of Upper and Lower Liberties divisions are £4,059 and £6,139, respectively, there being of the former division, £834 inside the borough—that is part of Ballymagowan, £164, and part of Creggan, £80, and of the latter division the townlands of Pennyburn and Craigavon, valued at £1,106, are also within the borough. The present municipal borough is divided for municipal purposes into three wards, east, north and south.

62. Are there the same wards for poor law purposes?—No; the city division alone is the area for poor law purposes.

63. What is the total valuation of Waterside and Upper and Lower Liberties outside the borough?—£4,153 for Waterside electoral division, for Upper Liberties, £3,955, and Lower Liberties £5,333.

64. Are you in a position to say—when the extended boundary in 1864 was made—what prompted the Corporation to choose the extension they did?—As well as I recollect they selected it on the report of their surveyor, and they thought it would be a sufficiently wide area for municipal and parliamentary purposes.

65. I believe the surveyor took a radius of one mile all round, from the centre of the town?—Yes. I think he wanted to make the Corporation Hall the centre. At any rate I remember that that was the idea.

66. Have you any suggestion to make as to the boundary of Londonderry?—It would, in my opinion, be very desirable that the boundaries of the electoral divisions of the city and Waterside should be made coterminous with the parliamentary boundary or with the wards.

67. For what purpose?—For the convenience of striking the rates and for other purposes.

68. Do you think that is the feeling of the Board of Guardians?—They have never taken it into consideration.

69. Would you propose to create poor law wards?—Yes; by dividing the representation on the poor law board, and making it by wards the same as in Belfast.

70. Is there anything more you would add?—Yes. There are four elected Poor Law Guardians for the city division; two for the Waterside, two for Lower Liberties, and one for Upper Liberties. I might mention with regard to the wards, that I think a re-arrangement of them would be desirable.

71. The South ward is much smaller than either of the other two—do you think the city is not equally distributed?—I look upon the area as not being a test at all of the valuation and importance of the place. For instance, the valuation of the South ward of the city in 1859 was £9,378, and its present valuation is £17,169 10s.

72. Mr. William J. Robinson.—Perhaps Mr. Russell is not aware that in the South ward, at present, there are a very large number of buildings being erected.

Mr. Russell.—In the South ward the valuation in 1859 was £18,318, whereas now it is £28,434; in the East ward in 1859 the valuation was £16,616; at present it is £25,164. The number of municipal voters in 1859 for the South ward was 108, now it is 170; for the North ward it was 203 in 1859, now it is 300; and for the East ward the number of municipal voters in 1859 was 183, and the present number is 304. It is clear from this that the city is extending in a northerly and easterly direction.

73. The East ward is at present the largest?—No, the North ward is the largest in point of valuation. I don't look upon the area as of much consequence. It is generally made up of pasture lands in the North ward, but the city is extending to the north and east. I would suggest that a fourth ward should be created from portions of the north and south, that is to say, by creating a West ward, or by readjusting the present wards, and giving a large portion from the north and east to the South ward. The South ward, at present, in my opinion, has an undue representation at the council, and the North and East wards not a proper representation.

74. Mr. William J. Robinson.—I may explain that within the last twelve months there has been a larger increase in the number of buildings in the South ward than in the other two put together.

75. Mr. Robinson.—Would these buildings be rated at the full rate?—Oh, certainly. They are within a hundred yards of a public lamp. There are about 44 acres in the South ward, at present, being laid out for building purposes. There has been a tendency to build in the South ward within the past eight years.

76. Do you think there is any change required in the existing wards?—I think not, but there is at the same time a good deal of force in what Mr. Russell has said.

[The inquiry terminated.]

LIMERICK—JULY 4TH, 1879.

Before Messrs. EXHAM, Q.C., C. P. COTTON, C.E., and HENRY A. ROBINSON.

MR. JOHN ELLARD, Town Clerk, examined.

1. MR. EXHAM.—How long have you been Town Clerk?—Twenty-two years.

2. The queries that we sent down to you were submitted, I presume, to the Town Council?—Yes, first of all they were submitted to a Committee, and the report of the Committee was brought before the Council and approved of by them.

3. Was that approval unanimous?—The report was adopted, there may have been one or two Councillors who did not approve of it, but only one or two.

4. The present boundaries are those adopted in 1840?—Yes. As marked out by the Corporation Act.

5. Are the wards the same?—No.

6. When was the alteration made in the wards?—In 1853, under the Limerick Improvement Act.

7. Can you now say whether, suppose there was no alteration in the boundary, those wards are considered satisfactory?—They are.

8. How many members of the Town Council are there?—Forty. There are eight wards, eight aldermen, and thirty-two councillors.

9. Was the boundary before 1840 much larger than the present?—Yes.

10. Were the old town boundary coterminous with the parliamentary boundary?—Yes; and the parliamentary boundary remained the same since 1840.

11. How far does that parliamentary boundary extend?—It extends in various directions—not equally.

12. What is the furthest extent it goes beyond the centre of the town?—I should say about six miles, but it is not the same in every direction.

13. How long was that the parliamentary boundary?—From the time of the Down Survey.

14. That was the old city of Limerick?—Yes. We have a map showing it, and the city surveyor will be here and he can speak to it.

15. What is the area of the parliamentary boundary?—According to the report before me 16,848 Irish acres, but there was a doubt as to the exact correctness of that.

16. MR. EXHAM.—As I understand from the reply to the queries of the Commissioners, it is proposed by the Town Council to extend the municipal boundary to the entire of the parliamentary boundary?—Yes.

17. That would make it about 26,000 statute acres in extent?—It would be more than that.

18. You say that the recommendation of the Committee was adopted?—Yes; according to the minute of the Council of the 10th of January, 1879, at a meeting at which nineteen members were present, "it was proposed and adopted unanimously that the report of the Committee be adopted."

19. As a matter of fact was it adopted unanimously?—Well, there may have been an individual member who did not agree to it, but if any one wished to have had his dissent recorded it would have been taken down.

20. Did the Corporation or the Committee consider whether they proposed to light and water the entire of that district?—No.

21. Surely they did not propose to take in people six or seven miles off and not give them any of the advantages enjoyed by those residing in the city, and yet make them pay the same rate?—Well, they held in recollection that they could only levy one-third of the rate for land under the Limerick Improvement Act, and in that way they would be only subject to one-third of the improvement rate.

22. Did the Corporation consider in that proposal the question of their taking up all the roads within that district?—They did.

23. And what did they do with regard to that—did they, for one-third, propose to maintain all the roads?—Yes.

24. Then according to that the people living in this district would derive a very great advantage, for at present they pay county cess. Do the roads in the city cost more than those in the county?—Well, I could not say.

25. Do they propose that they should only pay one-third of the cost of keeping up the roads?—No. They directed Mr. Corbett, the surveyor, to prepare an estimate and take a measurement of the roads in the county which he did—of the part proposed to be taken up—and he was to form an estimate of what the cost of maintenance would be. They also got him to prepare a statement, showing what the rate would be likely to produce, to guide them as to the advantages or disadvantages attendant on extending the borough boundary.

26. Did he report on that to the Committee?—Yes, Mr. Corbett has that. We have a special Act making the rate one-third, "the Limerick Improvement Act, 1853." The Corporation Act altered the wards, and increased them from five to eight.

27. Have the Corporation considered this question, whether in anything to be brought in, if they take up the management of the roads, the parties should remain liable to the same county cess they pay at present and then pay something towards the city rate?—They took into consideration they would have to pay the general purposes rate and also one-third of the improvement rate, and they calculated that our general purposes rate would be smaller than what the county Grand Jury rate is.

28. Is there any difference between the county of the city and the municipal boundary—are they not one and the same?—Yes; and the county of the city of Limerick is a county in itself.

29. The jurisdiction of the fixing judge sitting in Limerick is coterminous with the municipal boundary?—I believe so. At the commencement I understand there was some doubt about it, but the practice has been to use it as such, and the magistrates of the North Liberty locally are county magistrates, and exercise jurisdiction as county magistrates between the present municipal boundary and the parliamentary boundary. The municipal boundary only goes to Kilrush—Little Kilrush—but the whole district of Caherdavin votes in the city.

30. They are part of the county, I take it, except for parliamentary purposes?—Yes, exactly.

31. The general purposes rate you have is analogous to Grand Jury cess in the county?—Yes, exactly.

32. What is the maximum of the improvement rate here under your Act?—Five shillings.

33. What is that rate applicable to?—Lighting, watching, cleansing, scavenging, and repairing the roads. The sewerage is included in it now, under the Public Health.

34. Have you a separate rate for it?—No; we use the improvement rate for it.

35. What was the improvement rate since 1874?—1874, 3s. 10d.; the general purposes, &c., in 1875, 4s. 9d. and 1s. 11½d.; in 1876, 3s. 7d. and 1s. 3d.; in 1877, 4s. 1d. and 1s. 10d.; and in 1878, 3s. 6d. and 1s. 6d.

36. How was it that in 1874 the general purposes rate was 2s., in 1876, 1s. 11½d.; in 1877, 1s. 10d.; and in the other two years only 1s. 3d.?—The amount for each rating would be different.

37. I am confining myself to the general purposes, how is it that the "fixed" charges varied so much?—There was the lunatic asylum and the expiration

LIMERICK. July 4, [illegible]. Mr. John Ellard.

grant given by Government towards the support of lunatics, that, in the years it was given, would reduce the rate very much.

38. Did it vary so much each year?—Yes; it was at the rate of 4s. per head.

39. How, exactly, would that make a difference?—According to the numbers in the house. The Government advanced out of the consolidated fund the amount to the governors of the lunatic asylum to carry them on, and we subsequently passed presentments for that money to refund it. Then, when these Acts came into force, the Government did not advance the money, and we were called on for one or two presentments to repay what they advanced, and to advance money to carry on the asylum, and that added considerably to our general purposes rate in those years.

40. What will be your general purposes rate on the new area, having got rid of the presentments, and so on?—About 4d. or 6d. in the pound, we calculate it at that; it would be very low. Another reason for the general purposes rate increasing is, that there were some industrial schools established, and we entered into arrangements with some of them to receive persons there—there was one in Cork—another where fifty were arranged for.

41. Still your calculation is that paying for reformatories, public schools, and those things, you would be able to do it at the 6d. rate?—That was considered what eventually it will be.

42. Was it considered your improvement rate would remain the same, 3s. 6d.?—It would be about that; 3s. 6d. would be the maximum, because in those rates we include sewerage and matters connected with sanitary purposes.

43. Have the Corporation considered this, that at present the portion you propose to bring in, which is inside the parliamentary boundary, is in the hands of the rural sanitary authority, and that the rates the occupiers pay—the sanitary rate under the Act of last year—are divided between the occupier and the landlord which does not apply to those within the city. Now, what do you propose as to that. If they were added, would you be prepared to scavenge, cleanse, and sewer, and all for them, and become the nuisance authority for the whole of that district, they paying you only a certain proportion?—The Corporation propose that the incidence of taxation should be made the same as the poor rate, even in the city, and at the present moment we have sent forward petitions to Parliament about it.

44. That is that the whole district should be on the same footing, and the landlord pay one-half, and the tenant one-half?—Yes.

45. For sanitary purposes?—Yes, poor law and sanitary, and, indeed, the Corporation think it should be for all rates.

46. You have given us in your reply to the queries returns of the three baronies, North Liberty, Clanwilliam, and Pubblebrien. Clanwilliam appears to pay the highest county cess. It amounted up to 1s. 3½d., the others were as low as 1s. 6d., do you propose to have only one uniform rate for these in respect of county-at-large charges. If you bring them into the city, I understand you to say, you want them to pay only one-third of the improvement rate?—No, the whole of the general purposes rate, and one-third of the improvement rate.

47. What do you propose to do with the roads, do you put them under the improvement rate, and make the occupiers pay only one-third for them?—Yes, that is all we would have the power to do, it is under the improvement rate we maintain our own roads and streets. We don't take one shilling out of the general purposes fund.

48. If you do it on that footing the public outside would get a great advantage from it. It would lessen taxation on them?—Yes, but the Corporation were under the impression it would be an advantage to the Liberties to be joined, and an advantage to the city to have a larger area of taxation, and our Grand Jury cess being so much lower than the county cess would give them an advantage without injury to the city.

49. What is the view of the people with regard to owners of houses in that district, is it that they should pay full taxation?—Yes, the houses should be liable for the full value.

50. Would you give those houses the benefit of lighting, watering, and so on?—No, that could not be done.

51. Why then make them pay the full rate the city pays, if you don't put water up to their door, or light or scavenge for them?—We would only do what is required under the Act.

52. Do the Corporation consider that fair—remembering that if you take the case of a resident, three miles from the centre of the city, and outside the present boundary—his land, of course, would only pay one-third, but there is no exemption in favour of his house?—No taxation would compensate for extending gas mains and water-pipes out miles in a purely rural district.

53. Have the Corporation considered their being put on a differential scale?—Well, perhaps it would be equitable to make some difference.

54. In other places they proposed to take in gentlemen's houses, and I asked the owners if they considered it right to be taxed for that, and they said, "No, they should not be taxed for the full, inasmuch as they want give us water or light; if they give that we will be delighted, but if they don't it would not be fair to make us pay the same as men in the town." In some places the idea was that they ought to pay one-half rating?—My own individual opinion is that it would be equitable they should not pay the same as those who are getting the advantage of light and water, but in respect of the land they get the benefit of only paying one-third.

55. But he would not get off so far as his house and demesne proper is concerned, paying only one-third on that; he would be compelled—if the Act of Parliament remained the same—to pay the same as the gentleman whose place is within the boundary. He will get the benefit of light, water, sewers, &c., in the present boundary, though I question the great advantage of the water if it has not very much improved of late, but if you go two miles off there are several places which I see on the map—one is Mr. Delmege's—would it be fair or right to make them pay the same taxes, unless you supply them with equal advantages to those enjoyed by those within the boundary?—Well, the parties residing near the town have the advantage of the streets, of the lighting and watering to a certain extent, their horses and cars come in and cut up our roads and streets, and it is but fair that they should pay something towards that.

56. Why should market gardeners, who use the city very largely, be let off with one-third and not pay more, while the gentlemen who get no greater advantage pay in full for their houses?—But the market gardener would pay in full for his house.

57. From your knowledge and experience can you say whether land in the immediate vicinity of Limerick derives exceptional advantages and benefit from its proximity to the town, and are higher rents paid for it?—There is not a doubt of it.

58. Does that apply to land six or seven miles off?—Not to such an extent, but to a certain extent. Of course, land six or seven miles off is not of the same value as land one mile off.

59. Then comes in the question, why make the man, whose land is five or six or seven miles off, and who does not get anything like the same benefit that is, pay the one-third, the same as the man within two miles of the town?—Except on the principle that you cannot do a general good without doing some individual wrong. In every Act of Parliament some one will be aggrieved by it.

60. But you are making a great boundary, we have not been asked anywhere to take in land to a distance of three miles off, that is land property so called. In

[illegible] Sir Peter Tait's residence, and Strabane [illegible] about three miles [illegible] from the town [illegible]

61. Would it be fair to take in a distance of six miles [illegible] an illegible number of miles away?—I should mention that an [illegible] of circumstances has arisen regarding the position of the citizens in relation to the inhabitants of [illegible] [illegible] Waterford and Limerick Railway Company [illegible] and finally it was decided [illegible]. That placed the city at very great disadvantage [illegible] the city would have the benefit of these [illegible].

62. [illegible] they should fix that boundary [illegible] miles [illegible]

63. But the principle of extending boundaries appears to be this [illegible] the purposes of residences [illegible] the Corporation [illegible] the city [illegible] from Limerick on one side and [illegible] on the other. [illegible] Corporation [illegible] their ancient rights and privileges.

64. That is [illegible] by Act of Parliament?—[illegible]

65. Have you made a calculation as to what the additional taxation would be by bringing in that district?—Mr. Cussen will be able to give you that.

66. Have the Corporation considered the question [illegible] Limerick Corporation [illegible] lighting, watching [illegible] and so on.

67. What great advantage would it be to the [illegible] Limerick?—It would go to other purposes [illegible] the roads and streets [illegible] Now I don't use a vehicle or horse, and I know a gentleman outside whose horse and carriage [illegible] in all my life [illegible]

68. You can understand the difference of which I [illegible] the difference between the persons fairly called a residential occupier living within a mile and a half or two miles of the city [illegible] they have [illegible] for shopping, for amusement, and for other purposes. I can understand the Corporation saying they ought to be brought in; but I can

[illegible] the centre of the town [illegible] advantages [illegible] They have the advantage of lighting [illegible]

69. Yes, I know; but could you fairly go as far as six miles?—Well, [illegible] people [illegible] in Limerick, and some of them [illegible]

70. Would [illegible] be brought in?—No, it was never in. You will see that [illegible] would be included, and [illegible] would be excluded.

71. I see by the map that the parliamentary boundary [illegible] a mile in one direction, and [illegible] the county and there is not half a mile. The county Clare is on the other side.

72. Would you propose to go into the county Clare in that direction?—No. There are [illegible] Little [illegible], that formerly belonged to the Liberties, and is in no way connected with the county, and to go from the county Limerick to there you must pass over the city of Limerick and over the Shannon [illegible] the North Liberty. It is lying exactly between the county of Clare and the city of Limerick; but, though [illegible] as it were, as an island of land, it was taken from the city and given to the county.

73. Mr. Curtis.—Would you wish to take that in, in that which I am to understand?—Yes; that was part of the Old Liberties.

74. Chairman.—Does it belong to the county Clare?—No; it belongs to the county Limerick, but is not connected with it. It is on the Clare side of the river.

75. What was the poor rate for the past five years?—In 1874, [illegible]; in 1875, [illegible]; in 1876, [illegible]; in 1877, [illegible]; and in 1878, [illegible].

76. Now, what [illegible], in the North Liberty [illegible] in 1874, [illegible]; in 1875, [illegible]; in 1876, [illegible]; in 1877, [illegible]; and in 1878, [illegible].

77. In [illegible]?—In 1874, [illegible]; in 1875, [illegible]; in 1876, [illegible]; in 1877, [illegible]; and in 1878, [illegible].

78. And in [illegible]?—In 1874, [illegible]; in 1875, [illegible]; in 1876, [illegible]; in 1877, [illegible]; and in 1878, [illegible].

79. Do the people living five or six miles off [illegible] into the city [illegible] people do close to the city?—No; but they [illegible]. If they live near at hand, and they find out that the prices are up, they have the advantage of [illegible] in the city [illegible] advantage of it, whereas, if they lived [illegible] miles away, they would not have the same advantage. They [illegible] the city, and [illegible]

80. What are the present debts of the Corporation?—There are debts on the improvement rate, general purposes rate, and borough fund.

81. What is the present debt on the improvement rate?—[illegible] on the improvement rate is a sum of £3,788 [illegible] St. Michael's Parish Commissioners [illegible] bonds.

82. What is the next?—The next is £3,000, balance of a loan of £10,000, of which we paid off £6,000, and we have enough in hand by the sinking fund to pay off this £2,000 this month.

83. Then, we may consider that as paid off?—I think so.

84. What is the next item?—£6,000, the balance of £10,000, for the purchase of gas works; this was originally £10,000, and we have reduced it by providing a sinking fund for it.

85. What is the sinking fund for that?—£468 15s.

6d. a year; in point of fact, in between nine and ten years that will be wiped off.

86. What is the next?—£4,600, which was for the improving of the Corkanree slob lands. The produce of that pays the interest on that, and it is worth the money; we have the land for it.

87. Have you the land in your own hands?—Yes; the original sum was £5,400, but we paid off £800.

88. That is a charge on the Corkanree Embankment as well?—Yes; and the borough boundary was extended to take in that land under the Corkanree Act.

89. What year was that in?—In 1865.

90. Then there was a small extension of the borough boundary to take in that slob land?—Yes.

91. What else is there?—£3,293 6s. 8d. that was borrowed for sewerage purposes under the late Act—that is to be repaid by instalments. It was £3,600, but we borrowed more since—there was £1,000 more borrowed since.

92. That is payable in so many years?—Yes; in thirty years. The interest on the £4,894 is paid out of the proceeds of the gas, out of the profits, the Corporation are never called on to pay the interest on that.

93. So the improvement fund is only a collateral security in fact?—Yes.

94. Is there any charge on the general purposes rate?—There is £283 1s. 5d. for building the jails and other small things. The are some small instalments paid out of that.

95. Are these the only city debts proper?—Yes; on the rates. There is £37,500 due on the lands—a separate mortgage.

96. What is the rental of the city estate?—About £1,300 a year, in 1878 it realized £1,319; there was from that a deduction for taxes and repairs, and so on, £378 10s.

97. And the mortgage on that is £37,500, will it realize it.

Mr. Kenny (Solicitor).—I think it will.

98. I want to get the charges on all the city property, to see that the people to be brought in would not be injured by being liable for debts, so if necessarily there are no debts the question would not arise. Now, is the city to be pledged in any way to the gas-works under the new arrangement with them?

Mr. Ellard.—It is; we got power under the Act to borrow money for the purpose of the gas-works, and to pay off any liability they have incurred; the improvement rate would be liable or subject to that.

99. How much are your borrowing powers?—£34,000.

100. What is the estimated value?—Perhaps the gas-works will be in round numbers £30,000.

101. Then you will never want to exercise your borrowing powers?—Yes; to the extent of the purchase-money.

102. But what I mean to say is, will there be any charge on the improvement rate in aid of the gas-works?—So far as I can, not.

103. That is, the gas-works will be worth what they cost you?—Yes, and we expect to make a large profit.

104. The improvement rate is only collateral security?—Yes, that is so. The purchase of the gas-works will be, say £30,000, then there was a sum of £14,000 odd due to the National Bank, that has been reduced to £11,000 about, for which they have a mortgage for, I think, £6,700.

105. That is, they have a mortgage on the gas-works?—Yes; then there is the difference due on an overdraw. I may mention that Mr. Spillane made £3,600 last year of the gas-works, and the same for the past two or three years. It is calculated, that when the two companies are in the hands of one party, with one set of pipes, it will bring the profit up to £8,000 a year.

106. May we take it then, that according to the best estimates, the improvement rate will never be called on to contribute one farthing towards the gas-works?—There are the figures to show that the Limerick Gas Company made so much last year. Mr. Pelly, the Government auditor, certified it.

107. Mr. Connolly (Solicitor).—As is the maximum price, and there are places that are paying 10s.

108. Chairman.—What about the waterworks, is there a debt for water?—No.

109. You have given us now all the debts that could by possibility be placed on the improvement fund?—Yes.

110. They amount to about £88,000, including Corkanree, if you were to put it all together?—That is including what is in the prospective.

111. That is the greatest amount, however, that any gentleman's estate, within these two and a half or three miles, would be liable to the full rate for, to pay his quota?—Yes, there is some of that too that could not be called in—the £6,000 and odd.

112. The valuation of Limerick at present is £65,397 15s., that is the return you gave us?—Yes. I would say £64,610, for there are exemptions. It varies over this.

113. Mr. Connolly (Solicitor).—There is another thing, we get a contribution from the Government for their buildings which is not included in that.

Mr. Ellard.—Yes; they give a contribution on the valuation of their own, which lessens the improvement rate.

114. Chairman.—How much did the Government give last year?—£346 10s. 8d. for the improvement rate.

115. As their proportion?—Yes; and general purposes, £153 15s. 8d.—hitherto the Government paid no rates whatever.

116. Mr. Connolly.—That would represent a valuation of about £3,000 a year. Of course if Government buildings were included the valuation would be so much more.

117. Chairman.—What is the population?—44,209 by the last census.

118. And the area?—The area at present is 2,074a. 2r. 37p., which includes Corkanree Embankment.

119. Are the citizens generally satisfied with the wards—with their area, supposing no alteration was made in the boundaries?—Yes.

120. If we report in favour of any extension of the municipal boundaries, what are the views of the Town Council as to the alteration of the existing wards, or the number of the Town Councillors, have they considered the matter—would they propose to have the number increased, or to remain as it is, forty?—I don't think they took it into consideration.

121. That would be an important thing for us to know?—I could give you my own individual opinion.

122. Are you able to say how many electors would be brought into the municipality by either or both of the extensions proposed?—I cannot say at present, but can get it for you.

123. We would want to consider how you would give them representation—whether you would give separate wards, or add to the existing wards portions of the outlying districts?—That was spoken of in the committee room, and the opinion appeared to be that the rural interests should be represented by separate wards.

124. Mr. Cotton.—Was that all that was said about it?—Yes; that appeared to be the opinion.

125. What about the number of Councillors—did they seem to think the number should be increased?—From what I heard spoken in the committee room and otherwise, I gathered that the view was that the rural district should be formed into rural wards, and be represented by distinct members, but that the number of the Council was sufficient.

126. Chairman.—How many wards did you propose to give the rural people and take away from the city?—Oh, it was not gone into as closely as that.

127. As Town Clerk you will be able to give us the best idea of that—if the members are to remain the same and if the rural wards are to receive separate representation, what would you do?—Well, I would

LIMERICK. July 4, 18[illegible]. Mr. John Ellard.

say they should be guided more by the proportions of the valuations and population—to take the two together.

128. Can you give the number of voters for each existing ward?—I can procure them for you.

129. At present are the wards in the city coterminous for municipal and Poor Law purposes?—Yes.

130. Then in the district to be annexed we should, if possible, try to make them coterminous with Poor Law boundaries?—The Union electoral division goes beyond the present municipal boundary, and for Poor Law purposes; they have wards—the north and south suburbs—have wards for municipal purposes. The present parliamentary boundary runs outside the Poor Law electoral division.

Mr. Connolly.—The red line on the map shows the electoral boundary. The parliamentary boundary—pink—is very much larger.

131. CHAIRMAN.—What would be your view as to making the electoral division the boundary?—In some instances it would scarcely alter the present boundary.

132. Mr. COTTON.—Would not the electoral division take in Gurrogh?—Yes.

133. Mr. ROSEBERRY.—Was it under the Act of 1853 the wards were altered?—Yes.

134. What is the area of the electoral division?—6,221 acres.

135. And the valuation?—£78,763.

136. CHAIRMAN.—There is only a difference of £13,000 or 11,000 between that and the valuation of the municipal district?—Yes.

137. Can you tell us, Mr. Wilson, what electoral divisions are there outside the present municipal boundary, and within the parliamentary boundary.

Mr. Wilson.—The whole or parts of six.

138. We could hardly, in this case, make the electoral divisions and municipal boundary coterminous?—Oh, no.

139. How many townlands are included in the present parliamentary boundary, without cutting electoral divisions?—I could not say.

140. Now, Mr. Ellard, if the extension over the entire parliamentary boundary appears too large altogether, independent of the difficulty arising of cutting those electoral divisions—now what would you say to including the whole electoral division of Limerick?—My evidence before, as I recollect it, was in favour of an extension of the boundaries from a mile or a mile and a half to two miles, but I think that an extension merely to the electoral division of Limerick would be entirely too limited, it would be scarcely worth the alteration.

141. What electoral division would you add on to the electoral division of Limerick which would not cause the cutting of electoral divisions, and yet would not go as far as the parliamentary boundary?—I would not like to say at present, but, looking over the map, I would be able to let you know later on. Mr. Corbett has marked on the map what would be a mile to a mile and a half.

142. Would an extension to a mile and a half meet the question?—Yes, it would be fair.

143. Well, from looking at the map, the electoral division would go beyond two miles in some directions, and in others it would go nearly three miles?—Yes, if my memory serves me right, the measurement made was from the present boundary.

144. How many townlands would an extension of two miles cut?—I could not say.

145. It is evident the intention was to keep poor law voting and municipal voting the same. There are so many electoral divisions it is hard to make a boundary without going through some of them—and that is what we are told not to do.

Mr. *Ellard.*—There is an opinion in Limerick that the electoral division of Limerick is too limited.

146. Is it your opinion that the valuation of Limerick is too low—what I mean is that it is not fairly apportioned to the different classes of houses?

Mr. Connolly, Solicitor.—I can answer that. It is very uneven. I know one case where a man spent £10,000 on a house, and it is valued at £90, and my house is valued at £52.

Town Clerk.—Yes, in the old town, where property is decaying, the old valuation has remained.

147. CHAIRMAN.—Should there then not be a revaluation for the purpose of a fair adjustment of the taxes?—Yes, it would be better. The general scale here has been two-thirds of the annual rent. There are exceptions, but that is about the average.

148. Do you say of your own personal knowledge that there is a general feeling that there should be an extension of the boundary?—Yes, I think that is the general wish.

149. Has there been any meeting of the ratepayers to hear their views?—No.

150. Mr. *Kenny*, (Solicitor.)—I appear for the Marquis of Lansdowne, an extensive proprietor on the Clare side of the river, to oppose the extension.

151. Mr. *Delmege.*—I also oppose it.

152. CHAIRMAN.—Your taxation is 4*d.* or 5*d.* in the pound, and their proposition is virtually to lessen it.

Mr. *Delmege.*—"Timeo Danaos et dona ferentes."

153. The *Mayor.*—I have only to say that I quite concur in everything that has been said by the Town Clerk. I think the members of the Council are unanimous on the subject.

154. *Town Clerk.*—It is felt in the city that parties within the parliamentary boundary who pay no taxes exercise all the privileges in reference to the elections, and the citizens feel that a hardship. The citizens, on the 1st July, if they don't pay the rates are disqualified, while men who have nothing to do with the city and pay not sixpence of rates will be left in, in the other part.

155. CHAIRMAN.—What do you think, Mr. Connolly?

Mr. Connolly.—I am strongly of opinion myself, not speaking as law adviser of the Corporation, that the borough boundaries ought to be extended, but I don't know that they should be extended so far as the Town Clerk says.

156. Is it not the fact that in some cases the houses on one side of the roads in the city are rated, whilst those on the opposite side are not?—Yes, and that is the complaint I make. If you take the new street, Eden terrace, there are twelve or sixteen large mansions, they pay no taxes towards the city, but the people who live in them make all their money by the city, and contribute in no way towards its support by paying taxes for the houses they live in. This and other roads are lighted, cleansed, and all maintained by the city, and the people in the city have to pay for doing it. I only express my own individual opinion in saying it would be absurd to ask places at Adare to be included. If you take the electoral division, and one or two townlands, I think it would do.

157. Mr. *Kenny*, (Solicitor.)—I would ask, Mr. Commissioner, is it not a hardship to capitalists who have laid out their money on Eden-terrace that they should be brought in.

158. CHAIRMAN.—That is what was said in other places, that it was a hardship to bring in people who had laid out their money on the faith of an existing state of things.

159. Mr. *Kenny.*—There is a great difference between men laying out money in the city and knowing the taxes that are to be met and calculated for, and in the outlying districts where there are none, and where they build on that understanding.

160. *Town Clerk.*—Before the Municipal Act of 1840 was passed, the whole of the new town of Limerick was free from the Grand Jury cess. It contributed £500 in lieu thereof to the Grand Jury for Grand Jury purposes, and up to the passing of that Act there was no Grand Jury cess. That was in St. Michael's parish, which comprised the whole of the new town of Limerick, and it was on the faith of that arrangement that very elegant houses were built there. They were

LIMERICK, July 4, 1879.

Mr. John [illegible].

obliged, however, to submit to the infliction, if it was an imposition, though they built their houses under the impression that they would not be taxed.

161. CHAIRMAN.—What is the valuation of the different wards, and the number of persons on the burgess roll?

Town Clerk.—In Castle ward the valuation in 1878 was £3,578 10s.; in 1879, £3,681; and the number of voters, 65. In Abbey ward, in 1878, £3,170 16s., in 1879, £6,767 5s.; number of voters, 78. Irishtown ward, 1878, £5,164 10s.; 1879, £5,164 16s.; number of voters, 67. Custom House, 1878, £9,303 10s.; 1879, £9,193; number of voters, 108. Market ward, 1878, £9,167; 1879, £9,308, number of voters, 124. Shannon ward, 1878, £9,661; 1879, £10,006, number of voters, 155. Glentworth ward, 1878, £9,125; 1879, £9,148 10s.; number of voters, 123. And Dock, 1879, £11,390 15s., 1878, £11,430 15s.; number of voters, 165. Total valuation in 1878, £65,357 15s.; in 1879, £65,359 5s. Total number on the burgess roll, 917.

162. *Mr. Connolly.*—I would be for keeping the electoral division on the north-east up to the corner of Ballysheedy East. I would take in Ballysheedy West, Dooradoyle, Ballykeefe, and Rossbrien, where it reaches the river. The result would be to make it almost uniform all round.

163. What electoral division would that be in?—It would make it tolerably equal all round. It would be (taking from the present boundary of the city and running a mile all round) would be taking a bit of Ballysimon, and a little of Roxborough.

164. Would you see any objection to leaving out Ballysheedy West?—No. If you left that out you would only be obliged to cut one electoral division. It would certainly make it more equal all round.

165. It would have the advantage of not cutting the electoral division of Roxborough?—Yes.

166. Would that take in all the villa residences?—Yes.

Mr. ROBERT M'DONNELL, J.P., examined.

Mr. Robert M'Donnell, J.P.

167. CHAIRMAN.—You are a member of the Town Council?—Yes, for some years.

168. What is your view with reference to the extension or otherwise of the boundaries of Limerick?—I have always been of opinion that there should be an extension, and have advocated it. The city is growing all round, and the property adjoining it derives very great advantage from its proximity to the city, and should contribute to the taxation. I agree with Mr. Connolly's view on the matter. The line adopted or suggested some five or six years ago is the best, but the Council recently were under the impression it would be better to go for a further extension. I yielded to the majority, but my own impression was and is, that the line suggested some five or six years ago, and which you have before you, is the best.

169. What is your view as to the payment of the sanitary rate, by the people in the increased area. At present in the rural sanitary district the landlord pays half; should that remain still?—Certainly, the same incidence of taxation.

170. With regard to the same rate in the city, is it your opinion that one half of the sanitary rate should be paid by the landlord?—Yes, it would be a great advantage—it would be only fair.

171. I am confining it to the sanitary as well as poor rate?—Yes. I would be one of the last to take in the rural persons if it would increase their taxation, but in my opinion the result would be to lessen it.

172. Does the line you are in favour of adopting take in land—property so called?—No, it only takes in gentlemen's houses, terraces of houses, gentlemen's seats, demesnes, and they should fairly contribute. It also takes in the portion of the county to which the city is rapidly extending.

173. Does the land adjacent to the city derive exceptional advantage from its proximity to the town?—Yes. No doubt about it. The landlord receives a higher rent, and the tenant from the advantage he derives from his proximity to the city is better able to pay it. They supply all the people inside Limerick with milk, butter, and all that, of course the land is much better. The North Liberty district is in the electoral division of Limerick. The North Liberties are peculiarly situated, they are in the county Limerick though not in any way connected with the county Limerick—they are completely detached from the county. My impression is that the taxation would be decreased, certainly 3d. or 4d. in the pound, by taking an increased area. Some of my nearest friends would be affected by it, for their lands lie just outside the present boundary.

174. Is it your opinion they should be brought in, paying the same improvement rate?—Well that is a question of detail.

175. You don't propose that lands should pay?—No.

176. Would you bring in Mr. Delmege's place?—Yes.

177. Is it your proposition that Mr. Delmege should pay the full improvement rate?—No.

178. Would it be fair to charge Mr. Delmege the full improvement rate unless you were prepared to give him gas and water up to his door?—It would be scarcely fair if we did not give him corresponding advantages. That is a matter of detail that could be arranged.

179. Would it be fair in this outside district to make them pay one half?—Well, I would not like to commit myself to what the proportion should be, but I do think that if they did not get the full benefit of the various city advantages and improvements, it would be scarcely fair to charge them the whole improvement rate. They will get no doubt the full advantages of the roads and of scavenging but not, I think, of lighting up to their doors.

180. Supposing the legislature took this view of it, that in any future legislation it was to be provided that every part of a township was to get equal advantage, that the farthest point should be lighted as well as the nearest, would you then be in favour of extension?—No, for I do not think it would be fair to lay mains so far out. I would not tax Mr. Delmege without giving him at least full benefit for what he would be asked to pay.

181. Are you satisfied with the wards as they are at present?—Oh no.

182. If there was to be no alteration in the boundaries?—Well, as they exist at present it might do well enough.

183. Suppose there was to be an alteration, would you suggest that the eight city wards should remain as they are, and that the new district should be formed into two new wards. Do you suggest that?—That probably would be a fair arrangement.

184. You cannot bring them in without representation?—No.

185. Would you think it better to add the new districts to the existing wards or give them separate representation?—I think it would probably be as well to give them separate representation, as they have in the new law.

186. How would you arrange it so as to give equivalent representation?—I could not say, for I do not know the exact valuation. I would give them the full number of representatives they would be entitled to according to valuation.

187. If the extension was carried out as suggested would there be any difficulty in the way of the Corporation taking that increased district under their management?—No, besides a good many of the Corporation are members of the Board of Guardians

[illegible]

limit the parliamentary boundary ?—Of course, we have no any objection to rural voters.

Mr. William Spillane, examined.

[illegible]

Mr. *M'Donnell*.—I think not; I see no great objection.

206. Mr. *Spillane*.—I am prepared to give eight representatives under the rearrangement.

207. Mr. *Kearney* (Solicitor).—The north side is not as large as the south.

208. CHAIRMAN.—That could be arranged in this way—five could be given to one and three to the other. At present it is divided into two wards for Poor Law purposes, north and south suburbs, but if it was found there was any substantial difference, of course you could give three members to one and five to the other.

Mr. *Spillane*.—If we give eight members out of the city we don't care of course how you subdivide it.

209. *Town Clerk* (to Mr. Spillane).—Do you propose to cut off Shannon View, Newcastle Hill, Mount Cashel, Roselands? All these elegant residences are owned by gentlemen who would make most desirable representatives in the council?

Mr. *Spillane*.—Yes; but if they are outside the line what is to be done. Some line must be adopted.

210. CHAIRMAN.—If we go further outside we must cut ever so many electoral divisions.

Mr. *Kearney*.—I would ask Mr. Connolly to go through the townlands, at the north side of the river, he proposes to be added.

211. CHAIRMAN.—At the north side he proposes to leave the electoral division the boundary.

Mr. *Kearney*.—A good deal of that is purely agricultural.

212. They are market gardens?—

Mr. *Kearney*.—No. There is Coonagh that is all grass.

213. Mr. *Delmege*.—There is not in the whole north a market garden.

214. *Town Clerk*.—All the city bricks are manufactured there—We all know the brickfields.

215. CHAIRMAN.—The land that is brought in there would only have to pay one third of the taxes of the city.

Mr. *M'Donnell*.—There is Rahanagh, there is the same class of land in the city.

216. *Town Clerk*.—There is land there which pays £10 an acre, and if it were now taken out it would not pay £5.

217. CHAIRMAN.—I think there may be some misunderstanding about this. In bringing in any of the outlying district do you propose they shall pay one third of the improvement rate?—Yes.

218. And the whole of the general purposes?—Yes.

219. So that taking 1878 they would pay 1s. 8d. and 1s. 3d. that is 2s. 8d.; now in the North Liberty barony they only pay one-third, so that would be putting 1s. 3d. on them?—Yes that is two years, it would be making them pay 1s 3d. extra. What I would say as to the general purposes rate being reduced is that it would reduce the rate if you extended the boundary.

220. Your general purposes rate you say would be reduced to about 9d.?—About that. As to the North Liberty, in the Spring Assizes, 1878, the Grand Jury cess was 6½d. and for the Summer it was 8½d.—that is just 1s. 3d.

221. Could you tell me what were the county at large charges last year?—No, not now.

Mr. *Corbett*.—At the Summer Assizes £310 1s. 6d.

222. Then so far as I can see their taxation would be increased.

Mr. *Corbett*.—Yes, according to the document I made out it would increase the taxation to 1s. 6d.

223. Mr. *Spillane*.—As Mr. Delmege is here, and as he may make some observations touching the mortgage, I would ask you to allow me to reply.

224. CHAIRMAN.—Has not the legislature settled the matter?—

Mr. *Delmege*.—I would allude to the mortgage only to show my brother rate-payers in the Liberties that there is looming in the distance additional taxation in respect of that gas purchase. As surely as the sun sets so surely will we in the Liberties be called upon at some future period to pay additional taxation for that mortgage. I am prepared to show that the Corporation property is all gone—is frittered away.

Mr. Connolly, &c., examined.

225. CHAIRMAN.—What is the difference in the acreage between the parliamentary and municipal boundary?—I find the lands in the parliamentary boundary cover 31,153a. 1r. 1p., and the valuation of that is £33,261. The municipal boundary contains, between townlands and portions of townlands, 2,074a. 2r. 37p., and the valuation is £54,612.

226. Have you seen the map on which is marked the boundary, as proposed by Mr. Connolly, and that the others have approved of?—Yes.

227. What is the acreage and valuation of the electoral division?—It comprises forty-three townlands, 6,614a. 3r. 32p., and the valuation is £13,208. The city comprises twenty-eight townlands.

228. Does the electoral boundary take in all that can be properly called suburban residences and building ground?—Yes; a large quantity of it.

229. Is the whole of that occupied by residences and building ground?—It is occupied both by residences and building ground, and arable land too.

230. Is the arable land, land in the nature of town-parks, market gardens, and that class of land?—There is a great deal of it plain arable land.

231. Mr. COTTON.—You say the valuation of the electoral division is £13,208—how much of that is applicable to houses?—I could not say that. The city valuation I made out to be £54,612, and the electoral division or north and south suburb, £13,208; and the valuation of houses in that is, as I make it out, £2,963.

232. And the rest I take it is agricultural land and would pay one third?—Yes. On that I find the improvement warrant of 1878 in the city £10,798. I find that the county roads' contract taking in the north and south suburban wards is £716 18s., and I added to that, the amount of increase of salaries that would come to the officers, about £400 a year, or about £11,876 18s., which would be met by the present improvement rate levied on the whole electoral division.

233. That £11,879 18s., would be a 3s. 6d. rate for the year?—Yes; that is making houses pay the full and land one-third.

234. Would that give roads and all?—That would take in county roads.

235. What was the general purposes rate in 1878 in the city?—£4,033 8s. 7½d., and the proportion of county expenses £281 in that electoral division, and that would be £4,370 8s. 7½d., or a 1s. 1d. rate. I see the Grand Jury cess in Castleconnell for 1878 was 1s. 11½d.; then taking the general purposes and the improvement rate as 1s. 9d. or a difference of 9½d. in addition. In Pubblebrien the Grand Jury cess was 1s. 6d. and the general purposes and improvement rate 2s. 3d. in the year, and 10d. would be the addition; and in the North Liberty 1s. 6d. would be the addition.

236. Charging houses at the full?—Yes; in the improvement rate houses at the full, and land one-third.

237. Mr. COTTON.—How many miles of road are there to be maintained in the electoral division?—I did not make that up, but I could do so.

238. CHAIRMAN.—Are the roads in the county kept better than in the city?—I don't think they are.

239. Mr. COTTON.—Do you know the amount of contracts in each?—I know that for that portion within the electoral division the amount £758 18s. 6d.

[illegible] great difference in the rating between the baronies of [illegible] and North [illegible]?—I suppose it is in consequence of the valuation.

241. [illegible] that it should be [illegible] in the one more than in the other [illegible] ?—In [illegible] they are [illegible] in the other.

242. Are there more roads to keep up?—Oh yes; more in [illegible] than in the North [illegible].

243. [illegible]—There are only [illegible] roads [illegible].

244. CHAIRMAN.—What advantages have the [illegible] people in the north [illegible] for bringing them [illegible] to make them pay the full increase?—Well, certainly they will gain [illegible] by [illegible] there is no [illegible] than [illegible].

244. You [illegible]?—Yes.

245. Are the houses on each side of the [illegible] private property?—Yes, and the borough boundary runs down the centre of it.

246. MR. [illegible]—Is that a public road?—Yes, but it is not repaired by the city.

247. Are there lights along it?—There are lights on both sides, as it contains [illegible].

248. CHAIRMAN.—Is there any public [illegible] through it?—No.

249. How are the houses [illegible] lighted? [illegible] The lights stop exactly at the boundary.

250. [illegible] there are [illegible] buildings [illegible] outside?—Yes.

251. At one side do not the people pay for gas?—Yes.

252. And for city taxation?—Yes.

253. And the people on the other side don't pay anything?—No; I think they ought to be brought in.

254. What boundary would you suggest [illegible] [illegible] all suburban residences and [illegible] building land?—I think a mile outside the present boundary would be fair enough.

255. [illegible] Would you mark on the map what you would propose, with the boundaries kept as nearly as possible within the electoral [illegible]?—I would leave out part of the parish of [illegible].

256. Would you not take in the union workhouse?—Yes.

257. MR. [illegible]—[illegible] you take in that?—Yes.

258. Do you think the [illegible] would be too high?—[illegible] I would think about a [illegible] would be fair.

259. What would you think about the wards?—I would [illegible].

260. [illegible] ?—Yes; there are a great many of [illegible] [illegible] [illegible] to be [illegible].

261. CHAIRMAN.—Would you [illegible]?—Yes; [illegible] I would [illegible].

262. You would then [illegible] eight?—Yes; I would [illegible] that way.

263. How would you [illegible] with the new [illegible]?—I would put [illegible] the North [illegible] ward and the South [illegible] ward. In fact I would put in three wards, [illegible], and North Liberty.

264. [illegible] the number of [illegible]?—[illegible] population is generally taken into consideration in [illegible] wards. There [illegible] the entire [illegible]. There would be no difficulty about that. The valuation of the North Liberties is 26,[illegible], and of the South [illegible].

265. [illegible] by Mr. [illegible] on the map—would you say that it fairly represents the [illegible] likely to be [illegible] building ground?—I think so.

266. Do you think it represents the land that [illegible] to the city [illegible]?—I think it does.

267. Would there be any difficulty on the part of the Corporation in [illegible]?—I don't think so.

268. MR. [illegible]—There would be no difficulty about collecting the [illegible], but one point that I [illegible] would be [illegible]. Mr. [illegible] of Limerick, but if he had dealings with the [illegible], as I have, he would see it in a different light.

Mr. [illegible], J.P., examined.

269. Are you opposed to [illegible]?—Indeed I am. I am not against an extension to [illegible] places of the kind [illegible] I think if they were included it would be an [illegible] and an act of justice, and it would give them an opportunity of [illegible] the place [illegible] and [illegible]—which would be a [illegible].

270. But they have all these [illegible]?—They have light only up to the borough boundary.

271. Half the road is in the county?—Yes; but it is lighted in such a way at present that it is of little advantage to anyone, but if it was included it would be as well lighted as any of the streets.

272. What do you say as to [illegible]?—Well, I am not so [illegible] with that. I know there are [illegible], a road over the [illegible] up there about a mile beyond the present boundary. If that were [illegible] I believe it would be for the benefit of those people.

273. Would you go for an extension of a mile, following a proper boundary from the present boundary?—Yes, under particular circumstances; but it is not to be forgotten that if I go a mile from the boundary, in certain directions, I may as well go twenty miles into the country, for there is no prospect whatever of residences being built there, except [illegible] valued [illegible] from £1 to £3.

274. You would not say that land twenty miles away, bought anything like the rent of land within a mile of the town?—I am the occupier of about 250 Irish acres, and I may tell you that I pay the land six or seven miles away from [illegible], as much as any land around Limerick is worth to me.

275. Is the land six or seven miles away of the same quality?—Yes; and better. It is not, it would not fetch the price. I hold land for grazing purposes, [illegible] eight or ten miles off, and it is of the very same or better quality than the land I hold at Limerick. I am the occupier of [illegible] acres, a quarter of a mile outside the present boundary. I [illegible] for that land thirty years ago, [illegible] the [illegible] of the then existing state of things continuing—on the [illegible] of what I was then to pay. I never [illegible] to pay city taxes, for the lighting, cleansing, sewerage, &c., of Limerick. If those gentlemen in the Corporation who are seeking an extension of the boundary get the parties interested in the value of property in Limerick to pay equal proportion of taxation according to [illegible] it would be an act of justice. If that were done, [illegible] that every one interested in property in the city should pay a fair proportion of taxation we would not be ever [illegible] and there would be no necessity for extending the boundaries.

MR. [illegible]—We tried to do what Mr. [illegible] suggests, and a [illegible] with that object was [illegible].

MR. [illegible]—As to the land being more valuable near the town, I can tell you the contrary that [illegible] in a [illegible], as I can prove in my own case.

276. CHAIRMAN.—Yours must be a very exceptional case then. We know that in the case of most people having land around a city, they have greater advantages and facilities for sending in milk and butter, and turning money in that way.

277. Mr. Elliott.—Is it not a fact, Mr. Kelly, that they do supply milk to the workhouse and the asylum, and is not their proximity an advantage to them?—In some cases, yes; in others not. I believe the man who is a dairy farmer, and has his cattle seven or eight or ten miles off, can make as much, if not more, as the man within a mile of the city.

278. CHAIRMAN.—Well there may be something exceptional in the circumstances of the land around Limerick, but I can only say that it is directly contrary to what has been proved everywhere else. We have heard that there is no more profitable way of having land than as a market garden or for grazing, the produce of which is sent in every day to the town and sold, and we have found that lands convenient to the town are very much increased in value.

Mr. Kelly.—I believe that houses, residences and building land outside the present boundary might be brought in fairly, and with advantage to the parties.

279. If you bring in those would you make them pay what the citizens pay?—Yes; and I would give them all the advantages.

280. But the land only pays one-third now?—But I don't mean to include the lands, only the market gardens and places attached to residences. That is all I want to include.

Mr. JOHN CHRISTOPHER DELMEGE, examined.

281. In the first place I don't at all object to the statement of Mr. Spillane. On the contrary, I quite agree with it—with part of it at least—namely, that all those suburbs should be brought into the taxation of the city, and also the ground that is being used, or is intended finally to be used for building ground. As to Eden-terrace, the state of things that prevails with reference to it has been mentioned, and I think it is most unjust that one side should be obliged to pay taxes, whilst the other, obtaining nearly equal advantages, gets off scot free.

282. CHAIRMAN.—In your direction, Mr. Delmege, how far do you think the boundary should go. I see, for instance, a place called Whitfield, a little above the girls-home—should it go as far as that?—I may say that I have written some letters in the public prints, and have rather studied the subject. I would rather speak on the general question than on any personal grounds, but as you ask me the question I may tell you that in my part of the country—the North Liberty barony—it is not at all a suburban district. I am living there for more years than I would like to say, and I don't know of a single house having been built, except by the rent-paying farmers, who pay large rents and are subject to pretty smart taxation, who have taken from large landed proprietors, like the Marquis of Lansdowne and others, and who have these lands leased to them under certain conditions of taxation, which they and I consider as vested rights which should not wilfully be overthrown. If you extend the municipal boundary and its consequent taxation to them, I do not see how it would be justice, and I do not think the borough boundary of the North Liberty ought to be extended an inch more than it is. I should say, as regards the other side towards the poor-house and Eden-terrace, Kilrush and that, those are suburban districts, and where you see new residences springing up, I do think that it is only justice that people in those districts should be included in city taxation.

283. The union workhouse is not included?—No.

284. Do you think it ought to be?—Yes.

285. I see places marked Thereville, are they in the city?—Yes.

286. Thereville is not. It is in the county, it is on the same line of road with Eden-terrace, and Barbrow House is in the county. Now, Mr. Delmege, do you think those places ought to be taken in?—Yes; because these are suburban building districts. I am of opinion that every house or suburb, where houses can and are likely to be built, ought to be taken into the municipal boundary, but I am as strongly of opinion that land of a purely agricultural nature, farmed by tenants without gardens or anything of that sort, should be left out.

287. Yes, but you could not draw a line merely to take in buildings or houses—otherwise Parliament would probably have provided that no township be formed to take in any arable land, but the way they get rid of that difficulty is this, provided that arable land should only pay one-fourth of the rate—houses properly so called pay the full rate, and arable land, market gardens and so on, are not excluded altogether, but are only asked to pay a proportion. Some gentlemen say "take in all ground likely to be built on, so don't take me in." How then are we to draw the line so as to make a proper boundary whilst doing no serious injustice?—

Mr. Delmege.—I am prepared to say this, that every bargain to be legal and binding should have a consideration. Now the Corporation give no consideration of any kind, and there is very little affection between the Liberties and the Corporation. If they gave us lamps or anything of that kind for increased taxation there might be some advantage. I say to them "are you prepared to give them" and they reply that they are not. Then I say, why ask us to pay so much for such advantages as you say we derive, in going to the town for the purposes of schools, markets, and so on.

288. Would it be fair to ask them to pay one-half for the advantages they derive in that way?—Well we do use their streets, but they would be very badly off without us, if we did not come in and spend our money in their shops. I was going to wind up with one observation about the streets. They cost, I am informed, about £1,000 a year, and what I would suggest is that they should be repaired by the county-at-large. The people at Rathkeal use the streets as much as anyone else does, and leave as large a deposit behind. I make that suggestion because I think it is rather unfair that the people in the city should have the entire responsibility of the taxation for the repairs of the streets, cleansing, &c., the cost of which amounts to about £4,000. Now as to another point concerning the question of political influence, I am satisfied that if the Liberties were polled tomorrow they would be glad to give up their power of voting for a member provided there was no taxation imposed upon them. Another thing I would say is this. If we are brought into the municipal boundary and if we are obliged to pay taxes for municipal purposes—then I say, that property has its rights as well as its duties, and should have its representation. I think if you do bring the country element in, we ought to have a representation according to property, so that we would not be merely a myth on the Corporation, borne down by the votes of the majority. Another thing is I think the Corporation is a great deal too large, forty members is a great deal too much.

289. What is your view as to the division of taxes between landlord and tenant, particularly the sanitary taxes—do you think what is applied to the rural should be applied to the city districts, that the tenant should deduct the half from the landlord?—I think it would be very unfair to put all the tax on the tenants.

290. Would you divide the sanitary tax?—Yes; it would be unfair to put it on the tenants—they have to bear quite enough, but as regards the financial part of the matter, it is evidently in not, for our good that the Corporation seek to put us in. The object of extending the boundary is not to do benefit to us in the least

the purposes [illegible] of the Corporation. They are at present in a most unfortunate [illegible] to [illegible] their [illegible], which nobody has [illegible] to them.

[illegible]. Mr. Connolly.—If Mr. Delany really [illegible] [illegible] individuals [illegible], I think he will speak of what he knows of his own knowledge, to the [illegible], and not quote [illegible]. You have told us [illegible] Mr. [illegible] one [illegible] [illegible] to the [illegible] of all the [illegible] on the Corporation property.

[illegible]. Mr. Delany.—I know Mr. Connolly's feelings as representing the Corporation, but I will [illegible] before the Commissioners and the public, if Mr. Connolly, or any member of the Corporation [illegible] my words.

[illegible]. Mr. Connolly.—I only want Mr. Delany to state facts, which he knows to be facts.

[illegible]. Mr. Delany.—My facts are taken from the [illegible], and if that [illegible] they are also taken from what I [illegible] of my own knowledge and from [illegible] with members of the Corporation. I [illegible] in writing [illegible], and in the following [illegible] I [illegible] and from [illegible]:—

"[illegible] Mr. [illegible] says—'[illegible] the city [illegible], if the Corporation [illegible] £[illegible] the Commissioners [illegible] to [illegible] for the purpose of paying the Corporation debts.' [illegible] and evidence before the [illegible] in 1876. The total [illegible] of the Corporation was £[illegible]; [illegible] £27,000 for the gas and other [illegible] and other [illegible] property in the Landed Estates Court, some of which have been sold. This [illegible] does not include any moneys due to the National Bank on [illegible] accounts, which amounted in 1876 to £[illegible]."

Mr. Connolly.—[illegible] is a grossly [illegible] statement.

Mr. Delany.—[illegible] of the Corporation [illegible] that they are [illegible] in debt.

Mr. Connolly.—I [illegible] think it is necessary to [illegible] Mr. Delany's letter to the newspapers.

[illegible]. Mr. Delany.—I pledge myself to every statement I make, being [illegible] upon the blue book. I have the [illegible] here, and I can say this, that "that £[illegible] does not include any moneys due to the National Bank on overdrawn accounts, which amounted in 1876 to £[illegible]."

[illegible]. Chairman.—I think you are in error in saying you [illegible] from the report of the Committee.

[illegible]. Mr. Delany.—The statements I make in the letter to the public press [illegible] which I [illegible] on that report. They are in the blue book. I go on to say:—

"But, in December, 1877, the overdraft on the gas account was reduced to £[illegible], but the Commissioners said, '[illegible] to add that [illegible] have been made.' The [illegible]."

And this in my mind [illegible]:—

"They have [illegible] every shilling which they could [illegible]. They have mortgaged all their landed property [illegible] the city, and also their [illegible] and their property in [illegible] held in fee-simple; also the [illegible], all of which was, [illegible], or have been sold. [illegible] the improvement rate has been [illegible] mortgaged, and yet we are '[illegible] of £[illegible],' and yet [illegible] that the Corporation [illegible] the £[illegible] or £[illegible] to purchase the Limerick Gas Company's Works, so as to have the entire monopoly of the lighting of the city."

I say that is the financial state of the city.

[illegible]. Mr. Connolly.—Now, of this £[illegible], there is £27,000 charged on property in Limerick belonging to the Corporation [illegible] independent of all city [illegible] whatever, and Mr. [illegible], solicitor, the gentleman who has the money, is suing in the Landed Estates Court, and it is [illegible] that the property will realise that £27,000, so that the city is [illegible]. As to the gas, Mr. [illegible], out of the [illegible] of the Corporation [illegible] the [illegible] on the £[illegible], and not a [illegible] of that comes out of the improvement rate. The next item is £[illegible]. In [illegible] there was a large [illegible], in respect of which the Corporation borrowed £[illegible], and the [illegible] been that [illegible] the Corporation to [illegible] pay the £[illegible]; so that the only charge the Corporation [illegible] for all the improvement rate is £[illegible], [illegible] on the [illegible], and £[illegible] [illegible] on the 1st of July for the credit of the Corporation, to pay [illegible], so that the total liability of the Corporation on the Limerick improvement rate does not [illegible] £[illegible]. So that, in point of fact, you will find that the [illegible] £[illegible] at the [illegible] £[illegible] or £[illegible], the [illegible] charge on the improvement rate. It is right to say that there is not £[illegible] due to the National Bank. It has been reduced to £[illegible], and it will soon be only £[illegible] or £[illegible].

Mr. Delany.—Mr. Connolly [illegible] that [illegible], the Corporation [illegible] no [illegible] property [illegible] "[illegible]." Their property is sold. I know the [illegible] of it. Their [illegible] is sold, or nothing—everything is sold. That is why [illegible] are so badly [illegible]. The [illegible] up to [illegible], and they spend [illegible] a day [illegible] and [illegible] of [illegible] [illegible] [illegible]. What have they done to get rid of debt? They have sold, mortgaged, and got rid of everything; and now they are [illegible] the Limerick [illegible]. They [illegible] don't look after their property as carefully as an ordinary individual would. For [illegible] Hospital, by their own [illegible], they pay £[illegible] a year out of the [illegible] of the city, because, I am informed, they have no [illegible], and are unable to pay this high [illegible] of the city.

[illegible]. Mr. Connolly.—This £[illegible] a year was a matter [illegible] with the present Corporation, [illegible] as the [illegible]. It [illegible] which was [illegible] when Mr. Delany had charge of the city.

[illegible]. Mr. [illegible].—I should mention, Mr. Chairman, that it was proved before you, at your former inquiry, that the £27,000 was [illegible] borrowed to pay off the debts of the old Corporation, and not by the present body at all.

[illegible]. Chairman.—At page [illegible] of our former report it is fully set out, and it appears from that, and I think it is quite clear, that the debt of the Corporation is really very little. [illegible] is [illegible] by the Government auditor.

[illegible]. Mr. [illegible].—There is a sum of £[illegible] due to the gas works. That is due by the city at present.

Sir [illegible].—Now, Mr. Delany, in [illegible] your opinion there should be any increase, and, if so, what increase would you recommend?—There ought to be an increase to bring in suburban districts, where there have been built, or are about being built, but no other increase of any kind. I think it right, however, to point out that the Corporation are in their [illegible] position that they have no other means of [illegible] than by borrowing these large sums of money, and by way of [illegible] their [illegible] than by [illegible] their property, and [illegible] to force the [illegible] to [illegible] these [illegible]. How are these moneys expended—they are [illegible] taken from the improvement rate for the purpose of [illegible] up what Mr. [illegible] called this [illegible] [illegible], [illegible] concern.

[illegible]. It is generally admitted that land within a mile or two miles [illegible] derive such exceptional advantages, shared in by the landlord and tenant, that they ought to pay something. Is that your opinion?

LIMERICK. July 5, 1892. Mr. John C. Delaney.

305. Mr. *Delaney*.—If a radius of a mile all round were agreed on, and if it would be possibly managed, that we should have a fixed sum to pay as a contribution to the city, and that it was not left to the power of the Council to tax it, as they wish, I would not object to it. The way to manage that would be by giving the added district adequate representation in the Corporation. As I understand, the suggestion would be to give them [illegible] representation, and then you would get gentlemen like Mr. [illegible] to do the work, and the Corporation, as a body, would be [illegible] or afraid to increase the taxation, for if they increased it on others they would increase it on themselves.

306. Mr. *Smith*.—I would ask you to get out how this debt of £21,000 was contracted?

307. [illegible].—It is all in the blue book here.

308. Mr. Murray (Solicitor).—I am authorised, on the part of the Marquis of Lansdowne, to say, that so far as the extension into villa and suburban districts is concerned, we offer no opposition, but we would be strongly opposed to taking in any purely agricultural land.

309. Are you opposed to taking in anything beyond a mile from the city?—Yes, certainly it, if it is exclusive agricultural land.

310. You must know that it would be impossible for us to fix a boundary cutting out a bit here because it was agricultural, and taking in a bit there that was not. Does not the owner of land outside and adjacent to the town get a much higher rent for his land than if it was further off?—Yes, he does, I dare say.

311. Does he not get that higher rent from the mere reason of the proximity of the land to the city, which enables the tenant to pay that higher rent. Why then should he not pay his quota towards the taxation of the town, from the proximity to which he derives such advantage?

312. Mr. *Murray*.—As to this property, very little of it pays a higher rent than the lands five or six miles from Limerick.

313. Mr. *Delaney*.—It is a difficulty to think that land, near the city is not of greater value than land further off. We admit only this. The only thing I would say is this, if you would kindly take a note of it—my objection is this—that it is not fair for the citizens of Limerick to tax themselves for £4,000 for drainage, widening, and repairing the streets, for all the country people living within one mile or twenty miles to use. On the same ground as the county pays for the bridges, there ought to be contributions for these streets—it would not be more than [illegible] of a farthing on the whole county.

Mr. *Cunningham*.—The gentleman's, Mr. Delaney, proposals to represent are not taking them at all.

Mr. *Delaney*.—I can only say that we are prepared to give up our political power for the sharing of a member for the city if we are not additionally taxed. The Government ought to leave us as we are.

Mr. John Glennon.

Mr. JOHN GLENNON examined.

314. Where do you live?—At Clonlisheen, within the electoral division.

315. What land do you hold?—Forty-five acres.

316. Is it your opinion that land within the electoral division is more valuable, from its proximity to the city of Limerick, than if it were further off?—I don't think the myself than where I am situated it is.

317. As you are situated—but take your land, supposing your forty-five acres were to be let, and forty-five acres of similar land, say three or four miles off from Limerick, which would the farmer give more for?—I think there would be no difference.

318. Then you don't think land near the city is more valuable?—No.

319. Then you don't agree with Mr. Delaney?—No. I am only made to pay more for it in regard to the rates.

320. But you are not paying a penny?—I am paying sixty rates.

321. Then you ought to wish to bring others in to help you?—It is the city poor rate I mean.

322. The electoral division rate?—Yes.

323. Do you send in your produce to the city?—I do, sir.

324. Any milk or butter?—Yes; milk.

325. Don't you think it of advantage to be so near the town?—No; not the least. If it was further from the city I would turn to a different style of farming that would pay as well.

326. Do you think you contribute to the wear and tear of the roads of the city?—To some extent, but very little.

Mr. John Byrne.

Mr. JOHN BYRNE examined.

327. I live outside the city but within the electoral division. I farm thirty-nine acres.

328. Is it your opinion the land near the city is not more valuable on that account?—I am pretty sure it is not. I pay 30 per cent. over the valuation. That is a rack-rent.

329. Is that on account of the land being better or more valuable?—I suppose so.

330. But you say it is not more valuable?—Well, I have no benefit by it.

Mr. *Cunningham*.—Their view is, that if the landlord were to pay all the rates they would be better off.

Mr. *Byrne*.—I only know this, that I am paying more than I am able.

The inquiry terminated.

WESTPORT—6TH SEPTEMBER, 1879.

(Before Messrs. C. P. Cotton, C.E., and H. A. [illegible].)

Mr. [illegible], examined.

1. Mr. COTTON.—You are Town Clerk?—Yes.
2. How long did you hold Town Clerk's position?—[illegible].
3. Under what Act is the town constituted?—The Towns Improvement Act, 1854.
4. When was it placed under that Act?—In 1856.
5. Was it under any Act previously?—Yes, the 9th George 4th, chap. 82.
6. Was it entirely under that Act for all purposes?—Yes, for all purposes except water and light. These provisions were not adopted; subsequently the water provisions were adopted; now the guardians are the sanitary authority, and within a month they adopted the lighting powers; the present boundary is that adopted in 1856.
7. Did it differ from the previous boundary?—Under the 9th George 4th it was somewhat wider; but the Commissioners of Valuation curtailed the boundary on the application of Lord John Browne and the Marquis of Sligo. I have a map here which from the Commissioners of Valuation at the time the boundary was decided. The Commissioners of Valuation excluded the yellow portion to be the boundary, but the Marquis of Sligo and Lord John Browne made a very strong representation and the white portion inside the red line and outside the yellow line was added all round. The population by the Census of 1871 was 4,417. That is the town proper, and I think it has increased. The buildings have increased.
8. Are the buildings within the constituency?—They are. Mr. Livingstone, the Chairman of the Commissioners, has put up some buildings and so has the Vice-chairman.
9. You say the population is 4,417, exclusive of the [illegible] portion?—I mean that the town proper is 4,417.
10. What do you mean by the rural portion?—The population on the [illegible] on the rural district, and not included in the 4,417. It is the excess of the [illegible] only [illegible] up [illegible].
11. Where did you get the 4,417?—From "Thom's Directory."
12. And what makes you think that only includes the [illegible] as the population for the population and I came to the conclusion that the town alone has a population of 4,417. I may be wrong but I don't think I am.
13. What was the area of the township?—3,018 a. 0r. 31 p.
14. What is the valuation of the buildings in the town?—£8,887 15s.
15. And of land?—£1,[illegible] 10s., altogether £[illegible].
16. Are there no [illegible]?—No.
17. In what electoral division is the town situated?—Westport.
18. Altogether in Westport?—Altogether.
19. Can you give me the municipal rates from 1874 to 1879?—In 1874, 1s. on houses, and 3d. on land.
20. What is the [illegible]?—In 1874, 9d., since they were the sanitary authority. In 1875, 6d.; in 1876, 6d.; in 1877, 3d.; and in 1879, 2d.
21. What was the [illegible] for the same years?—In 1874, 2s. [illegible]; in 1875, 1s. [illegible]; in 1876, 2s. [illegible]; in 1877, 2s. [illegible]; in 1878, 1s. [illegible]. The borough rate in 1874 was 3s. [illegible]; in 1875, 3s. 6d.; in 1876, 3s.; in 1877, 1s. [illegible]; in 1879, 2s. 4d.
22. How much of the borough rate in 1879 was the sanitary rate?—There was no special sanitary rate since the separation.
23. Have the Board of Guardians struck a special sanitary rate?—They have struck a rate extending over the entire union of one penny, and to supplement that they borrowed £30,000.

24. But have they struck any special sanitary rate that was confined to the collecting-district? How much of it was the sanitary rate, say in 1878, when the rate was 2s. [illegible]?—The sanitary rate would be 3d. in the pound.
25. On what district was that struck?—On the whole electoral division. The guardians made the whole electoral division the contributory district for the sanitary purposes of the town of Westport, instead of placing it on the owners of the township.
26. What was the nature of the sanitary works?—It consisted of [illegible], which has been done [illegible] and completely covered in the town [illegible], and they would have to pay heavy rates for water were it not that the Marquis of Sligo, of his own free will and of his own generosity, supplied an unlimited water supply for all time, and [illegible] the [illegible] the cost of it [illegible] twelve or fourteen hundred pounds.
27. How is the town lighted?—The lighting of the town commenced partially in November, 1877, when Mr. Livingstone, the Chairman of the Commissioners, [illegible] were [illegible] twenty lamps, and paid for the lighting of them up to last April. When he was going to the cost, and he wrote a letter to the Commissioners, a letter which I think urged on them the desirability and [illegible] the necessity of providing lighting for the town, as a town like Westport should not be without lighting. It was a reflection on its civilization, and a [illegible]. The Commissioners [illegible] Mr. Livingstone's [illegible]. They took preliminary steps by applying to the Local Government Board to get power, and on the 23rd July, a public meeting was held and the lighting powers adopted, and £[illegible] was contracted with [illegible] for forty-four lamps.
28. Have you a contract for the lighting for the ensuing winter?—We have, [illegible] per thousand feet.
29. Is the gas supplied to the inhabitants at the [illegible]?—The cost up to the present has been 8s. 4d., but in consequence of the lighting powers we adopted, the contractors reduced it to 7s. 6d. for private lighting.
30. In the drainage of the town good?—Yes, I may unhesitatingly state the Board of Guardians have brought the drainage of the town into a condition not surpassed by any town in the empire. We have got splendid sewage pipes all round the town, which they got from Glasgow, and the water is the best that could be found outside Dublin, which we believe is the best in Ireland.
31. How many Commissioners are there?—Eighteen. Lord John Browne sometime ago retired from the Board, and the Town Commissioners.
32. How many municipal voters are there?—Altogether 350 persons qualified to vote.
33. How many are qualified to sit as Commissioners if elected?—I have not made that out, but there are about sixty—fully that.
34. Have the Commissioners considered these queries sent down to them?—When they got these queries they met, and they thought it right to give them the fullest possible publicity, and they ordered me to get one hundred copies printed and circulated, and I did so. And we sent them round to every proprietor, and every poor law guardian, and all the principal ratepayers. That circular intimated that the Town Commissioners would consider this question, on the 13th January, 1879. The Commissioners met after six weeks' notice of the meeting, and their chairman, Mr. Livingstone, was not there, but he wrote a letter recommending an extension of the boundaries.
35. Did they come to a resolution?—They did.

Westport. [illegible], 1879.

Mr. John Egan.

The Commissioners present were six in number, and the resolution passed was—

"Referring to the circular of the Municipal Boundaries Commissioners, of the 11th November, 1878, and the queries, copies of which have been [illegible], as directed by the minutes of the Commissioners it is now unanimously resolved that the Town Commissioners recommend that the boundaries of the town be extended, so as to be coterminous with the electoral division of Westport, with the exception of the townland of [illegible], for reasons stated in the queries' sheet now adopted."

The date of that resolution, was the 13th January, 1879.

36. Was it passed unanimously?—It was.

37. And the chairman, who was not there, wrote a letter, approving of it [illegible].

38. Did the Commissioners ever consider the question of becoming the urban authority?—[illegible].

39. What was their view of it?—[illegible] when the Public Health Act was passed in 1878, [illegible] Board of Guardians [illegible] sanitary authority, and they had [illegible] the town, and they gave the Commissioners [illegible]. They asked them to take into consideration whether they would become the sanitary authority or not. The Commissioners [illegible] Board of Guardians [illegible] competent body, [illegible].

40. Lord John Browne [illegible] Chairman, and the Board of Guardians offered to assist the Commissioners if they wished to become the urban authority.

Examination of Mr. Egan continued.

41. Did the Commissioners ever consider whether they would become the road authority?—They did wish to become the road authority, and they applied for a provisional order, which came before the Grand Jury, and was opposed, and Mr. [illegible], Queen's Counsel, argued the case [illegible]; but when the Town Commissioners brought it before the Grand Jury, the latter decided, that they did not give to the Town Commissioners the authority over the roads and streets, and buildings.

42. Are the Commissioners aware that if they become the urban authority, they might, by permission of the Local Government Board, become the road authority, whether the Grand Jury liked it or not?—[illegible] it was the [illegible] of rating, and the inequality of rating in the town that weighed [illegible] on the people, because the buildings must be always rated at four times the rating on the land. The valuation of land in the town is £1,120, and that land would pay comparatively nothing. For instance, on a rate of [illegible] in the £ for all purposes, land would be only paying [illegible], and that [illegible] the other rate under the Poor Law Board, where land and houses are equally rated. It weighed very much, [illegible] the Commissioners [illegible] the Chairman of the Board, Lord John Browne, and the guardians. We said if we took the road authority, the land would be comparatively free, and the buildings of the town would have to pay the greater portion.

43. You are speaking on the assumption that if they became the road authority, the rate would still be in the proportion of one-fourth?—I am.

44. That is not clear, because if you became the road authority, the question as to the rating would be settled at the time by the Local Government Board. However, you declined to become the urban authority, and so it is out of your power to become the road authority?—Yes.

45. What is the valuation of the electoral division?—The whole area is [illegible], and the valuation on the houses is, £3,620 [illegible]; half annual rents, £348 14s. The valuation of land is, £3,973 4s., making in all, £7,930 10s.

46. Mr. Robinson.—Is there land within the present municipal boundary available for building?—There is.

47. Is there much land?—There is.

48. In which direction?—There is scarcely an end of the town where there is not land available for building.

49. Is building going on outside the boundary?—Not at present, but it is very probable there will be.

50. Mr. Cotton.—Supposing the electoral division was brought in, how many additional voters would it add?—It would bring in 250, valued over £4, qualified to vote in the election of Commissioners, but there are other voters who have the power to vote at the adoption of lighting power, of £8 value.

51. How many would be qualified to become Commissioners?—Thirteen qualified to sit in the proposed extension.

52. Mr. Robinson.—Adopting the electoral division gives you an increased valuation of £4,658, and an increased area of 3,334 acres.

53. Mr. Cotton.—How far does the present boundary extend from the centre of the town?—It is not exactly uniform. I call the market-house the centre of the town, and roughly, it is scarcely a mile.

54. It is about a mile in every direction?—No; it is not a mile.

55. What is it to the north?—It is very nearly a mile—about three quarters.

56. To the east?—It is more than a mile.

57. To the south?—Seven-eighths of a mile.

58. To the west?—It is over a mile.

59. What is the distance of the most remote part of the electoral division from the centre of the town, in English statute miles?—Two and a half miles to the east.

60. How much to the north-west?—Two and three-quarters.

61. That is the farthest distance?—It is.

62. What are the items of your income and expenditure?—The income consists of town rates, dog tax and fines at petty sessions.

63. You have no land?—No property of any kind, but what we get from the rates and fines, and our items of expenditure are for the cleansing of the town.

64. Mr. Robinson.—Do the people carrying on business in the town mostly live in the town, or have they residences outside?—Some few have residences outside, but the great majority of them live in town.

65. Do they live outside from any desire to avoid taxation?—By no means to avoid taxation.

66. Mr. Alfred A. Kelly (on the part of those opposing the extension).—There was a resolution passed exempting the townland of [illegible]?—Yes. That is the most southerly townland. It is separated from the other parts of the electoral division by a good sized river, and the opinion is that it should never have formed part of the electoral division at all.

67. What reasons were given why the township should be extended to be co-extensive with the electoral division?—The reasons stated in the query sheet.

68. What are the reasons?—There was a long discussion on the matter, and some wanted different boundaries.

69. Mr. Cotton.—The reason given in reply to the queries is, the population of the entire electoral division of Westport is benefited by the accommodation that the town affords them for fairs, markets, &c., and consequently they should contribute to the town improvement rates.

70. Mr. Kelly.—But that doesn't give any reason for exempting [illegible]?—The vice-chairman of the Commissioners who presided on that occasion, said there was a natural separation of [illegible] from the other portions of the electoral division by a large river. Moreover, that as the townland is very poor and so far away, it would not be right to include it. By resolution, passed on Friday last, the 10th, day

resolved to include the whole electoral division. On that day I laid before them your communication, and there were nine Commissioners present. I read the letter from the Municipal Boundaries Commissioners, stating they would attend at the Town Hall, Westport, at eleven o'clock, for the purpose of hearing evidence as to the existing boundaries, and then it was proposed and resolved unanimously "That Mr. Thomas J. Gibbons be employed, at a fee of two guineas, to represent the Commissioners and others in favour of the extension of the township boundaries, so as to include the entire electoral division of Westport." Mr. Gibbons, being now in Dublin, cannot attend.

70. Mr. *Kelly*.—Only six Commissioners thought it worth their while to attend at the former meeting?—Yes; and the Chairman apologised for not attending.

71. Were the nine unanimous?—Yes.

72. But at the former meeting, out of eighteen only six attended?—Yes.

73. Mr. Cotton.—Are your meetings open to the public?—They are.

74. Mr. *Kelly*.—Was it only to the Commissioners you gave notice of the meeting in January, 1873?—I gave notice to all the guardians having property in the electoral division. I distributed fifty copies of the notice, and gave copies of it here.

75. You did not give notice to all the ratepayers interested in the extension?—I looked through the list, as far as I could see, of Parliamentary voters, and I sent a copy of the notice to each of them.

76. But you only sent these notices to parliamentary voters?—Yes.

77. Why didn't you send them to the electors entitled to vote under the Towns Improvement Act?—The press was present and reported the meeting, and I sent round fifty of the notices.

78. But you did not send them to those who had votes and would be eligible to be Commissioners if the area was extended?—I did a thing that was not done elsewhere—sending round circulars at all.

79. When did the Commissioners get powers first?—Under the 9 Geo. IV., they had powers in 1853.

80. When did they apply for an extension of powers?—The Towns Improvement Act was passed in 1854, and when it was about a year and a half passed they applied for powers under that Act.

81. What powers?—They applied for all the powers of the Act, except as to light and water.

82. They didn't think the lighting of any consequence?—They did, and they applied for it subsequently.

83. But the first time they didn't think the lighting at all necessary?—Oh, I am not competent to interpret what they meant or what they thought.

84. What was the population then?—It was the same as now.

85. And there was no application for light?—There was an application for light in 1857.

86. Was that thrown out and refused?—It was not adopted by the ratepayers.

87. Was it opposed and thrown out unanimously, both by the ratepayers of the town, and every member of the district?—I speak from records. When you ask me was it rejected unanimously, I say decidedly not.

88. Who was in favour of it?—There was no poll taken.

89. Therefore, without a poll, it was refused?—It was refused.

90. How soon after that did you again apply for these powers?—I think, in 1874 or 1876.

91. What became of the application then?—The application was not adopted. There was no poll taken then either.

92. What state of facts exists now that did not exist then, that would give more benefit to the people if the area be now extended?—The state of facts remains pretty much the same, except that we have got the railway into the town.

93. Had you not the railway in 1876?—Yes; the lighting are placed by a far more competent authority—the Chairman of the Commissioners.

WESTPORT.
Nov. [illegible]
Mr. John Kean.

94. The rates at both times were very much the same as at the two occasions when lighting was opposed?—Yes. The Commissioners ordered me to write to every town in Ireland of the population of Westport, or of half the size; and I did write to every town where there were Commissioners, and every where there were no Commissioners, and I found no town in Ireland, with a third of the population, without light.

95. And you did that on the two occasions when they rejected the proposal?—No, only on the last occasion it was rejected.

96. As it stands, it was rejected twice by the Commissioners, and by the ratepayers, and it is utterly what took place at the meeting—no poll was taken, because people who had no votes at all swamped the meeting, and those who had votes did not vote at all.

97. Then the voice of the people was what governed the question and decided the death knell of the application?—The voice of the people, those living outside the boundary, and those who had no votes. There was no poll taken.

98. The people outside the boundary—have they any votes?—I know individuals myself who are not in the township at all, and they came in there clamouring and making their voices.

99. But they came from near the town?—They lived outside the boundary.

100. Was it outside the electoral division of Westport?—Yes, and some of them came from other electoral divisions.

101. What was proposed in January was to light as far as Westport extends, was it?—That is true, entirely.

102. Was it the police?—Those proposed to go as far as that.

103. Did any of your outside people go taken in then?—No.

104. At the last meeting of the Commissioners when lighting was adopted, are you aware of any idea of what changed the spirit of the friends of the Commissioners?—I have stated this emphatically and distinctly, that when the Commissioners at their meeting proposed an extension of the boundary to the electoral division, there was no talk whatever of the lighting of the town.

105. There was nothing then talked of it?—No; nor for two months afterwards.

106. Why was it then they wanted to extend the township?—I speak from records. The population of the entire electoral division are benefited by the town, in the accommodation it affords them for fairs, markets, &c., consequently, they should contribute to the town rate.

107. That is the only ground you have on record?—Yes; because there was no room in the paper to write any more. If I wrote down all the grounds it would take much space.

108. With regard to the accommodation for fairs, markets, &c., what distance do the people come?—I dare say they come from Mullingar and Liverpool, and all parts of the kingdom.

109. Tell me how far the fairs and markets are availed of by the people in the rural districts?—They are availed of by all the surrounding parishes, and I think on the fair day in Westport we have all the farmers of the seven parishes around about.

110. How many miles would that be?—It is an extremely wide area.

111. They come from all parts?—Yes.

112. How far is Louisburgh from Westport?—Ten miles, Irish.

113. How far is it from Louisburgh to the Killeries?—It is more than forty miles, for it is a very bad road. From here to the Killeries is about twenty miles.

114. Do the inhabitants of that district avail themselves of the town of Westport as much as those

Westport. Sept. 4, 18[illegible]. Mr. John [illegible].

actually living in the town?—They do, and from Clare Island also.

115. Mr. Cowton.—In fact, the advantages of the town, so far as fairgrounds are concerned, is not confined to people of three or four miles away, but extends to a very much wider area?—As regards fairs it is a very wide area, but if you ask as to markets I can define it.

116. Mr. Kelly.—You think, so far as fairs go, this extension would be unfair and unreasonable?—I don't say that.

117. Don't you think it would be unfair as regards fairs to extend the district to the extent of the present application?—I don't think it would be fair to extend the boundary beyond the electoral division of Westport.

118. Do you say it would be fair or reasonable, considering the advantages derivable from the fairs, to extend the present boundaries to the extent proposed? —If you take it on the ground of the advantages derived from the fairs, you might extend the area over the whole parish. There are six fairs in Westport in the year, and these are attended by people from all parts of Mayo and outside Mayo.

119. You have a weekly market, every Thursday, and you see a good many people in the town?—Yes, I am looking at them for thirty-five years.

120. You say they come a very long distance?—Yes.

121. What distance do they come for the markets? —You may fairly estimate that for market purposes, the people attend from six or seven miles all round.

122. Do they come from Newport?—They do.

123. And Castlebar?—Yes.

124. And Louisburgh and Percy?—Yes.

125. And are not the advantages of the market as great to these people as to those within half-a-mile of the town?—These people living within the electoral division come in larger proportion than those living outside it.

126. I am speaking of people coming here to transact business. Don't people from Newport, Louisburgh, and Partry derive as much benefit as people here?—Yes, and Clew Bay too.

127. So that the people you want to tax derive just the same benefit as those living outside, and in the outlying districts?—They do, because the town is nearer to them. You must diminish the extent of the accommodation by the distance which they live from the town—the nearer the town the greater the accommodation.

128. Mr. Rosseter.—Is land within the electoral division more valuable because of its proximity to the town?—I should imagine it is.

129. Mr. Kelly.—What is the rateable valuation of the division of Killeencoursh?—313 acres, and the valuation on land is 467 10s., and on houses 411 6s.

130. Take Derrygorman?—Yes, it contains 234 acres, and the valuation is £102.

131. Take Carlecross?—It is one of the townlands included; it contains 11a. 3r. 29p., and the valuation is £37 10s.

132. That is nearly 10s. an acre?—Yes.

133. And in the other case it is not a half-a-crown. Take Drumindoff with an area of 273a. 1r. 1p., what is the valuation of it?—£146 18s.

134. What is Ardgowan valued at?—It is not in the electoral division of Westport at all.

135. I know that?—It is in Ardgowan north.

136. Isn't it rated at a greater valuation than Derrygorman?—It is in the electoral division of Ardgowan north, and I have not got the valuation of it.

137. Who is the owner of Ardgowan?—The Marquis of Sligo.

138. Are not the lands of Ardgowan of higher valuation than those of Derrygorman?—I don't know the valuation of the townland of Ardgowan, because I thought I was only to bring the rate book of the electoral division here.

139. I'll take your opinion of it; you know both these places?—I do.

140. Do you say that Derrygorman bears an increased valuation from its proximity?—I think Ardgowan and Derrygorman are nearly equally distant.

141. Take Tourmaney—and isn't the valuation of the land of Ardgowan greater than Tourmaney, which is much nearer the town?—The land of Mount Browne and all the townlands out towards Knockbrack are very valuable.

142. As you have no valuation of these places, do you say that Tourmaney bears an increased value from its proximity to the town?—I consider that townlands near the town, and within a mile or two miles of the town, are from their proximity to the town more valuable for that very reason, because of the ready market they have at Westport.

143. Your statement is that what is a mile from the town is more valuable than two miles, and therefore is less value than two miles?—The further you go from the town the worse, and the nearer town the better for the markets.

144. Does the town derive greater benefits and emoluments from the markets than the country districts?—The town has no tolls; they are payable to the proprietor.

145. Mr. Cowton.—The town derives no advantage? —No.

146. Mr. Kelly.—But the inhabitants of the town, the traders and merchants of the town, derive more benefit from the markets than the country districts two miles away?—They derive benefit in this way—they are the sellers, and the others are the buyers.

147. They have greater benefits than the country people?—They have the benefit there is between buyer and seller. The people from the country sell their wares in the town, and buy the town wares.

148. The publicans of the town are generally sellers; they are not buyers?—They buy food in the market, such as butter and eggs.

149. That is small compared with what they sell? —I think so, I am sorry to say.

150. There was a meeting here for the lighting of the town?—There was recently.

151. Was that attended by all the Town Commissioners?—They did not all attend. It was the time of the market, and as many as could come did.

152. And had they a meeting to have the town lighted?—They had.

153. And didn't you propose to make the people living two miles out pay for the lighting?—If the boundaries are extended the people living within it must pay their proportion of it.

154. They would be called upon to pay their proportion of the light?—Certainly, for lighting and cleansing—that means the scavenging of the town.

155. The sewers have been made by the Guardians? —Yes, and most generously made.

156. And it was paid for by the district you wish to saddle with the other expenses?—Yes; the Board of Guardians justly merit and have received the gratitude of the town for the way they carried out that work.

157. Some of the sewers were made by the Grand Jury?—Some of them, but they found they could not make any more of them, and the Guardians took it up.

158. Then the people of the electoral division of Westport didn't make any objection to pay for the sewerage of the town?—No, the Guardians very fairly considered it on full notice—for we admit they acted very fairly in the matter—and the people did not object. Public notice was given to the people of the district, and they were perfectly aware of what was about to be done; for all the acts of the Guardians are very public.

159. And they did not object?—No.

160. On the contrary they allowed the sewerage to be carried out?—It was altogether carried out without discussion and division. Some Guardians were [illegible]

favour of restricting the contributions to the townlands of the town.

161. But the money was carried out in the way you have mentioned, and the rates paid by the people of the electoral division?—Yes.

162. I don't object to that, but I do object to the light that we will never see?—Will you not be coming to the town?

163. At that meeting the Commissioners were represented?—They were professionally represented.

164. Mr. Burke, solicitor, and Mr. Thomas J. O'Adams, were there?—Yes.

165. They were the mouthpieces of the Commissioners and the people?—One of the most eloquent mouthpieces was Mr. William Livingstone.

166. Didn't professional gentlemen here represent the Commissioners and the people in endeavouring to get light for the town?—Yes.

167. And, I assume put forward the views and wishes of the people?—Yes.

168. And there were one or two opponents at that time?—The opposition was exceedingly insignificant.

169. Was that insignificant opposition withdrawn owing to the representations made by those professional gentlemen, and by the Chairman of the Town Commissioners?—If you tell me the incidents I will tell you.

170. Was it not through the representations made by them that the opposition was withdrawn?—They stated the expense on land and the expense on building.

171. Was it through the representations made by these gentlemen, as to the benefits the township would derive, and the small sum they would have to pay for it, that it was agreed to light the town?—The majority in favour of lighting was so overwhelming that there was no use in refusing it.

172. But was not the opposition withdrawn?—A few in the rural portion of the town came in and made a fuss, but they made no case, and the Chairman asked what their cause of complaint was, and they said increased taxation, and he explained to them what the taxation would be, and they said "all right."

173. Did he explain the area to be taxed?—There was no talk of area.

174. Didn't he say there was so much per thousand cubic feet?—Yes.

175. Did he say a word about the extension of the boundary?—No, but it was stated that if the Municipal Boundaries Commissioners increased the boundary it would diminish the taxation.

176. Was the opposition given to the lighting by some of the people in the town?—What I would call opposition, in proposing amendments.

177. Was it by the people of the town the opposition was given?—There came some six or eight people from the town, but the question is whether they were voters.

178. It was in consequence of a statement made by the professional gentlemen that the opposition was withdrawn?—The opposition in no case would have had any effect, because it was so slight.

179. Mr. *Kelly*.—We don't object to the lighting, but there was an undertaking given that the people of Westport were to pay for all this, and in contravention to that this application for extension was made and having got one end of the wedge in they want to have it further inserted. One of my grounds for opposing this extension is that we have no benefits and that we should not be taxed. This is a matter got up by the Commissioners themselves, the most of them being occupiers of houses in the town, and if they can get the tax extended over the electoral division, it eases their own pockets and relieves them from certain charges. All their action is in bad faith and contrary to express undertakings and arrangement made a year previously. (To witness.)—Did the people of Westport who are now to be benefited by this extension undertake to pay for the light?—Yes, lighting powers were applied for by the inhabitants within the present boundary, and the inhabitants within the present boundary adopted the lighting powers, and of course those outside had no voice in it.

Westport, Sept. 6, 18[illegible]

Mr. John Lynn.

180. And did they undertake to pay for it?—They did.

181. If the boundaries are extended those outside will have to pay for it?—If the boundary is extended, 8*d*. will not be required, a 7*d*. rate will do and this extension will increase the rates by about £30 a year or something like that.

182. At what time do the fairs and markets be over?—Strictly speaking they close when the public houses close at nine o'clock.

183. What time do the fairs commence?—About eight or nine o'clock in the morning, and finish about two o'clock. The cattle go away about two or three o'clock, but the people don't.

184. The benefit that is derived then from the markets and fairs after two o'clock is confined to the publicans?—By four or five o'clock the cattle are all gone off.

185. And the people having transacted their business generally begin to go home then?—They remain in the town as long as the houses keep open.

186. Would not some of those people remain until one o'clock in the morning if they were allowed [illegible] them in.

187. Therefore the benefit of the lighting would be to drunken class of people who are rather too fond of drink?—Yes.

188. Do well-disposed people go home in the daylight?—Well-inclined people of the best class are to be seen in Westport at nine o'clock at night.

189. Do you know that Lord John Browne opposes this?—Yes.

190. Won't it necessitate serving him to pay rates than he will not otherwise have to pay?—His lordship's assessment will remain as it is if extension is granted, and it will remain as it is if it is not granted.

191. Therefore he is opposing as a benefactor of the people?—His opposition is perfectly disinterested. Both at public meetings and through private individuals and others, there is but one general expression in the town amongst all classes, that they would make any sacrifice or do anything rather than clash in any way with Lord John Browne.

192. And is not the same opinion held by the people in the part you wish to bring in?—I know the respect for him is most universal.

193. Mr. *Bourke*.—When the Commissioners suggested this extension were there any improvements they had in contemplation?—No, sir.

194. The question of lighting was not then mooted?—The question of lighting was by no means in conjunction with the extension of the boundaries. They did not think of the extension until your queries arrived, and they then said it would be very good to get an extension of area.

195. Are there any improvements they would carry out if they had extension?—Light is very good, and they would employ additional scavengers and have the town properly cleansed.

196. Has there been no complaint made by themselves as to the cleansing of the town?—Yes, there have been complaints.

197. When?—They are of weekly occurrence. People say the town is not sufficiently cleansed.

198. Extension will not help that?—They will have more funds.

199. Would not the scavengers you have do well enough if they minded their business?—We have on the average above three men, but the town is too large for them; they have to go down to the quay.

200. And you have too large an area to manage it?—No; if we took in the boundary along the shore it will not increase the scavenging.

201. Do the lines on the map represent the electoral division and the municipal boundary?—The green line is the municipal boundary, and the blue line is the electoral division boundary.

Mr. WILLIAM LIVINGSTONE examined.

Westport. Sept. 5, 18[illegible]. — Mr. William Livingstone.

302. You are Chairman of the Commissioners?—Yes. Before answering any questions I wish to state publicly on behalf of the Commissioners that we have in no way applied for this inquiry. There is an idea abroad that it was on the application of the Commissioners that you attend here.

303. Mr. COTTON.—There was no such application whatever. (To witness.)—How long have you been Chairman?—Nearly three years.

304. And you have been Commissioner for a long time before?—I was not a Commissioner at all before. My father was.

305. What is your opinion as to the extension of the boundaries?—I am in favour of extension.

306. To the extent of the whole electoral division?—Yes.

307. Upon what ground?—On the ground that I think property, and especially the district along the shore at Rosbeg and Streamstown, which I may call the residential district of Westport, in which considerable improvements have taken place. A number of houses have been built of a very good class, inhabited by people who use the town very largely, and to whom the town is a benefit; that district I think should form part of the town. In fact it has become a suburb of Westport to a large extent, and in future years I expect that that district will be very largely built over. Hardly any extension of the town takes place except in that district. Personally I have property in that district, and I would suffer by taxation, but still I am in favour of the extension. My property there is valued at £377, principally mills, and the house and some land.

308. Do you know the opinion of the rest of the Commissioners?—As far as I can judge, I think they are all in favour of extension. I never had an opportunity of meeting them together, so I cannot say accurately. The majority are in favour of extension, so far as I know.

309. The Clerk has said that the Commissioners have no wish whatever to become the sanitary authority?—None whatever. The Commissioners are extremely well pleased at the treatment the town received at the hands of the Guardians. They thought all the sanitary work was very well done, and they thought it was very liberal treatment of the Guardians to place the taxation for town sanitary purposes on the electoral division, and when the offer was made to the Commissioners to undertake the work they disclaimed any wish to do so, very much preferring that the Board of Guardians should continue it, as they had every reason to be satisfied with the manner in which the work was done and the means taken for the payment of it.

310. Does the same reason that influences you in taking in that portion down by the sea influence you in taking in a large part of the electoral division that lies to the south at Killeencoff?—Certainly not. I think the other district is first of all ten times more valuable, and in future years it will be a great deal more valuable. It was under discussion to leave out one or two of the portions that are inhabited by very poor people, and Killeencoff or Killeencorb was one of them. It was thought subsequently that if the extension went to the whole electoral division there should be no exception. Of course the incidence of taxation of such a district would be so small it would not hurt them much, possibly from 1s. to 1s. 6d. a year.

311. Do you think Derrygorman derives such advantage that it should contribute something?—I consider that all the lands in close proximity to the town derive certain benefit.

312. And that view seems to be adopted inasmuch as all land close to the town is rented as townparks and produces a very considerable rent?—I think Derrygorman derives more advantage than places further off.

313. To Mr. ROBINSON.—I was not aware of the recommendation about the electoral division when considering the question. During the time this question was under discussion I was absent, but I quite endorse the view of my brother Commissioners when I heard they had applied for an extension. Great stress was put on the gas question by Mr. Kelly that it was a hard case that the people outside should be called upon to pay for gas.

314. You mean people outside the present boundary?—Yes. I confess I am entirely in favour of lighting the town with gas, and I think it was a discredit and a disgrace to Westport to remain so long as they did without having that benefit which almost every town of every station throughout the whole country enjoys. I think gas is essential for the preservation of property, cleanliness, &c. I think those gentlemen who live outside the town, and who have occasion to come into town, and passing to and from the railway station, must have felt the greatest inconvenience from having to drive through a dark town. The district of Rosbeg is one which I think deserves especially to be included in the extension, for I think the small amount that the highest valued of those gentlemen would have to pay, would be a bagatelle to the advantages they would derive by having the town well kept and well lighted, and altogether made a satisfactory place for frequent use. With regard to another statement of Mr. Kelly's, which he dwelt upon, the Commissioners are in a very unfortunate position. We have no professional advice; we are merely here to speak for ourselves upon the merits of the case, and having two able professional gentlemen opposed to us, is, of course, a great disadvantage; and we hoped that a professional gentleman would have been here to represent us, but he did not attend. At the same time, the Commissioners disclaim having any personal feeling in the matter. They put it forward purely on public grounds, and they are glad to put forward their views before you, but they have not the slightest desire to go in contravention to the Guardians in any way.

Cross-examined by Mr. *Malachi Kelly*.

315. You said you consider gas essential for the preservation of property and cleanliness?—These are some of the reasons amongst many.

316. Take the preservation of property in particular, your observation applied to the preservation of property in the town of Westport?—Certainly.

317. And doesn't that portion of your observations in reference to cleanliness also apply to the town?—Yes, and to those who use the town; and the same about lighting.

318. And you consider it a hardship to gentlemen who come from time to time to the town, and find some difficulty in passing through the dark town, and not having the benefit of light?—I don't consider it a hardship, but I think it would be a great convenience to have light.

319. Your observation is confined to the resident gentry in and about Rosbeg?—Not exclusively; but everybody who uses the town.

320. Was not portion of your observations principally applicable to the resident gentry in and about Rosbeg?—It was so far applicable that they would be called upon to pay more, and I would expect greater intelligence from them in seeing the advantage of the gas.

321. Has there ever been complaint made by country people within this proposed extension as to the want of gas in the town?—I never heard any complaint.

322. As a matter of fact, are you not aware that the people, one and all, within the proposed area, are opposed to annexation?—I am not aware of that. I am aware there are a good many opposed to it, but I think it is only natural that small country farmers

Wednesday, Sept. 4, 1878.

Mr. William Livingstone.

would be opposed to it, because I think it is very much owing to the fact that they don't know the amount they would be called upon to pay; but if they knew it was only 1s. or 1s. 6d., they would not object to it.

223. Winter would be the time when the great benefit would be specially conferred?—Yes.

224. And during the summer they don't light in other places for five or six months?—Yes.

225. And that would be the rule, I hope, in Westport?—No.

226. That is the rule in other towns?—I have heard it is the rule in some other places.

227. You consider the district of Rossbeg should be principally annexed?—I think so, on account of the class of inhabitants there.

228. As a matter of fact, only that you are aware that the desire was to include the entire electoral division, would not you have recommended to exclude the rural portion of Killaseeff and the other townlands named?—I don't think I would.

229. Would not you exclude Killaseeff?—In the first place, it was considered right to exclude them, as the amount of taxation to be derived from them was hardly worth speaking of.

230. Would that not apply to the adjoining townland?—To a certain extent it would but not to the same extent.

231. You told us there was a great deal of improvement in and about Strangetown, as a matter of fact, have more than two gentlemen built in that district?—I think only two gentlemen as yet have built, but one of these gentlemen is desirous of building more, I am happy to hear, and the other, I hear, also.

232. Are you not aware that one of the gentlemen who built seems wishes he built less?—I should be sorry to think so.

233. And, as a matter of fact, are not there a number of houses only tenanted for the summer season?—Yes.

234. And are not there a great number of gentlemen in other parts of the county owners of houses there?—Not many.

235. Are not there some?—At the moment I cannot say.

236. Will you swear there are not twelve?—I have not the slightest idea.

237. Are there not a greater number of untenanted than tenanted houses during the winter season?—No, I think not.

238. Will you swear there are not an equal number?—Your observation applies to any bathing place, and the district you refer to is occupied by summer residences.

239. Principally by summer residences?—No; a good many summer residences.

240. I think you told us you had property there valued at £287?—Yes.

241. I am happy to say there is not a more respected or more extensive merchant than the gentleman I have the honour of questioning. Would you give us the valuation of the property you are interested in in the town?—That our firm have directly?

242. Yes. I'll put my question in this way: What is the valuation of the property that you and your firm are interested in the town?—About £800 a year.

243. While the proportion in the outlying district is £287, against £800 in the town?—Yes.

244. What is the valuation of your property in the town for which your tenants pay rates?—About £200 a year.

245. That is about £1,000 a year in round numbers?—Yes.

246. Do you recollect the town since '34?—I do.

247. You have heard that in '34 it availed itself of the provisions of the Act of '34?—Yes.

248. Did you hear that the area at that time was about the same as it is now?—I heard it to-day.

249. As a matter of fact, have the limits of the town been extended since '34?—Not that I am aware of.

250. Are you aware that the Commissioners of Valuation came down to Westport some time subsequent to '34?—I was not aware.

251. You heard it to-day?—I did.

252. And did you hear that the area of the township as established in '34 was limited by them?—Yes.

253. And that Lord Sligo, with his usual desire to benefit the town, considered the proper area was that made in '34?—Well, that was his view in '34, but the world's ideas have enlarged very much since then.

254. You believe that land in the proximity of the town derives benefit—doesn't your opinion extend to all lands adjacent to the town?—I think all lands the nearer the town they are benefit more or less by it, and I am borne out in that opinion by finding it in the rents.

255. Do you consider that the lighting and cleansing increases the value of the property lying near it?—I think if the town is well kept it is an attractive place to come in and live in its neighbourhood.

256. Do you consider now that the lighting and cleansing of Westport would make Killaseeff an attractive place to come and live at?—In my wildest imagination I could not imagine that.

257. Do you consider the lighting of Westport would induce people to come and live at Buckwards?—No.

258. And the same applies to a good many other places?—Yes.

259. The observation is general?—Yes, and I believe especially to the residential districts.

260. And in addition to your other holdings you have a farm?—I have reason to regret it.

261. As a matter of fact, taking the fairs of Westport, they are as early as ordinary fairs, except Balla?—No; it is a late fair.

262. Mr. Egan told us that all the cattle was out of town by three or four o'clock?—It all depends on the fair.

263. Do you consider it would be for the benefit of the people that facilities should be afforded to remain in the town and drink to a late hour?—I don't think that would be desirable.

264. You are aware that in the district there are two hundred and fifty burgesses qualified to vote in the election of Commissioners in the district proposed to be brought in?—Yes.

265. And five hundred and fifty-five in the town?—Yes, I heard Mr. Egan say so. I have no knowledge myself on the subject. I wish to correct a misapprehension. The time the gas meeting was held there was no undertaking whatever given that the area of taxation should not be extended.

Mr. Eustace Lynch, Town Commissioner, examined.

Mr. Eustace Lynch.

266. It was I that seconded Mr. Livingstone in proposing the gas. There was no undertaking given at all to the meeting. A few parties came who were really not voters at all. One of them said he represented his mother and had no vote or interest in the matter at all. There was no undertaking given. It was put to the vote whether there would be a poll taken, and when it was understood that the losing party might have to pay for the poll, they all walked out of the courthouse.

267. You heard the Chairman express his opinion as to the extension, do you coincide with him?—I am a very small proprietor, and I believe it would benefit the town to extend the district. Some of the districts are continually building, something like Blackrock and Kingstown.

Westport.
Sept. 8, 1891.
Mr. Patrick O'Dowd.

Mr. PATRICK O'DOWD examined.

268. You are Vice-Chairman of the Town Commissioners?—Yes.

269. You were chairman of the meeting at which these queries were considered?—Yes.

270. And you came to the unanimous conclusion to extend the district to the electoral division except Kilbeggan?

271. What were your reasons for fixing the electoral division?—The town is peculiarly situated. They have no townparks as in other towns, very few of the shopkeepers have townparks, and consequently they have to depend for the supply of milk and butter and vegetables on the surrounding districts of Attireash, Derrygorman, and Tonnasny. Women come in every morning with cans of milk from these outlying districts, to supply the town people; and it is calculated that the town has to pay at least £1,500 to the surrounding districts, and it comes from Sruwaddacon, Knockfinn, Carrowsallagan, and these outlying districts; vegetables come from the same districts. For these reasons, I believe that land is very much increased in value, I would say ten shillings an acre. Another reason is that Mr Livingstone is one of the largest merchants in Ireland. He has extensive mills at Brilskra, and gives extensive employment to people working in these mills, and labourers, and five-sixths of these live in this district. Mr. Livingstone has thirty or forty carts employed, and they come from all parts of the town. There are carriers employed by him in the outlying districts, and they are all being benefited by it, so it is not in one way the district is benefited from the proximity to the town. I live in Rosbeg myself, and that neighbourhood is largely benefited by the proximity to the town. People within the present boundary go outside and take patches of ground, and pay four or five pounds an acre for it. I have to pay a very high price for land myself outside.

272. Mr. [illegible].—They think the advantages of proximity to the town are so great it would not be any hardship for these people to have to pay 1s. 6d. taxation?—It would be a mere bagatelle compared with the advantages they have.

273. Cross-examined by Mr. *Kelly*.—Do you pay rates yourself where you reside in Rosbeg?—I do.

274. What is your valuation?—£12.

275. What is your valuation in town?—£100 a year.

276. You have built a very fine house or two in the town?—Yes.

277. What do you expect the probable valuation of them will be?—About £100 a year.

278. You carry on the most of your business in Westport?—Yes.

279. Would not you derive benefit in the town from lighting and scavenging?—If I was going to the railway, or leaving town at night, I would derive benefit by it.

280. And don't you derive more benefit from the gas in the town, having your business in the town, than you would derive by passing through the town?—No. I derive no benefit from it in the town, so far as my business is concerned, for it is over by six o'clock.

281. Of course, by the extension now proposed, you would lessen the expense of the town?—Very little. It would be a difference of about 2s. in the year to you.

282. It would be important to you, at all events?—It would be about 2s. in the year.

283. You say people in the town are supplied with milk and butter from these outlying districts?—Yes.

284. You think, that having that benefit derived from these townlands, it would be an advantage to extend the district?—I think, as they derive great benefit from the town, they have a right to pay their small share of the expense of it.

285. Are you aware that these townlands are within the municipal boundary?—Portions of them are, and portions are not. Portion of Attireash is within, but Slogger is not.

286. What benefit does Slogger derive?—It is not more than half a mile from the town.

287. Has it as much benefit as Attireash?—Of course it has.

288. And it is outside the proposed boundary?—It is not.

289. Isn't Carrowsallagan within the boundary?—No; the southern portion is outside.

290. With regard to the fairs and markets of the town, don't the people living at Louisburg derive as much benefit as we do?—No, I think not. If a man lives close to the market he has the benefit of going into the market over the man who has to go a distance.

291. Tell me any advantage from fairs or markets that the residential community gain?—I think it is a convenience to them to have a market so near them.

292. What benefit is it to Mr. John William Kelly?—If it was not for the closeness of the town to the railway, his place would not be so valuable.

293. What has he to say to the market?—It was convenient for him and his tenants to be so close to the market. Mr. Kelly is a large farmer.

294. Doesn't he live only half a year there?—He is a large grazier, and he can bring in his cattle to the fair close to his own house, and he is free to dispose of his own property.

295. Has he ever disposed of his property out of Rosbeg in Westport?—I believe so. I don't see what other place he could go to.

296. What produce does he dispose of?—I don't know, but if he has any to dispose of he certainly does not go to Castlebar with it.

297. Don't all the residents that come during the summer months spend money in the town?—There are a number of bathing places around the bay. People come to Rosbeg in preference, because there is a railway station here, and a market.

298. Isn't Rosmoney a favourite bathing place at present?—It is not.

299. Have there not been more residents in Rosmoney than in Rosbeg?—In Rosbeg, by all means. One house at Rosbeg is of more value than all the houses in Rosmoney and Carrowsallagh together.

300. And they set at more rent?—They are set at very much more rent. There is one house let at Rosbeg higher than all the houses at Rosmoney.

301. Isn't the description of the house different?—There is one very good house at Rosmoney.

302. Is it not a fact that the cottages at Rosmoney are to a great extent set higher than the same class of houses at Rosbeg?—No, that is not the case. I know one that is set at £13 in Rosmoney, which would bring £30 at Rosbeg.

303. Isn't that a new slated house?—Yes, therefore I say Rosbeg is benefited by the neighbourhood of Westport, and the railway station.

304. Are the people in Derrygorman benefited?—They are.

305. They are more benefited than those living outside the boundary?—Yes, carters living at a mile or two outside the town come in and get employment in the town. People in Derrygorman bring in their produce, and people come from the other districts and have a ready market for their milk and so on.

306. You say there is only a ditch between Derrygorman and Dom Castle, which is just outside the line—take a person living on the other boundary, what benefit has the Derrygorman man over the Dom Castle man?—I never heard any Dom Castle man come in for milk.

307. You know the bridge of Attireash?—Yes.

308. What benefit would a person on the Attireash side have over any person on the Slogger side?—That was not asked to be included in the new township, because it was beyond the electoral division. We

to the other extreme. The demesne parks of the Marquis of Sligo are on that side, and there are no small farmers. The Commissioners considered it would not be fair to include that district, because it is demesne lands.

Lord *John Browne*.—In my opinion the onus probandi rests with the Commissioners who propose the extension; they should show some good reason and make out a good case. At present taxation is extremely light. If it was heavy they could have said, "here's a fair matter to bring under consideration," and I believe the people of the country around would be willing to consider it, but when it is extremely small, the last rate was 3d., and we may assume it to be 6d. generally without lighting, but that is much smaller than the tax in Castlebar and Ballina and other towns of the same class; and, of course, as to the benefit of proximity to the town, we know that there is a certain amount of benefit derived from it, but I don't believe it is to any appreciable extent. The lands that do derive benefit are generally already within the town. As to the reasons stated that if they had more money they would do more in the cleansing way, there are few towns in Ireland, on the whole, better cleansed than it is. They have those old men that they don't want to discharge, as they have been a great many years in their service, but if they were young men they could do double the work. The application to light the town with gas would also be taken into consideration, and I think that matter should be adjourned until after this inquiry, but it would be unfair to decide the question of gas by the votes of people in the town if the people outside, who have no votes are to be immediately taxed for it. I don't care whether it is large or small, it is a great injustice to tax people outside for the lighting that they don't derive any benefit from whatever. I kept away from the meeting, I was not in favour of it in a bad year like this, and I don't think it would be a judicious season to go on with that expenditure. If the tax is merely levied on the present district, it is very well, but I think it would be an injustice to make other people pay for it.

309. Mr. *Nathan Lynch*.—Don't you think that Streamstown, and even other places, are greatly improved by being near Westport, and have you ever heard it said by any gentleman in Westport or Rosbeg that it was a disgrace not to have light.

Lord *John Browne*.—I heard those who wish to have gas say it was a disgrace not to have it.

310. Mr. *Kelly*.—And what did you hear those who oppose it say?

Lord *John Browne*.—That it would be a great injustice, and very unfair.

311. Mr. *Lynch*.—Did you hear any gentleman travelling by the railway say it was a disgrace there was no gas up to the railway station?

Lord *John Browne*.—I never heard a stranger say it.

312. Mr. *Lynch*.—Do you consider that the lands near Belclare are not increased in value by proximity to the town and the railway station?

Lord *John Browne*.—Near the railway station, undoubtedly.

313. Mr. *Lynch*.—And by proximity to the town also?

Lord *John Browne*.—Well it may be some slight benefit, but then this district is occupied by summer visitors, who come there, not for the sake of living near the town of Westport, but to get the fresh air by the seaside, and they are there at a time when the gas would not be lighted.

314. Mr. *Kelly*.—At the quay at Westport there is a very nice little village, and the people of Rosbeg and Streamstown get their provisions there without going to Westport at all. WESTPORT, Sept. 6, 1887. — Mr. [illegible] [illegible]

Lord *John Browne*.—I think occasionally there would be something they could not get, but to a fair extent they could be supplied there.

315. Mr. *Lynch*.—And isn't the quay within the present boundary?

Lord *John Browne*.—Yes.

316. Mr. CURRAN.—Is it proposed to light Westport quay?

Mr. *Kelly*.—I don't think it is. I think it is intended to confine the lighting to the town.

Lord *John Browne*.—There is no gas at present on the quay.

317. Mr. *Kelly*.—Is not it your opinion that the benefits derived by the residents of Rosbeg to Westport is due to the railway communication?

Lord *John Browne*.—To a great extent certainly.

318. Mr. *Livingstone*.—Do you think that all the building extensions will probably take place in what are called the residential districts, where it has already commenced?

Lord *John Browne*.—There is some extension of building there, but I cannot say whether that is in connexion with Westport. It is totally separate and independent of it, and I don't think there will be a great deal of building there. I don't think the profits there have been so great as to induce the people to carry out more buildings.

319. Mr. *Livingstone*.—Isn't it a fact that Lord Sligo retains a large portion of building ground there for building only?

Lord *John Browne*.—I think he has only very little indeed. I know he would be more glad to see more buildings put up by you, Mr. Kelly.

320. Mr. *Patrick Egan*, T.C.—Do you consider the land to the north more valuable than on the other side of the town?

Lord *John Browne*.—Yes; for the sake of sea-side lodgers.

321. And don't you think that people who have money to lay out are more calculated to lay it out there on account of its being near a town?—Yes; because it is a more profitable place to build upon, but they are fairly inclined to build in the town too.

322. Isn't the land there nearly double the value of what it is on the other side?—Perhaps so. A house there would bring more money as a residence than at Westport; but I am not prepared to say that of business houses.

323. Mr. CURRAN.—I understand you to say that the desirability of that place was on account of its own nature, and not its proximity to the town?—Yes.

324. And if it was transferred away two miles further it would be still as valuable?—Yes; and it is affected very little by the proximity to the town.

325. Mr. *Egan*.—Is land let at the enormous rate of £10 an acre there?—I cannot answer that; but I said that a house there will let for a great deal more. More than ten houses could be squeezed into an acre.

326. Mr. *Kelly*.—Are you aware whether the people having lodgings at Rosbeg are generally people from Westport?—No; I think they are generally people from a distance.

327. Mr. *Egan*.—And if it was not for the town being so close do you think they would come there at all?—They come down for the sea air.

Westport. Sept. [illegible] 18[illegible]

Mr. John W. Kelly, J.P.

Mr. John W. Kelly, J.P., examined.

328. I am a resident of Rosbeg. I am very glad that Lord John Browne has given a practical turn to the discussion. He went directly on the merits and challenged the merits, and although they are very ably advocated by Mr. Livingstone, they have failed to make out any case at all for extension. I quite go with the Commissioners about the gas. I think it is of great importance to the town, and they deserve great credit for it, considering all the difficulties they had to contend with. But the people who live out in the country fail to see in what respect gas is a benefit to Rosbeg and such places, for they hardly ever see it. If Mr. Livingstone guarantees to bring the gas down there, I'll vote for the extension, but I don't expect that. The whole case appears to be as to the equity of the expense, and I would like to call your attention to the map. You will see that the boundary is just what it might be expected to be. It extends regularly for a mile or so all round the town, and the proposed extension is perfectly incongruous. They don't propose a boundary equal all round at all. They extend it at some places, and curtail it at others. The whole of the extensions are nearly in two directions, east and south-west. To the north there is no extension at all. I don't know why this should be, for there are lands in the north that should be included as well. I don't propose that you should extend it to the north, but I am only showing the incongruity of the extension proposed. It appears to me to be the most ridiculous extension that could be imagined. As to Rosbeg I think Mr. Livingstone did not make a good case. I was sorry to see him engaged in such a bad case at all. His argument went to show that the people of Westport ought to extend their boundary to lessen their taxation, but he takes great care to drop the places that would not be worth taking in.

329. Mr. *Egan*.—We agreed afterwards to bring in all these districts, we don't exclude any district.

Witness.—They have given no reason for not bringing in certain places, but they think they would not be worth fleecing. Instead of taking the rational principle of a radius all round they have dived off at a tangent, and because there are a few houses they fasten upon a place to be included as it would benefit the town. The whole question is really whether it would lessen the taxation of the town, and they don't care what they do. I object to be taken in at all, because I think we derive no benefit, and I say that as having a place of business in the town myself.

330. By Mr. *Malachi Kelly*.—Do the residents at Rosbeg or Carrowmore at all themselves of the fairs and markets at Westport at all?—I think the resident proprietors have nothing to do with the fairs, but with the markets they have, and no doubt it is a benefit to them to have a good market, for Westport has a very good market. That benefit extends through the whole country, and the question is not whether they derive any benefit, but where is the line to be drawn, and if it is to be drawn at all, it should be equitably done.

331. Mr. Cotton.—That is at the same distance all round?—Yes, practically, but in the present instance they rush off in one direction.

332. Supposing they extended it in a circle from Rosbeg the whole way round, would you have any objection?—If they ventured to do it they would certainly have a good deal of moral courage.

333. Do you think you should contribute anything at all to the town of Westport?—No, certainly not. On the contrary, I think the taxation of those houses they have been talking of has given very bad encouragement to build more houses. They are trying to make them in every way, and these houses have been a very bad speculation, and they want now to put more taxation on them without the slightest reason. What has Rosbeg to do with the town. It is separated by a demesne and river, and there is a little village between it, and we are cut at one, and they want us to pay the taxes for the lighting and cleansing of the town, and on the whole, I say that the principle of extension put forward here, are certainly the crudest I ever saw. It is very unlike the present boundary, which is nearly equal all round.

334. Mr. Robinson.—You don't think the town derives any advantage from the residents down there?—Yes, of course, the principal customers are down there. I don't think that could be gainsaid by any one.

335. You are opposed to this extension?—Yes.

336. Mr. *Livingstone*.—What is the valuation of your house. I know that the taxation or valuation of my house is very high. Your valuation is £31. Upon the taxation proposed that would amount to £3 1s. I would think that a gentleman of your intelligence and broad views, would consider that a town well kept, and well cleansed, and lighted, which you often use, and at night, would be worth £3 1s. for yourself and family?

Witness.—I assure you it is not for the amount of the probable taxation, but I object on principle and as unnecessary, and I think we should never have been asked. The people down there never objected as far as drainage and sanitary proceedings went, and they bore the burdens of the town, although they might have declined to do so, and it is because they are generous in this respect, that the people of Westport think there is no end to what they will give.

337. Mr. Cotton.—With your present views, I don't know why you didn't object to the drainage charge?—I didn't happen to be here at the time.

338. Mr. Robinson.—You think if the people within the electoral division have to pay their share of the municipal taxation it would affect building?—I believe one way or other, building will come down there, for it is a very bad speculation. I don't think it will affect it much one way or the other.

339. Mr. *O'Donel*.—Isn't it a fact that notwithstanding the sanitary expenses the poor rates are lower than they have been for a dozen years?—I believe it is, and it is very satisfactory.

Mr. *Egan*.—The sewers constructed were paid direct from the rates before the loan was obtained, but if they get a loan it will be very light, and not more than 1½d. in the pound.

340. Mr. Cotton.—On what terms used they to get a loan?

Mr. *Egan*.—For thirty-five years.

Witness (Mr. Kelly).—In conclusion, I submit that the only reason assigned for extending the town is to reduce the taxation of the town, and I deny that it is necessary when the rates are so favourably low at present.

Mr. Cotton.—I did not understand that that was the reason put forward.

Mr. *Livingstone*.—No. I think it would only make a difference of 1d. in the pound.

Mr. *Malachi Kelly*.—After the evidence of Lord John Browne, who is largely interested, and understands the question, and the evidence of Mr. Kelly, we close our case. We have a number of people who are ready and willing to give evidence, but I don't think it necessary to detain the Commissioners by calling them. We have heard the evidence of Mr. Alfred Kelly, representing the people in these rural districts outside the boundary which is proposed to be included by the Commissioners, and I am free to admit that if any advantage would accrue to the people of these districts they would be the first to come forward and take their share in the burdens; but I ask you on the evidence to come to the conclusion that there is no advantage directly or indirectly. The only reason put forward was that there was an advantage derived by the lands near the town, but that is no reason why they should be brought in, for all lands that lie adjacent to towns are enhanced in value. But because they are enhanced in value are the people bound to relieve the townspeople of some of the taxation that on pay at present, and before you come to the conclusion that the town should have the benefit of the taxation of these people outside, you must convince yourself that there are special advantages conferred by the town upon those lands outside; and, as Mr. Kelly has pointed out, when it was proposed to them to have gas in the town, one of the gentlemen whose property was situated on the part of the people of Westport used the observation that "If you give us gas we are prepared to pay for it," and then we have a meeting of the Commissioners in January, and out of eighteen only six attended, and it is alleged, I believe [illegible], that the [illegible] was [illegible], and two of them were not [illegible] at all; but of the fifteen Commissioners who [illegible] at home only six attended. The people [illegible]. They did not appear [illegible] it was a matter of very great importance, and I don't think there is much weight to be attached to what the Commissioners decided upon there, for two months after they had come to the conclusion to have the area extended they adopted these lighting powers. There was an unanimous understanding there, though not a legal undertaking, at the meeting on the 31st July, that if the lighting powers were granted, and if the vote of the people of Westport was to be obtained, they would pay for the convenience themselves, but it was never suggested that the people of the outlying districts were to contribute any expense, and the opposition was withdrawn on that understanding, and two months afterwards the Commissioners, having secured the lighting powers, then come and say, "You must extend the area and relieve us of the burden of taxation, and you must ask the people of Kilmeena and Belclare to contribute to the comforts and advantages which the town people would derive from the light. The proposal to extend is based on two grounds—first, that the lighting of the town would benefit the people in Belclare and the outlying districts; and secondly, that if an extension was granted, instead of [illegible], you will have additional scavengers, so that the whole reason for which you are asked to extend the area is that they may have four instead of three scavengers and have the town lighted, and they ask you to do that, and to make the outlying people pay for no benefit whatever. It is not [illegible] that the people coming into market to the town would benefit, for, on the evidence of Mr. Egan, [illegible] make it a rule not to stay after three or four o'clock in the day, and the people go home, except those who are inclined to drink. [illegible] they have contributed to the resources of the town, and when they enlivened the people to that extent they thought they would not [illegible] to do more. You have the Commissioners refusing to undertake the sanitary care of the town, and you have [illegible] the [illegible] of the people of Westport, and as to the water supply, I don't think the [illegible] should be allowed to pass without [illegible] with which the Marquis of Sligo [illegible] over the interests of the town. The water supply, for which his lordship contributed a large sum, has been most successful, and there is a copious supply of water to every part of the town. There would be no advantage whatever to the poor people, and if the people of Kilmeena and Belclare are so [illegible] in hospitality that they would keep their friends until a late hour, they cannot expect the poor people to pay for the giving them the advantage of gas home, or to the railway station in town. I therefore ask you, confidently, not to recommend any extension of the town.

Westport. Sept. 4, 1879.

Mr. Egan recalled.

Mr. Egan.

341. What is the valuation, and what portion of the demesne comes in the electoral division of Westport?—The valuation of the land is £31 10s. and the buildings £5, and the area 26a. 1r.

[The inquiry then terminated.]

OMAGH—23RD JULY, 1879.

Omagh. July 23, 1879.

(Before Mr. Cotton, C.E., and Mr. Henry A. Robinson.)

Mr. Samuel [illegible] examined.

Mr. Samuel [illegible].

1. Mr. Cotton.—Are you the Town Clerk?—Yes.
2. How long have you held that post?—Since 1872.
3. Is Omagh under the Towns Improvement Act?—No; under the 9th of George IV. Since 1845.
4. How many Town Commissioners are there?—Twenty-one.
5. Can you give me the area?—It is in or about 500 acres.
6. Do you know anything about the description of the boundary?—The only map for it is the Ordnance survey map.
7. What is the population?—Last census it was 3,744, but I am of opinion it is considerably increased since then.
8. And has the town itself shown signs of improvement?—Yes; a good many respectable dwellings have been erected within that period.
9. Have you any idea of the number of houses in the town?—No.
10. What is the valuation?—£7,237.
11. And the poundage on that?—£361 8s. 7d.
12. What rates have you struck within the past five years?—The municipal rate has been 1s., 9d., 8d., and 1s.
13. One shilling was the highest?—Yes.
14. Those were the only rates you struck?—Yes.
15. Can you tell me the poor rate for those years?—Yes; in 1874, 1s. 2d.; in 1875, 1s. 4d.; in 1876, 1s. 1d.; in 1877, 1s.; and in 1878, 1s. 11d.
16. Was any portion of that 1s. 11d. for special sanitary rate?—Yes; I think the sanitary rate is included in that.
17. How much was it?—I could not tell.
18. Can you give me the county cess for that period?—In 1874, 2s. 1½d.; in 1875, 2s. 3d.; in 1876, 2s.; in 1877, 1s. 10d.; in 1878, 1s. 10½d.
19. You have no wards in the town?—No.
20. What electoral division is the town in?—In Omagh.
21. Mr. Robinson.—Is the entire town in the Omagh electoral division?—Yes.
22. Mr. Cotton.—Have the Commissioners considered this question, as to whether any alteration was needed in the municipal boundary?—Yes; they have.
23. And what is their opinion?—They do not consider it necessary to make any alteration at present.
24. Why do you say "at present"?—Because at their first meeting they were determined to apply for a small increase, but circumstances altered them. They did want an increase of taxation and would have wished an increased area for it, but they do not now.
25. And now that they don't wish for an increase of funds, they don't want an increased area?—Yes.
26. Have the Commissioners considered the question

whether they wished to become the urban sanitary authority instead of the Guardians ?—No; I don't think so. I think they would be inclined to leave it as it at present stands, in the hands of the Guardians.

27. How many municipal electors are there ?—Upwards of 100.

28. They vote for Commissioners ?—Yes—125 or 126 is the number I think.

29. How many are legally qualified to act as Town Commissioners ?—Forty-six.

30. How is the town supplied with light ?—By gas supplied by a private company.

31. How many public lamps are there ?—Sixty-three.

32. And what do they cost ?—£2 17s. 6d. per lamp.

33. What is the charge to private consumers ?—Seven shillings and six pence per thousand I think.

34. What are the rules or terms of the contract for lighting ?—To light from the 15th of August to the 15th of May, inclusive, each year, for the sum of £2 17s. 6d. per lamp. The lamps to be extinguished during the first fifteen nights in August, and the last fifteen nights in May, at 12 o'clock, and to be lighted every dark night during the lighting season—the company to have liberty to extinguish them on every clear moonlight night. The contract was entered into for three years from July, 1877.

35. Mr. Robinson.—Can you give us a description of the existing municipal boundary ?—The municipal boundary of the town of Omagh extends—

"From the cross-roads at the Rev. Mr. Clement's to the railway bridge on the old Dromore-road—length 66 chains or 264 perches; and from railway bridge on the old Fintona-road to the end of Horkins Holme—70 chains or 318 perches. Extent about 300a. 2r. 8p. The townland of Omagh proper, thirty-one acres or thereabouts. The other portions are situate in Dergmoney Lower, Mountjoy Hill, Cashelgerd Lower; Gortmore, Lisnamallard, Campsie, and a small part of Crevenagh."

36. That is the original boundary ?—Yes. This was the boundary recommended by Sir Richard Griffith. (Witness handed in a document.)

37. Was it adopted ?—So I understood when I came here.

38. But this is under the Town Improvement Act of 1854 ?—Yes.

39. And was that Act adopted ?—No; but he recommended that as our boundary.

40. Were you in office in 1854 ?—No, I only came into office in 1872.

41. At any rate it would appear that, on the 1st April, 1870, there was a proposed boundary submitted by Sir Richard Griffith.

42. Mr. Cotton.—Read that description, entitled "Description of the boundary of the town of Omagh, as proposed by Sir Richard Griffith, for the approval of His Excellency the Lord Lieutenant, under the provisions of the above Act the—Towns Improvement Act:—

"Commencing on the north, where the boundary of the townland of Lisnamallard joins the river Camowen first—thence along said townland boundary, in a north-easterly direction to the fence which joins the workhouse grounds from Glencordangal—thence along the said fence, in a southerly direction, to the road leading to Killyclogher; third—thence along said road in a westerly direction, for the distance of about thirty-three yards, to a fence running through the holding of H. P. Buchanan, Esq.; fourth—thence, southerly, along said fence, and continuing in the same direction along the eastern boundary of the gardens of Lisnamallard House, to the mill-race; fifth—thence, easterly, along the mill-race to the weir; sixth—thence, southerly, across the river Camowen to the fence which divides the gardens and the field of the late Mr. J. Greer, and along said fence, to the road leading to Armagh; seventh—thence, easterly, along said road and southerly along the road leading to Dervaragh to the Ulster Railway; eighth—thence, westerly, and along the southern fence of said railway, to Cassidy's bridge over said railway; thence, in a straight line, to Mr. Aiken's, crossing the highroad between the railway, and thence along the southern fence of said lane to the bridge leading to Dromore; ninth—thence, north-easterly, along the road leading to the workhouse, to the fence dividing the holdings of R. C. Hill, of Knockmoyle; tenth—thence, northerly, and along said fence to its junction with the Newtownstewart road, and across said road, continuing in the same direction by the fence that divides the holdings of John MacEvaum, and Knockmoyle, and Francis Magee, to the north side of the river Strule; thence along the said river in an easterly direction to the point first described."

43. Do you know is that anything like the present boundary ?—It is the one we are acting on.

44. Is there any resolution in your books adopting that ?—Not that I am aware of. I was not in office.

45. What about the water supply of Omagh ?—It is supplied by the Guardians.

46. Is it supplied at high pressure ?—Yes.

47. Can you tell us the contributory district ?—All these townlands—the townland of Gortmore, the townland of Cashelgerd (Lower), the townland of Mountjoy Hill, the townland of Omagh, the townland of Lisnamallard, and Dergmoney (Lower).

Mr. James Smyth examined.

48. Mr. Cotton.—Are you a Commissioner ?—Yes; I have been Chairman of the Board.

49. How was the boundary extended from the original one ?—On one occasion the Chairman, Mr. M. [illegible], upon the Dromore-road, wished to erect buildings, and would not do it unless by the leave of the Commissioners. The County Surveyor would not let him erect the buildings on the road side, and consequently we extended the boundaries along the Dromore-road to enable him to erect these buildings.

50. At what time was that ?—I am not sure.

51. Mr. Robinson.—Under what power did you get the boundaries extended ?—Under the Act of George IV., we have the power. The boundary was defined and we merely made an extension to it. It was defined in 1848 when it was placed under the 9th of George IV.

52. Mr. Cotton.—Is that definition, I would like to see ?—It has been extended from time to time since then.

53. Mr. Robinson.—Under what section did you consider you had the power of so extending it ?—Under the 31st section of the ninth of George IV.

55. Do you know the valuation of the contributory district mentioned by the Town Clerk ?—£9,[illegible]

56. What rate is now struck over it for the water works ?—1s. 4d. in the pound.

57. What was the loan you obtained in respect of those works ?—£8,000. We are repaying it by a sinking fund—it is repayable in thirty years.

58. Mr. Cotton.—How is the town of Omagh drained ?—Badly.

59. Is there any project on foot for draining it ?—None at present.

60. Have the guardians expended any money on drainage in late years ?—None.

61. And there are complaints about it ?—Well I suppose there are. I believe, indeed, a scheme of drainage is in contemplation.

62. Have you any idea of the cost of it ?—There is no estimate of it yet.

63. Mr. Robinson.—Are there any buildings upon them going on in the town ?—Yes.

64. Are there any going on outside ?—Yes.

65. In which direction ?—In the direction of the south-east and east.

66. What class of houses ?—Very fair; two-story houses. In fact the townland of Campsie has become almost a village.

67. Is that within the boundary ?—Yes. Within a few years it was homogeneous.

Mr. William Mullan examined.

Omagh. [illegible] Mr. William Mullan.

69. Mr. Cowan.—You are Chairman of the Town Commissioners?—Yes.

70. You have a strong feeling on the part of the Town Board that an extension of the boundary is necessary?—Yes.

71. As I understand that was the unanimous opinion of the Commissioners?—When we got the powers, in [illegible], we came to the conclusion, on the powers of taxation we [illegible] 1s., 2s., and 3s., we had not enough of money to carry out improvements, and that with the extension, taking in some [illegible] fields, and some gentlemen's residences near up into the boundary, [illegible], and under that consideration we found that we would have to extend our lighting as far and to those places if we took them into our boundary, and that the [illegible] of lighting would be more than we could get from them. There is no suburb lighting [illegible], and under the circumstances we thought it better to keep our boundary and we were the more disposed to do that in consequence of the Grand Jury dealing very fairly with us, and taking the cleaning of the streets.

72. The Grand Jury have taken up the cleaning of the streets of Omagh?—Yes, we thought we were entitled to that as we were paying over £700 county cess and were getting only what represented £200 or £300.

73. I presume then you never contemplated taking up the control of the streets and roads yourselves?—Yes, we did.

74. Did you ever think about becoming the urban sanitary authority?—Yes.

75. Were you then in the first instance considered, if you would wish to become the urban sanitary authority?—Yes, some time ago we would have been disposed to have got the entire management of the town, from the fact that we considered it would enable us, by not having any additional expenses, to provide [illegible], but ultimately the Commissioners were [illegible] with regard to [illegible] the control of the sanitary matters in the guardians, and the roads to the Grand Jury. There is one thing I would say, I think, that all the Commissioners would be in favour of uniform rating. I think my opinion of rating in you [illegible].

76. Would your own opinion be in favour of putting the town under the Towns Improvement Act?—Well I don't say I am disposed to make any change.

77. But would not uniform rating be a change?—Well, yes.

78. Well, with the exception of uniform rating, how would the adoption of the Towns Improvement Act affect you differently?—It would give us [illegible] as the Commissioners entertained the exact notions of being careful of the funds of the town. It would give more extended power of rating, and the people of the town would be dissatisfied with that.

79. It would not give power beyond the maximum which you have at present?—I thought it would give us power up to 1s. 6d.

80. It would be 1s., without dealing with the water?—That would give us scope for the management of the town.

81. The Towns Improvement Act was not adopted?—No, it was very strongly opposed.

82. On what ground?—On the ground of not giving power of rating higher than at present.

83. That was on the part of those who were rated at 3s.?—Yes.

84. Mr. Robinson.—Are there any improvements required here, and which the Commissioners have been prevented from making through want of funds?—I don't think there are. The sewerage is what is most required.

85. Mr. Cowan.—Is the Board of Guardians ever asked to do anything about sewerage which they have declined?—They have not exactly declined, but we have only just finished with the water works, and it would meet with a good deal of opposition to put on new taxation for sewerage.

86. You know the sanitary district for the water rate?—Yes.

87. Would it be fair to have the same district put to the town rate?—Yes, I think so.

88. They are the townlands which are [illegible] in this town?—Yes, the same.

89. As persons you wish for an alteration of the boundary?—Yes, I think it would be an advantage to such places.

90. And is that the feeling of the majority as well as the Commissioners?—I think so.

91. Do you know the feeling of any of the people living outside on this subject, the way it would affect to be brought in?—On the contrary, I believe they would strongly wish to be kept out and would oppose being brought in.

92. Mr. Robinson.—Would the extension of the boundary to the electoral division give you a population sufficient to constitute you the urban sanitary authority?—I am not aware of that.

93. You know the electoral division?—I do.

94. It extends, I believe, from a mile to a mile and a half—would you consider that would be too much to go into within the municipal area?—Well, I think there would be very strong objections to it by the parties living out of the town. They would think they got no advantage whatever to justify them.

95. Mr. Cowan.—Do you yourself think that the persons living say a mile or a mile and a half from us [illegible] interest in the condition of the town, as having it well kept, the streets properly lighted and so on. Don't they all use Omagh as a market and a post and [illegible]?—Yes, but as far as I know them they would be very much opposed to paying anything towards the lighting or anything else of Omagh.

96. Have they not an interest in it?—I am sure they would be glad to see it improve, to use the markets [illegible].

97. Would it not be fair that they should pay something towards the expense of the town?—Well, perhaps so, but it would be very strongly opposed.

98. Do you not think that the lands outside derive exceptional advantages from their proximity to the town?—Yes.

99. There are schools and places of worship to which the people outside come to, or send their children?—Yes, they do that. [illegible] two or three or four miles. I would say this, that if it was forced on them they would say nothing, but if proposal be laid they would be opposed to it.

100. Mr. Robinson.—You think yourself that it would be only fair that people living within a reasonable distance should contribute something towards the maintenance of the town they live so nearly, from which they derive exceptional advantages and in the welfare of which as you say they are much interested?—Yes, I think so.

101. Mr. Cowan.—Can you tell me roughly how many gentlemen's places are within the electoral division?—About thirty.

102. How much would it add to the population?—It would bring us nearly up to the 6,000.

103. Has the land about the town increased very much in value owing to its proximity to the town?—Yes, and the gentlemen around the town and the people more than the gentlemen in the town.

104. Do you think if there was to be an extension at all it should be to the electoral division?—Yes.

105. You don't know what the drainage scheme would cost?—No, I would not form any [illegible].

106. Are there complaints as to the sewerage?—Yes; great complaints.

107. Have any complaints been made to the Guardians?—Yes; repeatedly.

Omagh. July [illegible], 1879.

Mr. William [illegible].

107. Have the Guardians ever done anything?—I never knew them. I brought it before them last winter—in going round with the coal fund we found places flooded with every kind of filth.

Mr. [illegible].—I have brought it twice before the Sanitary Board. They certainly appointed committees to investigate the subject.

108. But they took no further steps?—No.

[illegible].—You were asking a question about the people outside wishing an extension. I have been speaking to gentlemen at [illegible], which would be taken in—and they said it would destroy their [illegible] rights.

109. Whatever opinions we ask it is on the understanding that there would be no alteration in any one's rights?—I should say that they would oppose it. I may also add that the feeling of the people is against the Towns Improvement Act.

110. Mr. Robinson.—Why?—They imagine that power would be taken out of their hands, and that things would be so manipulated that outsiders would govern their town and drive the trade away.

111. Do you mean that the Commissioners would not be elected by the same class of people?—No; but that it would be divided into wards, and that instead of the present gentlemen having the rule, others who would not be so useful or proper would be in their place.

112. You are not in favour of auxiliary rating?—I am if it could be done under the 9th of George IV., but not otherwise.

113. You say the Towns Improvement Act in the opinion of some people would drive the trade away. How is that?—It would drive it out of the streets.

114. Do you mean into the fair green?—They have no fair green, but a place for cattle. There are some of the men who have carts in the streets. Mr. M'Crystal took up the part of the countrymen who did so, and there was a dispute about it. Few were put on carts, and boxes, and barrels, in the streets, and they drove the carts out of the streets and there was a great agitation; in fact we held a sort of indignation meeting, because the turf carts and the hay and straw carts were of more advantage to the town than all the gentlemen's carriages or that, that drove through the town.

Mr. John M'Crystal, j.p.

Mr. John M'Crystal, c.e., examined.

115. Mr. Cotton.—You have heard the evidence given to-day?—Yes.

116. Have you anything to add to it?—No; except to say that any gentleman within four miles, having property within the boundary, would be able to vote under the Towns Improvement Act for Commissioners, and it would be throwing ourselves into the hands of the tyrants to adopt it.

The inquiry terminated.

Mr. Smith handed in the following returns:—

	£	s.	d.
Valuation of electoral division of Omagh,	15,811	10	0
Do. of constituency district,	9,787	17	0

Area of electoral division, 4,330 statute acres.

Population of same in 1871, 8,443.

Number of gentlemen's residences in same, about 14.

In the year 1841, the population of the Omagh Union was 80,[illegible]; in 1851, 66,477; in 1861, 58,[illegible]; in 1871, 57,[illegible]. A decrease in the Omagh Union in thirty years of 23,[illegible].

ANTRIM—19th JULY, 1879.

(Before Mr. H. A. Robinson.)

Antrim. July 19, 1879.

Mr. John Young.

Mr. John Young examined.

1. Mr. Robinson.—You are the Town Clerk?—Yes.

2. How long have you held that position?—About six years.

3. You are therefore well acquainted with the town?—Yes.

4. Antrim is under the Towns Improvement Act of 1854?—Yes.

5. Previous to the adoption of that Act, was the government of the town under any other Act?—No.

6. And the present boundary of Antrim was at that time adopted?—Yes.

7. Would you describe the boundary to me. How far does it extend in a northerly direction?—Not more than twenty perches from the centre of the street between the workhouse and the town.

8. On the south how far does it extend?—On the south it extends further on one side; I suppose a quarter of a mile.

9. And on the east and west?—On the east there are houses up to very near the boundary, but the street stops before it goes altogether up that length; I suppose within about ten or twenty perches.

10. Can you tell me on what principle the Commissioners adopted the boundary which now exists?—I cannot.

11. It appears to me that Antrim consists of one long street, and the boundaries, as far as possible, took in that street and nothing more, and a piece on each side of the street?—Yes, that is so.

12. There are no wards in Antrim?—No.

13. How many townlands is the municipality in?—It is all in the townland of Antrim; the townparks of Antrim, and a portion of Balloo.

14. Is it all within one electoral division?—Yes; all within the electoral division of Antrim.

15. Can you give me the area of the town?—Mr. Scott will give you that. I can give you the valuation.

16. Give me the valuation?—The valuation of houses is £3,312 3s.

17. And the valuation of lands alone?—The valuation of lands alone is £[illegible] 18s. That is the present year's valuation. It is somewhat less than last year. Some changes have been made which have had the effect of making the amount less.

18. What is the population of Antrim?—In 1871 it was 2,030.

19. Are you of opinion that it is an increasing population?—No; it is a decreasing population.

20. Is Antrim a thriving town?—It is not.

21. And is there any building going on outside the municipal boundary?—There has been one new house erected lately near the railway station.

22. Is there any of the land about the town taken on building leases?—Not very much. There is no encouragement to build, for the lord of the soil will not give long leases.

23. Are there any buildings being erected within the present boundary?—I do not know of any going on at present within the boundary.

24. Will you now give me the municipal rates for the last few years?—We have not had a rate every year; we have missed some years, and have had no

rate. In 1870 we had a rate of 1s.; in 1872, 10d.; in 1876, 6d.; there was no rate in 1877; in 1878, 10d.; in 1879, 6d. The average for the last eight years has been a yearly rate of 7d. in the pound of a township rate.

35. Can you give me the county cess?—In 1872 we had two cesses of 10d. each, making 1s. 8d. in the pound for that year; in 1876, one cess of 8d. and the other of 10d., making for the year 1s. 6d.; in 1877 the two cesses amounted to 1s. 6d.; in 1878 the cesses for the year were again 1s. 6d., one cess being of 11d., and the other of 7d.; and in 1879, the present year, there are two cesses of 10d., making again 1s. 8d.

36. Are there fairs held in Antrim?—There are.

37. And markets?—Yes.

38. And do the people resident outside the boundary come into the town to buy large quantities of the [illegible] of the markets?—We have good fairs, but the market is not a good one, in point of its [illegible]. We have good monthly fairs.

39. Is the town well lit?—It is fairly lighted for its size. There are thirty-three lamps.

40. Was the Towns Improvement Act when adopted, adopted for all purposes?—It was adopted on the 3rd of September, 1850, and the water clauses were excluded.

41. Are there schools in the town?—There are.

42. And do the people from outside the boundary come in and avail themselves of these schools?—They do, largely. We have got an Intermediate school here now, and a good many attend it—even people from four and five miles off.

43. There were some queries sent down here to you by the Municipal Boundary Commissioners in Dublin?—Yes.

44. Were the questions contained in that document submitted to your Board?—They were.

45. Was there a special meeting of the Board summoned to consider them, or did they come before the Board at one of its ordinary meetings?—Before the ordinary monthly meeting on the ordinary fixed day.

46. Can you give me a copy of any resolution that was passed on the subject, if there was a resolution?—I have not got it here. In substance it was to the effect that there was no necessity for a change in the boundary.

47. And was that passed unanimously?—It was by the Commissioners present.

48. How many Commissioners were present at that meeting?—Not less than five. It takes five to form a quorum.

49. And they were of opinion that no extension was necessary?—They were.

50. And did they not think that any people who reside outside the present boundary derive certain advantages from the proximity of the town?—That was not considered I think.

51. Have the Commissioners considered the question of becoming the urban sanitary authority?—No, I don't think they have considered that question officially.

52. Can you tell me what is the feeling of the Board on the subject?—I think a great many of the Commissioners would prefer things to remain as they are, in the hands of the guardians.

53. Do you think a radius of one mile from the centre of the town would make you an urban sanitary authority—would bring the population up to 6,000?—I don't think it would.

54. Have the Town Commissioners ever considered the question of taking up the roads?—That has been thought of, but not officially considered. There has been no motion on the subject. It has been talked of by the Commissioners amongst themselves, and some of the members are favourable to it. However, others think it would be a mistake—that it would cost them more money than they now pay, and that the work would not be so well done as at present. The Board are divided so far as I know on the subject.

55. Do you know the extent of the electoral division?—I do.

56. Have there been any sanitary rates struck lately by the Board of Guardians?—There has been one of 2d.

57. What was the particular district on which that rate was struck?—The townland of Townparks, Antrim—that was one portion; and there was another portion on the outward[illegible] more extended area.

58. What was that rate for?—For making sewers.

59. Is the town well sewered now?—I don't think it is. It could be improved. Still on the main street here it is pretty well sewered.

60. As you have stated the views of the Town Commissioners, may I now ask you your individual opinion as to the present boundary—do you think the present municipal boundary of Antrim, includes land enough for building for many years to come?—At present the demand for building land is not a very bright one. I don't think there is much probability of building taking place to any great extent about the town.

61. And do you agree with your board, that no extension is required for the town?—I do.

62. And I suppose that any extension that might be made in any direction whatever would only bring in land that could be rated, as agricultural?—It might bring in one or two houses. For instance, it would bring in the new house I have spoken of as the workhouse hospital.

63. Is there any other statement you would wish to make bearing on the subject of this inquiry?—No.

Mr. Henry C. Scott examined.

64. Mr. [illegible].—You are the Clerk of the Union, I believe?—Yes, I am.

65. Do you know the electoral division?—Yes.

66. What is the valuation of it?—The valuation is £17,473 17s.

67. And the population?—2,020 is the population of the town. The population of the electoral division is, I think, about 4,700.

68. And for how many miles does the electoral division extend in the most remote direction from the town?—I think not more than two miles.

69. I may tell you that my reason for asking the question, is that the Select Committee of the House of Commons have in their report [illegible] told us that, as far as possible, it is desirable that the boundaries of towns should be made conterminous with Poor Law electoral divisions?—Yes.

70. From your knowledge of the electoral division of Antrim, do you think it would be advisable to adopt its boundary as the new boundary of the town?—I do not.

71. You think it is too large?—Yes, quite too large.

72. And the land it would bring in would be mainly arable land, in fact nearly all of that description?—Yes, nearly all of it.

73. There is no working population or mills in Antrim?—Very little.

74. Do you think the people living in the most remote part of the electoral division derive any advantages from the proximity of the town?—Only [illegible] advantages.

75. They come and make use of the town and its markets?—Just so.

76. Antrim is their natural town?—Yes.

77. They make use of the streets of the town and they send their children to the schools of the town, do they not?—Only to a limited extent.

78. You think they do not get advantages, which [illegible]

Antrim.
[illegible]
Mr. [illegible] Young.

Mr. Henry C. Scott.

would entitle them to pay for their use of the town?—I am sure they would not consider it so.

69. Is not the land in the electoral division more valuable from its proximity to the town of Antrim?—Yes, it would be in proportion to its proximity.

70. Do you approve of a boundary cutting townlands, the way the present boundary does. The present boundary, I understand, goes through townlands, taking it from point to point. Have you considered that?—I don't think I have.

71. Can you give me the valuation of the townlands included within the boundary; into how many townlands does it go?—I don't think there is an entire townland within the boundary.

72. There is not an entire townland?—No; only portions.

73. Into how many portions of townlands does it go?—Into the Towparks of Antrim and those of Ballee.

74. Would it not be desirable to include the whole of these townlands, so as to give a better defined boundary?—It might.

75. Could you tell me what would be the area of the town if that was done?—I could, 1,800 acres.

76. What would be the valuation of those two townlands?—The valuation of those two townlands would be £6,667 2s.

77. The townland of Ballee I believe extends a good distance to the south of the town?—Not very far—an English mile I should say.

78. Would it be too far to take in the whole of that townland?—The extremity of it is not more distant than it would be to the extremity of the Towparks on the north side. It is generally regarded as Towparks under another name.

79. Are you resident in the town?—I am.

80. And I am sure you take an interest in it?—Yes.

81. Do you think any change is required in the existing boundaries of the town?—Well, I find it difficult to give you an answer to that, as the question has not exactly come before me.

82. I am asking for your individual opinion?—An extension might be useful in the way you have described.

83. An extension so as to give a better defined boundary, so as to go by townland boundaries?—Yes.

84. Would you now give me the poor rate for a number of years, say from 1873?—Yes. In 1873 it was 1s. 8d.; in 1876 1s. 8d.; in 1877 1s. 5d.; and in 1878 1s. 3d.; but in the last-named year there was an additional rate of 2d. in the pound on the townland of Towparks, Antrim, for sanitary purposes.

Mr. William Vance, jun., examined.

85. You are one of the Town Commissioners of Antrim?—I am.

86. How long have you been living in the town?—I was born here, and have resided here ever since.

87. Were you a member of the Town Commissioners when the town first came under the Act?—I was one of the first appointed.

88. Were you one of the committee appointed to draw out the present boundary of Antrim as it now exists?—Yes.

89. The boundary was never, I believe, modified or altered since?—Never.

90. Can you tell me what it was that prompted you to adopt the boundary which you now have?—Well, the mode in which we adopted the boundary was this. We took in only land very close to the town. We did not extend, inasmuch as we thought a great many were getting accommodations. We confined the boundary to a very short distance from the town. We did not extend more than a quarter of a mile from any extreme point. But I was just observing that if you take in the whole of the townland of Antrim and Ballee, and the Grange of Muckamore, which lies very close by, be left out, it would be putting too heavy a tax upon those two townlands, without getting more. Muckamore Abbey, Mr. Thompson's place, we should take that in, because we run close by it. The townland of Antrim, I may mention, runs four miles away up over the hills.

91. Since 1854 have many new buildings been erected in the town?—Very few.

92. The town, then, appears to have been very much at a stand-still since that time?—Yes, at very much of a stand-still.

93. Are there any manufactories in the town of Antrim?—None at present. We had a paper mill and a brewery, but both have ceased working, and all we have now is a flour mill, which is near the railway station.

94. Is there any tendency to build in more than one direction?—The inducements to build here are almost nil. Parties would be willing enough to build if they could get leases, but the landlord has not seen his way to give leases such as would be acceptable to them.

95. Would there then be an inclination to build if satisfactory leases were granted?—Yes.

96. In which direction?—In all directions. I think if the people got good leases there would be houses to grow up.

97. Do you know any place outside the present boundary where it is likely, under the circumstances referred to, there would be an inclination to build?—I do not. All the people are looking for are satisfactory leases, and Lord Massereene is not willing to give long leases, and they won't build on twenty-one years' leases.

98. Do you think that the people living in proximity to the town should be made to contribute towards the maintenance of the town?—Well, I hold seventy-two acres of Towparks myself. If you only go a certain distance you put a heavy tax upon me, but if you go out over the whole townland, and the townland of Ballee, that would have the effect of reducing the rate. If you only go a mile it would increase the present charge on gentlemen holding land near the town.

99. Are there any improvements which you have been deterred from carrying out for want of funds?—I have heard no one complain of that. All they want are leases. I think money could be got on the spot if they had leases. It is for want of leases they won't spend their money.

100. What I mean is, have the Town Commissioners been cramped in their operations for want of funds?—We had to get a loan for footpaths and a town clock, but we will be able to wipe that out in another year.

101. Then the funds of the Town Commissioners are in a satisfactory condition?—They are.

102. Were you present at the meeting of the Town Commissioners at which the queries sent you by us from Dublin were considered?—No. I happened to be away at the time.

103. The majority of the Commissioners were not favourable to an extension?—I would be in favour of an extension if you take in the whole townland, but I think if you only take in half a mile you would punish the present ratepayers.

104. You think then for the purpose of rectifying the boundary satisfactorily, the townland of Towparks should be taken in, and part of the townland of Muckamore should also be included?—Yes, and I am reminded by a gentleman near me that the townland of Moylinny which intervenes between those two should also be included.

105. If that boundary which you propose was to be adopted it would be about a little more than half a mile radius from the centre of the town, as nearly as possible?—Yes.

106. And do you think that people living within

[illegible] derive advantages from the proximity of the town?—Certainly they do.

107. They come in and enjoy the benefit of the markets, and if the town is kept clean and well lit they have the advantage of those benefits too?—Yes; and [illegible]

108. In the town, well lit?—Yes, splendidly. [illegible]

109. Mr. Young.—There is a very small population [illegible] the [illegible] that would be found.

Examination of Mr. Vance resumed.

110. Mr. Robinson.—Are there many houses of business in the town—good shops?—Well, I suppose you would count twenty average shops.

111. Do these people live on their premises in the town or have they residences outside?—They all live in the town.

112. There are no villa residences outside Antrim?—None at all.

Mr. Henry M'Lorinan continued.

113. Mr. Robinson.—You are one of the Town Commissioners, I presume?—Yes.

114. Have you lived long here?—I was born here and have resided here all my life.

115. Were you a member of the committee that adopted the general boundary?—No, I am not a Commissioner so long as that. There was one matter you referred to in the course of this inquiry—as to the Sanitary Act—whether it was properly carried out in this town. I wish to state that I think it is very badly carried out here.

116. You think the Guardians do their duty badly?—Yes.

117. Is it your opinion that the sanitary work would be better carried out if it was in the hands of the Town Commissioners?—Decidedly.

118. And have you ever expressed that opinion at meetings of the Board?—I have.

119. And in what spirit has it been met?—The question has never [illegible] brought up; but we have proposed and carried resolutions and they have been forwarded to the Sanitary Board and they have taken very little notice of them; and in the matter of water and drainage and things of that sort, they don't seem to me to expend any money.

120. I am afraid those matters are not within the scope of the present inquiry. You think then it is desirable that you should become the sanitary authority?—Yes, I do think that is desirable.

121. Are you of opinion also that the maintenance of the roads would be better carried out under your supervision?—Yes, I think so.

122. You think that all the authority over the town of Antrim should be in your own hands and not in the hands of three divided authorities?—That is my opinion.

123. Have you heard the suggestion to take in the whole of the townlands of Townparks, Balloo, and the townland of Muckamore?—Yes, and if you think of making an extension of the boundary, it would be my opinion that you should extend it in that way.

124. It would add considerably to the valuation of the town and make the rates lighter?—It would.

125. And you think the people living on those townlands derive advantages from the proximity of the town that they should in fairness pay for?—Yes, I do.

126. Have you heard the views of any of the ratepayers on the subject?—I have heard the [illegible] of [illegible] a fair proportion of the county cess.

127. If you had adopted the increased area suggested, do you think the people living within the townlands of Townparks, and Muckamore, would be glad to have the roads in the hands of the Town Commissioners?—I think the roads would be kept in a better state if we had the collecting of the county cess and the management of it.

Mr. William Atkinson examined.

128. Mr. Robinson.—Have you heard the suggestion with reference to an extension of the boundary?—I have.

129. Have you lived long in Antrim?—I have been away for a number of years, but I have lived here for twenty years.

130. Do you think that there is any likelihood of any building going on in the vicinity of the town?—I see no possibility of it at present, and I quite agree with the observations of Mr. Vance and Mr. M'Lorinan.

131. Namely, that you would like to have an extended area, the care of the roads, and the direction of the sanitary business within that area?—Quite so.

132. And you do not approve of a divided authority?—I do not; I think all these matters should be in the hands of the Town Commissioners.

133. Do you know the electoral division boundary at all?—I have paid very little attention to it, but I should know it.

134. Are you a Guardian?—No.

135. Do you think that a mile in one direction and two in another would be too large an area?—Yes. I think Mr. Vance was quite correct in what he said in reference to that matter.

The inquiry then terminated.

Aughnacloy.
July 24, 1879.

Mr. Foster M'Kay.

AUGHNACLOY—THURSDAY, 24TH JULY, 1879.

(Before Mr. H. A. Robinson.)

Mr. Foster M'Kay examined.

1. Mr. Robinson.—You are the Town Clerk?—I am.

2. This town is under the Towns Improvement Act, I believe?—Yes.

3. How long has that Act been adopted?—Since 1864.

4. Then the Act was adopted the year it became law?—Yes.

5. Was that Act adopted for all purposes?—I think so.

6. Do you remember the town at that time?—No.

7. Will you kindly give me the population of Aughnacloy?—At the last census it was 1,432; below the statutory limit.

8. Do you think that the population has increased since then?—I think it has not. I dare say it would be about the same.

10. Is your population a working or farming population?—A good deal of it is commercial.

11. Are there any manufactures carried on in the town?—No.

12. What is the area of the town?—349 acres.

13. And the valuation?—£1,879—indeed it is now £1,900.

14. Will you now tell me on how much of that the full rate is struck, and on how much the one-fourth?—Upon £1,807 the full rate is struck, and on £73 10s. the one-fourth rate is struck.

15. In how many electoral divisions is the town of Aughnacloy?—One.

16. And what electoral division is that?—Aughnacloy.

17. Of the Clogher union?—Yes.

18. Does the municipal boundary of Aughnacloy cut through townlands or take in only whole townlands?—It cuts through townlands.

19. How many townlands are wholly included or how many are divided?—None of them are wholly included.

20. And how many does it intersect?—Dernagh, Lisnahill, Tully, Ravella, and also a portion of Glenk.

21. And if you were to include the whole of these townlands, so as to give a well-defined townland boundary for the town of Aughnacloy, would it give you a very much increased valuation?—We would not I think take in any houses, perhaps, except the Archdeaconry, but I think it would be unfair to do that, because there is only a very little piece of Glenk in the boundary.

22. The district brought in would then be all liable to the one-fourth rate?—There would be some houses.

23. Would the class of houses brought in be farmers' houses?—The archdeaconry would be one; the manse would be another, and there would be a few farmers' houses. Indeed, there would be a good many farmers' houses in Ravella, Tully. In all the townlands.

24. What have the municipal rates been for the last five years, commencing 1874?—They were 1s. in 1874; 8d. in 1875, 8d. in 1876, 8d. in 1877, 10d. in 1878, and 10d. in 1879.

25. And what was the poor rate in the same period?—In 1874, it was 1s. 3d.; in 1875, 1s. 6d.; in 1876, 1s. 6d.; in 1877, 2s.; and in 1878, 1s. 6d.

26. Have there been any sanitary rates struck by the guardians of late years?—I don't know.

27. Do you know if the sanitary work done is carried on to the satisfaction of the Commissioners?—Well, the Commissioners have made no complaint.

28. Can you tell me whether or not there have been any special rates for sanitary purposes?—I cannot.

29. When we sent you down the queries was there a special meeting of the Commissioners to consider them, or were they considered at an ordinary meeting?—At an ordinary meeting.

30. And they were of opinion that no extension was required?—Yes.

31. And were they unanimous in coming to that conclusion?—They were. I may, however, mention that there was a special meeting of the Commissioners the other day in view of this inquiry, and at that meeting they adopted a resolution stating, as follows,

"That there is no necessity for any change to be made in the existing boundaries of the town of Aughnacloy, and that there is no special matter to be submitted to the Commission."

32. Are you acquainted with the boundary of the electoral division in which Aughnacloy is situated?—I know the townlands.

33. Do you know the extent of the electoral division?—I do not. I have an idea of it. I know the townland.

34. Would it be your opinion that the electoral division of Aughnacloy would be too large to be adopted for the new boundary of the town?—Certainly.

35. I asked the question, because the Select Committee of the House of Commons have told us that, so far as possible, town boundaries should be made coterminous with the boundaries of poor law electoral divisions. In some cases we find that can be done; in others we find that the extent of arable land and country that would be brought in by such an arrangement, would be quite too much, and that is what I understand your opinion with regard to Aughnacloy?—Certainly.

36. Are there markets here?—Yes.

37. How many?—One weekly market.

38. And the people who live outside the town, I understand, bring in their produce for sale here?—Yes; it is a good general market.

40. Do you think that the people in all these townlands which are partly intersected by the municipal boundary, avail themselves of the town to a great extent?—They do.

41. Is the town lighted?—It is.

42. With gas?—Yes.

43. How much do the Commissioners pay per lamp?—About 33s. a year.

44. The people outside the town also have the advantage of the lighting in the town?—They do, of course.

45. And of the cleansing of the roads?—Yes.

46. And of the scavenging?—Yes.

47. And if the townlands were to be wholly taken in, parts of which are now included, would it not be fair that they should contribute their portions towards the maintenance of the town of which they enjoy the benefits. Can you say if that is the opinion of your board?—I don't know, indeed.

48. Would they have any objection to bring in these remaining portions of the townlands, in order to have a well-defined boundary?—I suppose those Commissioners who hold land outside would not like that.

49. Has that question ever been considered at the board?—No, it has not.

50. Are there schools in the town?—Yes.

51. And the children, I understand, from the districts all around the town attend these schools?—Yes.

52. And make use of the roads from day to day?—Yes.

53. Has it ever been considered at this board whether it would be desirable to make the Town Commissioners the urban sanitary authority?—I think the Commissioners would have preferred retaining that power.

54. But the Commissioners have not passed any definite resolution on the subject?—They have not.

55. As far as you can ascertain, the opinion of your Board is, that the sanitary control would be better managed in your own hands?—Yes.

56. As they live on the spot and have better facilities for seeing the wants derived?—Yes.

57. You are aware, I presume, that they can, by the 7th section of the Public Health Act, ask and obtain a provisional order from the Local Government Board giving them the sanitary control?—Yes.

58. Have they ever considered the question of taking up the control of the roads from out of the hands of the Grand Jury, and of managing them themselves?—They have talked of it, but it was never formally considered.

59. There was no resolution on the subject?—No.

60. Do you know the feeling of the Board on that subject—is it adverse to or in favour of it?—I don't know.

61. You say they have talked over the subject, what do you think is their feeling?—I think most of them would prefer having the control of the roads.

62. Some of the Commissioners prefer that the town should be under one undivided authority?—Yes.

63. Have you talked over the question of the extension of the boundary with the people resident in the town?—I have not.

64. Nor with the people resident outside?—No.

65. Then you have had no opportunity of ascertaining the feelings of the people on the subject?—None except the Commissioners.

66. And we may take it, I suppose, that the Commissioners represent the people in this matter?—I think they do.

67. Have you given the present inquiry any publicity in the shape of advertisements or placards?—No.

68. And they have had no opportunity of seeing any reference to it, except the advertisements I put in the newspapers?—I suppose not.

69. How long have you lived here?—For fifteen years.

70. And you know, I presume, the circumstances of the town pretty well?—Yes.

71. Having stated the opinion of the Commissioners as far as you know them, may I ask is it your individual opinion that any change is necessary?—I don't know of any being necessary.

72. Are there any buildings going on in the town?—I think Mr. Abraham is building.

73. In which direction is the building progressing?—In the Lisnadevil and Glenk direction.

74. Is the present boundary large enough to allow space for all the buildings that are likely to be constructed within the next few years?—Yes, it is.

75. Are there any buildings going on outside the present boundary?—Not close to the town.

76. Is the land more valuable which is outside the town from its proximity to it?—It is.

[illegible], July 26, 1878.

Mr. Foster M'Kay.

Dr. William Scott examined.

Dr. William Scott.

77. Mr. Robertson.—You are one of the Town Commissioners?—I am.

78. Have you been a Commissioner for a very long time?—Since the commencement of municipal operations. I got up the township.

79. When you first came under the Act at a special meeting of the Commissioners you adopted a certain boundary?—We did.

80. Had you a committee to draw up and arrange that boundary?—Yes.

81. Can you tell me the motives that prompted you to take the present boundary?—The principle upon which we went was of getting certain known points, points that were known to everyone and that ran in straight lines in certain directions. The Fever Hospital gate was one, the gate of the Bruseen South school was another, making the boundary between two townlands, and the river wale at the cross roads another point, and making a wall a point, and then straight lines from one to another. It was really the best, well defined, well known boundaries we selected without consideration as far as I can recollect of any other question.

82. You have had no extension of the boundary since that time?—No, we have had no extension since.

83. You heard the question I asked Mr. M'Kay—if the Commissioners had ever proposed to include the whole of the townlands, portions of which were now inside the boundary. The reason I put that question is because it is so desirable to have a properly defined boundary, and much inconvenience is caused by anomalies in that respect. For instance, a point to point boundary sometimes goes through the dining-room of a man's house, leaving one part of the building inside and the other part outside the boundary. It is also most desirable to have permanent marks by means of which the boundary can be hereafter recognised. You mentioned the gate of the Fever Hospital. Well, supposing that gate was removed, how would your boundary be ascertained?—As to townlands, a portion of Glenk is in the town, and yet there is another portion of it so far away that it makes the adoption of that suggestion undesirable. Owing to the peculiar shape of that townland it goes away more than a mile from the town, and is rather narrow in one direction. I think it would not do very well with Tully, nor is the townland of Ravella of that kind that it would be practicable in that case. Derramukes is a very large townland, and you would have to take land a great distance off if you included it in the town boundary. On account of the entire Derramukes is not intersected by the municipal boundary. All Derrygush would be better to be in the town.

83. Do you think that the people living in these townlands derive advantages from the proximity of the town of Aughnacloy?—Yes, great advantages.

84. The land is rendered more valuable?—There is not the least doubt of that.

85. If they had to pay a one-fourth rate—if they had to pay a three-halfpenny rate, do you think they have advantages commensurate with that?—Yes. It would certainly apply to the townland of Derrygush, but I think there are portions of the other townlands which are too far from the town.

86. How far does the boundary extend to the north?—Northward it only extends to the Fever Hospital gate, very close to the town—for instance, to the new market, and that extends to the very boundary.

87. How far does the boundary extend to the south?—On the south it extends no great distance either. On the Monaghan-road, which is south-east, it extends some little way, but taking it to the south it is very close to the town, nearly to the gardens of the town.

88. And how far does it go to the east?—It goes further out in that direction than the other directions—it goes to a greater distance—to the mill race, or rather the lands of Mill view, and the lands of a person named M'Mahon, adjoining. It is not far, certainly; not more than twenty perches from where the houses included in the town are.

89. And to the west, how far does the town extend?—And on the west it is not more than twenty perches from the houses in the town—I suppose about fifteen perches. The boundaries are very narrow as far as that is concerned.

90. Do you know the electoral division?—I know it pretty well.

91. Do you know it sufficiently well to be able to say that it would be wholly impossible to adopt the electoral division as the boundary for the town?—It

[illegible]. July 10, 1872. Mr. William [illegible].

would be a hardship on some of the inhabitants in the far off portions of the electoral division.

92. What is the distance from the most remote part of the electoral division to the centre of the town? — Not further than two statute miles from the centre of the town. Without seeing the map I could not answer that question with accuracy.

93. Do you recollect the town when it first came under the Act? — I do, very well.

94. Is it much changed since then? — It is changed in two ways. It is changed in the first place in that there are better houses now in the town than then, and in the next place it has become a most peaceful place instead of being a riotous one, and all through the operation of the Towns Improvement Act. And though the town has changed very much in those respects, there is not much loss of a population. In 1861 we had exactly 1,841 inhabitants, and now there are under 1,800.

95. What sources of income have the Town Commissioners besides the rates? — Dog tax and fines.

96. Are there any improvements in the town which you would carry out if you had larger funds? — There are several connected with drainage.

97. That is a matter that is in the hands of the Board of Guardians? — But there are very many others.

98. Of what nature? — Principally with respect to the markets. There are a good many that we want.

99. There are a good many improvements that you are in need of? — Yes, very many. We are very badly off as regards market accommodation.

100. Are you under the impression that the sanitary work would be better done if it was in the hands of the Commissioners rather than under the control of the Board of Guardians? — I am sure of it, because it is not done at all. We attended strictly to sanitary matters until they were taken out of our hands. We had an inspector of nuisances and took a great deal of trouble about it. There is literally no one in the present system, and I may tell you that I am intimately conversant with it.

101. Do you think that you do not get value for the money you pay? — Certainly not.

102. Is the town well sewered? — No.

103. But there are I suppose some good sewers? — Yes.

104. And are they well looked after? — Yes; there is perpetual flushing from the surface drains, and that keeps them pretty clear.

105. Are any complaints you may have occasion to make to the Guardians promptly attended to? — Well I suppose I may say they are; but really as a matter of fact we do not make many complaints, because we know the difficulty there is in carrying out what we require.

106. How far is the union from here? — About eight Irish miles, which is eleven and a half or twelve English miles.

107. Have you ever considered the question of taking up the control of sanitary matters in the town? — Yes, I have often considered it personally. Have you ever brought the subject before your fellow Commissioners? — Yes.

108. And was it favourably received? — Yes.

109. Have you ever thought of the desirability of taking up the management of the roads? — Yes, we have often thought of it, but the Commissioners are divided on that question.

110. Do you think you get from the Grand Jury value for the county cess you pay? — I am sure we do.

111. Do you think it would be desirable to have the town under one undivided authority? — I think the work would be better done, although I have no complaint to make of the Grand Jury. I distinctly wish to guard against being understood to find fault with the Grand Jury. We got a good deal of the money of the Grand Jury — as much as we are entitled to, I think. They have made one very important drain for us — a very important sewer.

112. Do you know what the contributory district is for sanitary work? — I don't know, I am not able to say. Although I am a member of the Board of Guardians I rarely go to their meetings.

113. Are there any residences outside the present municipal boundary? — The [illegible] is a very fine house. That is the only place which could with any reason be brought into the municipal boundary.

114. I suppose there is no tendency to build outside the boundary for the purpose of avoiding municipal rates? — None whatever.

115. Do you think any building that is likely to go on for some time to come will be inside the present municipal boundary? — I think so.

116. And there is sufficient land for that? — I think there is.

117. Still the lands outside the present boundary are rendered more valuable by reason of the proximity of the town? — Certainly.

118. Is there anything you would wish to add bearing on the subject of this inquiry? I think not; I think you have worked out all the points.

Mr. Peter Sullivan.

Mr. Peter Sullivan, examined.

119. Mr. Robinson. — You are a Town Commissioner? — I am. And I understand you have some property outside the present boundary? — Yes, a little.

120. In which direction? — Both in the north and in the west.

121. Of what nature is your property? — Buildings.

122. And what is the nature of the land you hold? — Pasture and farming both.

123. And do you bring in your produce for sale at the market in the town here? — Yes.

124. And is not your land more valuable from the fact of its being situated close to the town? — Well it is, to a certain extent.

125. Bearing in mind that it would be desirable to have a well defined boundary, would you object if the whole of the townland was included, which would bring you within the municipal limits? — I believe that would make it too large a boundary.

126. Have you any objection to the manner in which the Town Commissioners carry on their work? — I have not.

127. Then you would not mind being under their rule? — It is not with reference to that that I would object to the extension you refer to, but I would not put all the townlands into the boundary, because that would have the effect of making it too large.

128. The only reason then that you give for not wishing to be included, is that if the townlands were brought in, it would make the boundary too large, but you would have no objection to be under the rule of the Town Commissioners? — Oh no; I would not.

129. Don't you think you derive exceptional advantages from being so close to the town? — I think so.

130. Did you object to any extension of the boundary? — I think it is large enough. There is quite enough of building ground.

131. Is there any tendency to build in the direction in which your property is situate? — Not much.

132. Still you have heard that if there was a larger boundary and all those townlands were taken in and there was an increased valuation for the Commissioners to strike a rate on, the Commissioners would have more funds at their disposal to enable them to carry out improvements which they are now prevented from effecting? — I don't think there would be much gained by it, for there are not many houses in it.

133. Do you think that the boundary of the electoral division would be too large to adopt as the municipal boundary?—Indeed I am quite sure it would. The electoral division extends, I suppose, nearly three miles from the town.

134. Would the people living outside the present boundary be opposed to being brought in?—I don't know.

135. They have no objection to avail themselves of the town, but they don't like to be rated for it?—Yes, I think you may assume that that statement is perfectly true. [illegible] Mr. Peter Sullivan.

Mr. Samuel M'Caffrey examined. Mr. Samuel M'Caffrey.

136. Mr. Robinson.—You are a Town Commissioner also, I understand?—I am.

137. Do you think that the sanitary work of this town would be better managed in your own hands?—I do, sir.

138. And do you think that there are no improvements wanted in the town?—I presume that sanitary improvements are what are most essential to the town.

139. And you think that if you were the sanitary authority, you would carry out certain improvements which the guardians are not doing at present?—I think we would have a better supply of water.

140. And have you not a good water-supply?—We have not.

141. What is the supply obtained from at present?—We have pumps in the town, and also wells, and both are inadequate to give the supply required.

142. May I ask you has the water been analysed?—I cannot say, but it is known to be bad.

143. And is dissatisfaction felt by the people at not having a proper water-supply?—The supply is very unsatisfactory, and there is a stoppage by a frost in a great many cases, and there is no means of getting it repaired as quickly as would be essential I believe.

144. Have you facilities for getting a better supply?—I could not answer that question. The pumps are very good—what there are of them, but there is too much difficulty in getting water from them.

145. Are there any drains near the wells, or graveyards, with offensive matter percolating through the soil?—I believe there are drains which are not properly framed, so as to prevent a certain amount of surface nuisance.

146. Do you know the town well?—I have some local knowledge of it.

147. Do you coincide with the views expressed by Mr. Sullivan and Dr. Scott that there are likely to be no buildings outside the present limits of the town for some time to come?—If you take the future as the past, I think there is not. I don't think there is a probability of there being much extension for a time, at all events, in buildings.

148. Do you think it would be fair to rate those people just outside the town who come in and avail themselves of the markets, roads, schools, lights, and so forth of the town—to rate them at the one-fourth rate?—I question if it would be justice to them. Such a proceeding might be of advantage to the people of the town, but I do not believe they would derive much benefit. My impression is that persons who live convenient to the town have not much more interest in it than persons living at a greater distance, in a certain way.

149. Is it not the fact in the case of the people who live close to the town that their land is rendered more valuable?—I have some doubts about that, for this reason—that I think our markets are not such as to draw people to them from a considerable distance, owing to causes which I cannot here explain.

150. What are the causes—would it be difficult to explain them?—One of the causes is that our markets are not in a satisfactory state. There are a good many complaints concerning them, and the people say that they prefer going to other markets.

151. To Clogher, I suppose?—Yes.

152. Do you think that one of the results would be—if the boundary was extended, and you had an increased valuation on which to strike rates—that you would have more income to spend on the repair and improvement of the markets?—It strikes me that that source of income should arise from the town itself, and I don't think it would be fair to tax people outside the town for the purpose.

153. I think, in reference to the people who live far away, that if the markets here are required for the convenience of those that they should also contribute towards such expenditure?—I say that the person who lives at three miles distance from the town frequents it as often as the person who resides only two miles away. I say as regards any person who lives within two miles of the town, that I do not see why he should be taxed if he does not derive any more benefit than a person at five miles distance.

154. Have you any other observations to add to your evidence, or any suggestions to make?—No; I think you have already received testimony strong enough in reference to the sanitary matter.

Mr. Joseph Abraham examined. Mr. Joseph Abraham.

155. Mr. Robinson.—Do you think the present boundary requires alteration?—I think not.

156. Have you been living in the town for some time?—Yes.

157. The town is, so far as I can understand, generally a flourishing town, but is somewhat at a standstill at present?—Yes.

158. You think the boundary is large enough for all purposes?—Yes.

Dr. Scott re-examined. Dr. William Scott.

159. Mr. Robinson.—I understand you wish to add something to your evidence?—Yes. In reference to the water supply, I would not wish that there should be any misapprehension from what Mr. M'Caffrey said. There is no reason to apprehend in the world that there is anything injurious in our pumps. That is simply impossible, as there is no sewer or sewers near the wells. I think his observations referred to a well in low ground. There are no impurities in the water as far as my rough analysis would lead me to form an opinion—nothing except lime to a most prodigious extent. There is nothing about the supply except that you are drinking simply lime mixed with water. Our wells are very deep—two of them something over sixty-five feet. I am not quite sure, but it must be something near that; judging from my own pump I think it must be that depth. It is impossible that these pumps could be contaminated in any way except something is thrown into the wells from above. The supply is, however, I must say, very imperfect and by no means continual in hot weather; but we have not suffered in that respect this year as yet. Last summer we were at a standstill altogether. I may mention that the town is an exceedingly healthy one, and has a singularly low death-rate.

160. In the event of your becoming the sanitary authority, do you think if you had an increase of the funds in consequence of an extension of the boundary you would apply the additional income so obtained to the improvement of the water supply?—I should advise such a course, certainly.

161. Mr. Abraham.—And I would go in for that too.

[The inquiry then terminated.]

BALLINASLOE—2ND OCTOBER, 1879.

(Before Mr. H. A. Robinson.)

Mr. Edward B. Stack examined.

1. You are the Town Clerk of Ballinasloe?—Yes.

2. Do you hold any other appointment under the Town Commissioners?—I am Clerk of the Gas Company. I am fifteen years connected with the Town Council.

3. Were you residing in Ballinasloe before that?—A short time.

4. Under what Act is it constituted?—The Towns Improvement Act of 1854.

5. Was it under any Act previous to that?—Yes; the 9th Geo. IV.

6. In what respect did the boundary of the 9th of Geo. IV. differ from the present?—I think it was a smaller boundary.

7. Do you know in what way exactly it differed?—Well, Garbally House was excluded under the old Act—now it is included.

8. What was the original boundary?—This is a copy of it (produced).

9. Since the town came under the Towns Improvement Act has there been any extension?—No.

10. What is the area of the town?—4,326a. 15p.

11. Does it include entire townlands?—It takes in fourteen whole townlands, and portions of some.

12. It goes right through Garbally demesne?—Yes.

13. What is the population?—In 1871, it was 4,619.

14. Then you are not the urban sanitary authority?—No.

15. From your knowledge of the trade of the town, would you say it is increasing—would you say it is increasing in population?—It has increased during the past ten years.

16. Will the census of 1881 show an increase, do you think?—I think not.

17. What is the valuation of the township?—£9,809 5s.

18. On how much of that is the full rate assessed?—On £3,800, and the balance the one-fourth.

19. What does your full rate produce?—£360 18s. 1d.

20. What is the full rate?—1s.

21. You have always struck the full rate?—Yes; since 1874.

22. What other source of income have you, besides fines from Petty Sessions Court and dog tax?—We get a majority of Petty Sessions fines.

23. Have you any works?—We have gasworks.

24. When were they commenced?—They were started in 1841 by shareholders. They were, however, bought out from time to time, and the only one who has any money in it now is Lord Clancarty. The Commissioners, who have been managing it, out of the profits arising from the gasworks, bought out the shareholders.

25. Is the town well lighted?—Yes; with forty-seven lamps, lighted at all seasons of the year when the night requires it.

26. It is not restricted to particular months, as is the case in some towns?—No.

27. Is the town divided into wards?—No.

28. How many Commissioners are there?—Fifteen.

29. In what electoral division is it?—Portion in the county Galway, in the electoral divisions of Ballinasloe, Creagh and Kilcooley (Roscommon).

30. The entire of the portion south of the river is not in the Creagh division?—No. All west of the river is in the county Galway; all east of the river in Roscommon.

31. Would the extension relate to the replies to our queries and into another electoral division?—No.

32. How far does the electoral division of Ballinasloe extend on the south?—I don't know, but it is a long distance—miles.

33. And on the north?—I am not quite sure.

34. Have you the area and valuation of these electoral divisions?—Yes.

35. Give them, please?—Creagh, 6,383a. 2r. 3p.; valuation, £4,730 1s.; Ballinasloe, 7,872a. 2r. 34p.; valuation, £9,973 17s.

36. Do you know the population of Creagh?—1,938.

37. And of Ballinasloe?—6,812.

38. Do you know the poor rates?—No; I do not.

39. Do you know of any special sanitary rate having been struck?—No; there has been no special rate for sanitary purposes.

40. Are any sanitary works carried on in your town?—No; except a small thing.

41. Are they paid for out of the general rate of the union?—Yes.

42. Do you know the county cess?—I think it was 10½d. or 10¾d.—that is my impression—for the half year.

43. Have the Commissioners ever considered the question of becoming the sanitary authority?—Yes; they would like it, but according to the Act of Parliament they would require to pay the officers.

44. Had they that in view—the desire of becoming the sanitary authority—in asking for this extension?—No.

45. Are sanitary improvements required in the town?—The town is in a tolerably good state, so far as that is concerned.

46. Are there any improvements the Commissioners would carry out if they had an increased income?—I don't know.

47. I understand the Commissioners do not ask this two-mile extension because they want increased income, but rather because they wish to have a better defined boundary?—They think the boundary is too irregular, and that the people living outside derive benefits from being near the town, for which they ought fairly to pay.

48. Do they consider that people living two miles out, derive benefits from the town?—Yes.

49. Do they think that it is the people living outside who support the town?—Of course they have an influence on the town.

50. Were the Commissioners aware when they were seeking this extension that they were proposing what would only give them a very small increase of income, probably only £8 or £10?—Well, indeed, my own opinion was that it would only be about £10, but the opinion of the gentleman moving in the matter was that there would be £50.

51. This proposed extension would not, I presume, enable them to carry out any improvements they cannot do now?—I think not, they could become the sanitary authority by putting the Local Government Board in motion.

52. Has the question of becoming the authority over the roads ever been discussed?—It has been spoken of.

53. Is it the opinion of the Board they will be likely to seek it hereafter?—I don't think so.

54. Have you ever heard the opinion of the ratepayers on the subject?—No, I have not.

55. Have you heard the opinion of the people outside as to extension?—Well, there are so few to be brought in.

56. How many would it bring in?—Well, I cannot say exactly, but I can give you an idea. There are two tolerably good houses.

57. Would it bring in any persons qualified to vote?—Yes.

58. Are any buildings going on outside the town?—No.

59. Is the town itself extending?—Not very much. A few years ago some four or five very good houses were put up.

60. I should have asked you to read the conclusion of the Commissioners so as to have it on the notes?—

"That after examining the boundary map of Ballinasloe, the Town Commissioners are of opinion that the present boundary is a most irregular one, and believe that the more equitable mode of defining same would be by a circle drawn [illegible] from the centre of the town, and extending two miles from thence."

BALLINASLOE. Mr. Edward S. Black.

The Right Hon. the Earl of Clancarty examined.

The Right Hon. the Earl of Clancarty.

61. What is your view on the subject of the proposed extension?—I am the Chairman of the Board of Town Commissioners, and I did not know the question was to be raised until I heard some account of it some days ago. I was, in fact, not made aware that the meeting was to be held, and, consequently, I was not here, so that I have only been able within the last few moments to gather the views of those who were here. But in my opinion, the question of the alteration of the boundary was answered in the negative—that there was no necessity for it—and I do not myself see that there is any necessity for it. I do not see that there is any public work being done by the Town Commissioners, and none of the work we [illegible] has been taken from us. If we had any extra work to do there might be reason for altering the boundary, which has existed, I think, since the passing of the Towns Improvement Act, or since its adoption by this town. I must say I do not see any special reason for altering it now. Besides, if there were grounds stated on which it seemed necessary to have such a change effected, and that those grounds were presented to the Government there is power, under the provisions of the Towns Improvement Act, enabling us to have it done. It would make much difference to me personally. I pay heavily towards the taxes of the town at present.

Mr. Thomas Carroll examined.

Mr. Thomas Carroll.

62. The extension of the boundaries was first suggested by me. My first reason was the belief that those who would be brought in by this extension derived exceptional advantages from their being near the town. They frequent the town almost every day. These people have the benefit of the markets, and derive the great advantage of the high prices they get [illegible] for all their marketable produce in the town. The imposition of a tax would only result in [illegible]. Another reason is the fact of the very great irregularity of the boundary, and the necessity of extending it over a larger area, so that the consideration may be [illegible], lightened on the townspeople, who, for thirty years, have been at the maximum rate of 1s. in the pound—never less than that. If the people living outside are asked to contribute towards reducing this maximum rate, it will be only just and right. There is another reason why I would be an advocate. The corn [illegible] [illegible], that we would in all probability increase our population, so as to bring it up to the limit necessary to [illegible] to have the sanitary laws carried out by the Town Commissioners.

63. Are you aware that it does not depend upon your being up to the number of 6,000 to enable you to obtain those powers; and that, under the seventh section of the Act, you may, by a provisional order, obtain the jurisdiction in sanitary matters?—I did not know that.

64. Are there any improvements which you think you would carry out if you had those increased powers?—I think there is one very great improvement, suggested some time ago by our chairman, Lord Clancarty—the adoption of water works.

65. Yes; but that is a sanitary matter. Is there anything under your own jurisdiction, in the way of lighting say, that you would be inclined to carry out?—No; unless we had the sanitary work in our own hands.

66. Then you don't propose to confer additional benefit on them, but to tax the people whom you bring in for the benefits they receive at the present?—Precisely.

67. And you consider that they do derive exceptional advantages from their proximity to the town?—Yes.

68. But does not the money that they get for their produce find its way into the pockets of the tax-payers of the town?—No.

69. The town is not self-supporting?—No, but there is a mutual advantage; but at the same time I think that the advantages are greater on those outside and within the limits of the proposed extension than their appropriation of the advantages the town derives from those outside.

70. You think the advantage tends on your own side?—Yes; that is, it is conferred to a larger extent on those outside by us.

71. What would you say are the advantages they derive?—They have the light of forty or forty-two lamps, lighted seven or eight months in the year.

72. Are the markets held daily or less?—The [illegible] [illegible] when the people bring in their marketable produce, except on [illegible] as on other [illegible].

73. Your chief reason, I take it, for what you think is your reason for wishing this extension, is that it would be the means of lightening the taxation of the people within the town?—Yes.

74. Is there any municipal debt at present contracted by the Town Commissioners?—Yes, we are in debt.

75. To what extent?—Mr. [illegible].—£1,[illegible]. There is £1,[illegible] due to Lord Clancarty—having for his security a second claim on the property. There is then due the Bank of Ireland, account No. 2, £[illegible], having as security a first claim on the property. The overdraft in bank on current account, No. 1, is £[illegible] [illegible]s. [illegible]d.; credit, No. 2 account, £[illegible] [illegible]s. [illegible]d.; leaving £[illegible] [illegible]s. [illegible]d., due on current accounts.

Examination of Mr. Carroll resumed.

76. Are there any building operations likely to extend outside of the town boundary?—I am not aware.

77. Is there sufficient land available within the present limits for building for some time to come?—Yes.

78. And do the people who carry on business in the town mostly live in their places of business, or do they live outside?—They generally live in their places of business.

79. The lands you propose to include by the two-mile extension are they mostly owned by people residing in the town?—No; on the contrary, they are nearly all held by people living outside the present boundary.

80. Have you considered what the annual increment in the town funds would be by this extension?—Not much. It would not be more than £50 a year.

81. There appears to me—looking at the Ordnance map—to be a large amount of bog land in the districts

Ballinasloe, Oct. [illegible], 187[illegible].

Mr. Thomas Carroll.

you propose to bring in, have you made any calculation of the acreage or valuation of the proposed added area?—No.

82. Are you in favour of this hard and fast boundary of a circle, or would you not prefer to limit a definition by bounds or something of that sort?—I would prefer a circle.

83. Are you aware that such a hard and fast boundary is very inconvenient; for instance, it may cut through a man's house—you might have a man's dining-room in and another part of the building outside the limits?—In that case I would take in the entire house. I would take a circle unless it was to be defined with by a house.

84. Were you a Commissioner when the town came under the Towns Improvement Act?—I was a Commissioner at the time, the Commissioners applied to the Local Government for the adoption of the Act under which they at present act. At the election that ensued I did not become a Commissioner.

85. Were you aware what steps the Commissioners took to determine the boundaries of the town?—No; for I did not become a Town Commissioner.

86. Are you aware that the Commissioners now could obtain by Provisional Order the sanitary powers and control over the roads, lighting, &c.?—We are not at all satisfied with the execution of the sanitary law; it would be better under the supervision of the Town Commissioners, and it would be a great advantage to the township too if we got control over the roads.

87. You are of opinion, then, that the entire sanitary of the town of Ballinasloe should be vested in the Town Commissioners?—Yes.

88. Is there any probability of the Commissioners applying [illegible] to the Local Government Board for them which the [illegible] section of the Public Health Act of last session gives you?—The matter was under consideration, and since then the application was made to the Board of Guardians, and I think they would [illegible] as to [illegible] the [illegible] of the sanitary authority, but would not give to the Board of the money. The Board of Town Commissioners [illegible] and are still of opinion that it would be a great privilege if we had the sanitary laws in our control.

89. Then you would be in favour of having the larger area on which to work your plan?—Yes.

90. Have you any property outside the present boundary?—None.

91. Have you had an opportunity of ascertaining the feelings of the ratepayers?—It has been talked of since the receipt of your communication, and I have not heard that there was any one who was indisposed to adopt the project. I heard that Mr. [illegible] would oppose it, and Mr. [illegible]. I may remark that the Commissioners are not remunerated.

Mr. John Ward.

Mr. John Ward examined.

92. Are you a Town Commissioner?—Yes.

93. How long have you resided in Ballinasloe?—For the last twenty years.

94. Do you believe the town is increasing or diminishing in population?—I believe it has increased for the last seven or eight years, but I think there was a decrease before that.

95. Do you think the census of 1881 will show an increase or decrease as compared with that of 1871?—I think an increase.

96. Are there any building operations going on within the town?—Not many.

97. Are there a better class of houses being built than formerly?—The improvement is in that direction.

98. Are there any unoccupied houses in the town at present?—Very few.

99. Were you present when the question of extension was discussed at the first instance?—Yes, I was.

100. When the resolution was [illegible]?—Yes.

101. The Commissioners then were unanimously in favour of having the boundary as it was?—Yes, not having that map before us. I for one suggested that the line was certain, and on that condition I agreed, but had I known it was drawn, not only in that irregular manner, but seemingly partial manner, I would not have agreed to it.

102. Are you aware of the inconvenience of a circular hard and fast line?—I am—of cutting through houses.

103. Or through a holding—through a field?—I don't think that is a great inconvenience—going across a field, but it certainly would be going through houses.

104. Do you contemplate a considerable increase of income by this extension?—Yes, in some respect.

105. To what extent?—I would say between £30 and £40. I was never before called last Tuesday when our present boundaries were, I always thought our boundary was circular.

106. Were you aware of the 7th section of the Public Health Act enabling you to acquire by provisional order the sanitary authority?—I am now.

107. Were you aware of it at the time of the meeting?—No.

108. Then am I to understand it is for the two purposes of seeing the mains on the town that you favour the proposed extension?—Yes, and of equalising the boundary.

109. You heard the **evidence given by Mr. Carroll?** —Yes.

110. Do you concur with him?—Yes, and as to the desirability of having this Board the Sanitary Board I think it ought to be. I am a member of the Sanitary Board of which Lord Clancarty is chairman, and since that Act was passed we were paying 5d. in the pound for everything to act, and there was nothing at all done, the town was neglected. I again and again called the attention of the Committee to the [illegible].

111. What was the nature of the sanitary improvements most required?—Sewerage. The sewerage was neglected—[illegible] of [illegible], absence of [illegible] and so forth.

Mr. [illegible] Larkin.

Mr. [illegible] Larkin examined.

112. You are a member of the Town Board?—Yes, I was elected on the last day, and I have really nothing to say in addition to what has been put forward. I endorse the expressions of Mr. Ward, and Mr. Carroll. They speak my sentiments.

113. You have made no calculation as to the probable number of voters to be brought in?—No. I was struck on the last day when that map was produced, by the inequality of the boundary, and I saw that some people were left out and that ought to be brought in.

Mr. M'C[illegible] examined.

BALLYCASTLE. Oct. [illegible], 18[illegible]. Mr. [illegible] M'C[illegible].

114. Are you in favour of extension?—Yes. I reside in the town.

115. To the extent proposed by the Commissioners, are you in favour of their suggestion?—No; I think the electoral division would be a good boundary for sanitary purposes.

116. You are aware the Rural Sanitary Authority can assess any district they like for sanitary purposes as a contributory district?—Yes.

Mr. F[illegible] J. H[illegible] examined.

Mr. F[illegible] J. H[illegible].

117. What is your view on the subject of the proposed extension?—I refused to accede to the proposal on principle, because when the Commissioners got your queries they decided that an extension was not necessary, and I did not wish to undo that—in fact I did not think it was legal to do so, but as an individual I would be glad of an extension if there was any benefit to be derived from it, but I do not see that there is.

Captain Thornhill examined.

Captain Thornhill.

118. I have a place of business in the town [illegible] and I keep a place outside.

119. This extension would include the place where you live?—Yes; I believe it, but I do not [illegible] what the extension is.

120. It is a hard and fast circle of one mile from the centre?—I cannot understand what [illegible] purpose it would be to [illegible] the boundary.

121. They don't say they propose to confer any benefit, but [illegible] for the advantages you are enjoying, and for which you contribute nothing, so far as your premises outside are concerned?—[illegible] I cannot see what benefit I derive.

122. You come into the town?—Yes.

123. And spend your money in it?—Yes.

124. Do you sell anything in it?—[illegible]

125. You consider then that the advantages [illegible] of it?—Yes.

126. And you object to the [illegible]?—Yes.

127. Would any improvements in the town be a benefit to you [illegible]?

128. If the town was well lighted and [illegible]

129. Lord C[illegible].—I wish to say a word or two. There is a great deal of [illegible], and there are a great many [illegible] I am sorry to say, [illegible] would not be benefited by any increase in taxation, unless the extension which would bring [illegible]. Another instance is this, Mr. Lancaster's house is on one side of the [illegible], and Mr. [illegible]'s is on the other; Mr. [illegible]'s would be taxed and Mr. Lancaster's would not. I cannot see why that should be. [illegible] Mr. Lancaster's house would not be benefited [illegible]. There would [illegible] brought in [illegible]. As I said before I am against any extension of the present boundary, I [illegible] that there is any necessity for it.

The inquiry terminated.

BALLYMONEY—18TH JULY, 1879.

BALLYMONEY. July 18, 1879.

(Before Mr. H. A. ROBINSON.)

Mr. THOMAS HAMILTON examined.

Mr. Thomas Hamilton.

1. Mr. ROBINSON.—You are Clerk of the Union and also Town Clerk?—I am.

2. How long have you held those positions?—I have been thirteen years Clerk of the Union, and seventeen years Town Clerk.

3. Was the Towns Improvement Act adopted for all purposes?—No, only for lighting and cleansing.

4. Do you know when the town came under the operation of that Act?—It was adopted on the 20th of May, 1856.

5. And it was then that the present boundary of Ballymoney was defined?—It was.

6. And with the consent of the ratepayers?—Yes.

7. How far does the boundary extend to the north?—About a quarter of a mile.

8. To the south how far does it extend?—Rather more than a quarter of a mile.

9. And to the east?—About half a mile.

10. And to the west?—About a quarter of a mile.

11. Were you the clerk to the Town Commissioners when the town first came under the operation of the Towns Improvement Act?—I was not.

12. Are you aware what it was which prompted the Town Commissioners to adopt the boundary which now exists?—No, I am not.

13. Does the present boundary sub-divide townlands, or does it include whole townlands?—It cuts townlands. You have the whole of Glebe townland in it; you have portion of Ballybrakes, portion of Drumahoe, a portion of Millquarter, and the remainder a portion of Townparks.

14. What is the area of the present boundary?—About 170 acres.

15. What is the population of Ballymoney?—Under 3,000—3,[illegible] I think at the last census. I should think there would be an increase of 200 since that was taken.

16. Is it your opinion then, when the next census is taken there will be found to be an increase of the population as compared with the last?—I think there will.

17. Is Ballymoney a thriving town?—I may say it is.

18. Is there any desire to build houses outside the present boundary?—Not very much.

19. The building that is going on in Ballymoney is going on within the present municipal limits?—It is.

20. What is the valuation—I will take the total valuation first?—£6,[illegible] 15s.

21. Can you now give me the valuation on which the one-fourth rate is struck?—£[illegible] 3s.

22. And on the balance of £5,[illegible] 12s. the full rate is struck?—Yes.

BALLYMONEY. July 24, 1879. — Sir Thomas Boulton.

24. Are there fairs in Ballymoney?—There are.

25. How many in the year?—Three fairs, and in addition to that there is a good cattle market on the first and third Thursday of each month.

26. Do the people living outside the present boundary come in and out from a distance, for the purpose of attending those markets?—Yes, in large numbers.

27. From outside the present boundary?—Yes.

28. From what distance outside the present boundary do they come in—do the people living out a mile all round derive advantages from the proximity of the town of Ballymoney?—Yes, certainly they do.

29. Are the lands more valuable on that account within a radius of say a mile?—I would not say that.

30. Can you tell me what the municipal rates for the last five years have been?—I can give you them for the last three years.

31. That will do?—In 1878 the municipal rate was 1s.; in 1877, 6d., and in 1876, 6d.

32. And what was the poor rate?—The poor rate for 1878 was 1s. Do you wish me to include in that the sanitary rate?

33. No, kindly keep the sanitary rate separate?—The rate for sanitary purposes in that year was 7d.

34. And what was the sanitary rate for?—For making new sewers.

35. What was the contributory district upon which that rate was struck?—Townparks and Glebe.

36. Then it was struck over a considerable portion of the radius outside the present municipal limits?—It was.

37. Now as to Townparks. Are there any buildings in the townland of Townparks? Is the townland of Townparks much built over?—Not very much.

38. Is it mostly arable land?—Mostly.

39. And the portion of Townparks which is outside the present municipal limits, is it much built over?—Very little.

40. Will you now please give me the poor-rate for 1877 and the following years?—The poor-rate for 1877 was 1s. and the sanitary-rate 6d., and in 1878 it was 1s., with a sanitary-rate of 4½d.

41. What was the county cess for the same years?—The county cess in 1877 was 2s.; in 1878, 2s. 6d.; and in 1879, 2s. 1d.

42. When our queries were sent down to you, were they submitted to your Board?—They were.

43. Was there a special meeting to consider the question, or did it come before an ordinary meeting of the Board?—I fancy it came before an ordinary meeting of the Board, as we generally have very nearly the whole of the members present at all the meetings.

44. And what was the opinion they expressed in reference to the queries?—Their opinion was that no change in the boundaries was required.

45. Was that a unanimous opinion?—It was.

46. Was any resolution passed on the subject?—I don't think there was.

47. Has the boundary since first formed ever been altered?—No, it has not.

48. Then the boundary adopted when you came under the Act is the existing boundary?—It is.

49. Can you give me a description of that boundary? Would not your first minute show it?—I believe the way in which that boundary was first laid out was that there was a small committee of the Commissioners appointed to lay out the boundary, and they gave in a report to the ratepayers of Ballymoney, and I believe it was on the recommendation of that committee that those boundaries were adopted.

50. And the Town Commissioners are of opinion that no extension is required?—Yes.

51. Is it their opinion that all the buildings likely to be carried on by people who have their business in the town is likely to be within the present municipal limits?—Yes, for many years.

52. Can you give me the names of the townlands at present included in the electoral division?—Yes, they are, [illegible], [illegible], [illegible], [illegible], Newhill, Greenville, Prospect, Ballyratrick, Drumaquillagh, Ballymoney, Carnany (Lower), Townparks, Ballybrakes, Millquarter, Bravallen, Lislagan (Lower), and Glebe.

53. Can you give me the total valuation of the electoral division?—£[illegible].

54. Can you say if it is the opinion of your Board that the electoral division would be too large for a new municipal boundary for Ballymoney? In other words, do you think it would be the opinion of the Town Commissioners of Ballymoney that the boundary of the electoral division would be too large for the town?—I am sure it is their opinion that it would.

55. But the Commissioners are at the same time of opinion that the people who live on the most remote part of the electoral division derive advantages from their proximity to Ballymoney?—Oh yes, certainly.

56. Have the Town Commissioners ever considered the question of becoming the urban sanitary authority?—They have.

57. And is it their opinion that it would be desirable and advantageous to the town of Ballymoney that they should become the urban sanitary authority?—They are of opinion that such would not be desirable. There are three Guardians for the electoral division of Ballymoney, and they think that their interests are very well looked after.

58. Have the Town Commissioners considered the question of obtaining the control over the roads?—No, they have not.

59. Do they think for the money they pay in county cess that they get adequate value for it from the Grand Jury?—No.

60. Has the question ever been discussed by the Board?—Yes. It has been discussed by the Board, and they are of opinion that they don't get a due proportion of the amount they pay, but I don't know that they ever formally considered the question of taking the roads into their own hands.

61. Are there any buildings houses outside the present municipal boundary?—Yes, a few.

62. In which direction?—Indeed upon reflection I don't think there are any.

63. Is there any tendency to build inside the municipal boundary in one direction more than another?—There is certainly. In Glebe, there is quite a number of new houses being built there in consequence of leases being given in perpetuity, but outside that there is very little building.

64. Do you know the town well?—I was born here.

65. Do you think the boundary large enough for the requirements of the town for many years to come?—Yes, I do.

66. And are you of opinion that no extension is desirable?—I don't think so.

67. And that such would not be likely to be beneficial to the town in future?—No.

Mr. Thomas M'Elderry examined.

Ballymoney, July 18, 1878. Mr. Thomas M'Elderry.

68. Mr. Robertson.—You are Chairman of the Town Commissioners, and also of the Board of Guardians?—Yes.

69. And I presume you are well acquainted with the town?—Yes.

70. You have lived here, I suppose, for a considerable number of years?—Yes, I have.

71. Do you know the present municipal boundary?—Yes, I do.

72. And do you think it large enough?—I do.

73. Were you present when the question which was sent down by us to your Board were discussed?—Yes, I was.

74. Did you move in the matter?—Well, the Board discussed the matter, and we arrived at the conclusion that there was no necessity for any change as far as we were concerned.

75. Are there schools in this town?—Yes, we have a number of schools in the town.

76. And I suppose the people living in the districts for a mile round send their children into your schools?—Yes, especially in the Model school.

77. Is the town well lighted?—Pretty well.

78. With gas?—Yes.

79. Are there fairs and markets in the town?—Yes.

80. And I suppose the people living in the districts around the town bring in their produce to the town and dispose of it?—Yes.

81. Is it not, therefore, an advantage to them to have the town of Ballymoney kept well cleansed and lighted?—I think they don't see that exactly.

82. But do you see it?—Well, it is a question upon which I would not like to say much. On the one side we have Coleraine, six miles off, and the people in that part of the country desire to take goods from our market.

83. Because, I suppose, Coleraine is a larger market?—I think our market is as good a market as Coleraine.

84. You don't think that the people living outside the town derive sufficient advantages that they should be called upon to pay town rates?—I don't think it desirable that they should be called upon to pay town rates.

85. Are there any improvements required in the town which the Commissioners are unable to carry out for want of funds?—I think the only improvement that is very pressing is a supply of pure water.

86. If there was a larger valuation, and the rates coming into the hands of the Town Commissioners, larger in amount than at present, do you think that there would be any improvements you would effect?—I don't think there are any improvements required.

87. They strike the full rate, now, do they not?—This last year there was only six-pence rate.

88. Do you know the electoral division?—Yes.

89. You heard what I asked Mr. Hamilton here, as to whether the Commissioners would be favourable to adopting it as the municipal boundary—do you think that would be desirable?—I don't think it would.

90. You think it would be too large?—Yes.

91. And you are afraid you would be compelled to give the people living in Ballymoney, Ballygobbin, and those other townlands, the advantage of lighting?—I think we would. Since the sanitary matters have been put in the hands of the Board of Guardians, I think there is less necessity for it.

92. Are there any people having businesses in town, who have residences outside the present municipal boundary?—I don't know of any. There are a few farmers in the neighbourhood who deal in the markets, but none who have business places in the town.

93. Then there are no villa residences outside the present boundary?—No, we have none.

94. And if the electoral division were to be adopted for the municipal boundary, would that bring the population within these boundaries up to 6,000?—I am not aware what the population is. I am sure it would bring it over 6,000.

95. And still you don't think that is desirable?—I think not.

96. And the Town Commissioners are of opinion that the sanitary work is perfectly well managed by the Guardians?—Well I think it is only right to say that there was a division of opinion among the Town Commissioners at the time that the sanitary matters were taken out of their hands. On thinking over the matter, a good many of the Commissioners are very well satisfied with the arrangement, because there is a moiety of the poor rate that we get back from the landlords, whereas we don't get back any of the town rate.

97. In reference to the sanitary rate struck by the Guardians, one half is paid by the landlord, and the other half by the tenant, and if a municipal rate was struck it would be all paid by the tenant?—Yes.

98. Is there any other matter upon which you would wish to tender evidence?—I don't think so.

99. You are of opinion with Mr. Hamilton that the present boundary includes land enough to be built over for the next two years?—I am quite sure of it unless something goes on that we are not aware of at present.

Mr. Andrew Todd examined.

Mr. Andrew Todd.

100. Mr. Robertson.—You have heard the views expressed by Mr. Hamilton and Mr. M'Elderry, does your opinion as to the questions touched upon by them coincide with theirs?—Yes.

101. Have you lived long in Ballymoney?—Thirteen or fourteen years.

102. Do you consider it an increasing town?—I do.

103. Are there any manufactures peculiar to Ballymoney?—Not any immediately in the town. There is a spinning mill about two miles outside the town.

104. Were you present at the meeting of the Commissioners at which the question of the boundaries was considered?—Yes, I think I was.

105. And you coincide with the views already expressed?—Yes. I have a strong opinion that we are in want of a good water supply.

106. And would you like to take that matter out of the hands of the Guardians?—No.

Mr. James Cramsey examined.

Mr. James Cramsey.

107. Mr. Robertson.—Your views I suppose coincide with the evidence that has been given by the previous witnesses?—Yes.

Ballybay.
July 25, 1879.

Mr. Thomas M'[illegible].

BALLYBAY—25th JULY, 1879.

(Before Mr. C. P. Cotton, c.e.)

Mr. Thomas M'[illegible] examined.

1. You are Town Clerk of Ballybay?—Yes.

2. How long have you been Town Clerk?—Since the town came under the Act.

3. What is the area of the town?—Something under seventy acres.

4. You have given it in the return to us as twenty-six, but I think that is a mistake?—That is a mistake. I had no opportunity of ascertaining the area until we got this map (produced), from which I took the answer I have given you now. I don't think it could be just so large as I have said—seventy acres.

5. It will be about sixty acres?—Yes, about sixty acres.

6. What is the population of the town?—At the last census in 1871 it was 1,714.

7. Has it been increasing since that?—I think so. I think there has been considerable increase since, judging from the number of new buildings erected for the poorer or labouring class of the town, I would say there has been an increase.

8. Are there any buildings erected outside your boundary?—No, I think not.

9. Where have the new buildings been within the last ten years?—From Corrybrannan bridge there has been a considerable number of buildings, and a number have been erected at the end of the Main street near the bridge. The fowl market has been built and a very excellent building has been erected there.

10. What class of houses have been built?—A superior class of houses.

11. Of what value for rating purposes?—About £[illegible].

12. Has there been any buildings above the railway station?—Yes; the opening north of the railway station has been filled up. Some three houses have been built there, and at the fair green, the old shambles have been knocked down and a new range of buildings have been erected where the shambles stood.

13. What is the valuation of the town?—The valuation is £[illegible] 10s.

14. It is increasing?—Yes; in 1871 it was £2,417 10s. showing an increase of £167 since then.

15. It is not very much?—No; I may mention that this new range of buildings is not included in the valuation. I have not got this year's certified copy of the tenemental valuation yet.

16. You have no wards?—No.

17. What electoral division is the town in?—In the Ballybay electoral division.

18. What number of Commissioners have you?—Nine.

19. How many ratepayers are there in the town who have a right to vote?—One hundred and forty-four on the last burgess roll.

20. How many are qualified to be Commissioners if elected?—About thirty.

21. Will you give me the rates struck since 1874?—In 1874 there was 10d.; in 1875, 10d.; in 1876, 9d.; in 1877, 8d.; and in 1878, 8d.

22. Give me the poor rate and county cess for each of those years?—In 1874 the poor rate was 11d., in 1875, 1s. 8d.; in 1876, 1s.; in 1877, 1s. 8d.; and in 1878, 1s. 6d.

23. What is the county cess for each of those years?—It averages about 10½d. in the pound for each half year.

24. That is, the two half years together make 1s. 9d. a year?—Yes, or 1s. 9d.

25. Perhaps you know what the levy this year was? It was a fraction over 10d.

26. Then 1s. 6d. would be a fair average?—Yes.

27. Have the Commissioners considered the question whether they wish for extension or not?—They have had a meeting.

28. Have they adopted a resolution?—Yes.

29. When was it adopted?—There was a meeting yesterday but there was an informal resolution adopted previous to the return being filled up. There was an informal meeting and there was a resolution which was not written on the minutes.

30. What was the resolution adopted yesterday?—It was unanimously in favour of a moderate extension of the boundary. Some of the Commissioners wished for a greater extension than others, but after a discussion there was a give and take compromise agreed upon.

31. How many Commissioners were present at that meeting?—There were seven.

32. Can you describe what that moderate extension was?—It commences at Corrybrannan bridge and goes about 260 yards along the south side of the [illegible] road (the road leading to [illegible]), then across to the [illegible] road at a lane; along that lane and on to the lake; then along the northeast side of the lake for two fields beyond the mill river; then northward to the Clones road along the southern boundary of the Clones road for 100 yards; then north by the base of the railway, and along the river to the [illegible] stream for a distance of 600 feet, and then to a lane leading into the Monaghan road including one field in width from the road; then north along a lane for a distance of 100 yards, and then in a south-westerly direction to the [illegible] road, and then to [illegible] stream again at 300 yards away from the public road; then south along a fence for 150 yards, and then along a fence including a large demesne field to the railway; thence by a stream to the lake; thence along the north-west side of the lake to the Corrybrannan bridge.

33. Have the Commissioners considered how much land that would add?—No.

34. Or what value it would add?—No; but it was not so much for the additional value as to bring the different approaches to the town under the jurisdiction of the Commissioners for the purpose of carrying out the market regulations, and also for the purpose of gaining something from the police force.

35. If it was for that purpose why should they not

go further? — There seemed to be unwillingness to tax people, and to create ill-feeling on their minds, which would naturally follow their being taxed.

36. When was the Improvement Act adopted? — In November, 1870.

37. Was it adopted wholly or only in part? — Wholly.

38. How is the town lighted? — With gas.

39. By a company? — Yes.

40. And you make an agreement with the company? — Yes; 8s. 4d. per 1,000 feet. That was the contract price last year.

41. I suppose it was the same price to the public? — Yes.

42. How many lamps are there? — I think it is nineteen we have now.

43. What was the amount paid for gas last year? — £41 0s. 11d.

44. Was that the gas bill for the year? — Yes; and the cost of lighting. There was something for erecting a shed; but that is the cost of the lighting and incidentals.

45. How is the town supplied with water? — The town is supplied with water by pumps.

46. Is the supply sufficient and of good quality? — There are complaints about the quantity.

47. The pumps are in charge of the Guardians? — Yes; they are the sanitary authority.

48. Are there complaints about the quality? — About the quality of some there are complaints.

49. Are there enough pumps? — They are sufficiently numerous, but they don't give sufficient water. We have only two pumps that are really good for the supply of water in the town.

50. And are they of good quality? — Yes; the water is of good quality.

51. Has there been any talk of doing anything more in the way of supplying water? — Yes; it was under consideration to apply to have some additional sinking done to increase the supply of water.

52. How is the town drained? — By sewers.

53. Are there enough of them and in good order? — The sewerage is pretty fair, with the exception of one portion of the town, beyond the railway bridge on the north side of the town.

54. It is insufficiently drained? — Yes.

55. Have the Guardians ever been asked to do anything in that way that they have not done? — Their attention has been called to the defective state of the drainage there, and I believe they did something to remedy it.

56. Do you know whether any of the 1s. 6d. poor rate for last year was a special rate for sanitary purposes? — I think there was 2d. in the pound, or 1½d. or 1d. special.

57. You don't know the amount? — It was 1d.

58. What was the 1d. for — was it for the payment of sanitary officers? — I think so; but they have never done any sanitary work for which the special rate was struck. I think there was a sanitary rate struck for the sinking of the pump at Corrybrannan.

59. Do you know whether it was struck upon any special district or over the whole of the electoral division? — I think it was over the whole electoral division.

60. Do the Commissioners do anything in the way of scavenging? — They do; they cleanse the town.

61. You have not struck the entire of your rate of late years, so I suppose you don't want any more money to spend in the town? — The Commissioners contracted with the Board of Works for a loan of £800.

Ballybay, July [illegible], 1879.

Mr. Thomas [illegible].

62. For what purpose? — To pay the expenses incurred in the construction of new footpaths in the town at a cost of something over £400.

63. Did the Board of Works lend the money to pay off a loan? — They did.

64. When was that? — About three years ago the Commissioners contracted for a loan of £800, but they have only drawn £400 to pay off the debt incurred by the footpaths. Having the privilege of borrowing they availed themselves of it.

65. But borrowing for the purpose of paying off a debt is very different from borrowing for the construction of works? — The works were constructed four or five years before the loan was obtained.

66. You have commenced to pay that off? — No; we don't commence to pay principal until May, 1881.

67. At what rate do you then pay it off? — We pay 5 per cent.

68. For how many years? — Until the money is paid off. I think it is twenty-five years.

69. Have the Commissioners ever considered whether they would wish to be the sanitary authority themselves? — They have discussed the matter, and the feeling of the Commissioners was that they were very well pleased at being relieved from the disagreeable duties in connexion with sanitary affairs.

70. They would rather not have the authority? — No; particularly as the Board of Guardians were pretty attentive to their suggestions. That is the feeling of the Board.

71. Do you know the feeling of the ratepayers of the town with regard to extension? — Yes; any I have spoken to were in favour of extension.

72. Such as you have described, or extension generally? — Extension generally.

73. Do you know the feeling of any of the people who are to be brought in? — The land that would be brought in by the proposed extension is in the occupation of residents in the town — it is all townparks.

74. Can you tell will the extension add to your voters' list? — Very slightly.

75. How many would you say at a guess? — I don't think the proposed extension would add a single voter to the list except Mrs. Leslie.

76. Have you considered the question yourself as to whether a larger extension would be desirable or not — I want your private opinion as a ratepayer of the town? — I would be in favour of a larger extension.

77. Even with that extension you would be left the smallest town in Ireland? — I would take in the four townlands of Derrynaloobinagh, Cashmeran, Corrybrannan, and Cornamucklaglass.

78. Is there any other townland you would take in? — No; those are all.

79. Cashmeran would run a long way off? — I have no desire to extend the town very far.

80. If you extend it so far as to take in the whole of a townland like Corrybrannan, why not take in Ballybay House? — I think there should be no objection to taking it in. I am not conversant with the boundary of the townlands out there, and my own idea was that the boundary should extend out on the Castleblayney road to the gate-house — about a short mile.

81. That is very nearly the townland boundary? — Yes; it is very much the same.

82. You would take in four townlands and the demesne? — Yes.

Mr. Benjamin [illegible], J.P., Chairman of the Town Commissioners, examined.

Mr. Benjamin [illegible], J.P.

83. What is the opinion of the Commissioners as regards the kind of extension they would desire? — [illegible] the boundary described.

84. Is that your own opinion, or would you be in favour of making a larger or smaller extension? — I would not be inclined for a larger extension, but it might give offence.

85. Do you think the one sketched out would be large enough? — I think it would meet the wants of the town at present.

86. What are the objects of the extension? — It was for the sanitary purposes principally. We found dangers were in the habit of getting outside the boundary to make [illegible] and escape the [illegible] of the

gation, as the Commissioners have no authority beyond the boundary.

87. Have you any market tolls?—Yes.

88. And they sell outside to escape the tolls?—Yes.

89. An extension of only a few hundred yards would not give you much more control?—It would add a good deal to the advantage of the town.

90. Would it add to your funds?—I think it would, as far as fines are concerned, on being convicted of selling outside the boundary.

91. If you only extend your radius 100 yards further on the road, it would appear as if the people had only to go 100 yards further out and escape you still. Is there any other reason—do you want to increase the funds of the town for any purpose?—No.

92. Is there anything you would do if you had more funds in the general improvement of the town?—No. We had in contemplation to get some accommodation for a butter and egg market at the rere of this court-house.

93. That is not a public necessity?—Well, it is. The butter and egg market is held on the street, which is a great obstruction on market and fair days.

94. Would you spend more money on keeping the town clean if you had it?—I don't know. We keep it pretty clean.

95. You spend as much as you want upon that work?—Yes.

96. Would you wish to be the sanitary authority?—No; I would not wish it. I found it very trouble-some when it was in the hands of the Commissioners.

97. Do you think the Guardians do their business fairly?—I think they do. They always attended to my letters.

98. What would you say to extending the boundary all round, taking in about three quarters of a mile, and including the five townlands named?—In my own opinion it would be an advantage. It would reduce the rate in the town.

99. And make the rates on the people outside something more?—Yes.

100. Of course you never discussed the question whether you wished to take charge of your own town or not?—Yes.

101. You were a Commissioner in 1871?—Yes.

102. What was the principle that guided them in forming the boundary then in that very contracted way?—I think it was, but it might give offence to make the boundary larger; but I understood from the arrangement that the boundary should be increased afterwards.

103. It was the general opinion that it would be increased?—Yes; that was the understanding of the Commissioners.

104. By making it so small at the commencement, you apparently did not shut out any one in particular?—No. Every one who owns land ... in the town.

Mr. John James M'Mahon examined.

105. I am a Commissioner. It was to disarm any opposition that might arise from the owner of the demesne being brought in that led to the adoption of the contracted boundary.

106. There was no bargain that the demesne was to be left out?—No, there was none, as far as I recollect.

107. What do you think yourself about the extension proposed?—I would extend the boundary to the five townlands mentioned.

108. What would be the value added by that?—I have no idea.

109. That would extend the valuation from £3,500 to £3,800?—Yes.

110. Would that be too much?—I think not.

111. What is your opinion as to the sanitary authority?—I think it would be better leave it as it is.

112. You think the guardians do the work fairly?—Yes.

113. Would you not be inclined with the increased boundary, to become the sanitary authority?—No, as long as the guardians do the work pretty fairly, I would be inclined to leave it to them.

114. Do you think you would raise more money on the increased area, or merely lower the rates in the town?—Unless we made a new market-house, we would not require more.

115. You don't require more for the lighting and cleansing of the town?—No.

116. That is all satisfactory?—Yes, and the reason for wishing extension is that our fairs go beyond our boundary a good deal.

117. And then they are out of your control?—That is the very reason. If a dispute occurred outside the boundary, our magistrates have no control. One horse fair goes beyond our boundary.

118. But you don't want any more money?—We don't want any more for ordinary purposes.

119. Do you know about the sanitary rate that was struck?—It was not much at any time.

120. What did they do with it?—Any rate struck lately, was for the payment of officials.

121. Have they constructed any drains, or done any work of that kind?—No. The only thing they have done is to make a pump.

122. I presume it had to be paid for?—Yes.

123. And it was paid for by the entire division?—Yes; I believe so.

124. Are any drains wanted to be constructed in the town?—Yes, there are some wanted. Dr. Burke was here four or five years ago, and reported that the town was very badly off for drains.

125. Have they been talking of making them?—No.

126. Have they been asked to make them?—No; we spoke about them, and they came and looked, but they have done nothing I heard of.

127. That is hardly doing the sanitary work satisfactorily?—It is only about a month or six weeks since we called their attention to the subject.

128. Have they not been asked before since 1874?—No, I think not; although Dr. Burke reported the town was very badly in need of drains, six or seven years ago.

129. You were the sanitary authority then?—We were.

130. Did you not do anything then?—We had not the means of doing it.

131. You have the means of doing it now, if you were the sanitary authority?—I am afraid not; not with our present rate.

132. But you have power to raise it, and you have only raised 6d.?—It would take a good deal more to construct drains through the town.

133. Do you expect that if the guardians took up that work, and spent a good deal of money on it, that it would be paid for by the entire electoral division?—They could lay it on as many townlands as they wished.

134. Do you expect it to be on the electoral division?—Yes.

135. Do you know the electoral division?—Yes.

136. Do you think it is too large to be the boundary of the town?—My own opinion is that it would not be a bit too large.

137. The acreage of the electoral division is 4,763, and the valuation £7,300?—We don't desire to extend it that much.

138. No, but the Parliamentary Committee thought that, if possible, the electoral divisions should be made the boundary of the towns?—We don't desire it.

Mr. WILLIAM M'KELVEY examined.

Mr. William M'Kelvey.

139. I am a Commissioner.

140. Would you be in favour of a considerable extension or a larger one?—I would be in favour of the proposed boundary that has been marked out and submitted by Mr. M'Henry. I think that would suit the purposes.

141. What are the purposes?—The extension of our market, especially our fair.

142. Which road is it that the town fair extends along?—Both the Monaghan road and the Keady road.

143. Then extending the boundary over 200 yards or so, would that give you control over the horse fair?—I would say it would, with very few exceptions; there might be a very few go beyond that; but that is the extent of the market ground, and as the Commissioners [illegible] to exhibition there, our cattle [illegible] exhibit fully as far up as the [illegible], and the boundary [illegible] there.

144. The boundary Mr. M'Henry submitted only goes up to, but doesn't include, the [illegible]?—Yes; but it would include enough for our purposes.

145. Is there anything else you wish to state?—I think the sanitary law is not carried out as it should be. I made application to the Guardians [illegible]. I made application there in the county to get part of the money, but I succeeded. I did not ask the Guardians at the time, but afterwards they added, to it; and that the Grand Jury was not applied to, as the man was not made for the county, and it was thrown [illegible] where it stands. The water is very deficient in [illegible], the [illegible] and [illegible] it, but I don't see a great deal needed out.

146. Would you be in favour of the Commissioners being the sanitary authority?—We were glad to get rid of it. It was too personal for us to be looking after our friends in the town.

147. But you would be the people who would have been [illegible] to [illegible]?

148. You think the Commissioners are pretty likely what is required of them?—Well, in some cases. They are rather deficient in the water. I think the last pump was quite insufficiently supplied, and the Guardians [illegible] it when they had no right.

149. And the rate of that was struck on the whole electoral division?—It is.

150. Is it not general to strike a pump rate on the whole electoral division?—It would be only in addition to it.

151. It is usual to put such a special rate on a much smaller district; as you have spoken in complaint of [illegible]—One thing I complain of is, that the pump is insufficient; they gave us water and charged money for it.

Mr. JOHN ENGLISH examined.

Mr. John English.

152. I live in the town.

153. You have property outside?—I have, one in the town, and one outside it.

154. You have one outside that would be taken in by the extension?—Yes.

155. And you object to the extension?—Yes; to the small extension. I think the town is rather limited for a township; and if it is to be extended I think it should be much larger than is proposed. I did not know the nature of the proposal until I heard of it now.

156. Would the two townlands be too much, or would that extension meet your view?—I think the two townlands would go far enough; what we call the Big House, Mr. French's [illegible] house, should be included.

157. The only land taken in would be the glebe house on the west?—Yes; there are some small houses not taxable to any great extent.

158. You don't think the two townlands would be too much?—It might be a little too much, but I have been thinking (only perhaps it doesn't come within your inquiry) that the boundary of the electoral division—which I think should be the boundary of the town—should be reduced in some cases in order to make the boundary of the electoral division the boundary of the town.

159. Do you think the electoral division, as it stands, is too large to be the boundary of the town?—I think it is; but it could be reduced a little.

160. That might be a very useful thing to apply for, but we have only to consider whether we can make the boundary of the town and the boundary of the electoral division?—I would hardly go to the length of adding more than four or five townlands, but the electoral division is twice as much. I object to the small addition proposed, but I would have no objection to the larger addition.

161. Mr. M'Kelvey.—I find that the loan alluded to was to be repaid in twenty-five years altogether; the first instalment to be paid at the end of five years after the [illegible] was executed, and the whole to be paid in forty half-yearly instalments.

162. Have your accounts been audited for this year?—Yes.

163. What are your sources of income?—We have no sources, except only dog taxes, water and tolls.

164. What are the dog taxes in the year?—About £6.

165. What are the pump [illegible]?—About £7.

166. You have tolls?—Yes, and [illegible].

167. What are they?—The tolls have been diminishing in point for the last five years. I would be in favour of having the sanitary authority transferred to the Commissioners, if the proposed extension was carried out, because it is inconvenient to have two authorities carrying out sanitary works in the town.

The inquiry then terminated.

BALLYSHANNON—6th OCTOBER, 1879.

(Before Mr. H. A. Robinson.)

Mr. John Ward examined.

1. What office do you hold in the town?—Clerk and collector of rates.

2. Under what Act is the town constituted?—Under the Towns Improvement Act, 1854.

3. Was it previously under the 9th of Geo. IV.?—No.

4. The boundary fixed in 1854 is the same as now exists?—We came under the Act in 1860, and the boundary then adopted still exists.

5. Was the Act adopted for all purposes?—For lighting and cleansing only.

6. What is the population of the town?—About 3,000.

7. It is not an urban sanitary authority?—No.

8. The Guardians are the sanitary authority?—Yes.

9. How many townlands are included in the town boundary?—Six.

10. Six entire townlands?—Yes; there are two wholly within, namely Ballyshannon and Carrickboy, and four partly within.

11. There appear to be two townlands wholly within?—Yes, and portions of the following, viz., Ballyhanna, Cooleholly, Dunmuckrum, Sheegys, and Portnason. The Abbey Island is not within the boundary.

12. What is the valuation of the town?—£2,989 11s.

13. You have given it to us as £3,738 7s.?—There are some items of valuation not rateable including the fishery.

14. Why is it exempt?—I do not know but we applied to have it rated and have not succeeded. The opinion of counsel was, I think, that we could not rate the fishery.

15. On how much of the valuation is the full rate assessed, and how much one-fourth?—The buildings are rated at £1,635 15s., and the lands at £348 1s.

16. Is the town divided into wards?—No.

17. Are there wards for poor law purposes?—No.

18. There was an island you alluded to?—That is Inishsamer.

19. Is that within the boundary?—It is, but it is used only for fishery purposes.

20. Is that paying there rates?—Yes; the house is on the valuation, but the fishery is not paying anything.

21. Do the Commissioners extend any of the advantages of the town to the island?—No; it is outside the quay.

22. In what electoral division is the town?—Ballyshannon, Carrickboy, and a small portion of Finner.

23. What do you consider the central point of the town?—I consider the court-house is the best centre.

24. Taking the court-house as the centre, and taking one mile all round, would it still be within these three electoral divisions?—It would.

25. Would an extension of two miles go into any other electoral division?—It would not.

26. What have been the municipal rates for the last five years?—One shilling on house property, and three-pence on land.

27. You have always struck the full rate?—Yes.

28. Is the income adequate for keeping up the town property?—It is adequate for lighting and cleansing, and we passed one year without taxes at all.

29. Are they in want of funds?—No; in 1877 we made the last rate. We have a rate made this year, but not put in force for the 1877 rate is still equal to our demand.

30. Are there any improvements which the Commissioners would carry out if they had increased funds?—I consider there are.

31. In what direction?—I think sanitary improvements are required.

32. Have the Commissioners ever considered the question of becoming the urban sanitary authority?—No.

33. Are they aware of the provisions of the seventh section of the Public Health Act, which enables to obtain a provisional order, transferring to them the sanitary powers whether the population is 6,000 or not?—No; I have often heard them complaining they were not the sanitary authority.

34. What does your full rate produce?—Between £135 and £145 a year, it seldom exceeds £145.

35. What are your principal sources of expenditure?—Lighting, cleansing, clerks' salary, and collector's salary. There is a fire engine, for which we pay £5 a year for caring.

37. Have you any source of income except the rates and fines from the Petty Sessions Court?—No.

38. There are no properties vested in the Commissioners?—No.

39. No tolls from the markets?—No; nothing but the rates.

40. At present you consider the income adequate?—The Commissioners are not able to carry out as many improvements as they would desire.

41. How many lamps are there?—Forty-one.

42. Are all the principal streets lighted?—Yes. A good many complaints are made of the side streets wanting more lights.

43. For what period of the year are they lighted?—From the 17th September to the 17th March.

44. Are the markets held late?—There are seldom any markets held earlier than eleven o'clock.

45. Do you consider that the lighting of the town is of advantage to the people going out in the evening?—I consider it of great advantage to the country people miles away from the town. They are very glad to have the light.

46. So that any improvements in the town would be of advantage to the people living close outside the town?—Yes, and to the people many miles away.

47. What markets have you?—Every Saturday there is a market for the sale of oats, wheat, and all farm produce. There is a Thursday market for flax and pork.

48. So that you have two markets a week?—Yes—during the winter season.

49. Ballyshannon is the market-town for these three electoral divisions?—Yes, for fifteen miles round.

50. What is the nearest market?—The nearest weekly market is Donegal. That is eleven miles from this, and it is the nearest proper market. The people of my neighbourhood, which is five miles away, all come into this market, and I have seen them come eight and ten miles along the Sligo road to this town.

51. Were our queries submitted to a general meeting of your board?—Yes.

52. And they sent a reply that they had come to the conclusion to let matters stand as they are. Was there a subsequent resolution?—Well, until this day there was not.

53. What is the resolution of to-day?—There was no formal resolution; but they think a circular boundary would be better than the one we have. I as collector, have found some dissatisfaction with ratepayers further from town than those nearer it.

54. Don't you think there would be more objection to a hard and fast line?—We have that at present. We have one part of some man's farm, and not the whole of them.

55. How far does the boundary extend on the North?—About three-quarters of a mile.

56. On the South, how far?—It is scarcely so much; but on the South-West it is very nearly a mile. On the East it is not more than half a mile from this house as the centre. On the West it goes to the sea.

57. Have you got a copy of the *Gazette* defining the original boundary, when you first came under the Act?—I have the *Gazette* of the 2nd February, 1860.

58. Is there not on the records of the Commissioners some description of the boundary, as determined by the ratepayers?—I have the book from the Valuation Office, and I see the boundary coloured on their map. They have sent it to us to revise.

59. But you must have had a written description of your boundary sent up to the Lord Lieutenant for approval?—I have not heard it. We have not passed the whole of the township [illegible].

60. How long have you lived in the town?—I have been Collector since 18[illegible].

61. Are there any improvements going on in the town?—Very few.

62. Has the town shown any tendency to extend in any direction?—No, it has not for the last ten years.

63. Are the houses being built of a better class?—There are very few being built at all; there are more going down than being built at all.

64. Are there any building operations going on?—I might know one or two buildings—a house.

65. Are there any important buildings outside the town?—No.

[illegible]

Mr. Robert Lowry, Chairman, Town Commissioners, examined.

Mr. Robert Lowry.

66. You have been resident in Ballyshannon for sometime?—Yes.

67. How long have you been a Commissioner?—For seven or eight years.

68. Did you occupy the position of chairman all that time?—No, I have been chairman for five or six years.

69. You are well acquainted with the town?—Yes, well acquainted.

70. The recommendation of the Select Committee, as to the electoral division boundaries, would give you a radius of four miles, and would not be applicable to this place?—I don't think it would.

71. Were you present when the question of extension was discussed?—I was.

72. Were you in favour of letting the boundaries remain as they were?—We were in favour of not giving ourselves any trouble about it; it was scarcely discussed at all.

73. Are you aware of the provisions of the 7th section of the Public Health Act?—Yes.

74. Are there any improvements required in the sanitary condition of the town?—I think the guardians are doing the work fairly.

75. What is the contributory district?—I believe it is inside the town boundary. We pay 1*d*. as a sanitary rate.

76. For all purposes?—For any improvements they make.

77. What have they done?—They have made some drains and some passages.

78. Is the town well supplied with water?—I think it is fair.

79. Is the quality of the water good?—Very good.

80. How is the town sewered?—The county does that. If the guardians are applied to in a proper way, they do everything of a sanitary kind required.

81. You think satisfaction is felt with the working of the sanitary business?—I think there would be dissatisfaction if you made any change at the present time. I don't think we would make any complaint about the sanitary work, or ask for any change at present.

82. You are not influenced by a desire to have this larger area of taxation?—No.

83. Do you think it is desirable that the roads should be in the hands of the Commissioners?—I don't think we care for change at present.

84. You would be content to leave things as they are at present?—Yes. The Town Commissioners go to the presentment sessions, and get anything fair and proper from them.

85. The county does the paving?—Yes; we have no power to contribute anything.

86. So that the extension would be in reference to powers you have already got?—It should be simply to equalize the rates.

87. That was the principal reason for desiring this extension?—The only reason.

88. Was the extension you put forward a mile from the limits of the town or from the centre?—I consider this court-house the centre, and a circle from this—I don't say a hard and fast line—but as near as possible to a circle from this would be a fair radius.

89. Have you ever calculated what the income from this proposed extension would be?—No.

90. You never calculated the cost either?—No.

91. What you have in view is more the equalizing of the rating?—It would be altogether to make a fair taxation and to have each person benefited equally rated.

92. Are you speaking the opinion of your Board or your own individual opinion?—We did not call a regular meeting, but all parties present agreed it would be a fair thing, and that each person benefited should contribute.

93. Would you be in favour of including the entire of those townlands portions of which are already included?—I would certainly say, go as near the circle as possible.

94. Taking this court-house as a centre, and taking a circle of a mile all round, are the lands mostly held as accommodation lands?—Yes, principally.

95. Held by people living in the town?—No. Some of them are held by farmers.

96. They derive benefit from the town?—No doubt about it.

97. And you consider that any improvements made in the town would be of advantage to them?—Yes.

98. The light is of especial benefit on market days?—Yes.

99. The paving is bad?—It is very much improved of late.

100. Where are your markets held?—We have a market yard.

101. Have you fairs in the town?—They are held in the upper end; mostly off the streets.

102. Have you a fair-green?—Yes, but when there is a large fair we have some cattle on the streets. We have thirteen fairs, one every month and one extra one.

103. What are the people living outside?—A good many of them are gentlemen having property.

104. How many gentlemen's places would be included by this extension?—I do not think there would be very many but what are in it at present.

105. Is Castlefinn thickly populated?—No.

106. You would not be enlarging the boundary very much by the proposed extension?—No, but it would equalize it.

107. You would not be inclined to make any further increase than you propose?—No, that would meet our present requirements.

108. Would you extend any advantages to the people you include?—We would give them additional lamps. The town is very scattered.

109. You would not propose to give lights to any district not thickly populated?—No.

110. Would you extend the lights out to Abbey

inland?—No. We could get on very well with our present income.

112. Have you heard complaints as to the irregularity of the present boundary?—Yes.

113. And it is with a view of rectifying that that this extension is proposed?—Yes. When I saw that some gentlemen living near the town were paying nothing, I thought it would be fair to the inhabitants to make equal rating.

114. Do you see any improvements in the town in the way of building?—I don't see very much.

115. Do you think the town is at a standstill?—Yes.

116. Is trade increasing?—I think so. It has been increasing for some years past.

117. Are there many unoccupied houses?—There are a good many tumbling down. All the houses are occupied that are in a habitable state. We don't get the petty sessions fines. I brought the matter before the magistrates some time ago, and there came a reply back that did not seem favourable to us, and we did not take any further steps in the matter. We have no town watch. We made every effort to get the fishery rated, and there was counsel employed, and the Commissioners of the Fishery Company decided that they would be bound by the decision of counsel. We would be very glad to make them pay if we could.

118. Don't you think it would be unfair to the people to be brought in, if you don't assess the town to the full extent?—Well, Mr. Alexander and Mr. Moore are the proprietors of the fishery; it is valued at over £1,000; it is within 300 yards, and so it must be within the town boundary.

119. You get no fines and you are not able to see your whole town?—Yes.

120. Was the fishery there when the town first adopted the provisions of the Act?—Yes. They would pay on the buildings, but they do not pay on the valuation of the fishery.

121. Do you think they should pay one-fourth or the full rate?—We only billed them with one-fourth. We consider that when the fishery is within the boundary we should get taxes on the valuation of it.

Mr. Robert Sweeney examined.

122. I am a Commissioner. I have nothing to add to what has been stated. I concur with Mr. Lipsett.

123. Do you consider that in order to get this scientific frontier an increase is desirable?—Yes.

124. You do not look so much to the increase in the income as to having a regular boundary?—No.

125. It is for the purpose of easing the rates on the people of the town you do that?—To some extent.

126. Are you aware of what would be the probable increment to the town funds?—It would be very small.

127. About £181?—Yes.

128. Are there any improvements which the Commissioners are unable to carry out for want of funds?—Not immediately, except lighting. We had to lessen the number of lamps some years ago, and then by applying to the promoters of the Gas Company we got them to lessen the price of the public lamps.

129. How much do you pay at present?—£3 10s. per lamp, and they are only lighted to ten or eleven o'clock at night, and we want them lighted up to twelve o'clock if we could pay for it.

130. Do you prefer leaving things as they are, so far as concerns the sanitary authority?—Yes.

131. Do you consider that the Grand Jury give you value for what they receive?—We are not exactly satisfied.

132. Do you think the money is expended on the town?—Not a third of it.

133. But you don't think you could do it cheaper?—This is a scattered town and it would require a good deal to keep it up.

134. Do you think the advantages the people outside derive are such that they should contribute their quota?—Considering that it is land I think they ought. There are some of the lands held as townparks and accommodation lands.

Dr. Simon Sheehan, J.P., examined.

135. Do you think the town should be extended for the purposes of rectifying the boundary?—That was discussed some years ago, some ratepayers proposed a radius of a mile and that was largely opposed at the time; one or two of them would have been here to-day to do the same if they had known.

136. Have you recognised the impracticability of adopting a hard and fast circle?—Yes. I think that is my recollection of the objection raised before.

137. Do you live in the town?—Yes, and I have property outside it; I am a large ratepayer within the present boundary.

138. Would you object to extension?—I think you ought to extend it in one or two directions, but the difficulty is to get an exact boundary.

139. Mr. *Lipsett.*—I would be brought in myself to a large extent, and my proposal is to rate myself, and I merely do it for the sake of doing what is fair for the inhabitants around.

Dr. *Sheehan.*—I object to the circular rating.

140. Would you have any objection to adopting equitable rating within a mile of the town following some well defined boundary?—The objection to that before was pressed by Mr. Dixon. He said it would take in people who have no benefit from the town, and they would get no value whatever.

141. Mr. *Sweeney.*—There was a dread then that if the Commissioners got the extension they would increase their powers and then be able to levy 5s. or 6s.

Mr. Edward M'Nulty examined.

142. Where do you live?—In Ballyshannon.

143. Have you any property outside?—I have.

144. In which direction?—The Abbey.

145. You are aware that the extension of one mile would take in portion of your property?—I am, and I think in the absence of the agent of that property it would be unfair to do anything of the kind. If the boundary was extended in that direction, the landlord might have to pay most of the rates for the great part of the buildings are under £4.

146. Your land is in the Abbey?—Yes.

147. And you object to be brought in?—I object on the part of the landlord, if he would be obliged to pay for those poor tenants.

148. On what ground do you object yourself?—That I am paying plenty at present, and that the rates in the town are well able to do all that is required.

149. You consider that the Commissioners do not require increased funds?—I do.

150. When these people outside the boundary come in they leave their money in the town?—Yes.

151. So that it is a mutual advantage?—Yes, it would be no town if the people did not come in and leave their money in it.

152. You are opposed to extension on behalf of your agent and on your own part?—Yes. There are a whole lot of the buildings on the Abbey valued at only £2 10s.

The inquiry then closed.

ARKLOW.—1st MAY, 1879.

(Before Mr. C. P. Cotton.)

Mr. Charles J. Fitzhenry examined.

Mr. Charles J. Fitzhenry.

1. Mr. Cotton.—You are the Town Clerk of Arklow?—I am.

2. What is the date of the order constituting this a township?—The [illegible] of July, 1870.

3. Was the Towns Improvement Act adopted in its entirety, or only in part?—Only in part.

4. Was it adopted for water?—Not for water.

5. Not for a water supply?—No.

6. How many Commissioners are there?—Fifteen; twelve for the Arklow ward, and three for Ferrybank.

7. There are two wards?—Yes.

8. Can you tell me the number of ratepayers qualified to vote in each of the wards?—Nearly everyone is rated at £4.

9. Can you give me the numbers?—I can give you them by-and-by.

10. Perhaps you will not only give me the numbers qualified to vote, but also the number qualified to sit as Commissioners if elected?—There are about twenty qualified to sit as Commissioners.

11. In each ward? I want them separately?—There are only three qualified in the Ferrybank ward, and we have those three, and there are seventeen others, beside the twelve we have, in the Arklow ward.

12. You have given me the population as 5,[illegible], but that is not divided into the two wards?—Well, I can give you them.

13. Please, give me the population of each ward?—I will do so.

14. And if you can give me the area of each ward, I shall be glad?—The area of the Ferrybank ward would be [illegible]a. 1r. 13p., and the balance in the Arklow ward is 1,01[illegible]a. 3r. 20p.

15. Can you tell me the valuation of each ward?—Well, I cannot just now.

16. Then tell me the total valuation?—£4,[illegible]—that is including the lands and the buildings together.

17. You have given it in the return to the "queries" as £[illegible]?—Well, if that [illegible] there was a mistake on the ratebook.

18. Are the municipal wards coterminous with the wards for poor law purposes?—Yes; I think so.

19. They are coterminous with the electoral division in fact?—Yes; we have two electoral divisions.

20. Arklow and Kilbride?—Yes.

21. You have struck no rate as yet?—We have.

22. I mean you did not for 1878?—We did not.

23. What rate have you struck now?—1s. in the pound on houses and 3d. on land.

24. That is a 1s. rate then?—Yes.

25. Now, will you kindly give me the poor law rate for five years, beginning at 1874?—In 1874 it was 1s. 10d.

26. You give it as 2s. 6d. here in the queries?—That cannot be right, because I have got the figures I am about to give you from the Clerk of the Union.

27. Then where do the figures in the queries come from?—At the time they were sent to you it was at a meeting of the Commissioners, and when they had not the poor law books.

28. You think the figures are right now?—Yes.

29. In 1874 what was the poor rate?—1s. 10d.; in 1875, it was 2s. 10d.; in 1876, 2s. 2d.; in 1877, 2s. [illegible]; and in 1878, 3s. 4d.

30. What was the county cess in 1874?—It has been, on an average for five years, [illegible].

31. On the half-year?—Yes, sir.

32. In reference to the poor rate that you have given me—does that include any special sanitary rate?—It includes the burial.

33. Of how much?—4d.

34. On what year?—4d. all through.

35. Every year?—Yes. It has been on for the last twelve or fourteen years, but it has been off for a couple of years.

36. But it is on at present?—I cannot say whether it was on in 1877, but it is in 1878.

37. And there is no other special rate?—No.

38. The Guardians are the sanitary authority of Arklow?—They are.

39. And they have struck no special sanitary rate?—No special sanitary rate to my knowledge.

40. These "queries" were submitted to the Commissioners?—Yes.

41. And did the Commissioners consider them at their meeting?—Yes.

42. At a special meeting or an ordinary meeting?—An ordinary meeting.

43. How many Commissioners attended?—Thirteen.

44. And were they unanimous in the replies that were given to these queries?—They were.

45. And I see, by one of them, that the Commissioners consider the area too small for the requirements of the town?—That was their opinion.

46. That was their opinion?—Yes; that was their opinion, unanimously.

47. Then, the particular grounds on which they suggest a change are put down as—

"The Town Commissioners consider that the valuation of the present area is insufficient to meet the necessary expenses of the township, and as the reservation of the harbour is a subject which closely concerns the town itself, and the property adjoining it, they think it desirable that as large an area as possible should be included with the town in order to place them in the position of undertaking any necessary guarantee required by Government for that purpose."

Those are the grounds upon which they suggest an extension of the area?—Yes, sir. Those are the grounds; but they have other grounds as well since then.

48. I shall be glad to hear them afterwards. Was any particular scheme of extension suggested?—There has been.

49. Was any particular extension suggested by your Commissioners on that day?—Not on that day.

50. They merely recorded the fact that they wanted an extension of some kind?—Quite so.

51. Have they considered the question since that at any meeting?—They have.

52. Have they come to any conclusion about a particular extension?—They have.

53. Can you describe that extension?—I can show it to you on the map, drawn by the solicitor for the Commissioners.

54. At what meeting did they consider that, and how many Commissioners were present?—The meeting was held on the 19th of April, and there were six Commissioners present.

55. And they had submitted to them a particular extension?—They had.

56. Did they approve of it?—They all approved of it.

57. Unanimously?—Yes.

58. Will you describe the extension—Was there a resolution giving it?—There was.

59. Read it please?—Witness reads:—

"It was proposed by Bernard Kearney, seconded by Mr. John Hennigan—'That the Commissioners be [illegible] at the evening meeting of the Municipal [illegible] Commissioners, on the 1st of May, 1878, by their solicitor, Mr. [illegible], to advocate an extension of the township; that the principle which they consider proper is that a circle should be struck [illegible], having its centre at the Arklow Post Office, and having a radius of one statute mile, and that all townlands within or partially within that circle should be included in the new township boundary."

That is the resolution.

60. Had the Commissioners before them at that time details of the quantity of land that would be taken in, and the valuation of it?—I may mention that the Commissioners had [illegible] meeting yesterday, at which this resolution was followed by a resolution that [illegible] should be taken in.

61. You had better give us that resolution. Tell me what the resolution was and you can give me a copy afterwards?—That one-half should be taken in, and only [illegible] partially within.

62. There was a meeting of the Commissioners yesterday?—There was.

63. And they came to the resolution to modify the proposed township to a radius of one mile?—Yes.

64. Which was the modification?—Not to take in all townlands within or partially within the circle, but to take in one-half.

65. One-half of what?—Any townland that one-half was not included within the one mile radius should be excluded. If more than one-half of a townland lay outside the one-mile radius it should be excluded.

66. If more than one-half of a townland lay outside the one-mile radius it should not be included?—Yes.

67. Do you know how much land that would bring in?—I cannot tell you that yet.

68. Mr. Edward T. C. Johnston.—I appear on behalf of the Earl of Wicklow and a great number of his tenants, and also on behalf of a great number of the Earl of Carysfort's tenants, and I have some observations which I shall make to you by-and-bye.

69. Mr. Mooney.—May I ask is Lord Wicklow totally opposed to this?

Mr. Johnston.—He is totally opposed, and I have the instructions of his lordship to oppose it, and also of a vast majority of his tenants—some tenants who hold [illegible] acres of land under the Earl of Wicklow.

Examination of Mr. [illegible] resumed.

70. Mr. Cotton.—You are not able to tell us how much land will be taken in by this proposal of the Commissioners?—No, sir.

71. I want you to furnish us, as soon as you possibly can, with a return of the quantity of land taken in by that proposal of the Commissioners yesterday, with the valuation of it, and the number as nearly as you can get it, of people which it would bring in, and the number of people that it would bring in eligible to act as Commissioners, if elected, people who are qualified?—I will give you those.

72. How many electoral divisions does the present town go into?—Two.

73. What are their names?—Arklow and Kilbride.

74. These electoral divisions I presume extend a very long way away from Arklow in different directions?—They do.

75. The boundary is the river, I believe?—It is.

76. Has the Board of Commissioners ever considered the question of becoming the sanitary authority for Arklow?—They have not yet considered it.

77. Nor by resolution?—No.

78. They are aware of the fact that they are entitled to become the urban sanitary authority?—They are.

79. They have struck no rates and done no work?—They have struck a rate.

80. They have done no work?—They have erected a number of lamps.

81. What arrangements are made at present for lighting in Arklow?—The lamps are lit with paraffin oil.

82. By the Commissioners?—Yes.

83. At what expense?—At an expense of [illegible] the lamp lighter [illegible] year, and about [illegible] for oil for the lighting.

84. That is the [illegible]?—It is.

85. How is Arklow supplied with water?—[illegible] The number of the lamps I may mention [illegible].

86. These lamps are under contract to you as well?—Yes. It is the [illegible] in each lamp.

87. Did the Commissioners consider the question of the [illegible] or otherwise of making any [illegible] by the present would?—They [illegible] the [illegible] of the [illegible] of the township.

88. But, in [illegible] of that, if the proposal to enlarge was carried, did they wish for any [illegible] to the [illegible] of the Commissioners [illegible] by them.

89. [illegible] what they propose to do about the [illegible] of [illegible] the new [illegible]?—The Commissioners have not expressed an opinion on that.

90. They have not said whether they propose anything in the way of new works, or to show our [illegible] and [illegible]?—They have not.

91. Mr. Johnston.—What year, under the present system, is the case which the Commissioners have put on [illegible]?—[illegible] paid [illegible] to the lighting.

92. And [illegible]?—[illegible].

93. What is the local rate [illegible] by the [illegible] £140 [illegible].

94. You say that the number of the lamps are [illegible]?—Yes.

95. What has the expense of lighting been?—The expense of lighting since December has been £13.

96. And [illegible]?—[illegible].

97. I believe the paraffin oil used by the lamps is purchased in large quantities [illegible] as the Commissioners require it.

98. The cost is cheap?—Yes, as cheap as it can be procured.

99. What is the present rate at which it is purchased?—The average of it [illegible] per gallon, and is it supplied at 1s. per gallon.

100. I believe the lamps are extinguished, or supposed to be extinguished, at eleven o'clock at night or at twelve, I believe.

101. Mr. Cotton.—What is the tendency of the [illegible]?—

Mr. Johnston.—The tendency of it is to increase what the present expenditure was, [illegible] the [illegible] which are imposed they have not sufficient to meet already their expenses.

102. Mr. Cotton.—You say that the [illegible] are suggested to be [illegible]?—

Mr. Johnston.—It is not [illegible] at all, and, other than that, I may tell you it would be the greatest possible hardship to impose taxation on [illegible] living outside the town who won't receive any of the benefits [illegible] from [illegible].

103. Mr. Cotton.—You are asking, Mr. [illegible], about the time the lamps are extinguished, and I mean as the [illegible] of that.

104. Mr. [illegible].—The case at present is quite inadequate to meet the demands of the Commissioners.

Cross-examination resumed.

105. Mr. Johnston.—On moonlight nights the lamps are not lit?—Yes.

106. And in every month there are at least one dozen moonlight nights?—A week only.

107. That would be then about three weeks in the month that the lamps would be lit, and extinguished at twelve o'clock?—Yes; and some kept lighting all night.

108. Some of them?—Yes.

109. How many?—Twenty-four. We don't light any lamps in the summer.

110. Mr. Cotton.—How long have the Commis-

[illegible] lighting the town?—Since the 13th of [illegible].

111. Mr. [illegible]—[illegible] of July.

112. Mr. [illegible]

[illegible]—Yes.

113. Mr. Johnston.—[illegible]

114. [illegible] £190 [illegible] twenty-eight [illegible]

115. Mr. [illegible]—[illegible]

116. Mr. Johnston.—[illegible] twenty-eight?—Yes.

117. [illegible] forty lamps, besides the twenty-eight.

118. [illegible] sixty-eight lamps in point of fact?—It would.

119. [illegible] forty lamps should be provided?—[illegible]

120. Do you consider forty additional lamps necessary?—I do.

121. Within what area is it contemplated to erect these forty additional lamps?—Within the area of the present township. I believe they are necessary.

122. Forty more lamps?—Yes.

123. Within the present area?—Yes.

124. [illegible] within the town?—Yes.

125. [illegible]

126. Mr. [illegible]

127. They consider they want more money for the purpose of increasing the lights?—Yes.

128. The Commissioners consider that they require any more money than they can raise on the [illegible]?—Yes, they do.

129. For what purpose?—For flagging the town of Arklow.

130. [illegible] the Grand Jury [illegible] for flagging purposes [illegible]?—Yes.

131. [illegible] the Commissioners [illegible]

132. Mr. Johnston.—The object of the proposed [illegible] additional lamps, and also to defray the expense of flagging the footways of Arklow?—Yes, and for other things which the Commissioners have not gone into yet.

133. What is the present distance between the [illegible]?—They differ very much.

134. What is the average distance?—[illegible]

135. Have there been complaints made that it is proposed by the Commissioners to increase the lamps [illegible]? [illegible] The Commissioners consider that the number of lamps at present provided for the town is quite inadequate.

136. Have there been any complaints?—I think there have been.

Mr. J. K. Tobias [illegible].

137. Mr. Cooper.—You are the solicitor to the Commissioners?—I am.

138. Are you authorised by them to represent their views on this inquiry?—I am.

139. Will you state what their views are in applying [illegible] Commission was about to be commenced at all, it was proposed that [illegible] They found very shortly after they commenced operations that their area was too limited, and it was proposed, and I was instructed to take proceedings under the 5th section of the Towns Improvement Act, for the extension; and in making inquiries about that, I ascertained from Mr. [illegible] that the present Commission was about to be [illegible] I thought that matter before the Earl of [illegible] and the other Commissioners, and they took up nothing until this Commission, reserving their views until they laid them before you now.

140. Can you tell me what the Commissioners took [illegible]?—The Commissioners [illegible] the ordinary small scale map of [illegible] townlands [illegible] should be included within a [illegible] radius.

141. Do you mean all townlands touched by that radius?—Yes, and when this came to be investigated afterwards, when it came to be put down on paper as I now lay it before you, it appeared that those were a number of townlands that would be just shaved by the line, and that would be extending almost a mile away again; and they came to the conclusion that it would not be fair and just, and they modified their proposition, as their meeting yesterday, and the map I have laid before you is a tolerably accurate map of the township and the townlands adjoining.

142. What is the area of the present township?—It would be very nearly included in an area of one mile, except the townland of Kilbride, which is not included within the present township, although it [illegible] within less than half a mile of the present township.

143. Excluding the townland of Kilbride, the township may be described as contained within a circle of one mile radius?—It may.

144. The Commissioners wish to extend it this mile, including those townlands of which a small portion only came within that radius?—Yes.

145. What are their grounds for seeking an extension?—They consider that persons residing within that distance [illegible] with the taxation that they propose to put upon them. They are having the town lighted to the last [illegible]. The streets of this township are very narrow, and the [illegible] of the different roads are very steep, and consequently they require lighting more than any town I have ever been in. It is now partially lighted, and they seek, as you have heard, to fully light the town. They also seek to flag the footpaths of the

Arklow [illegible] Mr. [illegible]

Mr. J. K. Tobias.

towns which are in a very bad state. They do not propose to interfere with the roadways, but they do propose going to the Grand Jury, and asking them for a contribution of one-half towards the flagging of the streets, and they think that the Grand Jury can scarcely now refuse that application. They did not [illegible] such a request when there were no means of [illegible], and now under the Act of Parliament we could get [illegible] from the Grand Jury, if they refused that reasonable proposition.

146. Do you mean to take up all the local presentments [illegible] the Grand Jury?—Yes; that could be done if they [illegible], but we do not wish to do that if it can be avoided.

147. You must know the urban sanitary authority [illegible]?—Yes, I know that. It is the intention of the Town Commissioners to become the sanitary authority, as Athlone is a little way behind [illegible] in sanitary matters. There is no such thing as a sewer in the town of Athlone. There is no drainage, and there are a great many houses [illegible] without any sanitary accommodation in the rear.

148. Have the Guardians done anything whatever in the way of sanitary matters for the township?—As far as I know, they have done some scavenging, but nothing more that I am aware of.

149. They have not made any special inquiry into the [illegible]?—I don't know. I am aware that the Commissioners think that they ought to have the administration of sanitary matters.

150. And they are going to apply for it?—They are; I believe they are. I will tell you also that Athlone is a place subject to epidemics. Whenever they have an epidemic, even with all the precautions taken by the most skilful people, they found great difficulty in controlling it until it ran its course, and of course in the cases of epidemics, proper drainage would greatly mitigate the danger, and would be as great a benefit to the persons resident within the districts proposed to be included as to the persons in the town, because they are equally [illegible] to be endangered by it.

151. How much land would be taken in by this extension?—I have not any idea. I made a calculation of the amount of land taken in by the first proposed extension. When the Commissioners only arrived at this conclusion so late as yesterday afternoon it was impossible for me to make a minute calculation, but I will have the information you require laid before you. I may say that the Commissioners have administered the funds entrusted to them [illegible] with as great economy as possible, and the cost of lighting has been very trifling indeed, and the cost of erecting the public lamps and other matters has been kept down; they advertised them and got tenders, and took the lowest tender, and in every way their desire has been and is to economise the funds entrusted to them. There is great unanimity on the board and I have never seen any want of unanimity upon it since they began to [illegible].

Cross-examined by Mr. Johnston.

152. You yourself are concerned with the locality proposed to be taken in, in this extended area?—I am.

153. And I understand that you have a number of gentlemen who reside in the proposed area?—Yes.

154. And you are aware they are large landowners?—Yes.

155. You know Mr. Robert Hudson, of [illegible]?—Yes, very well.

156. His property is proposed to be included in the two mile radius?—I don't think it would come in in the modified radius.

157. These gentlemen hold extensive property there?—They do there.

158. Well, the tax that it is proposed to put on them will be at the rate of 6d. in the pound on their lands?—Yes, that is the highest.

159. That would amount to a large sum?—Yes. It is for the purpose of getting that rate that the present extension is sought.

160. You stated that these gentlemen who reside outside the present area, and who will be within the proposed area, that they will derive [illegible] with the tax they will have to pay?—[illegible] much of them hold those lands so close to the town of Athlone that it would do them good, and any improvement in the town would beneficially affect them. Any improvement in the town of Athlone would [illegible] people who hold land so close to it.

161. What is the material benefit [illegible] [illegible]—[illegible] the danger of any collision.

162. Has Mr. Hudson complained about being [illegible]?—Yes, he does not want to be included.

163. Are you aware that he is going to oppose it?—Certainly; and I know that if I were him I would [illegible] very much like the [illegible] of Athlone should keep the town proper and at their own expense, and I would oppose it too.

164. This proposed flagging of the footways will cost a considerable sum?—I think.

165. A considerable sum?—Yes.

166. Supposing that the Grand Jury would [illegible] of the expense, yet the other moiety would be considerable?—It would be a substantial sum.

167. What would the material benefit be derived from the flagging of the footways—what would that be to those residing [illegible] miles outside of the town?—The material benefit that people now driving in carriages and other vehicles derive when they can get down off these vehicles and walk about the footways without danger of [illegible]; and of having their [illegible] kept clean—all the usual benefits of footways in other towns.

168. In other words, the contemplation of the Commissioners to have footways is, that they are [illegible] fashionable promenade for carriage people?—I didn't say that. Another point is that when people are beginning to build, one of the first things to be done is flagging, and in my opinion it should be done here too.

169. Yes, but not at the expense of those who reside at a distance of two miles from the town, and who have considerable property, and who are taxed [illegible] in proportion to those who are small householders in the town?

170. Mr. Gibson.—I don't understand that.

171. Mr. Johnston.—Mr. Hudson's valuation is £357 a year?

Witness.—Yes.

172. Threepence in the pound—how much would that be?—It would be about £5.

173. The land is a separate valuation, and is it [illegible] pound on that valuation?—That would be about £4 7s.

174. So that Mr. Hudson's valuation would be something like £8 10s.?—Yes; and it would not require to be levied, however if the Boundary Commissioners are pleased to recommend an extended area, there would be no necessity for levying the maximum amount of the taxation.

175. That would be merely fancy?—There would be no necessity. There would be a larger area and a smaller taxation.

176. But they would have the legal power of [illegible]?—They would of course.

177. Mr. [illegible].—In fact, [illegible] [illegible]—That is quite true.

178. Mr. Johnston.—The proposal is [illegible] [illegible] Mr. [illegible] [illegible].

179. Mr. Twomey.—I may also say that the Earl of Carysfort is represented here. [illegible] "yellow" [illegible] Earl of Wicklow, and [illegible] "pink" to the Earl of Carysfort. [illegible] the Earl of Carysfort [illegible] municipal boundary.

180. Mr. Wilson Anderson.—I appear also for the Earl of Carysfort, and I shall examine Lord Carysfort's agent.

Examination of Mr. Twomey resumed.

181. Mr. Johnston.—Mr. Fitzhenry has stated a number of items, [illegible] proposed flagging, [illegible] Commissioners, [illegible]

182. And what [illegible]—[illegible] Town Sergeant [illegible]

183. As a matter of fact [illegible] Town Sergeant [illegible]

184. Mr. [illegible].—[illegible] Commissioners [illegible] the Commissioners.

Mr. Stephen Halpin examined.

186. Mr. [illegible].—You are Chairman of the Town Commissioners, Dr. Halpin?—[illegible] Earl of Carysfort [illegible] Commissioners [illegible] Town Sergeant, [illegible]

187. What is your opinion as to that?—I think [illegible]

188. You are aware that this is a sanitary [illegible] Town Improvement [illegible] Public Health Act.

189. They can ask for it [illegible] Wicklow.

190. They are entitled to it as a matter of right?—Yes, sir. [illegible]

191. Do I understand you to say as Chairman of the Town Commissioners [illegible]

192. Does the question of a harbour [illegible] Dublin [illegible]

193. Mr. Johnston.—In reference to this [illegible] Earl of Carysfort [illegible]—He has not.

Examined by Mr. Twomey.

194. What is the sanitary condition of the town of Arklow?—It has improved very much of late years.

195. Is the sewerage of the town of Arklow in a satisfactory state?—It is very defective in the lower portion of the town.

196. You are the principal medical officer of the [illegible]?—Yes.

197. And you are acquainted very well with the [illegible]?—Very well, for the last [illegible] years.

198. Is there an [illegible] population?—[illegible] Lord Carysfort has improved [illegible]

199. Do you consider that sanitary [illegible] population?—There is no town in Ireland [illegible]

200. Is it your opinion that if the Town Commissioners [illegible] sanitary authority, it would [illegible] Board of Guardians [illegible]

201. You think they would deal with it more [illegible]?—Yes, more [illegible]

202. Is there difficulty in controlling an epidemic?—There is great difficulty in [illegible] epidemic.

203. And you [illegible] the epidemic of cholera—is it your opinion [illegible]?—Yes.

204. Have these persons that we seek to include [illegible] the town [illegible]

205. What is your opinion as to the necessity of it?—No town in Ireland [illegible]

206. Is it your opinion that the people outside the town would derive benefit from the flagging?—Yes; I

289. Mr. *Johnston*.—You don't think Lord Wicklow would oppose it?—No.

290. With reference to your holdings on both sides of the river—Ballyraymoyle under the Earl of Wicklow, and Ferrylands and Ballyduff under the Earl of Carysfort—are you adverse to the proposed extension?—Of course I am; naturally so.

300. Mr. *Cotton*.—State your grounds?—That is, personally I am. On the ground that I do not think that we have a right to be taxed for the improvements of the town, and in many ways; and I don't agree at all with a great many of the things stated. As to the lighting, it is no benefit to me. If I drive in on a dark night, I have lamps, I would never trust to the lighting of the town, coming to it and going home, so that it could be no benefit to me; and I'm sure there are others here who would say the same. In reference to the footpaths, I don't consider the footpaths to be in such a bad state at all as they are represented to be, and I don't think that the flagging would therefore be of any advantage to me at all.

301. You reside beyond the boundary suggested?—I do.

302. Supposing you resided at Ferrylands would you be of the same opinion?—I would.

303. Mr. *Johnston*.—With reference to the question put to Dr. Halpin with reference to the sewerage, Dr. Halpin has stated that there is a great engineering difficulty, and that the work could not be done without considerable expense—you know that?—I do.

304. That was one of the reasons why it was not done?—That was one of the reasons why they wanted a harbour.

305. If this proposed extension was carried out at the rate of 3d. in the pound on your landed property, would you be paying considerably more in proportion than those residing in the town?—I think it would be almost three times as much as the amount any ratepayer of the town would pay, according to the valuation of my property. I am including the houses, where we have to pay 1s., and 3d. on land.

Cross-examined by Mr. Tomkins.

306. How often do you come into the town, and people of your position?—I drive through the town on an average twice a week, that is on business, going from one farm to another to look after my business; and as for my family, perhaps they come in on an average twice a week.

307. Do you think there would be any material advantage to persons residing within a mile and a half of the town and having families, to have the town properly flagged, and in a good sanitary state?—Well within a mile and a half. I would say that people within a mile and a half would walk very much oftener than I would. I think though, there are people within a mile and a half, having some vehicles and horses.

308. Do you think they would derive benefit, supposing the Commissioners were now enabled to flag the town and put it in a sanitary state—would it not be a direct advantage to them?—Certainly. I am sure if the town was flagged it would be an improvement.

309. Would it not be an advantage to those residing within a mile and a half?—Of course, if they walk into the town it would.

310. Do you consider that the paving of the streets of the town would not be of advantage to those who drive in?—None, whatever, to those who drive.

311. Would not these people get off their cars sometimes?—My opinion is that the state of the footpaths, at present, is not so bad. I think they are in a very fair order and do not require improvement.

312. You have never resided near a town where flagging was carried out?—I have been in several towns.

313. Mr. *Anderson*.—Lord Wicklow would not oppose the addition of Killeagh?—I think he would not; he might, but I think he would not.

314. Do not the people derive as much benefit in Killeagh, from the town, as in the other townlands?—Yes, in the town, in the way of shopping, &c.

315. It is the nearest town to them?—Yes.

316. And then the people who live at Killeagh derive as much benefit as the people who live at Knockenrahan?—If you put it that way, I derive as much benefit as the people who reside at Killeagh.

316. Don't you think that the people who live at Killeagh should be excluded?—I cannot see why they should not be excluded.

317. Mr. *Johnston*.—Don't you oppose any extension?—I don't see why Killeagh should be included, if you take this view, more than any other common. There is no particular reason for including it; but if you say that there is to be a certain area on either side, I think Killeagh then should be included in that.

318. Mr. *Anderson*.—Do you find, as a matter of fact, that there is as much advantage gained on the north side as on the south?—I don't see that we get the same benefit on the north as you do on the south.

319. Mr. *Johnston*.—Is not the town of Arklow situated on the south side of the river?—Yes.

320. And on the north side there is only merely the little village of Ferrybank?—Yes.

321. So that as a matter of fact the different townlands on the south side of the river are in the immediate vicinity of the town?—Yes.

322. Because the townlands on the other side are away from it?—Yes.

323. Mr. *Anderson*.—The people of Killeagh have to come into the town?—Yes.

324. Mr. *Johnston*.—In the townland of Marsh there are three inhabitants?—Yes.

325. Mr. Tomkins.—Has not Lord Wicklow property in the village of Ferrybank?—I believe so.

326. Is it not improving?—Yes.

327. And building going on?—Yes, some houses are being built there at the present time.

328. Mr. *Johnston*.—It would improve if this town side was never thought of?—Yes.

329. And would have improved if the township had never been instituted?—I dare say.

330. What is the distance to Killeagh by road from the post office in Arklow?—About a mile and a quarter by road.

Mr. Robert M. Hudson examined.

331. Mr. *Johnston*.—You reside at Seabank?—Yes.

332. That is on the north side of the river?—Yes.

333. How far is Seabank from the town?—About a mile and a quarter.

334. How far is the most distant part of your property?—Some of it is close to the present boundary of the town.

335. You have property inside and outside the town?—Yes.

336. How much land do you hold?—About 170 acres in Seabank.

337. You have land in Johnstown?—I have.

338. What is the valuation of Seabank?—The valuation of Seabank is £237 a year.

339. Do you come into the town often?—Very often.

340. What do you come in?—Riding or driving.

341. You do not go on the footpaths?—Not very much.

342. Do you consider the lighting sufficient?—Yes.

343. These twenty-four lamps afford sufficient light as far as you are concerned?—Yes.

344. You never had any fault to find with the town with the mode of lighting, or the footpaths?—No.

345. If this proposed scheme for the extension of the township were carried into effect, you would have to pay a considerable amount in taxation on your holding at Seabank?—Yes.

346. How much would the increase amount to be—

between £4 and £5 not including the house. About £5 I think would be the extent to which it would affect me.

347. And for which you would have no benefit whatever?—I don't think I could.

348. What is the present condition of the footpaths of Arklow?—Better than I ever saw them for the last twenty years—by far better.

349. Mr. Anderson.—That is since the Commissioners were appointed?—They were very good before the Commissioners were appointed, very passable.

350. Then you most strenuously oppose this proceeding?—Yes.

351. You oppose everything within the two miles radius?—I do.

Mr. [illegible] Philpott examined.

[illegible]

ARKLOW.
May [illegible].
Mr. George [illegible].

as far as the boundary goes, it should be lighted, whatever be the boundary. I think if the boundary were a quarter of a mile, it should be lighted, and if the boundary was a mile, or half a mile it should be lighted, because I don't see what benefit a distant person gets if he does not get light. That is very important. If there is any enlargement of the boundary, there must be a change of wards and of representation.

372. What change would you propose?—I would propose a very sweeping change.

373. What is it?—That the north side get a fair share of representation. For instance, Mr. Anderson proposes on the part of Lord Carysfort that there should be an equal area taken in on the north side, and if you take in an equal area there should be equal representation.

374. Very good?—Then I also say, if I would not be going out of the scope of this inquiry, that I have known more or less for twenty years, agitation at times being raised to put the town under the Act, and time after time the balance of opinion appeared to be altogether that there would be no advantage to be got for coming under the Act in the way of management, that the town was better under the Guardians in the way of management.

375. Is it your opinion that if the township remains as it is, the wards should also be as they are?—Yes.

376. But if there is a change, what way should the wards be?—I think there should be at least three or four wards, because I think that the agricultural part of the ratepayers should be represented independently of the town part.

377. That if there is an extension including the agricultural land it should be represented independently of the present wards?—I think so.

378. Would you make that representation dependent on the valuation, or the population, or in what way?—Well, perhaps both might have a share of influence.

379. But you would not, if there was an extension, add partly to one ward and partly to another—you would make independent wards?—Ferrybank should be certainly severed, but there might be three wards added. We came to the conclusion that if it was severed it would lead to very costly expenditure, and I don't think the agricultural holdings should be brought in to pay any proportion of the sewerage of the town of Arklow.

380. I think, if you are aware of it, that the Guardians are compelled to carry out proper sewerage for the town of Arklow, it will be charged on the entire electoral division?—If the Guardians carry it out afterwards, the poor law management is expensive enough, and we would make it worse to give the power to the Town Commissioners.

381. You think the Guardians could carry out the sewerage?—I think if we want it it would be better in their hands. The township has been very lately formed, and I think the whole system ought not to be disturbed so soon. Then, again, so far as the Commissioners are concerned, they are really, so to speak, only apprentices at their work.

382. Mr. Fosman.—Don't you think that having this town under the Town Improvements Act is a mistake altogether, and are you not of opinion that independently of the business the town should not be under the control of the Commissioners at all?—Yes.

383. Did you hear the account given by the clerk of the disbursements for the first year?—I did.

384. Did you see a deficit?—I did.

385. You said it was probably made up of salaries and fees. Are you aware that there is only £20 and a lamplighter's salary?—I say that the lighting expenses—I said that the remainder was made up of preliminaries, incidental expenses and salaries and fees.

386. Tell me some of the preliminary expenses?—I am not aware. Can you tell me anything that does not come under any of my headings?

387. Have the farmers within the area the benefit, and do they derive benefit from the fair?—Not more so as all those classes at a radius of three miles.

388. But they have received some benefit?—Yes, they have received some, so also, have those who live at a distance of three miles, and for that reason I say if there is an extension there should be a liberal one. Those within a radius of three miles get as much benefit as those within a mile and a half.

389. Have you any substantial reason to give why you would be afraid that the Commissioners of the town of Arklow would not administer the funds with the same skill and care as other public bodies?—Not the slightest. I think the Commissioners have done very well.

390. Mr. Anderson.—You hold portion of Killbride yourself?—Yes.

391. And you naturally object to Kilbride being included?—I object naturally and on principle.

392. And the reason you give is that all the town-lands on the north side are held as townparks?—As a rule.

393. What is your idea of a townpark?—My idea of a townpark is where a party does not live on it, and it is held for the grass—for the purpose of grazing a cow, or for some purpose suitable, because it is near the town.

394. You say it is a townpark simply because the person does not live there?—A townpark is a piece of land that obtains an enhanced value from its proximity to the town.

395. Don't you know that the lands on the north side are agricultural lands?—I know no such thing, but I believe quite the contrary.

396. Would you be astonished to hear that you are wrong in that, and that they pay agricultural rents?—I can disprove it, because my father held a townpark at Kentchcurralow, and Major Peyly put on such an enormous rent that I can disprove your assertion.

397. Did you not say that as a general rule they pay an increased rent?—Yes.

398. Can you mention a case beside your father?—Yes, Andrew Byrne and Mrs. Kinsella.

399. Your only knowledge is about your father, because the rent was raised on him?—Yes.

400. Have you any knowledge of other tenants paying increased rent because the land is near the town?—Well I consider that when land——

401. I asked you to name any other tenant?—I consider that when land goes beyond £2 an acre and even to two guineas, that it is then at a fancy price—at townsland price.

402. Name any other tenant who pays an increased rent?—I believe, I cannot name it for a fact, that all those tenants pay above what I consider a fair rent—above £2—pay £3 and £4.

403. Do not the holders under Lord Carysfort live on the lands?—No, not within the present boundary—very few, if any.

404. Are there any houses upon the south side?—Yes.

405. Farmhouses of the people who till the land?—I think there may be two—Mrs. Aitken's and Mrs. Kearney's.

406. Are those the only two?—Those are the only two who carry on farming.

407. But is not farming also carried on in other portions of that side?—Yes; but if a man keeps a dozen cows and gets the milk in and sells the milk—that is not farming in the ordinary sense.

408. How many tenants are on the land at Kilbride?—I think four.

409. Do any of the tenants of Kilbride live in the town of Arklow?—If I saw the names of the persons I could tell you in a minute.

410. You said there were four persons who hold the land of Kilbride?—I know three, including myself.

411. Are there any others on the land?—If there are they live in the town.

412. How do you hold?—By lease.

[illegible] How do the others hold?—I believe they hold by lease [illegible].

[illegible] [illegible] would be liable to be taxed [illegible] [illegible] I believe Mr. Sherwood's [illegible] [illegible].

[illegible] Would it be unreasonable in extending the town at [illegible]?—The townpark portion; there is [illegible] park.

[illegible] With regard to the position which you describe as a townpark, is there any reason why it should be included [illegible] [illegible] a townpark [illegible] holding.

[illegible] There are portions of [illegible] that are townparks?—Only a comparatively small portion.

[illegible] [illegible] townpark [illegible] [illegible] Mr. Sherwood [illegible] holding [illegible].

[illegible] Supposing Mr. Sherwood were to live in Arklow, [illegible] [illegible] [illegible] small holdings.

[illegible] Supposing it was to be taxed, would [illegible] in Arklow?—[illegible].

[illegible] [illegible]?—Yes, of course.

[illegible] Are there any portions of townlands on the south side which are held by tenants, and which are not townparks?—Yes; I believe there are within the boundary.

[illegible] Will you tell me [illegible] [illegible] should be included within the township [illegible] [illegible] I think they should be taken out of the township. I think there should be no agricultural holding within the township, [illegible] with building ground and townparks, [illegible] the [illegible] [illegible].

[illegible] And the same rule should apply on the north and south sides of the town?—Yes; I don't see any distinction.

[illegible] Would you apply the same rule to the north side as to the south?—Not fully, for this reason, [illegible] the town of Arklow [illegible] on the south side of the river, [illegible] on the north side, [illegible] Ferrybank.

[illegible] The town of Arklow was on the south side?—Yes.

[illegible] But people living on either side have the [illegible] of the town?—Yes, they have the same benefits as the outside people on the north side. I say, that the inhabitants of Arklow and the holders of townparks on the [illegible] side [illegible] [illegible] [illegible] large. Those [illegible] ground for [illegible] [illegible].

Mr. Thomas Murray examined.

Mr. Thomas Murray.

[illegible] Mr. Johnston.—You reside I believe within two miles of the town of Arklow?—Yes.

[illegible] At what place?—[illegible].

[illegible] You have two holdings I believe under the Earl of Carysfort?—Yes.

[illegible] Is [illegible] outside the [illegible] [illegible]?—Yes, outside.

[illegible] You have a holding at the [illegible]?—Yes.

[illegible] What is the valuation of your holding at the [illegible]?—I think it is [illegible].

[illegible] You know the town of Arklow very well?—I do.

[illegible] [illegible] or more [illegible]?—Yes.

436. Do you consider the lighting of the town at present deficient?—I think not.

437. Do you consider that the footways or footpaths require in any way to be repaired or flagged?—I think not. I think they are in a very good state.

438. Are there any observations which you wish to make yourself?—The only thing I would wish to observe is that I think it is a very absurd thing for the Town Commissioners to strive to get any such area.

439. Mr. Andrews.—Don't you think there should be as much land in the boundary on the north as on the south side?—I think so.

440. That would be only fair?—I think that would be only fair.

Mr. Thomas Sherwood examined.

Mr. Thomas Sherwood.

441. Mr. Johnston.—You reside within a mile or two of the town?—About two miles.

442. Where do you reside?—At Kilbride.

443. What is the valuation of your holding there?—£[illegible].

444. Are you often in the town of Arklow?—Sometimes once a week, sometimes twice, and sometimes only once a month—sometimes not so often.

445. You consider that there is no defect in the lighting?—None whatever.

446. You consider that the town is quite sufficiently lit?—Yes; quite sufficiently lit.

447. And as regards the footways?—The footways are in good order, but in winter they would require [illegible].

448. As regards this proposed expenditure, this municipal [illegible] in flagging—what do you think about it?—I don't think it is required.

449. You don't consider it necessary?—No; I do not.

450. You don't consider that the Commissioners want any extended area for the purpose of getting more money?—No. As to the markets I don't think I have sold a penny's worth in them.

451. How do you dispose of your produce?—In Dublin.

452. By train?—I send it into Arklow by carrier.

453. It comes through the town?—It comes inside the bridge, and the [illegible] [illegible] it.

454. Is there a market [illegible] in the market?—There is a market for some fowls, and potatoes, but there is no butter or [illegible] market. I have been [illegible] in Arklow for years. There has been some improvement in the shape of [illegible], which the Commissioners have made arrangements with regard to.

455. You don't consider, Mr. Sherwood, that there is any necessity for this proposed improvement?—Not that I can see for myself. I think it would benefit the town of Arklow, and benefit the town people.

456. But you don't think it would benefit the outsiders?—I don't think so.

457. Assuming that the proposed extension were carried into effect, what would be the taxation that you would have to pay?—Threepence in the pound on land.

458. And would that be a considerable sum in proportion to what those residing inside the town would have to pay?—Yes, about double.

459. Mr. Andrews.—Your idea is that there should be no land outside the [illegible] included within the township?—Yes; unless to [illegible]—the better class of townspeople—the people who have land for their [illegible].

ARKLOW, May 2, 1879. — Mr. Thomas [illegible].

160. You think they should pay?—I do, certainly; and all townparks in the town, and I know there are townparks on this south side paying £3 an acre.

161. Mr. Cotton.—You think the townparks should contribute?—Yes; because the people who own them have all their trade in the town of Arklow.

162. You would exclude all land not townparks?—I would.

163. Do you think that the land occupied by the tenants on the north side should pay?—If they were nearer than townparks, stopping at [illegible] they are far removed from townparks. I think the townparks ought to pay, and the farmers ought not.

164. As a resident of [illegible] can you tell me why it was originally not included in the municipal boundary—why was it left out originally?—They considered that it was not necessary, and that the rates they would collect would be sufficient to meet all expenses. A marsh of which I hold part, was taken in, and I did not object to that.

Mr. Robert [illegible] — Mr. ROBERT [illegible] examined.

165. Mr. Johnston.—You reside within about two miles of the town of Arklow?—About two miles.

166. In what townland?—[illegible].

167. Is that within the two-mile radius?—I don't know.

168. Is any portion of it within the proposed extension?—I don't know.

169. Mr. [illegible].—It is not within it.

170. Mr. Johnston.—Then if you are not within it, it cannot affect you?—I see a great improvement since to what I have seen, and I don't know any improvement that the Commissioners have done since they got it, except to put up the lights.

171. Do you know that they propose an extension of the township?—Yes, I hear it.

172. Do you think they should get it?—I think they ought not.

Major Boyle. — MAJOR BOYLE examined.

173. Mr. [illegible].—You heard the evidence of Mr. Philpott, [illegible] townparks on the [illegible] side of the river?—Yes.

174. And as agent for the Earl of Carysfort you know the different holdings in all of them?

175. Is he right in saying that they are all held as townparks?—[illegible] Mr. Philpott's father held. That holding has been divided into [illegible] fields, and I think those [illegible] townparks on which was held by Mr. Philpott's father. These are the only townparks on Lord Carysfort's property.

176. [illegible]

177. And is there any [illegible] townparks?—[illegible]

178. [illegible] Kilbride?—Well, I cannot speak positively [illegible].

Mr. James Byrne. — MR. JAMES BYRNE examined.

179. Mr. Johnston.—You reside at [illegible]?—Yes.

180. And you [illegible]?—Yes.

181. [illegible]?—Yes.

182. You are frequently in the town of Arklow?—Frequently.

183. Have you any complaint to make about the present lighting of the town?—I think so far as I know, the lighting of the town is as good as any [illegible] town I have seen in any part of Ireland, north or south.

184. And what is the state of the [illegible]?—It is better than ever I knew it in all my life.

185. Does it require improvement?—I think it is quite good enough for the trade of the town, and better than ever I knew it before.

186. And you are decidedly opposed to any extension?—Decidedly; it is the greatest imposition and it is quite unnecessary.

The inquiry then closed.

BOYLE—30TH SEPTEMBER, 1879.

BOYLE, Sept. 30, 1879.

(Before Mr. H. A. ROBINSON.)

Mr. Patrick Coyne. — MR. PATRICK COYNE examined.

1. Mr. Robinson.—You are the Clerk to the Town Commissioners of Boyle?—I am.

2. Boyle is under the Towns Improvement Act of 1854?—It is.

3. When was it placed under that Act?—In 1857.

4. Was it previously under the 9th of George IV.?—No.

5. Was the Towns Improvement Act adopted for all purposes?—Yes.

6. For lighting, cleansing, and water?—Yes.

7. Have you got a map showing the boundaries of the town?—No, but I have one showing the extended boundary.

8. Has there been any alteration since the boundary was adopted in 1857?—None at all.

9. Can you give me a description of the boundary as then adopted?—Yes. Commencing on the [illegible] road, at the junction of the townlands of [illegible] and [illegible], thence eastward along [illegible] boundary of [illegible] to the Sligo [illegible] road, thence northward along Sligo-road to the [illegible] river, and south-eastward by [illegible] river to its confluence with the Boyle river, thence eastward along [illegible] of Boyle river to a point opposite the [illegible] boundary of Alexander [illegible]'s land [illegible] or Drum, thence southward along last-named boundary and by the fence which divides Miss Mary [illegible]'s land from that of Rev. John Magrath's to the junction of said fence with the Abbeytown-road, thence [illegible] ward along Abbeytown-road to the east boundary of the lands held by the representatives of Mr. [illegible] Judge, thence by eastern and southern boundaries of said lands to the Carrick-on-Shannon-road, thence southwards across said road, and by the [illegible] of Mr. Butler's house to the junction of said [illegible] with the boundary of the townland of [illegible] Park, thence

southward along said townland boundary to its junction with the fence which forms the southern boundary of Mr. John M'Dermott's land in Cloonshanagan, thence westerly along said fence, and by a fence passing through Mr. Alexander Arnold's land to the junction of the latter with the boundary of the townland of Great Meadow, thence southward along said townland boundary for about 200 yards to its junction with a fence which passes through Mr. Alexander Arnold's land in Great Meadow, thence westward along said fence to the Dublin road, thence northward along said road, and westward by the north boundary of Patrick Beckett's land in Great Meadow to the junction of the latter with the boundary of the townland of Tinny, thence southward, westward, and northward along said townland boundary to the Boyle river, thence northward in a straight line to the east boundary of Asylum graveyard, and continuing along said boundary to the Asylum Chapel, thence in a straight line to the eastern angle of Mr. John Fitzgerald's holding in Mocknagrea, thence westward along Ballymacurra, and northward by the fence which divides the holdings of Mr. John Fitzgerald and the representatives of Mr. Nicholas Mulhall to the junction of said fence with the townland boundary at Knocky, thence along north boundary of the townlands of Mocknagrea and Low Park to the point first described.

10. How many townlands are wholly or partially within the boundary?—Eight.

11. How many are wholly within the boundary?—Five are wholly included.

12. And how many partially?—Three are partially included.

13. Five wholly and three partially included?—Yes.

14. What is the valuation of the town?—£6,611.

15. And on how much is the full rate imposed, and on how much a fourth—how much on houses and how much on lands?—I cannot tell you that now, but I can send it to you.

16. Do you know what the whole rate produces?—The rate produces £84, and that includes the whole rate, and also one-fourth of the valuation on land.

17. What is the centre of the town?—The town bridge.

18. How far does the town extend to the north?—About half a mile to the north.

19. How far to the south?—All round the circumference of the town averages half a mile from the centre of the town.

20. In what electoral division is the town included?—Boyle.

21. How far does the Boyle electoral division extend?—To the north, about two and a half miles; to the south, about two miles; to the east, about a mile and a half; and to the west, about a mile.

22. Would not a two mile radius bring you into another electoral division?—Certainly.

23. What electoral division would that be?—I don't know what it might be. It would run into the Rockingham electoral division on the south, and the Tawnagh electoral division on the west. I hardly think that two miles would bring outside the Rockingham electoral division.

24. Yes it would?—I did not know that.

25. What is the area and valuation of the electoral division?—The valuation is £17,[illegible], and the area is [illegible],100 acres, statute.

26. Is Boyle, as a market town, much used by the people who reside within the electoral division?—Yes.

27. What are the towns closest to Boyle?—Frenchpark, Ballyfarnan, and Carrick-on-Shannon.

28. What were the municipal rates for the last five years?—In 1874, the rate was 10d.; in 1875, 10d.; in 1876, 11d.; in 1877, 6d.; and in 1878, 6d.

29. What were the poor rates for the same years?—In 1874, 4s.; in 1875, 2s. 10d.; in 1876, 1s. 1d.; in 1877, 2s.; and in 1878, 2s.

Boyle. Sept. 23, 1879. Mr. Patrick Coyne.

30. Did that include a sanitary rate?—No.

31. Has there ever been any special sanitary rate?—No.

32. Did the Guardians ever carry out the sanitary work?—They did.

33. What was the county cess in the years already referred to?—In 1874 it was 1s.; in 1875, 1s.; in 1876, 1s. 0½d.; in 1877, 1s.; and in 1878, 11d.

34. Is the town well lit?—Yes, it is well lit.

35. How many lamps are there?—74.

36. For what period of the year are they lit?—From the 1st of October to the 1st of April—six months.

37. Are the markets held late in the day?—Yes.

38. And are the lamps a necessity consequent upon that?—Yes, they are a convenience to those that require them.

39. Are there any improvements which the Commissioners are deterred from doing, or carrying out, from want of funds?—No, not that I know of.

40. Have they sufficient funds available for all purposes?—Yes.

41. Have the Commissioners ever considered the advisability of getting the jurisdiction of the sanitary authority?—I cannot say. I think they would wish to leave that work to the Board of Guardians.

42. Are there any building operations going on in the town?—Seven houses have been built within the last two years.

43. In which direction are those building operations extending?—They are going on in the centre of the town.

44. Are there any buildings outside in the immediate vicinity of the town, but outside the present municipal limits?—None.

45. If the two mile extension, which the Commissioners originally put forward was adopted it would include land liable to the one-fourth rate, and scarcely any houses?—Yes, they would include a great deal of land outside, but no houses of any consequence.

46. How many voters would they bring in by the two-mile radius?—I could not say.

47. Did you not go into any statistics concerning it?—No.

48. Did you calculate what the acreage would be?—No.

49. Or what increased income you would get?—No.

50. However, at the same time, you went in for a two-mile extension?—Yes.

51. Have you ascertained the feelings of the ratepayers on the subject?—They are well pleased with the boundaries as they now exist.

52. Then they have altered their opinion since November?—Yes; the Commissioners met last week.

53. I suppose I may take the Commissioners as representing the ratepayers?—Yes.

54. On the 30th of December the Commissioners were in favour of a two-mile extension?—Yes.

55. Did they pass any resolution on the subject?—Yes.

56. Can you give me a copy of it?—Yes.

57. What was the reason for that extension?—They consider at the present time that this is not the time to put on additional taxation.

58. Mr. William *Lawrence*.—On consulting the people we found that the people outside were opposed to any extension.

59. Mr. Robinson (To the *Town Clerk*).—Were the Commissioners aware of the recommendation of the Select Committee of the House of Commons that town boundaries should be made coterminous with electoral divisions?—They were.

Boyle, [illegible]. — Mr. W[illegible] Lawrence.

Mr. W[illegible] Lawrence examined.

60. You are a Town Commissioner?—I am.

61. Did you vote for the two-mile extension at the time it was suggested by the Commissioners?—I was not at the meeting at which it was considered.

62. Do you know the reasons that prompted the Board at the time to come to the conclusion that an area of two miles was a desirable one to include?—Not having been at the meeting I am not able to say.

63. Have you spoken to the members of the Board, who were present at that meeting, as to their reasons for coming to that conclusion? Did they consider that the people living within that radius derived such advantages from their proximity to the town that a [illegible] of the town taxation would not press unfairly upon them—was that the reason?—I think the Board came to the conclusion that it would not be desirable; that the people outside were quite satisfied for the present, and they did not wish to be taxed for the [illegible].

64. The people did not desire to be taxed?—Yes.

65. Do you consider that people living within the electoral division derive advantages from the proximity of the town?—Well, that is a question I could not answer, because one ratepayer might consider he ought, and another that he ought not, and the two might be of a different opinion.

66. Have you lived long in the town of Boyle?—All my life.

67. Do you consider it a thriving town?—Yes.

70. Is there any land within the present municipal limits available for building?—Yes.

71. If any building was likely to take place, the people would not have to go outside?—Yes.

72. They would be able to build within the present limits?—Yes.

73. Are the lands within the town principally accommodation lands and townparks?—Yes, mostly.

74. Held by people living within the town?—Yes; but that has been so for thirty years. They were originally townparks.

75. Are there any improvements which are required in the town which the Commissioners would carry out if they had a larger revenue from this increased taxation?—I don't know of any, now that the sanitary work is taken out of our hands.

76. Any improvements required in the way of lighting?—No.

77. Any sanitary improvements required for the present?—Well, from my own knowledge and experience, I think not. I think the town is well drained and well cleaned. As far as the streets are concerned, they might be better; but, for a country town, I think it is well cleaned.

78. Do you think that it is desirable to obtain the sanitary authority?—I would not be prepared to answer that question.

79. You don't like to give an opinion?—No, sir.

80. From your knowledge of your Board, do you know whether there are any members of it who are in favour of becoming the sanitary authority?—I am not aware.

81. I suppose you are aware that you can get a provisional order from the Local Government Board for the purpose?—I don't think we are.

82. The others are, also?—I would not answer for them. I don't think they are in favour of it.

83. Are you aware that you can get a separation from the Grand Jury—have you ever considered that desirable?—There was a time when we considered it desirable, but I don't think the Commissioners would do so now.

84. At that time were you of opinion that if you had jurisdiction over the roads, an extended area would be advisable, in which they would [illegible] the roads?—I don't think it came in that light before us.

85. You are aware that you [illegible] become the urban sanitary authority, before you can get control of the roads?—I know that.

86. Were you present at the meeting which was specially convened to consider the question of the boundaries [illegible]?—I was not; I was not [illegible].

87. I believe you heard considerable dissatisfaction [illegible]?—I have heard so.

88. And you consider that you have sufficient funds available for all your wants?—For the present purposes, [illegible] we have.

89. I suppose the people who have places of business in the town reside in the town. There are no villa residences outside the town?—None.

90. Do you know the electoral division?—Yes.

91. Do you consider that it would be advisable to adopt that as the municipal boundary, and that the recommendation of the Select Committee of the House of Commons should be carried out?—Well, if I were to speak for myself I might differ with them, but the Commissioners considering the people on whom the taxation would come, prefer to leave things as they are, and not to interfere with the boundary.

92. As an individual, what do you think?—I would say that we have quite enough money for our expenditure.

93. You consider the electoral division too large to be adopted as the town boundary?—Yes, I would.

94. And that the people living within it should not contribute to the works of improvement in the town?—I think they should not.

Cross-examined by Colonel King Harman, M.P.

95. Do you think the town has benefited by being brought under this Towns Improvement Act at all?—With the exception of water and light we have in no way benefited by it.

96. Mr. [illegible].—You don't approve of it then?—If I had had a voice in it when it was originated I would not have been a party to it.

97. Col. *King Harman*.—The town was not previously under the 9th of Geo. IV?—No.

98. Mr. [illegible].—It was not lit before that?—No. Those are the only two advantages we get from it.

99. Col. *King Harman*.—Don't you think it probable that they would have been brought into the town if there were no Commissioners?—It would be very hard to light except by Town Commissioners.

100. Is it lit by the Town Commissioners or by a private company?—By a private company, but the Town Commissioners pay for the lighting.

101. What description of light do you consider it to be?—We have had often to complain of it.

102. Mr. [illegible].—Do you consider it advisable that the municipal boundary should be limited in any way?—No.

103. Do you consider that the people living at the extreme point of [illegible]——? In one present boundary?

104. You—should contribute to the support of the town?—I would not be for limiting the town in any one way—certainly not for narrowing it. I would not alter it in any one way.

Colonel King-Harman examined.

[illegible] Colonel King-Harman.

105. Mr. Robinson.—Are you acquainted with the electoral division?—Yes.

106. You are the proprietor of a great portion of it?—Of the whole of it.

107. Is it your opinion that people residing in the remote part of the electoral division, who make use of the town—apart from deriving advantages from the proximity of the town—support the town and keep it up?—Certainly.

108. And you consider that if they make use of the lights coming into the town, yet the proceeds of their produce find their way into the pockets of the ratepayers of the town?—I don't think they use the lights.

109. But still that the result of the sale of their produce finds its way into the pockets of the ratepayers?—Yes, I would say so; but I disagree with the statement that they use the lights.

110. Are there not late markets?—Any late markets are usually well over before the lights are lit.

111. Do not the people who come to the early morning fairs use them?—As a matter of fact, the lamps are not lighted. They might be used in the winter time at early morning fairs, but in the evening they are not necessary for the country people.

112. Do I understand it to be your opinion that if the recommendations of the Select Committee were carried out here the effect would be, as there are no improvements contemplated, to bring in a lot of people who live in the outlying districts who would simply pay a rate for the purpose of raising the pockets of the ratepayers whom they themselves support?—Yes.

113. Has this always been your view?—Certainly. I say that improvements are required very much, and I say that the town, under the present system, is [illegible] most [illegible].

114. In what way are improvements required?—The owners of property in the town are not able to carry out designs of improvements which they would wish to do.

115. Because their estates are under the Town Council?—Yes. I would protest most strongly against any further extension of the municipal boundary, or [illegible] persons being subject to the Town Commissioners, [illegible] strongly.

116. I suppose you think the area of the electoral division too extensive to be adopted as the municipal boundary?—Yes; for the reasons given.

117. Are there many improvements required in the town?—A great many; but we are entirely thwarted and stopped by the town being in the hands of Town Commissioners.

118. In consequence of being in the hands of the Town Commissioners?—Yes; the Guardians and Town Commissioners are continually pulling in opposite directions.

119. You think the management of the town would be better carried out if it was vested in one individual authority?—Yes. I wish to say that if the Town Commissioners remain in the same as at present, I think the town ought certainly to take over the sanitary authority.

120. Is that your opinion or the opinion of the Board of Guardians?—That is my opinion.

Mr. Lawrence re-examined.

Mr. Lawrence.

121. If you included the electoral division would it, do you think, bring you up to the desirable 6,000?—I don't think it would.

122. Are there 3,000 residing in the electoral division in addition to those residing in the town?—I think not.

123. Colonel *King-Harman*.—Do you think a Grand Jury Board would be a better management for the town than the Town Commissioners?—Certainly not; I would hardly say that.

Major C. Robinson examined.

Major C. Robinson.

124. Mr. Robinson.—You are, I believe, agent for Colonel King-Harman?—I am.

125. Do you agree with the views he has expressed?—I quite coincide with what Colonel King-Harman has expressed. If the sanitary authority was vested in the Town Commissioners, I think it would make them a much more useful body, and it would be a smaller body that would have to deal with the subject than at present exists in the case of the Board of Guardians. Before the sanitary authority was vested in the Board of Guardians, we were in the habit of getting a good many county works done in the way of drains—covered drains. There is one very important one from the base of the town right up a steep hill, which was done at the expense of the county, and there is hardly a presentment sessions that I am aware of that we have not something done. Now if you go to the Grand Jury, you have then to go to the Guardians, and from the Board of Guardians you are jostled down to the Town Commissioners, all trying to shirk their business.

126. A regular conflict of authority?—Yes.

127. Well, is it your opinion that the entire management of the town should be in the hands of one body?—I think so, certainly.

128. Do you consider that if they do this, and the Commissioners are made the sanitary authority, and they should get a separation from the Grand Jury, that the present area is sufficient on which to assess the rates?—I think it should be slightly increased.

129. Please describe on the map the way in which you would suggest that it should be increased?—Take the extreme west of the boundary line, I would not go past that, and then work on. There is the Boyle river, there is a road that would run into the Sligo-road. I would bring it down there, and make that the northern boundary—that is the road connecting Boyle with the Sligo-road. Instead of going down the river to go down that road, I would take in both sides as there are houses on both sides. There is a road not marked on the map—a navigation road; I would bring the boundary up this navigation road, and I would cross the river and take in a very populous district there known as Drum or Warren—although there are only a few houses at the junction of Drum and Erris. I would then go along the old road—along the crossing between the Warren-bridge and the Boyle and Carrick-on-Shannon-road.

130. And then would you continue along the town-land boundary, and would you take in Lexford Park?—I would be inclined on the south side to extend to beyond Ozbert cross-road, and that would bring you round Doonyeane and bring it up to the back of the Gray Meadow.

131. Is that only on the understanding that the Commissioners become the sanitary authority?—Yes, on that understanding; otherwise, I think they have got too much.

132. Do you think there are any improvements required in the town?—I think there are improvements required.

133. But they do not go into the hands of the Town Commissioners?—They do not.

134. And that the conflict of authority operates to deter them from being carried out?—I think so.

You have referred to the Act of George IV. Perhaps you are not aware that Boyle is a very old borough town, with a "Borough Master." We had a charter of the Corporation of Boyle granted by King James I., on the 12th of February, in the eleventh year of his reign. There was an old borough court and a manor court.

135. Does that charter vest any property in the hands of the Town Commissioners?—I think not.

136. Are there any other matters you would wish to mention?—I might also add that I think from the class of people that are now Town Commissioners, that I believe there is a majority of them that would work the sanitary authority conscientiously, and for the wellbeing of the residents of the town—men of intelligence and men who would not fail to stick to their business, and not introduce politics and religion.

137. And that any improvements made in the town would directly benefit it, and be more than the Guardians could carry out?—Yes.

138. Colonel King-Harman.—The difficulty in connexion with the present state of the sanitary authority is how we are to act, and it prevents us from doing the work that we are anxious to do as landlords and as agents.

139. Mr. Robinson.—You are acquainted, Mr. Lawrence, with the electoral division?—Yes, but I have not got any statistics.

140. The recommendation of the Select Committee as regards Boyle being extended to that boundary would be out of the question?—Certainly.

Mr. Joseph Mulvall examined.

141. Mr. Robinson.—You have heard the evidence of the last witness?—Yes.

142. And you agree with it?—Yes.

Mr. William Dempsey examined.

143. Mr. Robinson.—Is this return correct that the valuation of the electoral division is £7,031?—I am not certain, but I think it is something like that.

144. Of the poor rate struck was any portion of it a sanitary rate?—In 1866 there was a sanitary rate of 1d. in the pound, and we have not had one since.

145. On what should be the minimum period sum for the union?

The Inquiry then closed.

BELTURBET—26th SEPTEMBER, 1879.

(Before H. A. Robinson, Esq.)

Mr. Thomas Charles examined.

1. You are Town Clerk?—Yes.

2. Under what Act is the town constituted?—The Towns Improvement Act.

3. Did you adopt the provisions of the Act for all purposes?—Yes; we were first under the 9th of George IV.

4. But the boundary then differed from the present boundary?—We had no boundary under the 9th of George IV. at all.

5. You ought to have had one?—But we had none; and under the 17th of Victoria we defined the boundary.

6. What steps did the Commissioners take to establish a boundary?—They then did it by perambulation. They brought in what they considered the most convenient and compact boundary they could devise.

7. Was the boundary you forwarded to the Government accepted by them, or did they make any change?—No; they made no change whatever.

8. Is the boundary composed of townlands or portions of townlands?—There is only one townland wholly in—Nugham.

9. And portions of how many?—Four.

10. What are their names?—Corporation Lands, Cromaughtan, Kilconny, and Derrinagland.

11. What is the area of the town?—We never levied any taxes, and all we required was to know the extent of our authority over the place.

12. But are you not aware of the area of the town?—We never required it.

13. What is the valuation of the town?—We never required a valuation of the town, but the amount prescribed by His Excellency was £12 a year occupancy to qualify for a commissioner. We never required any valuation or anything of the kind.

14. Then, so in this town, it is exceptionally circumstanced?—Yes.

15. There is property vested in the Commissioners?—Yes; there is only one or two other towns in the kingdom in similar circumstances.

16. What is the population?—In '61, 1,780; and in '71, 1,194.

17. Would you say that the town is thriving?—I think latterly it is.

18. And you consider the census of '81 will show an increase on the previous years?—I suppose it will.

19. Are there any houses not occupied in the town now?—Not one.

20. Are there building operations going on within the town?—There are. The fact of the matter is, the town is rather in an improving condition than anything else.

21. Are there building operations going on outside the town?—No.

22. Have you been resident here long?—About sixty years.

23. Do you see much difference in Belturbet now to what it was when you first became acquainted with it?—I do, so far as the independence of the people is concerned.

24. Are not the houses of a better class?—Far better.

25. Is there land within the municipal district available for building?—Plenty.

26. If building operations were required, the people would not have to go outside the boundary?—I don't know how they could require more land than the land inside. If they required it there is sufficient land inside.

27. Are you acquainted with the poor law electoral division of Belturbet?—I am.

28. How far does it extend?—It is bounded by the river.

29. The town is in two electoral divisions?—Yes.

30. What are they?—Belturbet and Kilconny.

31. How far does Kilconny extend?—More than a mile to the west.

32. And Balrgriet, how far?—It goes to Kingscourt.

33. What is the nearest market town?—Ballyconnell, to the west.

34. [illegible] Dunmanway(?).

35. [illegible]—Yes, many [illegible].

36. [illegible]—When they [illegible] they are ready.

37. Do people generally go away before it is dark?—Yes.

38. How is the town lighted?—By oil; we did not put up the lamps yet.

39. What are the months in which you light the lamps?—We begin in October, and end in April.

40. What is the cost per lamp?—The entire cost is £23 4s. 1d., which is the lighting and all the necessary repairs connected with it.

41. What are the gross rates?—Last year [illegible], but only 1s. 3d. now.

42. Was there any special sanitary work for which a rate was imposed?—No.

43. What was the amount of it?—10d. in the pound.

44. For what purpose?—Making drains.

45. Through the town?—Yes.

46. And what was the sanitary district over which it was charged?—It was [illegible] the town; there was a great [illegible] in that [illegible] and some of the drains were made through it.

47. Do you mean the position of [illegible] town?—Yes.

48. [illegible]—No, it was [illegible].

49. [illegible]—I am [illegible] of it, and what is most [illegible] is that [illegible] the town [illegible] to the extent of £50 or £60 [illegible].

50. The town is now well [illegible]?—There are no [illegible] now, every place is covered.

51. Have the Commissioners ever considered the question of becoming a sanitary authority?—Yes, I think they would be very anxious; they would rather have the management of it themselves than the Board of Guardians, it is so [illegible].

52. Are they aware that the seventh section of the Public Health Act enables them to obtain that power from the Local Government Board?—No, I did not get a copy of the Act [illegible].

53. How far is the Poor Law Union from this place?—The union house is [illegible].

54. And any sanitary matters would be transacted through the Guardians?—Yes.

55. And is it the opinion of your Board, that they would rather have the management in their own hands?—Yes, they are more interested in the matter and their arrangements would be attended with less expense.

56. Are there any sanitary arrangements required in the town?—No, they have been all done.

57. Do you know what the money spent is [illegible] this [illegible]?

58. Do you think the Commissioners would be in favour of having a separation from the Grand Jury?—We would [illegible], but the Grand Jury would not give their consent at all.

59. Are you aware that the same Act enables you to obtain that power whether the Grand Jury agree or not?—No, I was not aware of that.

60. Is it the opinion of the Commissioners that the municipal authority for the town should be in their own hands?—They endeavoured to procure that, and in consequence of [illegible], but the principal objection of the Grand Jury was that we have a large bridge near the town and Mr. [illegible] said we would have to pay if anything happened to the bridge.

61. Do you consider the advantages counterbalance [illegible] the money you pay in the Grand Jury cess?—No, that is why we made the application.

62. Is it still the opinion of the Commissioners that the sanitary work and the roads should be in their own hands?—Yes.

63. If the Commissioners had this power would they be in favour of having an enlarged area over which to [illegible]?—I think if we had that power it would be necessary to make the area larger.

64. Would you be in favour of including the whole of these townlands, portions of which are now included?—If they would not be too extensive.

65. Are the townlands included in the town occupied [illegible] principally by [illegible]?—Principally [illegible], except part of [illegible].

66. What is the nature of the property rated by the Commissioners?—Land and houses.

67. How did they acquire it?—By charter of Charles II., or one of them.

68. Another charter?—[illegible].

69. What does the property produce?—The rents for the last year were £182 9s. 5d.

70. What was your other source of income?—From under the Lighting Act, £17 3s.; dog licenses, £[illegible]; [illegible], £[illegible]; and the rent of the Town Hall, for exhibitions, £3 12s. 6d.

71. What was your expenditure?—£278 13s. 5d.

72. You have never struck any rate?—No.

73. Do you see any likelihood of your striking any rate?—No, if we go on as we are.

74. You have a balance of £[illegible] in hands?—That [illegible].

75. Do the Commissioners consider the question of enlarging the boundaries?—The Commissioners have never had much discussion on that subject. I was speaking to the Chairman this morning and he said he thought there was no change required; the area was large enough.

76. As to sticking [illegible] would it be an advantage to people living outside?—No advantage in the world.

77. That is your opinion of it?—Yes.

78. You don't see any likelihood of your rent being applied to [illegible]?—No.

Mr. Thomas Sheala(?) examined.

79. You are a Commissioner?—Yes.

80. You have heard the evidence of Mr. Clarke?—Yes.

81. And you agree with him, there is no necessity for extension?—Yes.

82. Are you in favour of having a transfer of the powers from the Grand Jury?—Yes.

83. You don't consider you receive full value from them?—Not a tenth of the value. The streets are in a most ridiculous manner at the present time, and with regard to footpaths they are never improved here at all.

84. You think it would be desirable to have these powers in your own hands?—Yes.

85. Were you aware of the 203rd section of the Act?—No.

86. Do you think the Commissioners are still in favour of the change?—I think they would be.

87. Are you in favour of having the management of the whole town in your hands?—Yes.

88. Under those circumstances would you be in favour of having a larger area for taxation than now exists?—I could not give a decided answer to that, for we have not had any meeting of the Corporation, but it would make it lighter on people in general.

89. Is it your opinion that if you had those powers vested in yourselves, an increased area would be desirable?—Yes.

90. Did you ever consider to what extent?—No.

91. Do you consider it would include the four townlands, portions of which are now included?—Yes.

92. Do you think the people there derive advantage from living so close to the town?—Yes, the produce is better and the facilities for disposing of it.

Stradbally. Aug. 20, 1879. — Mr. Thomas Smith.

92. They avail themselves of the light of the town? —Yes.

93. And there are schools in the town?—Yes, but the town people often send their children to schools outside also.

94. So that if these people had to pay their quota of a municipal rate it would not be a hardship on them, considering the advantages they enjoy?—No, it would make it lighter on others.

95. You don't in the future see any likelihood in the necessity of striking a rate?—No.

Mr. Thomas Devine.

Mr. Thomas Devine examined.

96. You are a Commissioner?—Yes.

97. And you concur in what has been stated?—Yes.

98. Are you in favour of having the management of the town in your own hands?—Yes.

99. And to have an enlarged area of taxation should you receive those powers?—If it was necessary.

Dr. Thompson.

Dr. Thompson examined.

100. You are sanitary officer for the district?—Yes.

101. Do you think there are any sanitary improvements required?—They always require sanitary improvements more or less; at present the town is in a very sanitary condition.

102. Did you find any difficulty in getting these improvements carried out with the Guardians?—Not in the least.

103. Do you think it would be better to have the sanitary works in the hands of the Commissioners?—Yes, I think it would be better.

104. How long does it take you to get anything done?—Well, about eight days; suppose I made a report to-day, it must go before the Guardians at their next meeting, which would be on next Tuesday.

105. Would you be in favour of including the portions of the townlands outside the boundary?—I think so. The Commissioners were unanimously in favour of having the sanitary work of the district carried out by themselves; but if taxation was necessary we would have to increase the area on which to assess the rate; that is supposing it was necessary, which I don't think at all likely.

Mr. James Mahaffy.

Mr. James Mahaffy examined.

106. You are a Commissioner?—Yes.

107. You also concur?—Yes, we were all anxious to get this grand jury power into our hands and we would like to try it again.

Mr. John Nash.

Mr. John Nash examined.

108. You are a Commissioner?—Yes.

109. Are you in favour of having the power vested in your hands?—Yes.

110. And increasing the area?—Yes, if it was required.

111. And you think that the people living in such proximity would have no objection to pay considering the advantages they get, and we getting their quota of the municipal property?—I don't think they would.

112. There is an advantage here, because the Commissioners strike no rate?—Just so.

Mr. Clarke.

Mr. Clarke recalled.

113. Is your property improving?—Well, I think it is not varying.

114. Is the rental the same every year?—Yes, pretty much the same. The lands are leased for thirty-one years.

The inquiry then terminated.

Callan. Aug. 21, 1879. — Mr. Thomas Ryan.

CALLAN—21st AUGUST, 1879.

(Before Mr. H. A. Robinson.)

Mr. Thomas Ryan, Town Clerk, examined.

1. How long have you been Town Clerk?—Since 1840.

2. Callan is constituted under the Towns Improvement Act, 1854?—Yes.

3. When did it come under the Act?—In 1855.

4. Did you adopt the provisions of the Act for all purposes?—Yes; watering, lighting, and cleansing.

5. When the town came under the Act, who were the committee who determined the boundary?—The Town Commissioners, nine in number.

6. Why did they adopt this boundary?—They considered it the most convenient boundary.

7. Has there ever been any revision of the boundary since that date?—No.

8. The boundaries then made exist now?—Yes.

9. Did it include whole townlands or take in parts of townlands?—I could not say how many townlands are included, they are what are called town parks adjoining dwellings.

10. When they adopted a boundary, did they follow any previously existing boundary; did they make the boundary coterminous with the townland boundary, or did they cut through fields, taking in parts of them?—Some small fields they cut through, taking in portions of them.

11. How far to the north does the boundary extend?—About a quarter of a mile from the cross.

12. And on the south how far?—About the same.

13. And on the east?—About the same, and to the west a little less.

14. Then it is about a quarter of a mile all round?—Yes.

15. Are the building operations extending without the municipal boundary?—No; there have been no buildings erected outside since the adoption of the Towns Improvement Act.

16. Are there any buildings going on towards the town boundary?—Not at present.

17. Previous to the adoption of the Act of 1854, was the town governed under any other statute?—Yes, the 9th George IV., cap. 82.

18. Were you Town Clerk then?—Yes.

19. What was the boundary of the town then?—Much the same; it was corrected by Mr. Griffith, and that was adopted then and sanctioned.

20. So I may take it that the town under the Act of 1854, subject to some few modifications, is the same as under the 9th George IV.?—Yes.

21. What is the area of the town?—[illegible] statute measure, and the net annual value, £3,630 [illegible]

22. On how much of that is the full rate struck

Callan, Aug. 21, 1880.

Mr. Thomas Ryan.

and how much one-fourth?—We have no rate struck for the last six or eight years.

23. What is the population?—In 1871 it was 2,357.

24. What was the population in 1881?—2,331. I take that out of "Thom's."

25. Do you consider Callan a thriving town?—I do.

26. Do you think any material increase in the population will be shown by the census of 1881?—I could not say; I really think there are no buildings outside from which we would derive much benefit, for in case we were to strike a town rate we would only get one-fourth on lands, so that suppose a rate of 1s. was struck to cover the expenses of the town, that 1s. would be levied on buildings alone, and only 1½d. on arable land.

27. In what electoral division is Callan?—In Callan.

28. What is the valuation of the electoral division?—9,700.

29. There have been no municipal rates?—No; for the last five years.

30. Have the Commissioners any property vested in them?—Yes, this was a corporate town, and the property we have passed into the hands of the people as a remnant of the former property.

31. What were the poor rates for the last three or four years?—I can't exactly say.

32. Of the poor rates struck in the last five years, was there any special rate for sanitary purposes?—No.

33. The Guardians are the sanitary authority?—Yes.

34. And has there been no special sanitary rate?—Yes, there has been 1d. in the pound.

35. What was the contributory district over which this rate was struck?—The entire electoral division.

36. What is the county cess?—It varies from 2s. 4d. to 2s. 2d. and 2s. 3d. That is taking the two half years together.

37. Are the Town Commissioners aware that under the 9th section of the Public Health Act of last session, they can apply to have the sanitary duty taken out of the hands of the Guardians and transferred to them?—Yes.

38. Would the Commissioners approve of the change, or do they consider that the sanitary work is sufficiently carried out by the hands of the Guardians?—They do, and I don't think the Commissioners would desire to take the duty into their own hands.

39. Are the Commissioners as a body satisfied with the sanitary management of the town?—As far as my judgment leads me, I think they are.

40. By the 200th section of the same Act, you can apply to get separation from the Grand Jury in respect of the roads, but you don't think the Commissioners would desire to get charge of the roads?—I don't think they would.

41. Did none of them ever express the opinion that the town would be better managed under one undivided authority?—I never heard them.

42. What is the nearest town to Callan?—Kilkenny is the nearest.

43. And how far is that away?—Eight Irish miles.

44. I may take it Callan is the market town for the entire electoral division?—Yes.

45. And all the farmers who have got land in the electoral division make use of it to dispose of their produce?—Yes, they generally do.

46. And it is of some advantage to them to have the town well kept?—Yes.

47. Do the people immediately outside the town make more use of it than people who are more remote?—Yes.

48. Do they pay any rate towards the town?—No.

49. Have the Commissioners ever considered whether it would be desirable that these people, owing the advantages they derive from the town, should pay something towards its rates?—I am not aware.

50. Do the people living outside make use of the schools in the town?—Yes; they come in from several parts of the country to the schools in town.

51. There are fairs held here?—Yes.

52. And I may take it that the town being well kept—well lighted, watched, and cleansed, besides being of advantage to the people in the town is of advantage to the people of the entire division?—Very much so.

53. We sent you down some queries for the purpose of ascertaining the opinion of your board, were they submitted to a special meeting of the Commissioners?—Yes.

54. Was there a resolution passed on the subject?—Yes; and they decided in favour of extension.

55. Was there any resolution put on the books?—No; the queries were simply filled up.

56. Were the Commissioners unanimous in deciding that extension was required?—Yes; they were at that meeting, which was held on the 2nd December, 1878.

57. They were in favour of extension, but no resolution was passed?—No; the queries were filled up and returned. Mr. Thomas Shelly was Chairman at that meeting.

58. Has there been any subsequent resolution passed?—No; there has been nothing more about it.

59. Are they still in favour of extension?—I can't say.

60. But the result of the meeting, as shown on the books, is that they were in favour of extension?—Yes.

61. Did the Commissioners, when they suggested that extension was desirable, specify any extension which they thought would be most appropriate?—No, but the question was discussed. When this town was under a corporate body it comprised about two miles from the centre of the town; that was the liberties of the town.

62. And were they discussing the advisability of including the liberties of Callan?—I don't exactly remember, but they had a general discussion about it. There was a general idea that extension would be desirable, but they did not point out what particular extension would be requested until you arrived. The present area is rather limited.

63. Is it your opinion that the reason they desired extension was that the people outside could use the town in every way as much as those living in it?—Exactly so.

64. And they considered that the land outside is more valuable by reason of its proximity to the town?—Just so.

65. You have hitherto been giving the opinion of your board, what is your own opinion, as a ratepayer, on this question?—I would not like to give my private opinion, but I think if anything occurred to increase the taxation that portion of the country outside which derives benefit from the town should share in the increased taxation.

66. There are no rates at present, but you think that if necessity arose for striking a rate there should be a larger area for taxation?—Yes.

Mr. MICHAEL MAHER examined.

Mr. Michael Maher.

67. You are Clerk of the Callan Union?—Yes.

68. And have been for sometime?—For the last twelve years.

69. You are acquainted with the electoral division?—Yes.

70. What is the valuation of it?—About £9,700.

71. How far on the north from the centre of the town does the electoral division extend?—It extends very nearly two miles on the north; on the south it goes exactly two miles; on the west scarcely two miles; and on the east not so far. On the average it is under two miles all round from the centre of the town to the limits of the electoral division.

72. Are you a resident in the town?—I am.

73. Do you take any interest in the affairs of the town?—Very little, I am sorry to say.

Mr. Patrick Coady examined.

74. You are one of the Town Commissioners?—Yes.

75. And have been so for some time?—Yes.

76. You have resided here for a long time?—All my life.

77. You are well acquainted with the statistics and circumstances of the town?—Yes; so far as my memory goes.

78. Can you tell me the nature of the property in the hands of the Commissioners?—Four small little houses.

79. Are there any tolls or dues?—Not exactly tolls, but when we established the monthly fair we made a small charge for cattle coming into the fair.

80. You derive property to such an extent that there has been no necessity for levying rates for the last five or six years?—No. We got our town almost all sewered by the Clifton family before the Commissioners took up the management. The Clifton family take great interest in the town.

81. Do you see any likelihood of any necessity for levying a rate for some time to come?—No.

82. Your income will be sufficient for many years to come?—Yes, with economy; but if there was extension it would alter the thing very much.

83. The town is lighted with oil?—Yes.

84. You light only in the winter months?—Yes; from 1st October to the 1st April.

85. Were you present when the question of extension was discussed?—Yes.

86. You were in favour of it?—Yes. My own opinion is that if the town was extended we might get the control of the roads out of the hands of the Grand Jury; because they are grossly neglected by the Grand Jury.

87. You think you don't get value commensurate with the money you pay?—I am of opinion the roads are eaten away.

88. You are aware you could not become the road authority unless you were the sanitary authority first?—I was not aware of that.

89. Do you think the management would be better under one undivided authority?—I am quite certain it would be.

90. You think the management of the roads, lighting, and cleansing, would be better in your own hands?—I think so.

91. Do you speak the feeling of the Commissioners in that matter?—I don't know that. If there was any idea of taxing the people outside they would oppose extension.

92. The people outside would be glad to receive any benefit so long as they had not to pay for it?—Yes; they have all the benefits; and I have even seen them come in here for water.

93. Taking into consideration the fact that the Select Committee have recommended that as far as possible town boundaries should be made coterminous with the electoral division—do you think it would be a hardship to ask the people in the entire electoral division to pay one-fourth of the town rates?—I think it would be an advantage to them, and no hardship at all.

94. You think they derive such advantage from having this place as a market town that the advantages would be increased by having the town better kept?—No doubt about it; and I have no doubt if they could foresee the result they would vote for this themselves.

95. You think the entire electoral division being a well-defined boundary might be adopted?—Yes.

96. It would give you an increased valuation of about £7,000 on which you could strike one-fourth of the rates?—It would be quite sufficient. We have not struck a rate for the last five years, and the reason is we did not want it. The town is pretty well kept.

97. Is there land within the municipal limits available for building purposes?—A good deal. We have another property in the fair green which is surrounded by a high wall. It contains twelve or thirteen English acres, and it is one of the best pieces of land in Ireland. We make a revenue from it by grazing cattle on it after the fairs. The grazing yields [illegible] a year, and the tolls come to £70 for the year.

98. I understand you to think the area altogether too limited?—Yes.

99. And if the people were of an enterprising turn of mind there is not much land available in the town to build upon?—As the boundary stands at present they are cramped in their action, and their ideas will not extend because they have no place to build. It is objectionable in other points. It is objectionable as regards the police law, for the moment a man passes the boundary he is out of the power of the town authority, in fact a man may go out about 100 yards and the town authority is powerless.

100. Is this a good business town?—It is one of the best in the south of Ireland.

101. Do the business people in the town occupy residences outside the town?—No; they generally live in the town.

102. There is no tendency to build outside the municipal boundary in order to avoid the town rates?—No.

103. If you adopted the electoral division boundary you would be prepared to take the roads into your charge—of course levying the rate which the county now levy for that purpose?—Yes. I would like to have control of the roads, and as a matter of absolute necessity. There has been a good deal done in the way of providing pumps, and that is the reason why we were not so anxious to become the sanitary authority; the union has acted rather generously with us, and made the cost of the pumps union charges.

Mr. Maher recalled.

104. What is the contributory district over which the sanitary rate is struck?—The union at large.

105. For works in the town?—For such matters as sewers in the town, the dispensary district is the area of taxation, but, for water, the union at large was made the contributory district.

106. How many electoral divisions are comprised in the Callan dispensary district?—Six.

107. And they levied the special sanitary rate over the whole of these divisions?—Yes; but for the water supply—it surprised everyone at the time—the Local Government Board, at the request of the majority of the Guardians, made the union at large chargeable. The Guardians evidently were of opinion that the people of the entire union derived advantage from town improvements.

108. Mr. Coady.—No doubt of it. The business of this town extends to the union at large. The people come from all parts to this market.

109. Are there any improvements in the town that the Commissioners would carry out if they had a larger income?—I think one of the first things required, more than anything else in the world, is labourers' cottages. The people are living here in houses in a state of the most absolute wretchedness. You could not punish a dog by putting him into the places these people occupy.

Mr. John [illegible] examined.

Castlebar. Aug. 23, 1879.

Mr. John [illegible].

111. Are you a Commissioner?—I am; and I wish to point out that, within a circumference of three or four miles there is not a school for paupers. The people from three or four miles come in here to attend school.

112. You think the town being kept in good condition is an advantage to the people out there?—Yes.

113. Are you in favour of extension?—I am not well posted up in it, but from what I have heard I think it would be advisable.

114. In case you had to strike a rate?—Yes.

115. And of course any people brought in now would have all the advantages and have nothing to pay?—Yes. There is no provision against fire.

115. You have no fire brigade?—No.

116. Do you think if you had a larger area you would take due steps to procure a fire brigade?—Yes.

117. Are there any other improvements required in the town?—Yes; we have no market-place. The markets are held on the streets.

118. But you have a fair green?—Yes.

119. Were you present at the meeting of the Commissioners when this subject was considered?—I was not.

120. Do you coincide in Mr. Coady's views?—I do.

Mr. James Malone examined.

Mr. James Malone.

121. You are a Commissioner?—Yes.

122. You have heard Mr. Coady's views on behalf of the Board and his own individual opinion; do you coincide with those?—I do.

123. Were you present at the meeting when this subject was discussed?—Yes.

124. And you approved of the decision arrived at?—Yes.

125. You are engaged in trade?—Yes.

126. Are you engaged in any farming?—No.

127. Do you consider that the people in the entire electoral division derive exceptional advantages from their proximity to so good a market town?—Yes.

128. And do you think if they were asked to pay one-fourth of the rates struck in the town, if rates were [illegible] necessary, they would not be hardly treated?—I think not.

129. Mr. Coady.—My evidence on the subject would be very disinterested, for any property I have is outside the boundary.

130. So that if this extension was made, as you [illegible], and rates were struck, you would be rated outside the boundary for municipal purposes?—Yes; considerably.

131. So that your personal interest is against yourself?—Yes.

The inquiry then closed.

CASTLEBAR—6th SEPTEMBER, 1879.

Castlebar. Sept. 6, 1879.

(Robert [illegible] A. Robinson, Esq.)

Mr. Joseph Robinson (Town Clerk) examined.

Mr. Joseph Robinson.

1. Do you hold any other office under the municipal authorities?—No. I am secretary to the Gas Company, but it is a private company.

2. How long have you been Town Clerk?—For fourteen years.

3. You are well acquainted with the town?—I am.

4. Is the town constituted under the Towns Improvement Act?—Yes.

5. When was it placed under that Act?—In 1863 or 1864.

6. Was the town previously under any other Act?—No.

7. Did you adopt the Act for all purposes?—Not in the first instance. The object in adopting the Act at first was to enable us to light the town, and to levy a rate sufficient to pay for that. It had to be incorporated subsequently, and regulating powers were sought in order to give us them, and when the Grand Jury refused to cleanse the streets, and we were driven to take the benefit of the cleansing powers of the Act.

8. What is the population of the town?—3,508.

9. Was that an increase or decrease compared with the census of 1861?—It was a decrease, but I would rather say it is stationary now.

10. And the Census of 1881 will not show any material increase?—I don't think it will.

11. What is the area of the town?—[illegible], 3r. 31p.

12. What is the valuation?—Buildings, £8,732 5s.; and lands, £1,387; total valuation, £[illegible].

13. Is there much land available within the town for building purposes?—Not within the town—in the town proper there is not much available.

14. How far does the town extend on the north from the centre of the town?—I would say half an English mile, and on the south half a mile.

15. In all directions, I am informed, it extends half a mile, except where they adopted the townland boundary?—Yes.

16. What principle the Commissioners in first adopting the present boundary?—They applied for a larger boundary, and the Lord Lieutenant sent back the application with a map marking a limited boundary, and as the Commissioners only wanted it for lighting purposes they accepted it, although their own selection was more in the nature of what they now seek.

17. Was any reason assigned for the curtailment?—No.

18. They simply defined a certain boundary?—Yes.

19. That boundary exists now?—Yes.

20. Does the town include whole townlands or portions only?—Portions of townlands principally.

21. And whole townlands also?—Yes.

22. Can you give me the names of townlands wholly and in part included?—Yes; we have the whole of [illegible], [illegible], [illegible], [illegible], and [illegible], and part of [illegible], [illegible], [illegible], and [illegible].

23. In what electoral division is the town situated?—The electoral division of Castlebar.

24. Entirely in that electoral division?—Yes.

25. Are the Commissioners aware that the Select Committee have suggested, as far as possible, to make the boundaries of the townships coterminous with the poor law division?—Yes, I think they are aware of it.

26. But in the case of Castlebar that would be impossible?—Yes, because it runs too far in one direction, while it is near enough in another.

27. There is such want of uniformity in the electoral division that it would be out of the question to adopt it as the township boundary?—Yes.

28. What are the rates struck in the town?—The last rate was 1s., and 6d. on land.

29. You struck the full rate in 1878?—Yes. In 1877, 10d.; in 1872, 1s.; 1875, 10d.; 1874, 1s.

30. What have been the poor rates in the same years?—In 1878 it was 2s. 1d.; in 1877, 1s. 10d.; in 1876, 1s. 6d.; in 1875, 1s. 9d.; and in 1874, 1s. 11d.

31. Does that include the rate made for special sanitary purposes?—It does. We assess 1d. on the entire union for sanitary purposes, &c., and it is at

Castlebar. [illegible]

Mr. Joseph Madden.

present about another penny, which is principally for waterworks in the town.

32. What is the contributory district?—The electoral division. In fact, all sanitary works in the division are assessed on the entire electoral division.

33. What was the county cess in 1876?—1s. 5½d. In 1877, 1s. 9½d.; 1876, 1s. 10d., 1875, 1s. 11½d.; 1874, 2s. 3½d.

34. Are there fairs held in the town?—There are.

35. And markets?—Yes.

36. I suppose it is the market for the people of the entire electoral division?—Yes, and more. They come from Galway, for this is one of the best pig markets in the country.

37. The people living within a mile of the town will derive benefit by having the town lighted when they come in to the market?—Yes.

38. I may take it that the lands within a mile are more valuable than those farther away from the town?—Yes.

39. And people living within that distance make considerable use of the streets?—Oh, yes.

40. And they come in every market day?—Yes, and all through the week.

41. And they send their children to school in the town?—Yes, within a mile they do.

42. The land is let at a higher value on account of its proximity to the town?—It is, I believe.

43. Is the town well lighted?—I am secretary to the Gas Company, and I consider it is well lighted.

44. It is lighted with gas?—Yes.

45. With reference to sanitary matters the Commissioners are aware, I suppose, that by the 7th section of the Public Health Act of last year they can get the sanitary matters taken out of the hands of the Guardians and placed in their own.

46. Have they ever discussed that matter?—No; but I think, having regard to the present state of their means, they would prefer leaving it to the Guardians.

47. They are influenced by the fact that half is paid by the landlord at present?—That has a good deal to do with it.

48. Have they ever considered the question of getting the care of the roads?—When Westport and Ballina sought it, the matter was discussed here, and it was considered there would be legislation on the subject.

49. Do you think it is the opinion of the Board, or of any section of it, that the management of the town should be under one undivided authority?—I think it is the opinion of individuals, but they never expressed it; but they are less complaining than other Boards. I think if you had their individual opinion they would say it ought to be.

50. The Commissioners are in favour of extension of the boundary?—Yes; they came to that conclusion.

51. Have they passed any resolution on the subject?—Yes.

"Resolved—That this Board is of opinion, that the present boundary as defined on the map should be extended by half a mile, and that the clerk do attend before the Commissioners and give effect to this resolution."

52. Was that adopted at an ordinary or a general meeting?—At an adjournment of an ordinary meeting; but the adjournment was made anticipating your arrival.

53. On what grounds did they wish the extension?—To increase their income. The rates at present press on the buildings in the town.

54. Are there any improvements in the town which you would carry out if you had a larger income from this extended area?—I don't think there are; but I think the application for the present extended area was not to enable them to do anything. Their object was to relieve the town rates.

55. Did the Commissioners specify any extension?—They did; an extension of half a mile from the present boundary, or about a mile from the centre of the town.

56. Can you form any opinion as to what would be the additional value of that extension?—The present valuation at 3d. on land (the rate being 1s.) gives £19 17s. 6d. My opinion is we would only derive the same amount from the extension of the town.

57. All the land to be brought in by the extension would be only liable to one-fourth?—Yes; the extension might, taking in two gentlemen's residences.

58. Are there any villa residences outside the present boundary?—No.

59. Do the people having business in the town live in the town and at their places of business?—They do; but they hope yet they will be able to live in fine villas.

60. I take it that the reason the Commissioners seek extension is, that they consider it would not be a hardship for the people outside within the extension to be asked to pay one-fourth of the town rate, considering the advantages they derive from their proximity to the town?—Yes; it would not be a hardship. The most of it will come upon Lord Lucan, Mr. Fulkiner, Mr. Irwin, and a few others.

61. Would you say the town is growing?—I think it is an improving town. I have watched it for a few years.

62. Do you notice much difference in the town since the Commissioners became the authority?—Yes; we have two banks and a gas works that we had not then.

63. Is there any tendency to build outside the present limits?—No.

64. And the people living outside the town do not do so for the purpose of avoiding taxation?—No; simply for convenience.

65. Are there building operations going on within the present area?—There are.

66. In which direction?—They built a new Roman Catholic chapel in a northerly direction.

67. Are there any houses being built?—Yes; one house in the same direction.

68. And there is not much land within the boundary available for building?—Oh, yes, a good deal, if Lord Lucan chooses to give it for the purpose.

69. Then there is sufficient within the township?—Yes; if we could get rid of private interests.

70. Do you consider that the town being well kept as to light and sewerage is an advantage to the people within a mile?—It is, and it is of importance to any one coming into it to have it well kept.

71. And those people come in regularly?—They do.

72. Do they stay in it after five o'clock on winter nights?—They do up to seven and eight o'clock.

73. And they contribute to the wear and tear of the roads?—They do.

74. And you think any increased income spent in the town would be of advantage to the people you propose to take in as well as to those in the town?—I think so. The increased boundary will not after all take in so many smaller people; but it will take in lands of those like Lord Lucan and others.

75. Do you think the Commissioners would have any objection in the event of this boundary being carried out to follow some well-defined boundary?—They would prefer uniformity, even at the expense of symmetry in the boundary.

76. The suggestion as to the electoral division boundary is out of the question?—Yes.

Mr. JAMES FITZGERALD examined.

Clonmel, Sept. 2, 1872. Mr. James Fitzgerald.

77. You are Chairman of the Commissioners?—Yes.

78. For how long have you been Chairman?—For about four years.

79. You have been a Commissioner for some time?—Yes; since the formation of the township.

80. Were you one of the Committee who submitted the boundary forwarded to the Lord Lieutenant?—I was one of the Committee.

81. And were you one of those who selected the boundary?—No.

82. Can you give me the reason why it was selected?—No. We only asked for lighting powers, and it appeared to us that was the reason why they gave us so small a boundary.

83. The boundary you now suggest was forwarded to the Lord Lieutenant and rejected by him?—Yes.

84. You applied afterwards for power to enlarge the area?—Yes, when the Grand Jury refused.

85. Do you think there is any likelihood of your endeavouring to get the town under the modified Schedule?—I cannot say.

86. Would it be desirable?—I think so. I think it is absurd to have three bodies in the town administering these small matters.

87. Do you think the work done by the Grand Jury is commensurate with the money you pay to the town?—I think if we took control of the whole area, we could effect a considerable saving.

88. Were you present when the question was discussed at the board?—Yes.

89. Are you in favour of the extension of half a mile?—Yes.

90. And you think the people within that radius derive advantage from the town?—Yes.

91. You are not asking to take in these lands on account of ratepayers?—[illegible] people have advantages and should pay their share?—The great reason is that our taxation is so high, and we want additional area of taxation to lessen it.

92. You think it will diminish taxation?—I think it will.

93. You would not be in favour of any further extension?—We might. The matter was discussed several times, and yesterday it was discussed at a special meeting and every one seemed in favour of extension. Mr. [illegible], who represents Lord Lucan, did not agree with us and he was absent yesterday.

94. Do you think building operations are likely to go on outside the present boundary?—I don't at present see any sign of it.

95. Do you think there is sufficient land available for building within the town?—There is a great deal.

96. Are there any improvements which you would carry out if you had additional income?—There are a great many required if we had powers and means.

97. Have you a fair-green?—Yes.

98. And how many fairs are held there?—There are twenty-four fairs held in the town annually. There is a good fair-green but we require increased market accommodation. We have no slaughter-house, and that is one thing that is necessary. We have a market-place but it might be improved vastly.

99. Have the Commissioners any income from tolls or customs?—No. Lord Lucan is proprietor of the town and tolls. He has them let to me, and the Commissioners have no control over them at all.

100. You would be able to improve the fair-green?—There is nothing required in the fair-green, but a market-house is wanted.

101. Would the better lighting accommodation be a convenience to the people who you propose to take in, as well as to the people within the town?—It would.

102. And these improvements which you anticipate from increased funds, would be of great advantage to the people you propose to bring in?—Our town will be better lighted; at present it is the lightest altogether in my jurisdiction, and it is principally from want of means we have not better light.

103. How many lamps are there?—Fifty or sixty, and on the principal road leading to the military we want two additional lamps, and on the road leading to the asylum we want another; it would be very desirable, but owing to the debt lately they have been to us more difficult to [illegible] it. Of course the better the town is lighted the more advantage for the people outside.

104. Is that your view or the view of your Board?—That is my own view and it was the view of the meeting yesterday without a single dissent, and not only that, but some of the large inhabitants—they are all unanimous—wish to extend the area to make the town in a better position.

It is the view of the ratepayers?—It is.

105. Have you heard any of the views of those outside?—No, they are generally agreeable; but the bulk of the land will be land held by Lord Lucan.

106. Are your fairs too dirty?—Yes; in winter particularly, and the markets are held here.

107. And the people attending them would derive advantage from the lighting of the town?—Very much.

108. Do you know the boundary of the electoral division?—I have an idea of it from the map.

109. Do you agree with Mr. Sheridan in saying that the recommendation of the Sidney Committee as to the electoral division could not be carried out?—It would not do at all. I quite agree with Mr. Sheridan.

Mr. JAMES DALY examined.

Mr. James Daly.

110. I am a member of the Board of Guardians and a Town Commissioner.

111. Have you been a Commissioner for some time?—For about four years.

112. You live in the town?—Yes.

113. And are pretty well acquainted with the circumstances of it?—Pretty fairly.

114. And you think it would be an advantage to the townspeople and to those outside it, to have additional income?—Great advantage.

115. Additional income is required?—Yes; there is a great deal to be done if we had means.

116. And in order to obtain means you think the people outside should contribute?—Yes, they come to buy and sell here; they come to Chapel in the town, and it is most essential that they should have the town well kept. These people contribute very largely to the state in which the town is left on Sunday mornings.

117. What is the income and expenditure of the town?—About £150 a year. We pay £77 for lighting, £40 for scavenging, and £15 for supervising the streets.

118. Have you incurred any debt?—No, we don't owe a penny.

119. Do you approve of the half-mile radius from the present limits?—Yes, and I would even prefer where the greater portion of a townland was within the radius to take in the whole of it.

120. You would endeavour to make it uniform as far as possible?—Yes.

121. You consider the land within a certain circle is more valuable?—Yes, the greater portion of it is in the hands of the lord of the soil, still it is more valuable.

122. What class of land is it?—Good grazing land.

123. Would the extension of the area to the pro-

posed limit bring up the population to 6,000?—I think if the town is improved it would bring it over it—there are as many as three or four families living in one house—there is a great want felt of more house property in the town.

124. Mr. *Sheridan*.—The extension would hardly bring the population over 6,000.

125. Mr. *Daly*.—There are several improvements that could be made, for instance, in the sanitary arrangements.

126. Is there difficulty in getting building land?—Yes.

127. Is it such that the people are building outside the town?—The land within a mile or two is held by the lord of the soil, and the people would build if they could get it.

Mr. Sheridan recalled.

128. What are the receipts and expenditure?—They are nearly equal. In round numbers, the income and expenditure are £200 a year.

129. Do you owe anything?—We owe nothing, because we paid off our liabilities yesterday.

130. The people outside would be liable to nothing except the rates?—Yes.

131. There are no debts?—No.

Mr. Daly recalled.

132. I coincide with Mr. Falkiner and Mr. Sheridan. I think the management should be in one body. There are several matters that come before the Board of Guardians, and they say it is not their duty but the duty of the Town Commissioners, and the Town Commissioners send it back to them, and they say it is the duty of the Grand Jury.

133. It has never been resolved to apply to the Local Government Board for a provisional order?—There was some time ago, but we thought it would be brought before the Parliament, and they deferred the matter until they saw the result of it and the Commission which preceded it. The markets are held on the streets, and there is great necessity for a market place. Produce of every kind is sold in the main streets, and it tends to the disfigurement of the place. The pig market is held in the public streets, and after a market they are nearly uninhabitable in some parts of the town. If the Commissioners had means they would prevent it, and as a member of the Board I would do whatever is requisite in the matter. If the lord of the soil would give a little more facilities they would improve the town materially.

134. Do you consider one-fourth is sufficient for the people outside to pay?—Yes.

135. It was said some places one-half should be paid?—I think they should pay one-fourth, and that is one of the reasons why I would be for extending the boundary further into the country. I would be in favour of extending it a mile from the outskirts of the town, and if I had been at the meeting yesterday, I would have proposed a larger extension.

136. And you are of opinion that if there was an extension of one mile from the present boundary it would not entail any hardship?—Not from the outskirts of the town. I mean a mile from the buildings, and that would be about the same as that proposed now.

Mr. Alfred H. Sheridan examined.

137. I am a Town Commissioner. I was present when this subject was discussed. I have heard Mr. Falkiner and Mr. Daly's evidence, and I agree with what they said.

138. Do you approve of the extension for a mile?—Yes. I was a sort of subcommittee that adopted that boundary, and it was afterwards adopted by the Board.

139. You do not adhere to this hard-and-fast boundary, but you would be prepared to adopt any well defined boundary?—Most decidedly. It would prevent confusion to have an entire townland in or out.

140. And there are improvements required for the town?—Very many.

141. And these would be of advantage to those outside?—As much as to those inside.

142. Do the people make use of the town to a considerable extent within a circle of half a mile?—All of them. It is the principal market town. There is no other within seven miles on any side. I might say ten English miles.

143. I suppose all the people living here make Castlebar their market?—Yes, they bring in corn, potatoes, milk, vegetables, &c.

144. Do the children attend school in town?—Almost in every case.

145. The markets are of great advantage?—No doubt.

146. In fact any improvements carried out in the town by this increased income would be felt by the people outside?—Yes, except that they would not share in the advantage of a water supply, so much as those living in the town, but in other respects they would. The want of market accommodation necessitates the holding of markets in the streets, and the consequence is that they cause a great deal of mud and filth on the streets every day of the week. If the mud is not removed on Saturday night it lies there on Sunday, and the country people who come into Mass have suffer. Except as to their residence and earning their bread, they use the town as much as ourselves. In striking upon the boundary we had no idea of leaving in one place or another. We just took the compass and made half a mile circle outside, but it would be desirable not to stick to a hard-and-fast line. Originally the Town Commissioners applied to have a larger boundary than the present.

147. Can you tell why it was refused?—No, except that they never like to give us as much as we ask.

148. And you think that if you asked a boundary twice as large you would have got what you now want?—I think so. Nearly every member of the Board, except myself, has land at present outside the boundary, which will come inside the proposed boundary, so that they also are disinterested in the matter. Mr Michael Quinn, who has taken a large interest in this will—except Lord Lucan—be the largest sufferer, and Mr. Falkiner in the same way; all I am sorry for is that I have no land either inside or outside.

149. Are you in favour of having one undivided authority?—At present I am not, for this reason: Under the Towns Improvement Act we have no authority to tax lands with more than one-fourth; at present the work is done, and well done so far as I [illegible] but, by the Guardians, who are the sanitary authority, and they have a right to tax to the full extent on lands equally with houses. They have power, and they have exercised it judiciously, to extend the sewerage over the whole division, which is a larger area than the township. In that way the Guardians have acted very

well, and unless the Commissioners had the same powers of putting the taxation equally on lands and houses, I think it would be a serious disadvantage to the town.

150. As well as I can see, what Mr. Falkiner said was, he was in favour of the broad principle of having an undivided authority in one body, but not to take the sanitary matters from the Board, under the circumstances, and looking to the large area over which the taxation was spread.

Mr. *Falkiner*.—Yes.

151. Mr. *Sheridan*, T.C.—I am not at present ready to say there would be a saving under the present system, but rather a loss to the town.

152. Mr. *Daly*.—If we got the additional powers, I think the tolls should be in the hands of the Commissioners.

153. Mr. *Sheridan*, T.C.—We are of opinion the market accommodation is bad.

154. Mr. *Daly*.—I concur with Mr. Sheridan it would be better to leave the matter in the hands of the Guardians rather than the Commissioners, so far as the sanitary matters are concerned. I know for the last term the Guardians have done more for this town than the Ballina Commissioners have done for that town. They have done everything they could do, without levying a 6d. rate on the town.

CASTLEBAR, Sept. 5, 1877. Mr. Albert H. Stevens.

155. Mr. *Falkiner*.—A great many of our Guardians are gentlemen living many miles away, and do you think these gentlemen have as much interest in the cleansing of the town as those living in it and having property in it?

156. Mr *Daly*.—I agree they have not, but they are disinterested in the taxation. Those living in the town are those who have to pay, but the Guardian in the country is quite disinterested, and does not inquire what he is to pay, and acts impartially. The town man is afraid to tax himself, or to incur the displeasure of taxing his neighbour.

157. Mr. *Falkiner*.—Who can have so much interest in the welfare of the town as the man living in it?

158. Mr. *Daly*.—For the last few years they have taken greater interest in advancing the town than the Town Commissioners ever did, or would have done, because they are simply the same as you are. They are impartial judges, and they are not looking whether they are taxing themselves or their friends, they are there and they are doing their duty above board, and levy the taxes over a more extended area.

Mr. ALEXANDER LARMINIE examined.

Mr Alexander Larminie.

159. You are agent for Lord Lucan?—Yes.

160. He is the owner of property both in the town and around it?—Yes; but I wish to state I have not got instructions from him to oppose extension in any way, and that what I say is entirely my own views, and I am not binding him to what I state.

161. He would be principally concerned if this extension was carried out?—He would be concerned more than any other individual, but I do not think his lordship would on those grounds object. Taking a valuation of £30, the charge on him would be £4 a year. As far as I could understand the real reason put forward is to decrease the taxation on the present area.

162. The principal reason was not so much to decrease their taxation as to enable them to carry on certain improvements in the town?—They are arguing on both lines.

163. They say taxation bears heavily on the people in the centre of the town?—But when they can show that by extending the area they can bring an increase of more than £11 in their income it would be worth considering, but with only that I don't see what improvements they could effect or how they could lower the taxation.

164. But you are assuming there are no buildings to be brought in?—The only buildings to be brought in are the houses of poor small farmers who have at present quite enough to do to live. I cannot see how the town can be said to confer a benefit on them to the same extent as upon those living in the town.

165. Do they confer a benefit on the town?—They support the town.

166. Would you be in favour of a larger extension?—Oh, no; I should not be at all in favour of that, for that would still more bring in small peasant occupiers.

167. Don't you mean to say they derive advantage from the town?—They derive convenience from the town, but the town derives advantage from them.

168. You think it is mutual?—More than mutual.

169. If they had not a town so close they would not so easily sell their produce?—If they were not so close the town would not exist.

170. That is your individual view?—Yes.

171. And you would not like to say whether Lord Lucan would object to the extension or not?—I don't think he is in favour of it.

172. Mr. *Sheridan*, T.C.—As far as we are concerned we have been mooting this thing for the last six months, and Mr Larminie, Lord Lucan's agent, was present at all our meetings, so that his lordship cannot be unaware of what the Commissioners state here now.

173. Mr. ROBINSON.—You do not object in *toto* to extension?

Mr. *Larminie*.—No; but I do not think the gain would be worth the candle; the expenses and trouble would swallow up the profit.

174. What expenses?—There are parliamentary expenses.

175. The expense in this case would be met by Act of Parliament?—Of course, I am aware, but there is some preliminary expense. If there is a prospect of all the powers being centred in one body with equal powers of taxation I think it would be advantageous to have an increased area. I am one of the Guardians of the electoral division, and it has always been on my motion that the taxation for sanitary purposes has been put on the entire electoral division. I do not wish to appear so entirely against extension.

The inquiry then closed.

CASTLEBLAYNEY—26TH JULY, 1879.

(Before HENRY A. ROBINSON, Esq.

MR. J. G. W[illegible] examined.

1. MR. ROBINSON.—You are clerk to the Town Commissioners?—I am.

2. Have you been clerk since the town first came under the Act?—No.

3. When did the town come under the Act?—On the 11th of September, 1855. The 10th of August was the date in the Gazette.

4. Are you an inhabitant of this town?—Yes.

5. Have you been so for any length of time?—Yes.

6. And are you well acquainted with its circumstances?—Yes, pretty well.

7. Before the adoption of the Towns Improvement Act, was the town under any other Act?—Yes, the 9th of George IV. It was in a very primitive state at the time.

8. Do you remember the town at the time?—Very distinctly.

9. Has the boundary that was then adopted been since changed?—I am not aware.

10. I suppose I may take it the same boundary still exists?—Yes.

11. The town is not divided into wards, I presume, for municipal purposes?—No.

12. Can you give me the population?—1,[illegible].

13. Would you say it was an increasing or a diminishing population?—I think it is increasing, but very gradually.

14. But you think the census of 1881 will show a perceptible increase on the present?—Yes, I think so.

15. Have buildings increased?—Well some time ago there were some houses empty, now however, there are no available houses to be had.

16. What is the area?—[illegible] acres.

17. And the valuation?—£[illegible].

18. Are you aware, when the Commissioners came under the Act, what steps they took to determine the boundaries now existing?—I think they had a surveyor who determined them.

19. And they fixed what they considered to be a proper boundary?—Yes.

20. Would you describe the boundaries?—I have the description here as they were approved of by the Lord Lieutenant.

21. Kindly read that description?—The entry is as follows:—

"The Lord Lieutenant has been pleased to approve of the boundaries as specified as aforesaid, that is to say—'Commencing on the north band of Derrygorry Bridge, thence south-east along the town boundary between Derrygorry and Drumnaffiard Big to Muckno Lough, thence southward and eastward along the townland boundary of Drumnaffiard Big and the western shore of Muckno Lough to junction of townland boundary of Drumnaffiard Little, thence southward and eastward and along said boundary to junction boundary of townland of Cargy [illegible], thence southward and eastward along said boundary to the eastern point of said boundary, eighty-five yards north east of Rent House in Castleblayney demesne, thence south-westward in a straight line to the eastern extremity of fence south west of Roman Catholic Chapel, thence south-westward along said fence to junction boundary, between townlands of Cargy and Conabury, thence north-westward along said boundary to junction with fence and boundary, the holding of Richard Mitchell, in the townland of Conabury, thence north-westward along said road to southern extremity of garden fence of Conabury Cottage, now held by [illegible], thence northward and westward along said garden fence to junction with garden fence of Conabury House, now held by Hugh Swanzy, esq., thence north-westward along said fence to western extremity of same, thence westward in a straight line to south-eastern extremity of boundary of Mr. Walker's holding, thence northward along said boundary to the boundary of townlands of [illegible] and Conabury, thence north-westward along said boundary across the Railway road to northern extremity of same crossing the Dundalk and Enniskillen Railway, thence across the Monaghan road, northward and eastward in a straight line along the fence to Mrs. Rule's holding to northern extremity of boundary between the lands of Drumnaffiard Little and Drumnaffiard Big, thence northward along said boundary to junction of boundary fence of Mrs. Rule's holding, thence northward in a direct line, and crossing the accommodation road in the townland of Drumnaffiard Big, to northern extremity of M'Carty's house on the Armagh road, thence north-eastward along the eastern boundary of said road, to the point first named.'"

22. We may take it that the boundary extends on an average of from a quarter to half a mile all round?—Yes, that is what I would say. It is more than half a mile in some places, but I would say from half to a quarter of a mile all round.

23. Does the town include whole townlands or parts of townlands. Are any whole townlands included?—I think from Mr. Ball Greene's return there is not a whole townland. It includes I know part of Conabury, Drumnaffiard Big, Drumnaffiard Little, [illegible], and Cargy.

24. Will you give me the rates for the last five years?—In 1878, 8d.; in 1877, 10d.; in 1876, 10d.; in 1875, 10d.; in 1874, 8d.

25. And the poor law rates?—In 1878, 1s. 1d.; in 1877, 1s. 4d.; in 1876, 1s.; in 1875, 1s.; and in 1874, 1s. 2d.

26. Does that include the rate for sanitary purposes?—Yes, from the time the sanitary law took effect.

27. You are not aware what the special rate was for sanitary purposes?—No, I am not, except what has been furnished in the return.

28. Are you aware what the contributory district was on which the sanitary rate was levied, what townlands it comprised?—No, I am not.

29. Can you give me the county cess for the past four or five years?—In 1878, it was 9d.; in 1877, 10d.; in 1876, 10d.; in 1875, 10d.; and in 1874, 11d.

30. Is there any property vested in the Town Commissioners?—No.

31. Your source of income is the rates?—Yes, and contributions arising from fines and dog tax.

32. Is the town well lighted?—It is very well lighted.

33. With gas?—No, not with gas. It was lighted with gas, but owing to a disagreement with the gas company, they resorted to burning oil.

34. And it answers the purpose?—Well, I don't say whether it does or not. There is a difference of opinion.

35. Is the whole town lighted?—Well, yes.

36. Up to the limits of the boundary?—Yes, except in the agricultural parts, or pastoral parts, where there are no habitable houses.

37. On how much of the valuation is the quarter rate, and on how much the full?—The full rate is on houses, and the one-fourth on land.

38. Can you tell me the valuation on which the full rate is struck?—I can give the full valuation, but cannot readily subdivide it—they are so interwoven.

39. Are there schools in the town?—Yes.

40. And I presume people from outside the present boundary send children to those schools?—Yes.

41. And I presume they make use of the market?—Yes.

42. Have the Commissioners ever considered the question of becoming the urban sanitary authority?—I am not aware.

43. You are aware that by provisional order they

Castleblayney, July [illegible]. Mr. J. G. Whitby.

not take the sanitary authority from the Board of Guardians, and become the sanitary authority themselves?—Yes.

44. Are the Commissioners aware of that fact?—I don't think so.

45. They do not know that the Commissioners can obtain a provisional order to become the urban sanitary authority?—No.

46. Is it the opinion of the Commissioners, do you think, that it would be advisable to have such a provision taken advantage of?—Yes, I would say so.

47. Would they be disposed if they had the extended area to take command of the roads, and to have the undivided authority of the town?—No, they would not take that on themselves.

48. Are there any markets in the town?—Yes.

49. Do the Commissioners derive any income from tolls from the markets?—No.

50. How often are the markets held?—Three days in the week.

51. Do the people who make use of these markets mostly reside in the town, or do they come from outside; are they small farmers and others of that class?—Yes; some of them come a considerable distance.

52. Do you think that all the farmers in the electoral division make use of the town of Castleblayney?—No.

53. Would you say they do for a mile round?—They may or may not according to circumstances.

54. What do you mean by according to circumstances?—Well, take it as a general rule they attend the next market.

55. Is Castleblayney the nearest town to farmers in the electoral division?—Yes.

56. Are there any manufactures in Castleblayney?—No.

57. Do the people in the town live in their shops or outside the limits of the town?—In their shops.

58. Can you tell what quantity of arable land there is in the town unbuilt on?—I could not.

59. But there is a considerable portion?—Yes; there must be about 100 acres.

60. There is a sufficiency of land inside the boundary for building purposes for many years to come?—I would not say that.

61. Is building extending in any one direction more than another?—Generally, it is on the southern end.

62. Are there any building leases outside the present boundary?—I don't know of any except the Almshouses.

63. Do the people carrying on business inside betray any tendency to live outside to evade the taxation?—No.

64. Are there any improvements that the Town Commissioners have been restrained from carrying out from want of funds?—I don't know that there are.

65. Are any improvements required that are under the Board of Guardians?—Well, I cannot say much—but any improvements that are required are under the supervision of the Board of Guardians.

66. Is the town well drained?—Very well. There are some parts, however, not so well drained. We are in a mountainous district.

67. That is in the hands of the Board of Guardians?—Yes.

68. Then, I may take it, there are no improvements required that come under the supervision of the Town Commissioners?—If they had the full authority of the Act of Parliament, which they at present have only adopted for lighting and cleansing, it would be better.

69. Is there a good water supply?—Yes, very good.

70. High pressure?—No.

71. Have the Commissioners considered the question of enlarging the boundaries of the town?—It was considered at a meeting.

72. Was it a special meeting?—An ordinary meeting.

73. And they are of opinion that no extension of the boundary was required?—They expressed that opinion at the time.

74. Did they pass any resolution on that occasion?—Not more than to say that they did not wish an extension of the boundaries.

75. Have you consulted the ratepayers on the subject?—No more than in casual conversation.

76. Do you know the feeling of the ratepayers?—They seem to be indifferent.

77. Do you think the Commissioners would have any objection, in order to get a better defined boundary, to adopt the whole of those townlands, portions of which are now included?—The principal Commissioners are here, and perhaps it would be better they should answer that.

78. An opinion to that effect has never been expressed at the board?—No.

79. You know the electoral division?—Yes.

80. Do you think, bearing in mind the recommendation of the Select Committee on the subject, that towns should be conterminous with poor law electoral divisions, that that would be desirable as a boundary?—No; it would be too large.

81. And do you think that people residing at the extreme ends of the electoral division do not derive sufficient advantages from the town to justify such an extension?—Quite so.

82. What is your own individual opinion on the subject of the extension of the boundary?—That any change of that kind would not be for the advantage of the town.

83. And do you think there is sufficient land within the limits of the town for some years to come?—Yes.

84. And you don't see any advantage that would follow from an extension of the boundaries in any direction?—No.

85. Have you any general observations that occur to you to make on the subject?—No.

Mr. John D[illegible] examined.

Mr. John [illegible].

86. You are a Town Commissioner?—Yes.

87. And have been, I understand, for a considerable time?—Yes.

88. Have you lived in the town for a number of years?—Yes; for twenty-four or twenty-five years.

89. And has the town within that period shown signs of improvement?—Yes; it has.

90. Have building operations gone on within that time?—Yes.

91. Is it your opinion that the Census of '81 will show an increase over the last Census taken?—Yes.

92. And are the people more prosperous?—Yes; I think the people are pretty well off. There are very few houses to let now.

93. What is your opinion as to the sanitary state of the town?—Well, there is certainly room enough for improvement. Between the Catholic and Protestant churches there is a place that is in a very bad way in wet or winter months, and the arrangements in that respect are not so good as if the Commissioners had power to make a sewer to the lake at the northern side. There is a large drain, too, that is a great nuisance, and is even dangerous.

94. Dangerous to health?—Yes; that is in the hands of the Board of Guardians.

95. If you were the urban sanitary authority, would you take steps to remedy it?—Yes.

96. And you think, therefore, that the sanitary business would be better managed if in the hands of the Town Commissioners than as at present?—Yes.

97. When the town came under the Act, I presume the present boundaries were fixed?—Yes.

98. Do you know what exactly they had in view in so fixing them?—No.

99. Do you think any extension is now required?—I do not know that.

100. Do you hold any land outside the municipal boundary?—Yes.

101. Of what character is the land?—It is not good. It is at Erne.

102. The boundary includes part of Cornaslary, Drumnailard Big, Drumnaliard Little, Moraghy, and Ouseny, would you see any objection to including the whole of these townlands?—No.

103. Do you think the lands in those portions of the townlands outside the boundary are more valuable from their proximity to the town?—I am sure they are.

104. And, if you were not bound to give them light and see to cleansing, you would have no objection to rate them at the threehalfpenny rate?—It would be the same people who would be rated, for they live in the town.

105. Are I to understand that all the portions of these townlands outside are held by people resident in the town?—Principally; I may say all.

106. Have you ever talked with any of the ratepayers on the subject and ascertained their feelings?—No.

107. According to the answers supplied to our queries the boundaries are regarded as satisfactory?—Yes.

108. And no change is required?—No.

109. And any buildings likely to take place for the next ten years, will they be inside or outside the boundary?—Inside.

110. There will be sufficient building ground inside for a considerable time to come?—Yes.

Mr. PATRICK SMITH examined.

111. You are a Commissioner?—Yes.

112. And you have lived here for a considerable time?—Yes.

113. And know the circumstances of the town?—Yes.

114. Do you think if the Commissioners had more funds they would carry out improvements that are now impracticable from want of means?—Yes; particularly sewerage.

115. That is now in the hands of the Guardians?—Yes.

116. And you think if the sanitary works were in the hands of the Commissioners they would do it better?—Yes.

117. But at present they are not cramped in any way?—No; not so far as their own work is concerned, but as you say, they would do better than the Guardians, so far as sanitary matters are concerned—cleansing and so on.

118. If the Commissioners were the urban sanitary authority an increased area of taxation would give them an increase of funds, which they would apply to sewerage purposes?—They certainly would apply part of it.

119. Then you think it would be desirable they should be the urban sanitary authority?—If they had that authority they would do more than at present.

120. Do the Guardians attend to any complaints that are made?—Yes, but there has been remissness.

121. Do you think there is likely to be any building operations extended outside the municipal limits?—I think not.

122. And I take it you corroborate the evidence already given?—Yes.

123. And you think you speak the feelings of the Board and of the ratepayers?—Yes.

124. The ratepayers, I presume, have had sufficient notice of the inquiry being held here?—Yes; ample notice.

125. And I take it they would have come here to express their views, if they differed from the Commissioners?—I think so.

126. Would you think it necessary to limit the boundary in any way?—No.

127. Do you know the electoral division?—Yes; pretty well.

128. Do you think, from what you know of the electoral division, that the size of it would deter the Commissioners from adopting it as a boundary?—Yes, it is altogether too large.

129. And it would be regarded as a hardship on people living in the most remote parts of the electoral division to be asked to contribute to the cleansing of the town?—Yes; they would not consent.

130. But they come in and carry on their marketing in the town?—Yes.

131. The land is more valuable from its proximity to the town?—Yes.

132. But they object to pay anything they can avoid?—Yes; I think so.

The inquiry terminated.

CAVAN—SEPTEMBER 27, 1879.

(Before Mr. H. A. ROBINSON.)

Mr. JOHN MOORE, Town Clerk, examined.

1. Under what Act is the town constituted?—The Towns Improvement Act, 1854.

2. Previous to that under what Act?—The 9th of Geo. IV., c. 82.

3. Does the boundary which was established when the Towns Improvement Act came into operation still exist?—No; the former boundary extended a mile in each direction.

4. Has there been any alteration in the boundaries since the Towns Improvement Act was adopted?—None whatever.

5. What was the boundary under the 9th of Geo. IV.?—A mile each way from the centre of the town.

6. A half-mile that is?—Yes.

7. Do think the present boundary is sufficiently large?—Yes; a great deal less, it extends only a quarter of a mile.

8. What is the area of the town?—[illegible]

9. How many townlands, whole and in part, are included in the boundary?—Twelve whole and [illegible] partly.

10. What are the townlands partly included?—Keady, Cagiam, Kilmore, Drumcrow, [illegible], Aughnaskerry, and Keenaghbeg.

11. What is the value of the town?—[illegible]

12. On how much of that is your rate assessed?—£8 10s. 10d. is all we get from land.

13. What is the valuation of it?—£158 6s. 6d.

14. And the valuation of the houses is the balance?—Yes.

15. Is there sufficient land within the boundary for building?—There is no ground within the town available.

16. Are there any building operations extending outside the boundary?—None that I know of.

17. Are there any within the boundary?—There is a new street now being built, [illegible], consisting of ten [illegible] houses.

18. In what direction is that? —North.

19. What class of houses are they? —Intended for tradespeople. Two of them are shops.

20. What is the population of the town? —3,033 at last census.

21. What was it the census before that? —3,171.

22. Can you say, from your own knowledge of the town, whether the census of 1881 is likely to show any sensible increase? —I think it will show an increase in the same ratio as between 1861 and 1871.

23. Were buildings going on to the same extent between 1861 and 1871 as at present? —I think not.

24. Do you see much improvement in the town now compared to when you first became acquainted with it? —I think so.

25. Are the houses of a better class? —They are; and many of the landlords have removed their old thatched houses and put on slate roofs.

26. Are there many unoccupied houses? —Few or none.

27. Are there any villa residences outside the municipal boundary? —I know of only two of that character; the Commissioners have obtained a large plot of ground on which they are to build twenty labourers' cottages, but that was within the boundary, just on the very confines of it. They got the land from Lord Farnham.

28. What power have they got to do that? —They have adopted the Artisans' Dwellings Act.

29. In what electoral division is the town? —Cavan.

30. Is it wholly within it? —Yes.

31. If an extension of one mile from the centre of the town was adopted, would that still be within the electoral division? —It would.

32. Would two miles? —No; it would go into [illegible] electoral division on the south.

33. What is the value of the electoral division? —£12,487 6s.

34. How far does it extend on the north from the centre of the town? —About three miles northwards, and on the south about a mile, and on the east about two miles, and a mile and a half on the west.

35. Cavan is the principal market town for the electoral division? —Yes.

36. What is the nearest town to Cavan? —The small village of Ballyhaise, three and a half miles away.

37. And you consider that the advantage of Cavan as a market town extends two miles? —Yes; and far more.

38. Is the land in the immediate proximity to the town more valuable? —I think so.

39. Does the increased value extend to the landlord? —I cannot say that.

40. The landlord gets higher rent? —Yes.

41. What have been the poor rates since 1874? —1874, 1s. 12d.; 1875, 2s. 8d.; 1876, 1s. 6d.; 1877, 1s. 8d.; 1878, 2s. 7d.

42. Does that include any rate for special sanitary purposes? —It includes a penny for general sanitary purposes. There never has been a higher sanitary rate than that only in one year; there was 1s. on Abbeyland.

43. For what purpose? —Sewering the town.

44. Was that assessed on the townland of Abbeyland? —It was put on a single street; they had to pay 1s. in the pound for it.

45. What is the contributory district for the 1d.? —The whole union.

46. There never has been any special sanitary work except in that instance of Abbeyland? —Yes, and even at present we have a contributory rate on the whole township since we have got liberty under the Act to divide townlands, it is struck on the township, and before that we had another charge on two townlands, and then on all the three townlands wholly within the township.

47. What has been the county cess since 1874? —1874, 1s. [illegible]; 1875, [illegible]; 1876, [illegible]; 1877, [illegible]; 1878, [illegible].

48. And the municipal rate? —1874, 1s.; 1875, [illegible]; 1877, [illegible]; 1878, [illegible].

49. And you think that census is correct? —Yes, I [illegible].

50. Have the Commissioners property vested in them? —No.

51. Is the town well lighted? —It is. I think thirty-nine or forty lamps.

52. The Commissioners adopted the Act for all purposes? —Yes.

53. What was the cost of the lighting? —[illegible] for the seven months of the winter, from the [illegible] September to [illegible] April.

54. Are your lamps kept lit [illegible] the people who come in are obliged to avail themselves of the light? —They are generally late leaving the town.

55. So that it is an advantage to those people residing outside to have those lights? —Most undoubtedly.

56. And the roads are good? —They are.

57. And to what extent do the people avail themselves of [illegible] about two miles.

58. And you think that the people within that distance derive exceptional advantages? —Yes.

59. Are there schools in the town? —Yes.

60. And do the people within that distance [illegible]; they have schools nearer [illegible].

61. Are the Commissioners likely to avail themselves of the 14th section of the Public Health Act, with reference to [illegible] of the sanitary works? —No; they have taken [illegible] sanitary authority [illegible].

62. Does that influence them in desiring to increase the area of taxation? —I do not think it does [illegible] sanitary authority they would wish to have an increased area.

63. What steps have they taken? —They have written to the Local Government Board.

64. Was a preliminary meeting [illegible]? —Yes.

65. Are they likely to ask for a [illegible] from the Local Government Board [illegible].

66. Were there any formal resolutions passed on the subject of extension? —When it first arose before them they considered it in a very limited way; they then would only have included those already paying [illegible], but since that they wish for a large extension [illegible].

67. They wish an extension of two miles from the centre of the town? —Yes.

68. Was this considered at a special meeting? —Yes, at a meeting on Wednesday last.

69. Did the ratepayers [illegible] a notice of it? —No.

70. Was an account of it published in the local papers? —Yes, it appears in this day's papers.

71. So that if any of the ratepayers had an interest in it they could have attended? —Yes.

72. What was the resolution? —That we ask for a [illegible] boundary in every direction from the market-house, and that was unanimously agreed to.

73. How many Commissioners were present? —Eight.

Cavan. [illegible] Mr. [illegible]

CAVAN. Sept. [illegible], 1879. Mr. J. [illegible], J.P.

Mr. J. [illegible], J.P., examined.

74. You are Chairman of the Town Commissioners?—Yes, and I have been a Commissioner for twenty-five years.

75. How long have you been Chairman?—For the past two years.

76. Were you a Commissioner when the town was under the previous Act?—No, shortly afterwards.

77. I believe the Commissioners under the [illegible] of George the Fourth had considerable property vested in them?—Under an ancient charter a wide [illegible] the centre of the town was given to the town for their special use.

78. And there was no necessity for [illegible]?—No, there was no [illegible].

79. How long is it since they enjoyed this property?—Not within my memory, and I don't believe it has been enjoyed for the last fifty years. It has been [illegible] in one way or another.

80. I understand you applied to the Local Government Board for a provisional order to become the sanitary authority; is that in accordance with the wishes of the ratepayers?—We would be bound under this Act to give notice to the ratepayers, and until we take preliminary steps we find it will cost little or nothing for there is no opposition, and as soon as we have got these cottages built we intend to apply for sanitary powers.

81. Do you consider you got sanitary work from the Guardians commensurate with the money you pay?—We have [illegible] to a considerable [illegible] action, but I am altogether of the firm belief that for all purposes of the Grand Jury, the sanitary, and local boards, the Commissioners are the proper body to exercise these powers.

82. You are of opinion that all the improvements of the town should be in the hands of one individual authority?—Decidedly.

83. Is there any likelihood of your applying for a separation from the Grand Jury?—Yes, [illegible], and if this were extended, we would be sure to do it, because we will keep the roads within it, and we would tax the town for that purpose.

84. And was it keeping this separation in view and having the sole authority that you asked for an extension?—Not immediately, but ultimately we had that in view. We would have asked for sanitary powers to be enforced independent of the Grand Jury powers being removed.

85. You are aware you cannot get the Grand Jury powers unless you first receive the sanitary authority?—I am aware.

86. What are the principal reasons you propose this extension for?—I will tax the people for the advantages they now enjoy. They would have the privilege of voting for Commissioners and might become Commissioners themselves; and we would look after their interests if they were amalgamated with us. It is principally first because of the fact that when we were extended, taking a great many of these gentlemen farmers living in the immediate vicinity having exceptional advantages in having the town kept clean, they think they are exempt from any of the expenses of it.

87. Are there any improvements required which you would effect if you had more funds?—Yes, we want an egg market which is sadly required, and we would commence it immediately if we had this extension. Our rate is very low [illegible] the pound; a mile extension would give us £44, a mile and a half £[illegible], and two miles about £100 a year. There is very little chance of our rates being higher because what we propose to do would be remunerative, and if it became necessary we would extend the lamps to the suburban buildings.

88. Assuming that you become the urban sanitary authority is it your opinion that any improvements you carried out in the town, would be of advantage to the people coming into it?—Yes, the first improvement will be the water supply.

89. How is the town supplied with water at present?—Very bad supply of pump water, although the Guardians submitted some of it to Dr. Cameron who thought it was not very good, but so far as the town, the purposes are [illegible] in dry seasons, we are very badly off.

90. Are there any facilities for supplying by gravitation?—The grandest you ever saw. There is a beautiful lake [illegible] acres, and with a very little engineering, we could bring that into a cistern that would reach the top of any house in the town.

91. Have the views of the Commissioners on this subject ever been laid before the Board of Guardians?—No, except on that very [illegible]. We have the power to adopt the works, and they ultimately will, however I look upon the water as the most essential for the health of the town. It would be cheaply done, and it would be one of the first things that would be done for the town.

92. And it would be an advantage to the people outside?—Yes.

93. The people would be taxed for the increased advantages they enjoyed?—There would be very little taxation; I think nothing more than 4d. or 5d.

94. Is the town well sewered?—Very well, there are a couple of good main sewers, but in dry seasons there is no water to carry off the sewage.

95. Do you think the Commissioners would [illegible] if they became the sanitary [illegible] in their own hands?—I think so, it is the first thing they would try to improve, the water supply, and then the sewerage.

96. And you think a larger area for taxation would be [illegible], because the people outside would enjoy the advantages of this improved water supply, and improved sewerage of the town itself?—Yes. And you must not abuse the Grand Jury power; we have nothing to complain of the county surveyor, but there are a great many byestreets in the town that require to be improved, and we cannot do it because we don't [illegible] it, and these things are totally neglected. There are some parts of the town which are a disgrace to civilization; the county surveyor is not bound and I believe he would not feel any [illegible] for them; the town Commissioners could not, and they are in a disgraceful state, but if the Commissioners had power they would immediately amend these places.

97. Are you aware of how many miles of road you would have in charge within the two mile radius?—Yes, we made a calculation of about eighteen miles of roads. Our solicitor, Dr. Babington, is [illegible] in favour of the two-mile radius. We calculated that we pay £400 a year out of this borough, and we don't get anything commensurately with that, of course I know there are a good many things we have to pay outside.

98. But taking these into consideration you don't consider that you get value for the cess?—No.

99. What would be the cost of the repairs, [illegible]?—We were entering into that, and some of the roads were [illegible] at a very high price—[illegible] we could do it as cheap as the county.

100. Do you think you would have any balance in hand by this?—Not by the cess now struck; we would have struck the same rate; I believe we could get work done cheaper than by the county.

101. Take the county cess last year, what income could you raise from the two-mile radius, the town alone is [illegible], would be £[illegible]. We did not calculate what it would be on the increased area; we calculated eighteen miles and that we could make them as cheap as the county would.

102. You resided in the town how long?—For twenty-five years.

103. Do you see any improvement in the town for [illegible]—[illegible] improvement. Our [illegible] has been increasing within the last four years [illegible], and I suppose our

[illegible] in Cavan within the last twenty years, there are thirty new houses; I don't think there is any town in the north of Ireland has improved more with so small a population, and except for the exceptional lines there is nothing in prospect for increasing it.

104. How many gentlemen's residences would this two-mile radius take in?—It would take in Cullies, a large residential establishment; Mr. Farnham's, Mr. Saunderson's and Mr. Kay's; about five or six.

105. You don't propose a local road line?—No.

106. You would be content to follow a well defined boundary keeping the two-mile in view?—Yes, we are not disposed to press for our limit to the two-mile boundary. Our original idea was [illegible], but we thought two-mile radius would be better.

107. Do you consider that those people would derive advantage from being brought in?—They have already derived an advantage from their proximity to the town.

108. Do you think it possible to include the extent of the townlands cut by the two-mile radius?—We are prepared to take the electoral division, as the two-mile radius goes outside it.

109. Have the Commissioners ever considered the question of including the electoral division in the township?—At one meeting that was the opinion, which was not [illegible].

110. Were they aware the Select Committee had made a recommendation as far as possible to make the boundaries of the town should be made coterminous with the electoral division?—Not then.

111. Do you think the people within the electoral division derive such advantage, that if they were made to pay their quota of municipal taxation it would not press injuriously upon them?—I think not. A mile and a half would only be 2s. 6d. and it [illegible] the rate is nearly 3s.

112. Would the Commissioners be in favour of taking the electoral division?—They are not bound to any hard and fast line. It would not make a deal of difference and it would scarcely be as far as the two-mile radius.

113. Is it not an equitable boundary if you adopt the electoral division?—It could be more equitable. For instance, Mr. Kay, a large merchant, lives within a mile and a half, and if you don't take the two-mile radius, you exclude him.

114. The proposed extension of two miles would embrace the four electoral divisions?—It would, but very slightly.

115. Could portions of them be left out?—Yes, we are not bound to any particular line, but whatever would be most equitable.

116. Would the Commissioners be prepared to take up the roads in the entire electoral divisions?—I do not see anything at all to prevent them. I don't think they would. The area of one mile would give an increase of 1,000 acres; one and a half miles would give an increase of 4,000 acres, and with an area of two miles we would become the sanitary authority, and without any parliamentary order, because it gives us an area of 8,000 acres, and an increase of the population.

117. Were you influenced by that?—We did not think of it. The additional income that would be brought in by the increase that one mile increase would be £24, at a mile and a half, £94, and at two miles only £100 at our present rates.

118. How many qualified voters are there in the borough?—Two hundred and thirty electors and eighty-eight qualified voters.

119. You gave the number of gentlemen's residences included by the proposed extension?—Yes, six.

120. How many are within the electoral division of Cavan?—There is only one outside.

Mr. Edward Fegan examined.

121. You are a Commissioner, and you have been resident in Cavan for some time?—Yes.

122. Were you a Commissioner under the 9th George IV.?—I am about twenty-eight or thirty years a Commissioner. I was not a Commissioner under the old Board. I was not one of the original Commissioners. I did not come upon the Board for two or three years afterwards.

123. Are you aware under what circumstances this boundary came to be adopted?—It came from the Castle. Mr. Griffith was here at the time.

124. Was the boundary, as transmitted by the Castle, adopted without modification?—It was. It was left to the hands of the gentleman who had it out, and the Commissioners did not interfere.

125. There have been no alterations or additions since?—No.

126. You have heard the evidence of the Town Clerk and of Mr. Crosson?—Yes.

127. Do you think an extension of two miles desirable?—It would be desirable, I think.

128. Were you present the other day when the matter was discussed at the Board?—I was. I proposed the extension.

129. Do you consider that the sanitary improvements you would carry out in the town would be of advantage to the people outside?—I believe they would.

130. Is the town in want of funds for any improvements?—No, we were never as well off for funds as at present. We have a large balance, and we have applied for a loan of £3,000 to build these houses.

131. Is it your opinion it would be desirable to take in the roads?—It is a question I have not given attention to.

132. Are you in favour of having the town make your own sanitary authority?—Yes.

133. And you would not give an opinion as to the roads?—No.

134. The two-mile boundary was not adopted looking to that point at all?—No.

135. Were you aware the two-mile boundary would bring you within the Act as sanitary authority?—No, we were not aware of that.

136. Do you consider that the people within the proposed area derive such advantage that they ought fairly to be asked to pay their quota?—I think so; they could have their vote in the town if they wished.

137. You consider it a growing town?—It is a very improving town; people equal upwards of twenty miles to the town.

138. What is the nearest town?—Ballyhaise, three miles off; it is not a very good market; it is a dear market, and Belturbet is seven miles away.

139. Do you think there is any likelihood of building operations extending beyond the present boundary?—I think there is.

140. If the town goes on improving as it has?—Yes, only for these bad times, I think building would improve.

141. It is your opinion that sanitary improvements of any nature are required in the town?—Yes.

142. Do you consider a water supply is required?—Yes.

143. And improved sewerage?—Yes.

144. And that the Commissioners if they had this extended area, and became the sanitary authority, thereby would carry out?—Yes.

Dr. William [illegible], J.P., examined.

CAVAN. April 27, 1[illegible]. Dr. William [illegible].

145. You have been for some time a [illegible]?—Yes.

146. Were you a Commissioner under the 9th George IV.?—No, I came in immediately after the Towns Improvement Act, and I was [illegible] the improvement of the town. I came here in 1819, and I can speak of the state of the town a great many years ago. The town of Cavan was a small [illegible] in my time.

147. Are there any houses unoccupied at the present time?—There is only [illegible].

148. There is no house unoccupied?—No.

149. And twenty years ago [illegible]?—No; we never had [illegible]. The moment a house was put up it was taken, [illegible].

150. Are you in favour of having the sanitary powers transferred from the Guardians?—I am, for I think it is a hardship [illegible]. [illegible] is no value for our money. The Commissioners could do it better.

151. Have you got any property outside the present boundary?—I have some, and my house is about a mile away.

152. And you propose to tax yourself?—Yes. Half of my property is only taxed at present.

153. The present boundary [illegible]?—Yes, and I am prepared to pay [illegible] additional.

154. And you think that is the feeling of the people outside?—Yes. I was speaking to Mr. Thompson, who [illegible] the improvement of the town. The [illegible] part of the business is the most important, but it is the worst conducted [illegible] I know of.

155. In the way of water supply?—In the way of everything. I asked Mr. Thompson [illegible] as he was, his property is at present [illegible].

156. Is your property within the [illegible]?—Yes, it is within a mile of the town.

157. Have you ever any opportunity of gathering the feeling of the rate payers on the subject?—[illegible] much.

158. Do you think if you had this [illegible] you would apply for a separation from the Grand Jury?—No, I would be against that. I would be for [illegible] the roads [illegible] we have at present to deal with.

159. Do you consider you get sufficient [illegible] with the money you pay to the Grand Jury?—No, it is very hard to get the Grand Jury to do anything for the town, even the [illegible], and it is [illegible] passed all the [illegible] in the Grand Jury [illegible] [illegible] the [illegible] houses for the [illegible].

160. Are there fairs and markets held in the town?—Yes, regularly.

161. In the streets of the town?—No, the fairs are held in [illegible], but the [illegible] in the [illegible].

162. And are the streets [illegible]?—Yes, the Commissioners [illegible] there is a great want of [illegible] [illegible] in the small houses. I [illegible] [illegible].

163. And all these [illegible] would be [illegible] by the Commissioners in time?—Yes, I [illegible] [illegible] condition.

Mr. [illegible] examined.

Mr. James Brady.

164. You are an engineer and you are borough surveyor?—Yes.

165. You are in favour of extension of the boundary?—Yes.

166. The two [illegible]?—Yes.

167. Have you gone into any calculations on the subject?—No.

168. Have you heard Mr. [illegible] estimate?—Yes, it is quite correct.

169. You consider that the sanitary matters would be better managed in the hands of the Town Commissioners?—I do.

170. You are not aware whether the [illegible] would bring you up to the statutory limit?—No.

171. Would you see any objection to leaving out portions of the electoral division to the [illegible]?—No, I think they might be left out without [illegible] to the town, I think [illegible] it should be included.

172. Are you aware whether [illegible] and Mr. [illegible] would have any objection to [illegible]?—No, I think only [illegible] in the [illegible] of the roads I think the [illegible] something like the [illegible]. It is [illegible] [illegible] to get a [illegible] like that.

173. Do you think it would be an advantage to have [illegible] of the roads?—If they got the [illegible] I do.

Mr. J. D. Greer.

Mr. J. D. Greer examined.

174. You are clerk of Cavan union?—Yes.

175. Do you know would the Board of Guardians have any objection to the Commissioners getting this Sanitary Authority?—I don't know, the question has never been before them.

The inquiry then terminated.

CLONMEL—26TH MAY, 1879.

(Before Mr. C. P. COTTON and Mr. ROBINSON.)

Mr. JOHN THOMAS LAFFAN examined.

1. Mr. COTTON.—You are the Town Clerk of Clonmel?—Yes.

2. How long have you occupied the position of Town Clerk?—Twenty-two years.

3. The town of Clonmel is under the third and fourth of Victoria?—It is under the second clause of the third and fourth of Victoria as amended, and we have also adopted the Towns Improvement Act.

4. When did you adopt that Act?—In 1859; on the 1[illegible] of [illegible], 1859.

5. Was the Towns Improvement Act adopted wholly or in part?—In its entirety.

6. What is the present area of the borough?—The present area of the borough is 33[illegible].

7. And the population?—According to the last census it was 10,112.

8. Has there been a diminution since the previous census of 1861?—Yes.

9. Is it increasing or diminishing now?—I don't think I could give you any accurate information on this point. The diminution has been since 1861. At that time it was 11,[illegible]; and in 1871 it was 10,112.

10. What is the present valuation?—£16,[illegible] [illegible]s.

11. There are two wards?—Yes; east and west. The east ward valuation is £8,[illegible] 10s.

12. And the west ward?—£8,[illegible] 10s.

13. Can you tell me the number of [illegible] in each ward?—I can, in a minute. Do you mean municipal voters?

14. Yes, municipal voters?—I can tell you that in a minute. The [illegible] that it might be mentioned that the valuation is [illegible] [illegible] as there is no unoccupied house in Clonmel at the present time.

15. What is the number of councillors?—Twenty-four. Six aldermen and eighteen councillors. Three aldermen in each ward.

16. And how many councillors?—Nine to each ward.

17. In what electoral division is Clonmel?—I stated in my answer to your question that it was in the electoral division of Clonmel. I wish to correct that. There is a small portion also in the electoral division of St. Mary's.

18. Mr. ROBINSON, to alter that query and make it correct?—Yes.

19. How much of the borough is in the electoral division of St. Mary's?—£[illegible] is in St. Mary's. That is in the eastern division, £[illegible] 10s.

20. Do you mean the east ward?—Well, I don't. The portion of St. Mary's in the borough of Clonmel, has a valuation of £7[illegible]. Now I will tell you what it is composed of. Of the eastern division £[illegible] 10s., and the western £75 5s.

21. What is the eastern division?—The poor law valuation, chiefly for the purposes of collection, the electoral division of Clonmel into Clonmel east and Clonmel west, Clonmel east and St. Mary's is £[illegible] 10s., and Clonmel west is £7[illegible] 5s.

22. In that division [illegible] east and west, dependent on the division between the east and west wards?—No; it is not. It is done merely for collection purposes. It is merely a local arrangement.

23. There are no such things as eastern and western electoral divisions?—It is a sub-distribution. The whole is £7[illegible].

24. Does St. Mary's lie altogether in the county of Waterford?—It does.

25. How much of the borough of Clonmel is in the county of Waterford?—£7[illegible] of valuation, and the [illegible] is [illegible] 2s.

26. Of St. Mary's, and the rest is altogether in the electoral division of Clonmel?—Yes; the rest is in the electoral division of Clonmel. There is £[illegible] 3s. in Clonmel—in the county Tipperary portion of the Clonmel electoral division; and £[illegible] in the county Waterford portion of the Clonmel electoral division.

27. Can you tell me what the rates have been for the last five years?—Yes; they are as follows:—

	Municipal		Poor Law		County	
	s.	d.	s.	d.	s.	d.
1875,	[illegible]	[illegible]*	[illegible]	[illegible]	[illegible]	[illegible]
1876,	[illegible]	[illegible]	[illegible]	[illegible]	[illegible]	[illegible]
1877,	[illegible]	[illegible]	[illegible]	[illegible]	[illegible]	[illegible]
1878,	[illegible]	[illegible]	[illegible]	[illegible]	[illegible]	[illegible]
1879,	[illegible]	[illegible]	[illegible]	[illegible]	[illegible]	[illegible]

* And a Towns Improvement rate of 6d.

28. How is the town of Clonmel supplied with water?—By pumps.

29. Has there ever been any project for increasing the water supply?—The matter was mooted from time to time before the Corporation, but they thought they had not sufficient powers at the time without getting a special Act to provide it, and I don't think there was unanimity on this subject, and it was apprehended that the expenditure would be very great.

30. Is there any complaint of the quantity and quality of the present water supply?—Some of the pumps are insufficient, and we have had them analysed and the water has been found to be good. The water is exceedingly hard. It is very suitable for mixing [illegible] with plenty of lime in it, and that may [illegible] account for the [illegible] [illegible] of the [illegible], but [illegible] people and those who are of a gouty and rheumatic habit [illegible] very much.

31. Is there any project suggested for a new supply of water?—It was desired that the water might be had easily from the county Waterford side lying in the [illegible] [illegible]. It is [illegible] [illegible] for quality of water, and we had it analysed by Professor Cameron [illegible] [illegible] for the purpose of seeing whether the water would be suitable for the purpose of supplying the town, and he said it was good and soft and most suitable for every purpose. Besides that there is great elevation, which would give high pressure, and in the [illegible] of [illegible] from the [illegible] we could avail of [illegible]. There was no estimate made by the county surveyor with the view of obtaining a supply from the Comeraghs, but that water is [illegible] on the ground of its [illegible] being spring water, and because that the borough authorities [illegible] [illegible] [illegible] [illegible] to [illegible] [illegible] [illegible] [illegible] the expense. Major Tulloch, the engineer officer, in charge of the department, did not think it would be a desirable scheme, because we had no power to get water from the Comeraghs, and they could not get high pressure. It would only give a pressure of thirty feet.

32. Has there been any estimate of the cost of the water supply to the county Waterford?—No; all those schemes have been merely in embryo and lay by until the Public Health Act was passed, and since then the Corporation have got other matters in progress; but the question of a water supply has not yet been considered. Some years ago Mr. [illegible] [illegible] brought forward a scheme before the Corporation, but we had not sufficient power at the time to proceed without going to Parliament. It suggests itself to me that one of the reasons that very likely made the Council [illegible] than they were deterred by the smallness of their area for taxation. I think they would have carried out some of these works, but that the area of taxation is too limited to incur expense, such as the procurement of a high pressure water supply is likely

Clonmel, May [illegible]

Mr. John T. [illegible].

to entail; but that if we had a more extended area there would be some inducement to embark on such undertakings.

33. Do you think if the area of taxation was extended it would lead to the taking up of such a scheme? —I think very likely it would.

34. How is the town lighted?—With gas. There is one company in Clonmel at present; there were two. The present company—the Clonmel Gas Consumers Company—bought up the old company.

35. Is the public lighting at so much per lamp?—We are now supplied at the rate of 6s. a thousand feet for the public lighting, and 6s. for the private lighting. It is on the basis of that that we are supplied at so much per public lamp per month. That was struck upon the basis of 6s. per thousand feet.

36. There is an agreement between the Corporation and the Gas Company?—Yes; the agreement is so much per lamp per month.

37. How much does that amount to?—It amounts to £430.

38. And how many lamps have you?—We have 187 lamps in winter, and 60 lamps in summer.

39. That was for four months?—Yes; we have 187 for eight months, and 60 lamps for four months—for May, June, July, and August.

40. How is Clonmel off in the way of sewerage?—As regards sewerage the town is fairly off with respect to some of the streets, but it is very indifferently off as regards others; but as regards sanitation, since we acquired powers under the Public Health Act of 1874, so far as the Corporation were capable of putting them in force, they have exercised them with very considerable diligence; but there was considerable difficulty in consequence of a conflict between the jurisdiction of the Grand Jury of the county of Waterford, and the Grand Jury of the county of Tipperary. We were not in a position to open up streets, because they were in the hands of contractors to the Grand Jury, and we would be liable to be summoned for trespass; and that was one of the things that moved the Corporation so strongly to apply for the separation of the borough from the county which is now nearly through Parliament. It has gone through the House of Lords.

41. And you had to go to the Local Government Board and get a provisional order for the separation of the borough from the county Waterford and the county of Tipperary?—Yes.

42. And is there no main drainage made by the Corporation?—Several sewers have been laid down—public sewers.

43. They all run into the river?—Yes, as a rule. In the Main-street there is no main sewer from Bridge-street up to the west gate. That is owing to an engineering difficulty. That is, that the levels are under the river. The levels of the rest of the houses in the Main-street are under the river, or below the level of the river.

44. The underground part of the street is below the level of the river?—Yes; accordingly it becomes flooded, in fact, if there was a sewer, it would be infiltrated into the walls.

45. Whatever main drainage there is is to the river? —Yes; the main drainage is to the river.

46. Are cesspools common in the town?—Cesspools, under the Public Health Act, are only a dernier ressort. When you can lead to main sewerage you are bound to do so. We have not main sewers to the extent that the town should be supplied with them. There was a very fine sewer in Johnston-street.

47. Does that go down to the river?—Yes; from Dunmore-street to the river.

48. Is there any objection from any of the riparian proprietors to the drainage going into the river?—I have heard of such a thing. It occurs to me that Mr. Thomas Grubb, who is a mill owner, did object to the sewer running into his tail-race. He is the owner of a large mill, and he certainly did object, finding the wheel of his mill clogged with foul matter.

49. Is there any project for the main drainage of the town now under consideration?—It is intended as soon as we have had the separation. The Royal assent is expected about the 15th of next month. It is intended to use all the powers of the Sanitary Act, for the purpose of thoroughly cleansing the town, and placing proper sewers throughout it—of course with a due regard to economy.

50. Have you had any systematic plan of main drainage laid down?—There has been no plan of main drainage laid down at present, by an engineer. All the drains that exist appear in the map marked in blue in the centre of the streets. You can see where the sewer is in any particular street laid down. There have been some made since the map was made.

51. Have you a borough surveyor?—We had a borough surveyor who was also the county surveyor, but only for one purpose. Formerly the county surveyor was the borough surveyor for all purposes, but the Grand Jury found fault and stated that they would insist on the entire of the duties being devoted to the discharge of the county business, and accordingly he was obliged to give them up, but he obtained permission from the Grand Jury to act as borough surveyor for one purpose, and that was in respect of dangerous buildings. It was necessary that a qualified man should certify every dangerous building, otherwise we could not pull them down. He resigned about a year and a half ago, Mr. Worrall, and we have no surveyor at present.

52. If you are going to lay out any new scheme of sewerage you would not be able to do it if you had no surveyor?—We have got a gentleman at present who is engaged just now on designs for a new Town Hall, Mr. Farrell. He is preparing plans. He is thoroughly qualified, and I dare say that probably if it were considered expedient to immediately prepare such a scheme, it would probably go into his hands the same as the Town Hall.

53. But at present you have no regular surveyor engaged?—None whatever.

54. Are you aware that under the Public Health Act you are bound to have a map showing all the sewers in the town, and which must be kept up, and whenever a new sewer is made it must be indicated on the map?—I am aware of that.

55. Can you do that without a surveyor?—I am aware that we are bound to that as soon as we get control of our streets, but we have not got control of our streets yet.

56. But you are bound to have that map?—There is the map, and there is the sewerage marked on it.

57. Are all the sewers in the town marked on that map?—All with the exception of those recently added.

58. And why are not they added?—I dare say they will be as soon as we get a surveyor.

[The Commissioner then read the section of the Act requiring the keeping of the map with the new sewers recorded from time to time].

59. As a matter of fact you are not keeping that up?—Substantially we do keep it up. We have a number of sewers marked on that.

60. Who is to put them up if you have no surveyor?—We have got an officer who must be called, if he is not in fact the borough surveyor. He is inspector of nuisances and inspector of the town, and he is thoroughly conversant with every sewer in the town, and he is in a position to point out, when anyone makes an application on the subject, the existence of a sewer—in the cases of those that are not marked on the map.

61. And why not get him to mark the new sewers on the map?—Mr. Brunskill is not a qualified man.

62. Can you give me any reason why you don't appoint a borough surveyor?—It is for this reason—that until quite recently we had no one in the town unless we imported some one who was qualified to discharge the duties. The county surveyor wrote a letter stating that he would resign his position as borough surveyor, which was as you will remember for one purpose only. There was a discussion about

Clonmel. May 18, 1878. Mr. John T. Lalor.

whether this tailor ought to be fixed or not; and [illegible] in any case, the question was carried, so that this [illegible] was never raised, but he [illegible] place.

62. The [illegible] would not [illegible] in [illegible] ... We have had no case of [illegible] in [illegible] within the last five [illegible], since Mr. Fitzell came.

63. Can you tell me when were the road assessment [illegible] made by the [illegible]?—Mr. Dunsdonald can give you evidence with respect to that better than I can. A good many [illegible] I may mention have been made under a peculiar system. They have been done by the Grand Jury, and yet at the same time they have been completely done under the Corporation, for the Corporation [illegible] by [illegible] the Grand Jury, and the [illegible] and the money was expended in that way.

64. Are you alluding to [illegible] for road purposes or sewerage [illegible]?—Well, I think the sewers there I [illegible] to be almost always [illegible] for [illegible] and not merely to carry off the surface water.

65. And the county [illegible] the [illegible]?—Yes; but I think that the legal reason for the [illegible] passed would indicate that [illegible] were [illegible] the [illegible] of the sanitary authority, and I don't think, even if we had not applied for a [illegible], that we would have got much more at it.—I think the county surveyor [illegible] that he did not believe it was legal.

66. Was your application to the Local Government Board to be [illegible] from the Grand Jury made with their assent?—Oh, yes. The [illegible] had to go up before the Grand Jury and apply for their consent.

67. And they agreed to it, yes; both Grand Juries agreed unanimously—Tipperary and Waterford.

68. With reference to the question of an extension of the boundary you say, in your replies to the queries that the Corporation are unanimous in desiring an extension of the boundary?—Yes. I can produce the minutes with reference to that.

69. You do? When was it a resolution passed?—On the 6th of May. The minute on the subject runs thus:—

"The Town Clerk stated that the Borough Boundary Committee, as directed at the last meeting of the Council, again took into consideration the subject of the extension of the borough boundary, with the view of ascertaining if it was advisable to increase the area of the borough by a larger extent than that recommended by the Committee in their report of the [illegible] of March, 1877, and that the Committee having had the subject before them at several meetings, and having devoted much time and attention to the matter, on the 29th of April last finally made the following report:—'At a meeting of the Borough Boundary Committee held in the Judges' Chambers at the Court-house, on the 29th of April, 1878, Alderman [illegible], Esq., in the chair, the Committee recommended the [illegible] of the proposed extension of the municipal boundary as marked out the map taking in the old bridge.'"

We will hand this map for you to refer to.

70. How many councillors and aldermen attended?—Fifteen out of the twenty-four.

71. They were unanimous?—They were.

72. Do you know any gentleman who was not present at that meeting?—I do not. I have no reason to believe there is any difference whatsoever, because I have never heard any expression of dissent from any of them.

73. Beginning, please, in such a way as we can put it on the notes, what is the extension proposed?—We will first take the extension on the [illegible] side of the river. On the north side of the river you propose to extend the boundary to the townland of Kilmacomma?—[illegible] do, but not taking it in.

74. Thence north to the railway, and thence along the railway by the northern side of the railway to the townland of Knockanaffrin?—[illegible] except.

75. Thence by the townland boundary to the townland of Glenbeg, and thence south to the west end of [illegible] Island [illegible].

76. Thence along the county boundary to the townland of Gilhulgh, and thence you take in a portion of [illegible]?—Yes.

77. And thence along the boundary of the townland of Raheen and the townland of [illegible]?—Yes; and then you come back to the original point.

78. Will you give me the acreage of the borough at the west on the north side?—I fear I cannot give you that.

79. Can you give me the increased area altogether? I can give it to you in the county Tipperary. I can give it to you in the valuation. In the county Tipperary the increase is £1,358 15s. 1d., and in the county Waterford, £2,[illegible] 3s.; total, £3,[illegible] 4s.

80. Taking a central point of the town of Clonmel, how far would that extension stretch in a northern direction?—I cannot say that. You can get that from Mr. Dunsdonald.

81. How many gentlemen's places would be taken in by that extension?—There would be from fifteen to twenty on the south side, and I would say about as many as that on the north side. From fifteen to twenty villa residences on the south side.

82. And how many on the northern side?—About the same; all Prior Park, but that is a suburban [illegible].

83. What have you to say about the old bridge or to the reason for taking that in?—The reason is this: that it is a most unsanitary place, and the whole of the people there are extremely poor, and the Council were not at all impressed with the idea of taking them in on grounds of economy, but on reflection they thought they should do so. One [illegible], who is on the committee, considered that we should not be allowed to take in the good bit and leave out the bad one, and on principle thought that we should take them in for the purpose of preventing disease or pestilence arising there spreading through the suburban portion of the town. For these reasons it was thought we should take that part in, put it into a perfectly sanitary condition, using the powers we possess as to improvement, &c., under the Act regulating artisans' dwellings, and so on, and under the Public Health Act.

84. The Artisans' Dwellings Act requires a population of 25,000?—Well, I am alluding to the Labourers' Cottages Act.

85. Because, I think, there are only three towns in Ireland that are able to avail themselves of the provisions of that Act?—There was another reason, too, that formed a portion of the argument of the [illegible] with regarding the taking in of the old bridge; it was this, that the property of the Corporation, or the bulk of it, is on the south side just bounding the old bridge, and a great number of the tenantry of the Corporation—many of them live on the old bridge, and are connected with the old bridge—are tenants, hold-[illegible] out of them.

86. What advantage would it be to them that that should be part of the borough?—Simply to keep it in a proper sanitary condition, so that the rest of the borough should not be affected injuriously by it in the event of sickness.

87. But surely that would apply whether they were tenants or not?—The Corporation thought that, as paternal landlords, they should have their tenants in a proper sanitary condition.

88. Would the extension on the south side extend into any new electoral division besides St. Mary's?—I am certain it would not, for this reason, that I find, on looking into the certificate of the Clerk of the Union, that that only goes into the old bridge.

89. I see that the line you have given me there extends into the townland of Carrigbrick on the north side?—Very slightly.

90. But it does go into it?—Yes.

91. And that townland is not in the electoral division of Clonmel?—I don't think it is.

92. What I want to know is, is there any particular

CLONMEL. May 28, 1878. Mr. John T. Larkin.

reason for including that townland—the townland of Gerrysbrane?—When making out the contemplated extension, directions were taken from the report of the Committee, to start from a point—that is from the northernmost fence of the railway, to a point nearly opposite the western extremity of the lunatic asylum, and to follow it, but he found that that would be highly inconvenient, because you would be going through tenemental boundaries.

93. I want to know is there any special reason for going out of our way to include a portion of that electoral division?—I don't think there is, except that I think it was for the purpose of uniformity that that was done, because if we had adopted the border of Cartmaloquin townland it would have been very zigzag.

94. There is no other reason?—I don't think there is.

95. Can you tell me how many additional municipal voters would be created by this extension?—I was not prepared for that question.

96. Will you be able to get that information for us? —I think I would; I can ascertain that for you.

97. I would like you to ascertain how many additional voters would be created by the extension, and how many of them would be qualified for the position of councillor and alderman—just the two things?—Quite so; you shall have that information.

98. With regard to the two wards—have the Council considered the question of whether it was desirable in any way to alter the extent of the wards?—Well, I think it appeared to them that there was no necessity.

99. Do you think there is?—I do not; I think the present arrangement is very satisfactory.

100. There is no dissatisfaction about it?—No.

101. Did the Council consider in laying down this extension, how they would deal with it as regards the wards? How they would distribute the new area among the wards?—I don't think that struck them.

102. Would they create new wards?—That never struck the Council. The point never arose then as to whether there was any necessity to add an additional ward. My own impression is that they would probably leave things as they are.

103. Surely, the new ground, if it is brought in, must be represented?—At any rate, it has not come on for discussion, and I have not been able to collect the sense of either the Council or the Committee on that point, for they have not discussed it.

104. You know the present division between the two wards?—I do.

105. What would you suggest yourself in dealing with the new area, if it is brought in?—On conferring with the Sheriff, he tells me—and I dare say it might meet the sense of the rest of the body—that we might dispose of the increase from the county Tipperary in the East and West wards, and create a new ward of the county Waterford portion.

106. That is your opinion?—It appears to me to be a reasonable proposition; but there has been no opportunity of discussing it.

107. Does the Corporation or do you know the opinion of the ratepayers with regard to this extension?—As far as I can judge, the matter has, I think, been under discussion since as far back as 1877.

108. Has anything that has taken place with reference to this question been extensively considered outside the Corporation?—There has been no ratepayers' meeting; but I have had an opportunity of freely speaking with the people, and they seem to consider that, whatever the Corporation in their wisdom think is right, that it should be acquiesced in, as they are the representatives of the people; and they also think that it is feasible and just that all the good villa residents and the suburban residents in the immediate neighbourhood of the town, all of whom derive nearly the entire of the advantages of the town—the shops, markets, lighting, and everything of that kind—that they should contribute fairly to the taxation of the town. I have had an opportunity of speaking to one of the principal gentlemen who would be most heavily affected by the change, and, notwithstanding that, he would be in favour of it; Mr. Fyfe considering that it is a reasonable thing to extend the boundary to that which really is a portion of the town.

109. That is the opinion of the ratepayers generally—that is what I want to get?—I have not directly been able to collect the opinion of great numbers; but I have heard it assented to and considered proper, and I have heard nothing against it.

110. Do you know the opinion of the gentlemen who would be taken in?—The gentlemen who are taken in, as a rule, do object; but, Mr. Fyfe, as I have told you, does not object.

111. But you think some others do?—I think it would be impossible to get perfect unanimity in a matter of this kind. For instance, the gentlemen present who occupy villa residences—I am sure they don't care about the [illegible] of Clonmel or any other place.

112. Does your Provisional Order deal with any question of a proposed extension at all?—No, sir, it does not. The committee that considered the matter thought it was quite right that they should extend the scope of their inquiry into the matter, and they prepared themselves, and they ascertained from the proper authorities what would be the cost of the roadways within the proposed extension, and I am prepared to give evidence upon that point.

113. And they are quite prepared to deal with it? —Yes. In the county of Tipperary there would be an addition of 1,071 perches of roadway.

114. Outside the present boundary?—Yes; and in the county of Waterford you would have an addition of 150 perches. We ascertained what the probable expense would be of maintaining those roads, and we found that we could maintain the roads in the county Tipperary at 1s. 11d. per perch. The particulars of these in perches and the amount of the proposed price I have before me, and I can furnish you with the details. We allowed very heavily on some of the roads.

115. Who had the commission to advise them in this matter?—Mr. Timothy Seery, who is one of the assistants to the County Surveyor. I will send you his report if you wish.

116. What is the scope of his report?—He has allowed an ample price for the county Tipperary portion, with which he is intimately acquainted, as those roads are under his charge, and he feels certain that in a few years the cost of maintaining these roads will be lessened by some thirty-five or forty per cent. As regards the county Waterford, he has put a price that will certainly also allow generally sufficient for [illegible] and sanitary purposes. In money, I may mention that the maintenance of the county Tipperary roads would be £293 6s. 8d., and the county Waterford would be £474 18s.

117. What would you have to meet that?—You would have the taxable area.

118. How much does that come to upon the valuation?—I have not the calculations with me; but, at any rate, at 3s. in the pound—that is including county-cess purposes and municipal purposes—it leaves a large margin over. That is, after our own municipal purposes have been provided for. I have not the exact calculation, but I can give it to you.

The Mayor.—I wish to ask the Town Clerk—Did he estimate the cost of lighting in the extended area? —I did not, for this reason—that I thought that that would be subsequent work after the extension was made; and also for this reason that we are quite satisfied from our knowledge of the requirements of the borough as it is at present that it would be quite possible for us to carry it on in the extended area, as there are no engineering difficulties in the way of supplying it with either water or gas.

119. And the Committee did contemplate a supply of water and gas to this extended area?—They

[illegible] a considerable supply; they do not consider an inadequate supply, they do not consider that it should be supplied in the principal streets of the town are supplied, but that they should be given a [illegible], and they consider that, with proper direction on the part of the council, that it should be laid down as a fixed and fast line that the people would be [illegible] as at present there are in the [illegible] municipal district and under the control of the municipal body.

121. They did not calculate the number of lamps required?—They did not. They considered that that was a proper matter to be considered afterwards by the council when we got the extension, but they did not consider that you as Commissioners, or Parliament afterwards, would oblige the municipal body to light the suburban roads to the same extent as the principal thoroughfares of the town—that is judging by your experience of other towns.

122. We put no weight upon any extension that we considered was anything of that kind. You will be governed by the law, whatever it is?—The Committee were unanimous on the subject, and they were perfectly willing to take the responsibility of everything they [illegible], and also of what they have done in the past. We are even now giving the ratepayers the benefit of seven lamps outside the borough boundary; at present we are giving them that which we purchased in them through the kindness of the Gas Company. We have [illegible] additional lamps, and we are lighting some of them outside the borough boundary.

123. Is the railway station at present within the boundary?—No, sir; it is outside.

124. It would be included within the proposed extension?—Yes.

125. Have you any by-laws regulating the hackney cars?—No, there are very few; in fact we have no stands. That does not apply as it did in Drogheda and other places. In the first instance to apply by-laws we must have cars that ply for hire.

126. Would it be an advantage that the municipal authority should have the control of the car traffic—would there be any object in bringing in the railway station for the purpose of having control over the cars that ply?—We have had a complaint from the borough authorities on that subject, and that is to the effect that they consider the charge for driving from [illegible] to the railway station—about half a mile or a quarter of a mile—that is that they have to pay 6d. It is [illegible]. I don't say that as a rule the drivers are independently of the employer, and that the driver frequently gets fully as much as the employer—1s. for the car and 1s. for the driver. But we have no rate [illegible] on him.

127. The railway traffic is not sufficient to create a regular supply of cars?—It is not sufficient.

128. Have the railway company expressed their opinion on this proposed extension at all?—They are a remarkably silent body. I never heard from them a word when they wrote to say that their lamp is out.

129. Do they know that two miles or more of the line is proposed to be taken into the borough?—I believe they read the papers, and these placards have been put up at the railway.

130. Are they aware that the extension proposed includes about two miles of their line?—They are perfectly aware of it, because, as I informed Mr. Chadwell, the station-master, of the fact.

131. Is there anything else you would wish to add to your evidence?—I would like to mention in connexion with question No. 4 in the queries—"Are the municipal and poor law boundaries, as at present arranged, coincident?"—No; all the townlands that constitute or form the borough are divided, a part of which is within and part without the municipal boundary."

132. That is the present boundary?—Yes, of course. With regard to No. 5, I did state, I believe, that each of the wards are coterminous now with those in existence for Poor Law purposes. I was under the impression that they were, and what led me astray was this, as regards the three local divisions of the electoral division of Clonmel.

133. Are the three any Poor Law wards, as a matter of fact?—There are no Poor Law wards in existence for Poor Law purposes, but there are certain electoral divisions which precisely align with our east and west wards. Here is a copy of the rate-book, and here it is described as the eastern division; and what completely led me astray was their own book, and they described them as the eastern and western electoral divisions, and anyone would mistake——

134. The Clerk of the Union does not divide them at all?—Well, I don't know about that.

135. How many miles of railway would be taken in by the extension?—You will get that better from Mr. Ramsey. As persons we have taken 1,014 and 2½ perches, about three miles of railway; but Mr. Ramsey will give you that. I think my evidence that would be pertinent to this question I have now given it.

136. Is there anything else which those queries that you wish to mention?—I believe you asked me what my opinion was as to the propriety of the extension?

137. Yes?—I think it would be highly desirable on the plainest principles of equity and justice.

138. The Mayor.—Would it not be well to remark to the Commissioners, that it is very desirable to regulate the cars and such matters, that the station should be brought under the jurisdiction of the borough magistrates?—Certainly.

139. Because there are disputes arising?—Frequent disputes occur, with respect to pigs particularly, and matters of that kind, and these are outside the jurisdiction of the local authority.

140. The Commissioner.—You are talking of the railway station?—Yes. Contracts are made in the town with respect to those matters and disputes arise at the railway station when loading, and yet they are outside the jurisdiction of the borough magistrates and it would be more expedient that the local authority should have the power of controlling those contracts.

141. What is the extent of the jurisdiction of the magistrates, could they adjudicate on cases over £2, for these contracts are generally over £20 or £40?—The Mayor has a very ancient jurisdiction on different matters, as clerk of the markets, and if it came within his province, he could certainly apply a useful jurisdiction.

142. Then you think it would be desirable to have the railway station included, for the purpose of giving the Mayor control on those fair days, under some Municipal Act?—He derives that power from ancient usage as followed in the charters, and that usage has now prevailed up to the present time. I believe he said several other Mayors had some doubts in their minds as to the propriety of that usage—it may make the usage still continue.

143. Will you kindly tell me the number of burgesses?—In the East ward they are 135, and in the West ward, 128—total 263.

144. And you will find out for me, the number of municipal ratepayers that would be brought in under the extension, at some time or other?—Yes, I will send it to you in Dublin.

CLONMEL.
Oct. 23, 1877.
Mr. O'Connell Hackett.

Mr. O'Connell Hackett examined.

145. You are Mayor of Clonmel?—I am. I wish to state as Chairman of the Committee and of the Municipal Council that, finding unanimity prevailing amongst the body, I did not enter my practical dissent from the line proposed to be adopted by them, nor do I at present, but I wish it to be understood that I do not believe that any such extension of the boundary is desirable in the interests of the ratepayers, for the reason that the roadways extend, I believe, four or five miles—the new area taken in—and suppose we impose a tax of 1s. in the pound, I think it would be impossible for us, taking into account the extent of the area, to maintain these roads and light them, and give them a proper water supply with a valuation of not more than £2,000 at 1s. in the pound, which would only bring in an income of about £100 a year. I don't think we could maintain the roads, light them and give a water supply for that amount. Therefore I think an extension would be prejudicial so far to the interests of the existing ratepayers at present. From another point of view—that the sanitary authority is the Board of Guardians—they have charge of the Old Bridge, that portion is contemplated to be taken in. They do their business fairly in a sanitary point of view. However I think under the Municipal Council the sanitation of Old Bridge would be better looked after, inasmuch as I think the municipal body exercises more vigilance and action in reference to sanitation than do the Board of Guardians.

146. Then you think it would require an increase in the Town Improvement rate if this addition was taken in?—Certainly.

147. Have you formed any opinion as to how much additional would be required?—I have not.

148. You have had no Town Improvement rate except in 1876?—We had one last year.

149. Was it put on for any special purpose?—It was.

150. You say you hadn't it before?—Our accounts got into arrears with our bankers, and we found it necessary to put on a new rate of 1d. in the pound.

151. Have you formed any idea of what the Town Improvement rate would have to be increased to?—No; but I have an idea of how far £100 a year will go.

152. How much more do you think would be required?—I asked the Committee to assess that. Say there are four miles of roads—how many lamps would those four miles require—and they would not come to a conclusion that would considerably strengthen us afterwards. I think the lamps outside the borough would cost £3 per annum, and where there were lamps outside the borough £5 was the cost of laying down pipes, and so on; and you must meet the extra labour placed on the local governing body by this extension.

153. Would it entail new salaries?—It would entail certainly an increase of salaries. For instance, our town inspector would have about twice as much work to do as he has at present.

154. Do you contemplate appointing any borough surveyor?—Certainly; we are bound to have a borough surveyor.

155. And his salary would be the same whether you had an extension or not?—I dare say it would. Any man we appoint we must pay, I should say, a considerable salary, unless we can get the services of a county surveyor.

156. Mr. *Luther*.—Do you think is it a fact that the same staff as we have now employed would not work the extension of the boundary at the same time as the present area?—It would, I think, require an increase. In fact, we have no staff at present.

157. You have no borough surveyor?—We have a town inspector and two sergeants.

158. Yes, you have?—And there is a medical officer and a sub-sanitary officer. The fact is we have no staff at present.

159. Is it in contemplation taking up the borough from the county?—Yes.

160. Then would you not want to have a staff?—Certainly.

161. And have you expressed an idea that the same staff would do?—I never expressed any such idea.

162. The CHAIRMAN.—What staff is contemplated when you take these roads up from the county?—We contemplate having a staff of men for the maintenance of the streets, and lanes, and thoroughfares.

163. And how many officers besides the borough surveyor?—It would increase the duties of our inspector, and it is difficult to say who would get an increase of salary, for the staff that would undertake six miles of roadways will not maintain ten miles. I am giving you now the opinion that I have held all through. We have been considering the subject for the these past two years. I wished to bring the Committee to details and particulars, and I could never do it, and I state that in the presence of the Committee now. They would never make estimates. In the first place they had an estimate made for the maintenance of the roadways, and I asked them to have an estimate made as to the cost of lighting, and I said that if they got twenty lamps it would cost them over £100, and they would not do that. I asked them also to get an estimate of the cost of a water supply, and they would not do either one or the other, and for that reason I hold, in the absence of the estimates, that it is so elusive that it was to a considerable extent a leap in the dark, even though, as Mr. Luther states, the Committee are prepared to take the responsibility of it.

164. Mr. *Luther*.—What I said was that the Committee were quite satisfied to take the responsibility on themselves as regards the water and the lighting supply, having had full experience as to the application of their powers in those respects in the present boundary. They were satisfied to do anything that the law required them to do, feeling that the discretion was with them as to the amount of lighting and water that was to be supplied.

165. The *Mayor*.—It was in consequence of that statement that I tendered myself as evidence.

166. The CHAIRMAN.—What arrangement would you make with regard to a supply of water?—I take it, that if we include the area, we are bound to supply the people with water.

167. In what way?—By pumps.

168. How is it supplied at present?—I don't know. I suppose, partly from pumps.

169. Would there be any obligation on the Corporation to go to additional expense if this area was taken in for a supply of water?—If it was required.

170. But is it required?—I don't know; as no estimate has been made, we are quite in the dark about it. That is what I complain of.

171. You have only generally come to the conclusion that it would cost more than they would receive from it at a 2s. rate?—Yes; that is my individual opinion on the matter, and that is the reason I tendered myself—because I wish that that matter would be cleared up by the Commission, as it has not been up to the present. I was the first person that originated the movement, although I do own property in the area to be taken in. I originated the movement in the Council, and it was only on analysis I came to the conclusion that it would be a losing concern; and, as I said, I was prepared to act myself in the interests of the ratepayers. I have more interest in the town now than I had when I introduced the matter. I wish to state that in explanation of the course I have adopted.

CLONMEL. May 21, 18..

Mr. Gerald Fitzgerald.

taxation—that is if the borough rate is not sufficient with the rents and so forth, then you go to the borough rate, and there if the maximum of the borough rate is not sufficient at present, you then estimate whatever would be required over and above that, and accordingly you are not tied down to any limited amount; and that is so in the case of the county cess, and then as regards sanitary matters the taxation is also without limit.

197. The COMMISSIONER.—I understand that from the 5s. rate you would derive sufficient to cover the expense of taking in this extension?—Mr. *Luther*.—Such a calculation as was made, was made on that basis.

198. The *Mayor*.—I say a calculation has not been made for the lighting or the water supply, and that is why I maintain that it is a leap in the dark. If a lamp was put for every quarter of a mile of the road on an average—that would make twenty lamps to be provided.

199. The COMMISSIONER.—Would a lamp be required for every quarter of a mile?

200. The *Mayor*.—I am not aware. I say that that question has not been examined, and has been studiously avoided, notwithstanding my protests to the contrary.

Examination of Mr. FITZGERALD resumed.

201. The COMMISSIONER.—You have made no calculation, Mr. Fitzgerald?—I made no calculation. The Corporation are prepared to supply every portion of the extended area with lamps where they should be supplied.

202. But not binding yourselves to put lamps at any particular places?

203. Mr. *Luther*.—Four lamps to the mile. That would be reasonable lighting for the rural portion of the proposed extension. The Committee thought that it would not be necessary to light it like a street.

204. *Witness*.—There was just a difference of opinion that that might do for one road and not for another, and that was the reason we came to no conclusion about it.

205. The COMMISSIONER.—There was a difficulty then with the Committee that examined into the question as to how many gas-lamps would be necessary for this extension?

206. Mr. *Luther*.—When the first report was made there were two for two against. The Mayor did not vote himself upon it, but he expressed his dissatisfaction with the condition of things, and accordingly the matter was referred to the Council, and the Council then referred it back again to the Committee with a request that the larger area might be disposed of, and that they should consider the advisability of taking in a lesser extended area. But the Committee, so far as I could see, were quite satisfied that lamps for each quarter of a mile would be desirable, but it appeared to me that the Mayor considered that the Corporation would be incurring the liability of being brought into the Court of Queen's Bench, if we did not light the roadways almost as efficiently as the streets of the town.

207. The *Mayor*.—I never gave such an absurd opinion at all.

208. At any rate you were of opinion that they should give plenty of lighting and water.

209. What was there to prevent the Committee going into the question and fixing what lamps the scheme would entail?—They did go into the subject and discussed the question of one every quarter of a mile, but in consequence of there not being unanimity on the subject it was not adopted.

210. You have stated, Mr Mayor, that you were informed that there were five miles of roads and that one lamp to every quarter of a mile would give twenty lamps?—Yes, that would cost £100, and that would leave £160 for the maintenance of five miles of roads, for the supply of water, and for the increase of salaries.

Examination of Mr. FITZGERALD resumed.

211. The COMMISSIONER.—Can you tell me anything about the water supply?—I cannot.

212. To your knowledge would there be any expense for a supply of water?—I should say there would.

213. Is there any part of the proposed extended area that is badly off for water now, and on which the town would have to spend money if it took it within the boundary?—I am not aware.

214. Mr. *Luther*.—Would we not get credit for these nine outside lamps out of the twenty. We are already provided with nine and then we would only want eleven. There are now nine lamps in what would be the extended area. Would those nine lamps form portion of the twenty, if there was one to every quarter of a mile?—Yes, I don't think twenty would be sufficient.

215. You were on that committee, I believe?—Yes.

216. Had you anything to say to the addition of the district called the old bridge?—Yes; I considered it fair, although it will entail a little more expense on the Corporation to take in that, because part of the Corporation property is situated within the old bridge, and they receive rents out of it. Two or three lamps outside the borough are at present lit there and paid for out of the borough rate—and also on the sanitary aspect it was thought desirable to include that district.

217. What right have the Corporation to pay for lamps outside their boundary?—They had no right to do it. It is very unfair that property outside the borough boundary, and that persons holding property outside the present boundary, should not contribute to it—people who are deriving benefit from the taxation of the town. We think so, but yet we pay for them.

218. On the subject of the water and on the subject of the gas lighting when these subjects were gone into, as far as you can remember, what was the view of the Committee on those subjects—was it that they were satisfied to give a reasonable and rational accommodation in both those respects?—The Committee did not come to a conclusion for a definite calculation, but they came to the conclusion that they would supply both water and gas-light wherever it was required at the time, taking each particular locality into consideration.

219. So that they would act equitably by them?—That was what was contemplated.

220. But they did not go into any exact calculation?—A rough estimate of a lamp for every quarter of a mile was given, and some of the Committee said that that would apply to one road and not to another, and they did not, for that reason, come to any definite conclusion on the subject; but it was considered that on an average that would be fair and reasonable.

Mr. Thomas Healy.

Mr. THOMAS HEALY examined.

221. You are a member of the Town Council of Clonmel?—I am.

222. And also a member of the Committee that inquired into the subject of the extension of the municipal boundary?—Yes.

223. You served on that committee I believe?—Yes; and attended nearly all its meetings.

224. Are you aware that that Committee was unanimous in recommending that extension?—Well, generally, they were.

225. You had a favourite scheme of your own?—Yes.

226. But you gave way in deference to the wishes of the majority?—I did.

227. The COMMISSIONER.—Did you think that the extension should be a larger or a smaller one?—I say

Clonmel. May 26, 1879. Mr. Thomas Roney.

as well explain to you the opinion I expressed to the committee now. This is a subject that I devoted a great deal of attention to. About some six or seven years ago I brought this subject under the notice of the Corporation, with a view to the extension of the [illegible] the present boundaries [illegible] of the present [illegible] it was very strange that Clonmel being the capital of the premier county in Ireland should be [illegible] of the present municipal boundary; and at that time I formed the opinion that it would be prudent to extend the area of the borough on [illegible] side east, west, north, and south [illegible]; and from that opinion I have not departed; but the subject has been so generally discussed by the committee, and all the [illegible] of it [illegible] I [illegible] my opinion, and I agreed with the committee in their [illegible] that [illegible] half a [illegible] my opinion.

238. And you agreed to what was finally adopted by the Corporation?—I did.

239. Personally do you consider the extension equitable and just?—Yes, I do.

240. On what ground?—The parties included within the proposed [illegible] is proposed [illegible] almost all the advantages and benefits that are possessed by a great many people actually living within the town. They have the advantage of the town, and if they have any garden produce [illegible] they have a market every day in the week for disposing of their market and farm produce; and I think the portion within the [illegible] more benefit than many people in the town.

241. [illegible] the advantages?—My opinion is that it extends about the full extent of my original plan, of about one Irish mile. They have a market every day in the week for all kinds of farm produce, butter, eggs, and milk, and it is my opinion that parties living within an Irish mile of the town derive all the advantages, and a great many more advantages, than people living in the town.

242. I believe you have experience with respect to the management of roads?—Yes.

243. I believe you are an engineer?—Yes.

244. Have you ever seen that [illegible] St. Mary's [illegible] Was that document [illegible] by the committee?—It was.

245. Are these prices reasonable and fair prices?—They are, generally speaking.

246. Are they sufficient?—They are little enough; there is no extravagance about them.

247. The Chairman.—Give an idea of the prices, take the road [illegible] for instance?—There are 207 perches [illegible] and the [illegible] road is 5s., that is too low, I would put 7s. for that road; 5s. is not half enough.

238. Mr. Roney, was not the sum of 7s. given as special repair and not as ordinary maintenance?—I don't know; under the present circumstances the Fethard road would require 5s. a perch as maintenance under a contract, because it is a very heavy road.

239. Are the rest of the prices fair enough?—Yes, they are, there are a few leading roads about the town that are very heavy.

240. The new road is. That is within the borough.

241. What is the price of that road?—7s. is the present price of all the public roads of Clonmel.

242. Have you looked into the county Waterford prices?—I am not at all acquainted with the Waterford side.

243. Mr. *Lasher*.—On the whole do you consider the prices about fair?—There might be a little addition made to them.

244. Did the committee take great trouble and care in considering this subject?—The greatest possible trouble and care, and went into all the details.

245. How long has the question been under the consideration of the Town Council are you aware?—I attended over half a dozen committees for it.

246. Are you aware that a committee of the Corporation considered this in the year 1877?—Yes.

247. And reported very fully on it?—Yes.

248. The Chairman.—Have you formed any conclusion as to how many additional lamps would be required in this district?—I think there is too much importance attached to the lamps in the discussion that has passed by. I really think that the rural portion of the intended district of the extension would require no lamps at all, as the inhabitants won't ask them.

249. Do you think that the Corporation will have to put up twelve additional lamps?—I don't think they will, it is my opinion that they will not.

250. Over six?—I don't think they will.

251. Will there be any indisposition to supply lighting upon a fair case being made to the council?—No, because the Corporation would be more than willing to do all that is reasonable, but my impression is that those lamps will not be required.

252. Are you aware of any instance where a fair case has been made to supply an additional lamp and the request been refused by the Council?—No, they are always most particularly attended to by the Corporation. The Corporation are most jealous in attending to their duties in this respect.

253. Do you consider Clonmel a friendly [illegible] town considering its area?—Yes, it is one of the best provincial towns in Ireland.

254. Have you any apprehensions in taking in this extension as to the liability to be contracted by the Corporation beyond their fair powers and scope?—Not a bit.

Mr. Benjamin Wright examined.

Mr. Benjamin Wright.

255. Mr. *Lasher*.—You have been, I believe, a member of the Town Council for a good many years?—Yes.

256. Have you also been one of the members of the committee that sat on this subject?—I have.

257. Are you aware that the committee gave great care and attention and consideration to it?—The greatest possible care.

258. What is your personal belief as to the extension, is it desirable or otherwise?—I am convinced that it is most desirable.

259. You have the facility of hearing the opinions of the townspeople very freely?—I have.

260. What has been, as far as you have had an opportunity of ascertaining it, the opinion of the townspeople with reference to the extension?—A unanimous opinion, so far as I know, in its favour.

261. And you have opportunities of knowing?—I have.

262. Have you any apprehension as regards the undertaking of this extension by the Corporation with respect to lighting and water?—None in life.

263. Do you believe the Corporation would listen to any reasonable application for the supply of both?—I am sure they will.

264. And that they will grant it?—Certainly. Furthermore, I might add what has not been touched upon as yet, that it is this: suppose in this portion of the town we intend to extend the area to, there was a fire—suppose a fire took place in any of those villas, what means have they, except the Borough Fire Brigade of Clonmel, of getting it extinguished?

265. The Chairman.—There is a fire brigade?—We have a staff for the purpose, and a very efficient one, and one that has been able to extinguish a great many fires in Clonmel.

266. Have you an engine?—We have, and a good one, and one of Clayton's Telescopic *Fire Escapes*. We have one of Captain Ingram's best men in charge, and he has drilled a number of people very successfully, and in case of fire they have proved of great advantage.

267. Are the men regularly employed as a fire brigade?—They are only paid by the day. It is composed of people who live in the vicinity, and who are ready to come to the call of the chief at any moment.

268. They are only paid when they are employed?—Yes. If a fire took place in any of these villas they would have no resource but our brigade to put it out, and I think therefore they should aid us in the expenses then. That is my view.

269. Supposing a fire occurred at Prior Park, where would you get a water supply from?—We have pumps in the neighbourhood and wells from which we would get our supply. I believe there is a large cistern immediately at hand there for railway purposes, and there is the Rocklish stream. It is also contemplated to increase our staff for the purpose of greater efficiency in encompassing all those places that we intend taking in as well as the town itself.

270. Do you mean that you would have an increased fire staff as well?—I think we will.

271. Mr. *Lather*.—With regard to the roadways, assuming the borough is not only extended for municipal purposes, but that also for county cess purposes we get a separation, do you apprehend any difficulty in dealing with the roadways?—No, I do not; we went carefully into that.

272. You had a large extension before you before this one?—Yes.

273. I believe it was sketched by Mr. Rogers on the map?—Yes.

274. I believe the Committee devoted considerable care and attention to it also?—They did, and it was only for the purpose of unanimity that we yielded to the lesser area.

275. Were you in favour of the larger?—Yes, I was.

276. With respect to the old bridge portion, is it a fact that the Corporation do not expect much value from that locality?—We expect none at all, but our opinion was that in taking it in we were but doing our duty, and fearing an epidemic might break out in that locality we did it for sanitary purposes.

Mr. James O'Halloran, T.C., examined.

277. Mr. *Lather*.—I believe you are a member of the Town Council?—Yes.

278. And also a member of the Committee that dealt with this question?—Yes.

279. I believe you are one of the largest ratepayers in Clonmel?—I am one of the largest in the Corporation.

280. How many did this Committee consist of?—I think the number was seven.

281. Will your property be affected by this extension?—I think my property will be considerably affected.

282. The Commissioners.—Do you hold property outside the borough that would be taken in?—No sir, my property is all within the borough, but it extends to the outside close to the limits.

283. Mr. *Lather*.—You have heard the questions that I have put to the other witnesses as to the great care and attention paid by the Committee to the investigation of this matter? Are you aware, of your own knowledge, that such is the fact?—No doubt of it, we went through the whole thing intelligently and from time to time we paid all the care and diligence we could, and we arrived at the conclusion that it would be both beneficial to the people of Clonmel and the people we would take in, both in a sanitary point of view and as regards the equalization of taxation; and with regard to the bridge, I may tell you that we did not contemplate more than about three bridges in addition to what we have at present. In my neighbourhood we do not require one at all.

284. The population there is very thin I believe?—Yes, very thin.

285. The Commissioners.—Would you think that one or three would fairly serve the purpose?—Yes, that is my notion.

286. You mean in addition to these nine bridges given gratuitously outside the borough boundary?—Yes, given indirectly gratuitously.

287. With regard to the supply of water, will there be any difficulty in satisfying the new rate-payers upon that point?—Not the slightest.

288. Is there an abundance of water?—Yes, and they know that we, as the Council of Clonmel, would give any persons who require it, fair accommodation in that respect.

289. You have great opportunities, as a public man, of ascertaining the sentiments of the rate-payers of the town upon this subject?—Well, I am looked up to by the rate-payers, as one of their best guardians or defenders, I suppose.

290. As far as you have been able, Mr. O'Halloran to learn, taking into account your large opportunities in that respect, what is the feeling of the people on the subject?—The feeling of the people is, that they do believe that they will be improved by it, after some short time.

291. Are you aware of any large section of the ratepayers, who would be affected by it, having expressed any strong dissent against it?—No, there were a few—the Mayor and a few others, they were not favourable to it, because it was taking in their property, but otherwise, the people outside were in favour of it.

292. I was asking you, is there any large section of the intended future rate-payers, opposed to the extension?—I never heard of it.

293. Are you aware that, on the contrary, there is a large number, and as far as you are aware, a majority in favour of it?—Of course, there was some believe it would be a benefit to the town and the ratepayers.

294. Do you consider that the taking in of the old bridge was a just and politic move on the part of the Corporation?—I was opposed to it at first and then I heard some of the Committee expressing it as their opinion, that we would be justified in doing so, in a sanitary point of view, and as a help to those poor people, in case of disease breaking out.

295. Was that purely for the sake of the public health?—Yes.

296. And not on account of the income derivable from it?—No, we don't want any income from the people at all.

join the county. I believe the people living in the proposed extension have a right to pay a portion of the expense of the town when they have all the advantages. They derive a great many advantages from being so close to the town.

304. Do you consider it equitable that those who enjoy those advantages should contribute?—I do; I believe there are a few who would object, but the great body of them have no objection to join us.

305. As regards the inhabitants, have you had an opportunity of learning their views as they are in favour of the extension?—[illegible] I may say with very few exceptions. There are a few of them who object, but you will never get the people to be unanimously in favour of any subject.

306. But the great bulk of the people, what is their opinion?—The great bulk of the people are anxious that the boundary should be extended.

307. Has the evidence that has been given by Mr. O'Halloran, the Sheriff, and others, with respect to the old bridge, been in accord with your opinion?—I coincide with what the members of the Council have said here.

308. You don't expect a large income from that?—No, it is from a sanitary point of view we would take them in.

309. With respect to the roads, lighting, and water —Do you apprehend any great difficulty, or expense?—No, I have no doubt we will overcome all these difficulties quite easily. We have paid great attention to this subject and there is not a point that we have not considered seriously and well.

[illegible]

310. I suppose the amount of lighting which would be given to a rural locality you do not consider should be the same or equal to what is given to a densely populated street?—No, but I think we will give more lamps than Mr. O'Halloran has said.

311. How many in addition to the ones already outside the boundary?—I think nine more would be amply sufficient.

312. Do you think there should be a lamp every quarter of a mile?—Ordinary rural districts don't require a lamp at all. Mr. O'Halloran's house on the Carrick road [illegible] down to his place, that is already in the Corporation boundary and there is no lamp on it, and it is not required, and there is a bit of the village below his place, it would want to have there [illegible] places, and I think they have never required it.

313. Do you consider that if any objection arises on any [illegible] for the supply of lighting and water that it will be given without your experience of the Council?—I am sure it won't. The Corporation only [illegible] the city and [illegible]

ALDERMAN PATRICK MURPHY examined.

Alderman P. Murphy.

314. Mr. *Luther*.—You are an alderman of the Town Council of Clonmel?—I am.

315. I believe you were not one of the members of the Committee that dealt with the question of extension?—No, I was not.

316. But you have heard the discussions in the Town Council on the subject?—Yes.

317. Are you in favour of this movement?—I am, indeed, but I think that the extension should be greater than it is intended, but still for the purpose of unanimity I consider that it would be well to adopt the present contemplated extension. If my personal ideas were consulted, I would have extended the area even further.

318. The COMMISSIONER.—To how much or such wide?—I would almost say a radius of a mile or a mile and a half.

319. But would it not go through agricultural land on the far side?—It would, but it is my idea that we would lose or gain nothing by that.

320. Mr. *Luther*.—Have you any apprehensions as regards the supply of gas and water?—As far as the south side is concerned, there is an abundant and pure supply of water.

321. As was suggested in the course of the evidence, I think it was by the Mayor, after laying out what would be required for the maintenance of the roads, there would be so little left to supply light and water that to give an adequate supply would entail a loss on the Corporation instead of a gain. Have you any apprehensions of that kind?—I have not, I am of the contrary opinion, I would not go so far as he has gone as regards lighting the roads and I believe as regards the provision of water it would be very trifling.

322. How many gas lamps would you say would be required?—I have taken upon myself to go and look over the places for my own private information and I consider that a dozen lamps would be sufficient.

323. Including the ones that are at present outside the boundary?—Including them. I don't think for one that it is advisable to run up lamps on a portion of the extended district where they are not necessary and are not required.

324. But if it ever became necessary do you think the Corporation would refuse to supply light?—It is my experience that the Corporation are very anxious to consult the wishes of the burgesses as well as their own.

325. From a sanitary point of view do you consider that it is better that the Town Council should be the local authority having charge of sanitary matters in that district?—I do.

326. I believe you have experience of the manner in which the sanitary business is conducted by the Town Council?—I have had some experience of it.

327. Have you ever been aware of an application having been refused, or of one having been made, or a matter having come under the notice of the authorities without having been attended to, in the way of sanitary matters?—I am quite sure there was nothing of the sort.

328. You are aware that there is machinery existing for the purpose—by the appointment of officers, sanitary officers, and consulting sanitary officer, and executive sanitary officer—in good working order?—Yes; they are in very good working order.

329. You are aware of prosecutions having been brought, if the complaints have not been attended to?—Yes; certainly.

330. Is it for this reason and on account of the activity with respect to sanitary matters by the Corporation, that you consider it would be well, on sanitary grounds, that this district should be taken under the control of the local authority—is that one of your reasons?—That is one of my reasons.

331. Do you concur—with respect to the old bridge—with the evidence of the other witnesses?—I do.

332. You believe the extension will be a boon to the people living there, and also an advantage, in a public health point of view, to the rest of the borough?—No doubt of it.

333. The old bridge is partly lit already, although it is outside the borough?—Yes. I wish to remark before I close my evidence that it has been asserted here by some of the witnesses, that our staff would have to be considerably increased. Now, I don't think it would. I think our staff when we would have a separation from the county and the management of the borough at large—I don't think our staff or the expenses would have to be increased by the extension, the staff that would work the present system would also work the proposed system.

334. Mr. *Luther*.—I may now state that there are a number of members of the Town Council who are of the same opinion, but it is not necessary to examine them as it would only be a repetition of the evidence already given.

Mr. [illegible] examined.

336. Mr. [illegible].—You are [illegible] to the County Surveyor of Tipperary?—I am—at Clonmel.

336. Take this document into your hand [illegible] to Wilcocks. Did you prepare this report?—Yes.

337. Are you conversant with all the roads then shaped in that report, as regards that portion of the proposed extension?—I am.

338. Do you consider those prices fair and correct and reasonable prices?—I do.

339. Are they sufficient for the maintenance of those roads?—Perhaps they would not be for the first year, but they would after the first or second.

340. Do you mean to say that they would be quite sufficient for a Corporation, who would, [illegible] the same money as those, but not quite sufficient for a contractor who would take his own profit out of it?—I think they are quite sufficient for any purpose. [illegible] at much less than these prices.

341. For these roads?—Yes.

342. Do you look upon those as sufficient prices?—I do.

343. If the Corporation expend the entire of the money upon the road, will a greater amount of capital be expended than could possibly be expended by a contractor?—[illegible]

344. The Commissioner.—But you must remember that the Corporation have to pay their officials?—

Mr. [illegible].—[illegible] road that was spoken of—the [illegible] road.—The [illegible] portion of that [illegible] is from this to [illegible] Hill, but the road as it [illegible] portion is from this through down to the railway bridge. I would rather include it for [illegible] a [illegible] than the other portion [illegible].

345. And this part is where you allowed [illegible]—that is only from the present municipal boundary to the limit of the proposed boundary [illegible] only to the railway bridge.

346. Is that sufficient to maintain that portion properly?—Amply sufficient as the quantity of material is taken, the a year's repair of that portion is taken in proportion to the other portion of that road.

347. You are not engaged on the county Waterford portion of the proposed extension?—No.

348. From the [illegible] have you a [illegible] knowledge of the prices paid on those [illegible] and they are referred to in the [illegible].

349. You live in Clonmel?—Yes.

350. Do you know the extension that is proposed?—Yes.

351. How many gas lamps would require to be lighted in addition to what they [illegible] here?—The only place I see that [illegible] to be lighted is the [illegible]-road.

352. How many lamps do you think would be sufficient there?—About eight lamps on the [illegible]-road.

353. You don't think any of the roads on the other side of the river require to be lighted?—I think also [illegible] the [illegible] road would be necessary.

354. The prices you have laid on for the repair of the roads in the county Waterford, do you think they are equal to what is paid at present?—They are at least thirty per cent. in excess, because I have [illegible] the [illegible] Waterford [illegible] [illegible] my report. With reference to the [illegible] road, it should be remembered that there are [illegible] roads—one in which we call the [illegible] road, that would require [illegible] a [illegible] to repair it.

355. Is that portion of what you have included?—No. There are [illegible] portion of it [illegible].

356. Is it not in your list?—It is not.

357. And why did you put it in [illegible] it is a somewhat [illegible] thing. I could not properly put it into the estimated sum. It was all in one line, going from [illegible]'s Hotel to the railway.—[illegible] [illegible] the various [illegible] and [illegible] that [illegible] portion. It was only afterwards that I [illegible] that that portion of it should be included in my list.

358. Then you would add to your estimate a certain portion of it?—Yes.

359. Can you give me the mileage in the county Tipperary?—Three miles [illegible] and [illegible], and in Waterford, three miles, two [illegible] and twenty-eight perches. [illegible] that is a total of six miles odd, including the county of Waterford.

Mr. [illegible] examined.

360. Mr. [illegible].—You are a member of the Town Council?—Yes.

361. And have belonged to it for a considerable time?—Yes.

362. And you have a pretty long experience of Council?—Yes.

363. Are you aware of this project for an extension of the municipal boundary? You have a knowledge of it?—Yes.

364. Not as a member of the committee, but as one of the Council?—Yes.

365. You are also aware of the unanimity of that body on the subject?—I am.

366. Do you consider yourself, that it would be a reasonable and expedient thing to do?—I do.

367. What are your reasons—what do you [illegible] them on?—I base my reasons on the very large amount of property lying close to the town, the owners of which derive all the benefits of the markets and fairs of the locality, and of the town, for the sale of their produce, and benefit by the proximity of the town and do their business in it, while they reside in the suburbs, and all the other reasons which exist to make property close to a town improved by its proximity, and I think that this applies here as well as to other places.

368. Do you approve of the taking in of the old bridge for sanitary purposes, and for the public health's sake [illegible] would do it for sanitary purposes, but not in point of profit to the Corporation.

369. But at the same time, you think the [illegible] would be [illegible] [illegible] the [illegible] of the old bridge?—On that score I would take it in.

370. And put it in a thoroughly healthy condition as regards sewerage, and everything of that kind?—Yes.

371. Have you any apprehension of loss to the Council with regard to the supply of water and gas that would have to be given to the extended area?—I heard part of the investigation here, but not the whole of it, and as I have not gone into the figures my answer would be [illegible] much the same as that of the others, but knowing the locality as I do, I have not any apprehension about it at all.

372. Do you consider that the additional area would have to be very extensively lit?—I do not, when you take into account that you have nine lamps already outside the area of the borough as it exists at present.

373. How many additional lamps do you think would be sufficient to light it adequately?—This is the very point I could not give you a decided answer on.

374. If you go in by mileage how many lamps per mile would you give the rural portion of it?—Portions of it, where the trees are not in the way would [illegible] very well as they are. I prefer leaving that to be explained by those who know the locality better.

375. Do you consider that the [illegible] would require lighting?—That is a place I think would require it.

376. Is there any other portion of the roadway [illegible]

the proposed extension that would require lighting?—The Richmond road.

378. Would you consider that a couple of additional lamps would be sufficient to light that road?—Yes, I think so; with the [illegible]

379. [illegible]

380. [illegible]

381. [illegible]

... separate appliances?—Yes; most decidedly; it would [illegible]

381. [illegible]

382. [illegible]

383. [illegible]

384. The Mayor.—[illegible]

385. [illegible]

386. Mr. Ladner.—Would it cost the Corporation [illegible]

387. [illegible]

388. Do you consider that £150 will pay for six miles of roads [illegible]

Mr. Benjamin Fayle examined.

Mr. Benjamin Fayle.

389. Mr. Ladner.—You are aware of the proposed extension?—I am.

390. I believe you will be one of those whose property will be affected?—Yes, my father's.

391. Do you consider it just and equitable that gentlemen of your position, whose property will be affected, should contribute something to the expenses of the town?—Well, I don't say I look upon it exactly in that light.

392. Do you derive convenience and advantages from the town, living in such close proximity?—Of course I do. I live on the other side of the gas house bridge, on the Waterford side.

393. Within a few hundred feet of the present boundary?—Yes, the property joins the Corporation bounds.

394. One of the lamps alluded to is not very far away from you?—Quite close.

395. That is one of the lamps outside the borough boundary?—Yes.

396. Do you think that lamp has a right to be there?—It was more than a public convenience, I think it is an absolute necessity.

397. Are any more lamps wanted?—There are, on the road up to Mr. Boyd's, the Raheen road, would want some.

398. How many would be wanted there?—Well, I think two at the outside, with what is already there.

399. How many would be required at the Coleville-road—how many would be sufficient to light it fairly?—I think if there were three additional lamps upon it it would be sufficient. The trees in it are very dangerous.

400. How many would be required in the vicinity of old bridge, up towards the [illegible]?—I think at the very outside two would be sufficient—I think one or two at the very outside.

401. Are there any other places of the districts outside the town that require lamps?—I don't know, I never saw this plan of extension until I heard of it here.

(The Town Clerk then explained to the witness, the nature of the extension sought by the Council.)

402. You have more than an ordinary knowledge I believe with respect to the gas?—Well I ought to know something about it, because I happen to be chairman of the gas company.

403. You are more skilled than ordinary people?—I have no technical skill on the subject.

404. But as regards the practical application for lighting purposes?—I believe the extension of the borough would be important to the town, as to the matter of civilization, and so on, but if it is done I have not the least doubt but it will be a very great increase in the taxation. I have not the least doubt about it; if you want things done you must pay for them, and it is utterly absurd to say you could keep six miles of road for £150 a year.

405. You don't pit your belief against the experience of a road contractor?—I don't pit my belief against anything, but I believe the borough extension would add considerably to the taxation of persons, not only in the boundary at present, but those added.

406. Notwithstanding that you are in favour of it?—I believe it would be of advantage to the town of Clonmel taking it in, but those persons who hold the views I do must be satisfied to put their hands into their pockets and to pay for it.

407. You heard the evidence of Mr. Carruthers and Mr. Besry, and you don't say they are erroneous in their views?—I do not.

408. Then you don't know anything about it?—I know my own common sense and I don't believe that £150 would pay the half of six miles of roads. Take the water supply—I have heard a great deal about the water to-day. I don't believe it is possible to put a water supply into Clonmel from the county Waterford. Some persons think it is very easy. I know every inch of the mountain, and I know of no supply of water, unless some enormous expense was gone to, and it is unnecessary, and on the other hand if you put in old bridge and the county Waterford side, if you give any water supply there—I suppose you will have to do it. Now from the new bridge corner down to the other end of the extension, there is hardly a good pump in the whole place. I believe there are only one or two pumps in the whole place.

409. Did you ever ask your rural sanitary authority to do anything in that way?—Oh, no; what could they

[illegible]. We had a well [illegible], and it [illegible], and it was [illegible] to [illegible]. The great bulk of Clonmel is comfortably well supplied with water, but there are special parts of Clonmel where the water is very hard to be got. The part that Alderman Hughes lives in is almost [illegible]—[illegible] Park—and Mr. [illegible] spent a heap of money trying to get water, and on our side the town is very much in the same way; but as regards the great bulk of the town there is no difficulty in our getting water.

410. In the great bulk of the town there is no difficulty?—Quite so; but it would be absurd to go to expense in getting another supply.

Mr. SEBASTIAN BRUNICARDI examined.

411. Mr. *Ludlow*.—How many years have you been in the service of the Council?—Eleven years now.

412. You formerly were in the employment of the Dublin Fire Brigade?—Yes.

413. Have you been at the extinguishing of a good many fires in Clonmel?—Yes, a number of them since I came here.

414. Do you find any difficulty in procuring the assistance of parties to work the engine?—No; none whatsoever. They always work very efficiently.

415. Have you reduced that matter to a system?—Quite so.

416. You have no difficulty on an alarm of fire being given in getting off to it?—I am able to turn out in a minute and a half to two minutes from the alarm. The parties live in the neighbourhood, and the moment they hear an alarm they are down at the station with myself.

417. Do they get paid?—Yes, at the time of fire.

418. Do those parties know they will be employed on going to the engine?—Yes, they do.

419. Is that what causes the activity?—They are willing to do it without money, and frequently refuse to take it, and would rather assist for the purpose of extinguishing the fire.

420. You have got one of Clayton's telescopic fire escapes?—Yes, one of the most improved fire escapes.

421. The COMMISSIONER.—Has it been often used?—We never had occasion to use it.

422. Mr. *Ludlow*.—Are you aware of the proposed extension?—I am.

423. Do you consider that with the appliances you have at present and with the dispersion of those to assist in the extinguishing of fires, that that area would be too great for you to attend to?—Under the present existing circumstances it would be.

424. In what way?—In this way:—taking into consideration the distance we would have to travel with the engine. The engine would scarcely be brought there within a reasonable time from the present station, but what I anticipate from my instructions is that they will then have horses and a proper fire brigade.

425. You mean that you will then have those whether the boundary is extended or not?—Yes, in the next few months we will have a permanent fire-brigade.

426. Would the extension of the boundary add anything more to that?—I think not.

427. Would you be able to cope with the proposed boundary?—I think so.

428. Would you consider yourself justified in going outside the Borough bounds?—I would not, nor do I without the permission of the mayor.

429. You have heard some observations with respect to the sewerage of the town—are the sewers fairly delineated on that map of the town?—They are.

430. How do you know that?—As Inspector of Nuisances and Town Inspector. The sewers are fully delineated in blue on the map, in the centre of the roadways. I think in that map they are all laid down, but the terminations are not accurately given, inasmuch as the sewers lately laid down have been put in the places of those formerly there, and they have been deepened and widened.

431. Are there any new ones, not on the map?—One only, the one through Bland-street and Garden-street, they are not on the map.

432. There is no difficulty in putting them on the map?—Not the slightest trouble in the world.

433. The COMMISSIONER.—This Bland-street sewer, where is that?—It runs through the centre of Bland-street.

434. And it brings the sewage of Bland-street in connexion with the river?—Yes, in one direction, and in connexion with Richmond-street in the other direction.

435. Wherever there is drainage, except in the case of cesspools, it is to the river?—Yes.

436. Are there any complaints of the cesspools?—No complaints.

437. There is no plan of dealing with drainage, otherwise than by cesspools, and the river?—There are some cesspools, but a few, in the town.

438. Is there any difficulty in getting them within a hundred feet of the main sewer, connected with it?—No, not much difficulty, some few instances did occur where we were obliged to summon, but only a few.

439. How many cesspools are there in the Main-street?—I don't know of one.

440. In Dublin-street?—None.

441. Where are the houses drained there from? Is there, in point of fact, a sewer in Dublin-street and in Main-street?—Yes; there is in Dublin-street.

442. Is there one in Main-street?—There is not, as it parallel with the houses, but at right angles. It would be impossible to drain the northern side of Main-street by a central sewer.

443. Would it be below the level of the river?—Yes, in some portions.

444. What becomes of the sewage then, that runs from the north of Main-street?—It is carried off to Johnson-street, and by Johnson-street, to Duncan-street, and thence to the river.

445. All the houses from there are drained by that system. Practically speaking, Main-street can be drained by the north and south?—The south is drained to the river. It is at present drained in that direction—into Johnson-street, and Bridge-lane.

446. So that there is no necessity for a main sewer in Main-street?—No, the sewage goes into the recent main sewer we have built, some 350 yards in length, and that sewer discharges into the river.

447. Do you consider, Mr. Brunicardi, from your experience as sanitary officer, that the sanitation would be more closely attended to in the proposed extension, than in leaving matters as they are under the individual control of either authority?—I am sure that if it was carried on as at present, under the borough of Clonmel, it would be much better attended to.

448. Would the sanitation of the old bridge district be better attended to there by the Guardians?—Undoubtedly so, it could not remain as it is; if the Corporation had it I am sure it would be improved.

449. Would the maintenance of the sanitary improvements there entail an expense that would be considerable or inconsiderable?—It would be considerable.

450. Is it absolutely necessary that it should be put in that condition?—Most undoubtedly.

451. If left as at present—would you consider if they are allowed to go on as at present, that from pestilence or disease arising there, injury would result to the rest of the town?—So I think. If disease broke out there it could not be prevented from extending to the town.

452. Do you consider that the management of the Corporation is better than that of the Guardians?—In consequence of having experienced men connected with the work, it must be evident that that is so.

453. Do you know that when a matter has been investigated and reported on and dealt with by the sanitary officer, and it is ordered to be done—are you aware whether the procedure has been proper or prompt as a rule?—I always found the notices very fairly served, and if the party did not comply he was summoned, and then he was dealt with by the magistrates.

454. Do you think the system of the Corporation is more prompt than that of the Guardians?—I think it is.

455. Mr. Luther.—That concludes the case for the Corporation.

Clonmel. May 1879. Mr. Sebastian Brunswick.

Mr. JOHN BAGWELL examined.

Mr. John Bagwell.

456. The COMMISSIONER.—What do you wish to say in reference to the proposition of the Town Council?—Without any communication or correspondence with the Mayor of the town, I wish to say that I entirely concur with what he said about the taxation, and the increase that the extension would cause. I have very little to add to what he said except to confirm from my long knowledge of the place both as a Grand Juror and magistrate, as a member of the Corporation, and member for the town, and as an owner of property in the town—I coincide with everything he said about it. We are now under a new regime, and that we are to govern ourselves as the result of the Provisional Order—I saw it down for 3rd reading the other day, and I suppose we shall have it over immediately.

457. There is no opposition to it?—No. The Grand Juries of both counties passed it. I have no doubt we shall be under increased taxation on account of that, and if this small valuation of £2,000 is added, to keep six miles of roads, and to get all the other applications, I think we shall have very much heavier taxation than we have now, being very heavy as it is. The town of Clonmel is very heavily taxed and I think it will be much increased by the new Bill, and if the increase on the roads of the new Bill is considerable, why these in these districts for us to take charge of? I differ in opinion with many of the gentlemen around me, when they talk about the increase of building. I don't think there has been a villa built in Clonmel for thirty years, and I think taking in these lands and putting us to heavier taxation in the town, would be probably the means of stopping building instead of increasing it. There has not been, I think, for thirty years, a villa built in the neighbourhood of Clonmel.

458. Mr. Luther.—If the additional taxation was not much, would you oppose the extension of the area? If the taxation was not to be heavier upon the town, I should not object to it at all, but I am sure it would be very much increased.

459. Would not the Colville and Raheen roads require lighting?—There are so near to the town that they might reasonably have been taken in long ago. It is all villas on both sides, there are villas on every part. I don't think it would be any advantage to them or the town, but a disadvantage to the town of Clonmel to take over the roads, and as to keeping the roads for £150 a year, I don't think Mr. Carruthers made his money by contracting for roads at that price. I don't think that sum would keep a gentleman's avenue properly. I think there might be changes made. I am not going to oppose anything. I merely come to give my opinion as a person concerned in the matter, and to give my opinion on the matter of taxation. I told gentlemen before, when they wished to separate from the county, that I thought it would increase the taxation, and I think so now; and I think this will further increase the taxation, and therefore I wish to give my opinion, but I don't wish to put a stoppage to any improvement that the people of Clonmel think they can do, but I give my opinion that this won't be an improvement so far as taxation is concerned.

460. The Mayor.—From my analysis of the matter I am quite satisfied that after the first year we will save considerably for the ratepayers, and we will have good streets in Clonmel, and that we have not had for a considerable time, notwithstanding that we have paid an enormous paving rate for it. Several of the most practical men of the Corporation have considered the matter very carefully, and that is the conclusion we have come to. It is simply in the interests of the ratepayers I am here, and not of factious opposition.

Mr. ALEXANDER BOYD examined.

Mr. Alexander Boyd.

461. The COMMISSIONER.—You live at [illegible]?—Yes.

462. That is within the proposed extension?—Yes.

463. Are you in favour of the extension or otherwise?—I think it is for the general good of Clonmel, and I would like my road, the [illegible] road, to be lit.

464. You would not object to pay something for it?—I would not.

465. Do you think that the extension would be beneficial generally to the inhabitants? I should say that it would.

Mr. JEREMIAH MORIARTY examined.

Mr. Jeremiah Moriarty.

466. The COMMISSIONER.—You reside at the old bridge?—Yes.

467. Mr. Luther.—You were, I believe, formerly a member of the Town Council?—I was.

468. And you are the owner of property in the old bridge district?—I am.

469. And you are in favour of the extension?—I am.

470. On the ground of the sanitary condition of the [illegible]?—Yes, and to include the cost of lighting

Mr. Lowry, re-examined.

479. The Commissioner.—Did the Grand Jury at the time they [illegible] to the [illegible], did they know that [illegible] of this kind was proposed?—I don't think they did; [illegible] might have [illegible] it from seeing that this Commission was going through the country, and that it was holding these inquiries. I don't think it was brought before them.

Mr. Richard Hastings examined.

[illegible] The Commissioner.—[illegible] Grand Juror, I believe?—Yes. On the [illegible] occasion, when the question was brought before the Grand Jury, I was [illegible]. There was a very [illegible] discussion and no [illegible] opposition, because [illegible] the Grand Jurors were [illegible] [illegible] [illegible] [illegible] to the town. I [illegible] upon social and political grounds, because I think the town should have its own management. But I think there would have been violent opposition if there had been any question of extension mooted. It was never mooted on the occasion I refer to, and it did not come to a vote, for the reason I tell you.

480. Mr. Lowry.—It never could have been in the mind of the Corporation to put on this increase to this territory at that time, for this reason: We considered this question in the year 1871. I doubt if your Commission was in being at the time. There was no [illegible] on the part of the Corporation. We had no conception of any extension at the time.

The enquiry then closed.

COOKSTOWN—SEPTEMBER 16TH, 1879.

(Before Mr. Henry A. Robinson.)

Mr. John Fleming examined.

1. Mr. Robinson.—You are clerk of the Town Commissioners?—Yes.

2. How long have you held that position?—For about twelve years.

3. Cookstown is under the Town Improvement Act?—Yes, since [illegible].

4. Was it adopted for all purposes?—Yes.

5. Give me the population of the town?—At the last census it was 3,303.

6. And would you say it is increasing or diminishing?—It is above 4,000 at present.

7. What is the area?—[illegible]

8. Does that include whole townlands or does it run through townlands?—There are portions of townlands running along the streets of the town.

9. [illegible], a portion of it, is included?—Yes, a small portion.

10. What is the acreage of [illegible]?—[illegible], and portions of Cookstown, [illegible], Gortalowry [illegible], Loy [illegible].

11. What is the valuation of the town?—[illegible]

12. And on how much of that is the full rate assessed, and on how much the one-fourth?—It is assessed the full rate on [illegible], and the one-fourth on the [illegible].

13. In what electoral division is the town included?—Cookstown.

14. Is it wholly included in Cookstown?—Yes.

15. If you take a radius of a mile from the centre of the town how many electoral divisions would it run?—It would still be in the Cookstown electoral division.

16. Are you certain of that?—Yes; perhaps it might go into [illegible].

17. What is the valuation of the electoral division?—[illegible]

18. And the area?—[illegible]

20. Has there been any alteration in the boundaries since they were first formed?—No.

21. Was the town of Cookstown under any Act previous to being constituted under the Town Improvement Act?—Yes, the 9th of George IV.

22. And the boundary under the 9th George IV., did it differ from the present?—I think it was the same, to a great extent.

23. What have been the municipal rates for the past five years?—In 1874 the municipal rate was [illegible] in the pound, and it has been [illegible].

24. You have always struck the full rate?—Yes, up to the present year.

25. What have been the poor law rates during the same period?—In 1874, 7d.; in 1875, 11d.; in 1876, 13d.; in 1877, 8d.; and in 1878 and 1879, 8d.

26. Did that include a special rate for sanitary purposes?—Yes, in 1876 there was 4d. in the pound for sewerage.

27. Eightpence additional?—Yes, and in 1878 10d.

28. What was the contributory district over which the sanitary rate was struck?—The contributory district took in the whole of Cookstown, Cookstown [illegible], Gortalowry and Loy.

30. No portion of Munreah?—No.

31. Is Cookstown a market town?—Yes, there is a market on Tuesday, and a general market on Saturday.

32. There are fairs?—Yes.

33. Have you a fair green?—Yes—a fair hill.

34. The fair is not held in the streets?—No, but the markets are.

35. For a radius of how far would you say the people derive advantage from the Cookstown fairs and markets?—Some come from an average of fifteen miles.

36. The whole of the electoral division avails itself of these advantages?—Yes.

37. Are there any villa residences outside the town?—Well, I can scarcely say there are.

38. Do the people carrying on business in the town live in their places of business or outside?—Nearly all reside in their places of business.

39. Are there building operations going on?—Yes, especially towards the railway.

40. Is there any tendency to build outside the municipal limits?—Not much.

41. Would you say there is sufficient land within the municipal boundary available for many years to come?—As to that I could scarcely say.

42. Is there difficulty experienced in getting building leases within the town?—Well, I can hardly say that.

43. Is the town well lighted?—Pretty well.

44. With gas?—Yes.

45. In what months of the year is it lighted?—In September—and usually kept lighting until April—sometimes until May.

46. Are the markets early or late?—They vary.

47. And the people who come in to these markets avail themselves of the lights?—Yes.

48. There are schools in the town availed of by the children of people living outside?—Yes.

49. Can you tell me how far the electoral division extends on all sides from the centre of the town?—The

Cookstown, Sept. 18, 18[illegible].

Mr. John Fleming.

farthest point would not be more than two miles. On the north it would be about a mile and a half to Claggan; on the south rather over a mile.

50. Are there any improvements which the Commissioners could carry on, if they had an increased area of taxation and a larger income?—There are a number of Commissioners here who would be better able to answer that question.

51. Have the Commissioners ever considered the question of becoming the urban sanitary authority?—I think they have, but we are under the statutory number at present.

52. But under the seventh section of the Act, you can obtain a Provisional Order, enabling you to become the urban sanitary authority?—A number of the Town Commissioners consider that the Poor Law Guardians do the work better than the Commissioners would.

53. Has the question ever been mooted of getting a separation from the Grand Jury as to roads?—The streets of Cookstown are very fairly repaired, and therefore we do not think it would be any advantage.

54. However there was no resolution passed on the subject?—No.

55. Now as to the question of extension; we submitted certain queries to you, were they considered at a special meeting or at an ordinary meeting?—At a general meeting.

56. We ask in query eight, "What is the opinion of the municipal body on the subject?" and they reply that they hold the existing boundary should be enlarged. Did they specify any particular extension?—Last Friday evening they held a meeting and came to the conclusion to take in the entire electoral division.

57. Did they intend to take in the entire of the townland of Drumgel?—It is in the electoral division and therefore it would come in.

58. On what ground do they suggest this?—They think it would be for the benefit of the town, and also that the people within the electoral division, or who live within a mile or so, derive advantage from the town.

59. You are a ratepayer in the town?—I am.

60. And have lived here some time?—Yes.

61. Have you formed any opinion yourself on the subject?—I would prefer not answering that.

Mr. Black, Solicitor.—I represent the landlords of a considerable portion of Cookstown—Messrs. James Moore and John Byers Gunning Moore.

62. *Mr. Black*.—As I understand you, Mr. *Fleming*, the present boundary contains 162 acres?—Yes.

63. And what now is the extended boundary proposed by the Town Commissioners, for I gather from your evidence that you yourself are not inclined to justify the proposed extension?—I did not say that.

64. No, but you preferred not answering the question put by the Commissioner?—I will explain the reason. I hold about 160 acres that will be within the proposed new boundary, and therefore I am not for it, on that account.

65. Now, as to the new area proposed, what does it comprehend, how many acres?—3,354a. 1r. 4p.

66. Something like twenty times the present area?—I suppose so.

67. And how many inhabitants are within the proposed extended area?—I do not know.

68. Look at that abstract of the valuation and say it is nearly correct (handing witness a paper)—do you see that there are scarcely any houses at all to be brought in?—There are not many.

69. How many over £10 valuation?—Well over £10 valuation not many.

70. Would there be half a dozen?—I think not.

71. Well, I am content to take that, and do you think it would be better for the town to take in this area?—Of course I have told you about my own farm, but it would make us pay less in the town.

72. So that it is simply to lessen the burthen of taxation on Cookstown that this is to be brought in?—I cannot say that.

73. How would the Commissioners in any way benefit this extended area?—They appear to think that it would lessen the taxation of Cookstown considerably.

74. And the express object is to lessen the taxation of Cookstown?—I don't know that.

75. Do you know of any other reason?—I do not.

76. Have you ever heard any other reason, but that it was to benefit Cookstown by lessening taxation?—I don't remember.

77. Would you have any sewerage or water to supply for this district?——

78. Mr. Bourgeois.—That is under the jurisdiction of the guardians.

79. Mr. *Black*.—Yes, but it is possible the guardians might become the sanitary authority, and I want to know if they could in any way benefit them.

Witness.—There is one thing certain that they don't want to be taxed, whether they would be lighted or not.

80. Do you think the Commissioners would propose to light any of this outlying district?—I cannot say really.

81. Is there any new building operations going on in these outlying districts?—The new buildings are all within the town.

82. And, therefore, there would be no reason for the Town Commissioners to interfere, so far as buildings are concerned, outside their boundary?—The only portions in my opinion that would be entitled to come into the town boundary are the buildings of the new railway here.

83. That is for the purpose of taxing them?—They will have to be lighted and, therefore, should be taxed.

84. Are they outside the boundary?—Yes.

85. Altogether, I gather from your evidence that it is for the purpose of benefiting the town of Cookstown and lightening the rates that this extended area would be brought in?—Yes.

Cross-examined by Mr. *Edward Young*, Solicitor, (appearing for Messrs. Adair, mill owners, who oppose the extension).

86. As to sixteen townlands, I have here a return, and from that it appears that there is no house at all in the first townland. There is no house at Ballymenna townland, none at Claggan?—I see the place I have my farm and house I don't see that valued there.

87. What I want to show is this, that as regards these sixteen townlands there would be taxation without representation, for there are only four houses in the whole sixteen townlands valued at more than £4?—That is so as to Ballymenna.

88. It applies to the whole sixteen townlands. There are only four houses valued above than £4, so that it would be taxation without representation?—Well I suppose it would.

89. Now you have already answered with regard to the benefit to be conferred on Cookstown by the extension. Do not the people who carry on business in Cookstown live for the most part in their places of business?—They do.

90. They do not live outside the boundary?—No.

91. Now have you read the queries sent down and the replies given by the Commissioners?—Yes.

93. Tell me what is the furthest distance these townlands run—would not some run two miles from the town?—Some would run about that distance.

94. Does not Dunmanbrie run two miles from where you are standing?—Scarcely.

95. Is it more than a mile and three quarters?—Of course, to the furthest part of it would be at least that.

96. Now you are the officers of the Commissioners, and you can tell us do they intend to expend any money on these townlands they wish to bring in to assist the rates?—If the town was extended I suppose they would have to do so.

97. Is there not plenty of building ground available in the town, and supplied at reasonable terms by our friends here?—Plenty.

Cookstown, Sept. 18, 1879.

Mr. John Fleming.

98. So far as you know, then, they do not intend to spend any money on building in this new boundary?——

99. Mr. Robinson.—What powers would the Commissioners have to do so?

100. Mr. Younge.—Well, yes; but what I want to bring out is that they are not contemplating doing anything for the new district. As to the sewerage of Cookstown, will it benefit any of these sixteen townlands?

101. Mr. Robinson.—But the Commissioners have nothing to do with it. It is the guardians who look after that.

102. Mr. Younge.—The Commissioners propose to light this district?—

Witness.—I think it would be ridiculous if they did.

103. Mr. Younge.—Now it is put forward that the fact of Cookstown being a baronial town requires them to get assistance from the surrounding country. Now what expense does it put them to—being a baronial town?—I don't know.

104. Nor anyone else. Is it not in fact an advantage to them—are there not four courts held in the court house—in consequence of its being a baronial town?—Yes.

105. And does not that bring farmers and others in here for the purpose of doing their business, four times in the year?—Yes.

106. And when they come to do not the shop windows here attract them to lay out their money to buy goods of different kinds?—I suppose so.

107. So that instead of its being a baronial town being prejudicial it is an improvement?—I suppose so.

108. You would not like all these people to be brought to Dungannon?—No. I would like to see as large a crowd in the town as I could.

109. Now is not Stewartstown only five miles away?—Yes.

110. Coalisland only six and a half miles?—Yes.

111. Dungannon only nine miles?—Yes.

112. Magherafelt only eight miles?—I suppose so.

113. And Pomeroy only seven miles?—I suppose so.

114. And is there not railway communication this minute with those towns?—Yes.

115. Now if the inhabitants of these sixteen townlands chose to go to those towns I have mentioned or any one of them would it not be a serious loss to Cookstown?—Yes.

116. So then we may take it that so far from Cookstown benefiting these sixteen townlands, these sixteen townlands benefit Cookstown by coming to the markets?—Yes.

117. Mr. Robinson.—You consider, I suppose, that it is a case of mutual benefit?—Yes, I think it is better for them to come here than to go far away.

118. Mr. Younge.—But it is to be remembered that if they were taxed they would go far away to avoid it—do you think the people of Cookstown carry on their business merely for the advantage of these sixteen outlying townlands?—No.

119. They are not such philanthropists as that, they carry it on, I should say for their own advantage?—Yes.

120. Now do you really think the outlying districts, proposed to be brought in, derive any advantage from the town?—I think they have a great many advantages.

121. Have they any more advantage than being able to use the roads of Cookstown?—In the first place they have good landlords.

122. But we have that in Dungannon; we have better, we have titled landlords. Now I ask you this, when the country people come in with their money—their ready money to spend here, do they derive any more advantage than simply to use the roads to enable them to walk in and out?—I suppose not.

123. And are not these roads kept up by the county?—Yes.

124. Now about the flagging, was not two-thirds of the cost of the flagging paid by the county?—It was.

125. Now in answer to the queries, allusion is made to the union workhouse, and it is given as a reason why there should be an extension, that the union workhouse is there, and that it affords a reason why county neighbours should assist them to pay taxation. In what manner does the union workhouse bring loss and to the expense of the town. Are not the persons holding the contracts for supplying the workhouse living in the town, and does not the town in that way get the benefit of those contracts?—Yes, but strangers can have those contracts if they tender lower.

126. Yes but the Scotch element is too strong here for that—do not the townspeople as a matter of fact get it?—Yes, I know they do.

127. And are not the contracts supplied by the shopkeepers for their own advantage?—Yes.

128. And are not the rates paid by the union?—Yes.

129. Now we are here met in this very comfortable Petty Sessions room—now that is made in some way a reason for this proposal—in the first place is not the rent paid by the county?—Yes.

130. And not out of the rate of the town—and is it not a great advantage to the town of Cookstown to have the litigants coming in twice every month, bringing in their money here to pay the professional men and to spend in the shops?—Yes.

131. Do you think it is right or fair to try to compel these sixteen townlands to bear any portion of the taxation of Cookstown?—As far as I am myself concerned, and from selfish motives, I would say not.

132. If you were not in office what would your opinion be?—Certainly I would think it hard to be taxed.

133. Mr. Robinson.—Do your clients say, Mr. Younge, that they derive no benefit whatever from Cookstown?

Mr. Younge.—Yes, they do—we say we confer benefit on it.

134. Do your clients come into the town frequently?—They do come in frequently.

135. Do they make use of the markets and shops?—Yes; but the roads are paid for by the grand jury.

136. Yes, but the scavenging is paid for by the Commissioners—do your clients maintain that they derive no benefit from the lights of the town?—They do not derive any benefit from them, because they all come in and go out when it is light.

137. Are your clients in every day?—Not every day.

138. But every day they come in of course they use those roads?—Of course they do, but it should not be forgotten that the roads are kept up by the county—the cleansing of the roads is done by the county—the lighting is done by the Town Commissioners. The Commissioners sweep the crossings.

139. They have a scavenging staff?—One man.

140. Do your clients say they have no advantage from the town?—They say that on the contrary they confer advantage on Cookstown. I pay rent for my office, and therefore I confer benefit on the town.

141. On the landlord rather?—Who is a Commissioner and lives in the town. My clients coming into the town do no injury and should not be asked to pay anything.

142. Do they not make use of the lights?—No; they don't come in at night.

143. Do they not do their marketing in the town?—Yes; but the town gets the benefit of that.

144. Well, so do they—you contend that they get no benefit from the town?—Yes, most solemnly and seriously we say we get no benefit, but confer benefit on the town every time they come in. There is no hotel here—I put my horse up there and give the ostler a shilling.

145. Well, it is a convenience to you to have the ostler there?—Yes, but he gets the shilling, and every one who comes in would lay out something. I would ask Mr. Fleming one question more—what does the scavenger who sweeps the crossings get?—

Mr. Fleming.—He gets 8s. a week for lighting the lamps and sweeping the crossings.

Cross-examined by Mr. Paige (Solicitor for gentlemen opposing the extension—Mr. Samuel Magill and Mr. John Murray).

146. You know Killymoon demesne?—Yes.

147. It comprises 500 acres?—I believe so.

148. It is shut in by a wall?—Yes.

149. Now has the proprietor of that demesne any interest beyond his own demesne wall?—I don't think so.

150. Can you say, or have you heard the Commissioners give any reason why the demesne should be included in the boundary, or how it would be benefited by being included? Did they propose to light the avenue to the house?—I am not sure.

151. Mr. *John Fair* (a ratepayer).—How many mills are situated within a mile of Cookstown?—There are four—yours is one and there are three others.

152. What is the distance of Mr. Adair's mills from the town?—About half a mile.

153. Mr. Romney.—How many gentlemen's residences are within the electoral division?—Not more than four at the outside.

154. I suppose the inclusion of the electoral division would not bring the population up to 6,000?—I think not.

155. Mr. *Fair*.—I would ask Mr. Fleming again how far is Mr. Adair's mill.

156. Mr. Romney.—It appears from the map to be about a quarter of a mile from the Main street.

157. Mr. Fair.—Exactly. Is there not a special lamp there for their works, on the edge of the boundary, paid for by the town?—I think it is specially for the benefit of the workers.

158. There is no other lamp in a similar position?—No.

159. Was not that lamp lit by the majority of the Commissioners taking charge, and by the influence of Messrs. Adair and others?—Yes.

160. And don't you think the Messrs. Adair and the other owners derive benefit from the lights of the town?—Yes.

161. Do not all the mills get an advantage from the lighting of the streets?—Yes.

162. Would it not be only fair that the new railway station should be brought in?—Yes.

163. Mr. Young.—Is not the lamp Mr. Fair has alluded to within the statutory boundary?—Yes.

164. It is not outside it?—No.

165. Now do you know of your own knowledge that it was at the solicitation of Mr. Adair that the lamp was put there?—Well, the lamp was some years in the town.

166. How many years ago?—It was taken away some years ago; it was taken away, and there was a new one raised up by some friends, and the lamp was put back.

167. Now is not a number of Mr. Adair's workers live in Cookstown and within the town?—The great majority of them live within the boundary.

168. And they may have found it to be an advantage, and pay rates for it?—Yes.

Mr. John Hammond examined.

169. Mr. Romney.—You are Chairman of the Town Commissioners?—Yes.

170. How long have you been a member of the Town Board?—Nearly since the commencement; in fact, I was only outside three years.

171. How long have you been Chairman?—I am in my third year at present.

172. You are a resident in the town?—Yes, and have been for forty years.

173. Were you present at the meeting when the question of the extension of the boundary was considered?—Yes.

174. And you are in favour of an extension?—Yes. Formerly it used to be. The original boundary, under the 9 Geo. IV., only went to Loughry; the Commissioners, then some years back.

175. Do you consider the people residing within the electoral division, but outside of the town, derive their principally to the town?—So far as having the town kept in good order, coming in to good shops—they certainly do.

176. And you think the improvements effected in the town in the way of lighting, sewerage, and so on, are of benefit, not only to the town, but to those living outside?—It should be an advantage for the town to be in good order, for the people coming in.

177. If the people outside had to pay municipal taxation, would it be too much—would it be a hardship?—Some farmers would feel it a hardship. I would rather myself—holding a good deal of property; but I think it would not be such a hardship on those so situated in close proximity to the town.

178. The landlords find their lands are better—is more valuable in fact, near the town?—No doubt. You can have rented grazing.

179. Does the land near the town fetch a higher rent on account of its proximity?—Generally.

180. Are you in favour of the area of the electoral division?—The Town Commissioners were under the impression, it could not be divided, as they would have left out some portions such as Drumgarrow and perhaps others.

181. Were you influenced by the fact that the Select Committee recommended the electoral divisions should be coterminous with towns?—Yes.

182. Otherwise you would not have taken in Drumgarrow?—No.

183. I suppose Cookstown is a very good market town?—Yes, very good.

184. And you don't see any advantage that would accrue to the people if they were to go off to Drumcorry or other places, as was suggested?—No. It is not probable that they would.

185. I understand you do not propose to light these outlying districts?—Oh, no.

186. And in, while these districts are within, you would not supply lights?—No. It would be quite impossible.

187. Is there any likelihood of the Commissioners applying for a provisional order to become the urban sanitary authority?—The general feeling is against it, on this ground, that we believe they would have their rights in a measure of the rates from the landlord.

188. The Select Committee have expressed an opinion that rates should be assessed equally. Are any like grievances of a similar nature experienced in this town?—I think not.

189. If you had a larger area is there any improvement that the Town Commissioners would try and effect in the way of paving?—We might put down more flagging, and put the streets in better order. There were complaints in winter about the crossings and flags.

190. Was your Board unanimous on the question of extension?—I called the meeting and there was no second opinion upon it, but we were misled, by the idea as to the electoral division, that we could not divide it.

191. We will accept any boundary you may recommend, provided it appears to be a fair and reasonable one. The Select Committee only made the suggestion as to the electoral division, but do you admit any boundary?—Well, anything within a mile would not be too far. It is providing against the contingency of any outside part on by the sanitary authorities at the extension.

192. They can strike that as they like?—That is looked upon as a great anomaly.

193. Do you think Killymoon should be brought in?—Well, it gets very well the guarding purposes.

194. Being so near the town?—Yes.

195. And therefore may be said to derive considerable advantages from its proximity to the town?—Yes; it makes it more valuable.

196. Mr. Brooke.—The income of the Commissioners is £300—how is it spent?—There is the lighting of the [illegible]........

197. What does the lighting cost?—£[illegible] [illegible] a [illegible].

198. What is the total amount?—£120 a year; about that.

199. And do you think the inhabitants of these townlands would be benefited by that lighting?—Yes, coming in to their business, they can see their way.

200. Do they generally come in at night?—No, but they very often stay.

201. How much is spent on keeping the crossings clean?—Not very much; the expenditure within the last few years has been principally on flagging and footpaths.

202. How much was spent on flagging?—There was £500 one year—we paid £200——

203. The county contributed largely to that?—Yes, they pay twice that towards the full sum of £1,300.

204. And do not the townlands pay their share of the county expenditure?—The same as we do.

205. Now I think you said necessity forced the extension on you?—Yes.

206. What has been the necessity?—There has been a sanitary rate and a poor rate.

207. How does the sanitary rate affect you, for the Commissioners do not levy that?—Is it any difference who levies it, when one's pocket has to suffer.

208. And will you tell me how the fact of the Guardians levying a sanitary rate forced an extension on the Commissioners?—There was great talk of a sanitary rate being levied for bringing water in with high pressure.

209. Well, and how will the Commissioners getting an extension help that?—Why, the thing will fall lighter on each person.

210. The Guardians put on a water tax, and the Commissioners put on a town tax, won't that be increased taxation?—Yes.

211. How will the Guardians putting on a water tax affect the Commissioners in getting an extension?—Why the Commissioners can prevail on us to equalize it, and make more parties than themselves feel it.

212. Is that what you call necessity forcing you to make an extension—you do not want to put your hands into your own pockets, but you do want to put your hands into the pockets of people outside?—No, I do not.

213. You have property in town?—Yes.

214. How much is your valuation in the town?—My own house is between £90 and £100, and connected with the hotel there is a valuation of £55, and——

215. Tell us in round numbers?—I think the whole is about £198.

216. Mr. Robinson.—Do you anticipate if you get an increased area for the municipal taxation, the contributory district on which the sanitary rates would be assessed would be enlarged also?—Yes.

217. That is a mistake then, for the Guardians can strike it upon what district they like. Do you anticipate becoming the urban sanitary authority yourselves?—Well, yes, that might be.

218. You selected the electoral divisions as the extended boundary, because you believed the Commissioners would adhere to it, and that it would not be deviated from?—Yes.

219. And as I understand, if you considered that it could be deviated from, you would of done so?—Yes, the extreme wings would have been left out. I will put it before them again.

220. In your private opinion as well as representing the Commissioners is that the only alteration you would propose to make?—It is at present the only one I see feasible. It would be difficult to form a circular boundary for Cookstown in one long street I may say —one mile long.

221. And the municipal district includes just that?—Very little else.

222. Mr. Black.—Suppose the electoral divisions was left out of the question altogether, what would you suggest as a proper boundary for the town?—Not more than a mile beyond the town—land or property within a mile of it is all benefited.

223. Do you not think the town benefits just as much from those properties as they do from it?—Well, we wish them to bear some of the burthens.

224. Your burthens?—Not personal burthens, but of the town.

225. Would you flag any of the outside district?—No.

226. Nor light it?—You may make as much logic as you like out of it, but you have it before you. They get benefits from the town as it is, and ought to pay something for that.

227. You want the people outside to pay for the flagging inside?—No, but just for the advantages they derive from coming into houses of worship, and houses of law, and schools, and markets, and using the roads and streets, and light and water and so on.

228. Mr. Fenegan.—I believe you are an advocate for no taxation without representation?—Yes.

229. Will you kindly tell the Commissioners what representation there would be in these sixteen townlands?—Certainly, they would have an opportunity of voting for Guardians and Commissioners, why not?

230. How many of the four people in the sixteen townlands would have a vote?—They are all rated over £4.

231. How many people would have a vote?—I could not say.

232. Four in sixteen townlands?—There are far more.

233. Mr. Fenegan.—You have given up Drumgarrell?—Well, I suppose so.

Mr. John L. Weir examined.

234. Mr. Robinson.—You are a ratepayer of Cookstown, I understand?—Yes.

235. You live inside the boundary?—Yes, and I have a mill outside.

236. You think the people outside derive advantage from the town?—Yes.

237. And if they had to pay one-fourth it would not be an undue hardship?—No. I would not go in for the boundary adopted by the Commissioners.

238. You would not be in favour of adopting the electoral divisions?—No—it would be unfair, and by no means a naturalistic frontier.

239. What do you consider would be a fair boundary to select?—I would include those townlands which touch the boundary.

240. The same in fact as the contributory district for sanitary purposes?—Yes.

241. How many townlands would you include?—There is Monrush, Cookstown, Loy, Coolnafranky, Sullenboy and Gortalowry.

242. Would you take in any portion of Mullans?—No.

243. Any portion of Coolreaghs?—Well, it is not much. I would take in those I have named.

244. The farmers in Coolreaghs derive advantage from the town?—Yes.

245. Now what are your reasons for this extension?—All the people in these townlands I have named derive benefit from the town.

246. And do any of these people pay anything towards the town?—No, and some of them have their mills three or four yards from the boundary. Mr. Young did not deny, and does not deny I suppose, that there is considerable traffic through the streets to the mills.

247. The Commissioners have always been obliged to strike the full rate?—This year it is reduced one halfpenny. The land near the town is double the value it would be if it was farther off. Land is let at £3 an acre here that farther away would not bring £1.

248. Is Cookstown considered a good market?—Yes, one of the best flax markets and general markets. It is one of the best markets in Ireland—people come here from fifteen to twenty miles.

249. And the extension you propose, would it take in any settlement?—Yes, there is Irongrove, for instance—Mr. Adair's mills and Mr. M'Clennen's.

250. Is it principally mill lands that are taken in?—There is a lot in the shape of mills that are taken in.

251. You do not propose to take in Killymoon demesne?—The approach to Killymoon demesne comes up to the town.

252. Is there anything you would like to suggest about the water?—The water there has been very bad, we endeavoured to get the town boundary extended for sewerage; there was an inquiry held, but it failed.

253. You think there are improvements required from a sanitary point of view?—Yes.

254. Would the sanitary jurisdiction be better in the hands of the Commissioners do you think?—No, it is better in the hands of the Guardians. The Town Commissioners are so dependent on the votes of the people, that they have to do what they are told.

255. You say the water is very bad?—Yes, there are surface wells of which ten have been condemned.

256. Were any representations made to the Guardians on this point?—Yes, and to the Local Government Board. One of the wells is now being puddled, and it is to be tested.

257. Are there facilities for a water supply?—Yes.

Cookstown, Sept. [illegible]

Mr. John L. Weir.

258. Mr. Black.—At what hour are the lamps put out?—At eleven o'clock.

259. Did that not reduce the rates from a shilling to ninepence?—Yes, I think it was fixed.

260. You want to include Mr. Adair's mills?—Yes.

261. You have perhaps the largest retail house in Cookstown?—One of the largest.

262. If the Messrs. Adair pay £10,000 in wages &c., I suppose you will admit a great portion of that goes into the shops of Cookstown and benefits the town?—No doubt, they do a great benefit to the town, but they also benefited by the town.

263. Do not a great majority of Mr. Adair's workers live in the municipal district?—Yes.

264. And contribute to the support of the town rates?—Yes.

265. Mr. Robinson.—Is your evidence, Mr. Weir, the expression of your individual opinion?—Yes. I have talked to a great many ratepayers and I believe that ninety per cent. would vote for an extension of the town. You will, of course, always get persons to vote in favour of taxing others.

Mr. Thomas M'Casland examined.

Mr. Thomas M'Casland.

266. Mr. Robinson.—You are a Town Commissioner?—Yes.

267. Were you present when the question of extending the boundary was discussed?—Yes.

268. Are you in favour of an extension?—Yes.

269. To the electoral division?—No.

270. How far?—Three quarters of a mile from the limits of the town.

271. Do you propose to follow townland boundaries?—I think there is a very good boundary around the town, there is a road.

272. Did you hear Mr. Weir's evidence?—Yes.

273. Would you approve of it?—Yes.

274. And do you think the people living in the outskirts do reap the same advantages from their proximity to the town?—Yes, more or less they do. The electoral division was chosen with a view to the expected expenditure for the water supply, and to have a larger area for taxation.

275. That is in anticipation of becoming the urban sanitary authority?—Yes.

276. Have you lived long in this town?—Eighteen years.

277. Do you notice any great difference in it now to what it was?—Yes, there is an increase of building, so that there is hardly any building ground now inside the boundary.

278. In what direction have building operations been most observable?—In the east.

279. What class of houses?—Shops and dwellings.

280. Mr. Black.—Those buildings are inside the boundary?—Yes.

281. There are some outside?—Those with Mr. Moore building.

282. Some labourers' houses?—Yes, and the railway station is outside; so that there is hardly any building ground inside the boundary.

283. How much land have you yourself outside the boundary?—None, except what I use for grazing.

284. For the season you have it?—No, by the year.

285. How much?—About four acres.

286. What benefit would that four acres derive from the extension?—I don't know it would, but the town would derive advantage.

287. That is your valuation in the town would have less rates to pay, for the county would have to contribute to the taxation of the town?—The county wants to use the town as much as they can. The Guardians are the sanitary authority, and so long as it does not touch their own pockets they don't care what is done to the town.

288. The Town Commissioners have no regard for the amount of taxes they put on?—They have.

289. If they were taxing people outside, they would have the same regard for the taxes they put on?—Yes.

290. Would they not be in exactly the same position as the Guardians are now—taxation without representation?

291. Mr. Robinson.—But they would have representation.

292. Mr. Black.—There are only four houses outside according to the return given to me.

293. Are there only four persons in this boundary qualified to be Commissioners?

Mr. Black.—That is all, four in the sixteen townlands, if such be the case there would be taxation without representation.

294. (To the witness.) You said the Commissioners wanted a larger area for taxation with a view to the water supply, what other reason was there for the extension?—For the general good of the town.

295. To get a rate in aid from the country?—Not exactly from the country, but from those who get advantage of all the improvements in the town.

296. To what extent are they benefited?—To a large extent.

297. Is the man living a mile out benefited by the town?—Yes.

298. Is the man living two miles out benefited by it?—Less or more he is.

299. Now the man living two miles out, is he benefited one bit less than the man living one mile out?—As I say to a greater or less extent he is. I would say less two miles out. What you say about going to Magherafelt and Pomeroy or those at all, nonsense, you might as well talk of Dublin or Derry.

300. I said nothing about it. Suppose now an extension of the kind proposed made no difference at all in respect of the water taxation, would you be of the same opinions you have expressed?—I would, because Cookstown is an improving town, and all persons outside the boundary enjoy its benefits without paying any taxation for it.

301. What benefit would you give those whom you would bring in, would you light those districts?—If the town progressed.

302. Would you light them if it did not?—Certainly, if they were inside the boundary.

303. Now you say you would light them if they were inside the boundary?—Yes, and if they paid the same rates.

304. Now take Drumgarrow, do you state here that you would light Drumgarrow?—I said I was in favour of a limited extension.

305. Mr. *Black*.—Would you light Loughry then?—If the houses were built.

306. Would you tax them till the houses were built?—I believe they do not go in for full taxation, only one-fourth.

307. But would you not tax them at once?—Yes to that extent.

308. You would tax them at once, but why would you not give them some advantage?—They have a return in the benefits they derive from the town.

309. Would you lay out a shilling now on Loughry? It is all grazing.

310. And yet, that is one of the townlands you would bring in?

311. Mr. Robinson. You think the people living in those townlands mentioned by Mr. Weir, derive such advantages at present from their proximity to the town that to ask them to pay one-fourth of the taxation would not be a hardship?—Exactly, that is it.

Mr. William [illegible] examined.

312. You are a ratepayer and ex-Commissioner I understand?—Yes.

313. You reside here and have done so for some time?—Yes.

314. And you are well acquainted with the town?—Yes.

315. You have considered this question of extension?—Yes.

316. What extension if any are you in favour of?—Something such as that proposed by Mr. Weir.

317. About half a mile, or so would you say?—Yes, I think it's there or thereabout, perhaps it would be better following some well-defined boundary that would go one half a mile round.

318. The electoral division you think would be too large?—Yes, I think so.

319. Do you hold property outside?—Yes, in the past.

320. Is it more valuable from its proximity to the town?—Yes.

321. And would you consider it a hardship on you if you had to contribute one-fourth?—No.

322. Would you be in favour of the military [illegible] being transferred?—No, I'd rather leave where it is.

323. Have buildings gone on within the limits of the town?—Yes, for the last twenty years, it is more nearly all built upon. There is some talk of [illegible] already, and these would go outside the boundary.

324. Is there not land available inside?—No.

325. Mr. Robinson.—Would it not be more advisable to extend the boundary when the necessity arose?—I think not, it is better done now.

326. Are you a Commissioner?—No.

327. You were unsuccessful in your effort to become one?—Yes, I am proud to say I was, because I opposed [illegible].

328. What is the extent of your interest outside?—Only four or five acres.

329. As yearly tenant?—Yes.

330. Mr. *Black*.—My case has been so fully developed that it is really unnecessary that I should burden the notes with additional matter. From the evidence you must see that the proposition to bring in these outside districts is one made in any way with a view to benefit these districts, in fact there is no argument to be carried on either within or without the town. The whole and sole object of bringing them in is to make them contribute to the expenditure of the town, I hold that that is not a fair or proper position for any public body to take. I can quite understand the desirability of getting additional powers if they were to be benefited by these powers, but it is simply with the object of making these people liable.

331. Mr. Robinson.—For the advantages they enjoy?

Mr. *Black*.—So they may, but I hold it is a mutual advantage, that the town receives as much advantage from the neighbourhood as the neighbourhood does from the town, and there must be a limit drawn in some one place, and the people outside think whatever [illegible], to draw it, would be drawing it so much [illegible] from the town as the parties inside and outside. I [illegible] not at all see why the town boundary here should be extended. There are no buildings going on outside to be controlled by the Commissioners.

332. Mr. Robinson.—But there is a likelihood of there being so?

Mr. *Black*.—There is really no evidence of that. The last witness I think said he had heard something about new streets being laid out, but from all we can gather from the town surveyor, [illegible], the gentleman himself, and therefore I say there is really no evidence of it. The evidence given to show that buildings have been taking place entirely within the present boundary. There are, take it, half a dozen houses outside, and is it not an extraordinary thing that even for the sake of these half dozen houses, the proposition should be made.

333. Mr. Robinson.—I think it was stated that it was in consequence of the advantages derived by the people living outside, that the boundary should be enlarged, and not because of those six houses?

Mr. *Black*.—I submit to you on the part of the [illegible]. Having, with one, the greater portion of the townland of Cookstown, and a great deal of the townlands adjoining, that in their opinion an extension for the purpose of making the outside people contribute to the rates of Cookstown would be unfair and unjust, and they are decidedly opposed to it. I do not think I have anything further to say, but I think it quite unnecessary to overload the notes with repetitions.

334. Mr. Robinson.—Is the land owned by your clients more valuable from its proximity to the town?—Some portion of course would be let as town parks, and in that way of course would bring a higher [illegible].

335. Do you allow that there is some advantage?—But portion of the land I speak of would be in the present boundary.

336. And portion of course not in the boundary?—Of course.

Mr. John Thompson examined.

337. You are a ratepayer of the town?—Yes.

338. And have resided here a good many years?—Yes.

339. Would it in your opinion be for the advantage of Cookstown to have the boundary extended?—Decidedly.

340. Would it be no hardship on those brought in?—No; I would be against it without giving them advantages. As to Killymoon demesne, I may say Foster Green, of Belfast, consulted me about it, and he considered that only for the isolated position, he would give more for it, if it was nearer to the town of Cookstown. It is located in a wilderness.

341. Are you in favour of an extension?—Yes.

342. And you would not consider it a hardship on those who would be brought in?—No—and who are benefited by their proximity.

343. Have you considered any specific extension to

Cootehill, Sept. 15, 1879. Mr. John Thompson.

be desirable? —I would say all property standing should be taken in.

344. I think you said you would not extend the boundaries unless you gave the people outside adequate advantages?—There is local [illegible], and there are [illegible] that would not be [illegible] more than [illegible] at all, it is only £[illegible] or [illegible] ... away.

345. And would the extension of the boundary be for the advantage of those [illegible]?—Yes; but [illegible] the [illegible] a great advantage from it.

346. You would give those people outside advantages, you say, if they were brought in?—Yes; what I say is they have great advantages and they don't pay anything for them.

347. Mr. Foreman.—Messrs. Adair's place of business [illegible] a quarter of a mile from the town. They spend £[illegible] a year on their workers. Surely it is evident

that that being spent so close to the town must be an advantage to the town. Must not a large proportion of that find its way into the pockets of the [illegible] [illegible]. Nine, six, more than half the workers in Messrs. Adair's live inside the present boundary and pay towards the taxation.

348. Mr Robinson.—Would Messrs. Adair wish to have their place, would they wish to have the boundary extended?—[illegible] says there is no occasion for extending, and that this is simply an attempt by the Town Commissioners of Cootehill to make their country neighbours contribute to their rates. Then he [illegible] [illegible] that the advocates of this—the [illegible], advocates of this extension, are not those people themselves.

349. Mr. Robinson.—So far we have not heard many expressing themselves against it.

Mr. Hugh Adair.

Mr. Hugh Adair examined.

350. You are the owner of this mill that has been spoken of?—Yes, one of the owners.

351. You say you derive no advantage from the town?—No, at least I would say it is no loss.

352. You [illegible] a [illegible] on the town [illegible].

353. And you say that the town does contribute some advantage to you?—Well, hardly that, but I don't wish to say much on that.

354. Is it not of advantage to you to be able to get your labour at [illegible] at hand?—No.

355. Are you opposed to the extension of the boundary?—Yes.

356. Your [illegible] through the town?—Yes.

357. And of course it is of advantage to them to have the lights?—Yes.

358. You say that is no advantage?—Yes, to a certain extent, but not [illegible] for that.

359. You pay some of the [illegible] taxes?—No, but I contribute to the [illegible] rate.

360. But you have [illegible] in the town?—There are [illegible] of the working [illegible] in the town, but I [illegible] pay [illegible] to property in the town. The workers [illegible] to the rates.

361. Your [illegible] have the advantage of the lights of the town?—Yes.

362. And you object to pay for that?—I do not like to pay for what I have no advantage from.

363. But you have just said you have the advantage of the lights?—Well, the lights are [illegible], but the [illegible] do not want the lights—the lights are not for the benefit of the [illegible].

364. However I think it is on the [illegible], that you [illegible] the advantage of having the lights?—I say the [illegible] would work as well without the lights—when they have the town boundary they can do without the lights. The lights are not for their benefit.

365. They are for the benefit of everybody who has need of them, is it not so?—I am opposed to any extension on the [illegible] that I derive no benefit from the town.

366. I thought you admitted you derived some benefit from it?—In one sense it is, to [illegible] perhaps; but as I say I really confer the benefit. My [illegible] is about £[illegible] a year.

367. How many hands do you employ?—[illegible] of about a thousand.

368. Do they all live in the town?—[illegible]. [illegible] say the result of this would be, I would derive no benefit whatever and that I would be paying more rates than all the Commissioners.

369. Are you of opinion that the sanitary matters would be better managed by the Town Commissioners than the Guardians?—I believe they would be better managed by the Town Commissioners.

370. Do you think there are any improvements required of a sanitary nature?—I think there have been too many improvements.

371. This is the first time I ever heard a complaint of that kind?—The county has been [illegible] fairly. I consider it has been [illegible] and [illegible] by the Board of Guardians.

372. And do you think if the Town Commissioners had the management of the sanitary matters it would not be necessary to have a larger class of [illegible]?—The [illegible] and [illegible] all the property that can possibly be [illegible] by any improvement that can possibly be carried out.

373. Would it not be of advantage to you to have the town well supplied?—My place is a quarter of a mile from it. I [illegible] my own [illegible] at my own expense, and light my own place. Great stress has been laid on the advantages derived or alleged from the gas of the town. When long before they had gas in Cootehill, we had it at our works and [illegible] the inhabitants of the town of Cootehill [illegible] to enable them to [illegible] gas cheaper we [illegible] our own works and [illegible] it from Cootehill.

The inquiry then terminated.

COOTEHILL.—15th SEPTEMBER, 1879.

Cootehill. Sept. 15, 1879.

Before Henry A. Robinson, Esq.

Mr. Peter Mongan.

Mr. Peter Mongan, Town Clerk, examined.

1. Mr. Robinson.—How is the town of Cootehill constituted?—It is constituted under the Town Improvement Act of 1854.

2. In what year was that Act adopted?—It was adopted in 1855 or 1856. But I should mention that the Commissioners' office was burned down some years ago, and a great many of the original papers were lost in consequence. I think it was in December 1871 that the office was burned.

3. And you have lost some of the original records?—We have, in fact all the original maps were burned.

4. But so far as you know, the Towns Improvement Act was adopted for Cootehill in 1856?—Yes.

5. Was the Act adopted for all purposes; lighting, cleansing, and water?—Yes.

6. What is the area of the town?—[illegible]a. [illegible]. [illegible]p.

7. Have you been Town Clerk since the commencement?—Yes.

8. How far does the town extend, taking a central point?—In some places it goes half a mile

COOTEHILL. Sept. 13, 1877. Mr. Paul [illegible]

9. What do you take as the centre?—The market house, which is not exactly the centre, but perhaps a quarter, or the Post Office.

10. How far does it extend to the north?—A quarter of a mile.

11. On the east?—Not so far, one-eighth of a mile.

12. On the south?—About half a mile.

13. Does the present boundary include whole townlands or parts of townlands?—It includes some whole townlands and some parts.

14. How many whole townlands does it include?—Six entire townlands, including part of Bellamont Forest.

15. Give their names?—Drumavaddy north, Glebe, Killycramph, Munnilly, Magheranure, and Bellamont Forest, part of.

16. Can you tell the valuations of each of these?—Yes.

17. And do you know their extent?—Yes.

18. And what is their valuation?—Drumavaddy, £139; Glebe, £80 15s.; Killycramph, £138 5s.; Magheranure, £1,725 17s.; Munnilly, £1,161 18s.; and that part of Bellamont Forest within the boundary, £22 10s.

19. That is five townlands and portion of Bellamont Forest?—Yes. The whole valuation is £3,239 2s.

20. What is the entire valuation of Bellamont Forest?—I do not know the entire valuation, the valuation of that part within the boundary is what I say.

21. How much of Bellamont Forest is within the boundary?—Twenty-five acres.

22. The total valuation you say is £3,000 odd?—Yes, £3,239 2s.

23. And on how much of that is the full rate assessed, and on how much the quarter rate?—The full rate is assessed on £4,... ; and the quarter rate on 399s. 3s. 1d.

24. Do you know the valuation of the latter portion—on land?—Yes, £241 14s.

25. And on the other, that is, on buildings?—£2,767 4s.

26. What is the population of Cootehill?—Under 3,000, according to the census of 1871.

27. Was that an increase upon the census taken before that?—Yes.

28. Will the census of 1881 show an increase, do you think?—I could not say that.

29. Is Cootehill a thriving town?—It is, rather thriving.

30. Are there any new buildings being erected in it?—Well, yes, some new buildings.

31. Are there many uninhabited houses?—Very few.

32. What electoral division is it in?—Cootehill.

33. Are you acquainted with the statistics of the electoral division?—Yes.

34. What is the entire valuation of it?—I do not know.

35. Are the Commissioners aware that the Select Committee have enjoined this Commission, as far as possible, to make the boundaries of the towns conterminous with the boundaries of the electoral division?—I do not know.

36. Was it not discussed?—No.

37. What have the rates been since 1874 or 1875?—In 1875, 1s. 4d.; in 1876, 10d.; in 1877, 6d.; 1878, 8d.; and for 1879 we have not struck it yet.

38. What were the poor rates for the same years?—1875, 10d.; 1876, 1s.; 1877, 1s.; 1878, 1s. 6d.

39. Does that include any special rate for sanitary purposes?—Yes, the last does, it was about twopence in the pound.

40. Was there any special sanitary work that was struck to defray the expense of?—Yes, drainage.

41. What was the contributory district over which that was assessed?—I do not exactly know.

42. Have you got all your accounts?—Yes.

43. What was the expenditure last year?—The expenditure was £114 13s. 6d., and the receipts were £177 13s. 10d.

44. Have the Commissioners any property vested in them?—No, their income is derived from rates, the dog tax, and Petty Sessions fines.

45. What are your principal items of expenditure?—Lighting and salaries of officers.

46. Is the town well lighted?—Very well, there are twenty-seven gas lamps.

47. In what months are they lighted?—For six months commencing in October.

48. Are your markets very late?—Pretty late in the winter.

49. So that people coming in from the country districts, to dispose of their produce here, get the benefit of the lighting?—Yes.

50. Is Cootehill a market town?—Yes.

51. Is it the market town for the people residing in the electoral division?—Yes, and outside of it; there are twelve fairs in the town.

52. How far do you say the advantages of Cootehill extend?—Well, the advantages of it go very far, the people say within a mile of it derive a good deal of advantage. They have an opportunity of coming in every day to make their purchases.

53. Would you say that people living within half a mile of Cootehill come into it every day?—Yes.

54. Are there schools in the town?—Yes.

55. And do the children of the people living outside attend those schools?—Yes.

56. And the people living within that distance derive exceptional advantages from their proximity to the town?—Yes.

57. Do you consider any improvement made in the town, is to the advantage of the people living outside?—Yes, for they have the privilege of coming into the markets held here.

58. And is land more valuable from its proximity to the town?—Yes, townparks are. I should mention that the townparks are mostly in the hands of the people in the town.

59. Do the landlords outside get higher rents in consequence of their lands being in proximity to the town?—Yes.

60. And the town of Cootehill is, therefore, an advantage to the landlords as well as to the tenants?—Yes.

61. Have the Town Commissioners ever considered the question of becoming the urban sanitary authority?—Yes, and their opinion was that it was better to leave it in the hands of the Guardians.

62. What was their reason for that—do the Guardians assess the poor rate on a larger area than the town?—Yes.

63. Has it ever been discussed at the Board publicly the question of the Commissioners becoming the urban sanitary authority?—Yes, but not much.

64. Was any resolution passed on the subject?—No.

65. Are the Commissioners aware that under the seventh section of the Public Health Act they can become the urban sanitary authority?—Yes.

66. And would their opinion be in favour of being separated from the Grand Jury, for the management of the roads?—Yes, we applied for that purpose, or were about to apply; it was discussed by the Commissioners here, but we found that other Commissioners who did apply, did not succeed.

67. That was before the passing of the Act of last session?—Yes.

68. But the Local Government Board can, if they consider it expedient, give a Provisional Order to an urban authority for the purpose, whether the Grand Jury like it or not?—Yes, so I understand.

69. Is it the opinion of your Commissioners that the whole management of the town of Cootehill should be under one undivided authority?—I am not sure of the opinion of the Commissioners on that subject, for my own opinion is caught.

70. They have never passed a resolution on the subject?—No.

71. Is the town well set in sanitary condition?—Fairly fairly.
72. Is it well sewered?—It should be better. The Commissioners when they were the sanitary authority did a good deal in the way of sewering.
73. What about the supply of water?—It is only middling.
74. What supply have you?—From pumps.
75. Was the water being analysed?—Yes.
76. And was a favourable opinion expressed on it?—I do not know.
77. Could you obtain a better supply by gravitation?—No.
78. Have you no facilities for procuring it [illegible], to get water supplied in that way?
79. Are there any improvements in the town that the Commissioners would bring out, if they had an increased area for taxation?—Yes.
80. What improvements are required?—Well, sewerage. If we increase the sanitary authority, we would apply the funds from the enlarged area of taxation, to the providing of a system of sewerage.
81. Is there any tendency to build within the present municipal limits?—The Commissioners have no power, but there have been houses recently by a landlord, Mr. Simpkin, to build.
82. In what direction?—In the upper part of the town.
83. Is there available land within the town for people to erect, for the purpose of building?—A great deal.
84. Is there a disposition manifested to build only in the municipal limits?—Well, there is.
85. In which direction?—[illegible]
86. Are there any buildings at present going on?—Yes, there is one just outside being built.
87. Are there [illegible] or anything of that kind outside the town limits?—No.
88. Now as to the question of extension, we understand [illegible] to you, [illegible], were they laid before your Board?—Yes.
89. Were they brought under the notice of the whole Board?—Yes, [illegible].
90. The Board are expressing the opinion of the ratepayers?—Yes.

91. What opinion did they form on the subject?—The opinion of the Board was, that the boundaries were extended far enough.
92. Was that opinion unanimous?—I do not know that it was, but it was the opinion of the Board.
93. Was there any resolution?—No.
94. Did you reply to those queries?—Yes, after consulting the Commissioners, and after having had a long consultation with Mr. Kilroy here.
95. Has the matter been since discussed?—Yes, very much since. I am of opinion that some of the Commissioners have changed their mind, and are now in favour of an enlarged area of taxation.
96. Has no resolution been passed on that subject?—No.
97. The population of Cootehill have never been altered?—[illegible].
98. Where was that map (pointing to a map on the table) taken from?—From a drawing made by Mr. Kelly, the engineer who assisted in marking out the boundaries originally; and it agrees with my own knowledge of the boundaries.
99. You have lived some time in this town?—Yes, thirty-five years at least.
100. And are, therefore, well acquainted with it?—Yes.
101. Do you notice any change in it now from what it was when you first became acquainted with it?—Yes, I see a spirit of improvement, and a number of buildings taking place, as the town will extend.
102. As your own individual opinion, do you think that the improvement of the town would confer advantages on those living outside?—Yes.
103. You know the river and Bridge?—Yes.
104. Do you think that would be too extensive to adopt as the boundary?—Yes.
105. You are aware that the Select Committee of the House of Commons expressed a recommendation in favour of adopting the electoral division as the boundary for municipal purposes?—I did not know that.
106. Well, as a general principle they did. What is your opinion about it?—I think it certainly would not do in this case.
107. You think it out of the question?—Yes.

Cootehill. Sept. 10, 1874. Mr. Peter Magee.

Mr. Robert Graham.

Mr. Robert Graham, Clerk of the Union, examined.

108. Mr. [illegible].—What is the valuation of the electoral division?—Over £3,000.
109. And the population?—I am not sure.
110. What is the area of it?—I am not sure.
111. Can you tell me what the special sanitary rate in '73 was for?—For sewering.
112. What was the contributory district?—The townlands in which the town is situated.
113. Was it on all the townlands, and even on the portion of one, it was assessed?—Yes.
114. On the town of Cootehill and on the Bellamont Forest demesne?—Yes.
115. But that goes out half a mile from the town?—Yes, but it is within the electoral division.
116. How far does the electoral division extend to the east?—About three miles.
117. And to the extreme west?—We are just on the borders of it.
118. And is it your opinion that the electoral division of Cootehill is too large to be adopted for the municipal boundary?—I do not think it would be a fair arrangement, as the town of Cootehill is all to one side.

131. Would it be judicious for the Commissioners to obtain control of sanitary matters, so as to have them in their own hands?—Our rates are so low that we consider the Poor-law Guardians can manage it better.

132. You are further influenced by the fact that the Guardians assess the rates on an area nearly double the size of the town?—Yes.

133. Were they influenced by the fact that the sanitary rate, being a poor rate, is divided equally between the landlord and the tenant, and the municipal rate is assessed wholly on the tenant?—I think the landlord pays it.

134. But if it was a municipal rate it would be all on the tenant?—Yes.

135. Would you be in favour of a separation from the Grand Jury for the management of your roads?—My opinion has always been that the Commissioners, when they had contracts for repairing the streets, they lost by it, but it would be a different thing if we had the entire control.

136. Do you think the entire control of the town should be in the Commissioners' hands?—Well, I do.

137. Well, bearing that in mind, would you not think it desirable to have an extended area upon which to assess the rates?—Yes; but in justice to the people at a distance from the town it would not be fair to extend it.

138. Then you are in favour of no extension?—Yes.

139. Do you think that the people living near the town derive benefit from it?—Yes.

140. Have you spoken to the ratepayers on the subject?—Yes.

141. And do they coincide with you?—Yes, the great majority of them.

142. Then some are opposed to your opinion?—I did not talk to more than one or two, and they were opposed to it.

143. Were you present at the meetings when this matter was discussed?—Yes.

144. Was there any reason advanced why the boundaries should be extended?—Only one gentleman advocated it, I think.

145. Are there many improvements required?—Yes, sewerage.

146. Then if you had the sanitary jurisdiction in your own hands you could carry out some improvements which are now required?—We should increase the taxation from what it is at present.

147. But if you had a large area of taxation you would be able to carry out improvements?—Yes.

148. And do you not think it would be advisable to increase the area of taxation?—No.

149. Would the sewerage be of advantage to those residing outside?—It would be to those living a short distance outside.

150. What is your opinion as to how far the advantages of the town of Cootehill are immediately felt. Would you say that the advantages are derived by those living within a quarter of a mile of the town, that the land is more valuable?—Yes, it is.

151. And solely on account of its proximity to the town?—Yes.

152. And not because it is better land?—Yes; it has been made better land.

153. Is it more valuable than the same quality of land would be three miles out?—Yes.

154. Does the landlord derive the same advantage from the improvement of Cootehill as the tenant would?—Yes.

155. He would get a higher rent if the town were well kept?—Yes.

156. Do you consider that the landlord should pay half the municipal rate?—I think people living in the town should; occupiers should pay a larger portion than landlords.

157. Are you then opposed to the recommendation of the Select Committee?—Yes, so far as that is concerned.

Mr. Edward County examined.

163. Mr. Robinson.—Are you a Town Commissioner?—No; I was. I am a ratepayer, one of the largest.

164. Is it long since you were a Town Commissioner?—Some years.

165. Have you been a resident here long?—Yes.

166. Do you see much difference as far as buildings are concerned in the town now, from what it was when you were first acquainted with it?—Not a large extension, but it is otherwise improved.

162. You mean a better class of houses?—Yes, and their being improved from what they were in my young days.

163. Do you consider that the advantages of Cootehill extend to a radius of half a mile?—Yes.

164. Would you say still further?—I would not like to say that; I would say about an English mile from the centre.

165. About half a mile from the limits of the town?—Yes.

166. And would you say that the people living within half a mile of the limits of the town have great facilities for the disposal of their products, and so on?—Yes.

167. And do you think they derive advantages to that extent that considerable taxation would not be a hardship on them?—Yes.

168. Have you considered any specific extension?—No more than this, there is a portion beyond Globe that pays rates, and I think people for the same distance all round should pay the same.

169. Now, suppose your recommendation was adopted, or rather what you seem to suggest, would the circle extend more than half a mile from the town, and would that circle comprise many houses?—I do not know.

170. It is principally land let at the quarter rate?—Yes.

171. Land within that circle might be considered more valuable than land further off?—Yes, it pays a higher rent than land further off, it is more than half again the value.

172. Then I take it the extreme corner of the electoral division is not as valuable as land within it?—No.

173. You heard the recommendation of the Select Committee as to electoral divisions.

174. And do you consider any improvement carried out in Cootehill is of advantage to the people living within that circle?—Yes.

175. Do you think it of advantage to have the town well sewered, well watered, and well lighted?—Certainly.

176. And you consider that in these respects the town is fairly well off?—Yes, the sewerage is fair, but not good enough.

177. And the people outside avail themselves of these advantages?—Yes, they do.

178. Are you satisfied with the management by the sanitary authorities?—I do not know exactly; that is a question I did not go into.

179. Is it your opinion that separation from the Grand Jury for the maintenance of the roads would be judicious—do you think the work would be better done by the Town Commissioners?—Yes.

180. Are you in favour of having the management of the town entirely under the one authority?—I do not know. If we have to pay the full rate I would not recommend it.

181. Are you influenced by the fact that the Guardians assess their rate on a larger area than the Town Com-

necessary one?—The Guardians can strike it in whatever district they wish.

184. If you had a separation from the Grand Jury for the roads would it be an advantage to have an increased area for taxation?—Yes.

185. Are you speaking your individual opinion?—I am speaking the opinion of [illegible], of [illegible] the majority of the [illegible], and I believe the majority of them would like to see the boundaries extended.

Mr. John M'Cabe examined.

186. Mr. Robinson.—Have you been long a Town Commissioner?—For fifteen years, I think.

187. And are you acquainted with the town?—Yes, for seventy-five years.

188. Have you got any property outside?—Yes, but it is not rated at present.

189. You are in favour of extension?—Yes.

190. Then your property is to contribute towards the maintenance of the town?—Yes.

191. I presume you think you derive each advantage outside from your proximity to the town, that if you had it anywhere else you would not consider it [illegible]?—No.

192. Where is your land situated?—At [illegible].

193. Are you tenant or a landlord?—A tenant.

194. Does your landlord get a higher rent in consequence of the proximity of his land to the town?—Yes, his rent is about £3 10s. an acre.

195. Is that higher than if it was four or five miles off?—It would not be more than £1 10s. further off.

196. Then the town is of incalculable advantage to the [illegible]?—Yes.

197. Have you heard the suggestion [illegible] in favour of the landlord paying half?—No, I never heard that suggestion.

198. You heard the evidence of Mr. Conroy?—Yes.

199. Does his suggestion appear good?—Well, I would go with him. The land he spoke of consists principally of [illegible] used by people living in the town.

200. Have you gone into the question of [illegible] taxation?—No.

201. Are you in favour of drawing a hard-and-fast line in selecting the boundary?—Well, I am.

202. Would it be a hard-and-fast line, the former one?—Yes.

203. Well, that is [illegible] a line which [illegible] right through the centre of his house?—Well, I would not go to that necessity.

204. Do you think that the people, having accommodation lands and [illegible], ought to pay the [illegible] rate?—Yes.

205. Can you tell me if the people [illegible] business in the town live mainly in their places of business?—Yes, almost all live in the town.

206. Then I may take it there are no, what I may call, villa residences?—No.

207. Are there many residences outside?—About half a dozen.

208. They do not live outside to avoid being taxed?—No.

209. But simply because their houses happen to be there?—Yes.

210. Are you in favour of having a separation from the Grand Jury?—Yes, if I thought the rate would cover the expense.

211. But if you had power, would you be in favour of a larger area of taxation?—I do not know, we would have a right to go, say half a mile.

212. Are you aware of the provisions of the 29th section of the Public Health Act?—No.

[illegible] You are aware that formerly separation from the Grand Jury was [illegible] but now that you may get it if you become a sanitary authority, whether they approve of it or not?—I would go into it under those circumstances.

Mr. Thomas Murphy, agent to the proprietor of [illegible] Forest demesne, examined.

213. Mr. Robinson.—I received a communication in which you stated that Mr. Smith, the proprietor of [illegible] Forest and a portion of [illegible], [illegible] that the boundaries require amendment?—Yes.

214. Now in what direction is it required?—Mr. Smith's view is this, that a portion of the demesne is in the town boundary, and he has no objection to this, but since the Guardians became the sanitary authority they tax the whole of his property outside; they have imposed upon it all the sanitary rates, and upon making inquiry from the clerk, he was informed that it was impossible to separate it from the small piece in the town boundary. Mr. Smith, therefore, does not like to have his demesne mixed up with the town at all. He does not object to having a portion of it in the town, only that it brings the [illegible] with it.

215. What is the acreage of [illegible] Forest?—About 200 acres in his demesne.

216. And the valuation?—About £170—it is £158 10s., besides the portion made to contribute to the town rates, and this part he objects to, and the [illegible] portion of the demesne is only valued at £20 altogether. He has no objection to the [illegible] part outside being asked to pay.

217. That is cut by Diamond Hill?—Yes.

218. Is Mr. Smith in favour of having the sanitary affairs of the town in the hands of the Town Commissioners?—Yes, I was on the Board myself, but the Commissioners would not undertake it.

219. Are there any sanitary improvements required in the town?—Yes, indeed there are.

220. Mr. Smith.—There is a [illegible], and all the [illegible] go into my [illegible], you cannot go [illegible] with the sewers. If they kept them all right, I [illegible].

221. Witness.—If Mr. Smith got the advantages to which he is entitled, he would have no objection to paying the rate, but they cannot do anything.

222. Does Mr. Smith [illegible] that he derives advantage from the sanitary works of the town?—No, the very [illegible] is [illegible] by it, as far as he is concerned.

223. Do you not think the people outside are benefited by the town?—No.

224. Is not the town well lighted?—No, it is not well lighted; they darken no [illegible].

225. When they come in when it is dark, do they not derive advantage from the lights?—Yes, in a dark night they would, but the [illegible] at such a time, and [illegible] the [illegible] greater part of [illegible]; [illegible] they were going home, and they go out of the light here, there is a dark [illegible] all the way home, [illegible] it is no benefit to them; it may be [illegible] in the town.

226. If the Commissioners became the Urban Sanitary Authority, what would you say to that?—All I say is, what do the Guardians care about [illegible]?

227. Are they not [illegible]?—There are many of them [illegible], [illegible] Guardians, and what do they care about [illegible]; it is [illegible] to have them there.

CARRICKMACROSS. Sept 14, 1879. Mr. Thomas Healy.

228. It would be better to leave this sanitary jurisdiction in the hands of the Commissioners?—Yes.

229. Are you in favour of leaving this matter in the hands of the Commissioners within the town?—Yes.

230. And leaving this in mind, should there be an extended area of taxation?—I think so.

231. Is there a difficulty in getting building leases?—Mr. Smith.—No, I will give anyone a lease.

232. On your property?—Yes.

233. Are building operations going on within the town?—There are just a few houses. There is every facility and no likelihood of people having to go outside.

Mr. Patrick Horan.

Mr. Patrick Horan examined.

234. Mr. Robinson.—You have heard the evidence of Mr. M'Cabe and others?—Yes.

235. And you corroborate it?—Yes.

236. You think that persons living outside the town derive such advantages from it, that one-fourth rating would not be too much for them to pay?—Yes.

237. Do you think that the landlord derives benefit from the proximity of his land to the town?—Yes.

238. Is it your opinion that if there was an extension of the boundary, that the landlord should pay one half of the rates?—I could not say that.

239. You think people living immediately outside, derive greater advantages than those living far off?—Yes, they are able to pay more for their land when it is near the town.

240. Are you in favour of sanitary matters being placed in the hands of the Town Commissioners?—No, I am not.

241. Would you rather have them in the hands of the Guardians?—Yes, for we only pay one-half now, and we would have to pay the whole then.

242. Do you think then it would be better to have the matter in the hands of the Guardians?—Yes, because we pay less rates.

243. Are you influenced in that opinion by the fact that there is a far larger area of taxation under the Guardians?—Yes. Even at present I may say we get very little benefit from the sanitary authority.

244. You think there is room for improvement, as Mr. Smith more than suggested?—Yes, certainly, there is nothing being done.

245. Would the Town Commissioners do more?—My opinion is that they are doing very little at present.

246. Do you think any improvement to the town would be an advantage to the people you propose to include?—Yes.

247. And any improvement in the way of lighting, cleansing, sewerage, and so on, would be an advantage to those near the town?—Yes.

Dr. M'Fadden.

Dr. M'Fadden examined.

248. Mr. Robinson.—Have you resided long in the town?—Yes, fifty years.

249. Do you see much difference in the town now, from what it was when you knew it first?—Yes.

250. Do you think the population at the next census will show an increase?—Yes, a considerable increase.

251. Do you know the townland proposed to be brought in—the townland adjoining the town?—I think the boundaries we have at present require revision.

252. More than extension?—I think anyone looking at the map will come to the same conclusion. You will see portions there adjoining the town wholly excepted, which I do not think they should be.

253. It would be better you think to include the land equidistant from the town?—Yes.

254. You would not be in favour of any very large extension?—No.

255. You would include all the townland?—Not all.

256. Would you want a properly defined boundary equidistant from the town?—Yes.

257. You would not I presume be in favour of a hard and fast circle?—Yes.

Mr. Peter Conolly.

Mr. Peter Conolly examined.

258. Mr. Robinson.—You have heard the views expressed at this inquiry?—Yes, and I agree with all that Dr. M'Fadden has said, as to the equitable extension.

259. Have you anything else to add?—No. I would like the sanitary authority to be in the hands of the Town Commissioners, who would carry out the sanitary arrangements better than the Board of Guardians, as they do nothing.

Mr. Thomas Healy.

Mr. Thomas Healy examined.

260. Mr. Robinson.—I have heard that you dissent from the proposed extension?—Yes.

261. Am I to understand that you are still unfavourable to it?—Yes. It has been said that the Guardians are doing nothing, but I would ask what the Commissioners are doing. If you take up that document you will find that, with the exception of the lamps, they have made no improvement in the town.

262. What improvements would you have the Commissioners carry out?—I would have [illegible].

263. [illegible] in the hands of the Guardians?—Well, there is [illegible]—and in fact they are doing very little, and something ought to be done for the sewerage.

264. Is there any other reason why you are opposed to the extension of the boundary?—I think the Commissioners ought to have power to improve the streets, though it is very difficult to get a presentment passed by the Grand Jury.

265. Am I to understand that you are entirely opposed to any extension of the boundary?—I would not like it to be extended outside the radius of a mile.

266. You would not object to the extension, say of half a mile?—No, that takes in the townparks.

267. You think they ought to be brought in?—Yes.

268. Mr. Robinson.—Then you are in favour of extension?—Yes.

Mr. Thomas Healy, B.C., junior.

Mr. Thomas Healy, B.C., junior, examined.

269. I am in favour of half a mile extension, which I consider to be reasonable.

270. Mr. Robinson.—You would be opposed to the suggestion to include the electoral division?—Yes.

271. You consider it is too large?—Yes, quite too large.

The inquiry then terminated.

DROMORE.—7th AUGUST, 1879.

Before Mr. Cotton, C.B.

Mr. Joseph [illegible] examined.

1. You are a Town Commissioner?—Yes.

2. And have been connected with the body of Commissioners for a long time?—I was [illegible] as Commissioner under their formation in 1854.

3. The town is now under the Towns Improvement Act?—It is. It was put under that Act in December, 1854.

4. That is the year of the passing of the Act?—Yes.

5. Prior to that time the town was under the 9th of Geo. IV., chap. 82?—Yes.

6. Was the town put under the Towns Improvement Act for all purposes?—No. Merely, in the first instance, the clauses relating to the cleansing of streets and the prevention of nuisances were adopted in the month of December, 1854, and afterwards—in January, 1855—we adopted the clauses relating to the lighting of the town and the supply of water.

7. That was in January, 1855?—Yes; the boundaries were settled in 1854 and were not changed in 1855, nor until April, 1867, when we had the boundary extended. At that time the boundary was extended to the present dimensions.

8. Have you any map showing the boundary of the town?—We have.

9. What is the present area of the town?—I cannot give you the area in acres.

10. What is the population?—The population, so far as I would say is about 2,500.

11. Is that more than it was in 1871?—Yes, the population has increased.

12. Is it increasing still?—It is increasing.

13. And are the houses increasing in number, too?—They are.

14. Are they increasing in any one particular direction?—No, I think not. They are increasing in this respect—in regard to the workers' houses. We are here in the midst of the linen manufacture, and the increase in buildings is principally in the way of workers' houses connected with the factories and other things in the linen trade; and the extension of the boundary in 1867 was with the view of taking in a large number, 40 or 50, of small houses which had been erected after the time that the Act was adopted, and also including the railway station and some bleach works.

15. They are all included now I suppose?—They are all included now, and at present I think there are no houses of any consequence outside the boundary that we would include our boundary in.

16. What is the valuation?—The rateable valuation of the town proper is £5,900 10s.

17. What do you mean by the town proper?—I mean what the town of Dromore comprised. We have land which is valued differently under the Towns Improvement Act; we have land adjoining the [illegible] of the valuation.

18. Do you mean that the amount you have stated is the valuation of the buildings?—Yes, the valuation of the buildings of the town.

19. That is the valuation of what is rated at the full rate?—Yes.

20. And have you the valuation of what is rated at a quarter?—Yes, the valuation of that is £350 [illegible].

21. That makes a total of, well above £6,250?—Yes, something like that, sir.

22. How many commissioners are there?—Nine.

23. And how many voters?—I think about 162.

24. How many of that number are qualified to sit as commissioners if elected?—I should say about 40.

25. Can you give me the rates for the last five years?—The rate has been a uniform rate of 6d. in the pound, except in one year, when it was only 5d.

26. Is that from 1874 to 1878?—From 1874 to 1878 it was only 6d.

27. When was the 5d. rate?—In 1873.

28. Then I may take it, that in 1874 it was 6d.; in 1875, 6d.; in 1876, 6d.; in 1877, 6d.; and, in 1878, 6d.?—Yes, quite so.

29. Do you know what the poor rates were for those five years?—The poor rates averaged from 1s. to 1s. 4d. in the pound. The poor rate in 1874 was 1s. 1d.; in 1875, 1s. 1d.; 1876, 1s. 3d.; 1877, 1s. 5d., and 1878, 1s. 2d.

30. Do you know whether any of that rate of late years was for sanitary work?—Yes, since the passing of the Act of 1874.

31. Since 1874 the guardians have been the rural sanitary authority?—Yes; less or so long, I think, sir.

32. In the year 1878 was any portion of that poor rate a special sanitary rate?—Yes; I think it was additional to about 1s. 2d.

33. Do you know that?—Yes, I believe it was 1s. 2d. with the poor rate and 2d. was the sanitary rate in 1878.

34. Do you know on what district the sanitary rate was levied?—I cannot tell you, sir. The Clerk of the union could tell you. There are three townlands that touch the town, and there it was levied even.

35. You think it was levied upon those townlands and the town?—Yes.

36. What are the names of those townlands?—I think Ballymacormick, Ballykeelmorly, Drumbroneth, and I think Ballymacate.

37. Was any of the special rate of Quilly is levied I think none of the townland of Quilly comes into the boundary. I think the Clerk of the union would be the only safe authority to give you information on that point.

38. At any rate it was **levied not upon the town** alone, but upon several **townlands around it?—I may** take that so. Yes.

39. Have the Commissioners considered the question as to whether or not any alteration of the boundary is desirable?—They have. We are unanimous. I think there is no difference of opinion—that there is no alteration of the boundary required.

40. What electoral division is the town in?—In the electoral division of Dromore.

41. Do you know the electoral division yourself; do you know the extent of it?—I do not.

42. How is the town of Dromore lighted?—Lighted by gas supplied by the Dromore Gas Company by contract.

43. Do you know the terms of the contract?—The terms of the contract are according to the quantity consumed at 7s. 1d. per thousand feet.

44. As a matter of fact, how are the lamps lit—are they lit all the night through?—I think not, sir.

45. You have not any special regulation?—Up to [illegible] o'clock at night is the general rule.

46. Except on moonlight nights, I suppose?—Yes; and they are kept alight until eleven o'clock on market day night, which is the principal market night.

47. Except, I suppose, full moon nights?—Yes, except full moon nights, when they are not lighted.

48. How is the town supplied with water?—It is supplied by pumps, public pumps.

49. How many public pumps are there?—Seven pumps, I think.

50. They are under the care of the guardians, I suppose?—They are under the care of the guardians as the sanitary authority.

51. How is the town drained?—As regards the drainage—I do not hear many complaints as to the

DROMORE. [illegible] Mr. [illegible]

drainage. It is true that occasionally we have the sanitary authority bringing people up and requiring them to provide proper sewerage, and to abate nuisances, and to remove anything that amounts to a nuisance, but there is no public complaint as to the sewerage.

52. Have you known of any works to be done by the guardians of late years?—Yes.

53. Of what kind?—Making pipe drains.

54. And it was for that, I suppose, that the sanitary rate was struck?—Yes, and similar works.

55. And for paying salaries?—Yes.

56. Have the Commissioners ever considered the question of whether they would wish to become the sanitary authority themselves?—We have not formally discussed it.

57. Can you give me the opinion of the Commissioners on the subject?—My opinion decidedly is this ——

58. Now, you are giving me only your own opinion?—Yes; my own opinion is that the sanitary authority had better remain in the hands of the guardians.

59. And, is that the opinion of the Commissioners, so far as you know?—I think they are in favour of the guardians remaining the sanitary authority.

60. You think the opinion of the Commissioners is that the Guardians are the proper sanitary authority?—Yes.

61. Do you know whether or not, the ratepayers of the town have ever considered the question as to whether a larger boundary is wanted?—It never has been mooted.

62. Or have they considered the question as to whether it would be better for the Commissioners to be the sanitary authority?—I don't think that has been considered at all publicly. There has not been any meeting to consider the subject, and I think there is no dissatisfaction at present.

63. Was the boundary extended in April, 1867?—Yes.

64. And how far—what was the description of the extended boundary?—The description is this:—

"To extend the boundary from Daniel M'Cauley's house in Hillsborough-street to the new houses erected in said street by Mr. Partridge, extending thence in a line down a field occupied by John Fagan, thence to the tenement and premises of William Backhouse, called Moss Vale, and to include the tenement and premises lately created on the Belfast road, and also the tenements lately created on the new road leading towards Ballinahinch, and thence to extend in a line to the Mount so as to include the new houses lately created at the head of said street, and to extend in a line from said Mount to the boundary at the entrance of John Watson's gate; from thence to the boundary at William Magorrel's house in Rampart-street, and from thence along the fields in the possession of William Sproat to the tenement, known as the Turnpike house, and the field adjoining same held by John Wardle, to the entrance at Quilly Road, and from thence along the river Lagan to the Viaduct of the Banbridge, Lisburn, and Belfast railway, to include Mr. M'Murray's Bleachworks, erected along said river, and from thence to the Bishop's bridge, and from thence to extend along James Quinn's field adjoining the railway to the Maypole bridge, and to include said railway from said viaduct to said bridge, and the several erections and buildings thereon, and from said Maypole bridge to a line drawn to the new houses, lately erected at the top of Hillsborough-street, as aforesaid."

That brings you back to where we started.

65. Have the Commissioners got any funded property?—None.

66. What income have they then besides the rates?—They have none.

67. They have fines I suppose?—They have the rates, dog tax, and court fines.

68. These are all the sources of income they possess?—These are all.

69. Do you know whether any of the people living immediately outside the town want to come in—would be desirous of being included within the municipal boundary?—None.

70. Is there any other subject that you would wish to refer to in your evidence?—There is one remark I wish to make. You asked a question as to how the town is lighted; and I replied "by the Gas Company of Dromore, by contract."

71. I did not ask you how many lamps there are; I would like to know that?—There are forty lamps; it occurred to me frequently, and I am of the same opinion still, that the gas works—the present system is not sufficient—the tank is not at all sufficient for the supply of the town, and the factories which have been erected since the Act was adopted. I was concerned as the solicitor in getting up the Gas Company, and also as a Town Commissioner, and I am aware personally of this fact—that at the time the gas works were built it was not contemplated by any means that they should be required to provide such a large quantity of gas, for such a large consumption as has since become necessary. We have had additional factories manufactories for the hemstitching of handkerchiefs, factories in which from 150 to 200 girls are employed, and in the winter months there is a very large consumption of gas. The works that have been constructed by us were on a small scale at first, the Company are having actually room to extend—but I think they have not the ground on which to erect additional works. It seems to me that the town will suffer from that fact—that there is the necessity for putting on an immense pressure upon the present works, in order to light the town at all.

72. Can you tell me what the measurement of the gas for one half year has been, as shown by your gas bills?—That is for the town lamps.

73. Yes, for the forty lamps?—Yes.

74. How many thousand feet were used in the forty lamps during the last year or six months?—I will give you the last six months.

75. Up to the 1st of April?—Yes.

76. That will do?—From the 1st of October to the 1st of May the quantity was 169,200 feet, and the cost of that was £59 17s. 6½d. No much dissatisfaction was expressed with the gas company in one season that the Town Commissioners decided on having oil lamps. I was not then a Commissioner, and I cannot tell the precise reason for that course, whether it was on account of the extreme price of gas, 7s. 1d., and dissatisfaction as the quality of the gas, or anything of that kind I am not aware; but I am aware that in one winter oil lamps were used instead of gas. That didn't prove satisfactory, and it was only in the one winter it was adopted.

77. Do you think it would be advantageous that the Commissioners should become the gas makers?—I don't think it would at all.

78. Then how does the matter bear upon this inquiry?—If you could put some pressure upon the gas company to increase their works.

79. The only thing we have to deal with is to see if the boundary could be extended, if you wanted funds for any particular purpose?—I don't think that would be desirable.

80. Then we have nothing to say to the gas question?—I merely throw out the suggestion as regards the gas, because the private consumers rather suffer in this respect.

81. Is there anything else you would wish to add?—I have this general remark to make—In small towns like Dromore, from my experience, we would be better without any Town Commissioners at all, if they could be done without. We have always dissatisfied people, and if a man undertakes office, even without any payment, he cannot satisfy his neighbours at all, and I know the present Town Commissioners and their predecessors have been unable to satisfy the objections and grumblings, and opposition of people, and I think it is a very desirable thing that public Boards, such as Poor Law Guardians, should have charge of the sanitary arrangements.

82. Do you think the Guardians should have charge of the lighting?—I don't see how they possibly could.

83. What would you do if you had no Town Commissioners (because it is the opinion expressed strongly by the Parliamentary Committee that there should be no Commissioners in a town with under 3,000 inhabitants)?—I am not prepared to say. As to the Guardians having the lighting of the town under their control, if they could do it, I think it would be desirable that they should.

84. But if not, how would it be?—If not, we should do without public lights.

85. Well, as regards the water supply?—I think there is a deficiency of water. I think there is a deficiency of water in some cases. I know that one of the pumps in the street in which I live [illegible] virtually useless, and the people go away to private pumps; they make use of one in my own yard.

86. With regard to that, have the Guardians been asked to do anything to these pumps that they have not done?—I cannot answer that question.

87. There evidently is something that might be done?—The town is not well supplied with water.

88. And still you think it is better to have the charge of the water and the sanitary matters in the control of the Guardians?—I do. They have sunk several pumps. I do not think they have referred to the pumps, but, unfortunately, they have not been kept in a state of sufficient supply. I don't know that the pump on the opposite side of the square here is useful either.

Mr. Joseph Dickson.

Mr. Edward Macartney examined.

Mr. Edward Macartney.

89. Upon what point do you desire to give evidence?—Mr. Dickson said that the people didn't want the Commissioners, and that they wanted to do away with them. They don't want to do away with them, but they say they cannot get light, and they could not get money, except by private subscription, and some would give and some would not.

90. You don't think there should be any extension of the boundary?—No. The ratepayers don't want any extension of the boundary.

91. Do you consider that a 6d. rate—which appears to be your maximum—gives you as much money as you want as Commissioners?—It has always done so; because we have a 3d. and 6d. sanitary rate along with that.

92. You pay for it, but you have not got it?—I mean we have been relieved of the sanitary duties, and the 6d. rate does us quite well for the lighting and cleansing.

93. But the county cleans the town?—Yes.

Mr. Dickson re-examined.

Mr. Dickson.

94. Do the Commissioners do anything but light?—Nothing now but that, and pay the clerk.

95. And the scavenging of the town, is that done by the Guardians?—It is done by the county and the Guardians. We have scavengers sent by the county.

96. Are these road contractors?—Yes. Regarding your question with reference to the sufficiency of the 6d. rate, I may mention, at the time of the adoption of the Act in 1854—and that was the reason for the adoption of the Act at all—the Commissioners—those who were to be elected Commissioners were pledged, and had to pledge themselves that they would not exceed a 6d. rate. I think Mr. Macartney himself proposed that, and we have not exceeded that rate. I don't think the 6d. rate was at all sufficient while we had the cleansing of the roads to do; we were beginning to be hampered on that account, but since the cleansing has been taken away by the Guardians, I think the 6d. rate was ample.

Mr. Macartney re-examined.

Mr. Macartney.

97. The point I want to get at is this—there is no reason for extending the boundary in order to get more rates?—No, sir.

Mr. Robert [illegible] examined.

Mr. Robert [illegible].

98. Upon what subject do you wish to give evidence?—I merely wish to speak about the water. We have a number of pumps in the town.

99. How many?—I think about seven, and in the summer time, particularly during a dry summer, many of these pumps run dry, and the water is bad. For instance, we have two pumps in this square and they cannot be used for cooking purposes safely at all.

100. Have any complaints been made of this state of things to the Guardians?—I think the water was analysed and found defective, and the Guardians know it.

101. And has anyone asked the Guardians to set the matter right?—

Mr. Macartney.—I went to the Guardians several times that the water was bad in the pump at the side of the square.

102. And they did nothing?—They sent a man down to examine it, and the man said that he could not sink it deeper, there was such a spring in it.

103. Mr. Dickson.—The sanitary officer, Dr. Weir, has frequently reported to the Guardians on the insufficiency of the water supply.

Examination of Mr. [illegible] continued.

104. Have you any further statement to make?—In consequence of the state of things I speak of, many people are much put about for the want of water. For instance, I know people, in fact my own family, have to go half way up to the railway for water.

105. And they would not have to do so, if the pumps were kept in proper order?—No.

106. Have you made any complaint to the Guardians yourself?—No, I have not. We are obliged almost always to go to private parties who have pumps, for water.

107. But you don't care to take the trouble to get the thing set right, and therefore what is the use of talking about it now?—But the Guardians are fully aware of the state of things.

108. Then you think that the Guardians don't do their duty?—I would not say that, but the thing is not done.

109. Do you think the water supply would be better looked after if the Commissioners were the sanitary authority?—I do think it would.

110. Are you a Commissioner yourself?—No, I am not; but I have been one. My own opinion about the matter is this—that the Commissioners are the best authorities in the town; they should have the whole management of the sanitary work and everything connected with the town in their own hands.

111. Do you know has there been any complaint about the drainage?—I don't know that there has. The Guardians have made some two or three drains since they got the sanitary work into their hands.

112. Have they done what was wanted?—I suppose they have, but there are many places about the town in very bad order. For instance, some of our streets are not paved or the sidepaths either, and there are no watercourses; we have only what nature made.

113. Has any application been made to the Grand Jury for a presentment?—I am not sure that there has.

Mr. Dugan re-examined.

114. I can answer that question. From time to time at special and at usual sessions applications have been brought forward for the paving and repairing of the footpaths and crossings in which the town was vitally interested. Invariably the County Surveyor has only recommended a small portion of the expense to be presented for—say one-half at the outside, and made the town supplement it if they chose. The consequence has been that in case after case the presentment has dropped through.

115. Because the one-half was conditional on the other?—The condition was that the presentment was simply passed for the half, on the understanding that the town subscribed the other half. When we were sitting as Town Commissioners we hadn't the power, because we had not adopted the clause for paving. That clause was not in operation, because we had not adopted the entire Act of Parliament, and our funds could not extend to the making of footpaths.

116. But nowadays you have never exercised more than half your powers of rating?—We have not, because it would be worth our while to exceed a 6d. rate. Well, sir, the consequence has been, as Mr. Herott says, that the footpaths are not what they should be. There is a great want of new footpaths, repairs of old footpaths and proper pavement, and proper flagging and crossings, and so on. We cannot get it done by the county unless we put our hands in our pockets, and supply the difference between something like half the cost and the entire cost of the work.

117. I don't see how an extension of the boundary can help you when you won't further exercise your powers of rating?—As we at present stand, the Guardians having charge of the sanitary affairs of the town; I don't think the Dungannon Town Commissioners would have power to impose a rate for the purpose of supplementing a Grand Jury presentment.

118. That is a legal question that I won't give an opinion on? We have discussed it frequently.

Examination of Mr. Stevens, continued.

119. Have you formed any idea that an alteration of the boundary would be desirable?—I don't think it would. I think our boundary takes in quite enough.

120. And you think that is the general opinion of the ratepayers?—Well, as far as I know it is; but I do think that if any plan could be adopted, by which several of our streets could be put in better condition, it would be exceedingly desirable—especially the footpaths.

121. But you must remember that this inquiry is limited to the question, as to whether or not any alteration of the boundary is desirable for any reason?—I was not aware that the scope of the Commission was so limited.

122. If you were able to show that the money the Commissioners have at present is not sufficient, and that they wanted more to do the paving, there would be something in it; but they do not appear to have exercised all their powers at present?—Quite so.

The inquiry then terminated.

ENNISKILLEN.—30TH JULY, 1879.

(Before Messrs. Cotton and Robinson.)

Mr. John Chapman examined.

1. Mr. Cotton.—You are town clerk of Enniskillen?—Yes.

2. For how long have you held that office?—For upwards of ten years.

3. What Act is the town under?—The 9th of George 4th and the Enniskillen Improvement Act.

4. What is the date of your Act?—The Enniskillen Borough Improvement Act, 1870.

5. What is the area of the town?—314a. 2r. 11p., including 60 acres of water.

6. What is the population?—About 6,000.

7. Are you the urban authority?—Yes, under the special Act.

8. What was your population in 1871?—It was about 6,000. We are the urban sanitary authority by virtue of the 60th section of the Public Health Act, 1878.

9. Then your population must have been over 6,000 in 1871?—It was not.

10. Then how can you be the urban authority?—Our special Act constitutes the Commissioners the urban authority.

11. You do not know what the population was in 1871?—It was under 6,000. It has slightly increased since 1861; in 1861 it was 5,761, and in 1871 it was nearly 6,000; and since then, I believe, the increase is going on but rather slowly. We have no means of ascertaining the increase exactly.

12. Mr. Robinson.—Are the buildings increasing?—Yes, the buildings are increasing, at least they are improving; a good many old houses are being thrown down and new ones erected.

13. Mr. Cotton.—The boundary of the town is the same as the parliamentary borough?—Yes.

14. It was extended in 1870 by this Act of Parliament?—It was.

15. What is the valuation of the town?—£11,393.

16. Is it increasing year by year?—Yes.

17. Can you give the valuation in the last few years?—Yes; in 1870 it was £10,[illegible]; in 1871, £10,[illegible]; in 1876, £11,[illegible] 10s.; and in 1878, £11,[illegible].

18. Is it slowly increasing?—From 1870 to 1878 the increase was [illegible].

19. What electoral division is the town in?—Enniskillen.

20. The electoral division extends to a great distance north and south, all round?—It does, I dare say, for two miles all round.

21. How many Commissioners are there?—Twenty-one.

22. How many wards?—Three.

23. How many are qualified to act as Commissioners, if elected?—I must find that out. The population in 1871 I find, according to Thom's Almanac, was 5,836.

24. Under your special Act what rates are you empowered to strike?—[illegible] borough improvement rate, and 1s. 6d. for water.

25. Is the improvement rate struck on houses and land?—Yes, houses and land.

26. Equally?—Yes.

27. No distinction?—No distinction, whatever.

28. And the water rate in the same way?—Yes.

29. What rates have you struck for the last five years?—In 1874, 1s. improvement rate and 1s. [illegible] for water; in 1875 it was the same, and all through the years. We never struck any other rate since the Act came into operation.

30. Your tickets are at what?—2s. 6d. and 1s. 6d.

31. What were the poor rates for these years?—In 1874, 1s. 2d.; in 1875, 1s. 2d.; 1876, 1s. 3d.; in 1877, 1s.; in 1878, 9d.

32. And the county cess?—In 1874, 1s. 10d.; in 1875, 1s. 10d. also; in 1876, the same; in 1877, the same; and in 1878, 2s.

33. That is the county cess upon the adjoining district?—Yes; the town is situated in two baronies, and it is the same in both.

34. Is that the average rate, or is it the same rate in both?—I think it is the average taken over the whole county.

35. That county cess you have given is the average over the whole county? So it would appear.

36. You are the road authority within your district?—Yes, within the borough.

37. What do you pay for county at large charges?—We pay our proportion.

38. Is it under this Act?—Yes, we pay our proportion of county at large charges.

39. Have the Commissioners come to any resolution on the subject of extending the boundaries?—Yes, they had a meeting immediately after receiving your papers.

40. How many Commissioners attended that meeting?—Eleven.

41. What conclusion did they come to?—It is not a regular resolution. My note of it is "Query about the Municipal Boundaries Commissioners having been discussed, and the several matters having been considered, it was decided that same be submitted to H. A. Robinson, Esq., Secretary of the Commissioners."

42. And the resolution was that an alteration was desirable or not?—Yes.

43. I suppose the reason is that as the rate was increased as late as 1876, there was no necessity for further increase?—Yes.

44. They were unanimous?—Yes.

45. What is the feeling of the ratepayers on the subject?—I never heard any feeling expressed by any ratepayers.

46. How is the town lighted?—By gas.

47. By a company?—Yes, the Ballyshannon Gas Company.

48. And you contract with them?—Yes.

49. What is your agreement?—For the last three years, £3 per lamp, for eighty-nine lamps. That is for lighting, cleaning, and extinguishing.

50. What are the Company to do for that?—To light the lamps from the 1st of [illegible] to the [illegible], except on nights [illegible] per lamp by meter.

51. Are there meter lamps?—No, but there are meters within the borough to determine what the lamps, and the quantity of gas consumed is by meter [illegible].

52. The water supply is from water works under this Act of Parliament?—Yes.

53. A full supply?—Unlimited and inexhaustible [illegible].

54. It is of good quality?—Yes, very good.

55. Are there any large sewage works undertaken by the Commissioners lately?—Well during the past four or five years they have made [illegible] sewage works.

56. What amount did they spend upon them?—During the last four or five years £1,000. I think on the same probably £1,500 or £1,600.

57. We have an application before us from Dr. Chilton, suggesting the including of the townland of Derryheny, has that been before the Commissioners?—No.

58. You do not know what they would say to this?—No.

59. Do you know the townland?—I do.

60. The Commissioners came to the conclusion there was no extension required?—Yes.

61. You have no wards?—No.

62. Has there been any suggestion there should be wards?—No.

63. Mr. Robinson.—Are there any debts due by the Commissioners?—Yes.

64. State the amount of them, and what they were for?—We owe the Public Works Loan Commissioners, London, £1,536. That was [illegible] for the water supply.

65. How is that debt discharged?—It is paid off by yearly instalments, [illegible] years. We also owe the Board of Works, Dublin, £2,300, and some old portion that was borrowed for town improvements.

66. When in 1876, but a [illegible] sum was borrowed in 1871?

67. How is the latter sum to be paid off?—In thirty years also. We pay 5 per cent. interest on the London loan, and on the other the Dublin loan 5 per cent. interest.

68. You owe nothing else?—No.

69. Mr. Cotton.—Can you let us have a copy of last year's audited accounts?—Yes.

70. What sources of income have you in addition?—We have houses and land property; amounting to something about £450 a year, and we have an income from water rents of £227 a year. That is for water supplied for other than domestic purposes; and to parties living outside the boundary, they pay so much per annum for water.

71. Have you a domestic and a public water rate?—No. Those who pay for other than domestic purposes, simply contract for it.

72. Have you any houses from tolls [illegible] or [illegible]?—No, Lord [illegible] has them. I don't know any [illegible] pressure [illegible] to the Commissioners.

73. If there was a small [illegible] of [illegible], would it take in many [illegible]?—No.

74. There are not many buildings?—No, very few.

75. Are building operations going on in Derryheny?—I am not aware of any going on at present.

Mr. Jeremiah Jordan, Chairman Town Commissioners, examined.

76. Mr. Cotton.—How long have you been Chairman?—Three years.

77. It is the opinion of the Commissioners there should be no alteration in the town boundaries?—It is.

78. Has the subject been discussed?—Yes, fully. I convened a special meeting when I received your circular for the purpose of discussing it, and we discussed the matter fully, and previous to our coming to the meeting, Mr. Ross and myself took the map, and we commenced with Derryheny, and went all round by Bunnahown, and Drumbar, Kilnamornagh, Cornagrade, and then Portnoo, and Drinduff, Windmill Hill, [illegible]'s Hill, and Mullaghmore, making a kind of circle in a radius, and then see the [illegible] we would have adopted if there was to be extension, but we should not have included anyone of them in the extension of the town.

79. Mr. Robinson.—That would make it the as possible a mile all round from the centre of the town, and taking in the whole of those townlands?—They were so situated it would have been very inconvenient.

80. What was the general opinion?—The persons were, that the valuation amounted to somewhat about £4,000, and in the first place we had some in some other places which was raised as to the amount that could be raised by taxation on land. We do not know whether this added that in any other place.

81. Under the Towns Improvement Act you can only levy one-fourth on land?—Yes.

82. But according to your Act you can levy equally off houses and land?—That was what the meeting saw

ENNISKILLEN. [illegible] Mr. [illegible] Enniskillen.

[illegible] in several places, and it [illegible] that our [illegible] only [illegible] would be [illegible].

83. Mr. Cotton.—[illegible] for [illegible] purposes, but [illegible] would [illegible] in a larger sum [illegible] [illegible]—We were [illegible] would [illegible] [illegible] with only [illegible] [illegible] [illegible] [illegible] the poor rate and water rate.

84. Mr. Robinson.—Are there any lands similar to those within the present boundary?—No, very little. We levy an equal rate on them.

85. Mr. Cotton.—Would that extension be desirable, suppose the full rate was levied?—If we had included in Enniskillen those lands the [illegible] rating would put off [illegible].

86. Yes, [illegible] [illegible] [illegible] [illegible] [illegible] If we had [illegible] [illegible] it is very likely we should have had very serious opposition [illegible] for the farmers would not have consented to have been included in the town at the rate of three-and-fourpence or four shillings in the pound as the case may be.

87. Is that of the county cess?—Yes. I think you would have had great opposition. After going into these things fully we decided by calculation, that supposing we could raise the full rate on this valuable property, it would not nearly make our roads and light the place, [illegible] [illegible] in water pipes or sewers.

88. Mr. Robinson.—Is your opinion that the land of these people living within this district was more valuable?—Yes, a very good deal of it is let for public works.

89. And the people use the streets of the town?—Yes, for instance [illegible] is [illegible] which [illegible] a very high rate being near the town, so in [illegible] [illegible], Cornagrade and Derrychara, it is at very high figures because it is all town-parks.

90. Would you advocate that extension if your [illegible] only the [illegible]?—No, the [illegible] [illegible] [illegible] for [illegible] it would not pay us to take it in. It would be very [illegible] in the [illegible] of the borough to take in these places, even if we were able to rate them to the full extent of our taxing powers; [illegible] [illegible] [illegible] [illegible]. Dublin road is a [illegible] heavy road to maintain, [illegible] the [illegible] and [illegible] road, and [illegible] road; the maintenance of these roads would nearly [illegible] the rate, and there would be no [illegible] and lighting of them out of the boundary.

91. Under [illegible] [illegible] would you propose to be included in?—Under no circumstances whatever; we discussed the matter and dismissed it together.

92. This same townland [illegible] [illegible] Dr. Collum has asked us to include, namely, Derrychara. I should say we should not include it at all on the inclusion of the plans.

93. Mr. Robinson.—There are two public roads running through Derrychara?—The Dublin road skirts it, and there is one [illegible] way through Derrychara.

94. Is there sufficient land within the borough for building purposes for some years to come?—For some years to come I think we have as much land within the boundary as is likely to be built upon, there is nothing to prevent our building outside the borough at present, and there is a very convenient place on the Dublin road on which to build.

95. Mr. Cotton.—Is there any tendency to build out towards your boundaries?—Only in one direction.

96. In which direction is that?—Convenient to the railway.

97. Beyond the railway?—Yes.

98. Mr. Robinson.—Does that tendency arise because it is easy to get there, or through a desire to get outside the boundary and avoid the rates?—No; there are no new buildings outside the borough at all.

99. Was there any application made to you to include this land of Derrychara by Dr. Collum?—No.

100. Then let me read you a letter we got from Dr. Collum:—

"9th December, [illegible]
"Rossorry House, Enniskillen, [illegible]

"To H. A. Robinson, Esq., Secretary,
"Four Courts, Dublin.

"Sir,—In answer to the advertisement in the Enniskillen newspapers requesting communication with a view to altering or enlarging the boundaries of the borough of Enniskillen, I have the honor to [illegible] herewith a map of the townland of Derrychara adjoining the borough of Enniskillen, and which I have had laid out in building plots for wharves and storehouses, and for private residences, for the accommodation of merchants and traders, and others connected with the town of Enniskillen. The map shows that this townland has for its boundary on one side the Dublin road and the large model schools erected by Government; on two sides it is bounded by the Lough Erne (where the water is deep); and on the fourth side it adjoins the town and borough of Enniskillen, the fair green, and the stations of the Irish North Western and the Enniskillen and Sligo Railways. There is no other locality where suitable accommodation can be found whereon to construct wharves and storehouses, to accommodate the traffic of Lough Erne and the railways, as Derrychara occupies a central position close to the town, with deep water *frontage* and land suitable for private residences for the merchants and such others as may be attracted by the [illegible] schools. The fact of Government having selected this particular neighbourhood for the site of the new schools for the education of the children of the town, and the Enniskillen and Sligo Railway also having brought its line to this, instead of the other side of the town, shows the special local advantages which it possesses. I beg, therefore, most respectfully to submit, for the consideration of your Commissioners, that the townland of Derrychara, lying between the Dublin road, the Sligo Railway and the Lough Erne, and offering so many conveniences, be incorporated within the boundaries of the borough of Enniskillen.

"I have the honour to be, &c.,

(Signed) "R. Collum, M.D."

I suppose you allow the advantages he claims this land possesses, that it is the only locality where suitable accommodation can be found to construct wharves and storehouses?—I do not think it would be suitable for storehouses at all. I don't understand what he means.

101. Have you any remarks to make on that letter?—Mr. Collum may be better able to explain it.

102. Mr Cotton.—If the application was made do you think the Commissioners would entertain it?—I think not.

103. And the ground is laid out in plots?—Of course there are plots, but they are not laid out yet in plots. There is not one house on it yet; and at 3s. 4d. in the pound, our present rating, which we intend soon to reduce to 2s. 6d., the amount derived from Derrychara would be only £44, and I believe £44 would not make the Dublin road alone. There is a clause in our Act which renders the whole of the road within our boundary, if you took the whole of the townland, and the boundary went through the centre of the road there, and yet that road is all in.

Mr. JAMES COLLINS examined.

Mr. James Collins.

104. Did you write this letter (produced)?—It is my father who really wrote it—I drew it.

105. Your father wanted to include the whole of the townland of Derrychara?—Yes.

106. Are there any remarks you wish to make in substantiation of the letter?—There is a very good road there, and as regards the lighting of it the Commissioners seem to be proud the light goes to the end of the borough boundary, close to the model school, so that the expense would not be very much more in carrying the light on further, for it is part of the way already, and there must be water on to the railway station, so that the whole expense would not be great.

107. Is the townland your father's property?—Yes, the whole of it.

108. Is he building on it at present?—He is not yet.

109. If the townland was included within the town would he commence building then?—That is his intention. When the Commissioners spoke of having some of my land for a cemetery, he strongly opposed it, and said he would never be any opposition to it; he did not wish to have the land thrown away for a graveyard.

110. Mr. [illegible].—Which was the portion that is valuable for which?—There is all water frontage.

111. But there is no public road down to that part?—No, but there would have been a road.

112. The road rises up and down, so that a new road should be constructed?—Yes.

113. What is to induce a man to build there?—It is principally the houses more than stores.

114. It seems to be a very distant prospect of stores and wharves being built there?—It is more with regard to building houses, and then more on the Dublin road.

115. Mr. ROBINSON.—What are the advantages your father expected to derive from coming within the jurisdiction of the Town Commissioners?—It would improve the value of land.

116. And is the land not equally valuable from its proximity to the town?—No; because we would have it laid out. When it was first bought it was the intention of my uncle, the late Mr. John Collins, to get it drained, but there has been one thing or another to interfere with it.

117. Has your father considered that there is a large sum due and owing by the Corporation which you would be liable for?—There does not appear much, and that what is owed to the Board of Works.

118. What advantage would you get in exchange for the £4?—We would hope to have lamps on it, and to lay them.

119. Mr. COTTON.—But elsewhere we have generally found that people are building more outside than inside the limits?—That might hold good for the other side of the town, but they are coming more and nearer to the railway station. The railway company got an Act of Parliament which gave them more trade, and whatever traffic is created would come to that side of the town.

120. Why should a man take land that is subject to rates rather than outside with the advantage those rates give?—No, I don't think it gives him any particular privilege to pay rates.

121. What advantage would the gas be on the roads?—I think it would induce people to take up houses if it was in the borough. Houses let far easier in the borough.

122. When you say borough you mean municipal and not Parliamentary borough?—I don't know there is any difference.

123. But if we recommended this to be added to the town, it would not add it to the Parliamentary borough?—I did understand that it would.

124. No, we have no control over the Parliamentary borough?—That is one of the things we were thinking of.

125. We have nothing to say to the Parliamentary borough?—I thought it was the Parliamentary borough.

126. Supposing it was not the Parliamentary borough, do you think that would affect your father's idea?—I don't see what advantage we would get in the municipal borough.

127. Mr. ROBINSON.—And then, under these circumstances, you would not wish to be included?—I don't think so.

Mr. JORDAN recalled.

Mr. Jordan.

128. We strongly opposed it. There is no—

129. Mr. COTTON.—What is the advantage in having the Parliamentary and the municipal area the same—is there any practical advantage?—I don't know, exactly.

130. Do you think there is any advantage in having them the same?—I have never thought of the subject; as it stands at present there is, because previously the Parliamentary borough extended further outside than the municipal, and then they were made the same all round, and we think there is an advantage in having them so again; it is confined to the inconvenience it hence those exports.

131. What is the convenience—does it save any work, or does it simplify matters?—I don't know.

132. Supposing, is there any reasons for thinking it is an advantage to have the boundaries of the towns complete townland boundaries, might there be any reason for not extending the boundary a little further, so as to take in the boundary of Windmill Hill townland?—I think we gave the matter our full consideration at the meeting of the Town Commissioners, and we unanimously decided we did not require any further extension.

133. We saw no advantage in taking in that small portion, and we would be glad to hear any objections there are to that—would you have any new roads to keep?—We would have some—about 400 yards additional.

134. The 10th section of your Act gives power, with the consent of the Grand Jury and the Lord Lieutenant, to extend the boundaries?—Yes.

135. Is there any such thing in the apparent conveniences in it?—I cannot tell.

136. There is some real convenience in having a municipal boundary consisting of entire townlands, and not portions of such, and here you have a boundary cutting up fields?—Yes; there are two lines that run that way. My idea is that there was an objection to the extension of the Parliamentary borough at one time, and the large proprietors who owned land opposed any inclusion in the direction of their property, and, when the Act of Parliament came, it caused an inconvenience by permitting the municipal and Parliamentary borough to go on.

137. You understand quite clearly that, when I spoke of the extension of Enniskillen taking in some of Windmill Hill, I don't mean the extension of the Parliamentary borough?—I was not aware until you mentioned it now. I don't see any reason why the whole of the townland should not be included for municipal purposes.

138. There are no special expenses connected with that townland?—No, except the road. If it would not increase the taxation on the ratepayers and the borough proper, we would have no possible objection. The only reason we opposed Derrychara and these other places was that it would increase the rates on the ratepayers, and we wished to avoid increasing the rates for tenants or landlords, and if it did not increase the rate on the borough, I see no objection, but it would be the greatest possible advantage.

Mr. Thomas Gordon, Town Commissioner, examined.

[illegible] July [illegible], 1877.

Mr. Thomas Gordon.

139. Have you considered this question?—I have, but I did not know the exact boundary proposed. The proposed extension to Windmill Hill would affect us very little.

140. Would there be any advantage in having the boundary altered at all?—No. I don't believe there would be any advantage.

141. You agree with the Chairman?—Yes. The matter came before the board at one time, and it was thoroughly discussed, and we agreed to remain as we are.

Mr. Jordan.

Mr. Jordan recalled.

142. I could see no possible objection to include Windmill Hill, as it does not affect the Parliamentary boundary, and does not increase the taxation on the ratepayers.

143. Are you satisfied it would not?—Mr. Rae is satisfied it would not. We are most anxious to protect the ratepayers against increased taxation, and we have no objection to include the whole area mentioned, except on the ground of taxation.

144. The boundary follows townlands?—Yes; but it excludes the infirmary.

145. You would get no rates from it?—No; but it should be in the boundary. It is a very awkward little bit, which stands in the midst of our property and we must go through the county road before we get to our property. It stands in the middle of our corporate property, and it is the road to the Sligo railway station.

Mr. John Rae.

Mr. John Rae examined.

146. You are surveyor of the town?—Yes.

147. Can you tell me the length of streets you have to maintain?—About five and a half miles.

148. You know Windmill Hill townland?—I do.

149. Do you think it would pay to bring it in?—I think it would pay the Commissioners.

150. And you know of no [illegible] objection to it?—No, I think it would be desirable to take it in.

151. You think the portion should be taken in including the county infirmary, up to the stream that runs to the south of the [illegible] road?—Yes, from the townland of Drumandoora.

152. What portion would you have to include the whole of Drumandoora?—I would certainly take it all in; but the Commissioners would have to supply water and light to the roads there, and it would not pay.

153. Would the town be at a loss by including the portion to which you refer, on which the county infirmary stands?—No, I think not.

154. There is a good length of road?—No, not very much, and we have to [illegible] pass it to get to the portion of our land which is north east of it.

155. What difficulty is there about this?—Not much, but when we go there with horses and carts, we have to use roads that are not our own, and there is a loss of time. It is very awkward to have it there.

156. What about water works?—An Act of Parliament was obtained for a supply of water and other benefits to the town in 1870, and it got the Royal assent in the August of that year. Water works were erected, and we have paid about half the cost of obtaining the Act. The works cost altogether about £[illegible], and they were completed within a year and a half from the day we entered into the contract, and from the day they were finished in 1873, they have not cost us a sixpence.

157. What is the supply?—Twenty-five gallons per individual, per day.

158. How many thousand gallons in the day?—[illegible] gallons in the day, or [illegible] gallons per head per day.

159. What actually goes into the town at present?—There are [illegible] gallons, for we use it liberally; that is [illegible] gallons per head for a population of [illegible], and about thirty-three gallons per head, with the present population.

160. How much is sold?—About £[illegible] worth, but I cannot tell you the quantity, for it is not sold by quantity.

161. You sell it to parties outside the town?—Yes.

162. What income do you get from them?—£[illegible] from the railway which is outside; £[illegible] from [illegible]; £[illegible] from the county infirmary; £[illegible] from the [illegible] schools which are outside the boundary.

163. Mr. Jordan.—That was one of the strong reasons for refusing to extend the borough, as we would have lost all those water rents by including them unnecessarily.

164. Mr. Robinson.—You would be liable to the rate.

165. Mr. Jordan.—But we would have to give them water.

Mr. Rae's examination resumed.

166. What pressure have you on the high parts of the town?—We have in the highest spot inhabited in the town [illegible] feet head of water, or [illegible] in the [illegible] tank.

167. Is that available for putting out fires?—Yes, and we are amply provided with machinery for that purpose.

168. What about drainage?—All the sewers of the town, except three, are designed by the Commissioners. They got the powers under their Act in 1870.

169. They all flow down into the river?—They do.

170. Are you spending much on the drainage at present?—No.

171. Why don't you drain these three streets?—It is contemplated to borrow money from the Board of Works at this moment.

172. Mr. Jordan wished to ask—Did you estimate the length of road there would be in those townlands?—I did not.

173. What would you put the maintenance of those roads at?—I could not say, but I think they would cost about £[illegible] a mile only.

174. Can you tell what is the area within the municipal boundary?—[illegible], I should say roughly, eighty acres.

175. Is that land let upon building leases?—A great deal is let on lease by the Commissioners.

176. Mr. Cotton.—This map shows in red the municipal boundary?—Yes, the red and yellow show the municipal boundary.

177. Portion is not within the Parliamentary borough?—They are outside the borough.

178. When was the Parliamentary borough changed?—In 1832.

179. Then the Act changed the Parliamentary as well?—Yes, it made them coterminous; the Parliamentary boundary was extended in 18[illegible].

180. This included in the Parliamentary boundary now?—Yes.

181. Do you see any objection to including that portion of Windmill Hill not included at present?—Not the slightest. I think it would be an improvement.

182. Would you not suggest any extension?—No, except to make the boundary more uniform by taking

[illegible] the county [illegible]. The source for water supply stands at a level of about 250 feet above the highest part of the town, and gives a working pressure of 125 feet at the highest spot.

182. Where is your service reservoir?—The [illegible] [illegible].

183. What is the working head?—It is about 115 feet above the [illegible].

184. Is there any navigation on the lake?—No, sir.

185. You say five miles is the length of the streets?—Yes, about five and a half miles.

186. What is the expense of maintaining them?—£311 1s. 6d. in 1878, and sweeping and cleansing £207 8s. additional, which includes cost of sweeping and cleansing [illegible], so that about £150 a year would pay for the sweeping; the town has paid about £150 each half year on an average of the county at large charges.

Mr. James Coulter, J.P., examined.

187. You heard the opinion given by Mr. Jordan that it was not desirable to extend the town—do you agree in that?—I do; from what the borough surveyor says, and what you say yourself that it would not increase the valuation to extend out this way, we thought it better not to have any extension.

The inquiry then terminated.

GILFORD—7TH AUGUST, 1879.

Before Mr. H. A. Robinson.

Mr. John Magennis examined.

1. Mr. Robinson.—You are Town Clerk of Gilford?—Yes.

2. How long have you been so?—Since 1865.

3. When was the town constituted under the Towns Improvement Act?—In 1859.

4. Previous to that was it under any Act?—No, not to my knowledge.

5. Was the Act adopted for all purposes?—For lighting and cleansing.

6. Were you a Commissioner previous to being Town Clerk?—Yes.

7. Were you one of the Commissioners who selected the boundary?—No.

8. I understand there has been no alteration in the boundary since that time?—Yes, there has been no alteration.

9. And the boundary remains the same?—Yes.

10. Are you aware what steps the Town Commissioners took to ascertain what the boundaries of the town should be?—No.

11. You were not one of the committee appointed?—No.

12. Was there a committee appointed?—Yes.

13. Does the boundary include parts of townlands, or whole townlands?—Parts.

14. What townlands, or parts of townlands, are included?—Loughans, Dunmahon.

15. And no other townlands?—No.

16. What are the areas of those townlands within the boundary?—Dunmahon is 83 acres, 3 roods, and 15 perches; Loughans is [illegible] acres, 3 roods.

17. Can you give me the areas of the portions of those townlands without the municipal limits?—No, I cannot.

18. I believe Loughans is [illegible] acres?—I will send them to you—the particulars.

19. Who fixed the present boundaries of Gilford?—[illegible] of [illegible] was there a committee of ratepayers appointed to fix on the boundaries?—There was a committee, I think Dr. M'Bride was one of them. I find (without having referred to a book) that a committee was appointed as follows:—Mr. Benjamin Dickson, Mr. Henry Heron, Mr. John Byers, Mr. John Dickson, Mr. Henry M'Bride, and Mr. Henry M'Donnell.

19. That was the committee appointed?—Yes.

20. You live in the town of Gilford?—Yes.

21. And you know all the circumstances connected with it?—Yes.

22. Are there large manufactures carried on in it?—Not within the boundary, but immediately adjoining the town there are.

23. Is the town a thriving one?—Yes, pretty fair.

24. Are you acquainted with the present boundary?—Yes.

25. How far in the northern direction does it extend?—To where you are sitting at present.

26. How far in the southern direction, from the centre of the town?—Well, Mr. Ben. Dickson's mills is immediately the extremity.

27. Not more than three hundred yards it appears to me?—Not more.

28. On the west?—It would be about five hundred yards.

29. On the east?—To the Roman Catholic Chapel, or about three hundred yards.

30. Well, I understand you to say that the principal business is carried on outside?—Yes, so far as [illegible] the mills and [illegible].

31. Do I understand that the mills have sprung up since the boundaries were fixed?—Oh, they were in existence then.

32. I see there is a large amount of building for such a small town, more here, [illegible] inhabited by the [illegible]?—They are outside.

33. In what townland are these mills situated?—In Loughans.

34. Are they wholly within the townland of Loughans or in the [illegible] of Gilford?—Yes.

35. Does the principal business of Gilford emanate from these mills?—Yes; there are other public works connected to the town, but the principal employers of the people are these mills.

36. Who is the landlord of the soil?—Partly Mr. M'Master and partly Mr. Ben. Dickson.

37. Can you tell me the present boundaries of the town, as mentioned in the minute?—Whereas these were the boundaries as follows:—

"On the north side of the Roman Catholic Chapel, in the townland of Loughans, thence along the fence of Mr. M'Master's lawn to Mr. Thompson's tenements, known as '[illegible]', [illegible] by said fence to the west corner of the Presbyterian Church; thence by the new Avenue made by Mr. M'Master's [illegible] entrance [illegible] by Mr. M'Master's lawn to opposite the north-west end of the Police Barrack opposite the road leading to [illegible], [illegible], and [illegible] to the end of what is known as the [illegible] [illegible] in the [illegible] Works; thence by the [illegible] at the back of the [illegible]'s shop, to [illegible] [illegible] by [illegible] [illegible] at the [illegible] of Mrs. M'Donnell's [illegible] [illegible], west and south, by the boundary between Mrs. M'Donnell's and Mrs. M'Creight's to the old road leading to [illegible], to the south; thence, in a straight line, to the garden [illegible] by Mrs. M'[illegible] house; thence along to the fence between [illegible] M'Creight's and Mrs. M'Creight's to the old road leading up by William Wilson's; thence, in a direct line, to the [illegible] between the Rev. William [illegible]'s orchard and field; thence to the road leading to Loughbrickland and Banbridge, and thence, in a straight line, across the river [illegible] to the [illegible] [illegible] Gilford-[illegible] [illegible] opening [illegible] [illegible] [illegible], thence by the [illegible] [illegible] James [illegible] [illegible] to

3 N 2

Gilford, July 1, 1879. — Mr. [illegible] Magenis.

the road leading to Banbridge on the west; thence, crossing the road in a direct line to John Byrne's ditch, in the townland of Drumaran; thence by the fence between John Byrne's and John Cromlean's to the small rivulet called the 'Pound' river; thence along to Thomas Allen's field; thence by the fence leading to Mr. Haran's march, first through Thomas Allen's farm then between John M'Cabe's and Thomas Allen's; thence by Mr. Haran's fence to the road leading past the Roman Catholic Chapel; thence across the road joining the chapel boundary, from which we commenced."

37. In what electoral division is the town?—Tullynaburn and the Banbridge Union.

38. What have been the poor rates for the past five years?—One shilling in the pound.

39. Do they include any sanitary rates?—Two pence in the pound this year.

40. Was that struck for any special purpose?—It was struck for a sanitary rate.

41. Have there ever been any sanitary rates struck for special purposes?—Yes; the previous year there was a sanitary rate of two pence in the pound.

42. What was that for?—For putting in these new [illegible].

43. What district was it levied on?—Loughans and Drumellen.

44. On the entire townlands?—Yes.

45. Can you give the county cess?—In 1874, one and eleven pence farthing; in 1875, twenty-two pence three farthings; in 1876, twenty-two pence; in 1877, twenty-two pence halfpenny; in 1878, two shillings and a penny; and the municipal rate in 1873 eleven pence; in 1874, the same; in 1875, seven pence; in 1876, five pence; in 1877, the same; and in 1878, two pence in the pound.

46. In addition to their income from the rates, have the Commissioners any source of income?—Yes; there are fines from the Court—all cases brought up within the boundary by the police.

47. There is no property vested in the Town Commissioners?—No.

48. Are there any markets held in the town?—No.

49. Or fairs?—No.

50. Is the town well lighted?—Yes.

51. The sanitary work is carried on by the Board of Guardians?—Yes.

52. Have the Commissioners ever expressed any wish to become the sanitary authority?—Yes.

53. Have they adopted any resolution on the subject?—I do not know whether there was any resolution which was adopted, but the opinion is general.

54. Is the idea favourable to it?—Yes.

55. As to the Commissioners becoming the sanitary authority?—Yes.

56. It is thought they would do the business better?—Yes; it was considered that the Guardians have not the same knowledge that the local authorities living in the place have.

57. Do the Commissioners consider that they receive full value from the rates levied by the Board of Guardians?—They do not.

58. Are they aware that under the Public Health Act of last Session they can apply to the Local Government Board for a provisional order to become the sanitary authority?—Yes.

59. Did they take steps in that direction?—I believe they will.

60. Are there any schools in the town?—Yes.

61. And do the people from the districts adjoining the town send in their children to take advantage of these schools?—Yes.

62. Do the people around the town make use of it for different purposes?—Yes.

63. Is the land more valuable from its proximity to the town?—Yes.

64. Do they dispose of their farming produce in Gilford?—Well, they do, to a certain extent; some people sell their potatoes in some months of the year, and some shopkeepers buy grain, but there is no real market.

65. What is the real market?—Portadown and Banbridge.

66. How far are you from Banbridge?—About five miles.

67. Do you know the electoral division?—Yes.

68. How far does the utmost limit of your electoral division extend?—About four miles.

69. The Select Committee instructed us as far as possible to make the towns coterminous with the electoral divisions, I presume that is one of the questions here?—It would be.

70. What is the valuation of Gilford?—£1,[illegible] 5s.

71. On how much of that is the full rate assessed, and on how much the quarter rate?—I cannot tell exactly that way, but I know that there are only forty-eight acres to which the quarter rate applies.

72. What was the population last census?—2,[illegible]

73. Would you say that the population is increasing or diminishing?—Decreasing, I would say.

74. Does the census of 1871 show a decrease or an increase over the one before that?—A decrease of about 100.

75. How long is this manufacturing colony in existence?—I do not know exactly.

76. Has that any population of its own?—Oh, yes.

77. And do they live distinct from Gilford?—Yes.

78. They have a colony of their own there outside, distinct from the town of Gilford?—Yes. Of course some of the work people reside in the town and surrounding district, but there is a large proportion of them who live apart from the town, and there are others scattered about here and there.

79. But those mills, as far as possible, as I understand it, feed the town of Gilford?—Yes.

80. Is there any other manufactory in Gilford?—No.

81. Are there no gentlemen's places close outside?—Well yes, Mr. Ben. Dixon has a castle a short distance outside.

82. If we were to include the entire of Drumaran and Loughans could you tell me what population would be brought in?—No.

83. You can get that for me perhaps?—Well no, I have not got it.

84. We sent you some queries with reference to the question of the proposed extension of the boundary?—Yes.

85. Were they submitted to a general meeting or a special meeting of the Commissioners?—To a general meeting of the Commissioners.

86. How many Commissioners were present?—There could not have been less than five.

87. You have nine Town Commissioners altogether I believe?—Yes. I know it was brought before the Commissioners here, and the question was fully discussed, and I got instructions to forward replies, but I think there was no resolution passed on the point.

88. The Commissioners expressed their belief that no alteration was required?—Yes.

89. Were the Commissioners unanimous in thinking that no alteration was needed?—Yes, but subsequently there were other Commissioners who said the boundaries should be extended.

90. In what direction?—They did not say that, they only said it was necessary.

91. And has any resolution been passed in favour of it?—No, this was a general conversation I am referring to, but there was no resolution passed on the point.

92. You are simply required to put the resolution on the book?—Yes, just with instructions to reply.

93. Have you had an opportunity of ascertaining the feeling of the ratepayers on the subject?—No, I made no inquiries when I got instructions to reply.

94. Are the ratepayers aware of the existence of this Commission, do they know that the inquiry was to be held to-day?—I think so, some of them knew it and some may not, I think it was pretty generally known.

95. You never heard the question mooted amongst

the ratepayers that an alteration was necessary?—I think I heard it spoken of that such should be the case.

94. Are there any improvements in the town which the Commissioners would carry out if they had additional powers?—I never heard of any.

95. They have not felt themselves restricted in carrying out any improvements?—No.

96. Have they ever considered the question of taking up the roads?—Yes, it has been talked of several times, but I think Dr. M'Bride can give you evidence as to that.

97. Is the land close outside the town let for building under building leases?—No.

98. It is mostly arable land?—Yes. Is there a good supply of water in Gilford?—Yes.

99. If the Commissioners became the Urban Sanitary Authority what way would they apply their power, would it be in the direction of draining?—The town is pretty well drained.

100. Do they think that the Guardians give perfect satisfaction?—Well, not altogether.

101. In what respect do they consider that the Guardians don't give full satisfaction?—Well, they think that things are not what they should be, particularly in the case of deeds.

102. As far as we can see, however, the town is pretty well looked after?—Yes.

103. Is there any place for building within the present boundary of the town?—No, I do not think so.

104. Does there seem to be any likelihood of the town extending in any one direction?—Not at present, it did some years ago in the direction of Mr. M'Master's works.

105. Have you any further general observations to make?—No.

Gilford, Aug. 1, 1877. — Mr. John Maguire.

Dr. Henry M'Bride examined.

Dr. Henry M'Bride.

106. I understand you have been one of the first Commissioners of this town?—Yes.

107. In fact you were one of the Commissioners who drew up the boundaries of Gilford as they now exist?—Yes.

108. What steps were taken originally to ascertain the boundaries that were to be adopted?—The principle that guided them originally was to only tax those who would be likely to receive benefit from the town, and the town is made as concentrated as possible.

109. Is there now no necessity for an alteration or rearrangement of the boundaries?—I would hardly say there is. It might be desirable, but is not absolutely necessary.

110. I notice in the description of the boundary, and on looking at the map there is a large rural suburb including Mr. M'Master's mill, which at the time the boundary was fixed appears to have been left out. Can you give me any reason for that?—I remember that matter was talked of very much at the time. Mr. M'Master, the present Mr. John's father, was very much interested at the time, but said he did not want his property to be included. He did not like the scavengers or any portion of that kind to be sent in by the Commissioners through his works. I believe he preferred doing it himself.

111. Then it was in consequence of Mr. M'Master's attitude in the matter that the district was left out?—Yes.

112. It seems to me that you left also the best part of the town out in doing that?—Yes.

113. Has it never been suggested that the bringing in of that district would double the valuation and population?—It has been frequently talked of, and a strong effort has been made once or twice, but still Mr. M'Master had the same wish. Mr. Ben Dickson wished to have it extended around by Glencliff's and around by Pritchard's, but Mr. M'Master had the same objection as formerly.

114. Is it not a fact that the town of Gilford has really originated and sprung from M'Master's mills?—Well, of course it was a very small village previous to the public works being established.

115. And it is now what it is on account of them?—Well, it has increased certainly.

116. Is it known that Mr. M'Master would be averse to extending the boundary to include it?—I never spoke to Mr. John's brother or any member of his family about it.

117. You have lived some time in this town?—Yes, thirty-seven years.

118. Is the town likely to extend in any one direction?—Well, in the present state of the prosperity of public works I do not think so. Things are rather at a stand-still.

119. But if there was an increase in the prosperity of trade there would be an extension of building outside the town?—Well, yes, very likely.

120. Is there sufficient land within the boundary for building purposes for more than to come?—No.

121. So that if any buildings had to be carried on near the town they could not be constructed within the municipal bounds?—No, they could not.

122. Whoever would erect such buildings should get land outside?—Yes.

123. Would the owners outside be disposed to let land at building leases?—I cannot say that.

124. But in recent years no buildings, except in the direction of M'Master's mills, have been erected?—None of any moment.

125. Do you attend the Board pretty regularly?—Yes.

126. And is it your opinion that the sanitary works would be better managed in your hands than in the hands of the Banbridge Union?—Yes.

127. When you apply to the Board of Guardians do they attend to you?—Well, as much as is convenient, but they really cannot do it. There is a good deal of roundabout work with them, a notice on one party, then notice on another, then an inspector comes and brings a sanitary officer, and he returns everybody else, and then it goes before the Guardians, and there is a roundabout way of doing things.

128. You are of opinion that it would be more satisfactory and more in accordance with the opinions of the ratepayers, if these powers were in your own hands?—I believe there would be some advantage in it. If there is a nuisance it is 10, 12 or 15 days before relief is provided by the Guardians, but it could be done at once by the Town Commissioners.

129. Is that the opinion of the Commissioners?—Certainly.

130. And the ratepayers?—Well, they have never been consulted on it.

131. And I presume the Commissioners may be said to represent the opinions of the ratepayers?—Yes.

132. Is it your opinion that the roads should be taken into the hands of the Commissioners?—Certainly, we made an effort in that direction once. We wished to have all the roads within the boundary cut off, and have the management of them, and have the streets and footpaths kept by us; however, it came out what was going to be done at the presentments, and the party who had been doing the work formerly offered to do it for a penny in the pound or so less, and the Commissioners were so annoyed at what took place, with the fact that they got no heed or help, they never made any movement since.

133. Then I take it, it is your opinion that the whole management of the town should be in one undivided authority?—Decidedly.

GILFORD. Aug. 1, 1879. Dr. Henry M'Bride.

131. That the sanitary authority, and everything, should be under one jurisdiction?—Yes.

132. Are you aware that the Local Government Board can, by a provisional order, give power for a separation from the Grand Jury to the Town Commissioners, who become the urban authority, without the consent of the Grand Jury?—No.

133. Well, they can, but you must first become the sanitary authority?—I know.

134. If we included the whole of that district in which M'Master's mills are, and that suburb, do you think the additional population would bring you up to the 6,000?—No.

135. If you took in the entire of those two townlands, would it bring you up to that population necessary to constitute you the Urban Sanitary Authority?—No, I do not think so; it would amount to more than 5,000.

Mr. John G. M'Master.

Mr. John Gordon M'Master examined.

136. Mr. Robinson.—I have been looking around the boundary, and I find your flourishing suburb springing up; would you have any objection, you or your partners, to its being included within the boundaries of the town of Gilford?—Well, I am not in a good position to state.

137. It has occurred to me here, having heard the evidence, that you would naturally be very much interested in this question, and it seems to me you would be in a better position to speak upon the subject if you consulted with your partners and find out their views on the matter?—Yes, my brother has been away.

138. Can you give me the valuation of this property of yours?—Not at present, but I can get it at the office. I do not carry these details about with me at all.

139. When this Commission was first started we inserted advertisements in all the papers in Ireland, stating that we would be glad to receive information. The people of Gilford and those interested in it were made aware of the circumstance through the Belfast papers, as there is no Gilford paper, and you seem to be taken somewhat by surprise. Now as I wish that every opportunity should be given to have the views of those most nearly interested in the question of the boundaries of Gilford expressed, I think it better that we should adjourn, and we will come down here again and hear what views you have to put forward on the subject, for it appears to me that you are unprepared with your evidence.

140. Mr. M'Master.—Thank you. I must say I have been taken by surprise, for I am not sufficiently posted in these matters. I am not quite acquainted with the business, but my eldest brother, could give you information that would no doubt affect any steps that you would take.

141. How many people are employed within your works?—I think about 1,250 at present.

142. And in consequence of your father objecting to the mills being included in the town, they were not included?—Yes.

143. I may take it as a fact however, that your mills really constitute the town of Gilford?—Well, I fancy that it is in consequence of their being situated here, the town of Gilford has attained its present position. The property is private property, we are our own sanitary authority, and we take proper care of it.

144. Do you carry on sanitary works in it?—Yes.

145. Do you drain it yourselves?—Yes.

146. At your own expense or the expense of the Guardians?—We have carts coming up every morning and we have pumps sufficient to supply that district with water.

147. And so in fact you have the management of the whole of this colony of yours?—Yes.

148. And you do it out of your own pocket?—Yes.

149. It appears to me it would be only fair to give you an opportunity of having your views properly expressed, and with this end it might be well to give you additional time, and I may say it will not be before the end of the present month that we will return. In the meantime you can prepare statistics and take steps to have the feeling of your partners put forward?—Yes, unanimous previous to the town being formed.

150. To Doctor M'Bride.—Do you remember the town when it first came under the Towns Improvement Act?—Well.

151. Do you notice any perceptible difference between it then and now?—It has increased.

152. There is a better class of buildings?—Yes, somewhat better.

The inquiry was then adjourned until the 15th September.

MONDAY.—15th SEPTEMBER, 1879.

Sept. 15, 1879.

Before H. A. Robinson, Esq.

Mr. Benjamin Dickson.

Mr. Benjamin Dickson examined.

153. You are Chairman of the Town Commissioners?—Yes.

154. You have resided a considerable time in Gilford, and are well acquainted with it, I presume?—Yes.

155. Were you one of the Commissioners when the town was originally formed?—Yes.

156. And did you determine, or were you one of those who determined the boundary now existing?—Yes, I was one of the Commissioners who agreed to the present boundary.

157. And I understand from the evidence given on the last day that Mr. M'Master's premises were left out of the boundary on account—was it that Mr. M'Master objected to the inclusion of his premises?—Yes; the late Mr. M'Master objected to the inclusion of his property in the town for the reason, principally that he thought lighted and kept the place clean, and he did not wish the interference of the Town Commissioners. He did everything himself.

157. That is, he kept his own property in order?—Yes; and he would most strenuously have opposed the town coming under the Towns' Improvement Act, if his place came within the municipal limits—he said so.

158. And under those circumstances, the Commissioners, the boundaries were made as they are now—leaving him out?—Yes.

159. What prompted you to adopt the boundary now existing—did you go as far as the buildings extended?—Yes, I think so.

160. The town consists mainly of buildings—there is not very much arable land about it; and if building operations were to take place, there is not much available land for the purpose?—No.

161. Now, if you were to include Mr. M'Master's premises it would confer a benefit on the town?—Well, it would have the effect of lowering the rates.

162. And it would nearly double the valuation of the town?—Yes; no doubt the valuation of Mr.

M'Master's property is probably as much outside of Gilford, and we would get an immense income by it [illegible] the whole town.

163. Messrs. M'Master's property would be all rated at the full rate?—Well, I don't know how far the proposed boundary would go, but the property [illegible] all buildings.

164. Do you consider the boundary of Gilford too circumscribed?—That was our opinion at first.

165. The present [illegible] any restriction on the [illegible]?—No.

166. Do you speak your own views or the views of the Commissioners?—Those are the views of the Commissioners, of whom I have been Chairman since the beginning.

167. Gilford is not, I suppose, a market town?—There is a market-day, but no market.

168. Would you say the town of Gilford conferred advantages on the people living within a radius of a mile of it?—Yes.

169. Do you think the land is more valuable within a mile of Gilford by reason of its proximity to it?—I think it is.

170. Where do the farmers dispose of their produce?—Some of them sell in Gilford, some in Tanderagee, and some in Portadown, and so on. Of course they go through Gilford to those markets.

171. The Commissioners, in considering the question of extension, did not specify anything in particular as a desirable extension?—No.

172. Did you form any opinion as to what would be a desirable extension?—No; inasmuch as I only heard of the thing since you were here before. The Commissioners at their meeting discussed the matter, and I think they are prepared to give their individual opinions.

Gilford, Sept. 23, 1878. Mr. Benjamin Dickson.

173. Are you of opinion that Messrs. M'Master's property derives any advantage from being so close to Gilford?—Well, except so far as regards the dwellings of the workmen, I don't know.

174. As I understand you, Mr. Dickson, you are in favour of an extension, but have not decided in your mind what extension would be most desirable?—Quite so.

175. You think that Messrs. M'Master's property should be included?—Yes, that was our view from the first.

176. Messrs. M'Master's property is part and parcel of the town—there are no fields between them?—None at all.

176. There is the public road between them?—No, there is his own lawn between it and the town.

177. If a wide extension was taken, can you say what houses would be taken in?—A very considerable number of houses.

178. Is your house within the municipal limits?—No.

179. Would you have any objection to be included?—No, not if it was for the benefit of the town.

180. Do you think you derive benefit from your proximity to the town of Gilford?—Yes, I think so. So far as certain produce is concerned I get better prices.

Mr. Hugh M'Connell.

Mr. Hugh M'Connell, examined.

181. You are a Town Commissioner of Gilford?—Yes.

182. Were you one of the original Commissioners?—Yes.

183. And were you at that time in favour of including Messrs. M'Master's mills when the town was formed?—[illegible]

184. And, like Mr. Dickson, and the others, thinking you would not get the Towns' Improvement Act if you did not do so, you agreed to the boundary?—Yes.

185. You are well acquainted with Gilford?—Yes, I have lived there for twenty years.

186. Do you see much improvement in Gilford in late years?—Yes.

187. Would you say it is a thriving town?—Yes, [illegible] the depression of trade for some years back has had its influence.

188. Your opinion is that the mill is the chief stay of the town?—Yes.

189. And that but for the labour given by the mill it would not be in so thriving a position?—Yes.

190. Are there other establishments or [illegible] in the town which, if the boundary was extended, would be also included—are you in favour of an extension?—Yes.

191. Are there any improvements required for the town which would be carried out if the Commissioners had an increased area and an increased income?—I think if the Commissioners had control of the sanitary affairs of the town it would be an improvement. The roads might be kept in better order. At present they are kept in a very bad and dirty state.

192. Then in proposing an extension you think it would be desirable to become the Urban Sanitary Authority?—Well, unless that were so there is no use in having Commissioners.

193. Would you then be in favour of having one individual authority over roads, sanitary matters, and all?—Yes.

194. Have you yourself any property outside the municipal limits?—Yes.

195. Do you believe it would confer a benefit on Gilford if the mill was included?—I do; indeed, I think it should be included.

196. The country people going to the mill use the streets, I presume, and take advantage of the lights?—Yes, they do.

197. And you think that any improvements effected in Gilford confer benefit on those living outside?—Yes, they come in so often that it is unquestionably of advantage to them to have a clean, well lighted town.

198. To what extent would you say those advantages fairly apply?—A mile, I think. I was thinking of extending the boundary to Madden's Bridge.

199. I suppose the greater portion of the property included within a mile radius would be only agricultural holdings?—Yes, of land, but there are many houses.

200. And do you think that if those people were asked to pay one-fourth, it would be only fair, considering the advantages they derive from their proximity to the town?—Yes; it would be only fair.

201. Do those people derive advantage from the lights of the town?—Yes.

202. And I presume they send in their children to school in the town?—Yes, and bring in their butter and eggs to be sold.

203. And the farmers have facilities for taking out manure?—Yes.

204. And you think the one-fourth rate would be no hardship?—No.

205. In considering the question of extension, have you ever considered what townland or townlands should be wholly included?—Well, I took it not by townlands, but by some well-marked boundary, such as streams or road.

207. Are you acquainted with the electoral division?—Yes.

208. Do you think it would be **too extensive to** select for a boundary?—Yes.

209. And, therefore, that the recommendation of the Select Committee cannot be carried out with regard to Gilford?—Yes.

210. What exactly is the boundary you would propose?—It would be about a mile in extent. The boundary I would propose is as follows:—

"Commencing at county drain, near Madden Bridge, keeping it as the boundary on the west side, until opposite the Vicar's Lane, in a direct line from drain to river Bann the line acting as a boundary, on the north side, then by the stream that divides the counties of Armagh and Down, following the course of that stream to John M'Cartin's Bridge in Ballinagarrick, thence along the road leading to Lurgan [illegible] to [illegible] corner, thence to M'Dowell's corner, thence by road leading to [illegible], until the road [illegible] past [illegible] Thompson's to [illegible], along behind Mr. [illegible], thence across [illegible] Cottage, across the [illegible] [illegible], [illegible], up to [illegible] thence by road leading from [illegible] past [illegible] [illegible] road, taking it as the boundary to [illegible] corner, thence [illegible] up the [illegible] road, [illegible] Mr. [illegible]'s [illegible], along [illegible] lane [illegible] in [illegible], following the [illegible] past [illegible] the [illegible] road, thence to the [illegible] opposite John [illegible] house, past Richard [illegible], and into John [illegible] in [illegible], [illegible] to [illegible] boundary, [illegible] from starting point of boundary commenced."

211. Mr. Tyrrell, Solicitor.—Have you had any opportunity of speaking to the ratepayers on the subject?—No.

212. And in giving your opinion, do you express the opinions of your Board or your own opinion?—My own.

213. Mr. Robinson.—I suppose you are aware that if you become the urban authority under the Public Health Act you can obtain a separation from the Grand Jury for your roads if you wish?—Yes.

214. Do you think the Grand Jury give you value for the money you pay?—No; I think the roads ought to be kept better than they are.

215. Would you be prepared to take the management of the roads?—Yes; so far as I am concerned I would.

Mr. William Whitworth examined.

216. Mr. Robinson.—Are you a Commissioner?—Yes.

217. You have heard the evidence given by Mr. Dickson and Mr. M'Connell?—Yes.

218. And are you in favour of an extension of the boundary?—Yes.

219. You think the people who would be brought in under the arrangement proposed by Mr. M'Connell, derive advantages from their proximity to the town?—Yes.

220. Do you think the land is more valuable?—Yes.

221. Have you any property outside?—Yes.

222. And your proposal, therefore, would be to tax yourself?—Yes.

223. What advantage do you think would accrue from this extension?—Well, in the first place, I think we would be likely to get a better class of Commissioners—a more influential body.

224. You would bring in gentlemen's residences?—Precisely.

225. Would you be anxious to get separation from the Grand Jury for the roads?—Yes.

226. Have you ever gone into any calculation on the subject of extension?—No.

227. Are you in favour of adopting a townland boundary?—I am, for an extension of about a mile.

228. But would you be in favour of following townland boundaries?—Yes.

229. Were you present at the meeting when the question of the boundaries was considered?—Yes.

230. How many Commissioners were present?—Six or seven.

231. Were there any dissentients—anyone opposed to the extension?—None that I heard.

232. And, I suppose, you consider the views of the Commissioners may be taken as representing those of the ratepayers?—Yes.

233. Have you heard anyone speaking against extension?—No.

Mr. Thomas Fox examined.

234. Mr. Robinson.—Are you a Commissioner?—Yes.

235. And you are well acquainted with the town of Gilford?—Yes.

236. Have you seen any improvements in Gilford in recent years?—Yes, there have been.

237. And do you anticipate greater improvements would follow from having a larger area and higher valuation on which to strike your rates?—If the boundary was larger, we would be able to get a good market into the town.

238. You think an extension of the boundary would confer a benefit on the town?—Yes.

239. And that a benefit to the town is felt by those living outside, and who take advantage of the town?—Quite so.

240. And on Mr. M'Master?—Yes, great benefit. We are getting very little benefit from Mr. M'Master. We get very little of his money—it is kept amongst themselves.

241. Have you considered the question of becoming the urban sanitary authority?—Yes.

242. Do you think this extension would confer advantage on the landlord and tenant outside?—Yes.

243. And do you think there are any improvements to which you would apply your increased income?—Yes.

244. Do you anticipate, if there is an extension, you will be able to live on the 1s. rate?—I am not sure if they would.

245. The people within the boundary, as proposed by Mr. M'Connell, all make use of the town?—Yes.

246. What is the opinion on the subject outside?—I cannot say.

247. Would it be opposed to paying the one-fourth the present improvement rate?—No; I don't think they would object to it. Mr. M'Master and others use the town bringing their horses and cars through it, and so on.

248. You think that the people outside derive such a benefit that the one-fourth rate would not press too heavily on them?—Yes.

249. Would you be in favour of a separation from the Grand Jury in respect of the roads?—Yes.

250. You think the whole town should be under the sanitary jurisdiction?—Yes.

Mr. Hugh Cochrane examined.

251. Mr. Robinson.—You have heard the opinions expressed here to-day?—Yes, and I wish to corroborate them in many instances.

252. In what regard do you dissent from the opinions expressed?—I don't know if it would be of much benefit to have such an extension as suggested.

253. Do you mean the extension which would include Messrs. M'Master's and those townlands?—Yes, it is too wide an extension.

254. You think a mile would be too much?—Yes.

255. Would you be in favour of any half a mile?—Yes.

256. You are in favour of extension to that extent?—Yes.

256. Do you not consider that the people living in the most remote parts within a mile of the town derive as much advantage from their proximity as those who reside within a radius of half a mile?—No, I do not.

257. How far do you think the advantages of the town extend?—About half a mile—it would vary some.

258. Is the land within half a mile of the town more valuable?—Yes.

259. And in the same way is not land within a mile more valuable than land further out?—Not so much as all the land within a half mile.

260. Are there schools in Gilford?—Yes; three.

261. And do people within a mile outside send their children to school there?—Yes.

262. Do you think this extension would confer a benefit on Gilford?—Well, I would not say it would.

263. Do you regard Gilford as being at a standstill as far as buildings are concerned?—Yes, unfortunately so.

264. There are no buildings going on?—No.

265. Is there land available for building in Gilford?—Yes, plenty.

266. Have buildings been erected there recently?—Not for years.

267. When you speak of half a mile extension do you mean from the present boundary or the centre of the town?—From the centre of the town.

268. That would just about go through Mr. Dickson's. Where that would end between you very well I don't know.

269. Generally speaking you are in favour of an extension, but not too large an extension?—Exactly.

270. Would you be in favour of dividing the urban sanitary authority?

272. Mr. Tyrrell, solicitor.—Would you be in favour of increasing the number of Commissioners if the boundaries were enlarged?—Yes, that might be.

273. Mr. Commissioner.—Gilford is not divided into wards?—No.

274. There are nine Commissioners?—Yes.

275. Would you think it desirable to give additional representation to the added district?—I have not considered that question. The place is very small.

276. In the event of the boundaries being extended would you, Mr. M'Connell, be in favour of increasing the number of representatives on the town board?

Mr. M'Connell.—Yes.

277. And that the place be divided into wards?—Well, yes, perhaps so.

278. Mr. [illegible].—I would object to that, because it would be bringing in those gentlemen who [illegible] the same interest in the town as the Commissioners have.

[illegible]

Mr. John George M'Master examined.

[illegible]

279. Mr. Robinson.—You were present at the last meeting?—Yes.

280. Could you tell me the principal reasons why you are opposed to an extension of the boundary?—Well, I don't say I am opposed to it.

281. Could you tell me the reason why, when the original boundary was decided on, your mills were not included?—I believe my father and his partners at the time looked after everything, the paving and everything connected with the district, [illegible] property in the same way as the Commissioners do the town of Gilford.

282. Do you light your property?—Yes.

283. At your own expense?—Yes.

284. Is it watered and paved in the same way?—Yes.

285. Lamplighters, horses and carts go through the town of Gilford?—Yes.

286. And otherwise use the town?—Yes.

287. Then do I understand you to convey that, whilst you are not strongly opposed to an extension of the boundary you question if it would be any advantage to you to be included?—I cannot see any advantage whatever in it again.

288. Would you be content if there was an extension to hand over the lighting, cleansing, and so on, to the Commissioners?—I believe we would have to do it ourselves, but I cannot give an opinion satisfactorily. We have done it ourselves, and I think the Commissioners will say it is as well done as Gilford. We have men and horses constantly looking after the cleansing and so on, of our schools.

289. Do you derive any advantage from proximity to Gilford?—I don't think so. I don't know. In fact, I would not like to say positively. I really don't know what benefit we've drawn.

290. But you believe you contribute to Gilford?—Yes; we employ a great many persons, and so on.

291. What is the total valuation of your property?—£3,088 10s., of that about £1,200 is within the town.

292. What is the population outside the boundary employed at your mills?—I could not exactly say. I don't think in one place there are 2,000.

293. Have you ever considered the question of extension?—No, not until we got notice of this inquiry.

294. Are you opposed, on behalf of yourself and your partners, to these mills being included?—I am, on the part of myself and partners.

295. But I understand from what you are personally concerned you do not express any strong objection to the extension?—Well; I cannot see what advantage to you there from being brought in. I consider the advantages we have are now at present sufficiently defined to make as well as be included, or make it quite preferable than we should be.

296. The Commissioners say it would be of advantage to Gilford?—Perhaps it would.

297. But you believe that your works at present confer advantages upon Gilford than Gilford does on you?—I should think so.

298. You consider that advantage of [illegible]?—Yes. I believe the fact of our mills being there is a greater advantage to Gilford than the fact of Gilford being near us is to us. I speak on the part of my partners.

299. Do you think the sanitary matters would be better carried on by the Commissioners in Gilford?—My own individual opinion is that it would. I am [illegible].

300. I understood you to say if the sanitary jurisdiction was vested in the Town Commissioners it would not affect this much if your property were in the district. I think you said you would still carry on your own sanitary arrangements?—Oh, no, I would not say that.

301. I asked you, and I thought your answer conveyed that?—We always have conducted our own sanitary arrangements.

302. Mr. Tyrrell, solicitor.—You and your predecessors have always carefully and adequately attended to the sanitary regulations of your concern?—Yes.

303. Paved, lighted, provided privies and all other matters coming under the head of sanitary arrangements?—Yes, I believe they did.

304. And paid for all this at their own expense?—Yes. We pay £100 a year for cleansing, &c.

305. And, notwithstanding that, you are obliged to contribute [illegible] to the sanitary rate?—Yes.

306. Is there a hospital provided by you in addition?—Yes.

Gilford. Sept. 22, 1879. Mr. John Rogers M'Master.

308. That is also maintained without any regard to the public rates?—Yes, by ourselves.

309. Is there a dispensary?—Yes.

310. And this very remarkable gentleman here, Mr. M'Bride, is the head of the place?—Yes.

311. Do you go to the cess of the county, or the union for the payment of Dr. M'Bride?—No, he is not the dispensary medical officer as far as we are concerned.

312. Lighting the place is at your own expense?—Yes.

313. Not imposed on the people of the village?—No.

314. Mr. Fox.—I would like to mention that it is the operatives, who keep up Dr M'Bride—they pay part of the money.

315. Mr. Tyrrell.—I was asking you whether you went to the county for these payments?—No.

316. And as to scavenging and so on, is that all done by you?—Yes.

317. You do not as I understand come forward here for the purpose of opposing anything as to this locality, in the way of extension; but to state the facts?—Yes.

318. Is it your opinion that if this extension took place you would be still obliged to perform these works yourself and also pay rates as well?—Yes, we would be liable.

319. Your opinion is that it would not be done in the same efficient style necessary for the health and comfort of your workpeople?—I don't wish to pass any opinion on the Commissioners as a sanitary authority.

320. Mr. Robinson.—But they are not the sanitary authority—I understand you to say you do not believe an extension of the boundary would confer any advantage on the town of Gilford?—Yes.

321. Mr. Tyrrell.—Put it this way, supposing this proposition was settled and that your establishment was thrown in, and having regard to the expense you were at for sanitary and other matters, if the Commissioners incurred these expenses would the town derive any benefit from it?—No, I don't think it would.

322. Mr. Robinson.—In the event of its being deemed advisable to recommend that the boundary be extended would your idea be that there should be a large extension?—Yes, I do think that there are people within a mile radius who derive as great and probably more advantages from the town than people nearer.

323. Then you allow that you do derive advantages from your proximity to the town?—Well I don't know I really don't see how we do. No doubt the Post Office is in the town and we derive advantage from that.

324. But you say, as I understand, that in the event of any extension being made, it should be a large one?—Yes, I think so.

325. A mile would you say that was sufficient?—Fully a mile.

326. Do you consider that the farmers within that radius derive advantage from being so near the town?—I am not aware.

327. Mr. Tyrrell.—If the extension should take place, would you be in favour of an increased number of Commissioners, and the creation of wards?—Yes.

Mr. J. Hutton.

Mr. J. Hutton examined.

328. Mr. Robinson.—Are you in favour of an extension?—Yes.

329. To what extent?—A large radius—a mile, if it was extended at all.

330. Have you heard the views of the Commissioners?—Yes.

331. And you coincide with them?—Yes.

332. Would you like to see the sanitary jurisdiction in their hands?—Yes.

333. On what grounds?—It would be an advantage to the town generally, and a saving of expense.

Mr. Samuel Mitchell.

Mr. Samuel Mitchell examined.

334. Mr. Robinson.—Are you a ratepayer of the town?—Yes, and I have property outside.

335. You have heard the evidence given by these gentlemen to-day?—Yes.

336. Do you think an extension desirable?—I don't see what great advantage it would be to the farmers outside.

337. But it would be a benefit to the town?—Yes.

338. And do you think the farmers derive no advantage from being near the town?—What advantage would it be to them to have to pay the rates.

339. I don't say it is an advantage to them, but is it fair they should be asked to contribute something for the advantages they do enjoy?—Well, I know if the farmers were notified of it they would oppose it. They have taxes enough.

340. Do they derive benefit from the lighting of the town?—No, they all go home in the daylight.

341. Mr. Fox.—Mr. M'Master said he paid £150 a year for cleansing, &c. Does he not take the stuff up to his place and use it on his own lands?—I would ask Mr. M'Master that. He says he derives no benefit from the town, but he receives £300 or £400 a year as head landlord out of houses in Gilford.

342. Mr. Tyrrell.—I would ask what revenue do the Town Commissioners get for the sweepings of Gilford?

Mr. M'Connell.—The Town Commissioners do not get it.

343. Mr. Tyrrell.—Have you ever made application to the Grand Jury to flag the streets of the town?

Mr. M'Connell.—No never.

The inquiry then terminated.

KELLS.—TUESDAY, APRIL 29, 1879.

Before Mr. C. P. Cotton, C.E.

Mr. John Nixon examined.

1. You are Clerk of the Town Commissioners?—Yes.

2. How long have you held that position?—About nine years and a half.

3. The town is constituted under the Towns Improvement Act?—Yes.

4. And when was it placed under that Act of 1854?—In the year 1854.

5. Have you any map of the town?—No.

6. Is there anything in the first minutes of the board showing when the boundaries were established by the Lord Lieutenant?—No; I have not.

7. What is the population of Kells, 2,822?—Yes, in 1871.

8. What is the area of the town?—361a. 1r. [illegible] perches.

9. What is the valuation?—£8,[illegible].

10. Is that the valuation of the town for rateable purposes?—Yes.

11. Where did you get the figure of the population?—It was up to 5,000 some time ago, and has been reduced, as much.

12. What do you mean by "some time ago"?—About seventy years ago the population was about 5,000.

13. It is returned in 1879, the valuation is returned as £8,[illegible], and you give it as £8,[illegible] or £8,[illegible]; has it increased?—I think it has, a little.

14. But where did you get your figure of £8,[illegible]?—I got it out of a [illegible].

15. Have you got a Town's Boundary Line?—No.

16. There are no wards in Kells?—No.

17. The town is all in the Electoral Division of Kells?—Yes.

18. There have been no municipal union?—No.

19. Have there ever been any [illegible]?—No.

20. Do you know what the poor rate is?—It is [illegible] in the pound.

21. Can you give me what it was for the past few years?—Well, it was generally an average of from 2s. 6d. to 3s. a year.

22. What is it this year?—2s. 6d.

23. What was it last year?—I think last year it was 2s. 11d.

24. And do you know anything about the years further back?—No.

25. What is the county cess in Kells?—[illegible] in the pound.

26. This half year?—Yes, for the half year.

27. And has it been the same for the past two or three years?—Yes.

28. The municipal body in Kells, I understand, did not require any extension of boundary?—No.

29. Have they authorised you to [illegible] in the [illegible] to any question to that effect?—Yes.

30. How many Commissioners are there?—Fifteen.

31. Was the question settled at any special meeting of the Commissioners?—Yes, at a monthly meeting on Thursday last.

32. How many attended?—I was not there. I will get the minutes. At that meeting some Commissioners attended, including the chairman.

33. Were they unanimous on that meeting?—Yes, they were.

34. Is that relating to a about the boundary?—They were without meaning.

35. Do you know the feeling of the absent Commissioners?—Well, a few of them were talking about it, and were of opinion that there ought to be a slight change in the boundary to have it extended.

36. Why were they of that opinion?—Well, there are a few wells outside the town, and they believe that it would be well to have them under the control of the Commissioners.

42. Is the boundary, generally speaking, a circle round the centre of the town—is it about the same distance in every direction?—No.

43. You have no map of it?—No.

44. How many acres are there?—361.

45. Of that number, how many were [illegible] by the Commissioners?—Well, I think about thirty.

46. About thirty?—Well, I am not quite certain, but I should think about thirty at least.

47. Was the Act adopted entirely, or in part?—Entirely.

48. How is Kells supplied with light?—Well we have a large property.

49. Have you any gasworks?—Yes.

50. They belong to the Commissioners?—No, they belong to a local company.

51. And you contract with them?—Yes.

52. For how many lamps?—We have about [illegible] lamps in the town.

53. How much do you pay for the gas—how much per lamp?—About £[illegible] a year it is.

54. Because in the return for 1879, you only put down £[illegible]?—Yes, but we got an increase of lamps since then—we got about twenty additional lamps since 1877.

55. What kind of water supply is there in Kells, how is it supplied?—It is supplied by pumps. It was considered good till a short time ago, when the Medical Officer of the district condemned the water, as unfit for use. They are thinking of getting up waterworks.

56. The pumps are under the control of the guardians?—Yes, at present, and have been since 1874.

57. Since 1874?—Yes, we have put before Parliament—before the House of Commons, the question of resuming the sanitary authority.

58. Then the Commissioners have considered that question?—Yes.

59. And have they sent in a memorial on the subject?—Yes, they have sent before Parliament.

60. Or to the Local Government Board?—Yes, and it is now before Parliament.

61. Was it been considered by the Local Government Board?—Yes, and the provisional order has been read for the first time in the House.

62. The Commissioners have no responsibility for cleansing and watering the streets?—Yes.

63. How is the town drained?—It is fairly drained.

64. The drainage has been looked after by the guardians?—Yes, at present.

65. What is the poor rate?—[illegible] in the pound.

66. How much of that was specially sanitary rate for sanitary purposes?—It was small.

67. And what was it for?—I think the sanitary rate was not more than [illegible], or [illegible] in the pound.

68. For what purpose?—For the purpose of cleansing the yards, and so on keeping the roads of the town clean.

69. When was the date of the memorial to the Local Government Board?—It was about the 10th of October, last.

70. How far does the boundary extend from the centre—from any the church—does it extend half a mile in any one direction?—Scarcely half a mile—little more than a quarter.

71. Well suppose a circle were struck round the central point, of say a mile radius, it would take in a very large tillage or cattle country?—Yes.

KELLS.
April 27, 1876.
Mr. John Spear.

72. And would there be many gentlemen's houses outside the present town, and within a mile radius?—No.

73. Would it add much to the number of voters who would have a vote?—Yes, a great many land-holders and ratepayers.

74. But you could not tell me roughly how many?—I could not.

75. Would it take in many who would be qualified to sit as Commissioners?—Oh yes, it would take in a good many.

76. But as far as I can see by the map, it does not take in many houses?—No, not very many, but there are a good deal of houses within a mile.

77. Outside of the present town?—Yes.

78. Have the Commissioners ever considered the question, if they take up the duties of, and become the sanitary authority—whether they would wish to take the charge of the roads from the Grand Jury?—No, they did not consider that.

79. But they were aware that they ought to do so?—Yes, likely they would do so.

80. Do you know how far the electoral division of Kells extends?—I do not.

81. Is the land in the immediate neighbourhood of and just outside the present boundary, in the nature of townparks or agricultural holdings?—Townparks.

82. And, of course, is let at a much greater value than land further away?—Yes.

83. Are there any schools in Kells to which farmers' children come from a distance?—Yes, there are.

84. How far would you say they come?—They come, I believe, about two miles.

85. What is the property of the Corporation—or you have no rates you must have some property?—Yes.

86. What does it consist of?—Landed property.

87. And what value is that at present—what are the receipts from it?—Our rental for last year was £1,[illegible] 11s. 2½d.

88. That is from rents?—Yes, rents out of the lands.

89. And houses?—No, we have no house property.

90. Is the land situated within the municipal district or outside it?—Outside it altogether.

91. Has it any particular denomination?—Yes, it is on the townland called Lloyd.

92. How far is it from the town?—The near part of it is about half a mile, and the more distant part about a mile and a half.

93. Do you know the acreage of it?—309 statute acres.

94. Is it under lease altogether?—No, it is fee-simple property.

95. Have you let it on lease?—Yes, about twenty-five acres are let on lease.

96. And the rest from year to year?—Yes.

97. I see that in 1874 the rental was only £1,040, and now it is £30 more?—Yes.

98. What is that from?—Since years the Commissioners have meadow land and it fetches different prices.

99. It is not from the falling in of any lease?—No.

100. And the only portion leased you say is twenty-five acres?—Yes, there are three leases for twenty-five acres.

101. That is, as I understand, about eight acres in each?—Yes, twenty-five acres altogether.

102. And the rest you say is held from year to year?—Yes.

103. And you don't expect any great increase from those leases falling in?—No.

104. What other receipts have you?—Well, we have dog tax.

105. What does that amount to?—£18 6s. 7d.

106. Have you anything from fines?—Yes, £40 10s. 9d.

107. Have you receipts from any other sources?—No.

108. You don't let the Town Hall?—No.

109. I see salaries, &c. returned at £163 12s. 6d. What do they consist of?—Salaries to clerk and surveyor, &c.

110. What is the clerk's salary?—£[illegible] a year.

111. And the surveyor's?—£30 a year.

112. What are the others?—There is herd and caretaker, £70.

113. That is on the land?—Yes, among the lands of Lloyd.

114. What else is there?—Steward, at or about £30.

115. Then there are a few pounds more?—Well, yes, a few pounds of salary to a few more went into arrear.

116. What is the next item?—Lighting, £[illegible] 3s. 10d.; cleansing, £77 12s. 6d.

117. That is cleansing and watering the streets?—Yes.

118. What is the next item?—Labour, £[illegible] 3s. 9d.

119. What is that for?—There is a good deal of labour improving the lands, ditching and fencing, and so on.

120. It represents work done outside the township?—Well, portion of the town work is included in that.

121. But it is principally outside?—Yes, on the borough lands.

122. How much of the borough lands is held by the Commissioners themselves?—All but the twenty-five acres—it is let from year to year to different people.

123. How then does it happen they require to have improvements effected and labour of that kind on the lands?—Well, a deal of it is meadow land, and if a man goes to draw away hay, he probably knocks down ditches and that, and the Commissioners have to build them up again.

124. Then there is not a great deal let from year to year to any one man, but by the season rather?—Yes.

125. And to different people?—Yes.

126. How much do you say is the item for labour?—£200 3s. 9d.

127. As to the water?—Pumps, cost £12 10s. 1d.

128. Is that for new pumps?—No.

129. What, then?—There was a balance for the pump contractor's salary which was handed over to the Board of Guardians. This £13 10s. 1d. remained, which was paid off.

130. Do you mean that it was due since 1874?—No.

131. Have the Commissioners had anything to say to the pumps since 1874?—No.

132. I see they spent in '74 £33 in watering?—Yes.

133. And this is the same sort of charge?—Yes.

134. Is it for new pumps or the maintenance and repairs of pumps, or what?—I think it is for salary of pump contractor.

135. How do the Commissioners come to pay him instead of the Guardians?—Well, I don't know.

136. The account is audited?—Yes.

137. You have a debt on the borough?—Yes.

138. How much?—We had a mortgage debt of £1,200 originally—about that.

139. In 1874 is it put down as £1,600?—Yes, it was £1,400 or £1,600 at that time.

140. And what is it now?—It is reduced to £[illegible].

141. What else was paid in 1876?—There was rent, £83 10s.

142. What was that for?—For some holdings the Commissioners have from Lord Headfort.

143. For what purpose?—For the purpose of the gas works.

144. I thought I understood you to say you contracted for the gas with a company?—Yes, but the Commissioners took it from Lord Headfort and let it to the company.

145. What other expenditure was there?—There was £31 8s. 11½d. paid for poor rate; county cess, £32 18s. 6d.; tithe rent, £16 18s. 3d.; and income tax, £7 5s. 6d. Total, £88 8s. 0½d.

146. Anything else?—Well, there was hay made—

expenditure, £38 6s. 9d.; percentage for levies, £33 6s. 8d.; shed for cattle, £9 16s.; town clock, £10; fence in Lloyd, £3 3s.; new gate for Corporation land, £1 10s.; printing, stationery, &c., £17 11s. 2d.; postage, £1 9s.; and for Town Hall, £9 7s.; election expenses, £5 5s. 7d.

147. Is that election expense municipal expense?—Yes.

148. Mortgage loan, £1,200—paid about £200.

149. What did you pay in '78?—£100.

150. Leaving £900 due?—Yes, after we paid another £100.

151. What else?—Discount on preliminary loan, and interest, £43 15s. 3d.—that is in connection with the land; Local Government Board for audit, £2 2s.; reward to constable in prosecutions, £5; miscellaneous expenses, £19 4s. 7d. Total, £1,171 18s. 6½d. Balance in hands of the treasurer at the close of the year, £261 5s. 8d. At the start of the year it was £112 13s. 8d.

152. When you become the sanitary authority, as you are in course of becoming, will you be able to carry on the sanitary work without striking a rate?—Yes.

153. And how will you provide the money for it?—Out of the Corporation land.

154. You are bound to carry on the reduction of the mortgage debt?—Yes.

155. Is it a payment that must be made?—Yes.

156. If you become the sanitary authority, will you have to strike a special rate?—We expect to have money enough.

157. You think you will have sufficient for the necessary expenditure?—Yes; the £1,171 18s. 6½d. will be enough.

158. What would be about the average for lay ord—you have mentioned that item?—About £38 6s. 9d. It varies. The present year I think it will be about £10 of the usual.

159. What will be the average?—Well, I think about £30.

160. Has the labour bill been always as large as you have given it?—No.

161. What was the labour expenditure in other years?—Sometimes it has been very low. It has been down as low as £30 in some years.

162. And altogether you don't expect to strike a rate when you become the sanitary authority?—We will not.

Kells. April 18, 1879.

Mr. John Kerin.

Mr. NATHANIEL LACY, Clerk of Kells Union, examined.

Mr. Nathaniel Lacy.

164. What is the area of the electoral division of Kells?—3,017 acres.

165. And the valuation?—£10,717.

167. How far can you say it extends?—About a mile and a half or more.

168. In every direction round?—Yes, about a mile and a half.

169. And it is that pretty evenly on all sides?—Yes.

170. Have you the valuation of the township separately?—Yes, it is £3,412.

171. And the acreage?—261 statute acres.

172. Could you tell me the names of the townlands comprised in it—in the township?—Yes, there is Archdeaconry Glebe, containing 9 acres 3 roods, and the rest is all comprised within the townland of Townparks—that is an enormous townland, taking in nearly 251 acres of the town and parks.

173. Have you a map showing the municipal boundary?—No, the Commissioners have maps.

174. Would you let me have the names of the townlands within the electoral division?—The names of the townlands in the electoral division are: Archdeaconry, Cakestown Glebe, Gallaghstown, Commonstown, Commons of Lloyd, Gardenrath, Grangegeeth Glebe, Headford Demesne, Kilmainham, Toltown, Lackwatch, Maudlin, Mountain Pole, Newrath Big and Newrath Little, Rockfield, Sydenarath, Sheeny, Townparks, and White Commons.

177. What has been the poor-rate for the past few years in Kells?—2s. 6d. in the pound.

178. What was it in '78?—2s. 6d.

179. And in '77?—2s. 6d.

180. And '76?—2s. 6d., and from that down to 1s. 3d., but the average was 2s. 6d.

181. Of that 2s. 6d., taking 1878, how much of it was for sanitary purposes?—There was £139 18s. 8d. included for sanitary purposes.

182. How much would that be in the pound?—3d.

183. On what district was that struck?—It was on the entire electoral division of Kells.

184. What was it struck for?—There is great dearth of water in the town, and the sanitary authority began to make improvements in the pumps. There is one in particular that cost a deal of money to get it sunk so as to keep the pollution by sewage away. A large sum was spent on the improvement of that pump.

185. And it was all for work done in the town of Kells, and the rate was struck on the whole electoral division?—Yes, there was one pump put down at Lisknetown.

186. That is outside the municipal district?—Yes, but in the division of Kells.

187. But with the exception of that, the whole of the special sanitary rate was expended on the town itself?—Yes, but of course that expenditure includes the officers' salaries as well, sanitary officer and sub-sanitary officer.

188. Their duties are not confined to the town?—No, they extend over the whole district.

Mr. JOHN HORNIG re-examined.

Mr. John Hornig.

187. I think you said there were schools used by the people for two and a half miles round?—I think so.

188. I suppose there are fairs in Kells?—Yes, twelve in the year.

189. Monthly fairs?—I think about six monthly fairs and six "old fairs."

190. But one in each month?—Yes, but there are old established fairs distinguished from the others, and which they don't call monthly fairs.

191. Well, do you happen to know, as a resident here, what the feeling of the inhabitants is, whether they wish for an extension of the municipal boundary or not?—No, except what I told you of a few gentlemen wishing to have a slight extension to take in the walls.

192. Has there ever been any scheme for a larger supply of water to your town?—No, there has not; but the ratepayers and guardians were talking about getting up waterworks, but the Commissioners have never had any scheme before them.

193. They never had it before them?—No, I believe they intended bringing water from the river, and forming a reservoir on the high grounds.

194. To get a high pressure supply?—Yes.

195. But they never had any estimate before them?—No.

196. Is there any information you wish to give in addition to what you have already said?—No, nothing.

KELLS.
April 20, 18[illegible].

Mr. Patrick Murtagh.

Mr. Patrick Murtagh examined.

196. You are Chairman of the Town Commissioners? —Yes.

197. What are your views on the subject of the extension of the township?—The Town Clerk has exactly stated all the facts.

198. It has been stated by the Town Clerk, that the Commissioners at a meeting last year gave expression unanimously to an opinion in favour of leaving the boundaries just as they are, that they did not in fact want any alteration?—Yes, I was at that meeting.

199. Has there been since then any change in opinion?—Except as to the wells that have been mentioned.

200. And what was the view entertained on that point?—Since the meeting, and as we were looking to get the sanitary authority into our hands again, we saw there were three wells immediately adjoining the boundary, and we believed that it would be well to get those under our control.

201. Can you describe those wells so that I can recognise them on the map?—There is Maltham's well to begin with. Our boundary runs to the left-hand side of it. Then there is St. Columba's well.

202. I understand you to say that it is to get control of those sources of water supply that you wish an extension to be made?—Yes.

203. In any case your object in desiring a slight extension is not to get an additional rate?—No.

204. You consider that you have at present money enough to carry on the work as sanitary authority, as you will do in a few months?—Yes.

205. And that you won't have to strike a rate at all?—No, it is not the wish of any party to strike a rate. We merely want control over those wells so as to keep them in proper order.

206. The Town Clerk I presume was correct in the information showing that the receipt from the borough property is not likely to alter much?—Not much.

207. Will it bring in this year as much as the average?—Well, this year there is rather a falling off, last rent-month. I think there will be some.

208. You know that if there was a falling off and a deficiency you would be obliged to strike a rate for sanitary purposes, when you would become sanitary authority?—I do not think we will.

209. But if you had not the money you would have no option?—I think the property would be well able to carry out the work without any special rate, but, as I stated before, this was an exceptional year and we had to expend more money.

Mr. George Mullen.

Mr. George Mullen examined.

210. You are Commissioner, Mr. Mullen?—Yes.

211. How long have you been a Commissioner?—About three years, or four.

212. Do you think that so long as there is no necessity for a rate, there is no necessity for increasing the boundary?—Yes.

213. But if the rate became necessary?—Yes. I think it would then be well to make some extension.

214. Do you think the people who live within, say a mile of the town, derive exceptional advantages from being so near the markets and fairs of Kells?—Certainly I do.

215. And do you think that if a rate was required for the maintenance of anything in the town—the maintenance of streets, sewers, or gas, they should be expected to pay something towards it?—Yes.

216. These outsiders get the advantages of the cleansing of the streets, the water of the town, and so on?—Yes.

217. And their children the advantages of the schools?—Yes.

218. You are aware, of course, that if any portion was taken into the town, as far as the town improvement expenditure is concerned, the lands would only be rated at one-fourth the valuation?—Yes.

219. And that you think would be fair?—Yes.

220. In some places they think they should pay one-half, they derive so much advantage?—I do not think we will ever have to strike a rate.

221. Was the expenditure of last year on the lands of Lloyd such an expenditure as will bring you an increased rental?—It will increase the value of the lands of Lloyd, and improve the rent.

222. Is the land let by auction or how?—Partly by auction, and the rents fixed by the Commissioners.

223. Why should it be partly by auction?—I will give an instance of what I mean. If there is a field going to be set in cuts in conacre, that is put up for competition, and if it is going to be set for the accommodation of the town, it is put up in that way, and an opportunity is given to people to set potatoes in small lots. Then the cattle—the usual way, the Commissioners go there and have a price on the cattle according to size. There are a great deal of complaints, no doubt—people saying the charges are too high.

224. Do you think if there was an extension—of what other towns have proposed in a great many instances—such as a mile all round the centre of the town—it would bring in many additional gentlemen who would be eligible to be Commissioners?—No, I do not; for there is a great deal of the land it would take in owned by people who live in the town, and others who cultivate it live in the town.

225. Would it add much to the number of voters?—No, I don't think so, where they all mostly live in the town.

226. One hundred and thirty-six, I think you said, was the number of voters?—Yes.

227. And would it increase that?—No, I don't believe so.

228. Is the railway station within the boundary?—It is just on the verge of the boundary.

229. Then you don't want an extension for the purpose of getting control over the cars at the station, or anything like that?—No; we have nothing to do with the cars. I don't think, about going a mile out, that it would be at all a good thing to do in Kells.

230. Supposing it was deemed to be right for the purposes of a rate, supposing that a rate was ever found to be necessary, what extension would you contemplate?—About half-a-mile from the centre of the town—no one, I believe, would object to that.

231. Would there be any objection on the part of the present inhabitants of Kells, or of the Commissioners, to such an extension?—No; I do not see that there would be any objection to it.

232. There is no reason against it?—No; and it would give us control of the stream running through the town, which is a drinking place for cattle. At present it is being polluted. It is a stream running through John-street.

233. And it is polluted outside the present boundary?—Yes.

234. For you will have control over it when you become sanitary authority in your own boundary?—Yes. As to the pollution, there are dead dogs thrown in it, and so on, and there should be put a stop to what is it running through the town.

235. I think I am right in saying that when you have the sanitary authority in your hands, you will have the power of stopping that, no matter whether the stream is in your own bounds or not; as you can compel the guardians to do the same as if you had control of it yourself?

236. Would all the wells that have been mentioned be taken in by a half-mile extension from the centre

of the town?—Yes, I think so; and I may say it might be of advantage in another way. [illegible]

[illegible] That is why I asked you [illegible]. Would it be desirable to extend the boundary for the purpose you have indicated?—Yes, for that reason.

[illegible] The Commissioners [illegible]?—No.

[illegible] Now have you the description of the boundary of the old [illegible] as it appeared in the [illegible], advertised [illegible] March 17, [illegible]; and was subsequently published [illegible] of April [illegible] [Witness handed in that copy of [illegible] with following extract [illegible]:—

"Boundary of Borough as advertised, March 17, [illegible].

"Commencing [illegible] [illegible]"

Mr. George Walters [illegible]

[illegible] I understand the Commissioners [illegible]?—No, never, because they always had sufficient to carry on the work [illegible].

[illegible] And if they are done, what would they do [illegible]?—They would borrow.

[illegible] They did not apply for an extension for police purposes or otherwise?—No; [illegible] [illegible]

Mr. John G. [illegible] examined.

Mr. John G. [illegible]

[illegible] You are a ratepayer?—Yes; and I would say, with reference to one [illegible], that it has been mentioned here that it was contemplated erecting waterworks for supplying the town with water; I wish to give it as my individual opinion that such a proceeding is quite unnecessary and would be a reckless [illegible] and likely to impose a serious burden on the ratepayers.

[illegible] [illegible] [illegible] [illegible]

[illegible] Then do you think there is to be derived any benefit from extending the present area?—I think it would certainly be of great importance that the Commissioners should have control [illegible] over these [illegible] wells. At present, I believe they have no legal control over [illegible].

[illegible] Do you [illegible] the wells [illegible]?—Yes. They have no control over the wells.

Do you [illegible] the wells [illegible], or do you contemplate the Commissioners [illegible] the wells? I think it would be [illegible] of very great importance, that the legal custody of the wells should vest in the Commissioners.

[illegible] Whatever may be the power you might obtain over them, it is quite clear you have no control over them as long as they are without the boundary?—Quite so.

Mr. Samuel A. [illegible], Town Commissioner and Poor Law Guardian, examined.

Mr. Samuel A. [illegible]

[illegible] With reference to the extension of the boundary, it has been stated that it would be advisable to have the area enlarged with a view of having certain wells brought within the municipal control of the Commissioners?—Yes, the Board of Guardians [illegible] have [illegible] one well, and [illegible] within the old boundary of the Corporation. That I believe, but there is no perfect proof of it. However, there was a boundary on a map within [illegible], so I think it would be well to have a new boundary and have [illegible] well, [illegible] well, at the end of [illegible] and [illegible] well brought in.

[illegible] Bring it [illegible]?—Yes.

The inquiry terminated.

LETTERKENNY.—AUGUST 11, 1879.

Before Mr. H. A. Robinson.

Mr. John Sweeney examined.

1. You are the Town Clerk of Letterkenny?—I am.

2. The town is constituted under the Towns' Improvement Act?—Yes.

3. Which was adopted, I understand, in 1854?—Yes.

4. Previous to that was it under any other Act?—No.

5. Was it adopted for all purposes, or only for lighting and cleansing?—Only for lighting and cleansing.

6. How many townlands does the town include?—Letterkenny only.

7. Are there no portions of other townlands included?—No—except one portion, which was then supposed to be part and portion of Letterkenny—anyway it was included.

8. Is that part now rated for municipal purposes?—Yes.

9. What prompted the Commissioners to select the present boundary?—Well, there were no Commissioners at the time.

10. Yes, but was there a meeting of ratepayers to consider the subject?—Yes. It originated with Mr. Sweeny, Mr. Murray, and myself, and one or two others, and the object then in view was to get lighting and cleansing—to get lighting, I may say, for we were in the dark then.

11. Did you adopt the townland boundary as now existing because you considered it to be a well defined boundary?—Yes, it was well defined, but the reason was, that as the gas was supposed to apply to the town, the town should pay for it.

12. How far from the centre of the town on each side does the municipal boundary extend?—Well, I can hardly say exactly.

13. Take the east and west, I should say (looking at the map), a little over a quarter of a mile?—I dare say, about that. You have the river firstly the boundary of the townland.

14. What is the area of the town?—401 a. 2r. 15p. That, I should say, includes the present holding of Mr. William Patterson, in Gortlee, outside the townland.

15. What is the area of Mr. Patterson's holding, do you know?—It is about 13a. 0r. 0p., statute measure.

16. And, can you tell me the population of Letterkenny?—The population, as far as I can make it out, is 2,116.

17. Would you say that that is an increasing population?—Well, I knew the time when it was more.

18. When it was more?—Yes, but that was owing to the union in the workhouse.

19. Did the census of 1871 show an increase or decrease as compared with the census of 1861?—I am not prepared to say, just now.

20. What is your opinion as to what it is likely to be in 1881—will it be greater or less. You can only give a surmise, of course?—Yes, well I am rather inclined to think it will show an increase, but it will be a very small one. There are a great many small houses going down, and a good many large ones springing up. I think, indeed, it will be very much the same.

21. Will you give me the valuation of the total municipal boundary? The total within the municipal boundary in land is £836 1s.

22. And in buildings?—In buildings it is £2,101. Then there are half annual rates amounting to £171 6s., giving a total of £3,179.

23. In what electoral division is the town of Letterkenny?—In Letterkenny division.

24. How far north of the town does the electoral division extend?—About a mile and a half.

25. On the south, how far?—That is very short, for it is met by the river—about a quarter of a mile.

26. If you took from the centre of the town a new boundary radius of, say a mile, how many electoral divisions would it go into if you included all the townlands hit by that circle?—You would cross the water there, and we would be in Corkey and Magheraboy.

27. I want to know the number of electoral divisions the radius would then touch?—All on the north would be in the electoral division of Letterkenny. On the south it would be in another—it would be in Carrigbreddy and Ballymacool.

28. Then it would touch two besides the present one of Letterkenny?—Yes.

29. What is the valuation of the electoral division of Letterkenny?—£3,531 14s.

30. I should mention to you that the Select Committee in their report suggested to us that it would be desirable to make towns coterminous with electoral divisions—to adopt electoral divisions in fact as the municipal boundaries.—In many cases, however, it was found that that would be altogether too much. Are there any districts around or nearly adjoining Letterkenny that you could describe as suburbs of the town?—No. There are residences, a few such as Mr. Boyd's and Major Patterson's.

31. But as far as I can see Mr. Boyd's is outside the electoral division?—Yes, you are quite right, but the other is inside.

32. Then if the electoral division was included there would be only a one-fourth rate struck, with one or two exceptions?—Yes, exactly; principally, nearly all agricultural land.

33. The municipal and Poor Law boundary is the same, with the exception of this small holding of Mr. Patterson's?—Yes.

34. Give me the municipal ratings for the past five years—from '74?—In '74, 10d.; '75, 10d., in '76, 10d.; '77, 10d.; '78, 8d.

35. And the county cess?—I had some difficulty in making out that, for it is twice in the year. For the same years it would run:—'74, 3s. 6d.; '75, 3s. 1d.; '76, 3s. 11d.; '77, 3s. 8d.; '78, 3s. 10d.

36. And the Poor Law?—It runs 1s. 6d., 1s. 3d., 1s. 6d., and 2s.

37. In that Poor Law rate was there anything for sanitary purposes?—There was in that last three years. There was a rate of 6d., and last year 8d., for water.

38. What are the contributory districts over which that is struck?—Simply the municipal boundary.

39. The guardians then were of opinion that any advantages which were derived from the supply of water did not extend to those outside the municipal boundary?—Yes.

40. Have the Commissioners ever considered the question of becoming the urban sanitary authority, under section 7 of the Public Health Act?—The subject was just broached, but there was nothing but a slight ventilation of it, for after mature consideration it was considered premature.

41. Are the Commissioners in any way dissatisfied with the way the guardians do the work entrusted to their jurisdiction?—I certainly never heard a complaint.

42. It is only in cases where the Poor Law Union is several miles from the town that we hear of dissatisfaction?—Yes, here the guardians meet more frequently than the Commissioners.

43. Are the Commissioners aware that under the provisions of the same Act (the Public Health Ire-

LETTERKENNY. Jan. 13, 1879.

Mr. John Ramsay.

land; do these powers are given to the Local Government Board by provisional order to grant a separation from the Grand Jury, and to take from them the control over the roads without the consent of the Grand Jury?—Well, I am not so sure that the Commissioners are aware of that.

45. Previous to the passing of that Act the Grand Jury could put their veto upon such a proposition and say they would not consent. Now, however, the Commissioners are enabled by the 206th section of the Act to effect the separation. Is it the opinion of the Board that the town would be better managed under one independent Board if they had the power vested in them?—They never considered that. It is a serious question to answer at once.

46. But it never came before them?—No.

47. Now as to extension, are the Commissioners satisfied with the present boundaries?—Yes.

48. Has the matter been formally before them?—Well, it has never been publicly agitated by the Commissioners.

49. We sent you down some queries. Were these submitted to a general meeting of the Board, or was there a special meeting?—There was no special meeting. The opinion was that no change was desirable.

50. Did they not think the people outside the present limits derive advantages from their proximity to the town?—Well, I think myself they ought to think so.

51. Is not the land outside more valuable from its proximity to the town?—Yes, in all cases I should say land is more valuable near a town.

52. Are there markets in the town?—Yes, weekly markets.

53. Are there schools in the town?—Yes, admirable schools.

54. What are your arrangements for lighting?—Well, we begin on the 1st of September, and light to the end of, or rather to the 12th of May. We do not continue to give light in the summer time.

55. How much do you pay the gas company?—We now pay a special rate. The amount per lamp would not be £2. We pay £70.

56. In the dark nights in summer do you light the lamps?—No, never.

57. I take it in fact then, that you don't light in the dark nights of summer, but you do light in the moonlight nights of winter?—Yes.

58. Do the people within the whole electoral division use the town as a market town?—Yes.

59. Do they dispose of their produce here?—Yes, except, perhaps, some that go with flax and pork to Strabane.

60. Do they send their children to school in the town?—Yes, I suppose the major part of them do.

61. You say all the people within the electoral division use the town of Letterkenny?—Yes.

62. You think the Commissioners would object to include the electoral division?—Well, yes.

63. As being unremunerative?—Yes, and being obliged to light out to the extreme ends.

64. But from their proximity, should they not be asked to contribute the one-fourth towards keeping up the lighting of the town, and so on?—I would not like to say that. They derive a little benefit no doubt if they walk in.

65. Is the entire town built on, within the municipal limits?—Oh, no.

66. Have you sufficient land within the municipal boundary for building operations to be carried on for many years to come?—Yes.

67. Does the town show a tendency to increase in any one direction?—I could hardly say it increased or was increasing much in any direction.

68. Is the supply of water in the town good?—Yes, splendid.

69. If under the 7th sec. of the Public Health (Ireland) Act the Commissioners were to become the urban sanitary authorities, are there any improvements they would carry out which the Guardians do not do at present?—No, I cannot anticipate any. I think the Guardians show every desire to do what they can.

70. Are there any improvements required which the Town Commissioners are deterred from carrying out from want of funds?—I don't see any that they would attempt if they had funds. Not at present, any way.

71. Have you ascertained the feelings of the ratepayers as to extension?—Well, I never heard any very decided expression on it.

72. Were they aware that this Commission was being held?—Yes, I published it, and you did so.

73. And do you think if there was any strong desire for extension entertained, they would have come here?—Well, I know they received every warning.

74. Now, take the townlands of Ballygrean, Ballyboedoonan, and Gortlee, would there be any objection to including them within the present boundary?—Well, I am not aware that there would be any objection on the part of the Commissioners.

75. It never suggested itself?—No.

76. Well, do you know who are the proprietors of those townlands?—Ballygrean is Lord Southwell's and Mr. Boyd.

77. And Ballyboedoonan?—I am agent for that. It is Mr. Fewsett's.

78. And Gortlee?—That is Major Patterson's, Mr. William Patterson's, Mr. Ramsay's, and others.

79. Do the people in these townlands come in very often to Letterkenny?—Oh, I think so.

80. And must it not be of advantage to them to keep the town well cleansed?—Well, yes.

81. Well cleansed and lighted?—Yes, to be well lighted must be of advantage to people coming into market, and well cleansed, is of course, good for any one who wants to walk cleanly.

82. Do the people living there or any of them possess holdings in the town?—Well, Mr. Boyd does, a vast deal. I don't know any one in Ballyboedoonan who has a holding in the town.

83. And in Gortlee?—Yes, there is Mr. Ramsay.

84. I may take it, however, that within these limits there are people who make considerable use of the town, and that some of them pay taxes, and some do not?—Yes.

Mr. John Robert Boyd examined.

Mr. John Robert Boyd.

85. You are the Chairman of the Town Commissioners?—Yes.

86. Were you one of the first Commissioners?—Yes.

87. And you have been a resident here?—Yes.

88. Can you tell the reason why this townland of Letterkenny was adopted as the boundary?—Principally because that was the whole of what derived any benefit from the town.

90. And is that your opinion?—Yes.

91. Do you think Letterkenny is a thriving town?—Yes.

92. Do you think as years come round there will be any villa residences or suburban seats built out beyond the town?—No. It is much more likely that there will be an increase within the town. Lately there have been some good buildings. The Hibernian Bank has built an excellent building. There is the police barrack and several good dwellings. It is a very improving town.

93. Were any of the buildings or villas outside built previous to the town coming under the Act, or after?—Previous.

94. So that I may take it, none of these houses were built to evade municipal taxes?—None.

95. Were you present when these queries were sent down, and were submitted to your Board?—No. I don't think they were submitted to any general meeting of the Commissioners.

96. Do you think, Mr. Boyd, that there is sufficient land available for building purposes within the boundary for many years to come?—Yes.

97. You live at Ballymacool?—Yes.

98. Outside the electoral division?—Yes.

99. If an extension were made in accordance with the recommendation of the Select Committee, would you have any objection to be included—to that townland being included?—Well, I don't think they derive any benefit from the town to justify that being done.

100. Do the residents there use the town for market purposes?—Yes.

101. And do they not use the schools—sending in their children to them?—Yes, some do.

102. And do they not dispose of their produce there in every way?—Yes.

103. But you think they should not be included within the municipal limits?—Well, I really do not see any occasion or ground sufficient for it. As to schools, I may say that most of those about there do not use the schools in the town, for I have a school there to which most of the children go.

104. You heard me say that under the Public Health Act the Commissioners can get a separation from the Board of Guardians?—Yes.

105. Would that, in your opinion, be desirable?—No, the Board of Guardians meet more regularly, and on the spot.

106. And you think the guardians being on the spot, they have every facility for keeping the town in a sanitary condition than the Commissioners who do not meet so often?—Yes.

107. Are you acquainted with the electoral division?—Yes.

108. Do you think the suggestion of the Select Committee can be carried out in this respect, that the electoral division boundary can be adopted as the boundary of the town; could that be done?—No, not with advantage to Letterkenny. I think the people in Carnamaugh Upper, for instance, do not derive sufficient advantages. They seldom come into the town when lighted.

109. But they come into the churches to worship, and so on, and should they not pay something towards the maintenance of the town?—Well, it is so very small.

110. The town is in a flourishing condition as to finance?—Yes.

111. You never exceed the full rate?—No.

112. And Mr. Storey says there is no occasion for expending more money?—No, there is no necessity for it.

113. This is your individual opinion?—Yes.

114. And the opinion of the Board of Commissioners?—I think it is probable that some of them will assent to it.

Mr. Edward M'Fadden examined.

115. You are a Commissioner?—Yes.

116. And you live in Letterkenny?—Yes.

117. And are well acquainted with it?—Pretty well.

118. Have you been a Commissioner for a length of time?—A good many years. With regard to the market I was going to say that one individual gets the entire produce of the town of Letterkenny.

119. Who is that?—Mr. Boyd, he gets the tolls and dues.

120. Well we have nothing to say to that. What is your opinion on the question?—I believe that if the town was taken into the hands of the Commissioners—the town generally and Mr. Boyd be offered a fair price for his expenditure and that, we could take care of ourselves.

121. Do you think the affairs of the town would be better managed under one authority than three?—I think so, certainly.

122. Did you hear about these queries being sent down to the Commissioners?—Yes, I knew of their being laid on the table.

123. Do you coincide with Mr. Storey and Mr. Boyd?—I have nothing to say against what they said, but if we had the town in our own hands and that Mr. Boyd would take a fair price we could place ourselves in a better position than at present.

124. Do you know the electoral division?—Pretty well.

125. If we adopt it as the boundary do you think the population would be brought up to 5,000?—No, not for ages or centuries to come.

126. You don't think any extension advisable?—No.

Dr. William Dunlop examined.

127. Have you any holdings outside the boundary?—No.

128. Do you think the people outside would object to be brought in?—I think so.

129. On account of coming under the management of the Town Commissioners?—I think so.

130. But they make every use of the town, they make no objection to come in and use the town, but they do object to pay the rates?—Quite right.

131. You think the present boundary suitable and well defined?—Yes.

Mr. William Patterson examined.

132. I see that the boundary is a [illegible] townland boundary, Mr. Patterson, plus a corner of your holding—what is the reason of that?—I cannot assign any reason. I know I pay town rates.

133. You acknowledge my reason?—No, my father before me paid rates and I [illegible] to pay municipal rates.

134. Do you know how it happened, Mr. Storey?—Mr. Storey.—No; the boundary was settled on the townland of Letterkenny, it was marked out on the map as it now stands with Mr. Patterson in, and was sent up to the Castle and adopted. I think myself it was a mistake of Mr. Montgomery. He thought the holding was within the townland.

135. Have you a copy of the Gazette defining the boundary?—No, but I will send it to you.

136. Have you (Mr. Patterson) ever asked to see the Gazette defining the boundary?—No.

137. If your holding was not included in the limits it does not matter what value they sent up to the Castle you are exempt from taxes I should say. Now would you have any objection to having the entire townland of [illegible] brought in?—Not if others are similarly included.

Major PATTERSON, [illegible], examined.

[illegible] — What would you say to including Ballygrain, [illegible] — I would have [illegible] objection.

[illegible] — I would have every objection.

[illegible] — [illegible] nothing to add.

The inquiry then terminated.

LIMAVADY.—JULY 15TH, 1879.

Before Mr. HENRY A. ROBINSON.

Mr. ALEXANDER M'KELVEY examined.

1. You are the Clerk of the Town Commissioners? —Yes.

2. How long have you held that position? —[illegible]

3. [illegible] — [illegible] in 18[illegible].

4. [illegible] — Yes, it was governed by the Act of George IV.

[illegible]

Limavady. May [illegible], 18[illegible]. Mr. Alexander [illegible].

[illegible], and along the said fence to Mr. M'Causland's plantation in [illegible]; thence along the boundary [illegible] and [illegible] land [illegible] belonging to William [illegible], Esq., to the old road leading from Newtown to [illegible] [illegible], and along the end of the [illegible] [illegible] Major [illegible] and Major M'Causland's [illegible] and along the said [illegible] to the new Coleraine road at [illegible] [illegible], thence across the new Coleraine road to the [illegible] [illegible] [illegible] of Lands [illegible] Alexander, Esq., and along said [illegible] to the [illegible] between Mr. [illegible] and [illegible] Hill and along said [illegible] to Mr. [illegible] Alexander's [illegible] of [illegible] Hill; thence along the fence at the top of [illegible] Hill to the [illegible] between the Rev. J. [illegible] field and Rev. J. [illegible] garden, along said fence to the [illegible] [illegible] across the [illegible] to the road leading from [illegible] to Dungiven; thence across the Dungiven road to a field in the possession of Edward Smith, Esq., and along the fence between said field of Edward Smith and [illegible], one belonging to William [illegible] and the other to [illegible] Boyle, Esq., to the [illegible] Mill road. Thence down the [illegible] Mill road and across the same to the boundary between the townlands of [illegible] and [illegible], and thence along said boundary to the [illegible] [illegible]."

42. Are there any suburbs within the present boundary?—There are.

43. And I presume that people from outside the boundary are in the habit of sending their children in, and taking advantage of these schools?—Yes.

44. And in that way, of course, make use of the town?—Certainly.

45. Are there any persons carrying on business or having their offices in the town of Limavady, and who have their residences outside?—I think just one or two, though I am not quite sure of that—there are certainly not many—very few.

46. At which side of the boundary are these few with residences?—They would be on the North side—but they are [illegible] [illegible] [illegible] [illegible] [illegible].

47. I may take it then, I suppose, that it is all [illegible] land outside the present boundary?—Yes.

48. And are there any building [illegible] of land outside that boundary?—Not any I would say.

49. Is there in point of fact any tendency to build in any direction outside the existing limits of the town?—No. I would say none—but any that there exist, or may exist, is in the direction of the railway, towards the North side. There have been very few new buildings erected.

50. Would you say the population of Limavady was an increasing population?—No, I would not.

51. Would you be inclined to think that when the census is [illegible] in 1891 it will be found there has kept up [illegible]?—Not much, very little, I should say.

52. Are there any mills or manufactories here?—No, practically none.

53. Then I may take it that all the people who have their daily avocations within Limavady, live within the town?—Yes, all do.

54. Are you in any way [illegible] with the Electoral division?—No, [illegible]. [illegible] [illegible] is [illegible], I think.

55. Have the Town Commissioners ever considered the question of [illegible] the [illegible] [illegible] in [illegible]?—Not to any [illegible] [illegible].

56. Have they ever, at their meetings passed any [illegible] on the subject?—No, but in [illegible] why the matter has been [illegible] amongst the local.

57. And do you know the feeling of the Commissioners on the subject?—Well, I believe there is [illegible] [illegible] on their part to increase the [illegible] [illegible] [illegible] [illegible] [illegible] [illegible], [illegible] that [illegible] [illegible] [illegible] [illegible] [illegible] [illegible] [illegible] [illegible], the landlord and [illegible] paying part.

58. Have you any idea as to the feeling of the people in [illegible]?—Well, I don't think they have any feeling on the subject.

59. What is the population?—About 3,000.

60. If you took the area that an extension of say a mile all round would give you, that would not, I presume, increase the population anything like 3,000, so as to constitute you an urban sanitary authority?—No, it would not.

61. Have the Town Commissioners ever considered the question of taking up the roads?—Yes, they have, and it is, perhaps, the only thing they would ask. They are [illegible] [illegible] to have control of the roads.

62. Do they think if they got the roads placed directly and entirely under their own control, they could manage them without difficulty?—Yes, they think they could manage them very much better than they are managed under the present system.

63. And more economically?—Yes, more economically.

64. They think that the town does not get value for the money they pay for the keeping of these roads [illegible]?—[illegible].

65. What is the county cess?—1s. to 1s. 6d.

66. And, have you any idea what it has been in the past five years?—On an average, almost 1s. 6d.—I don't think it has been less than 1s. 4d.

67. Have you lived long in this town?—More than thirty years.

67. And you therefore know it well, I suppose?—Yes.

68. What is your own opinion on the subject of extension; do you think an extension is required?—No, I think the present boundary, if anything, is rather too large.

69. Would your opinion be, then, that it is desirable in any way to shift the boundary?—No, I think it should be [illegible] as it is.

70. But, if you were obliging a boundary once again, you would not take in so much as is at present [illegible] within the limits of the present area?—No, if I could get a defined boundary without it.

Mr. W. P. Hunter. [margin note, partly illegible]

Mr. W. P. Hunter examined.

71. You are Clerk of the Union?—Yes.

72. How long have you held that position?—About thirty years.

73. Do you know the extent of the electoral division?—Yes.

74. How far does it extend on the north?—More than half a mile.

75. And on the south?—It would be, taking more, nearly a mile; but it is very irregular.

76. And on the east, how far?—About half a mile.

77. And on the west?—Well, much the same.

78. Can you give me the names of the townlands within the existing boundary?—Yes, there is [illegible], and [illegible] of [illegible]—some of [illegible] and [illegible].

79. What is the area of the electoral division?—[illegible] [illegible]. [illegible].

80. And what is the population?—I could not say that.

81. What is the valuation?—£7,[illegible] [illegible].

82. What have been the poor rates for the past five years?—Well the average has been 1s., or rather more, 1s. 3d.

83. Have you been long in Limavady?—Yes, all my lifetime.

84. Do you consider it a flourishing town?—Pretty fair. It is just a pretty fair business town.

85. Do you consider the town is extending, or do you think there is no tendency to straggle or sprawl, if I may use the term, beyond the borders of the boundary?—No.

86. Would it be, in your opinion, possible or not to make the electoral division the boundary?—No, it would be too large, I think. I would say it would be unfair to the farming classes outside.

87. Still, it is not your opinion that the persons residing within the limits of the electoral division derive

[illegible] advantages from their vicinity to the town?—Oh yes, no doubt.

89. And almost beyond it?—Yes, perhaps so.

90. To the extent of two miles would you say the inhabitants derive exceptional advantages from their proximity?—Well no, I would not say they derive great advantages.

91. Does the electoral division, in the town returned, extend more than over a mile from the Town Hall?—I don't think any part of it does.

92. I understand that portions of K[illegible], Bally[illegible], and Clonbrone are outside. Now, if the recommendation were brought in, would there be many holdings in that way added to the town?—No.

93. Take Clonbrone. Could you tell me the acreage of Clonbrone outside the present boundary?—It is nearly all outside.

94. We may take it roughly that there is 142 acres within the proposed boundary?—Yes.

95. Could you give the acreage of [illegible] outside the municipal boundary?—About 100 acres.

96. And of K[illegible]?—About 100 acres.

97. Can you let me have the valuation roughly of the portions of those townlands that are outside of the municipal boundary?—Of Clonbrone there are 142 acres outside, the valuation of which is £[illegible]; of [illegible], [illegible] acres, [illegible]; valuation £[illegible]; [illegible], [illegible] acres, valuation £[illegible].

98. Don't you think it would be of advantage to have townlands brought inside the boundary of the municipal district?—In my opinion, the present boundary is sufficient.

Mr. William Wilson examined.

Mr. William Wilson.

99. You are the Chairman of the Lismore Town Commissioners, I understand?—Yes.

100. And I believe you were a member of the Board for some time before you became the Chairman?—Yes.

101. You live within the present boundary?—Yes; I have my place in town.

102. Do you think Lismore, as a town, is likely to increase within the next few years?—No.

103. And do you think the present town of Lismore likely to be built on or extended outside its present limits?—No.

104. You have heard what I asked Mr. [illegible] relating to the recommendation of the Select Committee of the House of Commons, that the electoral division might be adopted as the municipal area?—The electoral division would be quite too large.

105. And are you, as Chairman of the Board, aware that is their opinion?—Yes. The Board are of opinion the boundaries should be left undisturbed. I should say that they have not considered the question of the electoral division in any detail; but, prior to the time of my becoming a Commissioner, the proposition of making a township boundary was considered, and that was rejected in consequence of its being utterly impracticable.

106. Would you be in favour of bringing in the portions of those townlands at present outside the boundary, and making them part of the municipal district?—I believe the Commissioners would have no objection to that, but that they feel they would be in [illegible] bound to give more benefits for the [illegible] [illegible] by such an extension, lighting, watering, and so on, and they could not do that.

107. Would they feel themselves bound to give light?—Well, they would consider it only fair to do the best they could.

108. Is every house of Lismore lighted to the limits, and to the limits of the town?—Nearly.

109. And out to Ballinamony?—Yes.

110. Bringing in the bits of those townlands I have mentioned would cause an addition of some 350 acres, and do I understand you to say that your Commissioners would be prepared to take in those outlying districts, provided they were not bound to supply them with those additional advantages enjoyed by the town?—There would be no objection to rectify the boundary if necessary, by taking in those little bits, if they did not think themselves bound in honour to extend those advantages.

111. And those benefits, I understand, you would not be prepared to give them?—We could not.

112. Are there any improvements you would like to carry out that are now not carried out [illegible] want of funds?—The chief improvements we desire is a change from having the streets vested in the Grand Jury.

113. But under the jurisdiction vested in you as the municipal body, there are no particular improvements you are unable to carry out?—I should say none, inasmuch as there is really no improvement that we wish, save with reference to the sanitary authority; we would much prefer to have the entire authority in ourselves.

114. Has your Board ever considered at their meetings the desirability of becoming the urban sanitary authority?—It was the general feeling that they should have more power than they have.

115. That is your independent opinion as an individual inhabitant of the town, and as Chairman of the Board?—Yes.

116. And do you anticipate that you will take steps to obtain the Provisional Order from the Local Government?—It is very probable.

117. You desire chiefly, I presume, that in order to get your separation from the Board, they as to get charge of the roads yourselves, you must first become the urban sanitary authority?—Yes.

118. And would you think that desirable?—Yes.

119. And therefore you would like to become urban sanitary authority as a preliminary to taking up the roads?—Yes.

120. You would like to have the full authority over everything within the town?—Yes.

121. Do you find the Guardians ready to do what is asked of them?—Well, they have never been asked. The thing hinges upon the powers vested in them too essentially; that was passed making them the sanitary authority.

122. Is the drainage of this town good?—It is good.

123. Are any gentlemen's mansions built outside the town, any demesnes?—Yes. Perhaps two or three.

124. And do they do marketing in Lismore or in Lismore?—Here.

125. And do you think it quite fair that those people outside should derive advantage from their proximity to the town and contributing nothing towards it, even if you gave them nothing in exchange?—We think that they might, perhaps, be asked to contribute for those advantages, but indeed I don't know that it would be quite fair to ask them if we did not extend the advantages.

LONGFORD. July 18, 1879.

Mr. R. H. Lane.

Mr. R. H. Lane examined.

125. Do you think it would be practicable or advisable to have the electoral division and the municipal boundaries the same?—No.

126. Do you think the boundary would be too large?—Much too large.

127. Do you think the people within that district derive an advantage from being so close to the town? —Nothing in such a degree as to justify their being taxed in connexion with the town.

128. You don't think they ought to be taxed?—No.

129. You think it perfectly fair that they should use the town and yet pay nothing?—Well, probably the same advantages you refer to would extend to people two miles off. If you extend the boundary two miles, or to the limits of the electoral division, I think it would be unfair.

130. Are not the lands adjoining the municipal boundary more valuable than lands further out?—For townparks, perhaps, yes, but not for agricultural purposes. Two miles out the land might be more valuable for townparks than three or four miles out.

131. Do you live in the town?—Yes.

132. And have you lived here for some time?—Yes.

133. And you don't think the present boundary likely to be built on to any extent for some time to come?—Certainly not.

Mr. W. R. Fawcett.

Mr. W. R. Fawcett, Deputy County Surveyor, examined.

134. You can say whether there are any buildings, or leases for buildings, likely to be commenced or effected towards the borders of the municipal area, or extending outside the present boundary?—I see no prospect of it.

135. For how many years, do you think, the area and district will, in all probability, remain without any further extension of buildings?—I don't believe it will ever be built on.

The inquiry then terminated.

LONGFORD. Oct. 1, 1879.

LONGFORD.—OCTOBER 1st, 1879.

Before Mr. Henry A. Robinson.

Mr. Christopher Cox.

Mr. Christopher Cox, Clerk to the Town Commissioners and Clerk of the Union, examined.

1. Longford is under the Town Improvement Act of 1854?—Yes.

2. When was the Act adopted?—I am thirteen years connected with the Commissioners, and during that time it was under it. It was since 1851, I think.

3. Was it adopted for all purposes?—Yes.

4. Previous to that was it under any other statute? —I believe it was under the 9th of George IV.

5. Are the boundaries now existing the same as existed under the 9th of George IV.?—No; there was some alteration made in it by the Towns Improvement Act.

6. Was the boundary under the 9 George IV. more extensive than the present?—I cannot tell.

7. Has there been alteration since 1854?—No, none.

8. What is the area of the town?—[illegible] 1r. 39p.

9. And how far does the town extend on the north from the centre of the town?—It does not extend half a mile on an average all round. In some directions it exceeds half a mile, but in others it does not go a quarter.

10. Does the town include any portions of townlands?—It includes three townlands, including the town proper and also portions of four others.

11. What are the names of the townlands partly included?—These are Townparks, Aghadegnan, Dean's Curragh, and Glack.

12. What is the area of the portions of these within the boundary?—In Aghadegnan I cannot give the area, but the valuation within the borough is only £35, and £156 10s. without. Dean's Curragh without the township, £15 15s. valuation, and within the township, £138. Glack, within the township, £43 15s., and without, £103 1s. Townparks, without the boundary, £79, and within, £5,468 15s.

13. What is the total valuation?—£8,886 15s.

14. And on how much of that is the full rate struck? —The 1s. rate on £5,923 12s., and the one-fourth rate on £263 17s.

15. Longford is divided into wards?—Yes, two wards, Abbeycartron and Longford.

16. In what electoral division is the town?—In Longford.

17. If a radius of one mile was taken all round from the centre of the town, would it cut into another electoral division?—Yes, it would.

18. In which direction?—It would cut into two—into Cloonfin and Oghil.

19. What is the valuation of the electoral division of Longford?—£11,712.

20. And the area?—7,349 acres.

21. Were your Board aware of the fact that the Select Committee made a recommendation that, so far as possible, the towns should be made coterminous with Poor Law boundaries?—Yes, and held a meeting after we got notice.

22. Are there any wards for Poor Law purposes?— No.

23. And what have been the poor rates since 1874?—In '74, 3s.; in '75, 3s. 6d.; in '76, 1s. 6d.; in '77, 3s.; in '78, 3s.; and the present rate is 2s. 6d.

24. Did that include any special rate for sanitary purposes?—There is a general sanitary rate for sanitary purposes.

25. But has anything been carried out by the Guardians?—Nothing requiring special sanitary rate.

26. Are any sanitary improvements required for the town?—The water question is pending.

27. Is the town well sewered?—I think fairly.

28. What is the municipal rate?—1s.—that is the full rate.

29. Have the Commissioners ever considered the question of becoming the sanitary authority?—Yes.

30. Have they passed a resolution on the subject? —Yes.

31. What was it?—On the 3rd of December they held a special meeting, at which it was resolved—

"That in the opinion of the Town Council the present boundary of the town is too limited, and should be extended about a mile or a mile and a half from the centre of the town; that they do not desire to have transferred to them from the Grand Jury the control over the roads, bridges, and so forth; nor do they wish to become the urban sanitary authority of the township."

32. Were they unanimous in that?—No, not quite. Mr. Fanning gave his adhesion to that only provided the extension of the boundaries did not convert the agricultural holdings in the proposed area into townparks within the meaning of the Land Act.

33. None of the Commissioners are desirous of becoming the sanitary authority?—No.

34. Are they influenced by the fact that at present the poor rates are assessed evenly on the landlord and tenant?—I have no doubt that has something to say to it.

35. Are they aware that the Select Committee have made a recommendation that in future all municipal rates should be assessed in the same way?—I am not aware.

36. Do you think if they were aware of that it would alter their opinion?—I am not aware, but it would, perhaps; some are opposed to becoming the sanitary authority.

37. Has any Commissioner expressed an opinion that it would be better if the whole management of the town was under the one undivided authority?—I have not heard that.

38. What does your poll rate produce?—Under £300.

39. And what is your entire income from all sources?—We have no other source of income.

40. You have dues from Petty Sessions and dog tax?—The fines did amount to something considerable; lately they have been about £14 a year.

41. Is the town well lighted?—Yes; there are fifty public lamps.

42. Between what periods are these lamps lighted?—From the 6th of September up to the 6th of April.

43. Are the markets here held early?—Well, the people don't leave very early, though the markets are held early enough.

44. Do the people coming in to sell their produce avail themselves of the lights, or do they, as a rule, leave early—I mean before the lights are turned on?—No, they do not leave before the town is lighted.

45. When is it lighted?—At dusk.

46. And continued until when?—Until ten, and on market nights until eleven; and seven lamps are kept lighted the whole night.

47. The Commissioners have no income from tolls?—No—nothing but the rates and Petty Sessions Court.

48. Is there sufficient land within the present municipal limits for building purposes?—Quite sufficient.

49. Is there any tendency to build outside?—There is some building going on at present.

50. Outside?—No, within the town.

51. In which direction?—In different parts of the town.

52. Are they showing a tendency to build in one direction more than another?—Well, I cannot say that—if at all it is in the workhouse direction.

53. Can you give me the heads of your expenditure for last year?—In the last audited accounts I find we paid £159 5s. 6d. for lighting the town, and £30 for sweeping.

54. Do you contribute towards the flagging?—No, we do very little because we are £300 in debt.

55. Are there any improvements the Commissioners cannot carry out from want of funds?—They would do more if they were not in debt, but I do not know of anything that is pressing at present.

56. Do the Commissioners consider that they get value from the Grand Jury commensurate with the county cess they pay?—Well, I don't think the Commissioners consider the amount collected from the township is expended within the town, but if they were to get a staff to do the work they would not do it as cheaply.

57. They are not in favour of becoming the road authority themselves?—No.

58. I suppose they are aware that under the 205th section of the Public Health Act it does not hinge upon the consent of the Grand Jury as formerly?—They are aware of that I think.

59. Have you lived in the town some years?—Yes, twenty years.

60. Do you think Longford shows signs of improvement?—Yes.

61. Are there a better class of buildings being erected?—Well, as to building it has not increased much within the last ten years.

62. As to extension—have they recently applied for an extension of the boundaries?—No.

63. When these queries were sent to them were they considered at a special meeting?—I think there was a special meeting. There was not any unanimity then upon it.

64. What are the reasons the Commissioners now get for this extension?—In the first place they are in debt, and they think that if they got an extended area they would be able to get out of debt, and that the people living adjacent to the town derive advantages for which they ought to contribute.

65. In point of fact is it the case that the income is not sufficient to maintain the town?—Yes.

66. What is the extension suggested?—About a mile.

67. From the centre of the town?—Yes.

68. Half a mile from the present limits?—Yes.

69. Do the Commissioners know of the recommendation of the Select Committee as to making towns coterminous with Poor Law electoral divisions?—Yes, but Longford is not situated centrally enough for that. They would not adopt the electoral division as the boundary.

70. Do they consider that any improvement carried out by them would be an advantage to the persons brought in by the proposed extension?—Yes, in this way—the people at present do derive advantage from the light and so on. They do not propose to give them any new benefits, but to tax them for the advantages they at present enjoy.

71. Would they extend the lamps outside the present boundary?—I don't know. I know in one place the lamps are much required, and if they had only the means they would erect lamps in the direction of the workhouse.

72. Is there a good market in Longford?—Yes.

73. And from what distance do the people avail themselves of it?—They come from ten to fourteen miles.

74. What is the nearest town to Longford?—Granard, Ballymahon, and Edgeworthstown. Then there is Mohill and Ballymahon is ten miles.

75. Longford is the market town for all the people within the electoral division?—Yes, and more.

76. Have you had any opportunity of ascertaining whether the people proposed to be included would object to pay one-fourth taxation for the advantages they enjoy?—I know that it might be very different suppose a large project, such as the water works, was taken up.

77. But at present you have no desire to become the sanitary authority; so if there was a large project the Guardians with the consent of the Local Government Board can arrange any contributory district they like?—I know, but from what it is likely they would do, I should say the people outside would object.

78. Would you like to give your own opinion on the subject generally?—I would rather not. I have no interest in the matter one way or the other.

79. Are there many buildings outside in this proposed area?—There are a few.

80. Could you tell me the number of voters—persons qualified to vote, brought in by the one-mile radius?—I suppose there would be forty or fifty—sixteen, perhaps—sixty.

81. Could you tell me the population that would be included?—I cannot tell you.

82. Can you tell me approximately?—The whole electoral division is 6,131, and of that Longford is 4,375, and the town.

83. What I want to know is how many would the one-mile radius bring you?—It would add, perhaps, 700 to it.

84. Has the population increased?—Well, since 1861 census to 1871, it showed a decrease of 297.

85. Can you form any opinion as to whether the census of 1881 will show a decrease or an increase?—I think a decrease.

86. Is the trade of Longford falling?—Well, there is a general depression which is, of course, felt here—it is temporary, let us hope.

87. Would you, by the increase, bring in any houses that would be liable to the full rate?—Yes, but they would be very few. A few gentlemen's places around the town.

Mr. Michael [illegible], T.C., examined.

88. You are a resident in the town of *Longford*?—Yes.

89. And have lived here, I presume, some time?—For sixty years.

90. Do you recollect the town of Longford when it first came under the Towns Improvement Act?—Yes.

91. It was under the 9th Geo. IV. before that time?—Yes.

92. What steps were taken to determine the present area?—I was treasurer to the Corporation at that time, and the area under the 9th of Geo. IV. was much larger than it is now.

93. Did you petition for the same area under the Towns Improvement Act as under the 9th Geo. IV.?—It was left to the residents in the town. It was the leading men struck it out. In one place it is not a quarter of a mile.

94. Were you present when the question of extension was discussed?—Yes.

95. Are you in favour of this extension of a mile from the centre of the town?—Yes, I am.

96. And on the grounds stated by Mr. Cox?—Yes.

97. He has represented the views of your Board?—Yes, that is my feeling.

98. Were there any dissentients?—No, we had a full meeting of the Commissioners.

99. You know the recommendation of the Select Committee, I presume, and I would ask you, do you think the electoral division could be, with fairness or advantage, adopted as the boundary of Longford?—No, I think not—the electoral division extends too far.

100. You think an extension of a mile would be fair?—Yes, a mile from the Courthouse.

101. Are you, as an individual, in favour of leaving the sanitary authority of the town?—No. I think it is better to leave it with the Guardians. I am a Guardian myself.

102. Are you not in favour of the principle that the entire management of the town would be better in one body?—No, under the circumstances no.

103. Is there no such thing as a conflict of the authorities here?—The Grand Jury and the Commissioners agree.

104. Do you find it inconvenient to have three different authorities?—No.

105. Can you say if there are any improvements required in the town, that you are unable to carry out from want of funds?—Yes, a great many. We have only the market, and we are in debt to the National Bank.

106. Would these improvements be of advantage to the people you propose to bring in?—Yes, no doubt about it, as I find those gentlemen outside come in, and have the use of the lamps, and everything, and indeed enjoy these things more in fact than the townspeople themselves.

107. Are any improvements required in the way of lighting?—I think the town is well lighted at present.

108. Have you sufficient lamps?—Yes, we have fifty lamps.

109. The town is not lighted out to the municipal limits?—At one side it is. It is not lighted down to the [illegible], but the town is very well lighted.

110. Were you influenced with regard to the sanitary matter by the fact that the sanitary rate is at present assessed equally on the landlord and tenant?—I would leave it in the hands of the Guardians.

Mr. [illegible] M'[illegible], T.C., examined.

111. Were you present at the meeting when the question was discussed?—Yes.

112. You heard the evidence given by the gentlemen who have just been examined?—Yes.

113. Do you agree with what they have said?—Yes.

114. With any reservations?—Well, the principal reason the Commissioners don't wish to become the sanitary authority, is that they don't wish the [illegible], and they think they are a little more independent of the people.

115. Are you in favour of having the entire management under one body?—Yes—if it could be managed.

116. Do you consider that those people living within a mile of the centre of the town ought to contribute to those improvements the Commissioners are unable to carry out?—I think so.

117. Would they have any objection do you think, if the rates would be small?—I don't think they would object.

118. Have you heard objections from the people outside?—Very few.

119. Do you consider there are improvements required in the town?—The only improvement required is the waterworks.

120. What difficulty is there in the way of procuring the water supply?—The expense.

121. Are there natural facilities for getting the supply?—Yes, but with a deal of expenditure.

122. Would you have to bring it from a great distance?—Yes.

123. How is the town supplied?—From wells, and there are pumps.

124. Has the water been analysed?—Yes, and condemned.

125. And of course you think it would be a great advantage to the town, and to those who come into it frequently to have a good and wholesome supply?—Decidedly.

Mr. Edward Farrell, examined.

126. You have heard the evidence given—have you anything to add to it?—The only thing I had to say is that in the case of the tenants outside, who would be taken in, their rights would be interfered with by the extension, and they would suffer.

127. You think their rights would be interfered with?—Yes.

128. You understand that I am taking all the evidence on the understanding that existing rights are not to be interfered with?—I am. Well, that is the chief thing I brought forward.

Mr. Patrick M'[illegible] examined.

129. Are you in favour of an extension of a mile from the centre of the town?—Yes.

130. Would you be in favour of any further extension?—Well, I would say a mile and a half would be the proper thing.

131. You think the people within a mile and a half should contribute to the improvement of the town?—Yes.

132. It is in fact of vital importance to them that the town should be well kept?—Yes.

Longford. Oct. 4, 18[illegible]

Mr. Patrick M'Garry.

133. And they derive full advantage from the improvements of the town without contributing towards those improvements?—Yes.

134. You are aware that the people outside aid in the support of the town?—Yes.

135. But still you think they are fairly entitled to pay something towards the advantages they enjoy?—Yes.

136. And you think it would not press unduly upon them?—No.

Mr. Michael [illegible] examined.

Mr. Michael [illegible].

137. Whereabouts do you reside?—About a mile and a half outside the town.

138. Are you taxed for municipal purposes?—Yes.

139. Would you be brought in by an extension such as is proposed?—I think so, by the extension of a mile and a half, just out of a mile.

140. Would you object to contribute towards the town funds if you thought it would tend to clear it from debt, and assist the Commissioners in carrying out useful improvements?—I would not be for contributing.

141. Would it not be an advantage to you to have the town well cleaned, and watched, and swept?—It is sufficiently done for my purposes, and of the people around me.

142. Have you ascertained the feeling of those around you?—Yes.

143. And are they all opposed to this extension?—Yes.

144. They use the town?—They do, for the benefit of the town.

145. Do you think that those who reside near the town derive no more advantage from the town than people living six miles away?—I don't see it.

146. Do you not think it would be of advantage to the people living outside to have the town well looked after, to have a good market close at hand, which they can [illegible] daily advantage of?—That looks very well, but take the quality of the land into account, it is high enough at present, and it is no great advantage that.

147. Is it let at a higher rent because it is near the town?—Yes.

148. And you say you echo the sentiments of those living around you?—Yes, they would object to it, and very properly.

149. If the Commissioners were constituted the sanitary authority, would you object to being brought in?—Yes, I would have the same objection.

150. Would it not be of advantage to you to live near to a well-governed and healthy town?—I believe we are coming into a well-governed town, and I believe, on the whole, it is well managed. It has stood the test of time up to this.

Mr. Harry M'Cann examined.

Mr. Harry M'Cann.

151. Are you in favour of extension?—Yes.

152. Do you live within the town?—I am inside and outside.

153. Then your proposal is to tax yourself?—Yes; I think it very unfair the people outside are not contributing, for they derive more benefit from the town actually than the people inside; but I am opposed to it unless they become the sanitary authority. I think they are entitled to a larger area if they become the sanitary authority. It is impossible for the Board of Guardians to do the work properly; we sit to look after our interests. We have only three or four members on it who have any interest in the town, and how can it be expected that men who have no interest in the town could be able to do the work as it ought to be done.

154. And your argument is that if the Town Commissioners became the sanitary authority there would be more members to take an interest in the affairs of the town?—Yes; for they would be taking care of themselves. Now, however, there are strangers taking care of them.

154. Do you think the town body ought to have control of the roads?—As far as drains are concerned, but we have to make the main drains.

155. Are there any signs of a disposition to build outside?—Well, sir; some buildings have been undertaken, but the buildings have been chiefly of an ornamental character.

156. Do you know the feeling of the Board of Guardians on this subject?—It is just divided—some are in favour of it.

157. Are they in favour of handing over the sanitary authority?—Yes.

Mr. John Dacre [illegible] examined.

Mr. John D. [illegible]

158. You are Lord Longford's agent?—Yes.

159. What is his lordship's view on the subject of extension of the boundary?—I don't think he cares very much one way or the other.

160. Do you think extension would be desirable considering that the people within the town are heavily taxed and in debt?—There are a good many things in Mr. Cox's evidence which I think may be answered. In the first place, I may say that I don't quite agree with Mr. M'Cann in thinking that it would be advisable to transfer the sanitary authority from the hands of the Board of Guardians to the Town Commissioners. The Local Government Board think we are badly off for water; in fact, they made an inquiry and pressed the Board of Guardians into it, but the Town Commissioners are satisfied with the present state of the water supply. The Town Commissioners have all their property in the town, and mostly house property, and it is more than you can expect from human nature that they should be inclined to tax themselves. The Local Government Board have used very strong language to the Board of Guardians for not carrying out the water supply, and the Town Commissioners have frequently expressed their satisfaction with it. Lord Longford employed the County Surveyor to investigate the subject, and the report was that the source which was ultimately deemed the one from which the supply could be got, and which was three miles away, would entail a cost of from £12,000 to £15,000, which would be double the valuation of the present township. As to sanitary matters, I think Mr. Cox considered that there were no sanitary improvements required. From my knowledge of Longford, I think you will find a very great amount of filth in it. The back lanes are almost as bad as Dublin. The main streets may look well, but they are as a sort of "Emmy" in what is behind. As to building operations, I must say that since I have been here—four and a half years—it has only been on a very limited scale indeed. As to drainage, Lord Longford agrees to pay one-third towards any improvement of the town which the Grand Jury and the Town Commissioners approve of.

161. Is the town well dragged?—Fairly.

162. Are there any improvements required in the way of lighting?—I can hardly say. I don't think

Lurgan, Jan. 1, 1879. Mr. Geo. D. Cochrane.

there are, with the exception perhaps of a few yards. As to the advantage to be derived by those brought in by the proposed extension, I do not quite agree with the gentlemen who have spoken.

163. What is proposed is to tax them for the advantages they already enjoy?—Yes; but I don't quite see what the advantage is for which they should be asked to pay.

164. Have they not got a market close at hand?—Yes; but I don't see what greater advantage that is to a man living a mile off than to a man say two miles off.

165. Well, we must draw the line somewhere.—Well, I think the present line is a very good line.

166. Then you would not be in favour of extension?—No.

167. Not even taking into account that the Commissioners' means are cramped, and that they are unable to carry on improvements because they have not funds?—I think they get the full benefit of what they do themselves. In the first place, the taxation would fall very heavily on those outside considering the class of people and the smallness of the streets.

168. The very utmost they would be rated at would be 3d. in the pound?—Yes, but Mr. [illegible] said I think there would be something like forty roads brought in; now I would not think there would be anything like so many.

169. You don't think it fair for the people outside to help the town out of debt, which they have contracted in a great measure by these people coming in?—No; I don't think they derive much greater advantage than people living farther out.

170. You think these people support the town?—Yes. I think the Town Commissioners seem to wish to be benefited by the change, and to obtain the benefit, whilst at the same time they shirk all responsibility regarding it. If you give rights you should give duties also.

LURGAN.—JUNE 13th, 1879.

Before Messrs. C. P. Cotton, C.E., and H. A. Robinson.

Lurgan, June 13, 1879. Mr. Thomas Lutton.

Mr. Thomas Lutton examined.

1. You are Town Clerk of Lurgan?—I am.

2. How long have you held that office?—For 12 years.

3. Lurgan is under the 17th and 18th Vic., cap. 103?—Yes.

4. When was it put under that Act?—In 1866.

5. Previously it was under what Act?—The 9th of Geo. IV., cap. 82.

6. Was the Towns Improvement Act adopted wholly or only in part?—Wholly.

7. What is the population of the town?—About 13,000 at present.

8. You have given it as 10,632; that was in 1871?—Yes.

9. Since that it has been increasing?—It has.

10. What is the acreage of Lurgan?—Mr. Hancock can tell you.

11. Two thousand and twenty acres?—That is up to the 1st of May last.

12. What is the valuation?—£15,2[illegible]; that is for 1879.

13. There are no wards in the town?—It is divided into drainage districts.

14. But there are no wards for electoral purposes?—No.

15. It is altogether in one electoral division?—Yes, the electoral division of Lurgan.

16. Do you know the size of that electoral division and how far it extends?—No, I can't tell you; but the town is comprised in a number of portions of townlands.

17. However, the town boundary and the electoral division are not the same?—No, they are not. The town boundary is all comprised within the electoral division.

18. It doesn't touch any other electoral division but that of Lurgan?—No.

19. What are the municipal rates for the last five years?—We had a general assessment of 1s. 4d. in the pound; in the north west district 2d. in the pound.

20. In addition?—Yes, we have four drainage districts, and we have drainage rates on them in addition to the general assessment.

21. Give me the general assessment for the five years first?—The highest rates in 1874 were 1s. 4d.; in 1875, 1s.; in 1876, 2s.; in 1877, 2s.; and in 1878, 1s. 6d.

22. Give me the drainage rates on each of the drainage districts for each of those five years?—For the north east special only 4d. in 1876.

23. In 1874 how much was it?—No rates on the north east special that year.

24. In 1875?—No rate.

25. In 1876?—4d. in the pound special.

26. In 1877?—None.

27. In 1878?—4d. in the pound.

28. Take the next district; what were the rates?—The south west district there was 6d. in the pound special in 1874; 6d. in 1875; 6d. in 1876; none in 1877, and 6d. in 1878. The north district is [illegible], and there there was 6d. special in 1874; 6d. in 1875, 6d. in 1876; 6d. in 1877; and 6d. in 1878. In the Ballyblagh district there was 1d. in 1874; 1d. in 1875; 1d. in 1876; 1d. in 1877; and 1d. in 1878.

29. How did these drainage districts come to be formed?—At the time of the adoption of the Act the town was divided into four drainage districts, the north east, the south west, [illegible], and Ballyblagh.

30. Can you tell me the boundaries of those districts; are they in the Ordnance maps?—No; they were prepared by the Town Surveyor at that time, but I know all about them from memory. I could not tell the acreage of them, but I can tell the whole acreage of the town—2020 acres, 3 roods, 33 perches.

31. You don't know how that is divided into drainage districts?—No, but I know the acreage from memory. I could not tell how much is in each district.

32. Can you get it for me afterwards?—Yes, our Surveyor will be able to give you that.

33. Will you give me the poor rates for the five years?—For 1874, 3s.; for 1875, 1s. 6d.; for 1876, 2s.; for 1877, 1s. 6d. The county cess in 1874 was 2s. 1d.; in 1875, 2s. 1d.; in 1876, 1s. 6d.; in 1877, 1s. 10d.; in 1878, 1s. 1d.

34. How many Commissioners are there?—Fifteen.

35. And how many voters?—[illegible].

36. How many are qualified to sit as Commissioners?—110.

37. Are the present municipal boundaries regarded with dissatisfaction by the ratepayers?—No, they are not.

38. Has the question of the extension of the boundaries been under the consideration of the Commissioners?—It has.

39. What conclusion did they come to on the question?—To decide the case.

40. That was in January last; have they altered their opinion since?—We had a special meeting on last Tuesday, and they came to the conclusion to leave the town as it is, as some of the residents who were to be included made some objections to the extension.

41. In consequence of the objection of the outsiders?—In consequence of the depression of trade they thought it would be better not to extend the

boundary at the present time. A great portion of the extension would have been land.

38. Do you know how much of the present area is agricultural land?—No, I could not tell; but it amounts to about £1,850 valuation.

39. Then the replies you sent us have been altered since?—They were altered at our special meeting, we came to the conclusion to let the boundary stand as it is for some time.

40. How is the town lit?—With gas; we have public lamps.

41. Do the Commissioners own the Gas Works?—The lamps belong to the Commissioners.

42. But the Gas Works do not?—No; they make a contract with the gas directors.

43. What is the contract?—We have fifteen lamps that burn all night at £3 per lamp.

44. At night the whole year round?—No; from the 1st September to the 1st May, from half an hour after sunset until daylight next morning. That is fifteen lamps, and then there are 110 lamps from half an hour after sunset until eleven o'clock at night, with the exception of Thursday and Saturday, when they are lit until twelve o'clock, at £1 14s. per lamp, with the exception of two nights before and two nights after full moon, when they are not lighted.

45. How is the town provided with water?—We have sixteen pumps.

46. Is there any complaint as to the quantity or quality of the water?—It is sometimes very scarce.

47. Has there been any scheme for bringing water from anywhere else?—It was in contemplation to get water from Lough Neagh, but some of the parties were against it, and it fell through.

48. How is the town drained?—We have two main sewers, and contributory sewers.

49. Have many new sewers been made of late years?—A number of contributory sewers have been made in the north-east, in 1856, and on the south west about twelve years ago. The two main sewers are very large.

50. Where do they drain to?—Lough Neagh.

51. Has there been any extension of them in contemplation, or the making of other contributory sewers?—We have made application for £1,000 to the Government for some sewers required in the town, and we have got a grant—it has been recommended to the Treasury.

52. Have the Commissioners ever considered whether they would like to take up the roads within this district?—It has been talked of at our board meeting that we wished to be divided from the county.

53. But they have come to no resolution on it?—No.

54. Nor taken any action towards getting the authority?—No; but they would be very desirous to have it.

55. I suppose they know they can ask for it?—Yes.

56. But they have not done so?—They have not done so yet. I could let you know what we have expended on sanitary purposes for the last year. Our income was £2,407 3s. 6d., and we expended £2,075 3s. 3d. for sanitary purposes; and for gas and other things, £338 19s. 6d. That is, with the repairs of lamps, £290 for gas alone, and then for repairs and lamps, the total cost is £338.

Lurgan, June 12, 1878. Mr. Thomas Lemon.

Mr. JOHN HANCOCK, J.P., examined. — Mr. John Hancock, J.P.

57. You are Chairman of the Town Commissioners of Lurgan?—I am.

58. Would you give us your opinion about the boundaries of Lurgan, and whether they should be altered or not?—Some time ago the Commissioners were almost unanimous in favour of having enlarged boundaries, such as are marked on the plan. That is, I think, the conclusion that was come to, under the impression that it should be a means of enabling us to take up the roads; but, since then, the Commissioners have come to a different conclusion, partly owing to the opposition of the gentlemen on the land outside, on which there are very few houses, and partly in doubt as to whether they had any chance of separation from the county. The Commissioners are now of opinion it would be better not to disturb the existing boundaries, but to let them stand as they are. They came to an unanimous vote on that question within the last fortnight.

59. Did they at all consider how many voters would be added by the extension?—No; but there would not be many.

60. Or many added to the number who might form the representative body?—I believe the entire income of rateable property would be only about £2,000 a year, and the greater portion of that would be on the low scale, and it is doubtful, supposing we could include such a large additional area, whether the additional expense we should be put to in providing lighting and drainage, would be covered by the additional funds.

61. The present area I may take to be from a half to three-quarters of a mile in every direction?—The surveyor will be able to give that information.

62. And the enlarged boundaries would be something like a quarter of a mile more?—Yes. The present boundary is 510 acres, and the proposed boundary would be 1,834 acres, and the increased valuation, something about £2,000.

63. In what direction does the building extend?—Rather towards the lake.

64. Is there any building going on outside the present boundaries?—A little; only one gentleman is building a number of houses, and he is carrying on business extensively.

65. But there are no streets extending from the town out beyond the boundaries?—No, not yet, but ultimately it will be a question of extension, if trade continues, and if the town continues to increase in buildings.

66. Is there any tendency to increase in any one direction more than another?—I think the tendency is to go towards Lough Neagh; that is on the north.

67. You have never applied to the Local Government Board, to get control of the roads?—We did not, because we knew we would meet with opposition from the Grand Jury; and we are not quite prepared to incur that, besides we get considerable assistance from the Grand Jury towards our local rates, and for the present we do not think it advisable.

68. Don't you think the people living within a certain distance, derive great advantages from the town?—They do.

69. And it is of great importance to them that the town should be well kept?—It is.

70. Don't you think it would be fair they should contribute something for that purpose?—But we understand we would be compelled to light, sweep, and drain, a very large additional area. As I say, ultimately extension must come to be a question of time.

71. When you were contemplating that extension it was under the supposition that the lighting should be extended fully to any new boundary?—Certainly. We have our lighting now extended to our present boundary, and we quite understand we would be bound to take the lamps out to the new boundary.

72. Along all the roads?—Along all the roads. In one case, Mr. Paul has to take out the lights at his own expense, and of course he could not be expected to continue that, and still to pay taxes.

73. But suppose you were only obliged to carry out lighting as far as there were buildings. Would that make any alteration in your opinion on extension?—Of course it would; that would lessen the expenditure of the town, but that would require a little

[illegible] Mr. John Hanbock, J.P.

[illegible] consideration as in the [illegible] [illegible] of [illegible] that the [illegible] of the [illegible] would not be [illegible] by the increase in the [illegible].

74. But if you were not obliged to supply the new district with these other improvements, the [illegible] might be equal to the expenditure. My view is that you are not compelled to take out [illegible] there are not buildings?—Under the old Act we were.

75. Yes; you were unable to [illegible], unless you did?—Yes, but unless we offered some benefits to the outside [illegible], they would be still [illegible] in their opposition to extension.

76. The proposed extension would so far as I can see, take in only two gentlemen's places?—[illegible]—Mr. [illegible] [illegible] of Lord Lurgan's demesne, Mr. [illegible] and the Rev. [illegible]. There is a school, and a couple of villas in the direction of the model school.

77. Would that extension go into any other electoral division?—Yes, it would go into [illegible] [illegible] and part of [illegible].

78. Would [illegible] House be in a different electoral division?—Yes, it is in the electoral division of Lurgan.

79. Bellevue?—Yes, that is in [illegible].

80. [illegible]?—That is in Lurgan; part of it. I think Mr. [illegible] is the owner of [illegible].

81. The reason I ask these questions, is that we are to take care to make the municipal boundaries [illegible] with the poor law division wherever possible. The present boundary is entirely inside the electoral division of Lurgan, and this [illegible] the proposed extension, would go into two other electoral divisions?—Yes.

82. And the present electoral division would not at all suit for town purposes?—It would not.

83. It would be going too far away?—It would.

84. Is there anything else you wish to state?—On the question of extension it may perhaps be interesting to know that, according to the census of 1841, the town was the sixty-seventh in Ireland, and in 1871, it became the [illegible]. So that in thirty years, it rose from the sixty-seventh to the [illegible] position as a town, and now there are only two other towns in Ulster, with a greater population.

85. Is that increase going on still?—No, since the depression of last year, building in the town has almost stopped.

86. Is much of the land within the town boundary of the nature of townparks?—Yes; it is gardens and grazing ground.

87. Is the lighting of the town sufficient?—Yes it is.

88. What is the state of the water supply?—It is not good. We have tried for many years to get better, but we have not succeeded, we are now depending on wells.

89. Has there been any scheme proposed that you consider feasible?—Yes, but the amount required was beyond what we considered our means would afford. The amount was for £14,000 to £16,000 or £17,000, and it involved further pumping, and the annual expense of steam engines. We had two schemes from two eminent engineers, one was by pumping from Lough Neagh and the other was from wells through chalk formation; the expense of pumping would be £300 a year and that would be too large a tax.

90. Is there much expenditure necessary for drainage?—I think the £1,000 we have got the sanction for will do the necessary work. All we want is contributory drains. The main drain is through two valleys, one on the north-east and the other on the south-west, and they carry out the object we have in view, but there are intermediate connecting drains required. You are aware we can't make the people of the house drain more than 100 feet; we must meet them and make the rest of the work; and now we are carrying out a system of contributory sewers.

91. Has there been any meeting of the ratepayers to consider this question?—No, but the question has been discussed here by the [illegible] themselves, and the Commissioners are according to the general feeling of the ratepayers. There is an annual election of one-third portion of the commissioners, and as a body, they, I think, represent the general feeling of the ratepayers fairly.

92. Is this resolution not to alter the boundaries unanimous?—It is.

Mr. John W. Greer, J.P.

Mr. John W. Greer, J.P., examined.

93. I have heard what Mr. Hanbock has stated and I agree with his view, but of course some parties may think different.

94. What is your own opinion?—I think the boundaries should not be extended at present, that it is not desirable to have too large a boundary to take care [illegible], and it is not necessary.

95. You think the Commissioners here, with their present powers, have enough money for this work?—They have enough work for their money.

96. Are there any things left undone that would be done if they had more funds?—No, I think not, except very expensive works.

97. You live outside the boundary?—I do towards Lough Neagh.

98. Are you one of the commissioners?—No I am not.

Mr. William Baird.

Mr. William Baird examined.

99. You are a town commissioner?—I am, I agree in what has been stated, and there is no necessity for going into the question more; I can only reiterate what has already been advanced. There were two meetings of the Commissioners. At one of the meetings they did decide to increase the town boundary and the principal reason for doing so was the impression that they would by that means have a better case to put before the Grand Jury to get separation from the county, but afterwards, in considering the matter, we thought that perhaps we would not be able to get separation, and if that was the case, they thought it better to remain as they were for two reasons:—The first was that at the meeting we had on Tuesday, a number of the ratepayers, who would have been taken in by the new boundary, attended, and expressed themselves dissatisfied. They stated that if they were taken in of course they would have to pay more rates, for which they would receive no advantage. As the boundary at present stands it contains an area of 848 acres; the proposed boundary would contain 1,634, taking in altogether 786 acres. There are only about eight gentlemen whose places would be brought inside that boundary, that is men of large property, whose houses would be taxed. They said if we took them in, we should be prepared to light and drain and perhaps sweep the streets for them, that is sweep and scavenge out to the extreme boundary and I made a calculation as to the amount we are likely to raise in rates on this increased area, and I found that from the land included, that is 786 acres, at the fourth of last year's rates we would only receive £40, because the value of the land taken in would be only £1,810, that is the poor law valuation, and then there would be houses, and the valuation of the houses within the new area would be £701, and that at the rate of the last rate which has been struck, would give us about £50 altogether for the increased area.

Lurgan. [illegible]

Mr. William [illegible].

We would, therefore, have £100 a year additional tax and the Commissioners are under the impression they would be compelled to light, drain and sweep, if I might use the term, the increased area, but the amount we would get for it in taxes would not compensate us, in fact the town instead of benefiting by the increase, would lose, and that was the reason why the Commissioners unanimously came to conclusion; of course whether the Commissioners are right in their supposition that they would be bound to light to the extreme point of the area, and that they would be compelled to drain and sweep the whole district, is another thing. If the Commissioners found they were not compelled to do these things of course it might alter the case very much.

100. Would it alter your own private opinion?—It would, for I have no doubt at all that some of those places that are now outside the boundary enjoy just as many advantages as the town, and that they would have a fair right to pay a proportion of the rates.

101. How far from the centre of the town would you say that advantage extends?—I should say that from the centre of the town it extends half a mile or three quarters.

102. Your present boundary is fully half a mile from the centre of the town, and you say that the people living in the neighbourhood, outside the present boundary, derive advantage from their proximity to the town?—Yes.

103. How far do you think the advantage extends?—I would say a mile.

104. Do people two miles away derive advantage from the town?—No, not two miles from the centre of the town.

105. But you would say a mile?—Yes.

Mr. James Livingstone.

Mr. James Livingstone examined.

106. Are you a Commissioner?—No. I live in the townland of Silverwood. That townland, Mr. [illegible] of Dublin has leased to [illegible]. I am Mr. [illegible] tenant, and I am bound so that I cannot build any, unless I have a written order from him. I built eleven cottages, twelve years ago, and I had them let at 2s. a week, but had to reduce them to 1s. 6d., and if I had to do it now I would not build a brick of them.

107. You are objecting to extension in that direction?—Yes. There is fully a quarter or half a mile between Lurgan and Silverwood without a house on it at all.

108. It is [illegible]; there are no houses.

109. Mr. [illegible].—I thought there was a house at Silverwood Bridge?—No. Mr. [illegible] holds almost every house in the same townland on the same terms, so that no portion of it would be fit for building.

110. Mr. [illegible].—You use Lurgan as a market, and everything of that kind?—It is no use to me for my business.

111. Don't you come into Lurgan often?—Sometimes. My principal market is Belfast.

112. You get your children educated in Lurgan?—Three [illegible] of them at school there, on the Lough-road. There is no prospect of any other house of mine being built along the Lough-road. In my time there have been only two houses built and the school, and I don't see any prospect of any other building going on. The direction in which the building is going on is about the workhouse.

113. What is the valuation of your holding in Silverwood?—[illegible]

114. William [illegible] O'Neill, Town Surveyor.—Mr. Livingstone's buildings are valued at £30 per annum.

115. What are the rents of the buildings?—I have not got the amount of land [illegible].

116. Does the boundary take in the small houses belonging to him?—Yes, all the buildings.

117. Mr. Livingstone.—I hold sixty-eight acres in the townland.

118. Mr. O'Neill.—And that would be valued at about £58 per annum.

Mr. James Usher.

Mr. James Usher examined.

119. I own two villas outside the boundary on the Lough road, in the townland of Derry. There is very little I can add to what has been said. I think the time has not come for extension, and I think we are not ripe for such a change. The map shows that on the face of it. There are only eight houses, leaving out those miserable houses of Mr. Livingstone's, let at 1s. 6d. a week, which the town could call upon to pay taxes. That is only eight houses outside the present boundary, but if the number was 800 we might have some reasonable and fair case to bring before you for extension; but in face of the fact which is proved by the map, I think the time has not arrived yet for enlargement of the boundary. The further fact exists that if we leave out these houses or country residences, taking the last fifteen years back, the town has not, as a matter of fact, extended at all, nor is the town showing at the present time any inclination to extend outside the present boundary. Of course there are a lot of weavers' houses up in Union-street, near the workhouse, which have been built.

120. But that increase of houses has been confined within the present boundary?—Yes; and that is part and parcel of what I say with regard to the other parts, and I think it shows powerfully that the town is not ripe for extension. If there were hundreds of houses outside the boundary there would be a fair case to say they should contribute to the taxation, but at present it would have a tendency to curtail the growth of the town, and to deter parties from erecting country residences and beautifying the outskirts of the town, if those places were brought in.

121. But at present they are not doing anything of the sort?—No; not of one kind or the other. In every direction they are prohibited from building. Mr. Livingstone has stated he is debarred from building without the sanction of his landlord. The same state of things exists in another direction. Mr. Samuel Hall, who lives at Bellvue, is hemmed up by a covenant from erecting even a chimney, which would injure the view from Bellvue-house. There is another fact. The demesne wall runs along there on one side, and, of course, no extension could take place at all out there. That is a very large section of the surrounding country.

122. You are confined altogether pretty well as to extension of buildings?—Yes.

123. Where do you live?—Between the two boundaries. With regard to this place outside the boundary, we enjoy what we want to enjoy; we don't want light; we have sufficient light; and as regards the important question of sewerage, we have our private sewers for our private purposes, to suit our premises, and if the Commissioners got this extension they would naturally be asked to lay part of the way, put up lamps, and erect sewers and all that, and they would lose by the transaction, for remember that there are at present only those few houses, eight, or nine altogether outside the boundary. Those buildings are, moreover, on the very verge of the boundary, and lamps would have to be erected if this extension was carried out.

124. Wouldn't that be an advantage to you?—I think not. We have got on very well for a number of years without it.

ROSCOMMON.—SEPTEMBER [illegible], 1879.

Before Mr. Henry A. [illegible].

Mr. John [illegible] examined.

Mr. John [illegible].

1. The Commissioner.—You are the Town Clerk of Roscommon?—I am.

2. Under what Act is the town of Roscommon constituted?—Under the Towns Improvement Act.

3. What Act, if any, was it under previous to the adoption of the Towns Improvement Act?—It was under the 9th of George IV.

4. Are the boundaries as they now exist under the Towns Improvement Act the same as they were under the 9th of George IV.?—I think they are.

5. Can you say positively that the boundaries are [illegible] as they were when the town was under the 9th of George IV.?—I cannot say positively, because I was not connected with the Commissioners then; but I believe they are the same.

6. When did you come under the Towns Improvement Act?—On the [illegible] of January, 1853.

7. What were the boundaries as then defined?—As defined in the notice for the public meeting, dated the 1st of January, 1853, they are as follows:—

"Commencing on the east side of the said town at the [illegible] bridge, on the road from Roscommon to Athlone, and boundary between Ballyphenan and [illegible]; thence westward by the main river to the [illegible] bridge; thence by the main river to the [illegible] bridge, running westward; thence by the centre of the [illegible] road and boundary between Ballyphenan and Ardnanagh, to the crossing of the [illegible] road; thence by the centre of the [illegible] behind the military barracks, and by the boundary between Ardnanagh and [illegible], to a point [illegible] the lands of Ardnanagh, [illegible], and [illegible]; thence turning north-east to follow the boundary between Ardnanagh and [illegible] to the crossing of the [illegible] road; thence by the centre of the [illegible] road and boundary between Ardnanagh and [illegible] to [illegible] at the [illegible] road [illegible]; thence by the boundary between Ardnanagh and [illegible] to the centre of the [illegible] at [illegible]; thence [illegible] by the boundary between [illegible] and [illegible] to the main drain from [illegible] and [illegible]; thence [illegible] to follow the main drain to the bridge at [illegible]; thence turning [illegible] by the boundary between [illegible] and [illegible], to the bridge on the [illegible] road; and thence [illegible] by the [illegible] and boundary between Ballyphenan and [illegible] to the [illegible] bridge aforesaid, comprising the townland of Ballyphenan, the townland of Ardnanagh, with the exception of the part [illegible], which lies south of the road from [illegible] to the bridge of [illegible], and including that part of [illegible] which lies north of the [illegible] from [illegible] to the bridge of [illegible] and [illegible] road, already described, containing [illegible] statute measure or thereabouts."

8. Has there been any alteration in the boundaries since that time?—No, sir.

9. What steps did the Commissioners at that time take to determine the boundary of the town of Roscommon as it is now defined?—I don't know, except so far as my own knowledge of the locality enables me to judge.

10. The Commissioners [illegible] their [illegible] with reference to the boundary to the [illegible] at the [illegible], in the usual way, I presume. Did the authorities make any [illegible] of the boundary as suggested by the Commissioners?—I can give you no information on that point, as the minute book of the period to which your question refers is not in my possession.

11. What is the area of the town?—[illegible] [illegible]. That is the present area.

12. Does the town include whole townlands, or does it subdivide them?—It contains one whole townland—Ballyphenan—and portions of two others—Ardnanagh and [illegible]. Part of the two last named townlands are inside the present municipal boundary.

13. Taking the [illegible] [illegible] as the centre of the town, how far does the boundary extend to the north?—About a quarter of a mile.

14. To the south how far does it extend?—Something more than that, nearly half a mile.

15. To the east?—About a quarter of a mile.

16. To the west?—About a quarter of a mile.

17. What is the valuation of the town?—£[illegible].

18. And upon how much of that is the full rate levied, and upon how much is the [illegible] levied?—The [illegible] is upon land.

19. Yes, but what is the valuation of the land upon which the [illegible] is assessed?—The valuation of houses within the boundary is £[illegible], and the valuation of land within the boundary is £[illegible] 12s.

20. What is the population of the town?—According to Thom's Almanac the population at the last census was [illegible].

21. Is it decreasing, or has it decreased, since the last census was taken?—I can form no accurate opinion with regard to that. I would be inclined to say that it had remained stationary. It is something about the same now that it was then.

22. Are there many houses unoccupied in the town?—There are some houses unoccupied, say about twelve.

23. The town, I understand, is not divided into wards for municipal or Poor Law purposes?—No.

24. In what electoral division is the town of Roscommon situate?—In the electoral division of Roscommon.

25. Is it wholly within that electoral division?—It is.

26. If a radius of a mile all round from the centre of the town was taken, would it still be within the electoral division of Roscommon?—It would.

27. How far does the electoral division extend in each direction?—It is about two miles in [illegible].

28. What is the valuation of the electoral division?—£[illegible] 7s.

29. And the area?—[illegible]a. [illegible]r. [illegible]p.

30. Are the Board of Town Commissioners aware of the recommendation of the Select Committee of the House of Commons that the boundaries of towns should, as far as possible, be made coterminous with those of Poor Law electoral divisions?—They are.

31. Were they aware of that recommendation when they made the replies to the queries submitted to them by the Municipal Boundaries Commissioners?—They were.

32. Is Roscommon a good market town?—Tolerably good.

33. Do the people of the entire electoral division of Roscommon use the town of Roscommon for [illegible] purposes?—They do.

34. What are the rates that have been struck within the past few years. I will take five years [illegible]?—In 1874 the poor rate was [illegible] in the pound; in 1875, [illegible]; in 1876, 2s. [illegible]; in 1877, [illegible]; in 1878, 2s. [illegible]; in 1879, [illegible].

35. Was any portion of those rates a sanitary rate, or was the sanitary rate included in them?—No.

36. Has there been any sanitary rate?—There was a sanitary rate of [illegible] in the pound in 1878, and the present sanitary rate is [illegible].

37. For what purpose was that rate struck?—For sanitary purposes.

38. Was it struck for any sanitary work in the way of drainage or water supply?—There was a tank put up by the Board of Guardians since they became the sanitary authority.

39. What is the sanitary district over which that sanitary rate is assessed?—Roscommon township.

40. The entire township?—No. The sanitary district comprises the entire townland of Ballyphenan, and the portions of the townlands of Ardnanagh and [illegible] within the municipal boundary.

[illegible] Sept. [illegible], 1879. Mr. John [illegible].

41. I understood you to say that the sanitary rate was struck over the entire of those three townlands, is that so?—No, sir.

42. Then it is only struck over the town?—Yes.

43. Would you now kindly give me the municipal rates for the same period as that for which you gave me the poor rate?—The municipal rate in 1874, was 6d.; in 1875, 1s.; in 1876, 1s.; in 1877, 1s.; and in 1878, 1s.

44. Have you got your rate for 1879 yet?—It has not yet been struck.

45. Was the Town Improvement Act of 1854 adopted for all purposes?—As I told you before, I have no record showing what course was pursued at the time of the adoption of the Act. There is no minute book of that period in my possession. The first minute recorded in the books given up to me by the late clerk, commenced in 1856 or 1853.

46. How long have you been in office?—About three years, or something more. As far as I could go over the old Act, and form a judgment, I believe the Act was adopted in its entirety.

47. Do you believe that the people residing within a mile of the town derive advantage from the proximity of the town?—It is my opinion that they do.

48. And do you know is that the opinion of the Board of Commissioners?—And that is the opinion of the Commissioners too.

49. Do your board consider that any improvements carried out for the good of the town are also for the advantage of the people residing outside?—They do, sir.

50. And I suppose the board consider that the people living outside should contribute towards the support of the town?—They are of that opinion.

51. Is the town all lighted?—It is lighted by twenty-two lamps.

52. During what months of the year are those lamps lit?—From the 1st of October to the 1st of April—six months. The winter six months of the year.

53. Are there any improvements in the town which are required, and which the Commissioners would carry out, if they had an increased income?—I don't know of any special improvements that they contemplate making, if they got an increase of revenue.

54. Have they ever considered the question of becoming the sanitary authority?—They have.

55. Have they passed a resolution on the subject?—They have.

56. Can you give it to me?—I can; I will send for it; but it is right for me to say that they are divided upon that subject.

57. Are they aware that by the 7th section of the Public Health Act of 1878, they can obtain a provisional order from the Local Government Board?—They are.

58. Have the Commissioners ever considered the question of a transfer of the Grand Jury powers?—They have, sir, and they are divided on that subject also.

59. Are they aware that under the Public Health Act of last session, by the 204th section, they can get a separation from the Grand Jury by a provisional order, whether the Grand Jury withhold their consent or not?—They are.

60. Do you think they have that in contemplation?—They are divided on that subject. They are unanimous with regard to the extension of the boundary, but they are divided with regard to the two other questions.

61. Can you say if it is the opinion of those people who are in favour of having the town controlled by one undivided authority, that if the town was so managed, they would require an increased area—if they had all those powers vested in them?—I can give no opinion with regard to the inhabitants of the town, what they think on the subject. The Chairman will probably be able to tell you as to that.

62. Have you lived in the town for any length of time?—No, sir. I live outside the town about a mile, but I have an office in the town.

63. Are the lands in the portions of the townlands of Ardnamagh and Cleenbrackan principally occupied as accommodation lands and townparks?—Some portions of them are, and some are not. They are chiefly held as large grass farms.

64. Can you say is it your opinion that the land close outside the town—within half a mile of the centre of the town—is more valuable, on account of its proximity to the town?—Certainly it is. I will give you a reason for that, sir. For instance, the grass of a cow on land that is adjacent to the town would be charged for at the rate of £4 or £4 10s., whereas, at a distance from the town, you will get it for £3 or £2 [illegible], and, therefore, the value of the land within a [illegible] of a mile of the town is very much enhanced.

65. That is an advantage to the landlord. The fact of the land being more valuable on account of its proximity to the town, is not that an advantage to the landlord and not to the tenant, as the municipal rates are assessed on the tenant?—It is of advantage to the landlords and to the tenants also, I think; both parties have [illegible].

66. Do the people who avail themselves of your markets have the advantage of the lights until they go out of the town?—They have, in the winter season as well as the townspeople.

67. Are there any sanitary improvements required for the town?—The late County Surveyor gave an estimate, according to which he estimated that a sum of £3,350 would be required for the sanitary improvement of the town. He drew a map of the necessary sewers that were required in the town.

68. Is not the town sewered at all?—It is only partially sewered.

69. Have you ever applied to the Guardians to have these sewers carried out?—No, sir, I don't think the Commissioners ever applied to the Guardians. The townspeople opposed the scheme, as they considered it too expensive.

70. If the Commissioners became the sanitary authority, and had an increased area of taxation, do you think they would carry out improvements in the town?—I think they would, if they had funds to do so.

71. If you had an increased area of taxation and larger funds, they would increase the gaslight?—Yes.

72. Hitherto you have struck the whole rate?—No, in 1874, only 6d.

73. In the last five years you have struck the whole rate of 1s.?—Yes; except in one year 1874, when we only struck a rate of 6d.

74. Did the Commissioners pass a resolution on the subject of an extension of the boundaries?—I summoned a meeting of the Commissioners to reconsider the matter on Friday last, and the minute book states that there was a special meeting of the Commissioners held, on Friday, the 26th of September, 1879—present, five Commissioners, including the Chairman—nine is the number, but there is one vacancy—and it was resolved—

"That we recommend an extension of the existing boundaries of the town of [illegible], so that the townlands of [illegible], [illegible], [illegible], [illegible], [illegible], [illegible], and [illegible], be added to the present area, together with the portions of the townlands of Ardnamagh and Cleenbrackan at present outside the municipal boundary."

That was the last resolution.

75. That would go to the north a mile from the centre of the town?—It would go more than that. It would go to the north a mile in addition to the former area—about an English mile to the north as nearly as possible.

76. Have the Commissioners considered what is the amount of the valuation for that additional area?—There are 1,935a. 2r. 39p. in the contemplated extension, and the valuation is £1,[illegible] [illegible].

77. What income would that produce at the one-fourth rate?—The revenue on a valuation of £1,[illegible] 15s., at 12d. in the pound, would be £[illegible] [illegible] 3d. The revenue on about 94 houses, at as near an approximation as I can make, on a valuation of £[illegible] 10s. each—some may be far more, and others may be far less, but striking an average—rated at 1s. the income would be £[illegible] 15s.,—that would make a total of £[illegible] [illegible] 3d., and that would be the probable revenue.

78. Do you consider that the people residing within this extended area derive as much advantage from the town, so that if they have to pay a quota of additional taxation it would not press unduly heavily on them?—That is the opinion of the Commissioners.

79. What is the reason for including these townlands?—The Commissioners [illegible] require funds to carry on works of improvement.

80. The Commissioners consider that they cannot adequately the necessary works of the town with the present income?—Yes.

81. And on this ground they argue that the people residing in close proximity to the town should contribute to the maintenance of the lands?—Yes.

82. On the understanding that any improvement in the town would be a benefit to them?—Yes.

83. Were there any other resolutions passed by the Commissioners?—Yes, there were.

84. I would like to get the previous ones passed on the subject of the extension?—Yes, you shall have them. There was a resolution passed on the [illegible] of November, 1876. That was a meeting assembled in order to reply to the series of queries sent by the Municipal Boundaries Commissioners for replies. There were seven Commissioners present, including the chairman.

"It was resolved—That a Committee, consisting of Messrs. Simpson, Finlay, and Dowley be appointed to draw up answers to the questions contained in the schedules then received from the Commissioners appointed to inquire into the state of the municipal towns in Ireland, so far as such questions relate to the town of Roscommon; and that an extension of the existing boundaries to about an English mile be recommended."

85. Is that the only resolution?—That and the other one I have read.

86. Was it unanimously adopted?—Yes.

87. Did the Committee furnish a report?—Yes, they did.

88. Will you hand me in a copy of that report?—I will send you one.

89. Are there any other sources of income that the Commissioners have beyond the rates?—Tolls, weighing machines, and [illegible]. [illegible] They derive income from both sources—from the petty customs and the borough rate—between £[illegible] and £[illegible].

90. And they are fixed?—Yes.

91. What was the entire municipal income for the last year?—£[illegible].

92. And what was the expenditure?—£130 17s. [illegible].

93. The Commissioners have not yet been able to light the centre of the town?—They have, but the suburbs are not lighted; but the chief parts of the town are lighted.

93. Is there land within the town available for building?—Yes, there is.

96. Is there any tendency to build outside the present municipal boundary?—No.

97. Are there any building operations going on within the town boundary, now?

98. In which direction?—In the direction of the railway.

99. Is the town fit to the extension limits?—It is, as far as the population and the houses go.

100. What opportunity have you had of ascertaining the feelings of the ratepayers on the subject of the proposed extension?—I have never had an opportunity of ascertaining the feeling of the ratepayers, and I can give no information on the subject.

101. Were the ratepayers aware that this inquiry was to take place here?—There were placards printed and posted up in the town.

102. On what day?—On the [illegible] they were posted up.

Cross-examined by Mr. *Holmes*.

103. You said that a person living within a mile of the town has the benefit of the town?—Yes, for certain.

104. Are they benefited by it?—Yes, they are benefited.

105. Where are the next market towns from Roscommon?—Ballygar is one, it is about seven Irish miles; Strokestown is another, about nine Irish miles; Athlone is another.

106. Do not people living half way between this and Ballygar and Strokestown get as much benefit as those within a mile of the town?—We do not propose to include them.

107. But they get just as much benefit as those who reside in the town, or within a mile of it?—Yes, they do; decidedly they do.

108. With regard to the present borough area, the whole of the buildings are within the area, there are none outside of it—there are no houses outside the area?—There are some farm houses.

109. But there are no villas?—No, sir, there are no houses of that kind.

110. The present boundary includes the whole of the real town of Roscommon?—It does.

111. Will you tell me in what way the Commissioners are improving the town, or do they ever do anything to improve it?—Oh, they do.

112. In what way?—Recently they made flagged footways—distance perches.

113. Where?—In Goff-street.

114. Out of their own funds?—Yes, at £3 a perch.

115. How?—They paid £2 themselves, and the Grand Jury contributed £1.

116. You say the people living about the town have the benefit of the gas?—Yes.

117. Have what benefit from the gas?—It is a benefit to have the town and the streets lighted.

118. What benefit does Ardsallagh-more get from this town?—If people come here to transact their business at night they derive benefit.

119. Do the people from Strokestown and Ballygar get equal benefit?—I have said so before.

120. Have the people of Ardsallagh-more any special benefit?—I don't think they have any special benefit.

121. I see that this meeting of the Commissioners on the 20th was signed by five Commissioners?—It is not signed; there were five present.

122. Was it approved of by the five Commissioners?—Yes.

123. There are eight Commissioners?—Yes.

124. How is it that the other three were not present at that meeting?—I cannot account for that; they were [illegible].

125. Is it because they were disapproving of the course pursued by the others that they did not attend?—No, sir.

Cross-examined by Mr. *Kelly*, B.L.

126. I think you stated that the total income of the Town Commissioners is about £180?—No, sir. The income from rates was £132.

127. What have you done with the balance—does that remain unexpended?—They have expended about £45 on footways, and £17 on water channels in Loughborough-street.

128. Do the Town Commissioners propose to put in lamps or to expend any money on the roadways of the extended district?—I think they do.

129. How much income do they expect to get from it—£30 a year?—Yes.

130. Do you know how much is laid out by the Grand Jury upon those roads and footpaths within a mile and a half of the town?—I do.

131. Do any of the Town Commissioners hold any land in this district over which they intend to extend the area?—I am not aware that any of them hold any land.

132. Is Mr. Greene's land outside the district to be taken in?—Not to my knowledge.

133. Is Mr. Dowley's?—Yes, it is.

134. Is the Chairman's land within the district proposed to be taken in?—No, I don't think it is.

135. How long do you know the town?—I have about eleven years experience of the town.

136. You have seen this map produced here—the Ordnance map?—I have not seen it.

[illegible]

Roscommon, Sept. 23, 1879. — Mr. John Lambert.

137. Do you know how many houses are in the town between the town leading to the old castle and the town boundary?—I don't know, but I can tell you how many houses there are in the different town-lands proposed to be added to the boundary.

138. Do you know how many old houses have been pulled down in Castle-street within the last few years?—I think there have been a great many.

139. Do you know that the valuation of Castle-street has diminished very much?—Yes, I know the valuation in houses has diminished very much.

140. Do you know the north of the town, what kind of land it is—is it not Lord Dunn's land, and is it not divided into demesne lands?—I believe so.

141. Are you aware that on a valuation of £400 a year, Mr. Kelly has two lords, two cottiers, and the houses?—I am not aware.

142. Do you know the townland of Lisgammon?—I do.

143. What benefit would that townland get from any extension or tax upon it?—I will tell you. That belongs to you, and you charge for the grass of a cow £4 10s. on the whole of that townland, and the grass of that cow outside that townland—two or three miles outside the town—you would get for £3.

144. How many grazing cows were on that land this year?—I cannot say.

Mr. L. M. Hynes.

Mr. L. M. Hynes, examined.

145. Mr. Romney.—You are Chairman of the Town Commissioners?—I am.

146. Have you been resident in Roscommon for any length of time?—Yes.

147. Were you a Commissioner before you were elected chairman?—Yes.

148. And were you a Commissioner when the town first came under the Towns Improvement Act of 1854?—No.

149. How many years have you been a Commissioner?—Fifteen.

150. And you were present, I understand, at the meeting at which this question of the municipal boundary was considered?—Yes.

151. And it is your opinion, I take it, that there should be an extension of the boundary?—I think so.

152. To what extent?—About a mile.

153. And what are your reasons for wishing an extension?—My reason is to give additional funds to our town, and with the view of decreasing the towns-people's taxation.

154. Do the taxes bear heavily on the townspeople at present?—Yes.

155. And the town funds at present available are insufficient for the purposes of the town?—Yes.

156. Are there any improvements which you would carry out in the town if you had increased funds?—Yes.

157. What are they?—Making paths and flaggings, and things like that.

158. Do you think that the people residing within the proposed extended area derive advantages from their proximity to the town?—I do.

159. Roscommon is a good market town?—It is.

160. Is Roscommon the market town for all the people you propose to bring in?—It is.

161. On the other hand all the money they get from the sale of the produce goes into the hands of the townspeople, so that they keep up the town to a certain extent?—Yes.

162. Do you think they would object to be assessed for the rates of the town?—I should think they would.

163. Do you think the sanitary work would be better done by the Commissioners?—Yes.

164. This extended area is simply for the purpose of enabling you to do your business as Commissioners under the Towns Improvement Act?—Yes.

165. Is there sufficient land within the town available for all purposes?—I think so.

166. Have you had an opportunity of ascertaining the feeling of the ratepayers on the subject of the proposed extension?—I have.

167. You have spoken to several of them?—I have.

168. Are they not in favour of the extension of the boundary?—Yes.

169. Does Mr. Lambert's evidence express your views?—Yes, it does, sufficiently.

170. And the views of your board?—Yes.

171. You were unanimous at the meeting of the Town Commissioners?—Yes.

172. And you think you represent the feeling of the ratepayers?—Yes.

Cross-examined by Mr. *Holmes*.

173. Is this inquiry attended by any independent people from the town, that is to say, by independent townspeople?—The town is represented by the Commissioners; they think that sufficient.

174. How many Commissioners are there here?—There are three Commissioners here.

175. I believe there has been no election of Commissioners since this notice came—since this Commission was appointed?—We thought it was not necessary.

176. Is it necessary or not? Has there been any election of Commissioners since this Commission has been in force?—No.

177. And there are none of those here?—No.

178. Did the townspeople authorize you as a body to tell the Commissioners here their opinion?—No, the townspeople did not.

179. How do you know that the ratepayers approve of it?—From conversation.

180. From casual conversation. Why didn't the the people who expressed these views come here?—I suppose they did not consider it necessary, in fact, I dare say, they did not think they would be allowed to come here.

181. Do you think that people living within a mile of the town get the benefit of the market here?—Yes.

182. May I ask you what they sell generally?—Hay, straw, turf, eggs.—

183. Where do the eggs go to?—I cannot answer that.

184. Are they bought for the English market?—I suppose so.

185. Then it is the English people get the benefit and not the townspeople?—Well, I don't know about that. Don't you know that the people coming to the market have the benefit of selling their eggs there.

186. Do they benefit more than the people two or three miles away?—Yes, they do.

187. What benefit do the people at the end of Ardsallagh get from the gaslight?—They do get benefit.

Cross-examined by Mr. *Kelly*.

188. Were you present at the meeting of the Commissioners when it was ordered that these placards should be printed?—When our clerk received notice from the Boundary Commissioners that the inquiry would be here on this day, he came to me with that notice, and I directed him to get placards printed, and some were sent to the principal people.

189. Did you send notices to the people whose property would be affected by the proposed boundary?—We posted them in the town.

190. Are you aware that nineteen years ago this matter was investigated before?—Yes.

191. Have you ever seen the records of the town containing the replies on the subject?—I have not.

192. Where are those records?—I don't know

Mr. [illegible] W. [illegible].

Mr. [illegible] W. [illegible]. 1st Aug., 18[illegible].

193. I appear here to represent myself. You have heard that the townland of [illegible] is sought to be included, and Mr. [illegible] says that the residents will be benefited. I wish to state that there is only a [illegible] house on that land, and the principal part of it is in the hand of a gentleman who farms and lives away from it, and he would have been here to-day if he had known anything about the inquiry. Now, I want to tell you what has occurred in the past with reference to this township. About the year 18[illegible], a memorial, of which this is a copy, was sent to the then Lord Lieutenant of the day. It stated:—

"That the highest rate allowed on the valuation of premises, within the present boundaries of the town, which amounts to £[illegible] [illegible]s., is wholly inadequate to afford the Commissioners the means of lighting [illegible] public lights for the town, which are now within their reach, in consequence of the establishment of a gas company under the Limited Liability Act. That your memorialists respectfully request that your Excellency may be graciously pleased under the powers vested in you by the [illegible] section of the [illegible] & [illegible] of Victoria, c. [illegible], to [illegible] the boundaries of the town, so as to include the townlands in the schedule hereunto annexed, being the townlands immediately adjoining the existing boundaries, whereby an increased revenue of £[illegible] [illegible]s. [illegible]d. would be afforded them, thus making their total revenue £[illegible] [illegible]s. [illegible]d., out of which they would be enabled to procure the benefit of public lights, [illegible] improvements, which would be an equal advantage to occupiers of the premises within the proposed limits, as well as to those within the present boundaries.

"Schedule referred to, being the proposed boundaries of the town of [illegible].

"The [illegible] limits of the following townlands:—[illegible], [illegible], that portion of [illegible] not included within the present boundaries, [illegible], [illegible], [illegible], [illegible], [illegible], [illegible], the portion of [illegible] not included within the present boundaries, [illegible], [illegible], [illegible], [illegible], [illegible], [illegible], [illegible], and [illegible]."

Well, we got up that memorial to the Lord Lieutenant of the day, and the answer we got from him was, that no lands would be included, save and except what would constitute the town, and the suburbs of the town. We got an answer to that effect, and of which the Town Commissioners should also be perfectly aware, that they could not sanction the change—that the original limits were carefully adopted, and meant to His Excellency fully adequate to the wants of the town, and were equally as extensive as those of other towns of a like population.

194. And you consider that ruling applies now?—Yes; you have the evidence of the Chairman before you—that they do not intend to avail themselves of any of the additional Acts; that they do not intend to avail themselves of the Sanitary Acts; they do not intend to abolish the [illegible]; but, they intend only to act under the old Towns Improvement Act—therefore they are in exactly the same position that they were in then.

195. Has the town increased since then?—It has increased to the extent of four or five public buildings. They have a gas works and a Presbyterian church, and [illegible]. There has been nothing of importance built in the town within the last eight or nine years to my knowledge. Those I have mentioned were built about that time, and subsequent to the memorial being sent. At that time the Lord Lieutenant considered that an income of £[illegible] [illegible]s. was ample. Now it is increased to £[illegible] odd, and they do not intend to do anything more than then. What right have they to go in now and take in my lands which are out in the country, and which constitute a farm? What good would the gaslights be to me? It would be no more be an improvement to my property. There are a number of farmers round the country who would be here to-day were it possible for them, for they were not expecting for this [illegible], which it was signed; and when I heard of this application, I was told by the officials of [illegible] [illegible] to get up a memorial, and it would be considered, and you will find there the reasons why the Lord Lieutenant refused to comply with their proposal. You have it on the evidence of the Chairman, that he does not intend to do anything except what was done under the old Towns Improvement Act; and under that Act the Lord Lieutenant was of opinion that £[illegible] [illegible]s. was an income quite sufficient for them. The Lord Lieutenant having said that the income was sufficient for that purpose in a town of [illegible] inhabitants, and would not interfere, I do not see any reason for a contrary course now. I would impress those things on you now, and I ask you, also, to consider that we are labouring under great difficulties from not having got sufficient notice of this inquiry. If we had, we would have got any number of people from the outside districts to tell you their story in opposition to the increase, and we would have got the proprietors to come forward. I can state that Lord [illegible], who is deeply interested in the welfare of the town, and his principal agent [illegible], is [illegible] opposed to this; almost every inch of the land is Lord [illegible]'s land, and he disapproves of these transactions. The Lord Lieutenant [illegible] [illegible] the change, and further, that the original limits were carefully adopted, and were to His Excellency fully adequate to the wants of the town; he evidently considered that there was no corresponding benefit given to any persons outside the town; and that the townspeople got all the benefits themselves; and that there was no benefit to the [illegible] and [illegible] of the outside district.

196. I understand that you consider an extension is desirable?—Certainly.

197. Do you consider that the people who come into the town of [illegible] are a benefit to the town?—Many of them are—in any case, they are the life of the town.

198. In your theory that, instead of the town giving them a benefit, they confer a benefit on the town?—It could not exist without them; the shops are altogether supported by the country people.

199. And you consider that, if they were brought in, it would be a hardship?—Yes.

Mr. J. J. [illegible] examined by Mr. [illegible], Barrister-at-Law.

Mr. J. J. [illegible].

199. Are you authorised to state what Lord [illegible]'s views are on the subject?—I am.

200. You have had a telegram from the head agent, stating that he is totally opposed to any extension of the boundaries of the town?—Yes, I have; and I am perfectly aware that that is his opinion.

201. Who is the owner of a portion of the land [illegible]?—He is the owner of almost all the land, and I myself am a tenant for [illegible] of what would come inside.

202. How many townlands do you hold surrounding the town?—Four portions of townlands.

203. Four of those [illegible]—the greater part of them—is in your own hands?—Yes.

204. And do you hold them under Lord [illegible]?—Yes.

205. What is your valuation in [illegible]?—£[illegible]

206. What is your valuation in the townland of [illegible]?—£[illegible] [illegible]s.

207. What is your valuation in the townland of [illegible]?—£[illegible] [illegible]s.

208. And what is your valuation in the townland of [illegible]?—£[illegible] [illegible]s.

209. These come to £[illegible] [illegible]s.?—Yes.

210. How many houses are there upon the whole of that belonging to whatever tenants there may be?—There are only five inhabited houses and two cabins that are valued for nothing. They are not in the valuation, and my own house and two [illegible] houses valued, one for [illegible] and the other for [illegible].

[illegible], Sept [illegible], 18[illegible].

Mr. E. T. Kelly.

211. Are these houses far from the town—about half a mile from the town?—All average half a mile from the town and more.

212. Mr. Rogers's, of Lismanagh, is £125 of a valuation?—Yes. There is only one herd's house in that.

213. Is the nearest of these denominations to the town. What part of Clonakeyne do you reside in?—I reside in that townland.

214. What is the part you reside in called?—I call it my demesne.

215. That is the demesne of Knox Lawn?—Yes.

216. Another townland, the whole of which is intended to be included within this district—Loughpasane—in which your valuation is £163 10s.—what is the nature or quality of that land?—Grazing; it is grazing land.

217. Is it at present partially flooded?—It is.

218. The portion near the town is under water?—Yes, there is two feet of water on it.

219. Do you get any benefit in the way of grazing stock from the town?—This year I have only two [illegible]. There are some people to whom I gave grass for nothing. I did not charge them anything as the season was not good.

220. The Commissioner.—You are opposed to the extension on your own behalf?—Yes, undoubtedly.

221. Is there any part of the whole district of the town, round about the town that is likely to be laid out in streets or built upon?—No, and I wish to say that for a mile on any side of the town the Grand Jury have made very good footpaths, and I don't think any improvement could be made in it, and on the road leading to the demesne there is a very good footpath there already.

Mr. Joseph Holmes.

Mr. Joseph Holmes examined.

222. The Commissioner.—Where do you reside?—Within the town.

223. Have you any property outside the town?—I represent some very large proprietors—[illegible] Lord [illegible], and Colonel [illegible], and they all object to the proposed extension of the boundary.

224. On what grounds are they all opposed to it?—Of the 1,[illegible] acres that it is proposed to add to the borough, at least 1,[illegible] acres or more of that are under grass, and in the occupation of large grass farmers who merely occupy them through their [illegible]. The rest of them are [illegible]; so that there is a very small population indeed that will have any benefit. They will pay for it.

225. You consider that the benefit is mutual?—They have no benefit at all. The benefit is for the town.

226. You have heard Mr. Rogers's evidence?—Yes.

227. And you coincide with what he has stated?—Yes; the town is altogether supported by the country and by the floating population.

228. Do you think that the country and the floating population would have any objection to pay a [illegible] of taxation, if it would improve the town?—I have no doubt they would.

229. Do you think it is an advantage for the people coming into the town to have it well lit and well kept?—It is well lit, but it is not well kept.

230. Do you think it is an advantage to the people to have the town well lit?—I don't think it is a great advantage, as long as they are in the town, and [illegible] the shops.

231. Supposing the town is well kept, don't you consider it an advantage to the country people?—I don't think it is. They spend their time on the land. They don't spend their time in the town.

232. You do not think it matters whether it is clean or dirty?—I don't think it does. It is not a town of a wonderfully enticing character.

233. You do not think it is right that the town people should tax them for the benefit they are enjoying?—The town, I am sorry to say, like every other town, has [illegible] in this way, that the people outside the town cannot buy cattle [illegible] as they used to do, and the consequence is that people are not in the same independent circumstances that they were, and it would not be fair to throw upon the [illegible] upon this 1,[illegible] acres, and so [illegible] than that of taxation of the landlords.

234. You consider the town a falling town. Do you consider that the people outside should assist in keeping it up?—I don't think so; this would be very [illegible]. It [illegible] is falling down since the rural population is decreasing. We have fewer houses and fewer tenants I am sorry to say.

235. Do you think that this extra [illegible] taken in the town might be [illegible]?—Do you mean to keep up the credit of the town?

236. I don't mean that?—It would not bring in more into the town.

237. Mr. Kelly.—Lord Kenmare [illegible] the [illegible] of [illegible], and is willing to [illegible] any sum of money that may be necessary for [illegible], in a proper sanitary condition, the portion of the town belonging to him.

Mr. Lambert.

Mr. Lambert, Town Clerk, re-examined by Mr. William Daly.

238. In the proposed area that you suggest should be annexed to the town of [illegible], how many persons qualified to vote, having the £4 qualification for the vote for a Town Commissioner?—There would be about forty-five [illegible] voters.

239. How many in the proposed area would be qualified to act as Commissioners, if elected?—One.

240. Who is that one?—Mr. Kelly, of Knox Lawn.

Mr. William Daly.

Mr. William Daly examined.

241. The Commissioner.—Upon what point do you desire to tender evidence?—I wish to submit that the feeling of the ratepayers of the town would be that the Town Commissioners should not take the sanitary powers into their management, provided that the present sanitary authority had power to include some of them and some of the large ratepayers of the town on a committee to inspect works and to carry them out. There is an objection because one-half of the expense should be paid by the landlords, and that the Board of Guardians are better qualified to carry out the work.

The inquiry then concluded.

NENAGH.—AUGUST 26th, 1879.

Before Mr. Henry A. Robinson.

Mr. Anthony Nolan, Chairman of the Town Commissioners, examined.

Nenagh.
Aug. 26, 1879.
Mr. Anthony Nolan.

1. How long have you been Chairman?—[illegible] years.

2. Previous to that you were a Commissioner for some time?—Yes.

3. And you are well acquainted with the requirements of the town?—Yes.

4. Were you present when the queries we sent down were submitted to your Board?—I think not.

5. The queries of this were submitted to a meeting of the Commissioners?—Yes.

6. Was a special meeting called?—Yes.

7. And the replies they gave us were to the effect that an extension was required?—Yes.

8. To what extent?—To extend the boundary two miles instead of one—the existing boundary is one mile.

9. Is the existing boundary [illegible]—It follows irregularly [illegible].

10. The existing boundary, I understand, is as near as possible a circle from [illegible]?—Yes, it is a circle.

11. And was it the general opinion of the Board that the proposed extension should be two miles?—It was unanimous.

12. Would you make the boundary coterminous with the Poor Law electoral division?—That was suggested by Dr. [illegible], a member of our board, and a Poor Law Guardian.

13. The Select Committee which referred us to report, suggested to us that as far as possible it would be desirable to make towns coterminous with Poor Law electoral divisions, so that if the proposed extension followed the lines of the electoral division it would be a gain in point?—Yes.

14. Nenagh is a market town?—Yes.

15. And the farming people from outside come in regularly to the market here?—Yes.

16. And is the land more valuable from its proximity to the town?—Yes.

17. Do the country people make use of the roads and lights?—Yes.

18. And send in their children to school?—Yes.

19. Do you think they derive advantages from the town being well and properly kept?—Yes.

20. And you think they ought to pay for it?—Yes.

21. Is it your opinion that the town would be better managed if the sanitary authority was vested in yourselves?—No, I would be for leaving it as it is, in the hands of the Poor Law Guardians; everything is very satisfactorily done by them.

22. You have no reason to complain, and every demand made on the sanitary authority has been complied to?—Yes.

23. Is it the opinion of your Board that separation from the Grand Jury for the management of roads would be desirable, as far as the town is concerned?—Some of the Board entertain a different opinion on the subject, and I think it is better to leave matters as they are.

24. Then you would not be in favour of having an individual authority over the town—you prefer to leave the sanitary work under the Guardians, and the roads under the Grand Jury, and the town under the Commissioners?—Precisely; that is my view.

25. You think the people outside derive such benefits from their proximity to the town that they ought fairly to be asked to contribute something towards it?—Yes.

26. You are under the Towns' Improvement Act of '54?—Yes.

27. What rate have you levied?—It is only 6d. in the pound.

28. Is there much land within the present boundary available for building?—There is very little.

29. In fact I suppose nearly the whole of the land within the boundary is built over to a certain extent?—With of course [illegible]. The people would extend the town by building in the suburbs.

30. Do you know the valuation of the electoral division?—I do not know; Mr. [illegible] will be better able to tell you.

31. What are the particular grounds on which you desire the extension?—We wish to have an increase in the boundary for this reason. People are out for extra light, and watching; they wish to have more watchmen employed than at present, and to have the town lighted during the whole of the night. The country people complain that it is at times in a state of darkness, and we are unable to raise the funds so as to meet the extra expense.

32. In fact certain improvements are needed for the people living out of them, you are deprived from want of means?—Yes.

33. And if you had an extended area of taxation it would be remedied?—Yes, I may mention that it is one of the great grievances that we have no fair green. The fairs are held in the streets, and it is deplorable to see the state of them in that respect.

34. If you had an increased income would you endeavour to obtain a fair green?—Yes.

35. Then I suppose I may take it that your chief reason in favour of the extension is a desire to carry out improvements in the town?—Yes.

36. And that any extension, giving an increased revenue and consequent improvements in the town, would be of advantage to those outside as well as those inside?—Yes.

37. Do you think the advantages of the town extend two miles?—Yes, and for several miles round.

38. Is there any large town near it?—No, not within [illegible] miles of it—there is Roscrea. [illegible] It is in fact in the centre of a district of [illegible] miles in which there is no other town of importance. There are villages, and for a radius of fifteen or sixteen miles, all the people would come in here.

39. And you think the people in the whole electoral division have all advantages from the town, nearly to the same extent as those in it?—Yes.

Mr. George [illegible], [illegible], examined.

Mr. George [illegible].

40. I was the first Chairman under the Town's Improvement Act, and the boundary was made out at the time.

41. Before the town came under the Towns' Improvement Act, was it under any other Act?—Yes, the 9th of George IV.

42. And which is now determined to adopt the Towns' Improvement Act was the boundary marked on the map mentioned, then fixed?—Yes, it was made out by Mr. [illegible] with my assistance.

43. And what steps did the Commissioners take to prepare a fair and just boundary being defined?—Mr. [illegible] and myself perambulated the entire boundary. I have heard Mr. Nolan's evidence. I may say that I reside in the neighbourhood, and have a good deal of property that would be taxed, but notwithstanding that I fully concur in Mr. Nolan's evidence. I think that the people around participate largely in the advantages of the town. I would strongly oppose any transfer of the powers from the

existing bodies—it would involve the appointment of an additional surveyor and staff and would be absurd. As to the sanitary body I would not have any such transfer, for it too would entail a separate staff, and we have a body that is now willing, and ready to give us every facility. I fully concur with Mr. Nolan, in saying that the people within the electoral division derive advantages from the town.

43. You think the electoral division would be a good boundary?—I have not studied it, and there are others more competent than I am to offer an opinion on it; but as far as I can form an opinion from what I have heard, and from my general knowledge of the neighbourhood, it would be well to have the boundaries of the town and the Poor Law electoral division coterminous.

44. You think that would result in advantage?—Well, not to myself, but to others.

45. Do you live outside the boundary?—I believe at present my place is outside the boundary. In my case the electoral division is a very well defined boundary, and I concur with Mr. Nolan.

46. Do you consider Nenagh a thriving town?—It is a very important town.

47. Do you think the census of 1881 will show an increase over the census of 1871?—I think it will show some improvement, perhaps, in point of population, but in point of buildings.

48. Are there any building operations going on at present within the town?—Yes, there are a large class of labourers' houses being erected. One gentleman and I are making arrangements with the Board of Works for some building operations.

49. Do people of business usually live in their places of business, or outside?—In their places of business.

50. There is no such thing as people living outside to avoid taxation?—No such idea.

51. How is it the full rate is never struck?—I have ceased to be a commissioner for a great many years, so that I don't know.

Mr. John O[illegible] examined.

52. You are Clerk of the Town Commissioners?—Yes.

53. How long have you been so?—About thirty years.

54. Nenagh is under the Towns' Improvement Act of 1854?—Yes.

55. When was it adopted?—In January, 1856.

56. Was it adopted for all purposes?—No.

57. Only for lighting and cleansing?—Yes; lighting and cleansing. We light, clean, water it, and supply water.

58. And the boundary then adopted is the one now existing?—Yes; there have been no alterations.

59. How far does that boundary extend on the north?—About a mile.

60. What is the area of the present boundary?—2,080 statute acres 3 perches.

61. And the population?—5,[illegible].

62. And do you consider it is increasing?—Yes.

63. And it is probable that after the next census Nenagh will be up to the number to constitute it the urban sanitary authority?—Yes. I think it is over 6,000 at present.

64. What is the valuation?—The full rate is on a valuation of £8,[illegible] 10s., that is the value of the buildings, and on £3,[illegible] we strike the one-fourth.

65. What are your receipts?—£[illegible].

66. And your expenditure?—It is nearly balanced.

67. Have you any other sources of revenue?—Yes, we have a dog tax, £13 or £14, and fines for drunkenness, which amount to about £15 in the year.

68. The town is not divided into wards?—No.

69. In what electoral division is the town?—Nenagh.

70. Is it entirely in the electoral division of Nenagh?—Yes.

71. Did the boundary chosen when the town came under the Towns' Improvement Act in 1856, follow the townland boundaries?—Yes, except where we met rivers and roads, and we made permanent boundaries wherever we could. In the case of a road or a river we sometimes deviated from the townland boundary.

72. To make it as nearly as possible a mile from the town?—Yes.

73. If the two-mile extension suggested was taken would the boundary run into more than one electoral division?—No. We have it sketched out here, and by making the electoral division of Nenagh the boundary, it would give nearly what we require by the two-mile extension.

74. Have the Town Commissioners any property vested in them?—No.

75. Have they no income from tolls, fairs, or otherwise?—No.

76. Will you give the poor rates and municipal rates since 1874?—The poor rate is about 2s. 6d., and municipal 6d.

77. I see you have given me here the poor rate for 1874 and 1876 as 2s. 6d.?—Yes; and 1877, 3s., 1878, 3s.

78. Does that include any special rate for sanitary purposes?—Yes. I think, indeed, there was something proposed.

79. Can you tell me the contributory district on which that special rate was assessed?—I cannot tell you that.

80. The county cess, what has it been for the same period?—For the last two years it has been about 9d. or 9½d.—lower than usual.

81. What markets have you in the town?—Every Thursday; a butter market on Monday.

82. And I suppose the people of the entire electoral division bring in their produce for sale?—Yes.

83. And make use of the roads?—Yes.

84. And it is generally considered that the town of Nenagh, being kept in a good condition, is of advantage to them?—Yes.

85. And they pay nothing towards the maintenance of the town?—No.

86. I see you only struck the one-half rate for the last four years, and it was stated by Mr. Nolan that there was no increase to your annual income desirable for the purposes of improvement—why, then, did they never strike the full rate?—They thought that the times were depressed, and the fact was that they did not want to put on the tax.

87. One of the purposes for which an increase of income would be desirable would be lighting?—Yes, they complain of that.

88. And the fair?—Yes.

89. The people always hold the markets and fairs in the streets, I understand?—Yes, and it is in a very wretched condition for a day or two afterwards; it is a very bad incident.

90. And do they expose their goods for sale in the streets?—Yes.

91. And you think it would be of advantage if proper arrangements were made to prevent this unpleasantness?—Yes; if you go through the town on such a day you will find cattle on the footpaths, and people are actually in danger of being knocked down and injured by the cattle.

92. Did you ever hear the objection raised that the limits of the borough are too small?—No.

93. When we sent these queries down to you, did you submit them to a special meeting of the Board or to an ordinary meeting?—I was away at the time.

and when I came back a special meeting was held yesterday, and the Commissioners adopted unanimously a proposition to have the area extended.

94. Did they specify to what extent they considered the increase of the area should be carried?—They did; they said a radius of two miles from the centre of the town would be most desirable.

95. Were any of the ratepayers present?—I am not sure.

96. But I suppose, after all, the Commissioners may be said to represent fairly the feeling of the ratepayers?—Yes; besides there was public notice given, and everybody was made acquainted with the fact that you would be here.

97. Was there any resolution passed for the enlargement?—There was.

98. Will you kindly give it to me?—I have not got the minutes, but it was proposed and seconded and put to the meeting and passed unanimously.

99. And was that resolution simply in favour of extension or in favour of extension of the electoral division?—They said about two miles, and the Clerk of the Workhouse said [illegible] found it would very nearly coincide with the electoral division.

100. I understood that the resolution you read spoke of an extension of about two miles, but does not specify that extension to be to the limits of the Poor Law electoral division?—Yes.

101. Were the Commissioners aware that the Select Committee, in their report, [illegible] suggested that wherever practicable the municipal areas and the Poor Law electoral divisions boundaries should be made coterminous?—Well, some said, [illegible] it might be too far from the town. They were not aware how far the boundaries would be, but I find that the boundary of the electoral division is just what they wanted it to be. They were not aware of that—I mean, they were not aware that the boundary which they expressed their desire to have would just be about the electoral division. I think that if I had had the boundaries marked out here yesterday, and had submitted them to the board, they would have adopted them.

102. And the reason the Commissioners gave for the enlarged boundary was, as I understand, that an increase of persons who [illegible] for the improvement of the town?—Yes.

103. And they think the enlargement of the town would be a benefit to the people residing outside the present limits?—Yes, they would derive some of the benefit in question.

104. Do those people come in [illegible] daily?—Yes.

105. And the [illegible] and lighting of the town is, I take it, an advantage to those people who come in as you say?—Yes.

106. Are there what you call villa residences outside the town?—Very few.

107. Do mostly all the inhabitants congregate in the town, as would be likely in any [illegible] ?—That is all.

108. In the town, extending in any one direction, does it [illegible]?—Well, there are [illegible] houses [illegible] cottages having [illegible] in one direction.

109. What direction is that?—Mainly to the south.

110. Do you remember the town twenty years ago?—Yes, there have been a great many new houses since then.

111. You consider it to be a thriving town?—I do.

112. Can you tell me the number of qualified voters that would be brought in if the area was extended?—No, I do not.

113. Would there be any gentlemen's residences included in this extension?—Yes.

114. About how many roughly?—Perhaps some three or four.

115. Is there a good water supply in the town?—[illegible].

116. Do the guardians carry out all the recommendations made to them?—Well, from my experience of them, since they are the sanitary authority they do all that is required of them.

117. If there was this extension of the area would it bring the population up to 6,000?—Yes, and they would become the sanitary authority, and I think they would become it now too.

118. Are there any sanitary improvements required in the town?—I suppose there are some.

119. Have you ever made any applications to the guardians for anything that was required which they have not carried out?—Well, I think not, [illegible], but I believe there have been [illegible] where such applications have been made.

120. Do the Commissioners know that they will have the [illegible]?—I suppose so.

121. Have they ever made application [illegible] from the Grand Jury?—There is nothing on the books to that effect.

122. By the 203rd section of the Public Health Act the Local Government Board can, when you first become the urban sanitary authority, give you exemption from the Grand Jury, even without their consent; are you aware of that?—I was not aware that they could do it without the consent of the Grand Jury.

123. Well, they can, by the Public Health Act of last session?—Individually I would be for separation, but if the Commissioners got the [illegible], and had the laying out of these [illegible], it would be between £500 and £700.

124. And if the Commissioners had the whole electoral division you think it would be better to have the Town Council with all the rights within themselves, and to be able to lay the rates themselves?—Yes, and I think it would lessen the rates.

Mr. [illegible], Clerk of the Union, examined.

125. How long have you been clerk?—Twenty years.

126. What is the population of the electoral division of [illegible]; do you know the population?—No.

127. Or the area?—No.

128. What is the valuation?—£11,204.

129. What is the present valuation of the town?—£5,[illegible].

130. Then you would add about £6,000 by taking in the electoral division?—Yes.

131. I suppose outside the present limits the occupiers are chiefly of the farmer class?—Yes, there are a good many gentlemen's residences surrounding the district.

132. Has there been any sanitary rate struck?—Yes, since the Sanitary Act was introduced.

133. But not a sanitary rate for special purposes?—Yes.

134. Applied to what?—Sewerage purposes.

135. What was the contributory district?—For the sewerage works of the town the union at large contributed one-seventh, and the electoral division the remainder; there was about £1,000 expended on that occasion.

136. The electoral division chiefly bore the expense?—Yes.

137. Do you live in the town?—Yes.

138. Did you hear the recommendation of Mr. [illegible]?—Yes.

139. And do you think that would be desirable?—I think [illegible] only have to pay a [illegible] rate, and they derive a very great advantage at present from their proximity to the town. I may say that the Guardians have always provided the sanitary works required at any particular time when recommended.

140. What is your opinion as to the advisability or otherwise of extending, curtailing, or otherwise altering the municipal limits?—I myself am in favour of the extension of the boundary.

Mr. John Johnston [illegible], Chairman of the Board of Guardians, examined.

141. I understand you are likely to have the military jurisdiction taken out of your hands in consequence of the population being up to the limits?—Yes.

142. You have heard the statement of Mr. [illegible]?—Yes.

143. And with reference to the suggestion to extend the boundary of the town so as to make the boundary coterminous with that of the electoral division, do the people in the electoral division derive advantage from the town of Newry?—Yes.

144. You think that to a large extent they make use of the town?—Decidedly.

145. And you think that they make such a use of it, that the rate that would be imposed on them could not fairly be considered a hardship?—No hardship.

146. It will reduce the rates in the town?—Yes; I am myself living within the present area, and have land outside the present area. It will make to a great deal of my land that is not as present taxed, but I do not object to it.

147. Have you any opportunity of ascertaining the feeling of the ratepayers, or the people who would be brought in by this extension?—Well, no; except in conversation with two of these gentlemen in the locality. They don't seem disposed to recommend it, however, I don't know that the matter was fully explained to them, and probably if it were they would make no opposition.

148. Were your Board aware of the matter, as to the electoral division being suggested?—No; I do not think the Board of Guardians were aware of that.

149. Do you think they would have made any objection to it?—I think that some gentlemen outside the area would, perhaps, object.

150. These gentlemen however, I presume, [illegible] they have the advantages of the town without paying for it?—They must do that.

151. You, yourself, do not think that electoral division is too large?—No; I think it is very fair. I was one of the parties who assisted in marking out the boundary of it from my knowledge of the district, and I have no objection to keeping to the electoral division.

152. Keeping to the electoral division would bring the population to considerably over 6,000; would your Board have any objection to the sanitary jurisdiction of the town being taken out of their hands?—I believe the townspeople are very well satisfied with the arrangements, and we have done the best for them we could; and, therefore, I don't think that it would be desirable. It would, perhaps, increase the staff, and a greater number of persons would be employed, but I do not think any great advantage would ensue from taking the sanitary jurisdiction from the Board of Guardians.

153. Do you think the Grand Jury have better appliances for carrying out the improvement of the roads?—I would leave the matter in the hands of the Grand Jury, and, presuming that if you make any change, you would have a surveyor, with a deputy surveyor, and a staff which we have not.

154. Do you think the Markets is a good regulation handing them to the board?—Well, I have considered myself in that place, and that they [illegible] as well as they might be. That, however, is a matter of opinion. In some places they are worse, and in some places better.

155. Have you anything further to add?—Nothing.

156. Are you of opinion that a fair-green ought to be established, instead of holding the markets in the streets of the town?—That is one of the things many people of wealth we have in complaint. I have heard persons living in the district saying they would not come to town, owing to the hurt [illegible] their cattle received, driving them through the streets.

157. Do I understand that the cattle are left on the footways?—They are left on the footways of the town, and that is the great objection.

158. You say the present arrangement in that respect may be described as a crying evil?—Yes.

159. I suppose it is impossible to carry out the proper cleansing of the town while this state of things goes on?—Yes; a great deal of the stuff goes into the sewerage, and in fact there is a great difficulty with it.

160. That is a matter, the correction of which is urgently needed?—I think when Mr. [illegible] [illegible] on a former occasion, it was hoped that something would be done. Some time ago there was a fair-green, and the fairs were held on it; but for some reason or another, the people of the town did not wish the people and the cattle to be separated. [illegible] made other, and they remained in the streets.

161. Do you think any other improvement might be for the town, and which the Town Commissioners did not carry out for want of money, is the lighting for instance, good?—The town [illegible] to be lighted. It is lighted from September to March, and the lights are shut off at eleven o'clock. Some nights, when there is a strong moon, the lights are not kept burning at the [illegible], but I think there would be an improvement in the lighting of the town if we had more money. I know they are very slow in paying the Gas Company, of which I am a director.

162. The town then is lighted with gas?—Yes.

163. Did I understand you to say it is lighted up to the limits of the boundary?—No; only to the [illegible] part of the town. During the [illegible] year the lights were put down a little lower than before, but they were [illegible]. [illegible].

164. You would I think, then you agree with Mr. [illegible], and you think that there are sanitary improvements, and improvements regarding the fair-green, lighting &c., which would be carried out if there was an increase of revenue?—Yes.

165. And that there should be an extension?—Yes, but I would recommend that the Grand Jury should remain in charge of the roads the Town Commissioners would have nothing to do according to the [illegible].

166. And your proposal is to take [illegible]?—Yes, for it is large for land at present [illegible].

Dr. Thomas Spair examined.

166. I have been a Commissioner for the past two years, and have resided in the town for the past sixty years.

167. Do you think with the Chairman that there are improvements which would tend to the better sanitary condition of the town, if there was an increase of funds, and you included in your new area a population of 6,000?—Yes.

168. Is the sanitary state of the town rendered bad by having the fairs held in the streets?—Yes, I am sure of it.

169. And would not your board be glad to have an increase of funds?—Yes.

170. And would they use these funds to procure a proper fairgreen?—Yes.

171. What increase would be required?—I cannot exactly say that.

172. Do you know the electoral division?—Yes.

173. It extends two miles from the centre of the town?—Yes.

174. And do you think the people living within that radius make use of the town of Newry?—Yes, and gain very great advantages from the town.

175. And pay nothing for it?—Yes.

176. And you think it would be no hardship if they paid one-fourth taxation?—No.

177. All the farmers come in on the market days?—Yes.

178. They use the roads, and make scavenging, &c., very necessary?—Yes.

179. Do you think the electoral division a well defined boundary?—Yes.

180. Have you any property outside?—Yes, something very small, not worth talking about.

181. And notwithstanding that you would be in favour of extension?—Yes.

182. Have the ratepayers had any opportunity of knowing that the Commission was to sit?—Yes, it was fully advertised.

Nenagh, Aug. [illegible]

Dr. Thomas Ryan.

Dr. B[illegible], a ratepayer, examined.

Dr. B[illegible]

183. Do you think the boundary of the town ought to be extended to the electoral division?—Yes.

184. And that all the people within the electoral division have very nearly the same advantages as in the town?—Yes.

185. They have the advantage of the lights and send their children in here to school, &c.?—Yes, except those that go to the National school outside.

186. Have you any property outside?—Yes.

187. And you would be taxed by the extension?—Yes.

188. And you don't object to that considering the advantages you derive from the town?—No.

189. I suppose the land is better and more valuable from its proximity to the town?—Yes.

Mr. Robert St. John, Town Commissioner, examined.

Mr. Robert St. John.

190. Were you present when the matter was discussed by your board?—Yes.

191. And have you had an opportunity of speaking with the people outside who would be taxed?—No.

192. Have you spoken to the ratepayers?—Well, any I spoke to have not expressed any objection to the extension.

193. Do you think Nenagh is improving?—I do. It is decidedly a very improving town.

194. And do you object to the fairs being held in the streets?—Yes.

195. Are the fairs held on the main streets, or on one street in particular?—There are three or four large fairs, and almost all the streets of the town are crowded with cattle.

196. And on market days I suppose the inconvenience is as great?—Well there are cattle exhibited on market days sometimes.

197. And the scavenging is a matter of difficulty?—Yes.

198. And do you think if nothing else was done with the additional funds derived from the extended area than to remedy this evil, it would be an advantage calculated to influence you in favour of the change?—Decidedly.

199. Are you acquainted with the electoral division?—Yes.

200. It is two miles from the centre of the town—do you think the people living within that area derive advantages from the town?—Yes. We decided on having a radius of as nearly two miles as possible.

201. I understand that on nearly every occasion it was unanimous?—On all occasions as to the extension.

202. The electoral division was not spoken of?—No, that was only an after-thought of Mr. Gleeson's.

203. You do not wish for a hard and fast line?—No, as near as possible. I think we could manage the sanitation of the town if it was placed in our own hands. There is a large water supply wanted here.

204. Are you in favour of the principle of having the entire undivided authority of the town in the hands of the Town Commissioners?—I would not take the roads.

205. Why?—I think the staff that would be required would, perhaps, run away with the money.

206. Do you know any other improvement besides that are required?—There is flagging. The flagging of the town is in a very bad way. We often thought of levying an extra rate, and by extending the township we will be able to do it better.

207. So there are a considerable number of improvements you would apply a larger income to?—Yes.

208. And all these you think would be equally applicable to the people outside?—Yes, I do. I may mention there are some mills out in the town, and they make use of the roads more than any one else.

209. Is the railway station in the township?—Yes.

Mr. John Ryan, Town Commissioner, examined.

Mr. John Ryan.

210. You are a ratepayer?—Yes.

211. Have you property outside?—Yes.

212. And do you make use of the fairs of the town?—Yes.

213. Do you object to their being held in the streets?—Yes.

214. And you think steps should be taken to procure a fair green?—Yes. There is a field at the end of the town offered ten or twelve years ago by Captain Holmes, the man who gave the squares.

215. Do you think the people of the entire electoral division would be in favour of a fair green?—I do.

216. And you don't think they would object to pay a very small rate for it?—No.

217. It would be a decided advantage to the people doing business at the fairs, and better for animals themselves to have a fair green?—Certainly. Captain Holmes would give the field still.

218. You say he offered it to them?—Yes, on account of getting the customs of the town.

219. And it was not taken?—No.

220. Can you tell me, Mr. Gleeson, why that was?

Mr. Gleeson.—The publicans and grocers think that by taking away the cattle from the streets they lose a good deal of custom.

221. Were those who so objected Commissioners?—They were. They think that if the people sold their cattle in a fair green they would go away.

Mr. St. John.—The publicans were the persons who succeeded in the opposition to the fair green?

Mr. Gleeson.—There are business people still in the town who think it better to have the cattle in the town. They think there would be more money circulated.

222. Would the fair green be inside or outside?—It is on the edge of the town, not 100 perches from here.

223. I have heard that it is considered by some people that, if any change were made, the revenues of the town would be lessened, inasmuch as there would be a likelihood of not so many people being fined for drunkenness?—Precisely. The fact is the belief was that they felt that if the fairs were held in a green the people would do their business and go home.

224. Is this proposed fair green suitable in every way?—In every way.

The inquiry adjourned.

STRABANE—JULY 14TH, 1879.

Before HENRY A. ROBINSON, Esq.

STRABANE. July 14, 1879.

Mr. Hugh Maguire.

Mr. HUGH MAGUIRE, Town Clerk, examined.

1. You are the Town Clerk?—Yes.
2. The town originally, I believe, was under 9th George IV?—Yes.
3. At what time did you come under the Towns' Improvement Act?—That Act was adopted in Strabane in the year 1874.
4. For all purposes?—Yes, I believe that was so, but I was not Town Clerk at that time.
5. What is the population of Strabane?—It is 5,369 now.
6. It is an increasing population?—Slightly.
7. Would you imagine that in 1871 it would number near 5,000 persons?—Well, I could hardly say.
8. What is the valuation?—£13,703 5s.
9. And the area is?—1,859 acres, 3 roods, and 33 perches.
10. Do you strike a full rate of one shilling on that?—Yes, sir.
11. I mean, how much is on the full, and how much on the one-fourth?—On the full, there is £10,132 15s., and on the one-fourth £2,600 7s.
12. What does that produce?—This produces on the full rate at one shilling in the pound £506 13s. 1½d.; and on the one-fourth, rating £35 1s. 11½d.—and the total of that is £542 15s. 10½d.
13. Is the electoral division of Strabane, and the townland of Milltown included in the present boundary?—It is not in the electoral division of Strabane.
14. What electoral division is it in?—Camus-juxta-Mourne. Milltown is outside the electoral division.
15. Could you give me the municipal rates for the last five years?—In 1874 there was 3s. in the pound, including water rate and the Public Health Act—a very high rate—the highest under the Act of the Act. In 1878 the rate was 2s. in the pound, and in 1879 it was 1s. and 6d. sanitary.
16. What was that for, had you any special rates then?—No, sir; the rate was for general purposes.
17. What was your rate in 1877?—None.
18. In 1878?—One shilling in the pound.
19. And in 1879?—One shilling in the pound.
20. Can you give me the county cess and poor-rates?—Well, the average is about 2s. 4d. with the county cess.
21. And the poor rates, how much?—Well, I think the average would be about 1s. 3d. in the pound. It is 3s. 6d. this year, including the rate for sanitary purposes.
22. How is the town of Strabane lighted?—It is lighted with gas.
23. Is there a good water supply?—It is good, at the present time.
24. Is it supplied from pumps or a reservoir?—It is from a reservoir. We have not made under the 9th of George IV., but we have another under a new scheme adopted by the Commissioners a higher elevation; and, in fact, they are both in use at the present time.
25. How many Commissioners have you?—We have got nine.
26. Was there ever any question raised about the boundary?—Yes, the question was entertained and the Commissioners were of opinion that an extension was required.
27. Did they pass a resolution, to that effect?—I cannot say that they did; but, at all events, they were unanimous that extension was not required; and I think probably there may be a resolution.
28. The land lying around Strabane is agricultural land?—Yes, and not much built upon.
29. Are there any villa residences outside the present boundary?—Not that I am aware of.
30. With reference to Milltown, have you the valuation of it?—The total valuation would be £309 12s.
31. What would be the feeling of the Board in reference to Milltown; would they object to have it excluded from the municipal area, in order to make the boundary coterminous with the Poor Law division?—The question has never been raised. The total cost involved in front is £3 7s. 10½d.
32. Chairman of Town Commissioners.—Mr. Humphreys is paying for the water in addition to that?—Yes.
33. Mr. ROBINSON.—Have the Commissioners considered the desirability of taking up the roads?—Yes, many times, and they have passed resolutions to that effect.
34. Do you think they would desire an extension, if they were the authorities for the roads?—I think they would be content to leave the jurisdiction within the present limits—that is, they think the burden of the money cess on the rates on the land would not pay the keeping up of the roads; that would be the difficulty.
35. And is it the feeling of the Board that they would like to have the superintendence of the roads in their own hands?—Yes—they have passed repeated resolutions to that effect.

Mr. James Kennedy.

Mr. JAMES KENNEDY, Chairman of the Town Commissioners, examined.

36. Mr. ROBINSON.—Have you lived long in the town of Strabane?—Nearly fifty years.
37. Were you a Commissioner under 9th George IV.?—No, I was not.
38. Have you any idea of the present limits of the town, and what they were then?—Yes.
39. Do you consider Strabane a growing town?—Yes.
40. Is it, would you say, increasing, or improving every day?—I would say yes.
41. Is there a tendency to build in any one direction?—Well, that tendency seems to have lapsed; and I would consider the taxation is a deterrent.
42. Is there a tendency to build outside the boundary?—Very little, or any, at the present time.
43. Have you fairs, markets, here?—Oh, yes.
44. And do the people around make use of the town for those purposes?—Yes, they come in here from four or five miles around.
45. Well, then, they derive certain advantages from the town being kept in good order and condition?—Yes.
46. And they, in a way, pay for that?—Yes, they do pay for the accommodation of the flax market and the corn market, but not the cattle market.
47. Have you any income from tolls and customs here?—Yes.
48. Is there any property vested in the corporate body?—No; except the gas.
50. And is there any profit derived to the Commissioners from the gas-works?—I could not say.
51. Is it your view then, that there is no extension required?—Yes, it is my view, and I believe it to be the view of the Board also. We had a matter under consideration with regard to the taking in of the town of Lifford.
52. Do you think it would be desirable to do so?—We have not had the matter before the Board, but I believe, in my own opinion, it would be desirable.
53. Would you, as a Board, be prepared to do everything for it as you have done for Strabane?—Yes.
54. You have the two towns lying almost together; and you think that under a joint management advantages might result for both?—Yes, but they might, of course, object to it.
55. Is Lifford lighted?—No.

56. Is the water supply there good?—I believe it is pretty good, but I am not certain of it.

57. What distance is Lifford from Strabane?—About an English mile from the Hall.

58. You cannot say, definitely, whether there is a good water supply there?—No; but I know it is supplied by the Board of [illegible].

59. And have you any method of recording your water supply in Lifford?—No, yes.

60. Then you think it would be desirable to take in Lifford?—Yes.

61. And do you think the Board is of the same opinion?—I could not say.

62. Is it the prevailing opinion that it ought to be brought within the boundary?—I think that would be popular, and I think it would lighten the taxation.

63. What about sewerage?—As the matter of sewerage, I think there would be no difficulty, as there is a fall to the river the whole way down.

64. Is Lifford in [illegible]?—[illegible].

65. Would Lifford derive any advantage from being annexed to Strabane?—I could not say.

66. Do you know the little townland of M'Ilroy's?—Yes.

Strabane. July 12, 1878.

Mr. [illegible] Kennedy.

67. How is it inhabited?—The principal house is that of Mr. Humphreys, the agent of the Duke of Abercorn; the rest are cottier houses. Mr. Humphreys is Chairman of the Board of Guardians.

68. Do you think the Commissioners would object to excluding M'Ilroy's, bearing in mind its isolated situation?—I think it should continue as it is.

69. Unless some adequate reason is given for putting it out of the boundary, you think the Commissioners would not like to part with it?—No; I think they would not, now that we have water and sewerage out to it, and gone to all such expense.

70. Do you extend the lights out to M'Ilroy's?—No, not quite so far; but the sewerage and water go out there.

71. Well, we may take it that your own individual opinion is the present town of Strabane is of sufficient extent?—Yes.

72. And that there is no extension required?—No, unless Lifford could be included.

Mr. Edward Gallagher, Town Commissioner, examined.

Mr. Edward Gallagher.

73. Mr. [illegible].—You have heard the evidence given by the Chairman of the Commissioners, and of Mr. Maguire, the Town Clerk?—Yes.

74. And do you coincide with their opinions?—Yes.

75. How long have you been a Commissioner?—Since the adoption of the Act in 187[illegible].

76. Is your Board well attended?—Yes.

77. You are few, and a very working body?—Well, there is rarely any difficulty in getting a quorum.

78. Do you think it would be desirable to take charge of the roads?—I know of several motions in regard to that, but we were afraid that we would have to go before Parliament for a bill, and then the last thing we [illegible] was that the Poor Law Guardians, becoming the sanitary authority, took the jurisdiction out of our hands altogether.

79. Do you think that it would be desirable for the Commissioners to become the urban sanitary authority?—Well, there is a division of opinion about it. The majority believe that that portion of the business would be better conducted here, because they consider there is a great deal of mismanagement, and that those who have the authority vested in them have not the interests of the ratepayers at heart. We have only two Guardians on the Board representing the people of Strabane.

80. They are in the minority then?—Yes, and the outside Guardians do as they please. The difficulty is this: as it is now, [illegible] the [illegible] is paid by the landlord, and they think that by [illegible] the sanitary authority the whole rate would be levied on the town. That is the only objection. The streets are kept in [illegible] repair and the Commissioners have to pay about £[illegible] a year for scavenging. They would like to have the roads, but [illegible].

81. What is your individual opinion?—Would it be better that the Commissioners were the urban sanitary authority?—I would like to see the road account [illegible] in the proportion [illegible] and [illegible] with the [illegible] additional [illegible] county; for I understand there is about £[illegible] paid in the support of the roads over what is expended—£[illegible] on the roads alone.

82. In thinking that it would be desirable to become the urban sanitary authority, do you think it would be desirable to bring in any other portion of other places within the boundary?—Lifford would be the only place that could be [illegible] for the purpose, as land would only be charged one-fourth.

83. Do you think it would be desirable to include Lifford?—Yes; I think it would be very desirable.

84. Have you ever gone into the matter financially?—No; we thought it would subject us to a great deal of trouble, Lifford being in another county.

85. The town appears to be very compactly built, from the one side the boundary appears to be about half a mile from the town, and in another place it is fully a mile and a quarter. Now, if we were to take in Lifford, within the boundary it would not extend on the [illegible] side more than the boundary does on the north?—No, it would not extend at all.

86. Then you would make [illegible] boundary?—I believe so. I had it measured to-day, not very accurately, but the distance out to Ballycolman is about the same as to Lifford. With regard to M'Ilroy's being included in the borough in the last arrangement, I think it was for the purpose of including Mr. Humphreys' house, but it is also included in the [illegible] boundary.

87. Is it within the [illegible] district?—No.

88. Is there any special sanitary rate levied by the Board of Guardians?—Yes, and M'Ilroy's is not included in the [illegible] district, although it is in the borough. Mr. Humphreys was Chairman of the Commissioners, and I may state that [illegible] his being connected with the Commissioners, it was included.

89. What was the special rate for?—It was for water and sewerage.

90. The [illegible] district was for the town of Strabane only, with the exception of M'Ilroy's?—Yes; the whole of the electoral division of Strabane only.

91. Would you see any objection to [illegible] M'Ilroy's?—Well, I think it would not be [illegible] for all the town [illegible]. Mr. Humphreys would be in favour of the water and the sewerage, although [illegible] which would subject him to a great deal of annoyance. He pays about 3d. in the pound for water, and he said that although he would be glad that M'Ilroy's should be comprised within the boundary, yet it would subject him to a great deal of annoyance.

92. Was the boundary of the town under the 9th George IV. much extended?—Yes, very much extended.

93. I suppose the boundary included only the town proper; simply the ground built upon?—Yes.

94. And when you adopted the Towns Improvement Act you adopted an extended boundary?—Yes.

95. You think if you had to strike the whole of the rate for sanitary purposes on the occupier, it would not be popular in Strabane?—I hardly think it would.

Mr. John Cunningham, Lifford, attended and said he was there to oppose the annexation of Lifford. He had not considered the matter financially, but he did not see that any advantage would accrue to Lifford by being brought under the rule of Strabane.

STRABANE.
July 14, 1879.

Mr. William M'Cullough, C.E.

Mr. William M'Cullough, C.E., examined.

96. Mr. Robinson.—How long have you been Town Surveyor of Strabane?—Three years.

97. Do you know the land pretty well within the boundary?—Yes.

98. Do you think there is any tendency to build any villa residences to avoid town taxes?—Well, I think not.

99. They who have their business and work in Strabane mostly live there?—Yes, that is generally so.

100. Is there a tendency to build of late years in Strabane?—Yes, a slight tendency, some two years ago, but I think it has decreased lately. I think this is owing to the heavy rates in the town for sanitary and other purposes.

101. Do you think there is any desirability of extension?—Well, I don't think there is.

102. You know Milltown?—Yes.

103. You see there is a difficulty arising about the contributory districts, and do you think it would affect the Commissioners if Milltown were excluded?—I quite concur in the opinion of Mr. Gallagher and Mr. Maguire, that is, I don't think it would much matter but they would rather retain it.

104. Would the Milltown people object?—Decidedly not.

105. Is the whole rate levied?—A portion of the £46 11s. 6d. pays full rate, and £24 18s. pays one-fourth rate. With regard to Lifford I would object to it coming under the Commissioners. I think we would not have a right to be taxed. A wide river intervenes between the two towns. It has its own water supply, but it is in the Strabane Union. I have had the opinion of some of the inhabitants of Lifford, and they would object decidedly.

106. There appears on this map to be no thickly populated district outside the town that the town could derive any advantage from?—No, there is no densely populated district.

107. You think that in 1874 they took in all that was desirable?—Yes.

This concluded the inquiry.

Sligo.
Sept. 1, 1879.

Mr. James M'Kim, Sligo.

SLIGO.—SEPTEMBER 1st, 1879.

Before Mr. C. P. Cotton, C.E.; and Mr. H. A. Robinson.

Mr. James M'Kim examined.

1. Mr. Cotton.—You are the Town Clerk of Sligo?—I am.

2. How long have you filled that post?—About thirteen years.

3. How is the municipality formed—under what Act?—Under the 3rd and 4th Victoria, chap. 108 and 109, and also by the Borough Improvement Act of 1869.

4. That is the Sligo Borough Improvement Act of 1869?—Yes.

5. What is the area of the Borough?—3,001 statute acres, 1 rood and 20 perches.

6. And what is the population?—The population in 1871 was 10,670.

7. Is that an increasing population?—I believe it is not, sir.

8. It is about stationary?—Yes; about stationary.

9. What is the valuation of the Borough?—£18,246 5s.

10. Has that been increasing?—Yes.

11. Can you give it to me—the amount for five or six years back?—I cannot give it to you now, but I will afterwards. I will go back two or three years.

12. Is Sligo divided into wards?—Yes.

13. How many?—Three.

14. What are their names?—The North, East, and West.

15. Can you divide the area—the 3,000 acres?—As to the wards?

16. Yes?—I have not got that.

17. Perhaps you can get me, bye-and-bye, the area and valuation of each ward?—Yes; I think I can.

18. Can you tell me the number of voters on the list of municipal voters?—Yes; I can give you them in the different wards now. In the North Ward there are 58 voters; in the East Ward 110; and in the West Ward, 163.

19. What is the representation?—£10.

20. No; I don't mean the qualification. How many councillors are there for each ward?—Six councillors and two aldermen for each ward.

21. That is 331 voters altogether. How many are qualified to sit as councillors, if elected?—I could not say. The qualification is £25.

22. Can you make that number out for me?—I think I can.

23. Can you give me the rates for the last few years, say from 1874?—The last rate was £3,330.

24. What is the municipal rate?—4s. 6d. for each year.

25. Mr. Robinson.—Is that the full limit?—That is the full limit.

26. Mr. Cotton.—Since 1874?—Since 1869.

27. Can you give me the poor rate from 1874 up?—Yes; in 1874, it was 2s. 5d.; in 1875, 2s. 5d.; in 1876, 2s. 1d.; in 1877, 2s. 1d.; in 1878, 2s.; and in 1879, 2s. 1d.; that includes everything.

28. The 4s. 6d. rate includes all rates in lieu of county cess?—Yes.

29. And is there any sanitary rate?—Yes; a 3d. rate.

30. In addition to the 4s. 6d.?—Yes.

31. Beyond the 4s. 6d.?—Yes; in addition to the 4s. 6d.

32. Does that the sanitary rate run back for the last few years?—Yes; it does, sir.

33. Can you tell me the county cess in the adjoining parts?—I cannot. I do not know what it is. I think I can give you the county cess in the barony of Carbury. I can give you that now from 1874. It is 1s. 2½d. for the summer of 1874, and 1s. 6d. for the spring; that is 2s. 8½d. for the two levies.

34. You had better give me the total for each year?—In 1875 it was 2s. 5½d.; in 1876, 2s. 1d.; in 1877, 2s. 1d.; and in 1878, 2s. 2½d.

35. In 1869 the boundary of the municipality was then increased?—It was, sir.

36. And made the same as the Parliamentary boundary?—Yes, made to be the same as the Parliamentary boundary.

37. What electoral division is the borough in?—In the electoral division of Sligo.

38. Mr. Robinson.—What was the area of the boundary before the Act of 1869?—The area was 60a. 2r. 18p.

Mr. Cotton.—And at the same time as the area was extended to the Parliamentary limit, you got the fiscal powers of the Grand Jury transferred to you?—Yes; they have been transferred by the Act of 1869.

40. What other object was there in getting the area extended at that time; or was there any special object?—Yes; there was the amalgamation of the two bodies—the Town and Harbour Commissioners—in managing the town.

41. That might have been independent of the area?—Well, it was considered ——

42. A good opportunity of extending the area?—Yes.

43. Has the question of altering the boundary again been before the Corporation?—It has.

44. And what conclusion did the Corporation come to?—They came to the conclusion that they are satisfied with the present boundaries.

45. Is that by formal resolution of the Council?—The queries you sent down were brought before the Council on the 11th of July.

46. And you were instructed to answer them as they appear before us, and there is no alteration required?—Yes.

47. Are the municipal wards coterminous with the Poor Law wards within the boundary?—They are.

48. Mr. Robinson.—Can you give us the area of the wards for Poor Law purposes.—No; I have not got a return at present showing that, but I think I will be able to find them out for you.

49. Mr. Cotton.—As far as you know is there any special advantage in having the Parliamentary boundary and the Municipal boundary the same—I mean for any purposes connected with the rate books or anything of that kind—any special advantage?—I think it saves a good deal of trouble in having the books and things of that kind the same.

50. In having them the same?—Yes, sir.

51. In opening these proceedings you heard me read out from the report of the Select Committee of the House of Commons, that part of what that Committee recommends is that the boundaries of towns should, where possible, be made coterminous with Poor Law electoral divisions. Well, I see that the Poor Law electoral division of Sligo is something larger than the present municipality. Has it been considered at all whether there would be any advantage or difficulty attending making the two the same. Do you understand me?—I do not.

52. Well, you see on the map that a green line marks the boundary of the town, and a blue line marks the boundary of the electoral division. You perceive that the electoral division is slightly larger than the town. Would there be any disadvantage attending an extension of the town boundary in order that it might be made coterminous with the blue line?—Well, we have not fully considered that, but I think there would.

53. What is your opinion?—My opinion is that the advantages we would derive from it would not be equal to the amount that would be expended upon the roads and other repairs.

54. You think that the valuation of the additional area would not compensate for the expense of the roads?—There are very few buildings outside, and these buildings are only valued at one-half for municipal purposes altogether between the two areas.

55. Between the old area and the new area?—Yes, they are only valued at one-half.

56. And that half if extended to the blue line would apply to the ring outside?—It would, I suppose.

57. You have not gone into any calculation on the subject?—No.

58. Nor the Corporation?—No.

59. Mr. Robinson.—The present boundary cuts through sixteen townlands. If the entirety of those townlands that are cut through were included, it would make the municipal boundary coterminous with that of the electoral division?—I think the electoral division is a coterminous boundary.

60. If the entire of the townlands partially cut were included, the boundaries would then be coterminous?—Yes, they would.

61. Mr. Cotton.—And except the additional expense of the roads you see no difficulty in making them coterminous?—Yes; there would be the additional injuries, the repairs of bridges, and other matters of that kind.

62. Do you extend the lighting out to the limits of the circle?—No, sir; only as far as the actual municipal boundary, and in some places not so far.

63. Is there sufficient land within the present boundary available for building purposes for many years?—Yes; I think so.

64. Has there been any opinion expressed about contracting the present area on account of its being too large?—No, sir; one of the objects for which the Act of 1869 was passed was to extend the municipal district.

65. Mr. Robinson.—Can you give me the area of the land upon which the entire rate is struck, and also that upon which only half is struck?—I may tell you that the land which is near the town, is that upon which 4s 6d. is paid. The rest is only valued at 2s. 3d.; and only 4s 6d. is paid on it within certain limits.

66. Mr. Cotton.—What is the valuation of buildings within the old area?—£12,807 11s.

67. Then half the rate upon the same area?—That is 1s. 6d., with certain deductions made under our Act.

68. What does each rate produce—being the entire rate?—The full amount of the rate is £8,850, that is about the gross sum. There is very little difference from year to year. Then comes the buildings between the two areas.

69. On which the 1s. 6d. rate is paid for buildings within the old area?—Yes. The amount is £12,807 11s.

70. And what is the next item?—£968.

71. That is the 2s. 6d. rate on buildings?—Yes. That is the half of the 5s. which we are empowered to levy in the event of striking an additional rate for water.

72. What is the valuation of the entire electoral division?—I could not tell you.

73. What is the rest of the items?—In the old municipal boundary the valuation of the land is £814 10s.

74. What rate is that?—That is the 2s. 3d. rate.

75. Then what is the amount outside that ring?—£3,047 5s., that also is half the 5s. rate.

76. That only makes £17,000?—But that is not all. Then there is half annual rents—Perhaps I had better give you them?

77. Yes?—Half annual rents inside the old municipal boundary is £713 8s., and the half annual rents between the two boundaries is £73 15s.

78. Do you know the opinion of the ratepayers within the town on the question of the boundary—has there been any expression of opinion?—There has been no expression of opinion.

79. Neither for or against?—No; not as far as I heard. I believe the people are satisfied with the present arrangement.

80. Do you know the opinion of the people living close to the present boundary—whether they would wish to be brought in?—I never heard any opinion expressed by them.

81. Mr. Norwood.—If the electoral division were included it would give you an increased valuation of £4,088, that would be only liable to the one-half rate?—Yes.

82. Would it bring in any buildings?—Very few, and even then it would be very little more than half.

Sligo.
Sept. 3, 1879.
—
Mr. James M'Kim.

Sligo.
Sept. [illegible] 1878.

Mr. Alexander Gillmor.

Mr. Alexander Gillmor, examined.

82. Mr. Cotton.—You are Mayor of Sligo?—Yes.

83. Will you kindly give us the opinion of the Corporation on the subject of the boundary of the borough?—That is on the subject of an extension?

84. Yes?—It was the unanimous feeling of the council, that there should not be any extension. I summoned a meeting of the Committee—which includes all the members of the Council—specially for the purpose of considering the matter. These queries were read out seriatim, and the answers to all approved of. That answer was afterwards approved of at a general meeting of the council, and I never heard any dissent to it from any member.

85. When they considered the question, I suppose it was not before you, as to whether an increase of the boundary to that of the electoral division would be desirable or not?—I don't think the point of the electoral division extension was before them; because I think it was generally understood that the same wards of the Borough and the Poor Law wards were coterminous, but I see now there is a little extension caused by the townlands.

86. The electoral division is larger, and it has a valuation of £4,000 more than the Borough of Sligo—you have not considered the question of whether it would or would not be desirable to extend the boundary to the electoral division?—I do not know the exact amount it would produce. We have not calculated it, but there seems to be the impression that the extension would not compensate for the additional duties that the Corporation would have to undertake.

87. Mr. Robinson.—The additional outlay necessary to keep up the enlarged district?—Yes.

88. Mr. Cotton.—Necessary for keeping up the roads?—Yes, I think it might create some bad feeling on the part of gentlemen having property; because we had a great difference of opinion with them when the Act of 1869 was obtained and it caused a great deal of bad feeling and I think an extension might lead to something of the same kind again, which I think with a view to the wellbeing of the town, it would be well to obviate if possible.

89. You don't think there would be any working advantage in having the electoral division and town areas the same?—No, I don't think there would, that is my impression.

90. The Committee of the House of Commons having expressed such a strong opinion about it, I am anxious to have recorded any reasons for or against it in the present instance. I may tell you there are very few cases where it would be possible, but it so happens that Sligo seems one of those cases where a slight extension would make the two the same, and that is why I would like to have on the notes, a reason for or against it.—In one direction such an extension would go out two miles.

91. Mr. Robinson.—It would go two miles from the centre of the town, but not two miles from the limit of the town?—Yes.

92. Mr. Cotton.—Have the Corporation considered the question whether or not a rearrangement of the wards would be desirable?—They came to the conclusion that they didn't think so, considering the position of the streets of the town. They are very nicely divided I should think.

93. And the ratepayers of the town generally are of the same opinion?—I have heard no objection. On the contrary, anyone outside the Corporation I have spoken to on the subject has been in favour of the present one remaining as it is.

94. And you have heard no opinion expressed by the people living near the boundary in favour of the boundary being contracted?—No.

95. Mr. Robinson.—Were you unaware of the wish of the Committee of the House of Commons to make the two boundaries coterminous?—I never heard of it before this morning. If we had known that that was the wish of the Committee of the House of Commons then we would have taken the sense of the Council on the subject. In fact I think very few members of the Council knew there was any difference. I think it was taken for granted that they were the same.

96. Has any inconvenience been experienced by the fact that the boundary is a hard and fast line cutting through townlands?—I have not heard of any; nor do I think it likely there would be any inconvenience experienced.

97. Do you know if it cuts through any house?—I don't think it does.

98. I suppose once the valuation was correctly adjusted there was no inconvenience after that?—I suppose people were bound to put up with it, even if it had caused inconvenience.

Mr. Alderman Kidd.

Mr. Alderman Kidd, examined.

99. Mr. Cotton.—May I ask what your view is on the subject of extending the municipal boundary?—I only wish to say that it was not considered by the Council—it was not put before them—the question as to whether any extension of the municipal boundary to that of the electoral division would be of advantage; I think the general feeling would be, and is, that any advantage that could be obtained by extending it and making it coterminous with the Poor Law boundary would be overborne by the cost of maintaining the roads and everything of that kind; and another thing, the Corporation would derive very little benefit for they would receive only 1s. 3d. in the pound on all that property, and it would make it very difficult to attend to the work for that, and the county cess itself would be about the same rate there, [illegible] the present boundaries are at present paying.

100. Why does that argument apply to the extension of the present boundary to the electoral division, and not apply to the extension of the old boundary to the present one; for it appears to me that there is just the same argument in both cases?—We thought the Parliamentary boundary would be a convenient one. I think that was really the reason it was adopted—that it would be equally convenient. The extension was from the municipal boundary to the Parliamentary boundary. The municipal boundary was a zigzag one, and the other was a mile radius from the centre of the town.

101. It was of advantage to the town to extend their boundary to the Parliamentary boundary?—Yes, we thought so.

102. The nature of the ground and the outline of the boundary appears to be just suitable for an extension to the electoral division. Why, therefore, would it not be equally of advantage to the town to extend the present boundary to that of the electoral division?—I really could not answer that question except in this way—that I think it never was considered. It was never suggested. Taking the Parliamentary boundary of a mile radius it was thought would be sufficient, and it was generally considered convenient, and the extension to that boundary brought in a valuation that was much more desirable.

Mr. M'Kim, Town Clerk, re-examined. Sligo. Sept. 1, 187[illegible]. Mr. M'Kim.

103. Mr. Cotton.—Can you give us the valuation between the two areas—the old area and the present one?—£3,301 3s. 3d.

Mr. Gillmor, Mayor, re-examined. Mr. Gillmor.

104. Mr. Cotton.—Do you wish to add anything to your previous evidence?—Yes; another reason for not extending the present boundary further has suggested itself to me. That is, that the Corporation would be bound to have sewerage, paving and all these, and it would be very expensive and would come to a large sum of money, and they would also have to pay [illegible] large charges [illegible].

105. In the same way when they extended their small area to the present large one, were they not bound to [illegible]?—There was a great deal done at the time.

106. The valuation you have stated, that was only £3,300, whereas if you included the whole of the electoral division you would have a valuation of £4,000 additional?—It would be a good deal larger no doubt.

Examination of Alderman [illegible] resumed. Alderman [illegible].

107. Mr. [illegible]—Would you take in the whole of the [illegible] division if you took in the [illegible] of the electoral division?—Yes.

108. [illegible]

109. [illegible]

110. [illegible]

111. [illegible]—Yes.

Mr. Edward Chisholm examined. Mr. Edward Chisholm.

112. Mr. Cotton.—What are the liabilities of the Corporation?—The total liabilities of the Corporation in the month of September last, the date of the last audit, amounted to £11,177 16s. 3d.

113. For what purposes was that debt incurred?—In 1869, before the Sligo Borough Improvement Act was introduced, there was a balance of about £1,000, and the origin of that, as far as I can see from the books, was at the time of the reformed corporations there was some change in the corporate bodies, and the Recorder and Town Clerk at that time were pensioned off. There was a sum given to him of several hundred pounds by way of compensation for loss of office and, also the expenses incurred by the Revising Barrister at the time. At all events, in 1869 there was about £1,000 incurred in that way. After the Improvement Act was passed in 1869—by that Act an outstanding debt of the Town Commissioners—which body was abolished by that Act, a debt of about £2,000 Irish, became the liability of the Corporation. That made the debt then about £3,000. The costs of the Improvement Bill itself were taxed at within a fraction of £3,000, making then a total of £6,000. There was also a debt at the time standing as between the Town and Harbour Commissioners. The result of an arbitration as between those two bodies, was that there was an award given for upwards of £800, which as having been due by the Town Commissioners to the Harbour Commissioners also became a liability of the Corporation who succeeded the Town Commissioners in their functions. That added nearly £1,000.

114. The Mayor.—I would desire to explain that last amount. That debt was incurred in this way. The Town and Harbour Commissioners opposed the Corporation in Parliament in getting the Act of 1869. Afterwards by a clause in that Act any matter in dispute between both parties was left to arbitration. The arbitration was held, and the amount was awarded by the arbitrator as against the Corporation, so that virtually the Corporation had to pay for the opposition against themselves. There was over £1,000 expended on engineering and other matters, and that was included in the parliamentary taxed costs.

115. That is in connexion with the waterworks portion of the Bill?—I am speaking with the Bill generally, and the waterworks especially.

116. Witness.—That would be about £6,000. Well, some few years ago there were two actions brought, resulting from the passing of that Bill, by Mr. Parke of Dunally and Mr. Wynne of Hazelwood, arising out of the water question; and those two actions with costs amounted to about £800, and the Corporation expended the balance of the debt incurred in completing the erection of this Town Hall.

117. Mr. Robinson.—How is the debt being paid off?—The amount of the debt now standing in debenture mortgages and bonds of the Corporation, on which they pay yearly interest, is £11,616 18s.

118. Mr. Cotton.—Has it been paid off at all?—No; there is none of it paid off. We are paying five per cent. interest on those bonds.

119. What property has the Corporation besides the rates?—A small rental of £75, Irish—nett about £72—deducting taxes.

120. That is all?—Yes, that is all; except this Hall.

121. Have they any other estates or markets?—

No, sir. Mr. Wynne of Hazelwood is the proprietor of the tolls and customs of the town. There are incomes in from the borough rate, from the sanitary rate, and also from the Petty Sessions fines.

122. What was the income of last year from the different items?—The actual amount of the borough rate lodged for last year was £2,334 0s. 5d. The Treasury paid in aid of local rates £100 4s. 3d. The dog tax last year was £31 13s. 10d., and the Petty Sessions fines for the borough amounted to £32 7s., and there was the rent, which I have already mentioned, £72. The sanitary rate—the actual lodgment last year, ending the 9th of September, was £205, and from the Treasury to that account £5 11s. 6d.—that is in all £210 11s. 6d. With reference to the income from the Town Hall, that will not be a source of profit to the Corporation now. The Grand Jury now occupy the new courts, but for three years we had apartments let here in the Town Hall for the purpose of holding assizes and sessions, and that produced £200 a year. We have not got that now, for, since March last, they have occupied their own courthouse. Speaking generally, there is not likely to be any profit to the Corporation from this Town Hall, because what we receive from lettings, and £25, the yearly rent from the commercial news rooms, will be expended in £40 ground rent for the site, about £40 the cost of the lights for the building, and about £40 caretaker's wages—at 15s. a week; so that we do not expect it will yield a surplus from the building itself, unless in the course of time they succeed in letting to advantage some of the apartments that can be spared for the purpose.

123. Can you tell me if you keep separate in the accounts the cost of the maintenance in the borough of the streets and roads?—Last year the payments to the Grand Jury by the Corporation amounted to £489 10s. 6d.

124. And what are the other items?—I can give you them all on a printed form. [The witness then handed in a printed statement of the receipts and expenditure of the Corporation.]

Mr. William Cochrane examined.

125. Mr. Cotton.—You are the Borough Surveyor of Sligo?—I am.

126. What is the length of the roads in the borough?—Twenty-two miles between the two.

127. Do you know what the length of the roads would be outside the present boundary, and within the electoral division?—I could let you know that in a few minutes. At present the roads cost us £30 per mile, but there are a great many very small ones. But the main roads that would be taken in would be rather expensive thoroughfares, and I think would cost a great deal more than that to keep up. We pay £675 a year for keeping that twenty-two and a half miles of streets and roads in order, but a great many of these are back streets, where there is very little traffic.

Mr. [illegible], Mayor, re-examined.

128. Mr. Cotton.—How does the question of the water supply stand at present?—It would be very difficult to answer that question. As you are probably aware a Provisional Order was granted in 1877, and it was then brought into the House of Commons, when a petition against it was lodged by Mr. Parke, of Dunally; and it was then discovered that there was a clause in the Public Health Act of 1875, prohibiting any public body from diverting water without the consent of all the parties connected with it, and Mr. Parke refusing to give his written consent, the Bill was consequently thrown out of the House—or for some reason or other it was withdrawn by the Government, and in 1878 the same clause was retained in it, and we hoped in the meantime that some action would be taken by the Legislature on the subject. It appears to me a monstrous thing that an Act of Parliament should give one man the opportunity and power of depriving a large community of a supply of water.

Examination of Mr. Cochrane resumed.

129. Is there any large expenditure contemplated in the matter of sewerage?—No, sir. We have completed our sewerage in Sligo now. All the main sewers are completed. You will see by this map (produced) that every street in Sligo is now supplied with a main sewer. We have completed our sewerage here.

130. Are there any building operations going on?—There have been twelve or thirteen houses built within the last two years.

131. In which direction do they extend?—They are all within the municipal boundary—all round the town.

The inquiry then terminated.

PORTADOWN.—JUNE 16TH, 1879.

PORTADOWN. June 16, 1879.

Before Mr. C. P. Cotton.

Mr. Robert M'Clatchey examined.

Mr. Robert M'Clatchey.

1. You are the Clerk to the Town Commissioners?—I am.

2. How long have you occupied that position?—Since 1878.

3. What Act is the municipality of Portadown under?—The Towns Improvement Act of 1854.

4. When was it put under that Act?—In December, 1854.

5. Had it been previously under any other Act?—Under 9th Geo. IV.

6. The boundaries of the town were fixed in 1854, when it was put under that Act. Have they been extended?—They were previously fixed, in September, 1828.

7. Were they altered when the Towns Improvement Act was adopted?—No, but in 1828 they were.

8. Have they altered since that?—No.

9. Have you a map of the town?—Yes.

10. Is the boundary of the town shown upon that map?—Yes.

11. Do you know what the previous boundary was?—I don't know at present what the boundary was in 1854.

12. Do you know, as a matter of fact, the extension in 1828 involved a large increase?—It was a large increase.

13. Do you know what was the object of it? Why was the increase sought for at that time?—I don't know.

14. What is the population of the town of Portadown?—In 1871 it was 6,735; at the present time I suppose it is nearly 8,000.

15. I see you have returned it as 8,000. Do you believe that to be about it?—Yes.

16. Do you know anything about the number of houses in Portadown?—There are 1,700 houses at present.

17. What is the area of Portadown?—407 acres, 2 roods, 7 perches, statute measure.

18. And the town valuation?—The valuation for this year is £16,616 10s. That is for 1879.

19. That is an increase upon the last year of a sum of £300?—Yes. It has risen by the increase since 1871—by the five years mentioned in the [illegible].

20. In what way can you give me the increase?—Year by year?—Yes. In 1874 it was £14,036 10s.; in 1875, £15,109 15s.; in 1876, £15,163 10s.; in 1877, £15,840; in 1878, £16,083; in 1879, £16,616 10s.

21. What is the number of municipal voters in Portadown? I think it is 417?—Yes; 417 is the number.

22. How many of those voters are qualified to sit on the Board of the Commissioners, if elected?—138. More than one-fourth.

23. What electoral divisions is Portadown in?—Portadown and Corcrevy [illegible].

24. Do you know how far these electoral divisions extend away from the town?—I think both extend outside the town.

25. They are not coterminous with the town?—No.

26. Do you know to what extent they go outside?—No, they do not.

27. Does not Portadown extend to Drumcree? The reason I ask that is, one of the recommendations of the Committee of the House of Commons was that, where it was possible, an electoral division should be coterminous with a town boundary. But in those cases in which it would be necessary to take the electoral division as the town boundary, it is necessary to [illegible] . You are quite clear about that?—Quite clear.

28. It extends so far?—Yes.

29. Will you give me the rates for the last five years—the municipal rates?—In 1874, 1s.; in 1875, 1s.; in 1876, 11d.; in 1877, 1s.; in 1878, 1s.

30. And have you struck any for this year?—Yes.

31. 1879 is a shilling also, is it?—Yes.

32. Will you give me the poor-rates for the same years?—In 1874 the poor-rate was 1s. 6d.; in 1875, 1s.; in 1876, 1s.; in 1877, 10d.; in 1878, 10d.; in 1879, 10d.

33. How would there be in the return you gave us for the year 1878 the poor-rate is rated at 10d. and [illegible]—was that a mistake?—That would be Corcrevy and Portadown, two electoral divisions.

34. Which is 10d.?—Portadown.

35. How much of the town is in the electoral division of Portadown, and how much in that of Corcrevy?—The greater portion of the town is in Portadown.

36. And is there much in Corcrevy?—No, not very much.

37. Can you divide the area between the two divisions?—Corcrevy is in Edenderry.

38. Was there a part of Edenderry included—you gave me the area 407 acres?—can you divide that between the two electoral divisions?—I can, but I have not got the figures just at present.

39. Could you point out on the map which is the portion that is in Portadown?—Yes.

40. Will you do so, please?—(The witness then pointed out the portion on the map)—133 acres, 3 roods, 3 perches, are in Corcrevy.

41. And the balance is in Portadown?—Yes.

42. Can you give me the county cess for the same years, beginning in 1874?—As taken from the collector's books it is as follows:—For the year '74, for spring and summer, 1s. 6d.; for '75, 1s. 8d.; for '76, 1s. 7d.; for '77, 1s. 6d.; for '78, 1s. 6d.

43. What was made this year for spring session?—I cannot say at present. I did not look for them.

44. Have the Commissioners had under consideration the question of extension of boundaries?—No. It has been talked about, but they have not had it under consideration.

45. Were these queries laid before them?—Yes.

46. And what instructions did they give you with regard to answering them?—I was directed to answer these queries as put in the return before you.

47. And the opinion of the municipal body is that they require no alteration at present?—Yes.

48. Was that done by a formal resolution, which is on the books?—It was not. Your letter was read, and the matter was talked over, and I was directed to reply to these queries as they are there.

49. The letter was read at the Board?—Yes; and the letter was entered on the minutes.

50. Can you tell me how many members were present at that meeting?—Yes.

51. Nine: was the meeting [illegible]?—Yes.

52. And you were directed by that meeting to say that no alteration was required?—I was.

53. Was that the unanimous opinion of the meeting?—I think there were some members who felt that they thought extension would be desirable, but that was what I was directed to reply to the question.

54. The decision was not by resolution?—No.

55. Do you know the opinion of the ratepayers of the town? Has the question been discussed among them?—I have not heard any opinion expressed by the ratepayers with reference to it.

56. Do you know the opinion of any of the residents outside the present limits, whether they would wish to be taken in?—I have heard of one that would not be very well pleased if he was included in the boundary.

57. You are the urban sanitary authority?—We are.

58. Have the Commissioners ever considered the

[illegible] Mr. [illegible] M'Closkey.

guidance as to whether they would wish to take up the ground over the roads within their district?—The Board have never had it under consideration, though I have heard it talked about.

58. Are they aware that they could petition to get it?—Yes, quite aware of that.

59. And that if the Local Government Board choose to give it to them they could get it?—Yes.

60. Did they have never taken any action?—They have not.

61. How is the town lighted?—By 121 lamps.

62. By gas?—Yes.

63. A contract with a gas company?—Yes, for the winter season.

64. How many lamps are there, and on what terms is the contract?—There are 121 lamps, which are lit for seven months at 50s. per lamp.

65. And what has been the effect of lighting?—Seven months.

66. And at what time in the evening are the lamps lit?—From half an hour before sunset to 12 o'clock at night. And this past year there was a certain number—35—lighted all night, at an additional cost.

67. Is there any agreement that they are not to be lit during full moon?—Yes. Some four nights before and four after.

68. Four nights before and four after?—Four nights altogether—two before and two after.

69. Do you consider that the town is fairly lighted?—I do.

70. Has there been any complaint about the lighting?—There were some complaints last winter in consequence of the frost.

71. Was anything done in consequence?—Yes.

72. Are there additional lights?—No. The complaints were in consequence of the frost.

73. I mean were there any complaints made officially to you as the Clerk of the Commissioners?—No.

74. How is the town supplied with water?—By pumps.

75. How many?—[illegible].

76. Have there been any complaints about the quantity or quality?—There have been complaints about the quality, and one pump was discontinued.

77. What action was taken?—It was closed and [illegible] from the [illegible] with [illegible], and it is not allowed to be used for domestic purposes, and there is a public notice up upon it to that effect.

78. How can you prevent the people using it for domestic purposes?—That's the only means of preventing that the Town Commissioners have.

79. That is, they can merely give notice that it is not to be used for domestic purposes?—Yes; there is a notice printed up on the wall.

80. Have you any water-works?—We have not.

81. Where do you get your water for them?—From the river [illegible].

82. Why was not that well to which you have referred closed altogether?—It was talked of being closed, but it was considered that it would be a pity to close it up, as it was good water, and it might after a time come right again. There was a generally

the people of the neighbourhood against closing it, and that if it was, it would be a great hardship. They would have no pump in place of that. Did [illegible] give them a sufficient supply, and the people said they would only use it for purposes other than domestic purposes.

83. Do you believe that it is not used for domestic purposes?—I believe it is not.

84. Has there ever been a scheme for a supply of water for the town?—No; it has not been under consideration yet.

85. How is the town drained?—By means of the main sewers.

86. Emptying into the river, I suppose?—Yes.

87. And are there distributing sewers from all the small streets?—Yes.

88. And are they connected with the houses?—[illegible].

89. Do you ever compel people to connect?—Yes, always.

90. And it is done?—Yes.

91. And could you give me a copy of the receipts and expenditure for the last year?—Yes.

92. Have you got a printed copy of the accounts as it has been audited, for the last year?—No, not until July it is generally audited.

93. Is there an additional drainage rate?—There is a drainage rate of [illegible] for the [illegible].

94. Under what Act of Parliament is that raised?—Under the Towns' Improvement Act.

95. And what is the amount of it limited to in the pound?

96. For what purpose [illegible]?

97. The main sewers?—Yes.

98. Is there anything that the Town Commissioners of this town think requires to be done, and which the Commissioners are not able to do on account of the want of funds?—Well, sir, at present the [illegible], but I don't think they have sufficient funds to complete them at present, but they are going on with them.

99. Is additional drainage wanted?—No sir; not at present.

100. The town is situated pretty much [illegible] a central point, extending about a similar distance in every direction?—Pretty much so, it is not exactly.

101. Do you know the size of the town before the last extension took place?

102. Have you got any old map of it?—I can [illegible] which there is any change in boundaries.

103. Have you the description of the original boundary here?

104. Would you let me look at them?—Yes.

105. Do your lamps extend up the roads, up to the present boundary?—Yes; with the exception of one road.

106. Have the Commissioners been asked in any case to extend the lighting beyond their boundary?—No.

107. Have you any other information to give me, or does anything occur to you that you would wish to add to your evidence?—No.

Portadown, June [illegible]. Mr. W. J. [illegible]

and a portion of [illegible] division. It was extended there, from where there was formerly a [illegible], beyond the present railway station.

118. It was extended there beyond the railway station?—Yes. It was.

119. Was the extension made for the purpose of bringing in land that had been built upon since [illegible] ?—Partly for that and partly to extend the boundary to land that was likely to be built upon.

120. And has that land been since built upon?—A great deal of it.

121. Are the buildings in [illegible], increasing as well as the population?—Yes.

122. In the building of new buildings do you tend in any particular direction?—Well we generally [illegible] with the exception of some forty-five houses.

123. Are there many villa residences close to, within any half a mile of the present boundary?—There are not. The villa residences were included at the time of the last extension.

124. On the [illegible] side of the town are there many buildings along the road? The Church (?) [illegible] and the other [illegible] the boundary, but just outside?—No. There have been no buildings recently

erected outside; none since that last extension of the boundary.

125. If there was an extension to say a quarter of a mile all round the present boundary, do you think it would bring in many additional voters?—It would.

126. Not many that would be eligible to sit as Commissioners?—No. It would not. [illegible] in a few, but very few.

127. Have you yourself [illegible] the question whether it would be desirable for the Commissioners to take up the roads [illegible] the Grand Jury, and [illegible] over the roads and so on?—Well, I have. I think for the present it would not be desirable for us to do so.

128. You think you get a fair return from the Grand Jury for the rates you pay?—We do not get a fair return.

129. But they contribute to your paving?—Yes. They contribute one-half of the flagging and crossings, which is the only [illegible] they make.

130. And they also charge of the principal streets under ordinary contracts?—They do.

131. Do they take charge of the [illegible]?—Yes, but in [illegible] instances they carry out contracts for doing them under the Grand Jury.

The Town Clerk re-examined. The Town Clerk.

132. Mr. M'Closkey, I forgot to ask you whether the Town Improvement Act was adopted in its entirety or not?—It was adopted in its entirety.

The examination of the Chairman resumed. The Chairman.

133. Is there anything that occurs to you that bears upon this question?—I may take it to be your private opinion as well as the Commissioners that an alteration of the boundary is required?—That is the opinion of the Commissioners generally.

134. Is that your opinion?—It is decidedly. I think the cost would be greater than the benefit. I think it would be a loss to the town to make such an addition.

135. In what way?—In the expense it would involve. We consider that were we to extend the town boundary we would be bound to give them light and supply water, and such things which at present come under the rural sanitary authority's care.

136. Yes, but supposing your supply of lighting was only to such portions of the roads going out of the town as are regularly built upon would that make any alteration in your opinion?—There are none which are regularly built upon beyond the town. There are not a dozen houses any where that would come in to a moderate area.

137. Supposing you had an extension and would not be bound to put gas lamps along the roads, would that alter your opinion?—No, it would not, because it would be taxing the people for no advantage to them, and to put money into the pockets of other ratepayers.

138. Do you think it would be any advantage if you had an increase of your funds arising from a rate levied on the people outside the present boundary leaving the Commissioners the beneficial use of it in addition to the present money they have?—No, we don't require it at present.

139. Don't you think the people who live outside the town or within three-quarters of a mile of the centre of the town, and especially a quarter of a mile or more outside the present boundary, derive great benefit from the town, living so near to it?—They do derive some benefit from it.

140. Are they not greatly interested in the question of the town being properly kept, well lighted, and cleaned?—I suppose any one who comes into the town is.

141. I suppose they do come into it, and they send their children into school, and come in on Sundays to Church and Chapel?—Yes, they do.

142. And still you think the town can be kept up without applying to them for additional funds?—Yes. We think that if the buildings were of such [illegible] we would be quite prepared to go in for an extension, but at present it would be taxing them and providing an extension for that [illegible] which might arise if they were built upon.

143. In the case of buildings?—Yes, that might arise.

144. Is building going on more inside than outside the town?—A great deal more inside.

145. You would not then [illegible] any building?—Yes, but those who would be [illegible] would be deterred from doing so if they were to be taxed. It would discourage them from building.

146. Is there anything else you would wish to add?—I don't think there is any matter in which the town is interested at present that I could refer to. We have got a considerable addition within the town boundary in the space for building ground owing to the opening of some property which had been closed and the opening up of a new street in the centre of the town.

147. Can you tell me if the 66? [illegible]—I don't know.

148. Can you tell me what value you [illegible] the [illegible]—how much of your valuation is only rated at three years?—I can get that for you, but I have not got it here.

149. I mean how much of the valuation that only pays three-quarters of the [illegible] rate?—The amount is [illegible].

150. Was there ever any project for supplying Portadown in any other way than by wells?—We have talked about it.

151. I mean have you ever got a plan for a new project laid before you?—We have not. We have thought about it; but you are aware that we can only tax the community at one-fourth of the [illegible] rate for supplying water; and that would not compensate us. It would take close upon a shilling in the pound to do it.

152. This can [illegible] for sanitary purposes or any [illegible]—there be no limit?—No. We think the amount of valuation is not sufficient to justify us in incurring the expenditure that would be involved.

PORTADOWN. June 16, 18[illegible]. The Chairman.

149. That is exactly what I want to know. Have you any idea what that expenditure would be?—We think we would be obliged to bring water from [illegible], and we consider that it would be equal to fully a shilling in the pound on the valuation.

150. What does a shilling rate bring in?—It brings in this year £224.

151. You think it would take that much to pay for the water supply?—Borrowing the money on [illegible] years at interest, it would be five per cent. on the amount.

152. Did you have [illegible] any [illegible] made?—We have not.

153. You consider that the drainage of the town is in a satisfactory state?—We do. We are [illegible] it satisfactorily. In some parts it is neglected; but on the whole it is very satisfactory.

154. And there is no special expenditure in any large amount wanted for the town?—No, except what we are carrying on at present. We have got a grant from the Board of Works for drainage. The town is progressing steadily, and, we think, owing to the fact that there is no attempt to force it in times of great prosperity more than in times of depression. We have been improving, and houses have been erected of a better character than formerly, and something like fifty-five buildings have been erected during the last two years, and several are in the course of erection at present. I mean, we have had no application for extension of the boundary from any one outside the boundary.

155. Do you know if there is any opposition—any feeling of the ratepayers inside the boundary in favour of the extension of the boundary or otherwise?—I am not aware of it.

Mr. John [illegible].

Mr. JOHN [illegible] examined.

156. You are a Town Commissioner?—Yes. I have been one for about seven and a half years.

157. What is your opinion about the boundaries of the town, having regard to the requirements of the town?—My opinion has always been that the boundaries should be extended.

158. Kindly say in what way to the best of your knowledge?—For several years, so far as I have seen, the town boundary extends in some directions only a short distance, and in other directions a much greater distance, so that the irregularity is very unsatisfactory.

159. Will you give it to us so that we can refer to the map afterwards?—Yes. At what is called [illegible] or [illegible] road, at Quarry's Farm—it is called here by the name of [illegible]-road. It leads out of the town towards [illegible].

160. Do you think the boundary should be extended along that road?—The town boundary ends there, at what is called Quarry's Farm. At that point we have a large villa and several houses, just on the very border of the town.

161. What is the name of the villa?—Eden Villa. And a number of houses go up along that direction, but particularly there is a large villa belonging to Mr. Wesley Atkinson, which is within one or two perches of the town boundary.

162. On that road?—Yes. The distance from this town hall (about the centre of the town) to there is about three-quarters of a mile.

163. To Mr. Atkinson's villa?—Yes.

164. Oh, it is not half a mile?—I say it is about three-quarters of a mile. It must be more than half a mile. In my opinion the boundary doesn't extend sufficiently far in that direction, looking at the extent in other directions.

165. Well, how far should it go in that direction?—I should take the road round by Eden Villa up, perhaps, a quarter or one-eighth of a mile.

166. A quarter of a mile outside the present boundary?—Yes; but I do not think there is much building going on there.

167. Take another direction?—Yes; I will take the [illegible] road, that leads up by the station facing the town hall here, up [illegible]. Then, when you go to the head of [illegible]-street, to what is called the Annagh-bridge——

168. The town boundary goes to the Annagh-bridge?—Yes.

169. And do you think it should be extended along that road?—In that direction I do not. I think it is more than a quarter of a mile from where you are now sitting, and I think we have houses built just a few perches outside the boundary. I think Mr. Paul said there was no house built there. However, in [illegible] a gentleman [illegible] lives who owns them. They have been built recently.

170. Mr. Paul said there were not many houses built there?—Well, there are not many.

171. How far do you think the boundary should be extended along that road?—About a quarter of a mile fully. It is a road likely to be built upon. The [illegible] [illegible] in that vicinity [illegible] the [illegible] of the town, as much so as [illegible] in the town, both in the matter of the lighting of the pathways, and also of the [illegible].

172. You'd not go beyond the town boundary?—No. It is not long since two gentlemen in that district suggested the extending the [illegible] [illegible] the [illegible]. They should be within a few yards of their buildings, and to be paid for by the people living in the town. It was very [illegible] to them to make suggestions.

173. We will take another direction towards Armagh road?—There that goes out by [illegible]—[illegible] through the [illegible] of the town. It is a continuation of the Main-street.

174. In the direction of Church-street, leading to [illegible], is [illegible] in two directions?—[illegible] I mean.

175. The present boundary goes a field beyond the railway in that direction?—At the [illegible] Weaving Factory.

176. How far do you think it should be extended in that direction?—Not very far. I don't think it is likely to be much built upon.

177. Are there any buildings there at present?—No. There are no buildings being erected in that direction.

178. Your object would be to take in the new buildings there?—Yes; because I believe it to be very likely to be built upon. It is a road much admired by the people of this town as being the best road, and houses are sought after in that locality. It is put down by us as being about three-eighths of a mile from where you sit to where the boundary of the town ends—that is a very short distance from the centre of the town. Then I refer to the Dungannon road.

179. Is that along Woodhouse-street?—No; along [illegible]-street. The present town boundary extends there to the [illegible] river.

180. That's a small stream?—Yes.

181. How far would you extend it in that direction?—About a quarter of a mile.

182. With what object?—With the object of taking in houses likely to be built there. This town is a rising town.

183. Would it take in any number of houses that are there now?—No; except some small ones.

184. I see a place here marked Oakfield House?—That is within the boundary.

185. And there is [illegible] Villa—it is near [illegible] House?—Yes; both of them are included within the boundary.

186. Have you any other map of the township but this one?

The *Town Clerk*.—No; I have never seen any other.

187. Does the map you have, show the drains in the entire township?—It does.

Examination resumed.

188. Is what you call Corkrain river, the same as what I see on the Ordnance map as Ballybay river?—I think it is.

189. How far beyond Corkrain river would you extend the town?—About a quarter of a mile.

190. That ground is not built upon at all?—No. I would extend it up to what is commonly known as Brankin's Hill.

191. Are there cross roads there?—Yes.

192. And, now, in any other direction?—And then here on the Loughall-road.

193. Is that along West-street?—Yes, that is a continuation of West-street.

194. How far would you go there?—Just where the town boundary breaks off. That is at the turn on the cross roads.

195. Near the Corkrain river?—I have it here entered down as near where the town sergeant lives, and where the town boundary breaks off at that point.

196. It breaks off at the cross roads?—Yes. I heard some one say there was no house to be taken in, but there are a number of houses.

197. What sort of houses?—Pretty good ones.

198. Houses that would bring in voters?—Yes.

199. How far would you extend it in that direction?—I would extend the boundary nearly half a mile on that road.

200. Generally speaking, I may take it that you think the boundary should be extended, in every direction, about a quarter of a mile?—No. There are some directions in which it is already a considerable distance out of the town.

201. In what direction?—On Garvaghy-road, along Castlestreet.

202. How far does the town extend there?—It extends up to a short distance beyond the nursery.

203. The nursery is not marked on the map. I see a house marked here called Woodside?—Yes, just there.

204. Does it take in Woodside? Yes.

205. And would you think of extending on that road?—No, I don't think beyond that there is much likelihood of building, for a great length of time at all events.

206. And you would not extend it there?—I would not, and also on the Lurgan-road it extends far out.

207. Which is the Lurgan-road?—Going on to Market-street and Bridge-street; the continuation of Bridge-street.

208. You think it should not be extended there?—No, because, so far as I can, it extends down far enough. I suppose it is fully three-quarters of a mile from this to where the town boundary ends there, and it is not a very eligible site for building beyond that, or likely to be much built on; but by the extension I have mentioned I believe a good many houses would be taken in.

209. Can you give me a rough guess at the number?—Perhaps it would take in between forty and fifty. I have not exactly counted them, or taken that subject into consideration.

210. Would they be valued at £4, and upwards?—Yes and more.

211. Would any of them be valued high enough to give the occupiers a seat at the Board?—Certainly.

212. How many do you think?—Seven or eight.

213. Have you formed any opinion, as a Commissioner, whether it would be desirable to take up the roads from the county?—I have formed an opinion from what I have read of the discussions in other parts of the country. Seeing then that there is something on antagonism between the Town Commissioners and the Grand Jury, in reference to the roads, it would be better if every town of the size of Portadown had control over their own roads.

214. You think the Grand Jury does not do as much as they ought for the town?—I think we could do the work better in every way, and that the town people would be satisfied.

215. Do you think you would be able to manage the roads yourselves as well?—I think better.

216. Do you think the drainage of Portadown is in a satisfactory condition?—I think it is pretty good.

217. And the lighting?—And the lighting is pretty good. Except last year, which has been a very great failure.

218. But that was exceptional. And the water supply, is that good?—It is pretty good.

219. Is there anything else you would wish to add that bears on the alteration of the boundary?—I heard you ask whether there was anything about the town that appeared to be wanted, and that was not carried out for the want of money. I cannot exactly say that it is for want of money, but we got from the Duke of Manchester several acres of land within the town boundary, for a fair green, nearly two years ago, and the Commissioners are paying a rent, I believe, of 30s. an acre for that. I have been one of the Commissioners who have urged that that should be put into a state of preparation long ago, as soon as we got control over it, and the cows got off the street, and I was very glad to see my suggestions supported by the Commissioners; and the town will be in a much more satisfactory state. And you know that heretofore in Parliament they have reported against the absurd practice of holding fairs upon the public streets. In this town it is utterly disgraceful to see it.

220. Are the Commissioners hampered for want of money?—I presume it is for the want of money. For instance, the Town Clerk has told me that we have not got the money borrowed yet that is intended to be borrowed for the purpose of the markets generally. Then this fair green has remained there for about two years, and nothing has been done to it, in direct opposition to myself as a Town Commissioner.

221. Have you made any motion?—I have. I have made motion after motion.

222. Have you been met with the answer that there are no funds?—No. It has been delayed for one purpose or another. It has never yet been stated publicly that it is for the want of funds.

223. Do you think if the Commissioners had more money they would do it at once?—I dare say they would, because it takes an outlay we could scarcely afford out of the rates, although it would be necessary.

224. You think want of funds has something to say to it?—Yes.

225. You have not gone into the question of what additional valuation you would bring in by the addition you propose?—I have not gone into a calculation, but I believe it would bring in more than the outlay, the extension I propose. I don't consider that there would be much expenditure.

226. Would you propose to extend the gas-lights the entire length of the roads, if the boundary was extended?—Partly. It would require only one additional lamp on any of the roads I have mentioned. One lamp would be enough.

227. That would be cross laid down altogether?—Yes.

228. With reference to this map of the sewerage that you are obliged to have under the Public Health Act, you add the additional drains as they are made?—Yes.

PORTADOWN. June 14, [illegible]. Mr. John Kelso.

Mr. M'Clatchey, Town Clerk, re-examined.

229. Can you give me a description of the boundary of 1835—the extended boundary?—I can.

230. Will you give me a copy of it?—Yes; I will send you a copy of it.

231. I would also like to have a copy of the one in 1840?—Yes; I can send that to you also.

232. Mr. *Jacob Seaton*.—With reference to the proposed extended boundary, in the whole of it, there have not been ten houses erected within the last ten years in the districts that Mr. Seaton has alluded to?

233. Mr. *M'Clatchey*.—Yes, there have been ten houses erected within the whole of the proposed extended area within the last seven years.

234. Mr. *Seaton*.—I don't agree with that.

235. Mr. *Seaton*.—I am stating that as a fact.

236. Mr. *Seaton*.—I am not sure of the number of houses, but the proposed extension will take in a great many houses.

Mr. James Hutton examined.

237. Where do you live?—At the Acre; I built the houses there that have been referred to.

238. Are they outside the present boundary?—They are.

239. How far from the present boundary?—I suppose about 100 perches.

240. What do you wish to state with reference to the extension of the boundary suggested?—I wish to say this: Mr. Seaton has made a remark that there is a likelihood of more houses being built. I don't think there will. I don't think there will be houses built there forty years along that road. And there is another thing I wish to ask particularly—how this extension of the boundary will affect our tenant-right? My land is held at will. It is a small island. By taking this property in I think it is a very serious consideration whether we are to be deprived of our tenant-right by the conversion of those lands into town-parks.

241. Our report will be based upon the assumption that no alteration will be made in any existing rights. The Legislature will deal with our report afterwards, and I cannot, of course, say what they will do?—It would be a great mistake if this wholesale extension was made without taking into consideration the value of the land, and whether it is likely to be built on. At the town boundary, in my direction, where the bridge is built there is ten feet of bog, and had it to be dug there would have to be fifty feet dug before a foundation could be got.

242. I may take it that you consider that there is no necessity for an extension in that direction?—There is no necessity. I may mention that I live out there near the town boundary, and from the sewer that passes into the Armagh river the stench is unbearable.

243. Where does the sewer come from?—From the town. It runs down the Armagh road, and goes into the Armagh river at the bridge.

244. And the nuisance from it is enough to prevent people building in the neighbourhood?—I would not say that altogether. And then, again, the year before last the whole country was flooded round about, and it has been known to be flooded before that.

245. You said there was effluvia from the sewer?—Yes.

246. Would that prevent building?—It might as well as anything else. It is not a likely locality for building.

247. Do you wish to give your opinion in favour of an extension in any other direction?—I do not. That is the only direction I know anything about. I think there is hardly any building likely to come in my neighbourhood, simply because of the low foundation, and everything is against it in that way. I have a large farm there, and I built those houses simply because the landlord would not give me any site to build there, and I built two or three houses, but I don't go in for that. I have no business in Portadown whatever. My business does not lie there.

248. Not in the market?—I make no use of the market in Portadown, except to buy a little—I make no business by the market.

249. You do not sell?—I do not, and the use I make of it is only the same facility that is extended to the farmers all round.

250. But you have considerable interest in the town, and make use of the roads which have to be maintained?—Yes, but the county do that under my circumstances. The Commissioners never lay out [illegible] on that.

251. Does it occur to you that the road should be lighted at the Armagh bridge?—Not a bit. It is the darkest place you could mention. They may put a lamp there if they like, but I do not want a lamp.

252. You have no interest in the pavements being kept clean—that is the business of yours?—Not the slightest.

253. Mr. *Seaton*.—The bridge is the very identical spot in which he suggested to me that there should be a lamp, but now when the question comes whether his lessors should pay a share of the cost of that lamp, he does not care whether there is a lamp or not; but previous to the suggestion that there should be an extension, he thought there should be a lamp.

254. Mr. *Seaton*.—That bridge is inside the present boundary.

255. The *Chairman*.—Mr. *Fard*.—With reference to this fair green that has been spoken of, there have been some matters in connexion with it that have delayed the work, but that fair green we expect to be open for the coming season in October. The delay in the work has not been caused by want of funds. We have got a grant of money from the Board of Works, and it is not from the want of funds, for they have funds, but some arrangement has been made with reference to the leases which have been carried out.

256. The question was whether or not the rates were sufficient or insufficient for the purpose?—We are not doing it with the rates.

257. It does not affect the rating question?—No; it is by the tolls we pay for it.

258. Then what you meant by funds was funds arising from the rates?—Yes.

Mr. James Greer examined.

259. Are you a ratepayer?—Yes.

260. What are your views with reference to an extension of the boundary?—My impression is that the Commissioners have their hands full of work at present.

261. Would you give your opinion as to whether any extension would be advisable?—It may be desirable in some directions.

262. Could you particularise them?—I really could not at present.

263. Are you aware of any ratepayer who is anxious for an extension?—I am not.

The inquiry then closed.

PARSONSTOWN.—MAY 31st, 1879.

Before Mr. C. P. Cotton, C.E.

Mr. Henry Barrow examined.

1. The Commissioner.—You are the Town Clerk of Parsonstown?—Yes.

2. How long have you occupied that post?—Since November, 1875.

3. The township is under the Towns Improvement Act?—Yes.

4. Was it under any Act previously?—Yes, under the 9th of George IV.

5. Was the Towns Improvement Act adopted wholly or in part?—In part.

6. What part was left out?—The water clauses.

7. Will you please tell me the area of the township?—1,585 acres.

8. And what is the population?—4,939.

9. Was that in the year 1871?—Yes.

10. Do you know whether the population is increasing or diminishing?—I should say it is increasing.

11. What was the last valuation?—£8,581 5s.

12. There are no wards here, I suppose?—No.

13. What is the number of Commissioners?—Twenty-one.

14. What is the number of voters?—233.

15. And of these 233 how many are qualified to sit as Commissioners if elected?—104.

16. Will you now give me the rates that have been struck; give me the municipal rates first?—In the year 1874 there was a shilling town rate, and a burial rate of fourpence.

17. I see there has been some dispute between you and the Guardians on the subject of the burial rate. How does that matter now stand?—There was a dispute between some of the ratepayers and the Town Commissioners, but not with the Guardians, but that has been all settled. They did object to pay the rate for some time, principally in the years 1873 and 1874, but they have all paid the last rates.

18. What was the rate for 1875?—There were no rates struck for our financial year of 1875. That was the time of the burial rate question, and owing to the dispute no rate was struck.

19. What was the rate for 1876?—One shilling, and a threepenny burial rate.

20. And in 1878?—Eightpence, and a three-halfpenny burial rate.

21. You don't strike a burial rate now?—There has not been one struck this year, and the Town Commissioners are seeking to become the urban sanitary authority.

22. But the burial rate of a town like Parsonstown would be struck by the Board of Guardians?—No, the sanitary authority was only the authority until the passing of the Public Health Act for this district outside the township, but the cemetery belongs to the Town Commissioners as a burial board. It was given to them by Lord Rosse, and they exercise full control over it.

23. Have you struck any rate this year?—Not for this financial year as yet.

24. What are the poor rates?—The poor rate for 1874 was 1s. 10d.; for 1875, 1s. 10d.; 1876, 1s. 4d.; 1877, 1s. 6d.; and 1878, 1s. 6d.

25. Were any parts of those poor rates special sanitary rates?—There was a penny included in that as a special sanitary rate each year, of course.

26. Is that for 1875, 1876, 1877, and 1878?—Yes.

27. What was that struck for?—For sanitary expenses.

28. Was it for salaries, or was there any special sanitary work necessary except the carrying out of the Public Health Act of 1874?—No.

29. And was the rate struck over the entire of the electoral division?—Yes.

30. What was the county cess in the same years that you have given me the other rates for?—For 1874 it was 1s. 6½d., 1875, 1s. 6½d.; 1876, 1s. 6½d.; 1877, 1s. 6d.; and 1878, 1s. 4½d.

31. How is the town supplied with water?—By pumps, over which the Guardians have control.

32. Has there ever been any complaint about the quantity or quality of the water?—No; not to my knowledge.

33. How is the town lit?—With gas.

34. By a company?—Yes, by a company.

35. And do you contract with the company?—Yes.

36. And what are the terms of your contract?—We pay the same as private consumers.

37. How much is that?—Eight shillings and fourpence per thousand feet. We pay by meter. There are three meters.

38. How many lamps have you?—Sixty. There are three meters, the average of which we take in computing the amount consumed.

39. What are your rules about lighting—the number of months that the lamps are lit?—They are lit from the 14th of September to the 15th of April.

40. Have you any rule about moonlight nights?—Well, the Gas Company arrange that. There is a resolution of the Gas Committee of the Town Commissioners that the manager of the Gas Company should use his discretion, and shut off the gas on moonlight nights. The Gas Committee used to order it before on some nights. They laid down a certain rule that the gas should be shut off at a certain time. Some nights before, and some nights after full moon, and then the Gas Company was directed to shut them off when they thought proper.

41. And it is now left to the discretion of the manager of the Gas Company?—Yes; but under the constant supervision of the Gas Committee. The three members of the Gas Committee look closely after that.

42. How much does the lighting come to in the year—what did each lamp cost last year about?—Each of the lamps cost about £3$\frac{1}{12}$. That is for the 17.

43. Is that the $\frac{1}{12}$ of a pound?—Yes.

44. Is there a system of sewers in the town?—There is.

45. Are there main sewers in each of the main streets?—Well, Mr. Garvey, the Chairman of the Town Commissioners, knows more about that than I do, and he would be better able than myself to give evidence as to that. I know myself that there are in some of the main streets.

46. The Guardians, of course, have hitherto attended to all that?—Yes, since 1874.

47. I understand that you have got a provisional order which is passing through the House now, to become the urban sanitary authority?—Yes.

48. Have you any map of the township?—Yes, we have the Ordnance map.

49. What electoral division is the township in?—Almost all in the electoral division of Parsonstown. There is a small portion in that of Eglish.

PARSONSTOWN. May 6, 1879. — Mr. Henry Bailey.

60. Chesterfield House is not in the electoral division of Parsonstown?—It is in the township.

61. The town is in the electoral division of Parsonstown, with the exception of a portion of the townland of Derrygarve?—Yes.

62. What electoral division is Derrygarve in?—That of Kilcolman. The portion of the townland of Derrygarve called Chesterfield, is in the electoral division of Kilcolman.

63. Were you the Town Clerk when the Towns Improvement Act was adopted?—No.

64. When was it adopted?—On the 25th of August, 1870, as published in the *Dublin Gazette*. It was adopted from and after that date.

65. What is the date of the *Gazette* that gives a description of the boundaries?—The 14th of June, 1870.

66. Have the Commissioners discussed the question as to whether when they become the urban sanitary authority, they would seek to take up the roads of the district?—They have.

67. Have they come to any resolution on the subject?—I could not say. It would be better to ask the chairman as to that.

68. They have come to the conclusion, at any rate, that they wish for no extension?—They do not wish for any extension.

69. I suppose I may take it that the Commissioners are unanimous in that view?—They are, there is no doubt about that.

60. As far as you know, what is the opinion of the ratepayers of the town on the subject?—As far as I know they are satisfied with the boundary as it exists at present.

61. Do you happen to know whether any of the people who live outside the township boundary, but near it, wish to be taken in?—I am not aware that they do.

62. Will you give me what the receipts and expenditure for the last year were?—I have a copy of the return made out for you. [Return handed in, see appendix.]

63. You have no funded property, I suppose?—No.

64. I see here in this return a subscription from the Earl of Rosse—I suppose that is a perpetual thing?—Yes; he gives annually the sum of £20 towards the funds of the Commissioners.

65. What do the Grand Jury do in the way of repairing the roadways in the town—have you ever applied for anything by way of presentments?—Yes, we have.

66. And have you got what you asked for?—They have been passed by the Road Sessions, but they never got any further than that. They were always thrown out by the Grand Jury.

67. Have you any staff for cleansing and watering the streets—I see you have an item in the account of £116 for that?—They have no staff regularly employed, but the same men are nearly always employed, and they are not kept constantly at work.

68. Then your town bailiff engages them when he wants them?—Yes; but sometimes the weather is such, that the streets do not require very much to be swept. There is, however, no regular permanent staff kept for that work by the Commissioners.

69. And is it at all considered that the sum of £16 is a sufficient amount to be expended on the cleansing of the streets?—Well, there has been a great increase in the expenditure under that head this year, that will end in liquidation. For instance, from November to the present time the sum of £40 has been expended in sweeping alone.

70. And will you be able to pay that amount and keep within your rates?—Well, we will so [illegible].

71. Then what do the Grand Jury do for you in the way of the streets?—They don't do anything worth speaking of.

72. All the streets are under contract, I suppose?—I think I am correct in saying all the streets of the town are in the charge of the County Surveyor. They have no contracts for them.

73. That is only the main streets, but what about the repair of the bye-streets?—The Town Commissioners do all the repairing of the bye-streets when required in any of the streets not contracted for.

74. Is there anything else that you have made a note of, that you desire to tell us?—No, except you wish to hear anything about the cemetery.

75. What is the reason of the burial rate being so high for the last three or four years as compared with other towns of similar circumstances and extent?—Well, there was a debt upon the cemetery; there was a loan of £100 got to lay out the cemetery and to build a wall.

76. And that was, I suppose, being paid off at a certain rate, £20 a year, or something of that kind?—Yes, £20 a year was being paid off, and during the time of the litigation there were not many burials in the cemetery. There was a Commission of Inquiry held here, and two old burial grounds—that is the two within the township—were closed, subject, of course, to certain rights of certain parties. Since that time the burials have largely increased in the new cemetery, and consequently the rate fell 50 per cent. from 1876 to 1878—it was 2d. in 1877, and 1½d. in 1878.

77. What was the area and valuation of the portion of Derrygarve?—£26.

Mr. Tyler R. Garvey.

Mr. TYLER R. GARVEY examined.

78. The TOWN COMMISSIONER.—You are the Chairman of the Town Commissioners?—I am.

79. Will you kindly give us your opinion with reference to the matters detailed by the Town Clerk?—With regard to the extension, I don't think there is any desire on the part of the Commissioners or the ratepayers for an extension.

80. Was there any wish expressed on the part of those who are living immediately outside the present boundary to be taken in?—No, I think not. We have taken every opportunity of giving publicity to the inquiry that was pending, and we have received no application from any outside whatever. The only persons who would probably be at all expected to desire to come in, or that one might suppose to be inclined to come in, are the inhabitants of the village of Crinkle and the barracks, and they have not expressed any desire to come in.

81. Crinkle is a mile and a half, I suppose, from the centre of Parsonstown?—I suppose it is.

82. What is the size of the village of Crinkle?—It is a village that consists of three small streets, with a population of about 400 or 500.

83. I find the population of Crinkle given in the return before me as 1,418, but I presume that that includes the barracks?—Yes; that number must have included the barracks, I think. Certainly in peace, and that number you have varies.

84. Of course the number varies according to the number of the troops stationed there?—Yes.

85. Would it be desirable to take the barracks in under your control?—I don't know that it would. I don't see that there would be any advantage in taking it in. They have their own arrangements for lighting the barracks, and their own sanitary arrangements altogether, and there is at the present moment a large project for the drainage of the barracks, under the consideration of the authorities.

86. And would there be any advantage in having the authority of the Commissioners extended over the roads about the barracks?—I think not. I think the extension at present in that direction is sufficient.

87. And as to the village of Crinkle, it would be an advantage to the town of Parsonstown to take that

Parsonstown, May 21, 1879.

Mr. Toler R. Garvey.

entirely relieved and maintained from the Grand Jury, although the amount of county cess contributed by the township exceeds its liability considerably.

114. You mean excepts which the Grand Jury spend on it?—Yes, excepts what the Grand Jury expend upon it. We get no help from the Grand Jury.

115. Are you thinking then of applying to have the present arrangement as you?—Yes, we are.

116. You are not aware you can get the transfer of the Local Government Board, approval of it?—Yes.

117. Of course it would be [illegible] for you to make application until you become the urban sanitary authority for you could not do it?—That is one of the reasons for our having made application to become the urban sanitary authority—with a view of getting the roads under our own control. If the Grand Jury would give us what we consider a reasonable amount of this, and if they would help us in the way that other Grand Juries do help other townships [illegible] all the towns I know of—we would not be disposed, perhaps, to look for the transfer.

118. The transfer that you would seek for would be merely the control over the streets, roads, and bridges?—Yes, merely that.

119. And do you think that if the sums that are now paid in county cess were transferred to you, [illegible] the money at [illegible] charges, you would be able to maintain the roads better than at present?—Yes, better than at present.

120. You would require a staff for the purpose?—Of course we would require a staff.

121. Have you gone into any figures as to what it would cost you, and as to what you would get for them?—We have; we know what the Grand Jury are able to maintain them for.

122. Are they maintained satisfactorily?—No.

123. Well then is that due to [illegible] something more?—It would cost them something more to put them into a satisfactory condition in the first instance, and then we think they would be easier maintained. I should like to explain the condition we are in with regard to the roads at the present time. In 1876 and 1877, all the [illegible] pieces of county roads, branching out from the [illegible], were given in charge of the County Surveyor, there not being contractors for them, and they were given into his charge by the Grand Jury for a term of five years. Until about a year ago these roads were tolerably well maintained, but the Town Commissioners felt rather aggrieved at the collection of road heaps in the town. The roads were scraped, and the road heaps were collected at the sides of the streets, and in many cases they were not removed for a considerable time.

124. Does not the removal of these become a sanitary matter?—It was considered that the person who scraped the material was the one who should clean it.

125. Were the Guardians asked to interfere?—I don't think the Guardians were asked to interfere in the matter, so well as I remember.

126. The state of things you speak of was since 1874. Then if these [illegible] on sanitary grounds, it would be by the Guardians as the rural sanitary authority?—Yes, probably on sanitary grounds, but it was more on the grounds of general inconvenience that we complained. The heaps of the road became hard and stiff, people driving through the town would have to drive over them, and that would be very disagreeable, if not dangerous.

127. We may possibly [illegible] that the road heaps in a town like this, much [illegible], a sanitary nuisance if they are not removed?—[illegible] an opinion was expressed here before Mr. Robin's Commission, that these heaps were a great nuisance, and I think Mr. Exham was of opinion that it was the duty of the County Surveyor to remove them. Very soon after that, the County Surveyor declined to scrape the roads and streets within the township at all, and he endeavoured to throw upon the Commissioners the duty of scraping the roads, and of what he called scavenging them. The Commissioners objected for some time to do this, because they considered that it was purely in the place of a road contractor whose duty, according to the terms of the specification, was to scrape the roads and to remove [illegible] all such material. However, in the [illegible], or rather gradually, without an [illegible] the roads when the [illegible], and [illegible] upon the Town Commissioners to do so, but not immediately at the time the roads [illegible] to put on the material, but he gave them to do it in such a way that whenever he scraped he was not rendered, [illegible], that they should be given to him in a proper shape to receive the material. The Commissioners consider this state of things a great hardship, and in fact that it would be impossible to carry on the work under such circumstances, because it would be dividing the work between the two authorities in a way that neither could act in any way. The Commissioners quite recognise their duty to the cleaning and to remove anything in the way of a nuisance, and to keep the [illegible] clean, but to scrape the [illegible] of the streets in order to prepare them for material, a [illegible] they have not recognised. However, for the sake of peace, and with the view of trying to preserve the streets of the town in good repair, the Commissioners agreed to the proposal of the County Surveyor to scrape the roads, and remove it all the streets—all the portion of the roads within the township so far as the houses go in each street, and asked him then to remove the road material beyond the houses but within the jurisdiction of the township, because the township extends out to a certain degree—indeed to a considerable extent where there are no houses.

128. Do you happen to know how many miles of roads there are contained [illegible] within the township?—I can tell you in perches.

129. That will do.—There are 3,611 perches of county roads within the township.

130. And what do they spend?—They are not under contract. I can tell you what the Grand Jury spend. The Grand Jury [illegible] extend beyond the township boundaries to the extent of 2,012 perches in addition to that, making altogether 5,623 perches under contract.

131. Under contract or in the County Surveyor's [illegible]?—In the County Surveyor's hands. Excluding [illegible], the Grand Jury spend upon these £341 3s. 4d., but in 1877 [illegible] charge on roads charged to the county at large making the cost of the roads [illegible].

132. Well, that is about 17 miles. Have the Commissioners ever considered what has been done in other towns of becoming themselves, not the Commissioners, but arranging so as to become contractors for the roads in the township?—Yes, we, and with the view of becoming contractors themselves, they made application at the last Presentment Sessions to take a portion of the roads into their own hands that are now worked by the County Surveyor.

133. Within, as well as without the municipal boundary?—No, only within; and we were told that whether the Grand Jury, having given them in charge for five years to the County Surveyor, would grant the application. At all events, we made the application and unfortunately, through an informality, the proceedings fell through. The County Surveyor had not been served with proper notice, and he raised an objection, and the application was consequently thrown out. But at the last Grand Jury, I [illegible] a resolution of the Grand Jury passed a resolution on the subject of those roads, and it was to this effect:—

"Proposed by Toler R. Garvey—That the County Surveyor having in 1876 and 1877 taken up for five years a number of roads partly within and partly without the town of Parsonstown, is hereby instructed to scrape and repair in same manner as heretofore, during the continuance of said term, all such portion of said roads as is beyond the [illegible] streets of the town, the Town Commissioners agreeing to scrape the dirt off the streets and remove same."

134. What became of it?—It was [illegible], and got

to the Grand Jury and back. The County Surveyor expressed an opinion that it should not pass, and it didn't. That, so far as [illegible] make reasons for wishing to become an urban sanitary authority—that we may have control over the [illegible]—in fact, there are three reasons why we desire to become the urban sanitary authority. One is, that we might have the roads under our own control [illegible] of the [illegible] state in which we consider they are now kept by the County Surveyor. Secondly, because we get no [illegible] towards carrying out any works of improvement, such as [illegible] and flagging, though [illegible] are [illegible] made, and it passed at Presentment Sessions, they are thrown out when they come before the Grand Jury; and thirdly, we think we might be able to carry out more efficiently, or perhaps more extensively, I should say, the sanitary operations, than they are at present carried out under the Board of Guardians, though we have no reason whatever to complain of the Board of Guardians because they have attended to everything [illegible] by them.

135. But you think that the Town Commissioners being on the spot and living in the town constantly—you would manage the [illegible] better?—Yes, we think that the local [illegible] would be a stronger and quicker [illegible] to do the work properly.

136. Taking in view the possibility of your having charge of the roads, and taking up the [illegible] of the Grand Jury, is there any alteration in the boundaries of the township that would be desirable—for instance, would it be desirable to include that portion of the road up to the new cemetery under the Commissioners' control?—I don't know any material enlargement or curtailment of the boundary, but is it your opinion that there would be any alteration in any way that would be desirable in view of taking the roads under your control?—That is a purely [illegible] road, though it passes out township boundary, and I don't think there would. I don't think it would be desirable to include them, as [illegible].

137. Or the road up to the [illegible]?—I don't think so. It is not very much used. As a rule, there can be no doubt—and it is only fair to [illegible] so—that the county roads are well [illegible].

138. And you would not include the road to the [illegible]?—I don't think so, unless we took in the [illegible] itself. I do not think there would be any object in having control over the road.

139. And you do not see any object in including the [illegible] itself?—I do not.

140. The railway station is within the limits of the township boundary at present?—It is.

141. Is there a large traffic going backwards and forwards to the railway?—Yes, a great deal of traffic.

142. Have you any by-laws regulating that traffic?—We have not.

143. Is there any necessity for them?—Well, we had a code of bye-laws prepared, and we did consider that there was a necessity for bye-laws, generally to apply to various matters, such as the regulation of [illegible] and things of that sort; but [illegible] understand that our powers are [illegible] and will be increased under the Public Health Act, it perhaps will render any bye-laws unnecessary.

144. It does not bear directly on the question of boundaries at all, but it just occurred to me that, as it is a frequent case with us and any [illegible] we have in many [illegible], on taking the question, that the boundary was made to include the railway yard, for the purpose of giving power to make bye-laws regulating the [illegible]?—Well, [illegible], that is not of much importance to us. The only thing as to which we have had some difficulty, in [illegible] the railway company keeping [illegible] upon the public [illegible] to the railway, until they have been [illegible].

145. Whatever that may be, your boundary does not need extending for that purpose?—No, it does not.

146. You say, then, there is no necessity for extending the boundary, in so far as to take in the new cemetery within the township?—I think not. When we become the urban sanitary authority, we shall have [illegible] over it, complete control over it.

147. I don't see any direct connexion between [illegible] and the town. In what way is it connected, so that it is especially desirable to get it in?—It is a very [illegible] from the [illegible] of the houses of the town, and I don't really know what other reason there is, except that the town supplies are very [illegible], and so on.

148. I see every reason why [illegible] should [illegible], if there [illegible]; the only objection to giving [illegible] a new electoral division for the sake of a [illegible]?—When the limits of the township were extended in 1870, the Commissioners proposed that a very large area should be taken in. That was met by Sir Richard Griffith making a report to the Lord Lieutenant, showing by the map that the boundaries proposed, extending into a rural district too much, would benefit no houses, and laying down other boundaries; and the boundaries laid down by Sir Richard Griffith are the boundaries that now exist. In fact, I may remark that we have been always accustomed to look upon [illegible] as a small [illegible] in itself, and I suppose in any [illegible] you may [illegible] it as quite being part of the township of [illegible], [illegible] are very few persons, except those who have to do with the [illegible], would know that it formed part of another electoral division.

149. At that time, no attention was paid to a township boundary being made identical with townland boundaries or electoral division boundaries?—It is so close to the town, that all the [illegible] are [illegible] for that [illegible] are [illegible] there free of expense to the owner. The Rev. Mr. [illegible] has made application for the pathways leading into the town to be put into proper repair.

150. How far does the lighting extend, particularly in the direction of the [illegible] of the railway station?—Just to the railway station. The lights within the boundary of the railway station are, of course, supplied by the company. The last lamp in the township goes to the top of the hill, just at the railway station.

151. Would it not be desirable, if it is not attended with any great expense to all parties, that the lamps should be extended up to the gate of the [illegible], and that would [illegible] the [illegible]; it is not a very long distance?—It is a considerable distance.

152. You will see by the map that it is not a quarter of a mile outside the township boundary?—Do you mean that we might go as far as the gate of the [illegible]?

153. Yes?—That would include the whole of the village of [illegible], and would render us liable for the lighting of the whole of it, and of looking after the sanitary arrangements of it altogether; and we thought, having given those matters consideration, that, I may state at once, that the Gas Company are not in a position to lay mains, and I don't think they would do so. I don't think they would lay mains for so so far, and I don't think we could lay it ourselves. There are no private connexions along that road.

154. Independently of the lighting question—would there be any objection, independently of that, to include the village of [illegible]?—I think that is the main objection. With the exception of the lighting, I don't think there would be any objection on the part of the Commissioners; but I understand that there would be an objection on the part of the people of [illegible].

155. Is there anything else you would wish to add to your evidence?—I would be glad if [illegible] you would take the [illegible] evidence, [illegible] Mr. [illegible], the Chairman of the Commissioners, who is [illegible] absent to-day, has to complain of [illegible], and anything [illegible] the [illegible] for excluding [illegible], it would be desirable to have explained, or [illegible] to consider the evidence, and asks why it was [illegible], there will be an explanation for that?—I don't think.

3 E 2

[illegible]
Mr. John M. Garvey.

there is anything else I have to add. I have already stated the ground of the objection to including Crinkle, as far as the Commissioners are concerned—the expense of lighting, and the difficulty in getting the Gas Company to lay mains.

156. How far apart, on such roads, do you consider it necessary to place the lamps—for instance, how many are there between this and the railway?—Between the entrance to the town and the bridge at the railway station there are five lamps.

157. That is very well lit, because that is just half a mile?—Yes; being a road where there is such a deal of traffic leading to the railway station it is necessary there should be good lighting.

158. How far do your lights extend on the south side and not towards Chesterfield?—But towards Chesterfield they only extend—

159. As far as the buildings go?—Yes, and nearly so far. As far as Oxmantown place.

160. How far along the [illegible] road?—Along the [illegible] road they extend as far as the corner of [illegible].

161. That is as far as [illegible]?—As far as the commencement of [illegible].

162. And then in other directions—towards Riverstown?—Towards Riverstown to Highstreet—part of Highstreet. What is down there on the map is [illegible], military, in that direction.

163. And on beyond to [illegible]?—As far as the [illegible] bridge.

164. These are the limits of lighting, all round, you may say?—Yes.

165. The part of the township down near Riverstown is not lit?—No, sir.

166. Are there many buildings down in that direction on the higher side of the river at Riverstown?—Only a few thatched cottages.

167. There seem to be a good many on the map, perhaps they are gone—at the cross roads?—Yes, there are some there, but a good many are gone. They are gone on the right hand side, but not on the left.

168. If there is no obligation to extend your lighting to Riverstown, what obligation would there be to light Crinkle?—Because there are better houses, and it is more in the nature of a town than those places. There are shops in the village of Crinkle.

169. Do you know if there has been anything decided as to how far the obligation on a Board of Commissioners extends as regards lighting. Is it not altogether in their own discretion?—Well, I don't know that, but upon the principle of justice and fair play, if there are a large number of ratepayers contributing to the rates, and a great amount of traffic and business going on in the way of shops, one would think there should be lighting.

170. Shops are a distinguishing element certainly, but along the road to Riverstown don't there seem to be a good number of ratepayers living there?—They are very small ratepayers, and most of them don't pay town rates. The entire rate paid by the whole of the people there—the last rate was 1s. 4d. on the [illegible] of [illegible]. We have had no application for any extension of lighting except in one direction, and that is in the direction of what you called the gaol road, and we have been asked to extend the lighting out as far as the houses go, and we have put on record upon the books that lights are required there, and we have asked the Gas Company to supply them, and we are quite prepared to pay for them when the Gas Company supply them. They are now laying new mains and they are to give us every facility for arranging the lights after this manner.

Mr. Henry Davis.

Mr. Henry Davis examined.

171. The Commissioner.—You are a Town Commissioner?—Yes.

172. You have heard what has been stated by the Town Clerk and by Mr. Garvey. Do you agree with the evidence they have given?—Quite so, I do.

173. Is there anything you would like to add?—The only remark I would wish to make is, that the Rev. Mr. Ewing—the proprietor of that large school to which reference has frequently been made in the course of the inquiry—has complained very much of the state in which the pathway of the road leading from Chesterfield into the town is allowed to remain, and not only that, but he complains of a want of lighting, because that part of the town is in total darkness. There is no light from Oxmantown Mall—from the Circle gate there, down towards his place—so that they are in complete darkness.

174. Along the road for over half a mile there is no light?—Quite so.

Mr. Adam Mitchell.

Mr. Adam Mitchell examined.

175. The Commissioner.—You are a Town Commissioner?—Yes.

176. Have you anything to add to the evidence already given?—Indeed I have nothing to say. In fact we discussed this matter at a meeting of the Town Commissioners as to the advisability of an extension of the boundary to the barracks, and I heard the main part of what Mr. Garvey has stated, and he is so thoroughly up to everything connected with the town, and so long acquainted with all its requirements, that I do not think it is necessary for me to add a single word. I have been at many meetings here, and we are all agreed on the one point, that if the lighting was not extended to the barracks they might be brought in.

177. Then you are also of opinion that when you become the urban sanitary authority it would be desirable to seek for getting the control of the roads?—I certainly feel that it would be desirable, unless the Grand Jury would come under some arrangement with the Town Commissioners. When I tell you that I am the solicitor to the Grand Jury, I need scarcely say that I would like everything to be done equitably as regards the town, because we contribute a very large amount, as has been stated, I fancy, by Mr. Garvey. I pay a good deal of rates in the town, and if it were in any way possible to extend the lighting in the direction of the school, it would be most desirable. As regards that part of the town, Lord Rosse has lately expended a large sum in putting up a good class of cottages. That might, by-and-by be lighted in all probability.

178. Is there any physical difficulty in lighting that part of the road towards Chesterfield?—None whatever, except the want of funds and the Gas Company. It is not convenient to them to lay down mains. It is a very poor district. From where Lord Rosse effected the improvements lately to the Model School there are a number of, I suppose, upwards of thirty five cabins there, which pay a head-rent to Lord Rosse, but they are let to a tenant under a lease of lives renewable for ever—fee-farm grant, and that tenant has re-let to another tenant who holds by lease of those cottages. Lord Rosse thought some time ago to get a conveyance of them, and he would have improved that part of the town, for it is a very bad part of the town, and those cabins would then have been removed and a better class of houses built. Though his lordship would lose £30 a year by that, he didn't mind that in order to improve the town, but he failed to get a conveyance.

Mr. Thomas Dooly examined.

Parsonstown, [illegible] Mr. Thomas Dooly.

179. The Commissioner.—You are the rate collector, I believe?—I am, and I know a good deal about [illegible] and know the village of Crinkle [illegible], I think, [illegible] the poorest place in the country—that is the village you were speaking about. I know the difficulty I have in getting rates of any sort out of the people there; [illegible] of them [illegible], the landlords [illegible] pay for them; they have all [illegible]. One half of this year the barracks [illegible] up, [illegible] in the village.

180. Do you think, [illegible] about lighting it, or any difficulty about dealing with the lighting—do you think it would be an advantage to Crinkle to be taken in?—I don't think it would. I don't see what advantage it would be.

181. Do you think the sanitary matters of Crinkle are looked after by the Guardians efficiently?—The sanitary matters—well, as far as the barracks are concerned, they are attended to by the Government, and the rest of the village is very badly done.

182. The Commissioners have not any control outside the barrack gates?—I know that.

183. And the Guardians look after the sanitary matters in Crinkle?—Yes.

184. Do they do so well?—I think so; they recently expended a good deal in putting down a good pump, and giving a good supply of water in the village.

185. I may take it that the Crinkle people have not applied to be taken in?—They have not, I believe.

Mr. William O'Meara, J.P., examined.

Mr. William O'Meara, J.P.

186. The Commissioner.—You are one of the Town Commissioners, I believe?—Yes.

187. Upon what points do you desire to give evidence?—I only wish to say that at the meeting of the Commissioners at which we considered the question, I understood we came unanimously to the conclusion of not wishing to include Crinkle, from the fact of feeling that we would have to light it, though we are not bound to include light. There would, I think, be a benefit to the town if the village of Crinkle were included within its boundary, and also the barracks since there was a depôt centre formed there. There would be always troops here, both in winter and summer, and the business portion of Crinkle will improve very much; being a business man myself I am able to form an opinion on the subject, and I must say I find that business there is improving, from the fact of the military being there, and I think if the barracks and village were included, it would be an advantage to us, provided we hadn't to light it with gas.

188. Have you formed any idea of what the expense of fairly lighting it would be—I don't mean, of course, to light it to the same extent as one of the streets of the town?—If the mains were laid down to Crinkle, I suppose four or five lights would be quite enough; we all settled that we would not have it included from the fact of believing that we would be bound to supply it with lights.

189. Is there any other point that strikes you, that you would give me your opinion on?—No, there is nothing else; I would imagine that if the new cemetery was included it would be an advantage; also to take in the cemetery and to make the bounds of the town up the cemetery road, and to include the cemetery.

190. In what way, Mr. O'Meara, do you think that would be an advantage to the town beyond having the control of the road?—It would bring in a small revenue, and I think it would be an advantage to have the cemetery within the township; it is only a very small distance from the town boundary.

Mr. Garvey re-examined.

Mr. Garvey.

191. The Commissioner.—Mr. Garvey, you don't think there is any special advantage in having the cemetery within the municipal boundary?—I cannot say that there is, for it is equally secure to us under the present Act the way it is; I don't see any objection to the boundary being extended along that road as far as the cemetery, provided that no persons residing at that place should be taken in; because, I think, it would be hardly fair to take them in.

192. I may tell you that I see an objection to taking in a piece of a townland like that into the boundary except there is some special reason for it?—Yes, no doubt.

193. Your present boundary is a road, and it is a very well defined boundary?—Yes, the present boundary certainly does divide a townland, but still a leading road and a public thoroughfare is the boundary, and that is the main reason for laying them down as such; if there be the smallest difficulty or doubt as to our control over the cemetery, I would then by all means say—"take it in"—but I don't think there is.

Mr. John Wright examined.

Mr. John Wright.

194. The Commissioner.—Would you kindly give us your views as to the present municipal boundary of Parsonstown?—I would be in favour of extending the boundaries of the town so as to include the village of Crinkle, as more or less the town is continuous on account of Mr. Davidson's houses being erected recently, and, moreover, I think it would increase the number of our population as a town. As a town I think we number under 5,000, but if Crinkle were included the number would be over 6,000, and I think that would give an increased status to the Town Commissioners, and I think it would reduce the taxation of the town—that is my private opinion, and in this manner: that it would extend it over that district as well, and the people there would have to bear a part of the burden that is imposed almost entirely now upon the people of Parsonstown.

195. You don't know at all, I suppose, even approximately, what the valuation is of the portion you would propose to take in at Crinkle?—No, I do not; I would take in the far boundary of the barrack wall, and run it on over across the fields, taking in the cemetery, and then it would be one complete addition to the town.

196. You don't know what valuation that would be?—No.

197. Or what the rates would be?—I do not; but it is my impression that it would be beneficial to the town, and that impression is nearly general, but I have no statistics to go upon; and as the Town Commissioners have, in a manner, jurisdiction over the cemetery, this would give them a uniform jurisdiction, for it is supplemental as it is now.

198. Is there anything else you would wish to add?—I have nothing additional to say.

Mr. Dooly re-examined.

Mr. Dooly.

199. The Commissioner.—What, Mr. Dooly, is about the valuation of the village of Crinkle?—I think it is about £400.

200. Does that include the barracks?—No; that includes all the ground to Mrs. Harburn's mills, which is £110.

201. Are you including in that a place called Rosevills?—Yes.

202. In fact all between the three roads, one of which goes to the barracks?—Yes, sir.

203. That is all about £400 valuation?—Yes.

204. Have you any idea of the population?—I think it is not more than about 240.

TIPPERARY.—MAY 30TH, 1879.

Before Mr. C. P. Cotton, C.E.

Mr. Jeremiah Dawson examined.

1. You are Town Clerk of Tipperary?—Yes.
2. How long have you filled the office?—For three years—three years last February.
3. The town is under the Towns Improvement Act?—Yes.
4. When was that Act adopted?—On the 6th of December, 1876.
5. Was that Act adopted in its entirety or only in part?—In its entirety.
6. This before me is a map of the township?—Yes.
7. And this is the boundary that was adopted (coloured yellow) when the township was put under that Act?—Yes.
8. Is that the same boundary as the town was previously under, when it was under the 9th of George IV.?—That boundary then was not struck out.
9. Have you anything showing the bounds then under the old Act?—No, sir; we have none of the books or papers of any kind belonging to the old body owing to some dispute between the Town Clerk acting under that body.
10. Do you mean to say that the books were not handed over to the new Commissioners?—Some of them were, but not all.
11. But no map? There was a copy of old writing.
12. Have you got that?—I think I have.
13. Well I would like to see it?—I shall show it to you directly.
14. What is the population of Tipperary?—It is stated in Thom's Almanac to be close on 6,000; 5,873 in 1861, and it is stated that in Thom's Almanac to be 6,636 in 1871 in one part, and under the head of County Statistics it is stated to be 5,623. I presume the latter is the correct one.
15. Yes, inasmuch as the Local Government Board didn't make you the urban sanitary authority?—It has been brought under the attention of the Local Government Board as to whether it should not be an urban sanitary authority.
16. Certainly, it is not an urban sanitary authority. The Board of Guardians is the rural sanitary authority?—Yes, and that is the reason why I am inclined to the opinion that 5,623 must be the correct population.
17. Is it in your opinion increasing or diminishing since 1871?—I think it is increasing.
18. Do you think that in 1881 the population would be over 6,000?—I should think so. I think there can be no doubt about it.
19. What is the area of the township?—79 acres, 3 roods, and 9 perches.
20. What is the valuation?—£3,916 [illegible]
21. Is that the last one?—Yes, according to the last division. That means land, buildings, and what is styled half-county rents.
22. There are no wards?—No, sir.
23. What electoral division is the township in?—That of Tipperary.
24. Do you know what the size of that electoral division is, how far it extends from the town?—It amounts to 1,033a. 3r. [illegible] It is 12½ times as large as the township.
25. How far does it extend from the centre of the town?—I don't know that. It must be over two miles from the centre of the town.
26. What have been the rates since the township was formed?—The rates under the Commissioners?
27. Yes?—In 1876 there was no rate; in 1876 the rate was 1s.; in 1877, 1s.; and 1878, [illegible]
28. Have you struck any rate this year?—Not yet.
29. What were the poor-rates in those years?—In 1874, 2s. 10d.; in 1875, 2s. 8d.; 1876, 2s. [illegible]; 1877, 1s. 6d.; 1878, 2s.
30. Do these include any special sanitary rates?—Yes, a small one for general purposes.
31. Of how much—about a ½d.?—Yes, I think so. There was nothing larger than that. There were no special sanitary rates for those years, but there must be a special rate this year.
32. It has not been struck yet?—I am not aware.
33. The special sanitary rate that was struck of ½d. was over the entire electoral division?—Yes, that was for general purposes.
34. Give me the county cess for those years?—In 1874 it was 1s. 7½d.; in 1875, 1s. 7½d.; in 1876, 1s. 8½d.; in 1877, 1s. 7½d.; and in 1878, 1s. 9½d.
35. What is the opinion of the Commissioners as to the present boundary?—That it is too small and too irregular, and that it should be extended.
36. Has that question been the subject of any special meeting?—Yes.
37. On what date?—On the 7th of March.
38. How many Commissioners attended on that day?—Thirteen.
39. What is the entire number of the Commissioners?—Eighteen.
40. Was there any resolution passed with regard to it?—Yes.
41. What were the terms of it?—I will read the resolution passed for you—

"Proposed by Mr O'Connor, seconded by Mr. [illegible], and unanimously agreed to—That anticipating the Municipal Boundaries Commission (Ireland) Inquiry, we hereby recommend an extension of the boundary, as the present one of the township is too small, and we hereby adopt a one and a half mile radius from the site of the old Town Hall, now the Munster Bank; but that that extension is subject to the preservation of the legal rights of farmers under the Land Act—that is to say, the farmers' legal rights as at present enjoyed by them shall be in no way prejudiced by the hereby intended extension of the boundary of this township."

42. That is the resolution passed by the Commissioners?—Yes, sir; and in addition to that they passed this resolution—

"Resolved—That the Commissioners are in favour of the transfer from the Grand Jury of the repairs and control of the roads, and so forth—provided that those powers would be as full as those now enjoyed by the Grand Jury."

43. Was that passed unanimously?—Yes, sir.
44. Do I understand from that that if the land rights could not be preserved they would not wish for an extension?—No, sir; they would not wish it.
45. Have the Commissioners ever considered the question as to whether they would wish to become the urban sanitary authority, and have the charge of the sanitary matters put upon them?—Yes; it would be their desire to become the responsible parties for that purpose.
46. And have they made any move towards becoming the urban sanitary authority?—No; the previous legislation being so much in favour of that, they have just bided their own time. They think the object will be attained by-and-by, without any cost or trouble.

Tipperary. May [illegible], 18[illegible].

Mr. Jeremiah [illegible].

47. Do they know they could, by application to the Local Government Board, become the urban sanitary authority ?—Yes.

48. Under the Public Health Act ?—Yes.

49. But they have not made application ?—No, sir; they considered it not worth their while. They will endeavour to become the sole authority over the town.

50. They were waiting for what course would be taken when this Commission reports ?—Yes.

51. How many voters are there in the town ?—263. That was the number last year.

52. How many of that 263 are qualified to sit on the board ?—About 117.

53. Had the Commissioners before them when they were considering the question of extension of a mile and a half—did they mean statute miles ?—I suppose so. They said "a mile and a half," without saying statute or otherwise. I think they mean statute miles.

54. Statute miles was the understanding ?—Yes.

55. Had they before them, or did they consider what the effect of that would be, in the way of taking any valuation of the extended area, or the number of voters it would bring in ?—Yes, they considered the proposition fully, and the facts.

56. Have you any idea as to how many voters it would bring in ?—I could not speak with absolute certainty, but I should think about 50.

57. And of those 50, how many would be qualified to sit on the Board of Commissioners ?—Not many; not more than half a dozen, or four or five.

58. Would it bring in any gentleman's place ?—I think none except Mr. Massy's.

59. It would bring in a place called "Rabbit's Walk House" ?—That is Mr. Massy's.

60. It would only bring in two gentlemen's places ? —Well, yes; I think so.

61. Have you any idea what the valuation of the extended area would be ?—The valuation of the area would be about £3,729 in round numbers.

62. What additional area would be brought in ?— The total area would be 4,523 acres. There would be £3,[illegible] additional valuation, and the 4,[illegible] acres would be the entire area.

63. How many additional acres would be brought in ?—About 3,[illegible].

64. Would that extension go into a new electoral division ?—Yes; a very small portion only of two electoral divisions—a very small portion.

65. What electoral divisions are these ?—[illegible] and Kilfeacle.

66. Looking at this map before me, can you tell me where these townlands you refer to as being in the new electoral divisions are. Is there anything special in the townlands of Friarsfield and Rabbit's Walk, that would make you go into those townlands, of the electoral divisions ?—Well, there are reasons for going into those townlands. There is a gentleman's residence in one place—Friarsfield—where Mr. St. George Massy lives. It would be well he was brought in; he would be a Commissioner.

67. With the exception of bringing in that house at Friarstown, there is no other reason for going into that particular townland ?—No.

68. You are aware, I suppose, that the Committee of the House of Commons suggested that, so far as possible, the electoral division boundaries should be made coterminous with township boundaries ?—Yes.

69. Then, there is no other special reason, except taking in that one house, for going into that new electoral division ?—No, sir.

70. How is the town of Tipperary lit ?—By gas, by public lamps.

71. By a private company ?—Yes.

72. And the Commissioners contract with them ?— Yes.

73. At so much a lamp ?—Yes.

74. How many lamps are there ?—90.

75. And what is the price ?—£3 [illegible].

76. And what are the terms of the contract ?— From the 1st of September until the 1st of May.

77. And are they kept lighting all night ?—From half an hour of sunset to half an hour before sunrise in the morning.

78. Whether moonlight nights or not ?—Yes; there are four nights in each month about full moon, when the lamps are not lit; but if any dark nights occur during those four nights, the Commissioners have power to light them.

79. At the contract price ?—Yes.

80. They have no extra to pay ?—They have extra to pay. It is no part of the contract to light on those nights, but the cost of lighting on those nights would be just in proportion to that paid on other nights.

81. If I understand you properly then, the Commissioners pay so much a year to light from the 1st of September to the 1st of May, except four nights about full moon, and if those nights happen to be dark, and the lamps are lit, they are paid for extra ?—Yes.

82. At what rate ?—At a proportionate rate.

83. What is the price to private consumers ?— 7s. 6d.

84. How is the town supplied with water ?—By wells; there are four wells in the town. There is a well called Church Well, which is able to supply the entire town.

85. Has there ever been any complaint about the supply of water made to the Commissioners ?—No.

86. Is it hard water ?—It is very good water. It contains a quantity of lime. It is good water.

87. For drinking purposes ?—Yes.

88. Is it good for washing ?—I am not "up" on that point.

89. How is the town off in the matter of drainage ?—There are pretty good main sewers in the town, but it should be better were it not that there is no control over them not being a sanitary board. There is a good main sewer in [illegible]-street, and another in Bridge-street.

90. Has anything been done by the sanitary authority in the way of making and repairing drains ?—They made one main drain and they endeavoured to saddle the cost of it on the township, but we had it put on the electoral division.

91. There should be a special sanitary rate for that ?—That will come in the next year.

92. Then it is not settled whether it is to be on the electoral division or not ?—It is settled. They endeavoured to put the entire cost on the township, but failed. It has been decided by the Board of Guardians to put it on the electoral division.

93. The Local Government Board must decide upon that ?—There was no objection made by the Local Government Board.

94. What were your receipts and expenditure for the last year—how much was received in 1878 on account of rates ?—£[illegible] 3s. 8d.

95. What have you received as dog tax, and your share of the fines ?—The dog tax amounted to £15 14s. 3d., and the fines to £35 0s. 1d.

96. Had you any other receipts ?—No, except from the Treasury £3 9s. 8d.

97. You have no funded property ?—No.

98. Have you any receipts from the letting of the Town Hall ?—None in that way. There was a bequest of £500 to the Commissioners to be invested by the Commissioners with interest.

99. Just state what is the nature of that bequest ?— Mr. Heardon bequeathed £400 to the Town Commissioners of Tipperary for the time being, and directed that that should be invested as they thought proper, and that the interest accruing on that should be divided among the poor of the town without religious distinction. That £400 has been received in the present year, and it has been invested in the Loan Fund Office in the town, and the interest which was £10 last year was distributed among the poor.

100. Did the Local Government Board Auditor bring that within the ordinary accounts ?—Yes, he did.

101. Kindly tell me now what the expenditure is— under the head of "salaries" first of all ?—The expen-

TIPPERARY. July 29, 1880. — Mr. Armstrong Dawson.

ditures for cleansing the crossings, channels, lanes, and so forth was £39 1s. 3d.; and for salaries was £80 10s.

102. What other expenditure had you?—Rents, £17 1s. for the Town Commissioners' office and also the manure depôt. This Town Hall was presented to the town by Mr. Smith Barry. The erection of new lamps cost £44 1s. 6d. With reference to the question of these new lamps, I may mention that the Commissioners thought the number too small, and increased them.

103. What did you pay for lighting?—£79 10s. Various expenses came to £18 1s. 11d., and that includes some hardware goods in addition.

104. What were they for?—Brushes for the scavengers. Then paving——

105. What is that paving—is it for crossings and channels?—Yes. It amounted to £19 12s. 2d. Some new flagging, and repairs of old ones cost £10 13s. 7d. Stationery and printing came to £25 7s. 6d., and incidental expenses to £10 11s. 10d.

106. What is the total?—£730 14s. 2d., including the [illegible]. The total amount of expenditure was £881 3s. 2d.

107. Do the Grand Jury do any works for you in the town?—The Commissioners from time to time present some presentments before the Grand Jury.

108. And do the Grand Jury accede?—And the work is carried out by us as contractors.

109. But they don't give what is asked?—Seldom what is asked, and sometimes we are refused altogether.

110. What did they give you last year?—A small sum—to the extent of something over £100.

111. Besides what they give in presentments they take charge of the streets?—Yes.

112. Do they take charge of the lanes?—They take charge of some of the lanes. They take charge of the streets so far as the repairing is concerned.

113. Do they clean the streets?—Very seldom.

114. The Commissioners take charge of cleaning the byelanes and channels and crossings?—Yes.

115. What staff does that take?—One. Only one man, but he is a very good one.

116. Have you an inspector of nuisances in the town?—We have a street inspector.

117. How many men has he under him?—Only one man.

118. Only one man to look after the whole town?—That is all.

119. At the time the last inquiry was held here you had five men and a clerk?—Yes, but it partook too much of the nature of sanitary business, and the Commissioners not being the sanitary body, they gave notice to the County Surveyor to keep the streets clean, and in a great measure they have done that.

120. What do they do with the street sweepings?—The contractors take them to some outskirt of the town.

121. Then you have no receipts from the sale of manure?—No.

122. And you have no expenditure in maintaining scavengers?—No.

123. And you have only one man?—Yes.

124. The object with which the Commissioners propose an extension of the municipal area, as I understand from the replies to the queries, is in order to get more rates?—Yes, and to have the population larger in order that they should become the sanitary body, and also in course of time to endeavour to have the transfer to them of the Grand Jury powers.

125. Have you or have the Commissioners considered how many miles of roads that extension to a mile and a half would take if they got those powers?—I could not say.

126. They have not considered whether it would pay them to take up the roads?—They are sure it would pay them. Supposing they got the amount of the county cess and the county at large charges, they believe they would do the same work better, and at less expense, including the county at large charges.

127. Have they calculated how much they would get for doing this from their increased rate?—They have not entered into any specific calculation with regard to that.

128. Because they might maintain the roads for less money than the present contractors, but they might not get so much money as that from the district, because the roads near the town are always much more expensive in the way of maintenance—they have not calculated that?—They did not in fact enter fully into any specific charges, but calculating £2,850 as the valuation, then the county cess on that at 1s. 6d. say——

129. Of the 1s. 6d. how much are county at large charges that would be paid in any case?—I don't know whether it would amount to 6d. in the pound.

130. Say 4d.; that would leave you 11d. What would an elevenpenny rate bring in?—About £175 14s.

131. Very well, and how many roads would you have to maintain for that—how much would an elevenpenny rate give you upon the entire present municipal area, and the extended area both; the two together would be a valuation of £14,000 is not that right, very nearly so at any rate; say £14,000; what would an elevenpenny rate on that give you?—About £642.

132. As far as I make it out something about fifteen miles of roads would be the amount you would have to maintain for that—how much a mile would that be?—It would be close on £43 a mile.

133. Could you do it for that?—Certainly, as the outlay is very small. The main street would take a good deal, about 6s. a perch or so, about that.

134. On the leading roads going out of the town, the road from the Junction for instance, the traffic is heavy, and the expense would be great?—Yes, there is heavy traffic there; but there are a good many byroads that would not cost much.

135. You have not gone fully into the figures relating to that, however?—The Commissioners have not fully gone into figures of that sort.

136. Is there anything else occurring to you bearing on the question that you would wish to add?—There is nothing more than their desire of increasing the present boundary, it being too small.

Mr. William Hurley.

Mr. WILLIAM HURLEY examined.

137. You are the Chairman of the Tipperary Town Commissioners?—Yes.

138. You have heard what Mr. Dawson has said about the meeting of the Commissioners, and their wish for an extension of the municipal boundary—is that correct?—Yes.

139. As you have an opportunity, being here, of ascertaining it, do you know what the feeling of the adjoining [illegible] is on the subject?—I think the [illegible] are favourable to the extension.

140. Have they considered the question of opposing it or anything of that kind?—I am not aware.

141. Have you heard any expression of opinion from those who live outside the boundary as it is at present, and who would be taken in if the extension you seek is granted?—I have heard no expression of opinion in opposition to it.

142. Or for it?—Or for it, from those outside the present boundary.

143. Who would of course have to pay something more than at present?—Certainly.

144. I see it is for the purpose of giving you more money the one thing, that you wish for the extension?—Yes, for that purpose, but we also wish to extend the

Tipperary. May [illegible], 18[illegible].

Mr. William [illegible].

[illegible] and to have the [illegible] influence [illegible] [illegible] on the Board, [illegible] I think it would be desirable.

145. But Mr. [illegible] says only a few would be brought in?—Even those few might be represented. [illegible] [illegible] [illegible] a number of gentlemen. There are farmers in the town who might be members of the Board if [illegible] [illegible] [illegible] [illegible], and I think it would be desirable that the farming interest should be represented in this place especially. It is very likely at no distant date that we shall have control of the [illegible], and it is no [illegible] to say that three-quarters of a million of those [illegible] is [illegible] of [illegible] [illegible].

146. There is a great [illegible] [illegible] [illegible]?—Yes, and for myself I would be very anxious to see the [illegible] [illegible], and the effect of that would be to give more confidence in the [illegible] [illegible].

147. With regard to the additional amount of [illegible] you have not exercised your full powers. You only [illegible] a rate of [illegible], so that you have money enough?—That was [illegible] [illegible] [illegible] [illegible], and I believe it [illegible], we are able to [illegible] [illegible] [illegible] [illegible] [illegible].

148. And I suppose you will strike the rate this year?—I think so.

149. Are there any things wanting to be done in the town that the Commissioners have power to do, and that they have not done for want of funds?—I should say not. They have not drained the town properly, nor is there sufficient lighting—we have not sufficient lamps. There are many things we would have done if we had had funds at our disposal.

150. That you would do as Commissioners without being the urban sanitary authority?—Yes. One reason that they do not want to [illegible] the urban sanitary authority is that they would not have a sufficient rate for [illegible]; and also that the rate levied by the present body—the present sanitary authority—is divided equally between the landlord and occupier, whereas if the Commissioners levied, the rate would be paid entirely by the occupier. That is an objection to taking over the sanitary duties.

151. Then you have not applied to be made the urban sanitary authority?—We have not, sir. The Commissioners thought it better, in their opinion, not to [illegible] such an application until their rate would be extended.

152. If your area was extended you would be disposed to take over those duties then?—Yes, I think so.

153. Do the Guardians do what you want in the town as regards sanitary matters?—They are very slow in doing anything we recommend.

154. But do they do it, even if they are slow?—Well, some things they have not done.

155. In what way?—With regard to the sewerage, draining [illegible] and putting in traps.

156. What kind of sewerage is there as a matter of fact?—Very good, I think. In the main street, and a number of streets I think it good, but there are other portions of the town unprovided with sewerage at all.

157. Are there main drains?—They should be extended in the west end. They only [illegible] [illegible] of the boundary, and not only of the boundary but very important houses.

158. Where does the sewage run to?—It is discharged into the river.

159. Then you think if you were made the urban sanitary authority you would not have money enough to take care of the town so far as sanitary purposes are concerned without an extended area?—I don't think we could do all that is necessary for the town even with the extended area.

160. And if you became the urban sanitary authority would you wish to take charge of the roads which [illegible] [illegible] from the Grand Jury?—Well, that is a question we have not fully considered. The [illegible] was [illegible] to that so far as we have inquired.

161. In fact you would not like to take those up if there should be a loss?—Yes, that there should not be a loss, as if there might be a gain, and that we would do the work better. However, we have not fully considered that or made the proper calculations.

162. Is there anything else you wish to add?—We think the people we would bring in should pay something towards the expenses of the town, considering what they gain by being so convenient to the town, and the [illegible] they have of the schools, that could not be maintained by any rural population, and that are maintained principally by the contributions of the people of the town.

163. How far do the people send their children in to the schools in the town?—From nearly the whole of the parish.

164. From two miles off?—They do; and then in marketing they have decided advantages over people living at a greater distance.

165. You think that advantage extends the entire mile and a half at least?—I should say beyond it. I may mention what has come under my own notice. I have known in the past spring and winter [illegible] selling for [illegible] at 6d. to 8d. a [illegible]. That is equivalent to from 5d. to 6d. a gallon for milk, at the very time that people living in the distance are getting from 5d. to 10d. a gallon for milk.

166. Do you think the rate payable on the [illegible] the present extension a fair rate for them to pay?—I think it is.

167. If they got the full value from the town being kept in a better state than it is?—Yes, and probably we would extend the lighting, though I don't think we would extend it beyond the present boundary, but even then the advantage would be a great deal.

168. Of course you don't contemplate extending the lighting to a mile and a half?—No, but without any prospect of advantage whatever, I think, from the town, they should pay their share towards the expenses of the town.

169. I suppose I may take it that the Commissioners who were not present on the day the special resolution on this subject was passed are of the same opinion as those who attended at that resolution?—I think so; they were specially summoned.

170. Is there anything else that occurs to you bearing on the subject of this inquiry?—I think not.

Mr. [illegible] [illegible] examined.

Mr. [illegible] [illegible].

171. You are one of the Town Commissioners of Tipperary?—I am.

172. What is your opinion with regard to the proposed extension?—I think it would be a great benefit to the town.

173. Do you think it right that the distance should be a mile and a half?—I think that is a fair distance.

174. You think the people living within a mile and a half derive advantage from the proximity of the town, and that they should be called upon to pay rates to the town?—I think so.

175. Do you think the poundage rate for land a fair one?—Yes, I think also that if we get the Grand Jury powers into our hands they would have less rate to pay—that we would maintain the roads and do the work, I think, at less rates than they pay at present.

176. But you have not gone into any figures?—I went into some myself, but I have not got them about me just now. I made a rough calculation some time ago. I think the Grand Jury do not expend more than about something like £150 a year at present on this township.

177. And how much do they get?—I think about £300 a year. According to the 11d. rate, they get about £280 a year. I don't think we had so low a rate as 11d. for many years.

178. One shilling and threepence three farthings for 1878—that was a low rate?—That is an exceptional rate. We hadn't so low a rate for years.

179. What is the last county cess for the half year of 1879?—I have not the 1879 rate, but I could procure it. I think it would enable us to employ a good staff to cleanse the town. At present if we had the Grand Jury powers we would not have work enough.

180. You would have to get a staff, and they would not be fully employed?—They would not be half employed. If we had an extended area, and the whole thing in our hands, we could get a good staff.

181. Are you of opinion that you would not wish to be the urban sanitary authority except you got an extension?—Certainly, I am of that opinion. However, I think we will have to take it in any case, because the Guardians are not doing their duty. They may only do anything.

182. The Guardians don't do anything?—Well, very little.

183. Are they asked?—They are asked repeatedly. They are taking some steps, but I hardly think they will carry them out. They talk a good deal, but do very little. I would be inclined to take up the roads from the Grand Jury.

184. According to the present state of the law, you cannot get the roads except you become the urban sanitary authority first, and you are not prepared to become the urban sanitary authority without you get an extension?—I think we will have to become so, because the population is certainly over 6,000 at present.

185. But except you ask to become it, you cannot become it before 1881?—Yes, but that period is only a short time away from us.

Mr. John O'Connor examined.

186. You are a Town Commissioner of Tipperary?—Yes.

187. At present you have no Surveyor for the town?—No; they cannot afford to pay him.

188. But you have nothing for him to do at present?—We would always find something for him to do, but we are not in a position to pay the salary.

189. You would not want him until you had charge of the roads?—There are a good deal of buildings being constructed here, and we should have a Surveyor to look after them in a good many cases.

190. If you got an extended area, anything like that which is now proposed, and became the urban sanitary authority, would you then appoint a Surveyor?—Certainly, and a good man.

191. What sort of salary would you give a man for that, before he had charge of the roads?—Well, I have not considered that.

192. You have not considered the question yet, whether it would pay to take up the roads?—We have made our minds up pretty well without going into figures, that it would pay, and we have a good local Surveyor here, if we had means to pay him.

193. If you do not get an extension, you would not wish to take up the present roads?—No; we would not be inclined unless we got an extension.

Mr. Dawson, Town Clerk, re-examined.

194. The taking up of the roads would be on the supposition that the people living in the extended area would pay the same amount as they do now to the county cess?—Exactly so. We also expect that if we got the butter market here under our control, we will be able to save so much from it, that eventually there will be no rates.

195. And by the tolls you would derive from that, you would benefit the people you take in, and also the people who pay the rates?—Yes.

196. What do the tolls amount to?—The present butter market is worth about £300 a year.

Mr. Hurley re-examined.

197. I wish to say that the butter market tolls are a little under £600 at present.

198. The butter market tolls are worth, you say, about £600 a year at present?—Yes. I think, in the hands of the Commissioners, the amount of the revenue derivable from that market would be very much increased. There is a great deal of butter sold outside in private, by people who pay no toll; but in the hands of the Commissioners, the tolls would, in my opinion, amount to considerably more—probably £1,000 a year.

199. How is it likely that the Commissioners would acquire the control of that market?—By purchase I should say. The present owner would be willing to sell to the Commissioners, but he has only a life interest, and it would be optional with those who appointed him—the Justices of the county—to recognise his necessity. We would be unwilling under those circumstances to purchase; but that objection being removed, I don't think there would be any difficulty in the matter.

200. If you purchased, you would have to borrow money for the purpose?—Yes.

201. And then you would have a charge upon that—interest and sinking fund?—Yes.

202. That would take a great deal away from the tolls?—It would take a considerable sum away from the tolls, but there would be a very large surplus. It would not cost, I should say, more than about £4,000 or £5,000 to purchase it. That at 4 per cent. would be £200 a year, say £250. If we could succeed in that, as I suppose, and bring in all the butter into the market, and charge the present toll, there would be £750 left surely.

203. And do you think it is possible to follow that out?—I think if the difficulty I have mentioned was removed, it would be done before twelve months.

204. Are any steps being taken about it?—No steps, except to make these inquiries indirectly. I know of my own personal knowledge that the present owner would be prepared to sell.

205. Supposing you had those tolls, and I suppose you are sure of getting them, the Town Commissioners are willing to expend the surplus to the advantage of the people in the extended area, as well as of those living within the present boundary?—Certainly, of all. Then we would have no rate at all to pay, and we would do a great deal more than we have been doing. Even if we had no rate, we would have more funds at our disposal than we have at the present time. I have nothing more to add of any importance, except what I have already said in reference to the butter market.

KILKENNY.—MARCH 6TH, 1879.

Before Mr. EXHAM, Q.C., and Mr. COTTON, C.E.

Mr. PATRICK WATTERS examined.

1. CHAIRMAN.—You are the Town Clerk of Kilkenny?—Yes.

2. And have been for a considerable time?—Yes.

3. The town is under the Towns Improvement Act?—Yes.

4. And was the entire Act adopted?—Yes; it came into operation on the 2nd of January, 1866.

5. Do you happen to have the Gazette fixing the boundaries?—The boundaries were fixed by the Corporation Act.

6. That is then, that the boundaries fixed by the Corporation Act were adopted under the Towns Improvement Act?—Yes, the boundaries were the same.

7. They were never altered?—No.

8. Is the Parliamentary boundary the same as the Municipal?—No, the Parliamentary boundary is much more extensive than the Municipal.

9. Can you tell me what is the area comprised within the Municipal boundary?—For rateable purposes, 878a. 0r. 30p.

10. How much of it is arable land as contra-distinguished from buildings on land?—I consider that the 871 acres represents the arable land, the agricultural land.

11. Yes, but how much of that pays only one-fourth of the rate under the Towns Improvement Act as contradistinguished from buildings on land?—Oh, it all pays the same at present.

12. Is there no land within that, no farming land?—Oh, yes, there is.

14. Could you tell me how much of the 800 and odd acres is land that only pays one-fourth?—Well, at present, I think it pays the entire tax.

15. Mr. *Dillon*.—Yes, for Grand Jury purposes.

16. CHAIRMAN.—Did you ever levy an Improvement rate.

WITNESS.—No, never; there was never any rate levied. It was the Grand Jury tax I was referring to. There was never any Borough rate levied in Kilkenny.

17. And the boundaries you say now remain the same as originally constituted?—They have been the same since the coming into operation of the Municipal Corporation Act.

18. What is the valuation of Kilkenny of the Municipal district?—The rateable valuation within the Municipal area is £17,158 5s.

19. How much of that represents land, and how much buildings, can you say?—No, I could not.

20. Now you are divided into two wards in Kilkenny?—Yes—St. Canice's and St. John's.

21. What is the valuation of each of those wards?—Well, the Municipal wards are not coterminous with the Poor Law wards, and, therefore, the valuations could not be separated under the Poor Law Act—there were three Poor Law wards, and they extended a good deal beyond the Municipal wards. The third ward is the East ward; so they are not coterminous, and the two Municipal wards have never been separately valued.

22. Do the Poor Law wards extend much beyond the Municipal?—Yes, considerably. The electoral division of Kilkenny extends beyond the Municipal boundary.

23. And the three wards are in that division?—Yes; the three Poor Law wards, and they include the Municipal division, but extend a good deal beyond it, and, of course, beyond the Municipal wards.

24. Then, I suppose, the portions of the Poor Law wards that are beyond the Municipal wards are not built on; they are mostly farming lands, I presume?—Yes. There are, of course, villa residences, but not streets or rows of houses.

25. There are, in fact, no streets outside the Municipal boundary?—No.

26. Is it considered that those wards are fairly divided in Kilkenny?—St. Canice's and St. John's?

27. Yes. Is any change in your opinion desirable?—I can tell you the number of burgesses in each ward. The total number of burgesses in Kilkenny is 379, of whom 267 are in St. Canice's, and 112 in St. John's; so that St. Canice's ward in point of number of burgesses is considerably larger, but as to the question of money value, I could not say. I should be inclined, however, to say that St. Canice's is the richer of the two on the whole.

28. Are there the same number of Town Councillors elected for each ward?—There are twenty-four members of the Town Council, and there are twelve from each ward, three Aldermen, and nine Councillors in each ward.

29. As far as you know, would it be desirable that any change should be made in those wards, that they be altered or divided in any way, or that they should be allowed to remain as they are?—Well, I can only say they have worked very well hitherto, and I would not like to suggest any change in their arrangement. The people here are very well contented with the two municipal wards as they at present stand.

30. What is the population?—Well, according to the census of 1871 it was 12,710.

31. And is the population increasing or diminishing as far as you know?—I should say it is not increasing. I see a great many houses in the vicinity that appear to be uninhabited, I would not say it is increasing at all.

32. Has there been or is there, do you know, any tendency or disposition to build outside the present municipal boundary?—No, there has not. There may have been two or three villas built within the last five years, but no general building at all.

33. The roads are in the management of the Grand Jury?—Yes, they are; the Corporation repair within the old city walls, and the difference or distance between the old city walls and the municipal district is repaired by the Grand Jury.

34. What area is there comprised within the old city walls?—Very small.

35. What fund do they do that with?—Their own funds.

36. Well, are not the portions kept by the Town Council or Corporation, are they not county roads, post roads, and so on?—They extend a very short distance. As long as I remember the Corporation repaired them within the old city walls formerly surrounding Kilkenny.

37. Out of the funds of the Corporation?—Yes.

38. What has the county cess been, can you tell, for the past five years?—In 1874 it was 3s. 10½d.; in '75, 3s. 9d.; in '76, 3s. 3½d.; in '77, 3s. 1d.; and in '78, 3s. 5½d. The average of that is 3s. 9¼d. on the five years.

39. Could you tell how much goes to the county at large charges, and how much to keeping up the roads within the municipality?—I have not the Grand Jury book here.

40. Can you give the poor rates?—For '74 it was 4s. 6d.; for '75, 3s. 6d.; for '76, 2s. 8d.; for '77, 3s. 6d.; '78, 3s. 9d.; and the average of that is 3s. 1½d.

41. Was there any sanitary work done in those years further back that made it so heavy?—No, the sanitary work has only been within the last two years.

42. Now, has there been any sanitary rate struck here at all?—No, never any rate at all struck.

3 H 2

KILKENNY.
Aug. 8, 1879.
Mr. Patrick Watters.

43. The Corporation then pays it out of its own property?—Yes.

44. The present boundaries—extend on an average to about three quarters of a mile from the centre of the town, do they not?—Yes, sir, about that.

45. Mr. Cotton.—That map does not agree with the Ordnance map in some points.

46. Chairman.—However, this map gives the boundary as fixed by the Municipal Corporations Act, 1843?—Yes, the boundaries were never altered since.

47. Do you know if the Corporation has considered the question, as to whether it would be advisable to extend the present boundaries?—Yes; they considered it very closely.

48. And has there been any resolution passed on the subject?—Yes, by the majority of the Corporation. They resolved that it should be extended to an area of two miles.

49. Two miles?—Yes, about that.

50. Mr. Cotton.—Is it a circular area?—No; I suppose they did not mean to say a hard and fast line, but one so arranged as not if possible to cut towards side. They followed roads and rivers as much as possible, and did not adopt any hard and fast line, but as consistent as could be on the average of two miles from the city.

51. Can you say the grounds on which the resolution was adopted?—Well, they think that by extending the area of taxation they could have greater public improvements; that there could be various things done by an extension of area of taxation, and bringing in more persons to contribute to the taxes.

52. But you never have struck any rate here?—Oh no; I don't mean to say by that a borough rate, but I mean the Grand Jury tax.

53. You but the persons living within that area pay the same Grand Jury tax as the people in the town?—No, the people outside the municipal boundary do not pay the same. The Grand Jury tax is not the same outside the municipal boundary as within. At present the persons outside do not pay as much Grand Jury cess as those within it, and the Corporation think if they extend the boundary of the municipal area they could effect more benefit and improvement by the extension of the area of taxation, and bring in more persons to contribute to their taxation.

54. Yes, but suppose they are brought in, your view would be that the taxation on them for Grand Jury cess would be higher than at present?—There would be more to contribute.

55. Yes, but what good would that do to the town, for that would go to the Grand Jury, except the Corporation would be prepared to take up the management of all the roads within their own district?—At present the opinion is it would be for the general good.

56. The effect would be, that the county cess would be higher but that would not go for the benefit of the Corporation but that of the Grand Jury?—No; but it would go for general purposes for the benefit of the city.

57. How would it go for the improvement of the city for you have never struck an improvement rate. I could understand if you had an improvement rate and if you wanted the outsiders to pay a fair share of it in borough rate or then, but you have not; would it not follow that if you bring them in you would be giving them advantages and that they would become more of burden on your rental and city funds than anything else?—Well, I don't think the Corporation ever contemplated a borough rate that I am aware. It was only what was to be got by Grand Jury tax.

58. But they would not hand that over to you unless the Corporation went in for being burdened to take over the roads and bridges, then I could understand their anxiety to bring in those people?—Well in the answers made to the queries which the Commissioners forwarded to us, the objections to the present boundaries are set forth. In answer to the question "Are the present Municipal boundaries regarded with dissatisfaction by the ratepayers generally, or by any section of them?" he had replied "Some of the ratepayers would wish for an extension of the present boundaries." To the query "If so, what are the objections entertained to them?" he answered "That the area of taxation is too limited." As to the query "What is the opinion of the Municipal body on this subject?" his answer was "A majority of the Municipal body is in favour of an extension to a radius of two miles, or thereabouts."

59. But why speak of an increased area of taxation when there has been no rate struck whatever?—There would be the Grand Jury tax. If the outlying districts were brought in they would participate in the advantages derived from it.

60. Yes, I can understand that, but if the outlying districts are brought in, the only effect would be that whereas they now pay a very small county cess, they then would pay a larger one, and that you know would go for the benefit of the borough inhabitants?—I am not prepared to say what the results would be; that would be a matter to be developed by degrees.

61. Have the Municipal body contemplated taking up the management of the roads themselves?—No, they have not entered into any ideas of that kind at all, but I believe it is understood it is the intention of the legislature that both Grand Juries and Corporation should be united in the management of the roads.

62. That is that there should be an undivided authority. It is in that view that the Town Council have come to the conclusion that it would be wise and proper to have the area extended and to bring in those who take advantage of the roads of the town?—Yes, it is considered to be a mutual benefit, and of course the outlying districts would participate in the advantages that would arise from the extension. Those living outside would have the advantages of being near the city here, of markets and fairs, and to these advantages they should contribute it is believed.

63. I suppose there is no doubt the owners and occupiers of land to a certain extent of distance beyond the Municipal boundary derive those exceptional advantages and that the land is more valuable on account of its proximity to the city?—Decidedly, of course it is a very great matter to have the land near to the town in order to have the advantages of fairs and markets.

64. I don't understand whether you intended to convey, that the Town Council considered if this outlying district was taken in they would contemplate in any way levying any taxation?—No, at present they never contemplated levying a tax.

65. Whether a rate should hereafter become necessary or not, I can't say, but unless the Corporation are compelled to do it, they will not, for they have certainly no intention whatever of doing it, I know it is contrary to their wish. They do everything—they light the city and repair it out of the Corporation property.

66. Well I asked you about the lands outside deriving exceptional benefits. Are there many gentry residing within the district you suggest?—Yes, there are from thirty to forty villa residences within the two mile radius.

67. That is outside the present municipal radius?—Yes, and within the boundary contemplated to be brought in.

68. How many persons would it add to the constituency supposing that district were brought in?—The present constituency of Parliamentary voters?

69. I mean for municipal purposes, say about how many?—Well it would come very close on the number of Parliamentary voters. I think the Parliamentary boundary is very much about two miles, there may be a difference in different parts, but I believe the Parliamentary boundary to be nearly two miles so that there is no great difference.

KILKENNY. Nov. [illegible]

Mr. [illegible] Walsh.

70. About how many municipal voters would you say would be brought in?—Some 300 I should say.

71. And how many would be eligible to be members of the Corporation?—I should say ninety. I am only ninety on it.

72. Mr. Cotton.—I think you may take it the two mile circle is exactly one half of the Parliamentary boundary, therefore you cannot, I think, make the valuation of it more.

73. Chairman.—You cannot however tell us what is the exact valuation of the increased area if we went for, say, a two mile area?—No.

74. In fact that is only going a mile and a half out?—Yes two miles from the place where you now are, which is the centre of the town.

75. Now suppose it is extended any distance beyond the present boundary are the Corporation prepared to light and water that district taken in?—Well I can't exactly say that.

76. Do you propose to give these people you bring in the same advantages the people in the present boundary have, or do you propose to bring them in at a differential rate?—That point has not been considered.

77. Mr. Simon Morris, T.C.—They did consider it, lighting your parishes, and they never intended to light it.

78. Chairman.—Was the matter discussed at a meeting of the Corporation?

Witness.—There was no resolution passed on that point, as to what would be done outside the municipal boundary. The only abstract resolution to which the Council came was that it would be of advantage to extend the boundary to a radius of two miles. There were however no particularities entered into at all as to what would be done hereafter.

79. Now with regard to the effect, the Public Health Act of last session or year, would have on the lands at present in the care of the rural sanitary authority if they were brought in?—No, no resolution on that point was come to.

80. To your own knowledge, do these people in the outside district proposed to be brought in, use the town largely?—Yes, very largely for markets and fairs. There is an extensive market here; there are fifteen fairs in the year; they avail in their purchases and take every advantage of these fairs and markets.

81. And there are schools used by the children of these persons living outside?—Yes, there are schools of all denominations.

82. And I suppose they use the houses of worship here on Sundays?—Yes, all the people within a radius of two miles, I should say, come in to the places of worship here.

83. And all I presume, may be said to frequent the railways more or less?—Yes, all use the railways.

84. It is within the municipal boundary, I believe?—Yes, the terminus is.

85. Now, the flagging here has it been done by the Grand Jury?—No, by the Corporation.

86. Out of their own property, I understand you to say, they do this?—Yes.

87. And all the sanitary arrangements other than taking off the surface water?—Yes.

88. They do it all themselves?—Yes, all the sanitary arrangements are done by the Corporation—everything in the way of improvement within the walls, everything for sanitary purposes, is done by the Corporation, including the cleansing of the streets. In the first instance the city Corporation were in the habit of repairing within the old city walls, and the difference between the city walls and the municipal boundary was done by the Grand Jury.

89. Have the Grand Jury, in that portion between the old city walls, and the municipal boundary made any sewers for you?—Well, there was one large sewer made for the benefit of the school-house—one of the new Industrial Schools established here. The Grand Jury gave £300, and we gave one.

90. The Grand Jury £300, and you one hundred?—Yes.

91. And with the exception of that, the flagging, sewerage, and all is done by the Corporation?—Yes, everything within the city walls is done by the Corporation, the roads outside the city walls are kept in repair by the Corporation.

92. Have you got high pressure water here?—No: we have no waterworks at all.

93. But there is plenty of water?—Yes; there are private wells.

94. And how about gas?—It is rather a vexed question, the present public lighting is by oil lamps, we have gone back to the olden time.

95. But there is a Gas Company?—Yes, and it supplies private individuals with gas.

96. I suppose the fact is you fell out about terms?—Yes, and there is an ejectment at law pending.

97. Mr. Cotton.—Can you describe the boundaries of the two wards generally—are they divided by the river?—No, not altogether; for instance we are now in St. Canice's ward, and so is the far side of the river.

98. How are they divided?—There is a long line—Kingsgreen, and one side is in St. John's—the right hand, and the left is in St. Canice's; it runs down to the extreme end of the town, and all to the right is St. John's, and to the left St. Canice's ward.

100. What I want is this, suppose that extension or any extension took place, how would you propose to throw in the additional ground into the wards, would you form a new ward or extend the present wards?—That is a question I suggested. My idea was to try and draw a straight line down through the centre, and let the new part go into each ward.

101. That is in other words to extend the present wards taking in on each side the portion of area added?—Yes, draw a line and give a certain portion to each ward.

102. Chairman.—Would you alter the present boundary of the wards?—No; I think they are at present arranged pretty fairly. There may be a little variance, but not much.

103. Then you would extend the divisions just straight out into two lines?—Yes; that I think would be better than making a third ward, to add to each ward portion of the increased radius.

104. Would your extension of two miles go into any other electoral division?—Yes; I consider it would.

105. You don't know though?—No.

106. I understand you to say the parliamentary boundary is all in one electoral division?—I am not quite sure.

107. The Mayor.—The two mile radius does not extend beyond the electoral division.

108. Chairman.—You have said fairly enough, that the municipal body here think it would be right that the people in that extended district should pay for the advantages they have, and there being such a large constituency as 300 to be brought in, would you not think it fair that that extended district should have one ward to look after the interest of the county?—That would be very fair.

109. Supposing you were to leave the two wards as they are, and out of the extended district form a new one giving it a representation of eight members, what would you say to such an arrangement as that?—I would see no objection to having a third ward.

110. You see if you are right in saying the valuation of the new district is anything like £17,000, and the present area £17,000 would it not be fair that the people taxed in that way on their valuation of £17,000 should get eight members on the Town Council to look after their interests?—Well, I think that would be the result in any case, for if there were a new district added to the existing wards every man rated at £10 would become a burgess, and of course they could in that way return their own friends to the Town Council, and they would have a voice in the matter of controlling the expenditure, and seeing to their own interests.

KILKENNY. Nov. 4, 18[illegible]. Mr. Patrick Waters.

111. Suppose you threw the new or extended area into the existing wards would you extend the number of your aldermen and town councillors?—Well, I don't say it would be absolutely necessary, but of course, there should be an Act of Parliament for that. I think that if there was an extended area it would be rational there should be an extension of the number of town councillors.

112. Do you think 24 quite enough?—I think, say, the town councils always do most work and do the business better. I think the highest number for a Grand Jury is 23, and they do their business well. I think 24 quite enough. The outside ratepayers were of course not represented on the town council when the resolution in favour of extension was passed.

113. Of course they could not [illegible] not having any votes on the council they could have put their views in another way, I suppose, if they were so inclined. In other places, for instance, there have been public meetings?—The resolution of the town council was of course confined to the Corporation, and does not bind anyone else.

114. Has any house [illegible] much building going on outside?—There has been very little building outside.

115. The Mayor.—I beg to state that after four days' debate the Corporation divided as to whether there should be an increase or not, and it was decided by a majority of 14 to 3 that we should support the two mile radius. There were 23 members present.

116. What was the resolution, Mr. Waters?—I find there were in fact 13 for and 4 against. First of all there was a motion moved by Mr. Fanning that the boundaries should be extended,—"That the municipal boundary should be extended to a radius of two miles or thereabouts." This was seconded by Mr. Quinn. Mr. McDermott moved an amendment that there be no extension made; this was seconded by Mr. McEvoy, and a division having been called for, the original motion was carried by 13 to 4.

Mr. Patrick J. [illegible].

Mr. Patrick Joseph [illegible], examined.

117. Chairman.—Do you hold any office under the Corporation?—Yes, borough surveyor and executive sanitary officer, and surveyor to the Grand Jury.

118. You heard already the question asked relative to the Grand Jury cess return?—Yes.

119. Well, immediately outside the present boundary and within the two mile radius, what is the Grand Jury cess?—The county Grand Jury cess for [illegible] is [illegible], and for Gowran 8d.

120. Is that for the half-year?—Yes, and Shillelogher [illegible].

121. How much of it is for county at large charges, because the difference would be for roads and bridges?—In Gowran, say, the county at large charges would be the same. The roads alone would in the city cost [illegible].

122. What would be the other charge making up the [illegible]?—The Lunatic Asylum, officers' salaries, the Industrial Schools, &c.

123. Mr. [illegible].—Would the two mile extension go beyond the county of Kilkenny?—It would extend into parts of three others. It is right that I should mention that the county cess would not be so heavy as formerly—since April last the Government pay for the support of prisoners at an average of £[illegible] per annum, and another thing, the Government pay [illegible] per head for lunatics, a saving to the city of £[illegible], so that we save a thousand a year by that.

124. If the county at large charges are, as I see, 1s. 4d. in the borough, how can the county cess be so little outside the borough, for the land outside should pay county at large charges?—But they vary between the county and the city, there is a difference between the county and the city. I don't understand how the county at large charges in the county are made up.

125. Well, at the present calculation, it would appear the valuation of the present borough is about £17,000, and the proposed increased area would be £17,000 more?—No, not that but £[illegible] more, and the increase in acreage would bring it to about [illegible] acres. The two would make in round numbers a valuation of about £[illegible].

126. Are we right in assuming as has been stated that the increased area would add about 300 to the constituency?—So I understand from what Mr. Waters says.

127. But you don't know yourself?—No.

128. As living here and being an engineer, and having a knowledge of the place, would you say that the people living in that district derive exceptional advantages from their proximity to the town—do they use the town largely?—I think they do.

129. Now, what advantage to the ratepayers in the town do you think there would be by bringing in this extended district, having regard to the fact that the Corporation pays so much?—I worked it out in this way: the total [illegible] for the years 1874, '75, '76, and '77 amounted to £10,[illegible] [illegible]s. [illegible]d. From this he deducted the amounts [illegible] in [illegible] accounts in three years, £[illegible] [illegible]s. [illegible]d., and further deducted Government allowances on account of lunatics, at [illegible] for 1874, twenty-nine at £10 4s. 8d. per head, £[illegible] [illegible]; for 1875, say thirty-two at £10 4s. 8d., £[illegible] [illegible]; [illegible], £[illegible] [illegible]. The average for four years would be £[illegible] [illegible], which would be half-yearly £[illegible] [illegible], and this would cause a tax of [illegible] under 1s. in the pound, if levied on the city on present valuation. If the area was extended to a radius of about two miles there was to be added [illegible] allowance, according to estimate made by Mr. Kelly, deputy surveyor, for roads and footpaths within the extended area, £[illegible]. For contingent expenses of additional [illegible] support of lunatics, according to Mr. [illegible]'s estimate, £[illegible], also for [illegible] upon increased [illegible] £[illegible], and you have a [illegible] of £[illegible] [illegible], which, upon the present city valuation of £17,[illegible], increased, according to Mr. [illegible]'s estimated valuation of [illegible] by £[illegible], would be a gross valuation of £[illegible], upon which [illegible] would be levied at a poundage rate of [illegible], while the addition of the [illegible] and which would affect the county [illegible] as follows:—Gowran, from 8d. to [illegible]; Shillelogher, [illegible] to [illegible]; and [illegible], [illegible] to [illegible].

130. That is a half-yearly calculation?—Yes.

131. Then the effect would be to reduce the city taxes, and to add to the others?—Yes.

132. So that it is no matter whether they get up the roads themselves, or continue under the Grand Jury, the citizens here would pay less cess, and the others would pay greater?—In that estimate I have added £[illegible] for maintaining the county roads in the area extended of about two miles. That is according to the estimate of Mr. Kelly, the deputy surveyor, for roads and footpaths.

133. Then the effect would practically be an extension of a radius of, say, two miles round. Suppose that is done, the effect would be that the ratepayers in the municipal boundary would be likely to have their rates reduced to [illegible] for [illegible] and that those between the half-mile or three-quarters would have theirs increased to about [illegible] or [illegible]?—Yes.

134. Now, is it your opinion they should fairly pay that, having regard to the fact that they use the roads much more largely than the others?—That is my opinion.

135. And I suppose an evidence of the very use they make of these roads is spoken to [illegible] on account of the use they make of [illegible] working in so often?—Yes.

136. The contractor's charges are more?—Yes.

137. They are at present only paying county cess

on the use of those roads to a certain extent, and [illegible] of paying anything, as I understand, for the use they make of the roads in the town?—Yes.

137. And that as a matter, therefore, whether you [illegible] up the roads, or they stay under the Grand Jury, the [illegible] would be [illegible] by the extension?—Yes.

138. In addition to which there is to be considered, I presume, the advantage to be derived by those outside from the improvements effected by the Corporation [illegible]—Undoubtedly. In the maintenance of the town we [illegible] and [illegible] in [illegible] £[illegible]; in 1877, £[illegible]; and in [illegible], £[illegible].

139. Then, Mr. Dillon, so far as [illegible], would the bringing in of this [illegible] affect the rates of the city, so as to make it likely you would have to put on an [illegible] rate if you brought them in?—I don't think so, unless for sanitary purposes. Of course if these people outside are brought in they have under the Public Health Act to pay whatever sanitary rate may be levied. The Corporation are called on now—I saw a paper from Mr. [illegible]—to alter the sewer in the town, and [illegible] and I think the Corporation would be very fairly [illegible] to make the [illegible] of the [illegible] contribute to that.

140. As far as you know, are the Corporation prepared, if this makes [illegible], to [illegible] the roads in the extended area, and to undertake all the sanitary arrangements?—They are prepared to undertake the repair of the roads as they are at present.

141. There is not traffic enough to make it necessary for the Corporation to do more than the road-contractor [illegible]?

142. And as to lighting?—Well, under the Municipal Corporation Act, section 121, I think they are bound only to light streets.

143. And would you say as to that that it was unnecessary to light those roadways, and so on?—Certainly.

144. Well, have you considered the feasibility of your being able to keep up the repair of the roads for the same as the Grand Jury do it at present?—Yes, I think so.

145. And that you would be able to do it as efficiently as at present?—Yes. There might be a small [illegible], because the portion of the roads near the town would be [illegible] than at a distance, and the contractor's prices would be more.

146. But what you say is this, in effect, that the ratepayers in the town would be prepared to undertake that responsibility?—Yes.

147. [illegible] they would have a saving?—Yes.

148. And you think that would more than pay for any extra work?—Yes.

149. And as to sanitary matters, of course, they would have to pay [illegible] sanitary works became necessary?—Yes, of course, if there was a case [illegible].

150. Now, have you considered the effect of the Public Health Act of last session. At present these [illegible] that are all outside the present municipal boundary pay the full sanitary rate, and they deduct one-half from their landlords?—Yes.

151. If they are brought within the boundary they are in the hands of the urban sanitary authority, and they only pay one-fourth, and deduct nothing from the landlord; now would the Corporation undertake all the sanitary work of this district, but they only [illegible] one-fourth?—As a matter of fact there would be very little sanitary work outside, for the houses are all good houses—in fact, the houses are few, and indeed the sanitary work in the [illegible] will [illegible] principally.

152. And even, though they should have to pay one-fourth towards the sanitary work of the town, in [illegible] your opinion they should fairly pay that, having regard to the fact that the town would be kept in good order [illegible] they come in from day to day?—Yes, and it would come small, because the one-fourth of £[illegible] (which would be the total valuation) would not be £[illegible] a year. It would be very trifling.

153. Suppose they were brought in and paid that one-fourth, is it your view that they should pay one-half of [illegible] from the landlord?—Yes, that would be my view, because the landlord gets a higher rent.

154. Well, now, have you, in view of the increased [illegible] that you would put on them on account of their proximity to the town, have you formed any opinion as to whether that [illegible] should any of it be borne by the landlord?—My opinion is that it should be divided, and that should [illegible] in such holdings the landlord should pay [illegible], as was intended by the Land Act, but the Land Act did not carry that into effect.

155. In other words, you hold that in the case where you bring in men who have to pay a larger Grand Jury cess on account of their proximity to the town, the land being valued [illegible] high from that reason, and the landlord getting an [illegible] rent, you think that the whole [illegible] of that increased valuation should not fall upon the landlord, but that it should be divided?—That is my opinion.

156. Are you able to say yourself that not only is the landlord enabled to get a better rent but that the land is valued higher?—Yes, considerably higher.

157. These lands [illegible] a similar character two or three miles off?—Yes.

158. Are there any debts on the town at present?—There are.

159. What are the total debts?—Well, there is £1,[illegible] for the building of this place, and about £[illegible] due to the National Bank on an over-draft. There is a market commenced recently which I must not give you.

160. And what is your income?—Rents and toll charges, £[illegible]; [illegible] weekly rents, £[illegible]. [illegible] £[illegible].

161. And your expenditure?—Since the Sanitary Act came into force, a [illegible] the income. We are [illegible] into it.

162. You have not levied any sanitary rate?—No.

163. Probably you will have to put it on to meet the new expenditure. Does that £[illegible], or whatever it is, represent your entire income?—The entire borough fund, but there is the fair green, and market income separately.

164. How much is that about?—The fair green is about £[illegible] or £[illegible].

165. Is that clear profit?—No, the expenses have to be deducted from that, leaving a surplus of about £[illegible].

166. Mr. COMMON.—On the fair-green?—Yes.

167. CHAIRMAN.—Can you give us the total income and total expenditure?—I can give them in detail. The total income is about £[illegible].

168. Can you give us altogether the entire income?—Yes, here are the accounts audited. Here is the gross income of the past year:—Corporation, £[illegible]; market, £[illegible]; fair green, £[illegible]; total, £[illegible], to annual numbers.

169. You have [illegible]?—That includes all.

170. I ask you have about £1,[illegible] now due, or about £1,[illegible]?—There is about £[illegible] balance of the loan due by the Corporation, about £[illegible] on current account, and about £1,[illegible] balance of £[illegible] debt for market purposes, but being paid off by sinking fund.

171. Practically there would be no difficulty as to that outside district, in making [illegible] if brought in?—No, for the market is able to meet its own liabilities.

172. £[illegible] a year I see is being paid?—Yes.

173. Do you expect any losses in the [illegible]?—Yes, in about [illegible] years we will have an increased rental.

174. Do you think it would be desirable to have any change in the wards as they exist at present?—No, I don't think you could divide them better.

175. You would not think of creating a new ward in the event of the extension being made?—No, I would not.

176. You would add on the increased area to each ward?—Yes.

Examined.
Mr. Patrick J. Dillon.

KILKENNY. Nov. [illegible] 18[illegible]. Mr. James S. Loughnan.

Mr. JAMES S. LOUGHNAN, Mayor, examined.

177. CHAIRMAN.—You are at present Mayor of Kilkenny?—Yes.

178. Well, I may take it, I suppose, that you can speak on the part of the thirteen gentlemen, including yourself, who voted in favour of that extension?—Yes.

179. And your view is, that that proposed extension is desirable?—Yes, I think it would be an advantage to the citizens.

180. Can you, of your own knowledge, say that the lands that are within the area you propose derive exceptional advantages from their proximity to the town?—Undoubtedly.

181. Are they valued more highly?—No, they are not valued up to anything like the rent.

182. Are they valued more highly than land of a similar character would be further off?—Oh, yes.

183. And even the landlords get the advantage of that increased value, and an increased rent?—Yes, very considerably.

184. On account of their being near the town?—Yes, town parks and town fields, for these they get three times, two or three times, more than they would produce outside.

185. I suppose you are aware that the farmers that occupy those grounds largely use the town as a fair and market town?—Yes, very largely.

186. And the farmers for selling their produce?—Yes.

187. And they get for their produce in that way?

188. You are aware of the recommendation of the Committee of the House of Commons, that you should assume the management of the roads?—I think so, but then would we be constituted as the Grand Jury?

189. Certainly, to adopt all the fiscal powers; this is the recommendation of the committee.

190. The *Mayor*.—Of course, that would make no difference to us.

191. You mean if you got the taxes of the Grand Jury transferred to you, you would be perfectly ready to undertake the management of the roads and so on?—Undoubtedly.

192. You have heard me pointing out, that if the people living in that extended district are brought into the city, they then become liable to pay one-fourth of the sanitary rate, and so on?—We have no sanitary rate; the Corporation does everything.

193. Well, then they will get the benefit of that; but if there was any sanitary rate imposed on them, do you think it ought to be divided between the landlord and the tenant?—Yes.

194. The sanitary rate?—I think it would be very fair; we pay one-half of the poor rates now.

195. And of course if they belonged to the Urban Sanitary Authorities, those lands would pay half of the sanitary rate, and you are of opinion that if brought in, the landlord and tenant should divide it?—I think so; I may say, that if the lands were brought in, if the extension were made, I myself would be a loser, for now I pay nothing, but I think it would be fair; I don't see any danger of there being a sanitary rate.

196. The principle would be right, you think?—Yes, the Corporation, with the exception of the £300 we received from the Grand Jury, did everything, and made large improvements.

197. In your opinion, would it be necessary now suppose that one district was brought in, to light it, in your opinion?—Certainly not, whatever advantage it might be to the suburban gentry, it would be impossible to keep the lamps, they would be broken.

198. Now you have heard the calculation of Mr. Dillon, that the city taxation would be reduced, and that of the people outside increased a little?—Yes.

199. Do you think that that increase that would be put on them, would be fairly more than they ought to bear, having regard to the advantages they have?—No, it would be only 1*d*. or 2*d*. in the pound.

200. It would be more, at present they pay from 1*s*. 3*d*. to 1*s*. 4*d*., from his calculation it would reach 1*s*. 6*d*.?—Well, I think it would be very well worth their while, for their property will soon be very much increased, and considering all the advantages they derive from town, and also, I may say that we would be very glad to see some of them in the Corporation, although I don't know if they would value that so much. Then I may mention there are some very large works; there is John's Bridge, we are very anxious to get it straightened, and if we get this extension of boundaries it would help to get it done, for if we have to pay our share of it out of what we have on the present rating of £16,000 or £17,000 a year it would come heavy, but with the new boundary it would give us a much larger rateable property to go on, and the county would join us and benefit by it.

202. Is it your opinion that the gentry and farmers living within that proposed extended district are even more interested than you in the straightening of that bridge?—Certainly, for the city people use it comparatively very little; it is the people in the suburbs and travellers from the railway who use the bridge. Certainly it would be useful to some of our local merchants, and it is much complained of by the hotel people, and so on, but the rural people would, in my opinion, benefit more by it than the city people.

203. Is the land valued higher on account of its proximity to the town, and the tenant better able to pay a higher rent by reason of having a near and ready market for the sale of his produce. But the landlord not only gets the rent on the higher valuation, but a great deal beyond that, do you think he should bear or pay any portion of the difference in the county cess that would be put on him?—Well, I would not like to give any opinion on that.

204. Would it, in your opinion, be fair?—Well, I don't think it would be fair. I will give my reason for saying so. My reason would be this. I said with regard to the sanitary rate, it would be fair, but as to the Grand Jury cess, I think it would not be fair, because why, the landlord has already let his land by the year or by lease to his tenants, with the perfect understanding that they would pay the whole of the county cess, and, therefore, I think anything of an *ex post facto* law might be considered unjust, for I consider it very hard to go behind existing rules and agreements.

205. That is all—binding agreements you would not interfere with?—Yes.

206. But as to the future?—Oh, that is quite another thing—that is all arranged, you know.

207. But you would not interfere with the present existing arrangements?—No.

208. CHAIRMAN.—I suppose we may now take it that we have as much information as to the views in favour of the extension as we require. There can be no use asking the gentlemen who coincide with the Mayor to give their views. I would be glad now to hear any of the gentlemen inside or outside the boundary who object to the extension.

Mr. Richard L[illegible].

Mr. RICHARD L[illegible], examined.

209. I have here a protest signed by the ratepayers, which, I suppose, I may hand in to the Secretary?

210. CHAIRMAN.—Certainly, if you are authorized to speak on behalf of these persons, and say they object to being brought within the boundaries of [illegible] you can do so.

WITNESS.—Well, a meeting of the ratepayers was held to take this subject of the proposed extension of the municipal boundaries into consideration and they

Kilkenny, Nov. 4, 1880. Mr. [illegible] [illegible].

adopted a protest, and signed it, which unanimously, as you may see. The resolution they came to was as follows:—

"We, the undersigned ratepayers of the baronies of Gowran, and Crannagh, and Shillelogher, in the county of Kilkenny, hereby protest against any application being made by the municipal corporation of Kilkenny, which would in the event of conceding the extension of our respective holdings, and would materially prove prejudicial to our interests."

Then follow the signatures.

211. How many would you say would be in favour of that?—Well, I think it was almost unanimous. There were about 130 persons present, and there is also a document signed by the County Grand Jury, protesting:—

"We, the undersigned members of the grand jury of the county of Kilkenny, assembled on the 5th of March, 1879, [illegible] most emphatically at the [illegible] of the [illegible] borough of Kilkenny, which, if carried into effect, would increase the rate of taxation of the county at large." (Appendix No. 8.)

212. How many members of the Grand Jury signed that?—It is signed by twenty-one members of the Grand Jury. The county of the city includes Kilkenny from the county of Kilkenny, and the latter bear the [illegible] for the purpose of taxation. The charges for the county at large are very heavy. In [illegible] the [illegible] of roughly [illegible] out of the expenses generally; nothing, in fact, but a few roads taken off them. I estimate the taxation on the district within the [illegible] of the Tholsel, and outside the present municipal boundary, to be got at in this way—the valuation of the municipal borough is £27,[illegible]; the valuation of the proposed extended area is £3,[illegible], or a total of £30,[illegible]. The amount of [illegible] which half year is £1,[illegible]; the cost for roads and footpaths in the proposed district for the half year, £[illegible]; the cost of [illegible] chargeable to that district for the half year, £[illegible], the total levy for the present half year being £1,[illegible], which would require a rate of 1s. [illegible]d. in the £, of £[illegible]. Now the city Grand Jury rate for the present half year, is at the rate of 1s. [illegible]d. in the £; the county Grand Jury rate for the same period, in the barony of Gowran, is [illegible], for Crannagh, [illegible], and for Shillelogher, [illegible].

213. Chairman.—What [illegible] that do you think was struck by the city Grand Jury last?—That is the county Grand Jury rate. The cess on those baronies include 1s. 2d. per pound for Ross bridge; this would still have to be levied on the new district. It produces, on a valuation of £3,500, exactly £[illegible] half yearly which could not be assessed on the remainder of the county of Kilkenny, nor on the present municipal borough; therefore, if the present Grand Jury rate on the city of Kilkenny, and the district proposed to be taken in were equalised there would be a further charge on said district of [illegible] owing to the grant for Ross bridge, so that the district would, consequently, be more highly taxed than the city of Kilkenny.

214. Mr. [illegible].—You are making the mistake of comparing the present area with what it is at present. You are considering it as it now is, and not as it would be on the extended valuation?

Witness.—I am taking it on a total valuation of £30,[illegible], whatever that is, and I think that will be found on the valuation with the extended district added. By the accounts I have mentioned, which are the sums actually to be paid at this Spring Assizes, it appears that the half-yearly cess on the present city or municipal borough if equalised would be at the rate of 1s. [illegible]d. per £1 for the present half-year, and on the district proposed to be taken, it would be 1s. [illegible]d. per £1, thus making [illegible] per half-year in Gowran, [illegible] per half-year in Crannagh, and [illegible] per half-year in Shillelogher baronies.

215. Chairman.—Are the two districts in the charge of Mr. [illegible]—Is he county surveyor for both?—Yes, of course the [illegible] does not come into his department; only the maintenance of the roads.

216. As to the terms of the [illegible] at present, [illegible] is small, I think, about [illegible] [illegible] [illegible] to be [illegible]. Now, all the opinions I have heard expressed have been to the effect that any action taken with reference to this subject, should not interfere with existing rights. I [illegible] here. I [illegible] the Corporation called meetings here, and had a meeting here last Friday evening at the [illegible], asking the citizens to support this movement. Yet no one seemed to be anxious for it, and the thing fell down almost entirely from members of the Corporation present. There is really no genuine feeling among the [illegible] persons to take into the boundary the outside people. It is those outside people after all who support them and by whom they live, and I may say that it is simply not a fact that the land in the immediate vicinity of the town is rendered more valuable by its proximity to the town that the [illegible] this way. But there is a keen competition among [illegible] to get these lands, and people who make a little money in the town are anxious to get a bit of land; but the great competition does not come from outside at all.

217. No doubt, then what gave the [illegible] may possess, is it not the fact in land that these lands are more productive or [illegible] to the [illegible]?—Yes, and the landlord gets the benefit of that. We don't deny that.

218. Are they not valued higher?—Yes, and the [illegible] [illegible] higher.

219. Is it not valued higher because it is closer to a market town, and affords a ready opportunity and facilities for disposing of produce and so on?—Yes, certainly.

220. And the facilities of coming to and using the railway and the places of worship, and sending children to the schools?—Yes, but they pay for those that support them.

221. Do they use the roads in that way?—Yes, but the same exists for the support of the [illegible], the [illegible] and markets are paid entirely by the [illegible] of those. The market [illegible] must be comparatively nothing. It is only a place for exchange. The Corporation make a large profit out of their [illegible], the farmers pay a large contribution by supporting the [illegible] in that and other ways. No doubt it is a convenience to have the town, but it is also they who [illegible]. They support the markets, and the Corporation benefit thereby.

222. The population of the municipal borough in 1871 was 12,[illegible], in 1861 it was 13,[illegible], in 1851 it was 14,[illegible], and in 1871 12,[illegible]. This is according to Thom's Almanac. Now you will see it decreased 10 per cent. from '61 to '71; and that rate of decrease appears to have continued. Therefore it may be assumed to have further diminished 1 per cent. since 1871 to the present time, which would give up a present population of 11,[illegible] in 1879. Now if the present town was considered to be large enough for 14,000 in 1841, surely it is large enough for 11,000 in 1879? The tradespeople in the town are supported by the people from the country coming in and buying their goods.

223. No doubt, but they have their profit?—Well if we use the town, we pay for it.

224. If there was sanitary work to be done, according to the law which at present, such persons outside would pay the full sanitary rate, and one-half would be paid by the landlord. If they were brought in they would only pay one-fourth, and no [illegible]?—The town is very badly supplied with water—there is nothing to supply it but pumps, the water of which has been pronounced to be very bad, it has been greatly condemned by Dr. [illegible]. There are only one or two of those [illegible]. Dr. [illegible] says it contains a large amount of sulphate of lime, which is very injurious, and if expensive waterworks were brought in we would have to pay largely for it.

225. As the law stands at present you would only

KILKENNY. May 8, 18[illegible].

Mr. Richard Langrishe.

have to pay one-fourth, and I was going to ask you do you think the landlords ought to pay a moiety of that? —My opinion is that it is as broad as it is long. The landlord, you may depend, will get the best rent he can. It is just a matter of pounds, shillings, and pence. I think that sentiment brought into it is absurd. A man can't give more for land than he can make out of it. There is a very strong feeling that the people don't want to be burgesses and members of the Corporation. They want to be let alone. They are very happy to come in and support the markets in the town, and buy what they want in the shops.

226. Don't they generally use the town for the places of worship, the trains, and so on?—Not much benefit do they get from lighting up to the railway. This week the town is lighted by moonlight. A lot of smoky paraffin lamps are not much good in the way of lighting up the road to the station or through the town.

227. Is there anything, in your opinion, exceptional in the city of Kilkenny to distinguish it so much from nearly all other places. We have about 113 towns to examine here, and we have already been at about 30, and, with the exception of two, there appears to be perfect unanimity about bringing in the people outside. It is only a question of terms, and do you think there is anything exceptional in the case of Kilkenny that would make a difference in the matter of legislation? —Well, unless you were intimately acquainted with those towns it is hard to answer that question.

228. Even in other towns every one of them has an improvement rate, then you see they would have the county question, the Grand Jury question, to face, the question of the sanitary rate and improvement rate, and which, as the law stands at present, may be up to 1s.; sanitary rate, water supply, and all. That being so, and there being no rate here in the nature of improvement rate, is there anything exceptional in the case of Kilkenny that would make the case one in which there should be rightly or fairly a difference of legislature from them. We have but to try and do the best we can. We want to know if there is anything exceptional here to make the views expressed here so different from what they have been elsewhere. There is perfect unanimity, or nearly so, in almost every place we have been.

229. Mr. Dillon.—It is right to say that the Commissioners have before expressed a most favourable opinion regarding the adoption of an extension. I may tell you in addition that there is a very strong feeling around among the people that their property has greatly deteriorated in value (I say that not to my own knowledge, but I hear it said), that the Corporation property has become dilapidated in a very great measure; houses have fallen into ruins, a great many of them are let at ridiculously low rents, and that the rental is greatly diminished within the past 25 years. That is not considered an encouraging prospect by the people who are now sought to be brought in.

230. The whole expenditure of the town does not appear to be much. If they had a couple of thousand a year more they would not want any rate at all, and then it would be a great advantage to those outside? —We can't know what the property would be leased at.

231. Chairman.—That is drawn attention to by the Select Committee's Report. They say no lease shall be made that is not first sanctioned by the chairman of the county, and also a calculation made and sanctioned by the treasurer?—These are very proper provisions.

232. If the Corporation property by good management was made more valuable, there would be almost no county cess required?—Oh, if there was no cess that would be all right, but it is too good to be true, I am afraid. The fact is the rural people object to the Corporation government altogether. They don't want to be brought in under the Corporation at all.

233. Mr. Cotton.—Do you know whether any of the people now within or just within the municipal boundary would like to have it contracted, would they like to have it put out of the city?—Well, I don't know; I would not like to say. But there are a great many people who live outside and hold some property inside, such as Mr. Smithwick and others, and they object very strongly to enlargement, and would prefer much to have it reduced.

234. Well, now about the wards, have you formed any opinion as to the question of the wards, and whether it would not be better to form a new ward or to increase the existing ones?—I have not considered it much, but I think if the country people were thrown into the present ward the town would be in the ascendant. The town people are too clever for the farmers.

235. You think it would be better to have three wards?—Certainly. If we were to be made burgesses against our will we would prefer to have one ward of our own. I should not like to be one. I don't pretend to be a town man and we want to be left alone in the country.

236. That money raised by the city Grand Jury here—do they not pay a considerable portion of it over to the county at large?—Not to the county of Kilkenny. The jail was a joint thing between them.

237. Do they not pay to Ross bridge?—No, and if we were brought in we would have to pay to Ross bridge.

238. Then in point of fact the county at large charges in the city are nothing?—No, they only pay for any lunatics or small things. The city pays share for the lunatics out of the same fund as the county.

239. Then they pay their own county surveyor and keep their own roads?—Yes, and their own secretary of the Grand Jury and so on.

240. And have nothing to pay otherwise?—Yes, they pay for half of the court-house. They were separated but were lately obliged to share. There is a separate Grand Jury called for the city.

241. How long does the contribution to Ross bridge last?—Twelve more years have to run. I may mention, with regard to John's bridge, I had something to do with that myself. My friend Mr. Burchael asked me to make a survey of it. The matter was brought before the Grand Jury, and the County Jury offered to give £2,000, I think. Tenders were got for it for £5,000, and they knocked it on the head. That sum did not even include the taking down of the present one. Well, this question of the bridge has started up. If they attempt it now, and they talk of an iron bridge, which I think would be a great mistake to put it up. With even a stone one they could get it done for say £6,000: then there would be a temporary bridge, and taking down the present one, you may say it would be £7,000. If the Grand Jury were still willing to give £2,000 that would leave to be levied about £5,000, which would be 2d. in the £ for 25 years; and if an extended area there would be 1d. in the £ for

242. Then the extended area would be paying 1d. in the £?—Yes.

243. And do you think the extended area should not have to pay it?—We would pay something, but that would be a terrible thing to add to all the other taxes. Of course the county ought to contribute.

244. But at present they are not bound to contribute anything?—Yes, the county offered £2,000. All we want is fair play.

KILKENNY May 6, 1879.

Mr. James [illegible].

Mr. JAMES [illegible], examined.

245. CHAIRMAN.—Are you at present living outside the boundaries?—Yes, I am.

246. And you are not a rate-payer of the city?—No.

247. How much land do you hold?—70 acres.

248. And would all that be taken in by the proposed extension?—Yes, every bit.

249. Were you ever living in the city?—Originally I was—the place where I lived was in the liberties of the city, and two miles about me.

250. What was your taxation in those days as compared with now?—It was a great deal more in the city. It was higher since '41 than before it.

251. For a series of years before you were put out of the city what was the county cess on the average would you say?—Well, I don't know. We used to pay twice more, I know.

252. And in point of fact your taxes have been considerably less for a series of years than they would be if you were in town?—Yes, I think so.

253. Do you think you get great advantages from the city?—Yes, and disadvantages, too. Everything is plundered and taken from you; everything is stolen, and you might as well live two miles out. It would be better to live three miles or more from Kilkenny than next it.

254. But then you would not have to pay so much for your lands—they would not be so highly valued?—That is just what Mr. Griffith said.

255. And is not the fact that you pay a higher rent, that the land is valued higher, caused by your being close to the town?—Yes, that is what Mr. Griffith told me, but I would rather be three miles away.

256. Do you use the town largely?—I don't know what you mean exactly.

257. Going into it frequently, buying and selling, getting manure, and so on?—Yes, but used pay very high for it.

258. Do you sell your produce in Kilkenny?—Not for the past 4 or 5 years. I bring it to Bagnalstown.

259. How—is it by rail?—Sometimes, and sometimes by road by horses.

260. Do the horses go through the town?—No, they go through the new soldiers' barracks, and go on to the hill to Bagnalstown.

261. But is so far as you use the railway you use the town?—Very little, indeed.

262. But those who live at the opposite or Kerdiffstown side, have to pass through the town to reach the railway?—Oh, yes, but I don't live on that side.

263. Do you not think that those people who pass through the town and sell their property, and derive advantages from the town, using the streets, and getting the benefits of the lighting, watering, &c., should contribute?—Well, I don't know. I don't know what advantage John's bridge is.

264. Do you send in produce every day?—No.

265. Are there not a number of people who send in milk and poultry, and so on?—Yes, people that drive all kind of farm produce—those people are in town, &c.

266. Then the people nearer the city are they not better off—is there not a saving of time to them?—Yes, they are nearer, no doubt.

Mr. Malone.

Mr. MALONE, Clerk of the Union, examined.

267. Mr. EXHAM.—Are the Poor Law Wards coterminous with the municipal?—No, the third portion of St. Mary's, in fact, goes into the other two—St. John's and St. Canice's.

268. But all comprised in the two municipal are within the three Poor Law Wards?—Yes. There are Guardians attached to each ward.

The inquiry then terminated.

LISBURN—14th JUNE, 1879.

(Before C. P. Cotton, Esq.)

Mr. John A. [illegible], examined.

1. You are the Town Clerk of Lisburn?—Yes.

2. How long is it since you were appointed?—I was appointed in August, 1874, when the town was put under the Towns Improvement Act.

3. Had it been previously under any other Act?—Yes, the old Municipal Act, 9 Geo. IV., chap. 82.

4. What is the population of Lisburn?—Over 8,000.

5. In 1871 what was it?—8,516. It is believed now to be about 11,000.

6. Has it been increasing since then?—It has.

7. Could you give me an account of the number of houses in the town?—Yes; the present number of houses is about 1,800.

8. Is building increasing in the town?—Yes. To give you an idea of the buildings, in 1874 the valuation was £15,030; in 1875 it was £15,376, that is an increase of £290; in 1876 it was £16,252; in 1877, £16,878; in 1878, £17,376; and in the present year, £17,869 18s.; that is a regular constant increase in it yearly since 1874.

9. What is the area of the township?—The present municipal boundary is 640 acres.

10. How is it you have given it in your return, in answer to the queries, as 604?—I made a mistake; I find from the survey it is 640; that was a clerical error. There is another slight mistake I find in the return that I wish to direct your attention to, in answer to query 8.

11. I would rather you would answer the questions I put to you, and speak of the queries afterwards. Are there wards?—There are no wards.

12. In what electoral divisions is the municipality?—It is in four electoral divisions; there are very small portions of the town in two of them.

13. Please give the names of the electoral divisions?—One is Drumbeg.

14. In what county is that?—It is partly in Antrim and partly in Down.

15. The principal portion of the electoral division is in what county?—Antrim.

16. And it comprises a very small portion?—Yes, a valuation of £31.

17. What is the fourth electoral division; you said there were four?—Lissue; that is a small portion also.

18. In what county is that?—Antrim, solely.

19. Can you give me the area in each of those electoral divisions?—I did give it to you.

20. Well, give it to me now?—You refer to the municipal area?

21. Certainly?—I suppose I may strike out the shillings.

22. Have you got the acres, or only the valuation?—I have the acres.

23. Well, then give me the acres, please?—I will send for them.

24. What is the acreage of the electoral division of Lisburn?—I can now give you the acreage in each of the electoral divisions. In Lissue, the acreage is 13a. 1r. 36p.; in Drumbeg, which is a portion, 6a. 0r. 25p.; Blaris, which is a portion only, 75a. 2r. 3p.; and in Lisburn there is an acreage of 545a. 2r. 3p., which gives a total of 640 acres.

25. What is the valuation of the portion of the electoral division of Lisburn?—£15,349 2s.

26. In the electoral division of Blaris what is the valuation?—£[illegible].

27. And in the electoral division of Drumbeg?—£31 10s.

28. And in Lissue?—£177 2s., making a total of £17,869 18s., which is the present valuation.

29. The boundaries of the town and those electoral divisions are coterminous?—No, they are not.

30. What were the municipal rates for the last five years?—In 1874 it was 1s.; 1875, 1s.; 1876, 1s.; 1877, 1s. 2d.; 1878, 1s. 2d.

31. Any rate struck for this year?—Not yet.

32. Give me the poor rate for each of those years?—1874, [illegible]; 1875, 1s. 9d.; 1876, 1s. 1d.; 1877, 1s. 2d.; 1878, 1s.

33. Now give me the county cess for the same years?—1874, 1s. 5d.; 1875, 1s. 11d.; 1876, 1s. 11d.; 1877, 1s. 10d.; 1878, 1s. 10d.

34. And in 1879, do you know what it is?—Well, it is much about the same; I think it is 1s. 10d.

35. How many Commissioners have you?—Fifteen.

36. And how many persons are entitled to vote at municipal elections?—983.

37. How many of those would be qualified to sit as Commissioners, if elected?—About one-fifth. I could not say the exact number, but it is over 100.

38. Have the Commissioners considered the question whether the municipal boundaries should be extended or altered in any way?—They have.

39. Have they come to any resolution on the subject?—They have.

40. On what day?—At the municipal meeting of the Commissioners, on the 7th April.

41. How many Commissioners were present at that meeting?—Seven. The following resolution was passed unanimously:—

"It was proposed by Mr. Reilly, seconded by Mr. [illegible], and unanimously passed, as an amendment to the resolution; [illegible] the proposed extension of the municipal boundary as recommended by the [illegible], that is, that the county Antrim portion [illegible] with the parliamentary boundary and the county Down portion be extended as described."

The following was the resolution:—

"That the proposed extension be adopted, and that the clerk insert the same in the queries to the Municipal Boundaries Commissioners."

42. And the extension that is alluded to there is the one marked in red on this map?—Yes.

43. On what ground do you consider that the boundaries should be extended?—That there have been a great many new houses built since the time the present boundary was fixed in 1874, when the town was put under the Towns Improvement Act. Those people, if brought within the municipal boundary, would receive the benefits arising from municipal supervision. It would also increase the rateable property of the town, which would enable the Commissioners to increase the municipal advantages.

44. Have you ascertained what additional number of houses would be brought in by that extension?—No.

45. Have you any idea what the increase would be?—I could not tell. It would not be many.

46. Would it bring in 200?—I could not say.

47. You don't know how many it would bring in who would be qualified to sit as Commissioners?—No.

48. Nor the number of voters brought in?—I could not say.

49. Would it bring in some of the villa residences?—It would bring in some good residences.

50. How many?—It would bring in Derryvolgie, Miss Gregg's, Lisnagarvy, which you have marked on the map, going to the left.

51. Yes?—There is then Avonmore Lodge, Mr. Barrett's and Brownlee's, Alpha Lodge, and the Union Workhouse.

52. With the exception of the workhouse these are all villas?—Yes; there are three on the Lisburn-road and on the Belfast-road, but they are not marked. There was one other, the Lambeg Glebe-house, which is marked there. These are the only ones of importance.

53. How many villas does that refer to altogether?—Nine or ten altogether.

54. How far would this new boundary proceed, extending from the centre of the town?—About one mile.

55. I see a place on the map marked "The Plantation" out in that direction (referring to the map), a great many houses are just at the boundary of the proposed extension; why was that left out—it is in the county Down?—I cannot give any particular reason for that; I think that a greater portion of the extension into the county Down coincides with the boundary of the townland of Lisnagarvy, and I think that formed one of the elements in the minds of the Committee when tracing it.

56. No, not at all; it does not coincide with it at all?—I thought it did.

57. How is the town of Lisburn lit, by gas?—Yes.

58. By a gas company?—Yes.

59. And the Commissioners contract with them?—Yes.

60. What are the terms of the contract?—£1 17s. 6d. per lamp for nine months' lighting, from 15th August to 15th May, nine months, and on the nights of full moon and two before they are not lighted; on two nights before full moon and the full moon they are not lighted.

61. That is three nights?—Yes.

62. And on other nights how long are they lighted?—From a quarter of an hour before sun-set, until an hour before sun-rise, and one half of the lamps are extinguished at half past ten.

63. That is in portions of the town where they are not required?—Every alternate lamp, and on Saturday night the lighting is extended for half an hour longer as it is market night.

64. How many lamps are there?—110.

65. How is the town supplied with water?—From a reservoir principally. It is the property of Sir R. Wallace, the landlord of the estate.

66. Is it a new work?—No; it is fifteen or twenty years old.

67. Is the supply of water considered good?—It is.

68. Or are there complaints about its quality or quantity?—It is good for domestic purposes.

69. And for drinking?—Yes.

70. Is there any deficiency of quantity?—It is not sufficient for sewerage or watering the streets, for which a larger supply would be desirable, but for domestic purposes it is quite sufficient.

71. Has there been any project before the Commissioners for getting an increased supply?—None.

72. How is the town drained?—By sewers. There is one sewer through the town, and there are a number of main sewers and drains from the houses.

73. Where is the main sewer discharged?—Into the river.

74. Is that considered a good state of drainage?—It is fair.

75. That 1s. 2d. rate struck in 1878, was any of it a sewerage rate?—No, not directly a sewer rate. The general assessment was a shilling, and that covered the sewer rate; and the two pence was a burial rate.

LISBURN.
June 16, 1879.
Mr. John A. [illegible]

76. And the same in 1877?—Yes.

77. Have the Commissioners considered the question whether they would take the roads from the Grand Jury?—It has never been directly before them.

78. They know they can apply for the power under the Public Health Act?—Yes.

79. That they can apply, and if they get the authority from the Local Government Board they can get the control over the roads?—They are aware of these powers.

80. But they have not taken any steps?—They have not.

81. Have you an increase of buildings in the Lisburn direction, or in what direction is it, or is it in more than one direction in which building has been carried on; in the first place is there much building outside the present limit?—A good deal.

82. Is it confined to one locality or is it being carried on equally all round?—Equally all round, principally in the Belfast direction and in the close vicinity of the town, that is of the present municipal boundary.

83. Do you know the opinion of the ratepayers of the town as regards the extension; I suppose it is known pretty well you are applying for an extension?—I don't know.

84. Have you heard anything said about it?—Nothing on one side or the other.

85. Have you heard any opinion expressed as from those you propose to include?—Nothing.

86. You have not got a valuation of the portion you propose to take in?—No.

87. Can you get it?—Except from the Valuation Commissioners. I don't see how I could get it; with some trouble I might get it.

88. I should like, if you could get it, to get the approximate number of the voters that would be brought in by the extension, and by which it would increase those qualified to sit as Commissioners if elected?—I could not get that at all, because there is one portion of the town, in the direction of Belfast, where houses are getting put up; in one district, I should say, at the rate of twenty per month.

89. Outside the present limit?—Yes; outside the present limit.

90. On what road is that, is it on the south side of the road leading to the fort?—Yes.

91. Can you let me have a copy of the receipts and expenditure for the last year?—Yes. I may state there would be about 200 additional voters in that district at least. I now beg to hand in a copy of the accounts audited by the auditor yesterday for the year ending 15th May, 1879.

92. Are there any things required to be done in the town the Commissioners are not able to do on account of being short of funds; you say in your answer that the addition to the rates would enable the Commissioners to increase the municipal advantages?—Yes.

93. In what way?—In flagging, sewerage, and general advantages.

94. I see the sum put down for flagging is very large, £948?—Yes.

95. Does the county contribute anything?—A little, about half; by the contract it was slightly under the half.

96. And is that a recurring expenditure. In other years is it nearly as large as that?—It is not.

97. Because it seems so very large?—It was one large contract, and the greater portion of it came in this year.

98. Besides additional flagging, what else is there that the Commissioners would do by additional rates if they got them?—Under the general expenditure they would extend the lighting.

99. Exactly; well, I want to know what portion of that comes under the head of general expenditure—is the lighting satisfactory?—It is.

100. Then that does not require improvement?—Well, except at present, lighting extends very close to the present municipal boundary.

Lisburn. June 14, 1878.

Mr. John A. Bownish.

101. Is it contemplated by the Commissioners that if they extended the boundary they would extend the lighting along the roads?—They would extend all the advantages.

102. They would light all the roads up to the limits of the boundary?—Not entirely up to the limits.

103. That is what I want to know; what would they propose; would they propose to light as far as there were buildings alongside of the road?—Yes. There is a great deal more sewerage and flagging to be done.

104. Sewerage and flagging are two things for which they want more money?—Yes. Flagging forms a very heavy item in the expenditure of the Commissioners.

105. Is there anything that occurs to you, you would wish to mention in addition to your previous evidence?—I don't know of anything.

Mr. John M'Henry.

Mr. John M'Henry examined.

106. You are the Borough Surveyor?—I am.

107. And you prepared this map before us, I suppose?—I did.

108. And this red line shows what the Commissioners wish by resolution to adopt as the extension?—That is marked according to my instructions, going over the ground with the Committee.

109. Could you explain what principle guided the Committee in extending the line in different directions, why was it not extended more out to take in large buildings and works I see at Lambeg?—I think they would have objected to that on account of their being so highly rated at the present time; the owners would object. That was the reason that guided them. I think that was one reason; it would have been an unnecessary extension owing to the fact that the taxation on those premises is very high at present.

110. I see there is a collection of houses that are marked on the map—a sort of village—The Plantation, why was not that taken in; you see you came by it?—That is occupied as far as I know by the weavers and manufacturers of linen. It was considered, being on an elevated position, and having what was considered a pretty fair means of carrying off the sewage and all that, it would be better to leave that portion out, and confine the boundary to a well-defined stream, which there is.

111. It is a stream in what townland?—Ballymacash.

112. In the townland of Ballymacash the boundary is defined by a stream. The boundary of the townland of Largymore, how is that cut?—That was by a straight fence from one road to the other, and also by another straight fence, so as to make it a well defined boundary.

113. You seem to have gone out of your way to leave out the house at Largymore?—Simply, it was considered, on account of its position, it was not desirable to take it in. That was the only ground so far as I know.

114. You actually put your boundary round it, and left it out?—Because that formed the boundary of the leased portion belonging to Mr. Ward.

115. Who is the owner of that house?—Yes, and another point I wish to explain is, that we did not wish to go on rateable property, leasehold; we wished to confine ourselves to what is termed townparks, and not to go into leasehold property at all. This is confined to townparks generally, with the exception of that one house of Derryvolgie.

116. It is in respect of townparks, except in the case of the house of Derryvolgie and Lisnagarvy?—Yes.

117. And, I suppose, Avonmore?—Yes, that is all leased too.

118. Well, then, on this road, the road going southward from that, it seems to have a good many houses on it, why was not that brought in—do you see where I mean?—I do, perfectly. It was mixed up with leasehold property and townparks, and there was very great difficulty in making the distinction, and it was considered that on that road, as buildings were not likely to extend, it would not be advantageous to take it in any further than the well-defined boundary at Townview.

119. Well, then, as to the rest of the boundary?—The parliamentary boundary on the north side, and the river Lagan on the south side, they are entirely in the county Antrim.

120. Have you calculated what additional area that would give you?—Yes, I did.

121. How much would it be?—1,000 acres, the boundary as now shown by the red line will contain 1,840 acres.

122. How many people would it be likely to bring in that would have a vote?—I should say it would bring in about 300 people.

123. And how many of those would be rated high enough to be Commissioners, if they were elected?—About eight.

124. And most of that extension would be agricultural?—Yes, but likely to fall in as villa sites and building ground, because in a certain portion our buildings are extending almost to the limits of our proposed new boundary.

125. On what roads?—On the Belfast-road, and also in the opposite direction—in the direction of Moira.

126. About the drainage of the town, how is that effected?—A large quantity of drainage flows into the stream that runs through the town, and it is generally carried off into the river Lagan.

127. Is it an open sewer?—It is.

128. Will you show me the course of it on the map?—(The witness showed it on the map).

129. That carries the drainage in what way?—Through the parliamentary section.

130. Is there any other main outlet for sewerage?—Yes; there is a barrel sewer that runs down to the river Lagan here; and there is another for Seymour-street, that is carried directly through the [illegible]. That is the sewer of that particular section of the town, and that is carried into the stream also.

131. Is it carried into the river or into the mill stream?—It is carried into the mill stream.

132. Has there ever been any objection to that?—No.

133. Then there was a question at a former Commission about sewering in that part of the stream?—That has been considered by the Commissioners.

134. Has anything been done since that time by the Commissioners?—Yes; they have kept it properly cleaned out every year, so that it is not so objectionable as it has been before the town came under the Towns Improvement Act.

135. It is dredged?—Yes.

136. Has it a paved bottom, that stream?—Part of it is, and part of it is not.

137. And what is done with what is taken out of it?—The refuse?

138. Yes?—Portion of it is thrown into an adjoining field, and the remainder where it could be got to be taken off.

139. Carried away?—Yes.

140. That is under your superintendence, is it not?—No, it is under the superintendence of a subsanitary officer.

141. The whole of the drainage of Lisburn goes straight into the river one way or the other?—It does.

141. Has any question ever been raised about it?—No.

142. Has there been any other scheme of drainage proposed for the town?—Not as yet.

143. What proposal has been made to improve that open drainage?—To cover it over by a large culvert.

144. Merely to cover it, and you are inclined to it?—Certainly.

145. Has there been any estimate as to the cost of that?—I believe there was.

146. Do you remember how much?—I don't remember exactly. It is a number of years since it was made out. I don't remember what the probable cost would be, but it was contemplated either to divert this by making a sewer through Anderlesbogie.

147. Anderson-street is a hill, then?—Yes, Anderson-street, and the case was before the Commissioners, but they did not see their way to burden the ratepayers with the amount at that time, and another objection was [illegible] and [illegible] water at the [illegible] to [illegible].

148. I see there was an objection to the [illegible] of Anderlesbogie in different counties?—Yes.

149. Just explain there why that [illegible] stink there?—It comes from the town [illegible], and the [illegible] [illegible] of an [illegible] description, and when there is heavy rain in winter, there is a great quantity of water necessarily thrown down by the [illegible] on the lower portion of the town, and we [illegible] a position that the outlet of the [illegible] in [illegible] is not sufficient to carry it. The [illegible] [illegible] through [illegible]-street is not sufficient, and the consequence of that is, it is [illegible] out on the lower portion of the town.

150. Could that be remedied?—That was one of the propositions in connexion with this proposed work, that a quantity of this water might be taken into the [illegible], and delivered below the bridge, [illegible] [illegible] [illegible].

151. And making the sewerage discharge higher [illegible] there?—Yes; through [illegible], [illegible] [illegible], which we have sufficient [illegible] to carry off [illegible] water [illegible] to [illegible] there.

152. Does the flooding in Anne-street [illegible] up the sewer there?—Yes, it does.

153. And the flood water is partly sewage at that particular time?—Yes.

154. Whereabouts is the reservoir which is in the [illegible] of [illegible]?

155. About a mile and a half from the quay.—Yes.

156. Do you know the date of its [illegible] [illegible] [illegible]?—It was constructed within the last eight years.

157. By the Commissioners?—No; by Sir Richard Wallace.

158. Do you know the cubic contents of it?—Yes; 10,000,000 gallons.

159. Does that supply high pressure to the town?—It does.

160. To the highest part of the town?—Yes.

161. And is it sufficient for domestic purposes, but not for the watering of the streets or sewerage?—It requires to be regulated in summer time, so that it has to be taken off one portion of the town and given to another. It does not give a sufficient supply during drought.

162. Does that partial supply last only about a month of the year?—About that.

163. How are the streets watered now?—When we have a supply of water running over at the reservoir, the Commissioners are allowed to draw water out, and I believe Mr. Chapman has intimated to the [illegible] that they could not [illegible] [illegible] them. But when it does not run over, and there is an apprehension of drought, the Commissioners must find some other means until we make arrangements for giving [illegible] to the reservoir.

164. Who is Mr. Chapman?—He is Sir R. Wallace's agent.

165. Do the Commissioners draw water from the river [illegible]?—They have had [illegible] [illegible] to [illegible] [illegible], and so [illegible] they would have to [illegible] new [illegible] they could not get it through the pipes.

166. Is the supply of water sufficient to [illegible] of [illegible] [illegible] in case of fire?—It has not been as good as we would like it.

167. That is, the pressure is not so good?—The pressure is very good if we had [illegible] [illegible] made [illegible] for the purpose of supplying them only.

168. But the working [illegible] are not sufficient for that supply?—In some parts of the town they are; in other parts they are not.

169. I see it stated there is a fire brigade here?—Yes.

170. What [illegible] have they?—They have two engines.

171. [illegible]?—Yes; a new pipe was laid about twelve years ago for a certain portion of the town, a six-inch main, and where they could come in contact with that for a supply in case of fire, it would be good. Unfortunately, in this part of the town, the old pipe is still in existence, and it is not what I would consider a proper supply.

172. Is the reservoir capable of being extended?—It is, to the extent of another half [illegible], but about half a mile higher up we have means of making it from, and there to [illegible] [illegible], so that we could [illegible] it and let it down to keep the reservoir always full. That is under consideration at the present moment.

173. Has there been anything about the [illegible] of that?—No, but I have got instructions to survey and make a report. It is a matter that [illegible] [illegible] the [illegible] it is properly [illegible].

174. That is not [illegible] under the [illegible] of the Town Commissioners at all?—No, it is not.

175. The Town Commissioners are interested in it because if it was not done by some one, the Town Commissioners will be called on to do it?—Certainly.

176. Is there anything you wish to add?—No; I shall be happy to answer anything.

Mr. David Beatty, J.P., examined. Mr. David Beatty, J.P.

177. You are Chairman of the Town Commissioners?—Yes.

178. You were unfortunately not able to attend when the question of the extension of the boundary was considered?—No; and I very much regretted that I was not.

180. I don't ask you for the opinion of the Commissioners, because I will get that from another Commissioner who was there, but I will be happy to have your own private view on the subject?—I heard you ask Mr. M'Henry, whether the people of the town generally were aware of what was contemplated.

181. That is what the Commissioners wish for?—Yes. I may remark particularly, if you refer to your notes, that the number of Commissioners who were present on that occasion was very small.

182. Well, there were seven out of fifteen. If you wish to give us what you think was the opinion of the absent Commissioners we will be happy to take it?—My being compelled to remain in my house for many months has prevented me from having the opportunity I would have of conferring with the general body, and it is only this morning, since I came into this court, that I have seen that map. I may say that if I had been in my usual health and in my proper place in the board-room when that was proposed, I certainly would have made strenuous objections against it. I will be glad to give you my reasons. I know that a great

number of persons in this town who are to a great extent humble, a great number of them are workers in the large mills here belonging to Mr. Barbour, Mr. Stewart, and the Island Spinning Co., and they call to me frequently about the question of their burdens; and I am quite convinced in my mind that if this goes up to the extent—mind you, I would not for an instant curtail it altogether, quite the contrary, because there are parts of the town in which it would be considered beneficial and great good would arise, but to add 1,000 acres to 600 acres to our town belonging.

183. It would be too heavy on the present ratepayers?—Yes.

184. What parts of the town could be extended beneficially?—I think there is very little room for extension on the Co. Antrim side. On the Co. Down side I have it from my brother Commissioners that they think it would be advisable to extend to a certain stream on the Hillhall road in the Co. Down.

185. That is Mr. Barbour's stream that Mr. M'Ilveeny alluded to?—Yes.

186. In the townland of Ballymullan and Largymore?—Yes.

187. Have you ever considered the question whether it would be advisable for the Commissioners to take up the care of the roads from the Grand Jury?—Indeed I would be sorry they should do anything of the kind.

188. You would be against it?—Yes.

189. Has it been the subject of consideration by the Commissioners as a body?—No; I cannot recollect any occasion on which it was considered.

190. Do you think the roads well kept by the county?—Very well.

191. And that you would be no gainers by becoming the road custodians?—Quite the contrary, in my opinion.

192. Do you think the town is fairly lighted and that the gas is sufficient?—Very well lighted.

193. And that no more lamps are wanted at present?—We have put them in when necessary; I don't know at the present time that there is any wanted.

194. Do you consider the water supply sufficient?—It is, with the exception that they cannot spare so much as to water the streets.

195. But with that exception there is enough for the [illegible], and it is excellent water. The Commissioners have had it tried by competent persons in Belfast, and they all say it is first rate.

196. Are you satisfied with the state of the drainage?—Yes; we have done a good deal, many hundred feet of drainage for the town within the last few years.

197. You know the open stream that has been talked of as receiving the drainage of a great part of the town?—I know it well. It goes by my garden where I have lived all my lifetime.

198. Are you of opinion it could be covered in easily in some way?—Yes; if the expenditure would not be too great.

199. Have the Commissioners ever considered the question of the expense of it?—No, they have never done so. They have always thought it was too large a job for them to take in hands.

200. If they have never asked the expense they could never know?—I have not gone into that. I should be very glad to see it done, however.

201. Is it in the present state a nuisance to you?—I don't find it so to me, though, I believe, some other people do.

202. Is there any smell from it?—Yes, in the heat of summer.

203. Surely that is a nuisance?—No doubt of that. A good deal of that comes from Messrs. Barbour's mill, which lies on the very verge of it. I recollect the time when the water which flows along there, when there was no other place to take the cattle to get water, except this water which came along what is called now Antrim-street, and it was good, pure, and it was coming from the same source as the general reservoir which supplies the town. There has been a great deal [illegible] by the persons and former proprietors with regard to supplying the town with water—very great, and I should say there has been paid here more than from £2,000 to £3,000 spent in that direction. I was glad to hear the observations made by Mr. M'Ilveeny speaking of the water. There is a place about three miles from the town, where there might be three or four acres got that would raise as much water as would [illegible] along the great basin, personally, [illegible]. Of course the property would have to be purchased from the owners.

204. Is there anything else you wish to add?—I have no doubt on my mind that there would be a great outcry amongst the humble people.

205. The ratepayers inside the town?—Yes; the ratepayers that would come within it if the boundary was extended.

206. Is it merely outside or within those living in the town?—Those living outside as well as in.

Mr. William Savage, examined.

207. You are a Commissioner?—I am.

208. And you are cognizant of all these proceedings about this extension?—I am, most of them.

209. Tell us your opinion, and the opinion of your fellow Commissioners, so far as you know on that subject?—Well, my own opinion, and I believe the opinion of several who were not present, were in favour of an extension. Some of them may have differed as to the various points to which they should go, but I may say that taking the number of Commissioners who were present on that day, and on which the resolution was [illegible], there were other Commissioners who were absent that day——.

210. Besides the Chairman there were seven absent?—Yes; but there were some of these absent who were members of the Committee appointed to consider and define the boundary.

211. Then, of course, their feelings were known, although they were not present to join with the others in giving an opinion?—Those present were unanimous.

212. What is your view of the reasons for this particular extension?—My own opinion is that the present boundary is too limited, that there are several places immediately adjoining it, and in close proximity to it, that received all the advantages from being so closely adjacent to the town, and received the benefits of lighting, and much of their trade, and which do not contribute one penny of taxes; and I consider it would be only just to those living in the town that they should contribute their proportion to the rates.

213. That they should contribute something?—Yes.

214. And do you think, according to the principles of the Towns Improvement Act, by which agricultural land pays only one-fourth, that that is a fair contribution?—I do. I think the townparks, as they are called, and the value at which they are let, that a quarter of the value is a very fair proportion.

215. How far from the centre of the town could you say such advantages arise, that you would call on the people to be contributors?—I would say about a mile. There might be some cases where it would not extend to a mile, and there might be some places where we might go further along the leading road. We might go further all along the leading road, the advantages would go further.

216. Towards the north-east apparently where there are such large works do they derive much advantage from proximity to Lisburn?—Decidedly, they do

LISBURN. June [illegible]. Mr. William Savage.

217. You have not got them within your [illegible] boundary [illegible] would have been to have included them.

218. How far would you have gone in that direction?—I [illegible] as far as to [illegible] the [illegible] works, there was a feeling that as they had a good organization themselves in the sanitary arrangements. I think there was a feeling amongst some of the Commissioners that it might not be wise to take in them, in order.

219. Do you mean a kind of [illegible] opposition?—I don't know there would be opposition, though I am not certain. Mr. Barbour would not give much opposition, though I did not hear him saying so. The [illegible] Commissioners told me that he said he would not give us very decided opposition.

220. But in the other direction your present line is the boundary to a [illegible]?—Yes, I believe so.

221. But you did not go into details as to the number of votes that it would add, or the valuation?—No, we did not, but I think Mr. [illegible] has stated the number at 300. I think that is exaggerated, I don't think it would take in 300 at all. I would guess it at between 150 and 200.

222. Had the Commissioners before them the question of [illegible] additional cost the lighting of this extended area would be, or as they would light it?—I don't think they have gone into that matter, and knowing whether they are to get this extension or not, but I know from what I have heard that they would do it, that they would [illegible] a better lighting to the extended area than the present limits. The present lighting I consider very good, but there are points which they are not lighted.

223. And that requires to be lighted?—Yes.

224. In what direction?—Towards [illegible]. There is a [illegible] I don't know what the valuation is, but it is very large, and I consider that there ought to be lights there.

225. Is the gate lodge of that house in your present boundary?—No, it is not.

226. It is outside, but near it?—Yes, immediately at it.

227. Is there any lamp near it?—No, there is no lamp throwing light upon it. It is a house of good valuation. The persons who reside in the house receive the benefit of lights all the way as far as they go.

227. How far is that from the boundary?—[illegible] yards.

228. There is one lamp in the junction near the lodge house, and one half way between this and the nursery?—Yes.

229. How many lights do you think there ought to be there?—I think there should be two lights there along this way.

230. And in what other direction do you think there should be more lighting?—Along the Dublin road. It is a very dark road and there are a great number of houses there, extending along the road and outside the boundary. There is not enough lighting there.

231. In your observations [illegible] to any of the [illegible] roads?—[illegible]. There is a road leading to Hillsborough. There is not one on that road, and on the way is [illegible] the workhouse [illegible], and the new cemetery. I believe there should be some lights there. Then there is [illegible] lodge, these houses would be brought in by the extension, and I think from the additional value that would be got, that there should be lights put on those roads.

232. Is that very [illegible] going up along the Dublin road, outside the limits that requires lighting?—Yes; there are.

233. Don't you think there is an increase of the lighting required on all the roads at present?—Yes; an increase on the roads approaching the town in all directions.

234. Do you [illegible] giving any water supply to this extended area?—The Commissioners have not charge of the water.

235. Have they no control over it at all; for if it was not given by some one they would have to provide it?—Sir R. Wallace provides it. On a fine-day [illegible] at the time, there is a [illegible] and he gives them the water.

236. If there was no water supply the Commissioners would have to find one—have they considered this?—They have not hitherto. Sir R. Wallace has always [illegible] the [illegible] wants of the town.

237. That is so evident as possible, and they assume that whatever will be wanted will be supplied?—Yes.

Mr. Edward Jefferson.

Mr. Edward Jefferson examined.

238. You are a Town Commissioner of Lisburn?—I am. I may state that I was on the Committee that considered the question of an extension at first, but latterly I had not been able to attend its meetings.

239. You were not at the meeting on the 7th of April?—I was not, but I was at the Committee meeting.

240. And you approve of what was done?—Yes.

Mr. [illegible].

Mr. [illegible] examined.

241. Is there anything you would like to add to the evidence that has been already given?—Nothing, with this little exception. I may say that I also concur in the views that have been previously expressed, but with reference to what you have heard—that there were only seven who attended the meeting at which it was unanimously resolved to seek an extension of the town boundary, I may say that the subject had come up at other meetings before the Commissioners, who were then absent, and they all approved of it. Every thing [illegible] up [illegible] it, [illegible] they approved of it. It was talked of at several meetings.

Dr. Samuel Musgrave.

Dr. Samuel Musgrave examined.

242. What are your views on the subject of the extension?—I do not think I can add anything to what Mr Savage has said. There is just one thing that strikes me. One reason for not taking in those large works, and thickly populated districts beyond our boundary—Hilden, Glenmore, and Lambeg is, that the powers of the Commissioners are to some extent restricted by the Act of Parliament in reference to watching. Under the present law we cannot have watchmen for watching the streets of our own town except the police, and the cost would be so great that we would be quite precluded from having watchmen. If we cannot watch the town itself we could not watch the outlying districts, which are inhabited by the working people, and who would probably cause some trouble.

243. And it is now simply patrolled by the constabulary?—Yes; until twelve o'clock at night, and

LISBURN, June 14, 1877. — Dr. Samuel Musgrave.

in the case of the patrol the tramp of the police is heard a considerable distance away, and any disorderly persons get out of the way. I think if any amendment could be made in the law, under which we are appointed, it would be a very desirable one—that is, that the Commissioners should have the power to appoint watchmen other than the constabulary.

244. But not doing away with the patrolling at the same time?—By no means. For instance, if a fire took place after twelve o'clock at night the decent watchmen about the street would report it. Now, if a fire occurred, a person passing by and seeing it would go to the police office and report it.

245. And when that report is made is the fire escape available at once?—Yes. The report is generally made to the superintendent of the brigade, and not to the police office, but if there were watchmen on the streets we would know a great deal quicker, because it would be their duty to patrol the streets until six o'clock in the morning—when constabulary come out again.

246. To get the services of the constabulary would be too expensive?—We could not have less than a constable and four men, and the cost of these men would amount to about one-third of our rates. In 1874, an application was made to the constabulary authorities in Dublin, and we were told that the cost would be about £80 a man, and that would be about one-third of the rates at that time. I think that is a most important question to consider.

247. We have no power in the matter, but you can put it on the notes for the consideration of the Government?—I think that is one reason why I would not be an advocate for extending our boundary further than the Parliamentary boundary, which, I believe, is the natural boundary of this town.

248. That is on the north side?—Yes; that is what is recommended, and on the north side the addition is not very great. The south side is the natural boundary too, because it takes in townparks, and there is a watercourse, which seems to be also the natural boundary for the town.

249. Do you consider that any large sum is required to be expended in the town in the improvement of the drainage?—I do not.

250. You know that that is a matter that has been alluded to in the case of Mr. Beatty?—I do.

251. Ought not something to be done to remedy that?—With regard to that I think there might be a great improvement, and I think the money would be very well expended in remedying it; in culverting that stream, and probably to lower its level so as to make the fall more equal and more regular.

252. How is it that the Commissioners have never then ascertained what it would cost?—They have.

253. Do you remember what the estimate was?

254. Mr. *Houston*.—I do not remember any particular estimate being laid before the Commissioners?

255. *Witness*.—The report of our surveyor contained the cost, and I think it was about £800. The question was this, that the surveyor was requested to report upon certain floods that took place at certain times of the year after heavy rains in certain districts, and the reason assumed or given for the water accumulating was that this stream would not vent the water sufficiently quick. It was on that he reported the necessity of altering the bed of this stream, which runs through the town, and which is the main sewer of the town—to make another in another direction, to divert this flood water, and to empty it into the stream at a lower level—instead of giving it so much to do, where it is almost flat, to give another stream to the flooded district, and to make the sewer empty itself into the stream at a lower point, and that he estimated would have cost £800. That was what was proposed. It was not to culvert the byewash, but to relieve the byewash of this amount of water.

256. The Commissioners have not gone into the question of covering up this open sewer?—No; they have not. It is covered, or rather there is a good portion of it covered. There are other portions that it would be well to cover.

257. Has there been any complaint from the persons residing near the river of the sewage being discharged into the river?—No.

Mr. Wellington Young.

Mr. WELLINGTON YOUNG, examined.

258. What are your views with reference to the proposed extension?—I happen to be a ratepayer outside the boundary affected by the extension, because I own some houses at the boundary, and comprised in the extension in the Hillsborough direction. I have not any objection to the extension. I don't think it is correct to assume that any of the parties who are occupiers of the houses in the extended boundary would object, for this reason: that the majority will be paying no rates under the Act of Parliament. Our premises are rated under £4. It is the owners that will have to pay the rates, and I expect I will have to pay the rates for these houses; and the same rule will apply to most of those other small workmen's houses in the district lying towards Hilden.

259. With regard to the owners of arable land, their lands are all townparks?—I don't think it is unfair to ask them to pay the rate. The townparks will be converted into building ground ultimately, and the owners have them at very low rents.

260. And they derive such benefit that they ought to pay something?—Yes.

261. About the provision under the Public Health Act with reference to arable land paying one-fourth of the valuation, do you think that is a fair proportion?—I think they should pay something more—say one-half—and I will tell you why. A great number of these townparks are held by parties in the town who do not occupy them themselves, but sublet them, and make larger rents than what they would for land further out from the town, and they derive large profits owing to the proximity of these townparks to the town.

262. In that case who would pay the rates?—The tenant would pay the rates.

263. And not the sub-tenant?—No; the sub-tenant is an unknown individual who takes the land for six months or so. There is a reason why this extension should be given. Up to the year 1873 the town of Lisburn was at a perfect stand-still. There were good leases granted immediately afterwards under the present landlord. The town, at that time, was under the Act of 9th George IV., but, of course the powers of the Commissioners were very limited, and they were not required to be exercised, because the town was at a stand-still owing to there being no leases. Since 1874 an immense number of houses have been granted, and what were formerly townparks are now covered with buildings, particularly in the district now going to be extended towards the direction of Hilden. At that time that district was covered entirely with grass fields. It is all built on now. That is entirely owing to the leases granted. In another direction up higher on the Antrim-road direction—in the northward direction—it is all built in villas now in the present boundary, but away beyond that, and within the extended boundary, a large number of houses have been erected, and are in course of erection where there were formerly townparks, and in particular directions the houses are increasing. I agree with Dr. Musgrave as to not taking in Hilden. It would be a most troublesome district, and we would find it totally impossible to manage it without extra police, and the Town Commissioners would be held, to a certain extent, responsible.

264. Is it not kept in good order now?—The only

test of that is the number of cases tried here coming from Hilden. Taking that in connexion with the fact that there are no police at Hilden, it is only when the parties fall out among themselves, and come here that such cases are heard.

265. Are not any measures taken in the place to preserve order?—The Messrs. Barbour endeavour to exercise control. I know personally that the Messrs. Barbour, who are the owners of Hilden, would object to this—thinking that they are managing Hilden properly themselves—and it was merely a little village of their own, they would object to any extension, because they would get no benefit corresponding to it, and they would have to pay the tax out of their own pockets, most of the rated houses being under £4.

266. Do you know yourself the extent of the electoral division of Lisburn?—No; I cannot say what the extent of the electoral division is.

267. Do you know how far it extends from the town—the Poor Law electoral division?—It is a great portion of Lisburn.

268. How far does the electoral division of Lisburn extend from the present boundary?—In one direction it extends to Mr. Tully's, in the Moira direction—the west.

269. How far?—About a mile from the centre of the town.

270. How much further does the electoral division boundary go in other directions?—I could not say. It is a long way out.

271. Do you consider it completely out of the question to make the electoral division of Lisburn the municipal boundary of the town?—Clearly out of the question.

272. The reason I ask you is, because it is alluded to in the report of the Committee, out of which this Commission has arisen, as desirable where possible to make the electoral division boundary the boundary of the town?—It is totally impossible in this case. It is too far out. You asked a question—suppose this extension was granted, what would the Commissioners do with the money they would receive. Now, it has been given as a reason that they could sewer and flag; but I agree with Dr. Musgrave, and the report of the engineer, that it is absolutely necessary that there should be a sewer [illegible] to prevent this flooding of the Antrim-street district. Since the last flooding a great number of houses have been built within that district, and there are sewers made there, and that will, of course, increase the sewerage of the town, and unless there would be a separate sewer made to vent up any collection, that flooding would likely recur again. That could be done out of the surplus rates.

273. You must remember that for any works that are sanitary works the rates would be proportional?—There is a great deal of flagging to be done, in the way of side flagging, and as the Commissioners have no borrowing powers a resolution has been passed by them and forwarded to the proper quarter for the purpose of getting these borrowing powers.

274. Do you consider that there is a great deal of flagging to be done?—Yes, a great deal more to be done; a great deal of Castle-street and other portions of the town. The Commissioners have only flagged the business portions of the town.

275. Do you agree with Dr. Musgrave as to the want of watching?—Yes. I think the town is in a very bad state at present for the want of watching. It would be very wrong to pay so much money out of the rates to have extra police. Under the old Act of George IV. we had watchmen. Even if we had the powers under that old Act it would be sufficient, and they would pay watchmen themselves. Then, unfortunately, the Town Improvement Act has taken out of their hands. That is the only improvement out of the old Act that would be required to be put into the new.

The inquiry then closed.

NEWTOWNARDS—17TH JUNE, 1879.

(Before Mr. C. P. Cotton, C.E.)

Mr. William M'Gowan examined.

1. Mr. Cotton.—You are clerk to the Town Commissioners?—I am.

2. How long have you occupied that position?—For eight years.

3. The Town of Newtownards is under the Towns Improvement Act?—Yes.

4. At what time was it placed under that Act?—In 1866.

5. Was it under any other Act previously?—It was previous to that time under the 9th Geo. IV.

6. Was the Towns Improvement Act adopted in its entirety?—No.

7. The water clauses were not adopted?—No.

8. The boundary was fixed at that time?—It was.

9. Have you got a map showing the boundary?—Yes, we have.

10. Would you let me see it?—It is on the wall of this room.

11. The red line on this map shows the boundary of the town?—Yes.

12. What is the population of the town?—9,562.

13. That was in 1871?—Yes.

14. Has it been increasing since then?—No; I think not.

15. Do you know the number of houses in the town?—2,021.

16. Is there any building going on now—is the number of houses increasing?—No; there is not very much of an increase; still the number of houses is increasing a little.

17. Do you know how many acres there are in the town?—467.

18. And what was the valuation on the last revision?—£10,514.

19. That is the last valuation?—Yes.

20. You have no wards?—No.

21. What electoral division is the town in?—It is in the electoral division of Newtownards and Newtownards South.

22. Is there about one-half of the town in each of these electoral divisions?—I don't know about the proportions of the town in the electoral divisions.

23. You could not divide the acreage for me?—No, I could not.

24. Do you know the electoral division boundaries—how far they extend from the town?—No, I do not.

25. Do you know how far the electoral division of Newtownards extends from the town?—I do not.

26. Would you give me the rates that have been struck for the last five years—give me the municipal rates first?—In 1874 the municipal rate was 1s.; in 1875, 1s.; in 1876, 1s.; in 1877, 10d.; and in 1878, 9d.

27. Have you struck any rate this year?—No.

28. Would you now give me the poor rate for the same number of years?—In 1874 it was 27d.; in 1875, 27d.; in 1876, 1s. 6d.; in 1877, 28½d.; and in 1878, 21d.

29. Will you now give me the county cess for the same years?—The county cess in 1874 was 32d.; in 1875, 33½d.; in 1876, 30½d.; in 1877, 31d.; and in 1878, 32d.

30. Have the Commissioners had before them the question of whether or not any alteration is desirable

NEWTOWNARDS.
June 13, 1879.
Mr. William Wilson.

to the boundary of the town?—Yes, on the 12th of January.

31. How many Commissioners have you?—Thirteen.

32. How many attended the meeting held on that day?—Nine.

33. Did they come to any conclusion on that subject?—No. I was instructed to give the answers to the queries which I did give.

34. Then they are of opinion, I take it from you, that the boundaries should be extended?—No, they are not. They have had a subsequent meeting.

35. What meeting was that?—A meeting on the 13th of June.

36. How many Commissioners attended that meeting?—Six.

37. And what was the resolution that they came to?—"That the boundary be not extended at present." That is not just the words of the resolution, but it is the substance of it.

38. On what day was that passed?—On Friday, the 13th of June.

39. Were they unanimous—the six that were present at that meeting?—They were.

40. Were they present at the former meeting at which the Commissioners agreed to extend the boundary—those six?—I think they were.

41. Do you know the opinion of the Commissioners that did not attend?—No.

42. Can you tell me how many voters there are in the town—municipal voters?—305.

43. And how many are qualified to sit if elected as Commissioners?—231.

44. When the extension of the boundary was talked of originally, was any definite extension mentioned, or was it merely thought that it was desirable to extend the boundary?—Yes; it was thought desirable to extend it about half a mile all round.

45. Was the question gone into then as to how many voters it would add to the municipal list?—No, it was not.

46. Either voters, or population, or valuation?—No; that was not the object. The object was for the better regulation and direction of the market.

47. How would that be affected by an extension of the area?—As parties have gone to the limits of our boundaries, and there have established a kind of market.

48. To what place?—In some places that came.

49. In more than one place?—Yes.

50. They hold a sort of market outside the boundary on the roads?—Yes; and the Commissioners wish to have power over them and to control them.

51. Was that the object?—Yes.

52. Would not the simple result be that they would go on and hold them at the limit of the new boundary?—Well, that was the conclusion that the Commissioners came to—that if the boundary was extended that would be the result.

53. Then they think there would be nothing to be gained by an extension of the boundary?—Yes.

54. They don't want an extension of the boundary for the purpose of obtaining additional taxes?—No, they do not.

55. You are the Urban Sanitary Authority here?—Yes.

56. Have the Commissioners ever had under consideration the question of acquiring the control of the roads?—They have.

57. I believe they petitioned the Local Government Board once on the subject?—They did.

58. And the Grand Jury objected?—Yes.

59. And the application fell through?—Yes, in consequence of that.

60. Have they taken up that matter since the passing of the Act of 1878?—No.

61. They are doing nothing now about it at all?—Nothing at present. The matter is under consideration.

62. How is the town lighted?—By gas.

63. Have the Town Commissioners a contract with the gas company?—Yes.

64. What are the terms of that contract?—It is £3 per lamp.

65. For what period?—For eleven months of the year.

66. From what time?—From about the 1st of September until the end of April. It may not be eight months in the year.

67. And what are the hours of lighting?—From half an hour of sunset until half an hour after midnight, except when 11 o'clock intervenes, and they are put out at 11 o'clock.

68. That is an arrangement—11 o'clock?—Yes.

69. And is there not any arrangement as to dark full moon?—Yes; two nights before and two nights after full moon are exempted from the provisions of the lighting agreement.

70. What I understand about this half hour after midnight is this, that the lamps are put out at half past 11 o'clock?—Is that so?—Yes.

71. But suppose it is a new moon, and that there is no light from the moon, does that arrangement hold then?—No, then the lamps are put out at 11 o'clock.

72. Then it is not entirely a question of what the moon does?—No.

73. How many lamps have you?—One hundred and fifty-seven.

74. And what other lamps have you?—We have about twenty lamps that we let burn all night.

75. Additional to the 157?—No, portion of the 157.

76. And they are kept burning in the principal streets of the town?—Yes, in the principal streets.

77. What is the price of gas to the public?—Seven shillings and six pence a thousand.

78. And is the town fairly lit?—It is well lit.

79. There are no complaints about the lighting?—There have been no official complaints about it.

80. How is the town supplied with water?—It is well supplied with water.

81. In what way?—With pumps.

82. And how many public pumps are there?—Sixteen to eighteen.

83. Sixteen?—I think there are eighteen public pumps.

84. Are there any complaints about the quantity or quality of the water?—There have not been any complaints lately.

85. There were complaints made previously about the supply of water in dry seasons?—Yes.

86. Has that been remedied since?—It has, to a great extent.

87. How?—By new pumps?—Yes, by new pumps in those streets.

88. Of good quality?—Yes.

89. How is the town drained?—It is very imperfectly drained.

90. Is there any project of main drainage before the Commissioners at all?—No; that is the worst feature in Newtownards—its imperfect sewerage.

91. And have they had no complaints before them about that at all, or no plan before them for improving it?—Not that I am aware of.

92. Have you struck any special drainage rate?—No.

93. Have you spent any money on the sewers of late years?—Not much.

94. Will you let me have a copy of the accounts for 1878?—Have you got them printed?—I have.

95. You have not got them printed?—I have them in manuscript here.

96. The Town Commissioners are of opinion that the county should do a great deal more in the way of sinking sewers, and the county think that the Commissioners should do it?—The county make the sewers of the town. They are under the county surveyor

Newtownards. June 17, 18[illegible]. Mr. William [illegible].

but there are some streets in which there is no sewer to take off the surface water.

97. Why should the county make that?—Because there is nothing to take off the surface water.

98. And the Commissioners want them to attend to the drainage of the town?—Of course they do.

99. Then there is no item in the expenditure for sewers at all last year?—No.

100. Is it from want of funds that the Town Commissioners have not dealt with the sewerage question?—They don't want to increase the taxation.

101. And the taxation has not gone up to the shilling [illegible] any rate for the last two years?—They would rather keep it below the shilling than above it. Newtownards is very poor.

102. Has there ever been any representation made to the Local Government Board on the subject of the drainage?—I think not.

103. At the time of the inquiry as to the water?—What inquiry?

104. The one held by Dr. Owens?—What was that inquiry?

105. That was an inquiry as to the supply of water to Newtownards?—The conclusion that everyone came to was that the sewerage was defective and not the water supply.

106. Do you mean that the pumps were affected by the want of good drainage?—By the surface water.

107. That has not been remedied in any way then?—Yes it has been; but since these pumps were put down.

108. Because the pumps you put down were new ones?—Yes.

109. Have you got any map showing the system of drainage that you have in the town?—No.

110. Do you know that you are obliged to have one? Has your attention never been drawn to that clause in the Act—

"That the Urban Sanitary Authority shall provide a map exhibiting the system of sewerage that they have in their district and such map shall be kept at their office and be revised from time to time and shall at all reasonable times be open to the inspection of the ratepayers of the district."

—We have no system to supply.

111. I think in this case the section would be taken to apply to a map showing the want of a system of sewerage. Have you no drains of any kind in the town?—There are some drains.

112. Well it appears to me that you are bound to have, beyond all question, to have the map I have indicated, and I should advise you to have a map made of that sort as soon as possible?—Perhaps so.

113. There was surely a map made at the time you were applying for the control of the roads?—Yes, and that is the map, the map before you.

114. Do you know the opinion of the ratepayers on the question of whether there should be any alteration in the boundaries of the town?—No, I am not aware of the opinion of any of them.

115. Or of the opinion of any of the people who live outside the boundary but near to it, whether or not they would wish to be brought in?—No, the question has not been raised.

116. Are there many villa residences, or residences of that kind, close to the boundary, but outside it?—No.

117. Is it chiefly agricultural land all round the present limits?—Yes, chiefly townparks.

118. Townparks outside the present limits?—Yes.

119. Is that land principally held by residents in the town?—Principally.

120. Not by people living on it?—Yes.

121. Does that apply to the extent of half a mile outside the present limits?—Very few people live outside.

122. Take that half-mile extension that we mentioned before, would that add very few to the number of people?—Yes; very few, because they are mostly townparks.

123. And it would not add many houses?—No, it would not.

124. Can you tell me any particular road in which the market was ever held outside the boundary?—On the [illegible] road.

125. Can you tell me any other?—On the Donaghadee and Bangor road.

126. Any other?—On the William-street road.

127. Were there any on the Belfast road?—I am not sure.

128. If you are not sure it seems that there are not?—No; there may be a market and me not know of it.

129. You mean to say that you cannot prove that there was?—I mean to say that I don't know of it.

130. I presume that means to say that you cannot prove it. It is mere conjecture?—I don't know anything about it.

131. However, this does not bear on the question, and it is only at the request of a gentleman's present that these questions were put to you. Did you ever see a market on the Donaghadee road?—Yes.

132. What kind of market?—A fowl market.

133. I think there is nothing else that I have to ask you. Is there anything that occurs to you that you would wish to bring forward bearing on the subject of the present inquiry?—No, I don't think there is.

Mr. Andrew M[illegible] examined.

Mr. Andrew M[illegible].

134. Mr. Cotton.—You are the Chairman of the Town Commissioners?—I am.

135. How long have you presided over the board?—For five or six years.

136. And I suppose you were a Commissioner prior to that time?—Yes, for four or five years.

137. The opinion of the Commissioners, I take it to be, is that no extension of the present boundary is required?—That is the opinion of the Commissioners.

138. Would you say that that is the unanimous opinion of the Commissioners?—Indeed I might almost go the length of saying that they are unanimous on the point, and I have asked every ratepayer to whom I had an opportunity of speaking on the subject too, so that we are quite free to say that an extension would not be desirable at the present time.

139. Why at the present time?—They qualified it in that way, and I can scarcely answer for why except that I presume that they might have in view, at some time not far in the distance, a separation from the county. I construe it in that way, but I am not certain it is the fact.

140. If you were separated from the county do you think it would be of advantage to the town to have an extension?—Well, it has been the impression of the Commissioners, as well as of a large number of ratepayers heretofore, that it would be very much to the advantage of Newtownards if they were separated from the county.

141. What I want to know is—if you were separated from the county would an extension be of advantage then?—Well, I don't know that it would be of advantage exactly, for taking into account that we would probably have to light the extension—all the roads along, and give it town privileges, I believe it would be a disadvantage. I am not prepared to answer that one way or the other at the present moment, because it is one of those things that I have not considered.

142. You have not made up your minds about the consideration of that question?—It is under consideration at the present time.

143. You have not made any application to the Local Government Board?—No, we have not moved in the matter more than to consider it.

144. What is the reason the Town Commissioners

Newtownards. June 17, 1879. Mr. Andrew [illegible].

have not taken up the drainage question?—Well, the great matter has been heretofore that the county had no one, and that though they were imperfect the town tried to utilize those sewers as best they could. The Commissioners were almost unanimous to try and keep down the town expenses and rates as low as they possibly could, and while, as the town clerk has said, and I quite agree with him, the sewerage is imperfect, except in some isolated cases it answers pretty well, but the sewerage is not perfect, or what it should be.

145. Do the sanitary officers complain?—Sometimes they do.

146. And you have not expended anything last year on the drains?—As far as the sewerage is concerned the expense has been very trifling.

147. It was nothing last year?—There may have been some repairs done, and that may have come under a special head—probably it did—but we have no special tax for that particular purpose.

148. But you have taken no steps for the preparation of a system of sewerage?—We have not; we have tried to utilize the sewers of the county, in order to make use of the system of drainage that is existing in the town.

149. Are you waiting in the hope that the county will do it for you?—I am not, for I think it is more than likely that if we had the management of the streets the town of Newtownards could do the business a great deal more satisfactorily, and to better advantage than the county has done it heretofore, for I may say that for a period of years, as far as my knowledge extends, the county has done very little, except the sewers already constructed.

150. In other respects, do you think that the county has expended as much money as you had a right to expect from them?—I think for the last two or three years, probably they have been doing something, only what is fair in that respect. If they had only done so in years gone by—I go back ten or twelve years—the town of Newtownards would be much better off in the way of sewerage; but this last two or three years, since the question of separation has been occupying the mind of the Grand Jury and other officials, I think they are disposed to be a little more friendly to the town of Newtownards than heretofore.

151. You are not applying for it at present?—No; we have it under consideration.

152. Is the town fairly lighted?—Yes, it is perfectly well lit, and the gas is very good.

153. Do you consider the water supply of the town good?—I think there is a very fair supply all over town.

154. There are no complaints?—Not one word for sometime past. The Commissioners have recently put down pipes from the Square to [illegible]-street, and a pump which cost £14 in the Square, that supplies that quarter, and there has not been a word said since that time.

155. You consider that the pumps are sufficient for the town?—Yes, for the private supply, a great number of residents of the town have their private supply.

156. Is there anything else you would like to put on the notes?—I don't know anything more than that at the present time, more than to say what the chairman has said about the question of an extension, and the decision that was come to.

157. The extension that you suggested, when you replied to the queries we sent you, was with a view to controlling the markets outside the town?—That was the intention that the Commissioners had in view.

158. And it was only when they saw that it would be practically useless that they then changed their mind?—They changed their mind as far as that point was concerned. They thought it better to control the markets. The Commissioners thought that if they extended the boundary the people would go still further outside.

159. Do you know the electoral division?—I am not at all acquainted with it.

160. I want to ask you do you know it sufficiently to say whether it would or would not be a desirable boundary for the town—that is to make the electoral division the boundary of the town—whether that would be out of the question or not. Do you know it sufficiently well for that?—I would not like to say that just now.

161. I may tell you that it extends somewhere about three miles away?—I thought it extended about five miles away.

162. Would it not be absurd to make that the boundary?—It would; quite absurd.

163. I may tell you that the reason I asked you the question is that a Committee of the House of Commons has mentioned that it is desirable to make towns conterminous with Poor Law electoral divisions, and it is evidently out of the question here, and I wish to put it on the notes. The town of Newtownards only extends to the north, from the centre of the town, about a quarter of a mile; and I would suppose not more than about half a mile to the east and west?—Well, yes; I should say so.

164. A quarter of a mile to the north, a quarter of a mile to the south, and half a mile to the east and west, from the centre of the town?—Yes.

Mr. William Henry.

Mr. William Henry examined.

165. Mr. Cotton.—You are a Town Commissioner of Newtownards?—Yes; I think our Chairman has fairly represented our views on these questions.

166. Both as regards the question of extension and as regards the application for the roads?—Yes.

167. The question of making the control of the roads is under consideration?—Yes; and I am one of the Committee considering the question, and we would wish to have it; and the application will be made even if we do not have it.

Mr. Robert B. Caughey.

Mr. Robert B. Caughey examined.

168. Mr. Cotton.—You are a Town Commissioner?—I am, and I am also one of the Committee in charge of this matter, and I quite agree with Mr. Henry that there is hardly a doubt that we will make another application to have the town separated from the county, for I think that is very desirable.

169. Have you considered whether or not an alteration of the boundary would be desirable, supposing you did get the separation?—We have not.

170. Mr. Henry.—The Commissioners are unanimous that there should be a separation.

171. Mr. Caughey.—And the Commissioners have only deferred making the application.

Mr. Edward M'Call examined.

Newtown-ards. June 17, 1877. Mr. Edward M'Call.

172. The Commissioners are of opinion that if we had the control of the town we would be able to take up the question of sewerage in a much better manner than is possible at present. We think that if we had the county cess in our hands we could apply it to drain the town thoroughly, and with that advantage to the town we would not have to strike such more municipal rate.

173. You have gone into the figures and have considered that with the same amount of money that represents county cess—less county-at-large charges—you would be able to do the roads, and do them better than they are now done?—Yes; those accounts we went into before and they stand good still—that we are charged too much on county cess, owing to the weight of the county cess and poor rate together. In fact the town is not able to strike a clear rate to do the work for the town.

174. Have you considered the question as to what staff it would take?—We look upon the matter that it would be really useful for the town to get a separation. I think the sewerage question hinges upon that.

Mr. James Lafory.

Mr. James [illegible] examined.

175. Mr. Cotton.—You are a Town Commissioner?—Yes. I fully agree with what Mr. M'Call has said in regard to the sewerage. I believe that although the county is doing a great deal, it is not done in the right direction; and much the community a great deal has [illegible] in bringing the [illegible] and the sewerage, and for one reason I think it should be done, and first [illegible] that under the bed of our town there is layers of about eight feet of gravel, and all the bad matter sinks down through the gravel and contaminates the pumps, and if we had sewerage we would be saved the complaints that crop up about the water.

176. There have been complaints about the drainage [illegible] [illegible] some time ago. The cause is what I have stated.

177. We have been receiving evidence on the question of separation, and I should be glad to learn from you, if in your opinion, supposing there was separation, the boundary of the town should be larger?—I think not; there is nothing to induce us to think about pushing our boundary larger, more and except for the better government of our districts.

Rev. Joseph [illegible].

The Rev. Joseph [illegible] examined.

178. I wish to say that I think it would be perfectly absurd to make the boundary of the town coterminous with the two electoral divisions. The parish of Newtownards proper, and Newtownards South, is about seven and a half miles right through—it extends about three and a half miles in one direction, and three and a half miles in another, whilst the town extends to within a quarter of a mile on the [illegible], and [illegible] on the north comes within half a mile, on either side.

Mr. Martin.

Mr. Martin cross-examined.

179. Mr. *James Norland* (who appeared for the Grand Jury).—How much does the town pay annually for county cess?—That is a question I did not anticipate would arise here to-day.

180. Well what I want to know is have you considered that?—We have not.

181. So that you are not in a position to form a correct opinion yet as to that?—No.

182. Do you know how much has been expended by the county on improvements in the town?—We have not gone into that yet.

183. Have you considered this in reference to applying for a separation—that the Local Government Board has power to make provision for the fixing and payment of any contribution to the cost of making and maintaining the roads, bridges, and footpaths in the barony or baronies, surrounding or adjoining such district?—We have considered a great many cases.

184. Have you considered what effect that would have upon you?—No, we have not.

185. You have not considered these matters?—We have not.

186. Do you say that if you were separated from the county, that you should be exempt from the county-at-large charges?—Not at all.

187. Well I merely suggest that you should consider those things?—We have not considered those things severally, but we have heretofore. We have considered the matter this far—that if we had a separation no doubt we would be held liable for a certain amount of county-at-large charges that we would be disposed to pay.

188. You tell me you have not come to any conclusion on the subject, and I only want to mention these facts, which may be worthy of consideration, because you will find them very valuable?—Yes, our views are not very perfectly formed, or formed sufficiently for me to make a very clear and definite statement here to-day on the subject; but we are far enough and clearly enough that it would be much to the advantage of the town to have a separation.

189. Even though it would cost you more?—That is the reason why we want to be clear—because it would cost us less.

190. How can you come to that conclusion when you have not considered these matters?—At a rough approximation.

191. Mr. Cotton.—Although it comes in incidentally in this inquiry it is evident you are going to apply for it?—There is no doubt about that.

192. Then I would like an answer to this question—supposing you do get this separation—whether any alteration of the boundary would be of advantage to the town?—I should say it would not be of advantage. That is my present opinion, without giving it that consideration which the question requires. I think that if the boundary was extended, say a quarter of a mile further than it is at present, as a matter of course the town would be obliged to light out to the new boundary. That is the difficulty—the rates would be small as against the expense of lighting.

193. Except in the matter of lighting, if the area of the town was extended half a mile round do you think what you would receive would be more than sufficient to keep up the additional roads brought in?—That is a question for consideration; I fear it would not.

194. You have not gone into that question?—We have not.

Mr. James Finlay examined.

195. There is not a market day in Newtownards that there are not fowl bought at the corner of the Donaghadee and Bangor road. That is so nearly every market day—just opposite my house.

196. Mr. Cowan.—Is that outside the jurisdiction of the Commissioners?—No; it is inside the boundary.

Mr. Caughey re-examined.

197. Mr. Cowan.—I understand that on the Mill-road there is a market held outside the boundary, at a short distance from the centre of the town?—So I understand.

198. If the boundary was extended would it have any effect in keeping that market within the town, or would the market go out as the boundary went out?—I think people who are inclined to evade would [illegible] travel outside the boundary.

199. And you don't think an extension of the boundary would have anything to say to it?—I don't think it would.

Mr. Robert Jackson examined.

200. Mr. Cowan.—You live near the town?—Yes, within half a mile of the town, or a quarter of a mile of the boundary.

201. I believe you wish to express an opinion as to the drainage of the town?—Yes; I wish to state that the town is very improperly drained.

202. And I suppose you are interested in its being kept well drained?—I would like to see it well drained, and I think the principal reason that it is not so is that there is a want of sufficient [illegible] to take the water from the town of [illegible] the [illegible].

203. We have heard it stated that there has been no systematic plan of drainage proposed?—Well, I think I heard Mr. Smyth, the county surveyor, say that there might be a plan that would meet approbation. It is to have the outlet [illegible] to be not a canal, because the bottom is higher than the land round about, so strictly speaking it is not a canal—If that canal was [illegible] to twice its size, and two gates put on it instead of one, the water would get away at once.

204. You are against an extension of the boundary?—I don't hold an idea about that at all. I didn't think of coming to make any statement about that; but I would object to any extension in the belief that they would get a separation from the county.

205. Well, the drainage comes into the question in this way—if the Commissioners require more rates to improve the drainage of the town it would be one element for consideration as to whether they should not have an extended area, and I question very much whether the Town Commissioners would change their opinion on that. I do not think the town could afford to open the sewers and drain them in the way the sewers should be made.

206. Change their opinion on what?—On the [illegible] sewering of the town.

207. They have given no opinion on it at all?—Oh, Mr. Marrow said they would drain the town themselves if they got it from the county.

208. He said they might?—I do not think they could, because they could not get sufficient to do so.

209. However, that does not affect the boundary question. Do you think more funds are wanted for drainage purposes?—I hold that neither the county nor the town should do the whole of that work. I hold that Lord Londonderry should do part of the work, and I have no doubt that the late Marquess of Londonderry intended to do so. I may remark that when the tide is in, the mouth of the sewer in South-street—one of the main sewers of the town is filled up—the whole mouth of that sewer is filled up.

210. Do you wish to convey that the boundary should be altered for the purpose of remedying that state of things?—I do not think that matter has anything to do with an extension of the boundary.

211. Do you think the town is insufficiently drained for want of funds?—I think they have not funds, nor could they waste funds to do it.

212. If they got an additional area could they not do it?—I do not think it would be fair to ask them to do it.

The inquiry then closed.

TANDERAGEE—16TH SEPTEMBER, 1879.

(Before Henry A. Robinson, Esq.)

Mr. Robert Tavener examined.

1. You are Town Clerk of Tanderagee?—Yes.

2. How long have you filled that office?—For about twenty years.

3. Tanderagee is under the **Town Improvement** Act of 1854?—Yes.

4. When was it adopted?—In 1855.

5. Was it adopted for all purposes?—Yes.

6. For lighting, cleansing and watering?—Yes.

7. How was the present boundary adopted?—A Committee was formed to determine what should be the boundaries.

8. Do you know what steps they took to determine the boundaries—to determine what rule they were to strike the rates on?—The Commissioners themselves formed the area and applied to the Lord Lieutenant. Then there was a person sent down here, and he went over the same ground.

9. What had they in view in selecting this boundary?—To choose what they considered represented the district deriving advantage from the town.

10. What is the area of the town?—[illegible] a. [illegible] r. [illegible] p.

11. And the population?—1,500, I think.

12. What is the valuation?—Lands, £2,[illegible] [illegible] and houses, £[illegible]—total, £3,[illegible] [illegible].

13. Is the population, so far as you can tell, increasing or diminishing?—It has increased, I would say. Some years ago it increased by the building of the mills here.

14. And have houses been built for the accommodation of persons engaged at the mills?—Yes.

15. Do you think the census of 1881 will show an increase over that of 1871?—I don't know.

16. Are there any buildings of any other sort going on?—There are just some building operations, but not much.

17. Do you see any tendency to build in any particular direction?—Not much.

18. Is there sufficient land within the present boundary limits, available for some years to come, for building purposes?—Oh, abundance.

19. I suppose the "Castle" and its surroundings occupy a large proportion of the townland upon which the town lies, the Duke of Manchester's estate.

20. Is the whole of the demesne in the municipal boundary?—No; the greater part is.

21. In what electoral division is Tanderagee?—In Tanderagee.

22. If a circle of one mile from the centre of the town is adopted as a boundary, would it be within the electoral division of Tanderagee?—Oh, I am wrong, there is a small portion of [illegible] included. That is to the north-west.

23. Well, if a radius of a mile were taken, how many electoral divisions would be included?—Three or two.

24. How far does the town extend on all sides?—Half a mile.

25. And how many townlands are included entirely, and how many partly within the municipal limits?—There are seven townlands altogether or partly in it.

26. Are you acquainted with the boundary of the electoral division at all?—Well, I know it pretty well.

27. How far does it extend?—From a mile to a mile and a half on either side.

28. And can you tell me the population of it?—No, I don't know that.

29. Do you know the valuation?—No.

30. Have the Commissioners ever had it under their consideration to include the electoral division in the boundary of the town?—Never.

31. Are they aware that the Select Committee of the House of Commons made it a recommendation that as far as possible that should be done—that municipal boundaries should be made coterminous with poor law electoral divisions?—No; I never heard it.

32. Have you a copy of the accounts?—Yes; of last year.

33. What are your total receipts and your total expenditure?—The expenditure last year was £80 5s. 0d., and the receipts £85 3s. 11d.

34. What was the rate for this year?—6d., and 1½d.

35. What have been the rates for the past five years?—In 1874, 7d.; in 1875, 6d.; in 1876, 4d.; in 1877, 6d.; and in 1878, 5d.

36. And one-fourth of that on land?—Yes.

37. What have been the poor rates for the same period?—In 1874, 3d.; in 1875, 2d.; 1876, [illegible] (incl. arrears); 1877, 9d.; 1878, 1s. (3d. arrears).

38. For what purposes were these sanitary rates struck?—For water and cleansing.

39. And what were the constituency districts?—The [illegible] of those townlands, portions of which are now included.

40. Give the names of those townlands?—[illegible], [illegible], [illegible], Derryallen, Ballymore, Tullyhugh, [illegible]. [illegible] is in the electoral division of [illegible], the others are in Tanderagee.

41. Portions of every one of them, as I understand, are in the municipal boundary?—Yes.

42. And if you were to include the whole of them within the municipal boundary what valuation would it give?—I don't know.

43. Not the area?—No.

44. Was the 6d. in 1878 for water only?—Yes.

46. Your principal source of income are the rates, the dog tax, and petty customs?—Yes.

47. What staff have you in the town?—The clerk and a man for cleansing the town.

48. For scavenging?—Yes.

49. Are there any improvements which the Town Commissioners are prevented from carrying out from want of funds?—No; our rates are low, and they will be lower still—they will be only 4d.

50. If the Commissioners had an increased income at their disposal is there anything they would be likely to do for the town, and which is now required?—I don't know of anything.

51. Have the Commissioners ever expressed an opinion as to the desirability or otherwise of becoming the urban sanitary authority?—At first they did, but now they are satisfied with being in the Banbridge Union, and under the Guardians. TANDERAGEE, Sept. 18, 1879. Mr. Robert Troter.

52. Is any improvement of a sanitary nature required?—No.

53. Is the town well sewered?—Yes.

54. And well lighted?—Yes.

55. With lamps?—Yes.

56. How many lamps?—Twenty-five.

57. Costing I suppose about £1 a lamp?—Yes.

58. Between what periods are they lit?—Between September and April.

59. They are not lit through the summer?—No.

60. Now as to the question of extension, have the queries sent down to you been submitted to a meeting of the Board of Commissioners?—Yes; there was a meeting held at which they were considered.

61. When was that?—About the 22nd of November. I don't indeed think the matter was formally considered at a meeting, but I asked all the Commissioners about it.

62. There was no resolution then recorded?—No.

63. But you were desired by the Commissioners to come forward and state that no extension was required?—Quite so.

64. Do you think the Commissioners were unanimously of that opinion?—Yes.

65. And when you filled in the answers to the queries, was it your own individual opinion you expressed, or the view of the Commissioners?—It was the opinion of the Commissioners.

66. Are the Commissioners of opinion that the town of Tanderagee does not confer benefit on the people who reside within reach of say a mile from the centre of the town?—Well, I don't know.

67. Do these people living outside bring in their produce for sale here?—Some do.

68. It is a market town?—Yes. The market, I am sorry to say, has fallen off.

69. I suppose if you were burdened with taxes, you would like to have a large area?—Well, I think the area is large enough.

70. If you became the sanitary authority, would you be satisfied with the present boundary of the town?—I think so.

71. You have never heard any objections to the boundaries, by ratepayers or others?—No.

72. There have been no alterations in these boundaries since they were first decided on?—No. I may say that there are only half a dozen people who live outside the boundary proper.

73. And they don't live outside to evade taxation?—No.

74. Are there any building operations going on outside the town?—No.

75. And none inside?—None, except a couple of houses.

76. Is the town at a stand-still in trade?—Well, I think so; it is rather on the down hill.

77. Would the Commissioners be anxious to have the boundaries increased?—No; they are quite satisfied with them.

78. Are they satisfied with the way the roads are cared within their boundary?—I think so; we always get what we want.

79. You never heard the opinion expressed by the Board that it would be well to have care of the roads?—No, we are satisfied.

80. Would a mile radius take in any gentleman's residences?—No; I don't know that it would.

81. Are you a resident of the town?—Yes.

82. And have been I suppose for a good many years?—Yes, for fifty years.

83. And you are therefore intimately acquainted with it?—Yes.

84. Do you notice any difference now in the general aspect of the town as compared with what it was when

4 A

PORTADOWN. Sept. 24, 1879.

Mr. Robert Trotter.

you knew it first?—Well, I may say the market has gone completely.

85. How do you account for that, is it in consequence of its proximity to Portadown?—Partly, but principally in consequence of the failure of the flax crop. The flax ceased to grow, and there were other markets from which it used to come.

86. Was there, in fact, a more thriving trade then than now?—Yes. The opening of the mill here has given a certain impetus to trade.

87. When was it opened?—About ten years ago.

88. Do the people carrying on business in the town live in the town?—Yes.

89. There are no villa residences?—No.

Mr. J. Hardy.

Mr. J. HARDY, Chairman of the Town Commissioners, examined.

90. How long have you occupied your seat at the Board?—Only since October last.

91. Are you a resident of the town?—Yes.

92. You have heard Mr. Trotter's evidence, do you agree with it?—Yes.

93. He was authorized by you and your brother Commissioners to attend here and state that no alteration of the boundary was required?—Yes.

94. Do you think it would not be advantageous to the town to have a larger area of taxation?—Yes.

95. You think there are sufficient funds at present to enable you to carry on whatever improvements are required?—Yes.

96. You never struck the full rate?—No.

97. You are content to leave matters as at present in the hands of the Guardians?—Yes; I think so.

98. There is no desire, as I understand, to get a separation from the Grand Jury?—No; I think not at present.

99. The Select Committee have recommended that, as far as possible, towns should be made coterminous with Poor Law electoral divisions. The electoral division of Tanderagee extends about a mile and a-half outside. In our report we must show some strong reason for not adopting the electoral division—do you think it would be too large?—Yes, altogether too large.

100. Do you think that people within the electoral division derive exceptional advantages from their proximity to the town?—No; I don't think they do.

101. You think, perhaps, that fifty years ago they might have done so, but not now, in consequence of the altered circumstances as explained by Mr. Trotter?—Exactly.

102. Then, I may take it, you consider the electoral division is out of the question as regards Tanderagee?—Yes.

103. Have you ever had an opportunity of talking to the ratepayers on the subject?—Yes.

104. Are they of opinion that no alteration is necessary?—Yes; all to whom I have spoken are of that opinion.

105. If we thought it necessary to include the entire of townlands now partly included, would that meet with the disapprobation of residents within and without the boundary?—Decidedly.

106. And of the Commissioners?—Yes.

107. Do the Commissioners hold land outside the boundary?—Some do, I think.

108. Do many residents within the town hold land outside?—Well, they have townparks, and the like of that.

109. You agree with Mr. Trotter, that there are no improvements required for the town, and that if there were you are enabled to strike double the rate you do now, to carry them out?—Yes.

The inquiry terminated.

MONAGHAN. Sept. 25, 1879.

Mr. James Mitchell.

MONAGHAN—25TH SEPTEMBER, 1879.

(Before H. A. ROBINSON, Esq.)

Mr. JAMES MITCHELL examined.

1. You are the Town Clerk?—I am.

2. Monaghan is constituted under what statute?—Ninth George IV., chap. 82.

3. What is the area?—67A. 2R. 24P.

4. In the return which you transmitted to us you say 67A. 3R. 8P. How do you account for that discrepancy?—I took down a very few days ago, 67A. 2R. 24P.

5. Then I may take it that the 67A. 2R. 24P. is correct?—Yes.

6. How far does the town extend to the north?—To the end of this street.

7. And on the south?—To the end of the lake near the convent.

8. To the east?—To Roosky hill.

9. And to the west?—To the bridge at Mr. Young's, Kilnacloy.

10. The boundary is well defined?—It is.

11. Is there land within the boundary sufficient for building for some years to come?—No.

12. Is there any tendency to build in any one direction?—Yes.

13. In which direction?—In the north-east.

14. And what class of houses are being built there?—Houses from £10 to £20 valuation.

15. Are these houses occupied by residents in the town?—Yes. There are at present eight new houses. They are not all occupied.

16. Are there any buildings going on inside the town?—Yes.

17. Would you say that the buildings outside the town are carried on from any tendency to avoid municipal taxation, or simply as a matter of convenience?—Merely as a matter of convenience.

17. What is the population of the town?—3,632.

18. Would you, as an inhabitant, say that Monaghan was an increasing town?—I am not prepared to say, but there are not only no houses in the town unoccupied, but building operations are going on rapidly.

19. The valuation of the town is what?—For taxation purposes it is £4,980 10s.

20. You have given us the valuation in one of your answers to these queries as £5,920 10s.?—The entire valuation of the town is £5,970 5s., but there are a number of tenants valued under £5, which are not liable to be taxed under the 9th George IV., cap 82. When these were deducted it left the valuation of the town liable to rates, £4,980 10s.

20. The town is not divided into wards?—No.

21. In what electoral division is the town included?—In Monaghan.

22. The Commissioners are desirous for an extension of the boundary?—They are.

23. If you took for the proposed boundary a radius of a mile from the centre of the town, would you get into another electoral division?—Yes.

24. What electoral division?—Kilmore.

25. How many townlands are wholly included in the present municipal boundary?—None, wholly. But there were four partly.

26. What are these?—Portions of Kilnacloy, part of Mullaghmonaghan, part of Roosky, and part of Tullybrenna.

27. What is the extent of the town included in those portions of the four townlands?—Kilnacloy, the Great Northern Railway Station; Mullaghmonaghan.

[illegible]; and Tedavnet [illegible].

28. Are the fever hospital, the new workhouse, the barracks, Rossmore Lodge, and the buildings on the other side of the railway within the boundary?—No, outside.

29. It is in there, **that the new houses are being built?**—Yes.

30. You **are Clerk of the Union also, I believe?**—Yes.

31. Are you acquainted with the Poor Law electoral division of Monaghan?—Yes.

32. What is the valuation?—It is [illegible].

33. What is the area?—[illegible].

34. How far does the electoral division extend to the north from the centre of the town?—I very [illegible] distance, about half a mile.

35. On the north?—I suppose three miles.

36. And on the east and west?—To the east it would be a mile and a half, and on the west it would extend a mile or more.

37. Were the Commissioners, when they considered the question of extending the boundary, aware of the fact that the Select Committee had recommended that the boundaries should be as far as possible coterminous with the electoral division?—No.

38. I suppose it would be the opinion of your Board that, in the extension of the boundary, this would be impracticable?—Yes.

39. You think it would be injurious to the town?—It would not bring in any additional buildings which would be rated.

40. I suppose the people residing in the electoral division of Monaghan derive, from their proximity to the town of Monaghan, substantial benefit?—I think the town of Monaghan derives benefit from the people living outside. I think those people living outside support the town to a certain extent.

41. For the purposes of a county rate, I understand the whole of the four townlands are taken in?—Yes.

42. And also in the constabulary duties dealt by the Poor Law Commissioners?—Yes.

43. The municipal rates, please?—The municipal rates have been 12d., 9d., and 6d., [illegible] on houses valued at and over £[illegible] on houses valued at £[illegible] and under £[illegible], and the houses valued at £[illegible] and under £[illegible].

44. You have always assessed **the full rate?**—Except last year.

45. When was **it there?—3d., 6½d. and 10d. per** pound.

46. The poor rate, please?—The poor rate in 1878 has been 14d., including a union rate of nine pence, all over.

47. The rates have been in 1874 and 1876, 13d.; 1876, 12d.; 1877, 13d.; and in 1878, 14d.

48. The 1878 rate, that included nine pence, was there any special sanitary work carried out then?—Nothing special.

48. Have the Guardians, within the last ten years, carried out any special sanitary works, such as a sewerage scheme?—Nothing. The only thing was the keeping the town pumps in order.

49. The county cess, please?—The county cess—I am not prepared to say exactly; but from a note I took in the courthouse, I believe it to be in 1878, 2s. 1½d.; 1877, 2s. 6½d.; 1876, 2s. 1½d.; 1875, 2s. 3½d.; and in 1874, 2s. 8d.

50. The markets are held in this town?—They are.

51. Are they held in the streets?—They are.

52. Whereabouts are they held?—All through the streets.

53. Are the fairs held in the town?—Yes.

54. Is Monaghan the principal market town for all the people residing in the electoral division?—Certainly.

55. What is the nearest market town?—The nearest is Ballybay.

56. Are there any markets in Glaslough?—Glaslough is in the County Tyrone.

57. Within a radius of a mile do the people bring in their produce to Monaghan?—The greater portion.

58. Are there schools in the town?—Yes.

59. And the people sending them to the town make use of the town for that purpose?—Yes.

60. Is the town well lighted?—Very well.

61. Is it with gas?—With gas.

62. How many lamps are there?—Sixty-four.

63. Is there any necessity for any other lamps?—The commission who considered that, did not consider so.

64. Are the markets large?—The markets are from eleven o'clock till three or four o'clock generally. When it is a very large market it may be later in the day.

65. Do the country people, who come in to dispose of their produce, make use of the lights of the town?—Not much, the principal portion of the people are all away before the town is lighted.

66. How is the town drained?—It is very well drained.

67. Have there been any drainage works carried out lately?—Not lately.

68. Is there a good supply of water?—Well, very good.

69. From where?—From town pumps.

70. Are there any sanitary inconveniences requiring to be remedied in the town?—I should say there is very little to be complained from time to time. The Commissioners do not feel they have power as to themselves to go outside the boundary.

71. Are there any improvements in the town which the Commissioners are deterred from carrying out from want of funds?—I am not prepared to say.

72. Have the Commissioners considered the question of becoming the sanitary authority?—They have.

73. Have they applied for a provisional order?—They have.

74. Are they also likely to consider the question of becoming the authority over the roads?—They are.

75. Are you aware that the Select Committee recommended the opinion that each town, as far as possible, should be under one undivided authority?—I think the Commissioners would be the best authority to do everything about the town.

76. Is that the feeling of your Board?—I believe it would be.

77. Now, with reference to the question of extension. We sent these queries to you; were they considered at a general meeting of the Board?—I think they were, we considered it in general meeting.

78. Did you reply to them as directed by the Board?—I asked them considering them.

79. Are those the views of your Commissioners?—"The Town Commissioners would be desirous to extend the boundaries, on the north side of the town, so as to take in new houses, the owners and occupiers being anxious to avail themselves of the provisions of 9 Geo. IV., cap. 82." Is that the view of your Board?—Yes. The matter has been discussed about bringing certain houses under assessment.

80. Was there any resolution passed on the subject?—Yes.

81. Will you give me that resolution, please?—I cannot tell you at present.

82. Will you send me a copy of it?—Yes.

83. The Commissioners are in favour of the extension of the boundary?—Yes.

84. In which direction?—To the north side.

85. Do they propose to take in the barracks and the new workhouse?—They must, if they go in that direction.

86. Had they any maps before them specifying the proposed extension?—No.

87. What was their reason for making the proposed extension?—Well, I think the first thing that was done was, application was made by the proprietors of these houses here.

MONAGHAN. Sept. 26, 18[illegible]

Mr. James Mitchell.

87. Who wished to have his houses lighted?—Yes; and he wanted to have the scavenger working the length.

88. The district you wish to bring in, is it thickly populated?—About the lower end. This is all covered with water at present. (Witness here pointed to a district on the map.)

89. Can you point me out the district you propose to include?—Yes. That road running along there, beyond Rossmore Lodge up to the Asylum Bridge, and to the turn at Tully, to take in the Mall-road and the ground inside that boundary.

90. Mr. William Swan, Commissioner.—The postal delivery extends at present as far as Rossmore Lodge.

Examination resumed.

91. Have you considered, Mr. Mitchell, what the increased valuation would be?—Well, it would be between £280 and £290 a year; of course the public buildings, if included, would make it a good deal more. I do not include the barracks or the union workhouse.

92. Do you bring in the asylum?—We do.

93. Have you gone into any calculation as to what the area, and the income produced by this proposed extension would be?—I have not.

94. Have the Commissioners entertained the question at all?—They have not, no.

95. Have you lived in the town of Monaghan any length of time?—Yes.

96. Do you see a great tendency to increase in the buildings of the town?—Yes, there is a vast difference from the time I came to the town first.

96. How long ago is that?—Forty years.

97. In what was the difference?—A great many houses have been rebuilt, and old thatched houses have been removed. Now there is not more than one or two thatched houses in the town.

98. Do I understand you to say that the people whom you propose to include in the boundary, are in favour of being included?—Yes; the landlord is.

99. Is the landlord aware that the Select Committee recommended that the municipal rates should be assessed half on the landlord and half on the tenant?—I do not know.

100. Suppose he was not, do you think he would be favourable?—I am not aware. (Witness here pointed out on the map the several districts to be taken in by the proposed extension.)

101. When do you expect to become the sanitary authority?—Next season.

102. Are there any special improvements you require?—Well, the Commissioners wish to have the control in their own hands of the sanitary work which they have not at present, but they have not taken into consideration any further improvements.

103. You will be taking the rate off a smaller area than the Guardians at present?—Certainly, so far as the water is concerned.

104. Have the Commissioners ever expressed an opinion as to adopting the provisions of the Towns Improvement Act?—No; it was brought before the Board, and they objected to it, at least a majority did.

105. Then you cannot strike a one-fourth rate, as they do under the Towns Improvement Act?—No.

106. Was there any special meeting of the inhabitants called, to consider this question of the extension of the boundary?—No; not that I am aware of.

Col. James Lloyd.

Colonel James Lloyd examined.

107. You have heard the opinions expressed by the Town Clerk. Do you agree that there should be an extension of the boundary?—I think it is absolutely necessary.

108. Would you go in for any further extension?—Only with regard to the Mall road and Rossmore Lodge.

109. Taking into consideration the question that you are likely to become the sanitary authority would it not be necessary to have a larger area than this?—No, I think not.

110. They simply wish to include all the buildings that are lying outside?—Yes.

111. I understand that the buildings are not built outside to avoid taxation but merely as a matter of convenience?—Yes, as a matter of convenience.

112. In your opinion would it be advisable to adopt the Towns Improvement Act?—I think it is doubtful. At one time I considered it would be for the benefit of the locality and I brought the matter forward, but the Board seemed to think not.

113. Was this matter also brought before the ratepayers in any way—the question of the extension of the boundary?—No.

113. I may take it no one objects?—I think no one objects.

114. This seems to have been done at the instance of the landlord?—Of the landlord.

115. You have known Monaghan for a lengthened time?—For over twenty years.

116. Do you think it is an improving town?—Yes.

117. The people within a distance of one mile have an advantage from their proximity to the town?—Yes.

118. It is the market town for an area of at least five miles round.

119. Would you think the municipal rates being equally assessed on landlord and tenant satisfactory?—I think it would be satisfactory.

120. Is the land lying close to the town the more valuable?—Certainly.

121. Portions of the land outside the boundary are town parks?—Yes, within a certain area.

122. What are the relative values of the lands?—The townparks were let from £2 to £3 an acre and the land outside them from 14s. to 20s. an acre.

123. The holders of townparks derive advantage from their proximity to the town?—Yes.

124. I suppose the town is well lighted all over?—Yes.

125. The increase of funds arising from the extension, will it be applied to lighting this district up here?—(pointing to a district on the map) Yes, that is the principal object of the extension.

126. In your opinion would it be desirable if the town would get separation from the Grand Jury?—I think so.

127. Do you think it would be desirable that the town should be under one undivided authority?—Yes.

128. Do you think the Grand Jury gave you value for what you paid?—Yes.

129. But you think it would be better to have a separation?—Yes.

Mr. William Swan.

Mr. William Swan examined.

130. Mr. Swan you are a Commissioner?—Yes.

131. You have heard the views expressed by Colonel Lloyd, and the Town Clerk?—Yes.

132. I may take it that you corroborate the opinions expressed?—Yes.

133. Have you ever heard of any objection to the proposed extension of the boundaries?—No.

134. I take it it is your opinion that the management of the town would be better under one undivided authority?—I think so.

135. Are the roads leading into the town well kept up by the Grand Jury?—There have been complaints made about them.

136. Do you think if the Commissioners had the

[illegible] of them, they would [illegible]?—[illegible] in their [illegible] [illegible].

137. The [illegible] Commissioners have recommended that the [illegible] should be equally [illegible] on the landlord and tenant; do you think that a fair distribution?—I think so. I think the tenants would agree to that. When [illegible] [illegible], who [illegible] the landlord, agrees, I don't see why we should not agree.

138. Have you got any land outside the present boundary [illegible] [illegible] of [illegible] under Lord [illegible]. [illegible] [illegible] [illegible]. Sir William [illegible].

Dr. [illegible] examined. Dr. [illegible].

139. Do you wish to make any [illegible]?—I [illegible] [illegible] [illegible] the general feeling of the [illegible] that both the residents and [illegible] [illegible] [illegible]. It would [illegible] very much to the prosperity of the town if they were [illegible]. [illegible] [illegible] [illegible] [illegible] [illegible] [illegible] [illegible] [illegible] [illegible] [illegible]. I think they should be [illegible].

140. The Commissioners.—I [illegible] [illegible] [illegible] [illegible], but I [illegible] I quite agree with you.

Mr. Richard J. [illegible], Commissioner, examined. Mr. Richard J. [illegible].

141. Do you corroborate what Mr. Mitchell and the other witnesses have said?—I think the Commissioners are unanimous with regard to the question of extension. That is all I wish to say.

Mr. Thomas Cunningham.—I think the people have not had an opportunity of expressing their opinion on the subject of extension.

142. Were they aware that the Commission would sit to-day?—I cannot say.

Well, we had it advertised in all the papers.

Mr. [illegible] [illegible].—There was a [illegible] made by the Town Clerk, [illegible] [illegible] of the [illegible] was not [illegible]. The [illegible] of that is that they are not [illegible]. I know very well that they are already engaged as soon as they are [illegible].

143. The Commissioners.—Mr. Cunningham, do you think if the ratepayers had had an opportunity of expressing their views they would have expressed an opinion against the extension?—I think not.

The inquiry then closed.

NEWRY—MONDAY, JULY 26, 1879.

(Before Mr. C. P. Cotton and Mr. H. A. Robinson).

Mr. Robert H. Doherty, Town Clerk, examined.

Newry. July 28, 1879. Mr. Robert H. Doherty.

1. Mr. Cotton.—You are Town Clerk of Newry?—I am.

2. Newry is, I believe, under a special Act?—Yes.

3. And also under the Towns Improvement Act?—Under the Towns Improvement Act, and also a special Act of 1871—the Newry Improvements and Water Act of 1871—the 34 and 35 Victoria, chapter 192.

4. What is the area of the town?—The area of the town is 711a. 2r. 4p.

5. Was that area fixed by the special Act?—No, sir, it was fixed by the Act of 1854—the Towns Improvement Act.

6. When was the Towns Improvement Act adopted?—In 1853.

7. Was it adopted wholly or in part?—Wholly.

8. Have you got a description of the boundary, or have you got a map showing the boundary?—The town surveyor has marked out the boundary on the map.

9. What is the population of Newry?—The population last census was 14,078 within the municipal boundary.

10. And is that increasing?—I consider it is largely increasing; it has very largely increased within the last twelve years.

11. What has been the extent of the increase?—I will say there are 16,000 inhabitants at present.

12. Mr. Robinson.—Was that the population in 1861?—There is a difficulty about that. The census of 1861 embraces the whole of the parliamentary boundary, and that is a very large area, 3,803 acres, and it did not distinguish the population within the municipal boundary. The population of the town has increased from 1861 to 1871.

13. Was Newry under any municipal government before 1853?—It was under the 9th of George IV.

14. Mr. Cotton.—Do you think the boundary under the 9th of George IV. was much the same as the parliamentary boundary?—No, it was not. The boundary under the 9th of George IV. was very ill-defined. It was for lighting and cleansing. I was not connected with the Commissioners then, but I know this historically. But for census purposes the whole parliamentary boundary was taken in. It made a difference of some 800 or 900 against the town in 1871, or upwards of 1,000.

15. You have no map showing the boundary under the 9th of George IV.?—I don't think there was such a thing in existence at all; I am not aware of it.

16. Have you got the minute books of that period, the time of George IV.?—Yes; I have the minute books.

17. When was the town put under the 9th of George IV.?—It was one of the earliest towns put under that Act in Ireland. In fact the 9th of George IV. was specially originated for Newry. It was introduced for the town of Newry as a local Act, and was afterwards taken by the Government, and adopted for the whole of Ireland. Newry was one of the first towns that adopted the 9th of George IV.

18. Have you got the first volume of minutes under the 9th of George IV.?—I believe I have.

19. Would you kindly look for it by-and-by?—I will.

20. What is the valuation of the town?—The present valuation is £30,468 2s.

21. And is that increasing year by year?—It is, sir. It has largely increased.

22. Can you give me any previous valuation of late years—say 1874?—The valuation has been going up since 1853, at the rate of from £700 to £800 a year.

23. What was it in 1865?—Something like £24,000; in 1871 it was £28,000 odd.

24. Is building increasing?—Largely increasing.

25. Specially in any one direction?—No, sir; principally filling up vacancies through the town.

26. And not extending the town out through suburbs?—It is not.

27. And not extending in any one direction?—No, sir; except in the case of some villas immediately adjoining the town, but to a very slight extent.

28. There is no tendency to extend beyond the pre-

NEWRY.
July 30, 1878.
———
Mr. Robert E. Dowdall.

west boundary?—No, not at present, sir. The principal reason for that is that leases are difficult to get, and the principal portions of the property are in townships. The custom of the Kilmorey property gives leases for thirty-one years for building purposes and twenty-one years for agricultural leases.

29. The town is divided into three wards?—Yes.

30. What are they called?—The North, South, and West.

31. Can you divide the valuation and the population of these wards at all for me?—Well, I might. The valuation of the county Armagh side of the town, which comprises the West Ward, is something like £2,800 at the least.

32. Is the West Ward wholly in Armagh?—None of the North and South; the North and South are in the town.

33. Can you give me any particulars about the West Ward?—The West Ward valuation is some £3,800.

34. Do you know anything about the population?—5,800 it was in round numbers. It has increased since, I should say.

35. Have you any idea of the area of the West Ward?—The area is 26a. 1r. 17p.

36. Can you tell me how many voters there are in the West Ward?—In the West Ward for municipal purposes there are 151 voters.

37. Can you give me the same particulars regarding the North and South Wards?—The North and South, you will have to take the two combined.

38. Well, give it to me in that way.—The North and South Wards combined have an area of 337a. 3r. 32p.

39. Can you separate the population of the wards?—The population is much larger on the Down side than on the Armagh side.

40. Can you separate the population of the North and South Wards?—The population of the wards has been put down at 6,500 and 5,000.

41. 6,500 in the two wards together?—Yes, sir; that was in 1871.

42. And the valuation of the two wards would be about £17,000?—The valuation of the two wards is £17,398.

43. And the number of voters for the North Ward?—577.

44. And for the South Ward?—334.

45. How many Commissioners are there?—Eighteen.

46. That is six to each ward?—Yes, six to each ward.

47. Out of the 14,000 voters, how many are qualified to be Commissioners?—About 250, as well as I can make out, seventy in the West Ward, ninety-eight in the North, and ninety in the South Ward.

48. That is 258?—Yes, sir, 258.

49. When were the wards divided?—In 1853 at the time of the introduction of the Towns Improvement Act into this town.

50. What electoral division or divisions is the town in?—The West Ward is in the electoral division of Ballybot.

51. And Newry?—The North and South Wards are in the electoral division of Newry.

52. I suppose both electoral divisions run very much further than the town boundary?—Yes. The west, or Ballybot, runs in a line nearly four Irish miles and the south three English miles, as far as I can learn.

53. And how far does the Newry division run?—The Newry division runs about three miles from the centre of the town.

54. Are there any wards for poor law purposes?—No, sir; nothing only the two electoral divisions.

55. Can you give me the municipal rates, please?—The municipal rate is 3s. in the pound.

56. That includes county cess?—No. The borough rate in 1874 was 1s. 6d.; in 1875, 1s. 3d.; in 1876, 1s.; in 1877, 1s.; and in 1878, 1s. 6d.

57. The Town Commissioners are the road authority?—Yes, sir.

58. They have control over the roads?—Yes.

59. Is that under any special Act?—Yes, under a special Act for lighting purposes, &c.

60. What do they contribute to the county at the present time, of the county charge, for lunatic asylum, and so forth?—£1,[illegible].

61. On what scale?—A proportionate sum on the whole county. The valuation of the townlands in the valuation of the county.

62. That is the valuation of Newry to the valuation of the county?—Yes, the one as to the other.

(At this stage Mr. Henry, town surveyor, handed in a map to the Commissioners, showing the boundary as defined in the Newry when the town was put under the Towns Improvement Act.)

Examination of Mr. Dowdall resumed.

63. Mr. Cotton.—Then you pay your share in the county expenses?—Yes, we are to contribute to the costs of extra and assistant [illegible] salaries.

64. That is an [illegible] including the [illegible] county?—It does, sir.

65. What is the contribution to the county at present?—About 1½d. in the pound.

66. For two years?—Yes.

67. And what was your contribution to the county in 1877?—Do you mean the entire sum, sir?

68. No. How much in the pound?—About 2d. and a fraction. The sum in 1877 was a fraction over 2d. in the pound.

69. Have the Commissioners had these [illegible] before them?—They have.

70. Did they come to any resolution?—They did not come to any resolution on the subject, they left the matter in the hands of the Town Chairman and myself to express their opinion.

71. And you have no instructions to [illegible] instructions?—Yes.

72. As a matter of fact is it the wish of the Commissioners that there should be any alteration whatever in the present boundary?—They are desirous of having an extension of the boundary.

73. Was the question of the extension of the whole town discussed?—It was merely discussed.

74. So far as you know, there is no dissatisfaction with the present arrangement?—Well, I would not like to say that.

75. The Commissioners have never said anything about it beyond?—No, sir. They have never said anything about it themselves. There is some dissatisfaction in the townships. There is one square, known as the [illegible], a very awkward arrangement; it is not quite a square.

76. Mr. Robinson.—What square is that?—It is Market-square.

77. Mr. Cotton.—Has any change been made since?—There has been no change valued or otherwise that I am aware of. I understand that it was done to get the valuation of one of the wards. There is a difference of over a thousand pounds in the valuation of the North and South wards.

78. Can you separate the valuation of those—you have already given them in bulk?—The valuation of the North ward is £7,443 10s., and of the South ward £9,111 10s.

79. You gave me the two together at £17,398?—No, the three came to that sum.

80. No; the whole three amount to £20,[illegible]—£17,093 what I gave you as the amount of the two together.

81. £17,398 you gave me as the valuation of the two wards together?—I said that in round numbers the valuation of the North ward was £8,800; South, £8,500; West, £3,800; that is £20,000 for the whole town. There is a difference of over £1,700.

82. How much do you make them?—The entire Down side is £16,800.

83. Take them separately?—The North ward, £7,183 5s.

84. How much for the South ward?—£9,111 15s.

85. The West?—£13,108 5s.

86. That is £900 less than the present valuation?—Well, sir, that has increased between 1876, and the present year's rating, the summary I have been using was one that was made out for Mr. Lawless, when he held his inquiry here in connexion with the Local Government and Taxation of Towns Commission.

87. Mr. Cotton.—In fact the valuation you have given me for the wards is that of 1876, and the valuation of the whole town you have given me is for 1879?—Yes. The summary was made out for Mr. Lawless's inquiry, and it would be some difficulty to go into the matter again.

88. So that you gave me the valuation as £30,403 5s.?—Yes.

89. For 1876?—No, for 1879. That is the rate we are at present collecting.

90. Then the town has gone up £900 in the valuation in one year?—It has, sir.

91. That is all right; I understand now. How is the town lighted?—With gas.

92. Do the Commissioners own the gasworks?—The Commissioners have owned them since the 1st of January last.

93. And the water—is there a large water supply?—Yes; the water supply is also under the control of the Commissioners.

94. It is a very large scheme?—It is a very large scheme.

95. The supply is 833,000 gallons a day?—Yes.

96. Has there been any expression of opinion on the part of the ratepayers, independently of the Commissioners, as to whether or not any alteration should be made in the boundaries?—There has not, sir.

97. And you have heard no expression of opinion from people living in places adjoining the township as to whether they would wish to be brought in [illegible], sir.

98. Mr. [illegible].—Was the question ever brought before the ratepayers in any way?—Well it was.

99. Was any meeting convened?—Well, I [illegible] the meeting [illegible] and it was talked of generally [illegible] and it was published in the ordinary proceedings of the Board.

100. [illegible]

101. [illegible]

102. [illegible]

103. [illegible]

104. [illegible]

105. [illegible]

106. [illegible]

107. [illegible]

108. [illegible]

109. Mr. Cotton.—We have no [illegible] with the [illegible].

Mr. James Francis [illegible] examined.

110. Mr. Cotton.—You are the Chairman of the Town Commissioners?—I am.

111. How long have you occupied the position?—I was the last appointed.

112. For three years?—No; for one year.

113. How long are you a Commissioner?—I am a Commissioner since 1866.

114. There is no wish, on the part of the Commissioners, to have any extension or alteration of the boundary whatever?—I communicated with several of them, and they all agreed that there should not be any change.

115. And that is your opinion too?—Yes; that is my opinion. I do not see any object in making the change, and several ratepayers agree in the same view.

116. And do you think there is no necessity or desirability to change the wards in any way?—I think not, I think they work very well.

117. Can you tell me what guided the original framers of the area of the municipality?—I really could not give you any information as regards that.

118. Did you assist in forming the township?—I did not.

119. Is there any tendency as to building about the town in either villas or otherwise?—Not at present. Mr. Doherty mentioned that the building consisted of filling up vacancies through the town. Perhaps there are one or two cases where building is not extending out, and one difficulty is that of obtaining extended leases. I suppose it is due to that in great measure; but the facts are that it is not extending in that way.

120. Mr. Rennell?—Are you a poor law guardian?—I am.

121. Of the Newry Union?—Yes.

122. Are you acquainted with the electoral divisions of Newry?—I am not.

123. Do you think the land within the Newry electoral division is more valuable from its proximity to the town?—No doubt about it.

124. And the people living in it come in and make use of the streets of the town, and use the town for market purposes?—Yes; no doubt.

125. And are you of opinion that for the use they make of the town they should be made to contribute to the municipal rates?—Well, I think we do not require that. I think it would be reasonable, probably; but any further taxation would not be desirable.

126. Do you think it would be possible to adopt the electoral division boundary of Newry as the boundary of the town?—I think it would not be possible for the people in the vicinity of the town; if it were adopted, the electoral division would not probably pay as much as they actually pay at present, because they would then be free of county cess, and that would not incur much more expense to them. Probably it would be about the same as at present.

127. Mr. Cotton.—It would be no benefit to them?—Little or nothing.

128. Do you think the electoral divisions—the two of them would be too large to form a township out of?—I think they would. I think it would not be wise at present to make any alteration.

129. Would there be any object in bringing the union workhouse, and the district about there, within the boundary of the town?—I do not think there would.

130. In some places we find they wish to take in the workhouse in order to bring it under the authority of the borough magistrates?—Well, we have a Bench

NEWRY, July 21, 1870.

Mr. James F. Erskine.

him to have authority over them. We sit once a week here, and take all such cases as may come before us.

130. Mr. ROBINSON.—Do you know the valuation of the electoral division?—I do not. We should have had the Clerk of the Union here. We gave him notice to come.

Mr. James Fagan.

Mr. JAMES FAGAN examined.

131. Mr. COTTON.—You are a member of the Town Commissioners?—I am.

132. Were you a Commissioner when the Act of the 9th Geo. IV. was first adopted for Newry?—I was not.

133. Were you a Commissioner at the time the Act was adopted in 1860?—I was.

134. Did you take any part in having the town put under the Towns Improvement Act?—I did.

135. Did you take any part in striking out the boundaries then adopted?—I did.

136. Can you give me any idea as to what principle guided you in that?—We were very much guided by the houses that were outside regular streets, to see whether it would be worth while to bring them in or not; and we took old fences for our limits. We did not cut through any fields whatever; we took either streets or old fences.

137. In some directions, I see you stretched a great deal more than others; for instance, in the north-west you have gone half a mile beyond any building according to this map—beyond the union workhouse?—North of the union workhouse. We don't take in the union workhouse at all.

138. You left it out, but you went north of it into the country a great distance?—Not very far.

139. I suppose what guided you was to take in all the land built upon or likely to be built upon?—And we did.

140. But you do not consider it should extend beyond that?—We do not. It would be no advantage to the town to have it extended further; quite the contrary, for there is no prospect whatever of any houses being built outside the present municipal boundary for some years.

141. Then you have no wish for an extension in the present boundary?—I think there should be none.

142. With regard to the wards, do you think they are in a satisfactory condition?—I think they are. The only thing I would suggest would be to put in a block off Hill-street. It is just for uniformity sake. You could run down the boundary from the North to the South ward from Needham-bridge.

143. From Margaret-street to Market-street ought to be thrown into a different ward?—Yes.

144. What ward is it in now?—The North.

145. Do you think it should be put into the South?—Yes.

146. On what ground?—On the ground that there is more in the South than in the North. I believe that the first Chairman, under the Act of 1834, resided in that, and it was more out of compliment to him that the arrangement was made as it now exists, because he took a great deal of trouble in getting the Act introduced here; so that when they left him in the North ward it was at his own special request.

147. What difference does it make?—Not much. Instead of having it going along Hill-street, you would have it going down Margaret-street to the Needham-bridge.

148. There is no difference whatever, except that it would be a more natural division?—Yes.

149. It is not for the sake of utilizing the valuation of the property or anything of that sort?—Not at all. I may mention there are a great deal of new buildings erected during the last two years, in the North ward, particularly in Sandy's-street close by here, that will increase the valuation of the North ward; and there have been some new buildings erected in Church-street, in the North ward. I think two new houses have been erected there.

150. There are new buildings erected in Church-street, off Pound-street?—Church-street they are in.

151. Pound-street is an extension of Church-street?—A continuation of Church-street.

152. These buildings go out to the very limit of the town?—They do not.

153. They are shown on the map as?—They are between Cowramount and High-street. I think there were one or two erected there, but they are not very good.

154. They are not anything to induce you to go out along that road any farther?—Not at all. I may mention that a great deal better fields outside the boundary are townparks, and there is not a great prospect of any buildings being erected upon them, particularly because, as I said before, the leases are against building.

155. And the occupiers of the townparks reside in the town?—Yes.

156. And are ratepayers?—Yes; ratepayers.

157. So that it would not increase the number of ratepayers to make a moderate extension outside the town?—I think not.

158. Have you any other improvements which the Commissioners would carry out if they had means?—We want more drainage. We have done a great deal of drainage, but we want more.

159. Mr. ROBINSON.—If you included the two electoral divisions do you think the area of taxation would be sufficient to meet this difficulty?—I think it would.

160. Do you think it would be desirable?—I think it would. We want to borrow money to make the drainage, and the two electoral divisions would be sufficient to pay the money to the Government, and the interest, if they give us the money.

161. Mr. COTTON.—I do not understand you to advocate an increase of the town to the size of the two electoral divisions?—Oh, not at all. I may mention also, that the greater portion of the building for manufacturing purposes is taking place in the West Ward.

162. In the West Ward the number has increased?—Yes; there are a great many mills erected there within the past two years.

163. Has the opening of the docks at Greenore had any effect on it?—Not yet. A great deal of our merchants live in Rostrevor and Warrenpoint. A large number of merchants go down there; and that is one reason why there are not many villas erected in the town. They go down there for the sake of the sea bathing.

Mr. John K. Todd.

Mr. JOHN K. TODD examined.

164. Mr. COTTON.—You have heard what was said by the Chairman of the Town Commissioners—do you agree with the views he has expressed?—I do; I agree with every word said by Mr. Erskine and Mr. Fay. It would be perfectly absurd to think of including the electoral division of Newry. It extends miles out into the country—on the north side four Irish miles and nearly three Irish miles on the west side. It goes away to Bessbrook.

165. Well, you see that a Committee of the House

[illegible] expressed an opinion that, in dealing with this question, care should be taken to make municipal wards conterminous with wards for Poor Law purposes, and towns with Poor Law electoral divisions, so that we have to inquire into the question in each case, whether it is desirable or not?—I think it would be absurd in this case; I think it would be out of the question altogether. Messrs. [illegible], Mr. John K. [illegible]

Mr. Thomas [illegible] examined. Mr. Thomas [illegible]

166. Mr. Cotton.—You are a Town Commissioner?—Yes.

167. It has been stated here by the Chairman of the Commissioners that the general feeling is that no alteration whatever is desirable of the present boundaries—do you agree in that?—Yes, I don't see any change that could be made at present.

168. Do you think there should be any alteration where the wards lie [illegible]?—I think not. If the electoral boundary was changed in some way, but I don't think you are going to interfere with that.

169. Do you mean the parliamentary boundary?—Yes.

170. We have nothing to say to that?—I have heard no complaint about the borough boundary.

171. Mr. Robinson.—Were you a Commissioner when the town was put under the Act of 1848?—Yes.

172. Have you any idea what was the boundary of the town under the 9th of George IV.—whether it was larger than the present limits?—Under the 9th of George IV. it only took in the best houses where they were built. They collected only 6d. in the pound on houses rated under £10, and that would not pay much for either cleansing or lighting. There was a local valuation which the Commissioners had under the 9th of George IV., and when the Government valuation came in it knocked it all to pieces.

Mr. [illegible] examined. Mr. [illegible]

173. Mr. Cotton.—You are the Borough Surveyor?—Yes, I am.

174. The town is supplied with water under a special Act?—Under the Newry Borough Improvement Act.

175. Can you give me any idea where the waterworks are?—There was originally a supply of water [illegible] two small reservoirs.

176. Those are situated on the Ouleaera [illegible]?—Yes. In 1871 there was an Act got for the purpose of the borough improvement and water, and the Camlough lake was [illegible] and the drainage area [illegible] very nearly doubled.

177. How far is Camlough lake from the town?—A little under four English miles from the town—about three and three quarter English miles.

178. And what is the supply now?—The Town Commissioners didn't carry out the works themselves. They paid a sum of £12,000 to a company, or [illegible] who were called the Camlough Waterworks Trust, and they carried out the works. They were bound to make a dam, lay pipes from the lake into the town, and construct a small service reservoir, and to supply daily 535,000 gallons, and maintain the works in [illegible] and so on.

179. Is that 535,000 gallons supplied now?—Yes, it is.

180. Is that for domestic purposes?—They are only bound to deliver that quantity for the Commissioners into the [illegible] reservoir, and they can do what they like after that, and for that the Commissioners paid the trustees the sum of £12,000, which did not cover the cost of the whole of the works of the town.

181. This £12,000 was raised by the town on loan?—Yes.

182. Is it being paid off?—Yes.

183. By sinking fund?—Yes.

184. At what rate?—Fourpence including, I think. There were other loans for [illegible] and so on, and this £12,000 was part of them. I may mention that 535,000 gallons is the daily supply of water.

185. In what state is the sewerage of the town?—There has been a great deal of money expended on it, and if we get the loan of £2,500 we contemplate making a main sewer to run up [illegible]-street, and [illegible]-street, and then, with other branch sewers, this side of the town will be perfect. There is a large open drain which must be covered, because at present it is more or less of a nuisance in dry weather.

186. Besides this £2,500 do you contemplate any other expenditure?—The £2,500 is for the county Down side of the town. We have been laying out about £150 or more every year on drainage, and we calculate that the interest on that £2,500 to the Board of Works would be saved, and that we should not expend more than that £150. If we borrowed that £2,500 at a low rate, that £150 a year would more than pay the interest upon it and pay it off, and we need not go into any large expense. We have not increased the expenses, because we have at present been laying out £150 a year, and that would more than cover the interest and sinking fund.

187. How many miles of roads and streets are there?—Eleven miles.

188. What is the cost of road maintenance per mile to maintain them all [illegible]?—We, we break the stone; we have a stone breaker and several workmen.

189. And I suppose a large proportion of that eleven miles is country roads?—There are five of these outside the town boundary, but there is very heavy traffic through the central streets of the town. They are mostly laid [illegible]. There are five and a half miles of streets, mostly paved, over which has heavy traffic—main streets in the mills, railway, and canal.

190. Do you think it beneficial that the Commissioners should be the road authority?—I think so. I think the county cess will be something over 1s. in the pound, and we do not expend 1s. on the roads.

191. It used to be 1s.?—Yes.

192. Can you tell me what the maintenance of the main roads is?—About £150 a year on the average for point of the roads, but we lay out other money in lighting and [illegible].

193. Previously you paid a sum of £10,[illegible]?—Yes.

194. It was in 1871 you became the road authority?—Yes; I was not surveyor until 1875.

195. You don't know what the Grand Jury did before that in the way of town works?—They did expend some money on drainage in the County Down side. I live on the County Armagh side, and the streets were also under contract with different road contractors for the streets, and the same contract had not expired when I took charge of the County Armagh side, and I was very glad to take them up.

196. You think the roads come to ——?—Between £700 and £800 at the outside.

197. Were you resident in Newry before 1871?—I was.

198. Do you think they are better kept now than before?—Yes.

Newry. July 22, 1878. Mr. Joseph [illegible]

199. In these [illegible] observations that occur to you as to the boundaries, whether they should be altered at all or not?—Well, no; I would not alter them from an engineering point of view. We do not want any extension of the boundary so far as sewerage is concerned.

200. Are any of your streets laid out so as to benefit any extent of country beyond the boundary [illegible]?—No; the only [illegible] [illegible] is [illegible] a house which has been rated. There are no houses outside the boundary [illegible], perhaps, half a dozen [illegible]. I [illegible] close to it.

201. And does the gas-lighting extend to the boundary in all roads along the [illegible]?—In all the streets it does. There are a couple of suburban roads where it does not extend.

202. But those suburban roads are not built on?—Not built on. There are one or two small [illegible] houses on back roads, but wherever it is crossed by a number of houses it [illegible].

203. The whole of the town is fairly lit?—Yes; [illegible] they are putting up a [illegible] lamps. This year they are improving the lighting of the town. The Commissioners have only had charge of the gas works since the beginning of the year. There were [illegible] lamps and they are putting up eighty more now.

204. What is the charge to private consumers for gas?—5s.—4s. 6d. up to the 1st of July; 4s. 6d. per 1,000. We contemplate a reduction in the price as soon as we get into working order. In reference to the water, I may remark that we are consuming that [illegible] gallons; we are wasting it.

205. That is something more than forty gallons a head?—Yes.

206. Does that include water for manufacturing purposes?—Yes.

207. How much of that quantity would you put as going to manufactures?—Well, I think that the special supplies come to something about £400 a year, or something near it.

208. What rate do you charge manufacturers?—It depends; from 1s. a thousand down to 6d., and the railway company have a special rate on account of large consumption.

209. Taking away all that, how much would it leave—thirty gallons a head?—There is a great deal of waste, there is no question about that.

210. It would take about twenty gallons for the consumption?—Twenty gallons would be about the consumption, and there is nearly as much more going to waste.

The inquiry then closed.

Templemore. March 18, 1879. Mr. G. C. Fitzgerald.

TEMPLEMORE—18TH MARCH, 1879.

(Before Mr. C. P. Cotton, C.E.)

Mr. G. C. Fitzgerald, J.P., examined.

1. I appear at the request of Sir John Carden, who regrets very much he is unable to wait upon you for the purpose of opposing any extension which would include his mansion house. He asked me because I believe I am the only survivor of the first board who were incorporated under the Act in Templemore [illegible] Sir John Craven Carden, [illegible], to state his objections to the proposed extension of the boundary. It was within my own knowledge, for I was a party to the arrangement. Sir John Carden, [illegible] the same reasons of which I [illegible], opposed the introduction of the Act, but finding that the great majority of the ratepayers were in favour of the Act, he yielded, but on the understanding that his mansion house was not to be included within the area of taxation. I was a party to that as one of the first Commissioners; Sir John as proprietor of the town gave consent on the condition that the body of which I speak would never take any step that would include his mansion house, or render it liable to be taxed. That is within my own knowledge, and therefore I speak of it as a fact; I was a party to the arrangement, and I was the person who carried on the communications at the time with Mr. Bell [illegible] who was then superintendent of valuation. I learned from Sir John, that the town has been twice extended since that period, but in no case was it contemplated to include his house. He never would have given his [illegible] to the introduction of the Act, and [illegible] would have been fatal, but for this arrangement, and therefore if any proposal be made to the Commissioners to include his demesne, it would involve a breach of the arrangement that was honourably entered into with him by the board who were the predecessors of the existing town Commissioners, and he asked me to hand you this letter (produced), regretting at the same time that he was prevented by circumstances from waiting upon you. This is a copy of some minutes he refers to in his letter.

2. Does he wish them to be put in evidence?—I fancy so; certainly.

"Templemore Abbey,
March 12th, 1879.

"Gentlemen,—I regret that circumstances prevent me from attending before you to oppose any extension of the boundaries of the township of Templemore; I however beg to lay before you a copy of the minutes of a meeting held by the Town Commissioners on the 6th July, 1868. You will [illegible] that you have the power to recommend the alteration of any agreement previously made; but I [illegible] that had I opposed the formation of the town commissioners, I could have done so by a large majority. It may be said by some that I [illegible] in the town of Templemore, and I should pay accordingly; but I [illegible]. [illegible]

"I am, gentlemen, yours obediently,
John Craven Carden.

"To the Municipal Boundaries Commissioners."

"Templemore, [illegible] March, 1879.

"Sir John C. Carden, Bart.

"Sir,—[illegible] of a [illegible] meeting held by the Commissioners on the 6th July, 1868.—John Kennedy, Esq., Chairman, [illegible] Martin, J. Connolly, O'Meara, Bergin, Ryan, Bohan and Glass.

"Extension of Boundary.

"In pursuance of notice given at last meeting by Mr. V. O'Meara, moved 'That the boundary of the township be extended so that same will run in a straight line from the [illegible] Lodge to [illegible] cross-road, thence to [illegible] Lodge, thence [illegible] through [illegible] to the [illegible] at [illegible], thence [illegible] to the present boundary at [illegible], all as [illegible] in the Commissioners' [illegible], and that in making this [illegible] the residence of Sir John Carden, should be [illegible] exempted, when the boundary of the township was originally formed, and as a [illegible] when Sir John Carden had it in his power to oppose successfully the introduction of the Towns Improvement Act into the town of Templemore.'

"Mr. John [illegible] proposed the following amendment on Mr. O'Meara's motion:—

[illegible] the division for the present boundary [illegible] Sir John Cradock's [illegible] the [illegible] [illegible] the [illegible] [illegible] the Liquidators' [illegible] [illegible] the [illegible] [illegible] Tipperary [illegible] the [illegible] boundary [illegible] Sir John Carden's [illegible] [illegible] agreed upon by the majority of the Council. [illegible] the portion of his resolution relating to the Abbey, the residence of Sir John Carden, being excluded from the proposed extension be adopted. [illegible]

(Signed) "[illegible], Chairman.
"[illegible] Carey, Clerk."

"[illegible] the [illegible] in the [illegible] The [illegible]

the Municipal Boundary Commissioners, [illegible] Templemore is changed, as you will see by the [illegible].

"I have the honour to be, Sir John,
"Your obedient servant,
"John Carey."

3. Mr. Corcoran.—[illegible] Templemore will be dealt with [illegible] the [illegible] rates in other towns—[illegible] town will be dealt with [illegible]—Yes, but Sir John will expect [illegible] that his representations will be considered. [illegible] in his letter that he [illegible] the [illegible] of the land round the town.

4. And I take your [illegible] the same as if Sir John was here to state his own views?—Yes. He asked me to represent his views, and I [illegible] an [illegible] the opinion he expressed in the letter that he considers any [illegible] [illegible] for the purposes of the town [illegible] that the present Commissioners have [illegible] the full extent of the town which they are empowered to levy.

Mr. John Carey examined.

Mr. John Carey.

5. You are Clerk to the Town Commissioners of Templemore?—Yes.

6. How long have you held that office?—[illegible] years.

7. Under what Act is the town?—The Towns Improvement Act of 1854.

8. When was it put under that Act?—In June, 1860, I think.

9. Perhaps by referring to the books you could tell accurately?—Yes, these are the minutes of the first meeting of the Commissioners, held on the 22nd October, 1860.

10. Were there any Commissioners before that of any kind?—Never to my knowledge.

11. Was the Act adopted in its entirety or only in part?—Only in part.

12. Was the town ever enlarged from the original size?—Not to my knowledge. It was [illegible] it should have been extended.

13. When?—I find the resolution in the minutes of 6th July, 1868.

14. Just turn to the minutes of the 6th July, 1868, and read the resolution?—(Reads as follows.)

"In [illegible] of notice given at last meeting by Mr. V. O'Meara, moved 'That the boundary of the township be extended [illegible] Liquidators' [illegible] through [illegible] present boundary at [illegible] as described on the map by the Commissioners' [illegible] the Abbey, the residence of Sir John Carden, should be included, [illegible] being [illegible] when the boundary of the township was originally formed, and at a time when Sir John Carden had it in his power to [illegible] the introduction of the Towns Improvement Act into the town of Templemore.'"

15. I see there was an amendment moved and carried [illegible] in the boundary?—Yes, and then Mr. O'Meara moved:—

"That the portion of his resolution relating to the Abbey, the residence of Sir John Carden, being excluded from the proposed extension be adopted."

16. "The motion having been seconded was agreed upon"?—Yes.

17. That is in the minute book?—Yes.

18. As far as you know the boundary has never been altered since the original boundary was fixed?—Never.

19. I see that in the replies to the queries you have not given the population of the town—do you know what it is?—It is 3,[illegible].

20. What census was that?—In 1881.

21. What is the area of the township?—1,[illegible]a. 3r. 10p.

22. What is the valuation?—£[illegible] 12s.

23. There are no wards in the town?—No.

24. In what electoral division is the town situated?—In Templemore electoral division.

25. What were the municipal rates in 1874?—[illegible] in the pound.

26. In 1875 what were they?—Sixpence.

27. And in 1876?—Nothing.

28. And in 1877?—Eightpence.

29. And last year?—Eightpence also.

30. What were the poor rates during the same years?—In 1874, 1s. [illegible] in the pound; 1875, 1s. [illegible]; 1876, 1s.; 1877, 1s. [illegible]; and 1878, 1s. [illegible]

31. What was the county cess for the same periods?—In 1874 it was 2s. [illegible] in the pound; in 1875 it was 2s. [illegible]; in 1876, [illegible]; in 1877, 1s. [illegible]; and in 1878, 1s. [illegible] in the pound.

32. Of that poor rate was any portion a sanitary rate?—None whatever, except in 1876.

33. The Poor Law Guardians are the sanitary authority of Templemore?—Yes.

34. Did they strike any special sanitary rate?—Yes, in 1876.

35. How much?—Fourpence in the pound on [illegible] of [illegible].

36. But only on that townland?—Yes.

37. What was it for?—For sewerage in the town.

38. The whole of the town proper lies within that townland?—Yes.

39. Was there any sanitary rate struck except that since 1871?—Yes, in 1877.

40. What was it for?—I could not really say.

41. What was the amount of it?—Fourpence.

42. Was it on the same townland?—On the whole [illegible].

43. And not outside it?—No; and there was a [illegible] rate of a penny in 1876.

44. How far does the township of Templemore extend from the centre of the town on the north?—A very small distance. I never measured it.

45. Is it half a mile?—It is less than half a mile.

46. To the west how far does it extend from the market house?—Nearly a mile.

47. And to the south how far?—Under a mile.

48. To the east?—Under a mile a little.

49. Is there in the military [illegible]?—It is.

50. And all the [illegible] connected with it?—Yes.

51. What sources of income have the town besides the rate?—None whatever.

52. Haven't they the dog tax?—They have.

53. How much does it come to?—About £[illegible] annually.

54. Have they anything from fines?—Yes; they have half the fines.

[illegible] Corcoran, [illegible] 15. [illegible]

EXAMINATION, MARCH 15, 1888. Mr. John Deeg(?).

55. How much does that come to?—One year it was £75, and this year I should think more.

56. What are the total expenditure and receipts of the township?—The total expenditure was £[illegible], and the total receipts £[illegible] 14s., and there is a balance of £[illegible] in hands.

57. Has there been any meeting of the Commissioners held to consider the question of the boundary extension?—Yes, there has.

58. And they authorised you to give these answers?—Yes. It was in this form I wrote them under their instructions.

59. Did they come to any resolution on the subject?—There is a resolution on that body on the 2nd December.

60. How many Commissioners were there?—Fifteen.

61. And how many attended that meeting?—Eight.

62. There was no resolution pointing to any particular boundary?—No.

63. But they were in a unanimous wish?—Yes.

64. Was that resolution unanimous?—Yes; unanimous amongst the Commissioners present there.

65. It is upon the minutes of that body?—No. The Commissioners only present were there at the time.

66. Your answer to the query, whether you consider the present boundary satisfactory is, "It is too small and unequally divided"?—Yes.

67. That was the opinion of the Commissioners present on that day?—Yes.

68. What do you mean by "unequally divided"?—That it doesn't extend to the same distance all round.

69. They did not come to the conclusion of extending any particular radius?—Some were for the electoral division, and some were for the mile radius.

70. No. 4 of our questions is, "Are there any changes in the existing boundaries which they would suggest as desirable, whether in the direction of excluding, dividing, or otherwise altering them?" And your answer to that is, "Taking the market house as a centre, and the utmost point of present boundary at Greenwood as a radius, and a circle described thereby as the extension." That was the unanimous wish of the Commissioners then?—Yes.

71. And you got directions from them at that meeting to return that answer?—Yes; and it was in their presence, and it was read a second time for them.

72. How many inhabitants of Templemore are qualified to vote for Commissioners at the elections?—One hundred and seventy-five. That is not rated at £12, and there are 60 rated at £12 and upwards.

73. That is, that there are 235 qualified to vote for the Commissioners, and 60 qualified to be Commissioners?—Yes; but amongst the 60 there are some women. There are 55 houses rated up to £12.

74. In considering this question of extension, did they consider how many additional votes would be brought in?—They did not.

75. Or how many gentlemen in addition would be qualified to become Commissioners?—They did not consider that. There was no reference to that.

76. Did they consider the area or the valuation that would be brought in?—They did.

77. How much did they consider the additional area would be?—They considered it would be one-third additional.

78. And the additional valuation would be how much?—Nearly the same—one-third.

79. Since 1874, the guardians have been the sanitary authority?—Yes.

80. Have the Commissioners considered in any way whether they would wish to become the sanitary authority again themselves?—They have.

81. Have they arrived at any conclusion?—Yes, they have. They have a provisional order from the Local Government Board.

82. There is a provisional order?—Yes, it is going to be passed into Parliament.

83. Have they considered this question at all—supposing they do get this provisional order confirmed, whether they would wish to take up the roads and bridges from the Grand Jury?—Yes, we have. They think that they would if they could.

84. You are aware it is possible to do so when they become the Urban Authority?—When sanctioned by the Grand Jury.

85. Do they not know that it is possible under the Act of last year to get possession of the roads and bridges, whether the Grand Jury like it or not?—I don't think they do.

86. The Act of last year, empowers the Local Government Board, after receiving a memorial from the Urban Authority (Templemore would be an Urban Authority, when they get the provisional order confirmed), praying to have transferred to them the powers of the Grand Jury over roads and bridges—whether the Grand Jury consent or not—the Act empowers the Local Government Board, to hear it they can, on a further provisional order conferring the powers. That order has to receive law, and might be opposed of course. Have the Commissioners considered the matter in that light?—No, sir. It would be very beneficial to the town, I think to have the change.

87. How is the town lighted?—By oil, and public use of the street.

88. Is it considered well lit?—Yes.

89. There is no general wish for an extension of the lighting?—Not that I heard.

90. Of what description is the water-supply?—Very poor.

91. What is the supply from?—Only pumps.

92. Are they public pumps?—They are.

93. Kept in repair by the guardians?—Very badly kept in repair.

94. Do the guardians refuse to do the work which the Commissioners consider necessary?—Not so far that they pay no request to repairs sent to them from time to time.

95. How is the town off for drainage?—It wants to be drained.

96. It is not well drained?—It is not.

97. Could the Commissioners out of their present income do anything towards drainage?—Very little indeed. The income is small; only 6d. in the pound.

98. Is there anything else the Commissioners would do if they had a larger income?—I am sure there is.

99. What?—They would drain the town thoroughly.

100. Anything except drainage?—They would bring water in.

101. Was there any project to bring water to the town?—There was a suggestion between the Commissioners regarding it.

102. But there they ever gone into any detailed project involving an estimated expense?—Partially.

103. What was that proposal?—To bring water from the John's Well, known as the Black Well, into the town, there was a probable estimate of about £[illegible].

104. Only £[illegible]?—Yes.

105. Are there any other sources from which water could be brought?—Yes; the War Department were in contemplation sometime ago, of bringing water from a hill called the Devil's Pit to the garrison.

106. Independent of this town?—Yes, and they would let or sell to the town as soon as they brought it to the end of the town, and give the Commissioners an opportunity of supplying the town from that source.

107. How are the barracks supplied with water at present?—By pumps.

108. The Black Well is the private property of the Lady Carden?—Yes.

109. And has he ever been asked to allow this supply of water?—Yes; and he says if pipes are brought under ground sufficiently deep he has no objection.

110. In fact, if the thing was once brought forward to

king, or a stabilizing, he would have no objection?—No; it is overflowing at the source.

Mr. Fitzgerald.—I have known Sir John to refuse water from that well for any purpose, and even when the town was threatened with a removal of the troops he declined to give this consent to the supply of the barracks, which are very badly supplied with water, and I might almost say he would not allow this well to be used for the purpose of supplying the town, or allow pipes to be laid down in his demesne.

111. There is no other project talked of?—Not that I know of.

112. Would the extension now pending in this reply have been asked for by the Commissioners at the meeting, go into any other electoral division than Templemore?—The extension from some parts of the boundary would be beyond the electoral division, but the water Mr. Fitzgerald is speaking of is directly coming into the town. It is already flowing into the town at the bridge, and the whole thing would be to make it. The Commissioners said sometime they would put a pump there, and throw the water again, because it is overflowing on the surface, and is not considered the best water on that account. The water is still there, and it is from the old source.

113. Mr. Fitzgerald.—It has been found that the [illegible] could not be utilised, because the military authorities have failed to supply themselves with water from that source, and the town has been severed, [illegible] with the removal of the troops, and they have under consideration at this moment a proposal to bring water from a greater distance—the Devil's Bit Mountain.

114. Would that extension that is pending in bring in any gentleman's place?—Yes. It would bring in the Abbey, that is the only place I know of.

115. That is Sir John's own house?—Yes.

116. Would it bring in other gentlemen's residences?—No.

117. Have you any idea how many additional voters it would bring in?—I think it would bring in eight.

118. Do you mean voters as Commissioners?—Two qualified to be Commissioners and eight voters.

Mr. Joseph S. Whittaker examined.

119. You are Chairman of the Templemore Town Commissioners?—I am.

120. How long have you held that post?—For eight years.

121. Were you at the meeting of the 2nd December last?—Yes.

122. When the question of the extension of the boundary was talked of?—Yes.

123. What was the opinion of the Commissioners who attended that meeting?—My opinion was that there was a necessity for the extension of the boundary.

124. "Taking the market-house as a centre and the utmost point of the present boundary at Greenwood as a radius and a circle described thereby to be the extension"?—Yes.

125. What was the feeling of the Town Commissioners not present that day?—I think the general feeling is for extension.

126. For that extension?—Yes.

127. We have had Sir John Carden's opinion on the subject. Do you happen to know the feeling of anyone else who would be brought in by that extension?—I have heard one man express a wish for a greater extension.

128. Was he a ratepayer of the town?—No.

129. Does he live within the extension?—He would be within the extension I mentioned taking the whole of the electoral division.

130. You were of opinion that the whole of the electoral division should be taken in?—Yes.

131. Have you any idea of the size of that?—I have not.

132. Have you any idea how far it extends from the town?—It extends a very small distance at one side.

133. At which side?—At Sir John's side.

134. That is the west?—Yes.

135. How far could you say it extends on the west?—I think a mile.

136. And how far does it extend to the north?—I think it extends about a mile.

137. And to the east how far?—To near Loughmore—about two miles.

138. And in the other direction—to the south?—It takes about the same.

139. You don't consider two miles too far?—I would not.

140. You consider that people living outside the boundary derive advantage from their proximity to the town?—Decidedly.

141. From the markets?—And from other sources which the town is able to supply and which they require. For instance, manure collected in the town.

142. You mean the manure of the town?—Yes.

143. Do they derive any other advantages? Are there any schools to which the children from the outside districts come?—Yes, they come to the National schools.

144. How far do you think the children come from the outlying districts to these schools?—About a mile and a half.

145. The electoral division would go beyond that distance?—It would. My reason for speaking of the electoral division is, that if a law is taken, or if the radius is taken which has been described, taking the market-house as a centre and Greenwood as the furthest point, and a radius struck round it will cut up farms and there would be no proper defined boundary on any map to describe the townships.

146. You are of opinion, for instance, that the boundaries should be by townlands or something of that kind?—Yes, by townlands.

147. With regard to the sanitary authority you have already got a provisional order from the Local Government Board?—Yes.

148. And with regard to the question of taking up the roads from the Grand Jury, if you could do it what would be the feeling of the Commissioners?—I have heard some of them express a wish that the roads were under the control of some local authority.

149. What other local authority could there be but yourselves?—No other.

150. Then it means yourselves?—Yes.

151. In what way do they think they would manage the roads better?—They would keep the roads better. They are kept in a very bad state. The principal street when there is an outpour of wet can't be crossed from one side to the other.

152. Do you know how much the Grand Jury get out of the town?—I think they get between £400 and £500 a year.

153. Have you ever calculated what they expend on it?—I could not do that.

154. The Commissioners have not gone into that?—No.

155. They have not really gone into the question of figures as to the roads?—No.

156. In fact they were not aware they could get the control in spite of the Grand Jury?—No; I should have stated that we made inquiries as far as I can recollect, at one time about it, and we found it could not be, but we have heard of another board getting the control.

157. Have the Town Commissioners ever made application to the Grand Jury, by presentment or otherwise, for any works?—We have got some assistance from the county for flagging.

158. Have you got in print all your rules?—[illegible]

159. What have you raised in 1879 and was it [illegible]?—I could not tell you but the clerk could.

Town Clerk, re-examined.

160. What applications were made to the Grand Jury in the last two years, [illegible], for works in the town?—We made applications for about [illegible] for flagging, and £50 was allowed; and for gravel [illegible] for the wall of the bridge, and they were allowed.

161. To what amount?—[illegible]

162. Nothing else?—No.

163. In fact, then, you got what you asked for from the county for flagging?—Yes.

164. Do you know what the Board [illegible] spent in the town?—I do not. They have made [illegible] their own hands this year, they could not get a [illegible] contractor for them at the price they offered.

Mr. Whittaker's examination resumed.

165. Is there anything else you wish to state?—No, except as to the water. We have had hardly any water supply for the past four months or five, and we have made several applications to the present sanitary authority, and they have put the pumps once in repair, and done nothing since, and one is out of repair for the last two months.

166. You are becoming the sanitary authority yourselves now, so that that is not of much importance?—I got the clerk to write to the Local Government Board asking would they give authority to expend something in getting water for the town, and we got an answer that it could not be done.

167. Are there any other things in the town that ought to be done, and that you can't do for want of funds?—There is the drainage of the town.

168. That is when you become the sanitary authority?—Yes.

169. You will want additional funds for that?—Yes, if it was not for the funds we derive from them, and some small portion we get from the Government for the barracks, and the dog tax, we could not get along.

170. How much do the Government pay?—I think it was £13 for the last year. Even the shilling rate would not do, we could do nothing with it.

171. I see you have never exercised your full power of rating?—No, we considered that the town was so heavily taxed for poor rates and county cess that we would not be doing justice to the [illegible] if we imposed that extra money on it, or taxed them to the full extent of our taxing power.

172. In fact you want to get money from the outside district to relieve your taxation, your own rates in your full power?—We want the outside district to bear a proportion, which I think they should do.

173. Still it is a matter of fact that you have not raised your own rate to a shilling?—No.

174. Not within the last five years?—No, nor the last three years.

175. Three years ago you struck the rate at [illegible]?—Yes.

176. The outlying lands, with the exception of the [illegible], are all agricultural lands?—Yes, nearly all.

177. You think it should be fair [illegible] the town to pay for the advantages they derive from the town?—Yes, I do think it fair.

178. Is there anything else you wish to add on the subject of this inquiry?—I don't know of anything else that I wish to say.

Mr. James Quinn examined.

179. You are one of the Town Commissioners of Templemore?—I am.

180. You agree with what was said by the Chairman as to extension?—I do.

181. You have nothing to add?—No, sir.

Mr. William Fogarty examined.

182. You are one of the Commissioners?—Yes.

183. You heard the Chairman's evidence?—Yes.

184. Do you agree with him?—I do.

185. How long have you been a Commissioner?—A great many years. I am the oldest Commissioner.

186. Were you one of those present at the meeting on the 2nd of December?—I was.

Mr. Joseph Davy examined.

187. You are one of the Commissioners?—I am.

188. Were you present at the meeting on the 2nd December?—No, sir.

189. You heard the evidence of the Chairman with regard to the extension of the boundary?—Yes, sir.

190. Do you agree with that?—I do.

191. Have you anything additional to add?—No, sir.

Mr. Daniel Magee examined.

192. You are a Commissioner?—I am.

193. Do you agree with what was said as to the extension considered necessary?—Yes.

194. On the grounds the Chairman stated?—Yes.

Mr. George Patterson—continued.

Thurles. [illegible] Mr. George Patterson.

192. You are a Commissioner?—I am.

193. Were you one of the members present at the meeting on the 2nd December?—I was.

194. And the resolution that was come to by the Commissioners was, that extension was desirable in the terms embodied in the reply?—Yes.

195. On what grounds did you do that?—On the ground that it would take in persons who thought derived benefit from proximity to the town. There are a number of parties there who derive more or less benefit from the town, and we thought it fair they should bear portion of the rates, and the trade brings us here they should share.

196. How many persons besides Sir John Carden would be taken in—twenty or thirty people. Nothing [illegible] on the property, perhaps, but [illegible] [illegible].

197. And those people, you thought, derived such benefit that they should be asked to contribute?—I think it only fair they should bear some portion of the taxes.

198. You think a mile is about the distance to which the benefit you feel would not limit it to a mile. I would adopt the plan of the Guardians and [illegible] [illegible].

199. You would not go to the extent of two miles?—No; I don't think I would.

200. You think that all being agricultural holdings, except Sir John Carden's, on which it's a fair proportion for them to pay for the advantages they derive?—I think it is very fair.

201. Do you know what is the opinion of the Commissioners who were not present at that meeting?—I think the general opinion is in favour of extension.

202. Do you know the opinion of any of those outsiders who would be taken in?—Of course very few people like to be taxed.

203. Have you heard them express any opinion?—No; I heard one gentleman express himself anxious to be taxed.

204. Is he here to-day?—No; he is in Dublin to-day. I would not agree with the Chairman about taking up the roads. I don't think that would be desirable.

205. You think the roads are better left in the Grand Jury?—I do.

206. Do you think you get a fair return from the county for the rate you pay?—Not for the town alone, but we do for the neighbourhood.

207. A good deal of the town is on the outside 1,000 acres in the township?—I think they could do a good deal more, but at the same time, they do as well as the Commissioners could. They have expensive work done which the Commissioners could not afford to have. They have the County Surveyor and a Deputy County Surveyor. The Commissioners could not be able to manage it.

208. Is there anything else you wish to add?—No; except, that as to the urban sanitary authority in [illegible] I think it is very desirable we should have that.

209. But you have got it?—We have a provisional order for it.

210. You think it desirable that the provisional order should be confirmed?—Decidedly.

211. And that is the opinion of the other Commissioners?—Yes; and of the people in general.

212. You think you could do the sanitary works better?—Far better.

213. Are there any other works which the Commissioners would do which they are prevented from doing now, if they had money?—Except the supply of water; the town is badly supplied with water; indeed not at all supplied.

214. Has any estimate ever been prepared of the cost of drainage of the town?—No, because the Commissioners knew it would be far beyond their power; it would be idle work.

215. Have they considered that when they become the urban sanitary authority they may be obliged to do it?—They may consider it then, but it would cost a very large sum.

216. Did they contemplate that being thrown on them when they applied to become the urban sanitary authority?—Yes, they did; and that I think was one of the reasons that induced them—that and the water supply. They expect to be able to borrow money as soon as they get authority.

217. And they would rather do it than they have it in the Guardians?—Yes.

218. Mr. Fitzgerald (Chairman, Town Commissioners).—We had taken the contract for the repairs of the pumps and keeping them in order from the Board of Guardians, and we did so for two or three years.

219. The Commissioners became contractors to the Board of Guardians?—Yes, and we kept the town very fairly from that time, but they then refused to give us the contract at a little additional to what we had before.

220. And since then they have kept it themselves?—Yes; and the people are actually starved from the water for the last five months.

221. Did the Guardians oppose the provisional order?—No, they sanctioned it. It was mentioned to me that the Government authorities wished the Sanitary Board of Templemore to take water from them, and that they would be glad to give it, but we were not in a position to give us money, not being the sanitary authority of the town.

222. The bridge that Mr. Fitzgerald stated at the opening of the inquiry?—Yes.

223. Have you any remark to make upon that—namely that there was an agreement between the Commissioners originally and himself, that no future extension should take in Mr. Alcey?—Yes, we have a recollection of that.

224. Were you an original Commissioner?—Yes, sir.

225. Mr. Fitzgerald.—Sir John expressed himself to me that according to this effect, that if it was the intention of the Commissioners to extend the present boundaries, that he would not oppose their wish so extend them to such an extent as would bring in parts of his land, but he would decidedly object to bringing in his residence, inasmuch as he would look upon it as a breach of faith. I used no pressure to you than I don't appear in any capacity except to deliver a message from Sir John Carden, as he was not able to come himself, for I am no doubt interested in the town in any particular manner.

The inquiry terminated.

TULLAMORE—13TH MAY, 1879.

(Before Mr. C. P. COTTON, C.E.)

MR. [illegible] LYNCH examined.

1. You are clerk to the Town Commissioners of Tullamore?—Yes.

2. How long have you held that office?—Since 1872.

3. When was the township formed?—The Towns Improvement Act was adopted on the [illegible], 1860, and approved of by the Lord Lieutenant [illegible] of August in the same year.

4. Was it previously under any municipal authority?—No.

5. Was the Act adopted wholly or in part?—Only in part.

6. The water provisions were not adopted?—No, they were not.

7. What was the population of the town in 1871?—[illegible].

8. Has it decreased or increased since?—I believe the population has increased since then.

9. Do you think it has increased beyond [illegible] [illegible]?

10. What is the rate of the town?—[illegible].

11. And the valuation?—£5,[illegible].

12. Have you a map of the town?—No; this map (produced) was furnished by the [illegible] county surveyor. In it he sketches the boundaries of the town within the [illegible] lines.

13. You have no map of your own?—No. The only thing we have of the old bounds is the Lord Lieutenant's order, and the [illegible] of the [illegible] August, 1860.

14. Is the town pretty equally divided all round the central point?—Not exactly.

15. It is pretty much half a mile all round?—Yes. I think the extreme point is half a mile, if not more.

16. In what electoral division is the town situated?—The electoral division of Tullamore.

17. Do you know the electoral division?—I do.

18. Does it stretch very far away from the town to the north?—I should say it extends at least a distance of two miles.

19. And to the west how far?—Pretty much the same distance.

20. And to the south how far?—Well, I should say about two miles to the south.

21. To the east how far does it extend?—It is not more than half a mile to the east.

22. What is the number of Commissioners?—There are fifteen.

23. How many ratepayers are there?—[illegible].

24. Of these [illegible] how many would be qualified to sit as Commissioners?—Forty-seven would be qualified to sit.

25. Are there any wards in the town?—No wards.

26. Can you give me the municipal rates for the last five years?—Yes. In 1874 it was [illegible] in the pound; in 1875, [illegible]; in 1876, [illegible]; in 1877, [illegible]; and in 1878, [illegible].

27. What was the poor-rate in the same years?—In 1874 the poor-rate was [illegible]; in 1875, [illegible]; in 1876, [illegible]; in 1877, [illegible]; and in 1878 [illegible] in the pound.

28. Do you know whether any portion of that was a special sanitary rate?—Yes, [illegible] was.

29. What was the special sanitary rate for?—For carrying on sanitary matters in the town; that is in the way of opening old sewers and reconstructing them and making new ones.

30. On what contributory district was that rate struck?—On the electoral division.

31. On the whole division?—Yes, on the whole division.

32. Was there any previous special sanitary rate?—As soon as the Act came into operation there was a sanitary rate. It has been from [illegible] to [illegible] since for sanitary purposes.

33. Were these ordinary rates always struck on the whole electoral division?—Yes.

34. Can you tell me the county cess for those years?—Yes; in 1874 it was [illegible].

35. That is for the whole year?—Yes.

36. In 1875 how much was it?—It was [illegible]; in 1876 it was [illegible]; in 1877, [illegible]; and in 1878, [illegible].

37. Have the Commissioners formed any opinion whether any extension of the town, or any alteration is desirable?—On receipt of your queries, a circular embodying the substance of the queries was sent to the Commissioners, as a matter to be considered at their next meeting. I put it this way, "Two extension [illegible] of queries from the Municipal Boundaries Commissioners," so as to give them an idea that there was such a thing in existence. They each read through and [illegible] this came before them, and I have answered the queries here with the answers given thereto at the meeting.

38. Then the [illegible] of the replies is that the Commissioners wish for extension on the south side for a particular reason?—So it would appear from the answer expressed in the replies.

39. How many Commissioners were present at that meeting when the queries were considered?—Eight.

40. Were they unanimous?—Quite so.

41. Do you know the opinion of the others who were not there?—I do not. I believe some of the [illegible] Commissioners are here to-day and they will answer for themselves.

42. How is the town supplied with gas at present?—By the Gas Company; the Town Commissioners paying for the same [illegible] as ordinary consumers.

43. By the thousand feet?—Yes, so much by the thousand cubic feet.

44. What rate do they pay?—[illegible] per thousand.

45. It is by contract?—Yes, it is measured by meter.

46. How many lamps are there in the town?—Fifty-[illegible].

47. How is the town supplied with water?—There are four public pumps within the township, and there is one nearly on the border, and this one, although outside the boundary, is practically within the town, so that there are five public pumps.

48. In which direction is that one outside the boundary?—On the [illegible] side.

49. Would it be included in the extension that is alluded to?—It certainly would.

50. The pumps are under the care of the Commissioners?—Yes, of course; I may add that there are a large number of private pumps.

51. Is the public supply of water considered sufficient, or has any question been raised about it?—[illegible].

52. Either as to the quantity or the quality?—[illegible] occasionally the water becomes muddy, and then the pumps undergo the process of cleansing.

53. By the Guardians?—Yes.

54. And that is done by them when required?—It is.

55. Have the Commissioners considered the question—the wish of becoming the urban authority?—My own opinion is they would not do the work so efficiently, and they would not wish to have the [illegible] arrangements vested in them. At present they [illegible]

everything as [illegible] by the [illegible] but, of course, that is [illegible] by the fact that [illegible] of the Commissioners on the Board of Guardians already.

[illegible]. To this extension you have alluded to, was there any particular [illegible] mentioned?—I think not, nothing [illegible].

[illegible]. Is the railway station inside the township boundary?—It is the boundary; the township ends there.

[illegible]. Have the Commissioners control over the road to the railway station?—They have not.

[illegible]. Is that outside the town?—No; it is within the township boundary.

[illegible]. Then, it is in private property?—Yes, that is the railway property. The [illegible] belongs to the railway company.

[illegible]. Is the [illegible] on the [illegible] at the [illegible] side?—It is on the [illegible] side.

[illegible]. There are [illegible] in the town?—Yes, two [illegible] principally [illegible] Tullamore and those [illegible] in [illegible].

[illegible]. Are there any schools in the town?—There are [illegible] schools in the town.

[illegible]. Then, it is a place to which the children of the neighbouring districts come for school purposes?—Certainly, from a considerable distance.

[illegible]. From how far, would you say?—About a mile perhaps, not much farther.

[illegible]. Are there people scattered about the country further out?—There are.

[illegible]. But, within a mile, they come into school in the town?—I [illegible] quite sure they do.

[illegible]. What [illegible] have you?—Twelve in the year.

[illegible]. What is the character of the country; say within half a mile all round outside the present boundary?—It is principally an agricultural district.

70. Are there many gentlemen's places within that distance?—Not, taking you out to Charleville Castle.

71. That is a good deal more than half a mile?—[illegible].

72. This map represents the boundary going thirty?—Pretty fairly.

73. Do you know the opinion of any of the people living outside and adjoining the present boundary as to whether they wish to be taken in?—I am not aware; I have no opportunity of knowing.

74. Is there anything else you wish to have included?—No. I think you have got everything I am interested in.

Tullamore, [illegible]. Mr. [illegible] Lyman.

Dr. MICHAEL JOSEPH MOORHEAD examined.

Dr. Michael J. Moorhead.

75. You are Chairman of the Tullamore Commissioners?—Yes.

76. Have you been long a Commissioner?—I became a Commissioner about 1870, and in 1879 I became Chairman of the Board.

77. Mr. Lyman says it is the feeling of the Commissioners that they would rather not become the urban authority?—That is my opinion too.

78. You think the other Commissioners agree in that view?—I never heard one of them dissent from it. They may have their own opinions upon it, but I never heard it. I take it that the feeling is so in consequence of the satisfaction they seem to feel at the mode in which the business is conducted by the Guardians.

79. How is the town off as regards sanitary arrangements?—I think it is very well off. There were some [illegible] defective, but they are repaired now, and I think it is as well off as any town I know.

80. Is anything that is wanted in the way of repairs attended to by the Board of Guardians?—Certainly. Of course, sometimes they may not be able to undertake work as quickly as necessary in a sanitary point of view, but they don't lose sight of it.

81. They do it as efficiently as the Commissioners would?—They do.

82. Is there any contemplated large expenditure for a system of main drainage?—No.

83. Or for waterworks?—No. There are no waterworks, save the public pumps.

84. You consider the water supply good?—I do. Occasionally it has become impure, but it has always been attended to. The water is analysed, and when it is found impure steps are taken to remedy it. I consider the water supply better than in any other inland town I know of.

85. Have you yourself considered the question of extension or alteration of the boundaries?—Well, I have not considered it a great deal, but some of the Commissioners have considered it much more, and they seem to be of opinion that extension on the south side is desirable so as to include the three townlands of [illegible], Spollanstown, and Ballyrogh; one of them is only a field, there are two residences on it.

86. Do you coincide in the opinion about the extension?—Well, I do.

87. With what object is extension contemplated?—My brother Commissioners seem to think it would make the area more uniform and make the taxation more equitable. There is one of the gentlemen who has considered the matter more fully than I have, and he seems to think it would be an advantage in that respect.

88. Had the Commissioners before them any details of the additional area, or of the additional valuation, that would be brought in by the extension?—They had none. There would be an addition, I think, of 700 or 800 acres, with £100 increase in valuation.

89. Mr. Lyman, Town Clerk.—Of the Spollanstown townland we have 66 acres with a valuation of £104 in the town already. The total of it is 128 acres, and the valuation £[illegible]. Ballyrogh comes near, but it is outside the town. It contains 5[illegible] acres, and the valuation is £45 10s. Of Kilcruttin we have 35a. 1r. 3p., valued at £37 5s. The whole of Kilcruttin is 43a. 1r. 7p., and the valuation of it is £125 15s.

Dr. MOORHEAD'S examination continued.

90. You see that the extension to the extent of those townlands would make the boundary go much farther to the south than to the north?—Yes; I see that, and that is objectionable if it could be avoided.

91. Do you know of any reason why it should not be extended to the north to the same extent?—I don't know.

92. As you don't wish to become the urban authority for sanitary matters, of course you have not considered the question whether you would wish to take up control of the roads, and become the authority over the roads also, within your district?—That is a question that was considered a long time ago.

93. You can't get control over the road without first becoming the urban sanitary authority?—The Commissioners were not aware of that or they might have taken another view of the matter. The roads was a subject that occupied attention two or three years ago, and it was very anxiously and warmly debated, and steps were taken to get the Grand Jury to consent to the transfer.

94. The Act of last year gives the Local Government Board power, under certain circumstances, to give the control of the roads, and to take all the fiscal powers from the Grand Jury and give them to the Commissioners, but it only enables the Local Government Board to give the powers to urban sanitary authorities?—I don't think that was considered by the Board; they were not aware of that.

95. Supposing you were in a position, as no doubt you will be at the next census, to get that authority, being a town of over 5,000 inhabitants, would it be your private opinion that it would be desirable to

Portarlington, Sep. 14, 1879. Dr. Michael L. Moorhead.

take up the control of the roads?—It would, and, I think, that opinion is shared in by the other Commissioners.

96. Do you know what is the opinion of the ratepayers about any extension of this kind, or has it been before the ratepayers?—I think not.

97. Then I don't suppose you know the opinion of any of the outsiders in these townlands?—I have not the least idea.

98. Are the receipts of the Commissioners sufficient at present, or do they want more income?—They have plenty of money. We have money to our credit in bank, and we are proud of it, and all with a 6d. rate.

99. Is there anything else that occurs to you bearing on the question of the extension of the boundaries?—No.

Mr. William Adams.

Mr. William Adams examined.

100. I am a Commissioner of the town. I agree fully in what the Chairman has said as to the extension.

101. Do you know those particular townlands alluded to?—Yes, I do.

102. What reason is there for including Ballyrogan, and not extending the boundary to the north?—Well, we think that by taking in those three townlands the boundary would be more uniform, and prevent the land occupiers to the north saying the boundaries extend too far on that side, and only went so far on the opposite side.

103. But if you put in Spollanstown, the boundary will extend much farther to the south than to the north?—I think you will find it not very much; it is a long tail of poor land. It may appear long on the map, but there is some bog, and it is poor. The small amount at which it is valued shows it is not worth much, and it is included principally for uniformity sake and to prevent other people grumbling.

104. What is the difference in the quality, is the land on the north; is it much richer than on the south?—It is, and there are more residences. We don't think it would be worth while, for the small amount of rates we would get, to alter the boundaries on the north, but we think by altering the boundary on the south we are only doing what is businesslike and for the sake of uniformity. The value of the land on the north would be still equal to that on the south.

105. The valuation of what lies to the north of the town now, would be fully equal to what lies to the south with the additions proposed?—Yes.

106. Take Ballyrogan—why should it be brought in?—Because it lies between Kilgraigue and Spollanstown.

107. No, not at all?—Then it must extend farther south than I thought.

108. Ballyrogan is to the west of Kilgraigue altogether?—Well, could we have the other two and leave out Ballyrogan. We could leave out Ballyrogan; it was merely for appearance sake we proposed to take it in, and not so much coveting the valuation of it, for it is only £35 a year.

109. Was there any special reason?—No, it is only for uniformity. It would not give us £2 in the year, for the rate would be only half.

110. You want to have the boundary more uniform?—That is the only reason, and to take away the ground from under the feet of some in the north who say we did not do them justice.

111. You mean you did not do them justice in fixing the original boundary?—Yes, in taking them in and leaving others on the south out.

112. Whereabouts is this complaint made, for the northern gentlemen appear to be as near the town as the others?—We have northerns, but we have none of the southerns in at all.

Dr. Moorhead.

Dr. Moorhead recalled.

113. In saying that we did not want any more money, what I meant was that we had enough money without over-drawing any account in the bank, but if we had an opportunity of getting more money, we would know how to lay it out.

114. Are there any works which are necessary and ought to be done, which the Commissioners are not able to do for want of funds?—I think the footpaths would be a matter of great importance and the crossings and matters of that kind.

115. Do the Grand Jury help you in these matters?—They show a disposition to help us in the crossings, but unfortunately the scale of remuneration allowed by the county surveyor is so small that contractors refuse to put in tenders, and the work fell to the ground. I was under the impression that the Grand Jury passed the presentment for the crossings but I'm told that is not so.

116. Is the town well lighted, or are you restricted in the lighting for want of funds?—So far as we go we are restricted in nothing of our present requirements, but there are additional requirements which we have not entered upon.

117. Are these essential matters?—No, I don't think they are, but of course the town would be nicer, and neater, and be attended with a smarter appearance and all that sort of thing, if what I speak of was done.

118. But you have not exceeded one-half your rating powers at any time?—No. For the last few years it has been fluctuating between 6d. and 9d. in the pound.

119. Then you are not only out of debt, but you are not wanting money?—Yes.

Mr. Lynam.

Mr. Lynam, Town Clerk, examined.

120. The Commissioners in adopting the Act did not adopt that portion of it having reference to the streets, and they would not have power to expend anything on the streets, so that if they had the money tomorrow they could not spend it.

121. Then have you no power to control building, [illegible] buildings, and what is more, we have not even power to number the houses.

122. Then you have no by-laws of any kind?—No. There were a lot of things omitted from the order, which would have cost nothing, and which would have been very useful, but there was great opposition at the time, and there was difficulty in getting the order.

123. Have you ever considered the question of applying for an extension of the powers under the order?—We have, and we applied to the Local Government Board to have an opportunity of paving the streets and numbering the houses, and they met us by saying that the Commissioners should fall back upon the usual way of giving effect to the views of the ratepayers.

124. Do you mean that they thought the ratepayers would not consent?—Not exactly that, but they would not go raise the question again.

Mr. PATRICK EGAN examined.

Tullamore, June 14, 18[illegible]. — Mr. Patrick Egan.

122. You are a Town Commissioner of Tullamore?—I am.

123. You know the extension talked of?—I do.

124. Do you know the townland of Ballyduff?—Yes.

125. Do you know any special reason for bringing it in?—No, except to square the boundaries.

126. If you look at the map, and take the pink line to be the present boundary, and the red line to be the proposed extension, it doesn't appear to me to be squaring the boundary?—If I was asked my own private opinion, I would say the other boundary would be sufficient.

128. But you would not extend the boundary to the north at all?—No, I don't think there is any necessity.

130. And there is no necessity for extending it on the south, except to make the boundary uniform?—That is the only reason.

131. Where do you take the central point of the town to be?—Charleville-square.

132. Except the town has altered very much since the map was made, the north appears to be as near the centre of the town as any other part of it. There is no town north of the canal?—No.

Mr. ROBERT JAMES GOODBODY examined.

Mr. Robert J. Goodbody.

133. You are a ratepayer in the town?—Yes.

134. Have you formed any opinion as to whether extension or any alteration in the boundaries is required?—Yes; I think there is extension required.

135. What is that extension?—I think the lands on the southern side are increased in value by the position with relation to the town more than those on the northern side; particularly those on the north of the canal. You see the canal separates those lands very much from the town. It cuts them off.

136. They have several bridges?—Well, they have; but they are to the northeast, and those lands are comparatively speaking cut off. They might as well be two miles from the town as where they are; but the lands on the southern side are all increased in value by the position they hold.

137. When you say the lands on the southern side do you mean within or without the boundary?—Without.

138. They are increased in value?—Yes; but I think towards the north the boundary doesn't extend far enough. I am speaking of the northeast when I speak of the canal. I don't know exactly how far the boundary extends in that direction; but I certainly think the boundary should be extended, so as to bring in those quarries of Ballyduff within the town, if not even farther.

139. Do you consider that the boundaries should be extended, so as to include those quarries to the northwest?—Yes. The land that runs round is all increased in value in consequence of its contiguity to the town, and I think it only fair that lands that are made more valuable by their position should pay part of the town expenses.

140. On account of the advantages they get from the town being well lighted and well kept when they come into it, and on account of their children being sent into school in the town?—Yes.

141. How far do you think these advantages extend, so as to make it fair to expect that contribution?—I think those quarries would be a very natural boundary, and I think a circle from that point would be a very fair boundary to take.

142. But you think the boundary on the north-east should not be extended?—Yes. When we were originally getting this Act there was a good deal of opposition by the ratepayers and from country people, and the promoters of the Act did not feel themselves strong enough to go in for a large boundary, because every one of those men would have come in to vote against it. They had merely a bare majority in favour of it, and I conceive it was just considered that the railway made a kind of natural boundary that would be easily defined, and the consequence was that this district of Spollanstown was all left out, which would have been included then if the promoters had been strong enough to carry it. Everyone who lives there would have come in to vote against it.

143. And so far as you know would that be the feeling of the inhabitants now?—I should say it would. Mr. Egan is one of the owners there. They would be opposed to it merely for self-interest.

144. Sometimes we have found them anxious to come in. Is there any general feeling among the ratepayers of the town wishing to have this extension, or has it been before the ratepayers at all?—No, it has not, but I think, as a ratepayer, that it is only fair to the ratepayers of the town that those people should contribute. After all it is a very small tax upon them; it would only be those halfpence when we pay sixpence.

145. Then the object of extending the township and bringing in the new area would be to reduce the expense you are paying?—Yes.

146. And not to bring in additional money?—No, but the same reason—that the want of strength amongst the promoters to carry the Act with full powers at the time alone prevented their making full powers; that the Commissioners ought to have powers to pave, because there are a great many little things that would be done in the town that the Grand Jury cannot be reasonably be called upon to do, and which they won't do.

147. Do you think it would be an advantage that the Town Commissioners should have the fiscal powers of the Grand Jury?—That would be going a little further.

148. Well, say the control of the roads?—I think it would be an advantage. Of course it would give them a great deal more responsibility.

149. Do you mean that they would be able to manage the roads as well as the Grand Jury?—I don't see why they should not be, unless it would involve a great deal of expense.

150. How would it involve any additional expense, except as to the staff of overseers?—There would be a staff of surveyors. I think it would be a great advantage to the town if the representatives of the town had power to do anything that ought to be done in the way of keeping it in proper order. I think it is a great advantage to a town to be kept looking well, if for nothing else than to give us a thriving appearance, whether we are thriving or not. It makes a town thrive to give it a thriving look.

151. What benefit is shared in by the people living round?—I think they share in a variety of benefits. I think they ought to have the right to apply for powers to supply water and paving. They have no power to do anything in the way of supplying water. Anything that has been done in the way of supplying water has been done by private subscriptions.

152. Is that not done by the Guardians?—No. Mr. Egan says it is done by the Guardians since the sanitary powers were given, but I did not know that. The pumps at present in the town were all put down by private subscriptions.

153. That was previous to 1874?—Yes.

154. But they are repaired and kept in order now by the Guardians?—Yes, I suppose they are.

155. Have the Guardians power to put down a new pump now?—I did not know that before, but at all events, I think the Commissioners should have power to pave and keep the town in proper order.

Mr. Lahan, Clerk, recalled.

156. What are the receipts of the Commissioners for the year 1878?—£294 19s. 1d.

157. Of what does that consist?—The rates amounted to £111 8s. 1d.; the contribution from the Government in lieu of rates, £1 3s. 11d.; dog tax, £13 10s. 6d.; fairs, £34 10s. 6d.; petty sessions court, £19 7s.; and there was a sum of £10, rent received for this house, portion of which is let to a tenant. That makes altogether £294 19s. 1d. The total expenditure for the year 1878 was £204 13s. 8d., leaving a balance in favour of the Commissioners at the end of the year of £90 1s. 6d.

158. How did you start at the beginning of the year?—£104 18s. 4d. to our credit. Our year commences on the 1st October, so that last October we had this £90 1s. 6d. on hand. I take this from the audited abstract of accounts.

159. What did the expenditure consist of generally?—Salaries, £47. There was a sum of £4 for audit to the Local Government Board; rent of the hay-banks, fuel, &c., £17 6s. 10d.; gas and lighting for 1878, £83 7s. 10d.

160. Was that a complete year's lighting?—Yes. New lamp posts, £16 16s.; painting, £10 1s. 9d.; total, £37 0s. 7d. for the lamps and lighting of the year; fire engine, coal and repairs, £18 17s.; watering the streets, £3 10s.; printing, stationery, &c., £1 13s. 6d.; advertising and postage, £4 3s. 1d.; sundries, £3 10s.

161. The rent you received was for portion of this house?—Yes, the portion let to a tenant. We receive a profit rent of £10, and pay a rent of £14 ourselves.

Mr. John Tallentire examined.

162. You are a Commissioner of [illegible]?—Yes.

163. You have heard what the Chairman has said about extending; do you agree with him in the desirability of there being an extension of the township?—Yes.

164. For what reason?—That I think it would just bring it on near an equal radius on every side of the town. The south side at the railway is not in the town.

165. You consider that the town goes up to the railway?—Yes.

166. Do you know the townland of Ballynagh?—I do. I never heard of it until I came here today.

167. Where do you live?—I live in [illegible] square, and I have lived outside, as we all know.

168. Mr. [illegible].—Would it be possible to include only half way across a townland, taking in that of [illegible]?

169. Mr. [illegible].—The only reason we take in [illegible] is not to divide a townland.

170. You think none of the townland should be taken in, and that it is just as well to take it all in?—Just so.

Mr. [illegible] recalled.

171. You think the town to the north ought to go to the Bog of [illegible]?—Yes. It is a very natural boundary, and in fact it is the direction that is always looked upon as forming part of the town; and there is a road here along by the very road, and it would form a good natural boundary both ways.

172. Mr. [illegible].—In fixing the portion of Ballyduff as a boundary, we must not forget that we have not the whole nor portion of that townland within the township, and that you would have to cut up that townland by going out as far as Ballyduff, for that portion not in, from [illegible].

173. Mr. [illegible].—The question is precisely on the edge of the boundary, but the owner lives in Ballyduff. I think the boundary should run up to Mr. Boyd's [illegible], not to include Boyd's farm, but to run on there and thence, which would form the boundary of the town.

174. Mr. [illegible].—That is the very first time we [illegible] the townland of Ballyduff, and crossing [illegible].

175. Mr. [illegible].—You think that the boundary should run so as to include the townland of [illegible] and part of Ballyduff?—Yes. It appears that the [illegible] of the man who holds those quarries is just over the boundary. But there is Mr. Boyd. He has a large farm there on both sides of the [illegible], and his view was that the township boundary should pass as far as it, but not to include any part of Mr. Boyd's farm in the area immediately adjoining [illegible].

176. Mr. [illegible].—It is the very first time I have seen.

Mr. [illegible] [illegible] examined.

177. You are a Commissioner?—Yes. At first it was not proposed to extend the boundary for the purpose of making money at all.

178. You consider the extension proposed is right, in order to make a uniform boundary?—That is the only motive from first to last.

179. You don't think the boundary ought to be extended on the north side at all?—No.

180. Nor to the north-west?—It would not add much to the funds of the Commissioners, and it is only to make it look more uniform that extension is proposed at all.

181. And to distribute the rates more fairly?—Well, only in a small way.

182. What you anticipate from extension is not a great increase of money, but a more fair distribution of what is received?—Not only; to make the boundary more like a circle.

The inquiry then terminated.

Dublin: Printed by Alex. Thom & Co., 87, 88, & 89, Abbey-street,
The Queen's Printing Office.
For Her Majesty's Stationery Office.

www.ingramcontent.com/pod-product-compliance
Lightning Source LLC
Chambersburg PA
CBHW021934110726
47901CB00003B/830

* 9 7 8 3 7 4 2 8 0 5 5 6 0 *